POPULARMMOS

Popular MMOs (aka Pat) is one of the most popular YouTubers in the world. Pat and his wife, Jen (aka Gaming With Jen), created their *Minecraft*-inspired channel, PopularMMOs, in 2012. Since then, they have entertained millions of fans around the world with their gaming videos and original characters.

Pat and Jen live in Florida with their cat, Cloud. *PopularMMOs Presents: Enter the Mine* is their second book.

To my Nana. Can't wait for our next adventure.—D.J.

A special thanks to Joe Caramagna for all his creative help!

Popular MMOs Presents: Enter the Mine Copyright © 2019 by Popular MMOs, LLC. All rights reserved. Printed in the United States of America. No part of this book may be used or reproduced in any manner whatsoever without written permission except in the case of brief quotations embodied in critical articles and reviews. For information address HarperCollins Children's Books, a division of HarperCollins Publishers, 195 Broadway, New York, NY 10007.
www.harpercollinschildrens.com

Library of Congress Control Number: 2018966562
ISBN 978-0-06-289428-1 (trade bdg.)
ISBN 978-0-06-291529-0 (special edition)
ISBN 978-0-06-294024-7 (special edition)
ISBN 978-0-06-293357-7 (special edition)
ISBN 978-0-06-295022-2 (special edition)

The artist used an iPad Pro and the app Procreate to create the digital illustrations for this book.
Typography by Erica De Chavez 19 20 21 22 23 PC/LSCC 10 9 8 7 6 5 4 3 2 1 ❖ First Edition

PopularMMOs

PRESENTS
ENTER THE MINE

By **PAT+JEN** from **POPULARMMOs**
Illustrated by **DANI JONES**

HARPER
An Imprint of HarperCollinsPublishers

Hey, what's going on, guys!

It's Pat and Jen, and we're so thrilled that you're reading our second book. It's another exciting adventure where you'll get to meet all your favorite characters from our YouTube channel. Of course, there's me and Jen and Bomby and Cloud, but this time, Bob, Hoss, the Mayor, Valentine, and more get in on the action. We all band together to stop Evil Jen's evilest plot yet—and worse, this time she has Evil Pat along for the ride!

We can't tell you how much we appreciate your support. Writing this book has been a totally amazing experience, and we can't wait to tell you how much it means to us both that you've decided to Enter the Mine along with us. We think you'll really enjoy this "explosive" new adventure—watch out for all the zombies and holes. We just hope you enjoy reading it as much as we enjoyed writing it. Being creative is what we are all about, and we hope that this book inspires you to be creative, too!

Have fun! Read on! And thanks for being a fan.

PAT & JEN

Pat is an awesome dude who's always looking for an epic adventure with his partner, the Super Girly Gamer Jen. Pat loves to have fun with his friends and take control of every situation with his cool weapons and can-do attitude. Jen is the sweetest person in the world and loves to laugh, but don't let her cheeriness fool you—she's also fierce. In fact, she could be an even greater adventurer than Pat . . . if she weren't so clumsy. Together, along with their cat, Cloud, they have a bond that can never be broken.

CARTER

Carter is Jen's best friend and biggest fan, but he doesn't seem to like Pat very much at all. Carter is also not very smart and sometimes carries a pickle that he thinks is a green sword!

CAPTAIN COOKIE

No one is quite sure if Captain Cookie is a real sea captain or if he just dresses the part. He doesn't seem to be very good at anything, but that doesn't stop him from bragging about how great he is! He's rude to everyone he meets but always in a funny way.

CLOUD

Cloud is Pat and Jen's white Persian cat. He may have a fluffy exterior, but underneath, he's all *savage*.

HONEY BOO BOO

Honey Boo Boo is a golem of iron on the outside but is all softy on the inside!

BOMBY

Bomby is somewhat of a pet to Pat and Jen but also Pat's best friend. You can usually find him by following the craters left by the TNT that he loves to watch explode.

THE MAYOR

The Mayor loves being the mayor and loves reminding everyone that he's the mayor, but doesn't seem to have much authority over anyone or anything.

VALENTINE

An elf and a master archer, he leads the revolt against Evil Jen's rule in the Underworld.

BOB

Bob is Valentine's best friend. After he is imprisoned by Evil Jen, he becomes the unofficial leader of the miners.

HOSS

Hoss claims to be a doctor but doesn't seem to know anything about what a doctor actually does. He's better at being a chef. Actually, he's better at doing anything than he is at being a doctor!

EVIL JEN

Evil Jen's favorite thing is chaos. She lives for wreaking havoc on the world. What makes her truly evil, however, is that she would take someone as sweet as Jen and become an evil version of her. She even looks *exactly* like her (just don't tell Jen we said that!).

LATER...

PAT, DO YOU THINK BOMBY WILL BE ALL RIGHT?

LATER...

HMM...

...WHERE IS THAT **NEW** HOLE AGAIN?

WHOOPS!

THAT WAS CLOSE!

I WAS HOPING TO TELL YOU **AND** JEN **TOGETHER,** BUT I'LL JUST COME OUT WITH IT.

OUR COMMUNITY OWES YOU A LOT OF **GRATITUDE** FOR ALL YOU'VE DONE TO SAVE OUR VILLAGERS FROM THE HORRORS OF EVIL JEN—

—SO I'VE DECIDED TO AWARD YOU EACH WITH A **MEDAL** AS A TOKEN OF MY APPRECIATION!

I MUST NOT BE AS GOOD AT READING LIPS AS I THOUGHT.

IT LOOKED LIKE YOU SAID YOU WERE GONNA GIVE US **MEDALS!**

THAT'S **EXACTLY** WHAT I SAID!

DUDE! THAT IS **EPIC!** WE HAVE TO FIND JEN AND TELL HER **RIGHT AWAY!**

STOP WITH YOUR **MIND** GAMES!

AAAAAAHHH!

SHE'S BROUGHT THIS ON **HERSELF.** SHE'S GOT **ONE JOB** AND SHE WON'T DO IT.

"EVIL JEN'S BEEN TRAPPING FOLKS FROM THE REAL WORLD TO MINE AN ORE SHE DISCOVERED CALLED 'BOOMIUM,' WHICH SHE USES TO MAKE SUPERPOWERFUL TNT."

SHE HAS ALL OF THESE ZOMBIES DOWN HERE, CARTER. WHAT DOES SHE WANT WITH US?

"THESE ZOMBIES ARE CLODS. BOOMIUM'S VERY DELICATE. ONE FALSE MOVE COULD SET OFF A CHAIN REACTION OF POCKET EXPLOSIONS THAT WILL COLLAPSE THE WHOLE MOUNTAIN, WITH US INSIDE!"

"SO CHIP IT OUT CAREFULLY AND PLACE IT IN THE MINE CARTS TO BE TAKEN... WHEREVER SHE STORES THIS STUFF."

—THIS!

MAYOR!
HONEY BOO BOO!
FOLLOW M—

ME?

I **ALREADY** HELPED YOU. YOU SAID THAT IN RETURN YOU WOULD HELP **ME** FIND MY WAY **HOME.**

I **HAVE** TO GET BACK TO MY **LIFE.** I MISS PAT—MY **FRIENDS.** MY CAT, **CLOUD,** CAN'T SURVIVE **WITHOUT** ME.

BUT, JEN, IF YOU **DON'T** HELP US, ALL OF THOSE THINGS YOU CHERISH WILL CEASE TO EXIST AS YOU KNOW THEM!

HUH?

EVIL JEN IS TRYING TO MAKE A BOMB SO POWERFUL IT'LL BLAST A HOLE TO THE **OVERWORLD** SO BIG THAT REALITY WILL FOLD IN ON ITSELF. IF **THAT** HAPPENS, BOTH THE UNDERWORLD AND **YOUR** WORLD...

...WILL BECOME **ONE** AND THE **SAME!**

AND EVIL JEN WILL RULE US **ALL.**

UNLESS WE **STOP** HER...

WHAT THE HECK? I IMITATED EVIL JEN ONCE— I CAN DO IT **AGAIN.**

LET'S DO IT!

WAK WAK!

KRAKK!

ALL CLEAR.

SO FAR, SO **GOOD.** EVERYTHING'S AS THE BLUEPRINT SAYS IT IS—

RAGGLE-RAZ!

CHUNK!

RAZZLE!

RIP-RABBLE!

RIZ-RAGGLE!

KRAKK!

CLUNK!

BUNK!

UNDERSTANDABLE. BOB'S BEEN IN HERE FOR A **LONG TIME** NOW.

VALENTINE IS KINDA...**INTENSE.** ISN'T HE?

START

MEANWHILE...

HUFF... HUFF...

OW! WATCH YOUR **SPEAR**, DUDE!

I'M **WORKING**, I'M **WORKING**! SHEESH!

RIBBLE-RAG!

WHAT NOW?

THERE'S A **RIOT** IN THE **MINE?** THE PRISONERS HAVE BROKEN THEIR CHAINS AND ARE TRYING TO ESCAPE?

I'D BETTER GO SEE WHAT'S HAPPENING.

GIVE HER THE **HUMAN FINGER CHEESE SANDWICH** AND MAKE SURE SHE EATS IT **ALL**— I WANT HER FULLY TRANSFORMED BY MORNING!

ZOMBIES— BLOCK THE EXIT TUNNEL! **NO ONE GETS OUT!**

HUH?

RAGGLE-FRAGGLE!

WHO NEEDS AN ELECTRIC FENCE WHEN THEY'VE GOT A **WALL OF ZOMBIES?**

HOW ARE WE EVER GONNA GET THROUGH **THAT—?**

HONEY BOO BOO!

NOOOO!

NO! I DIDN'T **MEAN** TO DO THAT!

COME ON, JEN, WE GOTTA FIND A WAY OUT **NOW!**

I'M SORRY—

CLUNG!

UFF!

WHERE HAVE **YOU** BEEN?

WELL?! DON'T JUST STAND THERE **STARING** AT ME—

—WE CAN STILL **CATCH** THEM, **EVIL PAT!**

Featured Applications in This Book

Oregon Decides Which Medical Treatments to Provide 2
Tax on Fast-Food Containers 4
Income Threshold Model and China 4
Putting Saturn in Orbit 9
Aggregating the Demand for Cling Peaches 20
American Steel Quotas 35
Gas Lines 37
Minimum Wage Law in Puerto Rico 40
Web Fee 50
Demanding Rail Safety 55
Discouraging Smoking 62
Gasoline Taxes as a Revenue Source 65
Incidence of Federal Ad Valorem Taxes 70
Indifference Curves Between Food and Clothing 83
Taxes and Internet Shopping 96
Food Stamp Experiments 101
Income Elasticities of Demand for Cars 116
Why the Wealthy Buy More Houses 122
Does Inflation Hurt? 125
The Total CPI Bias 129
Leisure-Income Choices of Textile Workers 135
Estimated Labor Supply Curves 136
Effects of Tax Cuts 139
Malthus and Mass Starvation 154
A Semiconductor Integrated Circuit Isoquant 159
Returns to Scale in Manufacturing 166
German Versus British Productivity 170
Nonneutral Technical Change in Pin Manufacturing 172
Automobile Manufacturing Innovations 173
Opportunity Cost of Waiting Time 179
Swarthmore College's Cost of Capital 180
Internet Firms' Fixed Costs 183
Short-Run Cost Curves of a Printing Firm 189
Rice Milling on Java 199
Average Cost of Cement Firms 207
Long-Run Cost Curves in Printing and Oil Pipelines 210
Choosing an Ink Jet or a Laser Printer 213
Learning by Doing in Computer Chips 217
Dead End 220
Breaking Even on Christmas Trees 229
Shutting Down Oil Wells 243
Threat of Entry in Shipping 249

The Naked Truth about Costs and Entry 250
Upward-Sloping Long-Run Supply Curve of Cotton 252
Slope of Long-Run Market Supply Curves 256
Consumer Surplus from Television 269
Deadweight Loss of Christmas Presents 279
Taxicab Medallions 283
Discriminating Against Groups 284
Barriers to Protect Our Way of Life 286
Job Termination Laws 287
International Cost of Agricultural Subsidies 293
Japanese Nontariff Barriers 300
Sin Taxes 310
Living-Wage Laws 313
Auto Trade Barriers 330
Wealth Distribution in the United States 332
Humana Hospitals 354
Airport Monopolies 355
Deadweight Loss of the U.S. Postal Service 359
Electric Power Utilities 366
Government Sales of Monopolies 368
A Drug Patent 369
Monopoly in Names 378
Disneyland Pricing 386
A Hot Sale of Coke 391
Tagamet Revisited 393
Generics and Brand-Name Loyalty 401
Getting Consumers to Identify Themselves 404
Taking Women to the Cleaners 406
Warehouse Stores 410
IBM 411
Automatic Savings 413
Oligopoly Competition among Governments 423
A Government-Created Cartel 429
Vitamin Price Fixing 428
Bail Bonds 430
Airline Mergers 430
Appliances 440
Airbus and Boeing 448
Deadweight Losses in the Food and Tabacco Industries 451
Entry and Airline Prices 455
Toothbrushes 460
Welfare Gain from New Cereals 461
Government Deterrence 473
Hitting Rivals Where It Hurts 486
Preventing Customers from Switching 487

Evidence on Strategic Entry Deterrence 489
Drug Commercials 492
O. J. Trial Effect 494
Pink Toothbrush 495
Secret Ingredients 496
Thread Mill 507
Record Prices 516
Union Monopoly Power 517
Baseball Salaries and Ticket Prices 520
Monopsony Wage Setting 524
Monopsony Price Discrimination 527
Outsourcing 529
Aluminum 531
Cutting Off Oxygen 533
Usury 538
Power of Compounding 542
Saving for Retirement 546
Winning the Lottery 549
Comparing Two Contracts 550
Durability of Telephone Poles 555
Redwood Trees 563
Taking from Future Generations 568
Gambling 583
Bond Ratings 586
Laws Limiting Diversification 589
Flight Insurance 592
Natural Disasters 593
Premium for a Riskier Investment 595
Loans, Defaults, and Usury Laws 598
Michael Jordan's Positive Externalities 604
Waste Not 607
Taxes on Fuels 611
Emissions Standards for Ozone 614
Sulfur Dioxide Market 623
Extensive Overfishing 625
For Whom the Bridge Tolls 626
Free Riding on Water 632
Risky Hobbies 641
Recycling Lemons 646
College Guarantee 649
Multiple Brand Names 651
Advertising Lowers Prices 654
Contracts and Productivity in Agriculture 678
Lawyers' Contingent Fees 683
Pleased to Be Paid by the Piece 686
Increasing Use of Incentives 687
Abusing Leased Cars 695
Savings and Loans Moral Hazards 696
Performance Termination Contracts 698

CONGRATULATIONS!

As a student purchasing Perloff's *Microeconomics*, Second Edition, you are entitled to a prepaid subscription to premium services on the Companion Web Site! You will have online access to useful Web features such as the *Student Resource Kit*.

The duration of your subscription is 6 months.

To activate your prepaid subscription:

1. Launch your Web browser and go to the Companion Web Site at www.awlonline.com/perloff

2. Enter the Student Resources area. When you select a protected section of the Web site, you will be asked to log in.

3. Follow the instructions on the screen to register yourself as a new user. Your preassigned Access Code is:

Activation ID: PFWNST06007337

Activation Password: MOUNTAINEER

4. During registration, you will choose a personal User ID and Password for use in logging into the Web site.

5. Once your personal User ID and Password are confirmed, you can begin using the Web site.

This Access Code can be used only once to establish a subscription. This subscription is not transferable.

If you did not purchase this product new and in a shrink-wrapped package, this Access Code may not be valid!

MICROECONOMICS

Second Edition

Jeffrey M. Perloff
University of California, Berkeley

Boston   San Francisco   New York
London   Toronto   Sydney   Tokyo   Singapore   Madrid
Mexico City   Munich   Paris   Cape Town   Hong Kong   Montreal

To my mother, Mimi Perloff

Executive Editor	DENISE CLINTON
Executive Development Manager and Development Editor	SYLVIA MALLORY
Managing Editor	JAMES RIGNEY
Senior Production Supervisor	NANCY FENTON
Marketing Manager	DARA LANIER
Cover and Interior Design	REGINA HAGEN
Senior Media Producer	MELISSA HONIG
In-house Composition	SCOTT SILVA, SALLY SIMPSON
Senior Manufacturing Buyer	HUGH CRAWFORD
Illustrator	JIM MCLAUGHLIN
Project Management	ELM STREET PUBLISHING SERVICES, INC.
Cover Image	© HIDEKI KUWAJIMA/PHOTONICA

Photo credits appear on page A-60, which constitutes a continuation of the copyright page.

Library of Congress Cataloging-in-Publication Data
Perloff, Jeffrey M.
    Microeconomics / Jeffrey M. Perloff. — 2nd ed.
        p.   cm.
    Includes bibliographical references and index.
    ISBN 0-201-63773-1 (alk. paper)
    1. Microeconomics.
    HB172.P39 2001
    338.5—dc21   00-033190

3 4 5 6 7 8 9 10 — RNT — 04 03 02 01

CONTENTS

Preface   xiii

CHAPTER 1   *Introduction*   1

1.1   **Microeconomics: The Allocation of Scarce Resources**   1

Trade-Offs   2

Who Makes the Decisions   2

APPLICATION   Oregon Decides Which Medical Treatments to Provide   2

Prices Determine Allocations   3

APPLICATION   Tax on Fast-Food Containers   4

1.2   **Models**   4

APPLICATION   Income Threshold Model and China   4

Simplifications by Assumption   5

Testing Theories   6

Positive Versus Normative   7

1.3   **Uses of Microeconomic Models**   8

Uses of Microeconomics by Individiuals and Governments   8

APPLICATION   Putting Saturn in Orbit   9

Summary   12

PART ONE   SUPPLY AND DEMAND

CHAPTER 2   *Supply and Demand*   13

2.1   **Demand**   14

The Demand Curve   15

The Demand Function   18

Summing Demand Curves   20

APPLICATION   Aggregating the Demand for Cling Peaches   20

2.2   **Supply**   21

The Supply Curve   22

The Supply Function   24

Summing Supply Curves   24

Effects of Government Import Policies on Supply Curves   25

SOLVED PROBLEM 2.1   26

2.3   **Market Equilibrium**   27

Using a Graph to Determine the Equilibrium   27

Using Math to Determine the Equilibrium   27

Forces That Drive the Market to Equilibrium   28

2.4   **Shocking the Equilibrium**   30

Effects of a Shift in the Demand Curve   30

Effects of a Shift in the Supply Curve   31

SOLVED PROBLEM 2.2   31

2.5   **Effects of Government Interventions**   32

Policies that Shift Supply Curves   32

SOLVED PROBLEM 2.3   34

APPLICATION   American Steel Quotas   35

Policies that Cause Demand to Differ from Supply   35

APPLICATION   Gas Lines   37

APPLICATION   Minimum Wage Law in Puerto Rico   40

Why Supply Need Not Equal Demand   41

2.6   **When to Use the Supply-and-Demand Model**   41

Summary   43

Problems   44

Math Problems   45

CHAPTER 3   *Applying the Supply-and-Demand Model*   46

3.1   **How Shapes of Demand and Supply Curves Matter**   47

3.2   **Sensitivity of Quantity Demanded to Price**   48

Price Elasticity of Demand   48

APPLICATION   Web Fees   50

Elasticity Along the Demand Curve   50

Other Demand Elasticities   53

APPLICATION   Demanding Rail Safety   55

3.3   **Sensitivity of Quantity Supplied to Price**   56

Elasticity of Supply   56

Elasticity Along the Supply Curve   57

3.4 **Long Run Versus Short Run** 58
Demand Elasticities over Time 58
Supply Elasticities over Time 59

3.5 **Effects of a Sales Tax** 59
Two Types of Sales Taxes 59
Equilibrium Effects of a Specific Tax 60
APPLICATION   Discouraging Smoking 62
Tax Incidence of a Specific Tax 63
SOLVED PROBLEM 3.1 64
APPLICATION   Gasoline Taxes as a
Revenue Source 65
The Same Equilibrium No Matter
Who Is Taxed 66
The Similar Effects of Ad Valorem and
Specific Taxes 67
SOLVED PROBLEM 3.2 68
APPLICATION   Incidence of Federal Ad
Valorem Taxes 70

Summary 70
Problems 71
Math Problems 72

PART TWO   CONSUMER THEORY

CHAPTER 4 *Consumer Choice* 73

4.1 **Preferences** 74
Properties of Consumer Preferences 75
Preference Maps 76
SOLVED PROBLEM 4.1 79
APPLICATION   Indifference Curves Between
Food and Clothing 83

4.2 **Utility** 84
Utility Function 84
Ordinal Preferences 84
Utility and Indifference Curves 85
Utility and Marginal Utility 85
Utility and Marginal Rates of Substitution 87

4.3 **Budget Constraint** 87
Slope of the Budget Constraint 89
Purchasing Fractional Quantities 89
Effect of a Change in Price on Consumption 89
Effect of a Change in Income on
Consumption 90
SOLVED PROBLEM 4.2 91

4.4 **Constrained Consumer Choice** 92
The Consumer's Optimal Bundle 92
SOLVED PROBLEM 4.3 95

APPLICATION   Taxes and Internet Shopping 96
★Optimal Bundles on Convex Sections of
Indifference Curves 96
Buying Where More Is Better 97
SOLVED PROBLEM 4.4 98
Food Stamps 99
APPLICATION   Food Stamp Experiments 101

Summary 102
Problems 103
Math Problems 104

CHAPTER 5 *Applying Consumer Theory* 105

5.1 **Deriving Demand Curves** 106

5.2 **How Changes in Income Shift
Demand Curves** 109
Effects of a Rise in Income 109
SOLVED PROBLEM 5.1 111
Consumer Theory and Income Elasticities 112
APPLICATION   Income Elasticities of
Demand for Cars 116

5.3 **Effects of a Price Change** 117
Income and Substitution Effects with a
Normal Good 117
Income and Substitution Effects with an
Inferior Good 119
SOLVED PROBLEM 5.2 121
APPLICATION   Why the Wealthy Buy
More Houses 122

5.4 **Cost-of-Living Adjustments** 123
Inflation Indexes 123
APPLICATION   Does Inflation Hurt? 125
Effects of Inflation Adjustments 126
APPLICATION   The Total CPI Bias 129

5.5 **Deriving Labor Supply Curves** 130
Labor-Leisure Choice 130
Income and Substitution Effects 133
SOLVED PROBLEM 5.3 134
APPLICATION   Leisure-Income Choices of
Textile Workers 135
Shape of the Labor Supply Curve 136
APPLICATION   Estimated Labor
Supply Curves 136
Income Tax Rates and Labor Supply 138
APPLICATION   Effects of Tax Cuts 139

Summary 140
Problems 141
Math Problems 142

PART THREE THEORY OF THE FIRM

CHAPTER 6 *Firms and Production*   143

6.1 **The Ownership and Management
      of Firms**   144
      The Ownership of Firms   145
      The Management of Firms   145
      What Owners Want   146

6.2 **Production**   146
      Production Functions   147
      Time and the Variability of Inputs   147

6.3 **Short-Run Production: One Variable
      and One Fixed Input**   148
      Total Product   148
      Marginal Product of Labor   149
      Average Product of Labor   150
      Graphing the Product Curves   150
      Law of Diminishing Marginal Returns   153
      APPLICATION Malthus and Mass Starvation 154

6.4 **Long-Run Production:
      Two Variable Inputs**   155
      Isoquants   155
      APPLICATION A Semiconductor Integrated
                   Circuit Isoquant   159
      Substituting Inputs   161
      SOLVED PROBLEM 6.1   163

6.5 **Returns to Scale**   164
      Constant, Increasing, and Decreasing
        Returns to Scale   164
      SOLVED PROBLEM 6.2   165
      APPLICATION Returns to Scale in
                   Manufacturing   166
      Varying Returns to Scale   168

6.6 **Productivity and Technical Change**   168
      Relative Productivity   169
      APPLICATION German Versus British
                   Productivity   170
      Innovations   171
      APPLICATION Nonneutral Technical Change
                   in Pin Manufacturing   172
      APPLICATION Automobile Manufacturing
                   Innovations   173

Summary   174
Problems   174
Math Problems   176

CHAPTER 7 *Costs*   177

7.1 **Measuring Costs**   178
      Economic Cost   178
      APPLICATION Opportunity Cost of
                   Waiting Time   179
      Capital Costs   179
      APPLICATION Swarthmore College's Cost
                   of Capital   180

7.2 **Short-Run Costs**   181
      Short-Run Cost Measures   181
      APPLICATION Internet Firms' Fixed Costs 183
      Short-Run Cost Curves   183
      Production Functions and the Shape of
        Cost Curves   186
      APPLICATION Short-Run Cost Curves for
                   a Printing Firm   189
      Effects of Taxes on Costs   189
      SOLVED PROBLEM 7.1   191
      Short-Run Cost Summary   192

7.3 **Long-Run Costs**   193
      Input Choice   193
      APPLICATION Rice Milling on Java   199
      SOLVED PROBLEM 7.2   201
      How Long-Run Cost Varies with Output   202
      SOLVED PROBLEM 7.3   204
      The Shape of Long-Run Cost Curves   204
      APPLICATION Average Cost of Cement Firms 207
      Estimating Cost Curves Versus Introspection 208

7.4 **Lower Costs in the Long Run**   209
      Long-Run Average Cost as the Envelope
        of Short-Run Average Cost Curves   209
      APPLICATION Long-Run Cost Curves in
                   Printing and Oil Pipelines 210
      APPLICATION Choosing an Ink-Jet or a
                   Laser Printer   213
      Short-Run and Long-Run Expansion Paths   214
      How Learning by Doing Lowers Costs   214
      APPLICATION Learning by Doing in
                   Computer Chips   217

7.5 **Cost of Producing Multiple Goods**   218
      APPLICATION Dead End   220

Summary   220
Problems   220
Math Problems   221

PART FOUR   PERFECT COMPETITION

CHAPTER 8   *Competitive Firms and Markets*   **223**

8.1   **Competition**   224
   Price Taking   224
   Why the Firm's Demand Curve Is Horizontal   224
   ★Derivation of a Competitive Firm's Demand Curve   226
   Why We Study Perfect Competition   227

8.2   **Profit Maximization**   228
   Profit   228
   APPLICATION   Breaking Even on Christmas Trees   229
   Two Steps to Maximizing Profit   230

8.3   **Competition in the Short Run**   233
   Short-Run Competitive Profit Maximization   233
   SOLVED PROBLEM 8.1   235
   SOLVED PROBLEM 8.2   238
   Short-Run Firm Supply Curve   239
   Short-Run Market Supply Curve   241
   APPLICATION   Shutting Down Oil Wells   243
   Short-Run Competitive Equilibrium   244

8.4   **Competition in the Long Run**   246
   Long-Run Competitive Profit Maximization   246
   Long-Run Firm Supply Curve   246
   Long-Run Market Supply Curve   248
   APPLICATION   Threat of Entry in Shipping   249
   APPLICATION   The Naked Truth About Costs and Entry   250
   APPLICATION   Upward-Sloping Long-Run Supply Curve for Cotton   252
   APPLICATION   Slope of Long-Run Market Supply Curves   256
   Long-Run Competitive Equilibrium   256
   SOLVED PROBLEM 8.3   258

8.5   **Zero Profit for Competitive Firms in the Long Run**   259
   Zero Long-Run Profit with Free Entry   259
   Zero Long-Run Profit When Entry Is Limited   260
   The Need to Maximize Profit   262

Summary   262
Problems   263
Math Problems   264

CHAPTER 9   *Applying the Competitive Model*   **265**

9.1   **Consumer Welfare**   266
   Measuring Consumer Welfare Using a Demand Curve   266
   APPLICATION   Consumer Surplus from Television   269
   Effect of a Price Change on Consumer Surplus   269
   SOLVED PROBLEM 9.1   271

9.2   **Producer Welfare**   273
   Measuring Producer Surplus Using a Supply Curve   273
   Using Producer Surplus   274
   SOLVED PROBLEM 9.2   275

9.3   **Competition Maximizes Welfare**   276
   Why Producing Less than the Competitive Output Lowers Welfare   276
   Why Producing More than the Competitive Output Lowers Welfare   278
   APPLICATION   Deadweight Loss of Christmas Presents   279

9.4   **Policies that Shift Supply Curves**   280
   Restricting the Number of Firms   281
   APPLICATION   Taxicab Medallions   283
   Excluding Certain Groups from Owning Firms   284
   APPLICATION   Discriminating Against Groups   284
   Raising Entry and Exit Costs   285
   APPLICATION   Barriers to Protect Our Way of Life   286
   APPLICATION   Job Termination Laws   287

9.5   **Policies that Create A Wedge Between Supply and Demand**   287
   Welfare Effects of a Sales Tax   287
   Welfare Effects of a Price Floor   289
   SOLVED PROBLEM 9.3   291
   APPLICATION   International Cost of Agricultural Subsidies   293
   Welfare Effects of a Price Ceiling   293
   SOLVED PROBLEM 9.4   294

9.6   **Comparing Both Types of Policies: Imports**   295
   Free Trade Versus a Ban on Imports   296
   Free Trade Versus a Tariff   296
   Free Trade Versus a Quota   300
   APPLICATION   Japanese Nontariff Barriers   300
   Rent Seeking   301

Summary   302
Problems   303
Math Problems   304

CHAPTER 10 *General Equilibrium and
                Economic Welfare*   305

10.1 General Equilibrium   306
      Feedback Between Competitive Markets   307
      APPLICATION   Sin Taxes   310
      Minimum Wages with Incomplete
         Coverage   311
      APPLICATION   Living-Wage Laws   313
      SOLVED PROBLEM 10.1   313

10.2 Trading Between Two People   314
      Endowments   315
      Mutually Beneficial Trades   315
      SOLVED PROBLEM 10.2   319
      Bargaining Ability   319

10.3 Competitive Exchange   319
      Competitive Equilibrium   320
      The Efficiency of Competition   322
      Obtaining Any Efficient Allocation
         Using Competition   322

10.4 Production and Trading   323
      Comparative Advantage   323
      SOLVED PROBLEM 10.3   325
      Efficient Product Mix   328
      Competition   328
      APPLICATION   Auto Trade Barriers   330

10.5 Efficiency and Equity   331
      Role of the Government   331
      APPLICATION   Wealth Distribution in the
                    United States   332
      Efficiency   334
      Equity   335
      Efficiency Versus Equity   339

Summary   340
Problems   341
Math Problems   341

**PART FIVE   MARKET POWER AND
              MARKET STRUCTURE**

CHAPTER 11 *Monopoly*   343

11.1 Monopoly Profit Maximization   344
      Marginal Revenue   344
      Choosing Price or Quantity   348

      Graphical Approach   349
      Mathematical Approach   350

11.2 Market Power   352
      Market Power and the Shape of the
         Demand Curve   352
      Lerner Index   353
      APPLICATION   Humana Hospitals   354
      Sources of Market Power   354
      APPLICATION   Airport Monopolies   355

★11.3 Effects of a Shift of the Demand Curve   356

11.4 Welfare Effects of Monopoly   357
      Graphing the Welfare Loss   357
      APPLICATION   Deadweight Loss of the
                    U.S. Postal Service   359
      SOLVED PROBLEM 11.1   360
      ★Welfare Effects of Ad Valorem Versus
         Specific Taxes   362

11.5 Cost Advantages that Create Monopolies   364
      Sources of Cost Advantages   364
      Natural Monopoly   364
      SOLVED PROBLEM 11.2   366
      APPLICATION   Electric Power Utilities   366

11.6 Government Actions that Create
      Monopolies   367
      Barriers to Entry   367
      APPLICATION   Government Sales
                    of Monopolies   368
      Patents   368
      APPLICATION   A Drug Patent   369

11.7 Government Actions That Reduce
      Market Power   372
      Regulating Monopolies   372
      SOLVED PROBLEM 11.3   374
      Increasing Competition   378
      APPLICATION   Monopoly in Names   378
      Dominant Firm and Competitive Fringe   379

Summary   380
Problems   381
Math Problems   382

CHAPTER 12 *Pricing*   383

12.1 Why and How Firms Price Discriminate   384
      Why Price Discrimination Pays   384
      APPLICATION   Disneyland Pricing   386
      Who Can Price Discriminate   387
      Preventing Resales   388

Not All Price Differences Are Price
   Discrimination   388
Types of Price Discrimination   389

12.2 **Perfect Price Discrimination**   389
How a Firm Perfectly Price Discriminates   389
   APPLICATION   A Hot Sale of Coke   391
Perfect Price Discrimination: Efficient
   but Hurts Consumers   391
   APPLICATION   Tagamet Revisited   393
   SOLVED PROBLEM 12.1   394
Transaction Costs and Perfect Price
   Discrimination   395

12.3 **Quantity Discrimination**   396

12.4 **Multimarket Price Discrimination**   397
Multimarket Price Discrimination
   with Two Groups   398
   SOLVED PROBLEM 12.2   400
   APPLICATION   Generics and Brand-Name
                 Loyalty   401
Identifying Groups   403
   APPLICATION   Getting Consumers to Identify
                 Themselves   404
Welfare Effects of Multimarket Price
   Discrimination   405
   APPLICATION   Taking Women to the Cleaners   406

12.5 **Two-Part Tariffs**   406
A Two-Part Tariff with Identical Consumers   407
A Two-Part Tariff with Nonidentical
   Consumers   408
   APPLICATION   Warehouse Stores   410

12.6 **Tie-in Sales**   410
Requirement Tie-In Sales   410
   APPLICATION   IBM   411
Bundling   411
   APPLICATION   Automatic Savings   413

Summary   413
Problems   414
Math Problems   415

CHAPTER 13 *Oligopoly and Monopolistic
                Competition*   416

13.1 **Market Structures**   417

13.2 **Game Theory**   419
A Single-Period, Two-Firm, Quantity-Setting
   Game   419
Why Firms Do Not Cooperate in a
   Single-Period Game   421

Collusion in Repeated Games   422
   APPLICATION   Oligopoly Competition
                 Among Governments   423

13.3 **Cooperative Oligopoly Models**   423
Laws Against Cartels   424
Why Cartels Form   425
Why Cartels Fail   426
Maintaining Cartels   427
   APPLICATION   Vitamin Price Fixing   428
   APPLICATION   A Government-Created Cartel   429
Entry and Cartel Success   430
   APPLICATION   Bail Bonds   430
Mergers   430
   APPLICATION   Airline Mergers   430

13.4 **Cournot Model of Noncooperative
       Oligopoly**   431
Cournot Model of an Airline Market   431
Comparing the Cournot and Cartel Models   436
The Cournot Equilibrium and the Number
   of Firms   438
   APPLICATION   Appliances   440

13.5 **Stackelberg Model of Noncooperative
       Behavior**   440
Stackelberg Game Tree   440
Stackelberg Graphical Model   442
Why Moving Sequentially Is Essential   444
Strategic Trade Policy   444
   APPLICATION   Airbus and Boeing   448
   SOLVED PROBLEM 13.1   449

13.6 **Comparison of Collusive, Cournot,
       Stackelberg, and Competitive Equilibria**   450
   APPLICATION   Deadweight Losses in the
                 Food and Tobacco Industries   451

13.7 **Monopolistic Competition**   451
Monopolistically Competitive Equilibrium   452
Fixed Costs and the Number of Firms   452
   SOLVED PROBLEM 13.2   455
   APPLICATION   Entry and Airline Prices   455

13.8 **Bertrand Price-Setting Model**   456
Bertrand Equilibrium with Identical
   Products   456
Bertrand Equilibrium with Differentiated
   Products   459
Differentiating Products   459
   APPLICATION   Toothbrushes   460
   APPLICATION   Welfare Gain from
                 New Cereals   461

Summary 462
Problems 463
Math Problems 464

CHAPTER 14 *Strategy* 465

14.1 **Preventing Entry: Simultaneous Decisions** 466
Room for Two Firms 467
Room for Only One Firm 468
Summary of the Simultaneous-Decision
Entry Game 469
SOLVED PROBLEM 14.1 469

14.2 **Preventing Entry: Sequential Decisions** 470
To Act or Not to Act? 471
APPLICATION Government Deterrence 473
Commitment and Entry Prevention 473
SOLVED PROBLEM 14.2 477
Commitment and Fixed Costs 477
SOLVED PROBLEM 14.3 482

14.3 **Creating and Using Cost Advantages** 484
Lowering Marginal Cost While Raising
Total Cost 484
Learning by Doing 485
Raising Rivals' Costs 485
APPLICATION Hitting Rivals Where It Hurts 486
APPLICATION Preventing Customers from
Switching 487
Raising All Firms' Costs 488
Advantages and Disadvantages to
Moving First 489
Preventing Entry: Summary 489
APPLICATION Evidence on Strategic
Entry Deterrence 489

14.4 **Advertising** 491
Monopoly Advertising 491
APPLICATION Drug Commercials 492
APPLICATION O. J. Trial Effect 494
Strategic Advertising 495
APPLICATION Pink Toothbrush 495
APPLICATION Secret Ingredients 496

Summary 498
Problems 499
Math Problems 500

PART SIX FACTOR MARKETS

CHAPTER 15 *Factor Markets and*
Vertical Integration 501

15.1 **Competitive Factor Market** 502

Short-Run Factor Demand of a Firm 502
SOLVED PROBLEM 15.1 507
APPLICATION Thread Mill 507
Long-Run Factor Demand 508
Factor Market Demand 509
Competitive Factor Market Equilibrium 511

15.2 **Effect of Monopolies on Factor Markets** 512
Market Structure and Factor Demands 512
A Model of Market Power in Input and
Output Markets 514
APPLICATION Record Prices 516
APPLICATION Union Monopoly Power 517
SOLVED PROBLEM 15.2 519
APPLICATION Baseball Salaries and
Ticket Prices 520

15.3 **Monopsony** 521
Monopsony Profit Maximization 521
APPLICATION Monopsony Wage Setting 524
Welfare Effects of Monopsony 524
SOLVED PROBLEM 15.3 524
Monopsony Price Discrimination 526
APPLICATION Monopsony Price
Discrimination 527

15.4 **Vertical Integration** 528
Stages of Production 528
Degree of Vertical Integration 529
APPLICATION Outsourcing 529
Produce or Buy 530
APPLICATION Aluminum 531
APPLICATION Cutting Off Oxygen 533

Summary 534
Problems 534
Math Problems 535

CHAPTER 16 *Interest Rates, Investments,*
and Capital Markets 537

16.1 **Comparing Money Today to Money
in the Future** 538
Interest Rates 538
APPLICATION Usury 538
Using Interest Rates to Connect the Present
and Future 541
APPLICATION Power of Compounding 542
Stream of Payments 543
SOLVED PROBLEM 16.1 545
APPLICATION Saving for Retirement 546
Inflation and Discounting 547
APPLICATION Winning the Lottery 549

16.2 Choices over Time   550
    APPLICATION   Comparing Two Contracts   550
    Investing   551
      SOLVED PROBLEM 16.2   552
      SOLVED PROBLEM 16.3   554
    Rate of Return on Bonds   554
    Durability   555
    APPLICATION   Durability of Telephone Poles   555
    Human Capital   556

16.3 Exhaustible Resources   559
    When to Sell an Exhaustible Resource   559
    Price of a Scarce Exhaustible Resource   560
    APPLICATION   Redwood Trees   563
    Why Price May Be Constant or Fall   564

16.4 Capital Markets, Interest Rates, and
     Investments   566
    Increased Savings, More Investment   566
    Increased Government Demand, Less Private
     Investment   567
    APPLICATION   Taking from Future Generations   568

Summary   569
Problems   569
Math Problems   570

PART SEVEN   UNCERTAINTY, MISSING MARKETS,
              AND LIMITED INFORMATION

CHAPTER 17   Uncertainty   571

17.1 Degree of Risk   572
    Probability   572
    Expected Value   574
      SOLVED PROBLEM 17.1   574
    Variance and Standard Deviation   575

17.2 Decision Making Under Uncertainty   577
    Expected Utility   577
    Risk Aversion   578
      SOLVED PROBLEM 17.2   580
    Risk Neutrality   581
    Risk Preference   582
    APPLICATION   Gambling   583

17.3 Avoiding Risk   585
    Just Say No   586
    Obtain Information   586
    APPLICATION   Bond Ratings   586
    Diversify   587
    APPLICATION   Laws Limiting Diversification   589
    Insure   589

    SOLVED PROBLEM 17.3   590
    APPLICATION   Flight Insurance   592
    APPLICATION   Natural Disasters   593

17.4 Investing Under Uncertainty   593
    How Investing Depends on Attitudes
     Toward Risk   594
    APPLICATION   Premium for a Riskier
               Investment   595
    Investing with Uncertainty and Discounting   596
    Investing with Altered Probabilities   597
    APPLICATION   Loans, Defaults, and
               Usury Laws   598

Summary   599
Problems   600
Math Problems   601

CHAPTER 18   Externalities, Commons,
            and Public Goods   602

18.1 Externalities   603
    APPLICATION   Michael Jordan's Positive
               Externalities   604

18.2 The Inefficiency of Competition with
     Externalities   604
    Supply-and-Demand Analysis   605
    APPLICATION   Waste Not   607
    SOLVED PROBLEM 18.1   611
    APPLICATION   Taxes on Fuels   611
    Cost-Benefit Analysis   612
    APPLICATION   Emissions Standards
               for Ozone   614

18.3 Market Structure and Externalities   616
    Monopoly and Externalities   616
    Monopoly Versus Competitive Welfare
     with Externalities   617
    SOLVED PROBLEM 18.2   618
    Taxing Externalities in Noncompetitive
     Markets   618

18.4 Allocating Property Rights to Reduce
     Externalities   619
    Coase Theorem   619
    Markets for Pollution   622
    APPLICATION   Sulfur Dioxide Market   623

18.5 Common Property   624
    Overuse of Common Property   624
    APPLICATION   Extensive Overfishing   625
    Solving the Commons Problem   626
    APPLICATION   For Whom the Bridge Tolls   626

18.6 **Public Goods**   627
    Types of Goods   627
    Markets for Public Goods   629
    Reducing Free Riding   631
    APPLICATION Free Riding on Water   632
    Valuing Public Goods   633

Summary   635
Problems   635
Math Problems   636

CHAPTER 19 *Asymmetric Information*   637

19.1 **Problems Due to Asymmetric Information** 638

19.2 **Responses to Adverse Selection**   639
    Controlling Opportunistic Behavior
      Through Universal Coverage   639
    Equalizing Information   640
    APPLICATION Risky Hobbies   641

19.3 **How Ignorance About Quality Drives
    Out High-Quality Goods**   641
    Lemons Market with Fixed Quality   642
    SOLVED PROBLEM 19.1   644
    Lemons Market with Variable Quality   645
    Limiting Lemons   646
    APPLICATION Recycling Lemons   646
    APPLICATION College Guarantee   649

19.4 **Price Discrimination Due to False
    Beliefs About Quality**   650
    APPLICATION Multiple Brand Names   651

19.5 **Market Power from Price Ignorance**   651
    Tourist-Trap Model   652
    SOLVED PROBLEM 19.2   654
    Advertising and Prices   654
    APPLICATION Advertising Lowers Prices   654

19.6 **Problems Arising from Ignorance
    When Hiring**   655
    Information About Employment Risks   655
    Cheap Talk   656
    Education as a Signal   658
    SOLVED PROBLEM 19.3   660
    Screening in Hiring   663

Summary   664
Problems   665
Math Problems   666

CHAPTER 20 *Contracts and Moral Hazards*   667

20.1 **Principal-Agent Problem**   668
    A Model   669
    Types of Contracts   669
    Efficiency   670

20.2 **Production Efficiency**   671
    Efficient Contract   671
    Full Information   672
    SOLVED PROBLEM 20.1   677
    Asymmetric Information   677
    APPLICATION Contracts and Productivity
      in Agriculture   678

20.3 **Trade-Off between Efficiency in
    Production and in Risk Bearing**   679
    Contracts and Efficiency   680
    Choosing the Best Contract   682
    APPLICATION Lawyers' Contingent Fees   683
    SOLVED PROBLEM 20.2   684

20.4 **Payments Linked to Production or Profit** 685
    Piece-Rate Hire Contracts   685
    APPLICATION Pleased to Be Paid by
      the Piece   686
    Contingent Contract Rewards Linked to
      a Firm's Success   687
    APPLICATION Increasing Use of Incentives 687

20.5 **Monitoring**   688
    Bonding   689
    SOLVED PROBLEM 20.3   690
    Deferred Payments   691
    Efficiency Wages   692
    After-the-Fact Monitoring   694
    APPLICATION Abusing Leased Cars   695
    APPLICATION Savings and Loans
      Moral Hazards   696

20.6 **Checks on Principals**   697
    APPLICATION Performance Termination
      Contracts   698

20.7 **Contract Choice**   700

Summary   701
Problems   702
Math Problems   703

Chapter Appendixes

Appendix 2A: Regressions   A–1
Appendix 3A: Effects of a Specific Tax on Equilibrium   A–3
Appendix 4A: Utility and Indifference Curves   A–4
Appendix 4B: Maximizing Utility   A–6
Appendix 5A: The Slutsky Equation   A–8
Appendix 5B: Labor-Leisure Model   A–9
Appendix 6A: Properties of Marginal and
    Average Product Curves   A–10
Appendix 6B: Cobb-Douglas Production Function   A–11
Appendix 7A: Minimum of the Average Cost Curve   A–11
Appendix 7B: Norwegian Printing Firm's Short-Run
    Cost Curves   A–12
Appendix 7C: Minimizing Cost   A–13
Appendix 8A: The Elasticity of the Residual Demand   A–15
Appendix 8B: Profit Maximization   A–15
Appendix 9A: Demand Elasticities and Surplus   A–16
Appendix 11A: Relationship Between a Linear
    Demand Curve and Its Marginal
    Revenue Curve   A–17
Appendix 11B: Incidence of a Specific Tax on
    a Monopoly   A–17

Appendix 12A: Perfect Price Discrimination   A–18
Appendix 12B: Quantity Discrimination   A–19
Appendix 12C: Multimarket Price Discrimination   A–19
Appendix 12D: Two-Part Tariffs   A–20
Appendix 13A: Cournot Equilibrium   A–20
Appendix 13B: Stackelberg Equilibrium   A–23
Appendix 13C: Bertrand Equilibrium   A–24
Appendix 14A: Mixed Strategies   A–25
Appendix 14B: Profit-Maximizing Advertising
    and Production   A–25
Appendix 15A: Factor Demands   A–26
Appendix 15B: Monopsony   A–27
Appendix 16A: Perpetuity   A–28
Appendix 18A: Welfare Effects of Pollution in a
    Competitive Market   A–29
Appendix 20A: Nonshirking Condition   A–30

Answers to Selected Problems   A–31
Definitions   A–41
References   A–47
Sources for Applications   A–53
Credits   A–60
Index   A–61

PREFACE

When I was a student, I fell in love with microeconomics because it cleared up many mysteries about the world and provided the means to answer new questions. I wrote this book to show students that economic theory has practical, problem-solving uses and is not an empty academic exercise.

This book shows how individuals, policy makers, and firms can use microeconomic tools to analyze and resolve problems. For example, students learn that

- individuals can draw on microeconomic theories when deciding about issues such as whether to invest and whether to sign a contract that pegs prices to the government's measure of inflation;
- policy makers (and voters) can employ microeconomics to predict the impact of taxes, regulations, and other measures before they are enacted;
- lawyers and judges use microeconomics in antitrust, discrimination, and contract cases;
- firms apply microeconomic principles to produce at least cost and maximize profit, select strategies, decide whether to buy from a market or to produce internally, and write contracts to provide optimal incentives for employees.

My experience in teaching microeconomics for the departments of economics at MIT, the University of Pennsylvania, and the University of California, Berkeley; the Department of Agricultural and Resource Economics at Berkeley; and the Wharton Business School has convinced me that students prefer this emphasis on real-world issues.

FEATURES

This book differs from other microeconomics texts in three main ways. First, it integrates real-world "widget-free" examples throughout the exposition, in addition to offering extended applications. Second, it places greater emphasis than other texts on modern theories—such as industrial organization theories, game theory, transaction cost theory, information theory, and contract theory—that are useful in analyzing actual markets. Third, it employs a step-by-step approach to demonstrate how to use microeconomic theory to solve problems and analyze policy issues.

Widget-Free Economics

To convince students that economics is practical and useful, not just a textbook exercise, this text presents theories using real-world examples rather than made-up analyses of widgets, those nonexistent products beloved by earlier generations of textbook writers. These real economic "stories" are integrated into the formal presentation of many economic theories, discussed in featured Applications, and analyzed in what-if policy discussions.

Integrated Real-World Examples. The book uses real-world examples throughout the narrative to illustrate many basic theories of microeconomics. Students learn the basic model of supply and demand using estimated supply-and-demand curves for Canadian processed pork. They analyze consumer choice employing typical consumers' estimated indifference curves between beer and wine and mill workers' indifference curves between income and leisure. They learn about production and cost functions using evidence from a Norwegian printing firm. Students see monopoly theory applied to a patented pharmaceutical, Tagamet. They use oligopoly theories to analyze the rivalry between United Airlines and American Airlines on the Chicago–Los Angeles route and between Coke and Pepsi in the cola industry.

Applications. The text also includes many featured Applications to illustrate the versatility of microeconomic theory. One such Application derives an isoquant for semiconductors using actual data. Other Applications look at measures of the pleasure consumers get from television, and the amount by which recipients value Christmas presents relative to the cost to gift givers. Applications analyze the impact of government subsidies on the rivalry between Boeing and Airbus and the effects of the coverage of the O. J. Simpson trial on television advertising. One Application investigates whether buying flight insurance makes sense.

What-If Policy Analysis. In addition, the book uses economic models to probe the likely outcomes of changes in public policies. Students learn how to conduct what-if analyses of policies such as taxes, subsidies, barriers to entry, price floors and ceilings, quotas and tariffs, zoning, laws limiting diversification, pollution controls, licensing laws, and laws governing pensions. The text analyzes the effects of taxes on virtually every type of market.

The book also reveals the limits of economic theory for policy analysis. For example, to illustrate why attention to actual institutions is important, the text uses three different models to show how the effects of minimum wages vary across types of markets and institutions. Similarly, the text illustrates that a minimum wage law that is harmful in a competitive market may be desirable in certain noncompetitive markets.

| **Modern Theories** | The first half of the book (Chapters 1–10) examines competitive markets and shows that competition has very desirable properties. The second half (Chapters 11–20) concentrates on imperfectly competitive markets, where firms have market power, firms and consumers are uncertain about the future and have limited information, and there are externalities and public goods. |

The book goes beyond basic microeconomic theory to look at theories and applications from many important contemporary fields of economics. Extensive coverage of problems from resource economics, labor economics, international trade, public finance, and industrial organization is featured throughout.

This book differs from other microeconomics texts by using game theory throughout the second half rather than isolating the topic in a single chapter. Game theory and decision trees are used to study oligopoly quantity and price setting, strategic trade policy, strategic behavior in multiperiod games (such as collusion and preventing entry), strategic advertising, investing when there's uncertainty about the future, and pollution (the Coase Theorem). Unlike most texts, this book covers pure and mixed strategies and analyzes both normal-form and extensive-form games.

The last two chapters draw from modern contract theory to analyze adverse selection and moral hazard extensively, instead of (as other texts do) mentioning these topics only in passing, if at all. The text covers lemons markets, signaling, preventing shirking, and the revelation of information (including through contract choice).

Step-by-Step Problem Solving	Many professors report that their biggest challenge in teaching microeconomics is helping students learn to solve new problems. This book is based on the belief that the best way to teach this important skill is to demonstrate problem solving repeatedly and then to give students exercises to do on their own. Each chapter (except Chapter 1) provides several Solved Problems showing students how to answer qualitative and quantitative problems using a step-by-step approach. Rather than empty arithmetic exercises demanding no more of students than to employ algebra or a memorized mathematical formula, the Solved Problems focus on important economic issues such as analyzing government policies and determining firms' optimal strategies.

One Solved Problem uses game theory to examine the competition between Netscape and Microsoft in the Internet browser market. Another shows how a monopolistically competitive airline equilibrium would change if fixed costs (such as fees for landing slots) rise. Others examine why firms charge different prices at factory stores than elsewhere, and when markets for lemons exist, among many other topics.

The Solved Problems illustrate how to approach the two sets of formal end-of-chapter problems. The first set of problems poses questions that students can solve using graphs or verbal arguments; the second set requires the use of math. The answers to selected end-of-chapter problems appear at the end of the book, and the solutions to the remaining problems may be found in the Instructor's Manual and at **www.awlonline.com/perloff**.

CHANGES IN THE SECOND EDITION

This Second Edition is substantially updated and reorganized based on the very helpful suggestions of faculty and students who used the First Edition. In addition, I have made numerous small changes throughout the book in response to their insightful comments.

Because adopters of the First Edition said that one of the main reasons that they chose the book was its up-to-date examples, I have added 21 new Applications. Most of these are based on 1998–2000 newspaper and journal articles, as well as other sources. These Applications cover taxes on the Internet, the end of the monopoly in obtaining Internet addresses, the living wage, the latest methods used by Coke to price discriminate, and baseball ticket-pricing strategies, among others. Also, I have integrated several new, longer examples in the text. For example, I analyze why Sony has set a different price in Japan than in the United States for its robot dog, Aibo, and study the effect of taxes in the American market for roses. In addition, I have revised and updated 29 other Applications and added new problems (many based on recent events) at the end of chapters. To make room for this new material, I moved some of the older Applications to the book's companion Web site at **www.awlonline.com/perloff**, where they are easily accessible.

I also reorganized the book slightly, in response to feedback from several adopters of the First Edition who recommended that the former Chapter 13 (Pricing) be moved up to follow immediately after Chapter 11 (Monopoly). So the new sequence is Monopoly (Chapter 11), then Pricing (Chapter 12), and then Oligopoly and Monopolistic Competition (Chapter 13). Further, in this edition, Chapter 13 examines *all* the standard oligopoly models, including Bertrand, which I formerly covered in the chapter on pricing.

ALTERNATIVE ORGANIZATIONS

Because instructors differ as to the order in which they cover material, this text has been designed for maximum flexibility. The most common approach to teaching microeconomics is to follow the sequence of the chapters in the first half of this book: supply and demand (Chapters 2 and 3), consumer theory (Chapters 4 and 5), the theory of the firm (Chapters 6 and 7), and the competitive model (Chapters 8 and 9). Many instructors then cover monopoly (Chapter 11), price discrimination (Chapter 12), oligopoly (Chapter 13), input markets (Chapter 15), uncertainty (Chapter 17), and externalities (Chapter 18).

A common variant is to present uncertainty (Sections 17.1 through 17.3) immediately after consumer theory. Many instructors like to take up welfare issues between discussions of the competitive model and noncompetitive models, as Chapter 10, on general equilibrium and economic welfare, does. Alternatively, that chapter may be covered at the end of the course. Faculty can assign material on factor markets earlier (Section 15.1 could follow the chapters on competition, and the remaining sections could follow Chapter 11). The material in Chapters 14–20 can be presented in a variety of orders, though Chapter 20 should follow Chapter 19 if both are covered, and Section 17.4 should follow Chapter 16.

Many business school courses skip consumer theory (and possibly some aspects of supply and demand, such as Chapter 3) to allow more time for consideration of the topics covered in the second half of this book. Business school faculty may want to place particular emphasis on strategies (Chapter 14), vertical integration (Section 15.4), capital markets (Chapter 16), and modern contract theory (Chapters 19 and 20).

Technically demanding sections are marked with a star (★). Subsequent sections and chapters can be understood even if these sections are skipped.

SUPPLEMENTS TO ACCOMPANY *MICROECONOMICS*

Excellent supplements for this textbook are available for students and faculty. These supplements have been updated for the Second Edition. The **Study Guide,** by Charles F. Mason of the University of Wyoming and Robert Whaples of Wake Forest University, provides students with a quick guide to Key Concepts and Formulas, as well as additional Applications, and it walks them through the solution of many problems. Students can then work through a large number of Practice Problems on their own and check their answers against those in the Guide. At the end of each Study Guide chapter is a set of Exercises suitable for homework assignments. Also available to students is the **Student Resource Kit** by Gautam Sethi of the University of California, Berkeley. It features a review of the main text concepts, some sample Solved Problems, and handy flash cards to aid in the review of key terms and ideas. And at **www.awlonline.com/perloff,** students will find the text figures in downloadable form, self-assessment chapter quizzes, a sample midterm and final exam, and additional Applications and Solved Problems.

The **Instructor's Manual,** by Peter von Allmen of Moravian College, has many useful and creative teaching ideas. It also offers additional Applications, as well as extra problems and answers, and it provides solutions for the end-of-chapter text problems for which answers are not given at the end of this book. The **Test Bank,** by Hayley Chouinard of the University of California, Berkeley, and Peter Zaleski of Villanova University, has been substantially revised. It features many different types of problems of varying levels of complexity, suitable for homework assignments and exams. A computerized testing program for Windows users, **TestGen-EQ,** provides the same questions as the print Test Bank in a versatile electronic format.

Additionally for instructors, all the text figures are available both as full-color **PowerPoint Presentation** slides and as separately bound black-and-white **Transparency Masters.** The perforated and three-hole-punched book containing the masters also includes convenient **Student Graph Worksheets** reproducing all the text figures; these may be photocopied and distributed to students for class note taking.

Finally, a set of original **Microeconomics Experiments** for instructors who opt to use active classroom learning to help their students grasp key principles is available at **www.awlonline.com/perloff.**

ACKNOWLEDGMENTS

My greatest debt is to my students and to the two best development editors in the business, Jane Tufts and Sylvia Mallory. My students at MIT, the University of Pennsylvania, and the University of California, Berkeley, patiently dealt with my various approaches to teaching them microeconomics and made useful (and generally polite) suggestions. I received constructive student and faculty comments on early versions of this book when it was used by faculty members at Berkeley and by Jerome Culp at the Duke University Law School.

Jane Tufts reviewed drafts of this book for content and presentation. By showing me how to present the material as clearly, orderly, and thoroughly as possible, she greatly strengthened this text. Sylvia Mallory worked valiantly to improve my writing style and helped to shape and improve every aspect of the book's contents and appearance. In addition, Jane and Sylvia collected the views and advice of many reviewers from around the world.

My excellent research assistants—Hayley Chouinard, R. Scott Hacker, Nancy McCarthy, Enrico Moretti, Asa Sajise, Gautam Sethi, Zhihua Shen, Klaas van't Veld, and Ximing Wu—worked hard to collect facts, develop examples, and check material. I am particularly grateful to Klaas, Scott, and Zhihua for helping to produce many of the best examples in the book. Nancy, Enrico, Hayley, Ximing, and Asa showed flair in collecting facts. Hayley and Gautam carefully checked the book and made very helpful suggestions.

Many people were very generous in providing me with data, models, and examples, including the following: Alan Auerbach, University of California, Berkeley: generational differences in tax burdens; Peter Berck, University of California, Berkeley: exhaustible resources and investments; James Brander, University of British Columbia: American Airlines and United Airlines; Richard Garbaccio, Brandeis University: China; Farid Gasmi, Université des Sciences Sociales, Toulouse: Coke and Pepsi; Claudia Goldin, Harvard University: income distribution; Rachel Goodhue, University of California, Davis: incentives; William Greene, New York University: power plants; Nile Hatch, University of Illinois: semiconductors and learning by doing; Gloria Helfand, University of Michigan: ozone example; Charles Hyde, University of Melbourne: demand estimates; Fahad Khalil, University of Washington: contract theory; Jean-Jacques Laffont, Université des Sciences Sociales, Toulouse: Coke and Pepsi; Karl D. Meilke, University of Guelph: pork; Giancarlo Moschini, Iowa State University: pork; Michael Roberts, University of California, Berkeley: exhaustible resources; Peter von Allmen, Moravian College: various applications; Quang Vuong, Université des Sciences Sociales, Toulouse, and University of Southern California: Coke and Pepsi.

Writing a textbook is hard work for everyone involved. I am grateful to the many teachers of microeconomics who spent untold hours reading and commenting on proposals and chapters. Many of the best ideas in this book are due to them. I particularly thank W. Bruce Allen of the Wharton School of Business, who read every single word in the First Edition at least twice (and commented productively on nearly each one) and James Brander, University of British Columbia, who made insightful comments on both editions. James Dearden, Lehigh University; Steven Goldman, University of California, Berkeley; Charles F. Mason, University of Wyoming; David Reitman, Department of Justice; Nora Underwood, University of California, Davis; and Robert Whaples, Wake Forest University, read many chapters and offered particularly useful comments. Peter Berck made major contributions to

Chapter 16. I also thank the following reviewers, who provided valuable comments at various stages:

M. Shahid Alam, Northeastern Univ.
Niels Anthonisen, Univ. of Western Ontario
S. Brock Blomberg, Wellesley College
Vic Brajer, California State Univ., Fullerton
Cory S. Capps, Univ. of Illinois,
    Urbana–Champaign
Leo Chan, Univ. of Kansas
Joni S. Charles, Southwest Texas State Univ.
Kwang Soo Cheong, Univ. of Hawaii at
    Manoa
Dean Croushore, Federal Reserve Bank of
    Philadelphia
Andrew Daughety, Vanderbilt Univ.
Carl Davidson, Michigan State Univ.
John Edgren, Eastern Michigan Univ.
Roy Gardner, Indiana Univ.
Rod Garratt, Univ. of California, Santa
    Barbara
Wei Ge, Bucknell Univ.
J. Fred Giertz, Univ. of Illinois,
    Urbana–Champaign
Srihari Govindan, Univ. of Western Ontario
Thomas A. Gresik, Pennsylvania State Univ.
Jonathan Gruber, MIT
Claire Hammond, Wake Forest Univ.
John A. Hansen, State Univ. of New York,
    Fredonia
L. Dean Hiebert, Illinois State Univ.
Kathryn Ierulli, Univ. of Illinois, Chicago
D. Gale Johnson, Univ. of Chicago
Charles Kahn, Univ. of Illinois,
    Urbana–Champaign
Alan Kessler, Providence College
Kate Krause, Univ. of New Mexico
Fred Luk, Univ. of California, Los Angeles
Robert Main, Butler Univ.
David Malueg, Tulane Univ.
Steve Margolis, North Carolina State Univ.

James Meehan, Colby College
Claudio Mezzetti, Univ. of North Carolina,
    Chapel Hill
Janet Mitchell, Cornell Univ.
Babu Nahata, Univ. of Louisville
Kathryn Nantz, Fairfield Univ.
Patrick B. O'Neil, Univ. of North Dakota
John Palmer, Univ. of Western Ontario
Christos Papahristodoulou, Uppsala Univ.
Sharon Pearson, Univ. of Alberta
Ingrid Peters-Fransen, Wilfrid Laurier Univ.
Sunder Ramaswamy, Middlebury College
Luca Rigotti, Tillburg Univ.
S. Abu Turab Rizvi, Univ. of Vermont
Bee Yan Aw Roberts, Pennsylvania State
    Univ.
Nancy Rose, Sloan School of Business, MIT
Joshua Rosenbloom, Univ. of Kansas
David Sappington, Univ. of Florida
Richard Sexton, Univ. of California, Davis
William Doyle Smith, Univ. of Texas at
    El Paso
Philip Sorenson, Florida State Univ.
Peter Soule, Park College
Shankar Subramanian, Cornell Univ.
Beck A. Taylor, Baylor Univ.
Wade Thomas, State Univ. of New York,
    Oneonta
Judith Thornton, Univ. of Washington
Kay Unger, Univ. of Montana
Peter von Allmen, Moravian College
Eleanor T. von Ende, Texas Tech Univ.
Lawrence J. White, New York Univ.
John Whitehead, East Carolina Univ.
Colin Wright, Claremont McKenna College
Peter Zaleski, Villanova Univ.
Mark Zupan, Univ. of Arizona

In addition, I thank Bob Solow, the world's finest economics teacher, who showed me how to simplify models without losing their essence. I've also learned a great deal over the years about economics and writing from my coauthors on other projects, especially Dennis Carlton (my coauthor on *Modern Industrial Organization*), Jackie Persons, Steve Salop, Michael Wachter, Larry Karp, Peter Berck, and Dan Rubinfeld (whom I thank for still talking to me despite my decision to write this book).

It was a pleasure to work with the good people at Addison-Wesley, who were incredibly helpful in producing this book. Marjorie Williams and Barbara Rifkin signed me to write it. Denise Clinton, Executive Editor for Economics and Finance, was instrumental in making the entire process work. Nancy Fenton supervised the production process and assembled the extended publishing team. Bruce Emmer ably copyedited the book. Scott Silva did a masterful job of typesetting the book. Gina Hagen designed the handsome interior and cover, and Jim McLaughlin skillfully prepared the figures. Ingrid Mount and the rest of the staff at Elm Street Publishing Services have my sincere thanks for keeping the project on track and on schedule. I also want to acknowledge, with gratitude, the efforts of Melissa Honig in developing the Web site and Dara Lanier in marketing the entire program.

Finally, I thank my family, Mimi Perloff, Jackie Persons, and Lisa Perloff (p. 386), for their great patience and support during the nearly endless writing process. And I apologize for misusing their names—and those of my other relatives and friends—in the book!

J. M. P.

Introduction

I've often wondered what goes into a hot dog. Now I know and I wish I didn't.
—William Zinsser

If each of us could get all the food, clothing, and toys we want without working, no one would study economics. Unfortunately, most of the good things in life are scarce—we can't all have as much as we want. Thus scarcity is the mother of economics.

Microeconomics is the study of how individuals and firms make themselves as well off as possible in a world of scarcity and the consequences of those individual decisions for markets and the entire economy. In studying microeconomics, we examine how individual consumers and firms make decisions and how the interaction of many individual decisions affects markets.

Microeconomics is often called *price theory* to emphasize the important role that prices play. Microeconomics explains how the actions of all buyers and sellers determine prices and how prices influence the decisions and actions of individual buyers and sellers.

1. **Microeconomics: the allocation of scarce resources:** Microeconomics is the study of the allocation of scarce resources.
2. **Models:** Economists use models to make testable predictions.
3. **Uses of microeconomic models:** Individuals, governments, and firms use microeconomic models and predictions in decision making.

IN THIS CHAPTER,

WE EXAMINE

THREE MAIN

TOPICS

1.1 | MICROECONOMICS: THE ALLOCATION OF SCARCE RESOURCES

Individuals and firms allocate their limited resources to make themselves as well off as possible. Consumers pick the mix of goods and services that makes them as happy as possible given their limited wealth. Firms decide which goods to produce, where to produce them, how much to produce to maximize their profits, and how to produce those levels of output at the lowest cost by using more or less of various inputs such as labor, capital, materials, and energy. The owners of a depletable natural resource such as oil decide when to use it. Government decision makers—to benefit consumers, firms, or government bureaucrats—decide which goods and services the government produces and whether to subsidize, tax, or regulate industries and consumers.

Trade-Offs

People make trade-offs because they can't have everything. A society faces three key trade-offs:

- **Which goods and services to produce:** If a society produces more cars, it must produce fewer of other goods and services, because there are only so many *resources*—workers, raw materials, capital, and energy—available to produce goods.
- **How to produce:** To produce a given level of output, a firm must use more of one input if it uses less of another input. Cracker and cookie manufacturers switch between palm oil and coconut oil, depending on which is less expensive.
- **Who gets the goods and services:** The more of society's goods and services you get, the less someone else gets.

Who Makes the Decisions

These three allocation decisions may be made explicitly by the government or may reflect the interaction of independent decisions by many individual consumers and firms. In the former Soviet Union, the government told manufacturers how many cars of each type to make and which inputs to use to make them. The government also decided which consumers would get a car.

In most other countries, how many cars of each type are produced and who gets them are determined by how much it costs to make cars of a particular quality in the least expensive way and how much consumers are willing to pay for them. More consumers would own a handmade Rolls-Royce and fewer would buy a mass-produced Ford Taurus if a Rolls were not 21 times more expensive than a Taurus.

Application   **OREGON DECIDES WHICH MEDICAL TREATMENTS TO PROVIDE**

In 1989, to restrain the skyrocketing costs of Medicaid, which provides health care for low-income people, Oregon excluded some previously covered poor people. Almost immediately, state decision makers changed their mind. They decided that rather than reduce the number of poor people who receive aid, the government would further limit the range of services provided.

After a great deal of debate, the new plan went into effect in 1994. The state ranked 688 medical procedures using factors that included a treatment's medical effectiveness, its cost, and subjective social values about which treatments or conditions are most important to treat.

Medicaid covered only the top 568 of these procedures. Treatments were provided for all major diseases of women and children; all preventive and screening services; some treatments not currently covered by Medicaid requirements, such as dental procedures, hospice services, prescription drugs, most transplants, and routine physicals; preventive services such as maternity and newborn care and immunizations; and comfort care and diagnostic services. The plan did not pay to treat conditions that get better on their own, such as a viral sore throat, dizziness, and benign cysts in the eye; conditions for which home treatments are effective; and conditions for which treatment is generally ineffective, such as aggressive medical intervention for advanced cancer.

By 1999, the plan was being severely criticized on the grounds that there was little medical evidence to support the government's choice of which procedures to cover, that only half of the originally uninsured population was being covered, and that costs had risen 160% in the five years since the plan took effect. To avoid bankruptcy, the state further reduced the number of covered conditions by 32 and started requiring that recipients pay a fixed amount per year.

Thus Oregon's government makes two of the three main allocation decisions itself rather than leaving these decisions to individuals. The government decides who gets medical care: It provides some care to more Oregonians than just the poorest of the poor. The government also decides which services are provided.[1]

Prices Determine Allocations

An Economist's Theory of Reincarnation: If you're good, you come back on a higher level. Cats come back as dogs, dogs come back as horses, and people—if they've been real good like George Washington—come back as money.

Prices link the decisions about *which goods and services to produce, how to produce them,* and *who gets them.* Prices influence the decisions of individual consumers and firms, and the interactions of these decisions by consumers, firms, and the government determine price.

Interactions between consumers and firms take place in a **market**, which is an exchange mechanism that allows buyers to trade with sellers. A market may be a town square where people go to trade food and clothing, or it may be an international telecommunications network over which people buy and sell financial securities. Typically, when we talk about a single market, we refer to trade in a single good or group of goods that are closely related, such as soft drinks, movies, novels, or automobiles.[2]

Most of this book concerns how prices are determined within a market. We show that the *number of buyers and sellers* in a market and the amount of *information* they have help determine whether the price equals the cost of production. We also show that if there is no market—and hence no market price—serious problems, such as high levels of pollution, result.

---

[1] Sources for Applications appear at the end of the book.

[2] We use the term *market* loosely to illustrate economic concepts rather than to provide a legal definition. For example, when we say that "an increase in the price of gasoline in the Chicago market affects the price of gasoline in the St. Louis market," we mean that gasoline prices in the two cities are related. Lawyers use a more explicit definition of a market that turns on exactly how closely these prices are related. Whether there are two separate markets or a single combined market is a key issue in many legal cases.

TAX ON FAST-FOOD CONTAINERS

In 1994, the German Federal Administrative Court upheld the right of cities to impose taxes on disposable containers. One city, Kassel, requires snack bars and fast-food restaurants to pay a tax of 30¢ for each paper plate they use, 25¢ for each can or nonreturnable bottle, and 6¢ for each plastic spoon, fork, or knife. Such a large tax changes *how fast-food meals are produced*, as restaurants substitute from the now relatively more expensive disposable products to nondisposable products. After the tax, many fast-food outlets in Kassel began serving cream in reusable metal pitchers, jam in glass jars, and french fries on plates made of edible wafers.

Because the tax raised its costs of production, McDonald's raised its prices. In response to the higher prices and reduced convenience, consumers began eating at home and in regular restaurants more often. As a result, McDonald's contemplated closing its outlet in Kassel. Thus changes in how fast-food meals are produced and the cost of producing them change the decision as to *what to produce*.

Kassel now produces 500 fewer tons of garbage than it did in the year before the tax was imposed. People who buy from fast-food firms and vending machines bear the cost of cleaning up the environment through higher fast-food prices. Relatively more fast food is consumed in cities that do not tax disposable products and less in cities that do. Thus this tax affects *who gets the goods*.

1.2   MODELS

> *Everything should be made as simple as possible, but not simpler.*
>
> —Albert Einstein

To *explain* how individuals and firms allocate resources and how market prices are determined, economists use a **model**: a description of the relationship between two or more economic variables. Economists also use models to *predict* how a change in one variable will affect another.

INCOME THRESHOLD MODEL AND CHINA

According to an *income threshold model*, no one who has an income level below a threshold buys a particular consumer durable, which is a good that can be used for long periods of time such as a refrigerator or car. The theory also holds that almost everyone whose income is above the threshold does buy the durable.

If this theory is correct, we predict that, as most people's incomes rise above that threshold in less-developed countries, consumer durable purchases will go from near zero to large numbers virtually overnight. This prediction is consistent with evidence from Malaysia, where the income threshold for buying a car is about $4,000.

Given such evidence from other countries, many firms believe that this model's predictions will apply to China. Incomes are rising rapidly in China and are approaching the threshold levels for many types of durable goods. As a result, these companies are predicting that the greatest consumer durable goods sales boom in history will take place there over the next decade. Anticipating this boom, these companies have greatly increased their investments in durable goods manufacturing plants in China. Annual foreign investments went from $916 million a year in 1983 to more than $4 billion in 1991 and $52 billion in 1998. Anticipating this growth potential, even traditional political opponents of the People's Republic—Taiwan, South Korea, and Russia—have been investing in China.

Simplifications by Assumption

We stated the income threshold model verbally, but we could have presented it using graphs or mathematics. Regardless of how the model is described, an economic model is a simplification of reality that contains only its most important features. Without simplifications, it is difficult to make predictions because the real world is too complex to analyze fully.

By analogy, if the manual accompanying your new videocassette recorder (VCR) has a diagram showing the relationships between all the parts in the VCR, the diagram will be overwhelming and useless. In contrast, if it shows a photo of the buttons on the front of the machine with labels describing the purpose of each button, the manual is useful and informative.

Economists make many *assumptions* to simplify their models.[3] When using the income threshold model to explain car purchasing behavior in Malaysia, we *assume* that factors other than income, such as the color of cars, are irrelevant to the decision to buy cars. Therefore, we ignore the color of cars that are sold in Malaysia in describing the relationship between average income and the number of cars consumers want. If this assumption is correct, by ignoring color, we make our analysis of the auto market simpler without losing important details. If we're wrong and these ignored issues are important, our predictions may be inaccurate.

Throughout this book, we start with strong assumptions to simplify our models. Later, we add complexities. For example, in most of the book, we assume that consumers know the price each firm charges. In many markets, such as the New York Stock Exchange, this assumption is realistic. It is not realistic in other markets, such as the market for used automobiles, in which consumers do not know the prices

---

[3]An economist, an engineer, and a physicist are stranded on a desert island with a can of beans but no can opener. How should they open the can? The engineer proposes hitting the can with a rock. The physicist suggests building a fire under it to build up pressure and burst the can open. The economist thinks for a while and then says, "*Assume* that we have a can opener. . . ."

each firm charges. To devise an accurate model for markets in which consumers have limited information, we need to add consumer uncertainty about price into the model, as we do in Chapter 19.

Testing Theories

Economic *theory* is the development and use of a model to test *hypotheses*, which are predictions about cause and effect. We are interested in models that make clear, testable predictions, such as "If the price rises, the quantity demanded falls." A theory that said "People's behavior depends on their tastes, and their tastes change randomly at random intervals" is not very useful because it does not lead to testable predictions.

Economists test theories by checking whether predictions are correct. If a prediction does not come true, they may reject the theory.[4] Economists use a model until it is refuted by evidence or until a better model is developed.

A good model makes sharp, clear predictions that are consistent with reality. Some very simple models make sharp predictions that are incorrect, and other more complex models make ambiguous predictions—any outcome is possible—which are untestable. The skill in model building is to chart a middle ground.

The purpose of this book is to teach you how to think like an economist in the sense that you can build testable theories using economic models or apply existing models to new situations. Although economists think alike in that they develop and use testable models, they often disagree. One may present a logically consistent argument that prices will go up next quarter. Another, using a different but equally logical theory, may contend that prices will fall. If the economists are reasonable, they agree that pure logic alone cannot resolve their dispute. Indeed, they agree that they'll have to use empirical evidence—facts about the real world—to find out which prediction is correct.

Although one economist's model may differ from another's, a key assumption in most microeconomic models is that individuals allocate their scarce resources so as to make themselves as well off as possible. Of all affordable combinations of goods, consumers pick the bundle of goods that gives them the most possible enjoyment. Firms try to maximize their profits given limited resources and existing technology. That resources are limited plays a crucial role in these models. Were it not for scarcity, people could consume unlimited amounts of goods and services, and sellers could become rich beyond limit.

As we show throughout this book, the maximizing behavior of individuals and firms determines society's three main allocation decisions: which goods are produced, how they are produced, and who gets them. For example, diamond-studded pocket combs will be sold only if firms find it profitable to sell them. The firms will make and sell these combs only if consumers value the combs at least as much as it costs the firm to produce them. Consumers will buy the combs only if they get

---

[4]We can use evidence on whether a theory's predictions are correct to *refute* the theory but not to *prove* it. If a model's prediction is inconsistent with what actually happened, the model must be wrong, so we reject it. Even if the model's prediction is consistent with reality, however, the model's prediction may be correct for the wrong reason. Hence we cannot prove that the model is correct—we can only fail to reject it.

more pleasure from the combs than they would from the other goods they could buy with the same resources.

Positive Versus Normative

The use of models of maximizing behavior sometimes leads to predictions that seem harsh or heartless. For instance, a World Bank economist predicted that, if an African government kept the price of food low during a drought, food shortages would occur and people would starve. The predicted outcome is awful, but the economist was not heartless. The economist was only making a scientific prediction about the relationship between cause and effect: Price controls (cause) lead to food shortages and starvation (effect).

Such a scientific prediction is known as a **positive statement**: a testable hypothesis about cause and effect. "Positive" does not mean that we are certain about the truth of our statement—it only indicates that we can test the truth of the statement.

If the World Bank economist is correct, should the government control prices? If the government believes the economist's predictions, it knows that the low prices help those consumers who are lucky enough to be able to buy as much food as they want while hurting both the firms that sell food and the people who are unable to buy as much food as they want, some of whom may die. As a result, the government's decision whether to use price controls turns on whether the government cares more about the winners or the losers. In other words, to decide on its policy, the government makes a value judgment.

Instead of first making a prediction and testing it and then making a value judgment to decide whether to use price controls, the government could make a value judgment directly. The value judgment could be based on the belief that "because people *should* have prepared for the drought, the government *should* not try to help them by keeping food prices low." Alternatively, the judgment could be based on the view that "people *should* be protected against price gouging during a drought, so the government *should* use price controls."

These two statements are *not* scientific predictions. Each is a value judgment or **normative statement**: a conclusion as to whether something is good or bad. A normative statement cannot be tested because a value judgment cannot be refuted by evidence. It is a prescription rather than a prediction. A normative statement concerns what somebody believes *should* happen; a positive statement concerns what *will* happen.

Although a normative conclusion can be drawn without first conducting a positive analysis, a policy debate will be more informed if positive analyses are conducted first.[5] Oregon's Health Services Commission, in deciding which medical treatments to provide poor people, used both positive analyses—scientific evidence on the cost and effectiveness of treatment—and normative judgments—subjective judgments about which treatments or conditions were more important.

---

[5]Some economists draw the normative conclusion that, as social scientists, we economists *should* restrict ourselves to positive analyses. Others argue that we shouldn't give up our right to make value judgments just like the next person (who happens to be biased, prejudiced, and pigheaded, unlike us).

Suppose your normative belief is that the government should help the poor. Should you vote for a candidate who advocates a higher minimum wage (a law that requires that firms pay wages at or above a specified level), a European-style welfare system (guaranteeing health care, housing, and other basic goods and services), an end to our current welfare system, a negative income tax (in which the less income a person has, the more the government gives that person), or job training programs? Positive economic analysis can be used to predict whether these programs will benefit poor people but not whether they are good or bad. Using these predictions and your value judgment, you can decide for whom to vote.

Economists' emphasis on positive analysis has implications for what we study and even our use of language. For example, many economists stress that they study people's *wants* rather than their *needs*. Although people need certain minimum levels of food, shelter, and clothing to survive, most people in developed economies have enough money to buy goods well in excess of the minimum levels necessary to maintain life. Consequently, in wealthy countries, calling something a "need" is often a value judgment. You almost certainly have been told by some elder that "you *need* a college education." That person was probably making a value judgment—"you *should* go to college"—rather than a scientific prediction that you will suffer terrible economic deprivation if you do not go to college. We can't test such value judgments, but we can test a hypothesis such as "One-third of the college-age population *wants* to go to college at current prices."

1.3 | USES OF MICROECONOMIC MODELS

Have you ever imagined a world without hypothetical situations?   —Steven Wright

Because microeconomic models *explain* why economic decisions are made and allow us to make *predictions*, they can be very useful for individuals, governments, and firms in making decisions. Throughout this book, we consider examples of how microeconomics aids in actual decision making. Here we briefly look at some uses by individuals and governments and then examine a series of recent decisions by General Motors.

Uses of Microeconomics by Individiuals and Governments

Individuals use microeconomics to make purchasing and other decisions. In Chapter 5, we examine how inflation and adjustments for inflation affect individuals. In Chapter 16, we show how to determine whether it pays financially to go to college.

Another use of microeconomics is helping you decide for whom to vote based on candidates' views on economic issues. Does your candidate advocate increasing government spending on education or reducing regulation of businesses to stimulate growth? Will these policies actually stimulate growth? Will they have other desirable or undesirable side effects?

Your government's elected and appointed officials use (or could use) economic models in many ways. Recent administrations have placed increased emphasis on economic analysis. Today, economic and environmental impact studies are required before many projects can commence. The President's Council of Economic Advisers and other federal economists analyze and advise national government agencies on the likely economic effects of all major policies.

Indeed, probably the major use of microeconomic models by governments is to predict the probable impact of a policy before it is adopted. In Chapter 3, we show how to predict the likely impact of a tax on the prices consumers pay and on the tax revenues raised.

In some cases, microeconomic analysis suggests solutions to problems, such as how countries may protect themselves against harmful coordinated actions of firms. Groups of firms—including many international groups of producers of commodities such as oil, mercury, peppers, and diamonds—try to coordinate their activities to raise prices. Some of these organizations, called *cartels*, keep prices above noncartel levels for years, while others fail miserably. Microeconomic theory predicts which cartels will succeed and which will fail. By using this theory, governments can act to undermine cartels by prohibiting certain actions by firms or by altering their buying behavior, as we discuss in Chapter 13. For example, how governments let firms bid on major projects may determine whether a cartel succeeds or fails.

Application   PUTTING SATURN IN ORBIT

Many firms have staffs of economists to make predictions and evaluate policies. In Chapter 5, we discuss how General Motors (GM) uses a study by one of its staff economists to predict consumer demand for its cars.

Microeconomic analysis was particularly important to GM when it started selling its line of Saturn cars in 1991. The company broke a lot of its old rules. It built Saturns differently from the way it built its other cars and changed its relationship with its dealers so that they would sell and service the cars in a new way. Did GM's gamble work?

Manufacturing Costs. Starting up the Saturn line was a major risk; GM spent an estimated $5 billion to get Saturn going. (We examine investment policies in Chapter 16.) To keep manufacturing costs down, GM built a new plant that uses modern technology and a team approach and other Japanese-style management methods to assemble cars. One of these, just-in-time inventories, allows GM to keep its inventory costs down by having suppliers ready to deliver parts almost immediately when needed. The Saturn plant produces relatively few models, and its sharing of engines and other major parts reduces production costs. (We analyze how firms minimize costs in Chapter 7.)

In building its new plant and designing its new car, GM had to take into account the federal government's emissions standards and other pollution regulations. (In Chapter 18, we analyze how firms react to such regulations and the effects of the regulations.)

Some industry experts believe that GM lost $500 million a year in the first few years because it couldn't make enough cars to cover its investment. Does it make sense to run a plant at a loss for a while? (We first examine this issue in Chapter 8.) In keeping the plant operating, GM was counting on Saturn managers' and workers' gaining experience in producing cars, which would lower the costs of production in the future. (In Chapter 7, we discuss learning by doing.)

Pricing.   GM does not sell Saturns the way it sells its other cars. Knowing consumers' tastes with respect to the cars' features, service, and purchasing negotiations was an essential part of GM's new strategy. (Consumer decision making is analyzed in Chapters 4 and 5.)

Saturn's most striking marketing innovation was the "no-dicker sticker." Saturn dealers charge a fixed price for a car—they don't negotiate with customers as do most dealers. Why? One reason is that, according to a J. D. Power survey, 78% of American car buyers dislike negotiating for a new car. At the very least, this negotiation process is time consuming.

Why do traditional firms want to bargain with customers? It allows them to charge customers different prices. Such price discrimination can raise a firm's profits. (We discuss price discrimination in Chapter 12.)

In the past, some consumers who did not bargain well or had little information about costs and prices paid substantially more than the dealer's cost for a car. One dealer claims that car dealers often marked up their price over cost by 24% in the 1960s. Now, information about dealers' costs is available on the Internet. Using such information, some consumers are able to strike better deals than they could previously. (In Chapter 19, we discuss the roles of unequal information on the prices consumers pay.) As a result, price markups have fallen to about 6.7% over cost.

Saturn's approach is slowly winning converts. A few dealers of other brands have used no-dicker prices. In 1999, Mercedes-Benz USA announced to its dealers that they should use a "negotiation-free process" to turn dealers into "retailers" and customers into loyal, satisfied "clients."

Dealers.   GM wanted its Saturn dealers not only to charge a fixed price, but also to provide superior service. With superior service, they could compete more effectively with dealers of high-quality imported cars and attract repeat customers. How could GM induce its dealers to provide superior service? (Chapter 20 discusses how one firm gives another incentives to ensure the desired behavior.)

Because of its pricing method and its emphasis on service, by the end of the millennium, Saturn was one of consumers' top-rated brands for service, along with Cadillac, Jaguar, Volvo, Land Rover, Land Rover, Mercedes-Benz, and Lexus. When Saturn held a "homecoming" in its fifth year of operation, between 30,000 and 40,000 Saturn owners, including a contingent from Japan, convened at the company's factory south of Nashville.

GM ensured that its dealers would earn unusually high profits by limiting the number of Saturn dealers. Initially, GM had only 230 Saturn dealers nationally, compared with 5,000 Chevy dealers. As a result, a Saturn dealer's markup of its price above its costs is greater than it would be if the dealer had to compete with many other local Saturn dealers (see Chapter 13). According to one expert, the typical Saturn price markup is 13% over dealer costs, whereas traditional dealer markups average about half that.

Are higher dealer prices and profits good for GM? On the one hand, the higher retail price cuts current sales of Saturns, which hurts GM. On the other hand, the resulting high profits give dealers an incentive to provide superior service. As one dealer said, "If there were more Saturn dealers, with more competition among ourselves, we couldn't afford to give extra service. The trouble with non-Saturn GM dealers is that they cut their own throats by charging too little and taking most profit out of deals." Extra service should increase the demand for Saturns, which helps GM.

Because its sales staff does not have to spend time negotiating with each customer, Saturn dealers need fewer salespeople. Some dealers calculate that traditional dealers need 30% to 40% more sales staff. Thus the ratio of labor to capital in traditional dealers is different from that in fixed-price dealers. (Chapters 6 and 7 analyze substitution between inputs.)

At traditional dealerships, a salesperson gets a commission of about a quarter of the markup on a final sale. Because they make money from each extra sale, these salespeople use cold calls (phone calls to strangers) and personal contacts to attract customers. In contrast, Saturn sales staff are paid a salary. As a result, Saturn salespeople have less incentive to pursue customers aggressively than salespeople who earn a commission (see Chapter 20). To offset this effect, some Saturn dealers boost advertising to generate showroom traffic (see Chapter 14).

Strategy. Why did GM change the way it did business? The reason was that its old approach was not working: GM was losing business and profits to other auto manufacturers.

By the very way it designed the Saturn, GM went after a particular type of customer. Only relatively short customers can fit comfortably in a Saturn. Customers who want sporty or other special features are not going to buy a Saturn. Saturn was apparently designed for customers who want to minimize the hassles in their life. A Saturn customer does not have to negotiate over price and is assured a well-built, well-serviced car (with a loaner available if repairs take a long time). (Chapter 13 discusses how firms aim at specific market niches.) Noting that consumers were switching to larger cars, Saturn decided in 1999 to extend its line to include full-size cars and sport utility vehicles.

Other dealers and auto manufacturers did not stand still. In picking its strategies, a firm forms beliefs about how its rival will react to its actions (see Chapters 13 and 14). When GM drops its wholesale price, Ford and Honda respond to prevent the loss of sales and profits. When GM started selling Saturns and some of its other cars at fixed prices, Ford began using fixed prices on two of its vehicles. Rival manufacturers have also aimed for the customer profile that Saturn targeted. (Chapter 13 examines how large firms compete with each other in setting their prices or quantities. Chapter 14 looks at more complex investment strategies that firms use to gain at the expense of their competitors.)

Thus GM made many production, marketing, and strategy decisions based on microeconomic models and predictions. The test that GM uses to determine whether its models and predictions are correct is whether Saturn makes a profit.

Summary

1. **Microeconomics: the allocation of scarce resources:** Microeconomics is the study of the allocation of scarce resources. Consumers, firms, and the government must make allocation decisions. The three key trade-offs a society faces are which goods and services to produce, how to produce them, and who gets them. These decisions are interrelated and depend on the prices that consumers and firms face and on government actions. Market prices affect the decisions of individual consumers and firms, and the interaction of the decisions of individual consumers and firms determines market prices. The organization of the market, especially the number of firms in the market and the information consumers and firms have, plays an important role in determining whether the market price is equal to or higher than marginal cost.

2. **Models:** Models based on economic theories are used to predict the future or to answer questions about how some change, such as a tax increase, affects various sectors of the economy. A good theory is simple to use and makes clear, testable predictions that are not refuted by evidence. Most microeconomic models are based on maximizing behavior. Economists use models to construct *positive* hypotheses concerning how a cause leads to an effect. These positive questions can be tested. In contrast, *normative* statements, which are value judgments, cannot be tested.

3. **Uses of microeconomic models:** Individuals, governments, and firms use microeconomic models and predictions to make decisions. For example, to maximize its profits, a firm needs to know consumers' decision-making criteria, the trade-offs between various ways of producing and marketing its product, government regulations, and other factors. For large companies, beliefs about how a firm's rivals will react to its actions play a critical role in how it forms its business strategies.

Supply and Demand

Talk is cheap because supply exceeds demand.

When asked, "What is the most important thing you know about economics?" many people reply, "Supply equals demand." This statement is a shorthand description of one of the simplest yet most powerful models of economics. The supply-and-demand model describes how consumers and suppliers interact to determine the *quantity* of a good or service sold in a market and the *price* at which it is sold. To use the model, you need to determine three things: buyers' behavior, sellers' behavior, and how they interact. After reading this chapter, you should be adept enough at using the supply-and-demand model to analyze some of the most important policy questions facing your country today, such as those concerning international trade, minimum wages, and price controls on health care.

After reading that grandiose claim, you may ask, "Is that all there is to economics? Can I become an expert economist that fast?" The answer to both these questions is no (of course). In addition, you need to learn the limits of this model and what other models to use when this one does not apply. (You must also learn the economists' secret handshake.)

Even with its limitations, the supply-and-demand model is the most widely used economic model. It provides a good description of how many markets function and works particularly well in markets in which there are many buyers and many sellers, such as in most agriculture and labor markets. Like all good theories, the supply-and-demand model can be tested—and possibly shown to be false. But in markets where it is applicable, it allows us to make accurate predictions easily.

IN THIS CHAPTER,

WE EXAMINE

SIX MAIN

TOPICS

1. **Demand:** The quantity of a good or service that consumers demand depends on price and other factors such as consumers' incomes and the price of related goods.
2. **Supply:** The quantity of a good or service that firms supply depends on price and other factors such as the cost of inputs firms use to produce the good or service.
3. **Market equilibrium:** The interaction between consumers' demand and firms' supply determines the market price and quantity of a good or service that is bought and sold.
4. **Shocking the equilibrium:** Changes in a factor that affect demand (such as consumer's income), supply (such as a rise in the price of inputs), or a new government policy (such as a new tax) alter the market price and quantity of a good.
5. **Effects of government interventions:** Government policies may alter the equilibrium and cause the quantity supplied to differ from the quantity demanded.
6. **When to use the supply-and-demand model:** The supply-and-demand model applies only to competitive markets.

2.1 | DEMAND

Potential consumers decide how much of a good or service to buy on the basis of its price and many other factors, including their own tastes, information, prices of other goods, income, and government actions. Before concentrating on the role of price in determining demand, let's look briefly at some of the other factors.

Consumers' *tastes* determine what they buy. Consumers do not purchase foods they dislike, artwork they hate, or clothes they view as unfashionable or uncomfortable. Advertising may influence peoples' tastes.

Similarly, *information* (or misinformation) about the uses of a good affects consumers' decisions. A few years ago when many consumers were convinced that oatmeal could lower their cholesterol level, they rushed to grocery stores and bought large quantities of oatmeal. (They even ate some of it until they remembered that they couldn't stand how it tastes.)

The *prices of other goods* also affect consumers' purchase decisions. Before deciding to buy Levi's jeans, you might check the prices of other brands. If the price of a close *substitute*—a product that you view as similar or identical to the one you are considering purchasing—is much lower than the price of Levi's jeans, you may buy that brand instead. Similarly, the price of a *complement*—a good that you like to consume at the same time as the product you are considering buying—may affect your decision. If you eat pie only with ice cream, the higher the price of ice cream, the less likely you are to buy pie.

Income plays a major role in determining what and how much to purchase. People who suddenly inherit great wealth may purchase a Rolls-Royce or other luxury items and would probably no longer buy do-it-yourself repair kits.

Government rules and regulations affect purchase decisions. Sales taxes increase the price that a consumer must spend for a good, and government-imposed limits on the use of a good may affect demand. If a city's government bans the use of skateboards on its streets, skateboard sales fall.

Other factors may also affect the demand for specific goods. Consumers are more likely to have telephones if most of their friends have telephones. The demand for small, dead evergreen trees is substantially higher in December than at other times of the year.

Dr. David A. Kessler, former U.S. Commissioner of Food and Drugs, alleged that Brown & Williamson Tobacco Corporation developed a genetically engineered tobacco with more than double the amount of nicotine that some other cigarettes deliver to the smoker. Higher levels of nicotine may increase smokers' addiction and thus boost the demand for cigarettes.

Although many factors influence demand, economists usually concentrate on how price affects the quantity demanded. The relationship between price and quantity demanded plays a critical role in determining the market price and quantity in a supply-and-demand analysis. To determine how a change in price affects the quantity demanded, economists must hold constant other factors such as income and tastes that affect demand.

The Demand Curve

The amount of a good that consumers are *willing* to buy at a given price, holding constant the other factors that influence purchases, is the **quantity demanded**. The quantity demanded of a good or service can exceed the quantity *actually* sold. For example, as a promotion, a local store might sell music CDs for $1 each today only. At that low price, you might want to buy 25 CDs, but because the store ran out of stock, you can buy only 10 CDs. The quantity you demand is 25—it's the amount you *want*, even though the amount you *actually buy* is only 10.

We can show the relationship between price and the quantity demanded graphically. A **demand curve** shows the quantity demanded at each possible price, holding constant the other factors that influence purchases. Figure 2.1 shows the estimated demand curve, D^1, for processed pork in Canada (Moschini and Meilke 1992). (Although this demand curve is a straight line, demand curves may also be smooth curves or wavy lines.) By convention, the vertical axis of the graph measures the price, p, per unit of the good—here dollars per kilogram (kg). The horizontal axis measures the quantity, Q, of the good, which is usually expressed in some *physical measure* (million kg of dressed cold pork carcass weight) *per time period* (per year).

The demand curve hits the vertical axis at $14.30, indicating that no quantity is demanded when the price is $14.30 (or higher). The demand curve hits the horizontal

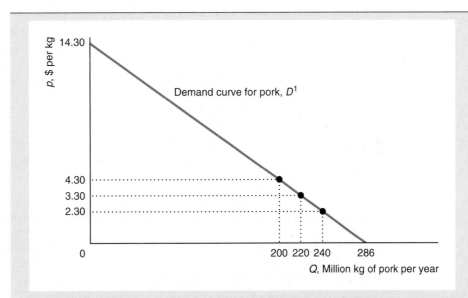

Figure 2.1 A Demand Curve. The estimated demand curve, D^1, for processed pork in Canada (Moschini and Meilke, 1992) shows the relationship between the quantity demanded per year and the price per kg. The downward slope of the demand curve shows that, holding other factors that influence demand constant, consumers demand less of a good when its price is high and more when the price is low. A change in price causes a *movement along the demand curve*.

quantity axis at 286 million kg—the amount of pork that consumers want if the price is zero. To find out what quantity is demanded at a price between these extremes, pick that price on the vertical axis—say, $3.30 per kg—draw a horizontal line across until you hit the demand curve, and then draw a line straight down to the horizontal quantity axis: 220 million kg of pork per year is demanded at that price.

One of the most important things to know about a graph of a demand curve is what is *not* shown. All relevant economic variables that are not explicitly shown on the demand curve graph—tastes, information, prices of other goods (such as beef and chicken), income of consumers, and so on—are held constant. Thus the demand curve shows how quantity varies with price but not how quantity varies with tastes, information, the price of substitute goods, or other variables.[1]

Effect of Prices on the Quantity Demanded. Many economists claim that the most important *empirical* finding in economics is the **Law of Demand**: Consumers demand more of a good the lower its price, holding constant tastes, the prices of other goods, and other factors that influence the amount they consume. According to the Law of Demand, *demand curves slope downward*, as in Figure 2.1.[2]

A downward-sloping demand curve illustrates that consumers demand more of this good when its price is lower and less when its price is higher. What happens to the quantity of pork demanded if the price of pork drops and all other variables remain constant? If the price of pork falls by $1 from $3.30 to $2.30 in Figure 2.1, the quantity consumers want to buy increases from 220 to 240.[3] Similarly, if the price increases from $3.30 to $4.30, the quantity consumers demand decreases from 220 to 200. These changes in the quantity demanded in response to changes in price are *movements along the demand curve*. Thus the demand curve is a concise summary of the answers to the question "What happens to the quantity demanded as the price changes, when all other factors are held constant?"

Effects of Other Factors on Demand. If a demand curve measures the effects of price changes when all other factors that affect demand are held constant, how can we use

---

[1]Because prices, quantities, and other factors change simultaneously over time, economists use statistical techniques to hold the effects of factors other than the price of the good constant so that they can determine how price affects the quantity demanded. (See Appendix 2A.) Moschini and Meilke (1992) used such techniques to estimate the pork demand curve. As with any estimate, their estimates are probably more accurate in the observed range of prices ($1 to $6 per kg) than at very high or very low prices.

[2]Theoretically, a demand curve could slope upward (Chapter 5); however, available empirical evidence strongly supports the Law of Demand.

[3]Economists, being lazy, typically do not state the relevant physical and time period measures unless they are particularly useful. They refer to *quantity* rather than something useful such as "metric tons per year" and *price* rather than "cents per pound." Being as lazy as the next economist, I'll follow this sloppy convention when no confusion is likely to arise. To keep from driving us all nuts, from here on, I'll usually refer to the price as $3.30 (with the "per kg" understood) and the quantity as 220 (with the "million kg per year" understood).

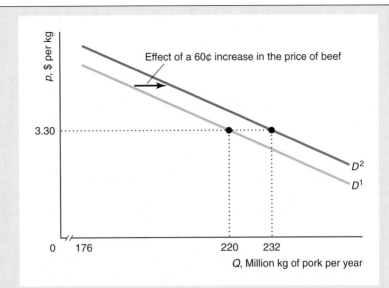

Figure 2.2 A Shift of the Demand Curve. The demand curve for processed pork shifts to the right from D^1 to D^2 as the price of beef rises from \$4 to \$4.60. As a result of the increase in beef prices, more pork is demanded at any given price.

demand curves to show the effects of a change in one of these other factors, such as the price of beef? One solution is to draw the demand curve in a three-dimensional diagram with the price of pork on one axis, the price of beef on a second axis, and the quantity of pork on the third axis. But just thinking about drawing such a diagram probably makes your head hurt.

Economists use a simpler approach to show the effect on demand of a change in a factor that affects demand other than the price of the good. A change in any factor other than price of the good itself causes a *shift of the demand curve* rather than a *movement along the demand curve*.

Many people view beef as a close substitute for pork. Thus at a given price of pork, if the price of beef rises, some people will switch from beef to pork. Figure 2.2 shows how the demand curve for pork shifts to the right from the original demand curve D^1 to a new demand curve D^2 as the price of beef rises from \$4.00 to \$4.60 per kg. (The quantity axis starts at 176 instead of 0 in the figure to emphasize the relevant portion of the demand curve.) On the new demand curve, D^2, more pork is demanded at any given price than on D^1. At a price of pork of \$3.30, the quantity of pork demanded goes from 220 on D^1, before the change in the price of beef, to 232 on D^2, after the price change.

Similarly, a change in information can shift the demand curve. The average number of eggs per year each American eats has fallen steadily since 1955, even though the price of eggs has fallen relative to the price of other goods during this period. Brown and Schrader (1990) found that new information about the link between cholesterol (eggs are high in cholesterol) and heart disease caused the demand curve for eggs to shift to the left. This shift was largely responsible for the per capita decline in fresh egg consumption of 16% to 25% by 1987. Per capita egg consumption fell another 6% between 1987 and 1997.

To properly analyze the effects of a change in some variable on the quantity demanded, we must distinguish between a *movement along a demand curve* and a *shift of a demand curve*. A change in the *price of a good* causes a *movement along a demand curve*. A change in *any other factor besides the price of the good* causes a *shift of the demand curve*.

The Demand Function

In addition to drawing the demand curve, you can write it as a mathematical relationship called the *demand function*. The processed pork demand function is

$$Q = D(p, p_b, p_c, Y), \tag{2.1}$$

where Q is the quantity of pork demanded, p is the price of pork, p_b is the price of beef, p_c is the price of chicken, and Y is the income of consumers. This expression says that the amount of pork demanded varies with the price of pork, the price of substitutes (beef and chicken), and the income of consumers. Any other factors that are not explicitly listed in the demand function are assumed to be irrelevant (the price of llamas in Peru) or held constant (the price of fish).

By writing the demand function in this general way, we are not explaining exactly how the quantity demanded varies as p, p_b, p_c, or Y changes. Instead, we can rewrite Equation 2.1 as a specific function:

$$Q = 171 - 20p + 20p_b + 3p_c + 2Y. \tag{2.2}$$

Equation 2.2 is the estimated demand function that corresponds to the demand curve D^1 in Figures 2.1 and 2.2.[4]

When we drew the demand curve D^1 in Figures 2.1 and 2.2, we held p_b, p_c, and Y at their typical values during the period studied: $p_b = 4$ (dollars per kg), $p_c = 3\frac{1}{3}$ (dollars per kg), and $Y = 12.5$ (thousand dollars). If we substitute these values for p_b, p_c, and Y in Equation 2.2, we can rewrite the quantity demanded as a function of only the price of pork:

$$Q = 171 - 20p + 20p_b + 3p_c + 2Y$$
$$= 171 - 20p + (20 \times 4) + \left(3 \times 3\tfrac{1}{3}\right) + (2 \times 12.5)$$
$$= 286 - 20p \tag{2.3}$$

The straight-line demand curve D^1 in Figures 2.1 and 2.2—where we hold the price of beef, the price of chicken, and disposable income constant at these typical values —is described by the *linear* demand function in Equation 2.3.

---

[4]The numbers are rounded slightly from the estimates to simplify the calculation. For example, the estimate of the coefficient on the price of beef is 19.5, not 20, as the equation shows.

The constant term, 286, in Equation 2.3 is the quantity demanded if the price is zero. Setting the price equal to zero in Equation 2.3, we find that the quantity demanded is $Q = 286 - (20 \times 0) = 286$. Figure 2.1 shows that $Q = 286$ where D^1 hits the quantity axis at a price of zero.

This equation also shows us how quantity demanded changes with a change in price: a movement *along* the demand curve. If the price increases from p_1 to p_2, the change in price, Δp, equals $p_2 - p_1$. (The Δ symbol, the Greek letter delta, means "change in" the following variable, so Δp means "change in price.") As Figure 2.1 illustrates, if the price of pork increases by $1 from $p_1 = \$3.30$ to $p_2 = \$4.30$, $\Delta p = \$1$ and $\Delta Q = Q_2 - Q_1 = 200 - 220 = -20$ million kg per year.

More generally, the quantity demanded at p_1 is $Q_1 = D(p_1)$, and the quantity demanded at p_2 is $Q_2 = D(p_2)$. The change in the quantity demanded, $\Delta Q = Q_2 - Q_1$, in response to the price change (using Equation 2.3) is

$$\begin{aligned}
\Delta Q &= Q_2 - Q_1 \\
&= D(p_2) - D(p_1) \\
&= (286 - 20p_2) - (286 - 20p_1) \\
&= -20(p_2 - p_1) \\
&= -20\Delta p.
\end{aligned}$$

Thus the change in the quantity demanded, ΔQ, is -20 times the change in the price, Δp. If $\Delta p = \$1$, $\Delta Q = -20\Delta p = -20$.

The slope of a demand curve is $\Delta p / \Delta Q$, the "rise" (Δp, the change along the vertical axis) divided by the "run" (ΔQ, the change along the horizontal axis). The slope of demand curve D^1 in Figures 2.1 and 2.2 is

$$\text{Slope} = \frac{\text{rise}}{\text{run}} = \frac{\Delta p}{\Delta Q} = \frac{\$1 \text{ per kg}}{-20 \text{ million kg per year}}$$

$$= -\$0.05 \text{ per million kg per year.}$$

The negative sign of this slope is consistent with the Law of Demand. The slope says that the price rises by $1 per kg as the quantity demanded falls by 20 million kg per year. Turning that statement around: The quantity demanded falls by 20 million kg per year as the price rises by $1 per kg.

Thus we can use the demand curve to answer questions about how a change in price affects the quantity demanded and how a change in the quantity demanded affects price. We can also answer these questions using demand functions.

To answer the question about how a change in quantity affects price, we use algebra to rewrite Equation 2.3 so that price is a function of quantity. We call this rewritten demand curve an *inverse demand curve*. Subtracting Q from both sides of Equation 2.3 and adding $20p$ to both sides, we find that $20p = 286 - Q$. Dividing both sides of the equation by 20, we obtain the inverse demand function:

$$p = 14.30 - 0.05Q. \tag{2.4}$$

Equation 2.4 shows that if the quantity increases by ΔQ, price falls by $\Delta p = -0.05 \Delta Q$ (where -0.05 is the number multiplied by Q in the equation).[5] For consumers to demand one million more kg of pork per year, the price must fall by nearly 5¢ a kg, which is a *movement along the demand curve*.

Summing Demand Curves

If we know the demand curve for each of two consumers, how do we determine the total demand for the two consumers combined? The total quantity demanded *at a given price* is the sum of the quantity each consumer demands at that price.

We can use the demand functions to determine the total demand of several consumers. Suppose that the demand function for Consumer 1 is

$$Q_1 = D^1(p)$$

and the demand function for Consumer 2 is

$$Q_2 = D^2(p).$$

At price p, Consumer 1 demands Q_1 units, Consumer 2 demands Q_2 units, and the total demand of both consumers is the sum of the quantities each demands separately:[6]

$$Q = Q_1 + Q_2 = D^1(p) + D^2(p).$$

It makes sense to add the quantities demanded only when both consumers face the same price. Adding the quantity Consumer 1 demands at one price to the quantity Consumer 2 demands at another price would be like adding apples and oranges.

Application   **AGGREGATING THE DEMAND FOR CLING PEACHES**

We illustrate how to combine individual demand curves to get a total demand curve graphically using estimated demand curves for cling peaches (French and King, 1986). Cling peaches are used for canning. The total demand for cling peaches in the figure is the sum of the demand for cling peaches for use in cans of peaches and the demand for cling peaches for use in cans of fruit cocktail.

Farmers sold cling peaches for $183 per ton in 1984. At that price, fruit cocktail canners demanded $Q_f = 4$ tons per 10,000 consumers per year and peach canners demanded $Q_c = 18$, so the total quantity demanded was $Q = Q_f + Q_c = 4 + 18 = 22$.

---

[5]Let the quantity increase from Q_1 to Q_2 so that $\Delta Q = Q_2 - Q_1$. The change in price is $\Delta p = p_2 - p_1$:

$$\Delta p = (14.30 - 0.05Q_2) - (14.30 - 0.05Q_1) = -0.05(Q_2 - Q_1) = -0.05\Delta Q.$$

[6]We can generalize this approach to look at the total demand for three or more consumers. In each case, the total demand is the sum of the individual demands for each consumer at a specific price. For example, at price p, the total demand, Q, for three consumers is

$$Q = Q_1 + Q_2 + Q_3 = D^1(p) + D^2(p) + D^3(p).$$

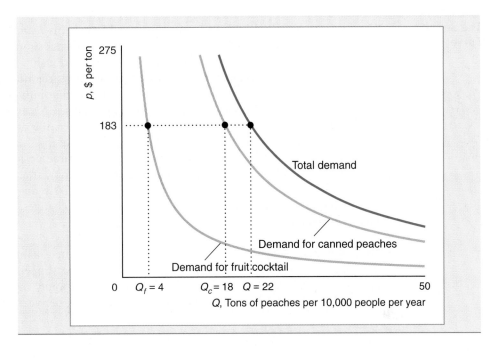

2.2 | SUPPLY

Knowing how much consumers want is not enough, by itself, to tell us what price and quantity are observed in a market. To determine the market price and quantity, we also need to know how much firms want to supply at any given price.

Firms determine how much of a good to supply on the basis of the price of that good and other factors, including the costs of production and government rules and regulations. Usually, we expect firms to supply more at a higher price. Before concentrating on the role of price in determining supply, we'll briefly describe the role of some of the other factors.

Costs of production affect how much firms want to sell of a good. As a firm's cost falls, it is willing to supply more, all else the same. If the firm's cost exceeds what it can earn from selling the good, the firm sells nothing. Thus, factors that affect costs, also affect supply. A technological advance that allows a firm to produce a good at lower cost leads the firm to supply more of that good, all else the same.

Government rules and regulations affect how much firms want to sell or are allowed to sell. Taxes and many government regulations—such as those covering pollution, sanitation, and health insurance—alter the costs of production. Other regulations affect when and how the product can be sold. In Germany, retailers may not sell most goods and services on Sundays or during evening hours. In the United States, the sale of cigarettes and liquor to children is prohibited. New York, San Francisco, and many other cities restrict the number of taxicabs.

The Supply Curve

The **quantity supplied** is the amount of a good that firms *want* to sell at a given price, holding constant other factors that influence firms' supply decisions, such as costs and government actions. We can show the relationship between price and the quantity supplied graphically. A **supply curve** shows the quantity supplied at each possible price, holding constant the other factors that influence firms' supply decisions. Figure 2.3 shows the estimated supply curve, S^1, for processed pork (Moschini and Meilke, 1992). As with the demand curve, the price on the vertical axis is measured in dollars per physical unit (dollars per kg), and the quantity on the horizontal axis is measured in physical units per time period (millions of kg per year). Because we hold fixed other variables that may affect the supply, such as costs and government rules, the supply curve concisely answers the question "What happens to the quantity supplied as the price changes, holding all other factors constant?"

Effect of Price on Supply. We illustrate how price affects the quantity supplied using the supply curve for processed pork in Figure 2.3. The supply curve for pork is upward sloping. As the price of pork increases, firms supply more. If the price is $3.30, the market supplies a quantity of 220 (million kg per year). If the price rises

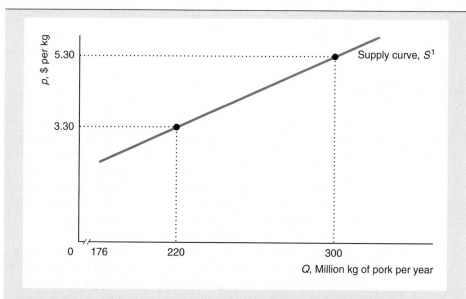

Figure 2.3 A Supply Curve. The estimated supply curve, S^1, for processed pork in Canada (Moschini and Meilke, 1992) shows the relationship between the quantity supplied per year and the price per kg, holding cost and other factors that influence supply constant. The upward slope of this supply curve indicates that firms supply more of this good when its price is high and less when the price is low. An increase in the price of pork causes a movement *along the supply curve*, resulting in a larger quantity of pork supplied.

to $5.30, the quantity supplied rises to 300. An increase in the price of pork causes a *movement along the supply curve*, resulting in more pork being supplied.

Although the Law of Demand requires that the demand curve slope downward, there is *no* "Law of Supply" that requires the market supply curve to have a particular slope. The market supply curve can be upward sloping, vertical, horizontal, or downward sloping. Many supply curves slope upward, such as the one for pork. Along such supply curves, the higher the price, the more firms are willing to sell, holding costs and government regulations fixed.

Effects of Other Variables on Supply. A change in a variable other than the price of pork causes the entire *supply curve to shift*. Suppose the price, p_h, of hogs—the main factor used to produce processed pork—increases from $1.50 per kg to $1.75 per kg. Because it is now more expensive to produce pork, the supply curve shifts to the left, from S^1 to S^2 in Figure 2.4. Firms want to supply less pork at any given price than before the price of hogs rose. At a price of processed pork of $3.30, the quantity supplied falls from 220 on S^1, before the increase in the hog price, to 205 on S^2, after the increase in the hog price.

Again, it is important to distinguish between a *movement along a supply curve* and a *shift of the supply curve*. When the price of pork changes, the change in the quantity supplied reflects a *movement along the supply curve*. When costs, government rules, or other variables that affect supply change, the entire *supply curve shifts*.

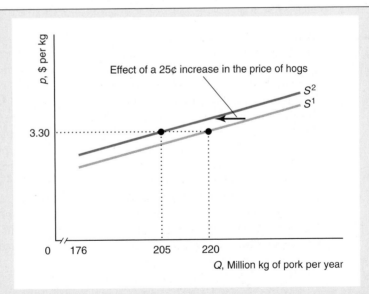

Figure 2.4 **A Shift of a Supply Curve.** An increase in the price of hogs from $1.50 to $1.75 per kg causes the supply curve for processed pork to shift from S^1 to S^2. At the price of processed pork of $3.30, the quantity supplied falls from 220 on S^1 to 205 on S^2.

The Supply Function

We can write the relationship between the quantity supplied and price and other factors as a mathematical relationship called the *supply function*. Written generally, the processed pork supply function is

$$Q = S(p, p_h), \tag{2.5}$$

where Q is the quantity of processed pork supplied, p is the price of processed pork, and p_h is the price of a hog. The supply function, Equation 2.5, may also be a function of other factors such as wages, but by leaving them out, we are implicitly holding them constant.

Based on Moschini and Meilke (1992), the linear pork supply function in Canada is

$$Q = 178 + 40p - 60p_h, \tag{2.6}$$

where quantity is in millions of kg per year and the prices are in Canadian dollars per kg. If we hold the price of hogs fixed at its typical value of $1.50 per kg, we can rewrite the supply function in Equation 2.6 as[7]

$$Q = 88 + 40p. \tag{2.7}$$

What happens to the quantity supplied if the price of processed pork increases by $\Delta p = p_2 - p_1$? Using the same approach as before, we learn from Equation 2.7 that $\Delta Q = 40\Delta p$.[8] A $1 increase in price ($\Delta p = 1$) causes the quantity supplied to increase by $\Delta Q = 40$ million kg per year. This change in the quantity of pork supplied as p increases is a *movement along the supply curve*.

Summing Supply Curves

The total supply curve shows the total quantity produced by all suppliers at each possible price. For example, the total supply of rice in Japan is the sum of the domestic and foreign supply curves of rice.

Suppose that the domestic supply curve (panel a) and foreign supply curve (panel b) of rice in Japan are as Figure 2.5 shows. The total supply curve, S in panel c, is the horizontal sum of the Japanese *domestic* supply curve, S^d, and the *foreign* supply curve, S^f. In the figure, the Japanese and foreign supplies are zero at any price equal to or less than $\underline{p}$, so the total supply is zero. At prices above $\underline{p}$, the Japanese and foreign supplies are positive, so the total supply is positive. For example, when price is p^*, the quantity supplied by Japanese firms is Q_d^* (panel a), the quantity supplied by foreign firms is Q_f^* (panel b), and the total quantity supplied is $Q^* = Q_d^* + Q_f^*$ (panel c). Because the total supply curve is the horizontal sum of the domestic and foreign supply curves, the total supply curve is flatter than either of the other two supply curves.

---

[7]Substituting $p_h = \$1.50$ into Equation 2.6, we find that

$$Q = 178 + 40p - 60p_h = 178 + 40p - (60 \times 1.50) = 88 + 40p.$$

[8]As the price increases from p_1 to p_2, the quantity supplied goes from Q_1 to Q_2, so the change in quantity supplied, $\Delta Q = Q_2 - Q_1$, is

$$\Delta Q = (88 + 40p_2) - (88 + 40p_1) = 40(p_2 - p_1) = 40\Delta p.$$

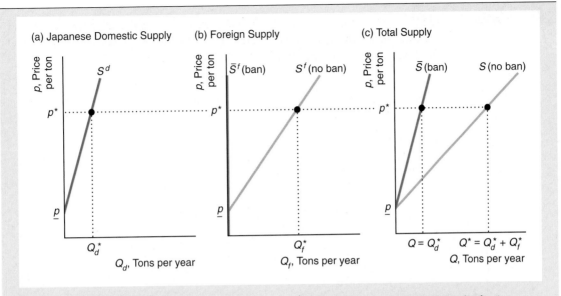

Figure 2.5 Total Supply: The Sum of Domestic and Foreign Supply. If foreigners may sell their rice in Japan, the total Japanese supply of rice, S, is the horizontal sum of the domestic Japanese supply, S^d, and the imported foreign supply, S^f. With a ban on foreign imports, the foreign supply curve, $\bar{S}^f$, is zero at every price, so the total supply curve, $\bar{S}$, is the same as the domestic supply curve, S^d.

Effects of Government Import Policies on Supply Curves

We can use this approach for deriving the total supply curve to analyze the effect of government policies on the total supply curve. Traditionally, the Japanese government banned the importation of foreign rice. We want to determine how much less is supplied at any given price to the Japanese market because of this ban.

Without a ban, the foreign supply curve is S^f in panel b of Figure 2.5. A ban on imports eliminates the foreign supply, so the foreign supply curve after the ban is imposed, $\bar{S}^f$, is a vertical line at $Q_f = 0$. The import ban has no effect on the domestic supply curve, S^d, so the supply curve is the same as in panel a.

Because the foreign supply with a ban, $\bar{S}^f$, is zero at every price, the total supply with a ban, $\bar{S}$, in panel c is the same as the Japanese domestic supply, S^d, at any given price. The total supply curve under the ban lies to the left of the total supply curve without a ban, S. Thus the effect of the import ban is to rotate the total supply curve toward the vertical axis.

The limit that a government sets on the quantity of a foreign-produced good that may be imported is called a **quota**. By absolutely banning the importation of rice, the Japanese government sets a quota of zero on rice imports. Sometimes governments set positive quotas, $\bar{Q} > 0$. The foreign firms may supply as much as they want, Q_f, as long as they supply no more than the quota: $Q_f \leq \bar{Q}$.

We investigate the effect of such a quota in Solved Problem 2.1. In most of the solved problems in this book, you are asked to determine how a *change* in a variable or policy *affects* one or more variables. In this problem, the policy *changes* from no quota to a quota, which *affects* the total supply curve.

Solved Problem 2.1

How does a quota set by the United States on foreign steel imports of $\overline{Q}$ affect the total American supply curve for steel given the domestic supply, S^d in panel a of the graph, and foreign supply, S^f in panel b?

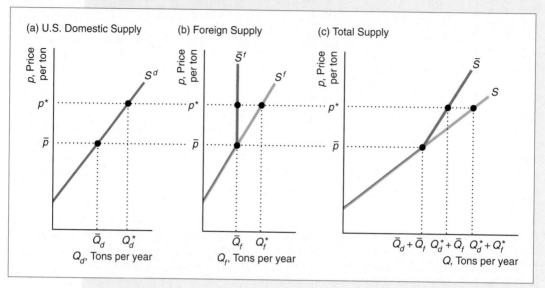

(a) U.S. Domestic Supply   (b) Foreign Supply   (c) Total Supply

Answer

1. *Determine the American supply curve without the quota:* The *no-quota* total supply curve, S in panel c, is the horizontal sum of the U.S. domestic supply curve, S^d, and the no-quota foreign supply curve, S^f.

2. *Show the effect of the quota on foreign supply:* At prices less than $\overline{p}$, foreign suppliers want to supply quantities less than the quota, $\overline{Q}$. As a result, the foreign supply curve under the quota, $\overline{S}^f$, is the same as the no-quota foreign supply curve, S^f, for prices less than $\overline{p}$. At prices above $\overline{p}$, foreign suppliers want to supply more but are limited to $\overline{Q}$. Thus the foreign supply curve with a quota, $\overline{S}^f$, is vertical at $\overline{Q}$ for prices above $\overline{p}$.

3. *Determine the American total supply curve with the quota:* The total supply curve with the quota, $\overline{S}$, is the horizontal sum of S^d and $\overline{S}^f$. At any price above $\overline{p}$, the total supply equals the quota plus the domestic supply. For example at p^*, the domestic supply is Q_d^* and the foreign supply is $\overline{Q}_f$, so the total supply is $Q_d^* + \overline{Q}_f$. Above $\overline{p}$, $\overline{S}$ is the domestic supply curve shifted $\overline{Q}$ units to the right. As a result, the portion of $\overline{S}$ above $\overline{p}$ has the same slope as S^d.

4. *Compare the American total supply curves with and without the quota:* At prices less than or equal to $\overline{p}$, the same quantity is supplied with and without the quota, so $\overline{S}$ is the same as S. At prices above $\overline{p}$, less is supplied with the quota than without one, so $\overline{S}$ is steeper than S, indicating that a given increase in price raises the quantity supplied by less with a quota than without one.

2.3 | MARKET EQUILIBRIUM

The supply and demand curves determine the price and quantity at which goods and services are bought and sold. The demand curve shows the quantities consumers want to buy at various prices, and the supply curve shows the quantities firms want to sell at various prices. Unless the price is set so that consumers want to buy exactly the same amount that suppliers want to sell, either some buyers cannot buy as much as they want or some sellers cannot sell as much as they want.

When all traders are able to buy or sell as much as they want, we say that the market is in **equilibrium**: a situation in which no participant wants to change its behavior. A price at which consumers can buy as much as they want and sellers can sell as much as they want is called an *equilibrium price*. The quantity that is bought and sold at the equilibrium price is called the *equilibrium quantity*.

Using a Graph to Determine the Equilibrium

This little piggy went to market . . .

To illustrate how supply and demand curves determine the equilibrium price and quantity, we use our old friend, the processed pork example. Figure 2.6 shows the supply, *S*, and demand, *D*, curves for pork. The supply and demand curves intersect at point *e*, the market equilibrium, where the equilibrium price is $3.30 and the equilibrium quantity is 220 million kg per year, which is the quantity firms want to sell *and* the quantity consumers want to buy.

Using Math to Determine the Equilibrium

We can determine the processed pork market equilibrium mathematically, using the supply and demand functions. We use these two functions to solve for the equilibrium price at which the quantity demanded equals the quantity supplied (the equilibrium quantity).

The demand function, Equation 2.3, shows the relationship between the quantity demanded, Q_d, and the price:

$$Q_d = 286 - 20p.$$

The supply function, Equation 2.7, tells us the relationship between the quantity supplied, Q_s, and the price:

$$Q_s = 88 + 40p.$$

We want to find the *p* at which $Q_d = Q_s = Q$, the equilibrium quantity. Because the left-hand sides of the two equations are equal in equilibrium, $Q_s = Q_d$, the right-hand sides of the two equations must be equal:

$$286 - 20p = 88 + 40p.$$

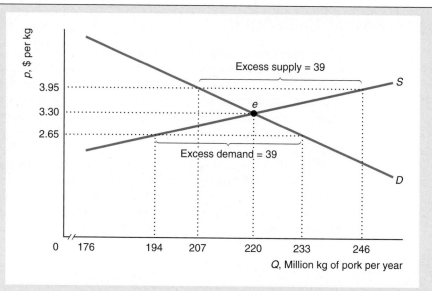

Figure 2.6 **Market Equilibrium.** The intersection of the supply curve, *S*, and the demand curve, *D*, for processed pork determines the market equilibrium point, *e*, where *p* = $3.30 per kg and *Q* = 220 million kg per year. At the lower price of *p* = $2.65, the quantity supplied is only 194, whereas the quantity demanded is 233, so there is excess demand of 39. At *p* = $3.95, a price higher than the equilibrium price, there is excess supply of 39 because the quantity demanded, 207, is less than the quantity supplied, 246. When there is excess demand or supply, market forces drive the price back to the equilibrium price of $3.30.

Adding 20*p* to both sides of this expression and subtracting 88 from both sides, we find that 198 = 60*p*. Dividing both sides of this last expression by 60, we learn that the equilibrium price is *p* = $3.30. We can determine the equilibrium quantity by substituting this *p* into either the supply or the demand equation:

$$Q_d = Q_s$$
$$286 - (20 \times 3.30) = 88 + (40 \times 3.30)$$
$$220 = 220.$$

Thus the equilibrium quantity is 220.

Forces That Drive the Market to Equilibrium

A market equilibrium is not just an abstract concept or a theoretical possibility. We can observe markets in equilibrium. Indirect evidence that a market is in equilibrium is that you can buy as much as you want of the good at the market price. You can almost always buy as much as you want of such common goods as milk and ballpoint pens.

Amazingly, a market equilibrium occurs without any explicit coordination between consumers and firms. In a competitive market such as that for agricultural goods, millions of consumers and thousands of firms make their buying and selling decisions independently. Yet each firm can sell as much as it wants; each consumer can buy as much as he or she wants. It is as though an unseen market force, like an *invisible hand*, directs people to coordinate their activities to achieve a market equilibrium.

What really causes the market to move to an equilibrium? If the price is not at the equilibrium level, consumers or firms have an incentive to change their behavior in a way that will drive the price to the equilibrium level, as we now illustrate.

If the price were initially lower than the equilibrium price, consumers would want to buy more than suppliers want to sell. If the price of pork is $2.65 in Figure 2.6, firms are willing to supply 194 million kg per year but consumers demand 233 million kg. At this price, the market is in *disequilibrium*, meaning that the quantity demanded is not equal to the quantity supplied. There is **excess demand**—the amount by which the quantity demanded exceeds the quantity supplied at a specified price—of 39 (= 233 – 194) million kg per year at a price of $2.65.

Some consumers are lucky enough to buy the pork at $2.65. Other consumers cannot find anyone who is willing to sell them pork at that price. What can they do? Some frustrated consumers may offer to pay suppliers more than $2.65. Alternatively, suppliers, noticing these disappointed consumers, may raise their prices. Such actions by consumers and producers cause the market price to rise. As the price rises, the quantity that firms want to supply increases and the quantity that consumers want to buy decreases. This upward pressure on price continues until it reaches the equilibrium price, $3.30, where there is no excess demand.

If, instead, price is initially above the equilibrium level, suppliers want to sell more than consumers want to buy. For example, at a price of pork of $3.95, suppliers want to sell 246 million kg per year but consumers want to buy only 207 million, as the figure shows. At $3.95, the market is in disequilibrium. There is an **excess supply**—the amount by which the quantity supplied is greater than the quantity demanded at a specified price—of 39 (= 246 – 207) at a price of $3.95. Not all firms can sell as much as they want. Rather than incur storage costs (and possibly have their unsold pork spoil), firms lower the price to attract additional customers. As long as price remains above the equilibrium price, some firms have unsold pork and want to lower the price further. The price falls until it reaches the equilibrium level, $3.30, where there is no excess supply and hence no more pressure to lower the price further.

In summary, at any price other than the equilibrium price, either consumers or suppliers are unable to trade as much as they want. These disappointed people act to change the price, driving the price to the equilibrium level. The equilibrium price is called the *market clearing price* because it removes from the market all frustrated buyers and sellers: there is no excess demand or excess supply at the equilibrium price.

2.4 | SHOCKING THE EQUILIBRIUM

Once an equilibrium is achieved, it can persist indefinitely because no one applies pressure to change the price. *The equilibrium changes only if a shock occurs that shifts the demand curve or the supply curve. These curves shift if one of the variables we were holding constant changes.* If tastes, income, government policies, or costs of production change, the demand curve or the supply curve or both shift, and the equilibrium changes.

Effects of a Shift in the Demand Curve

Suppose that the price of beef increases by 60¢, and so consumers substitute pork for beef. As a result, the demand curve for pork shifts outward from D^1 to D^2 in panel a of Figure 2.7. At any given price, consumers want more pork than they did before the price of beef rose. In particular, at the original equilibrium price of pork, $3.30, consumers now want to buy 232 million kg of pork per year. At that price,

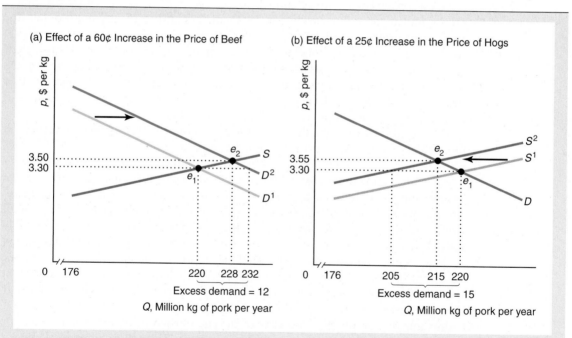

(a) Effect of a 60¢ Increase in the Price of Beef

(b) Effect of a 25¢ Increase in the Price of Hogs

Figure 2.7 Effects of a Shift of the Demand Curve. (a) An increase in the price of beef by 60¢ causes the demand curve for processed pork to shift outward from D^1 to D^2. At the original equilibrium, e_1, price, $3.30, there is excess demand of 12. Market pressures drive the price up until it reaches $3.50 at the new equilibrium, e_2. (b) An increase in the price of hogs by 25¢ causes the supply curve for processed pork to shift to the left from S^1 to S^2, driving the market equilibrium from e_1 to e_2.

however, suppliers still want to sell only 220. As a result, there is excess demand of 12. Market pressures drive the price up until it reaches a new equilibrium at $3.50. At that price, firms want to sell 228 and consumers want to buy 228, the new equilibrium quantity. Thus the pork equilibrium goes from e_1 to e_2 as a result of the increase in the price of beef. Both the equilibrium price and the equilibrium quantity of pork rise as a result of the outward shift of the pork demand curve. Here the increase in the price of beef causes a *shift of the demand curve*, causing a *movement along the supply curve*.

Effects of a Shift in the Supply Curve

Now suppose that the price of beef stays constant at its original level but the price of hogs increases by 25¢. It is now more expensive to produce pork because the price of a major input, hogs, has increased. As a result, the supply curve for pork shifts to the left from S^1 to S^2 in panel b of Figure 2.7. At any given price, firms want to supply less pork than they did before the price of hogs increased. At the original equilibrium price of pork of $3.30, consumers still want 220, but suppliers are now willing to supply only 205, so there is excess demand of 15. Market pressure forces the price of pork up until it reaches a new equilibrium at e_2, where the equilibrium price is $3.55 and the equilibrium quantity is 215. The increase in the price of hogs causes the equilibrium price to rise but the equilibrium quantity to fall. Here a *shift of the supply curve* results in a *movement along the demand curve*.

In summary, a change in an underlying factor, such as the price of a substitute or the price of an input, shifts the demand or supply curve. As a result of this shift in the demand or supply curve, the equilibrium changes. To describe the effect of this change in the underlying factor on the market, we compare the original equilibrium price and quantity to the new equilibrium values.

Solved Problem 2.2

Mathematically, how does the equilibrium price of pork vary as the price of hogs changes if the variables that affect demand are held constant at their typical values?

Answer

1. *Solve for the equilibrium price of pork in terms of the price of hogs:* The demand function does not depend on the price of hogs, so we can use Equation 2.3 from before,

$$Q_d = 286 - 20p.$$

To see how the equilibrium depends on the price of hogs, we use supply function Equation 2.6:

$$Q_s = 178 + 40p - 60p_h.$$

The equilibrium is determined by equating the right-hand sides of these demand-and-supply equations:

$$286 - 20p = 178 + 40p - 60p_h.$$

Rearranging terms in this last expression, we find that $60p = 108 + 60p_h$. Dividing both sides by 60, we have an expression for the equilibrium price of processed pork as a function of the price of hogs:

$$p = 1.8 + p_h. \tag{2.8}$$

(As a check, when p_h equals its typical value, $1.50, Equation 2.8 says that the equilibrium price of pork is $p = \$3.30$, which we know is correct from our earlier calculations.)

We find the equilibrium quantity as a function of the price of hogs by substituting this expression for the equilibrium price, Equation 2.8, into the demand equation (though we could use the supply function instead):

$$Q = 286 - 20p = 286 - 20(1.8 + p_h) = 250 - 20p_h.$$

(Again, as a check, if p_h equals its typical value of $1.50, $Q = 220$, which we know is the original equilibrium quantity.)

2. *Show how the equilibrium price of pork varies with the price of hogs:* We know from Equation 2.8 that $\Delta p = \Delta p_h$. Any increase in the price of hogs causes an equal increase in the price of processed pork. As panel b of Figure 2.7 illustrates, if the price of hogs increases by $\Delta p_h = \$0.25$ (from $1.50 to $1.75), the price of pork, p, increases by $\Delta p = \Delta p_h = \$0.25$ (from $3.30 to $3.55).

2.5 | EFFECTS OF GOVERNMENT INTERVENTIONS

A government can affect a market equilibrium in many ways. Sometimes government actions cause a shift in the supply curve, the demand curve, or both curves, which causes the equilibrium to change. Some government interventions, however, cause the quantity demanded to differ from the quantity supplied.

Policies That Shift Supply Curves

As we saw earlier, quotas on imports affect the supply curve. We illustrate the effect of quotas on market equilibrium.

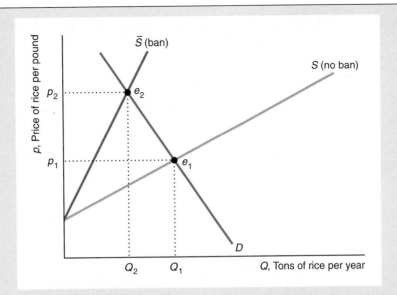

Figure 2.8 A Ban on Rice Imports Raises the Price in Japan. A ban on rice imports shifts the total supply of rice in Japan without a ban, S, to $\bar{S}$, which equals the domestic supply alone. As a result, the equilibrium changes from e_1 to e_2. The ban causes the price to rise from p_1 to p_2 and the equilibrium quantity to fall to Q_1 from Q_2.

The Japanese government's ban on rice imports raised the price of rice in Japan substantially. Figure 2.8 shows the Japanese demand curve for rice, D, and the total supply curve without a ban, S. The intersection of S and D determines the equilibrium, e_1, if rice imports are allowed.

What is the effect of a ban on foreign rice on Japanese demand and supply? The ban has no effect on demand if Japanese consumers do not care whether they eat domestic or foreign rice. The ban causes the total supply curve to rotate toward the origin from S (total supply is the horizontal sum of domestic and foreign supply) to $\bar{S}$ (total supply equals the domestic supply).

The intersection of $\bar{S}$ and D determines the new equilibrium, e_2, which lies above and to the left of e_1. The ban causes a shift of the supply curve and a movement along the demand curve. It leads to a fall in the equilibrium quantity from Q_1 to Q_2 and a rise in the equilibrium price from p_1 to p_2. Because of the Japanese ban on imported rice, the price of rice in Japan has at times been over seven times higher than the price in the rest of the world.

A quota of $\bar{Q}$ may have a similar effect to an outright ban; however, a quota may have no effect on the equilibrium if the quota is set so high that it does not limit imports. We investigate this possibility in Solved Problem 2.3 and the application that follows it.

Solved Problem 2.3   **What is the effect of a United States quota on steel of $\overline{Q}$ on the equilibrium in the U.S. steel market?** *Hint:* The answer depends on whether the quota binds (is low enough to affect the equilibrium).

Answer

1. *Show how a quota, $\overline{Q}$, affects the total supply of steel in the United States:* The graph reproduces the no-quota total American supply curve of steel, S, and the total supply curve under the quota, $\overline{S}$ (which we derived in Solved Problem 2.1). At a price below $\overline{p}$, the two supply curves are identical because the quota is not binding: It is greater than the quantity foreign firms want to supply. Above $\overline{p}$, $\overline{S}$ lies to the left of S.

2. *Show the effect of the quota if the original equilibrium quantity is less than the quota so that the quota does not bind:* Suppose that the American demand is relatively *low* at any given price so that the demand curve, D^l, intersects both the supply curves at a price below $\overline{p}$. The equilibria both before and after the quota is imposed are at e_1, where the equilibrium price, p_1, is less than $\overline{p}$. Thus if the demand curve lies near enough to the origin that the quota is not binding, the quota has no effect on the equilibrium.

3. *Show the effect of the quota if the quota binds:* With a relatively *high* demand curve, D^h, the quota affects the equilibrium. The no-quota equilibrium is e_2, where D^h intersects the no-quota total supply curve, S. After the quota is imposed, the equilibrium is e_3, where D^h intersects the total supply curve with the quota, $\overline{S}$. The quota raises the price of steel in the United States from p_2 to p_3 and reduces the quantity from Q_2 to Q_3.

Application   AMERICAN STEEL QUOTAS

The U.S. government has repeatedly limited imports of steel into the United States. In some years, the U.S. government negotiated with the governments of Japan and several European countries to limit the amount of steel those countries sold in the United States. Various agreements were in effect from 1969 through 1974. But the quotas were often set so high that they had no effect.

In 1971 and 1972, however, the quotas were apparently binding for most steel products. In those years, the quotas raised average U.S. steel prices between 1.2% and 3.5%.

In 1984, President Ronald Reagan announced a new set of *voluntary* quotas, which covered most steel-exporting countries and limited finished steel imports into the United States to 18.5% of the total U.S. sales for 1985–1989. These limits on imports drove up prices above what they would have been without the quotas. In 1979–1980, in the absence of quotas, the average U.S. price of steel was approximately the same as the market price in Antwerp, Belgium. In 1984 and 1985, under the Reagan quotas, the average U.S. price was about 25% higher than the corresponding price in Antwerp.

In 1980, pig iron and semifinished steel imports accounted for only 3.5% of domestic steel use, a share that remained virtually unchanged through 1992. Thereafter, in the absence of quotas, imports rose substantially, and the share of imports reached 26.4% by 1998. In 1999, the U.S. House of Representatives passed a bill calling for a 30% reduction in steel imports; however, the Senate rejected this legislation in the face of a threatened veto by President Bill Clinton.

Policies That Cause Demand to Differ from Supply

Some government policies do more than merely shift the supply or demand curve. For example, governments may control prices directly, a policy that leads to either excess supply or excess demand if the price the government sets differs from the equilibrium price. We illustrate this result with two types of price control programs. When the government sets a *price ceiling* at $\bar{p}$, the price at which goods are sold may be no higher than $\bar{p}$. When the government sets a *price floor* at $\underline{p}$, the price at which goods are sold may not fall below $\underline{p}$.

Price Ceilings. Price ceilings have no effect if they are set above the equilibrium price that would be observed in the absence of the price controls. If the government says that firms may charge no more than $\bar{p} = \$5$ per gallon of gas and firms are actually charging $p = \$1.30$, the government's price control policy is irrelevant. However, if the equilibrium price, p, would be above the price ceiling $\bar{p}$, the price that is actually observed in the market is the price ceiling.

To keep prices from rising in wartime, the United States government has used price ceilings. During World War II, for example, the prices of all staples (such as sugar and gasoline) were controlled. To limit inflation, President Richard Nixon instituted wage and price controls on many goods in 1971–1972. Since 1992, there have been periodic debates in Congress about whether to apply price controls to medical services.

The U.S. experience with gasoline illustrates the effects of price controls. In the 1970s, the Organization of Petroleum Exporting Countries (OPEC) reduced supplies of oil (which is converted into gasoline) to Western countries. As a result, the total supply curve for gasoline in the United States—the horizontal sum of domestic and OPEC supply curves—shifted to the left from S^1 to S^2 in Figure 2.9. Because of this shift, the equilibrium price of gasoline would have risen substantially, from p_1 to p_2. In an attempt to protect consumers by keeping gasoline prices from rising, the U.S. government set price ceilings on gasoline in 1973 and 1979.

The government told gas stations that they could charge no more than $\bar{p} = p_1$. Figure 2.9 shows the price ceiling as a solid horizontal line extending from the price

Figure 2.9 Price Ceiling on Gasoline. Supply shifts from S^1 to S^2. Under the government's price control program, gasoline stations may not charge a price above the price ceiling $\bar{p} = p_1$. At that price, producers are willing to supply only Q_s, which is less than the amount $Q_1 = Q_d$ that consumers want to buy. The result is excessive demand, or a shortage of $Q_d - Q_s$.

axis at $\bar{p}$. The price control is binding because $p_2 > \bar{p}$. The observed price is the price ceiling. At $\bar{p}$, consumers *want* to buy $Q_d = Q_1$ gallons of gasoline, which is the equilibrium quantity they bought before OPEC acted. However, firms supply only Q_s gallons, which is determined by the intersection of the price control line with S^2. As a result of the binding price control, there is excess demand of $Q_d - Q_s$.

Were it not for the price controls, market forces would drive up the market price to p_2, where the excess demand would be eliminated. The government price ceiling prevents this adjustment from occurring. As a result, an enforced price ceiling causes a **shortage**: a persistent excess demand.

At the time of the controls, some government officials argued that the shortages were caused by OPEC's cutting off its supply of oil to the United States, but that's not true. Without the price controls, the new equilibrium would be e_2. In this equilibrium, the price, p_2, is much higher than before, p_1; however, there is no shortage. Moreover, without controls, the quantity sold, Q_2, is greater than the quantity sold under the control program, Q_s.

With a binding price ceiling, the supply-and-demand model predicts an *equilibrium with a shortage*. In this equilibrium, the quantity demanded does not equal the quantity supplied. The reason that we call this situation an equilibrium, even though a shortage exists, is that no consumers or firms want to act differently, given the law. Without the price controls, consumers facing a shortage would try to get more output by offering to pay more, or firms would raise prices. With effective government price controls, they know that they can't drive up the price, so they live with the shortage.

What happens? Some lucky consumers get to buy Q_s units at the low price of $\bar{p}$. Other potential customers are disappointed: They would like to buy at that price, but they cannot find anyone willing to sell gas to them.

What determines which consumers are lucky enough to find goods to buy at the low price when there are price controls? With enforced price controls, sellers use criteria other than price to allocate the scarce commodity. Firms may supply their friends, long-term customers, or people of a certain race, gender, age, or religion. They may sell their goods on a first-come, first-served basis. Or they may limit everyone to only a few gallons.

Another possibility is for firms and customers to evade the price controls. A consumer could go to a gas station owner and say, "Let's not tell anyone, but I'll pay you twice the price the government sets if you'll sell me as much gas as I want." If enough customers and gas station owners behaved that way, no shortage would occur.

Application   GAS LINES

The 1973 and 1979 price controls on gasoline led to gas shortages and long lines of cars at service stations as consumers waited to buy scarce gasoline. Some stations sold their gas on a first-come, first-served basis. Others rationed the amount of gasoline they would sell to an individual, sometimes to as little as one or two gallons. After selling all their gasoline, stations closed. Few stations opened on weekends or in the evenings.

Customers waited hours in long lines of cars to buy gas. Some lined up as early as 4:00 A.M. on the Saturday of the long Washington's Birthday weekend. Some stations reported lines of over 75 cars by 7:00 A.M. It was estimated that a mile-long line of idling six-cylinder cars burns up 150 gallons of gasoline per hour. Thus the lines worsened the shortage.

Some retailers ignored the price controls and raised their prices. Others evaded the controls by using *tie-in sales*: customers could buy gasoline if they also purchased another high-priced item, such as an expensive car wash. U.S. Attorney General William B. Saxbe threatened to bring criminal and civil actions against gas station operators who used either of these approaches to evade the price controls.

Americans respected the price control laws more in some cities than in others. A study of 92 major U.S. cities found no gasoline lines in 52 of them. However, in cities such as Chicago, Hartford, New York, Portland, and Tucson, potential customers waited in line for an hour or more before getting to the pump.

Some stations posted "Out of Gas" signs early every morning. But people who had a dealer-supplied red plastic strip in their window, identifying them as regular customers, could buy gasoline.

In response to this tactic, Federal Energy Director William F. Simon prohibited gas stations from discriminating against buyers by practices such as selling gasoline only to regular customers or to those who purchased large amounts of gasoline in advance. Director Simon was operating under his authority to control prices and allocate motor fuels during this crisis. He urged motorists to contact the Internal Revenue Service immediately if they believed they were being discriminated against in violation of his order. A station owner who was convicted of violating the regulation under the criminal code could be fined up to $5,000.

Generally, the government acted to protect consumers from having to pay high prices for oil. But in so doing, it created shortages and incurred substantial enforcement costs. Deacon and Sonstelie (1989) calculate that for every dollar consumers saved during another episode of gasoline price controls in 1980, they lost $1.16 in waiting time and other factors.

Would you prefer to pay a relatively high price and be able to buy as much gasoline as you want at that price or to pay a low price and have to stand in line to buy a restricted amount? Consumers differ on the answer to this question. Presumably, consumers who put a relatively low value on their time are more likely to favor controls than consumers who value time and convenience more highly.

Price Floors. Governments also commonly use price floors. One of the most important examples of a price floor is the minimum wage in labor markets.

The minimum wage law forbids employers from paying less than the minimum wage, $\underline{w}$. Currently, the federal minimum wage is $5.15 an hour. If the minimum wage binds—exceeds the equilibrium wage, w^*—the minimum wage creates *unemployment*, which is a persistent excess supply of labor.[9]

For simplicity, suppose that there is a single labor market in which everyone is paid the same wage. Figure 2.10 shows the supply and demand curves for labor services (hours worked). Firms buy hours of labor service—they hire workers. The quantity measure on the horizontal axis is hours worked per year, and the price measure is the wage per hour.

With no government intervention, the market equilibrium is e, where the wage is w^* and the number of hours worked is L^*. The minimum wage creates a price floor, a horizontal line, at $\underline{w}$. At that wage, the quantity demanded falls to L_d and the quantity supplied rises to L_s. As a result, there is an excess supply or unemployment

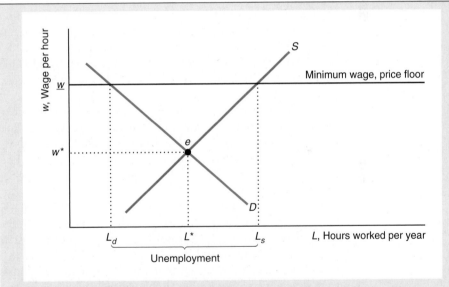

Figure 2.10 **Minimum Wage.** In the absence of a minimum wage, the equilibrium wage is w^* and the equilibrium number of hours worked is L^*. A minimum wage, $\underline{w}$, set above w^*, leads to unemployment—persistent excess supply—because the quantity demanded, L_d, is less than the quantity supplied, L_s.

[9]Where the minimum wage applies to only a few labor markets (Chapter 10) or where only a single firm hires all the workers in a market (Chapter 15), a minimum wage may not cause unemployment (see Card and Krueger, 1995, for empirical evidence). The U.S. Department of Labor maintains at its Web site (**www.dol.gov**) an extensive history of the minimum wage law, labor markets, state minimum wage laws, and other information.

of $L_s - L_d$. The minimum wage prevents market forces from eliminating this excess supply, so it leads to an equilibrium with unemployment.

It is ironic that a law designed to help workers by raising their wages may harm some of them by causing them to become unemployed. A minimum wage law benefits only those who remain employed.[10]

Application   MINIMUM WAGE LAW IN PUERTO RICO

In 1938, the Fair Labor Standards Act established a $\underline{w}$ = 25¢ per hour minimum wage for many U.S. industries engaged in interstate commerce. This rate was at or below the equilibrium wage in most of these industries, so this price floor had little effect. Unfortunately, the same minimum wage was applied to Puerto Rico, a self-governing island commonwealth in free association with the United States, whose residents are U.S. citizens. Puerto Rico's average wage was much lower: only about 7¢ (= w^* in Figure 2.10) in tobacco and coffee industries, 12¢ in fruit canning, 14¢ in laundries, and 18¢ in apparel industries.

Employers in several important Puerto Rican industries screamed bloody murder. Employers in the tobacco-stemming industry would not comply with the law and practically locked out workers, making them unemployed.

The needlework export industries were decimated. A comparison of 1939–1940 to 1940–1941 shows that exports fell by 61% in cotton manufacturing and linen manufacturing, 71% in silk manufacturing, and 47% in other needlework manufacturing.

This loss of jobs and output devastated Puerto Rico. In response, the U.S. Congress established special minimum wages for specific Puerto Rican industries. For example, by the end of 1940, the rate fell to as low as 12.5¢ in some parts of the needlework industry. Starting in 1974, the Puerto Rican minimum wage was raised gradually to the U.S. level. By 1983, both minimums were the same, $3.35.

In 1998, the minimum wage was nearly two-thirds (61%) of the average hourly earnings in manufacturing in Puerto Rico but only about one-third (37%) on the mainland. Castillo-Freeman and Freeman (1992) estimate that island employment would have been 8% to 10% higher in 1987 if the minimum wage had been set so that the ratio of the minimum to the average wage was comparable to that in the United States. They find that the change in the minimum wage was responsible for one-third of the drop in the employment rate (the ratio of employment to population) in Puerto Rico from 1975 to 1987.

---

[10]The minimum wage could raise the wage enough that total wage payments, wL, rise despite the fall in demand for labor services. If the workers could share the unemployment—everybody works fewer hours than he or she wants—all workers could benefit from the minimum wage.

Why Supply Need Not Equal Demand

The price ceiling and price floor examples show that the quantity supplied does not necessarily equal the quantity demanded in a supply-and-demand model. The quantity supplied need not equal the quantity demanded because of the way we defined these two concepts. We defined the quantity supplied as the amount firms *want to sell* at a given price, holding other factors that affect supply, such as the price of inputs, constant. The quantity demanded is the quantity that consumers *want to buy* at a given price, if other factors that affect demand are held constant. The quantity that firms want to sell and the quantity that consumers want to buy at a given price need not equal the *actual* quantity that is bought and sold.

When the government imposes a binding price ceiling of $\overline{p}$ on gasoline, the quantity demanded is greater than the quantity supplied. Despite the lack of equality between the quantity supplied and the quantity demanded, the supply-and-demand model is useful in analyzing this market because it predicts the excess demand that is actually observed.

We could have defined the quantity supplied and the quantity demanded so that they must be equal. If we were to define the quantity supplied as the amount firms *actually* sell at a given price and the quantity demanded as the amount consumers *actually* buy, supply must equal demand in all markets because the quantity demanded and the quantity supplied are *defined* to be the same quantity.

It is worth pointing out this distinction because many people, including politicians and newspaper reporters, are confused on this point. Someone insisting that "demand *must* equal supply" must be defining demand and supply as the *actual* quantities sold.

Because we define the quantities supplied and demanded in terms of people's *wants* and not *actual* quantities bought and sold, the statement that "supply equals demand" is a theory, not merely a definition. This theory says that the equilibrium price and quantity in a market are determined by the intersection of the supply curve and the demand curve if the government does not intervene. Further, we use the model to predict excess demand or excess supply when a government does control price. The observed gasoline shortages during the period when the U.S. government controlled gasoline prices are consistent with this prediction.

2.6 WHEN TO USE THE SUPPLY-AND-DEMAND MODEL

As we've seen, supply-and-demand theory can help us to understand and predict real-world events in many markets. Through Chapter 10, we discuss competitive markets in which the supply-and-demand model is a powerful tool for predicting what will happen to market equilibrium if underlying conditions—tastes, incomes, and prices of inputs—change. The types of markets for which the supply-and-demand model is useful are described at length in these chapters, particularly Chapter 8. Briefly, this model is applicable in markets in which:

■ **Everyone is a price taker:** Because no consumer or firm is a very large part of the market, no one can affect the market price. Easy entry of firms into the market, which leads to a large number of firms, is usually necessary to ensure that firms are price takers.

- **Firms sell identical products:** Consumers do not prefer one firm's good to another.
- **Everyone has full information about the price and quality of goods:** Consumers know if a firm is charging a price higher than the price others set, and they know if a firm tries to sell them inferior-quality goods.
- **Costs of trading are low:** It is not time consuming, difficult, or expensive for a buyer to find a seller and make a trade or for a seller to find and trade with a buyer.

Markets with these properties are called *perfectly competitive markets.*

Where there are many firms and consumers, no single firm or consumer is a large enough part of the market to affect the price. If you stop buying bread or if one of the many thousands of wheat farmers stops selling the wheat used to make the bread, the price of bread will not change. Consumers and firms are *price takers*: They cannot affect the market price.

In contrast, if there is only one seller of a good or service—a *monopoly* (see Chapter 11)—that seller is a *price setter* and can affect the market price. Because demand curves slope downward, a monopoly can increase the price it receives by reducing the amount of a good it supplies. Firms are also price setters in an *oligopoly*—a market with only a small number of firms—or in markets where they sell differentiated products so that a consumer prefers one product to another (see Chapter 13). In markets with price setters, the market price is usually higher than that predicted by the supply-and-demand model. That doesn't make the model generally wrong. It means only that the supply-and-demand model does not apply to markets with a small number of sellers or buyers. In such markets, we use other models.

If consumers have less information than a firm, the firm can take advantage of consumers by selling them inferior-quality goods or by charging a much higher price than that charged by other firms. In such a market, the observed price is usually higher than that predicted by the supply-and-demand model, the market may not exist at all (consumers and firms cannot reach agreements), or different firms may charge different prices for the same good (see Chapter 19).

The supply-and-demand model is also not entirely appropriate in markets in which it is costly to trade with others because the cost of a buyer's finding a seller or of a seller's finding a buyer are high. **Transaction costs** are the expenses of finding a trading partner and making a trade for a good or service other than the price paid for that good or service. These costs include the time and money spent to find someone with whom to trade. For example, you may have to pay to place a newspaper advertisement to sell your gray 1990 Honda with 137,000 miles on it. Or you may have to go to many stores to find one that sells a shirt in exactly the color you want, so your transaction costs includes transportation costs and your time. The cost of a long-distance call to place an order is a transaction cost. Other transaction costs include the costs of writing and enforcing a contract, such as the cost of lawyers' time. Where transaction costs are high, no trades may occur, or if they do occur, individual trades may occur at a variety of prices (see Chapters 12 and 19).

Thus the supply-and-demand model is not appropriate in markets in which there are only one or a few sellers (such as electricity), firms produce differentiated products (music CDs), consumers know less than sellers about quality or price (used cars), or there are high transaction costs (nuclear turbine engines). Markets in which the supply-and-demand model has proved useful include agriculture, finance, labor, construction, services, wholesale, and retail.

Summary

1. **Demand:** The quantity of a good or service demanded by consumers depends on their tastes, the price of a good, the price of goods that are substitutes and complements, their income, information, government regulations, and other factors. The *Law of Demand*—which is based on observation—says that *demand curves slope downward*. The higher the price, the less of the good is demanded, holding constant other factors that affect demand. A change in price causes a *movement along the demand curve*. A change in income, tastes, or another factor that affects demand other than price causes a *shift of the demand curve*. To get a total demand curve, we horizontally sum the demand curves of individuals or types of consumers or countries. That is, we add the quantities demanded by each individual at a given price to get the total demanded.

2. **Supply:** The quantity of a good or service supplied by firms depends on the price, costs, government regulations, and other factors. The market supply curve need not slope upward but usually does. A change in price causes a *movement along the supply curve*. A change in the price of an input or government regulation causes a *shift of the supply curve*. The total supply curve is the horizontal sum of the supply curves for individual firms.

3. **Market equilibrium:** The intersection of the demand curve and the supply curve determines the equilibrium price and quantity in a market. Market forces—actions of consumers and firms— drive the price and quantity to the equilibrium levels if they are initially too low or too high.

4. **Shocking the equilibrium:** A change in an underlying factor other than price causes a shift of the supply curve or the demand curve, which alters the equilibrium. For example, if the price of beef rises, the demand curve for pork shifts outward, causing a movement along the supply curve and leading to a new equilibrium at a higher price and quantity. If changes in these underlying factors follow one after the other, a market that adjusts slowly may stay out of equilibrium for an extended period.

5. **Effects of government interventions:** Some government policies—such as a ban on imports—cause a shift in the supply or demand curves, thereby altering the equilibrium. Other government policies— such as price controls or a minimum wage—cause the quantity supplied to be greater or less than the quantity demanded, leading to persistent excesses or shortages.

6. **When to use the supply-and-demand model:** The supply-and-demand model is a powerful tool to explain what happens in a market or to make predictions about what will happen if an underlying factor in a market changes. This model, however, is applicable only in markets with many buyers and sellers; identical goods; certainty and full information about price, quantity, quality, incomes, costs, and other market characteristics; and low transaction costs.

Problems

If you ask me anything I don't know, I'm not going to answer.   —*Yogi Berra*

Answers to selected problems appear at the back of the book.

1. In 1998, a virus killed more than half the oysters used to produce pearls in the world's busiest undersea factory. Use a diagram to indicate why the price of pearls rose 18%. How did the equilibrium quantity change?

2. Increasingly, instead of advertising in newspapers, individuals and firms use Web sites that offer free classified ads, such as Realtor.com, Jobs.com, Monster.com, and portals like Yahoo and America Online. Using a supply-and-demand model, explain what will happen to the equilibrium levels of newspaper advertising as the use of the Internet grows. Will the growth of the Internet affect the supply curve, the demand curve, or both? Why?

3. What was the effect on the worldwide market for alcoholic beverages of the Eighteenth Amendment to the U.S. Constitution, which banned the sale or production of alcohol in the United States? Explain what happened to the supply curves, demand curves, and the equilibrium prices and quantities.

4. The U.S. supply of frozen orange juice comes from Florida and Brazil. What is the effect of a freeze that damages oranges in Florida on the price of frozen orange juice in the United States and on the quantities of orange juice sold by Floridian and Brazilian firms?

5. What is the effect of a quota $\overline{Q} > 0$ on equilibrium price and quantity? (*Hint:* Carefully show how the total supply curve changes.)

6. Usury laws place a ceiling on interest rates that lenders such as banks can charge borrowers. Low-income households in states with usury laws have significantly lower levels of consumer credit (loans) than comparable households in states without usury laws (Villegas, 1989). Why? (*Hint:* The interest rate is the price of a loan, and the amount of the loan is the quantity measure.)

7. In 1999, after nearly 20 years of rent control in Berkeley, California, the elimination of the law led to an estimated rise in rents of nearly 40%. Using supply-and-demand models, illustrate how the law and then its elimination affected the rental housing market. Discuss the effects on the equilibrium rental price and the quantity of housing rented.

8. After a major earthquake struck Los Angeles in January 1994, several stores raised the price of milk to over $6 a gallon. The local authorities announced that they would investigate and that they would enforce a law prohibiting price increases of more than 10% during an emergency period. What is the likely effect of such a law?

9. Is it possible that an outright ban on foreign imports will have no effect on the equilibrium price? (*Hint:* Suppose that imports occur only at relatively high prices.)

10. If certain jurisdictions ban the use of skateboards on city streets, what is the likely effect on the market for skateboards? How do such laws affect the supply curve, the demand curve, and equilibrium price and quantity?

11. *The New York Times* reported in 1997 that a crackdown on a cocaine-smuggling ring caused cocaine prices in Manhattan to rise from $20,000 to $30,000 a kilogram. Illustrate in a supply-and-demand diagram why this happened, and explain in words.

12. In 1996, a group of American doctors called for a limit on the number of foreign-trained physicians permitted to practice in the United States. What effect would such a limit have on the equilibrium quantity and price of doctor services in the United States? How are American-trained doctors and consumers affected?

13. Suppose that cotton is produced only in the United States and China. The U.S. government says that if an American farmer sells a bale of cotton at the world price, p, the government will give the farmer $(p^* - p)$ per bale, where $p^* > p$. What happens to the quantities sold by American and Chinese growers and the world price of cotton?

14. Use a supply-and-demand diagram to explain the statement "Talk is cheap because supply exceeds demand." At what price is this comparison being made?

Math Problems

15. Using the estimated demand function for processed pork in Canada (Equation 2.2), determine how price changes as the quantity demanded increases by one unit (that is, the quantity demanded increases by 1 million kg per year). (*Hint:* Rewrite the demand function so that price is a function of quantity.)

16. Using the estimated demand function for processed pork in Canada (Equation 2.2), show how the quantity demanded at a given price changes as per capita income, Y, increases by $100 a year.

17. Suppose that the price of beef, p_b, in Canada increased by 30%, from $4 to $5.20. How does the demand curve for processed pork shift?

18. The supply of corn by the United States is $Q_a = a + bp$, and the supply by the rest of the world is $Q_r = c + ep$. What is the world supply?

19. The demand function for a good is $Q = a - bp$, and the supply functions is $Q = c + ep$, where a, b, c, and e are positive constants. Solve for the equilibrium price and quantity in terms of these four constants.

20. Show how the equilibrium quantity of pork varies with income.

21. Using the equations for processed pork demand (Equation 2.2) and supply (Equation 2.6), solve for the equilibrium price and quantity in terms of the price of hogs, p_h; the price of beef, p_b; the price of chicken, p_c; and income, y. If $p_h = 1.5$ (dollars per kg), $p_b = 4$ (dollars per kg), $p_c = 3\frac{1}{3}$ (dollars per kg), and $y = 12.5$ (thousands dollars), what are the equilibrium price and quantity?

Applying the Supply-and-Demand Model

Few of us ever test our powers of deduction, except when filling out an income tax form.
—Laurence J. Peter

How large a tax would be necessary to reduce the number of teenagers who smoke by half? If the phone company starts charging users 10¢ per minute to connect to the Internet, would use fall enough that we would no longer call the World Wide Web the "World Wide Wait"? If the government were to intercept half the cocaine smuggled into New York City, how much would the price of cocaine rise in the short run and in the long run? We can use supply-and-demand analysis to answer such questions.

When an underlying factor that affects the demand or supply curve changes, the equilibrium price and quantity also change. Chapter 2 showed that you can predict the direction of the change—the *qualitative* change—in equilibrium price and quantity even without knowing the exact shape of the demand and supply curves. In the examples in Chapter 2, all you needed to know to give a qualitative answer was the direction in which the supply curve or demand curve shifted when an underlying factor changed.

To determine the exact amount the equilibrium quantity and price change—the *quantitative* change—you can use estimated equations for the demand and supply functions, as we demonstrated using the pork example in Chapter 2. This chapter shows how to use a single number to describe the shape of a demand or supply curve at a given price and how to use these summary numbers to obtain quantitative answers to what-if questions.

1. **How shapes of demand and supply curves matter:** The effect of a shock (such as a new tax or an increase in the price of an input) on market equilibrium depends on the shape of demand and supply curves.
2. **Sensitivity of quantity demanded to price:** The sensitivity of the quantity demanded to price is summarized by a single measure called the price elasticity of demand.
3. **Sensitivity of quantity supplied to price:** The sensitivity of the quantity supplied to price is summarized by a single measure called the price elasticity of supply.
4. **Long run versus short run:** The sensitivity of the quantity demanded or supplied to price varies with time.
5. **Effects of a sales tax:** How a sales tax increase affects the equilibrium price and quantity of a good and whether the tax falls more heavily on consumers or suppliers depend on the shape of the supply and demand curves.

3.1 | HOW SHAPES OF DEMAND AND SUPPLY CURVES MATTER

The shapes of the demand and supply curves determine by how much a shock affects the equilibrium price and quantity. We illustrate the importance of the shape of the demand curve using the processed pork example (Moschini and Meilke, 1992) from Chapter 2. The supply of pork depends on the price of pork and the price of hogs, the major input in producing processed pork. A 25¢ increase in the price of hogs causes the supply curve of pork to shift to the left from S^1 to S^2 in panel a of Figure 3.1. The *shift of the supply curve* causes a *movement along the demand curve*, D^1, which is downward sloping. The equilibrium quantity falls from 220 to 215 million kg per year, and the equilibrium price rises from $3.30 to $3.55 per kg. Thus this supply shock—an increase in the price of hogs—hurts consumers by raising the equilibrium price 25¢ per kg. Customers buy less (215 instead of 220). Table 3.1 summarizes these effects.

A supply shock would have different effects if the demand curve had a different shape. Suppose that the quantity demanded were not sensitive to a change in the price, so the same amount is demanded no matter what the price is, as in vertical demand curve D^2 in panel b. A 25¢ increase in the price of hogs again shifts the supply curve from S^1 to S^2. Equilibrium quantity does not change, but the price consumers pay rises by 37.5¢ to $3.675. Thus the amount consumers spend rises by more when the demand curve is vertical instead of downward sloping.

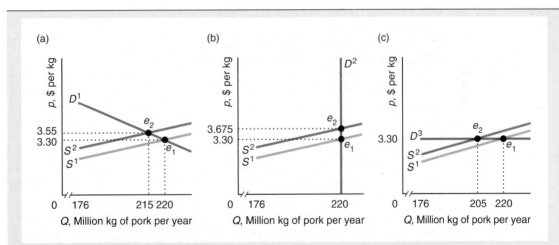

Figure 3.1 How the Effect of a Supply Shock Depends on the Shape of the Demand Curve. A decrease in the price of hogs shifts the supply of processed pork outward. (a) Given the actual downward-sloping linear demand curve, the equilibrium price rises from $3.30 to $3.55 and the equilibrium quantity falls from 220 to 215. (b) If the demand curve were vertical, the supply shock would cause price to rise to $3.675 while quantity would remain unchanged. (c) If the demand curve were horizontal, the supply shock would not affect price but would cause quantity to fall to 205.

Table 3.1	How the Effect on the Processed Pork Market of a 25¢ Increase in the Price of Hogs Depends on the Shape of the Demand Curve	
Shape of Demand Curve	Change in Price, Δp, cents per kg	Change in Quantity, ΔQ, million kg per year
Downward sloping (actual demand)	25	–5
Vertical	37.5	0
Horizontal	0	–15

Now suppose that consumers are very sensitive to price, as in the horizontal demand curve, D^3, in panel c. Consumers will buy virtually unlimited quantities of pork at $3.30 per kg (or less), but, if the price rises even slightly, they stop buying pork. Here an increase in the price of hogs has *no* effect on the price consumers pay; however, the equilibrium quantity drops substantially to 205 million kg per year. Thus how much the equilibrium quantity falls and how much the equilibrium price of processed pork rises when the price of hogs increases depend on the shape of the demand curve.

3.2 SENSITIVITY OF QUANTITY DEMANDED TO PRICE

Knowing how much quantity demanded falls as the price increases, holding all else constant, is therefore important in predicting the effect of a shock in a supply-and-demand model. We can determine how much quantity demanded falls as the price rises using an accurate drawing of the demand curve or the demand function (the equation that describes the demand curve). It is convenient, however, to be able to summarize the relevant information to answer what-if questions without having to write out an equation or draw a graph. Armed with such a summary statistic, the pork firms can predict the effect on the price of pork and their revenues from a shift in the market supply curve.

In this section, we discuss a summary statistic that describes the shape of a demand curve at a given point. This statistic tells us how much the quantity demanded changes in response to an increase or a decrease in price. In the next section, we discuss a similar statistic that summarizes the shape of the supply curve. At the end of the chapter, we show how the government can use these summary measures for demand and supply to predict the effect of a new sales tax on the equilibrium price, firms' revenues, and tax receipts.

Price Elasticity of Demand

The most commonly used measure of the sensitivity of one variable, such as the quantity demanded, to another variable, such as price, is an **elasticity**, which is the percentage change in one variable in response to a given percentage change in another variable. We can use the *price elasticity of demand* (or simply *elasticity of demand*) to describe the shape of the demand curve. The **price elasticity of demand** is the percentage change in the quantity demanded, Q, in response to a given percentage change in the price, p. The price elasticity of demand (represented by ε, the Greek letter epsilon) may be calculated as

$$\varepsilon = \frac{\text{percentage change in quantity demanded}}{\text{percentage change in price}} = \frac{\Delta Q/Q}{\Delta p/p}, \tag{3.1}$$

where the symbol Δ (the Greek letter delta) indicates a change, so ΔQ is the change in the quantity demanded; $\Delta Q/Q$ is the percentage change in the quantity demanded; Δp is the change in price; and $\Delta p/p$ is the percentage change in price. For example, if a 1% increase in the price results in a 3% decrease in the quantity demanded, the elasticity of demand is $\varepsilon = -3\%/1\% = -3$.[1] Thus the elasticity of demand is a pure number (it has no units of measure).

It is often more convenient to calculate the elasticity of demand using an equivalent expression,

$$\varepsilon = \frac{\Delta Q/Q}{\Delta p/p} = \frac{\Delta Q}{\Delta p}\frac{p}{Q}, \tag{3.2}$$

where $\Delta Q/\Delta p$ is the ratio of the change in quantity to the change in price.[2]

We can use Equation 3.2 to calculate the elasticity of demand for a linear demand curve, which has a demand function (holding fixed other variables that affect demand) of

$$Q = a - bp,$$

where a is the quantity demanded when price is zero, $Q = a - (b \times 0) = a$, and $-b$ is the ratio of the fall in quantity to the rise in price, $\Delta Q/\Delta p$.[3] Thus for a linear demand curve, the elasticity of demand is

$$\varepsilon = \frac{\Delta Q}{\Delta p}\frac{p}{Q} = -b\frac{p}{Q}. \tag{3.3}$$

As an example, we calculate the elasticity of demand for the linear pork demand curve D in panel a of Figure 3.1. The estimated linear demand function for pork,

---

[1]Because demand curves slope downward according to the Law of Demand, the elasticity of demand is a negative number. Realizing that, some economists ignore the negative sign when reporting a demand elasticity. In the example, instead of saying the elasticity is –3, they would say that the elasticity is 3 (with the negative sign understood).

[2]When we use calculus, we use infinitesimally small changes in price (Δp approaches zero), so we write the elasticity as $(dQ/dp)(p/Q)$. When discussing elasticities, we assume that the change in price is small.

[3]As the price increases from p_1 to p_2, the quantity demanded goes from Q_1 to Q_2, so the change in quantity demanded is

$$\Delta Q = Q_2 - Q_1 = (a - bp_2) - (a - bp_1) = -b(p_2 - p_1) = -b\Delta p.$$

Thus $\Delta Q/\Delta p = -b$. (The slope of the demand curve is $\Delta p/\Delta Q = -1/b$.)

which holds constant other factors that influence demand besides price (Equation 2.3, based on Moschini and Meilke, 1992), is

$$Q = 286 - 20p,$$

where Q is the quantity of pork demanded in million kg per year and p is the price of pork in dollars per kg. For this demand equation, $a = 286$ and $b = 20$. Using Equation 3.3, we find that the elasticity of demand at the equilibrium e_1 in panel a, where $p = \$3.30$ and $Q = 220$, is

$$\varepsilon = b\frac{p}{Q} = -20 \times \frac{3.30}{220} = -0.3.$$

The negative sign on the elasticity of demand of pork illustrates the Law of Demand: Less quantity is demanded as the price rises. The elasticity of demand concisely answers the question "How much does quantity demanded fall in response to a 1% increase in price?" A 1% increase in price leads to an ε% change in the quantity demanded. At the equilibrium, a 1% increase in the price of pork leads to a -0.3% fall in the quantity of pork demanded: A price increase causes a less than proportionate fall in the quantity of pork demanded.

Application   WEB FEES

Currently, most U.S. users pay a flat fee per month to connect to the Internet. Once connected, they can surf to their heart's content, downloading as much information as they want, at no additional cost. A typical user may download large numbers of files—Web pages, music, movies, and other information-rich material. This heavy usage slows the entire system, leading some disgruntled users to dub the World Wide Web the "World Wide Wait."

How high a price would Internet providers have to charge to substantially reduce connect time? We have some idea of the answer from observing what happened in December 1996, when America Online (AOL) and most other Internet providers switched from charging $9.95 per month for the first five hours of connect time and $2.95 per hour for every additional hour to a flat monthly rate of $19.95 for unlimited access. By 1998, average use rates for AOL had risen from 6.4 to 22.1 hours per week.

Edell and Varaiya (1999) conducted an experiment to determine how the elasticity of demand for hours of connect time with respect to the price per minute of connect time varies with the speed of the connection. Based on their experiment, Varian (1999) found that the price elasticity of demand is -1.71 at a connection speed of 64 kilobits per second (kbps) and -3.34 at 96 kbps.

Elasticity Along the Demand Curve   The elasticity of demand varies along most demand curves. In this section, we show that the elasticity of demand is different at every point along a downward-sloping linear demand curve. Then we point out that the elasticities are constant along horizontal and vertical linear demand curves.

Downward-Sloping Linear Demand Curve. On strictly downward-sloping linear demand curves—those that are neither vertical nor horizontal—the elasticity of demand is a more negative number the higher the price is. Consequently, even though the slope of the linear demand curve is constant, the elasticity varies along the curve. A 1% increase in price causes a larger percentage fall in quantity near the top (left) of the demand curve than near the bottom (right).

The linear pork demand curve in Figure 3.2 illustrates this pattern. Where this demand curve hits the quantity axis ($p = 0$ and $Q = a = 286$ million kg per year), the elasticity of demand is $\varepsilon = -b(0/a) = 0$, according to Equation 3.3. Where the price is zero, a 1% increase in price does not raise the price, so quantity does not change. At a point where the elasticity of demand is zero, the demand curve is said to be *perfectly inelastic*. As a physical analogy, if you try to stretch an inelastic steel rod, the length does not change. The change in the price is the force pulling at demand; if the quantity demanded does not change in response to this pulling, it is perfectly inelastic.

For quantities between the midpoint of the linear demand curve and the lower end where $Q = a$, the demand elasticity lies between 0 and –1: $0 \geq \varepsilon > -1$. A point along the demand curve where the elasticity is between 0 and –1 is *inelastic* (but not perfectly inelastic). Where the demand curve is inelastic, a 1% increase in price leads to a fall in quantity of less than 1%. For example, at the competitive pork equilibrium, $\varepsilon = -0.3$, so a 1% increase in price causes quantity to fall by –0.3%. A physical

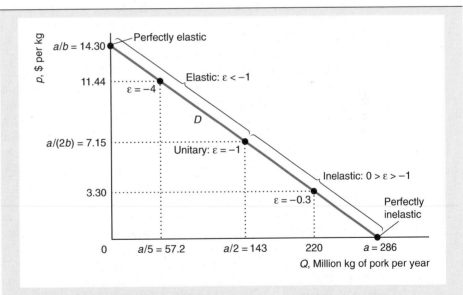

Figure 3.2 Elasticity Along the Pork Demand Curve. With a linear demand curve, such as the pork demand curve, the higher the price, the more elastic the demand curve (ε is larger in absolute value—a larger negative number). The demand curve is perfectly inelastic ($\varepsilon = 0$) where the demand curve hits the horizontal axis, is perfectly elastic where the demand curve hits the vertical axis, and has unitary elasticity ($\varepsilon = -1$) at the midpoint of the demand curve.

analogy is a piece of rope that does not stretch much—is inelastic—when you pull on it: Changing price has relatively little effect on quantity.

At the midpoint of the linear demand curve, $p = a/(2b)$ and $Q = a/2$, so $\varepsilon = -bp/Q = -b(a/[2b])/(a/2) = -1$. Such an elasticity of demand is called a *unitary elasticity*: A 1% increase in price causes a 1% fall in quantity.

At prices higher than at the midpoint of the demand curve, the elasticity of demand is less than negative one, $\varepsilon < -1$. In this range, the demand curve is called *elastic*. A physical analogy is a rubber band that stretches substantially when you pull on it. A 1% increase in price causes a more than 1% fall in quantity. The figure shows that the elasticity is -4 where $Q = a/5$: A 1% increase in price causes a 4% drop in quantity.

As the price rises, the elasticity gets more and more negative, approaching negative infinity. Where the demand curve hits the price axis, it is *perfectly elastic*.[4] At the price a/b where $Q = 0$, a 1% decrease in p causes the quantity demanded to become positive, which is an infinite increase in quantity.

The elasticity of demand varies along most demand curves, not just downward-sloping linear ones. Along a special type of demand curve, called a *constant-elasticity demand curve*, however, the elasticity is the same at every point along the curve.[5] Two extreme cases of these constant-elasticity demand curves are the strictly vertical and the strictly horizontal linear demand curves.

Horizontal Demand Curve. The demand curve that is horizontal at p^* in panel a of Figure 3.3 shows that people are willing to buy as much as firms sell at any price less than or equal to p^*. If the price increases even slightly above p^*, however, demand falls to zero. Thus a small increase in price causes an infinite drop in quantity, so the demand curve is perfectly elastic.

Why would a demand curve be horizontal? One reason is that consumers view this good as identical to another good and do not care which one they buy. Suppose that consumers view Washington apples and Oregon apples as identical. They won't buy Washington apples if these sell for more than apples from Oregon. Similarly, they won't buy Oregon apples if their price is higher than that of Washington apples. If the two prices are equal, consumers do not care which type of apple they buy. Thus the demand curve for Oregon apples is horizontal at the price of Washington apples.

Vertical Demand Curve. A vertical demand curve, panel b in Figure 3.3, is perfectly inelastic everywhere. Such a demand curve is an extreme case of the linear demand curve with an infinite (vertical) slope. If the price goes up, the quantity demanded is

---

[4]The demand curve hits the price axis at $p = a/b$ and $Q = 0$, so the elasticity is $-bp/0$. As the price approaches a/b, the elasticity approaches negative infinity. An intuition for this convention is provided by looking at a sequence, where -1 divided by $1/10$ is -10, -1 divided by $1/100$ is -100, and so on. The smaller the number we divide by, the more negative is the result, which goes to $-\infty$ (negative infinity) in the limit.

[5]Constant-elasticity demand curves all have the form $Q = Ap^\varepsilon$, where A is a positive constant and ε is a negative constant, which is the demand elasticity at every point along these demand curves.

Figure 3.3 Vertical and Horizontal Demand Curves. (a) A horizontal demand curve is perfectly elastic at p^*. (b) A vertical demand curve is perfectly inelastic at every price. (c) The demand curve of an individual who is diabetic is perfectly inelastic below p^* and perfectly elastic at p^*, which is the maximum price the individual can afford to pay.

unchanged ($\Delta Q/\Delta p = 0$), so the elasticity of demand must be zero: $(\Delta Q/\Delta p)(p/Q) = 0(p/Q) = 0$.

A demand curve is vertical for *essential goods*—goods that people feel they must have and will pay anything to get. Because Jerry is a diabetic, his demand curve for insulin could be vertical at a day's dose, Q^*. More realistically, he may have a demand curve (panel c of Figure 3.3) that is perfectly inelastic only at prices below p^*, the maximum price he can afford to pay. Because he cannot afford to pay more than p^*, he buys nothing at higher prices. As a result, his demand curve is perfectly elastic up to Q^* units at a price of p^*.

Other Demand Elasticities

We refer to the price elasticity of demand as *the* elasticity of demand. There are, however, other demand elasticities that show how the quantity demanded changes in response to changes in variables other than price that affect the quantity demanded. Two such demand elasticities are the income elasticity of demand and the cross-price elasticity of demand.

Income Elasticity. As income increases, the demand curve shifts. If the demand curve shifts to the right, a larger quantity is demanded at any given price. If instead the demand curve shifts to the left, a smaller quantity is demanded at any given price.

We can measure how sensitive the quantity demanded at a given price is to income by using an elasticity. The **income elasticity of demand** (or *income elasticity*) is the percentage change in the quantity demanded in response to a given percentage change in income, Y. The income elasticity of demand may be calculated as

$$\xi = \frac{\text{percentage change in quantity demanded}}{\text{percentage change in income}} = \frac{\Delta Q/Q}{\Delta Y/Y} = \frac{\Delta Q}{\Delta Y}\frac{Y}{Q},$$

where ξ is the Greek letter xi. If quantity demanded increases as income rises, the income elasticity of demand is positive. If the quantity does not change as income rises, the income elasticity is zero. Finally, if the quantity demanded falls as income rises, the income elasticity is negative.

We can calculate the income elasticity for pork using the demand function, Equation 2.2:

$$Q = 171 - 20p + 20p_b + 3p_c + 2Y, \tag{3.4}$$

where p is the price of pork, p_b is the price of beef, p_c is the price of chicken, and Y is the income (in thousands of dollars). Because the change in quantity as income changes is $\Delta Q/\Delta Y = 2$,[6] we can write the income elasticity as

$$\xi = \frac{\Delta Q}{\Delta Y} \frac{Y}{Q} = 2\frac{Y}{Q}.$$

At the equilibrium, quantity $Q = 220$ and income is $Y = 12.5$, so the income elasticity is $2 \times (12.5/220) \approx 0.114$. The positive income elasticity shows that an increase in income causes the pork demand curve to shift to the right. Holding the price of pork constant at \$3.30 per kg, a 1% increase in income causes the demand curve for pork to shift to the right by 0.25 ($= \xi \times 220 \times .01$) million kg, which is about one-ninth of 1% of the equilibrium quantity.

Income elasticities play an important role in our analysis of consumer behavior in Chapter 5. Typically, goods that society views as necessities, such as food, have income elasticities near zero. Goods that society considers to be luxuries generally have income elasticities greater than one.

Cross-Price Elasticity. The **cross-price elasticity of demand** is the percentage change in the quantity demanded in response to a given percentage change in the price of another good, p_o. The cross-price elasticity may be calculated as

$$\frac{\text{percentage change in quantity demanded}}{\text{percentage change in price of another good}} = \frac{\Delta Q/Q}{\Delta p_o/p_o} = \frac{\Delta Q}{\Delta p_o} \frac{p_o}{Q}.$$

When the cross-price elasticity is negative, the goods are *complements* (Chapter 2). If the cross-price elasticity is negative, people buy less of the good when the price of the other good increases: The demand curve for this good shifts to the left. For example, if people like cream in their coffee, as the price of cream rises, they consume less coffee, so the cross-price elasticity of the quantity of coffee with respect to the price of cream is negative.

If the cross-price elasticity is positive, the goods are *substitutes* (Chapter 2). As the price of the other good increases, people buy more of this good. For example, the quantity demanded of pork increases when the price of beef, p_b, rises. From

---

[6]At income Y_1, the quantity demanded is $Q_1 = 171 - 20p + 20p_b + 3p_c + 2Y_1$. At income Y_2, $Q_2 = 171 - 20p + 20p_b + 3p_c + 2Y_2$. Thus $\Delta Q = Q_2 - Q_1 = 2(Y_2 - Y_1) = 2(\Delta Y)$, so $\Delta Q/\Delta Y = 2$.

Equation 3.4, we know that $\Delta Q/\Delta p_b = 20$. As a result, the cross-price elasticity between the price of beef and the quantity of pork is

$$\frac{\Delta Q}{\Delta p_b} \frac{p_b}{Q} = 20 \frac{p_b}{Q}.$$

At the equilibrium where $p = \$3.30$ per kg, $Q = 220$ million kg per year, and $p_b = \$4$ per kg, the cross-price elasticity is $20 \times (4/220) \approx 0.364$. As the price of beef rises by 1%, the quantity of pork demanded rises by a little more than one-third of 1%.

Taking account of cross-price elasticities is important in making business and policy decisions. General Motors wants to know how much a change in the price of a Toyota affects the demand for its Chevy.

Application   **DEMANDING RAIL SAFETY**

In 1992, in response to the deaths of four people in rail accidents in the previous year, British Rail spent £215 million ($373 million) on new safety precautions. To cover this expenditure, fares were increased by 7%.

Were these safety expenditures a good idea? Some people argue that saving lives is worth "any price." If we assume that these new safety precautions will save four lives a year, the cost per life saved is $93.25 million. But that expenditure might not be the only cost of this policy.

British Rail's economists estimated the demand for rail travel as a function of the price. They found that a 7% increase in price reduced the number of passenger-kilometers traveled by rail by 1 billion kilometers, or roughly 3.5%. Thus the demand elasticity is

$$\varepsilon = \frac{\text{percentage change in quantity}}{\text{percentage change in price}} = \frac{-3.5\%}{7\%} = -\frac{1}{2}.$$

In response to the rail price increase, what do these discouraged passengers do instead of taking a train? If they travel the same distance by car, accident statistics suggest that 4.9 of them will die. If so, the expected effect of this extra spending on rail safety is to kill nearly an extra person per year! Therefore, if the estimated demand elasticity and probabilities of accidents are accurate, making the additional safety expenditures was a bad idea.

To conduct this analysis properly, one would want to know the cross-price elasticity of auto travel with respect to a change in the price of rail travel. An increase in the rail travel price does not necessarily cause demand for automobile travel to increase by as much as demand for rail travel falls.

Not everyone is comfortable with considering such a trade-off between reduced rail deaths and increased deaths by car; however, if one believes that this type of cost-benefit analysis is appropriate, elasticities play a crucial role. For example, if the rail travel demand elasticity were close to zero (and not the −0.5 that British Rail estimates), there would be no trade-off of deaths from rail and road accidents from this expenditure.

3.3 | SENSITIVITY OF QUANTITY SUPPLIED TO PRICE

To answer many what-if questions, we need information about the sensitivity of the quantity supplied to changes in price. For example, to determine how a sales tax will affect market price, a government needs to know the sensitivity to price of both the quantity supplied and the quantity demanded.

Elasticity of Supply

Just as we can use the elasticity of demand to summarize information about the shape of a demand curve, we can use the elasticity of supply to summarize information about the shape of a supply curve. The **price elasticity of supply** (or *elasticity of supply*) is the percentage change in the quantity supplied in response to a given percentage change in the price. The price elasticity of supply (η, the Greek letter eta) is

$$\eta = \frac{\text{percentage change in quantity supplied}}{\text{percentage change in price}} = \frac{\Delta Q/Q}{\Delta p/p} = \frac{\Delta Q}{\Delta p}\frac{p}{Q}, \qquad (3.5)$$

where Q is the *quantity supplied*. If $\eta = 2$, a 1% increase in price leads to a 2% increase in the quantity supplied.

The definition of the elasticity of supply, Equation 3.5, is very similar to the definition of the elasticity of demand, Equation 3.1. The key distinction is that the elasticity of supply describes the movement along the *supply* curve as price changes, whereas the elasticity of demand describes the movement along the *demand* curve as price changes. That is, in the numerator, supply elasticity depends on the percentage change in the *quantity supplied*, whereas demand elasticity depends on the percentage change in the *quantity demanded*.

If the supply curve is upward sloping, $\Delta p/\Delta Q > 0$, the supply elasticity is positive: $\eta > 0$. If the supply curve slopes downward, the supply elasticity is negative: $\eta < 0$.

To show how to calculate the elasticity of supply, we use the supply function for pork (based on Moschini and Meilke, 1992), Equation 2.7,

$$Q = 88 + 40p,$$

where Q is the quantity of pork supplied in million kg per year and p is the price of pork in dollars per kg. This supply function is a straight line in Figure 3.4. (The horizontal axis starts at 176 rather than at the origin.) The number multiplied by p in the supply function, 40, shows how much the quantity supplied rises as the price increases: $\Delta Q/\Delta p = 40$. At the equilibrium where $p = \$3.30$ and $Q = 220$, the elasticity of supply of pork is

$$\eta = \frac{\Delta Q}{\Delta p}\frac{p}{Q} = 40 \times \frac{3.30}{220} = 0.6.$$

As the price of pork increases by 1%, the quantity supplied rises by slightly less than two-thirds of a percent.

We use the terms *inelastic* and *elastic* to describe *upward-sloping* supply curves, just as we did for demand curves. If $\eta = 0$, we say that the supply curve is *perfectly inelastic*: The supply does not change as price rises. If $0 < \eta < 1$, the supply curve is

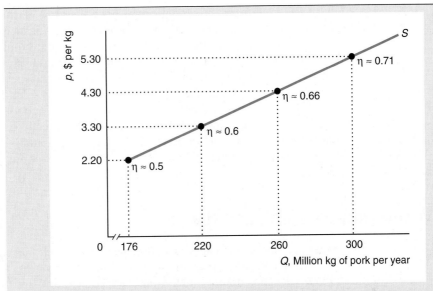

Figure 3.4 Elasticity Along the Pork Supply Curve. The elasticity of supply, η, varies along the pork supply curve. The higher the price, the larger is the supply elasticity.

inelastic (but not perfectly inelastic): A 1% increase in price causes a less than 1% rise in the quantity supplied. If η = 1, the supply curve has a *unitary elasticity*: A 1% increase in price causes a 1% increase in quantity. If η > 1, the supply curve is *elastic*. If η is infinite, the supply curve is *perfectly elastic*.

Elasticity Along the Supply Curve

The elasticity of supply may vary along the supply curve. The elasticity of supply varies along most linear supply curves.

The supply function of a linear supply curve is

$$Q = g + hp,$$

where g and h are constants. By the same reasoning as before, $\Delta Q = h \Delta p$, so $h = \Delta Q / \Delta p$ shows the change in the quantity supplied as price changes.

The supply curve for pork is $Q = 88 + 40p$, so $g = 88$ and $h = 40$. Because $h = 40$ is positive, the quantity of pork supplied increases as the price of pork rises.

The elasticity of supply for a linear supply function is $\eta = h(p/Q)$. The elasticity of supply for the pork is $\eta = 40p/Q$. As the ratio p/Q rises, the supply elasticity rises. Along most linear supply curves, the ratio p/Q changes as p rises.

The pork supply curve, Figure 3.4, is inelastic at each point shown. The elasticity of supply varies along the pork supply curve: It is 0.5 when $p = \$2.20$, 0.6 when $p = \$3.30$, and about 0.71 when $p = \$5.30$.

Only *constant elasticity of supply curves* have the same elasticity at every point along the curve.[7] Two extreme examples of both constant elasticity of supply curves and linear supply curves are the vertical and the horizontal supply curves.

The supply curve that is vertical at a quantity, Q^*, is perfectly inelastic. No matter what the price is, firms supply Q^*. An example of inelastic supply is a perishable item such as fresh fruit. If the perishable good is not sold, it quickly becomes worthless. Thus the seller accepts any market price for the good.

A supply curve that is horizontal at a price, p^*, is perfectly elastic. Firms supply as much as the market wants—a potentially unlimited amount—if the price is p^* or above. Firms supply nothing at a price below p^*, which does not cover their cost of production.

3.4 | LONG RUN VERSUS SHORT RUN

The shapes of demand and supply curves depend on the relevant time period. Short-run elasticities may differ substantially from long-run elasticities. The duration of the *short run* depends on how long it takes consumers or firms to adjust for a particular good.

Demand Elasticities over Time

Two factors that determine whether short-run demand elasticities are larger or smaller than long-run elasticities are ease of substitution and storage opportunities. Often one can substitute between products in the long run but not in the short run.

When oil prices rose rapidly in the 1970s and 1980s because of actions by OPEC, consumers in most Western countries did not greatly alter the amount of oil they demanded. Someone who drove 27 miles to and from work every day in a 1969 Chevy could not easily reduce the amount of gasoline purchased. In the long run, however, this person could buy a smaller car, get a job closer to home, join a car pool, or in other ways reduce the amount of gasoline purchased.

Gallini (1983) estimated long-run demand elasticities that are more elastic than the short-run elasticity for gasoline in Canada. She found that the short-run elasticity is –0.35; the 5-year intermediate-run elasticity is nearly twice as elastic, –0.7; and the 10-year, long-run elasticity is approximately –0.8, which is slightly more elastic. Thus a 1% increase in price lowers the quantity demanded by only about a 0.35% in the short run but by more than twice as much, 0.8%, in the long run. Similarly, Grossman and Chaloupka (1998) estimate that a rise in the street price of cocaine has a larger long-run than short-run effect on cocaine consumption by young adults (aged 17–29). The long-run demand elasticity is –1.35, whereas the short-run elasticity is –0.96.

For goods that can be stored easily, short-run demand curves may be more elastic than long-run curves. If frozen orange juice goes on sale this week at your local supermarket, you may buy large quantities and store the extra in your freezer. As a result, you may be more sensitive to price changes for frozen orange juice in the short run than in the long run.

---

[7]All constant elasticity of supply curves are of the form $Q = Bp^{\eta}$, where B is a constant and η is the constant elasticity of supply at every point along the curve.

Supply Elasticities over Time	Supply curves too may have different elasticities in the short run than in the long run. If a manufacturing firm wants to increase production in the short run, it can do so by hiring workers to use its machines around the clock, but how much it can expand its output is limited by the fixed size of its manufacturing plant and the number of machines it has. In the long run, however, the firm can build another plant and buy or build more equipment. Thus we would expect this firm's long-run supply elasticity to be greater than its short-run elasticity.

Similarly, Adelaja (1991) found that the short-run elasticity of supply of milk is 0.36, whereas the long-run supply elasticity is 0.51. As a result, the quantity response to a 1% increase in price is about 42% (= [0.51 − 0.36]/0.36) more in the long run than in the short run.

3.5 | EFFECTS OF A SALES TAX

Before voting for a new sales tax, legislators want to predict the effect of the tax on prices, quantities, and tax revenues. If the new tax will produce a very large increase in the price consumers pay, legislators who vote for the tax may lose their jobs in the next election. Voters' ire is likely to be even greater if the tax does not raise significant tax revenues.

In this section, we examine three questions about the effects of a sales tax:

1. What effect does a sales tax have on equilibrium prices and quantity?
2. Is it true, as many people claim, that taxes assessed on producers are *passed along* to consumers? That is, do consumers pay for the entire tax?
3. Do the equilibrium price and quantity depend on whether the tax is assessed on consumers or on producers?

How much a tax affects the equilibrium price and quantity and how much of the tax falls on consumers depend on the shape of the demand and supply curves, which is summarized by the elasticities. Knowing only the elasticities of demand and supply, we can make accurate predictions about the effects of a new tax and determine how much of the tax falls on consumers.

Two Types of Sales Taxes	Governments use two types of sales taxes. The most common sales tax is called an *ad valorem* tax by economists and *the* sales tax by real people. For every dollar the consumer spends, the government keeps a fraction, α, which is the ad valorem tax rate. As of 1997, Japan's national sales tax was $\alpha = 5\%$. If a Japanese consumer buys a CD player for \$100, the government collects $\alpha \times \$100 = 5\% \times \$100 = \$5$ in taxes, and the seller receives $(1 - \alpha) \times \$100 = \$95$.[8]

---

[8]For specificity, we assume that the price firms receive is $p = (1 - \alpha)p^*$, where p^* is the price consumers pay and α is the ad valorem tax rate on the price consumers pay. Many governments, however, set the ad valorem sales tax, β, as an amount added to the price sellers charge, so consumers pay $p^* = (1 + \beta)p$. By setting α and β appropriately, the taxes are equivalent. Here $p = p^*/(1 + \beta)$, so $(1 - \alpha) = 1/(1 + \beta)$. For example, if $\beta = \frac{1}{3}$, then $\alpha = \frac{1}{4}$.

The other type of sales tax is a *specific* or *unit* tax, where a specified dollar amount, τ, is collected per unit of output. The federal government collects $\tau = 18.4\mathrm{¢}$ on each gallon of gas sold in the United States. Many communities charge a fixed filing fee or tax on every house sold.

Equilibrium Effects of a Specific Tax

To answer our three questions, we must extend the standard supply-and-demand analysis to take taxes into account. Let's start by assuming that the specific tax is assessed on firms at the time of sale. If the consumer pays p for a good, the government takes τ and the seller receives $p - \tau$.

Specific Tax Effects in the Pork Market. Suppose that the government collects a specific tax of $\tau = \$1.05$ per kg of processed pork from pork producers. Because of the tax, suppliers keep only $p - \tau$ of price p that consumers pay. Thus at every possible price paid by consumers, firms are willing to supply less than when they received the full amount consumers paid. Before the tax, firms were willing to supply 206 million kg per year at a price of $2.95 as the pretax supply curve S^1 in Figure 3.5 shows. After the tax, firms receive only $1.90 if consumers pay $2.95, so they are not willing to supply 206. For firms to be willing to supply 206, they must receive $2.95 after the tax, so consumers must pay $4. As a result, the after-tax supply curve, S^2, is $\tau = \$1.05$ above the original supply curve S^1 at every quantity, as the figure shows.

We can use this figure to illustrate the answer to our first question concerning the effects of the tax on the equilibrium. *The specific tax causes the equilibrium price consumers pay to rise, the equilibrium quantity to fall, and tax revenue to rise.*

The intersection of the pretax pork supply curve S^1 and the pork demand curve D in Figure 3.5 determines the pretax equilibrium, e_1. The equilibrium price is $p_1 = \$3.30$, and the equilibrium quantity is $Q_1 = 220$. The tax shifts the supply curve to S^2, so the after-tax equilibrium is e_2, where consumers pay $p_2 = \$4$, firms receive $p_2 - \$1.05 = \$2.95$, and $Q_2 = 206$. Thus the tax causes the price that consumers pay to increase ($\Delta p = p_2 - p_1 = \$4 - \$3.30 = 70\mathrm{¢}$) and the quantity to fall ($\Delta Q = Q_2 - Q_1 = 206 - 220 = -14$).

Although the consumers and producers are worse off because of the tax, the government acquires new tax revenue of $T = \tau Q = \$1.05$ per kg $\times$ 206 million kg per year $= \$216.3$ million per year. The length of the shaded rectangle in the figure is $Q_2 = 206$ million kg per year, and its height is $\tau = \$1.05$ per kg, so the area of the rectangle equals the tax revenue. (The figure shows only part of the length of the rectangle because the horizontal axis starts at 176.)

How Specific Tax Effects Depend on Elasticities. The effects of the tax on the equilibrium prices and quantity depend on the elasticities of supply and demand. The government raises the tax from zero to τ, so the change in the tax is $\Delta\tau = \tau - 0 = \tau$. In response to this change in the tax, the price consumers pay increases by

$$\Delta p = \left(\frac{\eta}{\eta - \varepsilon}\right)\Delta\tau, \qquad (3.6)$$

where ε is the demand elasticity and η is the supply elasticity at the equilibrium (this equation is derived in Appendix 3A). The demand elasticity for pork is $\varepsilon = -0.3$, and the supply elasticity is $\eta = 0.6$, so a change in the tax of $\Delta\tau = \$1.05$ causes the price consumers pay to rise by

$$\Delta p = \left(\frac{\eta}{\eta - \varepsilon}\right)\Delta\tau = \frac{0.6}{0.6 - [-0.3]} \times \$1.05 = 70¢,$$

as Figure 3.5 shows.

For a given supply elasticity, the more elastic demand is, the less the equilibrium price rises when a tax is imposed. In the pork equilibrium in which the supply elasticity is $\eta = 0.6$, if the demand elasticity were $\varepsilon = -2.4$ instead of -0.3 (that is, the linear demand curve had a less steep slope through the original equilibrium point), the consumer price would rise only $0.6/(0.6 - [-2.4]) \times \$1.05 = 21¢$ instead of 70¢.

Similarly, for a given demand elasticity, the greater the supply elasticity, the larger the increase in the equilibrium price consumers pay when a tax is imposed. In the pork example, in which the demand elasticity is $\varepsilon = -0.3$, if the supply elasticity were $\eta = 1.2$ instead of 0.6, the consumer price would rise $1.2/(1.2 - [-0.3]) \times \$1.05 = 84¢$ instead of 70¢.

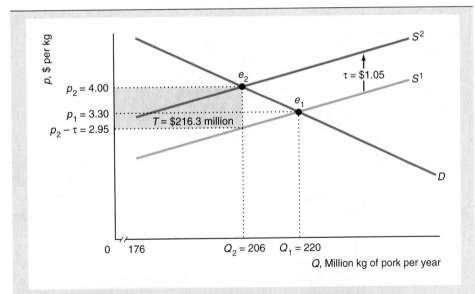

Figure 3.5 Effect of a \$1.05 Specific Tax on the Pork Market Collected from Producers. The specific tax of $\tau = \$1.05$ per kg collected from producers shifts the pretax pork supply curve from S^1 to the posttax supply curve, S^2. The tax causes the equilibrium to shift from e_1 (determined by the intersection of S^1 and D) to e_2 (intersection of S^2 with D). The equilibrium price increases from \$3.30 to \$4.00. Two-thirds of the incidence of the tax falls on consumers, who spend 70¢ more per unit. Producers receive 35¢ less per unit after the tax. The government collects tax revenues of $T = \tau Q_2 = \$216.3$ million per year.

Application

DISCOURAGING SMOKING

If the government really wants to stop people—especially teenagers—from smoking, how should it do so? It could spend millions on education programs and public service ads. Alternatively, the government could raise the tax on cigarettes, which would reduce smoking and raise revenues rather than cost money.

TOM the DANCING BUG   BY RUBEN BOLLING

The more elastic the demand, the more a tax on cigarettes discourages smoking. Keeler, Hu, Barnett, and Manning (1993) estimate that the short-run demand elasticity for cigarettes is inelastic, between –0.3 and –0.5, but that the long-run elasticity is slightly more elastic, between –0.5 and –0.6. One possible reason for the difference in short-run and long-run elasticities is that cigarettes are addictive. Few addicted users stop smoking when the price rises in the short run; however, some potential smokers do not start if the price rises in the long run. Keeler, Hu, Barnett, and Manning conclude that the 1989 increase in the California cigarette tax from 10¢ to 35¢ per pack reduced cigarette consumption by 10% to 12%.

Other studies show that taxes have a greater impact on teenagers than on older people, so an increase in cigarette prices reduces teenage smoking by twice as much as for the population as a whole. For example, as the price of cigarettes in Canada increased 158% between 1979 and 1991 (after adjusting for inflation and including taxes), teenage smoking dropped by 61% and overall smoking fell by 38%.

Thus a moderate tax that raises the price of cigarettes can reduce smoking significantly. In addition to federal taxes, states add their own taxes. The rates differ substantially across states. In 1999, the tax was 2.5¢ per pack in Virginia, 3¢ in Kentucky, 5¢ in North Carolina, 58¢ in Illinois, 65¢ in the District of Columbia, 76¢ in Massachusetts, 82.5¢ in Washington, and $1 in Alaska.

Because of this difference in rates across states, a tax increase in one state may not lead to a substantial price increase for all consumers in that state. When Michigan raised its cigarette tax from 25¢ to 75¢ in 1994, taxable cigarette sales fell nearly 27%, while sales over the Indiana border, where the tax is 15.5¢, jumped 40%. According to one estimate, cigarette smuggling grew 250% from 1980 to 1994 as state taxes differentials grew. Cigarettes are smuggled from low-tax states, Mexico, untaxed tribal reservations, and military bases to high-tax states. As a consequence, if one wants to discourage smoking in a given state, a national tax is more effective than high taxes in that state alone. The Canadian tax was recently decreased substantially, in part to reduce cross-border shopping and smuggling from the United States.

The U.S. tax burden on cigarettes is the lowest of all industrialized countries. As of 1997, the U.S. tax per pack ranged from 34¢ to $1.24 (depending on state taxes) and averaged 66¢. The average in Canada was $1.97, ranging from $1.12 to $2.97. Taxes in other countries were $2.61 in France, $2.76 in New Zealand, $3.13 in Sweden, $4.16 in Ireland, $4.30 in the United Kingdom, and $5.23 in Norway.

Adjusting for inflation, the U.S. federal tax is currently about half its level 20 years earlier. The federal specific tax was 8¢ per pack from 1951 through 1982, 16¢ from 1983 to 1989, 20¢ from 1991 to 1992, and 24¢ from 1993 on. It is scheduled to rise progressively to 39¢ by 2002, though some current proposals call for raising it to 55¢ or even $2. According to one study, the proposed settlement of the Medicaid lawsuits against the tobacco industry (rejected by the U.S. Senate in 1998) would have raised the price of a pack of cigarettes by approximately one-third and reduced the number of teenage smokers by approximately 24%, resulting in 1.3 million fewer smoking-related premature deaths.

Tax Incidence of a Specific Tax

We can now answer our second question: Who is hurt by the tax? The **incidence of a tax on consumers** is the share of the tax that falls on consumers. The incidence of the tax that falls on consumers is $\Delta p/\Delta \tau$, the amount by which the price to consumers rises as a fraction of the amount the tax increases.

In our pork example in Figure 3.5, a $\Delta \tau = \$1.05$ increase in the specific tax causes consumers to pay $\Delta p = 70¢$ more per kg than they would if no tax were assessed. Thus consumers bear two-thirds of the incidence of the pork tax:

$$\frac{\Delta p}{\Delta \tau} = \frac{\$0.70}{\$1.05} = \frac{2}{3}.$$

Firms receive $(p_2 - \tau) - p_1 = (\$4 - \$1.05) - \$3.30 = \$2.95 - \$3.30 = -35¢$ less per kg than they would in the absence of the tax. The incidence of the tax on firms—the amount by which the price to them falls, divided by the tax—is $\$0.35/\$1.05 = \frac{1}{3}$. The sum of the share of the tax on consumers, $\frac{2}{3}$, and that on firms, $\frac{1}{3}$, adds to the entire tax effect, 1. Equivalently, the increase in price to consumers minus the drop in price to firms equals the tax: $70¢ - (-35¢) = \$1.05 = \tau$.

How Tax Incidence Depends on Elasticities. If the demand curve slopes downward and the supply curve slopes upward, as in Figure 3.5, the incidence of the tax *does not* fall solely on consumers. Firms do not pass along the entire tax in higher prices.

Firms can pass along the full cost of the tax only when the demand or supply elasticities take on certain extreme values. To determine the conditions under which firms can pass along the full tax, we need to know how the incidence of the tax depends on the elasticities of demand and supply at the pretax equilibrium. By dividing both sides of Equation 3.6 by $\Delta\tau$, we can write the incidence of the tax that falls on consumers as

$$\frac{\Delta p}{\Delta\tau} = \frac{\eta}{\eta - \varepsilon}. \tag{3.7}$$

Because the demand elasticity for pork is $\varepsilon = -0.3$ and the supply elasticity is $\eta = 0.6$, the incidence of the pork tax that falls on consumers is

$$\frac{0.6}{0.6 - (-0.3)} = \frac{2}{3}.$$

The more elastic the demand at the equilibrium, holding the supply elasticity constant, the lower the burden of the tax on consumers. Similarly, the greater the supply elasticity, holding the demand elasticity constant, the greater the burden on consumers. Thus as the demand curve becomes relatively inelastic (ε approaches zero) or the supply curve becomes relatively elastic (η becomes very large), the incidence of the tax falls mainly on consumers.

Solved Problem 3.1

If the supply curve is perfectly elastic and demand is linear and downward sloping, what is the effect of a \$1 specific tax collected from producers on equilibrium price and quantity, and what is the incidence on consumers? Why?

Answer

1. *Determine the equilibrium in the absence of a tax:* Before the tax, the perfectly elastic supply curve, S^1 in the graph, is horizontal at p_1. The downward-sloping linear demand curve, D, intersects S^1 at the pretax equilibrium, e_1, where the price is p_1 and the quantity is Q_1.

2. *Show how the tax shifts the supply curve and determine the new equilibrium:* A specific tax of \$1 shifts the pretax supply curve upward by \$1 to S^2, which is horizontal at $p_1 + 1$. The intersection of D and S^2 determines the after-tax equilibrium, e_2, where the price consumers pay is $p_2 = p_1 + 1$, the price firms receive is $p_2 - 1 = p_1$, and the quantity is Q_2.

3. *Compare the before- and after-tax equilibria:* The specific tax causes the equilibrium quantity to fall from Q_1 to Q_2, the price firms receive to remain at p_1, and the equilibrium price consumers pay to rise from p_1 to $p_2 = p_1 + 1$. The entire incidence of the tax falls on consumers:

$$\frac{\Delta p}{\Delta\tau} = \frac{p_2 - p_1}{\$1} = \frac{\$1}{\$1} = 1.$$

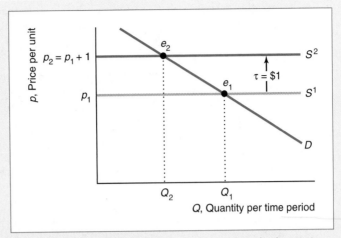

4. *Explain why:* The reason consumers must absorb the entire tax is that firms will not supply the good at a price that is any lower than they received before the tax, p_1. Thus the price must rise enough that the price suppliers receive after tax is unchanged. As consumers do not want to consume as much at a higher price, the equilibrium quantity falls.

Elasticity, Revenue, and Tax Strategy. Governments often use a sales tax to raise tax revenue. However, such a tax harms consumers and producers by reducing the equilibrium quantity.

Some economists and politicians argue that, all else the same, we should tax goods with relatively inelastic demands more heavily. They argue that the less elastic demand is, the less harm a sales tax does in terms of reduced consumption and the more revenue it raises (see Math Problem 21 at the end of the chapter). If the demand curve is vertical at Q_1, the quantity demanded is unchanged by a tax τ, and the revenue is τQ_1. With a downward-sloping demand curve (as in Figure 3.5), the tax reduces the quantity demanded from the original quantity Q_1 to Q_2, and the tax is only τQ_2, which is less than τQ_1.

Presumably, most voters would agree with the goal of reducing the harm of taxes. Whether they favor increasing tax revenues is less clear. Moreover, the less elastic the demand, the larger the incidence of the tax that consumers bear.

Application   **GASOLINE TAXES AS A REVENUE SOURCE**

Many governments rely heavily on gasoline taxes for revenues. Because the demand for gasoline is relatively inelastic, a tax on gasoline falls mainly on consumers and has little effect on the equilibrium quantity of gasoline consumed.

Gallini (1983) estimates that the short-run demand elasticity for gasoline in Canada is about –0.35. Another study concludes that the elasticity in Europe is about –0.2. Umberto Rastelli, an economist in the Italian Foreign Ministry, observed, "When the tax goes up again, we can measure a little reduction in traffic for a couple of weeks—but after that, it's back to normal." Because of this relatively inelastic demand, most developed countries (except the United States) apply very large specific taxes to gasoline to raise substantial revenues.

U.S. federal gasoline taxes are 18.3¢ per gallon, and average state and local taxes add another 22¢ per gallon. The U.S. federal government raises less than 1% of its budget from these taxes.

In Japan, the $1.63 tax raises 5% of government revenues. European taxes per gallon average 20 times U.S. federal rates. The U.K. tax is $2.76 per gallon and produces 17% of the government's budget revenue. Taxes are almost as high in Germany ($2.07), France ($2.38), and Italy ($2.20), where these taxes raise 4% to 5% of the national budget revenues.

The United States could raise substantially more revenues by increasing its gasoline tax. It is estimated that each extra 1¢ per gallon in gasoline tax yields an extra $1 billion in revenues. A 50¢ per gallon increase in the tax would cost the typical American household between $500 and $1,200 a year.

The Same Equilibrium No Matter Who Is Taxed

Our third question is "Does the equilibrium or the incidence of the tax depend on whether the tax is collected from suppliers or demanders?" Surprisingly, in a supply-and-demand model, the equilibrium and the incidence of the tax are the same regardless of whether the government collects the tax from consumers or producers.

We've already seen that, when the tax is collected from firms, they are able to pass on some or all of the tax to consumers. We now show that, if the tax is collected from consumers, they can pass the producer's share back to the firms.

Suppose the specific tax $\tau = \$1.05$ on pork is collected from consumers rather than from sellers. Because the government takes τ from each p consumers spend, sellers receive only $p - \tau$. Thus the demand curve as seen by firms shifts downward by $1.05 from D^1 to D^2 in Figure 3.6.

The intersection of D^2 and the supply curve S determines the after-tax equilibrium, e_2, where the equilibrium quantity is Q_2 and the price received by producers is $p_2 - \tau$. The price paid by consumers, p_2 (on the original demand curve D^1 at Q_2), is τ above the price received by producers.

Comparing Figure 3.6 to Figure 3.5, we see that the after-tax equilibrium is the same regardless of whether the tax is imposed on the consumers or the sellers. The price to consumers rises by the same amount, Δp, so the incidence of the tax, $\Delta p / \Delta \tau$, is also the same.

A specific tax, regardless of whether the tax is collected from consumers or producers, creates a *wedge* equal to the per-unit tax of τ between the price consumers pay, p, and the price suppliers receive, $p - \tau$. Indeed, we can insert a wedge—the vertical line labeled $\tau = \$1.05$ in the figure—between the original supply and demand curves to determine the after-tax equilibrium.

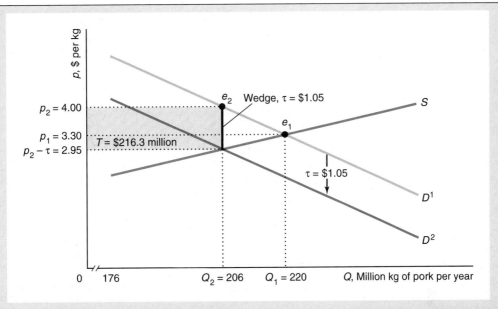

Figure 3.6 Effect of a $1.05 Specific Tax on Pork Collected from Consumers. The tax shifts the demand curve down by $\tau = \$1.05$ from D^1 to D^2. The new equilibrium is the same as when the tax is applied to suppliers in Figure 3.5. We can also determine the after-tax equilibrium by sticking a wedge with length $\tau = \$1.05$ between S and D^1.

In short, regardless of whether firms or consumers pay the tax to the government, you can solve tax problems by shifting the supply curve, shifting the demand curve, or using a wedge. All three approaches give the same answer.

The Similar Effects of Ad Valorem and Specific Taxes

In contrast to specific sales taxes, governments levy ad valorem taxes on a wide variety of goods. Most states apply an ad valorem sales tax to most goods and services, exempting only a few staples such as food and medicine. There are 6,400 different ad valorem sales tax rates across the United States, which can go as high as 8.5% (Besley and Rosen, 1999).

Suppose that the government imposes an ad valorem tax of α, instead of a specific tax, on the price that consumers pay for processed pork. We already know that the equilibrium price is $4 with a specific tax of $1.05 per kg. At that price, an ad valorem tax of $\alpha = \$1.05/\$4 = 26.25\%$ raises the same amount of tax per unit as a $1.05 specific tax.

It is usually easiest to analyze the effects of an ad valorem tax by shifting the demand curve. Figure 3.7 shows how a specific tax and an ad valorem tax shift the processed pork demand curve. The specific tax shifts the pretax demand curve, D, down to D^s, which is parallel to the original curve. The ad valorem tax shifts the demand curve to D^a. At any given price p, the gap between D and D^a is αp, which is greater at high prices than at low prices. The gap is $1.05 (= 0.2625 \times \$4)$ per unit when the price is $4, and $2.10 when the price is $8.

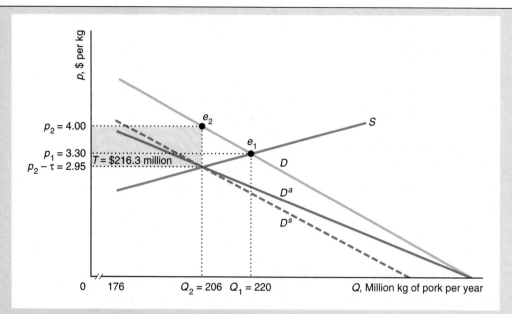

Figure 3.7 Comparison of an Ad Valorem and a Specific Tax on Pork. Without a tax, the demand curve is D and the supply curve is S. The ad valorem tax of $\alpha = 26.25\%$ shifts the demand curve facing firms to D^a. The gap between D and D^a, the per-unit tax, is larger at higher prices. In contrast, the demand curve facing firms given a specific tax of $1.05 per kg, D^s, is parallel to D. The after-tax equilibrium is the same with both of these taxes.

Imposing an ad valorem tax causes the after-tax equilibrium quantity, Q_2, to fall below the original quantity, Q_1, and the after-tax price, p_2, to rise above the original price, p_1. The tax collected per unit of output is $\tau = \alpha p_2$. The incidence of the tax that falls on consumers is the change in price, $\Delta p = (p_2 - p_1)$, divided by the change in the per unit tax, $\Delta t = \alpha p_2 - 0$, collected, $\Delta p/(\alpha p_2)$. The incidence of an ad valorem tax is generally shared between consumers and suppliers. Because the ad valorem tax of $\alpha = 26.25\%$ has exactly the same impact on the equilibrium pork price and raises the same amount of tax per unit as the $1.05 specific tax, the incidence is the same for both types of taxes. (As with specific taxes, the incidence depends on the elasticities of supply and demand, but we'll spare you going through that.)

Solved Problem 3.2   **If the short-run supply curve for fresh fruit is perfectly inelastic and the demand curve is a downward-sloping straight line, what is the effect of an ad valorem tax on equilibrium price and quantity, and what is the incidence on consumers? Why?**

Answer

1. *Determine the before-tax equilibrium:* The perfectly inelastic supply curve, S, is vertical at Q^* in the graph. The pretax demand curve, D^1, intersects S at e_1, where the equilibrium price to both consumers and producers is p^* and the equilibrium quantity is Q^*.

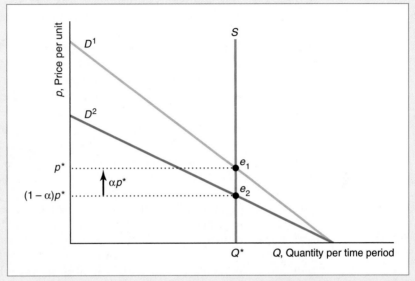

2. *Show how the tax shifts the demand curve, and determine the after-tax equilibrium:* When the government imposes an ad valorem tax with a rate of α, the demand curve as seen by the firms rotates down to D^2, where the gap between the two demand curves is αp. The intersection of S and D^2 determines the after-tax equilibrium, e_2. The equilibrium quantity remains unchanged at Q^*. Consumers continue to pay p^*. The government collects αp^* per unit, so firms receive less, $(1 - \alpha)p^*$, than the p^* they received before the tax.

3. *Determine the incidence of the tax on consumers:* The consumers continue to pay the same price, so $\Delta p = 0$ when the tax increases by αp^* (from 0), and the incidence of the tax that falls on consumers is $\$0/(\alpha p^*)$ $= 0\%$.

4. *Explain why the incidence of the tax falls entirely on firms:* The reason why firms absorb the entire tax is that firms supply the same amount of fruit, Q^*, no matter what tax the government sets. If firms were to raise the price, consumers would buy less fruit and suppliers would be stuck with the essentially worthless excess quantity, which would spoil quickly. Thus because suppliers prefer to sell their produce at a positive price rather than a zero price, they absorb any tax-induced drop in price.

Application

INCIDENCE OF FEDERAL AD VALOREM TAXES

Thanks to a change in federal law, we have a natural experiment that determines in which markets consumers bear the full incidence of sales taxes. On July 1, 1965, the federal ad valorem taxes on many goods and services were eliminated, and the 10% tax on automobiles was reduced to 7%. By the end of 1965, taxes on admissions to theaters, variety shows, and athletic and racing events, as well as on club dues and initiation fees, were also canceled.

Comparing prices before and after this change, we can determine how much the price fell in response to the tax's elimination. When the tax was in place, the tax per unit on a good that sold for p was αp. If the price fell by αp when the tax was eliminated, consumers must have been bearing the full incidence of the tax. Consequently, consumers got the full benefit of removing the tax from those goods.

Brownlee and Perry (1967) found that the entire amount of the tax cut was passed on to consumers immediately for many commodities. These commodities and services included all those studied for which the taxes were collected at the retail level (except admissions and club dues) and most commodities for which excise taxes were imposed at the manufacturer level. Goods for which consumers got essentially the entire tax cut included face powder, sterling silverware, wristwatches, and handbags. When the supply curve is nearly perfectly elastic, we would expect the full incidence of a tax—and hence the full benefit of the tax cut—to fall on consumers (as in Solved Problem 3.1). A perfectly elastic supply curve is likely when all firms have the same costs, as we might expect in retailing. The full incidence of the tax also falls on consumers if the demand curve is completely inelastic (end-of-chapter Problem 6).

Essentially none of the tax savings were passed on for motion picture admissions and club dues. We would expect this result either if the elasticity of demand were perfectly elastic (Problem 7 at the end of this chapter) or if the elasticity of supply were perfectly inelastic (Problem 8 at the end of the chapter).

The price decline was less than the amount of the tax cut for many lower-valued items on which manufacturers' taxes were reduced. The 10% reduction in taxes led to only a 6.3% drop in prices for portable TVs, 1.4% for golf clubs, and 0.9% for stereo records and golf balls. Thus for these goods, neither the demand curves nor the supply curves were perfectly elastic or perfectly inelastic.

Summary

1. **How shapes of the demand and supply curves matter:** The degree to which a shock (such as an increase in the price of a factor) shifts the supply curve and affects the equilibrium price and quantity depends on the shape of the demand curve.

Similarly, the degree to which a shock (such as an increase in the price of a substitute) shifts the demand curve and affects the equilibrium depends on the shape of the supply curve.

2. **Sensitivity of quantity demanded to price:** The

price elasticity of demand (or elasticity of demand), ε, summarizes the shape of a demand curve at a particular point. The elasticity of demand is the percentage change in the quantity demanded in response to a given percentage change in price. For example, a 1% increase in price causes the quantity demanded to fall by ε%. Because demand curves slope downward according to the Law of Demand, the elasticity of demand is always negative.

The demand curve is perfectly inelastic if $\varepsilon = 0$, inelastic if $0 > \varepsilon > -1$, unitary elastic if $\varepsilon = -1$, elastic if $\varepsilon < -1$, and perfectly elastic when ε approaches negative infinity. A vertical demand curve is perfectly inelastic at every price. A horizontal demand curve is perfectly elastic.

The income elasticity of demand is the percentage change in the quantity demanded in response to a given percentage change in income. The cross-price elasticity of demand is the percentage change in the quantity demanded of one good when the price of a related good increases by a given percentage.

3. **Sensitivity of quantity supplied to price:** The price elasticity of supply (or elasticity of supply), η, is the percentage change in the quantity supplied in response to a given percentage change in price. The elasticity of supply is positive if the supply curve has an upward slope. A vertical supply curve is perfectly inelastic. A horizontal supply curve is perfectly elastic.

4. **Long run versus short run:** Long-run elasticities of demand and supply may differ from the corresponding short-run elasticities. Where consumers can substitute between goods more readily in the long run, long-run demand curves are more elastic than short-run demand curves. If goods can be stored easily, however, short-run demand curves are more elastic than long-run curves. If producers can increase output at lower extra cost in the long run than in the short run, the long-run elasticity of supply is greater than the short-run elasticity.

5. **Effects of a sales tax:** The two common types of sales taxes are ad valorem taxes, by which the government collects a fixed percent of the price paid per unit, and specific taxes, by which the government collects a fixed amount of money per unit sold. Both types of sales taxes typically raise the equilibrium price and lower the equilibrium quantity. Both usually raise the price consumers pay and lower the price suppliers receive, so consumers do not bear the full burden or incidence of the tax. The effects on quantity, price, and the incidence of the tax that falls on consumers depend on the demand and supply elasticities. In competitive markets, for which supply-and-demand analysis is appropriate, the effect of a tax on equilibrium quantities, prices, and the incidence of the tax is unaffected by whether the tax is collected from consumers or producers.

Problems

1. If a 2% increase in the price of flame throwers results in a 3% decline in the quantity demanded, what is the elasticity of demand for flame throwers?

2. What section of a straight-line demand curve is elastic?

3. Give some examples of evidence that would convince you that the demand curve for a given product was inelastic. Similarly, what evidence would convince you that a supply curve was elastic? (*Hint*: Consider shocks caused by changes in factors that affect demand or by taxes.)

4. In 1997, the shares of consumers who had cable television service was 59% for people with incomes of $25,000 or less; 66%, $25,000–$34,999; 67%, $35,000–$49,999; 71%, $50,000–$74,999; and 78%, $75,000 or more. What can you say about the income elasticity for cable television?

5. A rent control law limits the price of an apartment. What is the likely effect of such a law in the short run? What is the likely effect of the law in the long run? Be sure to discuss the quantity and quality of apartments available for rent.

6. What is the effect of a $1 specific tax on equilibrium price and quantity if demand is perfectly inelastic? What is the incidence on consumers? Explain.

7. What is the effect of a $1 specific tax on equilibrium price and quantity if demand is perfectly elastic? What is the incidence on consumers? Explain.

8. What is the effect of a $1 specific tax on equilibrium price and quantity if supply is perfectly inelastic? What is the incidence on consumers? Explain.

9. What is the effect of a $1 specific tax on equilibrium price and quantity if demand is perfectly elastic and supply is perfectly inelastic? What is the incidence on consumers? Explain.

10. List as many conditions as you can for the incidence of a tax to fall entirely on consumers.

11. Do you care whether a 15¢ tax per gallon of milk is collected from milk producers or from consumers at the store? Why?

12. California supplies the United States with 80% of its eating oranges. In late 1998, four days of freezing temperatures in the state's Central Valley substantially damaged the orange crop. In early 1999, Food Lion, with 1,208 grocery stores mostly in the Southeast, said its prices for fresh oranges would rise by 20% to 30%, which was less than the 100% increase it had to pay for the oranges. Explain why the price to consumers did not rise by the full amount of Food Lion's price increase. What can you conclude about the elasticities of demand and supply for oranges? (*Hint:* Remember what determines the incidence of a tax.)

13. Consider the market for labor services. The state collects a tax of α (where $0 < \alpha < 1$) cents of every dollar a worker earns. If the state raises its minimum wage, what happens to the amount of tax revenues it collects? Must tax revenue necessarily rise or fall?

Math Problems

14. Calculate the price and cross-price elasticities of demand for coconut oil. The coconut oil demand function (Buschena and Perloff, 1991) is

$$Q = 1,200 - 9.5p + 16.2p_p + 0.2Y,$$

where Q is the quantity of coconut oil demanded in thousands of metric tons per year, p is the price of coconut oil in cents per pound, p_p is the price of palm oil in cents per pound, and Y is the income of consumers. Assume that p is initially 45¢ per pound, p_p is 31¢ per pound, and Q is 1,275 thousand metric tons per year.

15. Using the coconut oil demand function from Problem 14, calculate the income elasticity of demand for coconut oil. (If you do not have all the numbers necessary to calculate numerical answers, write your answers in terms of variables.)

16. The supply curve is $Q = g + hp$. Write a formula for the elasticity of supply in terms of p (and not Q). Now give one entirely in terms of Q.

17. Suppose that the demand function for apple cider is estimated to be $Q = 100 - p$, where p is the price paid by consumers in cents per bottle and Q is the quantity demanded in hundreds of thousands of bottles per day. The supply curve for cider is estimated to be $Q = \frac{1}{4}p$. Calculate the equilibrium price for bottles of cider and the equilibrium quantity sold. Illustrate using a diagram. An environmental group suggests that the government impose a specific tax per bottled beverage of 20¢, to be paid when consumers buy cider and to be used by the government to defray the costs of cleaning up bottle litter. Determine the effects of a 20¢ tax per bottle on the equilibrium price paid by consumers and on the equilibrium quantity sold. What price do the cider-producing firms receive? Discuss how the tax may improve the environment.

18. A constant elasticity supply curve, $Q = Bp^\eta$, intersects a constant elasticity demand curve, $Q = Ap^\varepsilon$, where A, B, η, and ε are constants. What is the incidence of a $1 specific tax? Does your answer depend on where the supply curve intersects the demand curve? Interpret your result.

19. A constant elasticity supply curve, $Q = Bp^\eta$, intersects a linear demand curve, $Q = a - bp$. What is the incidence of a $1 specific tax? Does your answer depend on where the supply curve intersects the demand curve? Interpret your result.

20. Use math to show that, as the supply curve at the equilibrium becomes nearly perfectly elastic, the entire incidence of the tax falls on consumers.

21. Use calculus to show that an increase in a specific sales tax τ reduces quantity by less and tax revenue more, the less elastic the demand curve. (*Hint:* The quantity demanded depends on its price, which in turn depends on the specific tax, $Q(p(\tau))$, and tax revenue is $R = pQ(p(\tau))$.)

Consumer Choice

If this is coffee, please bring me some tea; but if this is tea, please bring me some coffee.   —Abraham Lincoln

Alexx's employer wants to transfer him to the firm's Paris office. Although Alexx likes the idea of living in Paris, he's concerned about the high cost of living there. The firm offers to pay him enough in French francs that he can buy the same combination of goods in Paris that he is buying currently in the United States. In terms of what he can consume, will this higher income undercompensate, fully compensate, or overcompensate Alexx for the higher prices in Paris?

The government gives poor people food stamps, which they may use in retail stores only to buy food. Would the benefit to recipients be greater if they were given cash instead of food stamps? Would they buy less food?

As we saw in Chapters 2 and 3, the supply-and-demand model is useful for analyzing economic questions concerning markets. We could use the supply-and-demand model to examine the market price of croissants in Paris and New York or the effect of food stamps on the market price of donuts. However, the supply-and-demand model cannot be used to answer questions concerning individuals, such as Alexx's problem about whether to move to Paris or whether cash or food stamps would be better for a given individual.

To answer questions about individual decision making, we need a model of individual behavior. Our model of consumer behavior is based on the following premises:

- Individual *tastes* or *preferences* determine the amount of pleasure people derive from the goods and services they consume.
- Consumers face *constraints* or limits on their choices.
- Consumers *maximize* their well-being or pleasure from consumption, subject to the constraints they face.

Consumers spend their money on the products that give them the most pleasure. If you like music and don't have much of a sweet tooth, you spend a lot of your money on concerts, tapes, and CDs and relatively little on candy. By contrast, your chocoholic friend with the tin ear may spend a great deal on Hershey's Kisses and very little on music.

All consumers must choose which goods to buy because limits on wealth prevent them from buying everything that catches their fancy. In addition, government rules restrict what they may buy: young consumers cannot buy alcohol or cigarettes legally, and at any age, it is illegal to buy crack and other "recreational" drugs. Therefore, consumers buy the goods that give them the most pleasure, subject to the constraints that they cannot spend more money than they have and that they cannot spend it in ways that the government prevents.

In economic analyses designed to explain behavior (positive analysis—see Chapter 1) rather than judge it (normative statements), economists assume that *the consumer is the boss.* If your brother gets pleasure from smoking, economists don't argue with him that it is bad for him any more than they'd tell your sister, who likes reading Stephen King, that she should read Adam Smith's *Wealth of Nations* instead. Accepting each consumer's tastes is not the same as condoning the resulting behaviors. Economists want to predict behavior. They want to know, for example, whether your brother will smoke more next year if the price of cigarettes decreases 10%. The prediction is unlikely to be correct if economists say, "He shouldn't smoke; therefore, we predict he'll stop smoking next year." A prediction based on your brother's actual tastes is more likely to be correct: "Given that he likes cigarettes, he is likely to smoke more of them next year if the price falls."

IN THIS CHAPTER, WE EXAMINE FOUR MAIN TOPICS

1. **Preferences:** We can use three properties of preferences to predict which combinations, or bundle, of goods an individual prefers to other combinations.
2. **Utility:** Economists summarize a consumer's preferences using a *utility* function, which assigns a numerical value to each possible bundle of goods, reflecting the consumer's relative ranking of these bundles.
3. **Budget constraint:** Prices, income, and government restrictions limit a consumer's ability to make purchases by determining the rate at which a consumer can trade one good for another.
4. **Constrained consumer choice:** Consumers maximize their pleasure from consuming various possible bundles of goods given their income, which limits the amount of goods they can purchase.

4.1 PREFERENCES

We start our analysis of consumer behavior by examining consumer preferences. Using three basic assumptions, we can predict a great deal about preferences. Once we know about consumers' preferences, we can add information about the constraints consumers face, so we can answer many questions, such as the ones posed at the beginning of the chapter, or derive demand curves, as is done in the next chapter.

As a consumer, you choose among many goods. Should you have ice cream or cake for dessert? Should you spend most of your money on a large apartment or rent a single room and use the savings to pay for trips and concerts? In short, you must allocate your money to buy a *bundle* (*market basket* or combination) of goods.

How do consumers choose the bundle of goods they buy? One possibility is that consumers behave randomly and blindly choose one good or another without any thought. However, consumers appear to make systematic choices. For example, you probably buy more or less the same specific items each time you go to the grocery store.

To explain consumer behavior, economists *assume* that consumers have a set of tastes or preferences that they use to guide them in choosing between goods. These tastes differ substantially among individuals. Three out of four European men prefer colored underwear, while three out of four American men prefer white underwear.[1] Let's start by specifying the underlying assumptions in the economist's model of consumer behavior.

Properties of Consumer Preferences

Economists make three critical assumptions about the properties of consumers' preferences. For brevity, these properties are referred to as *completeness*, *transitivity*, and *more is better*.

Completeness. The completeness property holds that, when facing a choice between any two bundles of goods, a consumer can rank them so that one and only one of the following relationships is true: The consumer prefers the first bundle to the second, prefers the second to the first, or is indifferent between them. This property rules out the possibility that the consumer cannot decide which bundle is preferable.

It would be very difficult to predict behavior if consumers' rankings of bundles were not logically consistent. The next property eliminates the possibility of certain types of illogical behavior.

Transitivity. The transitivity (or what some people refer to as *rationality*) property is that a consumer's preferences over bundles is consistent in the sense that if the consumer *weakly prefers* Bundle z to Bundle y (likes z at least as much as y) and weakly prefers Bundle y to Bundle x, the consumer also weakly prefers Bundle z to Bundle x.[2]

If your sister told you she preferred a scoop of ice cream to a piece of cake, a piece of cake to a bar of candy, and a bar of candy to a scoop of ice cream, you'd probably think she'd lost her mind. At the very least, you wouldn't know which of these desserts to serve her.

More Is Better. The more-is-better property holds that, all else the same, more of a commodity is better than less of it (always wanting more is known as *nonsatiation*). Indeed, economists define a **good** as a commodity for which more is preferred to less, at least at some levels of consumption. In contrast, a **bad** is something for which less is preferred to more, such as pollution. We now concentrate on goods.

Although the completeness and transitivity properties are crucial to the analysis that follows, the more-is-better property is included to simplify the analysis—our most important results would follow even without this property.

---

[1] L. M. Boyd, "The Grab Bag," *San Francisco Examiner*, September 11, 1994, p. 5.

[2] The assumption of transitivity of weak preferences is sufficient for the following analysis. However, it is easier (and plausible) to assume that other preference relations—strict preference and indifference between bundles—are also transitive.

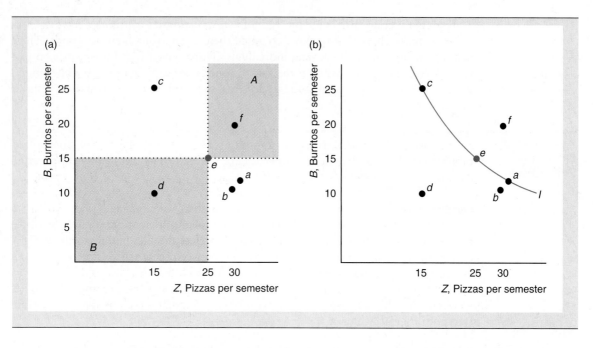

So why do economists assume that the more-is-better property holds? The most compelling reason is that it appears to be true for most people.[3] A second reason is that if consumers can freely dispose of excess goods, a consumer can be no worse off with extra goods. (We examine a third reason later in the chapter: Consumers buy goods only when this condition is met.)

Preference Maps

Surprisingly enough, with just these three properties, we can tell a lot about a consumer's preferences. One of the simplest ways to summarize information about a consumer's preferences is to create a graphical interpretation—a map—of them. For graphical simplicity, we concentrate throughout this chapter on choices between only two goods, but the model can be generalized to handle any number of goods.

Consider a choice between two goods. Each semester, Lisa, who lives for fast food, decides how many pizzas and burritos to eat. The various bundles of pizzas and burritos she might consume are shown in panel a of Figure 4.1, with (individual-size) pizzas per semester on the horizontal axis and burritos per semester on the vertical axis.

---

[3]When teaching microeconomics to Wharton M.B.A.'s, I told them about a cousin of mine who had just joined a commune in Oregon. His worldly possessions consisted of a tent, a Franklin stove, enough food to live on, and a few clothes. He said that he didn't need any other goods—that he was *satiated*. A few years later, one of these students bumped into me on the street and said, "Professor, I don't remember your name or much of anything you taught me in your course, but I can't stop thinking about your cousin. Is it really true that he doesn't want *anything* else? His very existence is a repudiation of my whole way of life." Actually, my cousin had given up his ascetic life and was engaged in telemarketing, but I, for noble pedagogical reasons, responded, "Of course he still lives that way—you can't expect everyone to have the tastes of an M.B.A."

Figure 4.1 **Bundles of Pizzas and Burritos Lisa Might Consume.** Pizzas per semester are on the horizontal axis, and burritos per semester are on the vertical axis. (a) Lisa prefers more to less, so she prefers Bundle *e* to any bundle in area *B*, including *d*. Similarly, she prefers any bundle in area *A*, including *f*, to *e*. (b) The indifference curve, I^1, shows a set of bundles (including *c*, *e*, and *a*) among which she is indifferent. (c) The three indifference curves, I^0, I^1, and I^2 are part of Lisa's preference map, which summarizes her preferences.

At Bundle *e*, for example, Lisa consumes 25 pizzas and 15 burritos per semester. By the more-is-better property, all the bundles that lie above and to the right (area *A*) are preferred to Bundle *e* because they contain at least as much of both pizzas and burritos as Bundle *e*. Thus Bundle *f* (30 pizzas and 20 burritos) in that region is preferred to *e*. By the same reasoning, all the bundles that lie in area *B*, below and to the left of *e*, such as Bundle *d* (15 pizzas and 10 burritos), Lisa likes less than *e*.

Bundles such as *b* (30 pizzas and 10 burritos), in the region below and to the right of *e*, or *c* (15 pizzas and 25 burritos), in the region above and to the left, may or may not be preferred to *e*. We can't use the more-is-better property to determine which bundle is preferred because these bundles each contain more of one good and less of the other than *e* does.

Indifference Curves. Suppose we asked Lisa to identify all the bundles that gave her the same amount of pleasure as consuming Bundle *e*. Using her answers, we draw curve *I* in panel b of Figure 4.1 through all bundles she likes as much as *e*. Curve *I* is an **indifference curve**: the set of all bundles of goods that a consumer views as being equally desirable.

Indifference curve *I* includes Bundles *c*, *e*, and *a*, so Lisa is indifferent between consuming Bundles *c*, *e*, and *a*. From this indifference curve, we also know that Lisa prefers *e* (25 pizzas and 15 burritos) to *b* (30 pizzas and 10 burritos). How do we know that? Bundle *b* lies below and to the left of Bundle *a*, so Bundle *a* is preferred to Bundle *b* by the more-is-better property. Both Bundle *a* and Bundle *e* are on indifference curve *I*, so Lisa likes Bundle *e* as much as Bundle *a*. Because Lisa is indifferent between *e* and *a* and she prefers *a* to *b*, she must prefer *e* to *b* by transitivity.

If we asked Lisa many, many questions, in principle, we could draw an entire set of indifference curves through every possible bundle of burritos and pizzas. Lisa's preferences are summarized in an **indifference map** or *preference map*, which is a complete set of indifference curves that summarize a consumer's tastes. Panel c of Figure 4.1 shows three of Lisa's indifference curves, I^0, I^1, and I^2.

We assume that indifference curves are continuous—have no gaps—as the figure shows. The indifference curves are parallel in the figure, but they need not be. All indifference curve maps must have four important properties:

1. Bundles on indifference curves farther from the origin are preferred to those on indifference curves closer to the origin.
2. There is an indifference curve through every possible bundle.
3. Indifference curves cannot cross.
4. Indifference curves slope downward.

First, we show that bundles on indifference curves farther from the origin (zero units of both goods) are preferred to those on indifference curves closer to the origin. By the more-is-better property, Lisa prefers Bundle f to Bundle e in panel c of Figure 4.1. She is indifferent among all the bundles on indifference curve I^2 and Bundle f, just as she is indifferent among all the bundles, such as Bundle c, on indifference curve I^1, and Bundle e. By the transitivity property, she prefers Bundle f to Bundle e, which she likes as much as Bundle c, so she prefers Bundle f to Bundle c. By this type of reasoning, she prefers all bundles on I^2 to all bundles on I^1.

Second, we show that there is an indifference curve through every possible bundle as a consequence of the completeness property: The consumer can compare any bundle to another. Compared to a given bundle, some bundles are preferred, some are enjoyed equally, and some are inferior. Connecting the bundles that give the same pleasure produces an indifference curve that includes the given bundle.

Third, we show that indifference curves cannot cross: A given bundle cannot be on two indifference curves. Suppose that two indifference curves crossed at Bundle e as in panel a of Figure 4.2. Because Bundles e and a lie on the same indifference curve I^0, Lisa is indifferent between e and a. Similarly, she is indifferent between e and b because both are on I^1. By transitivity, if Lisa is indifferent between e and a and she is indifferent between e and b, she must be indifferent between a and b. But that's impossible! Bundle b is above and to the right of bundle a, so Lisa *must* prefer b to a by the more-is-better property. Thus because preferences are transitive and more is better than less, indifference curves cannot cross.

Fourth, we show that indifference curves must be downward sloping. Suppose to the contrary that an indifference curve sloped upward, as in panel b of Figure 4.2. The consumer is indifferent between Bundles a and b because both lie on the same indifference curve, I. But the consumer prefers b to a by the more-is-better property: Bundle a lies strictly below and to the left of Bundle b. Because of this contradiction—the consumer cannot both be indifferent between a and b and strictly prefer b to a—indifference curves cannot be upward sloping.

Solved Problem 4.1   Can indifference curves be thick?

Answer

Draw an indifference curve that is at least two bundles thick, and show that a preference property is violated: Panel c of Figure 4.2 shows a thick indifference curve, *I*, with two bundles, *a* and *b*, identified. Bundle *b* lies above and to the right of *a*: Bundle *b* has more of both burritos and pizza. Thus by the more-is-better property, Bundle *b* must be strictly preferred to Bundle *a*. But the consumer must be indifferent between *a* and *b* because both bundles are on the same indifference curve. Because both relationships between *a* and *b* cannot be true, there is a contradiction. Consequently, indifference curves cannot be thick. (We illustrate this point by drawing indifference curves with very thin lines in our figures.)

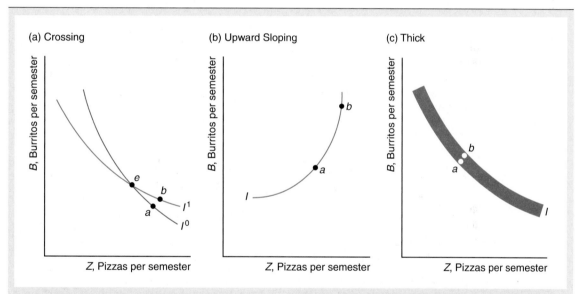

Figure 4.2 Impossible Indifference Curves.
(a) Suppose that the indifference curves cross at Bundle *e*. Lisa is indifferent between *e* and *a* on indifference curve I^0 and between *e* and *b* on I^1. If Lisa is indifferent between *e* and *a* and she is indifferent between *e* and *b*, she must be indifferent between *a* and *b* by transitivity. But *b* has more of both pizzas and burritos than *a*, so she *must* prefer *a* to *b*. Because of this contradiction, indifference curves cannot cross. (b) Suppose that indifference curve *I* slopes upward. The consumer is indifferent between *b* and *a* because they lie on *I* but prefers *b* to *a* by the more-is-better assumption. Because of this contradiction, indifference curves cannot be upward sloping. (c) Suppose that indifference curve *I* is thick enough to contain both *a* and *b*. The consumer is indifferent between *a* and *b* because both are on *I* but prefers *b* to *a* by the more-is-better assumption because *b* lies above and to the right of *a*. Because of this contradiction, indifference curves cannot be thick.

Willingness to Substitute Between Goods. Lisa is willing to make some trades between goods. The downward slope of her indifference curves shows that Lisa is willing to give up some burritos for more pizza or vice versa. She is indifferent between Bundles *a* and *b* on her indifference curve *I* in panel a of Figure 4.3. If she initially has Bundle *a* (eight burritos and three pizzas), she could get to Bundle *b* (five burritos and four pizzas) by trading three burritos for one more pizza. She is indifferent whether she makes this trade of not.

Lisa's willingness to trade one good for another is measured by her **marginal rate of substitution** (*MRS*): the maximum amount of one good a consumer will sacrifice to obtain one more unit of another good. The marginal rate of substitution refers to the trade-off (rate of substitution) of burritos for a marginal (small additional or incremental) change in the number of pizzas. Lisa's marginal rate of substitution of burritos for pizza is

$$MRS = \frac{\Delta B}{\Delta Z},$$

where ΔZ is the number of pizzas Lisa will give up to get ΔB more burritos or vice versa and pizza (*Z*) is on the horizontal axis. *The marginal rate of substitution is the slope of the indifference curve.*[4]

Moving from Bundle *a* to Bundle *b* in panel a of Figure 4.3, Lisa will give up three burritos, $\Delta B = -3$, to obtain one more pizza, $\Delta Z = 1$, so her marginal rate of substitution is $-3/1 = -3$. That is, the slope of the indifference curve is -3. The negative sign shows that Lisa is willing to give up some of one good to get more of the other: Her indifference curve slopes downward.

Curvature of Indifference Curves. Must an indifference curve, such as *I* in panel a of Figure 4.3, be *convex* to the origin (that is, must the middle of the curve be closer to the origin than if the indifference curve were a straight line)? An indifference curve doesn't have to be convex, but casual observation suggests that most people's indifference curves are convex. When people have a lot of one good, they are willing to give up a relatively large amount of it to get a good of which they have relatively little. However, after that first trade, they are willing to give up less of the first good to get the same amount more of the second good.

Lisa is willing to give up three burritos to obtain one more pizza when she is at *a* in panel a of Figure 4.3. At *b*, she is willing to trade only two burritos for a pizza. At *c*, she is even less willing to trade; she will give up only one burrito for another pizza. This willingness to trade fewer burritos for one more pizza as we move down and to the right along the indifference curve reflects a *diminishing marginal rate of substitution*: The marginal rate of substitution approaches zero as we move down and to the right along an indifference curve. That is, the indifference curve becomes flatter (less sloped) as we move down and to the right.

---

[4]The *slope* is "the rise over the run": how much we move along the vertical axis (rise) as we move along the horizontal axis (run). Technically, by the marginal rate of substitution, we mean the slope at a particular bundle. That is, we want to know what the slope is as ΔZ gets very small. In calculus terms, the relevant slope is a derivative. See Appendix 4A.

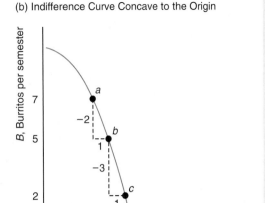

(a) Indifference Curve Convex to the Origin

(b) Indifference Curve Concave to the Origin

Figure 4.3 Marginal Rate of Substitution. (a) At Bundle *a*, Lisa is willing to give up three burritos for one more pizza; whereas at *b*, she is willing to give only two burritos to obtain another pizza. That is, the relatively more burritos she has, the more she is willing to trade for another pizza. (b) An indifference curve of this shape is unlikely to be observed. Lisa would be willing to give up more burritos to get one more pizza, the fewer the burritos she has. Moving from Bundle *c* to *b*, she will trade one pizza for three burritos, whereas moving from *b* to *a*, she will trade one pizza for two burritos, even though she now has relatively more burritos to pizzas.

It is hard to imagine that Lisa's indifference curves are *concave*, as in panel b of Figure 4.3, rather than *convex*, as in panel a. If her indifference curve is concave, Lisa would be willing to give up more burritos to get one more pizza, the fewer the burritos she has. In panel b, she trades one pizza for three burritos moving from Bundle *c* to *b*, and she trades one pizza for only two burritos moving from *b* to *a*, even though her ratio of burritos to pizza is greater. Though it is difficult to imagine concave indifference curves, two extreme versions of downward-sloping, convex indifference curves are plausible: straight-line or right-angle indifference curves.

One extreme case is **perfect substitutes**: goods that a consumer is completely indifferent as to which to consume. Because Bill cannot taste any difference between Coca-Cola and Pepsi-Cola, he views them as perfect substitutes: He is indifferent between one additional can of Coke and one additional can of Pepsi. His indifference curves for these two goods are straight, parallel lines with a slope of –1 everywhere along the curve, as in panel a of Figure 4.4. Thus Bill's marginal rate of substitution is –1 at every point along these indifference curves.

The slope of indifference curves of perfect substitutes need not always be –1; it can be any constant rate. For example, Charles knows from reading the labels that Clorox bleach is twice as strong as a generic brand. As a result, Charles is indifferent between

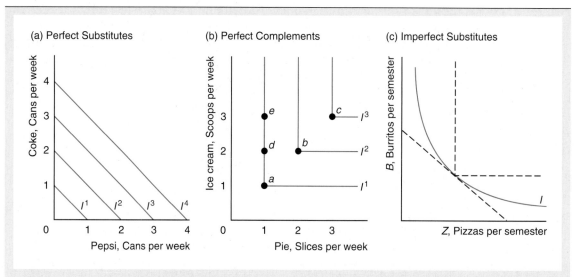

Figure 4.4 Perfect Substitutes, Perfect Complements, Imperfect Substitutes. (a) Bill views Coke and Pepsi as perfect substitutes. His indifference curves are straight, parallel lines with a marginal rate of substitution (slope) of −1. Bill is willing to exchange one can of Coke for one can of Pepsi. (b) Grace likes pie à la mode but does not like pie or ice cream by itself: She views ice cream and pie as perfect complements. She will not substitute between the two; she consumes them only in equal quantities. (c) Lisa views burritos and pizza as imperfect substitutes. Her indifference curve lies between the extreme cases of perfect substitutes and perfect complements.

one cup of Clorox and two cups of the generic bleach. The slope of his indifference curve is −2 (where the generic bleach is on the vertical axis).[5]

The other extreme case is **perfect complements**: goods that a consumer is interested in consuming only in fixed proportions. Grace doesn't like pie by itself or ice cream by itself but loves pie à la mode: a slice of pie with a scoop of vanilla ice cream on top. Her indifference curves have right angles in panel b of Figure 4.4. If she has only one piece of pie, she gets as much pleasure from it and one scoop of ice cream, Bundle *a*, as from it and two scoops, Bundle *d*, or as from it and three scoops, Bundle *e*. That is, she won't eat the extra scoops because she does not have pieces of pie to go with the ice cream. Therefore, she consumes only bundles like *a*, *b*, and *c* in which pie and ice cream are in equal proportions.

With a bundle like *a*, *b*, or *c*, she will not substitute a piece of pie for an extra scoop of ice cream. For example, if she were at *b*, she would be unwilling to give up an extra slice of pie to get, say, two extra scoops of ice cream, as at point *e*. Indeed,

---

[5]Sometimes it is difficult to guess what goods are close substitutes. According to Harper's Index (*San Francisco Examiner*, May 22, 1994, p. 6), flowers, perfume, and fire extinguishers rank 1, 2, and 3 among Mother's Day gifts that Americans consider "very appropriate."

she wouldn't give up the slice of pie for a virtually unlimited amount of extra ice cream because the extra ice cream is worthless to her.

The standard-shaped, convex indifference curve in panel c of Figure 4.4 lies between these two extreme examples. Convex indifference curves show that a consumer views two goods as imperfect substitutes.

Application   **INDIFFERENCE CURVES BETWEEN FOOD AND CLOTHING**

Using the estimates of Eastwood and Craven (1981), the figure shows the indifference curves of the average U.S. consumer between food consumed at home and clothing. The food and clothing measures are weighted averages of various goods. At relatively low quantities of food and clothing, the indifference curves, such as I^1, are nearly right angles: perfect complements. As we move away from the origin, the indifference curves become flatter: closer to perfect substitutes.

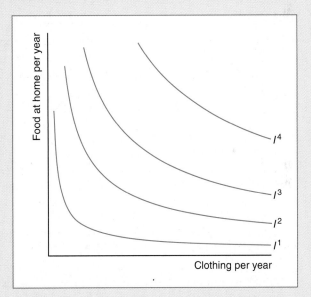

One interpretation of these indifference curves is that there are minimum levels of food and clothing necessary to support life. The consumer cannot trade one good for the other if it means having less than these critical levels. As the consumer obtains more of both goods, however, the consumer is increasingly willing to trade between the two goods. According to these estimates, food and clothing are perfect complements when the consumer has little of either good and perfect substitutes when the consumer has large quantities of both goods.

4.2 | UTILITY

Underlying our model of consumer behavior is the belief that consumers can compare various bundles of goods and decide which gives them the greatest pleasure. We can summarize a consumer's preferences by assigning a numerical value to each possible bundle to reflect the consumer's relative ranking of these bundles.

Following Jeremy Bentham, John Stuart Mill, and other nineteenth-century British economist-philosophers, economists apply the term **utility** to this set of numerical values that reflect the relative rankings of various bundles of goods. The statement that "Bonnie prefers Bundle x to Bundle y" is equivalent to the statement that "consuming Bundle x gives Bonnie more utility than consuming Bundle y." Bonnie prefers x to y if Bundle x gives Bonnie 10 *utils* (the name given to a unit of utility) and Bundle y gives her 8 utils.

Utility Function

If we knew the **utility function**—the relationship between utility measures and every possible bundle of goods—we could summarize the information in indifference maps succinctly. Suppose that the utility, U, that Lisa gets from burritos and pizzas is

$$U = \sqrt{BZ}.$$

From this function, we know that the more she consumes of either good, the greater the utility that Lisa receives. Using this function, we can determine whether she would be happier if she had Bundle x with 9 burritos and 16 pizzas or Bundle y with 13 of each. The utility she gets from x is 12 (= $\sqrt{9 \times 16}$) utils. The utility she gets from y is 13 (= $\sqrt{13 \times 13}$) utils. Therefore, she prefers y to x.

The utility function is a concept that economists use to help them think about consumer behavior; utility functions do not exist in any fundamental sense. If you ask your mother what her utility function is, she would be puzzled—unless, of course, she is an economist. But if you asked her enough questions about choices of bundles of goods, you could construct a function that accurately summarizes her preferences. For example, by questioning people, Rousseas and Hart (1951) constructed indifference curves between eggs and bacon, and MacCrimmon and Toda (1969) constructed indifference curves between French pastries and money (which can be used to buy all other goods).

Typically, consumers can easily answer questions about whether they prefer one bundle to another, such as "Do you prefer a bundle with one scoop of ice cream and two pieces of cake to another bundle with two scoops of ice cream and one piece of cake?" But they have difficulty answering questions about how much more they prefer one bundle to another because they don't have a measure to describe how their pleasure from two goods or bundles differs. Therefore, we may know a consumer's rank-ordering of bundles, but we are unlikely to know by how much more that consumer prefers one bundle to another.

Ordinal Preferences

If we know only consumers' relative rankings of bundles, our measure of pleasure is *ordinal* rather than *cardinal*. An ordinal measure is one that tells us the relative ranking of two things but not how much more one rank is than another.

If a professor assigns only letter grades to an exam, we know that a student who receives a grade of A did better than a student who received a B, but we can't say how much better from that ordinal scale. Nor can we tell whether the difference in performance between an A student and a B student is greater or less than the difference between a B student and a C student.

A cardinal measure is one by which absolute comparisons between ranks may be made. Money is a cardinal measure. If you have $100 and your brother has $50, we know not only that you have more money than your brother but also that you have exactly twice as much money as he does.

Because utility is an ordinal measure, we should not put any weight on the absolute differences between the utility associated with one bundle and another.[6] We care only about the relative utility or ranking of the two bundles.

Utility and Indifference Curves

We can use Lisa's utility function to construct a three-dimensional diagram that shows how utility varies with changes in the consumption of B and Z. Imagine that you are standing with your back against a corner of a room. Walking away from the corner along the wall to your left, you are tracing out the B axis: The farther you get from the corner, the more burritos Lisa has. Similarly, starting back at the corner and walking along the wall to your right, you are moving along the Z axis. When you stand in the corner, you are leaning against the utility axis, where the two walls meet. The higher the point along your back, the greater Lisa's utility. Because her utility is increasing (more is preferred to less) in both B and Z, her utility rises as you walk away from the corner (origin) along either wall or into the room, where Lisa has more B or Z or both. Lisa's utility or *hill of happiness* rises as you move away from the corner.

What is the relationship between Lisa's utility and one of her indifference curves, those combinations of B and Z that give Lisa a particular level of utility? Imagine that the hill of happiness is made of clay. If you were to cut the hill parallel to the floor at a particular height on the wall—a given level of utility—you'd get a smaller hill above the cut. Now suppose that you place that smaller hill directly on the floor and trace the outside edge of the hill. Looking down at the floor, the traced outer edge of the hill represents an indifference curve on the two-dimensional floor. Making other parallel cuts in the hill of happiness, placing the smaller hills on the floor, and tracing their outside edges, you could obtain a map of indifference curves on which each indifference curve reflects a different level of utility.

Utility and Marginal Utility

Using Lisa's utility function over burritos and pizza, we can show how her utility changes if she gets to consume more of one of the goods. We now suppose that Lisa has the utility function in Figure 4.5. The curve in panel a shows how

---

[6]Let $U(B, Z)$ be the original utility function and $V(B, Z)$ be the new utility function after we have applied a *positive monotonic transformation*: a change that increases the value of the function at every point. These two utility functions give the same ordinal ranking to any bundle of goods. (Economists often express this idea by saying that a *utility function is unique only up to a positive monotonic transformation*.) Suppose that $V(B, Z) = \alpha + \beta U(B, Z)$, where $\beta > 0$. The rank ordering is the same for these utility functions because $V(B, Z) = \alpha + \beta U(B, Z) > V(B^*, Z^*) = \alpha + \beta U(B^*, Z^*)$ if and only if $U(B, Z) > U(B^*, Z^*)$.

Figure 4.5 Utility and Marginal Utility. As Lisa consumes more pizza, holding her consumption of burritos constant at 10, her total utility, U, increases and her marginal utility of pizza, MU_Z, decreases (though it remains positive).

Lisa's utility rises as she consumes more pizzas while we hold her consumption of burritos fixed at 10. Because pizza is a *good*, Lisa's utility rises as she consumes more pizza.

If her consumption of pizzas increases from $Z = 4$ to 5, $\Delta Z = 5 - 4 = 1$, her utility increases from $U = 230$ to 250, $\Delta U = 250 - 230 = 20$. The extra utility ($\Delta U$) that she gets from consuming the last unit of a good ($\Delta Z = 1$) is the **marginal utility** from that good. Thus marginal utility is the slope of the utility function (Appendix 4A):

$$MU_Z = \frac{\Delta U}{\Delta Z}.$$

Lisa's marginal utility from increasing her consumption of pizza from 4 to 5 is

$$MU_Z = \frac{\Delta U}{\Delta Z} = \frac{20}{1} = 20.$$

Panel b shows that Lisa's marginal utility from consuming one more pizza varies with the number of pizzas she consumes, holding her consumption of burritos constant. Her marginal utility of pizza curve falls as her consumption of pizza increases, but the marginal utility remains positive: Each extra pizza gives Lisa pleasure, but it gives her less pleasure than the previous pizza relative to other goods.

Utility and Marginal Rates of Substitution

Earlier we learned that the marginal rate of substitution (*MRS*) is the slope of the indifference curve. The marginal rate of substitution can also be expressed in terms of marginal utilities. If Lisa has 10 burritos and 4 pizzas in a semester and gets one more pizza, her utility rises. That extra utility is the marginal utility from the last pizza, MU_Z. Similarly, if she received one extra burrito instead, her marginal utility from the last burrito is MU_B.

Suppose that Lisa trades from one bundle on an indifference curve to another by giving up some burritos to gain more pizza. She gains marginal utility from the extra pizza but loses marginal utility from fewer burritos. As Appendix 4A shows, the marginal rate of substitution can be written as

$$MRS = \frac{\Delta B}{\Delta Z} = -\frac{MU_Z}{MU_B}. \qquad (4.1)$$

The *MRS* is the negative of the ratio of the marginal utility of another pizza to the marginal utility of another burrito.

4.3 | BUDGET CONSTRAINT

You can't have everything. . . . Where would you put it? —Steven Wright

Knowing an individual's preferences is only the first step in analyzing that person's consumption behavior. Consumers maximize their well-being subject to constraints. The most important constraint most of us face in deciding what to consume is our personal budget constraint.

If we cannot save and borrow, our budget is the income we receive in a given period. If we can save and borrow, we can save money early in life to consume later, such as when we retire; or we can borrow money when we are young and repay these sums later in life. Savings is, in effect, a good that consumers can buy. For simplicity, we assume that each consumer has a fixed amount of money to spend now, so we can use the terms *budget* and *income* interchangeably.

For graphical simplicity, we assume that consumers spend their money on only two goods. If Lisa spends all her budget, Y, on pizza and burritos, then

$$p_B B + p_Z Z = Y, \tag{4.2}$$

where $p_B B$ is the amount she spends on burritos and $p_Z Z$ is the amount she spends on pizzas. Equation 4.2 is her budget constraint. It shows that her expenditures on burritos and pizza use up her entire budget.

How many burritos can Lisa buy? Subtracting $p_Z Z$ from both sides of Equation 4.2 and dividing both sides by p_B, we determine the number of burritos she can purchase to be

$$B = \frac{Y - p_Z Z}{p_B}. \tag{4.3}$$

According to Equation 4.3, she can buy more burritos with a higher income, a lower price of burritos or pizza, or the purchase of fewer pizzas.[7] For example, if she has one more dollar of income (Y), she can buy $1/p_B$ more burritos.

If $p_Z = \$1$, $p_B = \$2$, and $Y = \$50$, Equation 4.2 is

$$B = \frac{\$50 - (\$1 \times Z)}{\$2} = 25 - \tfrac{1}{2} Z. \tag{4.4}$$

As this equation shows, every two pizzas cost Lisa one burrito. How many burritos can she buy if she spends all her money on burritos? By setting $Z = 0$ in Equation 4.3, we find that $B = Y/p_B = \$50/\$2 = 25$. Similarly, if she spends all her money on pizza, $B = 0$ and $Z = Y/p_Z = \$50/\$1 = 50$.

Instead of spending all her money on pizza or all on burritos, she can buy some of each. Table 4.1 shows four possible bundles she could buy. For example, she can buy 20 burritos and 10 pizzas with $50.

Equation 4.4 is plotted in Figure 4.6. This line is called a **budget line** or *budget constraint*: the bundles of goods that can be bought if the entire budget is spent on those goods at given prices. This budget line shows the combinations of burritos and pizzas that Lisa can buy if she spends all of her $50 on these two goods. The four bundles in Table 4.1 are labeled on this line.

Table 4.1 Allocations of a $50 Budget Between Burritos and Pizza

Bundle	Burritos	Pizza
a	25	0
b	20	10
c	10	30
d	0	50

---

[7]Using calculus, we find that $dB/dY = 1/p_B > 0$, $dB/dZ = -p_Z/p_B < 0$, $dB/dp_Z = -Z/p_B < 0$, and $dB/dp_B = -(Y - p_Z Z)/(p_B)^2 = -B/p_B < 0$.

Lisa could, of course, buy any bundle that cost less than $50. The **opportunity set** is all the bundles a consumer can buy, including all the bundles inside the budget constraint and on the budget constraint (all those bundles of positive Z and B such that $p_B B + p_Z Z \leq Y$). Lisa's opportunity set is the shaded area in the figure. She could buy 10 burritos and 15 pieces of pizza for $35, which falls inside the constraint. Unless she wants to spend the other $15 on some other good, though, she might as well spend all of it on the food she loves and pick a bundle on the budget constraint rather than inside it.

Slope of the Budget Constraint	Every extra unit of Z that Lisa purchases reduces B by $-p_Z/p_B$, according to Equation 4.3, so the slope of the budget line is $\Delta B/\Delta Z = -p_Z/p_B$. The slope of the budget line is called the **marginal rate of transformation** (*MRT*): the trade-off the market imposes on the consumer in terms of the amount of one good the consumer must give up to obtain more of the other good. The marginal rate of transformation is the rate at which Lisa can trade burritos for pizza in the marketplace:

$$MRT = \frac{\Delta B}{\Delta Z} = -\frac{p_Z}{p_B}. \tag{4.5}$$

Because the price of pizza is half that of a burrito ($p_Z = \$1$ and $p_B = \$2$), the marginal rate of transformation Lisa faces is

$$MRT = -\frac{p_Z}{p_B} = -\frac{\$1}{\$2} = -\frac{1}{2}.$$

An extra pizza costs her half an extra burrito—or, equivalently, an extra burrito costs her two pizzas.

Purchasing Fractional Quantities	The budget constraint in Figure 4.6 is a smooth, continuous line, and the opportunity set includes all the points inside that constraint. Implicitly, this drawing implies that Lisa can buy fractional numbers of burritos and pizzas. Is that true? Do you know of a restaurant that will sell you a quarter of a burrito? Probably not.

Why then don't we draw the opportunity set and the budget constraint as points (bundles) of whole numbers of burritos and pizzas? The reason is that Lisa can buy a burrito at a *rate* of one-half per time period. If Lisa buys one burrito every other week, she buys an average of one-half burrito every week. Thus it is plausible that she could purchase fractional amounts over time, and this diagram concerns her behavior over a semester.

Effect of a Change in Price on Consumption	If the price of pizza doubles but the price of burritos is unchanged, the budget constraint swings in toward the origin in panel a of Figure 4.7. If Lisa spends all her money on burritos, she can buy as many burritos as before, so the budget line still hits the burrito axis at 25. If she spends all her money on pizza, however, she can now buy only half as many pizzas as before, so the budget line intercepts the pizza axis at 25 instead of at 50.

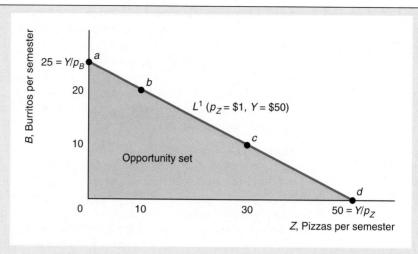

Figure 4.6 Budget Constraint. If $Y = \$50$, $p_Z = \$1$, and $p_B = \$2$, Lisa can buy any bundle in the opportunity set, the shaded area, including points on the *budget line*, L^1, which has a slope of $-\frac{1}{2}$.

The new budget constraint is steeper and lies inside the original one. As the price of pizza increases, the slope of the budget line, *MRT*, changes. On the original line, L^1, $MRT = -\frac{1}{2}$. On the new line, L^2, $MRT = p_Z/p_B = -\$2/\$2 = -1$. Lisa is unambiguously worse off (unless she wants to eat burritos only), because she can no longer afford the combinations of pizza and burritos in the shaded area.

A decrease in the price of pizza would have the opposite effect: The budget line would rotate outward around the intercept of the line and the burrito axis. As a result, the opportunity set would increase.

Effect of a Change in Income on Consumption

If the consumer's income increases, the consumer can buy more of all goods. Suppose that Lisa's income increases by $50 per semester to $Y = \$100$. Her budget constraint shifts outward—away from the origin—and is parallel to the original constraint in panel b of Figure 4.7. Why is the new constraint parallel to the original one? The intercept of the budget line on the burrito axis is Y/p_B, and the intercept on the pizza axis is Y/p_Z. Thus holding prices constant, the intercepts shift outward in proportion to the change in income. Originally, if she spent all her money on pizza, Lisa could buy $50 = \$50/\$1$ pizzas; now she can buy $100 = \$100/\$1$. Similarly, the burrito axis intercept goes from $25 = \$50/\$2$ to $50 = \$100/\$2$.

A change in income affects only the position and not the slope of the budget line. The slope is determined solely by the relative prices of pizza and burritos. If the prices of both pizza and burritos fall by half, Lisa can buy twice as much as

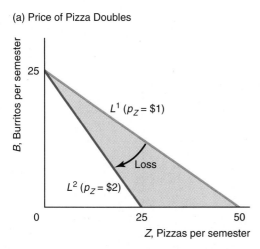

(a) Price of Pizza Doubles

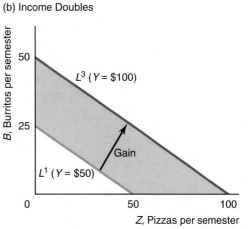

(b) Income Doubles

Figure 4.7 Changes in the Budget Constraint. (a) If the price of pizza increases from \$1 to \$2 a slice, Lisa's budget constraint rotates from L^1 to L^2 around the intercept on the burrito axis. The slope of the new budget line, L^2, is –1. The shaded area shows the combinations of pizza and burritos that she can no longer afford. (b) At the original prices, her new budget constraint moves from L^1 to L^2 if Lisa's income increases by \$50. This shift is parallel: Both budget lines have the same slope of $-\frac{1}{2}$. The new opportunity set is larger by the shaded area.

previously with the same budget. The budget line shifts outward parallel by the same amount as if her income doubles. Thus her opportunity set is identical if both prices drop by half *or* her budget doubles.

Solved Problem 4.2

During World War II, the U.S. and British governments rationed gasoline, setting quotas on how much a consumer could purchase. If a consumer could afford to buy 12 gallons a week but the government restricted purchases to no more than 10 gallons a week, what happened to the consumer's opportunity set?

Answer

1. *Draw the original opportunity set using a budget line between gasoline and all other goods*: In the graph, the consumer can afford to buy up to 12 gallons of gasoline a week if not constrained. The opportunity set, areas *A* and *B*, is bounded by the axes and the budget line.

2. *Add a line to the figure showing the quota, and determine the new opportunity set*: A vertical line at 10 on the gasoline axis indicates the quota.

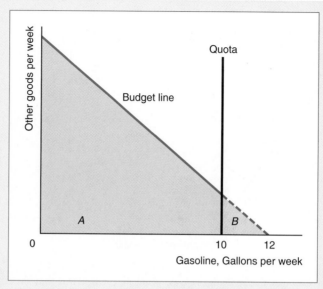

The new opportunity set, area *A*, is bounded by the axes, the budget line, and the quota line.

3. *Compare the two opportunity sets*: Because of the rationing, the consumer loses part of the original opportunity set: the triangle *B* to the right of the 10 gallons line. The consumer has fewer opportunities because of rationing.

4.4   CONSTRAINED CONSUMER CHOICE

My problem lies in reconciling my gross habits with my net income.   —Errol Flynn

Were it not for the budget constraint, consumers who prefer more to less would consume unlimited amounts of all goods. Well, they can't have it all! Instead, consumers maximize their well-being subject to their budget constraints. To complete our analysis of consumer behavior, we have to determine the bundle of goods that maximizes well-being subject to the budget constraint.

The Consumer's Optimal Bundle

To determine which of the points on the budget constraint gives Lisa the highest level of pleasure, we use her indifference curves in panel a of Figure 4.8.[8] We will show that her optimal bundle lies on an indifference curve that touches the budget constraint at only one point (*e* on I^2)—hence the indifference curve does not cross the constraint. We show this result by rejecting the possibility that the optimal bundle could be located off the budget constraint or that it lies on an indifference curve that intersects the budget constraint.

The optimal bundle must be on the budget constraint. Bundles that lie on indifference curves above the constraint, such as those on I^3, are not in the opportunity

---

[8]Appendix 4B uses calculus to determine the bundle that maximizes utility subject to the budget constraint.

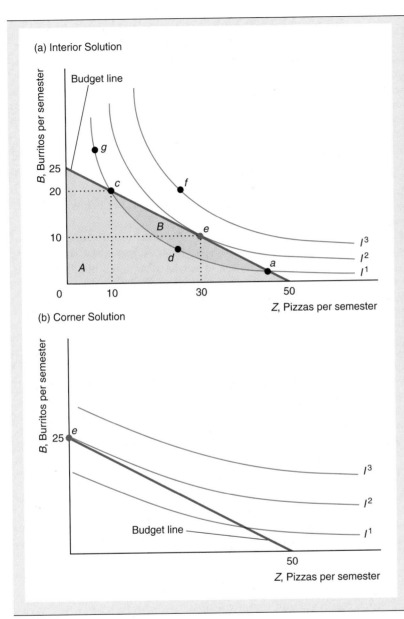

(a) Interior Solution

(b) Corner Solution

Figure 4.8 Consumer Maximization. (a) *Interior solution:* Lisa's optimal bundle is *e* (10 burritos and 30 slices of pizza) on indifference curve I^2. Any bundle that is preferred to *e* (such as points on indifference curve I^3) lies outside of the opportunity set—it can't be purchased. Bundles inside the opportunity set, such as *d*, are less desirable than *e*. (b) *Corner solution:* Spenser's indifference curves are relatively flat (he'll give up many pizzas for one more burrito), so his optimal bundle occurs at a corner of the opportunity set at Bundle *e*: 25 burritos and 0 pizzas.

set. So even though Lisa prefers *f* on indifference curve I^3 to *e* on I^2, *f* is too expensive and she can't purchase it. Although Lisa could buy a bundle inside the budget constraint, she does not want to do so, because more is better than less: For any bundle inside the constraint (such as *d* on I^1), there is another bundle on the constraint with more of at least one of the two goods, and hence she prefers that bundle. Therefore, the optimal bundle must lie on the budget constraint.

Bundles that lie on indifference curves that cross the budget constraint (such as I^1, which crosses the constraint at *a* and *c*) are less desirable than certain other bundles on the constraint. Only some of the bundles on indifference curve I^1

lie within the opportunity set: Bundles *a* and *c* and all the points on I^1 between them, such as *d*, can be purchased. Because I^1 crosses the budget constraint, the bundles between *a* and *c* on I^1 lie strictly inside the constraint, so there are bundles in the opportunity set (area *A* + *B*) that are preferable to these bundles on I^1 and affordable. By the more-is-better property, Lisa prefers *e* to *d* because *e* has more of both pizza and burritos than *d*. By transitivity, *e* is preferred to *a*, *c*, and all the other points on I^1—even those, like *g*, that Lisa can't afford. Because indifference curve I^1 crosses the budget constraint, area *B* contains at least one bundle that is preferred to—lies above and to the right of—at least one bundle on the indifference curve.

Thus the optimal bundle must lie on the budget constraint and be on an indifference curve that does not cross it. Such a bundle is the *consumer's optimum*. If Lisa is consuming this bundle, she has no incentive to change her behavior by substituting one good for another.

So far we've shown that the optimal bundle must lie on an indifference curve that touches the budget constraint but does not cross it. There are two ways that outcome can be reached. The first is an *interior solution*, in which the optimal bundle has positive quantities of both goods: The optimal bundle is on the budget line other than at one end or the other. The other possibility is called a *corner solution*, where the optimal bundle is at one end or the other of the budget line: It is at a corner with one of the axes.

Interior Solution. In panel a of Figure 4.8, Bundle *e* on indifference curve I^2 is the optimum bundle. It lies in the interior of the budget line away from the corners. Lisa prefers consuming a balanced diet, *e*, of 10 burritos and 30 pizzas, to eating only one type of food or the other.

For the indifference curve I^2 to touch the budget constraint but not cross it, it must be *tangent* to the budget constraint: The budget constraint and the indifference curve have the same slope at the point *e* where they touch. The slope of the indifference curve, the marginal rate of substitution, measures the rate at which Lisa is *willing* to trade burritos for pizza: $MRS = -MU_Z/MU_B$, Equation 4.1. The slope of the budget line, the marginal rate of transformation, measures the rate at which Lisa *can* trade her money for burritos or pizza in the market: $MRT = -p_Z/p_B$, Equation 4.5. Thus Lisa's utility is maximized at the bundle where the rate at which she is willing to trade burritos for pizza equals the rate at which she can trade:

$$MRS = -\frac{MU_Z}{MU_B} = -\frac{p_Z}{p_B} = MRT.$$

Rearranging terms, this condition is equivalent to

$$\frac{MU_Z}{p_Z} = \frac{MU_B}{p_B}. \tag{4.6}$$

Equation 4.6 says that the marginal utility of pizza divided by the price of a pizza (the amount of extra utility from pizza per dollar spent on pizza), MU_Z/p_Z, equals the marginal utility of burritos divided by the price of a burrito, MU_B/p_B. Thus Lisa's utility is maximized if the last dollar she spends on pizza gets her as much extra utility as the last dollar she spends on burritos. If the last dollar spent on pizza gave Lisa more extra utility than the last dollar spent on burritos, Lisa could increase her happiness by spending more on pizza and less on burritos.

Corner Solution. Spenser's indifference curves in panel b of Figure 4.8 are flatter than Lisa's. His optimal bundle lies on an indifference curve that touches the opportunity set only once, at the upper-left corner of the opportunity set, *e*, where he buys only burritos (25 burritos and 0 pizzas).

Bundle *e* is the optimal bundle because the indifference curve does not cross the constraint into the opportunity set. If it did, another bundle would give Spenser more pleasure.

Spenser's indifference curve is not tangent to his budget line. It would cross the budget line if both the indifference curve and the budget line were continued into the "negative pizza" region of the diagram, on the other side of the burrito axis.

Solved Problem 4.3   **Steven is indifferent between purchasing books from a local store and ordering them over the Internet because the price per book is *p* at either outlet. The local government introduces a tax on purchases from the local bookstore that raises the price per book to *p**, but Internet purchases remain untaxed. How will the tax affect the number of books Steven purchases and where he buys them?**

Answer

1. *Describe Steven's indifference curves for local and Internet books*: Because Steven views these books as perfect substitutes, his indifference curves, such as I^1 and I^2 in the figure, are straight lines with a slope of –1.

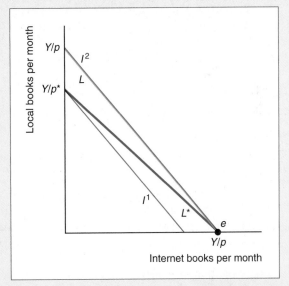

2. *Draw his initial budget line, and describe his optimum*: If Steven spends *Y* per week on books, he can buy *Y/p* books locally or *Y/p* over the Internet or any combination adding to *Y/p* from the two sources. Thus his initial budget constraint, *L*, is a straight line with a slope of –1 that hits each axis at *Y/p*. Because *L* is identical to his indifference curve I^2, any point along I^2 could be his optimal bundle.

3. *Draw the new budget line after the local tax is imposed, and show the new optimum:* After the tax is imposed, Steven's budget line L^* hits the Internet (horizontal) axis at Y/p and the local (vertical) axis at Y/p^*. Thus he can still buy Y/p books over the Internet but fewer books, Y/p^*, locally. He maximizes his utility by purchasing Y/p books over the Internet, point e, where I^2 hits L^* at the Internet axis.

Application   TAXES AND INTERNET SHOPPING

The 1998 Internet Tax Freedom Act put a three-year moratorium on e-commerce taxation. U.S. consumers who buy goods over the Internet (or by mail) are not liable for sales taxes on purchases from out-of-state vendors. Freedom from taxes has helped drive the 300%-per-year growth of online sales. Several of the major candidates for the U.S. presidency in the 2000 election campaign called for a permanent ban on Internet taxes.

As consumers shift their purchases to the Internet, state and local governments lose tax revenues. Consequently, the National Governors Association (NGA) called for a uniform tax of 5% on all Internet sales. In addition, many traditional retailers, including Wal-Mart, called for a change in the e-commerce taxation policy in 2000.

Some people are willing to pay a premium to shop locally. Others would pay more for the convenience of shopping over the Internet. However, those who are indifferent between the two means of shopping are sensitive to the higher local taxes.

Goolsbee (1998) finds that people who live in high-sales-tax areas are much more likely than other consumers to purchase over the Internet. He estimates that the NGA's flat 5% tax would lower the number of online customers by 18% and total sales by 23%. Alternatively, if each state could impose its own taxes (which average 6.33%), the number of buyers would fall by 24% and spending by 30%.

★Optimal Bundles on Convex Sections of Indifference Curves

Earlier we argued, on the basis of introspection, that most indifference curves are convex to the origin. Now that we know how to determine a consumer's optimal bundle, we can give a more compelling explanation about why we assume that indifference curves are convex. We can show that, if indifference curves are smooth, optimal bundles lie either on convex sections of indifference curves or at the point where the budget constraint hits an axis.

Suppose that indifference curves were strictly concave to the origin as in panel a of Figure 4.9. Indifference curve I^1 is tangent to the budget line at d, but that bundle is not optimal. Bundle e on the corner between the budget constraint and the burrito axis is on a higher indifference curve, I^2, than d is. Thus if a consumer had strictly concave indifference curves, the consumer would buy only one good—here, burritos. Similarly, as we saw in Solved Problem 4.3, consumers with straight-line

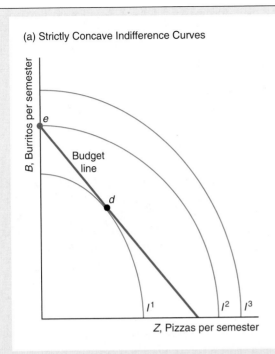

(a) Strictly Concave Indifference Curves

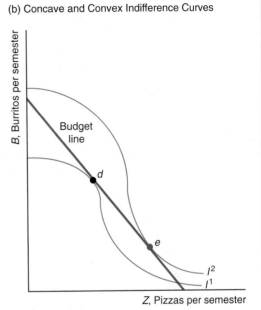

(b) Concave and Convex Indifference Curves

Figure 4.9 Optimal Bundles on Convex Sections of Indifference Curves. (a) Indifference curve I^1 is tangent to the budget line at Bundle d, but Bundle e is superior because it lies on a higher indifference curve, I^2. If indifference curves are strictly concave to the origin, the optimal bundle, e, is at a corner. (b) If indifference curves have both con- cave and convex sections, a bundle such as d, which is tangent to the budget line in the concave portion of indifference curve I^1, cannot be an optimal bundle because there must be a preferable bundle in the convex portion of a higher indifference curve, e on I^2 (or at a corner).

indifference curves buy only the cheapest good. Because we do not see consumers buying only one good, indifference curves must have convex sections.

If indifference curves have both concave and convex sections as in panel b of Figure 4.9, the optimal bundle lies in a convex section or at a corner. Bundle d, where a concave section of indifference curve I^1 is tangent to the budget line, cannot be an optimal bundle. Here, e is the optimal bundle and is tangent to the budget constraint in the convex portion of the higher indifference curve I^2. *If a consumer buys positive quantities of two goods, the indifference curve is convex and tangent to the budget line at that optimal bundle.*

Buying Where More Is Better   A key assumption in our analysis of consumer behavior is that more is preferred to less: Consumers are not satiated. We now show that, if both goods are consumed in positive quantities and their prices are positive, more of either good must be preferred to less. Suppose that the opposite were true and that Lisa prefers fewer burritos to more. Because burritos cost her money, she could increase her well-being by reducing the amount of burritos she consumes until she consumes no burritos—a scenario that violates our assumption that she consumes positive quantities of both goods.[9] Though it is possible that consumers prefer less to more at some large quantities, we do not observe consumers making purchases where that occurs.

In summary, we do not observe consumer optima at bundles where indifference curves are concave or consumers are satiated. Thus we can safely assume that indifference curves are convex and that consumers prefer more to less in the ranges of goods that we actually observe.

Solved Problem 4.4

Alexx doesn't care about where he lives, but he does care about what he eats. Alexx spends all his money on restaurant meals at either American or French restaurants. His firm offers to transfer him from its Miami office to its Paris office, where he will face different prices. The firm will pay him a salary in French francs such that he can buy the same bundle of goods in Paris that he is currently buying in Miami. Will Alexx benefit by moving to Paris?

Answer

1. *Show Alexx's optimum in the United States:* Alexx's optimal bundle, *a*, in the United States is determined by the tangency of his indifference curve I^1 and his American budget constraint L^A in the graph.

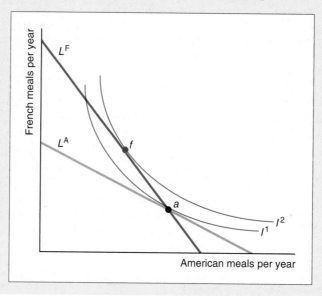

---

[9]Similarly, at her optimal bundle, Lisa cannot be *satiated*—indifferent between consuming more or fewer burritos. Suppose that her budget is obtained by working and that Lisa does not like working at the margin. Were it not for the goods she can buy with what she earns, she would not work as many hours as she does. Thus if she were satiated and did not care if she consumed fewer burritos, she would reduce the number of hours she worked, thereby lowering her income, until her optimal bundle occurred at a point where more was preferred to less or she consumed none.

2. *Discuss what happens if prices are higher in France but the relative prices between American and French meals are the same*: If the prices of both French and American meals are x times higher in France than in the United States, the relative cost of French and American meals are the same. If the firm raises Alexx's income x times, his budget line does not change. Thus if relative prices are the same in Miami and Paris, his budget line and optimal bundle are unchanged, so his level of utility is unchanged.

3. *Show the new optimum if relative prices in France differ from those in the United States*: Alexx's firm adjusts his income so that Alexx can buy the same bundle, *a*, as in the United States, so his new budget line in France, L^F, must go through *a*. Suppose that French meals are relatively less expensive than American meals in Paris. If Alexx spends all his money on French meals, he can buy more in Paris than in the United States, and if he spends all his money on American meals, he can buy fewer in Paris than in the United States. As a result, L^F hits the vertical axis at a higher point than the L^A line and cuts the L^A line at Bundle *a*. Alexx's new optimal bundle, *f*, is determined by the tangency of I^2 and L^F. Thus if relative prices are different in Paris and Miami, Alexx is better off with the transfer. He was on I^1 and is now on I^2. Alexx could buy his original bundle, *a*, but chooses to substitute toward French meals, which are relatively inexpensive in France, thereby raising his utility.[10]

Food Stamps

I've known what it is to be hungry, but I always went right to a restaurant.
— Ring Lardner

We can use the theory of consumer choice to analyze whether poor people are better off receiving food stamps or a comparable amount of cash. Currently, federal, state, and local governments work together to provide a food subsidy for poor Americans. Households that meet income, asset, and employment eligibility requirements receive coupons that can be used to purchase food from retail stores. The Food Stamps Program is one of the nation's largest social welfare programs with expenditures of $16.9 billion for nearly 19.8 million people per month in 1998.

Since the food stamp programs started in the early 1960s, economists, nutritionists, and policymakers have debated "cashing out" food stamps by providing checks or cash instead of coupons that can be spent only on food. Legally, food stamps may not be sold, though a black market for them exists. Because of technological advances in electronic fund transfers, switching from food stamps to a cash program would lower administrative costs and reduce losses due to fraud and theft.

Would a switch to a comparable cash subsidy increase the well-being of food stamp recipients? Would the recipients spend less on food and more on other goods?

---

[10]If French meals were relatively more expensive than American meals in Paris, the L^F budget line would cut the L^A budget line from below rather than from above as shown. However, the analysis would be essentially unchanged. Whether both prices, one price, or neither price is higher than in the United States is irrelevant to our analysis.

Cash Preferred to Food Stamps. Poor people who receive cash have more choices than those who receive a comparable amount of food stamps. With food stamps, only extra food can be obtained. With cash, either food or other goods can be purchased. As a result, a cash grant raises a recipient's opportunity set by more than food stamps of the same value do, as we now show.

In Figure 4.10, the price of a unit of food and the price of all other goods are both $1, with an appropriate choice of units. A person with a monthly income of Y has a budget line that hits both axes at Y: The person can buy Y units of food per month, Y units of all other goods, or any linear combination. The opportunity set is area A.

If that person receives a subsidy of $100 in cash per month, the person's new monthly income is $Y + \$100$. The budget constraint with cash hits both axes at $Y + 100$ and is parallel to the original budget constraint. The opportunity set increases by $B + C$ to $A + B + C$.

If the person receives $100 worth of food stamps, the food stamp budget constraint has a kink. Because the food stamps can be spent only on food, the budget constraint shifts 100 units to the right for any quantity of other goods up to Y units. For example, if the recipient buys only food, now $Y + 100$ units of food can be purchased. If

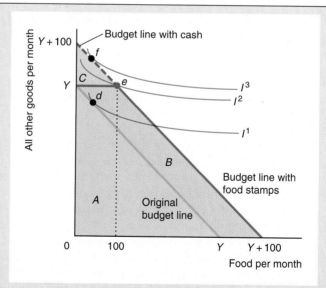

Figure 4.10 Food Stamps Versus Cash. The lighter line shows the original budget line of an individual with Y income per month. The heavier line shows the budget constraint with $100 worth of food stamps. The budget constraint with a grant of $100 in cash is a line between $Y + 100$ on both axes. The opportunity set increases by area B with food stamps but by $B + C$ with cash. An individual with these indifference curves consumes Bundle d (with less than 100 units of food) with no subsidy, e (Y units of all other goods and 100 units of food) with food stamps, and f (more than Y units of all other goods and less than 100 units of food) with a cash subsidy. This individual's utility is greater with a cash subsidy than with food stamps.

the recipient buys only other goods with the original Y income, that person can get Y units of other goods plus 100 units of food. However, the food stamps cannot be turned into other goods, so the recipient can't buy $Y + 100$ units of other goods, as can be done under the cash transfer program. The food stamps opportunity set is areas $A + B$, which is larger than the presubsidy opportunity set by B. The opportunity set with food stamps is smaller than that with the cash transfer program by C.

A recipient benefits as much from cash or an equivalent amount of food stamps if the recipient would have spent at least $100 on food if given cash. In other words, the individual is indifferent between cash and food stamps if that person's indifference curve is tangent to the downward-sloping section of the food stamp budget constraint.

Conversely, if the recipient would not spend at least $100 on food if given cash, the recipient prefers receiving cash to food stamps. Figure 4.10 shows the indifference curves of an individual who prefers cash to food stamps. This person chooses Bundle e (Y units of all other goods and 100 units of food) if given food stamps but Bundle f (more than Y units of all other goods and less than 100 units of food) if given cash. This individual is on a higher indifference curve, I^2 rather than I^1, if given cash rather than food stamps.

Application FOOD STAMP EXPERIMENTS

There are four effects of giving recipients cash instead of food stamps: (1) some individuals consume less food and more of other goods, (2) some individuals consume fewer nutrients, (3) the administrative costs of these welfare programs fall, and (4) each recipient's utility stays the same or rises.

According to a review of statistical analyses (Fraker, 1990), an additional dollar of income causes an average low-income household to increase its food expenditures by 5¢ to 10¢, and an additional dollar of food stamps leads to a 20¢ to 45¢ increase in food expenditures. Experiments (Moffitt, 1989; Fasciano, Hall, and Beebout, 1993; Carlson, 1993) show that responses to cashing out vary by area and demographic group. In Puerto Rico, giving cash instead of food stamps had no detectable influence on food expenditures; however, black market trafficking in food stamps was apparently widespread. In three out of four studies in the United States, researchers found that giving cash reduces household food expenditures, but the magnitude of the effect varies widely, from negligible to 17%.

Three studies of the nutrition effects of substituting cash for food stamps found no effect in Alabama, a 5% drop in San Diego, and a 6% to 11% decline in nutrients in Washington State. Even in Washington, however, cash recipients consumed far in excess of the recommended daily allowance of most nutrients.

A 1980 experiment involving elderly recipients in nine sites around the United States and a 1982 experiment in Puerto Rico show that the administrative costs and losses due to fraud and theft could be substantially reduced by switching to cash. Administrative costs fell from $2.05 to $1.03 per case per month in Alabama when checks were used. The government replaces lost or stolen checks but not clients' coupons that are lost or stolen, an additional benefit to recipients under the cash program.

If recipients spend less on food under the cash program, presumably they achieve higher utility from that program. Recipients report preferring cash. Of recipients in San Diego and Alabama, 4 out of 10 mentioned the greater choice of goods with cash. Other reported advantages of the cash program were a greater choice of stores and fewer feelings of embarrassment. Indeed, it is possible that the stigma of using food stamps may discourage participation in food stamp programs.

Why We Give Food Stamps. Two groups in particular object to giving cash instead of food stamps: some policymakers, because they fear that cash might be spent on booze or drugs, and some nutritionists, who worry that poor people will spend the money on housing or other goods and get too little nutrition.

In response, many economists argue that poor people are the best judges of how to spend their scarce resources. The question of whether it is desirable to let poor people choose what to consume is normative (a question of values), and economic theory cannot answer it. How poor people will change their behavior, however, is a positive (scientific) question, which we can analyze. Experiments to date find that cash recipients consume slightly lower levels of food but receive at least adequate levels of nutrients and that they prefer receiving cash.

Given that recipients are as well off or better off receiving cash than food stamps, why do we have food stamp programs instead of providing cash? The introduction to a report by the U.S. Department of Agriculture's Food and Nutrition Service, which administers the food stamp program (Fasciano, Hall, and Beebout, 1993, p. 6), offers this explanation:

> From the perspective of recipient households, cash is more efficient than coupons in that it permits each household to allocate its resources as it sees fit. . . . But in a more general sense, recipients' welfare clearly depends on public support for the program. And what evidence we have suggests that taxpayers are more comfortable providing in-kind, rather than cash, benefits and may consequently be more generous in their support of a coupon-based program. The question of which benefit form best promotes the welfare of financially needy households is thus more complex than it might appear.

Summary

Consumers maximize their utility (well-being) subject to constraints based on their income and the prices of goods.

1. **Preferences:** To predict consumers' responses to changes in these constraints, economists use a theory about individuals' preferences. One way of

summarizing consumers' preferences is with a family of indifference curves. An indifference curve consists of all bundles of goods that give the consumer a particular level of utility. On the basis of observations of consumers' behavior, economists assume that consumers' preferences have three properties: completeness, transitivity, and more is better. Given these three assumptions, indifference curves have the following properties:

- Consumers get more pleasure from bundles on indifference curves the farther from the origin the curves are.
- Indifference curves cannot cross.
- There is an indifference curve through any given bundle.
- Indifference curves have no thickness.
- Indifference curves slope downward.
- Consumers are observed purchasing positive quantities of all relevant goods only where their indifference curves are convex to the origin.

2. **Utility:** Economists call the set of numerical values that reflect the relative rankings of bundles of goods *utility*. Utility is an ordinal measure: By comparing the utility a consumer gets from each of two bundles, we know that the consumer prefers the bundle with the higher utility, but we can't tell by how much the consumer prefers that bundle. The marginal utility from a good is the extra utility a person gets from consuming one more unit of that good, holding the consumption of all other goods constant. The rate at which a consumer is willing to substitute Good 1 for Good 2, the marginal rate of substitution, *MRS*, depends on the relative amounts of marginal utility the consumer gets from each of the two goods.

3. **Budget constraint:** The amount of goods consumers can buy at given prices is limited by their income. As a result, the greater their income and the lower the prices of goods, the better off they are. The rate at which they can exchange Good 1 for Good 2 in the market, the marginal rate of transformation, *MRT*, depends on the relative prices of the two goods.

4. **Constrained consumer choice:** Each person picks an affordable bundle of goods to consume so as to maximize his or her pleasure. If an individual consumes both Good 1 and Good 2 (an interior solution), the individual's utility is maximized when the following four equivalent conditions hold:

- The indifference curve between the two goods is tangent to the budget constraint.
- The consumer buys the bundle of goods that is on the highest obtainable indifference curve.
- The consumer's marginal rate of substitution (the slope of the indifference curve) equals the marginal rate of transformation (the slope of the budget line).
- The last dollar spent on Good 1 gives the consumer as much extra utility as the last dollar spent on Good 2.

However, consumers do not buy some of all possible goods (corner solutions). The last dollar spent on a good that is actually purchased gives more extra utility than would a dollar's worth of a good the consumer chose not to buy.

Problems

1. Which of the following pairs of goods are complements, and which are substitutes? Are the goods that are substitutes likely to be perfect substitutes for some or all consumers?
   a. A popular novel and a gossip magazine
   b. A camera and film
   c. A gun and a stick of butter
   d. A Panasonic CD player and a JVC CD player

2. Gasoline was once less expensive in the United States than in Canada, but now gasoline costs less in Canada than in the United States due to a change in taxes. How will the gasoline-purchasing behavior of a Canadian who lives equally close to gas stations in both countries change? Answer using an indifference curve and budget line diagram.

3. Don is altruistic. Show the possible shape of his indifference curves between *charity* and *all other goods*.

4. Draw indifference curves with a good on one axis and a *neutral* product—one that the consumer is indifferent about whether or not to consume—on the other axis.

5. Give as many reasons as you can why we believe that indifference curves are convex.

6. What happens to a consumer's optimum if all prices and income double? (*Hint:* What happens to the intercepts of the budget line?)

7. In Spenser's state, a sales tax of 10% is applied to clothing but not to food. Show the effect of this

tax on Spenser's choice between food and clothing using indifference curves.

8. What happens to the budget line if the government applies a specific tax of $1 per gallon on gasoline but does not tax other goods? What happens to the budget line if the tax applies only to purchases of gasoline in excess of 10 gallons per week?

9. What is the effect of a 50% income tax on Dale's budget line and opportunity set?

10. A poor person who has an income of $1,000 receives $100 worth of food stamps. Draw the budget constraint if the food stamp recipient can sell these coupons on the black market for less than their face value.

11. Is a poor person more likely to benefit from $100 a month worth of food stamps (that can be used only to buy food) or $100 a month worth of clothing stamps (that can be used only to buy clothing)? Why?

12. Since 1979, recipients have been given food stamps. Before 1979, however, people bought

food stamps at a subsidized rate. For example, to get $1 worth of food stamps, a household paid about 15¢ (the exact amount varied by household characteristics and other factors). What is the budget constraint facing an individual if that individual may buy up to $100 per month in food stamps at 15¢ per each $1 coupon?

13. Show how much an individual's opportunity set increases if the government gives food stamps rather than sells them at subsidized rates.

14. *Review* (Chapter 2): The Clinton administration removed the ban that prevented U.S. companies from exporting personal computers to Eastern European countries. Companies in other countries also sell computers in those countries. What is the likely effect of this change in policy on the equilibrium price and quantity in Eastern Europe?

15. *Review* (Chapter 3): As a consumer, should you care whether a 15¢-per-gallon milk tax is collected from stores or from consumers? Use graphs to explain why or why not.

Math Problems

16. Julia consumes cans of anchovies, A, and boxes of biscuits, B. Each of her indifference curves reflects strictly diminishing marginal rates of substitution. Where $A = 2$ and $B = 2$, her marginal rate of substitution between cans of anchovies and boxes of biscuits equals -1 ($= MU_A/MU_B$). Will she prefer a bundle with three cans of anchovies and a box of biscuits to a bundle with two of each? Why?

17. Steve's utility function is $U = B + 2Z$. Describe the location of his optimal bundle (if possible) in terms of the relative prices of B and Z.

18. Linda loves buying shoes and going out to dance. Her utility function for pairs of shoes, S, and the number of times she goes dancing per month, T, is $U(S, T) = 2ST$. It costs Linda $50 to buy a new pair of shoes or to spend an evening out dancing. Assume that she has $500 to spend on clothing and dancing.
    a. What is the equation for her budget line? Draw it (with T on the vertical axis), and label the slope and intercepts.
    b. What is Linda's marginal rate of substitution? Explain.

    c. Solve mathematically for her optimal bundle. Show how to determine this bundle in a diagram using indifference curves and a budget line.

19. Jacob's utility function is $U = 10X^2Y$. The price of X is $p_X = \$10$, the price of Y is $p_Y = \$5$, and his income is $Y = \$150$. What is his optimal consumption bundle? Show in a graph.

20. Tara has a utility function $U(B, Z) = AB^\alpha Z^\beta$, where A, α, and β are constants, B is burritos, and Z is pizzas. If the price of burritos, p_B, is $2 and the price of pizzas, p_Z, is $1, what is Tara's optimal bundle?

21. If Jeremy's utility function is $U(B, Z) = B + AB^\alpha Z^\beta + Z$, what is his marginal utility of Z? What is his marginal rate of substitution between these two goods?

★22. Fiona requires a minimum level of consumption, a *threshold*, to derive additional utility: $U(X, Y)$ is 0 if $X + Y \leq 5$ and is $X + Y$ otherwise. Draw Fiona's indifference curves. Which of our usual assumptions are violated by this example?

Applying Consumer Theory

Median annual income Americans believe they would need to fulfill their "dreams": $102,000.   —Harper's Index, 1995

We used consumer theory in Chapter 4 to show how a consumer chooses a bundle of goods, subject to a budget constraint, so as to maximize happiness. Here we apply consumer theory to derive demand curves and examine their properties.

We start by using consumer theory to show how to determine the shape of a demand curve for a good by varying the price of a good, holding other prices and income constant. Firms use information about the shape of demand curves when setting prices. Governments apply this information in predicting the impact of policies such as taxes and price controls.

We then use consumer theory to show how an increase in income causes the demand curve to shift. Firms use information about the relationship between income and demand to predict which less-developed countries will substantially increase their demand for the firms' products.

Next, we show that an increase in the price of a good has two effects on demand. First, consumers would buy less of the now relatively more expensive good even if they were compensated with cash for the price increase. Second, consumers' incomes can't buy as much as before because of the higher price, so consumers buy less of at least some goods.

We use this analysis of these two demand effects of a price increase to show why the government's measure of inflation, the Consumer Price Index (CPI), overestimates the amount of inflation. Because of this bias in the CPI, some people gain and some lose from contracts that adjust payment on the basis of the government's inflation index. If you signed a long-term lease for an apartment in which your rent payments increase over time in proportion to the change in the CPI, you lose and your landlord gains from this bias.

Finally, we show how we can use the consumer theory of demand to determine an individual's labor *supply* curve. Knowing the shape of workers' labor supply curves is important in analyzing the effect of income tax rates on work and on tax collections. When he first ran for president, Ronald Reagan argued that if the income tax rates were cut, workers would work so many more hours that tax revenues would increase. If he was right, everyone could be made better off by a tax cut. If he was wrong, the deficit could grow to record levels. Before Congress adopted his tax cut, economists used empirical studies based on consumer theory to predict the effect of the tax rate cut on tax collections, as we discuss at the end of this chapter.

IN THIS CHAPTER,

WE EXAMINE

FIVE MAIN

TOPICS

1. **Deriving demand curves:** We use consumer theory to derive demand curves, showing how a change in price causes a shift along a demand curve.
2. **How changes in income shift demand curves:** We use consumer theory to determine how a demand curve shifts because of a change in income.
3. **Effects of a price change:** A change in price has two effects on demand, one having to do with a change in relative prices and the other concerning a change in the consumer's opportunities.
4. **Cost-of-living adjustments:** Using this analysis of the two effects of price changes, we show that the CPI overestimates the rate of inflation.
5. **Deriving labor supply curves:** Using consumer theory to derive the demand curve for leisure, we can derive workers' labor supply curves and use them to determine how a reduction in the income tax rate affects labor supply and tax revenues.

5.1   DERIVING DEMAND CURVES

We use consumer theory to show by how much the quantity demanded of a good falls as its price rises. An individual chooses an optimal bundle of goods by picking the point on the highest indifference curve that touches the budget line (Chapter 4). When a price changes, the budget constraint the consumer faces shifts, so the consumer chooses a new optimal bundle. By varying one price and holding other prices and income constant, we determine how the quantity demanded changes as the price changes, which is the information we need to draw the demand curve. After deriving an individual's demand curve, we show the relationship between consumer tastes and the shape of the demand curve, which is summarized by the elasticity of demand (Chapter 3).

We derive a demand curve using the information about tastes from indifference curves (see Appendix 4B for a mathematical approach). To illustrate how to construct a demand curve, we estimated a set of indifference curves between wine and beer, using data for American consumers. Panel a of Figure 5.1 shows three of the estimated indifference curves for a typical U.S. consumer, whom we call Mimi.[1] These indifference curves are convex to the origin: Mimi views beer and wine as imperfect substitutes (Chapter 4). We can construct Mimi's demand curve for beer by holding her budget, her tastes, and the price of wine constant at their initial levels and varying the price of beer.

The vertical axis in panel a measures the number of gallons of wine Mimi consumes each year, and the horizontal axis measures the number of gallons of beer she drinks per year. Mimi spends $Y = \$419$ per year on beer and wine. The price of beer, p_b, is \$12 per unit, and the price of wine, p_w, is \$35 per unit.[2] The slope of her budget line, L^1, is $-p_b/p_w = -12/35 \approx -\frac{1}{3}$. At those prices, Mimi consumes bundle e_1, 26.7

---

[1]My mother, Mimi, wanted the most degenerate character in the book named after her. She and I both hope that you do not consume as much beer or wine as the typical American in this example.

[2]To ensure that the prices are whole numbers, we state the prices with respect to an unusual unit of measure (not gallons).

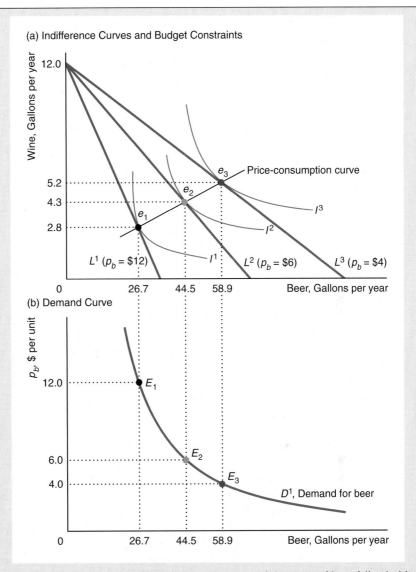

(a) Indifference Curves and Budget Constraints

(b) Demand Curve

Figure 5.1 Deriving an Individual's Demand Curve. If the price of beer falls, holding the price of wine, the budget, and tastes constant, the typical American consumer buys more beer, according to our estimates. (a) At the actual budget line, L^1, where the price of beer is $12 per unit and the price of wine is $35 per unit, the average consumer's indifference curve I^1 is tangent at Bundle e_1, 26.7 gallons of beer per year and 2.8 gallons of wine per year. If the price of beer falls to $6 per unit, the new budget constraint is L^2, and the average consumer buys 44.5 gallons of beer per year and 4.3 gallons of wine per year. (b) By varying the price of beer, we trace out the individual's demand curve, D_1. The beer price-quantity combinations E_1, E_2, and E_3 on the demand curve for beer in panel b correspond to optimal Bundles e_1, e_2, and e_3 in panel a.

gallons of beer per year and 2.8 gallons of wine per year, a combination that is determined by the tangency of indifference curve I^1 and budget line L^1.[3]

If the price of beer falls in half to $6 per unit, while the price of wine and her budget remain constant, Mimi's budget line rotates outward to L^2. If she were to spend all her money on wine, she could buy the same 12 ($\approx 419/35$) gallons of wine per year as before, so the intercept on the vertical axis of L^2 is the same as for L^1. However, if she were to spend all her money on beer, she could buy twice as much as before (70 instead of 35 gallons of beer), so L^2 hits the horizontal axis twice as far from the origin as L^1. As a result, L^2 has a flatter slope than L^1, about $-\frac{1}{6}$ ($\approx -6/35$). The slope is flatter because the price of beer has fallen relative to the price of wine.

Because beer is now relatively less expensive, Mimi drinks relatively more beer. She chooses Bundle e_2, 44.5 gallons of beer per year and 4.3 gallons of wine per year, where her indifference curve I^2 is tangent to L^2. If the price of beer falls again, say, to $4 per unit, Mimi consumes Bundle e_3, 58.9 gallons of beer per year and 5.2 gallons of wine per year.[4] The lower the price of beer, the happier Mimi is because she can consume more on the same budget: She is on a higher indifference curve (or perhaps just higher).

Panel a also shows the *price-consumption curve*, which is the line through the equilibrium bundles, such as e_1, e_2, and e_3, that Mimi would consume at each price of beer, when the price of wine and Mimi's budget are held constant. Because the price-consumption curve is upward sloping, we know that Mimi's consumption of both beer and wine increases as the price of beer falls.

We can use the same information in the price-consumption curve to draw Mimi's demand curve for beer, D^1, in panel b. Corresponding to each possible price of beer on the vertical axis of panel b, we record on the horizontal axis the quantity of beer demanded by Mimi from the price-consumption curve.

Points E_1, E_2, and E_3 on the demand curve in panel b correspond to Bundles e_1, e_2, and e_3 on the price-consumption curve in panel a. Both e_1 and E_1 show that when the price of beer is $12, Mimi demands 26.7 gallons of beer per year. When the price falls to $6 per unit, Mimi increases her consumption to 44.5 gallons of beer, point E_2. The demand curve, D^1, is downward sloping as predicted by the Law of Demand.

We can use the relationship between the points in panels a and b to show that Mimi's utility is lower at point E_1 on D^1 than at point E_2. Point E_1 corresponds to Bundle e_1 on indifference curve I^1, whereas E_2 corresponds to Bundle e_2 on indifference curve I^2, which is farther from the origin than I^1, so Mimi's utility is higher at E_2 than at E_1. Mimi is better off at E_2 than at E_1 because the price of beer is lower at E_2, so she can buy more goods with the same budget.

---

[3]These figures are the U.S. average annual per capita consumption of wine and beer. The numbers seem ridiculously high, given how many teetotalers are included in the average, but we've checked them in several sources. Apparently some heavy drinkers keep the average high. Average adult alcohol intake in the European Union is 2.4 times that of the United States; the British drink twice as much as Americans, and the French three times as much ("What a Lot of SterEUtypes," *The Economist*, October 23, 1999).

[4]These quantity numbers are probably higher than they would be in reality because we are assuming that Mimi continues to spend the same total amount of money on beer and wine as the price of beer drops.

5.2 | HOW CHANGES IN INCOME SHIFT DEMAND CURVES

To trace out the demand curve, we looked at how an increase in the good's price—holding income, tastes, and other prices constant—causes a downward *movement along the demand curve*. Now we examine how an increase in income, when all prices are held constant, causes a *shift of the demand curve*.

Businesses routinely use information on the relationship between income and the quantity demanded. For example, in deciding where to market its products, Whirlpool wants to know which countries are likely to spend a relatively large percentage of any extra income on refrigerators and washing machines.

Effects of a Rise in Income

We illustrate the relationship between the quantity demanded and income by examining how Mimi's behavior changes when her income rises, while the prices of beer and wine remain constant. Figure 5.2 shows three ways of looking at the relationship between income and the quantity demanded. All three diagrams have the same horizontal axis: the quantity of beer consumed per year. In the consumer theory diagram, panel a, the vertical axis is the quantity of wine consumed per year. In the demand curve diagram, panel b, the vertical axis is the price of beer per unit. Finally, in panel c, which shows the relationship between income and quantity directly, the vertical axis is Mimi's budget, Y.

A rise in Mimi's income causes the budget constraint to shift outward in panel a, which increases Mimi's opportunities. Her budget constraint L^1 at her original income, $Y = \$419$, is tangent to her indifference curve I^1 at e_1.

As before, Mimi's demand curve for beer is D^1 in panel b. Point E_1 on D^1, which corresponds to point e_1 in panel a, shows how much beer, 26.7 gallons per year, Mimi consumes when the price of beer is \$12 per unit (and the price of wine is \$35 per unit).

Now suppose that Mimi's beer and wine budget, Y, increases by roughly 50% to \$628 per year. Her new budget line, L^2 in panel a, is farther from the origin but parallel to her original budget constraint, L^1, because the prices of beer and wine are unchanged. Given this larger budget, Mimi chooses Bundle e_2. The increase in her income causes her demand curve to shift to D^2, in panel b. Holding Y at \$628, we can derive D^2 by varying the price of beer, in the same way as we derived D^1 in Figure 5.1. When the price of beer is \$12 per unit, she buys 38.2 gallons of beer per year, E_2 on D^2. Similarly, if Mimi's income increases to \$837 per year, her demand curve shifts to D^3.

The *income-consumption curve* through Bundles e_1, e_2, and e_3 in panel a shows how Mimi's consumption of beer and wine increases as her income rises. As Mimi's income goes up, her consumption of both wine and beer increases.

We can show the relationship between the quantity demanded and income directly rather than by shifting demand curves to illustrate the effect. In panel c, we plot an **Engel curve**, which shows the relationship between the quantity demanded of a single good and income, holding prices constant. Income is on the vertical axis, and the quantity of beer demanded is on the horizontal axis. On Mimi's Engel curve for beer, points E_1^*, E_2^*, and E_3^* correspond to points E_1, E_2, and E_3 in panel b and to e_1, e_2, and e_3 in panel a.

Figure 5.2 Effect of a Budget Increase on an Individual's Demand Curve. As the annual budget for wine and beer, Y, increases from $419 to $628 and then to $837, holding prices constant, the typical consumer buys more of both products, as shown by the upward slope of the income-consumption curve (a). That the typical consumer buys more beer as income increases is shown by the outward shift of the demand curve for beer (b) and the upward slope of the Engel curve for beer (c).

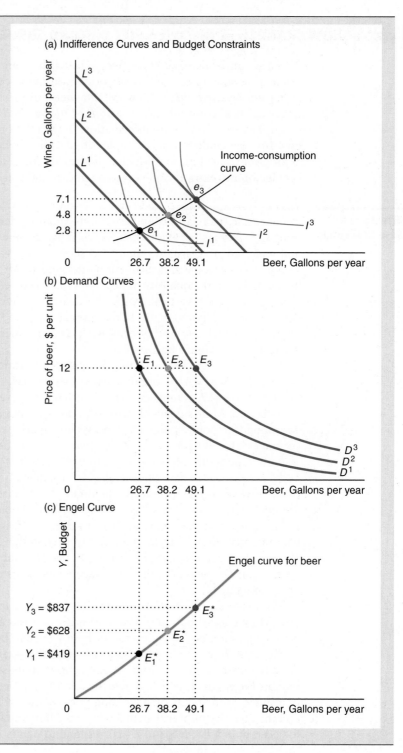

Solved Problem 5.1   Mahdu views Cragmont and Canada Dry ginger ales as perfect substitutes: He is indifferent as to which one he drinks. The price of a 12-ounce can of Cragmont, p, is less than the price of a 12-ounce can of Canada Dry, p^*. What does Mahdu's Engel curve for Cragmont ginger ale look like? How much does his weekly ginger ale budget have to rise for Mahdu to buy one more can of Cragmont ginger ale per week?

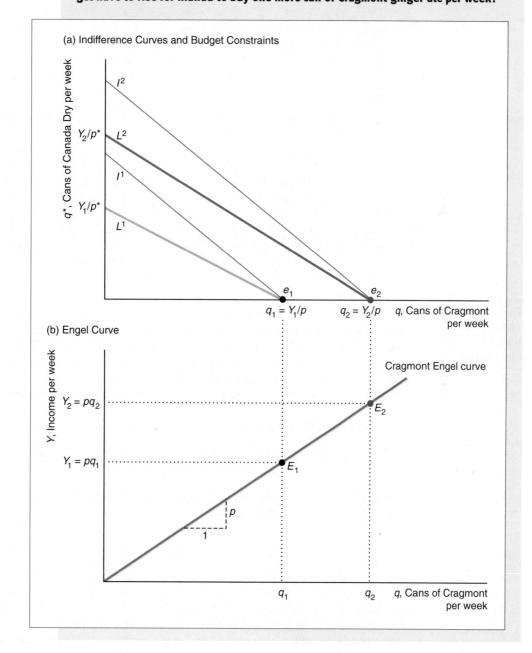

(a) Indifference Curves and Budget Constraints

q^*, Cans of Canada Dry per week

I^2

Y_2/p^* L^2

I^1

Y_1/p^* L^1

e_1 e_2

$q_1 = Y_1/p$ $q_2 = Y_2/p$ q, Cans of Cragmont per week

(b) Engel Curve

Y, Income per week

Cragmont Engel curve

$Y_2 = pq_2$ E_2

$Y_1 = pq_1$ E_1

p

1

q_1 q_2 q, Cans of Cragmont per week

Answer

1. *Use indifference curves to derive Mahdu's equilibrium choice*: Because Mahdu views the two brands as perfect substitutes, his indifference curves, such as I^1 and I^2 in panel a of the graphs, are straight lines with a slope of –1 (see Chapter 4). When his income is Y_1, his budget line hits the Canada Dry axis at Y_1/p^* and his Cragmont axis at Y_1/p. Mahdu maximizes his utility by consuming Y_1/p cans of the less expensive Cragmont ginger ale and no Canada Dry (corner solution). As his income rises, say, to Y_2, his budget line shifts outward and is parallel to the original one, with the same slope of $-p/p^*$. Thus at each income level, his budget lines are flatter than his indifference curves, so his equilibria lie along the Cragmont axis.

2. *Use the first figure to derive his Engel curve*: Because his entire budget, Y, goes to buying Cragmont, Mahdu buys $q = Y/p$ cans of Cragmont ginger ale. This expression, which shows the relationship between his income and the quantity of Cragmont ginger ale he buys, is Mahdu's Engel curve for Cragmont. The points E_1 and E_2 on the Engel curve in panel b correspond to e_1 and e_2 in panel a. We can rewrite this expression for his Engel curve as $Y = pq$. This relationship is drawn in panel b as a straight line with a slope of p. As q increases by one can ("run"), Y increases by p ("rise"). Because all his ginger ale budget goes to buying Cragmont, his income needs to rise by only p for him to buy one more can of Cragmont per week.

Consumer Theory and Income Elasticities

Income elasticities tell us how much the quantity demanded changes as income increases. We can use income elasticities to summarize the shape of the Engel curve, the shape of the income-consumption curve, or the movement of the demand curves when income increases. For example, firms use income elasticities to predict the impact of income taxes on consumption. We first discuss the definition of income elasticities and then show how they are related to the income-consumption curve.

Income Elasticities. We defined the income elasticity of demand in Chapter 3 as

$$\xi = \frac{\text{percentage change in quantity demanded}}{\text{percentage change in income}} = \frac{\Delta Q / Q}{\Delta Y / Y},$$

where ξ is the Greek letter xi. Mimi's income elasticity of beer, ξ_b, is 0.88, and that of wine, ξ_w, is 1.38 (based on our estimates for the average American consumer). When her income goes up by 1%, she consumes 0.88% more beer and 1.38% more wine. Thus according to these estimates, as income falls, consumption of beer and wine by the average American falls—contrary to frequent (unsubstantiated) claims in the media that people drink more as their incomes fall during recessions.

Most goods, like beer and wine, have positive income elasticities. A good is called a **normal good** if as much or more of it is demanded as income rises. Thus a good is a normal good if its income elasticity is greater than or equal to zero: $\xi \geq 0$.

Some goods, however, have negative income elasticities: $\xi < 0$. A good is called an **inferior good** if less of it is demanded as income rises. No value judgment is intended by the use of the term *inferior*. An inferior good need not be defective or of low quality. Some of the better-known examples of inferior goods are foods such as potatoes and cassava that very poor people typically eat in large quantities. Some economists—apparently seriously—claim that human meat is an inferior good: Only when the price of other foods is very high and people are starving will they turn to cannibalism.

A good that is inferior for some people may be superior for others. One strange example concerns treating children as a consumption good. Even though they can't buy children in a market, people can decide how many children to have. Willis (1973) estimated the income elasticity for the number of children in a family. He found that children are an inferior good, $\xi = -0.18$, if the wife has relatively little education and the family has average income: These families have fewer children as their income increases. In contrast, children are a normal good, $\xi = 0.044$, in families in which the wife is relatively well educated. For both types of families, the income elasticities are close to zero, so the number of children is not very sensitive to income.

Income-Consumption Curves and Income Elasticities. The shape of the income-consumption curve for two goods tells us the sign of the income elasticities: whether the income elasticities for those goods are positive or negative. We know that Mimi's income elasticities of beer and wine are positive because the income-consumption curve in panel a of Figure 5.2 is upward sloping. As income rises, the budget line shifts outward and hits the upward-sloping income-consumption line at higher levels of both goods. Thus as her income rises, Mimi demands more beer and wine, so her income elasticities for beer and wine are positive. Because the income elasticity for beer is positive, the demand curve for beer shifts to the right in panel b of Figure 5.2 as income increases.

To illustrate the relationship between the slope of the income-consumption curve and the sign of income elasticities, we examine Peter's choices of food and housing. Peter purchases Bundle e in Figure 5.3 when his budget constraint is L^1. When his income increases, so his budget constraint is L^2, he selects a bundle on L^2. Which bundle he buys depends on his tastes—his indifference curves.

The horizontal and vertical dotted lines through e divide the new budget line, L^2, into three sections. In which of these three sections the new optimal bundle is located determines Peter's income elasticities of food and clothing.

Suppose that Peter's indifference curve is tangent to L^2 at a point in the upper-left section of L^2 (to the left of the vertical dotted line that goes through e) such as a. If Peter's income-consumption curve is ICC^1, which goes from e through a, he buys more housing and less food as his income rises. (We draw the possible ICC curves as straight lines for simplicity. In general, they may curve.) Housing is a normal good, and food is an inferior good.

If instead the new optimal bundle is located in the middle section of L^2 (above the horizontal dotted line and to the right of the vertical dotted line), such as at b, his income-consumption curve ICC^2 through e and b is upward sloping. He buys more of both goods as his income rises, so both food and housing are normal goods.

Third, suppose that his new optimal bundle is in the bottom-right segment of L^2 (below the horizontal dotted line). If his new optimal bundle is c, his income-consumption curve ICC^3 slopes downward from e through c. As his income rises, Peter consumes more food and less housing, so food is a normal good and housing is an inferior good.

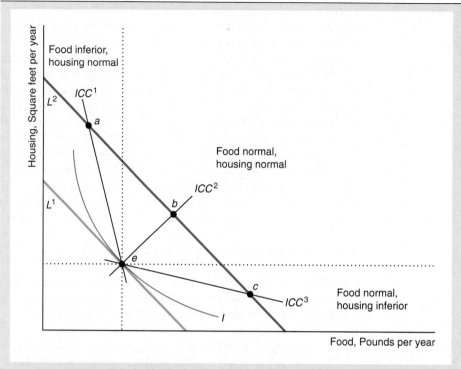

Figure 5.3 Income-Consumption Curves and Income Elasticities. At the initial income, the budget constraint is L^1 and the optimal bundle is *e*. After income rises, the new constraint is L^2. With an upward-sloping income-consumption curve such as ICC^2, both goods are normal. With an income-consumption curve such as ICC^1 that goes through the upper-left section of L^2 (to the left of the vertical dotted line through *e*), housing is normal and food is inferior. With an income-consumption curve such as ICC^3 that cuts L^2 in the lower-right section (below the horizontal dotted line through *e*), food is normal and housing is inferior.

Some Goods Must Be Normal. It is impossible for all goods to be inferior. We illustrate this point using Figure 5.3. At his original income, Peter faced budget constraint L^1 and bought the combination of food and housing *e*. When his income goes up, his budget constraint shifts outward to L^2. Depending on his tastes (the shape of his indifference curves), he may buy more housing and less food, such as Bundle *a*; more of both, such as *b*; or more food and less housing, such as *c*. Therefore, either both goods are normal or one good is normal and the other is inferior.

If both goods were inferior, Peter would buy less of both goods as his income rises—which makes no sense. Were he to buy less of both, he would be buying a bundle that lies inside his original budget constraint L^1. Even at his original, relatively low income, he could have purchased that bundle but chose not to, buying *e* instead. By the more-is-better assumption of Chapter 4, there is a bundle on the budget constraint that gives Peter more utility than any given bundle inside the constraint.

Even if an individual does not buy more of the usual goods and services, that person may put the extra money into savings. Empirical studies find that savings is a normal good.

Income Elasticities May Vary with Income. A good may be normal at some income levels and inferior at others. When Gail was poor and her income increased slightly, she ate meat more frequently, and her meat of choice was hamburger. Thus, when her income was low, hamburger was a normal good. As her income increased further, however, she switched from hamburgers to steak. Thus, at higher incomes, hamburger is an inferior good.

We show Gail's choice between hamburger (horizontal axis) and all other goods (vertical axis) in panel a of Figure 5.4. As Gail's income increases, her budget line

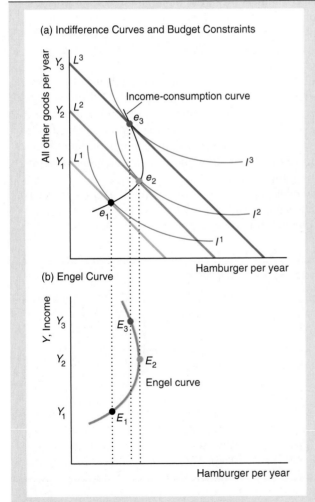

Figure 5.4 A Good That Is Both Inferior and Normal. When she was poor and her income increased, Gail bought more hamburger; however, when she became wealthier and her income rose, she bought less hamburger and more steak. (a) The forward slope of the income-consumption curve from e_1 to e_2 and the backward bend from e_2 to e_3 show this pattern. (b) The forward slope of the Engel curve at low incomes, E_1 to E_2, and the backward bend at higher incomes, E_2 to E_3, also show this pattern.

shifts outward, from L^1 to L^2, and she buys more hamburger: Bundle e_2 lies to the right of e_1. As her income increases further, shifting her budget line outward to L^3, Gail reduces her consumption of hamburger: Bundle e_3 lies to the left of e_2.

Gail's Engel curve in panel b captures the same relationship. At low incomes, her Engel curve is upward sloping, indicating that she buys more hamburger as her income rises. At higher incomes, her Engel curve is backward bending.

As their incomes rise, many consumers switch between lower-quality (hamburger) and higher-quality (steak) versions of the same good. This switching behavior explains the pattern of income elasticities across different-quality cars.

Application   INCOME ELASTICITIES OF DEMAND FOR CARS

As their incomes rise, some consumers buy their first car or an additional car, but others trade in their plain old car for a new sports car or luxury car. We expect that consumers will buy relatively more fancy cars than plain ones as incomes rise. In economic jargon, the income elasticity of demand is higher for sports cars and luxury cars than for other cars.

Bordley and McDonald (1993) estimated the income elasticity of demand for various types of cars. The income elasticity of demand is 1.8 on average across all cars, 1.5 for an economy car, 1.6 for small cars, 1.8 for compact and midsize cars, 1.9 for large and sporty cars, and 2.5 for luxury cars. Thus as expected, purchases of all types of cars rise faster than incomes, and purchases of large and sporty cars or luxury cars rise by more than purchases of economy, small, and compact and midsize cars.

The table shows the income elasticities for various cars. If average incomes increase by 1%, demand for small, utilitarian Chevettes grows by about the same amount (1.2%), but demand for sporty Corvettes grows more than three times as much (3.2%).

Car Model	Income Elasticity	Car Model	Income Elasticity
Accord	2.2	Maxima	2.5
BMW 700 Series	4.4	Mercedes 56	4.4
Camry	2.3	Mustang	1.9
Chevette	1.2	Nova 85	1.6
Civic	2.6	Olds 98	2.4
Corvette	3.2	Porsche 923	4.2
Eagle	1.7	Riviera	2.8
Festiva	1.4	Sprint	1.3
Grand Am	1.8	Taurus	2.1
Jaguar XJS	4.5	Volvo 760	3.4
Jetta	2.1	VW Fox	1.8
Mark VII	3.3	Yugo GV	1.2

Knowing these income elasticities, an auto manufacturer expects the demand for its fancy cars to rise more rapidly than demand for other cars during boom periods, when incomes are rising, and the demand for fancy cars to plummet more rapidly than the demand for other cars during busts, when incomes fall.

Do auto manufacturers really care about this information? Definitely. One of the authors of this study is employed by General Motors Research Labs.

5.3 | EFFECTS OF A PRICE CHANGE

An increase in a price of a good, holding other prices and income constant, has two effects on an individual's demand. One is the *substitution effect*: If utility is held constant, as the price of the good increases, consumers *substitute* other, now relatively cheaper goods for that one. The other is the *income effect*: An increase in price reduces a consumer's buying power, effectively reducing the consumer's *income* and causing the consumer to buy less of at least some goods. A doubling of the price of all the goods the consumer buys is equivalent to a drop in income to half its original level (Chapter 4). Even a rise in the price of only one good reduces a consumer's ability to buy the same amount of all goods as before. For example, if the price of food increases in China, the effective purchasing power of a Chinese consumer falls substantially because 39% of Chinese consumers' income is spent on food.[5]

When a price goes up, the total change in the quantity purchased is the sum of the substitution and income effects.[6] When estimating the effects of a price change on the quantity an individual demands, economists decompose this combined effect into the two separate components. By decomposing the change in demand into two effects, economists gain extra information that they can use to answer questions about whether inflation measures are accurate and whether an increase in tax rates will raise tax revenue, as we demonstrate at the end of this chapter.

Income and Substitution Effects with a Normal Good

We illustrate the substitution and income effects in Figure 5.5, which shows how Mimi changes her allocation of income when the price of beer falls from \$12 to \$4 per unit. With this decrease, Mimi's budget constraint rotates outward from L^1 to L^2. The new budget constraint is flatter, $-p_b/p_w = -4/35 \approx -\frac{1}{9}$, than L^1, $-12/35 \approx -\frac{1}{3}$, because beer is now less expensive relative to wine.

---

[5]Chinese State Statistical Bureau, *Statistical Yearbook of China* (Beijing: State Statistical Bureau Publishing House, 1998).

[6]See Appendix 5A for the mathematical relationship, called the Slutsky equation. See also the discussion of the Slutsky equation at **www.awlonline.com/perloff**, "Measuring the Substitution and Income Effects."

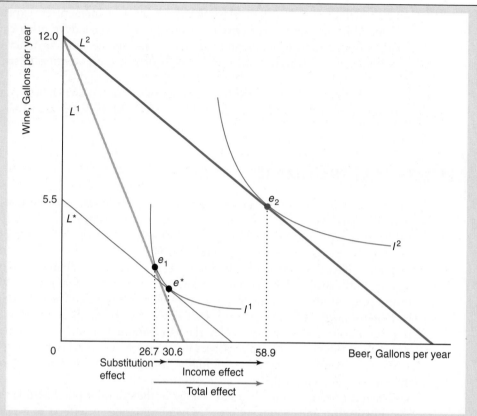

Figure 5.5 Substitution and Income Effects with Normal Goods. A decrease in the price of beer causes Mimi's budget line to rotate from L^1 to L^2. The imaginary budget line L^* has the same slope as L^2 and is tangent to indifference curve I^1. The shift of the optimal bundle from e_1 to e_2 is the *total effect* of the price change. The total effect can be decomposed into the *substitution effect*—movement from e_1 to e^*—and the *income effect*—movement from e^* to e_2.

Mimi can choose between more wine-beer bundles than she could at the higher price. The area between the two budget constraints is the increase in her opportunity set (Chapter 4) from the drop in the price of beer.

At the original price of beer and with a budget of $419, Mimi chooses Bundle e_1 (26.7 gallons of beer and 2.8 gallons of wine per year), where her indifference curve I^1 is tangent to her budget constraint L^1. When the price of beer drops, Mimi's new equilibrium bundle is e_2 (where she buys 58.9 gallons of beer), which occurs where her indifference curve I^2 is tangent to L^2.

The movement from e_1 to e_2 is the total change in her consumption owing to the fall in the price of beer. In particular, the *total effect* on Mimi's consumption of beer from the drop in the price of beer is that she now drinks 32.2 (= 58.9 − 26.7) more gallons of beer per year. In the figure, the arrow pointing to the right and labeled

"Total effect" shows this increase in beer consumption. We can break the total effect into a substitution and an income effect.

The **substitution effect** is the change in the quantity of a good that a consumer demands when the good's price changes, holding other prices and the consumer's utility constant. That is, the substitution effect is the change in the quantity demanded from a *compensated change in the price* of beer, when we decrease Mimi's income by enough to offset the drop in the price of beer so that her utility stays constant. To determine the substitution effect, we draw an imaginary budget constraint, L^*, that is parallel to L^2 and tangent to Mimi's original indifference curve, I^1. This imaginary budget constraint, L^*, has the same slope, $-\frac{1}{9}$, as L^2 because both curves are based on the lower price of beer. For L^* to be tangent to I^1, we need to reduce Mimi's budget from \$419 to \$194 to offset the benefit of the lower price of beer. If Mimi's budget constraint were L^*, she would choose Bundle e^*, where she consumes 30.6 gallons of beer.

Thus if the price of beer falls relative to that of wine and Mimi's utility is held constant by lowering her income, Mimi's optimal bundle shifts from e_1 to e^*, which is the substitution effect. She buys 3.9 (= 30.6 − 26.7) gallons more beer per year, as the arrow pointing to the right labeled "Substitution effect" shows.

The **income effect** is the change in the quantity of a good a consumer demands because of a change in income, holding prices constant. The change in income is due to the change in the price of beer, which allows Mimi to buy more with her same budget. The parallel shift of the budget constraint from L^* to L^2 captures this effective increase in income. The movement from e^* to e_2 is the income effect, as the arrow pointing to the right labeled "Income effect" shows. As her budget increases from \$194 to \$419, Mimi consumes 28.3 (= 58.9 − 30.6) more gallons of beer per year.

The *total effect* from the price change is the *sum of the substitution and income effects*, as the arrows show. Mimi's total effect (in gallons of beer per year) from a drop in the price of beer is

$$\text{Total effect} = \text{substitution effect} + \text{income effect}$$
$$32.2 \quad = \quad 3.9 \quad + \quad 28.3.$$

Because indifference curves are convex to the origin, *the substitution effect is unambiguous*: More of a good is consumed when its price falls. A consumer always substitutes a less expensive good for a more expensive one, holding utility constant.

The direction of the income effect depends on the income elasticity. Because beer is a normal good for Mimi, her income effect is positive. Thus both Mimi's substitution effect and her income effect go in the same direction.

Income and Substitution Effects with an Inferior Good

If a good is inferior, the income effect goes in the opposite direction from the substitution effect. For most inferior goods, the income effect is smaller than the substitution effect. As a result, the total effect moves in the same direction as the substitution effect, but the total effect is smaller. However, the income effect can more than offset the substitution effect in extreme cases. We now examine such a case.

Dennis chooses between spending his money on Chicago Bulls basketball games and on movies, as Figure 5.6 shows. When the price of movies falls,

Dennis's budget line shifts from L^1 to L^2. The total effect of the price fall is the movement from e_1 to e_2. We can break this total movement into an income effect and a substitution effect.

Dennis's income effect, the movement to the left from Bundle e^* to Bundle e_2, is negative, as the arrow pointing left labeled "Income effect" shows. The income effect is negative because Dennis regards movies as an inferior good.

Dennis's substitution effect for movies is positive because movies are now less expensive than they were before the price change. The substitution effect is the movement to the right from e_1 to e^*.

The total effect of a price change, then, depends on which effect is larger. Because Dennis's negative income effect for movies more than offsets his positive substitution effect, the total effect of a drop in the price of movies is negative.[7]

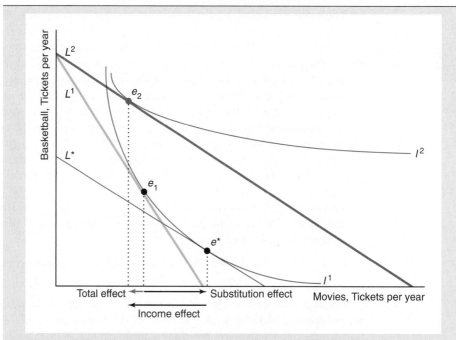

Figure 5.6 **Giffen Good.** Because a movie ticket is an inferior good for Dennis, the income effect, the movement from e^* to e_2, resulting from a drop in the price of movies is negative. This negative income effect more than offsets the positive substitution effect, the movement from e_1 to e^*, so the total effect, the movement from e_1 to e_2, is negative. Thus a movie ticket is a Giffen good because as its price drops, Dennis consumes less of it.

[7]Economists mathematically decompose the total effect of a price change into substitution and income effects to answer various business and policy questions: see **www.awlonline.com/perloff**, "Measuring the Substitution and Income Effects" and "International Comparison of Substitution and Income Effects."

A good is called a **Giffen good** if a decrease in its price causes the quantity demanded to fall.[8] Thus going to the movies is a Giffen good for Dennis. The price decrease has an effect that is similar to an income increase: His opportunity set increases as the price of movies drops. Dennis spends the money he saves on movies to buy more basketball tickets. Indeed, he decides to increase his purchase of basketball tickets even further by reducing his purchase of movie tickets.

The demand curve for a Giffen good has an upward slope! Dennis's demand curve for movies is upward sloping because he goes to more movies at the high price, e_1, than at the low price, e_2.

The Law of Demand (Chapter 2), however, says that demand curves slope downward. You're no doubt wondering how I'm going to worm my way out this apparent contradiction. The answer is that I claimed that the Law of Demand was an empirical regularity, not a theoretical necessity. Although it's theoretically possible for a demand curve to slope upward, economists have found few, if any, real-world examples of Giffen goods.[9]

Solved Problem 5.2   **Next to its plant, a manufacturer of dinner plates has an outlet store that sells plates of both first quality (perfect plates) and second quality (plates with slight blemishes). The outlet store sells a relatively large share of seconds. At its outlet stores elsewhere, the firm sells many more first-quality plates than second-quality plates. Why? (Assume that consumers' tastes with respect to plates are the same everywhere and that there is a cost, s, of shipping each plate from the factory to the firm's other stores.)**

Answer

1. *Determine how the relative prices of plates differ between the two types of stores*: The slope of the budget line consumers face at the factory outlet store is $-p_1/p_2$, where p_1 is the price of first-quality plates and p_2 is the price of the seconds. It costs the same, s, to ship a first-quality plate as a second because they weigh the same and have to be handled in the same way. At all other stores, the firm adds the cost of shipping to the price it charges at its factory outlet store, so the price of a first-quality plate is $p_1 + s$ and the price of a second is $p_2 + s$. As a result, the slope of the budget line consumers face at the other retail stores is $-(p_1 + s)/(p_2 + s)$. The seconds are relatively less expensive at the factory outlet than at other stores. For example, if $p_1 = \$2$, $p_2 = \$1$, and $s = \$1$ per plate, the slope of the budget line is -2 at the outlet store and $-3/2$ elsewhere. Thus the first-quality

---

[8]Robert Giffen, a nineteenth-century British economist, argued that poor people in Ireland increased their consumption of potatoes when the price rose because of a blight. More recent studies of the Irish potato famine dispute this observation, however.

[9]Battalio, Kagel, and Kogut (1991), however, showed in an experiment that quinine water is a Giffen good for lab rats!

plate costs twice as much as a second at the outlet store but only 1.5 times as much elsewhere.

2. *Use the relative price difference to explain why relatively more seconds are bought at the factory outlet*: Holding a consumer's income and tastes fixed, if the price of seconds rises relative to that of firsts (as we go from the factory outlet to other retail shops), most consumers will buy relatively more firsts. The substitution effect is unambiguous: Were they compensated so that their utilities were held constant, consumers would unambiguously substitute firsts for seconds. It is possible that the income effect could go in the other direction; however, as most consumers spend relatively little of their total budget on plates, the income effect is presumably small relative to the substitution effect. Thus we expect relatively fewer seconds to be bought at the retail stores than at the factory outlet. (Problem 9 at the end of the chapter asks you to illustrate this answer using graphs.)

Application WHY THE WEALTHY BUY MORE HOUSES

Why are high-income people more likely to buy houses than poor people are? One obvious explanation is an income effect: Richer people have more money, and housing is a normal good. A second, less obvious reason is a substitution effect: Housing is relatively cheap for high-income people due to tax exemptions. Thus the demand for housing rises with income due to both an income effect and a substitution effect.

A U.S. taxpayer can deduct mortgage interest payments from "taxable" income. Because high-income earners must pay a relatively large share of their taxable income to the government, this deduction saves them more than it does taxpayers whose tax rate is lower. Thus richer people pay less after taxes for their housing because every extra dollar spent on housing reduces their taxable income.

The following table, based on 1999 tax rates, shows the relative benefit to a lower-income person for every dollar of benefit to a taxpayer whose income exceeds $200,000:

Taxable Income	Relative Benefit
Less than $10,000	0.003¢
$10,000 to $20,000	0.1
$20,000 to $30,000	0.5
$30,000 to $40,000	2.0
$40,000 to $50,000	4.0
$50,000 to $75,000	9.0
$75,000 to $100,000	23.0
$100,000 to $200,000	42.0
Average of all groups with income under $200,000	6.0

> For every dollar of tax savings from buying housing to someone who earns over $200,000, the average person with less income saves only 6¢. Put another way, for every dollar in tax saved by the average taxpayer earning less than $10,000, an average taxpayer in the top income group saves $29,200.
>
> The substitution and income effects are large. Taube and MacDonald (1991) estimate that the income elasticity for housing is 0.76 and the pure substitution elasticity is –0.39. Thus if income rises by 10%, holding price constant, the quantity of housing demanded rises by about 7.6%. Similarly, holding income constant, a 10% decrease in the relative price of housing (after taxes) causes the demand for housing to rise by roughly 4%.

5.4 COST-OF-LIVING ADJUSTMENTS

By knowing both the substitution and income effects, we can answer questions that we could not if we knew only the total effect. For example, if firms have an estimate of the income effect, they can predict the impact of a negative income tax (a gift of money from the government) on the consumption of their products. Similarly, if we know the size of both effects, we can determine how accurately the government measures inflation.

Many long-term contracts and government programs include *cost-of-living adjustments (COLAs)*, which raise prices or incomes in proportion to an index of inflation. Not only business contracts but also rental contracts, alimony payments, salaries, pensions, and Social Security payments are frequently adjusted in this manner over time. We will use consumer theory to show that a cost-of-living measure that governments commonly use overestimates how the true cost of living changes over time. Because of this overestimate, you overpay your landlord if the rent on your apartment rises with this measure.

Inflation Indexes

The prices of most goods rise over time. We call the increase in the overall price level *inflation*.

Real Versus Nominal Prices. The actual price of a good is called the *nominal price*. The price adjusted for inflation is the *real price*.

Because the overall level of prices rises over time, nominal prices usually increase more rapidly than real prices. For example, the nominal price of a McDonald's hamburger rose from 15¢ in 1955 to 75¢ in 2000, a fivefold increase. However, the real price of a burger fell because the prices of other goods rose more rapidly than that of a burger.

How do we adjust for inflation to calculate the real price? Governments measure the cost of a standard bundle of goods for use in comparing prices over time. This measure is called the Consumer Price Index (CPI). Each month, the government reports how much it costs to buy the bundle of goods that an average consumer purchased in a *base* year (with the base year changing every few years).

By comparing the cost of buying this bundle over time, we can determine how much the overall price level has increased. In the United States, the CPI was 26.8 in

1955 and 168.7 in January 2000.[10] The cost of buying the bundle of goods increased 629% ($\approx 168.7/26.8$) from 1955 to 2000.

We can use the CPI to calculate the real price of a hamburger over time. In terms of 2000 dollars, the real price of a hamburger in 1955 was

$$\frac{\text{CPI for 2000}}{\text{CPI for 1955}} \times \text{ price of a burger} = \frac{168.7}{26.8} \times 15\text{\textcent} \approx 94\text{\textcent}.$$

If you could have purchased the hamburger in 1955 with 2000 dollars—which are worth less than 1955 dollars—the hamburger would have cost 94¢. The real price in 2000 dollars (and the nominal price) of a hamburger in 2000 was only 75¢. Thus the real price of a hamburger fell by about a fourth. If we compared the real prices in both years using 1955 dollars, we would reach the same conclusion that the real price of hamburgers fell by about a fifth.

Calculating Inflation Indexes. The government collects data on the quantities and prices of 364 individual goods and services, such as housing, dental services, watch and jewelry repairs, college tuition fees, taxi fares, women's hairpieces and wigs, hearing aids, slipcovers and decorative pillows, bananas, pork sausage, and funeral expenses. These prices rise at different rates. If the government merely reported all these price increases separately, most of us would find this information overwhelming. It is much more convenient to use a single summary statistic, the CPI, which tells us how prices rose *on average*.

We can use an example with only two goods, clothing and food, to show how the CPI is calculated. In the first year, consumers buy C_1 units of clothing and F_1 units of food at prices p_C^1 and p_F^1. We use this bundle of goods, C_1 and F_1, as our base bundle for comparison. In the second year, consumers buy C_2 and F_2 units at prices p_C^2 and p_F^2.

The government knows from its survey of prices each year that the price of clothing in the second year is p_C^2/p_C^1 times as large as the price the previous year and the price of food is p_F^2/p_F^1 times as large. If the price of clothing was \$1 in the first year and \$2 in the second year, the price of clothing in the second year is $\frac{2}{1} = 2$ times, or 100%, larger than in the first year.

One way we can average the price increases of each good is to weight them equally. But do we really want to do that? Do we want to give as much weight to the price increase for skateboards as to the price increase for automobiles? An alternative approach is to give a larger weight to the price change of a good as we spend more of our income on that good, its budget share. The CPI takes this approach to weighting, using budget shares.[11]

---

[10]The number 168.7 is not an actual dollar amount. Rather, it is the actual dollar cost of buying the bundle divided by a constant. That constant was chosen so that the average expenditure in the period 1982–1984 was 100.

[11]This discussion of the CPI is simplified in a number of ways. Sophisticated adjustments are made to the CPI that are ignored here, including repeated updating of the base year (chaining). See Pollak (1989) and Diewert and Nakamura (1993).

The CPI for the first year is the amount of income it takes to buy the market basket actually purchased that year:

$$Y_1 = p_C^1 C_1 + p_F^1 F_1. \tag{5.1}$$

The cost of buying the first year's bundle in the second year is

$$Y_2 = p_C^2 C_1 + p_F^2 F_1. \tag{5.2}$$

To calculate the rate of inflation, we determine how much more income it would take to buy the first year's bundle in the second year, which is the ratio of Equation 5.1 to Equation 5.2:

$$\frac{Y_2}{Y_1} = \frac{p_C^2 C_1 + p_F^2 F_1}{p_C^1 C_1 + p_F^1 F_1}.$$

For example, from 1996 to 1997, the U.S. CPI rose by $1.023 \approx Y_2/Y_1$ from $Y_1 = 156.9$ to $Y_2 = 160.5$. Thus it cost 2.3% more in 1997 than in 1996 to buy the same bundle of goods.

The ratio Y_2/Y_1 reflects how much prices rise on average. By multiplying and dividing the first term in the numerator by p_C^1 and multiplying and dividing the second term by p_F^1, we find that this index is equivalent to

$$\frac{Y_2}{Y_1} = \frac{\left(\dfrac{p_C^2}{p_C^1}\right) p_C^1 C_1 + \left(\dfrac{p_F^2}{p_F^1}\right) p_F^1 F_1}{Y_1} = \left(\frac{p_C^2}{p_C^1}\right)\theta_C + \left(\frac{p_F^2}{p_F^1}\right)\theta_F,$$

where $\theta_C = p_C^1 C_1 / Y_1$ and $\theta_F = p_F^1 F_1 / Y_1$ are the budget shares of clothing and food in the first or base year. The CPI is a *weighted average* of the price increase for each good, p_C^2/p_C^1 and p_F^2/p_F^1, where the weights are each good's budget share in the base year, θ_C and θ_F.

Application   DOES INFLATION HURT?

Due to inflation, the nominal prices of many goods have increased over time. But so have wages. Are consumers better off or worse off today than in the past?

Consumers today have a much wider choice of goods, most of which are of notably higher quality than the comparable items that their grandparents used. Today's color television set is much better than the old, unreliable black-and-white TVs of the 1950s. Even if we don't control for the quality difference, it takes a worker fewer hours to "earn" a television. In 1971, the typical worker toiled for 174 hours to have enough money to buy a 25-inch color set. In 1997, a much more reliable TV could be obtained after just 23 hours of work.

In 1900, an average worker could buy a 1.55-ounce Hershey chocolate bar for 5¢ after 19.9 minutes of work. In 1997, the bar's price was 45¢, but the worker could pay for it after only 2 minutes of work.

A Model T Ford could be had for $850 or 4,696 hours of work in 1908. In 1997, a Ford Taurus—a far superior vehicle—cost $17,995, or 1,365 hours of work.

Unfortunately, not everything is cheaper today. In 1926, a movie ticket cost 17¢, or 19 minutes of work. By 1997, the average ticket price was $4.25, which also cost a typical worker 19 minutes of work.

Effects of Inflation Adjustments

A CPI adjustment of prices in a long-term contract overcompensates for inflation. We use an example involving an employment contract to illustrate the difference between using the CPI to adjust a long-term contract and using a true cost-of-living adjustment, which holds utility constant.

CPI Adjustment. Klaas signed a long-term contract when he was hired. According to the COLA clause in his contract, his employer increases his salary each year by the same percentage as that by which the CPI increases. If the CPI this year is 5% higher than the CPI last year, Klaas's salary rises automatically by 5% over last year's.

Klaas spends all his money on clothing and food. His budget constraint in the first year is $Y_1 = p_C^1 C + p_F^1 F$, which we rewrite as

$$C = \frac{Y_1}{p_C^1} - \frac{p_F^1}{p_C^1} F.$$

The intercept of the budget constraint, L^1, on the vertical (clothing) axis in Figure 5.7 is Y_1/p_C^1, and the slope of the constraint is $-p_F^1/p_C^1$. The tangency of his indifference curve I^1 and the budget constraint L^1 determine his equilibrium consumption bundle in the first year, e_1, where he purchases C_1 and F_1.

In the second year, his salary rises with the CPI to Y_2, so his budget constraint, L^2, in that year is

$$C = \frac{Y_2}{p_C^2} - \frac{p_F^2}{p_C^2} F.$$

The new constraint, L^2, has a flatter slope, $-p_F^2/p_C^2$, than L^1 because the price of clothing rose more than the price of food. The new constraint goes through the original equilibrium bundle, e_1, because, by increasing his salary using the CPI, the firm ensures that Klaas can buy the same bundle of goods in the second year that he chose in the first year.

He *can* buy the same bundle, but *does* he? The answer is no. His optimal bundle in the second year is e_2, where indifference curve I^2 is tangent to his new budget constraint L^2. The movement from e_1 to e_2 is the *total effect* from the changes in the real prices of clothing and food. *This adjustment to his income does not keep him on his original indifference curve, I^1.*

Indeed, Klaas is better off in the second year than in the first. The CPI adjustment *overcompensates* for the change in inflation in the sense that his utility increases.

Klaas is better off because the prices of clothing and food did not increase by the same amount. Suppose that the price of clothing and food had both increased by *exactly* the same amount. After a CPI adjustment, Klaas's budget constraint in the second year, L^2, would be exactly the same as in the first year, L^1, so he would choose exactly the same bundle, e_1, in the second year as in the first year.

Because the price of food rose by less than the price of clothing, L^2 is not the same as L^1. Food became cheaper relative to clothing. So by consuming more food and less clothing, Klaas has higher utility in the second year.

Had clothing become relatively less expensive, Klaas would have raised his utility in the second year by consuming relatively more clothing. Thus it doesn't matter which good becomes relatively less expensive over time—it's only necessary for one of them to become a relative bargain for Klaas to benefit from the CPI compensation.

True Cost-of-Living Adjustment. We now know that a CPI adjustment overcompensates for inflation. What we want is a *true cost-of-living index*: an inflation index that holds utility constant over time.

How big an increase in Klaas's salary would leave him exactly as well off in the second year as in the first? We can answer this question applying the same technique we use to identify the substitution and income effects. We draw an imaginary budget line, L^* in Figure 5.7, that is tangent to I^1, so that Klaas's utility remains constant, but that has the same slope as L^2. The income, Y^*, corresponding to that imaginary budget constraint is the amount that leaves Klaas's utility constant. Had Klaas received Y^* in the second year instead of Y_2, he would have chosen Bundle e^* instead of e_2. Because e^* is on the same indifference curve, I^1, as e_1, Klaas's utility would be the same in both years.

The numerical example in Table 5.1 illustrates how the CPI overcompensates Klaas.[12] Suppose that p_C^1 is \$1, p_C^2 is \$2, p_F^1 is \$4, and p_F^2 is \$5. In the first year, Klaas spends his income, Y_1, of \$400 on C_1 = 200 units of clothing and F_1 = 50 units of food and has a utility of 2,000, which is the level of utility on I^1. If his income did not increase in the second year, he would substitute toward the relatively inexpensive food, cutting his consumption of clothing in half but reducing his consumption of food by only a fifth. His utility would fall to 1,265.

If his second-year income increases in proportion to the CPI, he can buy the same bundle, e_1, in the second year as in the first. His second-year income is Y_2 = \$650 ($= p_C^2 C_1 + p_F^2 F_1 = \$2 \times 200 + \$5 \times 50$). Klaas is better off if his budget increases to Y_2. He substitutes toward the relatively inexpensive food, buying less clothing than in the first year but more food, e_2. His utility rises from 2,000 to approximately 2,055 (the level of utility on I^2).

How much would his income have to rise to leave him only as well off as he was in the first year? If his second-year income is $Y^* \approx \$632.50$, by appropriate substitution toward food, e^*, he can achieve the same level of utility, 2,000, as in the first year.

We can use the income that just compensates Klaas, Y^*, to construct a true cost-of-living index. In our numerical example, the true cost-of-living index rose 58.1% ($\approx [632.50 - 400]/400$), while the CPI rose 62.5% ($= [650 - 400]/400$).

---

[12]We assume that Klaas has a utility function $U = 20\sqrt{CF}$, which we used to draw Figure 5.7.

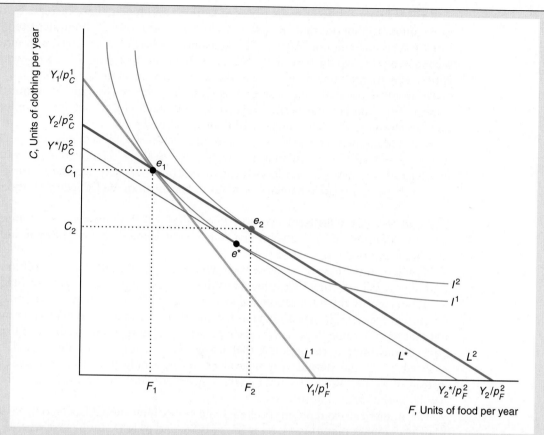

Figure 5.7 The Consumer Price Index. In the first year, when Klaas has an income of Y_1, his optimal bundle is e_1, where indifference curve I^1 is tangent to his budget constraint, L^1. In the second year, the price of clothing rises more than the price of food. Because his salary increases in proportion to the CPI, his second-year budget constraint, L^2, goes through e_1, so he can buy the same bundle as in the first year. His new optimal bundle, however, is e_2, where I^2 is tangent to L^2. The CPI adjustment overcompensates him for the increase in prices: Klaas is better off in the second year because his utility is greater on I^2 than on I^1. With a smaller true cost-of-living adjustment, Klaas's budget constraint, L^*, is tangent to I^1 at e^*.

Table 5.1 Cost-of-Living Adjustments

	p_C	p_F	Income, Y	Clothing	Food	Utility, U
First year	\$1	\$4	$Y_1 = \$400$	200	50	2,000
Second year	\$2	\$5				
No adjustment			$Y_1 = \$400$	100	40	$\approx 1,265$
CPI adjustment			$Y_2 = \$650$	162.5	65	$\approx 2,055$
True COLA			$Y^* \approx \$632.50$	≈ 158.1	≈ 63.2	2,000

Size of the CPI Substitution Bias. We have just demonstrated that the CPI has an *upward bias* in the sense that an individual's utility rises if we increase that person's income by the same percentage as that by which the CPI rises. If we make the CPI adjustment, we are implicitly assuming—incorrectly—that consumers do not substitute toward relatively inexpensive goods when prices change but keep buying the same bundle of goods over time. We call this overcompensation a *substitution bias*.

There is no substitution bias if all prices increase at the same rate so that relative prices remain constant. The faster some prices rise relative to others, the more pronounced is the upward bias caused by substitution to now less expensive goods.

Application   **THE TOTAL CPI BIAS**

Since 1995, members of both parties in the U.S. Congress have proposed changing the CPI. They argue that the upward bias in the CPI has been largely to blame for the rapid increases in costs for various government programs. The Senate Finance Committee commissioned a group of economists to determine how biased the CPI is. The commission (Boskin et al., 1997) concluded that the CPI overstated inflation by about 1.1 percentage points per year owing to three factors:

- The *substitution bias*: 0.4 %
- Failure to take proper account of *discount stores*, so that the wrong prices are used in the calculation: 0.1%
- Failure to account adequately for *quality improvements* or *new products*—particularly in drugs and computers—so that prices are overstated: 0.6%[13]

They concluded that for 1983–1986, the overestimate of the annual change in the CPI is 0.25% for housing (compared to an annual change of 4.20%), 1.00% for nonprescription drugs and medical supplies (annual change, 3.68%), 0.30% for furniture (0.72%), 0.30% for food (3.60%), 5.60% for computers (–2.39%), 1.00% for clothing (2.15%), and 0.59% for new cars (2.60%).

Although a 1.1 percentage point bias might sound small, the cumulative bias can be substantial over a number of years. Moreover, even small annual biases may matter to some firms. For example, the United States Postal Service (USPS) has a COLA based on the CPI in its union contracts. In 1997, a typical employee earned $48,793 a year, including benefits. A bias of 1.1% a year costs the USPS nearly $537 extra per employee. Because the USPS has about 893,000 employees, the bias costs the USPS over $479 million per year—and benefits its employees by the same amount.

According to the commission's final report, the CPI bias alone makes it the fourth-largest "federal program," after Social Security, health care, and defense. The commission calculated that $634 billion of the national debt would be eliminated in five years if the CPI rose 1% less rapidly per year. Offsetting the gain to the government is the loss to Social Security recipients

---

[13]See **www.awlonline.com/perloff**, "Quality Improvements, New Products, and the CPI."

and others who receive government funds, who would get smaller cost-of-living increases with an adjusted CPI. In 2000, the surviving members of the commission estimated that corrections by the government had reduced the total bias in the CPI from about 1.1 to about 0.8 percentage points per year.

5.5 | DERIVING LABOR SUPPLY CURVES

Throughout this chapter, we've used consumer theory to examine consumers' *demand* behavior. Perhaps surprisingly, we can use the consumer theory model to derive the *supply curve* of labor. We are going to do that by deriving a demand curve for time spent *not* working and then use that demand curve to draw the supply curve of hours spent working.

Labor-Leisure Choice

People choose between working to earn money to buy goods and services and consuming *leisure*: all time spent not working. In addition to sleeping, eating, and playing, leisure includes time spent cooking meals and fixing things around the house. The number of hours worked per day, H, equals 24 minus the hours of leisure or nonwork, N, in a day:

$$H = 24 - N.$$

Using consumer theory, we can determine the demand curve for leisure once we know the price of leisure. What does it cost you to watch TV or go to school or do anything for an hour other than work? It costs you the wage, w, you could have earned from an hour's work: The price of leisure is forgone earnings. The higher your wage, the more an hour of leisure costs you. For this reason, taking an afternoon off costs a lawyer who earns $250 an hour much more than it costs someone who earns the minimum wage.

We use an example to show how the number of hours of leisure and work depends on the wage, unearned income (such as inheritances and gifts from parents), and tastes. Jackie spends her total income, Y, on various goods. For simplicity, we assume that the price of these goods is $1 per unit, so she buys Y goods. Her utility, U, depends on how many goods and how much leisure she consumes:

$$U = U(Y, N).$$

Initially, we assume that Jackie can choose to work as many or as few hours as she wants for an hourly wage of w. Jackie's earned income equals her wage times the number of hours she works, wH. Her total income, Y, is her earned income plus her unearned income, Y^*:

$$Y = wH + Y^*.$$

Panel a of Figure 5.8 shows Jackie's choice between leisure and goods. The vertical axis shows how many goods, Y, Jackie buys. The horizontal axis shows both hours of leisure, N, which are measured from left to right, and hours of work, H,

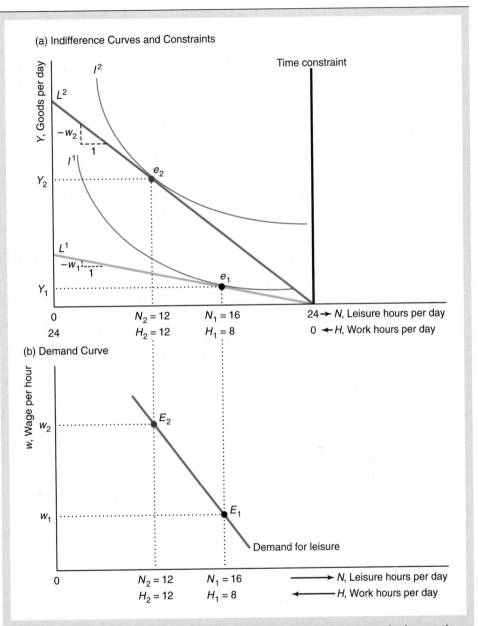

Figure 5.8 Demand for Leisure. (a) Jackie chooses between leisure, N, and other goods, Y, subject to a time constraint (vertical line at 24 hours) and a budget constraint, L^1, which is $Y = w_1 H = w_1(24 - N)$, with a slope of $-w_1$. The tangency of her indifference curve, I^1, with her budget constraint, L^1, determines her optimal bundle, e_1, where she has $N_1 = 16$ hours of leisure and works $H_1 = 24 - N_1 = 8$ hours. If her wage rises from w_1 to w_2, Jackie shifts from optimal bundle e_1 to e_2. (b) Bundles e_1 and e_2 correspond to E_1 and E_2 on her leisure demand curve.

which are measured from right to left. Jackie maximizes her utility given the *two* constraints she faces. First, she faces a time constraint, which is a vertical line at 24 hours of leisure. There are only 24 hours in a day; all the money in the world won't buy her more hours in a day. Second, Jackie faces a budget constraint. Because Jackie has no unearned income, her initial budget constraint, L^1, is $Y = w_1 H = w_1(24 - N)$. The slope of her budget constraint is $-w_1$, because each extra hour of leisure she consumes costs her w_1 goods.

Jackie picks her optimal hours of leisure, $N_1 = 16$, so that she is on the highest indifference curve, I^1, that touches her budget constraint. She works $H_1 = 24 - N_1 = 8$ hours per day and earns an income of $Y_1 = w_1 H_1 = 8w_1$.

We derive Jackie's demand curve for leisure using the same method that we used to derive Mimi's demand curve for beer. We raise the price of leisure—the wage—in panel a of Figure 5.8 to trace out Jackie's demand curve for leisure in panel b. As the wage increases from w_1 to w_2, leisure becomes more expensive, and Jackie demands less of it.

By subtracting her demand for leisure at each wage—her demand curve for leisure in panel a of Figure 5.9—from the 24, we construct her labor supply curve—the hours she is willing to work as a function of the wage—in panel b.[14] Her supply curve for hours worked is the mirror image of the demand curve for leisure: For every extra hour of leisure that Jackie consumes, she works one hour less.

Figure 5.9 Supply Curve of Labor. (a) Jackie's demand for leisure is downward sloping. (b) At any given wage, the number of hours that Jackie works, *H*, and the number of hours of leisure, *N*, that she consumes add to 24. Thus her supply curve for hours worked, which equals 24 hours minus the number of hours of leisure she demands, is upward sloping.

---

[14]Appendix 5B shows how to derive the labor supply curve using calculus.

Income and Substitution Effects

An increase in the wage causes both income and substitution effects, which alter an individual's demand for leisure and supply of hours worked. The *total effect* of an increase in Jackie's wage from w_1 to w_2 is the movement from e_1 to e_2 in Figure 5.10. Jackie works $H_2 - H_1$ fewer hours and consumes $N_2 - N_1$ more hours of leisure.

By drawing an imaginary budget constraint, L^*, that is tangent to her original indifference curve with the slope of the new wage, we can divide the total effect into substitution and income effects. The *substitution effect*, the movement from e_1 to e^*, must be negative: A compensated wage increase causes Jackie to consume fewer hours of leisure, N^*, and work more hours, H^*.

As the wage rises, if Jackie works the same number of hours as before, she has a higher income. The *income effect* is the movement from e^* to e_2. Because leisure is a normal good for Jackie, as her income rises, she consumes more leisure. When leisure is a normal good, the substitution and income effects work in opposite directions, so whether leisure demand increases or not depends on which effect is larger. Jackie's income effect dominates the substitution effect, so the total effect for leisure is positive: $N_2 > N_1$. Jackie works fewer hours as the wage rises, so her labor supply curve is backward bending.

If leisure is an inferior good, both the substitution effect and the income effect work in the same direction, and hours of leisure definitely fall. As a result, if leisure is an inferior good, a wage increase unambiguously causes the hours worked to rise.

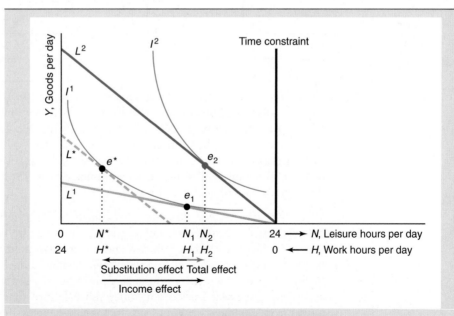

Figure 5.10 Income and Substitution Effects of a Wage Change. A wage change causes both a substitution and an income effect. The movement from e_1 to e^* is the substitution effect, the movement from e^* to e_2 is the income effect, and the movement from e_1 to e_2 is the total effect.

Solved Problem 5.3   **Enrico receives a no-strings-attached scholarship that pays him an extra Y^* per day. How does this scholarship affect the number of hours he wants to work? Does his utility increase?**

Answer

1. *Show his consumer equilibrium without unearned income:* When Enrico had no unearned income, his budget constraint, L^1 in the graphs, hit the hours-leisure axis at 0 hours and had a slope of $-w$.

2. *Show how the unearned income affects his budget constraint:* The extra income causes a parallel upward shift of Y^*. His new budget constraint, L^2, has the same slope as before because his wage does not change. The extra income cannot buy Enrico more time, of course, so L^2 cannot extend to the right of the time constraint. As a result, L^2 is vertical at 0 hours up to Y^*: His income is Y^* if he works no hours. Above Y^*, L^2 slants toward the goods axis with a slope of $-w$.

3. *Show that the relative position of the new to the original equilibrium depends on his tastes:* The change in the number of hours he works depends on Enrico's tastes. Panels a and b show two possible sets of indifference curves. In both diagrams, when facing budget constraint L^1, Enrico chooses to work H_1 hours. In panel a, leisure is a normal good, so as his income rises, Enrico consumes more leisure than originally: He moves from Bundle e_1 to Bundle e_2. In panel b, he views leisure as an inferior good and consumes fewer hours of leisure than originally: He moves from e_1 to e_3. (Another possibility is that the number of hours he works is unaffected by the extra unearned income.)

4. *Discuss how his utility changes:* Regardless of his tastes, Enrico has more income in the new equilibrium and is on a higher indifference curve after receiving the scholarship. In short, he feels that more money is better than less.

LEISURE-INCOME CHOICES OF TEXTILE WORKERS

Dunn (1977, 1978, 1979), using data obtained by questioning Southern cotton mill workers and examining their behavior, determined their indifference curves, which we can use to examine income and substitution effects. A typical worker's indifference curves are close to right angles (see the graph), indicating that leisure and all other goods are nearly perfect complements: The worker is relatively unwilling to substitute goods for leisure. (Workers' indifference curves vary only slightly by race and gender.)

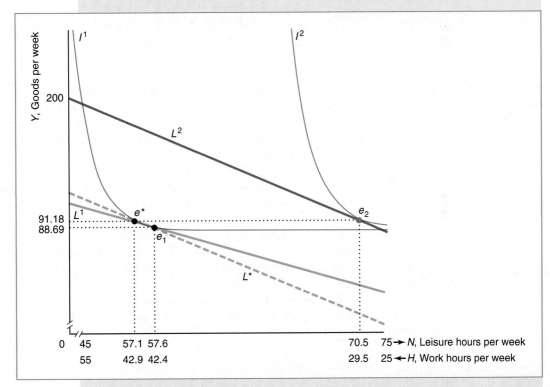

At the original wage, $2.09 per hour, the budget constraint is L^1 and a typical worker chooses to work 42.4 hours per week (assuming that there are 100 total hours to be allocated between work and leisure), Bundle e_1. An increase in the wage of $1 per hour causes the budget constraint to rotate outward to L^2.

An uncompensated increase in the wage increases the demand for leisure and reduces the hours worked to 29.5 per week, Bundle e_2. Thus workers' labor supply curves are backward bending: Workers decrease their hours as their wage rises. An increase in the wage from $2.09 to $3.09 leads to weekly earnings rising only from $88.69 to $91.18 because of the offsetting reduction in the hours worked.

What would happen if, when the wage increased, workers' incomes were reduced so that they remained on the original indifference curve, I^1? That is, what is the substitution effect for this $1 wage increase? The imaginary budget constraint L^* is parallel to L^2 but tangent to indifference curve I^1 at e^*. Thus the substitution effect—the movement from e_1 to e^*—due to a compensated wage increase is an increase in weekly hours by half an hour a week to 42.9 hours. The income effect (the movement from e^* to e_2) is to work 13.4 (= 29.5 − 42.9) fewer hours a week.

Shape of the Labor Supply Curve

Whether the labor supply curve slopes upward, bends backward, or has sections with both properties depends on the income elasticity of leisure. Suppose that a worker views leisure as an inferior good at low wages and a normal good at high wages. As the wage increases, the demand for leisure first falls and then rises, and the hours supplied to the market first rise and then fall.

The budget line rotates upward from L^1 to L^2 as the wage rises in panel a of Figure 5.11. Because leisure is an inferior good at low incomes, in the new optimal bundle, e_2, this worker consumes less leisure and more goods than at the original bundle, e_1.

At higher incomes, however, leisure is a normal good. At an even higher wage, the new equilibrium is e_3, on budget line L^3, where the quantity of leisure demanded is higher and the number of hours worked is lower. Thus the corresponding supply curve for labor slopes upward at low wages and bends backward at higher wages in panel b.

Do labor supply curves slope upward or backward? Economic theory alone cannot answer this question: Both forward-sloping and backward-bending supply curves are *theoretically* possible. Empirical research is necessary to resolve this question.

Application   **ESTIMATED LABOR SUPPLY CURVES**

Empirical studies find that the slopes of labor supply curves vary across demographic groups. Most studies find that the labor supply curves for British and American men are virtually vertical because the income and substitution effects offset each other almost exactly.

Studies find that the typical British man has a slightly backward-sloping supply of labor, with an estimated elasticity of supply ranging between –0.2 and –0.05. That is, as the wage rises by 1%, the number of hours these men work falls by at most –0.2%.

Most studies find that American male workers have virtually vertical supply curves, with estimated elasticities of supply ranging between –0.2 and 0.15. A very careful study of prime-age American males (MaCurdy, Green, and Paarsch, 1990), which controlled for income taxes, found that both substitution and income effects are essentially zero, so the total effect is zero and the labor supply curve is vertical.

Most studies report that female labor supply curves are upward sloping, averaging across married and unmarried women. Depending on the group and the country, the elasticities of supply range from 0 to relatively large positive numbers such as 4.0 and even higher for a few age groups of unmarried women. A number of studies of wives have found only that their supply curves are virtually vertical: slightly backward bending in Canada and the United States and slightly forward sloping in the United Kingdom and Germany.

Thus most studies conclude that the hours worked by typical men and married women are not sensitive to wages. Single women, however, tend to work more hours when their wage rises.

Figure 5.11 Labor Supply Curve That Slopes Upward and Then Bends Backward. At low incomes, an increase in the wage causes the worker to work more: the movement from e_1 to e_2 in panel a or from E_1 to E_2 in panel b. At higher incomes, an increase in the wage causes the worker to work fewer hours: the movement from e_2 to e_3 or from E_2 to E_3.

Income Tax Rates and Labor Supply

Why do we care about the shape of labor supply curves? One reason is that we can tell from the shape of the labor supply curve whether an increase in the income tax rate—a percent of earnings—will cause a substantial reduction in the hours of work. Taxes on earnings are an unattractive way of collecting money for the government if supply curves are upward sloping because the taxes cause people to work fewer hours, reducing the amount of goods society produces and raising less tax revenue than if the supply curve were vertical or backward bending. On the other hand, if supply curves are backward bending, a small increase in the tax rate increases tax revenue *and* boosts total production (but reduces leisure).

Presidents John Kennedy and Ronald Reagan argued that cutting the marginal tax rate (the percentage of the last dollar earned that the government takes in taxes) would stimulate people to work longer and produce more, both desirable effects. President Reagan claimed that tax receipts would increase due to the additional work.

Because tax rates have changed substantially over time, we have a natural experiment to test this hypothesis. The Kennedy tax cuts lowered the top personal marginal tax rate from 91% to 70%. The rate fell over the next couple of decades until in 1988, when the top rate for the highest income group dropped to 28%.

The effect of a tax rate of $\tau = 0.28$ is to reduce the effective wage from w to $(1 - \tau)w = 0.72w$.[15] The tax reduces the after-tax wage by 28%, so a worker's budget constraint rotates downward, similar to rotating the budget constraint downward from L^2 to L^1, in Figure 5.11.

As we discussed, if the budget constraint rotates downward, the hours of work may increase or decrease, depending on whether leisure is a normal or an inferior good. The worker in panel b has a labor supply curve that at first slopes upward and then bends backward, as in panel b. If the worker's wage is very high, the worker is in the backward-bending section of the labor supply curve.

If so, the relationship between the marginal tax rate, τ, and tax revenue, $\tau w H$, is bell-shaped, as in Figure 5.12.[16] At a zero tax rate, a small increase in the tax rate *must* increase the tax revenue, because no revenue was collected when the tax rate was zero. If the tax rate rises a little more, however, tax revenue must rise even higher, for two reasons. First, the government collects a larger percentage of every dollar earned because the tax rate is higher. Second, employees work more hours as

---

[15]Under a progressive income tax system, the marginal tax rate increases with income. The average tax rate differs from the marginal tax rate. Suppose that the marginal tax rate is 20% on the first $10,000 earned and 30% on the second $10,000. Someone who earned $20,000 would pay $2,000 (= 0.2 × $10,000) on the first $10,000 of earnings and $3,000 on the next $10,000. That taxpayer's average tax rate is 25% (= [$2,000 + $3,000]/$20,000). For simplicity in the following analysis, we assume that the marginal tax rate is a constant, τ, so that the average tax rate is also τ.

[16]We are assuming that the demand curve for labor is horizontal (the elasticity of demand is infinite), so the effect of the tax depends only on the elasticity of supply. In general, the effect of a tax on the labor market depends on both the elasticity of demand and the elasticity of supply. See Barlow and Sparks (1964), Head (1966), Allingham (1972), and Fullerton (1982) for a formal theoretical analysis on the necessary and sufficient conditions for a tax cut to increase hours worked and tax revenues.

the tax rate rises because workers are in the backward-bending section of their labor supply curves.

As the tax rate rises far enough, however, the workers are in the upward-sloping section of their labor supply curves. In this section, an increase in the tax rate reduces the number of hours worked. When the tax rate rises high enough, the reduction in hours worked more than offsets the gain from the higher rate, so tax revenue falls.

It makes little sense for a government to operate at very high marginal tax rates in the downward-sloping portion of this bell-shaped curve. The government could get more output *and* more tax revenue by cutting the marginal tax rate. Therefore, the question Congress faced when Reagan took office was whether we were on the downward-sloping section of the curve, where a tax cut would increase revenue. To answer this question, we need to know whether the tax rate before the cut was greater or less than the tax rate τ^* where the curve reaches its peak.

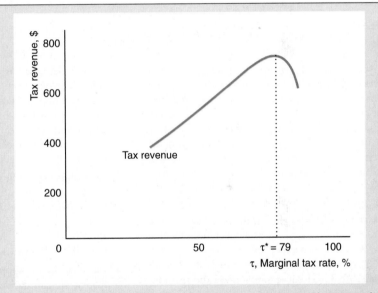

Figure 5.12 **Relationship of Tax Revenue to Tax Rates.** At marginal tax rates below τ^*, an increase in the rate leads to larger tax collections. At rates above τ^*, however, an increase in the marginal rate decreases tax revenue. These calculations (Fullerton, 1982, Table 1, p. 15) are based on the assumption that the labor supply elasticity with respect to the after-tax wage is 0.15.

Application   **EFFECTS OF TAX CUTS**

Economists have estimated the effects of tax cuts in many countries. As marginal tax rates vary substantially across countries, the effect of a tax cut on tax revenue also differs across countries.

Fullerton (1982) concluded that the marginal tax rate, τ^*, that maximizes tax revenue is very high for the United States. He calculated that $\tau^* = 79\%$ if the labor supply elasticity with respect to after-tax wages is 0.15. Stuart (1984) calculated that τ^* is close to 85%. Given that the American τ^* is between 79% and 85%, the Kennedy era tax cut (from 91% to 70%) raised tax revenue and increased the work effort of top-income-bracket workers, but a Reagan era tax cut (in which the actual rate was about half as big as τ^*) had the opposite effects.

In European countries with higher tax rates, a cut in the marginal tax rate is more likely to raise tax revenues. Stuart (1981) argued that Sweden's 80% marginal tax rate is greater than that country's τ^*. Van Ravenstein and Vijlbrief (1988) calculated that, in the Netherlands, τ^* is approximately 70%, which is just slightly above the actual tax rate of 67.4% in 1985.

Summary

1. **Deriving demand curves:** Individual demand curves can be derived by using the information about tastes contained in a consumer's indifference curve map. Varying the price of one good, holding other prices and income constant, we find how the quantity demanded varies with that price, which is the information we need to draw the demand curve. Consumers' tastes, which are captured by the indifference curves, determine the shape of the demand curve.

2. **How changes in income shift demand curves:** The entire demand curve shifts as a consumer's income rises. By varying income, holding prices constant, we show how quantity demanded shifts with income. An Engel curve summarizes the relationship between income and quantity demanded, holding prices constant.

3. **Effects of a price change:** An increase in the price of a good causes both a substitution effect and an income effect. The *substitution effect* is the amount by which a consumer's demand for the good changes as a result of a price increase when we compensate the consumer for the price increase by raising the individual's income by enough that his or her utility does not change. The substitution effect is unambiguous: A compensated rise in a good's price *always* causes consumers to buy less of that good. The *income effect* shows how a consumer's demand for a good changes as the consumer's income falls. The price rise lowers the consumer's opportunities, because the consumer can now buy less than before with the same income. The income effect can be positive or negative. If a good is normal (income elasticity is positive), the income effect is negative.

4. **Cost-of-living adjustments:** The government's major index of inflation, the Consumer Price Index, overestimates inflation by ignoring the substitution effect. Though on average small, the substitution bias may be substantial for particular individuals or firms.

5. **Deriving labor supply curves:** Using consumer theory, we can derive the daily demand curve for leisure, which is time spent on activities other than work. By subtracting the demand curve for leisure from 24 hours, we obtain the labor supply curve, which shows how the number of hours worked varies with the wage. Depending on whether leisure is an inferior good or a normal good, the supply curve of labor may be upward sloping or backward bending. The shape of the supply curve for labor determines the effect of a tax cut. Empirical evidence based on this theory shows why tax cuts in the 1980s did not increase the tax revenue of individuals as predicted by the Reagan administration.

Problems

1. Derive the demand curve for Coke for a person who views Coke and Pepsi as perfect substitutes.

2. Derive the demand curve for pie for Barbara, who eats pie only à la mode and does not eat either pie or ice cream alone (pie and ice cream are complements).

3. Michael views donuts and coffee as perfect complements: He always eats one donut with a cup of coffee and will not eat a donut without coffee or drink coffee without a donut. What does Michael's Engel curve for donuts look like? How much does his weekly budget have to rise for Michael to buy one more donut per week?

4. Don spends his money on food and on operas. Food is an inferior good for Don. Does he view an opera performance as an inferior or a normal good? Why? In a diagram, show a possible income-consumption curve for Don.

5. Under what conditions does the income effect reinforce the substitution effect? Under what conditions does it have an offsetting effect? If the income effect more than offsets the substitution effect for a good, what do we call that good?

6. Cora spends all her money on food and clothing. When the price of clothing decreases, she buys more clothing.

   a. Does the substitution effect cause her to buy more or less clothing? Explain. (If the direction of the effect is ambiguous, say so.)

   b. Does the income effect cause her to buy more or less clothing? Explain. (If the direction of the effect is ambiguous, say so.)

7. Bessie consumes only coffee and coffee cake and consumes them only together (they are complements). By how much will a CPI over these two goods differ from the true cost-of-living index?

8. Do you expect that relatively more high-quality navel oranges are sold in California or New York? Why?

9. Draw a figure to illustrate the verbal answer given in Solved Problem 5.2.

10. During his first year at school, Ximing buys eight new college textbooks at a cost of $50 each. Used books cost $30 each. When the bookstore announces a 20% price increase in new texts and a 10% increase in used texts for the next year, Ximing's father offers him $80 extra. Is Ximing better off, the same, or worse off after the price change? Why?

11. Under a welfare plan, poor people are given a lump-sum payment of L. If they accept this welfare payment, they must pay a high tax, $\tau = \frac{1}{2}$, on anything they earn. If they do not accept the welfare payment, they do not have to pay a tax on their earnings. Show that whether an individual accepts welfare depends on the individual's tastes.

12. If an individual's labor supply curve slopes forward at low wages and bends backward at high wages, is leisure a Giffen good? If so, at high or low wage rates?

13. Suppose that Roy could choose how many hours to work at a wage of w and chose to work seven hours a day. The employer now offers him time-and-a-half wages ($1.5w$) for every hour he works beyond a minimum of eight hours per day. Show how his budget constraint changes. Will he choose to work more than seven hours a day?

14. Jerome moonlights: He holds down two jobs. The higher-paying job pays w, but he can work at most eight hours. The other job pays w^*, but he can work as many hours as he wants. Show how Jerome determines how many hours to work.

15. Suppose that the job in Problem 14 that had no restriction on hours was the higher-paying job. How do Jerome's budget constraint and behavior change?

16. Suppose that Howard's wage varies with the hours he works: $w(H) = \alpha H$, $\alpha > 0$. Show how the number of hours he chooses to work depends on his tastes.

17. Nancy consumes only cookies and books. At her current consumption bundle, her marginal utility from books is 10 and from cookies is 5. Each book costs Alice $10, and each cookie costs $2. Is Alice maximizing her utility? Explain. If she is not, how can she increase her utility while keeping her total expenditure constant?

18. *Review* (Chapter 4): Is a wealthy person more likely than a poor person to prefer a government payment of $100 in cash to $100 worth of food stamps? Why or why not?

Math Problems

19. Nadia likes spare ribs, R, and fried chicken, C. Her utility function is

$$U = 10R^2C.$$

What is her marginal utility of spare ribs function? She pays $10 for a slab of ribs and $5 for a chicken. What is her optimal consumption bundle? Show her optimal bundle in a diagram.

20. Steve's utility function is $U = BC$, where B = veggie burgers per week and C = packs of cigarettes per week. What is his marginal rate of substitution if veggie burgers are on the vertical axis and cigarettes are on the horizontal axis? Steve's income is $120, the price of a veggie burger is $2, and that of a pack of cigarettes is $1. How many burgers and how many packs of cigarette does Steve consume to maximize his utility? When a new tax raises the price of a burger to $3, what is his new optimal bundle? Illustrate your answers in a graph.

21. Roger's utility function is Cobb-Douglas, $U = B^{1/4}Z^{3/4}$, his income is Y, the price of B is p_B, and the price of Z is p_Z. Derive his demand curves. (*Hint*: See Appendixes 4A and 4B.)

22. Derive Roger's Engel curve for B for the utility given in Problem 21.

★23. Using calculus, show that not all goods can be inferior.

24. Using calculus, show the effect of a change in the wage on the amount of leisure an individual wants to consume. (*Hint*: See Appendix 5A.)

25. Answer the same question as in Problem 24 when the utility function is $U = Y^\alpha L^{1-\alpha}$.

Firms and Production

Hard work never killed anybody, but why take a chance?

—Charlie McCarthy

The Ghirardelli Chocolate Company converts chocolate and other inputs into an output of 144,000 wrapped chocolate bars and 340,000 wrapped chocolate squares a day. The *material inputs* include chocolate, other food products, and various paper goods for wrapping and boxing the candy. The *labor inputs* include chefs, assembly-line workers, and various mechanics and other technicians. The *capital inputs* are the manufacturing plant, the land on which the plant is located, conveyor belts, molds, wrapping machines, and various other types of equipment.

Over time, Ghirardelli has changed how it produces its finished product, increasing the ratio of machines to workers. Several years ago, to minimize employees' risk of repetitive motion injuries, the company spent $300,000 on robots, which pack the wrapped chocolate and put it on pallets. The use of robotic arms resulted in greatly reduced downtime, increased production, and improved working conditions.

By using robotic equipment to pack finished, wrapped chocolate, the Ghirardelli Chocolate Company benefits from reduced downtime and increased production.

This chapter looks at the types of decisions that the owners of firms have to make. First, a decision must be made as to how a firm is owned and managed. Ghirardelli, for example, is a corporation—it is not owned by an individual or partners—and is run by professional managers. Second, the firm must decide how to produce. Ghirardelli now uses relatively more machines and robots and fewer workers than in the past. Third, if a firm wants to expand output, it must decide how to do that in both the short run and the long run. In the short run, Ghirardelli can expand output by extending the workweek to six or seven days and using extra materials. To expand output more, Ghirardelli would have to install more equipment (such as extra robotic arms), hire more workers, and eventually build a new plant, all of which take time. Fourth, given its ability to change its output level, a firm must determine how large to grow. Ghirardelli determines its current investments on the basis of its beliefs about demand and costs in the future.

In this chapter, we examine how a firm chooses its inputs so as to produce efficiently. In Chapter 7, we examine how the firm chooses the least costly among all possible efficient production processes. In Chapter 8, we combine this information about costs with information about revenues to determine how a firm picks the output level that maximizes profit.

The main lesson of this chapter and the next is that firms are not black boxes that mysteriously transform inputs (such as labor, capital, and material) into outputs. Economic theory explains how firms make decisions about production processes, types of inputs to use, and the volume of output to produce.

IN THIS CHAPTER,
WE EXAMINE
SIX MAIN
TOPICS

1. **The ownership and management of firms:** Decisions must be made as to how a firm is owned and run.
2. **Production:** A firm converts inputs into outputs using one of possibly many available technologies.
3. **Short-run production: one variable and one fixed input:** In the short run, only some inputs can be varied, so the firm changes its output by adjusting its variable inputs.
4. **Long-run production: two variable inputs:** The firm has more flexibility in how it produces and how it changes its output level in the long run when all factors can be varied.
5. **Returns to scale:** How the ratio of output to input varies with the size of the firm is an important factor in determining the size of a firm.
6. **Productivity and technical change:** The amount of output that can be produced with a given amount of inputs varies across firms and over time.

6.1   THE OWNERSHIP AND MANAGEMENT OF FIRMS

A **firm** is an organization that converts *inputs* such as labor, materials, and capital into *outputs*, the goods and services that it sells. U.S. Steel combines iron ore, machinery, and labor to create steel. A local restaurant buys raw food, cooks it, and serves it. A landscape designer hires gardeners and machines, buys trees and shrubs, transports them to a customer's home, and supervises the work.

Most goods and services produced in Western countries are produced by firms. In the United States, firms produce 84% of national production (U.S. gross domestic product); the government, 11%; nonprofit institutions (such as some universities and hospitals), 4%; and private households, less than 0.2% (*Survey of Current Business*, 1999). In developing countries, the government's share of total national production can be much higher, reaching 37% in Ghana, 38% in Zambia, 40% in Sudan, and 90% in Algeria, though it is as low as 3% in Bangladesh, Paraguay, and Nepal (United Nations, *Industry and Development: Global Report 1992/93*). In this book, we focus on production by for-profit firms rather than by nonprofit organizations and governments.

The Ownership of Firms

In most countries, for-profit firms have one of three legal forms: sole proprietorships, partnerships, and corporations.

Sole proprietorships are firms owned and run by a single individual.

Partnerships are businesses jointly owned and controlled by two or more people. The owners operate under a partnership agreement. If any partner leaves, the partnership agreement ends. For the firm to continue to operate, a new partnership agreement must be written.

Corporations are owned by *shareholders* in proportion to the numbers of shares of stock they hold. The shareholders elect a board of directors who run the firm. In turn, the board of directors usually hires managers who make short-term decisions and long-term plans.

Corporations differ from the other two forms of ownership in terms of personal liability for the debts of the firm. Sole proprietors and partners are personally responsible for the debts of their firms. All of an owner's personal wealth—not just that invested in the firm—is at risk if the business becomes bankrupt and is unable to pay its bills. Even the assets of partners who are not responsible for the failure can be taken to cover the firm's debts.

In contrast to sole proprietorships or partnerships, owners of corporations have **limited liability**: The personal assets of the corporation owners cannot be taken to pay a corporation's debts if it goes into bankruptcy. If the corporation fails, the shares become worthless. Because of the limited liability of corporations, the most that shareholders can lose if the firm goes bankrupt is the amount they paid for their stock. As a result, people are more willing to buy shares than they would be if they faced full liability.

In the United States, 90% of business sales are made by corporations, even though fewer than 20% of all firms are corporations. Nearly 73% of all firms are sole proprietorships. Sole proprietorships tend to be small, however, so they are responsible for only 5% of all sales. Partnerships account for 7% of all firms and make 5% of sales (*Statistical Abstract of the United States*, 1998).

The Management of Firms

In a small firm, the owner usually manages the firm's operations. In larger firms, typically corporations and larger partnerships, a manager or team of managers usually runs the company. In such firms, owners, managers, and lower-level supervisors are all decision makers.

The various decision makers may have conflicting objectives. What is in the best interest of the owners may not be the same as what is in the best interest of managers or other employees. For example, a manager may want a fancy office, a company car, a company jet, and other perks, but the owner would likely oppose these drains on profit.

The owner replaces the manager if the manager pursues personal objectives rather than the firm's objectives. In a corporation, the board of directors is supposed to ensure that managers do not stray. If the manager and the board of directors run the firm badly, the shareholders can fire both or directly change some policies through votes at the corporation's annual meeting for shareholders. Until Chapter 20, we'll ignore the potential conflict between managers and owners and assume that the owner *is* the manager of the firm and makes all the decisions.

Caves and Barton (1990) report that the average productivity of firms across U.S. manufacturing industries ranges from 63% to 99%. That is, in the manufacturing industry with the most diverse firms, the average firm produces slightly less than two-thirds as much as the most productive firm, whereas in the manufacturing industry with the most homogeneous firms, all firms are nearly equally productive.

Differences in productivity across markets may be due to differences in the degree of competition. In competitive markets, in which many firms can enter and exit the market easily, less productive firms lose money and are driven out of business, so the firms that are actually producing are equally productive (as Chapter 8 shows). In a less competitive oligopoly market, with few firms and no possibility of entry by new firms, a less productive firm may be able to survive, so firms with varying levels of productivity are observed.

In communist and other government-managed economies, in which firms are not required to maximize profits, inefficient firms may survive. For example, a study of productivity in 48 medium-size, machine-building state enterprises in China (Kalirajan and Obwona, 1994) found that the productivity measure ranges from 21% to 100%, with an average of 55%.

Application   GERMAN VERSUS BRITISH PRODUCTIVITY

Even within a single company, a plant in one country may be more productive than a plant in another country operating under different institutional rules and with a different workforce. The Ford Motor Company has virtually identical plants in Saarlouis, Germany, and Halewood, England. Each plant manufactured Escorts on production lines equipped with robot welders and automated presses that punch out parts.

Although the plants appeared to be identical, the German plant was much more productive in 1981. Whereas the German plant produced 1,200 cars a day (more than the 1,015 that Ford planners predicted) using 7,762 workers, the British plant manufactured only 800 cars a day using 10,040 workers. Equivalently stated, it took only about 21 hours of labor ($L/q = 1/AP_L$) to produce an Escort in Germany compared to about 40 hours in Britain.

Moreover, the German plant turned out the highest-quality cars of any Ford plant. The German Escorts averaged only half as many demerits from quality inspectors as British- or American-made Escorts.

According to Ford officials, the difference was due to the attitudes of the workers. In Britain, under pressure from labor, management used two daily shifts so that no one worked on Friday nights; in Germany, there was no such pressure. Labor unrest was more common in Britain. There were 20 strikes throughout Britain in the first nine months of 1981—though that was considerably fewer than the 300 strikes in 1976—whereas no strikes occurred in Germany.

British labor leaders argued that the German plant was unsafe. The British union summoned a company doctor to rule, for example, that two workers were required to lift the hood onto a body—a job that a single worker performed at the German plant. Rejecting this claim, a reporter contended that one worker lifted and the other merely watched at the British plant.

Because the British plant was less productive than its German counterpart, we could conclude that the British plant was operating inefficiently. An alternative interpretation is that the British plant was operating as efficiently as possible given the institutional and union rules.

Innovations

In its production process, a firm tries to use the best available technological and managerial knowledge. An advance in knowledge that allows more output to be produced with the same level of inputs is called **technical progress**. The invention of new products is a form of technical innovation. The use of robotic arms increases the number of automobiles produced with a given amount of labor and raw materials. Better *management or organization of the production process* similarly allows the firm to produce more output from given levels of inputs.

Technical Progress. A technological innovation changes the production process. Last year a firm produced

$$q_1 = f(L, K)$$

units of output using L units of labor services and K units of capital service. Due to a new invention that the firm uses, this year's production function differs from last year's, so the firm produces 10% more output with the same inputs:

$$q_2 = 1.1f(L, K).$$

This firm has experienced *neutral technical change*, in which it can produce more output using the same ratio of inputs. For example, a technical innovation in the form of a new printing press allows more output to be produced using the same ratio of inputs as before: one worker to one printing press.

Nonneutral technical changes are innovations that alter the proportion in which inputs are used. If a printing press that required two people to operate is replaced by one that can be run by a single worker, the technical change is *labor-saving*. The ratio of labor to other inputs used to produce a given level of output falls after the innovation. Similarly, the ratio of output to labor, the average product of labor, rises.

In our neutral technical change example, the firm's rate of growth of output was $10\% = \Delta q/q_1 = [1.1f(L, K) - f(L, K)]/f(L, K)$ in one year due to the technical change. Table 6.3 shows estimates of the annual rate at which output grew for given levels of inputs in the United States and Poland. The rates of productivity growth differ across industries within a country and across countries for a particular industry. The faster growth in Poland is due to playing catch-up: Starting with antiquated technology and little capital, Poland invested heavily in modern technologies and capital during this period.

Table 6.3 Annual Rates of Productivity Growth

United States, 1949–1983[a]		*Poland, 1962–1983*[b]	
Industry	*Growth Rate, %*	*Industry*	*Growth Rate, %*
Food and kindred products	0.7	Food and tobacco	4.9
Tobacco manufactures	0.2		
Lumber and wood products	1.3	Wood and paper	2.5
Paper and allied products	0.9		
Chemicals and allied products	1.5	Chemicals	8.0
Total manufacturing	1.1	Light industry	1.3

[a]Gullickson and Harper (1987) calculated the annual percentage change in output for various U.S. manufacturing industries, holding labor, capital, energy, material, and business service inputs constant.
[b]Terrell (1993) estimated the annual percentage change in output for various Polish industries, holding labor, domestic capital, and Western capital constant.

Application   **NONNEUTRAL TECHNICAL CHANGE IN PIN MANUFACTURING**

The history of the humble pin illustrates how nonneutral technological change caused the average product of labor to rise over several centuries (Pratten, 1980). According to Adam Smith, a factory of 10 highly specialized workers using only handheld tools could produce 48,000 pins per day in 1776, so the average product of labor was 4,800 pins per day.

In 1824, Samuel W. Wright patented a solid-head pin machine in England. In 1830, this machine produced 45 pins a minute. Machines were substituted for workers. As a consequence of this mechanization, the average product of labor rose 70%.

Thanks to further technical advances, machines in 1900 produced 180 pins a minute, and current machines can turn out over 500 per minute. The number of machines a single worker can control has also increased. Currently, one worker can control as many as 24 machines. As a consequence, 50 people are now employed in Britain producing more pins than thousands of workers could manufacture in the early 1800s. By 1980, the average product of labor at one plant in Britain was 800,000 pins per day, an increase of 167 times over the average product in Adam Smith's day. Stated another way, the average product of labor has increased by nearly 2.7% a year for two centuries.

Organizational Change. Organizational changes may also alter the production function and increase the amount of output produced by a given amount of inputs. Organizational innovations have been very important in automobile manufacturing.

Application | AUTOMOBILE MANUFACTURING INNOVATIONS

The automobile industry has experienced a sequence of major technological and organizational innovations. The first, and probably most important, innovations were due to the genius of Henry Ford. In recent years, Japanese manufacturers have made important organizational innovations.

In the early 1900s, Henry Ford revolutionized mass production through two organizational innovations. First, he introduced interchangeable parts, which cut the time required to install parts because workers no longer had to file or machine individually made parts to get them to fit.

Second, Ford introduced a conveyor belt and an assembly line to his production process. Before Ford, workers walked around the car, and each worker performed many assembly activities. In Ford's plant, each worker specialized in a single activity such as attaching the right rear fender to the chassis. A conveyor belt moved the car at a constant speed from worker to worker along the assembly line. Because his workers gained proficiency from specializing in only a few activities and because the conveyor belts reduced the

number of movements workers had to make, Ford could produce more automobiles with the same number of workers. By the early 1920s, Ford had cut the cost of a car by more than two-thirds and had increased production from fewer than a thousand cars per year to two million per year.

Organizational innovations continue in auto manufacturing. In recent years, Japanese auto manufacturers have introduced many new approaches. The Toyota production system uses teamwork, just-in-time delivery of parts, and great attention to detail. Each production worker is a "customer" of the previous worker in the assembly line. The worker takes only what is needed, and the previous worker replaces what was taken. Parts are delivered just in time for use, so the firm avoids the cost of maintaining large inventories. For example, the German carmaker Porsche, employing Japanese techniques, reduced its manufacturing time per car from 120 to 72 hours, reduced the number of managers it needs by 31%, and cut manufacturing flaws in half.

Summary

1. **The ownership and management of firms:** Firms are either sole proprietorships, partnerships, or corporations. In smaller firms (particularly sole proprietorships and partnerships), the owners usually run the company. In large firms (such as most corporations), the owners hire managers to run the firms. Owners want to maximize profits. If managers have different objectives than owners, owners must keep a close watch over managers to ensure that profits are maximized.

2. **Production:** Inputs, or factors of production—labor, capital, and materials—are combined to produce output using the current state of knowledge about technology and management. To maximize profits, a firm must produce as efficiently as possible: It must get the maximum amount of output from the inputs it uses, given existing knowledge. A firm may have access to many efficient production processes that use different combinations of inputs to produce a given level of output. New technologies or new forms of organization can increase the amount of output that can be produced from a given combination of inputs. A production function shows how much output can be produced efficiently from various levels of inputs. A firm can vary all its inputs in the long run but only some of them in the short run.

3. **Short-run production: one variable and one fixed input:** In the short run, a firm cannot adjust the quantity of some inputs, such as capital. The firm varies its output by adjusting its variable inputs, such as labor. If all factors are fixed except labor, and a firm that was using very little labor increases its use of labor, its output may rise more than in proportion to the increase in labor because of greater specialization of workers. Eventually, however, as more workers are hired, the workers get in each other's way or wait to share equipment, so output increases by smaller and smaller amounts.

This latter phenomenon is described by the law of diminishing marginal returns: The marginal product of an input—the extra output from the last unit of input—eventually decreases as more of that input is used, holding other inputs fixed.

4. **Long-run production: two variable inputs:** In the long run, when all inputs are variable, firms can substitute between inputs. An isoquant shows the combinations of inputs that can produce a given level of output. The marginal rate of technical substitution is the absolute value of the slope of the isoquant. Usually, the more of one input the firm uses, the more difficult it is to substitute that input for another input. That is, there are diminishing marginal rates of technical substitution as the firm uses more of one input.

5. **Returns to scale:** If, when a firm increases all inputs in proportion, its output increases by the same proportion, the production process is said to exhibit constant returns to scale. If output increases less than in proportion to inputs, the production process has decreasing returns to scale; if it increases more than in proportion, it has increasing returns to scale. All three types of returns to scale are commonly seen in actual industries. Many production processes exhibit first increasing, then constant, and finally decreasing returns to scale as the size of the firm increases.

6. **Productivity and technical change:** Although all firms in an industry produce efficiently, given what they know and the institutional and other constraints they face, some firms may be more productive than others: They can produce more output from a given bundle of inputs. Due to innovations such as technical progress or new means of organizing production, a firm can produce more today than it could in the past from the same bundle of inputs. Such innovations change the production function.

Problems

1. If each extra worker produces an extra unit of output, how do the total product of labor, average product of labor, and marginal product of labor vary with labor?

2. Each extra worker produces an extra unit of output up to six workers. After six, no additional output is produced. Draw the total product of labor, average product of labor, and marginal product of labor curves.

3. What is the difference between an isoquant and an indifference curve?

4. Why must isoquants be thin? (*Hint*: See the explanation of why indifference curves must be thin in Chapter 4.)

5. Suppose that a firm has a fixed-proportions production function, in which one unit of output is produced using one worker and two units of capital. If the firm has an extra worker and no more capital, it still can produce only one unit of output. Similarly, one more unit of capital does the firm no good.

   a. Draw the isoquants for this production function.

   b. Draw the total product, average product, and marginal product of labor curves (you will probably want to use two diagrams) for this production function.

6. To produce a recorded CD, $Q = 1$, a firm uses one blank disk, $D = 1$, and the services of a recording machine, $M = 1$, for one hour. Draw an isoquant for this production process. Explain the reason for its shape.

7. Michelle's business produces ceramic cups using labor, clay, and a kiln. She can manufacture 25 cups a day with one worker and 35 with two workers. Does her production process illustrate *diminishing returns to scale* or *diminishing marginal returns to scale*? What is the likely explanation for why output doesn't increase proportionately with the number of workers?

8. Draw a circle in a diagram with labor services on one axis and capital services on the other. This circle represents all the combinations of labor and capital that produce 100 units of output. Now draw the isoquant for 100 units of output. (*Hint*: Remember that the isoquant includes only the efficient combinations of labor and capital.)

9. In a manufacturing plant, workers use a specialized machine to produce belts. A new machine is invented that is laborsaving. With the new machine, the firm can use fewer workers and still produce the same number of belts as it did using the old machine. In the long run, both labor and capital (the machine) are variable. From what you know, what is the effect of this invention on the AP_L, MP_L, and returns to scale? If you require more information to answer this question, specify what you need to know.

10. Show in a diagram that a production function can have diminishing marginal returns to a factor and constant returns to scale.

11. If a firm lays off workers during a recession, how will the firm's marginal product of labor change?

12. During recessions, American firms lay off a larger proportion of their workers than Japanese firms do. (It has been claimed that Japanese firms continue to produce at high levels and store the output or sell it at relatively low prices during the recession.) Assuming that the production function remains unchanged over a period that is long enough to include many recessions and expansions, would you expect the average product of labor to be higher in Japan or the United States? Why?

13. Does it follow that, because we observe that the average product of labor is higher for Firm 1 than for Firm 2, Firm 1 is more productive in the sense that it can produce more output from a given amount of inputs? Why?

14. *Review* (Chapter 5): Melissa eats eggs and toast for breakfast and insists on having three pieces of toast for every two eggs she eats. If the price of eggs increases but we compensate Melissa to make her just as "happy" as she was before the price change, what happens to her consumption of eggs? Draw a graph and explain your diagram. Does the change in her consumption reflect a substitution or an income effect?

★15. *Review* (Chapters 4, 5, and 6): If we plot the profit of a firm against the number of vacation days the owner takes, we find that profit first rises with vacation days (a few days of vacation improve the owner's effectiveness as a manager the rest of the year) but eventually falls as the owner takes more vacation days. If the owner has usual-shaped indifference curves between profit and vacation days, will the manager take the number of vacation days that maximizes profit? If so, why? If not, what will the owner do and why?

Math Problems

16. Suppose that the production function is $q = L^{3/4}K^{1/4}$.

    a. What is the average product of labor, holding capital fixed at $\bar{K}$?

    b. What is the marginal product of labor? (*Hint*: Calculate how much q changes as L increases by 1 unit, or use calculus.)

    c. Does this production function have increasing, constant, or decreasing returns to scale?

17. What is the production function if L and K are perfect substitutes and each unit of q requires 1 unit of L or 1 unit of K (or a combination of these inputs that adds to 1)?

18. At $L = 4$, $K = 4$, the marginal product of labor is 2 and the marginal product of capital is 3. What is the marginal rate of technical substitution?

19. In the short run, a firm cannot vary its capital, $K = 2$, but can vary its labor, L. It produces output q. Explain why the firm will or will not experience diminishing marginal returns to labor in the short run if its production function is

    a. $q = 10L + K$
    b. $q = L^{1/2}K^{1/2}$

20. Under what conditions do the following production functions exhibit decreasing, constant, or increasing returns to scale?

    a. $q = L + K$
    b. $q = L^{\alpha}K^{\beta}$
    c. $q = L + L^{\alpha}K^{\beta} + K$

21. Firm 1 and Firm 2 use the same type of production function, but Firm 1 is only 90% as productive as Firm 2. That is, the production function of Firm 2 is $q_2 = f(L, K)$, and the production function of Firm 1 is $q_1 = 0.9f(L, K)$. At a particular level of inputs, how does the marginal product of labor differ between the firms?

Costs

An economist is a person who, when invited to give a talk at a banquet, tells the audience there's no such thing as a free lunch.

A semiconductor manufacturer can produce a chip using many pieces of equipment and relatively few workers' labor or many workers and relatively few machines. How does the firm make its choice?

The firm uses a two-step procedure in determining how to produce a certain amount of output efficiently. It first determines which production processes are *technologically efficient* so that it can produce the desired level of output with the least amount of inputs. As we saw in Chapter 6, the firm uses engineering and other information to determine its production function, which summarizes the many technologically efficient production processes available.

The firm's second step is to pick from these technologically efficient production processes the one that is also **economically efficient**, minimizing the cost of producing a specified amount of output. To determine which process minimizes its cost of production, the firm uses information about the production function and the cost of inputs.

By reducing its cost of producing a given level of output, a firm can increase its profit. Any profit-maximizing competitive, monopolistic, or oligopolistic firm minimizes its cost of production.

1. **Measuring costs:** Economists count both explicit costs and implicit (opportunity) costs.
2. **Short-run costs:** To minimize its costs in the short run, a firm adjusts its variable factors (such as labor), but it cannot adjust its fixed factors (such as capital).
3. **Long-run costs:** In the long run, a firm adjusts all its inputs because usually all inputs are variable.
4. **Lower costs in the long run:** Long-run cost is as low as or lower than short-run cost because the firm has more flexibility in the long run, technological progress occurs, and workers and managers learn from experience.
5. **Cost of producing multiple goods:** If the firm produces several goods simultaneously, the cost of each may depend on the quantity of all the goods produced.

IN THIS CHAPTER,

WE EXAMINE

FIVE MAIN

TOPICS

Businesspeople and economists need to understand the relationship between costs of inputs and production to determine the least costly way to produce. Economists have an additional reason for wanting to know about costs. As we'll see in later chapters, the relationship between output and costs plays an important role in determining the nature of a market—how many firms are in the market and how high price is relative to cost.

7.1 | MEASURING COSTS

To show how a firm's cost varies with its output, we first have to measure costs. Businesspeople and economists often measure costs differently.

Economic Cost   Economists include all relevant costs. To run a firm profitably, a manager acts like an economist and considers all relevant costs. However, this same manager may direct the firm's accountant or bookkeeper to measure cost in ways that are consistent with tax laws and other laws to make the firm's financial statement look good to stockholders or to minimize the firm's taxes this year.

Economists consider both explicit costs and implicit costs. *Explicit costs* are a firm's direct, out-of-pocket payments for inputs to its production process during a given time period such as a year. These costs include production workers' wages, managers' salaries, and payments for materials. However, firms use inputs that may not have an explicit price. These *implicit costs* include the value of the working time of the firm's owner and the value of other resources used but not purchased in a given period.

The **economic cost** or **opportunity cost** is the value of the best alternative use of a resource. The economic or opportunity cost includes both explicit and implicit costs. If a firm purchases and uses an input immediately, that input's opportunity cost is the amount the firm pays for it. If the firm uses an input from its inventory, its opportunity cost is not necessarily the price it paid for the input years ago. Rather, the opportunity cost is what it could buy or sell that input for today.

The classic example of an implicit opportunity cost is captured in the phrase "There's no such thing as a free lunch." Suppose that your parents offer to take you to lunch tomorrow. You know that they'll pay for the meal, but you also know that this lunch is not free for you. Your opportunity cost for the lunch is the best alternative use of your time. Presumably, the best alternative use of your time is studying this textbook, but other possible alternatives include what you could earn at a job or the value you place on watching TV. Often such opportunity costs are a substantial portion of total costs.

If you start your own firm, you should be very concerned about opportunity costs. Suppose that your explicit cost is $40,000, including the rent for your work space, the cost of materials, and the wage payments to your employees. Because you do not pay yourself a salary—instead, you keep any profit at the end of the year—the explicit cost does not include the value of your time. According to an economist, your firm's full economic cost is the sum of the explicit cost plus the opportunity value of your time. If the highest wage you could have earned working for some other firm is $25,000, your full economic cost is $65,000.

In deciding whether to continue running your firm or to work for someone else, you must consider both explicit and opportunity costs. If your annual revenue is $60,000, after you pay your explicit cost of $40,000, you keep $20,000 at the end of the year. The opportunity cost of your time, $25,000, exceeds $20,000, so you can earn more working for someone else. (What are you giving up to study opportunity costs?)

Application | OPPORTUNITY COST OF WAITING TIME

Canadian taxes pay for public health care. However, taxes do not cover the full cost of medical care. To contain costs, health care is rationed in part by having patients wait for treatment. People who are forced to wait are less likely to request treatment, some diseases clear up on their own during the wait, and some patients die while waiting. Are these additional waiting-time opportunity costs large?

Most Canadian patients remain on a waiting list less than two months. In one province, two-thirds of all inpatients and three-quarters of all outpatients reported waiting less than eight weeks for elective surgery. But 20% of inpatients and 14% of outpatients waited more than 12 weeks.

Many patients suffer or cannot work while waiting for treatment. Doctors estimate that 41% of all patients and 88% of cardiology patients have difficulty carrying on their work or daily duties as a result of their medical conditions.

As a proxy for the opportunity cost of waiting time for the 41% of people who experience difficulty while waiting, Globerman (1991) used average earnings. (Such a cost measure is an underestimate because it ignores pain and suffering.) He calculated that waiting-time cost was approximately $132 million in British Columbia, which amounted to 0.2% of that province's gross domestic product and about 8% of its total health cost.

Capital Costs

Determining the opportunity cost of capital, such as land or equipment, requires special considerations. Capital is a **durable good**: a product that is usable for years. Two problems may arise in measuring the cost of capital. The first is how to allocate the initial purchase cost over time. The second is what to do if the value of the capital changes over time.

Allocating Capital Costs over Time. Capital may be rented or purchased. For example, a firm may rent a truck for $200 a month or buy it outright for $18,000.

If the firm rents the truck, the rental payment is the relevant opportunity cost. By using the rental rate, we avoid the two measurement problems. The truck is rented period by period, so the firm does not have to worry about how to allocate the purchase cost of a truck over time. Moreover, the rental rate adjusts if the cost of a new truck changes over time.

Suppose, however, that the firm buys the truck. The firm's bookkeeper may *expense* the cost by recording the full $18,000 when it's made or may *amortize* the cost by spreading the $18,000 over the life of the truck according to an arbitrary rule set by the relevant government authority, such as the Internal Revenue Service (IRS). If the IRS approves of several approaches to amortizing expenses, a bookkeeper or an accountant may use whichever arbitrary rule minimizes the firm's taxes.

An economist amortizes the cost of the truck on the basis of its opportunity cost at each moment of time, which is the amount that the firm could charge others to rent the truck. That is, regardless of whether the firm buys or rents the truck, an economist views the opportunity cost of this capital good as a rent per time period: the amount the firm will receive if it rents its truck to others at the going rental rate.[1] If the value of an older truck is less than that of a newer one, the rental rate for the truck falls over time.

Actual and Historical Costs. Not only may the rental rate for a piece of capital fall over time as the capital ages, but it may also change because of shifts in supply and demand in the market for capital goods or for other reasons. A piece of capital may be worth much more or much less today than it was when it was purchased.

To maximize its profit, a firm must properly measure the cost of a piece of capital—its current opportunity cost of the capital good—and not what the firm paid for it—its historical cost. Suppose that a firm paid $30,000 for a piece of land that it can resell for only $20,000. Also suppose that it uses the land itself and the current value of the land to the firm is only $19,000. Should the firm use the land or sell it? As any child can tell the firm, there's no point in crying over spilt milk. The firm should ignore how much it paid for the land in making its decision. As the value of the land to the firm, $19,000, is less than the opportunity cost of the land, $20,000, the firm can make more by selling the land.

The firm's current opportunity cost of capital may be less than what it paid if the firm cannot resell the capital. A firm that bought a specialized piece of equipment with no alternative use cannot resell the equipment. Because the equipment has no alternative use, the historical cost of buying that capital is a **sunk cost**: an expenditure that cannot be recovered. Because this equipment has no alternative use, the current or opportunity cost of the capital is zero. In short, when determining the rental value of capital, economists use the opportunity value and ignore the historical price.

Application   **SWARTHMORE COLLEGE'S COST OF CAPITAL**

Many nonprofit institutions such as universities and governmental agencies are notorious for ignoring the implicit cost of their capital. When setting tuition and making other plans, Swarthmore College in Pennsylvania estimates its annual cost at $40,000 per student, based on the cost of salaries, academic and general institutional support, food, maintenance and additions to the physical plant, and other annual expenses such as student aid. This cost calculation is a gross underestimate, however, because it ignores the opportunity cost of the campus—the amount the college could earn by renting out its land and buildings. Including that opportunity cost of its land and buildings raises its true economic cost to about $50,000 annually per student.

---

[1]If trucks cannot be rented, an economist calculates an implicit rental rate for trucks taking account of both explicit and opportunity costs. If the firm could sell the truck for $5,000, the opportunity cost of keeping it is the interest that could be earned on $5,000 (Chapter 16). In addition, the firm incurs direct maintenance costs and the opportunity cost due to *depreciation*: the drop in value from wear and tear.

| 7.2 | **SHORT-RUN COSTS** |

To make profit-maximizing decisions, a firm needs to know how its cost varies with output. A firm's cost rises as it increases its output. A firm cannot vary some of its inputs, such as capital, in the short run (Chapter 6). As a result, it is usually more costly for a firm to increase output in the short run than in the long run, when all inputs can be varied. In this section, we look at the cost of increasing output in the short run.

Short-Run Cost Measures

We start by using a numerical example to illustrate the basic cost concepts. We then examine the graphic relationship between these concepts.

Cost Levels. To produce a given level of output in the short run, a firm incurs costs for both its fixed and variable inputs. A firm's **fixed cost** (*F*) is its production expense that does not vary with output. The fixed cost includes the cost of inputs that the firm cannot practically adjust in the short run, such as land, a plant, large machines, and other capital goods. The fixed cost for a capital good a firm owns and uses is the opportunity cost of not renting it to someone else. The fixed cost is $48 per day for the firm in Table 7.1.

A firm's **variable cost** (*VC*) is the production expense that changes with the quantity of output produced. The variable cost is the cost of the variable inputs—the inputs the firm can adjust to alter its output level, such as labor and materials. Table 7.1

Table 7.1 Variation of Short-Run Cost with Output

Output, q	Fixed Cost, F	Variable Cost, VC	Total Cost, C	Marginal Cost, MC	Average Fixed Cost, $AFC = F/q$	Average Variable Cost, $AVC = VC/q$	Average Cost, $AC = C/q$
0	48	0	48				
1	48	25	73	25	48	25	73
2	48	46	94	21	24	23	47
3	48	66	114	20	16	22	38
4	48	82	130	16	12	20.5	32.5
5	48	100	148	18	9.6	20	29.6
6	48	120	168	20	8	20	28
7	48	141	189	21	6.9	20.1	27
8	48	168	216	27	6	21	27
9	48	198	246	30	5.3	22	27.3
10	48	230	278	32	4.8	23	27.8
11	48	272	320	42	4.4	24.7	29.1
12	48	321	369	49	4.0	26.8	30.8

shows that the firm's variable cost changes with output. Variable cost goes from $25 a day when 1 unit is produced to $46 a day when 2 units are produced.

A firm's **cost** (or **total cost,** C) is the sum of a firm's variable cost and fixed cost:

$$C = VC + F.$$

The firm's total cost of producing 2 units of output per day is $94 per day, which is the sum of the fixed cost, $48, and the variable cost, $46. Because variable cost changes with the level of output, total cost also varies with the level of output, as the table illustrates.

To decide how much to produce, a firm uses several measures of how its cost varies with the level of output. Table 7.1 shows four such measures that we derive using the fixed cost, the variable cost, and the total cost.

Marginal Cost. A firm's **marginal cost** (MC) is the amount by which a firm's cost changes if the firm produces one more unit of output. The marginal cost is[2]

$$MC = \frac{\Delta C}{\Delta q},$$

where ΔC is the change in cost when output changes by Δq. Table 7.1 shows that, if the firm increases its output from 2 to 3 units, $\Delta q = 1$, its total cost rises from $94 to $114, $\Delta C = \$20$, so its marginal cost is $20 = $\Delta C/\Delta q$.

Because only variable cost changes with output, we can also define marginal cost as the change in variable cost from a one-unit increase in output:

$$MC = \frac{\Delta VC}{\Delta q}.$$

As the firm increases output from 2 to 3 units, its variable cost increases by $\Delta VC = \$20 = \$66 - \$46$, so its marginal cost is $MC = \Delta VC/\Delta q = \$20$. A firm uses marginal cost in deciding whether it pays to change its output level.

Average Costs. Firms use three average cost measures. The **average fixed cost** (AFC) is the fixed cost divided by the units of output produced: $AFC = F/q$. The average fixed cost falls as output rises because the fixed cost is spread over more units. The average fixed cost falls from $48 for 1 unit of output to $4 for 12 units of output in Table 7.1.

The **average variable cost** (AVC) is the variable cost divided by the units of output produced: $AVC = VC/q$. Because the variable cost increases with output, the average variable cost may either increase or decrease as output rises. The average variable cost is $25 at 1 unit, falls until it reaches a minimum of $20 at 6 units, and then rises. As we show in Chapter 8, a firm uses the average variable cost to determine whether to shut down operations when demand is low.

---

[2]If we use calculus, the marginal cost is $MC = dC(q)/dq$, where $C(q)$ is the cost function that shows how cost varies with output. The calculus definition says how cost changes for an infinitesimal change in output. To illustrate the idea, however, we use larger changes in the table.

The **average cost** (*AC*)—or *average total cost*—is the total cost divided by the units of output produced: $AC = C/q$. The average cost is the sum of the average fixed cost and the average variable cost:[3]

$$AC = AFC + AVC.$$

In Table 7.1, as output increases, average cost falls until output is 8 units and then rises. The firm makes a profit if its average cost is below its price, which is the firm's average revenue.

Application   **INTERNET FIRMS' FIXED COSTS**

Thanks to the Internet, the fixed costs of creating a small retail firm have dropped for many entrepreneurs. Before the Internet, a bookseller had to rent or buy a building, set up bookshelves, maintain an inventory, and incur other costs before selling any book. In contrast, today's Internet bookseller can operate on a small scale, with only minimal overhead expenses.

Linda and Lyle Bowlin started an Internet book company for about $2,500, using two personal computers in their home. They spent about $30 a month for Internet access and another $120 a month in other fixed expenditures (costs that do not vary with output). They could buy books from the same wholesalers as Amazon.com—the largest Internet bookseller—for about the same price as Amazon if they order at least five copies.

Though successful as a small firm, the Bowlins ran into trouble when they tried to expand and faced additional fixed costs. To achieve Amazon's huge sales, which were over a thousand times greater than the Bowlins', Amazon incurred large fixed costs for massive computers, enormous warehouses, and advertising. Amazon spent $50 million for advertising alone in 1998 and incurred other promotional expenses.

Short-Run Cost Curves

We illustrate the relationship between output and the various cost measures using curves in Figure 7.1. Panel a shows the variable cost, fixed cost, and total cost curves that correspond to Table 7.1. The fixed cost, which does not vary with output, is a horizontal line at $48. The variable cost curve is zero at zero units of output and rises with output. The total cost curve, which is the vertical sum of the variable cost curve and the fixed cost line, is $48 higher than the variable cost curve at every output level, so the variable cost and total cost curves are parallel.

Panel b shows the average fixed cost, average variable cost, average cost, and marginal cost curves. The average fixed cost curve falls as output increases. It approaches zero as output gets large because the fixed cost is spread over many units of output. The average cost curve is the vertical sum of the average fixed cost

---

[3]Because $C = VC + F$, if we divide both sides of the equation by q, we obtain

$$AC = C/q = F/q + VC/q = AFC + AVC.$$

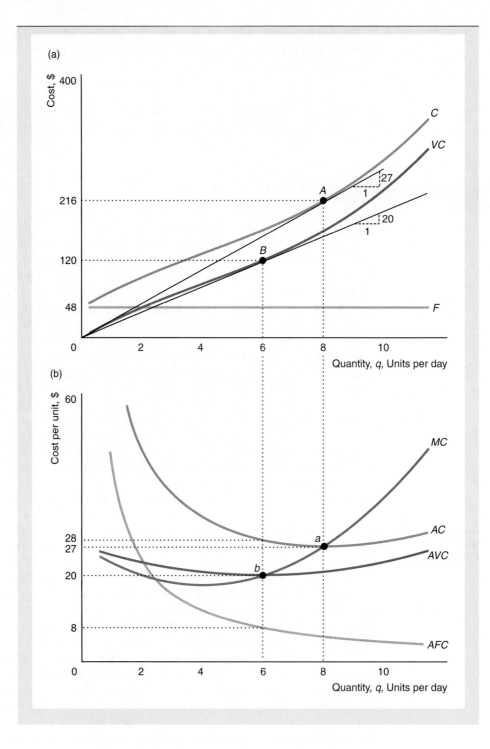

> Figure 7.1 **Short-Run Cost Curves.** (a) Because the total cost differs from the variable cost by the fixed cost, *F*, of $48, the total cost curve, *C*, is parallel to the variable cost curve, *VC*. (b) The marginal cost curve, *MC*, cuts the average variable cost, *AVC*, and average cost, *AC*, curves at their minimums. The height of the *AC* curve at point *a* equals the slope of the line from the origin to the cost curve at *A*. The height of the *AVC* at *b* equals the slope of the line from the origin to the variable cost curve at *B*. The height of the marginal cost is the slope of either the *C* or *VC* curve at that quantity.

and average variable cost curves. For example, at 6 units of output, the average variable cost is 20 and the average fixed cost is 8, so the average cost is 28.

The relationships between the average and marginal curves to the total curves are similar to those between the total product, marginal product, and average product curves, which we discussed in Chapter 6. The average cost at a particular output level is the slope of a line from the origin to the corresponding point on the cost curve. The slope of that line is the rise—the cost at that output level—divided by the run—the output level—which is the definition of the average cost. In panel a, the slope of the line from the origin to point *A* is the average cost for 8 units of output. The height of the cost curve at *A* is 216, so the slope is 216/8 = 27, which is the height of the average cost curve at the corresponding point *a* in panel b.

Similarly, the average variable cost is the slope of a line from the origin to a point on the variable cost curve. The slope of the dashed line from the origin to *B* in panel a is 20—the height of the variable cost curve, 120, divided by the number of units of output, 6—which is the height of the average variable cost at 6 units of output, point *b* in panel b.

The marginal cost is the slope of either the cost curve or the variable cost curve at a given output level. As the cost and variable cost curves are parallel, they have the same slope at any given output. The difference between cost and variable cost is fixed cost, which does not affect marginal cost.

The dashed line from the origin is tangent to the cost curve at *A* in panel a. Thus the slope of the dashed line equals both the average cost and the marginal cost at 8 units of output. This equality occurs at the corresponding point *a* in panel b, where the marginal cost curve intersects the average cost. (See Appendix 7A for a mathematical proof.)

Where the marginal cost curve is below the average cost, the average cost curve declines with output. Because the average cost of 47 for 2 units is greater than the marginal cost of the third unit, 20, the average cost for 3 units falls to 38. Where the marginal cost is above the average cost, the average cost curve rises with output. At 8 units, the marginal cost equals the average cost, so the average is unchanging, which is the minimum point, *a*, of the average cost curve.

We can show the same results using the graph. Because the dashed line from the origin is tangent to the variable cost curve at *B* in panel a, the marginal cost equals the average variable cost at the corresponding point *b* in panel b. Again, where marginal cost is above average variable cost, the average variable cost curve rises with output; and where marginal cost is below average variable cost, the average variable cost curve falls with output. Because the average cost curve is everywhere above the average variable cost curve and the marginal cost curve is rising where it crosses both average curves, the minimum of the average variable cost curve, b, is at a lower output level than the minimum of the average cost curve, a.

Production Functions and the Shape of Cost Curves

The production function determines the shape of a firm's cost curves. The production function shows the amount of inputs needed to produce a given level of output. The firm calculates its cost by multiplying the quantity of each input by its price and summing.

If a firm produces output using capital and labor and its capital is fixed in the short run, the firm's variable cost is its cost of labor. Its labor cost is the wage per hour, w, times the number of hours of labor, L, employed by the firm: $VC = wL$.

In the short run, when the firm's capital is fixed, the only way the firm can increase its output is to use more labor. If the firm increases its labor enough, it reaches the point of *diminishing marginal return to labor*, at which each extra worker increases output by a smaller amount. We can use this information about the relationship between labor and output—the production function—to determine the shape of the variable cost curve and its related curves.

Shape of the Variable Cost Curve. If input prices are constant, the production function determines the shape of the variable cost curve. We illustrate this relationship for the firm in Figure 7.2. The firm faces a constant input price for labor, the wage, of $5 per hour.

The total product of labor curve in Figure 7.2 shows the firm's short-run production function relationship between output and labor when capital is held fixed. For example, it takes 24 hours of labor to produce 6 units of output. Nearly doubling labor to 46 hours causes output to increase by only two-thirds to 10 units of output. As labor increases, the total product of labor curve increases less than in proportion. This flattening of the total product of labor curve at higher levels of labor reflects the diminishing marginal return to labor.

This curve shows both the production relation of output to labor and the variable cost relation of output to cost. Because each hour of work costs the firm $5, we can relabel the horizontal axis in Figure 7.2 to show the firm's variable cost, which is its cost of labor. To produce 6 units of output takes 24 hours of labor, so the firm's variable cost is $120. By using the variable cost labels on the horizontal axis, the total product of labor curve becomes the variable cost curve, where each worker costs the firm $120 per day in wages. The variable cost curve in Figure 7.2 is the same as the one in panel a of Figure 7.1, in which the output and cost axes are reversed. For example, the variable cost of producing 6 units is $120 in both figures.

Diminishing marginal returns in the production function cause the variable cost to rise more than in proportion as output increases. Because the production function determines the shape of the variable cost curve, it also determines the shape of the marginal, average variable, and average cost curves. We now examine the shape

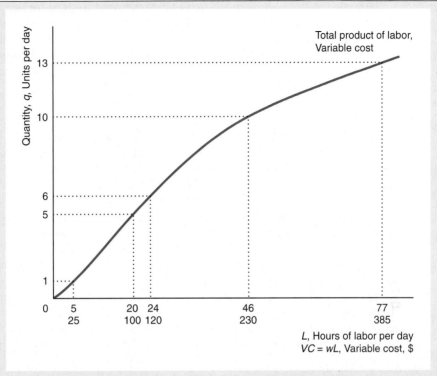

Figure 7.2 **Variable Cost and Total Product of Labor.** The firm's short-run variable cost curve and its total product of labor curve have the same shape. The total product of labor curve uses the horizontal axis measuring hours of work. The variable cost curve uses the horizontal axis measuring labor cost, which is the only variable cost.

of each of these cost curves in detail because in making decisions, firms rely more on these per-unit cost measures than on total variable cost.

Shape of the Marginal Cost Curve. The marginal cost is the change in variable cost as output increases by one unit: $MC = \Delta VC/\Delta q$. In the short run, capital is fixed, so the only way the firm can produce more output is to use extra labor. The extra labor required to produce one more unit of output is $\Delta L/\Delta q$. The extra labor costs the firm w per unit, so the firm's cost rises by $w(\Delta L/\Delta q)$. As a result, the firm's marginal cost is

$$MC = \frac{\Delta VC}{\Delta q} = w \frac{\Delta L}{\Delta q}.$$

The marginal cost equals the wage times the extra labor necessary to produce one more unit of output. To increase output by one unit from 5 to 6 units takes four extra workers in Figure 7.2. If the wage is $5 per hour, the marginal cost is $20.

How do we know how much extra labor we need to produce one more unit of output? That information comes from the production function. The marginal product of labor—the amount of extra output produced by another unit of labor, holding other inputs fixed—is $MP_L = \Delta q/\Delta L$. Thus the extra labor we need to produce one more unit of output, $\Delta L/\Delta q$, is $1/MP_L$, so the firm's marginal cost is

$$MC = \frac{w}{MP_L}. \tag{7.1}$$

Equation 7.1 says that the marginal cost equals the wage divided by the marginal product of labor. If the firm is producing 5 units of output, it takes four extra hours of labor to produce one more unit of output in Figure 7.2, so the marginal product of an hour of labor is $\frac{1}{4}$. Given a wage of $5 an hour, the marginal cost of the sixth unit is $5 divided by $\frac{1}{4}$, or $20, as panel b of Figure 7.1 shows.

Equation 7.1 shows that the marginal cost moves in the direction opposite that of the marginal product of labor. At low levels of labor, the marginal product of labor commonly rises with additional labor because extra workers help the original workers and they can collectively make better use of the firm's equipment (Chapter 6). As the marginal product of labor rises, the marginal cost falls.

Eventually, however, as the number of workers increases, workers must share the fixed amount of equipment and may get in each other's way, so the marginal cost curve slopes upward because of diminishing marginal returns to labor. Thus the marginal cost first falls and then rises, as panel b of Figure 7.1 illustrates.

Shape of the Average Cost Curves. Diminishing marginal returns to labor, by determining the shape of the variable cost curve, also determine the shape of the average variable cost curve. The average variable cost is the variable cost divided by output: $AVC = VC/q$. For the firm we've been examining, whose only variable input is labor, variable cost is wL, so average variable cost is

$$AVC = \frac{VC}{q} = \frac{wL}{q}.$$

Because the average product of labor is q/L, average variable cost is the wage divided by the average product of labor:

$$AVC = \frac{w}{AP_L}. \tag{7.2}$$

In Figure 7.2, at 6 units of output, the average product of labor is $\frac{1}{4}$ ($= q/L = 6/24$), so the average variable cost is $20, which is the wage, $5, divided by the average product of labor, $\frac{1}{4}$.

With a constant wage, the average variable cost moves in the opposite direction of the average product of labor in Equation 7.2. As we discussed in Chapter 6, the average product of labor tends to rise and then fall, so the average cost tends to fall and then rise, as in panel b of Figure 7.1.

The average cost curve is the vertical sum of the average variable cost curve and the average fixed cost curve, as in panel b. If the average variable cost curve is U-shaped, adding the strictly falling average fixed cost makes the average cost fall more steeply than the average variable cost curve at low output levels. At high output levels, the average cost and average variable cost curves differ by ever smaller amounts, as the average fixed cost, F/q, approaches zero. Thus the average cost curve is also U-shaped.

Application   **SHORT-RUN COST CURVES FOR A PRINTING FIRM**

The short-run average cost curve for the Norwegian printing firm (in Chapter 6) is U-shaped, even though its average variable cost is strictly upward sloping. The graph (based on the estimates of Griliches and Ringstad, 1971) shows the firm's various short-run cost curves, where the firm's capital is fixed at $\overline{K} = 100$. Appendix 7B derives the firm's short-run cost curves mathematically.

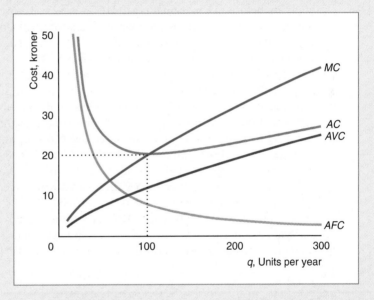

The firm's average fixed cost, as always, falls as output increases. The firm's average variable cost curve is strictly increasing. The average cost curve is the vertical sum of the average variable cost and average fixed cost curves. Because the average fixed cost curve falls with output and the average variable cost curve rises with output, the average cost curve is U-shaped. The firm's marginal cost lies above the rising average variable cost curve for all positive quantities of output and cuts the average cost curve at its minimum.

**Effects of
Taxes on Costs**   Taxes applied to a firm shift some or all of the marginal and average cost curves. For example, suppose that the government collects a specific tax of $10 per unit of output from the firm. This tax, which varies with output, affects the firm's variable cost but not its fixed cost. As a result, it affects the firm's average cost, average variable cost, and marginal cost curves but not its average fixed cost curve.

At every quantity, the average variable cost and the average cost rise by the full amount of the tax. The second column of Table 7.2 shows the firm's average variable cost before the tax, AVC^b. For example, if it sells 6 units of output, its average variable cost is $20. After the tax, the firm must pay the government $10 per unit, so the firm's after-tax average variable cost rises to $30. More generally, the firm's after-tax average variable cost, AVC^a, is its average variable cost of production—the before-tax average variable cost—plus the tax per unit, $10:
$AVC^a = AVC^b + \$10$.

The average cost equals the average variable cost plus the average fixed cost. Because the tax increases average variable cost by $10 and does not affect the average fixed cost, the tax increases average cost by $10.

The tax also increases the firm's marginal cost. Suppose that the firm wants to increase output from 7 to 8 units. The firm's actual cost of producing the third unit—its before-tax marginal cost, MC^b—is $27. To produce an extra unit of output, the cost to the firm is the marginal cost of producing the extra unit plus $10, so its after-tax marginal cost is $MC^a = MC^b + \$10$. In particular, its after-tax marginal cost of producing the eighth unit is $37.

A specific tax shifts the marginal cost and the average cost curves upward in Figure 7.3 by the amount of the tax, $10 per unit. The after-tax marginal cost intersects the after-tax average cost at its minimum. Because both the marginal and average cost curves shift upward by exactly the same amount, the after-tax average cost curve reaches its minimum at the same level of output, 8 units, as the before-tax average cost, as both panel a and Table 7.2 show. At 8 units, the minimum of the before-tax average cost curve is $27 and that of the after-tax average cost curve is $37. So even though a specific tax increases a firm's average cost, it does not affect the output at which average cost is minimized.

Similarly, we can analyze the effect of a franchise tax on costs. A *franchise tax*—also called a *business license fee*—is a lump sum that a firm pays for the right to operate a business. An $800-per-year tax is levied "for the privilege of doing

Table 7.2 Effect of a Specific Tax of $10 per Unit on Short-Run Costs

Q	AVC^b	$AVC^a = AVC^b + \$10$	$AC^b = C/q$	$AC^a = C/q + \$10$	MC^b	$MC^a = MC^b + \$10$
1	25	35	73	83	25	35
2	23	33	47	57	21	31
3	22	32	38	48	20	30
4	20.5	30.5	32.5	42.5	16	26
5	20	30	29.6	39.6	18	28
6	20	30	28	38	20	30
7	20.1	30.1	27	37	21	31
8	21	31	27	37	27	37
9	22	32	27.3	37.3	30	40
10	23	33	27.8	37.8	32	42
11	24.7	34.7	29.1	39.1	42	52
12	26.8	36.8	30.8	40.8	49	59

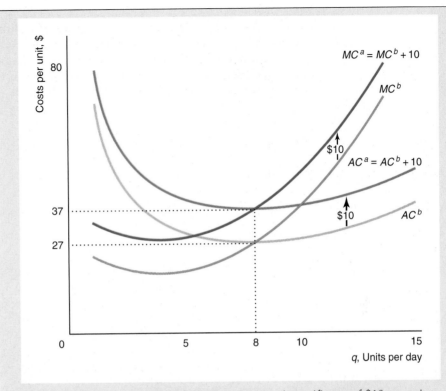

Figure 7.3 Effect of a Specific Tax on Cost Curves. A specific tax of $10 per unit shifts both the marginal cost and average cost curves upward by $10. Because of the parallel upward shift of the average cost curve, the minimum of both the before-tax average cost curve, AC^b, and the after-tax average cost curve, AC^a, occurs at the same output, 8 units.

business in California." A three-year license to sell hot dogs in front of New York City's Metropolitan Museum of Art costs $900,600. These taxes do not vary with output, so they affect firms' fixed costs only—not their variable costs.

Solved Problem 7.1 **What is the effect of a lump-sum franchise tax $\mathcal{L}$ on the quantity at which a firm's after-tax average cost curve reaches its minimum? (Assume that the firm's before-tax average cost curve is U-shaped.)**

Answer

1. *Determine the average tax per unit of output*: Because the franchise tax is a lump-sum payment that does not vary with output, the more the firm produces, the less tax it pays per unit. The tax per unit is $\mathcal{L}/q$. If the firm sells only 1 unit, its cost is $\mathcal{L}$; however, if it sells 100 units, its tax payment per unit is only $\mathcal{L}/100$.

2. *Show how the tax per unit affects the average cost*: The firm's after-tax average cost, AC^a, is the sum of its before-tax average cost, AC^b, and its average tax payment per unit, $\mathcal{L}/q$. Because the average tax payment per unit falls with output, the gap between the after-tax average cost curve and the before-tax average cost curve also falls with output on the graph.

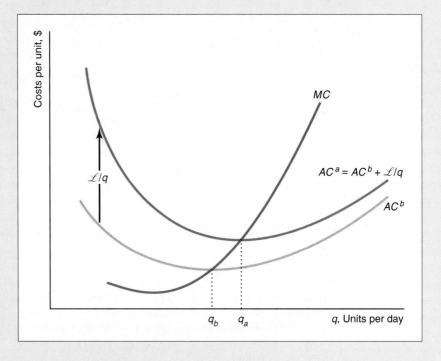

3. *Determine the effect of the tax on the marginal cost curve*: Because the franchise tax does not vary with output, it does not affect the marginal cost curve.

4. *Compare the minimum points of the two average cost curves*: The marginal cost curve crosses from below both average cost curves at their minimum points. Because the after-tax average cost lies above the before-tax average cost curve, the quantity at which the after-tax average cost curve reaches its minimum, q_a, is larger than the quantity, q_b, at which the before-tax average cost curve achieves a minimum.

Short-Run Cost Summary

We discussed three cost-level curves—total cost, fixed cost, and variable cost—and four cost-per-unit curves—average cost, average fixed cost, average variable cost, and marginal cost. Understanding the shapes of these curves and the relationships between them is crucial to understanding the analysis of firm behavior in the rest of this book. Fortunately, we can derive most of what we need to know about the shapes and the relationships between the curves using four basic concepts:

- In the short run, the cost associated with inputs that cannot be adjusted is fixed, while the cost from inputs that can be adjusted is variable.
- Given that input prices are constant, the shapes of the variable cost and cost curves are determined by the production function.
- Where there are diminishing marginal returns to a variable input, the variable cost and cost curves become relatively steep as output increases, so the average cost, average variable, and marginal cost curves rise with output.
- Because of the relationship between marginals and averages, both the average cost and average variable cost curves fall when marginal cost is below them and rise when marginal cost is above them, so the marginal cost cuts both these average cost curves at their minimum points.

7.3   LONG-RUN COSTS

In the long run, the firm adjusts all its inputs so that its cost of production is as low as possible. The firm can change its plant size, design and build new machines, and otherwise adjust inputs that were fixed in the short run.

Although firms may incur fixed costs in the long run, these fixed costs are *avoidable* (rather than *sunk*, as in the short run). The rent of F per month that a restaurant pays is a fixed cost because it does not vary with the number of meals (output) served. In the short run, this fixed cost is sunk: The firm must pay F even if the restaurant does not operate. In the long run, this fixed cost is avoidable: The firm does not have to pay this rent if it shuts down. The long run is determined by the length of the rental contract during which time the firm is obligated to pay rent.

In our examples throughout this chapter, we assume that all inputs can be varied in the long run so that there are no long-run fixed costs ($F = 0$). As a result, the long-run total cost equals the long-run variable cost: $C = VC$. Thus our firm is concerned about only three cost concepts in the long run—total cost, average cost, and marginal cost—instead of the seven cost concepts that it considers in the short run.

To produce a given quantity of output at minimum cost, our firm uses information about the production function and the price of labor and capital. The firm chooses how much labor and capital to use in the long run, whereas the firm chooses only how much labor to use in the short run when capital is fixed. As a consequence, the firm's long-run cost is lower than its short-run cost of production if it has to use the "wrong" level of capital in the short run. In this section, we show how a firm picks the cost-minimizing combinations of inputs in the long run.

Input Choice

A firm can produce a given level of output using many different *technologically efficient* combinations of inputs, as summarized by an isoquant (Chapter 6). From among the technologically efficient combinations of inputs, a firm wants to choose the particular bundle with the lowest cost of production, which is the *economically efficient* combination of inputs. To do so, the firm combines information about technology from the isoquant with information about the cost of labor and capital.

We now show how information about cost can be summarized in an *isocost line*. Then we show how a firm can combine the information in an isoquant and isocost lines to pick the economically efficient combination of inputs.

Isocost Line. The cost of producing a given level of output depends on the price of labor and capital. The firm hires L hours of labor services at a wage of w per hour, so its labor cost is wL. The firm rents K hours of machine services r per hour, so its capital cost is rK. (If the firm owns the capital, r is the implicit rental rate.) The firm's total cost is the sum of its labor and capital costs:

$$C = wL + rK. \tag{7.3}$$

The firm can hire as much labor and capital as it wants at these constant input prices.

The firm can use many combinations of labor and capital that cost the same amount. Suppose that the wage rate, w, is \$5 an hour and the rental rate of capital, r, is \$10. Five of the many combinations of labor and capital that the firm can use that cost \$100 are listed in Table 7.3. These combinations of labor and capital are plotted on an **isocost line**, which is all the combinations of inputs that require the same (*iso-*) total expenditure (*cost*). Figure 7.4 shows three isocost lines. The \$100 isocost line represents all the combinations of labor and capital that the firm can buy for \$100, including the combinations *a* through *e* in Table 7.3.

Along an isocost line, cost is fixed at a particular level, $\overline{C}$, so by setting cost at $\overline{C}$ in Equation 7.3, we can write the equation for the $\overline{C}$ isocost line as

$$\overline{C} = wL + rK.$$

Using algebra, we can rewrite this equation to show how much capital the firm can buy if it spends a total of $\overline{C}$ and purchases L units of labor:

$$K = \frac{\overline{C}}{r} - \frac{w}{r}L. \tag{7.4}$$

By substituting $\overline{C}$ = \$100, w = \$5, and r = \$10 in Equation 7.4, we find that the \$100 isocost line is $K = 10 - \frac{1}{2}L$. We can use Equation 7.4 to derive three properties of isocost lines.

First, where the isocost lines hit the capital and labor axes depends on the firm's cost, $\overline{C}$, and on the input prices. The $\overline{C}$ isocost line intersects the capital axis where the firm is using only capital. Setting $L = 0$ in Equation 7.4, we find that the firm

Table 7.3 Bundles of Labor and Capital That Cost the Firm \$100

Bundle	Labor, L	Capital, K	Labor Cost, $wL = \$5L$	Capital Cost, $rK = \$10K$	Total Cost, $wL + rK$
a	20	0	\$100	\$0	\$100
b	14	3	\$70	\$30	\$100
c	10	5	\$50	\$50	\$100
d	6	7	\$30	\$70	\$100
e	0	10	\$0	\$10	\$100

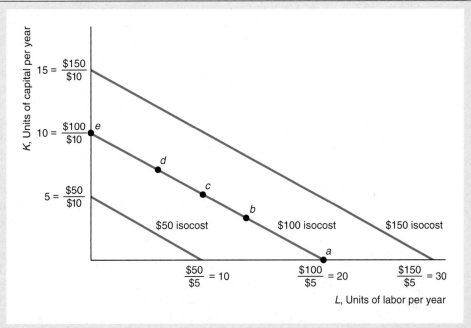

Figure 7.4 A Family of Isocost Lines. An isocost line shows all the combinations of labor and capital that cost the firm the same amount. The greater the total cost, the farther from the origin the isocost lies. All the isocosts have the same slope, $-w/r = -\frac{1}{2}$.

The slope shows the rate at which the firm can substitute capital for labor holding total cost constant: For each extra unit of capital it uses, the firm must use two fewer units of labor to hold its cost constant.

buys $K = \overline{C}/r$ units of capital. In the figure, the $100 isocost line intersects the capital axis at $100/$10 = 10 units of capital. Similarly, the intersection of the isocost line with the labor axis is at $\overline{C}/w$, which is the amount of labor the firm hires if it uses only labor. In the figure, the intersection of the $100 isocost line with the labor axis occurs at $L = 20$, where $K = 10 - \frac{1}{2} \times 20 = 0$.

Second, isocosts that are farther from the origin have higher costs than those that are closer to the origin. Because the isocost lines intersect the capital axis at $\overline{C}/r$ and the labor axis at $\overline{C}/w$, an increase in the cost shifts these intersections with the axes proportionately outward. The $50 isocost line hits the capital axis at 5 and the labor axis at 10, whereas the $100 isocost line intersects at 10 and 20.

Third, the slope of each isocost line is the same. From Equation 7.4, if the firm increases labor by ΔL, it must decrease capital by

$$\Delta K = -\frac{w}{r} \Delta L.$$

Dividing both sides of this expression by ΔL, we find that the slope of an isocost line, $\Delta K/\Delta L$, is $-w/r$. Thus the slope of the isocost line depends on the relative prices of the inputs. The slope of the isocost lines in the figure is $-w/r = -\$5/\$10 = -\frac{1}{2}$. If the firm uses two more units of labor, $\Delta L = 2$, it must reduce capital by one unit,

$\Delta K = -\frac{1}{2}\Delta L = -1$, to keep its total cost constant. Because all isocost lines are based on the same relative prices, they all have the same slope, so they are parallel.

The isocost line plays a similar role in the firm's decision making as the budget line does in consumer decision making. Both an isocost line and a budget line are straight lines whose slopes depend on relative prices. There is an important difference between them, however. The consumer has a single budget line determined by the consumer's income. The firm faces many isocost lines, each of which corresponds to a different level of expenditures the firm might make. A firm may incur a relatively low cost by producing relatively little output with few inputs, or it may incur a relatively high cost by producing a relatively large quantity.

Combining Cost and Production Information. By combining the information about costs contained in the isocost lines with information about efficient production summarized by an isoquant, a firm chooses the lowest-cost way to produce a given level of output. We examine how our Norwegian printing firm picks the combination of labor and capital that minimizes its cost of producing 100 units of output. Figure 7.5 shows the isoquant for 100 units of output (based on Griliches and Ringstad, 1971) and the isocost lines where the rental rate of a unit of capital is 8 kroner (the Norwegian monetary unit, abbreviated *kr*) and the wage rate is 24 kr.

The firm can choose any of three equivalent approaches to minimize its cost:

■ **Lowest-isocost rule:** Pick the bundle of inputs where the lowest isocost line touches the isoquant.
■ **Tangency rule:** Pick the bundle of inputs where the isoquant is tangent to the isocost line.
■ **Last-dollar rule:** Pick the bundle of inputs where the last dollar spent on one input gives as much extra output as the last dollar spent on any other input.

Using the *lowest-isocost rule*, the firm minimizes its cost by using the combination of inputs on the isoquant that is on the lowest isocost line that touches the isoquant. The lowest possible isoquant that will allow the printing firm to produce 100 units of output is the 2,000-kr isocost line. This isocost line touches the isoquant at the bundle of inputs *x*, where the firm uses $L = 50$ workers and $K = 100$ units of capital.

How do we know that *x* is the least costly way to produce 100 units of output? We need to demonstrate that other practical combinations of input produce less than 100 units or produce 100 units at greater cost.

If the firm spent less than 2,000 kr, it could not produce 100 units of output. Each combination of inputs on the 1,000-kr isocost line lies below the isoquant, so the firm cannot produce 100 units of output for 1,000 kr.

The firm can produce 100 units of output using other combinations of inputs beside *x*; however, using these other bundles of inputs is more expensive. For example, the firm can produce 100 units of output using the combinations *y* ($L = 24$, $K = 303$) or *z* ($L = 116$, $K = 28$). Both these combinations, however, cost the firm 3,000 kr.

If an isocost line crosses the isoquant twice, as the 3,000-kr isocost line does, there must be another lower isocost line that also touches the isoquant. The lowest possible isocost line that touches the isoquant, the 2,000-kr isocost line, is tangent to the isoquant at a single bundle, *x*. Thus the firm may use the *tangency rule*: The

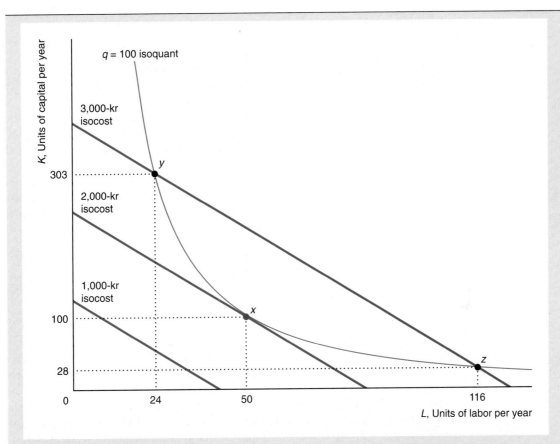

Figure 7.5 Cost Minimization. The Norwegian printing firm minimizes its cost of producing 100 units of output by producing at x ($L = 50$ and $K = 100$). This cost-minimizing combination of inputs is determined by the tangency between the $q = 100$ isoquant and the lowest isocost line, 2,000 kr, that touches that isoquant. At x, the isocost is tangent to the isoquant, so the slope of the isocost, $-w/r = -3$, equals the slope of the isoquant, which is the negative of the marginal rate of technical substitution. That is, the rate at which the firm can trade capital for labor in the input markets equals the rate at which it can substitute capital for labor in the production process.

firm chooses the input bundle where the relevant isoquant is tangent to an isocost line to produce a given level of output at the lowest cost.

We can interpret this tangency or cost minimization condition in two ways. At the point of tangency, the slope of the isoquant equals the slope of the isocost. As we showed in Chapter 6, the slope of the isoquant is the negative of the marginal rate of technical substitution (*MRTS*). The slope of the isocost is the negative of the ratio of the wage to the cost of capital, $-w/r$. Thus to minimize its cost of producing a given level of output, a firm chooses its inputs so that the marginal rate of technical substitution equals the relative input prices:

$$MRTS = \frac{w}{r}. \qquad (7.5)$$

The firm picks inputs so that the rate at which it can substitute capital for labor in the production process, the *MRTS*, exactly equals the rate at which it can trade capital for labor in input markets, *w/r*.

The printing company's marginal rate of technical substitution is 1.5*K/L*. At $K = 100$ and $L = 50$, its *MRTS* is 3, which equals the ratio of the input prices it faces, $w/r = 24/8 = 3$. In contrast, at *y*, the isocost cuts the isoquant so the slopes are not equal. At *y*, the *MRTS* is 18.9375, which is greater than the ratio of the input price, 3. Because the slopes are not equal at *y*, the firm can produce the same output at lower cost. As the figure shows, the cost of producing at *y* is 3,000 kr, whereas the cost of producing at *x* is only 2,000 kr.

We can interpret the condition in Equation 7.5 in another way. We showed in Chapter 6 that the marginal rate of technical substitution equals the ratio of the marginal product of labor to that of capital: $MRTS = MP_L/MP_K$. Thus the cost-minimizing condition in Equation 7.5 is

$$\frac{MP_L}{MP_K} = \frac{w}{r}. \tag{7.6}$$

This expression may be rewritten as

$$\frac{MP_L}{w} = \frac{MP_K}{r}. \tag{7.7}$$

Equation 7.7 states the *last-dollar rule*: Cost is minimized if inputs are chosen so that the last dollar spent on labor adds as much extra output as the last dollar spent on capital.

The printing firm's marginal product of labor is $MP_L = 0.6q/L$, and its marginal product of capital is $MP_K = 0.4q/K$.[5] At Bundle *x*, the printing firm's marginal product of labor is 1.2 (= 0.6 × 100/50) and its marginal product of capital is 0.4. The last krone spent on labor gets the firm

$$\frac{MP_L}{w} = \frac{1.2}{24} = 0.05$$

more output. The last krone spent on capital also gets the firm

$$\frac{MP_K}{r} = \frac{0.4}{8} = 0.05$$

extra output. Thus spending one more krone on labor at *x* gets the firm as much extra output as spending the same amount on capital. Equation 7.6 holds, so the firm is minimizing its cost of producing 100 units of output.

If instead the firm produced at *y*, where it is using more capital and less labor, its MP_L is 2.5 (= 0.6 × 100/24) and the MP_K is approximately 0.13 (≈ 0.4 × 100/303).

---

[5]The printing firm's production function, $q = 1.52L^{0.6}K^{0.4}$, is a Cobb-Douglas production function. The marginal product formula for Cobb-Douglas production functions is derived in Appendix 6B.

As a result, the last krone spent on labor gets $MP_L/w \approx 0.1$ more unit of output, whereas the last krone spent on capital gets only a fourth as much extra output, $MP_K/r \approx 0.017$. At y, if the firm shifts one krone from capital to labor, output falls by 0.017 because there is less capital and increases by 0.1 because there is more labor for a net gain of 0.083 more output at the same cost. The firm should shift even more resources from capital to labor—which increases the marginal product of capital and decreases the marginal product of labor—until Equation 7.6 holds with equality at x.

To summarize, we demonstrated that there are three equivalent rules that the firm can use to pick the lowest-cost combination of inputs to produce a given level of output when isoquants are smooth: the lowest-isocost rule, the tangency rule (Equations 7.5 and 7.6), and the last-dollar rule (Equation 7.7). If the isoquant is not smooth, the lowest-cost method of production cannot be determined by using the tangency rule or the last-dollar rule. The lowest-isocost rule always works—even when isoquants are not smooth—as we now illustrate.

Application   RICE MILLING ON JAVA

A dramatic change occurred in the process used for milling rice on Java in the early 1970s (Timmer, 1984). Experts believe that about 80% of that island's rice crop was hand-pounded in 1971. By 1973, less than 50%, and perhaps as little as 10%, was hand-pounded. During that period, thousands of new small, mechanical rice mills had been built. What prompted this change in technique? The change was due to a fall in the cost of capital, which increased the factor price of labor relative to capital.

Rice may be milled in five ways: by (1) hand pounding, (2) small-mill processing, (3) large-mill processing, (4) using a small bulk facility, or (5) using a large bulk facility. These methods vary in the amounts of labor and capital services required. Hand pounding, a technique that is at least a millennium old, is labor intensive: Workers use only a wooden pounding pole and pestle. Small-mill processing employs equipment to hull and polish the rice but relies on sun drying rather than mechanical drying equipment. Large mills (which are rare) hull, polish, and dry using a combination of machines and sunlight. Small and large bulk facilities mill and store high-quality rice; these were used elsewhere but not on Java.

What was the least expensive way to process rice on Java? The least-cost combination of laborers and capital is determined by finding the lowest isocost that touches the relevant isoquant.

The isoquant for 10 million rupees' worth of processed rice (see graph) has kinks. The point at each kink represents one of the five milling processes. The straight line connecting a pair of points shows how the same output could be produced by using a combination of those two processes. For example, at the midpoint of the line between hand pounding and small mills, half the rice is produced by hand pounding and half by the small mill.

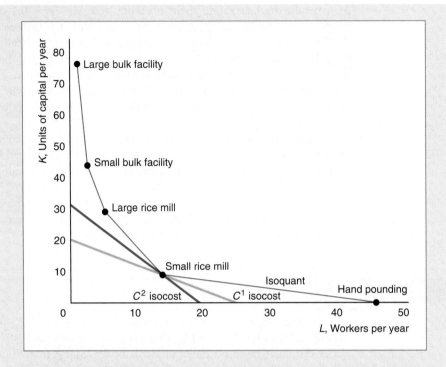

Because the isoquant has kinks, small changes in the relative cost of the two inputs do not necessarily lead to a change in technique. Two different sloped isocost lines, C^1 and C^2 (which reflect the range of relative factor prices in 1973), touch the isoquant at the same point: The small rice mill is the least expensive technique. The isocost line must be steeper than C^2 (the price of capital must fall relative to that of labor) for a more capital-intensive technique to be used.

Factor Price Changes. Once the Norwegian printing firm determines the lowest-cost combination of inputs to produce a given level of output, it uses that method as long as the input prices remain constant. How should the firm change its behavior if the cost of one of the factors changes? Suppose that the wage falls from 24 kr to 8 kr but the rental rate of capital stays constant at 8 kr.

The firm minimizes its new cost by substituting away from the now relatively more expensive input, capital, toward the now relatively less expensive input, labor. The change in the wage does not affect technological efficiency, so it does not affect the isoquant in Figure 7.6. Because of the wage decrease, the new isocost lines have a flatter slope, $-w/r = -8/8 = -1$, than the original isoquant lines, $-w/r = -24/8 = -3$.

The relatively steep original isocost line is tangent to the 100-unit isoquant at Bundle x ($L = 50$, $K = 100$). The new, flatter isocost line is tangent to the isoquant

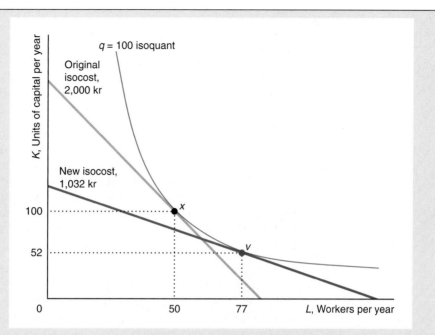

Figure 7.6 **Change in Factor Price.** Originally, the wage was 24 kr and the rental rate of capital was 8 kr, so the lowest isocost line (2,000 kr) was tangent to the $q = 100$ isoquant at x ($L = 50$, $K = 100$). When the wage falls to 8 kr, the isocost lines became flatter: Labor became relatively less expensive than capital. The slope of the isocost lines falls from $-w/r = -24/8 = -3$ to $-8/8 = -1$. The new lowest isocost line (1,032 kr) is tangent at v ($L = 77$, $K = 52$). Thus when the wage falls, the firm uses more labor and less capital to produce a given level of output, and the cost of production falls from 2,000 kr to 1,032 kr.

at Bundle v ($L = 77$, $K = 52$). Thus the firm uses more labor and less capital as labor becomes relatively less expensive. Moreover, the firm's cost of producing 100 units falls from 2,000 kr to 1,032 kr because of the fall in the wage.

This example illustrates that a change in the relative prices of inputs affects the mix of inputs that a firm uses. In contrast, if all prices increase by the same amount, so that the relative prices do not change, the firm continues to produce any given amount of output using the same input combination as it did originally, as we now show.

Solved Problem 7.2

When the input prices were $\hat{w}$ and $\hat{r}$, a firm produced $\hat{q}$ units of output using $\hat{L}$ units of labor and $\hat{K}$ units of capital. Suppose that the prices of both its inputs doubles. If the firm continues to produce $\hat{q}$ units of output, will it change the amount of labor and capital it uses? What happens to its cost of producing $\hat{q}$?

Answer

1. *Determine whether the change affects the slopes of the isoquant or the isocost lines*: A change in input prices does not affect the isoquant, which depends only on technology (the production function). Moreover, the doubling of the input prices does not affect the slope of the isocost lines. The original slope was $-\hat{w}/\hat{r}$, and the new slope is $-(2\hat{w})/(2\hat{r}) = -\hat{w}/\hat{r}$.

2. *Using a rule for cost minimization, determine whether the firm changes its input mix*: A firm minimizes its cost by producing where its isoquant is tangent to the lowest possible isocost line. That is, the firm produces where the slope of its isoquant, $-MRTS$, equals the slope of its isocost line, $-w/r$. Because the slopes of the isoquant and the isocost lines are unchanged after input prices doubled, the firm continues to produce $\hat{q}$ using the same amount of labor, $\hat{L}$, and capital, $\hat{K}$, as originally.

3. *Calculate the original cost and the new cost and compare them*: The firm's original cost of producing $\hat{q}$ units of output was $\hat{w}\hat{L} + \hat{r}\hat{K} = \hat{C}$. Its new cost of producing the same amount of output is $(2\hat{w})\hat{L} + (2\hat{r})\hat{K} = 2\hat{C}$. Thus its cost of producing $\hat{q}$ doubled when the input prices doubled. The isocost lines have the same slope as before, but the cost associated with each isocost line has doubled.

How Long-Run Cost Varies with Output

We now know how a firm determines the cost-minimizing output for any given level of output. By repeating this analysis for different output levels, the firm determines how its cost varies with output.

Panel a of Figure 7.7 shows the relationship between the lowest-cost factor combinations and various levels of output for the printing firm when input prices are held constant at $w = 24$ kr and $r = 8$ kr. The curve through the tangency points is the long-run **expansion path**: the cost-minimizing combination of labor and capital for each output level. The lowest-cost way to produce 100 units of output is to use the labor and capital combination x ($L = 50$ and $K = 100$), which lies on the 2,000-kr isocost line. Similarly, the lowest-cost way to produce 200 units is to use z, which is on the 4,000-kr isocost line. The expansion path goes through x and z.

The expansion path of the printing firm in the figure is a straight line through the origin with a slope of 2: At any given output level, the firm uses twice as much capital as labor.[6] To double its output from 100 to 200 units, the firm doubles the amount of labor from 50 to 100 workers and doubles the amount of capital from 100 to 200 units. Because both inputs double when output doubles from 100 to 200, cost also doubles.

The printing firm's expansion path contains the same information as its long-run cost function, $C(q)$, which shows the relationship between the cost of production

---

[6]In Appendix 7C, we show that the expansion path for a Cobb-Douglas production function is $K = [\beta w/(\alpha r)]L$. The expansion path for the printing firm is $K = [(0.4 \times 24)/(0.6 \times 8)]L = 2L$.

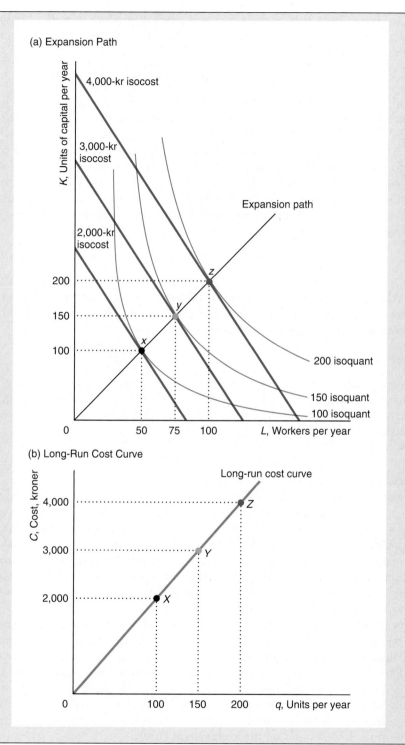

Figure 7.7 Expansion Path and Long-Run Cost Curve. (a) The curve through the tangency points between isocost lines and isoquants, such as *x*, *y*, and *z*, is called the expansion path. The points on the expansion path are the cost-minimizing combinations of labor and capital for each output level. (b) The expansion path shows the same relationship between long-run cost and output as the long-run cost curve.

and output. From inspection of the expansion path, to produce q units of output takes $K = q$ units of capital and $L = q/2$ units of labor. Thus the long-run cost of producing q units of output is

$$C(q) = wL + rK = wq/2 + rq = (w/2 + r)q = (24/2 + 8)q = 20q.$$

That is, the long-run cost function corresponding to this expansion path is $C(q) = 20q$. This cost function is consistent with the expansion path in panel a: $C(100) = 2,000$ kr at x on the expansion path, $C(150) = 3,000$ kr at y, and $C(200) = 4,000$ kr at z.

Panel b plots this long-run cost curve. Points X, Y, and Z on the cost curve correspond to points x, y, and z on the expansion path. For example, the 2,000-kr isocost line goes through x, which is the lowest-cost combination of labor and capital that can produce 100 units of output. Similarly, X on the long-run cost curve is at 2,000 kr and 100 units of output. Consistent with the expansion path, the cost curve shows that as output doubles, cost doubles.

Solved Problem 7.3   **What is the long-run cost function for a fixed-proportions production function (Chapter 6) when it takes one unit of labor and one unit of capital to produce one unit of output? Describe the long-run cost curve.**

Answer

Multiply the inputs by their prices, and sum to determine total cost. The long-run cost of producing q units of output is $C(q) = wL + rK = wq + rq = (w + r)q$. Cost rises in proportion to output. The long-run cost curve is a straight line with a slope of $w + r$.

The Shape of Long-Run Cost Curves

The shapes of the average cost and marginal cost curves depend on the shape of the long-run cost curve. To illustrate these relationships, we examine the long-run cost curves of a typical firm that has a U-shaped long-run average cost curve.

The long-run cost curve in panel a of Figure 7.8 corresponds to the long-run average and marginal cost curves in panel b. Unlike the straight-line long-run cost curves of the printing firm and the firm with fixed-proportions production, the long-run cost curve of this firm rises less than in proportion to output at outputs below q^* and then rises more rapidly.

We can apply the same type of analysis that we used to study short-run curves to look at the geometric relationship between long-run total, average, and marginal curves. A line from the origin is tangent to the long-run cost curve at q^*, where the marginal cost curve crosses the average cost curve, because the slope of that line equals the marginal and average costs at that output. The long-run average cost curve falls when the long-run marginal cost curve is below it and rises when the long-run marginal cost curve is above it. Thus the marginal cost crosses the average cost curve at the lowest point on the average cost curve.

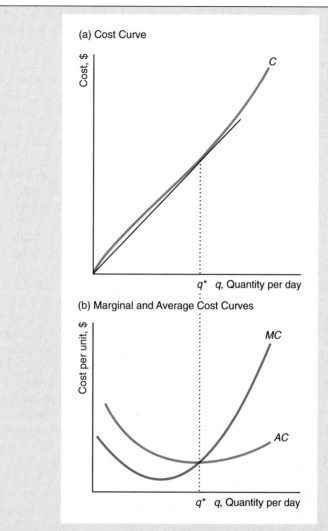

Figure 7.8 Long-Run Cost Curves. (a) The long-run cost curve rises less rapidly than output at output levels below q^* and more rapidly at higher output levels. (b) As a consequence, the marginal cost and average cost curves are U-shaped. The marginal cost crosses the average cost at its minimum at q^*.

Why does the average cost curve first fall and then rise, as in panel b? The explanation differs from those given for why short-run average cost curves are U-shaped.

A key reason why the short-run average cost is initially downward sloping is that the average fixed cost curve is downward sloping: Spreading the fixed cost over more units of output lowers the average fixed cost per unit. There are no fixed costs in the long run, however, so fixed costs cannot explain the initial downward slope of the long-run average cost curve.

A major reason why the short-run average cost curve slopes upward at higher levels of output is diminishing marginal returns. In the long run, however, all factors can be varied, so diminishing marginal returns do not explain the upward slope of a long-run average cost curve.

Ultimately, as with the short-run curves, the shape of the long-run curves is determined by the production function relationship between output and inputs. In the long run, returns to scale play a major role in determining the shape of the average cost curve and other cost curves. As we discussed in Chapter 6, increasing all inputs in proportion may cause output to increase more than in proportion (increasing returns to scale) at low levels of output, in proportion (constant returns to scale) at intermediate levels of output, and less than in proportion (decreasing returns to scale) at high levels of output. If a production function has this returns-to-scale pattern and the prices of inputs are constant, long-run average cost must be U-shaped.

To illustrate the relationship between returns to scale and long-run average cost, we use the returns-to-scale example of Figure 6.5, the data for which are reproduced in Table 7.4. The firm produces one unit of output using a unit each of labor and capital. Given a wage and rental cost of capital of $6 per unit, the total cost and average cost of producing this unit are both $12. Doubling both inputs causes output to increase more than in proportion to 3 units, reflecting increasing returns to scale. Because cost only doubles and output triples, the average cost falls. A cost function is said to exhibit **economies of scale** if the average cost of production falls as output expands.

Doubling the inputs again causes output to double as well—constant returns to scale—so the average cost remains constant. If an increase in output has no effect on average cost—the average cost curve is flat—there are *no economies of scale*.

Doubling the inputs once more causes only a small increase in output—decreasing returns to scale—so average cost increases. A firm suffers from **diseconomies of scale** if average cost rises when output increases.

Returns to scale in the production function are a sufficient but not necessary condition for economies of scale in the average cost curve. In the long run, a firm may change the ratio of capital to labor that it uses as it expands output. As a result, the

Table 7.4 **Returns to Scale and Long-Run Costs**

Output, Q	Labor, L	Capital, K	Cost, $C = wL + rK$	Average Cost, $AC = C/q$	Returns to Scale
1	1	1	12	12	
3	2	2	24	8	Increasing
6	4	4	48	8	Constant
8	8	8	96	12	Decreasing

$w = r = \$6$ per unit.

Table 7.5 **Shape of Average Cost Curves in Canadian Manufacturing**	
Scale Economies	Share of Manufacturing Industries, %
Economies of scale: initially downward-sloping *AC*	57
Everywhere downward-sloping *AC*	18
L-shaped *AC* (downward-sloping, then flat)	31
U-shaped *AC*	8
No economies of scale: flat *AC*	23
Diseconomies of scale: upward-sloping *AC*	14

Source: Robidoux and Lester (1992).

firm could have economies of scale in costs without increasing returns to scale in production or could have diseconomies of scale in costs without decreasing returns to scale in production.

Consider a firm that has constant returns to scale in production at every output level. At small levels of output, the firm uses lots of labor and commonly available tools. At large levels of output, the firm designs and builds its own specialized equipment and uses relatively few workers, thereby lowering its average cost. Such a firm has economies of scale in cost despite having constant returns to scale in production.

Average cost curves can have many different shapes. Competitive firms typically have U-shaped average cost curves. Average cost curves in noncompetitive markets may be U-shaped, L-shaped (average cost at first falls rapidly and then levels off as output increases), everywhere downward sloping, or everywhere upward sloping or have other shapes. The shapes of the average cost curves indicate whether the production process has economies or diseconomies of scale.

Table 7.5 summarizes the shapes of average cost curves of firms in various Canadian manufacturing industries (as estimated by Robidoux and Lester, 1992). The table shows that U-shaped average cost curves are the exception rather than the rule in Canadian manufacturing and that nearly one-third of these average cost curves are L-shaped.

Some of these apparently L-shaped average cost curves may be part of a U-shaped curve with long, flat bottoms, where we don't observe any firm producing enough to exhibit diseconomies of scale. Cement firms provide an example of such a cost curve.

Application   **AVERAGE COST OF CEMENT FIRMS**

Cement producers enjoy substantial economies of scale. The dots in the figure show the observed average costs for British cement firms (Norman, 1979). The estimated average cost curve (fitted through these dots) shows that the

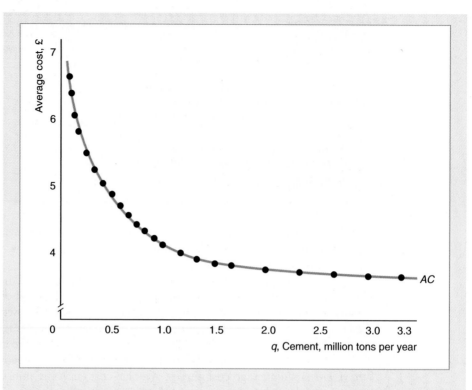

average cost curve is L-shaped: Average cost falls rapidly at first and then more slowly. Norman presented evidence that average cost curves have similar shapes in the United States and West Germany. Jha, Murty, Paul, and Sahni (1991) also found economies of scale in Indian cement, lime, and plaster plants. They estimated that a 1% increase in a plant's output lowers its average cost by 0.14%. Thus the long-run average cost in India is also L-shaped.

Estimating Cost Curves Versus Introspection

Economists use statistical methods to estimate a cost function. Sometimes, however, we can infer the shape by casual observation and deductive reasoning.

For example, in the good old days, the Good Humor company sent out fleets of ice-cream trucks to purvey its products. It seems likely that the company's production process had fixed proportions and constant returns to scale: If it wanted to sell more, Good Humor dispatched one more truck and one more driver. Drivers and trucks are almost certainly nonsubstitutable inputs (the isoquants are right angles). If the cost of a driver is w per day, the rental cost is r per day, and q quantity of ice cream is sold in a day, then the cost function is $C = (w + r)q$.

Such deductive reasoning can lead one astray, as I once discovered. A water heater manufacturing firm provided me with many years of data on the inputs it used and the amount of output it produced. I also talked to the company's engineers about the production process and toured the plant (which resembled a scene from Dante's *Inferno*, with staggering noise levels and flames everywhere).

A water heater consists of an outside cylinder of metal, a liner, an electronic control unit, hundreds of tiny parts (screws, washers, etc.), and a couple of rods that slow corrosion. Workers cut out the metal for the cylinder, weld it together, and add the other parts. "OK," I said to myself, "this production process must be one of fixed proportions because the firm needs one of everything to produce a water heater. How could you substitute a cylinder for an electronic control unit? Or how can you substitute labor for metal?"

I then used statistical techniques to estimate the production and cost functions. Following the usual procedure, however, I did not assume that I knew the exact form of the functions. Rather, I allowed the data to "tell" me the type of production and cost functions. To my surprise, the estimates indicated that the production process was not one of fixed proportions. Rather, the firm could readily substitute between labor and capital.

"Surely I've made a mistake," I said to the plant manager after describing these results. "No," he said, "that's correct. There's a great deal of substitutability between labor and metal."

"How can they be substitutes?"

"Easy," he said. "We can use a lot of labor and waste very little metal by cutting out exactly what we want and being very careful. Or we can use relatively little labor, cut quickly, and waste more metal. When the cost of labor is relatively high, we waste more metal. When the cost of metal is relatively high, we cut more carefully." This practice minimizes the firm's cost.

7.4 LOWER COSTS IN THE LONG RUN

In its long-run planning, a firm chooses a plant size and makes other investments so as to minimize its long-run cost on the basis of how many units it produces. Once it chooses its plant size and equipment, these inputs are fixed in the short run. Thus the firm's long-run decision determines its short-run cost. Because the firm cannot vary its capital in the short run but can vary it in the long run, short-run cost is at least as high as long-run cost and is higher if the "wrong" level of capital is used in the short run.

Long-Run Average Cost as the Envelope of Short-Run Average Cost Curves

As a result, the long-run average cost is always equal to or below the short-run average cost. Suppose, initially, that the firm in Figure 7.9 has only three possible plant sizes. The firm's short-run average cost curve is $SRAC^1$ for the smallest possible plant. The average cost of producing q_1 units of output using this plant, point a on $SRAC^1$, is $10. If instead the plant used the next larger plant size, its cost of producing q_1 units of output, point b on $SRAC^2$, would be $12. Thus if the firm knows that it will produce only q_1 units of output, it minimizes its average cost by using the smaller plant size. If it expects to be producing q_2, its average cost is lower on the $SRAC^2$ curve, point e, than on the $SRAC^1$ curve, point d.

In the long run, the firm chooses the plant size that minimizes its cost of production, so it picks the plant size that has the lowest average cost for each possible output level. At q_1, it opts for the small plant size, whereas at q_2, it uses the medium

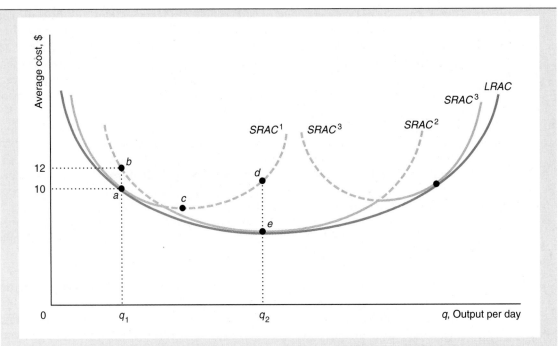

Figure 7.9 Long-Run Average Cost as the Envelope of Short-Run Average Cost Curves. If there are only three possible plant sizes, with short-run average costs $SRAC^1$, $SRAC^2$, and $SRAC^3$, the long-run average cost curve is the solid, scalloped portion of the three short-run curves. $LRAC$ is the smooth and U-shaped long-run average cost curve if there are many possible short-run average cost curves.

plant size. Thus the long-run average cost curve is the solid, scalloped section of the three short-run cost curves.

If there are many possible plant sizes, the long-run average curve, $LRAC$, is smooth and U-shaped. The $LRAC$ includes one point from each possible short-run average cost curve. This point, however, is not necessarily the minimum point from a short-run curve. For example, the $LRAC$ includes a on $SRAC^1$ and not its minimum point, c. A small plant operating at minimum average cost cannot produce at as low an average cost as a slightly larger plant that is taking advantage of economies of scale.

Application   **LONG-RUN COST CURVES IN PRINTING AND OIL PIPELINES**

Here we illustrate the relationship between long-run and short-run cost curves for our Norwegian printing firm and for oil pipelines. In the next application, we show the long-run cost when you or a firm chooses between a laser printer and an ink-jet printer, depending on how many pages will be printed.

Printing Firm

The first graph shows the relationship between short-run and long-run average cost curves for the Norwegian printing firm. Because this production function has constant returns to scale, doubling both inputs doubles output, so the long-run average cost, *LRAC*, is constant at 20 kr, as we saw earlier. If capital is fixed at 200 units, the firm's short-run average cost curve is $SRAC^1$. If the firm produces 200 units of output, its short-run and long-run average costs are equal. At any other output, its short-run cost is higher than its long-run cost.

The short-run marginal cost curves, $SRMC^1$ and $SRMC^2$, are upward sloping and equal the corresponding U-shaped short-run average cost curves, $SRAC^1$ and $SRAC^2$, only at their minimum points, 20 kr. In contrast, because the long-run average cost is horizontal at 20 kr, the long-run marginal cost curve, *SRMC*, is horizontal at 20 kr. Thus the long-run marginal cost curve is *not* the envelope of the short-run marginal cost curves.

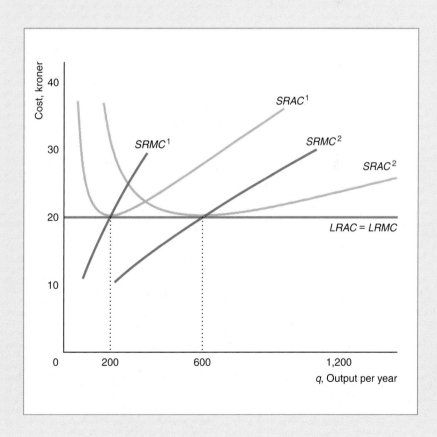

Oil Pipelines

Oil companies use the information in the second graph[7] to choose what size pipe to use to deliver oil. The 8" *SRAC* is the short-run average cost of a pipe with an 8-inch diameter. The long-run average cost curve, *LRAC*, is the envelope of all possible short-run average cost curves. It is more expensive to lay larger pipes than smaller ones, so a firm does not want to install unnecessarily large pipes. The average cost of sending a substantial quantity through asingle large pipe is lower than that of sending it through two smaller pipes. For example, the average cost per barrel of sending 200,000 barrels per day through two 16-inch pipes is 1.67 (= $50/$30) greater than through a single 26-inch pipe.

Because the company incurs large fixed costs in laying miles and miles of pipelines and because pipes last for years, it does not vary the size of pipes in the short run. In the long run, the oil company installs the ideal pipe size to handle its "throughput" of oil. As Exxon (1975, p. 16) notes, several oil companies share interstate pipelines because of the large economies of scale.

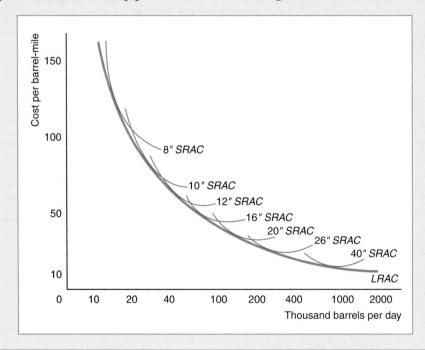

---

[7]Exxon Company, U.S.A., *Competition in the Petroleum Industry*, 1975, p. 30. Reprinted with permission.

CHOOSING AN INK-JET OR A LASER PRINTER

In deciding which piece of capital equipment to buy, firms take a long-run view. Suppose that you start a small firm and want to send nice-looking black-and-white letters to your customers. You can buy a personal laser printer for $400 or an ink-jet printer for $235 that both print eight pages per minute at the same density (600 dots per inch).

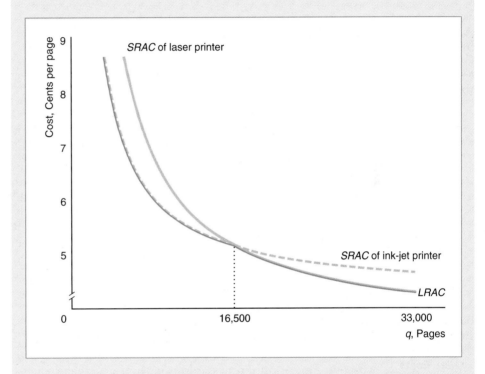

If you buy the ink jet, you save $165 right off the bat. The laser costs less per page to operate, however. The cost of ink and paper is about 3¢ per page for a laser compared to about 4¢ per page for an ink jet. That means that the average cost per page of operating a laser ($400/q + 0.03, where q is the number of pages) is less than that of an ink jet ($235/q + 0.04) after q reaches about 16,500 pages.

The graph shows the short-run average cost curves for the laser printer and the ink-jet printer. The lower-cost choice is the ink jet if you're printing fewer than 16,500 pages and the laser if you're printing more.

So should you buy the laser? Well, the typical ink-jet user averages only 15 pages per workweek. At that rate, to print 16,500 pages will take over 21 years (assuming that the ink jet will last that long). Thus if you print only a few pages per week, buy the ink jet. To print 16,500 pages in two years would take an average of over 158 pages per week, or about 33 pages per business day. Thus if you print 33 or more pages a day, the laser is cost effective (assuming that it lasts at least two years at this level of use).

Short-Run and Long-Run Expansion Paths

Long-run cost is lower than short-run cost because the firm has more flexibility in the long run. To show the advantage of flexibility, we can compare the short-run and long-run expansion paths, which correspond to the short-run and long-run cost curves.

The Norwegian printing firm has greater long-run flexibility. The tangency of the firm's isoquants and isocost lines determines the long-run expansion path in Figure 7.10. The firm expands output by increasing both its labor and its capital, so its long-run expansion path is upward sloping. To increase its output from 100 to 200 units (move from x to z), it doubles its capital from 100 to 200 units and its labor from 50 to 100 workers. Its cost increases from 2,000 kr to 4,000 kr.

In the short run, the firm cannot increase its capital, which is fixed at 100 units. The firm can increase its output only by using more labor, so its short-run expansion path is horizontal at $K = 100$. To expand its output from 100 to 200 units (move from x to y), the firm must increase its labor from 50 to 159 workers, and its cost rises from 2,000 kr to 4,616 kr. Doubling output increases long-run cost by a factor of 2 and short-run cost by approximately 2.3.

How Learning by Doing Lowers Costs

Two reasons why long-run cost is lower than short-run cost are that firms have more flexibility in the long run and that technical progress (Chapter 6) may lower cost over time. A third reason is **learning by doing**: the productive skills and knowledge of better ways to produce that workers and managers gain from experience.

In some firms, learning by doing is a function of the time since the product was introduced. In others, learning by doing is a function of *cumulative output*: the total number of units of output produced since the product was introduced. Learning is connected to cumulative output if workers become increasingly adept the more times they perform a task. As a consequence, workers become more productive if they make many units over a short period than if they produce a few units over a longer period. For example, the average labor cost of producing a C-141 plane (panel a of Figure 7.11) fell with cumulative output (based on Womer and Patterson, 1983).

If a firm is operating in the economies of scale section of its average cost curve, expanding output lowers its cost for two reasons. Its average cost falls today because of economies of scale, and for any given level of output, its average cost is lower in the next period due to learning by doing.

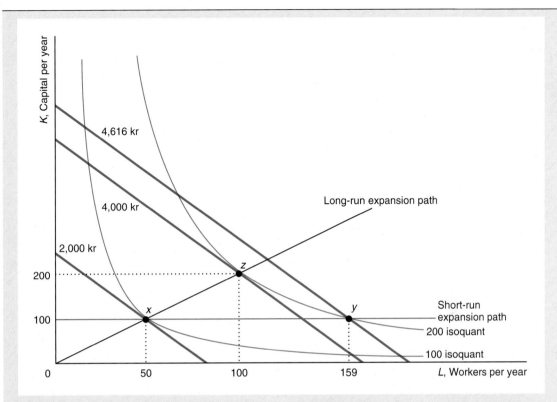

Figure 7.10 Long-Run and Short-Run Expansion Paths. In the long run, the Norwegian printing firm increases its output by using more of both inputs, so its long-run expansion path is upward sloping. In the short run, the firm cannot vary its capital, so its short-run expansion path is horizontal at the fixed level of output. That is, it increases its output by increasing the amount of labor it uses. Expanding output from 100 to 200 raises the printing firm's long-run cost from 2,000 kr to 4,000 kr but raises its short-run cost from 2,000 kr to 4,616 kr.

In panel b of Figure 7.11, the firm is currently producing q_1 units of output at point A on average cost curve AC^1. If it expands its output to q_2, its average cost falls in this period to B because of economies of scale. The learning by doing in this period results in a lower average cost, AC^2, in the next period. If the firm continues to produce q_2 units of output in the next period, its average cost falls to b on AC^2.

If instead of expanding output to q_2 in this period, the firm expands to q_3, its average cost is even lower in this period (C on AC^1) due to even more economies of scale. Moreover, its average cost in the next period is even lower, AC^3, due to the extra experience in this period. If the firm continues to produce q_3 in the next period, its average cost is c on AC^3. Thus all else the same, if learning by doing depends on cumulative output, firms have an incentive to produce more in the short run than they otherwise would to lower their costs in the future.

(a) Learning by Doing on C-141 Aircraft

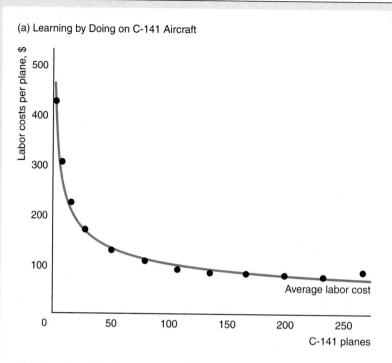

(b) Economies of Scale and Learning by Doing

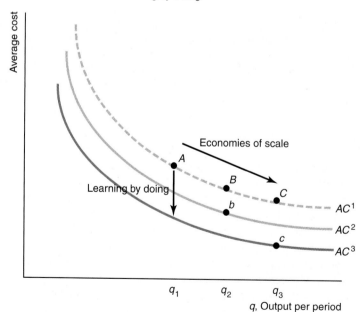

Figure 7.11 **Learning by Doing.** (a) As more C-141 aircraft were produced, the average labor cost per plane fell (Womer and Patterson, 1983). The horizontal axis shows the cumulative number of planes produced over time. (b) In the short run, extra production reduces a firm's average cost owing to economies of scale: because $q_1 < q_2 < q_3$, A is higher than B, which is higher than C. In the long run, extra production reduces average cost because of learning by doing. To produce q_2 this period costs B on AC^1, but to produce that same output in the next period would cost only b on AC^2. If the firm produces q_3 instead of q_2 in this period, its average cost in the next period is AC^3 instead of AC^2 because of additional learning by doing. Thus extra output in this period lowers the firm's cost in two ways: It lowers average cost in this period due to economies of scale and lowers average cost for any given output level in the next period due to learning by doing.

Application   LEARNING BY DOING IN COMPUTER CHIPS

The cost of producing a computer memory chip falls substantially due to learning by doing. There are several different types of MOS (metal oxide on silicon) memory chips: EPROM (erasable programmable read-only memory), DRAM (dynamic random-access memory), and fast SRAM (static random-access memory). From one generation to another, EPROM's storage capacity doubles, whereas the storage capacity of DRAM and SRAM increases by a factor of 4. Like clockwork, a new EPROM generation appears every 18 months; a new DRAM, every three years.

Gruber (1992) finds that the average cost of EPROM chips falls with cumulative output but does not decrease over time or with the scale of production. With each doubling in the cumulative output of an EPROM chip, its average cost falls by 22%. This effect may encourage firms to produce more EPROM chips in the first few months after a new generation is introduced

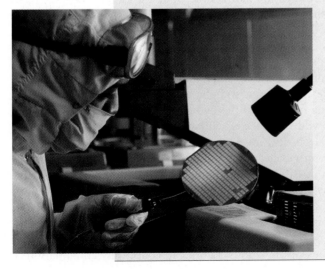

than they would without learning. By doing so, the firm gains experience more rapidly, which causes its average cost to fall more rapidly.

In contrast, the average cost of a DRAM chip does not fall with cumulative output but does fall with the time since introduction and exhibits economies of scale. With fast SRAM chips, only generation age affects average cost.

Although the type and speed of learning by doing vary across chips, they are the same across generations of the same chip. Thus firms know that they can count on their costs falling and build these predictable cost reductions into their planning over time.

7.5 | COST OF PRODUCING MULTIPLE GOODS

Few firms produce only a single good. We discuss single-output firms for simplicity. If a firm produces two or more goods, the cost of one good may depend on the output level of the other.

Outputs are linked if a single input is used to produce both of them. For example, mutton and wool both come from sheep, cattle provide beef and hides, and oil supplies both heating fuel and gasoline. It is less expensive to produce beef and hides together than separately. If the goods are produced together, a single steer yields one unit of beef and one hide. If beef and hides are produced separately (throwing away the unused good), the same amount of output requires two steers and more labor.

We say that there are **economies of scope** if it is less expensive to produce goods jointly than separately (Panzar and Willig, 1977, 1981). A measure of the degree to which there are economies of *scope* (*SC*) is

$$SC = \frac{C(q_1, 0) + C(0, q_2) - C(q_1, q_2)}{C(q_1, q_2)},$$

where $C(q_1, 0)$ is the cost of producing q_1 units of the first good by itself, $C(0, q_2)$ is the cost of producing q_2 units of the second good, and $C(q_1, q_2)$ is the cost of producing both goods together. If the cost of producing the two goods separately, $C(q_1, 0) + C(0, q_2)$, is the same as producing them together, $C(q_1, q_2)$, then *SC* is zero. If it is cheaper to produce the goods jointly, *SC* is positive. If *SC* is negative, there are diseconomies of scope, and the two goods should be produced separately.

To illustrate this idea, suppose that Laura spends one day collecting mushrooms and wild strawberries in the woods. Her **production possibility frontier**—the maximum amounts of outputs (mushrooms and strawberries) that can be produced from a fixed amount of input (Laura's effort during one day)—is PPF^1 in Figure 7.12. The production possibility frontier summarizes the trade-off Laura faces: she picks fewer mushrooms if she collects more strawberries in a day.

If Laura spends all day collecting only mushrooms, she picks 8 pints; if she spends all day picking strawberries, she collects 6 pints. If she picks some of each, however, she can harvest more total pints: 6 pints of mushrooms and 4 pints of strawberries. The product possibility frontier is concave (the middle of the curve is farther from the origin than it would be if it were a straight line) because of the diminishing marginal returns to collecting only one of the two goods. If she collects only mushrooms, she must walk past wild strawberries without picking them. As a result, she has to walk farther if she collects only mushrooms than if she picks both. Thus there are economies of scope in jointly collecting mushrooms and strawberries.

If instead the production possibility frontier were a straight line, the cost of producing the two goods jointly would not be lower. Suppose, for example, that mushrooms grow in one section of the woods and strawberries in another section. In that case, Laura can collect only mushrooms without passing any strawberries. That production possibility frontier is a straight line, PPF^2 in Figure 7.12. By allocating her time between the two sections of the woods, Laura can collect any combination of

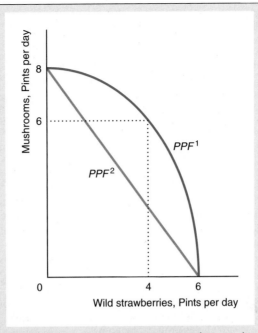

Figure 7.12 Joint Production. If there are economies of scope, the production possibility frontier is bowed away from the origin, *PPF*[1]. If instead the production possibility frontier is a straight line, *PPF*[2], the cost of producing both goods does not fall if they are produced together.

mushrooms and strawberries by spending part of her day in one section of the woods and part in the other.

A number of empirical studies show that some processes have economies of scope, others have none, and some have diseconomies of scope. Shoesmith (1988) found that there are economies of scope in refining. It is less expensive to produce gasoline, distillate fuels, and other refined products together than separately. Akridge and Hertel (1986) observed large economies of scope in producing various fertilizers together.

Friedlaender, Winston, and Wang (1983) found that for American automobile manufacturers, it is 25% less expensive (SC = 0.25) to produce large cars together with small cars and trucks than to produce large cars separately and small cars and trucks together. However, there are no economies of scope from producing trucks together with small and large cars. Producing trucks separately from cars is efficient.

Kim (1987) found substantial diseconomies of scope in using railroads to transport freight and passengers together. It is 41% less expensive (SC = −0.41) to transport passengers and freight separately than together. In the early 1970s, passenger service in the United States was transferred from the private railroad companies to Amtrak, and the services are now separate. Kim's estimates suggest that this separation is cost effective.

Application   **DEAD END**

Finally, dead people are pulling their weight—by providing "fuel" for heating thousands of homes in Sweden. The ovens of two high-tech crematoriums send power to local energy companies. The firms benefit from economies of scope because the costs of cremating and of producing energy are lower if the two activities are combined.

Summary

From all technologically efficient production processes, a firm chooses the one that is economically efficient. The economically efficient production process is the technologically efficient process for which the cost of producing a given quantity of output is lowest, or the one that produces the most output for a given cost.

1. **Measuring costs:** The economic or opportunity cost of a good is the value of its next best alternative use. Economic cost includes both explicit and implicit costs.

2. **Short-run costs:** In the short run, the firm can vary the costs of the factors that it can adjust, but the costs of other factors are fixed. The firm's average fixed cost falls as its output rises. If a firm has a short-run average cost curve that is U-shaped, its marginal cost curve is below the average cost curve when average cost is falling and above average cost when it is rising, so the marginal cost curve cuts the average cost curve at its minimum.

3. **Long-run costs:** In the long run, all factors can be varied, so all costs are variable. As a result, average cost and average variable cost are identical. The firm chooses the combination of inputs it uses to minimize its cost. To produce a given output level, it chooses the lowest isocost line that touches the rele-

vant isoquant, which is tangent to the isoquant. Equivalently, to minimize cost, the firm adjusts inputs until the last dollar spent on any input increases output by as much as the last dollar spent on any other input. If the firm calculates the cost of producing every possible output level given current input prices, it knows its cost function: Cost is a function of the input prices and the output level. If the firm's average cost falls as output expands, it has economies of scale. If its average cost rises as output expands, there are diseconomies of scale.

4. **Lower costs in the long run:** The firm can always do in the long run what it does in the short run, so its long-run cost can never be greater than its short-run cost. Because some factors are fixed in the short run, to expand output, the firm must greatly increase its use of other factors, which is relatively costly. In the long run, the firm can adjust all factors, a process that keeps its cost down. Long-run cost may also be lower than short-run cost if there is technological progress or learning by doing.

5. **Cost of producing multiple goods:** If it is less expensive for a firm to produce two goods jointly rather than separately, there are economies of scope. If there are diseconomies of scope, it is less expensive to produce the goods separately.

Problems

1. "There are certain fixed costs when you own a plane," [Andre] Agassi explained last week during a break in the action at the Volvo/San Francisco tennis tournament, "so the more you fly it, the more economic sense it makes. . . . The first flight

after I bought it, I took some friends to Palm Springs for lunch."[8] Discuss Agassi's statement.

2. The only variable input a janitorial service firm uses to clean offices is workers who are paid a wage, w, of $8 an hour. Each worker can clean

---

[8]Ostler, Scott, "Andre Even Flies like a Champ," *San Francisco Chronicle*, February 8, 1993, C1.

four offices in an hour. Use math to determine the variable cost, the average variable cost, and the marginal cost of cleaning one more office. Draw a diagram like Figure 7.1 to show the variable cost, average variable cost, and marginal cost curves.

3. Using the information in Table 7.1, construct another table showing how a lump-sum franchise tax of $30 affects the various average cost curves of the firm.

4. A firm builds shipping crates out of wood. How does the cost of producing a 1-cubic-foot crate (each side is 1 foot square) compare to the cost of building an 8-cubic-foot crate if wood costs $1 a square foot and the firm has no labor or other costs? More generally, how does cost vary with volume?

5. You have 60 minutes to take an exam with two questions. You want to maximize your score. Toward the end of the exam, the more time you spend on either question, the fewer extra points per minute you get for that question. How should you allocate your time between the two questions? (*Hint*: Think about producing an output of a score on the exam using inputs of time spent on each of the problems. Then use Equation 7.6.)

6. Boxes of cereal are produced by using a fixed-proportion production function: One box and one unit (8 ounces) of cereal produce one box of cereal. What is the expansion path?

7. Suppose that your firm's production function has constant returns to scale. What is the long-run expansion path?

8. The production process of the firm you manage uses labor and capital services. How does the long-run expansion path change when the wage increases while the rental rate of capital stays constant?

9. A U-shaped long-run average cost curve is the envelope of U-shaped short-run average cost curves. On what part of the curve (downward sloping, flat, or upward sloping) does a short-run curve touch the long-run curve? (*Hint*: Your answer should depend on where on the long-run curve the two curves touch.)

10. Suppose that the government subsidizes the cost of workers by paying for 25% of the wage (the rate offered by the U.S. government in the late 1970s under the New Jobs Tax Credit program). What effect will this subsidy have on the firm's choice of labor and capital to produce a given level of output?

11. Suppose in Solved Problem 7.1 that the government charges the firm a franchise tax each year (instead of only once). Describe the effect of this tax on the marginal cost, average variable cost, short-run average cost, and long-run average cost curves.

12. What can you say about Laura's economies of scope if her time is valued at $5 an hour and her production possibility frontier is PPF^1 in Figure 7.12?

13. *Review* (Chapter 6): What might cause the marginal product of capital to fall as output increases?

Math Problems

14. Give the formulas for and plot AFC, MC, AVC, and AC if the cost function is
    a. $C = 10 + 10q$
    b. $C = 10 + q^2$
    c. $C = 10 + 10q - 4q^2 + q^3$

15. What is the long-run cost function if the production function is $q = L + K$?

16. Gail works in a flower shop, where she produces 10 floral arrangements per hour. She is paid $10 an hour for the first eight hours she works and $15 an hour for each additional hour she works. What is the firm's cost function? What are its AC, AVC, and MC functions? Draw the AC, AVC, and MC curves.

17. A firm's cost curve is $C = F + 10q - bq^2 + q^3$, where $b > 0$.
    a. For what values of b are cost, average cost, and average variable cost positive? (From now on, assume that all these measures of cost are positive at every output level.)
    b. What is the shape of the AC curve? At what output level is the AC minimized?
    c. At what output levels does the MC curve cross the AC and the AVC curves?
    d. Use calculus to show that the MC curve must cross the AVC at its minimum point.

18. A firm has two plants that produce identical output. The cost functions are $C_1 = 10q - 4q^2 + q^3$

and $C_2 = 10q - 2q^2 + q^3$.

  a.   At what output levels does the average cost curve of each plant reach its minimum?

  b.   If the firm wants to produce 4 units of output, how much should it produce in each plant?

19. For a Cobb-Douglas production function, how does the expansion path change if the wage increases while the rental rate of capital stays the same? (*Hint*: See Appendix 7C.)

20. A firm has a Cobb-Douglas production function, $Q = AL^\alpha K^\beta$, where $\alpha + \beta < 1$. On the basis of this information, what properties does its cost function have?

21. A firm's average cost is $AC = \alpha q^\beta$, where $\alpha > 0$. How can you interpret α? (*Hint*: Suppose that $q = 1$.) What sign must β have if there is learning by doing? What happens to average cost as q gets large? Draw the average cost curve as a function of output for a particular set of α and β.

Competitive Firms and Markets

The love of money is the root of all virtue. —George Bernard Shaw

One of the major questions firms face is "How much should we produce?" To pick a level of output that maximizes its profit, a firm must consider its cost function and how much it can sell at a given price. The amount the firm thinks it can sell depends in turn on the market demand of consumers and its beliefs about how other firms in the market will behave. The behavior of firms depends on the **market structure:** the number of firms in the market, the ease with which firms can enter and leave the market, and the ability of firms to differentiate their products from those of their rivals.

In this chapter, we look at a competitive market structure, one in which many firms produce identical products and firms can easily enter and exit the market. Because each firm produces a small share of the total market output and its output is identical to that of other firms, each firm is a *price taker* that cannot raise its price above the market price. If it were to try to do so, this firm would be unable to sell any of its output because consumers would buy the good at a lower price from the other firms in the market. The market price summarizes all a firm needs to know about the demand of consumers *and* the behavior of its rivals. Thus a competitive firm can ignore the specific behavior of individual rivals in deciding how much to produce.[1]

IN THIS CHAPTER,

WE EXAMINE

FIVE MAIN

TOPICS

1. **Competition:** A competitive firm is a price taker, and as such, it faces a horizontal demand curve.
2. **Profit maximization:** To maximize profit, any firm must make two decisions: how much to produce and whether to produce at all.
3. **Competition in the short run:** Variable costs determine a profit-maximizing, competitive firm's supply curve, the market supply curve, and with the market demand curve, the competitive equilibrium in the short run.
4. **Competition in the long run:** Firm supply, market supply, and competitive equilibrium are different in the long run than in the short run because firms can vary inputs that were fixed in the short run.
5. **Zero profit for competitive firms in the long run:** In the long-run competitive market equilibrium, profit-maximizing firms break even, so firms that do not try to maximize profits lose money and leave the market.

---

[1] In contrast, each oligopolistic firm must consider the behavior of each of its small number of rivals, as we discuss in Chapter 13.

8.1 | COMPETITION

Competition is a common market structure that has very desirable properties, so it is useful to compare other market structures to competition. In this section, we describe the properties of competitive firms and markets. Next, we examine how competitive firms maximize profit to derive the short-run and long-run supply curves of competitive firms and competitive markets. Then we reexamine the competitive equilibrium.

Price Taking

When most people talk about "competitive firms," they mean firms that are rivals for the same customers. By this interpretation, any market that has more than one firm is competitive. However, to an economist, only some of these multifirm markets are competitive.

Economists say that a market is *competitive* if each firm in the market is a *price taker*: a firm that cannot significantly affect the market price for its output or the prices at which it buys its inputs. If any one of the more than 40,000 apple farms in the United States were to stop producing apples or to double its production, the market price of apples would not change appreciably. Similarly, by stopping production or doubling its production, an apple farm would have little or no effect on the price for apple seeds, fertilizer, and other inputs.

Why would a competitive firm be a price taker? It has no choice. The firm *has* to be a price taker if it faces a demand curve that is horizontal at the market price. If the demand curve is horizontal at the market price, the firm can sell as much as it wants at the market price, so it has no incentive to lower its price. Similarly, the firm cannot increase the price at which it sells by restricting its output because it faces an infinitely elastic demand (see Chapter 3): A small increase in price results in its demand falling to zero.

Why the Firm's Demand Curve Is Horizontal

Firms are likely to be price takers in markets that have some or all of four properties:

- Consumers believe that all firms in the market sell *identical products*.
- Firms *freely enter and exit* the market.
- *Buyers and sellers know the prices* charged by firms.
- *Transaction costs*—the expenses of finding a trading partner and making a trade for a good or service other than the price paid for that good or service—*are low*.

When the products of all firms are seen as perfect substitutes, no firm can sell its product if it charges more than others because no consumer is willing to pay a premium for that product. Consumers don't ask which farm grew an apple because they view apples as *homogeneous* or *undifferentiated* products. In contrast, consumers who know that the characteristics of a Jaguar and a Civic differ substantially view automobiles as *heterogeneous* or *differentiated* products. If some customers prefer one firm's product to those of other firms, the firm's demand curve has a downward slope. One firm can charge more than other firms without losing all its customers.

No firm can raise its price above the market price if other firms are able and eager to undercut another firm's high price to attract more customers. Even in markets with only a few firms, if other firms can quickly and easily enter, a firm cannot raise its price without other firms entering the market and undercutting its price. Moreover, ease of entry may cause the number of firms in a market to be large. The more firms there are in a market, the less the effect of a change in one firm's output on total market output and hence on the market price. If one of the 40,000 apple growers drops out of the market, market supply falls by only 0.0025% (assuming that the firms are of equal size), so the market price is unaffected.

If buyers know the prices other firms charge—the market price—a firm cannot raise its price without losing its customers. In contrast, if consumers do not know the prices other firms charge, a firm can charge more than other firms without losing all its customers, so its demand curve is downward sloping.

If transaction costs are low, it is easy for a customer to buy from a rival firm if the customer's usual supplier raises its price. Transaction costs are low if buyers and sellers do not have to spend time and money finding each other or hiring lawyers to write contracts in order to make a trade. The higher the transaction costs, the more likely it is that a firm's demand curve is downward sloping. Because finding a new, competent auto mechanic is very time consuming or involves traveling a great distance, some consumers continue to use their current auto repair shop even if it charges more than other firms. In some markets, buyers and sellers are brought together in a single room, so transaction costs are virtually zero. For example, transaction costs are very low at the auction in Amsterdam that the Verenigde Bloemenveilingen Aalsmeer cooperative holds daily for the 5,000 sellers who ship flowers from Zimbabwe, Colombia, Israel, Thailand, and Europe to 2,500 buyers around the world.

We call a market in which all these conditions hold a *perfectly competitive market*. In such a market, if a firm raised its price above the market price, the firm would be unable to make any sales. Its former customers would know that other firms sell an identical product at a lower price. These customers can easily find those other firms and buy from them without incurring extra transaction costs. If firms that are currently in the market cannot meet the demand of this firm's former customers, new firms can quickly and easily enter the market. Thus firms in such a market must be price takers.

The market for wheat is an example of an almost perfectly competitive market. Many farmers produce identical products, and transaction costs are negligible. Wheat is sold in a formal exchange or market such as the Chicago Commodity Exchange. Using a formal exchange, buyers and sellers can easily place buy or sell orders in person, over the telephone, or electronically, so transaction costs are negligible. No time is wasted in finding someone who wants to trade, and the transactions are made virtually instantaneously without much paperwork. Moreover, every buyer and seller in the market knows the market prices, quantities, and qualities of wheat available at any moment.

Even if some of these conditions are violated, firms and consumers may still be price takers. For example, even if entry of new firms is limited but the market has a very large number of firms and each can produce much more than its current output at about the same cost, firms are price takers. If one of these firms tries to raise its price, it will be unable to sell to consumers because other firms will expand their output if necessary to meet demand. A firm's demand curve is nearly horizontal as long as there are many firms in the market.

★Derivation of a Competitive Firm's Demand Curve

As a practical matter, are the demand curves faced by individual competitive firms flat? To answer this question, we use a modified supply-and-demand diagram to derive the demand curve an individual firm faces.

The demand curve that an individual firm faces is called the *residual demand curve*: the market demand that is not met by other sellers at any given price. The firm's residual demand function, $D^r(p)$, shows the quantity demanded from the firm at price p. A firm sells only to people who have not already purchased the good from another seller. We can determine how much demand is left for a particular firm at each possible price using the market demand curve and the supply curve for all *other* firms in the market. The quantity the market demands is a function of the price: $Q = D(p)$. The supply curve of other firms is $S^o(p)$. The residual demand function equals the market demand function, $D(p)$, minus the supply of all other firms:

$$D^r(p) = D(p) - S^o(p). \qquad (8.1)$$

At prices so high that $S^o(p)$ is greater than $D(p)$, the residual demand, $D^r(p)$, is zero.

In Figure 8.1, we derive the residual demand for a Canadian manufacturing firm that produces metal chairs. Panel b shows the market demand curve, D, and the supply of all but one manufacturing firm, S^o.[2] At $p = \$66$ per chair, the supply of other firms, 500 units (one unit being 1,000 metal chairs) per year, exactly equals the market demand (panel b), so the residual quantity demanded of the remaining firm (panel a) is zero.

At prices below $66, the other chair firms are not willing to supply as much as the market demands. At $p = \$63$, for example, the market demand is 527 units, but other firms want to supply only 434 units. As a result, the residual quantity demanded from the individual firm at $p = \$63$ is 93 (= 527 − 434) units. Thus the residual demand curve at any given price is the horizontal difference between the market demand curve and the supply of the other firms.

The residual demand curve the firm faces, panel a, is much flatter than the market demand curve, panel b. As a result, the elasticity of the residual demand curve is much higher than the market elasticity.

If there are n identical firms in the market, the elasticity of demand, ε_i, facing Firm i is

$$\varepsilon_i = n\varepsilon - (n-1)\eta_o, \qquad (8.2)$$

where ε is the market elasticity of demand (a negative number), η_o is the elasticity of supply of each of the other firms (typically a positive number), and $n - 1$ is the number of other firms (see Appendix 8A for a derivation).

---

[2]The figure uses constant elasticity demand and supply curves. The elasticity of supply, 3.1, is based on the estimated cost function from Robidoux and Lester (1988) for Canadian office furniture manufacturers. I estimate that the elasticity of demand is −1.1, using data from Statistics Canada, *Office Furniture Manufacturers*.

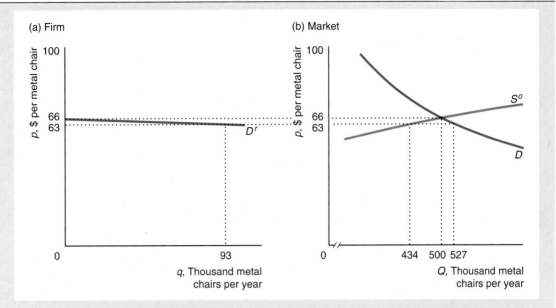

Figure 8.1 Residual Demand Curve. The residual demand curve, $D^r(p)$, a single office furniture manufacturing firm faces is the market demand, $D(p)$, minus the supply of the other firms in the market, $S^o(p)$. The residual demand curve is much flatter than the market demand curve.

There are $n = 78$ firms manufacturing metal chairs in Canada. If they are identical, the elasticity of demand facing a single firm is

$$\varepsilon_i = n\varepsilon - (n-1)\eta_o = [78 \times (-1.1)] - (77 \times 3.1)$$
$$= -85.8 - 238.7 = -324.5.$$

So even though the market demand elasticity is only -1.1, a typical firm faces a residual demand elasticity of -324.5. If a firm raises its price by one-tenth of a percent, the quantity it could sell would fall by nearly one-third. Therefore, the competitive model assumption that this firm faces a horizontal demand curve with an infinite price elasticity is not much of an exaggeration.

As Equation 8.2 shows, the residual demand curve a single firm faces is more elastic the more firms, n, in the market, the more elastic the market demand, ε, and the larger the elasticity of supply of the other firms, η_o.

Why We Study Perfect Competition

Economists spend a great deal of time discussing perfect competition, which takes place in markets in which firms are price takers because products are homogeneous, firms enter and exit the market freely, buyers and sellers know the prices charged by firms, and transaction costs are low.[3]

Perfectly competitive markets are important for two reasons. First, many markets can be reasonably described as competitive. Many agricultural and other commodity

---

[3]In addition, a perfectly competitive market has no externalities such as pollution (see Chapter 18).

markets, stock exchanges, retail and wholesale markets, building construction markets, and others have many or all of the properties of a perfectly competitive market. The competitive supply-and-demand model works well enough in these markets that it accurately predicts the effects of changes in taxes, costs, incomes, and other factors on market equilibrium.

Second, a perfectly competitive market has many desirable properties. Economists use this model as the ideal against which real-world markets are compared. Throughout the rest of this book, we show that society as a whole is worse off if the properties of the perfectly competitive market fail to hold. From this point on, for brevity, we use the phrase *competitive market* to mean a *perfectly competitive market* unless we explicitly note an imperfection.

8.2 PROFIT MAXIMIZATION

Economists usually assume that *all* firms—not just competitive firms—want to maximize their profits. One reason is that many businesspeople say that their objective is to maximize profits. A second reason is that firms—especially competitive firms—that do not maximize profit are likely to lose money and be driven out of business.

In this section, we discuss how any type of firm—not just a competitive firm—maximizes its profit. We then examine how a competitive firm in particular maximizes profit.

Profit

A firm's *profit*, π, is the difference between a firm's revenues, R, and its cost, C:

$$\pi = R - C.$$

If profit is negative, $\pi < 0$, the firm makes a *loss*.

Economists and businesspeople often measure profit differently. Because both economists and businesspeople measure revenue the same way—revenue is price times quantity—the difference in their profit measures is due to the way they measure costs (see Chapter 7). Some businesses use only explicit costs: a firm's out-of-pocket expenditures on inputs such as workers' wage payments, payments for materials, and payments for energy. *Economic cost* includes both explicit and implicit costs. Economic cost is the *opportunity cost*: the value of the best alternative use of any asset the firm employs.

Economic profit is revenue minus economic cost. Because explicit cost is less than economic cost, *business profit*—based on only explicit cost—is often larger than economic profit. The reason that this distinction is important is that a firm may make a costly mistake if it mismeasures profit by ignoring relevant opportunity costs.

A couple of examples illustrate the difference in the two profit measures and the importance of this distinction. First, let's return to the scenario in Chapter 7 in which you start your own firm.[4] You have to pay explicit costs such as workers' wages and the price of materials. Like many owners, you do not pay yourself a salary. Instead, you take home a business profit of $20,000 per year.

---

[4]Michael Dell started a mail-order computer company while he was in college. Today, it is the world's largest personal computer company. By 1999, his wealth reached $20 billion.

Economists (well-known spoilsports) argue that your profit is less than $20,000. Economic profit is business profit minus any additional opportunity cost. Suppose that you could have earned $25,000 a year working for someone else instead of running your business. The opportunity cost of your time working in your business is $25,000—your forgone salary. So even though your firm made a business profit of $20,000, you had an economic loss (negative economic profit) of $5,000. Put another way, the price of being your own boss is $5,000.

By looking at only the business profit and ignoring opportunity cost, you conclude that running your business is profitable. However, if you consider economic profit, you realize that working for others maximizes your income.

Similarly, when a firm decides whether to invest in a new venture, it must consider its next best alternative use of its funds. A firm that is considering setting up a new branch in Tucson must consider all the alternatives—placing the branch in Santa Fe, putting the money that the branch would cost in the bank and earning interest, and so on. If the best alternative use of the money is to put it in the bank and earn $10,000 per year in interest, the firm should build the new branch in Tucson only if it expects to make $10,000 or more per year in business profits. That is, the firm should create a Tucson branch only if its economic profit from the new branch is zero or positive. If its economic profit is zero, then it is earning the same return on its investment as it would from putting the money in its next best alternative, the bank. From this point on, when we use the term *profit*, we mean *economic profit* unless we specifically refer to business profit.

Application   BREAKING EVEN ON CHRISTMAS TREES

On the day after Thanksgiving each year, Tom Ruffino begins selling Christmas trees in Lake Grove, New York. The table summarizes his seasonal explicit costs.

Fixed Costs	
Permit	$ 300
Security (guard patrol when the lot is closed to prevent theft)	360
Insurance	700
Electricity	1,000
Lot rental (undeveloped land across from a major shopping mall)	2,500
Miscellaneous (fences, lot cleanup, snow removal)	2,000
Total fixed costs:	$6,860
Variable Costs	
Labor (two full-time employees at $12 an hour for 50 hours a week, plus some part-time workers)	$ 5,500
Trees (1,500 trees bought from a Canadian tree farm at $11.50 each)	17,250
Shipping (1,500 trees at $2 each)	3,000
Total variable costs:	$25,750
Total accounting costs:	$32,610

Mr. Ruffino sells trees for 29 days at the market price of $25 each. To break even, he has to sell an average of 45 trees per day, so his average cost is $25. If he can sell an average of 52 trees per day (1,508 trees total), he makes an accounting profit of $5,090 for the season.

To calculate his economic profit, he has to subtract his forgone earnings at another job and the interest he would have earned on the money he paid at the beginning of the month (on his fixed costs and the price of the trees, $27,110) if he had invested that money elsewhere, such as in a bank, for a month. Although the forgone interest is small, his alternative earnings could be a large proportion of his business profit.

Two Steps to Maximizing Profit

A firm's profit varies with its output level. The firm's profit function is

$$\pi(q) = R(q) - C(q).$$

A firm decides how much output to sell to maximize its profit. To maximize its profit, any firm (not just competitive, price-taking firms) must answer two questions:

- **Output decision:** If the firm produces, what output level, q^*, maximizes its profit or minimizes its loss?
- **Shutdown decision:** Is it more profitable to produce q^* or to shut down and produce no output?

The profit curve in Figure 8.2 illustrates these two basic decisions. This firm makes losses at very low and very high output levels and positive profits at moderate output levels. The profit curve first rises and then falls, reaching a maximum profit of π^* when its output is q^*. Because the firm makes a positive profit at that output, it chooses to produce q^* units of output.

Output Rules. A firm can use one of three equivalent rules to choose how much output to produce. All types of firms maximize profit using the same rules.

The most straightforward rule is

Output Rule 1: The firm sets its output where its profit is maximized.

The profit curve in Figure 8.2 is maximized at π^* when output is q^*. If the firm knows its entire profit curve, it can immediately set its output to maximize its profit.

Even if the firm does not know the exact shape of its profit curve, it may be able to find the maximum by experimenting. The firm slightly increases its output. If profit increases, the firm increases the output more. The firm keeps increasing output until profit does not change. At that output, the firm is at the peak of the profit curve. If profit falls when the firm first increases its output, the firm tries decreasing its output. It keeps decreasing its output until it reaches the peak of the profit curve.

What the firm is doing is experimentally determining the slope of the profit curve. The slope of the profit curve is the firm's **marginal profit**: the change in the profit

---

[5]The marginal profit is the derivative of the profit function, $\pi(q)$, with respect to quantity, $d\pi(q)/dq$.

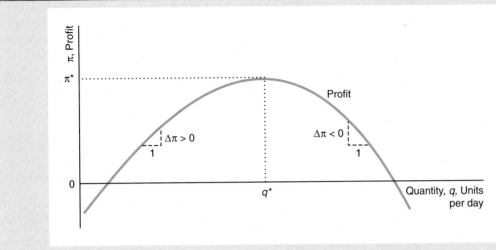

Figure 8.2 Maximizing Profit. By setting its output at q^*, the firm maximizes its profit at π^*.

the firm gets from selling one more unit of output, $\Delta\pi/\Delta q$.[5] In the figure, the marginal profit or slope is positive when output is less than q^*, zero when output is q^*, and negative when output is greater than q^*. Thus,

Output Rule 2: A firm sets its output where its marginal profit is zero.

A third way to express this profit-maximizing output rule is in terms of cost and revenue. The marginal profit depends on a firm's *marginal cost* and *marginal revenue*. A firm's *marginal cost* (MC) is the amount by which a firm's cost changes if it produces one more unit of output (Chapter 7): $MC = \Delta C/\Delta q$, where ΔC is the change in cost when output changes by Δq. Similarly, a firm's **marginal revenue**, MR, is the change in revenue it gets from selling one more unit of output: $\Delta R/\Delta q$, where ΔR is the change in revenue.[6] If a firm that was selling q units of output sells one more unit of output, the extra revenue, $MR(q)$, raises its profit, but the extra cost, $MC(q)$, lowers its profit. The change in the firm's profit is[7]

$$\text{Marginal profit}(q) = MR(q) - MC(q).$$

Does it pay for a firm to produce one more unit of output? If the marginal revenue from this last unit of output exceeds its marginal cost, $MR(q) > MC(q)$, the firm's marginal profit is positive, $MR(q) - MC(q) > 0$, so it pays to increase output. The firm

---

[6]The marginal revenue is the derivative of the revenue function with respect to quantity: $MR(q) = dR(q)/dq$.

[7]Because profit is $\pi(q) = R(q) - C(q)$, marginal profit is the difference between marginal revenue and marginal cost:

$$\frac{d\pi(q)}{dq} = \frac{dR(q)}{dq} - \frac{dC(q)}{dq} = MR - MC.$$

keeps increasing its output until its marginal profit = $MR(q) - MC(q) = 0$. There, its marginal revenue equals its marginal cost: $MR(q) = MC(q)$. If the firm produces more output where its marginal cost exceeds its marginal revenue, $MR(q) < MC(q)$, the extra output reduces the firm's profit. Thus a third, equivalent rule is (Appendix 8A):

> *Output Rule 3:* A firm sets its output where its marginal revenue equals its marginal cost
>
> $$MR(q) = MC(q).$$

Shutdown Rule. The firm chooses to produce if it can make a profit. If the firm is making a loss, however, does it shut down? The answer, surprisingly, is "It depends." The general rule, which holds for all types of firms in both the short run and in the long run, is

> *Shutdown Rule 1:* The firm shuts down only if it can reduce its loss by doing so.

In the short run, the firm has variable and sunk fixed costs (Chapter 7). By shutting down, it can eliminate the variable cost, such as labor and materials, but usually not the fixed cost, the amount it paid for its factory and equipment. By shutting down, the firm stops receiving revenue and stops paying the avoidable costs, but it is still stuck with its fixed cost. Thus it pays the firm to shut down only if its revenue is less than its avoidable cost.

Suppose that the firm's revenue is $R = \$2,000$, its variable cost is $VC = \$1,000$, and its fixed cost is $F = \$3,000$, which is the price it paid for a machine that it cannot resell or use for any other purpose. This firm is making a short-run loss:

$$\pi = R - VC - F = \$2,000 - \$1,000 - \$3,000 = -\$2,000.$$

If the firm shuts down, it loses its fixed cost, $3,000, so it is better off operating. Its revenue more than covers its avoidable, variable cost and offsets some of the fixed cost.

However, if its revenue is only $500, its loss is $3,500, which is greater than the loss from the fixed cost alone of $3,000. Because its revenue is less than its avoidable, variable cost, the firm reduces its loss by shutting down.

In conclusion, the firm compares its revenue to its variable cost only when deciding whether to stop operating. Because the fixed cost is *sunk*—the expense cannot be avoided by stopping operations (Chapter 7)—the firm pays this cost whether it shuts down or not. Thus the sunk fixed cost is irrelevant to the shutdown decision.[8]

In the long run, all costs are avoidable because the firm can eliminate them all by shutting down. Thus in the long run, where the firm can avoid all losses by not

---

[8]We usually assume that fixed cost is sunk. However, if a firm can sell its capital for as much as it paid, its fixed cost is avoidable and should be taken into account when the firm is considering whether to shut down. A firm with a fully avoidable fixed cost always shuts down if it makes a short-run loss. If a firm buys a specialized piece of machinery for $1,000 that can be used only in its business but can be sold for scrap metal for $100, then $100 of the fixed cost is avoidable and $900 is sunk. Only the avoidable portion of fixed cost is relevant for the shutdown decision.

operating, it pays to shut down if the firm faces any loss at all. As a result, we can restate the shut-down rule as:

> *Shutdown Rule 2:* The firm shuts down only if its revenue is less than its avoidable cost.

This rule holds for all types of firms in both the short run and the long run.

8.3 | COMPETITION IN THE SHORT RUN

Having considered how firms maximize profit in general, we now examine the profit-maximizing behavior of competitive firms, first in the short run and then in the long run. In doing so, we pay careful attention to the firm's shutdown decision.

Short-Run Competitive Profit Maximization

A competitive firm, like other firms, first determines the output at which it maximizes its profit (or minimizes its loss). Second, it decides whether to produce or to shut down.

Short-Run Output Decision. We've already seen that *any* firm maximizes its profit at the output where its marginal profit is zero or, equivalently, where its marginal cost equals its marginal revenue. Because it faces a horizontal demand curve, a competitive firm can sell as many units of output as it wants at the market price, p. Thus a competitive firm's revenue, $R = pq$, increases by p if it sells one more unit of output, so its marginal revenue is p.[9] For example, if the firm faces a market price of $2 per unit, its revenue is $10 if it sells 5 units and $12 if it sells 6 units, so its marginal revenue for the sixth unit is $2 = $12 − $10 (the market price). Because a competitive firm's marginal revenue equals the market price, *a profit-maximizing competitive firm produces the amount of output at which its marginal cost equals the market price:*

$$MC(q) = p. \tag{8.3}$$

To illustrate how a competitive firm maximizes its profit, we examine a typical Canadian lime manufacturing firm, which we assume is a price taker. Lime is a nonmetallic mineral used in mortars, plasters, cements, bleaching powders, steel, paper, glass, and other products. The lime plant's estimated cost curve, C, in panel a of Figure 8.3 rises less rapidly with output at low quantities than at higher quantities.[10] If the market price of lime is $p = $8, the competitive firm faces a horizontal demand curve at $8 (panel b), so the revenue curve, $R = pq = $8q$, in panel a is an upward-sloping straight line with a slope of 8.

---

[9]Because $R(q) = pq$, $MR = dR(q)/dq = d(pq)/dq = p$.

[10]Robidoux and Lester (1988) estimate the variable cost function. In the figure, we assume that the minimum of the average variable cost curve is $5 at 50,000 metric tons of output. Based on information from Statistics Canada, we set the fixed cost so that the average cost is $6 at 140,000 tons.

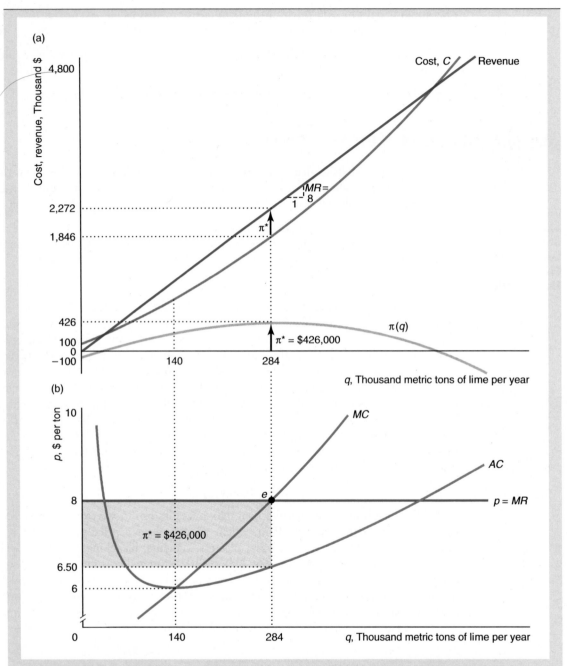

(a)

Cost, revenue, Thousand $

4,800

Cost, *C*   Revenue

MR = $\frac{8}{1}$

2,272

1,846

π^*

426

100

0

−100

$\pi(q)$

$\pi^* = \$426,000$

140   284

q, Thousand metric tons of lime per year

(b)

p, $ per ton

10

MC

AC

8   *e*   *p = MR*

$\pi^* = \$426,000$

6.50

6

1

0   140   284   *q*, Thousand metric tons of lime per year

Figure 8.3 How a Competitive Firm Maximizes Profit. (a) A competitive lime manufacturing firm produces 284 units of lime so as to maximize its profit at $\pi^* = \$426,000$ (Robidoux and Lester, 1988). (b) The firm's profit is maximized where its marginal revenue, *MR*, which is the market price, *p* = \$8, equals its marginal cost, *MC*.

By producing 284 units (one unit being 1,000 metric tons), the firm maximizes its profit at $\pi^* = \$426,000$, which is the height of the profit curve and the difference between the revenue and cost curves at that quantity in panel a. At the competitive firm's profit-maximizing output, its marginal cost equals the market price of $8 (Equation 8.3) at point e in panel b.

Point e is the competitive firm's equilibrium. Were the firm to produce less than the equilibrium quantity, 284 units, the market price would be above its marginal cost. As a result, the firm could increase its profit by expanding output because the firm earns more on the next ton, $p = \$8$, than it costs to produce it, $MC < \$8$. If the firm were to produce more than 284 units, so market price was below its marginal cost, $MC > \$8$, the firm could increase its profit by reducing its output. Thus the firm does not want to change its quantity only at output when its marginal cost equals the market price.

The firm's maximum profit, $\pi^* = \$426,000$, is the shaded rectangle in panel b. The length of the rectangle is the number of units sold, $q = 284$ units. The height of the rectangle is the firm's average profit, which is the difference between the market price, or average revenue, and its average cost:

$$\frac{\pi}{q} = \frac{R - C}{q} = \frac{pq}{q} - \frac{C}{q} = p - AC. \tag{8.4}$$

Here the average profit per unit is $\$1.50 = p - AC(284) = \$8 - \$6.50$.

As panel b illustrates, the firm chooses its output level to maximize its total profit rather than its profit per ton. By producing 140 units, where its average cost is minimized at $6, the firm could maximize its average profit at $2. Although the firm gives up 50¢ in profit per ton when it produces 284 units instead of 140 units, it more than makes up for that by selling an extra 144 units. The firm's profit is $146,000 higher at 284 units than at 140 units.

Using the $MC = p$ rule, a firm can decide how much to alter its output in response to a change in its cost due to a new tax. For example, one of the many lime plants in Canada is in the province of Manitoba. If that province taxes that lime firm, the Manitoba firm is the only one in the lime market affected by the tax, so the tax will not affect market price. Solved Problem 8.1 shows how a profit-maximizing competitive firm would react to a tax that affected only it.

Solved Problem 8.1   If a specific tax of τ is collected from only one competitive firm, how should that firm change its output level to maximize its profit, and how does its maximum profit change?

Answer

1. *Show how the tax shifts the marginal cost and average cost curves:* The firm's before-tax marginal cost curve is MC^1 and its before-tax average cost curve is AC^1. Because the specific tax adds τ to the per-unit cost, it

shifts the after-tax marginal cost curve up to $MC^2 = MC^1 + \tau$ and the after-tax average cost curve to $AC^2 = AC^1 + \tau$ (see Chapter 7).

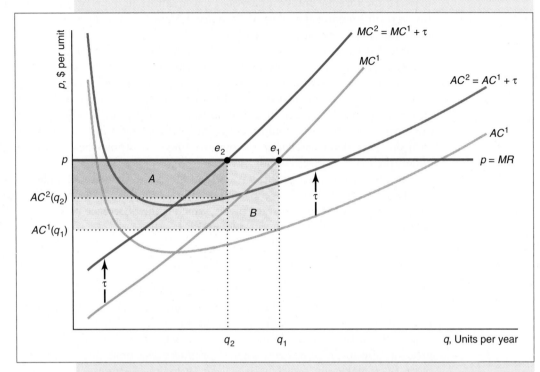

2. *Determine the before-tax and after-tax equilibria and the amount by which the firm adjusts its output*: Where the before-tax marginal cost curve, MC^1, hits the horizontal demand curve, p, at e_1, the profit-maximizing quantity is q_1. The after-tax marginal cost curve, MC^2, intersects the demand curve, p, at e_2 where the profit-maximizing quantity is q_2. Thus in response to the tax, the firm produces $q_1 - q_2$ fewer units of output.

3. *Show how the profit changes after the tax*: Because the market price is constant but the firm's average cost curve shifts upward, the firm's profit at every output level falls. The firm sells fewer units (because of the increase in MC) and makes less profit per unit (because of the increase in AC). The after-tax profit is area $A = \pi_2 = [p - AC^2(q_2)]q_2$, and the before-tax profit is area $A + B = \pi_1 = [p - AC^1(q_1)]q_1$, so profit falls by area B due to the tax.

Short-Run Shutdown Decision. Does the competitive lime firm operate or shut down? At the market price of $8 in Figure 8.3, the lime firm is making an economic profit, so it chooses to operate.

If the market price falls below $6, which is the minimum of the average cost curve, the price does not cover average cost, so average profit is negative (using Equation 8.4), and the firm makes a loss. (A firm cannot "lose a little on every sale but make it up on volume.") The firm shuts down only if doing so reduces or eliminates its loss.

The firm can gain by shutting down only if its revenue is less than its short-run variable cost:

$$pq < VC. \tag{8.5}$$

By dividing both sides of Equation 8.5 by output, we can write this condition as

$$p < AVC(q).$$

A competitive firm shuts down if the market price is less than the minimum of its short-run average variable cost curve.

We illustrate this rule in Figure 8.4 using the lime firm's cost curves. The minimum of the average variable cost, point *a*, is $5 at 50 units (one unit again being 1,000 metric tons). If the market price is less than $5 per ton, the firm shuts down. The firm stops hiring labor, buying materials, and paying for energy, thereby avoiding these variable costs. If the market price rises above $5, the firm starts operating again.

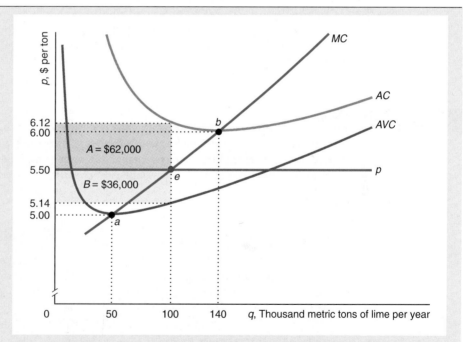

Figure 8.4 The Short-Run Shutdown Decision. The competitive lime manufacturing plant operates if price is above the minimum of the average variable cost curve, point *a*, at $5. With a market price of $5.50, the firm produces 100 units because that price is above *AVC*(100) = $5.14, so the firm more than covers its out-of-pocket, variable costs. At that price, the firm makes a loss of area *A* = $62,000 because the price is less than the average cost of $6.12. If it shuts down, its loss is its fixed cost, area *A* + *B* = $98,000. Thus the firm does not shut down.

In this figure, the market price is $5.50 per ton. Because the minimum of the firm's average cost, $6 (point *b*), is more than $5.50, the firm loses money if it produces.

If the firm produces, it sells 100 units at *e*, where its marginal cost curve intersects its demand curve, which is horizontal at $5.50. By operating, the firm loses area *A*, or $62,000. The length of *A* is 100 units, and the height is the average loss per ton, or 62¢, which equals the price of $5.50 minus the average cost at 100 units of $6.12.

The firm is better off producing than shutting down. If the firm shuts down, it has no revenue or variable cost, so its loss is the fixed cost, $98,000, which equals area *A* + *B*. The length of this box is 100 units, and its height is the lost average fixed cost of 98¢, which is the difference between the average variable cost and the average cost at 100 units.

The firm saves area *B* = $36,000 by producing rather than shutting down. This amount is the money left over from the revenue after paying for the variable cost, which helps cover part of the fixed cost.

In summary, a competitive firm uses a two-step decision-making process to maximize its profit. First, the competitive firm determines the output that maximizes its profit or minimizes its loss when its marginal cost equals the market price (which is its marginal revenue): $MC = p$. Second, the firm chooses to produce that quantity unless it would lose more by operating than by shutting down. The firm shuts down only if the market price is less than the minimum of its average variable cost, $p < AVC$.

Solved Problem 8.2   **A competitive firm's bookkeeper, upon reviewing the firm's books, finds that the firm spent twice as much on its plant, a fixed cost, as the firm's manager had previously thought. Should the manager change the output level because of this new information? How does this new information affect profit?**

Answer

1. *Show that a change in fixed costs does not affect the firm's decisions*: How much the firm produces and whether it shuts down in the short run depend only on the firm's variable costs. (The firm picks its output level so that its marginal cost—which depends only on variable costs—equals the market price, and it shuts down only if market price is less than its minimum average variable cost.) Learning that the amount spent on the plant was greater than previously believed should not change the output level that the manager chooses.

2. *Show that the change in how the bookkeeper measures fixed costs does not affect economic profit*: The change in the bookkeeper's valuation of the historical amount spent on the plant may affect the firm's short-run business profit but does not affect the firm's true economic profit. The economic profit is based on opportunity costs—the amount for which the firm could rent the plant to someone else—and not on historical payments.

**Short-Run
Firm Supply
Curve**

We just demonstrated how a competitive firm chooses its output for a given market price so as to maximize its profit. By repeating this analysis at different possible market prices, we learn how the amount the competitive firm supplies varies with the market price.

Tracing Out the Short-Run Supply Curve. As the market price increases from p_1 = \$5 to p_2 = \$6 to p_3 = \$7 to p_4 = \$8, the lime firm increases its output from 50 to 140 to 215 to 285 units per year in Figure 8.5. The equilibrium at each market price, e_1 through e_4, is determined by the intersection of the relevant demand curve—market price line—and the firm's marginal cost curve. That is, as the market price increases, the equilibria trace out the marginal cost curve.

If the price falls below the firm's minimum average variable cost at \$5, the firm shuts down. Thus *the competitive firm's short-run supply curve is its marginal cost curve above its minimum average variable cost.*

The firm's short-run supply curve, *S*, is a thick line in the figure. At prices above \$5, the short-run supply curve is the same as the marginal cost curve. The supply is zero when price is less than the minimum of the *AVC* curve of \$5. (From now on, we will not show the supply curve at prices below minimum *AVC*, to keep the graph as simple as possible.)

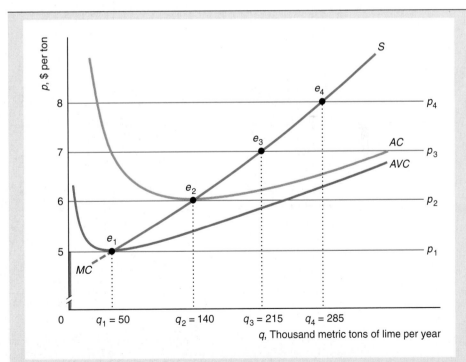

Figure 8.5 How the Profit-Maximizing Quantity Varies with Price. As the market price increases, the lime manufacturing firm produces more output. The change in the price traces out the marginal cost curve of the firm.

Factor Prices and the Short-Run Firm Supply Curve. An increase in factor prices causes the production costs of a firm to rise, shifting the firm's supply curve to the left. If all factor prices double, it costs the firm twice as much as before to produce a given level of output. If only one factor price rises, costs rise less than in proportion.

To illustrate the effect of an increase in a single factor price on supply, we examine a vegetable oil mill. This firm uses vegetable oil seed to produce canola and soybean oils, which customers use in commercial baking and soap making, as lubricants, and for other purposes. At the initial factor prices, a Canadian oil mill's average variable cost curve, AVC^1, reaches its minimum of $7 at 100 units (where one unit is 100 metric tons) of vegetable oil, as in Figure 8.6 (based on the estimates of the variable cost function for vegetable oil mills by Robidoux and Lester, 1988). As a result, the firm's initial short-run supply curve, S^1, is the initial marginal cost curve, MC^1, above $7.

If the wage, the price of energy, or the price of oil seeds increases, the cost of production rises for a vegetable oil mill. The vegetable oil mill cannot substitute between oil seeds and other factors of production. The cost of oil seeds is 95% of the variable cost. Thus if the price of raw materials increases by 25%, variable cost

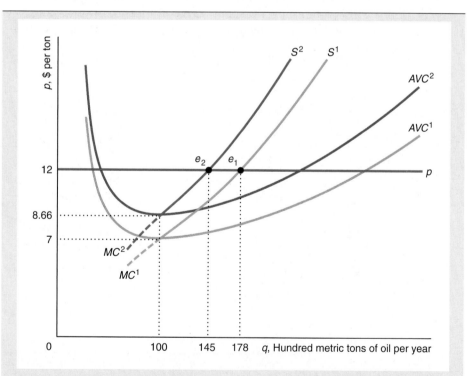

Figure 8.6 Effect of an Increase in the Cost of Materials on the Vegetable Oil Supply Curve. Materials are 95% of variable costs, so when the price of materials rises by 25%, variable costs rise by 23.75% (95% of 25%). As a result, the supply curve of a vegetable oil mill shifts up from S^1 to S^2. If the market price is $12, the quantity supplied falls from 178 to 145 units.

rises by 95% × 25%, or 23.75%. This increase in the price of oil seeds causes the marginal cost curve to shift from MC^1 to MC^2 and the average variable cost curve to go from AVC^1 to AVC^2 in the figure. As a result, the firm's short-run supply curve shifts upward from S^1 to S^2. The price increase causes the shutdown price to rise from $7 per unit to $8.66. At a market price of $12 per unit, at the original factor prices, the firm produces 178 units. After the increase in the price of vegetable oil seeds, the firm produces only 145 units if the market price remains constant.

Short-Run Market Supply Curve

The market supply curve is the horizontal sum of the supply curves of all the individual firms in the market (see Chapter 2). In the short run, the maximum number of firms in a market, n, is fixed because new firms need time to enter the market. If all the firms in a competitive market are identical, each firm's supply curve is identical, so the market supply at any price is n times the supply of an individual firm. Where firms have different shutdown prices, the market supply reflects a different number of firms at various prices even in the short run. We examine competitive markets first with firms that have identical costs and then with firms that have different costs.

Short-Run Market Supply with Identical Firms. To illustrate how to construct a short-run market supply curve, we suppose that the lime manufacturing market has $n = 5$ competitive firms with identical cost curves. Panel a of Figure 8.7 plots the short-run supply curve, S^1, of a typical firm—the MC curve above the minimum AVC—

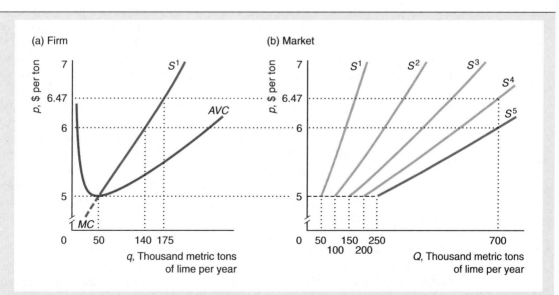

Figure 8.7 **Short-Run Market Supply with Five Identical Lime Firms.** (a) The short-run supply curve, S^1, for a typical lime manufacturing firm is its MC above the minimum of its AVC. (b) The market supply curve, S^5, is the horizontal sum of the supply curves of each of the five identical firms. The curve S^4 shows what the market supply curve would be if there were only four firms in the market.

where the horizontal axis shows the firm's output, q, per year. Panel b illustrates the competitive market supply curve, the dark line S^5, where the horizontal axis is market output, Q, per year. The price axis is the same in the two panels.

If the market price is less than $5 per ton, no firm supplies any output, so the market supply is zero. At $5, each firm is willing to supply $q = 50$ units, as in panel a. Consequently, the market supply is $Q = 5q = 250$ units in panel b. At $6 per ton, each firm supplies 140 units, so the market supply is 700 (= 5×140) units.

Suppose, however, that there were fewer than five firms in the short run. The light-color lines in panel b show the market supply curves for various other numbers of firms. The market supply curve is S^1 if there is one price-taking firm, S^2 with two firms, S^3 with three firms, and S^4 with four firms. The market supply curve flattens as the number of firms in the market increases because the market supply curve is the horizontal sum of more and more upward-sloping firm supply curves. As the number of firms grows very large, the market supply curve approaches a horizontal line at $5. Thus *the more identical firms producing at a given price, the flatter (more elastic) the short-run market supply curve at that price.* As a result, the more firms in the market, the less the price has to increase for the short-run market supply to increase substantially. Consumers pay $6 per ton to obtain 700 units of lime if there are five firms but must pay $6.47 per ton to obtain that much with only four firms.

Short-Run Market Supply with Firms That Differ. If the firms in a competitive market have different minimum average variable costs, not all firms produce at every price, a situation that affects the shape of the short-run market supply curve. Suppose that the only two firms in the lime market are our typical lime firm with a supply curve of S^1 and another firm with a higher marginal and minimum average cost with the supply curve of S^2 in Figure 8.8. The first firm produces at a market price of $5 or above, whereas the second firm does not produce unless the price is $6 or more. At $5, the first firm produces 50 units, so the quantity on the market supply curve, S, is 50 units. Between $5 and $6, only the first firm produces, so the market supply, S, is the same as the first firm's supply, S^1. At and above $6, both firms produce, so the market supply curve is the horizontal summation of their two individual supply curves. For example, at $7, the first firm produces 215 units, and the second firm supplies 100 units, so the market supply is 315 units.

As with the identical firms, where both firms are producing, the market supply curve is flatter than that of either firm. Because the second firm does not produce at as low a price as the first firm, the short-run market supply curve has a steeper slope (less elastic supply) at relatively low prices than it would if the firms were identical.

Where firms differ, only the low-cost firm supplies goods at relatively low prices. As the price rises, the other, higher-cost firm starts supplying, creating a stairlike market supply curve. The more suppliers there are with differing costs, the more steps there are in the market supply curve. As price rises and more firms are supplying goods, the market supply curve flattens, so it takes a smaller increase in price to increase supply by a given amount. Stated the other way, the more firms differ in costs, the steeper the market supply curve at low prices. Differences in costs are one explanation for why some market supply curves are upward sloping.

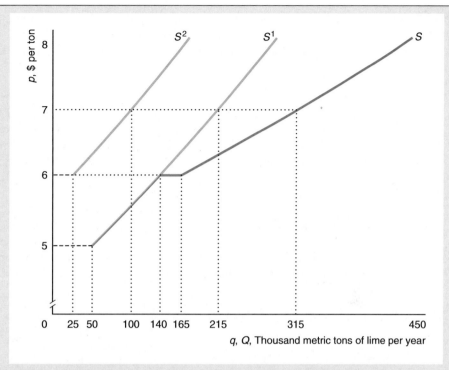

Figure 8.8 **Short-Run Market Supply with Two Different Lime Firms.** The supply curve S^1 is the same as for the typical lime firm in Figure 8.7. A second firm has a MC that lies to the left of the original firm's cost curve and a higher minimum of its AVC. Thus its supply curve, S^2, lies above and to the left of the original firm's supply curve, S^1. The market supply curve, S, is the horizontal sum of the two supply curves. When prices are high enough for both firms to produce, $6 and above, the market supply curve is flatter than the supply curve of either individual firm.

Application   SHUTTING DOWN OIL WELLS

The average variable cost of bringing underground oil to the earth's surface differs across wells, depending on the depth of the oil reserve, the quantity of oil, and other factors. Thus some oil wells may be shut down while others nearby still operate. In response to the drop in oil prices in 1998–1999, 136,000 of the 574,000 oil wells in the United States were shut down temporarily or permanently abandoned.

Terry Smith, the general manager of Tidelands Oil Production Company, shut down 327 of his company's 834 wells in response to sinking oil prices. He said that he would operate these wells at prices above $10 a barrel.

Short-Run Competitive Equilibrium

By combining the short-run market supply curve and the market demand curve, we can determine the short-run competitive equilibrium. We first show how to determine the equilibrium in the lime market, and we then examine how the equilibrium changes when firms are taxed.

Short-Run Equilibrium in the Lime Market. Suppose that there are five identical firms in the short-run equilibrium in the lime manufacturing industry. Panel a of Figure 8.9 shows the short-run cost curves and the supply curve, S^1, for a typical firm, and panel b shows the corresponding short-run competitive market supply curve, S.

In panel b, the initial demand curve D^1 intersects the market supply curve at E_1, the market equilibrium. The equilibrium quantity is $Q_1 = 1,075$ units of lime per year, and the equilibrium market price is $7.

In panel a, each competitive firm faces a horizontal demand curve at the equilibrium price of $7. Each price-taking firm chooses its output where its marginal cost curve intersects the horizontal demand curve at e_1. Because each firm is maximizing its profit at e_1, no firm wants to change its behavior, so e_1 is the firm's equilibrium. In panel a, each firm makes a short-run profit of area $A + B = \$172,000$, which is

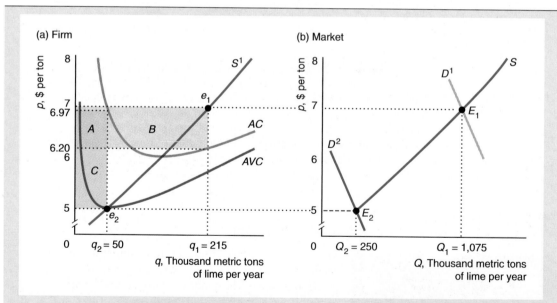

Figure 8.9 Short-Run Competitive Equilibrium in the Lime Market. (a) The short-run supply curve is the marginal cost above minimum average variable cost of $5. At a price of $5, each firm makes a short-run loss of $(p - AC)q = (\$5 - \$6.97) \times 50,000 = -\$98,500$, area $A + C$. At a price of $7, the short-run profit of a typical lime firm is $(p - AC)q = (\$7 - \$6.20) \times 215,000 = \$172,000$, area $A + B$. (b) If there are five firms in the lime market in the short run, so the market supply is S, and the market demand curve is D^1, then the short-run equilibrium is E_1, the market price is $7, and market output is $Q_1 = 1,075$ units. If the demand curve shifts to D^2, the market equilibrium is $p = \$5$ and $Q_2 = 250$ units.

the average profit per ton, $p - AC = \$7 - \$6.20 = 80¢$, times the firm's output, $q_1 = 215$ units. The equilibrium market output, Q_1, is the number of firms, n, times the equilibrium output of each firm: $Q_1 = nq_1 = 5 \times 215$ units $= 1,075$ units (panel b).

Now suppose that the demand curve shifts to D^2. The new market equilibrium is E_2, where the price is only $5. At that price, each firm produces $q = 50$ units, and market output is $Q = 250$ units. In panel a, each firm loses $98,500, area $A + C$, because it makes an average per ton of $(p - AC) = (\$5 - \$6.97) = -\$1.97$ and it sells $q_2 = 50$ units. However, such a firm does not shut down because price equals the firm's average variable cost, so the firm is covering its out-of-pocket expenses.

Effect of a Specific Tax on Short-Run Equilibrium. A tax that is applied to all firms in the market shifts the market supply curve, thereby altering the short-run equilibrium. In Figure 8.10, the government collects a specific tax of τ per unit from each of the identical firms in a competitive market. The specific tax causes both the marginal and average cost curves of each firm to shift up by τ in panel a (Solved Problem 8.1), which causes the firm's supply curve to move upward by τ.

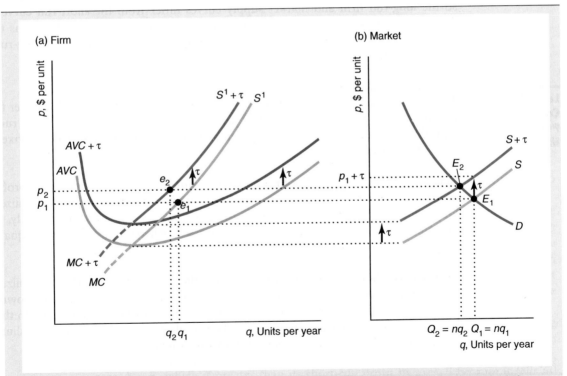

Figure 8.10 Short-Run Effect of a Specific Tax in the Lime Market. (a) A specific tax of τ per unit causes each identical firm's MC and AC curves to shift upward by τ, so the firm's short-run supply curve shifts upward from S^1 to $S^1 + \tau$. (b) As a result, the short-run market supply curve shifts from S to $S + \tau$. If the market demand curve is D, price rises by less than τ, and both market quantity and each firm's output fall.

Long-Run Market Supply Curve

The competitive market supply curve is the horizontal sum of the supply curves of the individual firms in both the short run and the long run. Because the maximum number of firms in the market is fixed in the short run, we add the supply curves of a known number of firms to obtain the short-run market supply curve. The only way for the market to supply more output in the short run is for existing firms to produce more.

In the long run, firms can enter or leave the market. Thus before we can add all the relevant firm supply curves to obtain the long-run market supply curve, we need to determine how many firms are in the market at each possible market price.

To construct the long-run market supply curve properly, we also have to determine how input prices vary with output. As the market expands or contracts substantially, changes in factor prices may shift firms' cost and supply curves. If so, we need to determine how such shifts in factor prices affect firm supply curves so that we can properly construct the market supply curve. The effect of changes in input prices is greater in the long run than in the short run because market output can change more dramatically in the long run.

We now look in detail at how entry and changing factor prices affect long-run market supply. We first derive the long-run market supply curve, assuming that the price of inputs remains constant as market output increases, so as to isolate the role of entry. We then examine how the market supply curve is affected if the price of inputs changes as market output rises.

Role of Entry and Exit. The number of firms in a market in the long run is determined by the *entry* and *exit* of firms. In the long run, each firm decides whether to enter or exit, depending on whether it can make a long-run profit.

In many markets, firms face barriers to entry or must incur significant costs to enter. Many city governments limit the number of cab drivers, creating an insurmountable barrier that prevents additional firms from entering. To enter other markets, a new firm has to hire consultants to determine the profit opportunities, pay lawyers to write contracts, and incur other expenses. Typically, such costs of entry or exit are fixed costs.

Even if existing firms are making positive profits, no entry occurs in the short run if entering firms need time to find a location, build a new plant, and hire workers. In the long run, firms enter the market if they can make profits by so doing. The costs of entry are often lower, and hence the profits from entering are higher, if a firm takes its time to enter. As a result, firms may enter markets long after profit opportunities first appear. For example, McDonald's announced that it would spend about $100 million to open 50 additional restaurants in Britain over four years.[11]

In contrast, firms usually react faster to losses than to potential profits. We expect firms to shut down or exit the market quickly in the short run when price is below average variable cost.

In some markets, there are no barriers or fixed costs to entry, so firms can freely enter and exit. For example, many construction firms, which have no capital and provide only labor services, engage in *hit-and-run* entry and exit: They enter the market whenever they can make a profit and exit when they can't. These firms may enter and exit markets several times a year.

---

[11] "McDonald's Plans 50 New Restaurants in Britain," *New York Times*, December 29, 1994:C4.

In such markets, a shift of the market demand curve to the right attracts firms to enter. For example, if there were no government regulations, the market for taxicabs would have free entry and exit. Car owners could enter or exit the market virtually instantaneously. If the demand curve for cab rides shifted to the right, the market price would rise, and existing cab drivers would make unusually high profits in the short run. Seeing these profits, other car owners would enter the market, causing the market supply curve to shift to the right and the market price to fall. Entry occurs until the last firm to enter—the *marginal firm*—makes zero long-run profit.

Similarly, if the demand curve shifts to the left so that the market price drops, firms suffer losses. Firms with minimum average costs above the new, lower market price exit the market. Firms continue to leave the market until the next firm considering leaving, the marginal firm, is again earning a zero long-run profit.

Thus in a market with free entry and exit:

- A firm enters the market if it can make a long-run profit, $\pi > 0$.
- A firm exits the market to avoid a long-run loss, $\pi < 0$.

If firms in a market are making zero long-run profit, they are indifferent between staying in the market and exiting. We presume that if they are already in the market, they stay in the market when they are making zero long-run profit.

Most transportation markets are thought to have free entry and exit unless governments regulate them. Relatively few airline, trucking, or shipping firms may serve a particular route, but they face extensive potential entry. Other firms can and will quickly enter and serve a route if a profit opportunity appears. Entrants shift their highly mobile equipment from less profitable routes to more profitable ones.

Application   **THREAT OF ENTRY IN SHIPPING**

Davies (1986) argued that in international ocean liner shipping, a market in which only a few firms serve a route, firms enter and exit frequently, so the threat of entry drives economic profits to zero. Only seven firms provide services between Canada and Japan, China, Korea, and Pacific Russia; only eight firms serve the Canada–Continental Europe route.

Existing firms can quickly shift ships from one route to another. With the increased use of internationally standardized container ships, liners can travel any route (in the past, the type of ship differed across routes). New and used vessels and equipment are sold on a world market that is accessible to all firms. As a result, potential entrants can easily rent equipment rather than have to raise large sums to buy liners. Similarly, exit is easy today. A firm exiting all markets can readily sell its used equipment.

As a result, firms engage in hit-and-run entry and exit to take advantage of fleeting profit opportunities. For example, for the nine principal trade routes to and from Canada, in a two-year period, the number of new services (152) on routes was 41% of the original number (373), while services terminated (109) were 29% of the original number. Thus even though relatively few firms serve any given route, firms can enter and exit easily and do so frequently.

market is $Q = nq = n \times 150$ units. Extra market output is obtained by new firms entering the market.

In summary, the long-run market supply curve is horizontal if the market has free entry and exit, an unlimited number of firms have identical costs, and input prices are constant. When these strong assumptions do not hold, the long-run market supply curve has a slope, as we now show.

Long-Run Market Supply When Entry Is Limited. If the number of firms in a market is limited in the long run, the market supply curve slopes upward. The number of firms is limited if the government restricts that number, if firms need a scarce resource, or if entry is costly. An example of a scarce resource is the limited number of lots on which a luxury beachfront hotel can be built in Miami. High entry costs restrict the number of firms in a market because firms enter only if the long-run economic profit is greater than the cost of entering.

The only way to get more output if the number of firms is limited is for existing firms to produce more. Because individual firms' supply curves slope upward, the long-run market supply curve is also upward sloping. The reasoning is the same as in the short run, as panel b of Figure 8.7 illustrates, given that no more than five firms can enter. The market supply curve is the upward-sloping S^5 curve, which is the horizontal sum of the five firms' upward-sloping marginal cost curves above minimum average cost.

Long-Run Market Supply When Firms Differ. A second reason why some long-run market supply curves slope upward is that firms differ. Firms with relatively low minimum long-run average costs are willing to enter the market at lower prices than others, resulting in an upward-sloping long-run market supply curve.

The long-run supply curve is upward sloping because of differences in costs across firms *only* if the amount that lower-cost firms can produce is limited. If there were an unlimited number of the lowest-cost firms, we would never observe any higher-cost firms producing. Effectively, then, the only firms in the market would have the same low costs of production.

Application   UPWARD-SLOPING LONG-RUN SUPPLY CURVE FOR COTTON

Many countries produce cotton. Production costs differ among countries because of differences in the quality of land, rainfall, costs of irrigation, costs of labor, and other factors.

The length of each steplike segment of the long-run supply curve of cotton in the graph is the quantity produced by the labeled country. The amount that the low-cost countries can produce must be limited, or we would not observe production by the higher-cost countries.

The height of each segment of the supply curve is the typical minimum average cost of production in that country. The average cost of production in Pakistan is less than half that in Iran. The supply curve has a steplike appearance because we are using an average of the estimate average cost in each

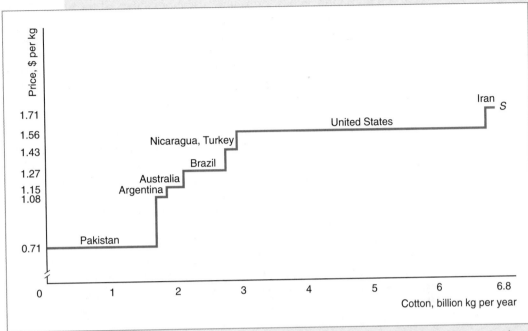

country, which is a single number. If we knew the individual firms' supply curves in each of these countries, the market supply curve would have a smoother shape.

As the market price rises, the number of countries producing rises. At market prices below $1.08 per kilogram, only Pakistan produces. If the market price is below $1.50, the United States and Iran do not produce. If the price increases to $1.56, the United States supplies a large amount of cotton. In this range of the supply curve, supply is very elastic. For Iran to produce, the price has to rise to $1.71. Price increases in that range result in only a relatively small increase in supply. Thus the supply curve is relatively inelastic at prices above $1.56.

Long-Run Market Supply When Input Prices Vary with Output. A third reason why market supply curves may slope is nonconstant input prices. In markets in which factor prices rise or fall when output increases, the long-run supply curve slopes even if firms have identical costs and can freely enter and exit.

If the market buys a relatively small share of the total amount of a factor of production that is sold, then, as market output expands, the price of the factor is unlikely to be affected. For example, dentists do not hire enough receptionists to affect the market wage for receptionists.

In contrast, if the market buys most of the total sales of a factor, the price of that input is more likely to vary with market output. As jet plane manufacturers expand and buy more jet engines, the price of these engines rises because the jet plane manufacturers are the sole purchaser of these engines.

To produce more goods, firms must use more inputs. If the prices of some or all inputs rise when more inputs are purchased, the cost of producing the final good also rises. We call a market in which input prices rise with output an *increasing-cost market*. Few steelworkers have no fear of heights and are willing to construct tall buildings, so their supply curve is steeply upward sloping. As more skyscrapers are built at one time, the demand for these workers shifts to the right, driving up their wage.

We assume that all firms in a market have the same cost curves and that input prices rise as market output expands. We use the cost curves of a representative firm in panel a of Figure 8.13 to derive the upward-sloping market supply curve in panel b.

When input prices are relatively low, each identical firm has the same long-run marginal cost curve, MC^1, and average cost curve, AC^1, in panel a. A typical firm produces at minimum average cost, e_1, and sells q_1 units of output. The market supply is Q_1 in panel b when the market price is p_1. The n_1 firms collectively sell $Q_1 = n_1 q_1$ units of output, which is point E_1 on the market supply curve in panel b.

If the market demand curve shifts outward, the market price rises to p_2, new firms enter, and market output rises to Q_2, causing input prices to rise. As a result, the marginal cost curve shifts from MC^1 to MC^2, and the average cost curve rises from AC^1 to AC^2. The typical firm produces at a higher minimum average cost, e_2.

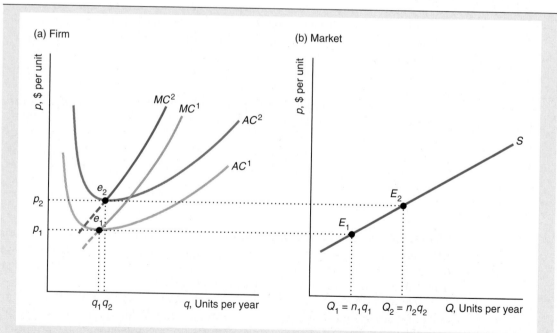

Figure 8.13 Long-Run Market Supply in an Increasing-Cost Market. (a) At a relatively low market output, Q_1, the firm's long-run marginal and average cost curves are MC^1 and AC^1. At the higher market quantity Q_2, the cost curves shift upward to MC^2 and AC^2 because of the higher input prices. Given identical firms, each firm produces at minimum average cost, such as points e_1 and e_2. (b) Long-run market supply, S, is upward sloping.

At this higher price, there are n_2 firms in the market, so market output is $Q_2 = n_2q_2$ at point E_2 on the market supply curve.

Thus in both an increasing-cost market and a constant-cost market—in which input prices remain constant as output increases—firms produce at minimum average cost in the long run. The difference is that the minimum average cost rises as market output increases in an increasing-cost market, whereas minimum average cost is constant in a constant-cost market. In conclusion, *the long-run supply curve is upward sloping in an increasing-cost market and flat in a constant-cost market.*

In decreasing-cost markets, as market output rises, at least some factor prices fall. As a result, *in a decreasing-cost market, the long-run market supply curve is downward sloping.*

Increasing returns to scale may cause factor prices to fall. For example, in the early 1980s, when the personal computer market was young, there was much less demand for floppy disk drives than there is today. As a result, those drives were partially assembled by hand at relatively high cost. As demand for floppy disk drives increased, it became practical to automate more of the production process so that drives could be produced at lower per-unit cost. The decrease in the price of these drives lowers the cost of personal computers.

Figure 8.14 shows a decreasing-cost market. As the market output expands from Q_1 to Q_2 in panel b, the prices of inputs fall, so a typical firm's cost curves shift

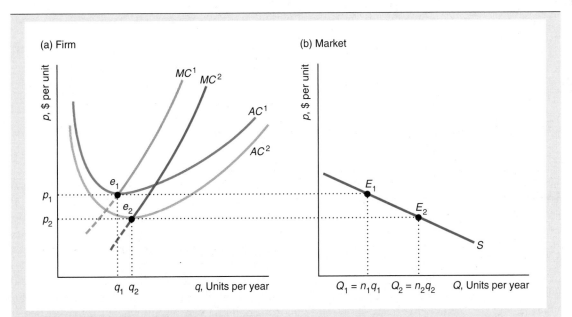

Figure 8.14 Long-Run Market Supply in a Decreasing-Cost Market. (a) At a relatively low market output, Q_1, the firm's long-run marginal and average cost curves are MC^1 and AC^1. At the higher market quantity Q_2, the cost curves shift downward to MC^2 and AC^2 because of lower input prices. Given identical firms, each firm produces at minimum average cost, such as points e_1 and e_2. (b) Long-run market supply, S, is downward sloping.

downward, and the minimum average cost falls from e_1 to e_2 in panel a. On the long-run market supply curve in panel b, point E_1, which corresponds to e_1, is above E_2, which corresponds to e_2. As a consequence, *a decreasing-cost market supply curve is downward sloping.*

To summarize, theory tells us that competitive long-run market supply curves may be flat, upward sloping, or downward sloping. If all firms are identical in a market in which firms can freely enter and input prices are constant, the long-run market supply curve is flat. If entry is limited, firms differ in costs, or input prices rise with output, the long-run supply curve is upward sloping. Finally, if input prices fall with market output, the long-run supply curve is downward sloping.

Application   **SLOPE OF LONG-RUN MARKET SUPPLY CURVES**

Determining the slope of the supply curve in a particular market requires careful studying of that market. Shea (1993) examined the slopes of the supply curves in 26 American manufacturing industries (which are assumed to be competitive). Only three of these industries have downward-sloping long-run supply curves: prepared feeds, construction equipment, and aircraft. Of the rest, more than twice as many are upward sloping as are flat. Sixteen industries have upward-sloping long-run supply curves, including lumber, drugs, paints, tires, cement, electronic components, and stone, clay, and glass. Seven industries, among them plumbing and heating products, floor coverings, and animal and marine fats and oils, have flat supply curves.

On average across all these industries, the long-run supply curves have a moderate upward slope. The supply elasticity is 5.5 on average across all these manufacturing industries, so a 1% increase in price leads to a 5.5% increase in quantity.

Long-Run Competitive Equilibrium

The intersection of the long-run market supply and demand curves determines the long-run competitive equilibrium. With identical firms, constant input prices, and free entry and exit, the long-run competitive market supply is horizontal at minimum long-run average cost, so the equilibrium price equals long-run average cost. A shift in the demand curve affects only the equilibrium quantity and not the equilibrium price, which remains constant at minimum long-run average cost.

The market supply curve is different in the short run than in the long run, so the long-run competitive equilibrium differs from the short-run equilibrium. The relationship between the short- and long-run equilibria depends on where the market demand curve crosses the short- and long-run market supply curves. Figure 8.15 illustrates this point using the short- and long-run supply curves for the vegetable oil mill market.

The short-run firm supply curve for a typical firm in panel a is the marginal cost above the minimum of the average variable cost, $7. At a price of $7, each firm produces 100 units, so the 20 firms in the market in the short run collectively supply 2,000 (= 20 × 100) units of oil in panel b. At higher prices, the short-run market

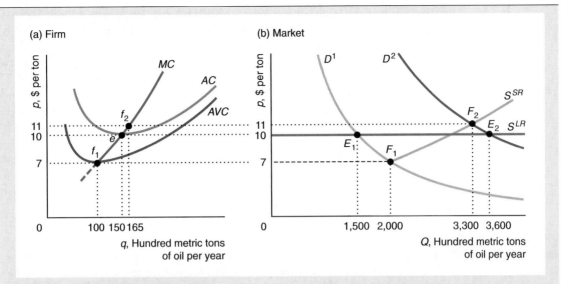

Figure 8.15 The Short-Run and Long-Run Equilibria for Vegetable Oil. (a) A typical vegetable oil mill is willing to produce 100 units of oil at $7, 150 units at $10, or 165 units at $11. (b) The short-run market supply curve, S^{SR}, is the horizontal sum of 20 individual firms' short-run marginal cost curves above minimum average variable cost, $7. The long-run market supply curve, S^{LR}, is horizontal at the minimum average cost, $10. If the demand curve is D^1, in the short-run equilibrium, F_1, 20 firms sell 2,000 units of oil at $7. In the long-run equilibrium, E_1, 10 firms sell 1,500 units at $10. If demand is D^2, the short-run equilibrium is F_2 ($11, 3,300 units, 20 firms) and the long-run equilibrium is E_2 ($10, 3,600 units, 24 firms).

supply curve slopes upward because it is the horizontal summation of the firm's upward-sloping marginal cost curves.

We assume that the firms use the same size plant in the short and long run so that the minimum average cost is $10 in both the short and long run. Because all firms have the same costs and can enter freely, the long-run market supply curve is flat at the minimum average cost, $10, in panel b. At prices between $7 and $10, firms supply goods at a loss in the short run but not in the long run.

If the market demand curve is D^1, the short-run market equilibrium, F_1, is below and to the right of the long-run market equilibrium, E_1. This relationship is reversed if the market demand curve is D^2.[12]

In the short run, if the demand is as low as D^1, the market price in the short-run equilibrium, F_1, is $7. At that price, each of the 20 firms produces 100 units, at f_1 in panel a. The firms lose money because the price of $7 is below average cost at 100 units. These losses drive some of the firms out of the market in the long run, so market output falls and the market price rises. In the long-run equilibrium, E_1, price is $10, and each firm produces 150 units, e, and breaks even. As the market

---

[12]Using data from *Statistics Canada*, I estimate that the elasticity of demand for vegetable oil is –0.8. Both D^1 and D^2 are constant –0.8 elasticity demand curves, but the demand at any price on D^2 is 2.4 times that on D^1.

demands only 1,500 units, only 10 (= 1,500/150) firms produce, so half the firms that produced in the short run exit the market.[13] Thus with the D^1 demand curve, price rises and output falls in the long run.

If demand expands to D^2, in the short run, each of the 20 firms expands its output to 165 units, f_2, and the price rises to $11, where the firms make profits: The price of $11 is above the average cost at 165 units. These profits attract entry in the long run, and the price falls. In the long-run equilibrium, each firm produces 150 units, e, and 3,600 units are sold by the market, E_2, by 24 (= 3,600/150) firms. Thus with the D^2 demand curve, price falls and output rises in the long run.

Because firms may enter and exit in the long run, taxes can have a counterintuitive effect on the competitive equilibrium. For example, as Solved Problem 8.3 shows, a lump-sum franchise tax causes the competitive equilibrium output of a firm to increase, although market output falls.

Solved Problem 8.3

If the government starts collecting a lump-sum franchise tax of $\mathscr{L}$ each year from each identical firm in a competitive market with free entry and exit, how do the long-run market and firm equilibria change?

Answer

1. *Show that the franchise tax causes the minimum long-run average cost to rise*: A typical firm's cost curves are shown in panel a and the market

(a) Firm

(b) Market

---

equilibrium in panel b. In panel a, a lump-sum, franchise tax shifts the typical firm's average cost curve upward from AC^1 to $AC^2 = AC^1 + \mathcal{L}/q$ but does not affect the marginal cost (see the answer to Solved Problem 7.1). As a result, the minimum average cost rises from e_1 to e_2.

2. *Show that the shift in the minimum average cost causes the market supply curve to shift upward, equilibrium quantity to fall, and equilibrium price to rise:* The long-run market supply is horizontal at minimum average cost. Thus the market supply curve shifts upward by the same amount as the minimum average cost increases in panel b. With a downward-sloping market demand curve, the new equilibrium, E_2, has a lower quantity, $Q_2 < Q_1$, and higher price, $p_2 > p_1$, than the original equilibrium, E_1.

3. *Show that the increase in the equilibrium price causes output of an individual firm to rise:* Because the market price rises, the quantity that a firm produces rises from q_1 to q_2. Thus if the firm remains in the market, it will produce more.

4. *Use the market quantity and individual firm quantity to determine how the number of firms changes:* At the initial equilibrium, the number of firms was $n_1 = Q_1/q_1$. The new equilibrium number of firms, $n_2 = Q_2/q_2$, must be smaller than n_1 because $Q_2 < Q_1$ and $q_2 > q_1$. Thus there are fewer firms but each remaining firm produces more output at the new equilibrium.

8.5 | ZERO PROFIT FOR COMPETITIVE FIRMS IN THE LONG RUN

Competitive firms earn zero profit in the long run whether or not entry is completely free. As a consequence, competitive firms must maximize profit.

Zero Long-Run Profit with Free Entry

The long-run supply curve is horizontal if firms are free to enter the market, firms have identical cost, and input prices are constant. All firms in the market are operating at minimum long-run average cost. That is, they are indifferent between shutting down or not because they are earning zero profit.

One implication of the shutdown rule is that the firm is willing to operate in the long run even if it is making zero profit. This conclusion may seem strange unless you remember that we are talking about *economic profit*, which is revenue minus opportunity cost. Because opportunity cost includes the value of the next best investment, at a zero long-run economic profit, the firm is earning the normal business profit that the firm could earn by investing elsewhere in the economy.

For example, if a firm's owner had not built the plant the firm uses to produce, the owner could have spent that money on another business or put the money in a bank. The opportunity cost of the current plant, then, is the forgone profit from what the owner could have earned by investing the money elsewhere.

The five-year median accounting return on capital across all retailing firms was 9.3%, indicating that the typical retailer earned a business profit of 9.3¢ for every dollar it invested in capital.[14] These firms were earning about what they would earn if they invested in other markets: The median return on capital for all markets was 9.4%. Thus these retailers were earning roughly zero economic profit but positive business profit.

Because business cost does not include all opportunity costs, business profit is larger than economic profit. Thus *a profit-maximizing firm may stay in business if it earns zero long-run economic profit but shuts down if it earns zero long-run business profit.*

Zero Long-Run Profit When Entry Is Limited	In some markets, firms cannot enter in response to long-run profit opportunities. One reason for the limited number of firms is that the supply of an input is limited. Only so much land is suitable for mining uranium, and only a few people have the superior skills need to play professional basketball.

One might think that firms could make positive long-run economic profits in such markets; however, that's not true. The reason why firms earn zero economic profits is that firms bidding for the scarce input drive its price up until the firms' profits are zero.

Suppose that the number of acres suitable for growing tomatoes is limited. Figure 8.16 shows a typical farm's average cost curve if the rental cost of land is zero (the average cost curve includes only the farm's costs of labor, capital, materials, and energy—not land). At the market price p^*, the firm produces q^* bushels of tomatoes and makes a profit of π^*, the shaded rectangle in the figure.

Thus if the owner of the land does not charge rent, the farmer makes a profit. Unfortunately for the farmer, the landowner rents the land for π^*, so the farmer actually earns zero profit. Why does the landowner charge that much? The reason is that π^* is the opportunity cost of the land: The land is worth π^* to other potential farmers. These farmers will bid against each other to rent this land until the rent is driven up to π^*.

This rent is a fixed cost to the farmer because it doesn't vary with the amount of output. Thus the rent affects the farm's average cost curve but not its marginal cost curve.

As a result, if the farm produces at all, it produces q^*, where its marginal cost equals the market price, no matter what rent is charged. The higher average cost curve in the figure includes a rent equal to π^*. The minimum point of this average cost curve is p^* at q^* bushels of tomatoes, so the farmer earns zero economic profit.

If demand falls, so the market price falls, these farmers will make short-run losses. In the long run, the rental price of the land will fall enough that, once again, each firm earns zero economic profit.

Does it make a difference whether farmers own or rent the land? Not really. The opportunity cost to a farmer who owns superior land is the amount for which that land could be rented in a competitive land market. Thus the economic profit of both owned and rented land is zero at the long-run equilibrium.

---

[14]Moukheiber, Zina, "Retailing," *Forbes*, January 1995:190–193.

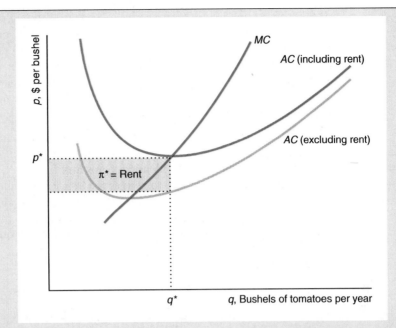

Figure 8.16 Rent. If it did not have to pay rent for its land, a farm with high-quality land would earn a positive long-run profit of π*. Due to competitive bidding for this land, however, the rent equals π*, so the landlord reaps all the benefits of the superior land, and the farmer earns a zero long-run economic profit.

Good-quality land is not the only scarce resource. The price of any fixed factor will be bid up in the same way so that economic profit for the firm is zero in the long run.

Another example is an industry in which the government requires that a firm have a license to operate and then limits the number of licenses. As we discuss at length in Chapter 9, the price of the license gets bid up by potential entrants, driving profit to zero.

Economists refer to the extra opportunity value of a scarce input as a "rent," even if the fixed factor is a person with high ability rather than land. Indeed, to economists, a **rent** is a payment to the owner of an input beyond the minimum necessary for the factor to be supplied.

Bonnie manages a store for the salary of $30,000, which is what a typical manager is paid. Because she's a superior manager, however, the firm earns an economic profit of $50,000 a year. Other firms, seeing what a good job Bonnie is doing, offer her a higher salary. The bidding for her services drives her salary up to $80,000: her $30,000 base salary plus the $50,000 rent. After paying this rent to Bonnie, the store makes zero economic profit.

Similarly, people with unusual abilities can earn staggering rents. Though no law stops anyone from trying to become a professional entertainer, most of us do not have enough talent that others will pay to watch us perform. The Rolling Stones earned $121.2 million from their 1994 concert tour, according to *Pollstar* magazine.

To put this amount in perspective, the 1993 gross national product (national income of the entire country) of Grenada, a country of a 100,000 people, was $215 million; that of Kiribati, $51.1 million; and that of Bhutan, $234 million.

In short, if some firms in a market make short-run economic profits due to a scarce input, the other firms in the market bid for that input. This bidding drives the price of the factor upward until all firms earn zero long-run profits. In such a market, the supply curve is flat because all firms have the same minimum long-run average cost.

The Need to Maximize Profit

In a competitive market with identical firms and free entry, if most firms are profit-maximizing, profits are driven to zero at the long-run equilibrium. Any firm that did not maximize profit—that is, any firm that set its output so that price did not equal its marginal cost or did not use the most cost-efficient methods of production—would lose money. Thus *to survive in a competitive market, a firm must maximize its profit.*

Summary

1. **Competition:** Competitive firms are price takers that cannot influence market price. Markets are likely to be competitive if all firms in the market sell identical products, firms can enter and exit the market freely, buyers and sellers know the prices charged by firms, and transaction costs are low. A competitive firm faces a horizontal demand curve at the market price.

2. **Profit maximization:** Most firms maximize economic profit, which is revenue minus economic cost (explicit and implicit cost). Because business profit, which is revenue minus only explicit cost, does not include implicit cost, economic profit tends to be less than business profit. A firm earning zero economic profit is making as much as it could if its resources were devoted to their best alternative uses. To maximize profit, all firms (not just competitive firms) must make two decisions. First, the firm determines the quantity at which its profit is highest. Profit is maximized when marginal profit is zero or, equivalently, when marginal revenue equals marginal cost. Second, the firm decides whether to produce at all.

3. **Competition in the short run:** Because a competitive firm is a price taker, its marginal revenue equals the market price. As a result, a competitive firm maximizes its profit by setting its output so that its short-run marginal cost equals the market price. The firm shuts down if the market price is less than its minimum average variable cost. Thus a profit-maximizing competitive firm's short-run supply curve is its marginal cost curve above its minimum average variable cost. The short-run market supply curve, which is the sum of the supply curves of the fixed number of firms producing in the short run, is flat at low output levels and upward sloping at larger levels. The short-run competitive equilibrium is determined by the intersection of the market demand curve and the short-run market supply curve. The effect of an increase in demand depends on whether demand intersects the market supply in the flat or upward-sloping section.

4. **Competition in the long run:** In the long run, a competitive firm sets its output where the market price equals its long-run marginal cost. It shuts down if the market price is less than the minimum of its average long-run cost because all costs are variable in the long run. Consequently, the competitive firm's supply curve is its long-run marginal cost above its minimum long-run average cost. The long-run supply curve of a firm may have a different slope than the short-run curve because it can vary its fixed factors in the long run. The long-run market supply curve is the horizontal sum of

the supply curves of all the firms in the market. If all firms are identical, entry and exit are easy, and input prices are constant, the long-run market supply curve is flat at minimum average cost. If firms differ, entry is difficult or costly, or input prices vary with output, the long-run market supply curve has an upward slope. The long-run market supply curve slopes upward if input prices increase with output and slopes downward if input prices decrease with output. The long-run market equilibrium price and quantity are differ-

ent from the short-run price and quantity.

5. **Zero profit for competitive firms in the long run:** Although firms may make profits or losses in the short run, they earn zero economic profit in the long run. If necessary, the prices of scarce inputs adjust to ensure that competitive firms make zero long-run profit. Because profit-maximizing firms just break even in the long run, firms that do not try to maximize profits will lose money. Competitive firms must maximize profit to survive.

Problems

1. Should a competitive firm ever produce when it is losing money? Why or why not?

2. Many marginal cost curves are U-shaped. As a result, it is possible that the *MC* curve hits the demand or price line at two output levels. Which is the profit-maximizing output? Why?

3. Suppose that the government imposes an ad valorem tax (Chapter 3) of α per dollar on a competitive firm. What happens to its long-run supply curve?

4. In Solved Problem 8.3, would it make a difference to the analysis whether the franchise tax were collected annually or only once when the firm starts operation? How would each of these franchise taxes affect the firm's long-run supply curve? Explain your answer.

5. Answer Solved Problem 8.3 for the short run rather than for the long run. (*Hint*: The answer depends on where the demand curve intersects the original short-run supply curve.)

6. Competitive firms in the United States and in France produce cheese. The French government gives each cheese manufacturer an annual subsidy (a negative tax) of s that is independent of the amount of cheese it produces. What happens to the long-run supply curve of cheese to the world?

7. How does the cheese subsidy in Problem 6 affect the world price, the amount sold by French and American firms, and the profits of both types of firms?

8. What is the effect on firm and market equilibrium of a law requiring a firm to give its workers six months' notice before it can shut down its plant?

9. Redraw Figure 8.11 showing a situation in which the short-run plant size is too large relative to the optimal long-run plant size.

10. Is it true that the long-run supply curve for a good is horizontal only if the long-run supply curves of all factors are horizontal? Explain.

11. Navel oranges are grown in California and Arizona. If Arizona starts collecting a specific tax per orange from its firms, what happens to the long-run market supply curve? (*Hint*: You may assume that all firms initially have the same costs. Your answer may depend on whether unlimited entry occurs.)

12. Americans used 33 million real Christmas trees and 40 million artificial trees in 1994. The number of tree producers fell by about a third over the previous 10 years, to about 2,000 in 1994, due to artificial tree sales. That year, trees sold for an average of $26.50, about 50¢ more than the previous year. Retailers' average cost was $20. In 1998, 33 million trees sold for an average of $29.25. Use graphs to illustrate this information.

13. *Review* (Chapters 2, 3, and 8): To reduce pollution, the California Air Resources Board in 1996 required the reformulation of gasoline sold in California. In 1999, a series of disasters at California refineries substantially cut the supply of gasoline and contributed to large price increases. Environmentalists and California refiners (who had sunk large investments to produce the reformulated gasoline) opposed imports from other states, which would have kept prices down. To minimize fluctuations in prices in California, Severin Borenstein and Steven Stoft suggest setting a 15¢ surcharge on sell-

ers of standard gasoline. In normal times, none of this gasoline would be sold, because it costs only 8¢ to 12¢ more to produce the California version. However, when disasters trigger a large shift in the supply curve of gasoline, firms could profitably import standard gasoline and keep the price in California from rising more than about 15¢ above prices in the rest of the United States. Use figures to evaluate Borenstein and Stoft's proposal.

14. *Review* (Chapters 7 and 8): Bribes paid by Swiss companies to foreign officials, which were tax deductible since 1946, are no longer deductible as of 1999. Use economic models from this chapter and Chapter 7 to show the likely effects of this ban on the bribing behavior of Swiss firms.

Math Problems

15. If a competitive firm's cost function is $C(q) = 100 + 10q - q^2 + \frac{1}{3}q^3$, what is the firm's marginal cost function? What is the firm's profit-maximizing condition?

16. If a competitive firm's cost function is $C(q) = a + bq + cq^2 + dq^3$, where a, b, c, and d are constants, what is the firm's marginal cost function? What is the firm's profit-maximizing condition?

17. Each firm in a competitive market has a cost function of $C = 16 + q^2$. The market demand function is $Q = 24 - p$. Determine the equilibrium price, quantity per firm, market quantity, and number of firms.

18. There are 10 identical competitive firms in a market. The linear market demand curve is $Q = 100 - p$, and the linear supply curve of each firm is $q = p$. What residual demand does a typical firm face?

19. There are n identical competitive firms in a market. The linear market demand curve is $Q = a - bp$, and the linear supply curve of each firm is $q = c + dp$, where a, b, c, and d are positive constants. What residual demand does a typical firm face?

20. At least 40,000 U.S. farms produce apples. The market demand elasticity of apples is about –0.2. At least how great must the residual demand elasticity that a single farm faces be?

Applying the Competitive Model

We've reached a compromise. We're going to raise the minimum wage by half a gallon of gas per hour.

In 1999, in response to the European Union's ban on imports of their beef, the U.S. and Canadian governments slapped 100% taxes on such European products as Roquefort cheese, foie gras, chocolate, and mustard. How does such a trade war affect consumers and producers? In this chapter, we show how the competitive model can answer this type of question. One of the major strengths of the competitive market model is that it can predict how trade wars, changes in government policies, global warming, and major cost-saving discoveries affect consumers and producers.

This chapter introduces the measure that economists commonly use to determine whether consumers or firms gain or lose when the equilibrium of a competitive market changes. Using such a measure, we can predict whether a policy change benefits the winners more than it harms the losers. To decide whether to adopt a particular policy, policymakers can combine these predictions with their normative views (values), such as whether they are more interested in helping the group that gains or the group that loses.

To most people, the term *welfare* refers to the government's payments to poor people. No such meaning is implied when economists employ the term. Economists use *welfare* to refer to the well-being of various groups such as consumers and producers. They call an analysis of the impact of a change on various groups' well-being a study of *welfare economics*.

1. **Consumer welfare:** How much consumers are helped or harmed by a change in the equilibrium price can be measured by using information from demand curves or utility functions.
2. **Producer welfare:** How much producers gain or lose from a change in the equilibrium price can be measured by using information from the marginal cost curve or by measuring the change in profits.
3. **Maximizing welfare:** Competition maximizes a measure of social welfare based on consumer and produce welfare.
4. **Policies that shift supply curves:** Government policies that limit the number of firms in competitive markets harm consumers and lower welfare.
5. **Policies that create a wedge between supply and demand:** Government policies such as taxes, price ceilings, price floors, and tariffs that create a wedge between the supply and demand curves reduce the equilibrium quantity, raise the equilibrium price to consumers, and lower welfare.
6. **Comparing both types of policies: imports:** Policies that limit supply (such as quotas or bans on imports) or create a wedge between supply and demand (such as *tariffs*, which are taxes on imports) have different welfare effects when both polices reduce imports by equal amounts.

IN THIS CHAPTER,

WE EXAMINE

SIX MAIN

TOPICS

9.1 | CONSUMER WELFARE

Economists and policymakers want to know how much consumers benefit from or are harmed by shocks that affect the equilibrium price and quantity. To what extent are consumers harmed if a local government imposes a sales tax to raise additional revenues? To answer such a question, we need some way to measure consumers' welfare. Economists use measures of welfare based on consumer theory (Chapters 4 and 5).

If we knew a consumer's utility function, we could directly answer the question of how an event affects a consumer's welfare. If the price of beef increases, the budget line facing someone who eats beef rotates inward, so the consumer is on a lower indifference curve at the new equilibrium. If we knew the levels of utility associated with the original indifference curve and the new one, we could measure the impact of the tax in terms of the change in the utility level.

This approach is not practical for a couple of reasons. First, we rarely, if ever, know individuals' utility functions. Second, even if we had utility measures for various consumers, we would have no obvious way to compare them. One person might say that he got 1,000 utils (units of utility) from the same bundle that another consumer says gives her 872 utils of pleasure. The first person is not necessarily happier—he may just be using a different scale.

As a result, *we measure consumer welfare in terms of dollars*. Instead of asking the rather silly question "How many utils would you lose if your daily commute increased by 15 minutes?" we could ask "How much would you pay to avoid having your daily commute grow a quarter of an hour longer?" or "How much would it cost you in forgone earnings if your daily commute were 15 minutes longer?" It is easier to compare dollars across people than utils.

We first present the most widely used method of measuring consumer welfare. Then we show how it can be used to measure the effect of a change in price on consumer welfare.

Measuring Consumer Welfare Using a Demand Curve

Consumer welfare from a good is the benefit a consumer gets from consuming that good minus what the consumer paid to buy the good. How much pleasure do you get from a good above and beyond its price? If you buy a good for exactly what it's worth to you, you are indifferent between making that transaction and not. Frequently, however, you buy things that are worth more to you than what they cost. Imagine that you've played tennis in the hot sun and are very thirsty. You can buy a soft drink from a vending machine for 75¢, but you'd be willing to pay much more because you are so thirsty. As a result, you're much better off making this purchase than not.

If we can measure how much more you'd be willing to pay than you did pay, we'd know how much you gained from this transaction. Luckily for us, the demand curve contains the information we need to make this measurement.

Marginal Willingness to Pay. To develop a welfare measure based on the demand curve, we need to know what information is contained in a demand curve. The demand curve reflects a consumer's *marginal willingness to pay*: the maximum amount a consumer will spend for an extra unit. The consumer's marginal willingness to pay is the *marginal value* the consumer places on the last unit of output.

David's demand curve for magazines per week, panel a of Figure 9.1, indicates his marginal willingness to buy various numbers of magazines. David places a marginal value of $5 on the first magazine. As a result, if the price of a magazine is $5, David buys one magazine, point *a* on the demand curve. His marginal willingness to buy a second magazine is $4, so if the price falls to $4, he buys two magazines, *b*. His marginal willingness to buy three magazines is $3, so if the price of magazines is $3, he buys three magazines, *c*.

Consumer Surplus. The monetary difference between what a consumer is willing to pay for the quantity of the good purchased and what the good actually costs is called **consumer surplus** (*CS*). Consumer surplus is a dollar-value measure of the extra pleasure the consumer receives from the transaction beyond its price.

David's consumer surplus from each additional magazine is his marginal willingness to pay minus what he pays to obtain the magazine. His marginal willingness to pay for the first magazine, $5, is area $CS_1 + E_1$. If the price is $3, his expenditure to obtain the magazine is area $E_1 = \$3$. Thus his consumer surplus on the first magazine is area $CS_1 = (CS_1 + E_1) - E_1 = \$5 - \$3 = \$2$. Because his marginal willingness to pay for the second magazine is $4, his consumer surplus for the second magazine is the smaller area $CS_2 = \$1$. His marginal willingness to pay for the third magazine is $3, which equals what he must pay to obtain it, so his consumer surplus is zero, $CS_3 = \$0$. He is indifferent between buying and not buying the third magazine.

At a price of $3, David buys three magazines. His total consumer surplus from the three magazines he buys is the sum of the consumer surplus he gets from each of these magazines: $CS_1 + CS_2 + CS_3 = \$2 + \$1 + \$0 = \$3$. This total consumer surplus of $3 is the extra amount that David is willing to spend for the right to buy three magazines at $3 each. Thus *an individual's consumer surplus is the area under the demand curve and above the market price up to the quantity the consumer buys.*

David is unwilling to buy a fourth magazine unless the price drops to $2 or less. If David's mother gives him a fourth magazine as a gift, the marginal value that David puts on that fourth magazine, $2, is less than what it cost his mother, $3.

We can determine consumer surplus for smooth demand curves in the same way as with David's unusual stairlike demand curve. Steven has a smooth demand curve for baseball trading cards, panel b of Figure 9.1. The height of this demand curve measures his willingness to pay for one more card. This willingness varies with the number of cards he buys in a year. The total value he places on obtaining q_1 cards per year is the area under the demand curve up to q_1, the areas *CS* and *E*. Area *E* is his actual expenditure on q_1 cards. Because the price is p_1, his expenditure is $p_1 q_1$. Steven's consumer surplus from consuming q_1 trading cards is the value of consuming those cards, areas *CS* and *E*, minus his actual expenditures *E* to obtain them, or *CS*. Thus his consumer surplus, *CS*, is the area under

Figure 9.1 Consumer Surplus. (a) David's demand curve for magazines has a step-like shape. When the price is $3, he buys three magazines, point *c*. David's marginal value for the first magazine is $5, areas $CS_1 + E_1$, and his expenditure is $3, area E_1, so his consumer surplus is $CS_1 = \$2$. His consumer surplus is $1 for the second magazine, area CS_2, and is $0 for the third (he is indifferent between buying and not buying it). Thus his total consumer surplus is the shaded area $CS_1 + CS_2 + CS_3 = \$3$. (b) Steven's willingness to pay for trading cards is the height of his smooth demand curve. At price p_1, Steven's expenditure is $E (= p_1q_1)$, his consumer surplus is CS, and the total value he places on consuming q_1 trading cards per year is $CS + E$.

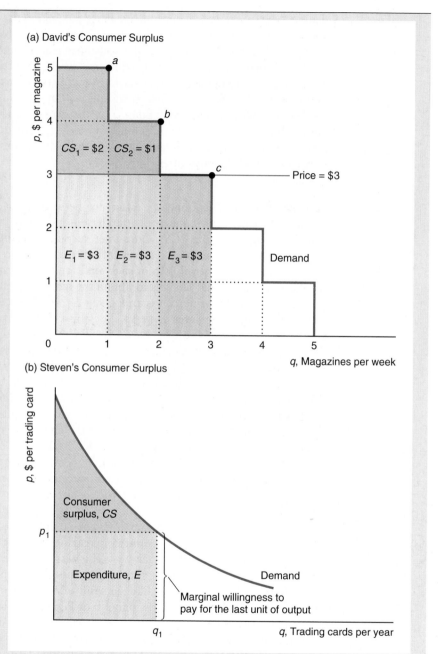

(a) David's Consumer Surplus

(b) Steven's Consumer Surplus

the demand curve and above the horizontal line at the price p_1 up to the quantity he buys, q_1.

Just as we measure the consumer surplus for an individual using that individual's demand curve, we measure the consumer surplus of all consumers in a market using the market demand curve. *Market consumer surplus is the area under the market demand curve above the market price up to the quantity consumers buy.*

To summarize, consumer surplus is a practical and convenient measure of consumer welfare. There are two advantages to using consumer surplus rather than utility to discuss the welfare of consumers. First, the dollar-denominated consumer surplus of several individuals can be easily compared or combined, whereas the utility of various individuals cannot be easily compared or combined. Second, it is relatively easy to measure consumer surplus, whereas it is difficult to get a meaningful measure of utility directly. To calculate consumer surplus, all we have to do is measure the area under a demand curve.

Application   CONSUMER SURPLUS FROM TELEVISION

Do you get consumer surplus from television? Fewer than one in four (23%) Americans say that they would be willing to "give up watching absolutely all types of television" for the rest of their lives in exchange for $25,000. Almost half (46%) say that they'd refuse to give up TV for anything under $1 million. One in four Americans wouldn't give it up for $1 million. Indeed, one-quarter of those who earn under $20,000 a year wouldn't give up TV for $1 million—more than they will earn in 50 years.

Thus if you ask how much consumer surplus people receive from television, you will get many implausibly high answers. For this reason, economists typically calculate consumer surplus by using estimated demand curves, which are based on actual observed behavior, rather than simply asking consumers.

Effect of a Price Change on Consumer Surplus

If the supply curve shifts upward or a government imposes a new sales tax, the equilibrium price rises, reducing consumer surplus. We illustrate the effect of a price increase on market consumer surplus using estimated supply and demand curves for sweetheart and hybrid tea roses sold in the United States.[1] We then discuss which markets are likely to have the greatest loss of consumer surplus due to a price increase.

---

[1] I estimated this model using data from the *Statisticsal Abstract of United States*, *Floriculture Crops*, *Floriculture and Environmental Horticulture Products*, and **usda.mannlib.cornell.edu/data-sets/crops/95917/sb917.txt**. The (wholesale) prices are in real 1991 dollars.

Consumer Surplus Loss from a Higher Price. Suppose that the introduction of a new tax causes the (wholesale) price of roses to rise from the original equilibrium price of 30¢ to 32¢ per rose stem, a shift along the wholesale demand curve in Figure 9.2. The consumer surplus is area $A + B + C = \$173.74$ million per year at a price of 30¢, and it is only area $A = \$149.64$ million at a price of 32¢.[2] Thus the loss in consumer surplus from the increase in the price is $B + C = \$24.1$ million per year.

Markets in Which Consumer Surplus Losses Are Large. In general, as the price increases, consumer surplus falls more (1) the greater the initial revenues spent on the good and (2) the less elastic the demand curve (Appendix 9A). More is spent on a good when its demand curve is farther to the right so that areas like A, B, and C in Figure 9.2 are larger. The larger $B + C$ is, the greater is the drop in consumer surplus from a given percentage increase in price. Similarly, the less elastic a demand curve is (the closer it is to vertical), the less willing consumers are to give up the good, so consumers do not cut their consumption much as the price increases, with the result of greater consumer surplus losses.

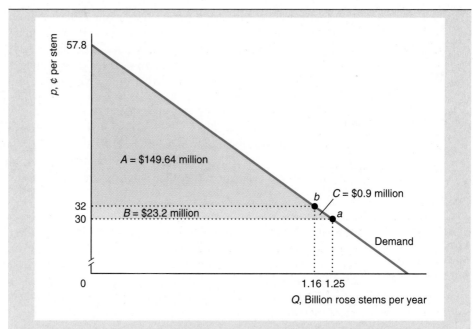

Figure 9.2 **Fall in Consumer Surplus from Roses as Price Rises.** As the price of roses rises 2¢ per stem from 30¢ per stem, the quantity demanded decreases from 1.25 to 1.16 billion stems per year. The loss in consumer surplus from the higher price, areas B and C, is $24.1 million per year.

---

[2]The height of triangle A is 25.8¢ = 57.8¢ − 32¢ per stem and the base is 1.16 billion stems per year, so its area is $\frac{1}{2} \times \$0.258 \times 1.16$ billion = $149.64 million per year. Rectangle B is $0.02 × 1.16 billion = $23.2 million. Triangle C is $\frac{1}{2} \times \$0.09 \times 0.09$ billion = $0.9 million.

Table 9.1 Effect of a 10% Increase in Price on Consumer Surplus (Revenue and Consumer Surplus in Billions of 1999 Dollars)

	Revenue	Elasticity of Demand, ε	Change in Consumer Surplus, ΔCS
Food	601	−0.245	−59
Housing	503	−0.633	−49
Medical	329	−0.604	−32
Transportation	283	−0.461	−28
Clothing	274	−0.405	−27
Utilities	145	−0.448	−14
Alcohol and tobacco	125	−0.162	−12

Source: Revenues and elasticities based on Blanciforti (1982). Appendix 9A shows how the change figures were calculated.

Higher prices cause greater consumer surplus loss in some markets than in others. Consumers would benefit if policymakers, before imposing a tax, considered in which market the tax is likely to harm consumers the most.

We can use estimates of demand curves to predict for which good a price increase causes the greatest loss of consumer surplus. Table 9.1 shows the consumer surplus loss in billions of 1999 dollars from a 10% increase in the price of various goods. The table shows that when the loss in consumer surplus is larger, the larger the initial revenue (price times quantity) that is spent on a good. A 10% increase in price causes a much greater loss of consumer surplus if it is imposed on food, $59 billion, than if it is imposed on alcohol and tobacco, $12 billion, because much more is spent on food.

At first glance, the relationship between elasticities of demand and the loss in consumer surplus in Table 9.1 looks backward: A given percent change in prices has a larger effect on consumer surplus for the relatively elastic demand curves. However, this relationship is coincidental: The large revenue goods happen to have relatively elastic demand curves. The effect of a price change depends on both revenue and the demand elasticity. In this table, the relative size of the revenues is more important than the relative elasticities.

If we could hold revenue constant and vary the elasticity, we would find that consumer surplus loss from a price increase is larger as the demand curve becomes less elastic. If the demand curve for alcohol and tobacco were 10 times more elastic, −1.62, while the revenue stayed the same—the demand curve became flatter at the initial price and quantity—the consumer surplus loss from a 10% price increase would be $1 million less.

Solved Problem 9.1 Suppose that two linear demand curves go through the initial equilibrium, e_1. One demand curve is less elastic than the other at e_1. For which demand curve will a price increase cause the larger consumer surplus loss?

Answer

1. *Draw the two demand curves, and indicate which one is less elastic at the initial equilibrium*: Two demand curves cross at e_1 in the diagram. The steeper demand curve is less elastic at e_1.[3]

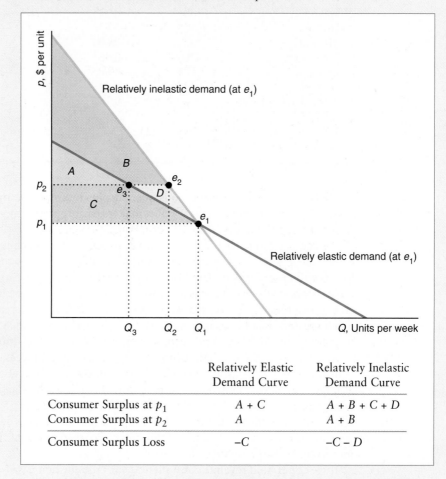

	Relatively Elastic Demand Curve	Relatively Inelastic Demand Curve
Consumer Surplus at p_1	$A + C$	$A + B + C + D$
Consumer Surplus at p_2	A	$A + B$
Consumer Surplus Loss	$-C$	$-C - D$

2. *Illustrate that a price increase causes a larger consumer surplus loss with the less elastic demand curve*: If the price rises from p_1 to p_2, the consumer surplus falls by only $-C$ with the relatively elastic demand curve and by $-C - D$ with the relatively inelastic demand curve.

---

[3]As we discussed in Chapter 3, the price elasticity of demand, $\varepsilon = (\Delta Q/\Delta p)(p/Q)$, is 1 over the slope of the demand curve, $\Delta p/\Delta Q$, times the ratio of the price to the quantity. At the point of intersection, where both demand curves have the same price, p_1, and quantity, Q_1, the steeper the demand curve, the lower the elasticity of demand.

9.2 | PRODUCER WELFARE

A supplier's gain from participating in the market is measured by its **producer surplus** (*PS*), which is the difference between the amount for which a good sells and the minimum amount necessary for the seller to be willing to produce the good. The minimum amount a seller must receive to be willing to produce is the firm's avoidable production cost (the shutdown rule in Chapter 8).

Measuring Producer Surplus Using a Supply Curve

To determine a competitive firm's producer surplus, we use its supply curve: its marginal cost curve above its minimum average variable cost (Chapter 8). The firm's supply curve in panel a of Figure 9.3 looks like a staircase. The marginal cost of producing the first unit is $MC_1 = \$1$, which is the area under the marginal cost curve

Figure 9.3 Producer Surplus. (a) The firm's producer surplus, $6, is the area below the market price, $4, and above the marginal cost (supply curve) up to the quantity sold, 4. The area under the marginal cost curve up to the number of units actually produced is the variable cost of produc- tion. (b) The market producer surplus is the area above the supply curve and below the line at the market price, p^*, up to the quantity produced, Q^*. The area below the supply curve and to the left of the quantity produced by the market, Q^*, is the variable cost of producing that level of output.

between 0 and 1. The marginal cost of producing two units is $MC_2 = \$2$, and so on. The variable cost, VC, of producing four units is the sum of the marginal costs for the first four units: $VC = MC_1 + MC_2 + MC_3 + MC_4 = \$1 + \$2 + \$3 + \$4 = \$10$.

If the market price, p, is $4, the firm's revenue from the sale of the first unit exceeds its cost by $PS_1 = p - MC_1 = \$4 - \$1 = \$3$, which is its producer surplus on the first unit. The firm's producer surplus is $2 on the second unit and $1 on the third unit. On the fourth unit, the price equals marginal cost, so the firm just breaks even. As a result, the firm's total producer surplus, PS, from selling four units at $4 each is the sum of its producer surplus on these four units: $PS = PS_1 + PS_2 + PS_3 + PS_4 = \$3 + \$2 + \$1 + \$0 = \$6$. Graphically, the total producer surplus is the area above the supply curve and below the market price up to the quantity actually produced. This same reasoning holds when the firm's supply curve is smooth.

The producer surplus is closely related to profit. Producer surplus is revenue, R, minus variable cost, VC:

$$PS = R - VC.$$

In panel a of Figure 9.3, revenue is $4 \times 4 = \$16$ and variable cost is $10, so producer surplus is $6.

Profit is revenue minus total cost, C, which equals variable cost plus fixed cost, F:

$$\pi = R - C = R - (VC + F).$$

Thus the difference between producer surplus and profit is fixed cost, F. If the fixed cost is zero (as often occurs in the long run), producer surplus equals profit.[4]

Another interpretation of producer surplus is as a gain to trade. In the short run, if the firm produces and sells its good—trades—it earns a profit of $R - VC - F$. If the firm shuts down—does not trade—it loses its fixed cost of $-F$. Thus producer surplus equals the profit from trade minus the profit (loss) from not trading of

$$(R - VC - F) - (-F) = R - VC = PS.$$

Using Producer Surplus

Even in the short run, we can use producer surplus to study the effects of any shock that does not affect the fixed cost of firms, such as a change in the price of a substitute or an input. Such shocks change profit by exactly the same amount as they change producer surplus because fixed costs do not change.

A major advantage of producer surplus is that we can use it to measure the effect of a shock on *all* the firms in a market without having to measure the profit of each firm in the market separately. We can calculate market producer surplus using the market supply curve in the same way as we calculate a firm's producer surplus using its supply curve. The market producer surplus in panel b of Figure 9.3 is the area above the supply curve and below the market price, p^*, line up to the quantity sold, Q^*. The market supply curve is the horizontal sum of the marginal cost curves of each of the firms (Chapter 8). As a result, the variable cost for all the firms in the market of producing Q is the area under the supply curve between 0 and the market output, Q.

---

[4]Even though each competitive firm makes zero profit in the long run, owners of scarce resources used in that market may earn rents (Chapter 8). Thus owners of scarce resources may receive positive producer surplus in the long run.

Solved Problem 9.2

If the estimated supply curve for roses is linear, how much producer surplus is lost when the price of roses falls from 30¢ to 21¢ per stem (so that the quantity sold falls from 1.25 billion to 1.16 billion rose stems per year)?

Answer

1. *Draw the supply curve, and show the change in producer surplus caused by the price change:* The figure shows the estimated supply curve for roses. Point *a* indicates the quantity supplied at the original price, 30¢, and point *b* reflects the quantity supplied at the lower price, 21¢. The loss in producer surplus is the sum of rectangle *D* and triangle *E*.

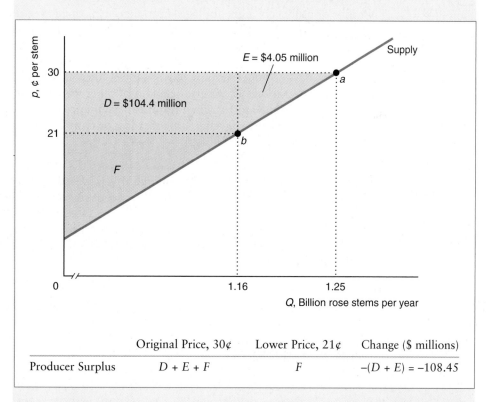

	Original Price, 30¢	Lower Price, 21¢	Change ($ millions)
Producer Surplus	*D* + *E* + *F*	*F*	−(*D* + *E*) = −108.45

2. *Calculate the lost producer surplus by adding the areas of rectangle D and triangle E:* The height of rectangle *D* is the difference between the original and the new price, 9¢, and its base is 1.16 billion stems per year, so the area of *D* (not all of which is shown in the figure because of the break in the quantity axis) is $0.09 per stem × 1.16 billion stems per year = $104.4 million per year. The height of triangle *E* is also 9¢, and its length is 0.9 billion stems per year, so its area is $\frac{1}{2}$ × $0.09 per stem × 0.9 billion stems per year = $4.05 million per year. Thus the loss in producer surplus from the drop in price is $108.45 million per year.

9.3 | COMPETITION MAXIMIZES WELFARE

How should we measure society's welfare? There are many reasonable answers to this question. One commonly used measure of the welfare of society, W, is the sum of consumer surplus plus producer surplus:

$$W = CS + PS.$$

This measure implicitly weights the well-being of consumers and producers equally. By using this measure, we are making a value judgment that the well-being of consumers and that of producers are equally important.

Not everyone agrees that society should try to maximize this measure of welfare. Groups of producers argue for legislation that helps them even if it hurts consumers by more than the producers gain—as though only producer surplus matters. Similarly, some consumer advocates argue that we should care only about consumers, so social welfare should include only consumer surplus.

We use the consumer surplus plus producer surplus measure of welfare in this chapter (and postpone a further discussion of other welfare concepts until the next chapter). One of the most striking results in economics is that competitive markets maximize this measure of welfare. If either less or more output than the competitive level is produced, welfare falls.

Why Producing Less than the Competitive Output Lowers Welfare

Producing less than the competitive output lowers welfare. At the competitive equilibrium in Figure 9.4, e_1, where output is Q_1 and price is p_1, consumer surplus equals areas $CS_1 = A + B + C$, producer surplus is $PS_1 = D + E$, and total welfare is $W_1 = A + B + C + D + E$. If output is reduced to Q_2 so that price rises to p_2 at e_2, consumer surplus is $CS_2 = A$, producer surplus is $PS_2 = B + D$, and welfare is $W_2 = A + B + D$.

The change in consumer surplus is

$$\Delta CS = CS_2 - CS_1 = A - (A + B + C) = -B - C.$$

Consumers lose B because they have to pay $p_2 - p_1$ more than at the competitive price for the Q_2 units they buy. Consumers lose C because they buy only Q_2 rather than Q_1 at the higher price.

The change in producer surplus is

$$\Delta PS = PS_2 - PS_1 = (B + D) - (D + E) = B - E.$$

Producers gain B because they now sell Q_2 units at p_2 rather than p_1. They lose E because they sell $Q_2 - Q_1$ fewer units.

The change in welfare, $\Delta W = W_2 - W_1$, is[5]

$$\Delta W = \Delta CS + \Delta PS = (-B - C) + (B - E) = -C - E.$$

The area B is a transfer from consumers to producers—the extra amount consumers pay for the Q_2 units goes to the sellers—so it does not affect welfare. Welfare drops

---

[5]The change in welfare is
$$\Delta W = W_2 - W_1 = (CS_2 + PS_2) - (CS_1 + PS_1) = (CS_2 - CS_1) + (PS_2 - PS_1) = \Delta CS + \Delta PS.$$

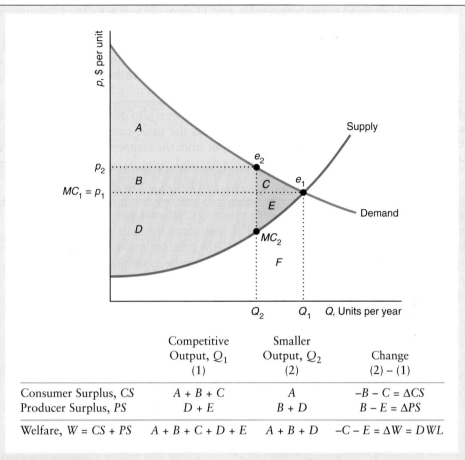

	Competitive Output, Q_1 (1)	Smaller Output, Q_2 (2)	Change (2) – (1)
Consumer Surplus, CS	$A + B + C$	A	$-B - C = \Delta CS$
Producer Surplus, PS	$D + E$	$B + D$	$B - E = \Delta PS$
Welfare, $W = CS + PS$	$A + B + C + D + E$	$A + B + D$	$-C - E = \Delta W = DWL$

Figure 9.4 Why Reducing Output from the Competitive Level Lowers Welfare. Reducing output from the competitive level, Q_1, to Q_2 causes price to increase from p_1 to p_2. Consumers suffer: Consumer surplus is now A, a fall of $\Delta CS = -B -$ C. Producers may gain or lose: Producer surplus is now $B + D$, a change of $\Delta PS = B - E$. Overall, welfare falls by $\Delta W = -C - E$, which is a deadweight loss (DWL) to society.

because the consumer loss of C and the producer loss of E benefit no one. This drop in welfare, $\Delta W = -C - E$, is a **deadweight loss** (DWL): the net reduction in welfare from losses of surplus by one group that are not offset by a gain to another group from an action that alters a market equilibrium.

The deadweight loss results because consumers value extra output by more than the marginal cost of producing it. At each output between Q_2 and Q_1, consumers' marginal willingness to pay for another unit—the height of the demand curve—is greater than the marginal cost of producing the next unit—the height of the supply curve. For example, at e_2, consumers value the next unit of output at p_2, which is much greater than the marginal cost, MC_2, of producing it. Increasing output from Q_2 to Q_1 raises firms' variable cost by area F, the area under the marginal cost (supply) curve between Q_2 and Q_1. Consumers value this extra output by the area under

Given holiday expenditures of about $40 billion per year in the United States, he concludes that a conservative estimate of the deadweight loss of Christmas, Hanukkah, and other holidays with gift-giving rituals is between a tenth and a third as large as estimates of the deadweight loss from inefficient income taxation.

The question remains why people don't give cash instead of presents. If the reason is that they get pleasure from picking the "perfect" gift, the deadweight loss that adjusts for the pleasure of the giver is lower than these calculations suggest. (Bah, humbug!)

9.4 | POLICIES THAT SHIFT SUPPLY CURVES

One of the main reasons that economists developed welfare tools was to predict the impact of government policies and other events that alter a competitive equilibrium, which we consider next. We focus on government policies rather than other shocks caused by random events or other members of society because we, as part of the electorate, can influence these decisions.

Virtually all government actions affect a competitive equilibrium in one of two ways. Some government policies, such as limits on the number of firms in a market, shift the supply or demand curve. Other government actions, such as sales taxes, create a wedge between price and marginal cost so that they are not equal, as they were in the original competitive equilibrium.

These government actions move us from an unconstrained competitive equilibrium to a new, constrained competitive equilibrium. Because welfare was maximized at the initial competitive equilibrium, the following examples of government-induced changes lower welfare. In later chapters, we examine markets in which welfare was not maximized initially, so government intervention may raise welfare.

Although government policies may cause either the supply curve or the demand curve to shift, we concentrate on policies that limit supply because they are frequently used and have clear-cut effects. The two most common types of government policies that shift the supply curve are limits on the number of firms in a market and quotas or other limits on the amount of output that firms may produce. We study restrictions on entry and exit of firms in this section and examine quotas later in the chapter.

Government policies that cause a decrease in supply at each possible price (shift the supply curve to the left) lead to fewer purchases by consumers at higher prices, an outcome that lowers consumer surplus and welfare. Welfare falls when governments restrict the consumption of competitive products that we all agree are *goods*, such as food and medical services. In contrast, if most of society wants to discourage the use of certain products, such as hallucinogenic drugs and poisons, policies that restrict consumption may increase some measures of society's welfare.

Governments, other organizations, and social pressures limit the number of firms in at least three ways. The number of firms is restricted explicitly in some markets, such as the one for taxi service. In other markets, some members of society are barred from owning firms or performing certain jobs or services. In yet other markets, the number of firms is controlled indirectly by raising the cost of entry.

Restricting the Number of Firms

A limit on the number of firms causes a shift of the supply curve to the left, which raises the equilibrium price and reduces the equilibrium quantity. Consumers are harmed: They don't buy as much as they would at lower prices. Firms that are in the market when the limits are first imposed benefit from higher profits.

To illustrate these results, we examine the regulation of taxicabs. Virtually every country in the world regulates taxicabs (except Sweden, which deregulated in 1991). Many American cities limit the number of taxicabs. To operate a cab in these cities legally, you must possess a city-issued permit, which may be a piece of paper or a medallion (a coinlike metal object).

Two explanations are given for such regulation. First, using permits to limit the number of cabs raises the earnings of permit owners—usually taxi fleet owners—who lobby city officials for such restrictions. Second, some city officials contend that limiting cabs allows for better regulation of cabbies' behavior and protection of consumers. (However, it would seem possible that cities could directly regulate behavior and not restrict the number of cabs.)

Whatever the justification for such regulation, the limit on the number of cabs raises the market prices. If the city doesn't limit entry, a virtually unlimited number of potential taxi drivers with identical costs can enter freely.

Panel a of Figure 9.6 shows a typical taxi owner's marginal cost curve, MC, and average cost curve, AC^1. The MC curve slopes upward because a typical cabbie's opportunity cost of working more hours increases as the cabbie works longer hours (drives more customers). An outward shift of the demand curve is met by new firms entering, so the long-run supply curve of taxi rides, S^1 in panel b, is horizontal at the minimum of AC^1 (Chapter 8). For the market demand curve in the figure, the equilibrium is E_1, where the equilibrium price, p_1, equals the minimum of AC^1 of a typical cab. The total number of rides is $Q_1 = n_1 q_1$, where n_1 is the equilibrium number of cabs and q_1 is the number of rides per month provided by a typical cab.

Consumer surplus, $A + B + C$, is the area under the market demand curve above p_1 up to Q_1. There is no producer surplus because the supply curve is horizontal at the market price, which equals marginal and average cost. Thus welfare is the same as consumer surplus.

Legislation limits the number of permits to operate cabs to $n_2 < n_1$. The market supply curve, S^2, is the horizontal sum of the marginal cost curves above minimum average cost of the n_2 firms in the market. For the market to produce more than $n_2 q_1$ rides, the price must rise to induce the n_2 firms to supply more.

With the same demand curve as before, the equilibrium market price rises to p_2. At this higher price, each licensed cab firm produces more than before by operating longer hours, $q_2 > q_1$, but the total number of rides, $Q_2 = n_2 q_2$, falls because there are fewer cabs, n_2. Consumer surplus is A, producer surplus is B, and welfare is $A + B$.

Thus because of the higher fares (prices) under a permit system, consumer surplus falls by

$$\Delta CS = -B - C.$$

The producer surplus of the lucky permit owners rises by

$$\Delta PS = B.$$

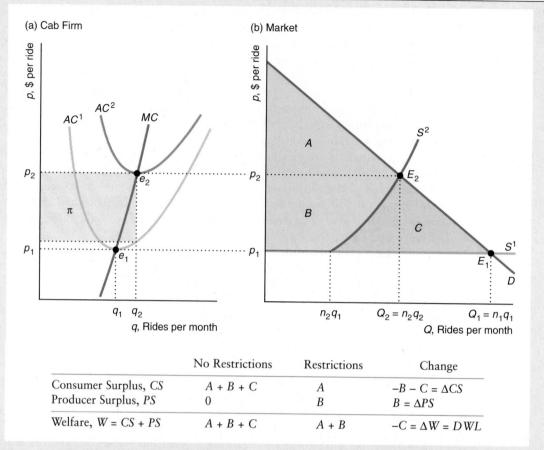

	No Restrictions	Restrictions	Change
Consumer Surplus, CS	$A + B + C$	A	$-B - C = \Delta CS$
Producer Surplus, PS	0	B	$B = \Delta PS$
Welfare, $W = CS + PS$	$A + B + C$	$A + B$	$-C = \Delta W = DWL$

Figure 9.6 Effect of a Restriction on the Number of Cabs. A restriction on the number of cabs causes the supply curve to shift from S^1 to S^2 in the short run and the equilibrium to change from E_1 to E_2. The resulting lost surplus, C, is a deadweight loss to society. In the long run, the unusual profit, π, created by the restriction becomes a rent to the owner of the license. As the license owner increases the charge for using the license, the average cost curve rises to AC^2, so the cab driver earns a zero long-run profit. That is, the producer surplus goes to the permit holder, not to the cab driver.

As a result, total welfare falls:

$$\Delta W = \Delta CS + \Delta PS = (-B - C) + B = -C,$$

which is a deadweight loss.

By preventing other potential cab firms from entering the market, limiting cab permits creates economic profit, the area labeled π in panel a, for permit owners. In many cities, these permits can be sold or rented, so the owner of the scarce resource, the permit, can capture the unusual profit, or *rent* (Chapter 8). The rent for the permit or the implicit rent paid by the owner of a permit causes the cab driver's average cost to rise to AC^2. Because the rent allows the use of the cab for a certain period of time, it is a fixed cost that is unrelated to output. As a result, it does not affect the marginal cost.

Cab drivers earn zero economic profits because the market price, p_2, equals their average cost, the minimum of AC^2. The producer surplus, B, created by the limits on entry go to the original owners of the permits rather than to the current cab drivers. Thus the permit owners are the *only* ones that benefit from the restrictions, and their gains are less than the losses to others.

In many cities, the rents and welfare effects that result from these laws are large. The size of the loss to consumers and the benefit to permit holders depend on how severely a city limits the number of cabs.

Application   TAXICAB MEDALLIONS

Too bad the only people who know how to run the country are busy driving cabs and cutting hair.
                                                                    —George Burns

Limiting the number of cabs has large effects in cities around the world. Some cities regulate the number of cabs much more severely than others. Only a tenth as many cabs have permits to operate legally in San Francisco as in Washington, D.C., which has fewer people but does not restrict the number of cabs. The number of residents per cabs is 757 in Detroit, 748 (soon to be 612) in San Francisco, 538 in Dallas, 533 in Baltimore, 350 in Boston, 301 in New Orleans, and 203 in Honolulu.

These cities allow only permit holders to operate cabs. Some cities, such as San Francisco, do not allow the permits to be resold, but others, including New York City, allow resales.

In San Francisco, permit holders lease their permits for up to $3,500 a month to taxi companies, which own only about a quarter of all permits. Thus each permit is worth up to $42,000 a year. This rent is the extra producer surplus of the lucky permit holders that would be eliminated if anyone could supply taxi services.

In 1937, when New York City started regulating the number of cabs, all 11,787 cab owners received permits in the form of medallions. Because New York City allows these medallions to be sold, medallion holders do not have to operate a cab to benefit from the restriction on the number of cabs. A holder can sell a medallion for an amount that captures the unusually high future profits from the limit on the number of cabs. Cab drivers who lease medallions certainly don't make these unusual returns: Some earn as little as $50 a day.

Even by the late 1940s, people must have believed that the number of cabs with permits was not much different from the equilibrium number in the absence of this law because permits sold for very little money. Apparently, this limit has become more binding over time: The price of a medallion nearly tripled from 1980 to 1989, to $140,000. The price of a medallion reached nearly a quarter of a million dollars by the end of 1999.

A 1984 study for the U.S. Department of Transportation estimated the annual extra cost to consumers from restrictions on the number of taxicabs throughout the United States at nearly $800 million. The total lost consumer surplus exceeds $800 million, because this amount does not include lost waiting time and other inconveniences associated with having fewer taxis.

Excluding Certain Groups from Owning Firms

By excluding certain groups, other groups can limit the number of firms or service providers in a market. If the favored group has so few firms that they earn economic profits, the exclusion of the other group restricts the total number of firms in the market. Such restrictions harm consumers and benefit members of the favored group who own firms.

Application   DISCRIMINATING AGAINST GROUPS

Sometimes by themselves and sometimes with the help of governments, certain groups have excluded other groups from owning firms or providing certain services. For example, unions and guilds have historically prevented outsiders from running certain types of firms or performing certain services (see **www.awlonline.com/perloff**, "Unions and Guilds"). Laws discriminating against a race or group are another example.

For years, apartheid laws denied black South Africans the right to own property, restricted where they could work, and made it difficult for them to obtain loans needed to start and run businesses. Since the repeal of the Group Areas Act in May 1991, which effectively ended apartheid, new black-owned businesses entered markets in previously white-only central business districts of South Africa.

For example, Africa Hut offers pap (a stiff corn porridge) served with malamagodu (tripe) or morogo (a leafy green vegetable), samp (a mixture of hominy and beans) and steak, skop (sheep heads), and fat cakes (fried dough) while "township jive" blares in the background. Until recently, these African foods were not available in downtown Johannesburg, where one found American-style chicken and burger shops on every corner.

Africa Hut has many customers. One reason is price: a large portion of pap with chicken stew and morogo costs about $1.60, half the price of a two-piece chicken dinner at a KFC outlet across the street. Because it is cost effective, this restaurant is thriving. By 1994, the black and white investors in Africa Hut already had three locations in Johannesburg, expected to open 10 franchises throughout South Africa soon, and were planning to acquire a U.S. trademark. The end of apartheid resulted in entry by many black-owned firms in a variety of markets. This new entry benefits consumers, who can buy more varied food at lower prices, and harms white-owned firms that were receiving unusually high profits under apartheid.

In the United States, Canada, the United Kingdom, and many other countries, barriers to various ethnic, racial, and gender groups are created by discrimination rather than by overt government acts. To the degree that discrimination keeps racial minorities, women, or other groups from fully participating in the market, it reduces the degree of competition in that market.

Raising Entry and Exit Costs

Instead of directly restricting the number of firms that may enter a market, governments and other organizations may raise the cost of entering, thereby indirectly restricting that number. Similarly, raising the cost of exiting a market discourages some firms from entering.

Entry Barriers. If its cost will be greater than that of firms already in the market, a potential firm might not enter a market even if existing firms are making a profit. Any cost that falls only on potential entrants and not on current firms discourages entry. A long-run **barrier to entry** is an explicit restriction or a cost that applies only to potential new firms—existing firms are not subject to the restriction or do not bear the cost.

At the time they entered, incumbent firms had to pay many of the costs of entering a market that new entrants incur, such as the fixed costs of building plants, buying equipment, and advertising a new product. For example, the fixed cost to McDonald's and other fast-food chains of opening a new fast-food restaurant is about $2 million. These fixed costs are *costs of entry* but are *not* barriers to entry because they apply equally to incumbents and entrants. Costs incurred by both incumbents and entrants do not discourage potential firms from entering a market if existing firms are making money. Potential entrants know that they will do as well as existing firms once they are in business, so they are willing to enter as long as profit opportunities exist.

Large sunk costs can be barriers to entry under two conditions. First, if capital markets do not work well, so new firms have difficulty raising money, new firms may be unable to enter profitable markets. Second, if a firm must incur a large *sunk* cost, which makes the loss if it exits great, the firm may be reluctant to enter a market in which it is uncertain of success.

If barriers to entry limit the ability of firms to enter a market in response to a profit opportunity, equilibrium price and firms' profits may remain high indefinitely. When a federal court declared unconstitutional a 50-year-old statute that allowed only five wholesalers to sell milk in New York City, a new firm entered the market, and the price per gallon fell 70¢, producing a savings to consumers of $80 million a year.[6]

---

[6]Oliver, Daniel, "Competition Deserves More than Lip Service," Center for the Study of American Business, Contemporary Issues Series 27, March 1988.

Application   **BARRIERS TO PROTECT OUR WAY OF LIFE**

Cities and countries commonly establish barriers to entry to protect existing firms or to achieve other goals. For example, many U.S. communities require that potential psychiatric hospitals incur the expense of proving the need for more hospitals in the community. Laws frequently stipulate that new factories be built with extra features to prevent pollution or earthquake damage, while exempting older factories.

Moratoriums and explicit bans are common. In the late 1990s, for example, Bermuda set a moratorium on new hotel beds. The ruling excluded major hotel chains from gaining a foothold, thereby protecting the business of smaller existing guest houses.

In 1997, the San Francisco Board of Supervisors passed an 18-month moratorium on new coffee shops in several neighborhoods. The board also has a long-standing rule allowing full-service restaurants to operate only in new buildings or in locations being vacated by other restaurants and has banned new liquor licenses for restaurants and bars in some districts.

Starting in 1998, to stem the "march of the superpub," Scottish publicans called for a three-year moratorium on new liquor licenses. The president of the Scottish Licensed Traders' Association warned that Scottish pub culture would be at risk if English chains were permitted to expand into Scotland. The outcome, he predicted, would be the closure of hundreds of existing pubs in a price-cutting war that would in turn lead to alcohol abuse and increased street crime. An alternative explanation is that his group fears competition.

Exit Barriers. Some markets have barriers that make it difficult (though typically not impossible) for a firm to exit by going out of business. In the short run, exit barriers can keep the number of firms in a market relatively high. In the long run, exit barriers may limit the number of firms in a market.

Why do exit barriers limit the number of firms in a market? Suppose that you are considering starting a construction firm with no capital or other fixed factors. The firm's only input is labor. You know that there is relatively little demand for construction during business downturns and in the winter. To avoid paying workers when business is slack, you plan to shut down during those periods. If you can avoid losses by shutting down during those periods, you enter this market if your expected economic profits during good periods are zero or positive.

Now suppose that a new law requires that you give your workers six months' warning before laying them off. Because the new law prevents you from shutting down quickly, you know that you'll regularly suffer losses during business downturns because you'll have to pay your workers for up to six months during periods when you have nothing for them to do. Knowing that you'll incur these regular losses, you are less inclined to enter the market. Unless the economic profits during good periods are much higher than zero—high enough to offset your losses—you will not enter the market.

If exit barriers limit the number of firms, the same analysis that we used to examine entry barriers applies. Thus exit barriers may raise prices, lower consumer surplus, and reduce welfare.

| *Application* | **JOB TERMINATION LAWS** |

Many government-imposed exit barriers are designed to protect workers who would be laid off in the event of a plant closure. How far in advance Canadian employers must give notice of termination varies by the size of the firm, reaching a maximum of 16 weeks for firms with more than 300 employees. In the United Kingdom, the amount of advance warning varies with length of service, ranging from 1 week to 8 weeks for workers with 15 or more years of service.

These warning periods may raise costs to firms enough to reduce the number of firms in markets in which downturns are frequent. So even though these warnings help workers in some markets prepare for layoffs, these exit barriers may reduce the number of employers in an industry—and hence the number of workers employed in that industry.

9.5 POLICIES THAT CREATE A WEDGE BETWEEN SUPPLY AND DEMAND

The most common government policies that create a wedge between supply and demand curves are sales taxes and price controls. Such policies frequently result in prices that are greater than marginal cost. Because consumers value the good more than it costs to produce it, these polices lower consumer surplus and welfare.

Welfare Effects of a Sales Tax

A new sales tax causes the price consumers pay to rise (Chapter 3), resulting in a loss of consumer surplus, $\Delta CS < 0$, and a fall in the price firms receive, resulting in a drop in producer surplus, $\Delta PS < 0$. However, the new tax provides the government with new tax revenue, $\Delta T = T > 0$ (if tax revenue was zero before this new tax).

Assuming that the government does something useful with the tax revenue, we should include tax revenue in our definition of welfare:

$$W = CS + PS + T.$$

As a result, the change in welfare is

$$\Delta W = \Delta CS + \Delta PS + \Delta T.$$

Even when we include tax revenue in our welfare measure, a specific tax must lower welfare in a competitive market. We show the welfare loss from a specific tax of $\tau = 11\cent$ per rose stem in Figure 9.7.

Without the tax, the intersection of the demand curve, D, and the supply curve, S, determines the competitive equilibrium, e_1, at a price of $30\cent$ per stem and a quantity of 1.25 billion rose stems per year. Consumer surplus is $A + B + C$, producer surplus is $D + E + F$, tax revenue is zero, and there is no deadweight loss.

The specific tax creates an $11\cent$ wedge (Chapter 3) between the price consumers pay, $32\cent$, and the price producers receive, $32\cent - \tau = 21\cent$. Equilibrium output falls from 1.25 to 1.16 billion stems per year.

The extra $2\cent$ per stem that buyers pay causes consumer surplus to fall by $B + C$ = \$24.1 million per year, as we showed earlier. Due to the $9\cent$ drop in the price firms

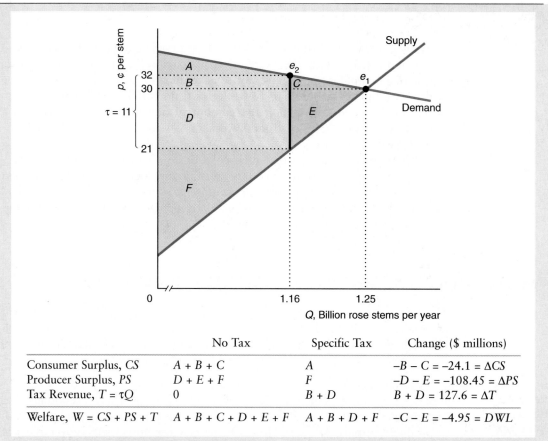

	No Tax	Specific Tax	Change ($ millions)
Consumer Surplus, CS	$A + B + C$	A	$-B - C = -24.1 = \Delta CS$
Producer Surplus, PS	$D + E + F$	F	$-D - E = -108.45 = \Delta PS$
Tax Revenue, $T = \tau Q$	0	$B + D$	$B + D = 127.6 = \Delta T$
Welfare, $W = CS + PS + T$	$A + B + C + D + E + F$	$A + B + D + F$	$-C - E = -4.95 = DWL$

Figure 9.7 Welfare Effects of a Specific Tax on Roses. The $\tau = 11¢$ specific tax on roses creates an $11¢$ per stem wedge between the price customers pay, $32¢$, and the price producers receive, $21¢$. Tax revenue is $T = \tau Q = \$127.6$ million per year. The deadweight loss to society is $\$4.95$ million per year.

receive, they lose producer surplus of $D + E = \$108.45$ million per year (Solved Problem 9.2). The government gains tax revenue of $\tau Q = 11¢$ per stem $\times$ 1.16 billion stems per year $= \$127.6$ million per year, area $B + D$.

The combined loss of consumer surplus and producer surplus is only partially offset by the government's gain in tax revenue, so that welfare drops:

$$\Delta W = \Delta CS + \Delta PS + \Delta T = -\$24.1 - \$108.45 + \$127.6 = -\$4.95 \text{ million per year.}$$

This deadweight loss is area $C + E$.

Why does society suffer a deadweight loss? The reason is that the tax lowers output from the competitive level where welfare is maximized. An equivalent explanation for this inefficiency or loss to society is that the tax puts a wedge between price and marginal cost. At the new equilibrium, buyers are willing to pay $32¢$ for one more stem of roses, while the marginal cost to firms is only $21¢$ (= the price minus τ). Shouldn't at least one more rose be produced if consumers are willing to pay nearly a third more than the cost of producing it? That's what our welfare study indicates.

Welfare Effects of a Price Floor

In some markets, the government sets a *price floor*, or minimum price, which is the lowest price a consumer can pay legally for the good. For example, in most countries, the government creates price floors under at least some agricultural prices to guarantee producers that they will receive at least a price of $\underline{p}$ for their good. If the market price is above $\underline{p}$, the support program is irrelevant. If the market price would be below $\underline{p}$, however, the government buys as much output as necessary to drive the price up to $\underline{p}$. Since 1929 (the start of the Great Depression), the U.S. government has used price floors or similar programs to keep prices of many agricultural products above the price that competition would determine in unregulated markets.[7]

We now show the effect of a price support using estimated supply and demand curves for the soybean market (Holt, 1992). The intersection of the market demand curve and the market supply curve in Figure 9.8 determines the competitive equilibrium, e, in the absence of a price support program, where the equilibrium price is p_1 = \$4.59 per bushel and the equilibrium quantity is Q_1 = 2.1 billion bushels per year.

With a price support on soybeans of $\underline{p}$ = \$5.00 per bushel and the government's pledge to buy as much output as farmers want to sell, quantity sold is Q_s = 2.2 billion bushels.[8] At $\underline{p}$, consumers buy less output, Q_d = 1.9 billion bushels, than the Q_1 they would have bought at the market-determined price p_1. As a result, consumer surplus falls by $B + C$ = \$864 million. The government buys $Q_g = Q_s - Q_d \approx$ 0.3 billion bushels per year, which is the excess supply, at a cost of $T = \underline{p} \times Q_g = C + D + F + G$ = \$1.283 billion.

The government cannot resell the output domestically because if it tried to do so, it would succeed only in driving down the price consumers pay. The government stores the output or sends it abroad.

Although farmers gain producer surplus of $B + C + D$ = \$921 million, this program is an inefficient way to transfer money to them. Assuming that the government's purchases have no alternative use, the change in welfare is $\Delta W = \Delta CS + \Delta PS - T = -C - F - G = -\$1.226$ billion per year.[9] This deadweight loss reflects two distortions in this market:

- **Excess production:** More output is produced than is consumed, so Q_g is stored, destroyed, or shipped abroad.
- **Inefficiency in consumption:** At the quantity they actually buy, Q_d, consumers are willing to pay \$5 for the last bushel of soybeans, which is more than the marginal cost, MC = \$3.60, of producing that bushel.

---

[7]My favorite program was the wool and mohair subsidy. The U.S. government instituted wool subsidies after the Korean War to ensure "strategic supplies" for uniforms. Congress later added the mohair subsidies, though mohair has no military use. In some years, the mohair subsidy exceeded the amount consumers paid for mohair, and the subsidies on wool and mohair reached a fifth of a billion dollars. (No doubt the end of these subsidies in 1995 has endangered national security.)

[8]In 1985, the period Holt studied, the price support was \$5.02. It has since ranged between \$4.92 and \$5.26.

[9]This measure of deadweight loss underestimates the true loss. The government also pays storage and administration costs. In 1999, the U.S. Department of Agriculture, which runs farm support programs, had 104,700 employees, or nearly one worker for every farm that received assistance (although many of these employees have other job responsibilities).

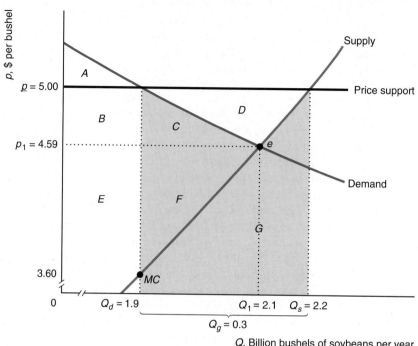

	No Price Support	Price Support	Change ($ millions)
Consumer Surplus, CS	A + B + C	A	−B − C = −864 = ΔCS
Producer Surplus, PS	E + F	B + C + D + E + F	B + C + D = 921 = ΔPS
Government Expense, −X	0	−C − D − F − G	−C − D − F − G = −1,283 = ΔX
Welfare, W = CS + PS − X	A + B + C + E + F	A + B + E − G	−C − F − G = −1,226 = ΔW = DWL

Figure 9.8 Effect of Price Supports in Soybeans. Without government price supports, the equilibrium is *e*, where p_1 = $4.59 bushel and Q_1 = 2.1 billion bushels of soybeans per year (based on estimates in Holt, 1992). With the price support at $\underline{p}$ = $5.00 per bushel, output sold increases to Q_s and consumer purchases fall to Q_d, so the government must buy $Q_g = Q_s − Q_d$ at a cost of $1.283 billion per year. The deadweight loss is C + F + G = $1.226 billion per year, not counting storage and administrative costs.

Price Floors and Quotas. Because of price supports, the government was buying and storing large quantities of food, much of which was allowed to spoil. As a consequence, the government started limiting the amount farmers could produce. Because there is uncertainty about how much a farmer will produce, the government set quotas or limits on the amount of land farmers could use, so as to restrict their output. However, a peanut or tobacco farmer whose acreage is limited could increase the amount of fertilizer and other inputs used to increase yields per acre. Thus the quotas can lead to inefficient production in which too much of noncontrolled inputs are used relative to controlled inputs.

Solved Problem 9.3

For simplicity, suppose that the government could put a binding quota, $\bar{Q}$, on the amount of soybeans farmers may produce (as opposed to a restriction on inputs), equal to the equilibrium quantity in the absence of a price support. What is the impact of such a quota on consumers, producers, the government purchases, and overall welfare in the soybean market, in which the price support is $5 per bushel?

Answer

1. *Describe the market if there is only a price support*: On the accompanying graph, at a price support of $5 per bushel, farmers sell Q_2, of which consumers buy Q_d and the government buys Q_g (= $Q_2 - Q_d$). Consumer

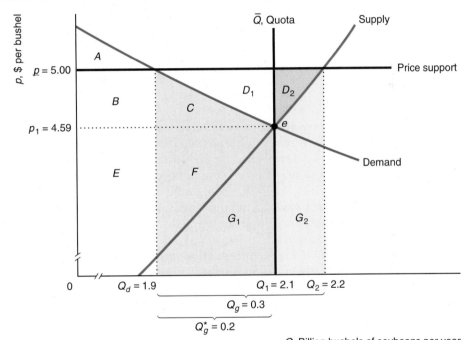

	Price Support	Price Support and Quota	Change: Support Alone Versus Support and Quota ($ millions)
Consumer Surplus, CS	A	A	$0 = \Delta CS$
Producer Surplus, PS	$B + C + D_1 + D_2 + E + F$	$B + C + D_1 + E + F$	$-D_2 = -16 = \Delta PS$
Government Expense, $-X$	$-C - D_1 - D_2 - F - G - G_2$	$-C - D_1 - F - G_1$	$D_2 + G_2 = 364 = \Delta T$
Welfare, $W = CS + PS - X$	$A + B + E - G_1 - G_2$	$A + B + E - G_1$	$G_2 = 348 = \Delta W$

surplus is A, producer surplus is $B + C + D_1 + D_2 + E + F$, and the loss from government expenditures is $-C - D_1 - D_2 - F - G_1 - G_2$.

2. *Show the effect of the quota*: The quota equals the equilibrium quantity in the absence of a price support, $\overline{Q} = Q_1$, so we add a vertical line showing the quota constraint at Q_1. The government now buys Q_g^* (= $Q_1 - Q_d$). Consumer surplus is A, producer surplus is $B + C + D_1 + E + F$, and loss from government expenditures is $-C - D_1 - F - G_1$.

3. *Compare prices, quantity, and welfare with and without the quota*: The quota reduces the amount the government buys by $Q_g^* - Q_g$, causing the government expenditures to fall by $D_2 + G_2$. Farmers' producer surplus drops by $-D_2$. Because the price to consumers is still p, consumers buy the same amount, Q_d, as before the quota, and their consumer surplus, A, is unchanged. The welfare is higher than it would be with price supports alone by G_2, but there's still deadweight loss. Compared to an unregulated market, welfare is lower with a price support and a quota by $-C - F - G_1$.

Recent Government Responses to Surpluses. In some years, the U.S. government paid to destroy some of a subsidized crop or some of the inputs. In the 1980s, the government was overwhelmed by the surpluses of butter and powdered milk due to subsidies. It sent some of these milk products to other countries by providing export subsidies. In 1986, though, the government announced that it would pay dairy farmers to kill 1.6 million cows. (As some of these slaughtered animals were sold for meat, this program lowered the price of cattle, thereby hurting cattle ranchers.)

Today, the U.S. government relies primarily on a different type of price support program, in which it adds a subsidy to whatever price consumers pay on the quantity actually sold to them. As a result of this change, the government buys no output at all, and the inefficiency of the programs has been substantially reduced.

Who Benefits. Presumably, the purpose of these programs is to help poor farmers, not to hurt consumers and taxpayers. However, the lion's share of American farm subsidies goes to large agricultural corporations, not to poor farmers. Nearly two-thirds (63%) of U.S. farms have sales of less than $20,000 per year, yet these farms received only 11.5% of the total direct government payments for agriculture in 1996.[10] In contrast, farms with over $1 million in annual sales are only 1.1% of all farms, yet they received 8.3% of all direct government payments. Farms with over a quarter of a million dollars in sales (top 8% of all farms) received 42.1% of the payments.

Application   INTERNATIONAL COST OF AGRICULTURAL SUBSIDIES

In some countries, government farm subsidies exceed the amount farmers receive from consumers. The Organization for Economic Cooperation and Development (OECD) collects information about such subsidies in its member nations, which include most European countries, Australia, Canada, Japan, New Zealand, and the United States. Farmers in OECD countries received $274 billion in producer support payments in 1999. Subsidies for major crops were 44% of the amount consumers paid in 1992 and 36% in 1996.

In 1998, support payments were $49 billion in Japan, $47 billion in the United States, and $129 billion in the European Union. As of 1999, farm programs constituted half of the EU budget.

Switzerland's farm supports are the largest fraction, 73%, of total receipts among the OECD nations. That is, the Swiss government gives farmers nearly $3 for every $1 a farmer earns from sales. The support shares are 70% in Norway, 69% in Iceland, 63% in Japan, 45% in the European Union, 22% in the United States, 16% in Canada, and 7% in Australia. Unlike other OECD countries, New Zealand has largely eliminated farm supports. Its support payments as a percentage of the value of farm production fell from 11% in 1986–1988 to 2% in 1991–1993 and only 1% in 1998.

The cost of farmer supports to the average taxpayer is substantial. In 1998, the average person in the European Union pays $381 a year to subsidize farmers. These per-person payments were $879 in Switzerland, $656 in Iceland, $449 in Japan, $363 in the United States, $140 in Canada, $92 in Australia, $63 in Mexico, and $26 in New Zealand.

Welfare Effects of a Price Ceiling

In some markets, the government sets a *price ceiling*: the highest price that a firm can legally charge. If the government sets the ceiling below the precontrol competitive price, consumers demand more than the precontrol equilibrium quantity and firms supply less than that quantity (Chapter 2). Producer surplus must fall because firms receive a lower price and sell fewer units.

Because of the price ceiling, consumers can buy the good at a lower price but cannot buy as much of it as they'd like. Because less is sold than at the precontrol equilibrium, there is deadweight loss: Consumers value the good more than the marginal cost of producing extra units.

In the 1970s, the U.S. government used price controls to keep gasoline prices below the market price (Chapter 2). This policy led to long lines at gas stations

---

[10]See **www.econ.ag.gov**, "Farm Business Economic Reports."

and large deadweight losses. Frech and Lee (1987) estimate that the loss in consumer surplus in California in 1985 dollars was $1.2 billion during the December 1973 to March 1974 price controls and $800 million during the May 1979 to July 1979 controls.

Solved Problem 9.4   What is the effect on the equilibrium and welfare if the government sets a price ceiling, $\bar{p}$, below the unregulated competitive equilibrium price?

Answer

1. *Show the initial unregulated equilibrium*: The intersection of the demand curve and the supply curve determines the unregulated, competitive equilibrium e_1, where the equilibrium quantity is Q_1.

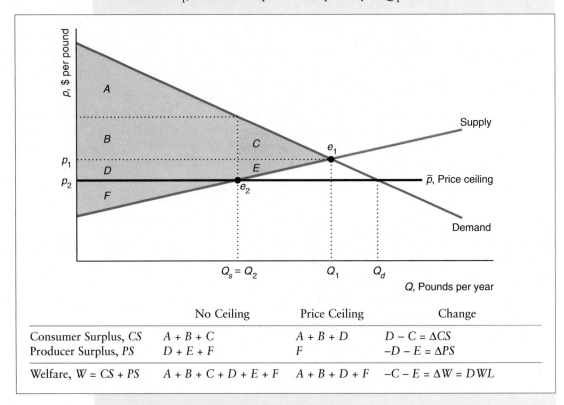

	No Ceiling	Price Ceiling	Change
Consumer Surplus, CS	$A + B + C$	$A + B + D$	$D - C = \Delta CS$
Producer Surplus, PS	$D + E + F$	F	$-D - E = \Delta PS$
Welfare, $W = CS + PS$	$A + B + C + D + E + F$	$A + B + D + F$	$-C - E = \Delta W = DWL$

2. *Show how the equilibrium changes with the price ceiling*: Because the price ceiling, $\bar{p}$, is set below the equilibrium price of p_1, the ceiling binds. At this lower price, consumer demand increases to Q_d while the quantity firms are willing to supply falls to Q_s, so only $Q_s = Q_2$ units are sold at the new equilibrium, e_2. Thus the price control causes the equilibrium quantity and price to fall, but consumers have excess demand of $Q_d - Q_s$.

3. *Describe the welfare effects*: Because consumers are able to buy Q_s units at a lower price than before the controls, they gain area D. Consumers lose consumer surplus of C, however, because they can purchase only Q_s instead of Q_1 units of output. Thus consumers gain net consumer surplus of $D - C$. Because they sell fewer units at a lower price, firms lose producer surplus $-D - E$. Part of this loss, D, is transferred to consumers because of lower prices, but the rest, E, is a loss to society. The total deadweight loss to society is $\Delta W = \Delta CS + \Delta PS = -C - E$.

9.6 | COMPARING BOTH TYPES OF POLICIES: IMPORTS

Traditionally, most of Australia's imports come from overseas.
—Keppel Enderbery, former Australian cabinet minister

We've examined examples of government policies that shift supply or demand curves and policies that create a wedge between supply and demand. Governments use both types of policies to control international trade.

Allowing imports of foreign goods benefits the importing country. If a government reduces imports of a good, the domestic price rises; the profits of domestic firms that produce the good increase, but domestic consumers are hurt. Our analysis will show that the loss to consumers exceeds the gain to producers.

The government of the (potentially) importing country can use one of four import policies:

- **Allow free trade:** Any firm can sell in this country without restrictions.
- **Ban all imports:** The government sets a quota of zero on imports.
- **Set a positive quota:** The government limits imports to $\overline{Q}$.
- **Set a tariff:** The government imposes a tax called a **tariff** (or a *duty*) on only imported goods.

We compare welfare under free trade to welfare under bans and quotas, which change the supply curve, and to welfare under tariffs, which create a wedge between supply and demand.

To illustrate the differences in welfare under these various policies, we examine the U.S. market for crude oil.[11] We make two assumptions for the sake of simplicity. First, we assume that transportation costs are zero. Second, we assume that the supply curve of the potentially imported good is horizontal at the world price p^*. Given these two assumptions, the importing country, the United States, can buy as much of this good as it wants at p^* per unit: It is a price taker in the world market because its demand is too small to influence the world price.

---

[11]We assume that the market is competitive. Our figures are based on short-run, constant-elasticity supply and demand equations for crude oil in 1988 using the short-run supply and demand elasticities reported in Anderson and Metzger (1991).

Free Trade Versus a Ban on Imports

No nation was ever ruined by trade.   —Benjamin Franklin

Preventing imports into the domestic market raises the price, as we illustrated in Chapter 2 for the Japan rice market. The estimated U.S. domestic supply curve, S^a, is upward sloping, and the foreign supply curve is horizontal at the world price of $14.70 in Figure 9.9. The total U.S. supply curve, S^1, is the horizontal sum of the domestic supply curve and the foreign supply curve. Thus S^1 is the same as the upward-sloping domestic supply curve for prices below $14.70 and is horizontal at $14.70. Under free trade, the United States imports crude oil if its domestic price in the absence of imports would exceed the world price, $14.70 per barrel.

The free-trade equilibrium, e_1, is determined by the intersection of S^1 and the demand curve, where the U.S. price equals the world price, $14.70, and the quantity is 13.1 million barrels per day. At the equilibrium price, domestic supply is 8.2, so imports are 4.9 (= 13.1 − 8.2). Consumer surplus is $A + B + C$, producer surplus is D, and welfare is $A + B + C + D$.

If imports are banned, the total U.S. supply curve, S^2, is the American domestic supply curve, S^a. The equilibrium is at e_2, where S^2 intersects the demand curve. The new equilibrium price is $29.04, and the new equilibrium quantity, 10.2 million barrels per day, is produced domestically. Consumer surplus is A, producer surplus is $B + D$, and welfare is $A + B + D$.

The ban helps producers but harms consumers. Because of the higher price, domestic firms gain producer surplus of $\Delta PS = B = \$132.5$ million per day. The change in consumers' surplus is $\Delta CS = -B - C = -\$163.7$ million per day.

Does the ban help the United States? The change in total welfare, ΔW, is the difference between the gain to producers and the loss to consumers, $\Delta W = \Delta PS + \Delta CS = -\$31.2$ million per day or −$11.4 billion per year. This deadweight loss is 24% of the gain to producers. Consumers lose $1.24 for every $1 that producers gain from a ban.

Free Trade Versus a Tariff

There are two common types of tariffs: *specific tariffs*—τ dollars per unit—and *ad valorem tariffs*—α percent of the sales price. In recent years, tariffs have been applied throughout the world, most commonly to agricultural products.[12] American policymakers have frequently debated the optimal tariff on crude oil as a way to raise revenue or to reduce "dependence" on foreign oil.

---

[12]After World War II, most trading nations signed the General Agreement on Tariffs and Trade (GATT), which limited their ability to subsidize exports or limit imports using quotas and tariffs. The rules prohibited most export subsidies and import quotas, except when imports threatened "market disruption" (the term that was, unfortunately, not defined). The GATT also required that any new tariff be offset by a reduction in other tariffs to compensate the exporting country. Modifications of the GATT and agreements negotiated by its successor, the World Trade Organization, have reduced or eliminated most tariffs.

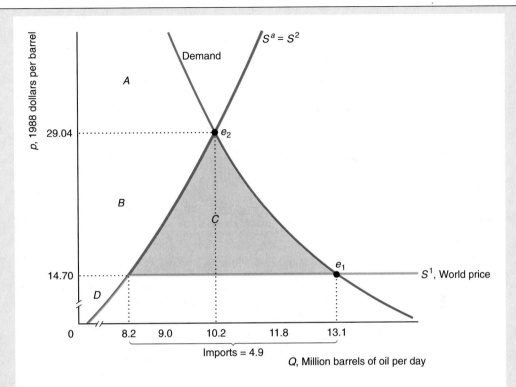

U.S.	Free Trade	U.S. Import Ban	Change ($ millions)
Consumer Surplus, CS	A + B + C	A	−B − C = −163.7 = ΔCS
Producer Surplus, PS	D	B + D	B = 132.5 = ΔPS
Welfare, W = CS + PS	A + B + C + D	A + B + D	−C = −31.2 = ΔW = DWL

Figure 9.9 **Loss from Eliminating Free Trade.** Because the supply curve foreigners face is horizontal at the world price of $14.70, the total U.S. supply curve of crude oil is S_1 when there is free trade. The free-trade equilibrium is e_1. With a ban on imports, the equilibrium e_2 occurs where the domestic supply curve, $S^a = S^2$, intersects D. The ban increases producer surplus by B = $132.5 million per day and decreases consumer surplus by B + C = $163.7 million per day, so the deadweight loss is C = $31.2 million per day or $11.4 billion per year.

You may be asking yourself, "Why should we study tariffs if we've already looked at taxes? Isn't a tariff just another tax?" Good point! Tariffs are just taxes. If the only goods sold were imported, the effect of a tariff in the importing country is the same as we showed for a sales tax. We study tariffs separately because a tariff is applied only to imported goods, so it affects domestic and foreign producers differently.

Because tariffs are applied to only imported goods, all else the same, they do not raise as much tax revenue or affect equilibrium quantities as much as taxes applied to all goods in a market. De Melo and Tarr (1992) find that almost five times more tax revenue would be generated by a 15% additional ad valorem tax on petroleum products ($34.6 billion) than by a 25% additional import tariff on oil and gas ($7.3 billion).

To illustrate the effect of a tariff, suppose that the government imposes a specific tariff of $\tau = \$5$ per barrel of crude oil. Given this tariff, firms will not import oil into the United States unless the U.S. price is at least $5 above the world price, $14.70. The tariff creates a wedge between the world price and the American price. This tariff causes the total supply curve to shift from S^1 to S^3 in Figure 9.10. Given that the world supply curve is horizontal at $14.70, a tariff shifts this supply curve upward so that it is horizontal at $19.70. As a result, the total U.S. supply curve with the tariff, S^3, equals the domestic supply curve for prices below $19.70 and is horizontal at $19.70.

The new equilibrium, e_3, occurs where S^3 intersects the demand curve. At this equilibrium, price is $19.70 and quantity is 11.8 million barrels of oil per day. At this higher price, domestic firms supply 9.0, so imports are 2.8 (= 11.8 − 9.0).

The tariff *protects* American producers from foreign competition. The larger the tariff, the less is imported, hence the higher the price that domestic firms can charge. (With a large enough tariff, nothing is imported, and the price rises to the no-trade level, $29.04.) With a tariff of $5, domestic firms' producer surplus increases by area $B = \$42.8$ million per day.

Because of the rise in the price from $14.70 to $19.70, consumer surplus falls by $61.9 million per day. The government receives tariff revenues, T, equal to area $D = \$14$ million per day, which is $\tau = \$5$ times the quantity imported, 2.8.

The deadweight loss is $C + E = \$5.1$ million per day, or nearly $1.9 billion per year.[13] This deadweight loss is almost 12% of the gain to producers. Consumers lose $1.45 for each $1 domestic producers gain. Because the tariff doesn't completely eliminate imports, the welfare loss is smaller than it is if all imports are banned.

We can interpret the two components of this deadweight loss. First, C is the loss from producing 9.0 million barrels per day instead of 8.2 million barrels per day. Domestic firms produce this extra output because the tariff drove up the price from $14.70 to $19.70. The cost of producing this extra 0.8 million barrels of oil per day domestically is $C + G$, the area under the domestic supply curve, S^a, between 8.2 and 9.0. Had Americans bought this oil at the world price, the cost would have been only $G = \$11.8$ million per day. Thus C is the extra cost from producing the extra 0.8 million barrels of oil per day domestically instead of importing it.

Second, E is a *consumption distortion loss* from American consumers' buying too little oil, 11.8 instead of 13.1, because the price rose from $14.70 to $19.70 owing to the tariff. American consumers value this extra output as $E + H$, the area under

---

[13]If the foreign supply is horizontal, welfare in the importing country *must* fall. However, if the foreign supply is upward sloping, welfare in the importing country may rise.

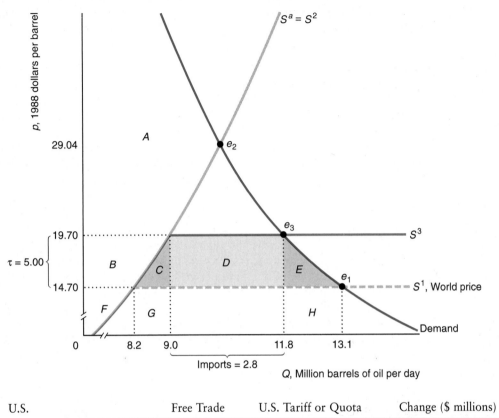

U.S.	Free Trade	U.S. Tariff or Quota	Change ($ millions)
Consumer Surplus, CS	A + B + C + D + E	A	B + C + D + E = 61.9
Producer Surplus, PS	F	B + F	B = 42.8
Tariff Revenues, T	0	D (tariff)	D = 14.0 (tariff)
		0 (quota)	0 (quota)
Welfare from a Tariff, W = CS + PS + T	A + B + C + D + E + F	A + B + D + F	C + E = 5.1 = DWL
Welfare from a Quota, W = CS + PS	A + B + C + D + E + F	A + B + F	C + D + E = 19.1 = DWL

Figure 9.10 Effect of a Tariff (or Quota). A tariff of τ = $5 per barrel of oil imported or a quota of $\overline{Q}$ = 2.8 drives the U.S. price of crude oil to $19.70, which is $5 more than the world price. Under the tariff, the equilibrium, e_3, is determined by the intersection of the S_3 total U.S. supply curve and the D demand curve. Under the quota, e_3 is determined by a quantity wedge of 2.8 million barrels per day between the quantity demanded, 9.0 million barrels per day, and the quantity supplied, 11.8 million barrels per day. Compared to free trade, producers gain B = $42.8 million per day and consumers lose $B + C + D + E$ = $61.9 million per day from the tariff or quota. The deadweight loss under the quota is $C + D + E$ = $19.1 million per day. With a tariff, the government's tariff revenue increases by D = $14 million a day, so the deadweight loss is only $C + E$ = $5.1 million per day.

their demand curve between 11.8 and 13.1, whereas the value in international markets is only H, the area below the line at $14.70 between 11.8 and 13.1. Thus E is the difference between the value at world prices and the value American consumers place on this extra 1.3 million barrels per day.

Free Trade Versus a Quota

The effect of a positive quota is similar to that of a tariff. If the government limits imports to $\bar{Q} = 2.8$ million barrels per day, the quota is binding because 4.9 million barrels per day were imported under free trade. Given this binding quota, at the equilibrium price, the quantity demanded minus the quantity supplied by domestic producers equals 2.8 million barrels per day. In Figure 9.10, where the price is $19.70, the gap between the quantity demanded, 11.8 million barrels per day, and the quantity supplied, 9.0 million barrels per day, is 2.8 million barrels per day. Thus a quota on imports of 2.8 leads to the same equilibrium, e_3, as a tariff of $5.

The gain to domestic producers, B, and the loss to consumers, $C + E$, are the same as those with a tariff. However, unlike with the tariff, with the quota the government does not receive any revenue (unless the government sells import licenses). Area D may go to foreign exporters. As a result, the deadweight loss from the quota, $19.1 million per day, or $7.0 billion per year, is greater than under the tariff. This deadweight loss is nearly half (45%) of the gains to producers.

Thus the importing country fares better using a tariff than setting a quota that reduces imports by the same amount. Consumers and domestic firms do as well under the two policies, but the government gains tariff revenues, D, only when the tariff is used.

Application   JAPANESE NONTARIFF BARRIERS

In recent years, Japan has used both formal trade barriers, such as tariffs and quotas, and informal measures, such as government "guidance" to firms, to limit imports in agriculture and several manufacturing industries. The table shows how much higher the prices that Japanese consumers paid were than

Product	Markup of Japanese Consumer Price over World Price, %	Tariff Rate, %	Implied Nontariff Barrier Rate, %
Milled rice	737.1	0	737.1
Soybeans	423.6	0	423.6
Tea and coffee	718.4	11.9	706.5
Wheat	477.8	0	477.8
Clothing	292.6	10.4	282.2
Cosmetics	661.6	2.0	659.6
Gasoline	229.0	5.5	223.5
Radio and televisions	607.0	0	607.0

the corresponding world prices for a number of goods. The price Japanese consumers paid for rice had more than a sevenfold (737%) markup over the world price, which would have been the Japanese price in the absence of trade barriers. The markup was six times for radios and televisions. Most of the markup is due to nontariff barriers such as quotas and informal barriers rather than tariffs. The 718.4% markup for tea and coffee represents an 11.9% markup due to tariffs and a 706.5% markup due to nontariff barriers.

One estimate of the cost of this protection to Japanese consumers is around $110 billion a year, or 3.8% of the Japanese national income. The net welfare loss is estimated to be 0.6% of Japanese national income.

Rent Seeking   Given that tariffs and quotas hurt the importing country, why do the Japanese, U.S., and other governments impose tariffs, quotas, or other trade barriers? The reason is that domestic producers stand to make large gains from such government actions; hence it pays for them to organize and lobby the government to enact these trade policies. Although consumers as a whole suffer large losses, most individual consumers face a negligible loss. Moreover, consumers rarely organize to lobby the government about trade issues. Thus in most countries, producers are often able to convince (cajole, influence, or bribe) legislators or government officials to aid them, even though consumers suffer more-than-offsetting losses.

If domestic producers can talk the government into a tariff, quota, or other policy that reduces imports, they gain extra producer surplus (rents), such as area B in Figures 9.9 and 9.10. Economists call efforts and expenditures to gain a rent or a profit from government actions **rent seeking**. If this rent-seeking behavior—such as hiring lobbyists and engaging in advertising to influence legislators—uses up resources, the deadweight loss from tariffs and quotas understates the true loss to society. The domestic producers may spend up to the gain in producer surplus to influence the government.[14]

Indeed, some economists argue that the government revenues from tariffs are completely offset by administrative costs and rent-seeking behavior. If so (and if the tariffs and quotas do not affect world prices), the loss to society from tariffs and quotas is all of the change in consumer surplus, such as areas $B + C$ in Figure 9.9 and areas $B + C + D + E$ in Figure 9.10.

Lopez and Pagoulatos (1994) estimate the deadweight loss and the additional losses due to rent-seeking activities in the United States in food and tobacco products. Table 9.2 summarizes their estimates for several industries in 1999 dollars. They estimate that the deadweight loss is $12.8 billion, which is 2.6% of the domestic consumption of these products. The gain in producer surplus is $46.3 billion, or 9.5% of domestic consumption. The government obtained $1.9 billion in tariff revenues, or 0.4% of consumption. If all of producer surplus and government revenues

---

[14]This argument is made in Tullock (1967) and Posner (1975). Fisher (1985) and Varian (1989) argue that the expenditure is typically less than the producer surplus.

Table 9.2 Welfare Cost of Trade Barriers (millions of 1999 dollars)

Industry	DWL	ΔPS	Government Revenues	ΔCS
Meat products	–27	2,227	64	–2,318
Dairy products[a]	–14,527	26,525	995	–38,902
Sugar confectionery[a]	–907	4,160	264	–5,329
Grain mill products	–9	1,083	9	–1,101
Fats and oils	–126	2,246	5	–2,377
Beverages	–8	1,038	139	–1,185
Tobacco	–194	3,625	90	–3,908
All food and tobacco	–12,798	46,308	1,878	–60,982

[a] Import quotas are the primary instrument of protection.

Notes: As estimated, ΔCS = DWL – ΔPS – government revenue. Dollar amounts were adjusted using the Consumer Price Index.

Source: Lopez and Pagoulatos (1994).

were expended in rent-seeking behavior and other wasteful activities, the total loss is $60.9 billion, or 12.5% of consumption, which is 4.75 times larger than the deadweight loss alone. In other words, the loss to society is somewhere between the deadweight loss of $12.8 billion and $60.9 billion. The largest deadweight losses were in milk products and sugar manufacturing, which primarily use import quotas to raise domestic prices.

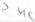

Summary

1. **Consumer welfare:** The pleasure a consumer receives from a good in excess of its cost is called *consumer surplus*. Consumer surplus equals the area under the consumer's demand curve above the market price up to the quantity that the consumer buys. How much consumers are harmed by an increase in price is measured by the change in consumer surplus.

2. **Producer welfare:** A firm's gain from trading is measured by its producer surplus. Producer surplus is the largest amount of money that could be taken from a firm's revenue and still leave the firm willing to produce. That is, the producer surplus is the amount the firm is paid minus its variable cost of production, which is profit in the long run. It is the area below the price and above the supply curve up to the quantity that the firm sells. The

effect of a change in a price on a supplier is measured by the change in producer surplus.

3. **How competition maximizes welfare:** One standard measure of welfare is the sum of consumer surplus and producer surplus. The more price is above marginal cost, the lower this measure of welfare. In the competitive equilibrium, in which price equals marginal cost, welfare is maximized.

4. **Policies that shift supply curves:** Governments frequently limit the number of firms in a market directly, by licensing them, or indirectly, by raising the costs of entry to new firms or raising the cost of exiting. A reduction in the number of firms in a competitive market raises price, hurts consumers, helps producing firms, and lowers the standard measure of welfare. This reduction in welfare is a

deadweight loss: The gain to producers is less than the loss to consumers.

5. **Policies that create a wedge between supply and demand:** Taxes, price ceilings, and price floors create a gap between the price consumers pay and the price firms receive. These policies force price above marginal cost, which raises the price to consumers and lowers the amount consumed. The wedge between price and marginal cost results in a deadweight loss: The loss of consumer surplus and producer surplus is not offset by increased taxes or by benefits to other groups.

6. **Comparing both types of policies: imports:** A government may use either a quantity restriction such as a quota, which shifts the supply curve, or a tariff, which creates a wedge, to reduce imports or achieve other goals. These policies may have different welfare implications. A tariff that reduces imports by the same amount as a quota has the same harms—a larger loss of consumer surplus than increased domestic producer surplus—but has a partially offsetting benefit—increased tariff revenues for the government. Rent-seeking activities are attempts by firms or individuals to influence a government to adopt a policy that favors them. By using resources, rent seeking exacerbates the welfare loss beyond the deadweight loss caused by the policy itself. In a perfectly competitive market, government policies frequently lower welfare. As we show in later chapters, however, in markets that are not perfectly competitive, government policies may increase welfare.

Problems

1. How would the quantitative effect of a specific tax on welfare change as demand becomes more elastic? As it becomes less elastic? (*Hint:* See Solved Problem 9.1.)

2. *Review* (Chapter 2): What were the welfare effects (who gained, who lost, what was the deadweight loss) of the gasoline price controls described in Chapter 2? Show these effects in a figure.

3. *Review* (Chapter 4): Use an indifference curve diagram (gift goods on one axis and all other goods on the other) to illustrate that one is better off receiving cash than a gift. (*Hint:* See the discussion of gifts in this chapter and the discussion of food stamps in Chapter 4.)

4. What is the long-run welfare effect of a profit tax (the government collects a specified percentage of a firm's profit) assessed on each competitive firm in a market?

5. What is the welfare effect of an ad valorem sales tax, α, assessed on each competitive firm in a market?

6. What are the welfare effects of a minimum wage? Use a graphical approach to show what happens if all workers are identical. Then verbally describe what is likely to happen to workers who differ by experience, education, age, gender, and race.

7. What effect does a per-unit subsidy (negative specific tax) have on equilibrium and on welfare?

8. What is the welfare effect of a lump sum tax, L, assessed on each competitive firm in a market?

9. What happens to welfare in Solved Problem 9.3 on soybeans if the government maintains a price support, p_2, but restricts output to Q_d using a quota?

10. The government wants to drive the price of soybeans above the equilibrium price, p_1, to p_2. It offers growers a payment of x to reduce their output from Q_1 (the equilibrium level) to Q_2, which is the quantity demanded by consumers at p_2. How large must x be for growers to reduce output to this level? What are the effects of this program on consumers, farmers, and total welfare? Compare this approach to (a) offering a price support of p_2, (b) offering a price support and a quota set at Q_1, and (c) offering a price support and a quota set at Q_2.

11. In 1995, the U.S. Congress debated various bills that would lower the federal price supports for sugar from 18¢ to 17¢ per pound. Given that the world wholesale price was 10¢ to 12¢, what would be the likely effect of this change?

12. By 1996, the world price for raw sugar, 11.75¢ per pound, was about half the domestic price, 22.5¢ per pound, because of quotas and tariffs on sugar imports. As a consequence, American-made corn sweetener, which costs 12¢ a pound to make, can be profitably sold. Archer-Daniels-Midland made

an estimated profit of $290 million in 1994 from selling corn sweetener. The U.S. Commerce Department says that the quotas and price support reduce American welfare by about $3 billion a year. If so, each dollar of Archer-Daniels-Midland's profit costs Americans about $10. Model the effects of a quota on sugar in both the sugar and corn sweetener markets.

13. A government is considering a quota and a tariff, both of which will reduce imports by the same amount. Which does the government prefer, and why?

14. Given that the world supply curve is horizontal at the world price for a given good, can a subsidy on imports raise welfare in the importing country? Explain your answer.

15. Canada has 20% of the world's known freshwater resources, yet many Canadians believe that the country has little or none to spare. Over the years, U.S. and Canadian firms have struck deals to export bulk shipments of water to drought-afflicted U.S. cities and towns. Provincial leaders have blocked these deals in British Columbia and Ontario. Use graphs to show the likely outcome of such barriers to exports on the price and quantity of water used in Canada and in the United States if markets for water are competitive. Show the effects on consumer and producer surplus in both countries.

Math Problems

16. If the inverse demand function is $p = 60 - Q$, what is the consumer surplus if price is 30?

17. If the inverse demand function is $p = a - bQ$, what is the consumer surplus if price is $a/2$?

18. If the supply function is $Q = Ap^{\eta}$, what is the producer surplus if price is p^*?

19. If the inverse demand function is $p = 60 - Q$ and the supply function is $Q = p$, what is the initial equilibrium? What is the welfare effect of a specific tax of $\tau = \$2$?

20. If the inverse demand function is $p = a - bQ$ and the supply function is $Q = c + dp$, what is the initial equilibrium? What is the welfare effect of a specific tax of $\tau = \$1$?

General Equilibrium and Economic Welfare

More than any time in history mankind faces a crossroads. One path leads to despair and utter hopelessness, the other to total extinction. Let us pray that we have the wisdom to choose correctly. —Woody Allen

A change in government policies, a natural disaster, or other shocks often affect equilibrium price and quantity in more than one market. To determine the effects of such a change, we must examine the interrelationships among markets. In this chapter, we extend our analysis of equilibrium in a single market to equilibrium in all markets.

We then examine how a society decides whether a particular equilibrium (or change in equilibrium) in all markets is desirable. To do so, society must answer two questions: "Is the equilibrium efficient?" and "Is the equilibrium equitable?"

For the equilibrium to be efficient, both consumption and production must be efficient. Production is efficient only if it is impossible to produce more output at current cost given current knowledge (Chapter 6). Consumption is efficient only if goods cannot be reallocated across people so that at least someone is better off and no one is harmed. In this chapter, we show how to determine whether consumption is efficient.

Whether the equilibrium is efficient is a scientific question. It is possible that all members of society could agree on how to answer scientific questions concerning efficiency.

To answer the equity question, society must make a value judgment as to whether each member of society has his or her "fair" or "just" share of all the goods and services. A common view in individualistic cultures is that each person is the best—and possibly only legitimate—judge of his or her own welfare. Nonetheless, to make social choices about events that affect more than one person, we have to make interpersonal comparisons, through which we decide whether one person's gain is more or less important than another person's loss. For example, in Chapter 9, we argued that a price ceiling lowers a measure of total welfare given the value judgment that the well-being of consumers (consumer surplus) and the well-being of the owners of firms (producer surplus) should be weighted equally. People of goodwill—and others—may disagree greatly about equity issues.

As a first step in studying welfare issues, many economists use a narrow value criterion, called the *Pareto principle* (after an Italian economist, Vilfredo Pareto), to rank different allocations of goods and services for which no interpersonal comparisons need to be made. According to this principle, a change that makes one person better off without harming anyone else is desirable. An allocation is **Pareto efficient** if any possible reallocation would harm at least one person.

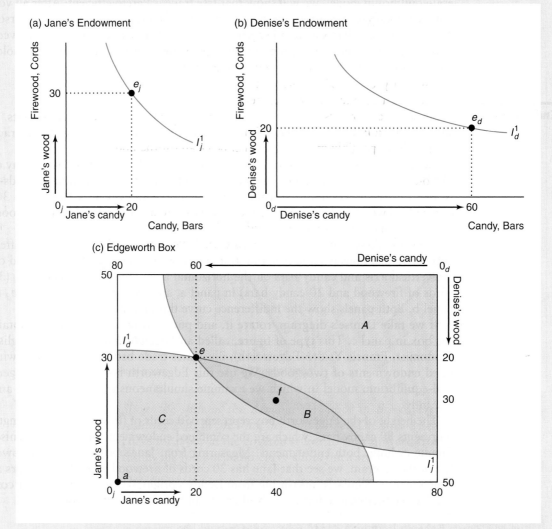

Figure 10.3 Endowments in an Edgeworth Box.
(a) Jane's endowment is e_j; she has 20 candy bars and 30 cords of firewood. She is indifferent between that bundle and the others that lie on her indifference curve I_j^1. (b) Denise is indifferent between her endowment, e_d (60 candy bars and 20 cords of wood), and the other bundles on I_d^1. (c) Their endowments are at e in the Edgeworth box formed by combining panels a and b. Jane prefers bundles in A and B to e. Denise prefers bundles in B and C to e. Thus both prefer any bundle in area B to e.

and neither person's consumption harms the other (one person's consumption of firewood does not cause smoke pollution that bothers the other person).

Figure 10.3 reflects these assumptions.

In panel a, Jane's indifference curve, I_j^1, through her endowment point, e_j, is convex to her origin, 0_j. Jane is indifferent between e_j and any other bundle on I_j^1. She prefers bundles that lie above I_j^1 to e_j and prefers e_j to points that lie below I_j^1. Panel c also shows her indifference curve, I_j^1. The bundles that Jane prefers to her endowment are in the shaded areas A and B, which lie above her indifference curve I_j^1.

Similarly, Denise's indifference curve, I_d^1, through her endowment is convex to her origin, 0_d, in the lower left of panel b. This indifference curve, I_d^1, is still convex to 0_d in panel c, but 0_d is in the upper right of the Edgeworth box. (It may help to turn this book around when viewing Denise's indifference curves in an Edgeworth box. Then again, possibly many points will be clearer if the book is held upside down.) The bundles Denise prefers to her endowment are in shaded areas B and C, which lie on the other side of her indifference curve I_d^1 from her origin 0_d (above I_d^1 if you turn the book upside down).

At endowment e in panel c, Jane and Denise can both benefit from a trade. Jane prefers bundles in A and B to e, and Denise prefers bundles in B and C to e, so *both* prefer bundles in area B to their endowment at e.

Suppose that they trade, reallocating goods from Bundle e to f. Jane gives up 10 cords of firewood for 20 more candy bars, and Denise gives up 20 candy bars for 10 more cords of wood. As Figure 10.4 illustrates, both gain from such a trade. Jane's indifference curve I_j^2 through allocation f lies above her indifference curve I_j^1 through allocation e, so she is better off at f than at e. Similarly, Denise's indifference curve I_d^2 through f lies above (if you hold the book upside down) her indifference curve I_d^1 through e, so she also benefits from the trade.

Now that they've traded to Bundle f, do Jane and Denise want to make further trades? To answer this question, we can repeat our analysis. Jane prefers all bundles above I_j^2, her indifference curve through f. Denise prefers all bundles above (when the book is held upside down) I_d^2 to f. However, there are no bundles that both prefer because I_j^2 and I_d^2 are tangent at f. Neither Jane nor Denise wants to trade from f to a bundle such as e, which is below both of their indifference curves. Jane would love to trade from f to c, which is on her higher indifference curve I_j^3, but such a trade would make Denise worse off because this bundle is on a lower indifference curve, I_d^1. Similarly, Denise prefers b to f, but Jane does not. Thus *any* move from f harms at least one of them.

The reason no further trade is possible at a bundle like f is that Jane's marginal rate of substitution (the slope of her indifference curve), MRS_j, between wood and candy equals Denise's marginal rate of substitution, MRS_d. Jane's MRS_j is $-\frac{1}{2}$: She is willing to trade one cord of wood for two candy bars. Because Denise's indifference curve is tangent to Jane's, Denise's MRS_d must also be $-\frac{1}{2}$. When they both want to trade wood for candy at the same rate, they can't agree on further trades.

In contrast, at a bundle such as e where their indifference curves are not tangent, MRS_j does not equal MRS_d. Denise's MRS_d is $-\frac{1}{3}$, and Jane's MRS_j is -2. Denise is willing to give up one cord of wood for three more candy bars or to sacrifice three candy bars for one more cord of wood. If Denise offers Jane three candy bars for one cord of wood, Jane will accept because she is willing to give up one cord of wood for two candy bars. This example illustrates that trades are possible where indifferent curves intersect because marginal rates of substitution are unequal.

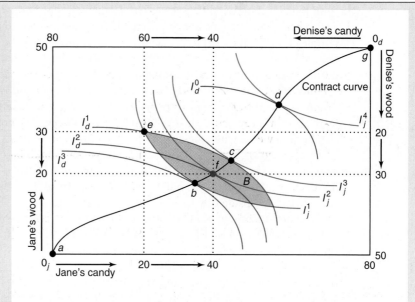

	Endowment, e		Trade		New Allocation, f	
	Wood	Candy	Wood	Candy	Wood	Candy
Jane	30	20	−10	+20	20	40
Denise	20	60	+10	−20	30	40

Figure 10.4 Contract Curve. The contract curve contains all the Pareto-efficient allocations. Any bundle for which Jane's indifference curve is tangent to Denise's indifference curve lies on the contract curve, because no further trade is possible, so we can't reallocate goods to make one of them better off without harming the other. Starting at an endowment of e, Jane and Denise will trade to a bundle on the contract curve in area B: bundles between b and c. The table shows how they would trade to Bundle f.

To summarize, we can make four equivalent statements about allocation f:

1. The indifference curves of the two parties are tangent at f.
2. The parties' marginal rates of substitution are equal at f.
3. No further mutually beneficial trades are possible at f.
4. The allocation at f is Pareto efficient: One party cannot be made better off without harming the other.

Indifference curves are also tangent at Bundles b, c, and d, so these allocations, like f, are Pareto efficient. By connecting all such bundles, we draw the **contract curve**: the set of all Pareto-efficient bundles. The reason for this name is that only at these points are the parties unwilling to engage in further trades or contracts—these allocations are the final contracts. A move from any bundle on the contract curve must harm at least one person.

Solved Problem 10.2 **Are allocations *a* and *g* in Figure 10.4 part of the contract curve?**

Answer

By showing that no mutually beneficial trades are possible at those points, demonstrate that those bundles are Pareto efficient: The allocation at which Jane has everything, allocation *g*, is on the contract curve because no mutually beneficial trade is possible: Denise has no goods to trade with Jane. As a consequence, we cannot make Denise better off without taking goods from Jane. Similarly, when Denise has everything, *a*, we can make Jane better off only by taking wood or candy from Denise and giving it to Jane.

Bargaining Ability

For every allocation off the contract curve, there are allocations on the contract curve that benefit at least one person. If they start at endowment *e*, Jane and Denise should trade until they reach a point on the contract curve between Bundles *b* and *c* in Figure 10.4. All the allocations in area *B* are beneficial. However, if they trade to any allocation in *B* that is not on the contract curve, further beneficial trades are possible because their indifference curves intersect at that allocation.

Where will they end up on the contract curve between *b* and *c*? That depends on who is better at bargaining. Suppose that Jane is better at bargaining. Jane knows that the more she gets, the worse off Denise will be and that Denise will not agree to any trade that makes her worse off than she is at *e*. Thus the best trade Jane can make is one that leaves Denise only as well off as at *e*, which are the bundles on I_d^1. If Jane could pick any point she wanted along I_d^1, she'd choose the bundle on her highest possible indifference curve, which is Bundle *c*, where I_j^3 is just tangent to I_d^1. After this trade, Denise is no better off than before, but Jane is much happier. By similar reasoning, if Denise is better at bargaining, the final allocation will be at *b*.

10.3 COMPETITIVE EXCHANGE

Most trading throughout the world occurs without one-on-one bargaining between people. When you go to the store to buy a bottle of shampoo, you read its posted price and then decide whether to buy it or not. You've probably never tried to bargain with the store's clerk over the price of shampoo: You're a price taker in the shampoo market.

If we don't know much about how Jane and Denise bargain, all we can say is that they will trade to some allocation on the contract curve. If we know the exact trading process they use, however, we can apply that process to determine the final allocation. In particular, we can examine the competitive trading process to determine the competitive equilibrium in a pure exchange economy.

In Chapter 9, we used a partial-equilibrium approach to show that one measure of welfare, *W*, is maximized in a competitive market in which many voluntary trades occur. We now use a general-equilibrium model to show that a competitive market has two desirable properties:

- **The competitive equilibrium is efficient:** Competition results in a Pareto-efficient allocation—no one can be made better off without making someone worse off—in all markets.
- **Any efficient allocations can be achieved by competition:** All possible efficient allocations can be obtained by competitive exchange, given an appropriate initial allocation of goods.

Economists call these results the *First Theorem of Welfare Economics* and the *Second Theorem of Welfare Economics*, respectively. These properties hold if everyone knows the preferences of all traders, there are no transaction costs, and indifference curves have the usual shapes.

Competitive Equilibrium

When two people trade, they are unlikely to view themselves as price takers. However, if there were a large number of people with tastes and endowments like Jane's and a large number of people with tastes and endowments like Denise's, each person would be a price taker in the two goods. We can use an Edgeworth box to examine how such price takers would trade.

Because they can trade only two goods, each person needs to consider only the relative price of the two goods when deciding whether to trade. If the price of a cord of wood, p_w, is $2, and the price of a candy bar, p_c, is $1, then a candy bar costs half as much as a cord of wood: $p_c/p_w = \frac{1}{2}$. An individual can sell one cord of wood and use that money to buy two candy bars.

At the initial allocation, e, Jane has goods worth $80 = ($2 per cord × 30 cords of firewood) + ($1 per candy bar × 20 candy bars). At these prices, Jane could keep her endowment or trade to an allocation with 40 cords of firewood and no candy, 80 bars of candy and no firewood, or any combination in between as the price line (budget line) in panel a of Figure 10.5 shows. The price line is all the combinations of goods Jane could get by trading, given her endowment. The price line goes through point e and has a slope of $-p_c/p_w = -\frac{1}{2}$.

Given the price line, what bundle of goods will Jane choose? She wants to maximize her utility by picking the bundle where one of her indifference curves, I_j^2, is tangent to her budget or price line. Denise wants to maximize her utility by choosing a bundle in the same way.

In a competitive market, prices adjust until the quantity supplied equals the quantity demanded. An auctioneer could help determine the equilibrium. The auctioneer could call out relative prices and ask how much is demanded and how much is offered for sale at those prices. If demand does not equal supply, the auctioneer calls out another relative price. When demand equals supply, the transactions actually occur and the auction stops. At some ports, fishing boats sell their catch to fish wholesalers at a daily auction run in this manner.

Panel a shows that, when candy costs half as much as wood, the quantity demanded of each good equals the quantity supplied. Jane (and every person like

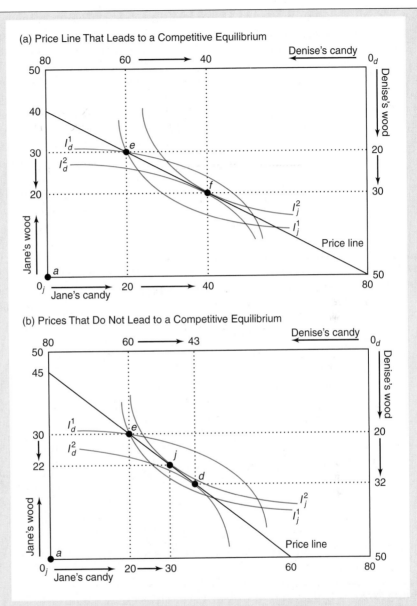

Figure 10.5 Competitive Equilibrium. The initial endowment is *e*. (a) If, along the price line facing Jane and Denise, p_w = $2 and p_c = $1, they trade to point *f*, where Jane's indifference curve, I_j^2, is tangent to the price line and to Denise's indifference curve, I_d^2. (b) No other price line results in an equilibrium. If p_w = $1.33 and p_c = $1, Denise wants to buy 12 (= 32 − 20) cords of firewood at these prices, but Jane wants to sell only 8 (= 30 − 22) cords. Similarly, Jane wants to buy 10 (= 30 − 20) candy bars, but Denise wants to sell 17 (= 60 − 43). Thus these prices are not consistent with a competitive equilibrium.

her) wants to sell 10 cords of firewood and use that money to buy 20 additional candy bars. Similarly, Denise (and everyone like her) wants to sell 20 candy bars and buy 10 cords of wood. Thus the quantity of wood sold equals the quantity bought, and the quantity of candy demanded equals that supplied. We can see in the figure that the quantities demanded equal the quantities supplied because the optimal bundle for both types of consumers is the same, Bundle *f*.

At any other price ratio, the quantity demanded of each good would not equal the quantity supplied. For example, if the price of candy remained constant at $p_c =$ $1 per bar but the price of wood fell to $p_w = \$1.33$ per cord, the price line would be steeper, with a slope of $-p_c/p_w = -1/1.33 = -\frac{3}{4}$ in panel b. At these prices, Jane wants to trade to Bundle *j* and Denise wants to trade to Bundle *d*. Because Jane wants to buy 10 extra candy bars but Denise wants to sell 17 extra candy bars, the quantity supplied does not equal the quantity demanded, so this price ratio does not result in a competitive equilibrium when the endowment is *e*.

The Efficiency of Competition	In a competitive equilibrium, the indifference curves of both types of consumers are tangent at the same bundle on the price line. As a result, the slope (*MRS*) of each person's indifference curve equals the slope of the price line, so the slopes of the indifference curves are equal:

$$MRS_j = -\frac{p_c}{p_w} = MRS_d. \tag{10.1}$$

The marginal rates of substitution are equal across consumers in the competitive equilibrium, so the competitive equilibrium must lie on the contract curve. Thus we have demonstrated the First Theorem of Welfare Economics:

Any competitive equilibrium is Pareto efficient.

The intuition for this result is that people (who face the same prices) make all the voluntary trades they want in a competitive market. Because no additional voluntary trades can occur, there is no way to make someone better off without making someone worse off in a competitive equilibrium. (If an involuntary trade occurs, at least one person is made worse off. A person who steals goods from another person—an involuntary exchange—gains at the expense of the victim.)

Obtaining Any Efficient Allocation Using Competition	Of the many possible Pareto-efficient allocations, the government may want to choose one. Can it achieve that allocation using the competitive market mechanism?

Our previous example illustrates that the competitive equilibrium depends on the endowment: the initial distribution of wealth. For example, if the initial endowment were *a* in panel a of Figure 10.5—where Denise has everything and Jane has nothing—the competitive equilibrium would be *a* because no trades would be possible.

Thus for competition to lead to a particular allocation—say, *f*—the trading must start at an appropriate endowment. If the consumers' endowment is *f*, a Pareto-efficient point, their indifference curves are tangent at *f*, so no further trades occur. That is, *f* is a competitive equilibrium.

Many other endowments will also result in a competitive equilibrium at *f*. Panel *a* shows that the resulting competitive equilibrium is *f* if the endowment is *e*. In that figure, a price line goes through both *e* and *f*. If the endowment is any bundle along this price line—not just *e* or *f*—the competitive equilibrium is *f*, because only at *f* are the indifference curves tangent.

To summarize, any Pareto-efficient bundle *x* can be obtained as a competitive equilibrium if the initial endowment is *x*. That allocation can also be obtained as a competitive equilibrium if the endowment lies on a price line through *x*, where the slope of the price line equals the marginal rate of substitution of the indifference curves that are tangent at *x*. Thus we've demonstrated the Second Theorem of Welfare Economics:

> *Any Pareto-efficient equilibrium can be obtained*
> *by competition, given an appropriate endowment.*

The first welfare theorem tells us that society can achieve efficiency by allowing competition. The second welfare theorem adds that society can obtain the particular efficient allocation it prefers based on its value judgments about equity by appropriately redistributing endowments (income).

10.4 PRODUCTION AND TRADING

So far our discussion has been based on a pure exchange economy with no production. We now examine an economy in which a fixed amount of a single input can be used to produce two different goods.

Comparative Advantage

Jane and Denise can produce candy or chop firewood using their own labor. They differ, however, in how much of each good they produce from a day's work.

Production Possibility Frontier. Jane can produce either 3 candy bars or 6 cords of firewood in a day. By splitting her time between the two activities, she can produce various combinations of the two goods. If α is the fraction of a day she spends making candy and $1 - \alpha$ is the fraction cutting wood, she produces 3α candy bars and $6(1 - \alpha)$ cords of wood.

By varying α between 0 and 1, we trace out the line in panel *a* of Figure 10.6. This line is Jane's *production possibility frontier* (PPF^j; Chapter 7), which shows the maximum combinations of wood and candy that she can produce from a given amount of input. If Jane works all day using the best available technology (such as a sharp ax), she achieves *efficiency in production* and produces combinations of goods on PPF^j. If she sits around part of the day or does not use the best technology, she produces an inefficient combination of wood and candy inside PPF^j.

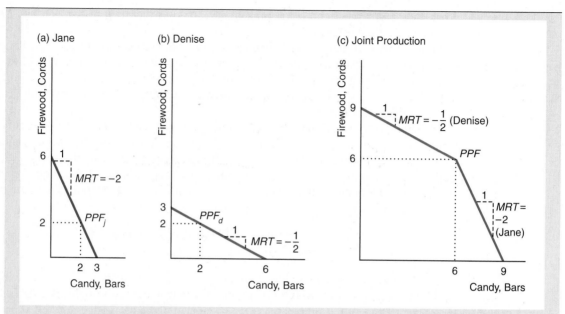

Figure 10.6 Comparative Advantage and Production Possibility Frontiers. (a) Jane's production possibility frontier, PPF^j, shows that in a day, she can produce 6 cords of firewood or 3 candy bars or any combination of the two. Her marginal rate of transformation (MRT) is –2. (b) Denise's production possibility frontier, PPF^d, has an MRT of $-\frac{1}{2}$. (c) Their joint production possibility frontier, PPF, has a kink at 6 cords of firewood (produced by Jane) and 6 candy bars (produced by Denise) and is concave to the origin.

Marginal Rate of Transformation. The slope of the production possibility frontier is the *marginal rate of transformation (MRT)*.[4] The marginal rate of transformation tells us how much more wood can be produced if the production of candy is reduced by one bar. Because Jane's PPF^j is a straight line with a slope of –2, her MRT is –2 at every allocation.

Denise can produce up to 3 cords of wood or 6 candy bars in a day. Panel b shows her production possibility function, PPF^d, with an $MRT = -\frac{1}{2}$. Thus with a day's work, Denise can produce relatively more candy, and Jane can produce relatively more wood, as reflected by their differing marginal rates of transformation.

The marginal rate of transformation shows how much it costs to produce one good in terms of the forgone production of the other good. Someone with the ability to produce a good at a lower opportunity cost than someone else has a **comparative advantage** in producing that good. Denise has a comparative advantage in producing candy (she forgoes less in wood production to produce a given amount of candy), and Jane has a comparative advantage in producing wood.

---

[4]In Chapter 4, we called the slope of a consumer's budget line the marginal rate of transformation. For a price-taking consumer who obtains goods by buying them, the budget line plays the same role as the production possibility frontier for someone who produces the two goods.

By combining their outputs, they have the joint production possibility frontier *PPF* in panel c. If Denise and Jane spend all their time producing wood, Denise produces 3 cords and Jane produces 6 cords for a total of 9, which is where the joint *PPF* hits the wood axis. Similarly, if they both produce candy, they can jointly produce 9 bars. If Denise specializes in making candy and Jane specializes in cutting wood, they produce 6 candy bars and 6 cords of wood, a combination that appears at the kink in the *PPF*.

If they choose to produce a relatively large quantity of candy and a relatively small amount of wood, Denise produces only candy and Jane produces some candy and some wood. Jane chops the wood because that's her comparative advantage. The marginal rate of transformation in the lower portion of the *PPF* is Jane's, –2, because only she produces both candy and wood.

Similarly, if they produce little candy, Jane produces only wood and Denise produces some wood and some candy, so the marginal rate of transformation in the higher portion of the *PPF* is Denise's, $-\frac{1}{2}$. In short, the *PPF* has a kink at 6 cords of wood and 6 candy bars and is concave (bowed away from the origin).[5]

Benefits of Trade. Because of the difference in their marginal rates of transformation, Jane and Denise can benefit from a trade. Suppose that Jane and Denise like to consume wood and candy in equal proportions. If they do not trade, each produces 2 candy bars and 2 cords of wood in a day. If they agree to trade, Denise, who excels at making candy, spends all day producing 6 candy bars. Similarly, Jane, who has a comparative advantage at chopping, produces 6 cords of wood. If they split this production equally, they can each have 3 cords of wood and 3 candy bars—50% more than if they don't trade.

They do better if they trade because each person uses her comparative advantage. Without trade, if Denise wants an extra cord of wood, she must give up two candy bars. Producing an extra cord of wood costs Jane only half a candy bar in forgone production. Denise is willing to trade up to two candy bars for a cord of wood, and Jane is willing to trade the wood as long as she gets at least half a candy bar. Thus there is room for a mutually beneficial trade.

Solved Problem 10.3 **How does the joint production possibility frontier in panel c of Figure 10.6 change if Jane and Denise can also trade with Harvey, who can produce 5 cords of wood, 5 candy bars, or any linear combination of wood and candy in a day?**

Answer

1. *Describe each person's individual production possibility frontier:* Panels a and b of Figure 10.6 show the production possibility frontiers of Jane and Denise. Harvey's production possibility frontier is a straight line that hits the firewood axis at 5 cords and the candy axis at 5 candy bars.

---

[5]Problem 9 at the end of this chapter asks you to prove that the joint production possibility frontier is concave, not convex (bowed toward the origin).

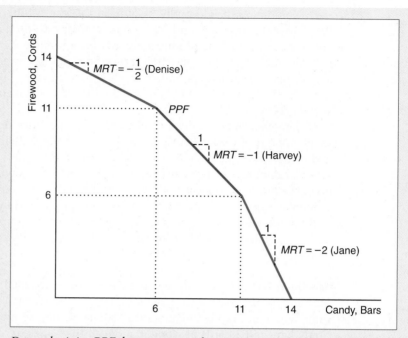

2. *Draw the joint PPF, by starting at the quantity on the horizontal axis that is produced if everyone specializes in candy and then connecting the individual production possibility frontiers in order of comparative advantage in chopping wood:* If all three produce candy, they make 14 candy bars (on the horizontal axis of the accompanying graph). Jane has a comparative advantage at chopping wood over Harvey and Denise, and Harvey has a comparative advantage over Denise. Thus Jane's production possibility frontier is the first one (starting at the lower right), then comes Harvey's, and then Denise's. The resulting *PPF* is concave to the origin. (If we change the order of the individual frontiers, the resulting kinked line lies inside the *PPF*. Thus the new line cannot be the joint production possibility frontier, which shows the maximum possible production from the available labor inputs.)

The Number of Producers. When there are only two ways of producing wood and candy—Denise's and Jane's methods with different marginal rates of transformation—the joint production possibility frontier has a single kink (panel c of Figure 10.6). If another method of production with a different marginal rate of transformation—Harvey's—is added, the joint production possibility frontier has two kinks (as in Solved Problem 10.3).

If many firms can produce candy and firewood with different marginal rates of transformation, the joint production possibility frontier has even more kinks. As the number of firms becomes very large, the PPF becomes a smooth curve that is concave to the origin, as in Figure 10.7.

Because the *PPF* is concave, the marginal rate of transformation decreases (in absolute value) as we move up the *PPF*. The *PPF* has a flatter slope at *a*, where the $MRT = -\frac{1}{2}$, than at *b*, where the $MRT = -1$. At *a*, giving up a candy bar leads to half

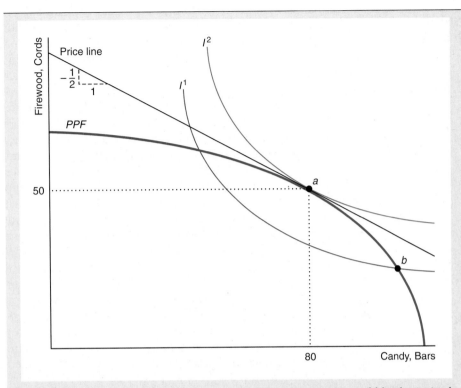

Figure 10.7 Optimal Product Mix. The optimal product mix, *a*, could be determined by maximizing an individual's utility by picking the allocation for which an indifference curve is tangent to the production possibility frontier. It could also be determined by picking the allocation where the relative competitive price, p_c/p_f, equals the slope of the *PPF*.

a cord more wood production. In contrast, at *b*, where relatively more candy is produced, giving up producing a candy bar frees enough resources that an additional cord of wood can be produced.

The marginal rate of transformation along this smooth *PPF* tells us about the marginal cost of producing one good relative to the marginal cost of producing the other good. The marginal rate of transformation equals the negative of the ratio of the marginal cost of producing candy, MC_c, and wood, MC_w:

$$MRT = -\frac{MC_c}{MC_w}. \tag{10.2}$$

Suppose that at point *a* in Figure 10.7, a firm's marginal cost of producing an extra candy bar is $1 and its marginal cost of producing an additional cord of firewood is $2. As a result, the firm can produce one extra candy bar or half a cord of wood at a cost of $1. The marginal rate of transformation is the negative of the ratio of the marginal costs, $-(\$1/\$2) = -\frac{1}{2}$. To produce one more candy bar, the firm must give up producing half a cord of wood.

Efficient Product Mix

Which combination of products along the *PPF* does society choose? If a single person were to decide on the product mix, that person would pick the allocation of wood and candy along the *PPF* that maximized his or her utility. A person with the indifference curves in Figure 10.7 would pick Allocation *a*, which is the point where the *PPF* touches indifference curve I^2.

Because I^2 is tangent to the *PPF* at *a*, that person's marginal rate of substitution (the slope of indifference curve I^2) equals the marginal rate of transformation (the slope of the *PPF*). The marginal rate of substitution, *MRS*, tells us how much a consumer is willing to give up of one good to get another. The marginal rate of transformation, *MRT*, tells us how much of one good we need to give up to produce more of another good.

If the *MRS* doesn't equal the *MRT*, the consumer will be happier with a different product mix. At Allocation *b*, the indifference curve I^1 intersects the *PPF*, so the *MRS* does not equal the *MRT*. At *b*, the consumer is willing to give up one candy bar to get a third of a cord of wood ($MRS = -\frac{1}{3}$), but firms can produce one cord of wood for every candy bar not produced ($MRT = -1$). Thus at *b*, too little wood is being produced. If the firms increase wood production, the *MRS* will fall and the *MRT* will rise until they are equal at *a*, where $MRS = MRT = -\frac{1}{2}$.

We can extend this reasoning to look at the product mix choice of all consumers simultaneously. Each consumer's marginal rate of substitution must equal the economy's marginal rate of transformation, *MRS* = *MRT*, if the economy is to produce the optimal mix of goods for each consumer. How can we ensure that this condition holds for all consumers? One way is to use the competitive market.

Competition

Each price-taking consumer picks a bundle of goods so that the consumer's marginal rate of substitution equals the slope of the consumer's price line (the negative of the relative prices):

$$MRS = -\frac{p_c}{p_w}. \tag{10.3}$$

Thus if all consumers face the same relative prices, in the competitive equilibrium, all consumers will buy a bundle where their marginal rates of substitution are equal (Equation 10.1). Because all consumers have the same marginal rates of substitution, no further trades can occur. Thus the competitive equilibrium achieves *consumption efficiency*: We can't redistribute goods among consumers to make one consumer better off without harming another one. That is, the competitive equilibrium lies on the contract curve.

If candy and wood are sold by competitive firms, each firm sells a quantity of a candy for which its price equals its marginal cost,

$$p_c = MC_c, \tag{10.4}$$

and a quantity of wood for which its price and marginal cost are equal,

$$p_w = MC_w. \tag{10.5}$$

Taking the ratio of Equations 10.4 and 10.5, we find that in competition, $p_c/p_w = MC_c/MC_w$. From Equation 10.2, we know that the marginal rate of transformation equals $-MC_c/MC_w$, so

$$MRT = -\frac{p_c}{p_w}.$$ (10.6)

We can illustrate why firms want to produce where Equation 10.6 holds. Suppose that a firm were producing at b in Figure 10.7, where its MRT is -1, and that $p_c = \$1$ and $p_w = \$2$, so $-p_c/p_w = -\frac{1}{2}$. If the firm reduces its output by one candy bar, it loses \$1 in candy sales but makes \$2 more from selling the extra cord of wood, for a net gain of \$1. Thus at b, where the $MRT < -p_c/p_w$, the firm should reduce its output of candy and increase its output of wood. In contrast, if the firm is producing at a, where the $MRT = -p_c/p_w = -\frac{1}{2}$, it has no incentive to change its behavior: The gain from producing a little more wood exactly offsets the loss from producing a little less candy.

Combining Equations 10.3 and 10.6, we find that in the competitive equilibrium, the MRS equals the relative prices, which equals the MRT:

$$MRS = -\frac{p_c}{p_w} = MRT.$$

Because competition ensures that the MRS equals the MRT, a competitive equilibrium achieves an *efficient product mix*: The rate at which firms can transform one good into another equals the rate at which consumers are willing to substitute between the goods, as reflected by their willingness to pay for the two goods.

By combining the production possibility frontier and an Edgeworth box, we can show the competitive equilibrium in both production and consumption. Suppose that firms produce 50 cords of firewood and 80 candy bars at a in Figure 10.8. The size of the Edgeworth box—the maximum amount of wood and candy available to consumers—is determined by point a on the PPF.

The prices consumers pay must equal the prices producers receive, so the price lines consumers and producers face must have the same slope of $-p_c/p_w$. In equilibrium, the price lines are tangent to each consumer's indifference curve at f and to the PPF at a.

In this competitive equilibrium, supply equals demand in all markets. The consumers buy the mix of goods at f. Consumers like Jane, whose origin, 0_j, is at the lower left, consume 20 cords of firewood and 40 candy bars. Consumers like Denise, whose origin is a at the upper right of the Edgeworth box, consume 30 (= 50 – 20) cords of firewood and 40 (= 80 – 40) candy bars.

The two key results concerning competition still hold in an economy with production. First, a competitive equilibrium is Pareto efficient, achieving efficiency in consumption and in output mix.[6] Second, any particular Pareto-efficient allocation between consumers can be obtained through competition, given that the government chooses an appropriate endowment.

---

[6]Although we have not shown it here, competitive firms choose factor combinations so that their marginal rates of technical substitution between inputs equal the ratios of the relative factor prices (see Chapter 7). That is, competition also results in *efficiency in production*: We could not produce more of one good without producing less of another good.

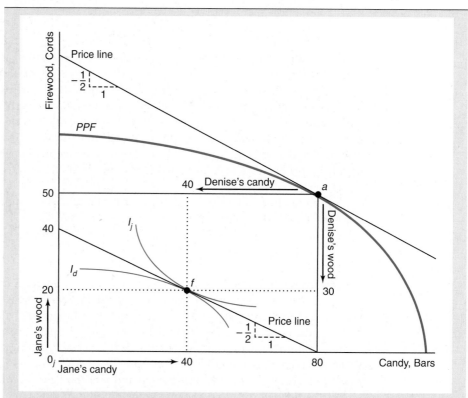

Figure 10.8 Competitive Equilibrium. At the competitive equilibrium, the relative prices firms and consumers face are the same (the price lines are parallel), so the *MRS* $= -p_c/p_w = MRT$.

Application   **AUTO TRADE BARRIERS**

Traditionally, customers in one European nation have not been able to buy cars easily from dealers in other countries. If they could, competition would equalize prices across countries. Without this competition, prices are much higher in some European nations than in others. In 1996, cars often sold for more in the country in which they were manufactured than in other European countries: A Mercedes-Benz S320 cost $72,614 in Germany and

$66,920 in Italy; a Renault Twingo went for $13,265 in France and $11,120 in Spain; a Peugeot 106 cost $12,129 in France and $11,532 in Spain; and a Volkswagen Polo priced at $8,562 in Italy sells for $1,250 more in Germany or Austria.

The European Commission was supposed to create a single European market for automobiles in the last quarter of 1994. With a single market and ultimately a single currency, the reasoning went, consumers could shop where they wanted, including across national borders. Allowing firms in various countries to compete would decrease price differentials across countries. However, various other restrictions (such as limits on the exchange of funds across countries) allowed large differentials to continue. There is some hope that the differentials will be eliminated in the next year or two.

Policies that create price differentials across countries reduce efficiencies (and hence welfare). In high-price countries, price is above marginal cost. Because consumers are willing to pay more for cars than they cost to produce, welfare is lower than if price equaled marginal cost. Moreover, because these price distortions are unequal across types of cars, the product mix is inefficient.

10.5 | EFFICIENCY AND EQUITY

How well various members of society live depends on how society deals with efficiency (the size of the pie) and equity (how the pie is divided). The actual outcome depends on choices by individuals and on government actions.

Role of the Government

By altering the efficiency with which goods are produced and distributed and the endowment of resources, governments help determine how much is produced and how goods are allocated. By redistributing endowments or by refusing to do so, governments, at least implicitly, are making value judgments about which members of society should get relatively more of society's goodies.

Virtually every government program, tax, or action redistributes wealth. Proceeds from a British lottery, played mostly by lower-income people, supports the "rich toffs" who attend the Royal Opera House at Covent Garden. Agricultural price support programs (Chapter 9) redistribute wealth to farmers from other taxpayers. Income taxes (Chapter 5) and food stamp programs (Chapter 3) redistribute income from the rich to the poor.

Application   WEALTH DISTRIBUTION IN THE UNITED STATES

Since the United States was founded, changes in the economy have altered the share of the nation's wealth concentrated in the hands of the richest 1% of Americans (see the figure). An array of social changes—sometimes occurring during or after wars and often codified into new laws—have led to new equilibria and new distributions of wealth. For example, the emancipation of slaves in 1863 transferred vast wealth—the labor of the former slaves—from rich Southern landowners to the poor freed slaves. Anti-immigration laws have helped the domestic poor, because immigrant labor is typically a

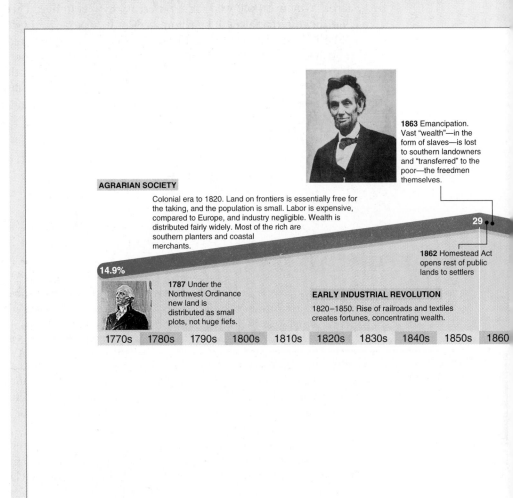

1863 Emancipation. Vast "wealth"—in the form of slaves—is lost to southern landowners and "transferred" to the poor—the freedmen themselves.

AGRARIAN SOCIETY

Colonial era to 1820. Land on frontiers is essentially free for the taking, and the population is small. Labor is expensive, compared to Europe, and industry negligible. Wealth is distributed fairly widely. Most of the rich are southern planters and coastal merchants.

29

1862 Homestead Act opens rest of public lands to settlers

14.9%

1787 Under the Northwest Ordinance new land is distributed as small plots, not huge fiefs.

EARLY INDUSTRIAL REVOLUTION

1820–1850. Rise of railroads and textiles creates fortunes, concentrating wealth.

| 1770s | 1780s | 1790s | 1800s | 1810s | 1820s | 1830s | 1840s | 1850s | 1860 |

---

[7]Bill Gates's personal wealth (as of January 2000) was estimated at $88 billion by **www.quuxuum. org/~evan/bgnw.html** and $126 billion by **www.webho.com/WealthClock**. Even at the lower

substitute for low-skilled domestic labor, and have hurt the middle and upper classes, because low-skilled immigrant labor is a complement to capital and high-skilled labor.

Until the Great Depression, the share of wealth held by the richest 1% generally increased,[7] then declined through the mid-1970s, when the trend reversed dramatically. By 1999, the richest 1% of Americans (2.7 million people, or 1 million families), had as much after-tax dollars as the poorest 100 million people—double the ratio a mere 22 years earlier.

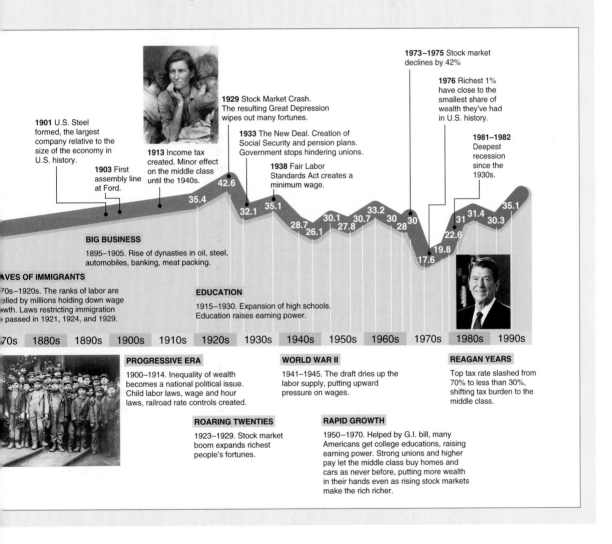

1973–1975 Stock market declines by 42%

1976 Richest 1% have close to the smallest share of wealth they've had in U.S. history.

1929 Stock Market Crash. The resulting Great Depression wipes out many fortunes.

1901 U.S. Steel formed, the largest company relative to the size of the economy in U.S. history.

1933 The New Deal. Creation of Social Security and pension plans. Government stops hindering unions.

1981–1982 Deepest recession since the 1930s.

1913 Income tax created. Minor effect on the middle class until the 1940s.

1903 First assembly line at Ford.

1938 Fair Labor Standards Act creates a minimum wage.

42.6   35.4   32.1   35.1   28.7   26.1   30.1   27.8   30.7   33.2   30   28   30   17.6   19.8   22.6   31   31.4   30.3   35.1

BIG BUSINESS
1895–1905. Rise of dynasties in oil, steel, automobiles, banking, meat packing.

WAVES OF IMMIGRANTS
1870s–1920s. The ranks of labor are swelled by millions holding down wage growth. Laws restricting immigration are passed in 1921, 1924, and 1929.

EDUCATION
1915–1930. Expansion of high schools. Education raises earning power.

1870s   1880s   1890s   1900s   1910s   1920s   1930s   1940s   1950s   1960s   1970s   1980s   1990s

PROGRESSIVE ERA
1900–1914. Inequality of wealth becomes a national political issue. Child labor laws, wage and hour laws, railroad rate controls created.

WORLD WAR II
1941–1945. The draft dries up the labor supply, putting upward pressure on wages.

REAGAN YEARS
Top tax rate slashed from 70% to less than 30%, shifting tax burden to the middle class.

ROARING TWENTIES
1923–1929. Stock market boom expands richest people's fortunes.

RAPID GROWTH
1950–1970. Helped by G.I. bill, many Americans get college educations, raising earning power. Strong unions and higher pay let the middle class buy homes and cars as never before, putting more wealth in their hands even as rising stock markets make the rich richer.

estimate, that's about *1/88th* of the U.S. gross domestic product (GDP), about the same as the GDPs of Israel and Colombia, and *1/337th* of the world GDP.

One reason for the increased concentration of wealth in recent decades was that the top income tax rate fell from 70% to less than 30% at the beginning of the Reagan administration, shifting more of the tax burden to the middle class. Since then, the top federal tax rate has increased to 41%.

The federal government transfers 5% of total national household income from the rich to the poor: 2% using cash assistance such as general welfare programs and 3% using in-kind transfers such as food stamps and school lunch programs. Poor households receive 26% of their income from cash assistance and 18% from in-kind assistance.

Efficiency

Many economists and political leaders make the value judgment that governments *should* use the Pareto principle and prefer allocations by which someone is made better off if no one else is harmed. That is, governments should allow voluntary trades, encourage competition, and otherwise try to prevent problems that reduce efficiency.

We can use the Pareto principle to rank allocations or government policies that alter allocations. The Pareto criterion ranks allocation *x* over allocation *y* if some people are better off at *x* and no one else is harmed. If that condition is met, we say that *x* is *Pareto superior* to *y*.

The Pareto principle cannot always be used to compare allocations. Because there are many possible Pareto-efficient allocations, however, a value judgment based on interpersonal comparisons must be made to choose between them. Issues of interpersonal comparisons often arise when we evaluate various government policies. If both allocation *x* and allocation *y* are Pareto efficient, we cannot use this criterion to rank them. For example, if Denise has all the goods in *x* and Jane has all of them in *y*, we cannot rank these allocations using the Pareto rule.

Suppose that when a country ends a ban on imports and allows free trade, domestic consumers benefit by many times more than domestic producers suffer. Nonetheless, this policy change does not meet the Pareto efficiency criterion that someone be made better off without anyone suffering. However, the government could adopt a more complex policy that meets the Pareto criterion. Because consumers benefit by more than producers suffer, the government could take enough of the gains from free trade from consumers to compensate the producers so that no one is harmed and some people benefit.

The government rarely uses policies by which winners subsidize losers, however. If such subsidization does not occur, additional value judgments involving interpersonal comparisons must be made before deciding whether to adopt the policy.

We've been using a welfare measure, W = consumer surplus + producer surplus, that weights benefits and losses to consumers and producers equally. On the basis of that particular interpersonal comparison criterion, if the gains to consumers outweigh the loss to producers, the policy change should be made.

Thus calling for policy changes that lead to Pareto-superior allocations is a weaker rule than calling for all policy changes that increase the welfare measure *W*. Any policy change that leads to a Pareto-superior allocation must increase *W*; however, some policy changes that increase *W* are not Pareto superior: There are both winners and losers.

Equity

All animals are equal, but some animals are more equal than others. —George Orwell

If we are unwilling to use the Pareto principle or if that criterion does not allow us to rank the relevant allocations, we must make additional value judgments to rank these allocations. A way to summarize these value judgments is to use a *social welfare function* that combines various consumers' utilities to provide a collective ranking of allocations. Loosely speaking, a social welfare function is a utility function for society.

We illustrate the use of a social welfare function using the pure exchange economy in which Jane and Denise trade wood and candy. There are many possible Pareto-efficient allocations along the contract curve in Figure 10.4. Jane and Denise's utility levels vary along the contract curve. Figure 10.9 shows the *utility*

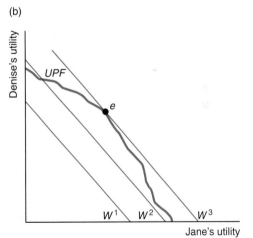

Figure 10.9 **Welfare Maximization.** Society maximizes welfare by choosing the allocation for which the highest possible isowelfare curve touches the utility possibility frontier, *UPF*. (a) The isowelfare curves have the shape of a typical indifference curve. (b) The isowelfare lines have a slope of –1, indicating that the utilities of both people are treated equally at the margin.

possibility frontier (UPF): the set of utility levels corresponding to the Pareto-efficient allocations along the contract curve. Point *a* in panel a corresponds to the end of the contract curve at which Denise has all the goods, and *c* corresponds to the allocation at which Jane has all the goods.

The curves labeled W^1, W^2, and W^3 in panel a are *isowelfare curves* based on the social welfare function. These curves are similar to indifference curves for individuals. They summarize all the allocations with identical levels of welfare. Society maximizes its welfare at point *b*.

Who decides on the welfare function? In most countries, government leaders make decisions about which allocations are most desirable. These officials may believe that transferring money from wealthy people to poor people raises welfare, or vice versa. When government officials choose a particular allocation, they are implicitly or explicitly judging which consumers are relatively deserving and hence should receive more goods than others.

Voting. In a democracy, important government policies that determine the allocation of goods are made by voting. Such democratic decision making is often difficult because people fundamentally disagree on how issues should be resolved and which groups of people should be favored.

In Chapter 4, we assumed that consumers could order all bundles of goods in terms of their preferences (completeness) and that their rank over goods was transitive.[8] Suppose now that consumers have preferences over allocations of goods across consumers. One possibility, as we assumed earlier, is that individuals care only about how many goods they receive—they don't care about how much others have. Another possibility is that because of envy, charity, pity, love, or other interpersonal feelings, individuals do care about how much everyone has.[9]

Let *a* be a particular allocation of goods that describes how much of each good an individual has. Each person can rank this allocation relative to Allocation *b*. For instance, individuals know whether they prefer an allocation by which everyone has equal amounts of all goods to another allocation by which people who work hard—or those of a particular skin color or religion—have relatively more goods than others.

Through voting, individuals express their rankings. One possible voting system requires that before the vote is taken, everyone agrees to be bound by the outcome in the sense that if a majority of people prefer Allocation *a* to Allocation *b*, then *a* is *socially preferred* to *b*.

Using majority voting to determine which allocations are preferred by society sounds reasonable, doesn't it? Such a system might work well. For example, if all

---

[8]The transitivity (or *rationality*) assumption is that a consumer's preference over bundles is consistent in the sense that if the consumer weakly prefers Bundle *a* to Bundle *b* and weakly prefers Bundle *b* to Bundle *c*, the consumer weakly prefers Bundle *a* to Bundle *c*.

[9]To an economist, love is nothing more than interdependent utility functions. Thus it's a mystery how each successive generation of economists is produced.

individuals have the same transitive preferences, the social ordering has the same transitive ranking as that of each individual.

Unfortunately, sometimes voting does not work well, and the resulting social ordering of allocations is not transitive. To illustrate this possibility, suppose that three people have the transitive preferences in Table 10.2. Individual 1 prefers Allocation *a* to Allocation *b* to Allocation *c*. The other two individuals have different preferred orderings. Two out of three of these individuals prefer *a* to *b*; two out of three prefer *b* to *c*; and two out of three prefer *c* to *a*. Thus voting leads to nontransitive preferences, even though the preferences of each individual are transitive. As a result, there is no clearly defined socially preferred outcome. A majority of people prefers some other allocation to any particular allocation. Compared to Allocation *a*, a majority prefers *c*. Similarly, a majority prefers *b* over *c*, and a majority prefers *a* over *b*.

If people have this type of ranking of allocations, the chosen allocation will depend crucially on the order in which the vote is taken. Suppose that these three people first vote on whether they prefer *a* or *b* and then compare the winner to *c*. Because a majority prefers *a* to *b* in the first vote, they will compare *a* to *c* in the second vote, and *c* will be chosen. If instead they first compared *c* to *a* and the winner to *b*, then *b* will be chosen. Thus the outcome depends on the political skill of various factions in determining the order of voting.

Similar problems arise with other types of voting schemes. Kenneth Arrow (1951), who received a Nobel Prize in Economics in part for his work on social decision making, proved a startling and depressing result about democratic voting. This result is often referred to as Arrow's Impossibility Theorem. Arrow suggested that a socially desirable decision making system, or social welfare function, should satisfy the following criteria:

- Social preferences should be complete (Chapter 4) and transitive, like individual preferences.
- If everyone prefers Allocation *a* to Allocation *b*, *a* should be socially preferred to *b*.
- Society's ranking of *a* and *b* should depend only on individuals' ordering of these two allocations, not on how they rank other alternatives.
- Dictatorship is not allowed; social preferences must not reflect the preferences of only a single individual.

Table 10.2 Preferences over Allocations of Three People

	Individual 1	Individual 2	Individual 3
First choice	*a*	*b*	*c*
Second choice	*b*	*c*	*a*
Third choice	*c*	*a*	*b*

Although each of these criteria seems reasonable—indeed, innocuous—Arrow proved that it is impossible to find a social decision-making rule that *always* satisfies all of these criteria. His result indicates that *democratic decision making may fail*—not that *democracy* must fail. After all, if everyone agrees on a ranking, these four criteria are satisfied.

If society is willing to give up one of these criteria, a democratic decision-making rule can guarantee that the other three criteria are met. For example, if we give up the third criterion, often referred to as the *independence of irrelevant alternatives*, certain complicated voting schemes in which individuals rank their preferences can meet the other criteria.

Social Welfare Functions. How would you rank various allocations if you were asked to vote? Philosophers, economists, newspaper columnists, politicians, radio talk show hosts, and other deep thinkers have suggested various rules that society might use to decide which allocations are better than others. Basically, all these systems answer the question of which individuals' preferences should be given more weight in society's decision making. Determining how much weight to give to the preferences of various members of society is usually the key step in determining a social welfare function.

Probably the simplest and most egalitarian rule is that every member of society is given exactly the same bundle of goods. If no further trading is allowed, this rule results in complete equality in the allocation of goods.

Jeremy Bentham (1748–1832) and his followers (including John Stuart Mill), the utilitarian philosophers, suggested that society should maximize the sum of the utilities of all members of society. Their social welfare function is the sum of the utilities of every member of society. The utilities of all people in society are given equal weight.[10] If U_i is the utility of Individual i and there are n people, the utilitarian welfare function is

$$W = U_1 + U_2 + \cdots + U_n.$$

This social welfare function may not lead to an egalitarian distribution of goods. Indeed, under this system, an allocation is judged superior, all else the same, if people who get the most pleasure from consuming certain goods are given more of those goods.

Panel b of Figure 10.9 shows some isowelfare lines corresponding to the utilitarian welfare function. These lines have a slope of −1 because the utilities of both parties are weighted equally. In the figure, welfare is maximized at *e*.

A generalization of the utilitarian approach assigns different weights to various individuals' utilities. If the weight assigned to Individual i is α_i, this generalized utilitarian welfare function is

$$W = \alpha_1 U_1 + \alpha_2 U_2 + \cdots + \alpha_n U_n.$$

---

[10]It is difficult to compare utilities across individuals because the scaling of utilities across individuals is arbitrary (Chapters 4 and 9). A similar rule that avoids this utility comparison is to maximize a welfare measure that equally weights consumer surplus and producer surplus, which are denominated in dollars.

Society could give greater weight to adults, hardworking people, or those who meet other criteria. Under South Africa's former apartheid system, the utilities of people with white skin were given more weight than those of people with other skin colors.

John Rawls (1971), a philosopher at Harvard, believes that society should maximize the well-being of the worst-off member of society, who is the person with the lowest level of utility. In the social welfare function, all the weight should be placed on the utility of the person with the lowest utility level. The Rawlsian welfare function is

$$W = \min \{U_1, U_2, \ldots, U_n\}.$$

Rawls's rule leads to a relatively egalitarian distribution of goods.

One final rule, which is frequently espoused by various members of Congress and by wealthy landowners in less-developed countries, is to maintain the status quo. Exponents of this rule believe that the current allocation is the best possible allocation. They argue against any reallocation of resources from one individual to another. Under this rule, the final allocation is likely to be very unequal. Why else would the wealthy want it?

All of these rules or social welfare functions reflect value judgments in which interpersonal comparisons are made. Because each reflects value judgments, we cannot compare them on scientific grounds.

Efficiency Versus Equity

Given a particular social welfare function, *society might prefer an inefficient allocation to an efficient one.* We can show this result by comparing two allocations. In Allocation *a*, you have everything and everyone else has nothing. This allocation is Pareto efficient: We can't make others better off without harming you. In Allocation *b*, everyone has an equal amount of all goods. Allocation *b* is not Pareto efficient: I would be willing to trade all my zucchini for just about anything else. Despite Allocation *b*'s inefficiency, most people probably prefer *b* to *a*.

Although society might prefer an inefficient Allocation *b* to an efficient Allocation *a*, according to most social welfare functions, society would prefer some efficient allocation to *b*. Suppose that Allocation *c* is the competitive equilibrium that would be obtained if people were allowed to trade starting from Endowment *b*, in which everyone has an equal share of all goods. By the utilitarian social welfare functions, Allocation *b* might be socially preferred to Allocation *a*, but Allocation *c* is certainly socially preferred to *b*. After all, if everyone is as well off or better off in Allocation *c* than in *b*, *c* must be better than *b* regardless of weights on individuals' utilities. According to the egalitarian rule, however, *b* is preferred to *c* because only strict equality matters. Thus by most of the well-known social welfare functions, but not all, *there is an efficient allocation that is socially preferred to an inefficient allocation.*

Competitive equilibrium may not be very equitable even though it is Pareto efficient. Consequently, societies that believe in equity may tax the rich to give to the poor. If the money taken from the rich is given directly to the poor, society moves from one Pareto-efficient allocation to another.

Sometimes, however, in an attempt to achieve greater equity, efficiency is reduced. For example, advocates for the poor argue that providing public housing to the destitute leads to an allocation that is superior to the original competitive equilibrium. This reallocation isn't efficient: The poor view themselves as better off receiving an amount of money equal to what the government spends on public housing. They could spend the money on the type of housing they like—rather than the type the government provides—or they could spend some of the money on food or other goods.[11]

Unfortunately, there is frequently a conflict between a society's goal of efficiency and the goal of achieving an equitable allocation. Even when the government redistributes money from one group to another, there are significant costs to this redistribution. If tax collectors and other government bureaucrats could be put to work producing rather than redistributing, total output would increase. Similarly, income taxes discourage people from working as hard as they otherwise would (Chapter 5). Nonetheless, probably few people believe that the status quo is optimal and that the government should engage in no redistribution at all (though some members of Congress seem to believe that we should redistribute from the poor to the rich).

Summary

1. **General equilibrium:** A shock to one market may have a spillover effect in another market. A general-equilibrium analysis takes account of the direct effects of a shock in a market and the spillover effects in other markets. In contrast, a partial-equilibrium analysis (such as we used in earlier chapters) looks only at one market and ignores the spillover effects in other markets. The partial-equilibrium and general-equilibrium effects can differ.

2. **Trading between two people:** If people make all the trades they want, the resulting equilibrium will be Pareto efficient: By moving from this equilibrium, we cannot make one person better off without harming another person. At a Pareto-efficient equilibrium, the marginal rates of substitution between people are equal because their indifference curves are tangent.

3. **Competitive exchange:** Competition, in which all traders are price takers, leads to an allocation in which the ratio of relative prices equals the marginal rates of substitution of each person. Thus *every competitive equilibrium is Pareto efficient.* Moreover, *any Pareto-efficient equilibrium can be obtained by competition, given an appropriate endowment.*

4. **Production and trading:** When one person can produce more of one good and another person can produce more of another good using the same inputs, trading can result in greater combined production.

5. **Efficiency and equity:** The Pareto efficiency criterion reflects a value judgment that a change from one allocation to another is desirable if it makes someone better off without harming anyone else. This criterion does not allow all allocations

---

[11]Letting the poor decide how to spend their income is efficient by our definition, even if they spend it on "sin goods" such as cigarettes, liquor, or illicit drugs. A similar argument was made regarding food stamps in Chapter 4.

to be ranked, because some people may be better off with one allocation and others may be better off with another. Majority voting may not allow society to produce a consensus, transitive ordering of allocations either. Economists, philosophers, and others have proposed many criteria for ranking allocations, as summarized in welfare functions. Society may use such a welfare function to choose among Pareto-efficient (or other) allocations.

Problems

1. What is the effect of a tax of t per hour on labor in only one sector of the economy on the equilibrium wage, total employment, and employment in the covered and uncovered sectors?

2. Suppose that the government gives a fixed subsidy of T per firm in one sector of the economy to encourage firms to hire more workers. What is the effect on the equilibrium wage, total employment, and employment in the covered and uncovered sectors?

3. A central city imposes a rent control law that places a binding ceiling on the rent that can be charged for an apartment. The suburbs of this city do not have a rent control law. What happens to the rental prices in the suburbs and to the equilibrium number of apartments in the total metropolitan area, in the city, and in the suburbs? (For simplicity, you may assume that people are indifferent as to whether they live in the city or the suburbs.)

4. Initially, Michael has 10 candy bars and 5 cookies, and Tony has 5 candy bars and 10 cookies. After trading, Michael has 12 candy bars and 3 cookies. In an Edgeworth box, label the initial Allocation A and the new Allocation B. Draw some indifference curves that are consistent with this trade being optimal for both Michael and Tony.

5. The two people in a pure exchange economy have identical utility functions. Will they ever want to trade?

6. Two people trade two goods that they cannot produce. Suppose that one consumer's indifference curves are bowed away from the origin—the usual type of curves—but the other's are concave to the origin. In an Edgeworth box, show that a point of tangency between the two consumers' indifference curves is not a Pareto-efficient bundle. (Identify another allocation that Pareto dominates.)

7. If Jane and Denise have identical, linear production possibility frontiers, are there gains to trade?

8. Suppose that Britain can produce 10 units of cloth or 5 units of food per day (or any linear combination) with available resources and Greece can produce 2 units of food per day or 1 unit of cloth (or any combination). Britain has an *absolute advantage* over Greece in producing both goods. Does it still make sense for these countries to trade?

9. In panel c of Figure 10.6, the joint production possibility frontier is concave to the origin. When the two individual production possibility frontiers are combined, however, the resulting *PPF* could have been drawn so that it was convex to the origin. How do we know which of these two ways of drawing the *PPF* to use?

10. Give an example of a social welfare function that leads to the egalitarian allocation that everyone should be given exactly the same bundle of goods.

11. Suppose that society used the "opposite" of a Rawlsian welfare function: It tried to maximize the well-being of the best-off member of society. Write this welfare function. What allocation maximizes welfare in this society?

Math Problems

12. The demand curve in Sector 1 of the labor market is $L_1 = a - bw$. The demand curve in Sector 2 is $L_2 = c - dw$. The supply curve of labor for the entire market is $L = e + fw$. In equilibrium, $L_1 + L_2 = L$.

    a. Solve for the equilibrium with no minimum wage.

    b. Solve for the equilibrium at which the minimum wage is $\underline{w}$ in Sector 1 ("the covered sector") only.

c. Solve for the equilibrium at which the minimum wage $\underline{w}$ applies to the entire labor market.

13. The demand functions for Q_1 and Q_2 are

$$Q_1 = 10 - 2p_1 + p_2$$

$$Q_2 = 10 - 2p_2 + p_1$$

and there are five units of each good. What is the general equilibrium?

14. The demands for two goods depend on the prices of Good 1 and Good 2, p_1 and p_2,

$$Q_1 = 15 - 3p_1 + p_2,$$

$$Q_2 = 6 - 2p_2 + p_1,$$

but each supply curve depends on only its own price:

$$Q_1 = 2 + p_1,$$

$$Q_2 = 1 + p_2.$$

Solve for the equilibrium: p_1, p_2, Q_1, and Q_2.

15. *Review* (Chapter 4): In a pure exchange economy with two goods, G and H, the two traders have Cobb-Douglas utility functions. Amos's utility is

$$U_a = (G_a)^\alpha (H_a)^{1-\alpha},$$

and Elise's is

$$U_e = (G_e)^\beta (H_e)^{1-\beta},$$

What are their marginal rates of substitution?

★16. Continuing with Problem 15: Between them, Amos and Elise own 100 units of G and 50 units of H. Thus if Amos has G_a and H_a, Elise has $G_e = 100 - G_a$ and $H_e = 50 - H_a$. Solve for their contract curve.

Monopoly

Monopoly: one parrot.

A **monopoly** is the only supplier of a good for which there is no close substitute. Monopolies have been common since ancient times. In the fifth century B.C., the Greek philosopher Thales gained control of most of the olive presses during a year of exceptionally productive harvests. Similarly, the ancient Egyptian pharaohs controlled the sale of food. In England, until Parliament limited the practice in 1624, kings granted monopoly rights called royal charters or patents to court favorites. Today, virtually every country grants a *patent*—an exclusive right to sell that lasts for a limited period of time—to an inventor of a new product, process, substance, or design. Until 1999, the U.S. government gave one company the right to be the sole registrar of Internet domain names.

A monopoly can *set* its price—it is not a price taker like a competitive firm. A monopoly's output is the market output, and the demand curve a monopoly faces is the market demand curve. Because the market demand curve is downward sloping, the monopoly (unlike a competitive firm) doesn't lose all its sales if it raises its price. As a consequence, the monopoly sets its price above marginal cost to maximize its profit. Consumers buy less at this high monopoly price than they would at the competitive price, which equals marginal cost.

IN THIS CHAPTER, WE EXAMINE SEVEN MAIN TOPICS

1. **Monopoly profit maximization:** Like all firms, a monopoly maximizes its profit by setting its price or output so that its marginal revenue equals its marginal cost.
2. **Market power:** How much the monopoly's price is above its marginal cost depends on the shape of the demand curve it faces.
3. **Effects of a shift of the demand curve:** A shift of the demand curve may have a wider range of effects on a monopoly than on a competitive market.
4. **Welfare effects of monopoly:** By setting its price above marginal cost, a monopoly creates a deadweight loss.
5. **Cost advantages that create monopolies:** A firm can use a cost advantage over other firms (due, say, to control of a key input or economies of scale) to become a monopoly.
6. **Government actions that create monopolies:** Governments create monopolies by establishing government monopoly firms, limiting entry of other firms to create a private monopoly, and issuing patents, which are temporary monopoly rights.
7. **Government actions that reduce market power:** The welfare loss of a monopoly can be reduced or eliminated if the government regulates the price the monopoly charges or allows other firms to enter the market.

11.1 | MONOPOLY PROFIT MAXIMIZATION

All firms, including competitive firms and monopolies, maximize their profits by setting *marginal revenue equal to marginal cost* (Chapter 8). We already know how to derive the marginal cost curve of a monopoly from its cost curve (Chapter 7). We now derive the monopoly's marginal revenue curve and then use the marginal revenue and marginal cost curves to examine the monopoly's profit-maximizing behavior.

Marginal Revenue

A firm's marginal revenue curve depends on its demand curve. We will show that a monopoly's marginal revenue curve lies below its demand curve at any positive quantity because its demand curve is downward sloping.

Marginal Revenue and Price. A firm's demand curve shows the price, p, it receives for selling a given quantity, q. The price is the *average revenue* the firm receives, so a firm's revenue is $R = pq$.

A firm's *marginal revenue*, MR, is the change in its revenue from selling one more unit. A firm that earns ΔR more revenue when it sells Δq extra units of output has a marginal revenue (Chapter 8) of

$$MR = \Delta R / \Delta q.$$

If the firm sells exactly one more unit, $\Delta q = 1$, its marginal revenue is $MR = \Delta R$.

The marginal revenue of a monopoly differs from that of a competitive firm because the monopoly faces a downward-sloping demand curve unlike the competitive firm. The competitive firm in panel a of Figure 11.1 faces a horizontal demand curve at the market price, p_1. Because its demand curve is horizontal, the competitive firm can sell another unit of output without dropping its price. As a result, the marginal revenue it receives from selling the last unit of output is the market price.

Initially, the competitive firm sells q units of output at the market price of p_1, so its revenue, R_1, is area A, which is a rectangle that is $p_1 \times q$. If the firm sells one more unit, its revenue is $R_2 = A + B$, where area B is $p_1 \times 1 = p_1$. The competitive firm's marginal revenue equals the market price:

$$\Delta R = R_2 - R_1 = (A + B) - A = B = p_1.$$

A monopoly faces a downward-sloping market demand curve, as in panel b of Figure 11.1. (We've called the number of units of output a firm sells q and the output of all the firms in a market, or market output, Q. Because a monopoly is the only firm in the market, there is no distinction between q and Q, so we use Q to describe both the firm's and the market's output.) The monopoly, which is initially selling Q units at p_1, can sell one extra unit only if the price falls to p_2.

The monopoly's initial revenue, $p_1 \times Q$, is $R_1 = A + C$. When it sells the extra unit, its revenue, $p_2 \times (Q + 1)$, is $R_2 = A + B$. Thus its marginal revenue is

$$\Delta R = R_2 - R_1 = (A + B) - (A + C) = B - C.$$

The monopoly sells the extra unit of output at the new price, p_2, so its extra revenue is $B = p_2 \times 1 = p_2$. The monopoly loses the difference between the new price

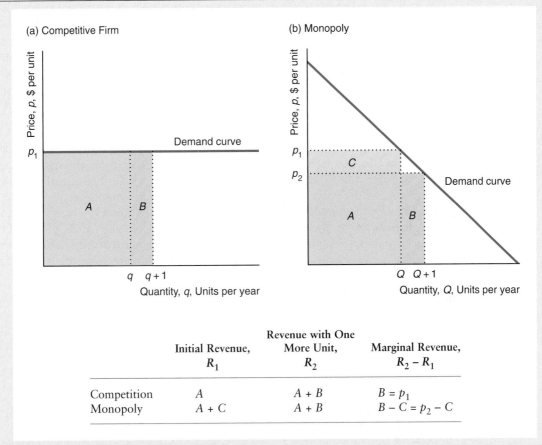

	Initial Revenue, R_1	Revenue with One More Unit, R_2	Marginal Revenue, $R_2 - R_1$
Competition	A	$A + B$	$B = p_1$
Monopoly	$A + C$	$A + B$	$B - C = p_2 - C$

Figure 11.1 **Average and Marginal Revenue.** The demand curve shows the average revenue or price per unit of output sold. (a) The competitive firm's marginal revenue, area B, equals the market price, p_1. (b) The monopoly's marginal revenue is less than the price p_2 by area C (the revenue lost due to a lower price on the Q units originally sold).

and the original price, $\Delta p = (p_2 - p_1)$, on the Q units it originally sold: $C = \Delta p \times Q$. Thus the monopoly's marginal revenue, $B - C = p_2 - C$, is less than the price it charges by an amount equal to area C.

The competitive firm in panel a does not lose an area C from selling an extra unit because its demand curve is horizontal. It is the downward slope of the monopoly's demand curve that causes its marginal revenue to be less than its price.

Marginal Revenue Curve. Thus *the monopoly's marginal revenue curve lies below the demand curve* at every positive quantity. In general, the relationship between the marginal revenue and demand curves depends on the shape of the demand curve.

For all *linear* demand curves, the relationship between the marginal revenue and demand curve is the same. The marginal revenue curve is a straight line that starts at the same point on the vertical (price) axis as the demand curve but has twice the slope of the demand curve, so the marginal revenue curve hits the horizontal (quantity) axis at half the quantity as the demand curve (see Appendix 11A). In Figure 11.2, the demand curve has a slope of −1 and hits the horizontal axis at 24 units, while the marginal revenue curve has a slope of −2 and hits the horizontal axis at 12 units.

★ **Deriving the Marginal Revenue Curve.** To derive the monopoly's marginal revenue curve, we write an equation summarizing the relationship between price and marginal revenue that panel b of Figure 11.1 illustrates. (Because we want this equation to hold at all prices, we drop the subscripts from the prices.) For a monopoly to increase its output by ΔQ, the monopoly lowers its price per unit by $\Delta p/\Delta Q$, which is the slope of the demand curve. By lowering its price, the monopoly loses $(\Delta p/\Delta Q) \times Q$ on the units it originally sold at the higher price (area C), but it earns an additional p on the extra output it now sells (area B). Thus the monopoly's marginal revenue is[1]

$$MR = p + \frac{\Delta p}{\Delta Q} Q. \tag{11.1}$$

Because the slope of the monopoly's demand curve, $\Delta p/\Delta Q$, is negative, the last term in Equation 11.1, $(\Delta p/\Delta Q)Q$, is negative. Equation 11.1 confirms that the price is greater than the marginal revenue, which equals p plus a negative term.

We now use Equation 11.1 to derive the marginal revenue curve when the monopoly faces the linear inverse demand function,

$$p = 24 - Q, \tag{11.2}$$

in Figure 11.2. Equation 11.2 shows that the price consumers are willing to pay falls $1 if quantity increases by one unit. More generally, if quantity increases by ΔQ, price falls by $\Delta p = -\Delta Q$. Thus the slope of the demand curve is $\Delta p/\Delta Q = -1$.

We obtain the marginal revenue function for this monopoly by substituting into Equation 11.1 the actual slope of the demand function, $\Delta p/\Delta Q = -1$, and replacing p with $24 - Q$ (using Equation 11.2):

$$MR = p + \frac{\Delta p}{\Delta Q} Q = (24 - Q) + (-1)Q = 24 - 2Q. \tag{11.3}$$

Figure 11.2 plots Equation 11.3. The slope of this marginal revenue curve is $\Delta MR/\Delta Q = -2$, so the marginal revenue curve is twice as steeply sloped as is the demand curve.

Marginal Revenue and Price Elasticity of Demand. The marginal revenue at any given quantity depends on the demand curve's height (the price) and shape. The shape of

---

[1]Revenue is $R(Q) = p(Q)Q$, where $p(Q)$, the inverse demand function, shows how price changes as quantity increases along the demand curve. Differentiating, we find that the marginal revenue is

$$MR = dR(Q)/dQ = p(Q) + [dp(Q)/dQ]Q.$$

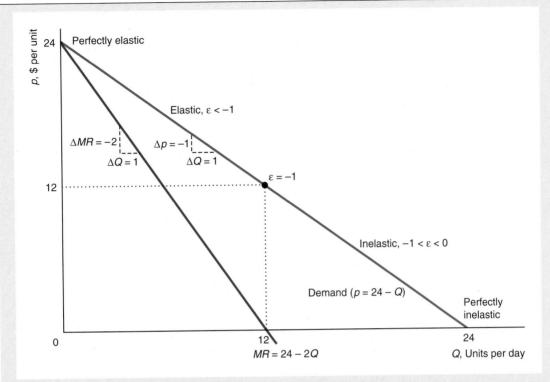

Figure 11.2 Elasticity of Demand and Total, Average, and Marginal Revenue. The demand curve (or average revenue curve), $p = 24 - Q$, lies above the marginal revenue curve, $MR = 24 - 2Q$. Where the marginal revenue equals zero, $Q = 12$, the elasticity of demand is $\varepsilon = -1$.

the demand curve at a particular quantity is described by the price elasticity of demand (Chapter 3), $\varepsilon = (\Delta Q/Q)/(\Delta p/p)$, which tells us the percentage by which quantity demanded falls as the price increases by 1%.

At a given quantity, the marginal revenue equals the price times a term involving the elasticity of demand:[2]

$$MR = p\left(1 + \frac{1}{\varepsilon}\right). \qquad (11.4)$$

According to Equation 11.4, marginal revenue is closer to price as demand becomes more elastic. Where the demand curve hits the price axis ($Q = 0$), the

---

[2]By multiplying the last term in Equation 11.1 by p/p (=1) and using algebra, we can rewrite the expression as

$$MR = p + p\frac{\Delta p}{\Delta Q}\frac{Q}{p} = p\left[1 + \frac{1}{(\Delta Q / \Delta p)(p / Q)}\right].$$

The last term in this expression is $1/\varepsilon$, because $\varepsilon = (\Delta Q/\Delta p)(p/Q)$.

Table 11.1 Quantity, Price, Marginal Revenue, and Elasticity for the Linear Inverse Demand Curve $p = 24 - Q$

Quantity, Q	Price, p	Marginal Revenue, MR	Elasticity of Demand, $\varepsilon = -p/Q$	
0	24	24	$-\infty$	↑
1	23	22	-23	more elastic
2	22	20	-11	
3	21	18	-7	
4	20	16	-5	
5	19	14	-3.8	
6	18	12	-3	
7	17	10	-2.43	
8	16	8	-2	
9	15	6	-1.67	
10	14	4	-1.4	
11	13	2	-1.18	
12	12	0	-1	
13	11	-2	-0.85	
14	10	-4	-0.71	less elastic
...	...	...	...	
23	1	-22	-0.043	
24	0	-24	0	↓

demand curve is perfectly elastic, so the marginal revenue equals price: $MR = p$.[3] Where the demand elasticity is unitary, $\varepsilon = -1$, marginal revenue is zero: $MR = p[1 + 1/(-1)] = 0$. Marginal revenue is negative where the demand curve is inelastic, $-1 < \varepsilon \leq 0$.

With the demand function in Equation 11.2, $\Delta Q/\Delta p = -1$, so the elasticity of demand is $\varepsilon = (\Delta Q/\Delta p)(p/Q) = -p/Q$. Table 11.1 shows the relationship among quantity, price, marginal revenue, and elasticity of demand for this linear example. As Q approaches 24, ε approaches 0, and marginal revenue is negative. As Q approaches zero, the demand becomes increasingly elastic, and marginal revenue approaches the price.

Choosing Price or Quantity

Any firm maximizes its profit by operating where its marginal revenue equals its marginal cost. Unlike a competitive firm, a monopoly can adjust its price, so it has a choice of setting its price *or* its quantity to maximize its profit. (A competitive firm sets its quantity to maximize profit because it cannot affect market price.)

The monopoly is constrained by the market demand curve. Because the demand curve slopes downward, the monopoly faces a trade-off between a higher price and a lower quantity or a lower price and a higher quantity. The monopoly chooses the

---

[3]As ε approaches $-\infty$ (perfectly elastic demand), the $1/\varepsilon$ term approaches zero, so $MR = p(1 + 1/\varepsilon)$ approaches p.

point on the demand curve that maximizes its profit. Unfortunately for the monopoly, it cannot set both its quantity and its price—thereby picking a point that is above the demand curve. If it could do so, the monopoly would choose an extremely high price and an extremely high output level and would become exceedingly wealthy.

If the monopoly sets its price, the demand curve determines how much output it sells. If the monopoly picks an output level, the demand curve determines the price. Because the monopoly wants to operate at the price and output at which its profit is maximized, it chooses the same profit-maximizing solution whether it sets the price or output. In the following, we assume that the monopoly sets quantity.

Graphical Approach	All firms, including monopolies, use a two-step analysis to determine the output level that maximizes its profit (Chapter 8). First, the firm determines the output, Q^*, at which it makes the highest possible profit—the output at which its marginal revenue equals its marginal cost. Second, the firm decides whether to produce Q^* or shut down.

Profit-Maximizing Output. To illustrate how a monopoly chooses its output to maximize its profit, we continue to use the same linear demand and marginal revenue curves but add a linear marginal cost curve in panel a of Figure 11.3. Panel b shows the corresponding profit curve. The profit curve reaches its maximum at 6 units of output, where marginal profit—the slope of the profit curve—is zero. Because *marginal profit is marginal revenue minus marginal cost* (Chapter 8), marginal profit is zero where marginal revenue equals marginal cost. In panel a, marginal revenue equals marginal cost at 6 units. The price on the demand curve at that quantity is $18. Thus the monopoly maximizes its profit at point *e*, where it sells 6 units per day for $18 each.

Why does the monopoly maximize its profit by producing 6 units where its marginal revenue equals its marginal cost? At smaller quantities, the monopoly's marginal revenue is greater than its marginal cost, so its marginal profit is positive. By increasing its output, it raises its profit. Similarly, at quantities greater than 6 units, the monopoly's marginal cost is greater than its marginal revenue, so it can increase its profit by reducing its output.

The profit-maximizing quantity is smaller than the revenue-maximizing quantity. The revenue curve reaches its maximum at $Q = 12$, where the slope of the revenue curve, the marginal revenue, is zero (panel a). In contrast, the profit curve reaches its maximum at $Q = 6$, where marginal revenue equals marginal cost. Because marginal cost is positive, marginal revenue must be positive where profit is maximized. Because the marginal revenue curve has a negative slope, marginal revenue is positive at a smaller quantity than where it equals zero. Thus the profit curve must reach a maximum at a smaller quantity, 6, than the revenue curve, 12.

As we already know, marginal revenue equals zero at the quantity where the demand curve has a unitary elasticity. Because a linear demand curve is more elastic at smaller quantities, *monopoly profit is maximized in the elastic portion of the demand curve.* (Here profit is maximized at $Q = 6$ where the elasticity of demand is –3.) Equivalently, *a monopoly never operates in the inelastic portion of its demand curve.*

Shutdown Decision. A monopoly shuts down to avoid making a loss in the long run if the monopoly-optimal price is below its average cost. In the short run, the monopoly shuts down if the monopoly-optimal price is less than its average variable cost. In our short-run example in Figure 11.3, the average variable cost, $AVC = \$6$, is less than the price, $p = \$18$, at the profit-maximizing output, $Q = 6$, so the firm chooses to produce.

Price is also above average cost at $Q = 6$, so the monopoly makes a positive profit.[4] At the profit-maximizing quantity of 6 units, the price is $p(6) = \$18$ and the average cost is $AC(6) = \$8$. As a result, the profit, $\pi = \$60$, is the shaded rectangle with a height equal to the average profit per unit, $p(6) - AC(6) = \$18 - \$8 = \$10$, and a width of 6 units.

Mathematical Approach

We can also solve for the profit-maximizing quantity mathematically. We already know the demand and marginal revenue functions for this monopoly. We need to determine its marginal cost curve. The monopoly's cost is a function of its output, $C(Q)$. In Figure 11.3, we assume that the monopoly faces a short-run cost function of

$$C(Q) = Q^2 + 12, \qquad (11.5)$$

where Q^2 is the monopoly's variable cost as a function of output and $\$12$ is its fixed cost (Chapter 7). Given this cost function, the monopoly's marginal cost function is[5]

$$MC = 2Q. \qquad (11.6)$$

This marginal cost curve is a straight line through the origin with a slope of 2 in panel a. The average variable cost is $AVC = Q^2/Q = Q$, so it is a straight line through the origin with a slope of 1. The average cost is $AC = C/Q = (Q^2 + 12)/Q = Q + 12/Q$, which is U-shaped.

We determine the profit-maximizing output by equating the marginal revenue (Equation 11.3) and marginal cost (Equation 11.6) functions:

$$MR = 24 - 2Q = 2Q = MC.$$

Solving for Q, we find that $Q = 6$. Substituting $Q = 6$ into the inverse demand function (Equation 11.2), we find that the profit-maximizing price is

$$p = 24 - Q = 24 - 6 = \$18.$$

At that quantity, the average variable cost is $AVC = \$6$, which is less than the price, so the firm does not shut down. The average cost is $AC = \$(6 + 12/6) = \$8$, which is less than the price, so the firm makes a profit.

---

[4]Because profit is $\pi = p(Q)Q - C(Q)$, average profit is $\pi/Q = p(Q) - C(Q)/Q = p(Q) - AC$. Thus average profit (and hence profit) is positive only if price is above average cost.

[5]By differentiating Equation 11.5 with respect to output, we find that the marginal cost is $MC = dC(Q)/dQ = 2Q$.

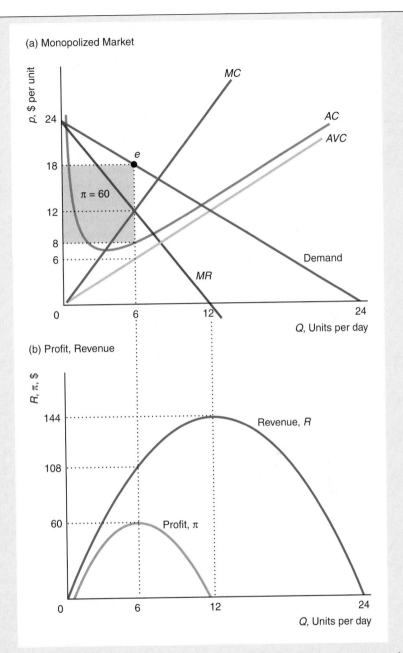

Figure 11.3 Maximizing Profit. (a) At $Q = 6$, where marginal revenue, MR, equals marginal cost, MC, profit is maximized. The rectangle showing the maximum profit $60 is average profit per unit, $p - AC = \$18 - \$8 = \$10$, times the number of units, 6. (b) Profit is maximized at a smaller quantity, $Q = 6$ (where marginal revenue equals marginal cost), than is revenue, $Q = 12$ (where marginal revenue is zero).

11.2 | MARKET POWER

A monopoly has **market power**: the ability of a firm to charge a price above marginal cost and earn a positive profit. We now examine the factors that determine how much above its marginal cost a monopoly sets its price.

Market Power and the Shape of the Demand Curve

The degree to which the monopoly raises its price above its marginal cost depends on the shape of the demand curve at the profit-maximizing quantity. If the monopoly faces a highly elastic—nearly flat—demand curve at the profit-maximizing quantity, it would lose substantial sales if it raised its price by even a small amount. Conversely, if the demand curve is not very elastic (relatively steep) at that quantity, the monopoly would lose fewer sales from raising its price by the same amount.

We can derive the relationship between market power and the elasticity of demand at the profit-maximizing quantity using the expression for marginal revenue in Equation 11.4 and the firm's profit-maximizing condition that marginal revenue equals marginal cost:

$$MR = p\left(1 + \frac{1}{\varepsilon}\right) = MC. \tag{11.7}$$

By rearranging terms, we can rewrite Equation 11.7 as

$$\frac{p}{MC} = \frac{1}{1 + (1/\varepsilon)}. \tag{11.8}$$

Equation 11.8 says that the ratio of the price to marginal cost depends *only* on the elasticity of demand at the profit-maximizing quantity.

In our linear demand example in panel a of Figure 11.3, the elasticity of demand is $\varepsilon = -3$ at the monopoly optimum where $Q = 6$. As a result, the ratio of price to marginal cost is $p/MC = 1/[1 + 1/(-3)] = 1.5$, or $p = 1.5MC$. The profit-maximizing price, $18, in panel a is 1.5 times the marginal cost of $12.

Table 11.2 illustrates how the ratio of price to marginal cost varies with the elasticity of demand. When the elasticity is −1.01, only slightly elastic, the monopoly's profit-maximizing price is 101 times larger than its marginal cost: $p/MC = 1/[1 + 1/(-1.01)] \approx 101$. As the elasticity of demand approaches negative infinity (becomes perfectly elastic), the ratio of price to marginal cost shrinks to $p/MC = 1$.[6]

This table illustrates that not all monopolies can set high prices. A monopoly that faces a horizontal, perfectly elastic demand curve, sets its price equal to its marginal cost—just like a price-taking, competitive firm. If this monopoly were to raise its price, it would lose all its sales, so it maximizes its profit by setting its price equal to its marginal cost.

The more elastic the demand curve, the less a monopoly can raise its price without losing sales. All else the same, the more close substitutes for the monopoly's good there are, the more elastic the demand the monopoly faces. For example,

---

[6]As the elasticity approaches negative infinity, $1/\varepsilon$ approaches zero, so $1/(1 + 1/\varepsilon)$ approaches $1/1 = 1$.

Table 11.2 Elasticity of Demand, Price, and Marginal Cost

Elasticity of Demand, ε	Price/Marginal Cost Ratio, $p/MC = 1/[1 + (1/\varepsilon)]$	Lerner Index, $(p - MC)/p = -1/\varepsilon$
−1.01	101	0.99
−1.1	11	0.91
−2	2	0.5
−3	1.5	0.33
−5	1.25	0.2
−10	1.11	0.1
−100	1.01	0.01
−∞	1	0

(left margin, top to bottom: ←more elastic   less elastic→)

Addison Wesley Longman has the monopoly right to produce and sell this textbook. Many other publishers, however, have the rights to produce and sell similar microeconomics textbooks (though you wouldn't like them as much). The demand Addison Wesley Longman faces is much more elastic than it would be if no substitutes were available. If you think this textbook is expensive, imagine what it would cost if no substitutes were published!

Lerner Index

Another way to show how the elasticity of demand affects a monopoly's price relative to its marginal cost is to look at the firm's **Lerner Index** (or *price markup*):[7] the ratio of the difference between price and marginal cost to the price: $(p - MC)/p$. This measure is zero for a competitive firm because a competitive firm cannot raise its price above its marginal cost. The greater the difference between price and marginal cost, the larger the Lerner Index and the greater the monopoly's ability to set price above marginal cost.

We can express the Lerner Index in terms of the elasticity of demand by rearranging Equation 11.8:

$$\frac{p - MC}{p} = -\frac{1}{\varepsilon}. \tag{11.9}$$

Because $MC \geq 0$ and $p \geq MC$, $0 \leq p - MC \leq p$, so the Lerner Index ranges from 0 to 1 for a profit-maximizing firm.[8] Equation 11.9 confirms that a competitive firm has a Lerner Index of zero because its demand curve is perfectly elastic.[9] As Table

---

[7]This index is named after Abba Lerner, the economist who invented it.

[8]For the Lerner Index to be above 1, ε would have to be a negative fraction, indicating that the demand curve was inelastic at the monopoly optimum. However, a profit-maximizing monopoly never operates in the inelastic portion of its demand curve.

[9]As the elasticity of demand approaches negative infinity, the Lerner Index, $-1/\varepsilon$, approaches zero.

11.2 illustrates, the Lerner Index for a monopoly increases as the demand becomes less elastic. If $\varepsilon = -5$, the monopoly's markup (Lerner Index) is $1/5 = 0.2$; if $\varepsilon = -2$, the markup is $1/2 = 0.5$; and if $\varepsilon = -1.01$, the markup is 0.99. Monopolies that face demand curves that are only slightly elastic set prices that are multiples of their marginal cost and have Lerner Indexes close to 1.

Application   **HUMANA HOSPITALS**

As the table shows, Humana hospitals in 1991 had very large price–marginal cost ratios and Lerner Indexes close to 1 on many supplies they sell to patients, apparently because they faced elasticities of demand close to –1. For example,

	Price Charged Patients, p	Hospitals' Marginal Cost, MC	p/MC	Implicit Demand Elasticity, ε	Lerner Index
Saline solution	$44.90	$0.81	55.4	–1.02	0.98
Rubber arm pads for crutches	$23.75	$0.90	26.4	–1.04	0.96
Rubber tips for crutches	$15.95	$0.71	22.5	–1.05	0.96
Heating pad	$118.00	$5.74	20.6	–1.05	0.95
Pair of crutches	$103.65	$8.35	12.4	–1.09	0.92
Esophagus tube	$1,205.50	$151.98	7.9	–1.14	0.87
Average, all supplies			2.3	–1.77	0.57

Humana's Suburban Hospital in Louisville charges patients $44.90 for a container of saline solution (salt water) that costs the hospital 81¢, so its price is more than 55 times higher than its marginal cost, implying a price elasticity of –1.02 and a Lerner Index of 0.98, which is close to the theoretical maximum. Although the table highlights some of the extreme cases—the price–marginal cost ratio for supplies averages "only" 227%—at least it doesn't show the markups at some of their hospitals on $9 Tylenol tablets and $455 nursing bras.

Sources of Market Power

When will a monopoly face a relatively elastic demand curve and hence have little market power? Ultimately, the elasticity of demand of the market demand curve depends on consumers' tastes and options. The more consumers want a good—the more willing they are to pay "virtually anything" for it—the less elastic is the demand curve.

All else the same, the demand curve a firm (not necessarily a monopoly) faces becomes more elastic as *better substitutes* for the firm's product are introduced, *more firms* enter the market selling the same product, or firms that provide the same service *locate closer* to this firm. The demand curves for Xerox, the U.S. Postal Service, and McDonald's have become more elastic in recent decades for these three reasons.

When Xerox started selling its plain-paper copier, no other firm sold a close substitute. Other companies' machines produced copies on special slimy paper that yellowed quickly. As other firms developed plain-paper copiers, the demand curve that Xerox faced became more elastic.

The U.S. Postal Service (USPS) has a monopoly in first-class mail service. Today, phone calls, faxes, and e-mail are excellent substitutes for many types of first-class mail. The USPS had a monopoly in overnight delivery services until 1979. Now Federal Express, United Parcel Service, and many other firms compete with the USPS in providing overnight deliveries. Because of this new competition, the USPS's share of business and personal correspondence fell from 77% in 1988 to 59% in 1996, and its overnight-mail market fell to 4%.[10] Thus over time the demand curves the USPS faces for first-class mail and overnight service have shifted downward and become more elastic.

As you drive down a highway, you may notice that McDonald's restaurants are spaced miles apart. The purpose of this spacing is to reduce the likelihood that two McDonald's outlets will compete for the same customer. Although McDonald's can prevent its own restaurants from competing with each other, it cannot prevent Wendy's or Burger King from locating near its restaurants. As other fast-food restaurants open near a McDonald's, that restaurant faces a more elastic demand.

What happens as a profit-maximizing monopoly faces more elastic demand? It has to lower its price. The next application illustrates how a monopoly adjusts its price as it changes its beliefs about the elasticity of demand it faces.

Application   AIRPORT MONOPOLIES

Most airports grant a single firm monopoly rights to sell food and other goods, a practice that evokes the oft-expressed sentiment that "the best way to avoid being robbed in an airport is to bring your own food." Host Marriott Corporation has had a monopoly on concessions at the San Francisco International Airport for 40 years. In 1995, however, it reduced its prices on hundreds of items. One interpretation of this cut is that Marriott changed its estimate of the elasticity of demand, ε, it faces for each of these goods.

We know Marriott's price and the corresponding prices at a 7-Eleven. Convenience stores like 7-Eleven typically charge more than grocery and other stores for the items they sell. Thus the 7-Eleven prices are probably above Marriott's marginal cost, MC. Nonetheless, we use the 7-Eleven prices as a conservative estimate of the true MC to calculate ε. (As a consequence, our estimates of the elasticities of demand in the table are too high in absolute

	7-Eleven Price	Original Airport Price	ε_O	New Airport Price	ε_n
Bottled water	0.49	1.69	−1.4	1.49	−1.5
Kodak FunSaver Camera (24)	9.99	14.95	−3.0	10.99	−11.0
Life Savers	0.59	0.85	−3.3	0.69	−6.9
Snapple	0.99	2.25	−1.8	1.59	−2.7

---

[10]Passell, Peter, "Battered by Its Rivals," *New York Times*, May 15, 1997:C1.

value—Marriott has more market power than our estimates indicate.) The table shows estimates of the original elasticity, ε_o, and the new elasticity, ε_n, of demand for several goods. Apparently Marriott decided that the demand curves for most of these goods were substantially more elastic than it previously believed.

Why does the airport grant a monopoly to a single firm? The airport authority captures these monopoly profits for itself by charging high rents. Marriott pays $48 per square foot per month for its space, while retail space in surrounding areas rents for as low as $1 to $3 per square foot. Though Marriott charges high prices, it may not make positive economic profits if the airport charges a high enough rent.

★11.3   EFFECTS OF A SHIFT OF THE DEMAND CURVE

Shifts in the demand curve or marginal cost curve affect the monopoly optimum and can have a wider variety of effects in a monopolized market than in a competitive market. In a competitive market, the effect of a shift in demand on a competitive firm's output depends only on the shape of the marginal cost curve (Chapter 8). In contrast, the effect of a shift in demand on a monopoly's output depends on the shapes of both the marginal cost curve and the demand curve.

As we saw in Chapter 8, a competitive firm's marginal cost curve tells us everything we need to know about the amount that firm will supply at any given market price. The competitive firm's supply curve is its upward-sloping marginal cost curve (above its minimum average variable cost). A competitive firm's supply behavior does not depend on the shape of the market demand curve because it always faces a horizontal demand curve at the market price. Thus if you know a competitive firm's marginal cost curve, you can predict how much that firm will produce at any given market price.

In contrast, a monopoly's output decision depends on the shapes of its marginal cost curve and its demand curve. Unlike a competitive firm, *a monopoly does not have a supply curve.* Knowing the monopoly's marginal cost curve is not enough for us to predict how much a monopoly will sell at any given price.

Figure 11.4 illustrates that the relationship between price and quantity is unique in a competitive market but not in a monopoly market. If the market is competitive, the initial equilibrium is e_1 in panel a, where the original demand curve D^1 intersects the supply curve, MC, which is the sum of the marginal cost curves of a large number of competitive firms. When the demand curve shifts to D^2, the new competitive equilibrium, e_2, has a higher price and quantity. A shift of the demand curve maps out competitive equilibria along the marginal cost curve, so for every equilibrium quantity, there is a single corresponding equilibrium price.

Now suppose there is a monopoly. As demand shifts from D^1 to D^2, the monopoly optimum shifts from E_1 to E_2 in panel b, so the price rises but the quantity stays constant, $Q_1 = Q_2$. Thus *a given quantity can correspond to more than one monopoly-optimal price.* A shift in the demand curve may cause the monopoly-optimal price to stay constant and the quantity to change or both price and quantity to change.

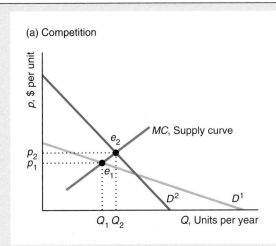

Figure 11.4 Effects of a Shift of the Demand Curve. (a) A shift of the demand curve from D^1 to D^2 causes the competitive equilibrium to move from e_1 to e_2 along the supply curve (the horizontal sum of the marginal cost curves of all the competitive firms). Because the competitive equilibrium lies on the supply curve, each quantity corresponds to only one possible equilibrium price. (b) With a monopoly, this same shift of demand causes the monopoly optimum to change from E_1 to E_2. The monopoly quantity stays the same, but the monopoly price rises. Thus a shift in demand does not map out a unique relationship between price and quantity in a monopolized market: The same quantity, $Q_1 = Q_2$, is associated with two different prices, p_1 and p_2.

11.4 | WELFARE EFFECTS OF MONOPOLY

Welfare, W (here defined as the sum of consumer surplus, CS, and producer surplus, PS), is lower under monopoly than under competition. Chapter 9 showed that competition maximizes welfare because price equals marginal cost. By setting its price above its marginal cost, a monopoly causes consumers to buy less than the competitive level of the good, so a deadweight loss to society occurs.

Graphing the Welfare Loss

We illustrate this loss using our continuing example. If the monopoly were to act like a competitive market and operate where its inverse demand curve, Equation 11.2, intersects its marginal cost (supply) curve, Equation 11.6,

$$p = 24 - Q = 2Q = MC,$$

it would sell $Q_c = 8$ units of output at a price of $16, as in Figure 11.5. At this competitive price, consumer surplus is area $A + B + C$ and producer surplus is $D + E$.

If the firm acts like a monopoly and operates where its marginal revenue equals its marginal cost, only 6 units are sold at the monopoly price of $18, and consumer surplus is only A. Part of the lost consumer surplus, B, goes to the monopoly; but the rest, C, is lost.

By charging the monopoly price of $18 instead of the competitive price of $16, the monopoly receives $2 more per unit and earns an extra profit of area $B = \$12$

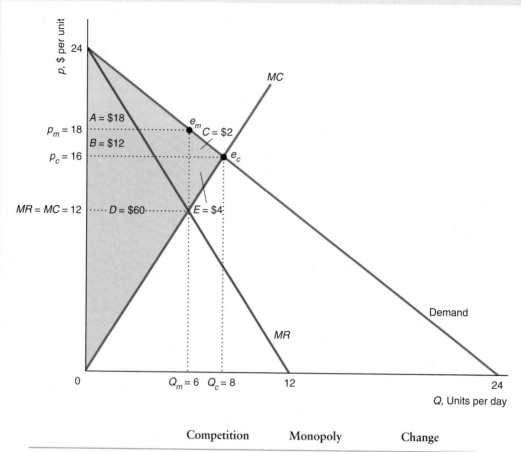

	Competition	Monopoly	Change
Consumer Surplus, *CS*	*A* + *B* + *C*	*A*	−*B* − *C* = Δ*CS*
Producer Surplus, *PS*	*D* + *E*	*B* + *D*	*B* − *E* = Δ*PS*
Welfare, *W* = *CS* + *PS*	*A* + *B* + *C* + *D* + *E*	*A* + *B* + *D*	−*C* − *E* = Δ*W* = *DWL*

Figure 11.5 Deadweight Loss of Monopoly. A competitive market would produce Q_c = 8 at p_c = $16, where the demand curve intersects the marginal cost (supply) curve. A monopoly produces only Q_m = 6 at p_m = $18, where the marginal revenue curve intersects the marginal cost curve. Under monopoly, consumer surplus is *A*, producer surplus is *B* + *D*, and the lost welfare or deadweight loss of monopoly is −*C* − *E*.

on the Q_m = 6 units it sells. The monopoly loses area *E*, however, because it sells less than the competitive output. Consequently, the monopoly's producer surplus increases by *B* − *E* over the competitive level. (We know that its producer surplus increases, *B* − *E* > 0, because the monopoly had the option of producing at the competitive level and chose not to do so.)

Monopoly welfare is lower than competitive welfare. The deadweight loss of monopoly is $-C - E$, which represents the consumer surplus and producer surplus lost because less than the competitive output is produced. As in the analysis of a tax in Chapter 9, the deadweight loss is due to the gap between price and marginal cost at the monopoly output. At $Q_m = 6$, the price, $18, is above the marginal cost, $12, so consumers are willing to pay more for the last unit of output than it costs to produce it.

Application | **DEADWEIGHT LOSS OF THE U.S. POSTAL SERVICE**

Lenard (1994) calculated the welfare losses from the monopoly of the USPS in delivering third-class mail, which includes advertising circulars and mail-order catalogs. The welfare cost of the postal service monopoly depends on how much higher the price is above the USPS's marginal cost and whether the USPS produces inefficiently. If the USPS produces efficiently, the deadweight loss is the reduction in consumer surplus not offset by a gain to the USPS or others. If the USPS is inefficient, the deadweight loss is even greater.

Private mail carriers may deliver fliers and other pieces of mail that do not have an individual's name in the address, but they may not deliver addressed mail such as third-class letters. On the basis of a survey of private mail carriers, Lenard calculated that the private companies could deliver third-class mail at a constant price of $p_c = 12.3¢$ per piece in 1992. Assuming that the private mail carriers are price takers, that price equals the marginal cost. This marginal cost was only about three-quarters of the USPS monopoly price for third-class mail, $p_m = 16.7¢$.

The USPS delivered $Q_m = 49.8$ billion pieces of mail in 1992. On the basis of the USPS estimate of the elasticity of demand for third-class mail of -0.625, $Q_c = 60.4$ billion pieces would have been delivered at the competitive price. Because the USPS is operating where demand is inelastic, $\varepsilon = -0.625$, its price is less than the profit-maximizing level.

On the basis of these numbers, customers lose consumer surplus of $2.46 billion dollars, which is 30% of the $8.3 billion they spend on third-class bulk mail. Of this lost consumer surplus, $237 million, the loss of area B in the graph, is a deadweight loss—a loss to customers that is not gained by the USPS—and the remaining $2.22 billion, area A, is the excess payment, $(p_m - p_c)Q_m$, the USPS gets by charging the monopoly price instead of the competitive price.

The USPS is obligated by statute to break even. Thus the $2.22 billion transferred from customers to the USPS due to the high price of mail is either wasted on inefficient production, used to subsidize other types of mail, or transferred to postal workers through high wages. Knowing that postal workers earn 21% more than comparable private-sector employees, Lenard calculated that postal workers get up to $1.51 billion of the third-class mail "profit." He inferred that $0.95 billion (= $2.46 billion – $1.51 billion) is wasted through inefficient production. Much of this inefficiency is due to the existence of post offices—especially in rural areas—that are

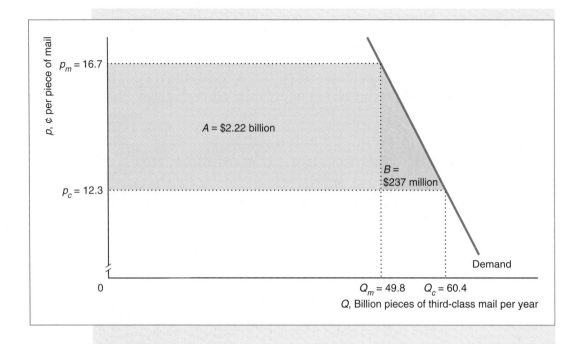

too small to use optical character readers and barcode sorters, so workers must sort by hand.

If the USPS produced efficiently, the deadweight loss would be B = $237 million, the amount customers lose that is not transferred to the USPS. Because the USPS produces inefficiently, however, the true deadweight loss to society is $1.19 billion: the sum of B and the $0.95 billion lost from production inefficiency.

Solved Problem 11.1

In our linear example, how does charging the monopoly a specific tax of τ = $8 per unit affect the monopoly optimum and the welfare of consumers, the monopoly, and society (where society's welfare includes the tax revenue)? What is the incidence of the tax on consumers?

Answer

1. *Determine how imposing the tax affects the monopoly optimum*: In the accompanying graph, the intersection of the marginal revenue curve, MR, and the before-tax marginal cost curve, MC^1, determines the monopoly optimum quantity, $Q_1 = 6$. At the before-tax optimum, e_1, the price is $p_1 = \$18$. The specific tax causes the monopoly's before-tax marginal cost curve, $MC^1 = 2Q$, to shift upward by $8 to $MC^2 = MC^1 + 8 = 2Q + 8$. After the tax is applied, the monopoly operates where $MR = 24 - 2Q = 2Q + 8 = MC^2$. In the after-tax monopoly optimum, e_2, the quantity is

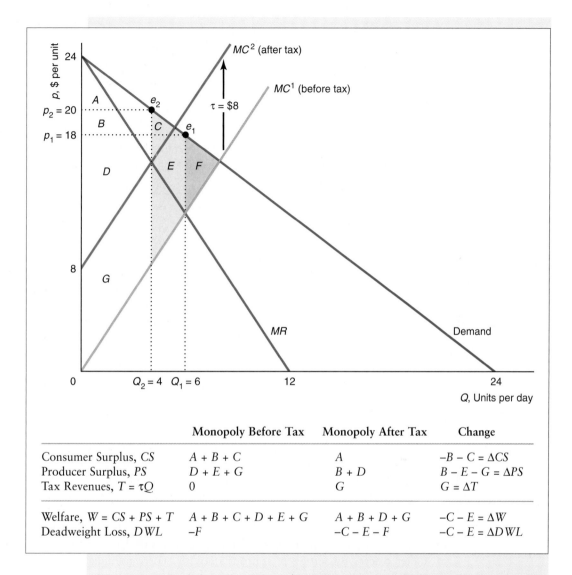

	Monopoly Before Tax	Monopoly After Tax	Change
Consumer Surplus, CS	$A + B + C$	A	$-B - C = \Delta CS$
Producer Surplus, PS	$D + E + G$	$B + D$	$B - E - G = \Delta PS$
Tax Revenues, $T = \tau Q$	0	G	$G = \Delta T$
Welfare, $W = CS + PS + T$	$A + B + C + D + E + G$	$A + B + D + G$	$-C - E = \Delta W$
Deadweight Loss, DWL	$-F$	$-C - E - F$	$-C - E = \Delta DWL$

$Q_2 = 4$ and the price is $p_2 = \$20$. Thus output falls by $\Delta Q = 2$ units and the price increases by $\Delta p = \$2$.

2. *Calculate the change in the various welfare measures:* The graph shows how the welfare measures change. Area G is the tax revenue collected by the government, $\tau Q = \$32$, because its height is the distance between the two marginal cost curves, $\tau = \$8$, and its width is the output the monopoly produces after the tax is imposed, $Q = 4$. The tax reduces consumer and producer surplus and increases the deadweight loss. We know that producer surplus falls because (a) the monopoly could have produced this reduced output level in the absence of the tax but did not because it was

not the profit-maximizing output, so its before-tax profit falls, and (b) the monopoly must now pay taxes. The before-tax deadweight loss from monopoly is −F. The after-tax deadweight loss is −C − E − F, so the increase in deadweight loss due to the tax is −C − E. The table below the graph shows that consumer surplus changes by −B − C and producer surplus by B − E − G.

3. *Calculate the incidence of the tax*: Because the tax goes from $0 to $8, the change in the tax is $\Delta\tau$ = $8. The incidence of the tax (Chapter 3) on consumers is $\Delta p/\Delta\tau$ = $2/$8 = $\frac{1}{4}$. (The monopoly absorbs $6 of the tax and passes on only $2.)[11]

★ Welfare Effects of Ad Valorem Versus Specific Taxes

Solved Problem 11.1 illustrates that a specific sales tax (the monopoly pays the government τ dollars per unit sold) provides tax revenue but reduces welfare below even the monopoly level. Governments use ad valorem taxes more often than specific taxes. Is there an advantage to using an ad valorem sales tax (the monopoly pays αp per unit of output, where α is a fraction and p is the price charged)? The answer is that a government raises more tax revenue with an ad valorem tax applied to a monopoly than with a specific tax when α and τ are set so that the after-tax output is the same with either tax, as we now show.[12]

In Figure 11.6, the before-tax market demand curve is D, and the corresponding marginal revenue is MR. The before-tax monopoly optimum is e_1. The MR curve intersects the MC curve at Q_1 units, which sell at a price of p_1.

If the government imposes a specific tax τ, the monopoly's after-tax demand curve is D^s, which is the market demand curve D shifted downward by τ dollars.[13] The corresponding marginal revenue curve, MR^s, intersects the marginal cost curve at Q_2. In this after-tax equilibrium, e_2, consumers pay p_2 and the monopoly receives $p_s = p_2 - \tau$ per unit. The government's revenue from the specific tax is area $A = \tau Q_2$.

If the government imposes an ad valorem tax α, the demand curve facing the monopoly is D^a. The gap between D^a and D, which is the tax per unit, αp, is greater at higher prices. By setting α appropriately, the corresponding marginal revenue

---

[11]In contrast to a competitive market, when a monopoly is taxed, the incidence of the tax on consumers can exceed 100%, as Appendix 11B demonstrates.

[12]Chapter 3 shows that both taxes raise the same tax revenue in a competitive market. The taxes raise different amounts when applied to monopolies or other noncompetitive firms. See Delipalla and Keen (1992), Skeath and Trandel (1994), and Hamilton (1999).

[13]Instead, we could capture the effect of a specific tax by shifting the marginal cost curve upward by τ, as in our answer to Solved Problem 11.1.

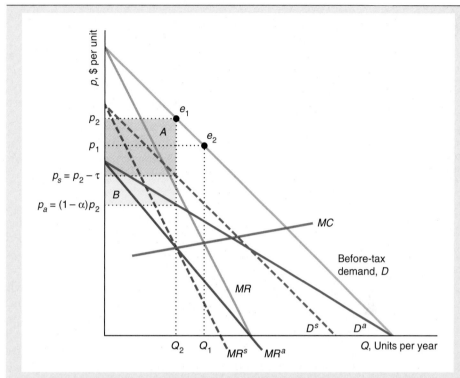

Figure 11.6 Ad Valorem Versus Specific Tax. A specific tax (τ) and an ad valorem tax (α) that reduce the monopoly output by the same amount (from Q_1 to Q_2) raise different amounts of tax revenues for the government. The tax revenue from the specific tax is area $A = \tau Q_2$. The tax revenue from the ad valorem tax is $A + B = \alpha p_2 Q_2$.

curve, MR_a, intersects the marginal cost curve at Q_2, where consumers again pay p_2. Although the ad valorem tax reduces output by the same amount as the specific tax, the ad valorem tax raises more revenue, areas $A + B = \alpha p_2 Q_2$.

Both sales taxes harm consumers by the same amount because they raise the price consumers pay from p_1 to p_2 and reduce the quantity purchased from Q_1 to Q_2. The ad valorem tax transfers more revenue from the monopoly to the government, so the government prefers the ad valorem tax and the monopoly prefers the specific tax. (Equivalently, if the government set τ and α so that they raised the same amount of tax revenue, the ad valorem tax would reduce output and consumer surplus less than the specific tax.)

Isn't that amazing! It makes sense for governments to employ an ad valorem tax rather than a specific tax, and they usually apply the ad valorem tax.

11.5 | COST ADVANTAGES THAT CREATE MONOPOLIES

Why are some markets monopolized? Two key reasons are that a firm has a cost advantage over other firms or that a government created the monopoly.[14] If a low-cost firm profitably sells at a price so low that other potential competitors with higher costs would make losses, no other firm enters the market.

Sources of Cost Advantages

A firm can have a cost advantage over potential rivals for a number of reasons. One reason is that the firm controls a key input.[15] For example, a firm that owns the only quarry in a region is the only firm that can profitably sell gravel to local construction firms.

A second important reason why a firm may have lower costs is that the firm uses a superior technology or has a better way of organizing production. Henry Ford's methods of organizing production using assembly lines and standardization allowed him to produce cars at lower cost than rival firms until they copied his organizational techniques.

When a firm develops a better production method that provides an advantage—possibly enough of an advantage for the firm to be a monopoly—the firm must either keep the information secret or obtain a patent, which provides government protection from imitation. According to a survey of 650 research and development managers of U.S. firms (Levin, Klevorick, Nelson, and Winter, 1987), secrecy is more commonly used than patents to prevent duplication of new or improved processes by other firms but less commonly used to protect new products.

Natural Monopoly

A market has a **natural monopoly** if one firm can produce the total output of the market at lower cost than several firms could.[16] With a natural monopoly, it is more efficient to have only one firm produce than more firms. Believing that they are natural monopolies, governments frequently grant monopoly rights to *public utilities* to provide essential goods or services such as water, gas, electric power, or mail delivery.

If a firm has economies of scale (Chapter 7) at all levels of output, its average cost curve falls as output increases for any observed level of output. If all potential firms

---

[14]In later chapters, we discuss three other means by which monopolies are created. One method is the merger of several firms into a single firm (Chapter 13). This method creates a monopoly if new firms fail to enter the market. A second method is for firms to coordinate their activities and set their prices as a monopoly would (Chapter 13). Firms that act collectively in this way are called a *cartel*. A third method is for a monopoly to use strategies that discourage other firms from entering the market (Chapter 14).

[15]Chapter 14 discusses in greater detail how one firm may control an *essential facility*: a scarce resource that a rival needs to use to survive.

[16]If the cost for Firm i to produce q_i is $C(q_i)$, the condition for a natural monopoly is

$$C(Q) < C(q_1) + C(q_2) + \cdots + C(q_n),$$

where $Q = q_1 + q_2 + \cdots + q_n$ is the sum of the output of any $n \geq 2$ firms.

have the same strictly declining average cost curve, this market has a natural monopoly, as we now illustrate.[17]

A company that supplies water to homes incurs a high fixed cost, F, to build a plant and connect houses to the plant. The firm's marginal cost, m, of supplying water is constant, so its marginal cost curve is horizontal and its average cost, $AC = m + F/Q$, declines as output rises.

Figure 11.7 shows such marginal and average cost curves where $m = \$10$ and $F = \$60$. If the market output is 12 units per day, one firm produces that output at an average cost of $\$15$, or a total cost of $\$180$ (= $\$15 \times 12$). If two firms each produce 6 units, the average cost is $\$20$ and the cost of producing the market output is $\$240$ (= $\$20 \times 12$), which is greater than the cost with a single firm.

If the two firms divided total production in any other way, their cost of production would still exceed the cost of a single firm (as the following question asks you to prove). The reason is that the marginal cost per unit is the same no matter how

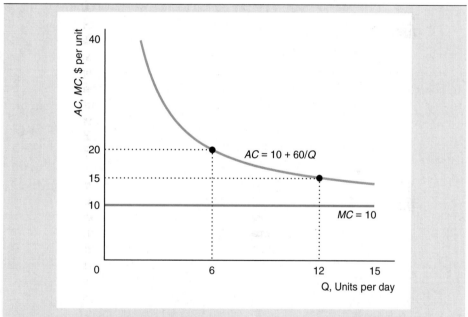

Figure 11.7 Natural Monopoly. This natural monopoly has a strictly declining average cost.

---

[17]A firm may be a natural monopoly even if its cost curve does not fall at all levels of output. If a U-shaped average cost curve reaches its minimum at 100 units of output, it may be less costly for only one firm to produce an output of 101 units even though average cost is rising at that output. Thus a cost function with economies of scale everywhere is a sufficient but not a necessary condition for natural monopoly.

many firms produce, but each additional firm adds a fixed cost, which raises the cost of producing a given quantity. If only one firm provides water, the cost of building a second plant and a second set of pipes is avoided.

Solved Problem 11.2

A firm that delivers Q units of water to households has a total cost of $C(Q) = mQ + F$. If any entrant would have the same cost, does this market have a natural monopoly?

Answer

Determine whether costs rise if two firms produce a given quantity: Let q_1 be the output of Firm 1 and q_2 be the output of Firm 2. The combined cost of these two firms producing $Q = q_1 + q_2$ is

$$C(q_1) + C(q_2) = (mq_1 + F) + (mq_2 + F) = m(q_1 + q_2) + 2F = mQ + 2F.$$

If a single firm produces Q, its cost is $C(Q) = mQ + F$. Thus the cost of producing any given Q is greater with two firms than with one firm, so this market has a natural monopoly.

Application   ELECTRIC POWER UTILITIES

According to the estimates of Christensen and Greene (1976), the average cost curve for U.S. electric-power-producing firms in 1970 was U-shaped, reaching its minimum at 33 billion kilowatt-hours (kWh) per year (see graph). Thus

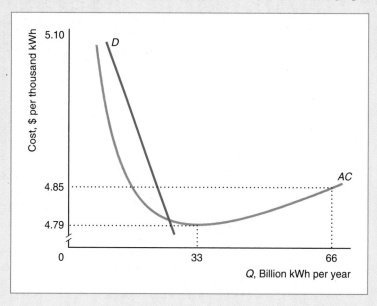

whether an electric power utility was a natural monopoly depended on the demand it faced.

For example, if the demand curve for an electric utility was *D* on the graph, the quantity demanded was less than 33 billion kWh per year at any price, so the electric utility operated in the strictly declining section of its average cost curve and was a natural monopoly. In 1970, most electric companies were operating in regions of substantial economies of scale. Newport Electric produced only 0.5 billion kWh per year, and Iowa Southern Utilities produced 1.3 billion kWh per year.

A few of these firms operated in the upward-sloping section of the average cost curve and were not natural monopolies. The largest electric utility in 1970, Southern, produced 54 billion kWh per year. It was not a natural monopoly because two firms could produce that quantity at 3¢ less per thousand kWh than a single firm could. As the graph shows, two firms producing 33 billion kWh each have an average cost of $4.79 per thousand kWh, while one firm producing 66 billion kWh has an average cost of $4.85, or 6¢ more per thousand kWh.

11.6 | GOVERNMENT ACTIONS THAT CREATE MONOPOLIES

Governments create many monopolies. Sometimes governments own and manage monopolies. In the United States, as in most countries, the postal service is a government monopoly. Indeed, the U.S. Constitution explicitly grants the government the right to establish a postal service. Many local governments own and operate public utility monopolies that provide garbage collection, electricity, water, gas, phone services, and other utilities.

Frequently, however, governments create monopolies by preventing competing firms from entering a market. For example, when a government grants a patent, it limits entry and allows the patent-holding firm to earn a monopoly profit from an invention—a reward for developing the new product.

Barriers to Entry

By preventing other firms from entering a market, governments create monopolies. Typically, governments create monopolies in one of three ways: by making it difficult for new firms to obtain a license to operate, by granting a firm the rights to be a monopoly, or by auctioning the rights to be a monopoly.

Frequently, firms need government licenses to operate. If governments make it difficult for new firms to obtain licenses, the first firm may maintain its monopoly. Until recently, many U.S. cities required that new hospitals or other inpatient facilities demonstrate the need for a new facility to obtain a certificate of need, which allowed them to enter the market.

Government grants of monopoly rights have been common for public utilities. Instead of running a public utility itself, a government gives a private company the monopoly rights to operate the utility. As discussed in the application on airport monopoly concessions, a government may capture some of the monopoly profits by charging a high rent to the monopoly. Alternatively, government officials may capture the rents for monopoly rights by means of bribes.

Governments around the world have privatized many state-owned monopolies in the past several decades. By selling its monopolies to private firms, a government can capture the value of future monopoly earnings today. However, for political or other reasons, governments frequently sell at a lower price that does not capture all future profits.

Application   GOVERNMENT SALES OF MONOPOLIES

Around the world, governments sell monopoly rights for money or promises of service. In 1984, the British government sold $4.9 billion worth of shares in British Telecom, the national telephone company. In 1995, France sold all but 10% of its tobacco monopoly, Seita, which makes Gauloise and Gitane cigarettes. In the United States, the Clinton administration auctioned off large parts of the airwaves for new wireless phone services and other uses. Recently, Mexico and Britain auctioned television stations.

Local governments frequently auction monopoly rights to the highest bidder. San Francisco auctioned the monopoly rights to store cars towed for illegal parking. The monopoly, City Tow, collects $40 per car, of which $15.03 goes to the city (the losing company had proposed to give the city only $7.50). Similarly, many localities award cable television monopolies to the highest bidder.

In recent years, nearly a dozen cities have sold a chosen cola company the exclusive rights to vend its products in city parks and on other municipal property. Huntington Beach, California, sold Coca-Cola 10 years of exclusive rights for nearly $6 million in cash and services, and San Diego granted Pepsi 12 years of exclusive rights for $6.7 million.

Sometimes monopoly rights are granted in exchange for other commitments. The United States granted a billionaire investor a 30-year monopoly on the cruise business to Hawaii in exchange for a commitment to buy two U.S.-built cruise ships for about $400 million each. In 1996, South Africa's parliament extended by five years the monopoly held by the telephone company Telkom on the condition that the firm install 2.8 million new lines and greatly improve service. If Telkom meets these goals, its reward is a sixth year of monopoly.

Patents

If a firm cannot prevent imitation by keeping its discovery secret, it may obtain government protection to prevent other firms from duplicating its discovery and entering the market. Virtually all countries provide such protection through a **patent**: an exclusive right granted to the inventor to sell a new and useful product, process, substance, or design for a fixed period of time. A patent grants an inventor the right to be the monopoly provider of the good for a number of years.

Patent Length. The length of a patent varies across countries. The U.S. Constitution explicitly gives the government the right to grant authors and inventors exclusive rights to their writings (copyrights) and to their discoveries (patents) for limited periods of time. Traditionally, U.S. patents lasted *17 years* from the date they were *granted*, but the United States agreed in 1995 to change its patent law as part of a GATT agreement. Now U.S. patents last for *20 years* after the date the inventor *files* for patent protection. The length of protection is likely to be shorter under the new rules, because it frequently takes more than three years after filing to obtain final approval of a patent.

Many European countries granted patent protection for very short periods of time, but these patents could be renewed upon the payment of a fee. The renewal fee was due in two years in France, three in Germany, and five in the United Kingdom. A patent could be renewed until it was 16 years old in Britain, 18 in Germany, and 20 in France.

Patents Stimulate Research. A firm with a patent monopoly sets a high price that results in deadweight loss. Why, then, do governments grant patent monopolies? The main reason is that inventive activity would fall if there were no patent monopolies or other incentives to inventors. The costs of developing a new drug or new computer chip are often hundreds of millions or even billions of dollars. If anyone could copy a new drug or chip and compete with the inventor, few individuals or firms would undertake costly research. Thus the government is explicitly trading off the long-run benefits of additional inventions against the shorter-term harms of monopoly pricing during the period of patent protection.

Application　　　**A DRUG PATENT**

In 1977, SmithKline Beckman (soon to be Glaxo-SmithKline) received a patent for its revolutionary anti-ulcer drug, Tagamet, which gave it the monopoly rights to sell Tagamet in the United States. It was sold as a prescription drug.

Tagamet blocks the histamine-2 (H_2) receptor on the cells of the stomach that produce gastric acid and thus reduces the amount of acid produced. This drug is much more effective than previous anti-ulcer drugs, which neutralize acids after they are produced. Three other H_2 drugs entered the market from 1983 to 1988: Zantac in June 1983, Pepcid in October 1986, and Axid in April 1988. After 1994, when Tagamet's patent expired, other firms started selling generic forms of Tagamet.

Thus from 1977 to late 1983, Tagamet was the only H_2 drug on the market and had no close substitute. From late 1983 to 1994, the market for H_2 drugs was oligopolistic. Today, there is a more complex market structure in which both branded goods (Tagamet, Zantac, Pepcid, and Axid) and unbranded, generic Tagamet copies are sold. In addition, Tagamet, Zantac, Pepcid, and Axid are now available without a prescription.

Using a few assumptions, we can calculate the pricing and welfare implications of SmithKline's monopoly in early 1983, just before Tagamet lost its monopoly. Before Zantac entered the market, about 1.3 million daily doses of oral Tagamet were sold at pharmacies at a price of about 75¢ per daily dose in 1983 dollars. Though the firm's cost data are not publicly available, some unofficial industry estimates put the marginal cost (and average variable cost) of an H_2 drug at about 10% of the price, or $MC = AVC = 7.5¢$. If we rearrange Equation 11.9, we can use this relationship between marginal cost and price to calculate the elasticity of demand that SmithKline faced if it were maximizing its short-run profits:

$$\varepsilon = -\frac{p}{p - MC} = -\frac{0.75}{0.75 - 0.075} \approx -1.11.$$

The demand it faced was only slightly elastic: A 1% increase in price caused quantity to fall by only a little more than 1%.

If we assume that the demand curve is linear and that the elasticity of demand is –1.11 at the monopoly optimum (1.3 million daily doses sold at 75¢ a dose), then the inverse demand function is

$$p = 1.43 - 0.52Q.$$

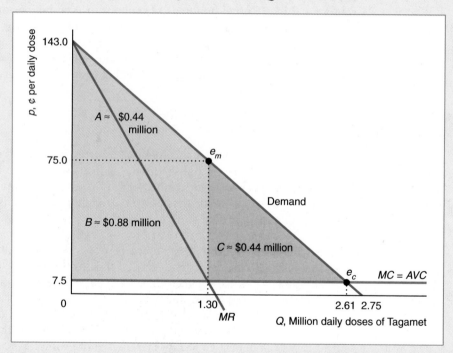

This demand curve (see graph) has a slope of –0.52, hits the price axis at $1.43 and the quantity axis at 2.75 million daily doses. The corresponding marginal revenue curve,

$$MR = 1.43 - 1.04Q,$$

strikes the price axis at $1.43 and has twice the slope, –1.04, as the demand curve.

The marginal revenue and marginal cost curves intersect,

$$MR = 1.43 - 1.04Q = 0.075 = MC,$$

at the profit-maximizing quantity of about 1.3 million daily doses. The corresponding price is 75¢.

Had Tagamet been sold at a price equal to its marginal cost, 7.5¢, consumer surplus would have equaled areas *A* + *B* + *C*, which, given our linearity and other assumptions, was about $1.77 million per day. At the higher monopoly price of 75¢, consumer surplus was only *A* ≈ $0.44 million per day, so consumers lost consumer surplus of *B* + *C*, or $1.33 million per day. Part of this loss to consumers, *B* = ($0.75 − $0.075) × 1.3 million daily doses ≈ $0.88 million per day, was a transfer from consumers to the firm, but the rest, *C* ≈ $0.44 million per day or $161 million per year, was the deadweight loss from monopoly pricing. SmithKline's profit was its producer surplus, *B*, minus its fixed cost.

SmithKline reported selling $14 billion of Tagamet during the 17 years its patent was in force. The gigantic rewards to be had from a successful drug provide a major incentive to firms to invest in developing new pharmaceuticals.

Were it not for patent protection, other companies could duplicate a new drug—as illustrated by the entry of generic copies of Tagamet when its patent expired—and competition would drive economic profits toward zero, reducing the financial incentive to engage in research.

It is extremely expensive to bring a new drug to market. Firms must pay for conducting research, winning patent approval, developing the product, performing clinical trials, and obtaining final approval from the Food and Drug Administration (FDA) to sell the drug, based on a demonstration of efficacy and safety. According to one U.S. government agency's estimate, the before-tax cost of developing a new pharmaceutical averages $359 million per drug (the after-tax cost is $194 million). Moreover, there's no guarantee that a drug will be successful. Tagamet was one of the most profitable drugs of all time; however, many other drugs, though costly to develop, produce minimal returns.

Thus the justification for letting patents create monopolies is that the monopoly profits spur new research. Many people benefit greatly from a drug like Tagamet. The monetary value of the relief from ulcers they received in the short run, when they bought Tagamet at the monopoly price, is area *A*; the value in the long run after the patent expired, when they buy the same drug at marginal cost, is area *A* + *B* + *C*.[18]

---

[18]According to some estimates, the rate of surgical operations for ulcers dropped from 155,000 in 1977, when Tagamet was introduced, to around 16,000 per year by 1991. Given that ulcer surgery costs $25,000 compared to H_2 drugs' cost of about $1,000, patients' net savings in out-of-pocket costs is over $3 billion per year.

Alternatives to Patents. Instead of using patents to spur research, the government could give research grants or offer prizes. Rather than trying these alternative approaches, Congress has modified the patent system. In the 1960s and 1970s, the effective life of a patent on a drug shrank because of the additional time it took to get FDA approval to sell the drug. By 1978, the average drug had patent protection for fewer than 10 years. The Drug Price Competition and Patent Term Restoration Act of 1984 restored up to three years of the part of the patent life that was lost while the firm demonstrated efficacy and safety to the FDA. At the same time, the act made it easier for generic products to enter at the end of the patent period. Thus the law aimed both to encourage the development of new drugs by increasing the reward—the monopoly period—and to stimulate price competition at the end of the period.

11.7 | GOVERNMENT ACTIONS THAT REDUCE MARKET POWER

Some governments act to reduce or eliminate monopolies' market power. Most Western countries have laws forbidding a firm from driving other firms out of the market so as to monopolize it. Many governments either regulate monopolies—especially those that the government has created—or destroy monopolies by breaking them up into smaller, independent firms or encouraging other firms to enter the market.

Regulating Monopolies

Governments limit monopolies' market power in a number of ways. Most utilities, for example, are subject to direct regulation. One method governments use to limit the harms of monopoly is to place a ceiling on the price that a monopoly charges.

Optimal Price Regulation. In some markets, the government can eliminate the deadweight loss of monopoly by requiring that a monopoly charge no more than the competitive price. We use our earlier linear example to illustrate this type of regulation in Figure 11.8.

If the government doesn't regulate the profit-maximizing monopoly, the monopoly optimum is e_m, at which 6 units are sold at the monopoly price of $18. Suppose that the government sets a ceiling price of $16, the price at which the marginal cost curve intersects the market demand curve. Because the monopoly cannot charge more than $16 per unit, the monopoly's regulated demand curve is horizontal at $16 (up to 8 units) and is the same as the market demand curve at lower prices. The marginal revenue, MR_r, corresponding to the regulated demand curve is horizontal where the regulated demand curve is horizontal (up to 8 units) and equals the marginal revenue curve, MR, corresponding to the market demand curve at larger quantities.

The regulated monopoly sets its output at 8 units, where MR_r equals its marginal cost, MC, and charges the maximum permitted price of $16. The regulated firm still

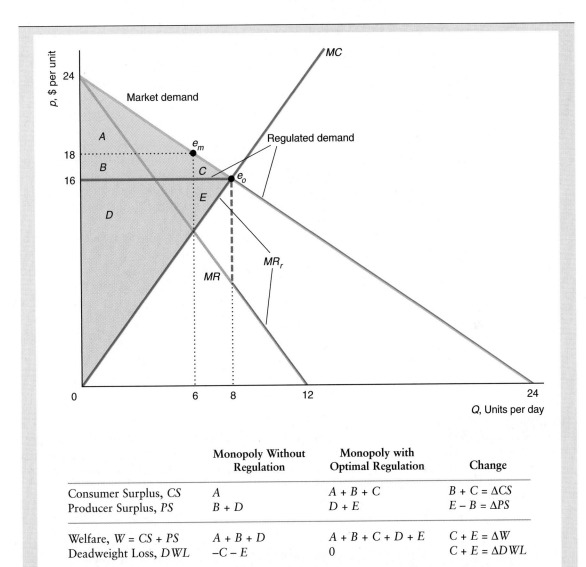

	Monopoly Without Regulation	Monopoly with Optimal Regulation	Change
Consumer Surplus, CS	A	$A + B + C$	$B + C = \Delta CS$
Producer Surplus, PS	$B + D$	$D + E$	$E - B = \Delta PS$
Welfare, $W = CS + PS$	$A + B + D$	$A + B + C + D + E$	$C + E = \Delta W$
Deadweight Loss, DWL	$-C - E$	0	$C + E = \Delta DWL$

Figure 11.8 Optimal Price Regulation. If the government sets a price ceiling at $16, where the monopoly's marginal cost curve hits the demand curve, the new demand curve the monopoly faces has a kink at 8 units, and the corresponding marginal revenue curve, MR_r, "jumps" at that quantity. The regulated monopoly sets its output where $MR_r = MC$, selling the same quantity, 8 units, at the same price, $16, as a competitive industry would. The regulation eliminates the monopoly deadweight loss, $C + E$. Consumer surplus, $A + B + C$, and producer surplus, $D + E$, are the same as under competition.

makes a profit, because its average cost is less than $16 at 8 units. The optimally regulated monopoly optimum, e_o, is the same as the competitive equilibrium, where marginal cost (supply) equals the market demand curve.[19] Thus setting a price ceiling where the *MC* curve and market demand curve intersect eliminates the deadweight loss of monopoly.

How do we know that this regulation is optimal? The answer is that this regulated outcome is the same as would occur if this market were competitive, where welfare is maximized (Chapter 9). As the table accompanying Figure 11.8 shows, the deadweight loss of monopoly, $C + E$, is eliminated by this optimal regulation.

Nonoptimal Price Regulation. Welfare is reduced if the government does not set the price optimally. Suppose that the government sets the regulated price below the optimal level, which is $16 in our example. If it sets the price below the firm's minimum average cost, the firm shuts down. If that happens, the deadweight loss equals the sum of the consumer plus producer surplus under optimal regulation, $A + B + C + D + E$.

If the government sets the price ceiling below the optimally regulated price but high enough that the firm does not shut down, consumers who are lucky enough to buy the good are better off because they can buy goods at a lower price than with optimal regulation. Some customers, however, are frustrated because the monopoly will not sell them the good, as we show next. There is a deadweight loss because less output is sold than with optimal regulation. (Problem 10 at the end of the chapter asks you to determine the effects of a regulated price that is above the optimal level.)

Solved Problem 11.3

Suppose that the government sets a price, p_2, that is below the monopoly-optimal level, p_1, but above the monopoly's minimum average cost. How do the price, the quantity sold, the quantity demanded, and welfare under this regulation compare to those under optimal regulation?

Answer

1. *Describe the optimally regulated outcome*: With optimal regulation, e_1, the price is set at p_1, where the market demand curve intersects the monopoly's marginal cost curve on the accompanying graph. The optimally regulated monopoly sells Q_1 units.

2. *Describe the outcome when the government regulates the price at p_2*: Where the market demand is above p_2, the regulated demand curve for the

---

[19]The monopoly produces at e_o only if the regulated price is greater than its average variable cost. Here the regulated price, $16, exceeds the average variable cost at 8 units of $8. Indeed, the firm makes a profit because the average cost at 8 units is $9.50.

	Monopoly with Optimal Regulation	**Monopoly with a Low Regulated Price**	**Change**
Consumer Surplus, CS	$A + B$	$A + C$	$C - B = \Delta CS$
Producer Surplus, PS	$C + D + E$	E	$-C - D = \Delta PS$
Welfare, $W = CS + PS$	$A + B + C + D + E$	$A + C + E$	$-B - D = \Delta W = DWL$

monopoly is horizontal at p_2 (up to Q_d). The corresponding marginal revenue curve, MR_r, is horizontal where the regulated demand curve is horizontal and equals the marginal revenue curve corresponding to the market demand curve, MR, where the regulated demand curve is downward sloping. The monopoly maximizes its profit by selling Q_2 units at p_2. The new regulated monopoly optimum is e_2, where MR_r intersects MC. The firm does not shut down when regulated as long as its average variable cost at Q_2 is less than p_2.

> 3. *Compare the outcomes*: The quantity that the monopoly sells falls from Q_1 to Q_2 when the government lowers its price ceiling from p_1 to p_2. At that low price, consumers want to buy Q_d, so there is excess demand equal to $Q_d - Q_2$. Compared to optimal regulation, welfare is lower by at least $B + D$.[20]

Problems in Regulating. Governments face several problems in regulating monopolies. First, because they do not know the actual demand and marginal cost curves, governments may set the price at the wrong level. Second, many governments use regulations that are less efficient than price regulation. Third, regulated firms may bribe or otherwise influence government regulators to help the firms rather than society as a whole.

Because of limited information about the demand and marginal cost curves, governments may set a price ceiling above or below the competitive level. Moreover, a regulatory agency may have to set the price higher than is optimal because it cannot offer a subsidy.

If the regulatory agency were to set the price equal to a natural monopoly's marginal cost, the price would be below the firm's average cost. The monopoly would threaten to shut down unless the regulatory agency were to subsidize it or raise the price.

To illustrate this problem, we calculate how setting the price too low would affect the electric power monopoly in Kyushu, Japan.[21] In the absence of regulation and in light of the curves in Figure 11.9, this firm maximizes its profit by operating where its marginal cost equals its marginal revenue, where it sells 23 billion kWh at ¥30.3 per hundred kWh and makes a profit equal to area A.

This firm would lose money if it faced a price ceiling of ¥19.5, where the demand curve intersects the marginal cost curve at 34 billion kWh. At that quantity, its average cost of ¥21.9 is greater than the price ceiling, and the firm loses an amount equal to area B. Thus if the government wants the firm to charge a price equal to marginal cost, it would have to subsidize the firm by at least B to keep it from shutting down.

Typically, it is politically infeasible for a government regulatory agency to subsidize a firm. Instead, the agency might set the price at ¥22.3, at which the demand curve intersects the average cost curve and the monopoly breaks even. There is still a deadweight loss because that price is above marginal cost, but the deadweight loss is smaller than if the monopoly were unregulated.

Unfortunately, regulation is often not effective when regulators are *captured*: influenced by the firms they regulate. Typically, this influence is more subtle than an

---

[20]The welfare loss is greater if unlucky consumers waste time trying to buy the good unsuccessfully or if goods are not allocated optimally among consumers. A consumer who values the good at only p_2 may be lucky enough to buy it, while a consumer who values the good at p_1 or more may not be able to obtain it.

[21]The cost curves in this example are based on the estimated short-run average cost curve in Nemoto, Nakanishi, and Madono (1993). To create an example of a possible demand curve, we assume that the demand is linear and that the electricity demand of Japanese consumers at the observed output is the same as that of American consumers (Maddock, Castano, and Vella, 1992).

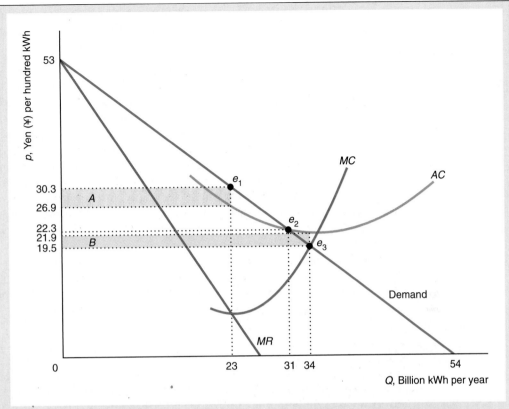

Figure 11.9 Regulating an Electric Utility. If the electric utility is an unregulated, profit-maximizing monopoly, e_1, it sets its output at 23 billion kWh and charges ¥30.3 per hundred kWh and makes a profit of area A. The government may regulate price so that the utility breaks even, e_2. Alternatively, the government may regulate the utility to behave like a price taker, e_3. If so, the government must subsidize the utility by area B to keep it from shutting down.

outright bribe. Many American regulators have worked in the industry before they became regulators and hence are sympathetic to those firms.[22] Many regulators hope to obtain good jobs in the industry eventually, so they don't want to offend potential employers. Other regulators, relying on industry experts for their information, may be misled or at least heavily influenced by the industry. For example, the California Public Utilities Commission urged telephone and cable companies to negotiate among themselves as to how they wanted to open local phone markets to

[22]For example, before his resignation in 1995, a California Public Utilities Commissioner (PUC) enjoyed friendly games of racquetball with a lobbyist for Southern California Edison Company, a utility that is regulated by the PUC. Another commissioner played golf with an Edison lobbyist as the pair toured England with top energy lobbyists on a trip paid for by a foundation with close ties to the California energy industry. California electricity rates were 50% above the national average at the time. (Sandoval, Ricardo, "PUC, Utilities: Too Close for Comfort?" *San Francisco Examiner*, March 26, 1995:B1.)

competition by 1997.[23] Arguing that these influences are inherent, some economists contend that price and other types of regulation are unlikely to result in efficiency.

Increasing Competition

Encouraging competition is an alternative to regulation as a means of reducing the harms of monopoly. When a government has created a monopoly by preventing entry, it can quickly reduce the monopoly's market power by allowing other firms to enter. As new firms enter the market, the former monopoly must lower its price to compete, so welfare rises. Many governments are actively encouraging entry into telephone, electricity, and other utility markets that were formerly monopolized.

Similarly, a government may end a ban on imports so that a domestic monopoly faces competition from foreign firms. If costs for the domestic firm are the same as costs for the foreign firms and there are many foreign firms, the former monopoly becomes just one of many competitive firms. As the market becomes competitive, consumers pay the competitive price, and the deadweight loss of monopoly is eliminated.

Governments around the world are increasing competition in formerly monopolized markets. For example, many U.S. and European governments are forcing former telephone and energy monopolies to compete. See www.awlonline.com/perloff, "Ending the Monopoly in Telephone Service" and "Deregulating Energy."

Application   **MONOPOLY IN NAMES**

The U.S. government established Network Solutions, Inc., as the exclusive registrar of Internet domain names in 1993. By 1999, this monopoly had registered 5 million names ending with **.com, .net,** and **.org** and was logging new domain names at a rate of 400,000 per month. It made large profits each year. In 1998 it posted an $11.2 million profit on revenue of almost $94 million. In the first half of 1999, its net income increased 135%, and its estimated value was $2.2 billion.

In the late 1990s, the U.S. government called for an end to this monopoly so as to lower price. Network Solutions struck a deal with the U.S. government whereby it retained control of the **.com** addresses, thought to be the crown jewel of Internet domains. The firm also agreed to pay the government $1.25 million, to reduce the wholesale price it charges rivals to enter new registrations into the Internet's main database from $9 to $6, and to provide public access to its directory.

In 1999, the U.S. government authorized some 70 registrar companies to compete with the original monopoly. One, Ipderdome, announced that it would charge $10 a year, well below Network Solutions' $35 annual fee ($70 fee for an initial two-year registration). Thus competition is expected to lower the monopoly pricing.

---

[23]Groves, Martha, "PUC Transfers Call on Open Phone Market," *Los Angeles Times*, December 22, 1994:D1.

> In the United Kingdom, the comparable registrar is the nonprofit Nominet (consisting of 1,000 members), which charges £80 per registration (about half again as much as the U.S. price) that ends in **co.uk**. A debate is raging as to whether to break up this organization and convert it to a competitive market.
>
> How important is a domain name, and how much is the monopoly right to use it worth? The right name is worth a lot. A 21-year-old named Eric MacIver, registered the name **Drugs.com**. After intensive bidding in 1999, he sold the name for $823,456. And the Internet search company AltaVista (owned by Compaq Computers), which did not own the Web address **www.altavista.com**, reportedly paid $3.3 million for that domain name in 1998.

Dominant Firm and Competitive Fringe

Sometimes when a monopoly ends, the former monopoly maintains a cost advantage over later entrants. Suppose that the government eliminates an import restriction and a number of foreign firms enter the market. These firms have higher costs than the domestic firm because of shipping costs. Each foreign firm is such a small part of the market that it acts as a price-taking competitive firm.

The former monopoly becomes a **dominant firm**: a price-setting firm that competes with price-taking firms. Small price-taking firms that compete with a dominant firm are called the **competitive fringe** (or *fringe*).

The dominant firm maximizes its profit given its cost curves and the demand curve it faces. Before the entry of the fringe, the monopoly faces the market demand curve, *D* in Figure 11.10. The fringe takes some of the market demand from the former monopoly. As a result, the demand curve the dominant firm faces after the fringe enters is a **residual demand curve**: the market demand that is not met by other sellers (the competitive fringe) at any given price (see Chapter 8).

The residual demand curve for the dominant firm is the horizontal difference between the market demand curve and the fringe supply curve: At any given price, p, the residual demand for the dominant firm, D^r, is

$$D^r(p) = D(p) - S^f(p),$$

where S^f is the supply curve of the fringe. As Figure 11.10 shows, the fringe supplies nothing at p_1 or any lower price, so the residual demand is the same as the market demand. At p^*, the residual demand is q_d^*, which equals the market demand, Q^*, minus the fringe supply, Q_f^*. At p_2, the fringe supplies as much as the market demands (S^f intersects D at p_2), so the residual demand is zero.

The dominant firm's marginal revenue curve is MR^r, which corresponds to the residual demand curve, D^r. The dominant firm maximizes its profit at point d by setting a price of p^*, where it sells q_d^* units—the quantity where MR^r intersects its marginal cost curve, MC^d. The fringe sells Q_f^* for p^*, at point f. At the market equilibrium, point e, the total amount that the dominant firm and the fringe sell, $q_d^* + Q_p^*$, equals the quantity the market demands at that price, Q^*, so neither consumers nor producers want to change their behavior.

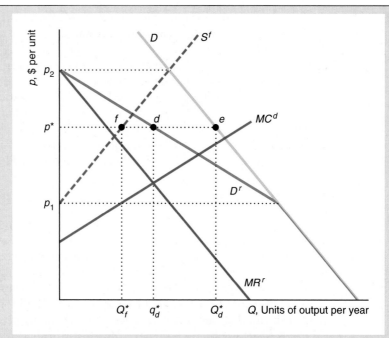

Figure 11.10 Dominant Firm–Competitive Fringe Equilibrium. The residual demand for the dominant firm, D^r, is the horizontal difference between the market demand curve, D, and the supply curve of the fringe firms, S^f. The dominant firm maximizes its profit at d by setting a price of p^* and selling q_d units where its residual demand curve, MR^r, intersects its marginal cost curve, MC^d. The fringe operates at point f, and the market equilibrium is point e.

Because of the upward-sloping supply curve of the fringe, the dominant firm's residual demand curve, D^r, lies below and is flatter than the market demand curve, D, that the monopoly faced. As a result, the dominant firm faces a more elastic demand than the monopoly did, which causes the dominant firm to set a lower price. At this lower price, consumers demand more, and the dominant firm and the fringe produce more collectively than the monopoly did alone. Thus the fringe erodes but does not eliminate the dominant firm's market power. Consumers benefit from the entry of the fringe, and some, but not all, of the deadweight loss under monopoly is eliminated.

Summary

1. **Monopoly profit maximization:** Like any firm, a monopoly—a single seller—maximizes its profit by setting its output so that its marginal revenue equals its marginal cost. The monopoly makes a positive profit if its average cost is less than the price at the profit-maximizing output.

2. **Market power:** Market power is the ability of a firm to charge a price above marginal cost and earn a positive profit. The more elastic the demand the monopoly faces at the quantity at which it maxi-

mizes its profit, the closer its price to its marginal cost and the closer the Lerner Index or price markup, $(p - MC)/p$, to zero, the competitive level.

3. **Effects of a shift of the demand curve:** Because a monopoly does not have a supply curve, the effect of a shift in demand on a monopoly's output depends on the shapes of both its marginal cost curve and its demand curve. As a monopoly's demand curve shifts, price and output may change in the same direction or different directions.

4. **Welfare effects of monopoly:** Because a monopoly's price is above its marginal cost, too little output is produced, and society suffers a deadweight loss. The monopoly makes higher profit than it would if it acted as a price taker. Consumers are worse off, buying less output at a higher price.

5. **Cost advantages that create monopolies:** A firm may be a monopoly if it controls a key input, has superior knowledge about producing or distributing a good, or has substantial economies of scale.

In markets with substantial economies of scale, the single seller is called a natural monopoly because total production costs would rise if more than one firm produced.

6. **Government actions that create monopolies:** Governments may establish government-owned and -operated monopolies. They may also create private monopolies by establishing barriers to entry that prevent other firms from competing. Nations grant patents, which give inventors monopoly rights for a limited period of time.

7. **Government actions that reduce market power:** A government can eliminate the welfare harm of a monopoly by forcing the firm to set its price at the competitive level. If the government sets the price at a different level or otherwise regulates nonoptimally, welfare at the regulated monopoly optimum is lower than in the competitive equilibrium. A government can eliminate or reduce the harms of monopoly by allowing or facilitating entry.

Problems

1. Show that after a shift in the demand curve, a monopoly's price may remain constant but its output may rise.

2. What is the effect of a franchise (lump-sum) tax on a monopoly? (*Hint*: Consider the possibility that the firm may shut down.)

3. What is the effect of a profit tax on a monopoly? Assume the government takes γ fraction of the before-tax economic profit, π, and the monopoly maximizes the after-tax profit, $(1 - \gamma)\pi$.

4. When is a monopoly unlikely to be profitable? (*Hint*: Discuss the relationship between market demand and average cost.)

5. A monopoly has a constant marginal cost of production of $1 per unit and a fixed cost of $10. Draw the firm's *MC*, *AVC*, and *AC* curves. Add a downward-sloping demand curve, and show the profit-maximizing quantity and price. Indicate the profit as an area on your diagram. Show the deadweight loss.

6. Can a firm be a natural monopoly if it has a U-shaped average cost curve? Why or why not?

7. Can a firm operating in the upward portion of its average cost curve be a natural monopoly? Explain.

8. *Review* (Chapter 8): Show why a monopoly may operate in the upward- or downward-sloping section of its long-run average cost curve but a competitive firm will operate only in the upward-sloping section.

9. When will a monopoly set its price equal to its marginal cost?

10. Describe the effects on output and welfare if the government regulates a monopoly so that it may not charge a price above $\overline{p}$, which lies between the unregulated monopoly price and the optimally regulated price (determined by the intersection of the firm's marginal cost and the market demand curve).

★11. *Review* (Chapter 10): Suppose that many similar price-taking consumers (like Denise in Chapter 10) have a single good (candy bars) and that Jane has a monopoly in wood. Thus Jane can set prices. Assume that no production is possible. Using an Edgeworth box, illustrate the monopoly optimum and show that it does not lie on the contract curve (isn't Pareto efficient).

12. A monopoly drug company produces a lifesaving medicine at a constant cost of $10 per dose. The demand for this medicine is perfectly inelastic at prices less than or equal to the $100 (per day) income of the 100 patients who need to take this drug daily. At a higher price, nothing is bought. Show the equilibrium price and quantity and the consumer and producer surplus in a graph. Now the government imposes a price ceiling of $30. Show how the equilibrium, consumer surplus, and producer surplus change. What is the deadweight loss, if any, from this price control?

13. The price of wholesale milk dropped by 30.3% in 1999 as the Pennsylvania Milk Marketing Board lowered the regulated price. The price to consumers fell by substantially less than 30.3% in Philadelphia. Why? (*Hint*: Show that a monopoly will not necessarily lower its price by the same percentage as its constant marginal cost drops.)

14. Today, drug companies spend large sums to determine additional uses for their existing drugs. For example, GlaxoWellcome PLC, a pharmaceutical giant, learned that its drug bupropion hydrochloride is more effective than the nicotine patch for people trying to quit smoking. That drug is now sold as Zyban, but it was introduced in 1997 as an antidepressant, Wellbutrin. Projected 1999 sales were $250 million for Zyban and $590 million for Wellbutrin. Using a graph, show the demand curves for Wellbutrin and Zyban and the aggregate demand for this drug, buproprion hydrochloride. On the graph, indicate the quantity of pills sold for each use and total use at the current price. Why does Glaxo, the monopoly producer, set the same price, $1.16 a pill, for both drugs?

15. Suppose that the competitive fringe's supply curve is horizontal in the long run. Show and describe the resulting dominant firm–competitive fringe equilibrium.

16. Show that the deadweight loss is higher in a monopoly optimum than in a dominant firm–competitive fringe equilibrium.

Math Problems

★17. Show mathematically that a monopoly may raise the price to consumers by more than the specific tax imposed on it. (*Hint*: One approach is to consider a monopoly facing a constant-elasticity demand curve and a constant marginal cost, m.)

18. The inverse demand curve a monopoly faces is

$$p = 100 - Q.$$

The firm's cost curve is $C(Q) = 10 + 5Q$. What is the profit-maximizing solution?

19. How does your answer to Problem 18 change if $C(Q) = 100 + 5Q$?

20. The inverse demand curve a monopoly faces is

$$p = 10Q^{-\frac{1}{2}}.$$

The firm's cost curve is $C(Q) = 5Q$. What is the profit-maximizing solution?

★21. *Review* (Chapters 6 and 7): A monopoly's production function is Cobb-Douglas: $Q = L^{\frac{1}{2}}K^{\frac{1}{2}}$, where L is labor and K is capital. As a result, the marginal product functions are $MP_L = \frac{1}{2}K^{\frac{1}{2}}/L^{\frac{1}{2}}$ and $MP_K = \frac{1}{2}L^{\frac{1}{2}}/K^{\frac{1}{2}}$. The demand function is $p = 100 - Q$. The wage, w, is $1 per hour, and the rental cost of capital, r, is $4.

   a. What is the equation of the (long-run) expansion path? Illustrate in a graph.

   b. Derive the long-run total cost curve equation as a function of q.

   c. What quantity maximizes this firm's profit?

   d. Find the optimal input combination that produces the profit-maximizing quantity. Illustrate with a graph.

Pricing

Everything is worth what its purchaser will pay for it.
—Publilius Syrus (1st century B.C.)

Why does Disneyland charge local residents $28 but out-of-towners $38 for admission? Why are airline fares less if you book in advance and stay over a Saturday night? Why are some goods, among them computers and software, sold bundled together at a single price? To answer these questions, we need to examine how monopolies set prices.

Monopolies (and other noncompetitive firms) can use information about individual consumers' demand curves to increase their profits. Instead of setting a single price, such firms use **nonuniform pricing**: charging consumers different prices for the same product or charging a single customer a price that depends on the number of units the customer buys. By replacing a single price with nonuniform pricing, the firm raises its profit.

Why can a monopoly earn a higher profit from using a nonuniform pricing scheme than from setting a single price? A monopoly that uses nonuniform prices can capture some or all of the consumer surplus and deadweight loss that results if the monopoly sets a single price. As we saw in Chapter 11, a monopoly that sets a high single price only sells to the customers who value the good the most, and those customers retain some consumer surplus. The monopoly loses sales to other customers who value the good less than the single price. These lost sales are a *deadweight loss*: the value of these potential sales in excess of the cost of producing the good. A monopoly that uses nonuniform pricing captures additional consumer surplus by raising the price to customers that value the good the most. By lowering its price to other customers, the monopoly makes additional sales, thereby changing what would otherwise be deadweight loss into profit.

We examine several types of nonuniform pricing including price discrimination, two-part tariffs, and tie-in sales. The most common form of nonuniform pricing is **price discrimination**, whereby a firm charges consumers different prices for the same good. Many magazines price discriminate by charging college students less for subscriptions than they charge older adults. If a magazine were to start setting a high price for everyone, many college student subscribers—who are sensitive to price increases (have relatively elastic demands)—would cancel their subscriptions. If the magazine were to let everyone buy at the college student price, it would gain few additional subscriptions because most potential older adult subscribers are relatively insensitive to the price, and it would earn less from those older adults who are willing to pay the higher price. Thus the magazine makes more profit by price discriminating.

Some noncompetitive firms that cannot practically price discriminate use other forms of nonuniform pricing to increase profits. One method is for a firm to charge a *two-part tariff*, whereby a customer pays one fee for the right to buy the good and another price for each unit purchased. Health club members pay an annual fee to join the club and then shell out an additional amount each time they use the facilities.

Another type of nonlinear pricing is a *tie-in sale*, whereby a customer may buy one good only if also agreeing to buy another good or service. Vacation package deals may include airfare and a hotel room for a single price. Some restaurants provide only full-course dinners: a single price buys an appetizer, a main dish, and dessert. A firm may sell copiers under the condition that customers agree to buy all future copier service and supplies from it.

IN THIS CHAPTER, WE EXAMINE SIX MAIN TOPICS	1. **Why and how firms price discriminate:** A firm can increase its profit by price discriminating if it has market power, can identify which customers are more price sensitive than others, and can prevent customers who pay low prices from reselling to those who pay high prices. 2. **Perfect price discrimination:** If a monopoly can charge the maximum each customer is willing to pay for each unit of output, the monopoly captures all potential consumer surplus, and the efficient (competitive) level of output is sold. 3. **Quantity discrimination:** Some firms profit by charging different prices for large purchases than for small ones, which is a form of price discrimination. 4. **Multimarket price discrimination:** Firms that cannot perfectly price discriminate may charge a group of consumers with relatively elastic demands a lower price than other groups of consumers. 5. **Two-part tariffs:** By charging consumers a fee for the right to buy any number of units and a price per unit, firms earn higher profits than they do by charging a single price per unit. 6. **Tie-in sales:** By requiring a customer to buy a second good or service along with the first, firms make higher profits than they do by selling the goods or services separately.

12.1 WHY AND HOW FIRMS PRICE DISCRIMINATE

Until now, we've examined how a monopoly sets its price if it charges all its customers the same price. However, many noncompetitive firms increase their profits by charging *nonuniform prices*, which vary across customers. We start by studying the most common form of nonuniform pricing: price discrimination.

Why Price Discrimination Pays

For almost any good or service, some consumers are willing to pay more than others. A firm that sets a single price faces a trade-off between charging consumers who really want the good as much as they are willing to pay and charging a low enough price that the firm doesn't lose sales to less enthusiastic customers. As a result, the firm usually sets an intermediate price. A price-discriminating firm that varies its prices across customers avoids this trade-off.

A firm earns a higher profit from price discrimination than from uniform pricing for two reasons. First, a price-discriminating firm charges a higher price to customers who are willing to pay more than the uniform price, capturing some or all of their consumer surplus—the difference between what a good is worth to a consumer and what the consumer paid—under uniform pricing. Second, a price-discriminating firm sells to some people who were not willing to pay as much as the uniform price.

We use a pair of extreme examples to illustrate the two benefits of price discrimination to firms—capturing more of the consumer surplus and selling to more customers. These examples are extreme in the sense that the firm sets a uniform price at the price the most enthusiastic consumers are willing to pay or at the price the least enthusiastic consumers are willing to pay, rather than at an intermediate level.

Suppose that the only movie theater in town has two types of patrons: college students and senior citizens. The college student will see the Saturday night movie if the price is $10 or less, and the senior citizens will attend if the price is $5 or less. For simplicity, we assume that there is no cost in showing the movie, so profit is the same as revenue. The theater is large enough to hold all potential customers, so the marginal cost of admitting one more customer is zero. Table 12.1 shows how pricing affects the theater's profit.

In panel a, there are 10 college students and 20 senior citizens. If the theater charges everyone $5, its profit is $150 = $5 × (10 college students + 20 senior citizens). If it charges $10, the senior citizens do not go to the movie, so the theater makes only $100. Thus if the theater is going to charge everyone the same price, it maximizes its profit by setting the price at $5. Charging less than $5 makes no sense because the same number of people go to the movie as go when $5 is charged. Charging between $5 and $10 is less profitable than charging $10 because no extra seniors go and the college students are willing to pay $10. Charging more than $10 results in no customers.

At a price of $5, the seniors have no consumer surplus: They pay exactly what seeing the movie is worth to them. Seeing the movie is worth $10 to the college students, but they have to pay only $5, so each has a consumer surplus of $5, and their total consumer surplus is $50.

Table 12.1 A Theater's Profit Based on the Pricing Method Used

(a) No Extra Customers from Price Discrimination

Pricing	Profit from 10 College Students	Profit from 20 Senior Citizens	Total Profit
Uniform, $5	$50	$100	$150
Uniform, $10	$100	$0	$100
Price discrimination*	$100	$100	$200

(b) Extra Customers from Price Discrimination

Pricing	Profit from 10 College Students	Profit from 5 Senior Citizens	Total Profit
Uniform, $5	$50	$25	$75
Uniform, $10	$100	$0	$100
Price discrimination*	$100	$25	$125

*The theater price discriminates by charging college students $10 and senior citizens $5.
Notes: College students go to the theater if they are charged no more than $10. Senior citizens are willing to pay up to $5. The theater's marginal cost for an extra customer is zero.

If the theater can price discriminate by charging senior citizens $5 and college students $10, its profit increases to $200. Its profit rises because the theater makes as much from the seniors as before but gets an extra $50 from the college students. By price discriminating, the theater sells the same number of seats but makes more money from the college students, capturing all the consumer surplus they had under uniform pricing. Neither group of customers has any consumer surplus if the theater price discriminates.

In panel b, there are 10 college students and 5 senior citizens. If the theater must charge a single price, it charges $10. Only college students see the movie, so the theater's profit is $100. (If it charges $5, both students and seniors go to the theater, but its profit is only $75.) If the theater can price discriminate and charge seniors $5 and college students $10, its profit increases to $125. Here the gain from price discrimination comes from selling extra tickets to seniors (not from making more money on the same number of tickets, as in panel a). The theater earns as much from the students as before and makes more from the seniors, and neither group enjoys consumer surplus. These examples illustrate that firms can make a higher profit by price discriminating, either by charging some existing customers more or by selling extra units. Leslie (1997) finds that Broadway theaters increase their profits 5% by price discriminating rather than using uniform prices.

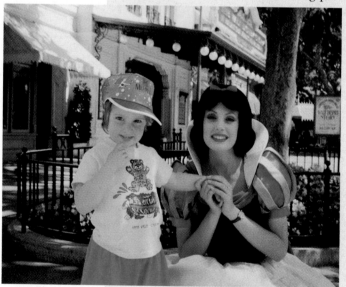

Application   DISNEYLAND PRICING

Disneyland, in southern California, is a well-run operation that rarely misses a trick when it comes to increasing profits. (Indeed, Disneyland mints money: When you enter the park, you can exchange U.S. currency for Disney dollars, which can be spent only in the park.)[1]

In 1998, Disneyland charged most adults $38 to enter the park but charged southern Californians only $28. This policy makes sense if visitors from afar are willing to pay more than locals and if Disneyland can prevent locals from selling discount tickets to nonlocals. Imagine a Midwesterner who's never been to Disneyland before and wants to visit. Travel accounts for most of the cost of the trip, so an extra $10 for entrance to Disneyland makes little percentage difference in the

[1]Studies show that it costs an average of $350,000 to raise a child from cradle through college. Parents can cut that total in half, however: They don't *have* to take their kids to Disneyland.

total cost of a visit and hence doesn't greatly affect that person's decision whether or not to go. In contrast, for a local who has gone to Disneyland many times and for whom the entrance price is a larger share of the cost of the visit, a slightly higher price might prevent a visit.

Charging both groups the same price is not in Disney's best interest. If Disney were to charge the higher price to everyone, many locals would stay away. If Disney were to use the lower price for everyone, it would be charging nonresidents much less than they are willing to pay.

By setting different prices for the two groups, Disney increases its profit if it can prevent the locals from selling discount tickets to others. Disney prevents resales by checking a purchaser's driver's license and requiring that the ticket be used for same-day entrance.

Who Can Price Discriminate

Not all firms can price discriminate. For a firm to price discriminate successfully, three conditions must be met.

First, a firm must have *market power*; otherwise, it cannot charge any consumer more than the competitive price. A monopoly, an oligopoly firm, a monopolistically competitive firm, or a cartel may be able to price discriminate. A competitive firm cannot price discriminate.

Second, consumers must *differ* in their sensitivity to price (demand elasticities), and a firm must be able to *identify* how consumers differ in this sensitivity.[2] The movie theater knows that college students and senior citizens differ in their willingness to pay for a ticket, and Disneyland knows that tourists and natives differ in their willingness to pay for admission. In both cases, the firms can identify members of these two groups by using driver's licenses or other forms of identification. Similarly, if a firm knows that each individual's demand curve slopes downward, it may charge each customer a higher price for the first unit of a good than for subsequent units.

Third, a firm must be able to *prevent or limit resales* to higher-price-paying customers by customers whom the firm charges relatively low prices. Price discrimination doesn't work if resales are easy because the firm would be able to make only low-price sales. A movie theater can charge different prices because senior citizens, who enter the theater as soon as they buy the ticket, do not have time to resell it.

Except for competitive firms, the first two conditions—market power and ability to identify groups with different price sensitivities—frequently hold. Usually, the biggest obstacle to price discrimination is a firm's inability to prevent resales. In some markets, however, resales are inherently difficult or impossible, firms can take actions that prevent resales, or government actions or laws prevent resales.

---

[2]Even if consumers are identical, price discrimination is possible if each consumer has a downward-sloping demand curve for the monopoly's product. To price discriminate over the units purchased by a consumer, the monopoly has to know how the elasticity of demand varies with the number of units purchased.

Preventing Resales

Resales are difficult or impossible for most *services* and when *transaction costs are high*. If a plumber charges you less than your neighbor for clearing a pipe, you cannot make a deal with your neighbor to resell this service. The higher the transaction costs a consumer must incur to resell a good, the less likely that resales will occur. Suppose that you are able to buy a jar of pickles for $1 less than the usual price. Could you practically find and sell this jar to someone else, or would the transaction costs be prohibitive? The more valuable a product or the more widely consumed it is, the more likely it is that transaction costs are low enough that resales occur.

Some firms act to raise transaction costs or otherwise make resales difficult. If your college requires that someone with a student ticket must show a student identification card with a picture on it before being admitted to a sporting event, you'll find it difficult to resell your low-price tickets to nonstudents, who must pay higher prices. When students at some universities buy computers at lower-than-usual prices, they must sign a contract that forbids them to resell the computer.

Similarly, a firm can prevent resales by *vertically integrating*: participating in more than one successive stage of the production and distribution chain for a good or service. Alcoa, the former aluminum monopoly, wanted to sell aluminum ingots to producers of aluminum wire at a lower price than was set for producers of aluminum aircraft parts. If Alcoa did so, however, the wire producers could easily resell their ingots. By starting its own wire production firm, Alcoa prevented such resales and was able to charge high prices to firms that manufactured aircraft parts (Perry, 1980).

Governments frequently aid price discrimination by preventing resales. State and federal governments require that milk producers, under penalty of law, price discriminate by selling milk at a higher price for fresh use than for processing (cheese, ice cream) and forbid resales. Government *tariffs* (taxes on imports) limit resales by making it expensive to buy goods in a low-price country and resell them in a high-price country. In some cases, laws prevent such reselling explicitly. Under U.S. trade laws, certain brand-name perfumes may not be sold in the United States except by their manufacturers.

Not All Price Differences Are Price Discrimination

Not every seller who charges consumers different prices is price discriminating. Hotels charge newlyweds more for bridal suites. Is that price discrimination? Some hotel managers say no. They contend that honeymooners, unlike other customers, always steal mementos, so the price differential reflects an actual cost differential.

The price for all issues of *PC Magazine* magazine for a year is $109.78 if you buy it at the newsstand, $49.97 for a standard subscription, and $27.96 for a college student subscription. The difference between the newsstand cost and the standard subscription cost reflects, at least in part, the higher cost of selling at a newsstand rather than mailing the magazine directly to customers, so this price difference does not reflect pure price discrimination. The price difference between the standard subscription rate and the college student rate reflects pure price discrimination because the two subscriptions are identical in every respect except price.

Types of Price Discrimination	There are three main types of price discrimination. With **perfect price discrimination**—also called *first-degree price discrimination*—the firm sells each unit at the maximum amount any customer is willing to pay for it, so prices differ across customers, and a given customer may pay more for some units than for others.

With **quantity discrimination** (*second-degree price discrimination*), the firm charges a different price for large quantities than for small quantities, but all customers who buy a given quantity pay the same price. With **multimarket price discrimination** (*third-degree price discrimination*), the firm charges different groups of customers different prices, but it charges a given customer the same price for every unit of output sold. Typically, not all customers pay different prices—the firm sets different prices only for a few groups of customers. Because this last type of discrimination is the most common, the phrase *price discrimination* is often used to mean *multimarket price discrimination*.

In addition to price discriminating, many firms use other, more complicated types of nonuniform pricing. Later in this chapter, we examine two other frequently used nonuniform pricing methods—two-part tariffs and tie-in sales—that are similar to quantity discrimination.

12.2 PERFECT PRICE DISCRIMINATION

If a firm with market power knows exactly how much each customer is willing to pay for each unit of its good and it can prevent resales, the firm charges each person his or her **reservation price**: the maximum amount a person would be willing to pay for a unit of output. Such an all-knowing firm *perfectly price discriminates*. By selling each unit of its output to the customer who values it the most at the maximum price that person is willing to pay, the perfectly price-discriminating monopoly captures all possible consumer surplus. For example, the managers of the Suez Canal set tolls on an individual basis, taking into account many factors such as weather and each ship's alternative routes.[3]

We first show how a firm uses its information about consumers to perfectly price discriminate. We then compare the perfectly price-discriminating monopoly to competition and single-price monopoly. By showing that the same quantity is produced as would be produced by a competitive market and that the last unit of output sells for the marginal cost, we demonstrate that perfect price discrimination is efficient. We then illustrate how the perfect price discrimination equilibrium differs from single-price monopoly by using the Tagamet application from Chapter 11. Finally, we discuss how firms obtain the information they need to perfectly price discriminate.

How a Firm Perfectly Price Discriminates	Suppose that a monopoly has market power, can prevent resales, and has enough information to perfectly price discriminate. The monopoly sells each unit at its

---

[3]Jehl, Douglas, "Trying to Revive a Canal That Is Out of the Loop," *New York Times*, April 30, 1997:A4.

reservation price, which is the height of the demand curve: the maximum price consumers will pay for a given amount of output.

Figure 12.1 illustrates how this perfectly price-discriminating firm maximizes its profit (see Appendix 12A for a mathematical treatment). The figure shows that the first customer is willing to pay $6 for a unit, the next is willing to pay $5, and so forth. This perfectly price-discriminating firm sells its first unit of output for $6. Having sold the first unit, the firm can get at most $5 for its second unit. The firm must drop its price by $1 for each successive unit it sells.

A perfectly price-discriminating monopoly's marginal revenue is the same as its price. As the figure shows, the firm's marginal revenue is $MR_1 = \$6$ on the first unit, $MR_2 = \$5$ on the second unit, and $MR_3 = \$4$ on the third unit. As a result, *the firm's marginal revenue curve is its demand curve.*

This firm has a constant marginal cost of $4 per unit. It pays for the firm to produce the first unit because the firm sells that unit for $6, so its marginal revenue

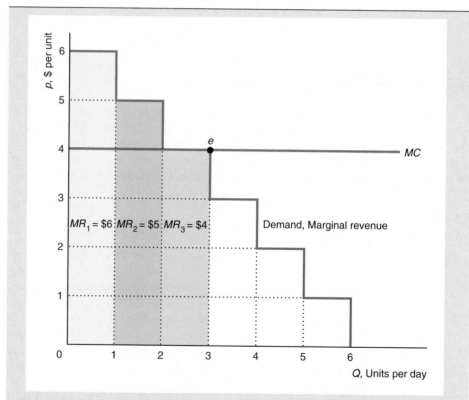

Figure 12.1 Perfect Price Discrimination. The monopoly can charge $6 for the first unit, $5 for the second, and $4 for the third, as the demand curve shows. Its marginal revenue is $MR_1 = \$6$ for the first unit, $MR_2 = \$5$ for the second unit, and $MR_3 = \$4$ for the third unit. Thus the demand curve is also the marginal revenue curve. Because the firm's marginal and average cost is $4 per unit, it is unwilling to sell at a price below $4, so it sells 3 units, point *e*, and breaks even on the last unit.

exceeds its marginal cost by \$2. Similarly, the firm certainly wants to sell the second unit for \$5, which also exceeds its marginal cost. The firm breaks even when it sells the third unit for \$4. The firm is unwilling to sell more than 3 units because its marginal cost would exceed its marginal revenue on all successive units. Thus like any profit-maximizing firm, a perfectly price-discriminating firm produces at point *e*, where its marginal revenue curve intersects its marginal cost curve.

This perfectly price-discriminating firm earns revenues of $MR_1 + MR_2 + MR_3 = $ \$6 + \$5 + \$4 = \$15, which is the area under its marginal revenue curve up to the number of units, 3, it sells. If the firm has no fixed cost, its cost of producing 3 units is \$12 = \$4 × 3, so its profit is \$3.

Application   **A HOT SALE OF COKE**

Firms continually seek new methods to achieve near-perfect price discrimination. Some vending machines in Japan use wireless modems to adjust their prices according to outside temperature. In 1999, the Coca-Cola Company started testing a vending machine with a computer-chip brain that can automatically raise drink prices in hot weather or lower prices during off-hours to boost sales.

Perfect Price Discrimination: Efficient but Hurts Consumers

A perfect price discrimination equilibrium is efficient and maximizes total welfare, where welfare is defined as the sum of consumer surplus and producer surplus. As such, this equilibrium has more in common with a competitive equilibrium than with a single-price-monopoly equilibrium.

If the market in Figure 12.2 is competitive, the intersection of the demand curve and the marginal cost curve, *MC*, determines the competitive equilibrium at e_c, where price is p_c and quantity is Q_c. Consumer surplus is $A + B + C$, producer surplus is $D + E$, and there is no deadweight loss. The market is efficient because the price, p_c, equals the marginal cost, MC_c.

With a single-price monopoly (which charges all its customers the same price because it cannot distinguish among them), the intersection of the *MC* curve and the single-price monopoly's marginal revenue curve, MC_s, determines the output, Q_s. The monopoly operates at e_s, where it charges p_s. The deadweight loss from monopoly is $C + E$. This efficiency loss is due to the monopoly's charging a price, p_s, that's above its marginal cost, MC_s, so less is sold than in a competitive market.

A perfectly price-discriminating monopoly sells each unit at its reservation price, which is the height of the demand curve. As a result, the firm's marginal revenue curve, MR_d, is the same as its demand curve. The firm sells the first unit for p_1 to the consumer who will pay the most for the good. The firm's marginal cost for that unit is MC_1, so it makes $p_1 - MC_1$ on that unit. The firm receives a lower price and has a higher marginal cost for each successive unit. It sells the Q_d unit for p_c, where its marginal revenue curve, MR_d, intersects the marginal cost curve, *MC*, so it just covers its marginal cost on the last unit. The firm is unwilling to sell additional

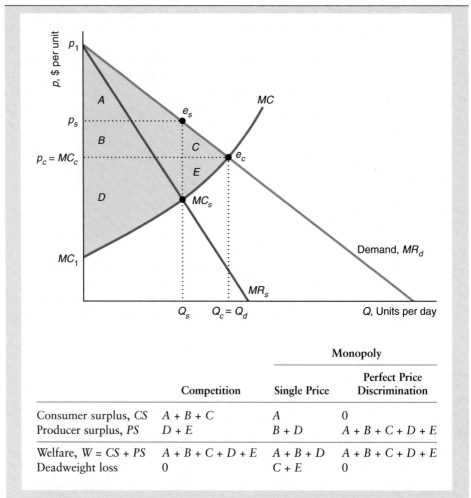

Figure 12.2 **Competitive, Single-Price, and Perfect Discrimination Equilibria.** In the competitive market equilibrium, e_c, price is p_c, quantity is Q_c, consumer surplus is $A + B + C$, producer surplus is $D + E$, and there is no deadweight loss. In the single-price monopoly equilibrium, e_s, price is p_s, quantity is Q_s, consumer surplus falls to A, producer surplus is $B + D$, and deadweight loss is $C + E$. In the perfect discrimination equilibrium, the monopoly sells each unit at the customer's reservation price on the demand curve. It sells Q_d ($= Q_c$) units, where the last unit is sold at its marginal cost. Customers have no consumer surplus, but there is no deadweight loss.

units because its marginal revenue would be less than the marginal cost of producing them.

The perfectly price-discriminating monopoly's total producer surplus on the Q_d units it sells is the area below its demand curve and above its marginal cost curve, $A + B + C + D + E$. Its profit is the producer surplus minus its fixed cost, if any. Consumers receive no consumer surplus because each consumer pays his or her

		Monopoly	
	Competition	Single Price	Perfect Price Discrimination
Consumer surplus, CS	$A + B + C$	A	0
Producer surplus, PS	$D + E$	$B + D$	$A + B + C + D + E$
Welfare, $W = CS + PS$	$A + B + C + D + E$	$A + B + D$	$A + B + C + D + E$
Deadweight loss	0	$C + E$	0

reservation price. The perfectly price-discriminating monopoly's equilibrium has *no deadweight loss* because the last unit is sold at a price, p_c, that equals the marginal cost, MC_c, as in a competitive market. Thus both a perfect price discrimination equilibrium and a competitive equilibrium are efficient.

The perfect price discrimination equilibrium differs from the competitive equilibrium in two ways. First, in the competitive equilibrium, everyone is charged a price equal to the equilibrium marginal cost, $p_c = MC_c$; however, in the perfect price discrimination equilibrium, only the last unit is sold at that price. The other units are sold at customers' reservation prices, which are greater than p_c. Second, consumers receive some welfare (consumer surplus, $A + B + C$) in a competitive market, whereas a perfectly price-discriminating monopoly captures all the welfare. Thus perfect price discrimination doesn't reduce efficiency—the output and total welfare are the same as under competition—but it does redistribute income away from consumers: consumers are much better off under competition.

Is a single-price or perfectly price-discriminating monopoly better for consumers? The perfect price discrimination equilibrium is more efficient than the single-price monopoly equilibrium because more output is produced. A single-price monopoly, however, takes less consumer surplus from consumers than a perfectly price-discriminating monopoly. Consumers who put a very high value on the good are better off under single-price monopoly, where they have consumer surplus, than with perfect price discrimination, where they have none. Consumers with lower reservation prices who purchase from the perfectly price-discriminating monopoly but not from the single-price monopoly have no consumer surplus in either case. All the social gain from the extra output goes to the perfectly price-discriminating firm. Consumer surplus is greatest with competition, lower with single-price monopoly, and eliminated by perfect price discrimination.

Application   TAGAMET REVISITED

We illustrate how perfect price discrimination differs from competition and single-price monopoly using the application from Chapter 11 of SmithKline's anti-ulcer drug, Tagamet. The graph shows a linear demand curve for Tagamet and a constant marginal cost (and average cost) of 7.5¢ per dose. If the market had been competitive (price equal to marginal cost at e_c), consumer surplus would have been $A + B + C \approx \$1.77$ million, and there would have been no producer surplus or deadweight loss.

In the single-price monopoly equilibrium, e_s, pharmacy customers paid 75¢ per daily dose, and 1.3 million daily doses of oral Tagamet were sold. The corresponding consumer surplus was $A \approx \$0.44$ million per day, producer surplus was $B \approx \$0.88$ million per day, and the deadweight loss was $C \approx \$0.44$ million per day.

Had SmithKline been able to perfectly price discriminate, its producer surplus would have nearly doubled to $A + B + C \approx \$1.77$ million per day, and consumers would have obtained no consumer surplus. The marginal consumer would have paid the marginal cost of 7.5¢, the same as in a competitive market.

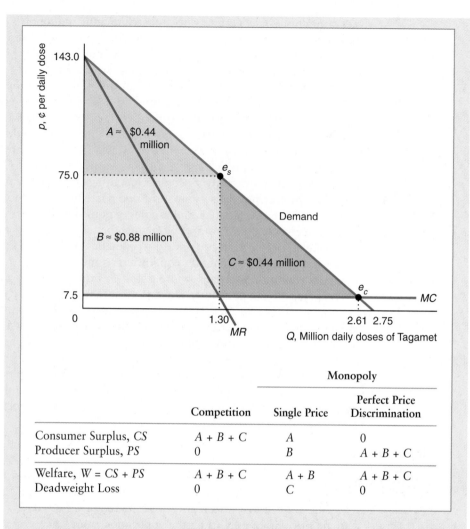

| | | Monopoly | |
	Competition	Single Price	Perfect Price Discrimination
Consumer Surplus, CS	A + B + C	A	0
Producer Surplus, PS	0	B	A + B + C
Welfare, W = CS + PS	A + B + C	A + B	A + B + C
Deadweight Loss	0	C	0

SmithKline's inability to perfectly price discriminate cost the company and society dearly. The profit of the single-price monopoly, $B \approx \$0.88$ million per day, is lower than that of a perfectly price-discriminating monopoly by about $A + C = \$0.88$ million per day, or $321 million per year. Similarly, society's welfare under single-price monopoly is lower than from perfect price discrimination by the deadweight loss of $0.44 million per day, or $161 million per year.

Solved Problem 12.1   How does welfare change if the movie theater described in Table 12.1 goes from charging a single price to perfectly price discriminating?

Answer

1. *Calculate welfare for panel a (a) if the theater sets a single price and (b) if it perfectly price discriminates, and (c) compare them*: (a) If the theater sets the profit-maximizing single price of $5, it sells 30 tickets and makes a profit of $150. The 20 senior citizen customers are paying their reservation price, so they have no consumer surplus. The 10 college students have reservation prices of $10, so their consumer surplus is $50. Thus welfare is $200: the sum of the profit, $150, and the consumer surplus, $50. (b) If the firm perfectly price discriminates, it charges seniors $5 and college students $10. Because the theater is charging all customers their reservation prices, there is no consumer surplus. The firm's profit rises to $200. (c) Thus *welfare is the same under both pricing systems where output stays the same.*

2. *Calculate welfare for panel b (a) if the theater sets a single price and (b) if it perfectly price discriminates, and (c) compare them*: (a) If the theater sets the profit-maximizing single price of $10, only college students attend and have no consumer surplus. The theater's profit is $100, so total welfare is $100. (b) With perfect price discrimination, there is no consumer surplus, but profit increases to $125, so welfare rises to $125. (c) Thus *welfare is greater with perfect price discrimination where output increases.* (The result that welfare increases if and only if output rises holds generally.)

Transaction Costs and Perfect Price Discrimination

Although some firms come close to perfect price discrimination, many more firms set a single price or use another nonlinear pricing method. Transaction costs are a major reason why these firms do not perfectly price discriminate: It is too difficult or costly to gather information about each customer's price sensitivity. Recent advances in computer technologies, however, have lowered these costs, causing hotels, car and truck rental companies, cruise lines, and airlines to price discriminate more often.

Private colleges request and receive financial information from students, which allows the schools to nearly perfectly price discriminate. The schools give partial scholarships as a means of reducing tuition to relatively poor students.

Many auto dealerships try to increase their profit by perfectly price discriminating, charging each customer the most that customer is willing to pay. These firms hire salespeople to ascertain potential customers' willingness to pay for a car and to bargain with them. Not all car companies believe that it pays to price discriminate in this way, however. As we saw in Chapter 1, Saturn charges all customers the same price, believing that the transaction costs (including wages of salespeople) of such information gathering and bargaining exceeds the benefits to the firm of charging customers differential prices.

Many other firms believe that, taking the transaction costs into account, it pays to use quantity discrimination, multimarket price discrimination, or other nonlinear pricing methods rather than try to perfectly price discriminate. We now turn to these alternative approaches.

12.3 | QUANTITY DISCRIMINATION

Many firms are unable to determine which customers have the highest reservation prices. Such firms may know, however, that most customers are willing to pay more for the first unit than for successive units: The typical customer's demand curve is downward sloping. Such a firm can price discriminate by letting the price each customer pays vary with the number of units the customer buys. Here the price varies only with quantity: All customers pay the same price for a given quantity.

Not all quantity discounts are a form of price discrimination. Some reflect the reduction in a firm's cost with large-quantity sales. For example, the cost per ounce of selling a soft drink in a large cup is less than that of selling it in a smaller cup; the cost of cups varies little with size, and the cost of pouring and serving is the same. A restaurant offering quantity discounts on drinks may be passing on actual cost savings to larger purchasers rather than price discriminating. However, if the quantity discount is not due to cost differences, the firm is engaging in quantity discrimination. Moreover, a firm may quantity discriminate by charging customers who make large purchases more per unit than those who make small purchases.

Many utilities use *block-pricing* schedules, by which they charge one price for the first few units (a *block*) of usage and a different price for subsequent blocks. Both declining-block and increasing-block pricing are common.

The utility monopoly in Figure 12.3 faces a linear demand curve for each customer. The demand curve hits the vertical axis at $90 and the horizontal axis at 90 units. The monopoly has a constant marginal and average cost of $m = \$30$. Panel a shows how this monopoly maximizes its profit if it can quantity discriminate by setting two prices. The firm uses declining-block prices to maximize its profit. It sells 40 units, charging $70 on the first 20 units (the first block) and $50 per unit for additional units (see Appendix 12B).

If the monopoly can set only a single price (panel b), it produces where its marginal revenue equals its marginal cost, selling 30 units at $60 per unit. Thus by quantity discriminating instead of using a single price, the utility sells more units, 40 instead of 30, and makes a higher profit, $B = \$1,200$ instead of $F = \$900$. With quantity discounting, consumer surplus is lower, $A + C = \$400$ instead of $E = \$450$; welfare (consumer surplus plus producer surplus) is higher, $A + B + C = \$1,600$ instead of $E + F = \$1,350$; and deadweight loss is lower, $D = \$200$ instead of $G = \$450$. Thus in this example, the firm and society are better off with quantity discounting, but consumers as a group suffer.

The more block prices that the monopoly can set, the closer the monopoly can get to perfect price discrimination. The deadweight loss results from the monopoly setting a price above marginal cost so that too few units are sold. The more prices the monopoly sets, the lower the last price and hence the closer it is to marginal cost.[4]

---

[4]Math Problem 16 at the end of the chapter examines what happens if the monopoly uses three block prices. In this example, the three prices are $75, $60, and $45.

(a) Quantity Discrimination

(b) Single-Price Monopoly

	Quantity Discrimination	Single Price
Consumer Surplus, CS	$A + C = \$400$	$E = \$450$
Producer Surplus or profit, $PS = \pi$	$B = \$1,200$	$F = \$900$
Welfare, $W = CS + PS$	$A + B + C = \$1,600$	$E + F = \$1,350$
Deadweight Loss, DWL	$D = \$200$	$G = \$450$

Figure 12.3 Quantity Discrimination. If this monopoly engages in quantity discounting, it makes a larger profit (producer surplus) than it does if it sets a single price, and welfare is greater. (a) With quantity discounting, profit is $B = \$1,200$ and welfare is $A + B + C = \$1,600$. (b) If it sets a single price (so that its marginal revenue equals its marginal cost), the monopoly's profit is $F = \$900$, and welfare is $E + F = \$1,350$.

12.4 | MULTIMARKET PRICE DISCRIMINATION

Typically, a firm does not know the reservation price for each of its customers. But the firm may know which groups of customers are likely to have higher reservation prices than others. The most common method of multimarket price discrimination is to divide potential customers into two or more groups and set a different price for each group. All units of the good sold to customers within a group are sold at a single price. As with perfect price discrimination, to engage in multimarket price discrimination, a firm must have market power, be able to identify groups with different demands, and prevent resales.

For example, first-run movie theaters with market power charge senior citizens a lower price than they charge younger adults because senior citizens are not willing to pay as much as others to see a movie. By admitting people as soon as they demonstrate their age and buy tickets, the theater prevents resales.

Multimarket Price Discrimination with Two Groups

Suppose that a monopoly sells to two groups of consumers and that resales between the two groups are impossible. The monopoly acts like a single-price monopoly with respect to each group separately and charges the groups different prices, thereby engaging in multimarket price discrimination.

We illustrate this behavior for a firm that sells to two groups of consumers, who are located in different countries. A patent gives Sony a legal monopoly to produce a robot dog that it calls Aibo ("eye-bo").[5] The pooch robot, which is about the size of a Chihuahua and has sensors in its paws and an antennalike tail, can sit, beg, chase balls, dance, and play an electronic tune. A camera and infrared sensor help the battery-powered pet judge distances and detect objects so that it can avoid walking into walls. Aibo has learning capabilities that enable the owner to influence its character by praising and scolding it. A sensor on its head can tell the difference between a friendly pat and a scolding slap. Aibo indicates that it's happy by wagging its tail or flashing its green LED eyes.

Sony started selling the toy in July 1999. At that time, the firm announced that it would sell 3,000 Aibo robots in Japan for about $2,000 each and a limited litter of 2,000 in the United States for $2,500 each. Why did it set different prices in the two countries? One possible explanation is that there are substantial extra costs to ship robots from Japan to the United States—but it is difficult to believe that the shipping costs amount to $500 more per pup.

An alternative and more plausible explanation is that Sony is engaging in multimarket price discrimination. That is, Sony is maximizing its profit by charging different prices in the two countries because it believes that the elasticities of demand differ.[6] Presumably, the cost to individuals of reselling Aibos purchased in Japan to customers in the United States is prohibitively high, so that Sony can ignore the problem of resales.

---

[5] Zaun, Todd, "Sony Unveils Robot Dog," www.sfgate.com/cgi-bin/article.cgi?file=/news/archive/1999/05/11/international1101EDT0557.DTL, May 11, 1999; Sullivan, Kevin, "Wonder Pup's Bark Depends on Byte; Robot Version of Man's Best Friend Is Japanese Techno-Sensation," *Washington Post*, May 13, 1999:A19; Guernsey, Lisa, "A Smart Dog with Megabytes," *New York Times*, May 13, 1999:G9; www.world.sony.com/robot; www.sony.co.jp/robot.

[6] Our belief that Aibo's U.S.-Japanese price differential is primarily due to unequal demand elasticities rather than to additional shipping costs is strengthened by observing that Sony sometimes charges lower prices for other products in Japan than in the United States. For example, a Sony Walkman AM/FM cassette player sold for 5.25 times as much in Japan as in the United States. (Sterngold, James, "Making Japan Cheaper for the Japanese," *New York Times*, August 29, 1993:6).

Sony charges Japanese consumers p_J for Q_J units, so its revenue is $p_J Q_J$. If Sony has the same constant marginal and average cost, m, in both countries, its profit (ignoring any sunk development costs) from selling robots in Japan is $\pi_J = p_J Q_J - mQ_J$, where mQ_J is its cost of producing Q_J units. Sony wants to maximizes its combined profit, π, which is the sum of its profits, π_J and π_{US}, in the two countries:

$$\pi = \pi_J + \pi_{US} = [p_J Q_J - mQ_J] + [p_{US}Q_{US} - mQ_{US}].$$

How should Sony set its prices p_J and p_{US}—or equivalently, its quantities Q_J and Q_{US}—so that its combined profit, π, is maximized? Appendix 12C gives a mathematical answer. Here we use our understanding of a single-price monopoly's behavior to answer this question graphically.

A multimarket-price-discriminating monopoly with a constant marginal cost maximizes its total profit by maximizing its profit to each group separately. The firm does so by setting its quantities so that the marginal revenue for each group equals the common marginal cost, m, which we assume is $500. Panel a of Figure 12.4 shows

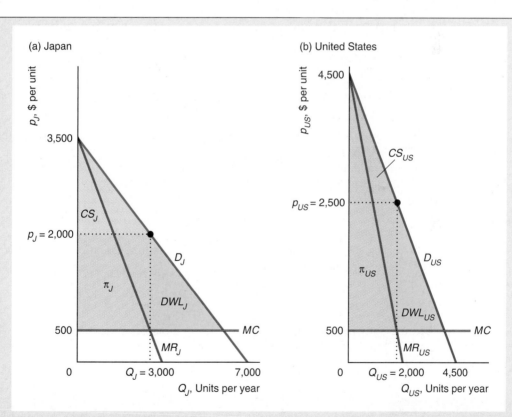

Figure 12.4 Multimarket Pricing of Aibo. Sony, the monopoly manufacturer of Aibo, charges more for its robot dog in the United States, $2,500, than in Japan, $2,000, presumably because the demand is relatively less elastic in the United States than in Japan. Sony operates where its marginal revenue in each country equals its marginal cost (assumed to be $500 in each country). As a result, in equilibrium, its marginal revenues are equal: $MR_J = \$500 = MR_{US}$.

that $MR_J = m = \$500$ at $Q_J = 3{,}000$ units and the resulting price is $p_J = \$2{,}000$ per robot. Similarly in panel b, $MR_{US} = m = \$500$ at $Q_{US} = 2{,}000$ units and the price is $p_{US} = \$2{,}500$, which is greater than p_J.

We know that this price-setting rule is optimal if the firm doesn't want to change its price to either group. However, would the monopoly like to lower its price and sell more output in Japan? If it did so, its marginal revenue would be below its marginal cost, so it would lose money. Similarly, if the monopoly sold less in Japan, its marginal revenue would be above its marginal cost. The same arguments can be made about the United States. Thus the price-discriminating monopoly maximizes its profit by operating where its marginal revenue for each country equals the firm's marginal cost.

Because the monopoly equates the marginal revenue for each group to its common marginal cost, $MC = m$, the marginal revenues for the two countries are equal:

$$MR_J = m = MR_{US}. \qquad (12.1)$$

We use Equation 12.1 to determine how the prices to the two groups vary with the price elasticities of demand, which reflect the shape of the demand curves. We can write each marginal revenue in terms of its corresponding price and the price elasticity of demand. For example, the monopoly's marginal revenue to Japan is $MR_J = p_J(1 + 1/\varepsilon_J)$, where ε_J is the price elasticity of demand for Japanese consumers. Rewriting Equation 12.1 using these expressions for marginal revenue, we find that

$$MR_J = p_J\left(1 + \frac{1}{\varepsilon_J}\right) = m = p_{US}\left(1 + \frac{1}{\varepsilon_{US}}\right) = MR_{US}. \qquad (12.2)$$

If $m = \$500$, $p_J = \$2{,}000$, and $p_{US} = \$2{,}500$ in Equation 12.2, the firm must believe that $\varepsilon_J = -4/3$ and $\varepsilon_{US} = -5/4$.

By rearranging Equation 12.2, we learn that the ratio of prices in the two countries depends only on the demand elasticities in those countries:

$$\frac{p_J}{p_{US}} = \frac{1 + 1/\varepsilon_{US}}{1 + 1/\varepsilon_J}. \qquad (12.3)$$

Substituting the prices and the demand elasticities into Equation 12.3, we confirm that Sony is pricing optimally:

$$\frac{p_J}{p_{US}} = \frac{\$2{,}000}{\$2{,}500} = 0.8 = \frac{1 + 1/(-5/4)}{1 + 1/(-4/3)} = = \frac{1 + 1/\varepsilon_{US}}{1 + 1/\varepsilon_J}.$$

Because Sony believes that the demand is one-ninth more elastic in Japan, it sets its price in Japan at only 80% of its U.S. price.

Solved Problem 12.2   A monopoly sells its good in the U.S. and Japanese markets. The American inverse demand function is $p_{US} = 100 - Q_{US}$, and the Japanese inverse demand function is $p_J = 80 - 2Q_J$, where both prices, p_{US} and p_J, are measured in dollars. The firm's marginal cost of production is $m = 20$ in both countries. If the firm can prevent resale,

what price will it charge in both markets? *Hint:* The monopoly determines its optimal (monopoly) price in each country separately because customers cannot resell the good.

Answer

1. *Determine the marginal revenue curve for each country*: The marginal revenue function corresponding to a linear inverse demand function has the same intercept and twice as steep a slope (Chapter 11). Thus the American marginal revenue function is $MR_{US} = 100 - 2Q_{US}$, and the Japanese one is $MR_J = 80 - 4Q_J$.

2. *Determine how many units are sold in each country*: To determine how many units to sell in the United States, the monopoly sets its American marginal revenue equal to its marginal cost, $MR_{US} = 100 - 2Q_{US} = 20$, and solves for the optimal quantity, $Q_{US} = 40$ units. Similarly, because $MR_J = 80 - 4Q_J = 20$, the optimal quantity is $Q_J = 15$ units in Japan.

3. *Substitute the quantities into the demand functions to determine the prices*: Substituting $Q_{US} = 40$ into the American demand function, we find that $p_{US} = 100 - 40 = \$60$. Similarly, substituting $Q_J = 15$ units into the Japanese demand function, we learn that $p_J = 80 - (2 \times 15) = \$50$. Thus the price-discriminating monopoly charges 20% more in the United States than in Japan.[7]

Application   **GENERICS AND BRAND-NAME LOYALTY**

We can apply what we've learned about how rival firms set prices and how firms with market power price discriminate to explain a phenomenon that otherwise is mysterious: *The prices of some brand-name pharmaceutical drugs rise when equivalent generic brands enter the market.* When a patent for a highly profitable drug expires, many firms produce generic versions. The government allows a firm to sell a generic product after a brand-name drug's patent protection expires only if the generic-drug firm can prove that its product delivers the same amount of active ingredient or drug to the body in the same way as the *brand-name* product.[8] Sometimes the same firm manufactures

---

[7]Using Equation 3.3, we know that the elasticity of demand in the United States is $\varepsilon_{US} = -p_{US}/Q_{US}$ and that in Japan it is $\varepsilon_J = -\frac{1}{2}p_J/Q_J$. At the equilibrium, $\varepsilon_{US} = -60/40 = -\frac{3}{2}$ and $\varepsilon_J = -50/(2 \times 15) = -\frac{5}{3}$. As Equation 12.3 shows, the ratio of the prices depends on the relative elasticities of demand:

$$p_{US}/p_J = 60/50 = (1 + 1/\varepsilon_J)/(1 + 1/\varepsilon_{US}) = (1 - \tfrac{3}{5})/(1 - \tfrac{2}{3}) = \tfrac{6}{5}.$$

[8]Generic drugs are a large and growing part of the pharmaceutical market. Forty percent of U.S. pharmaceutical sales by volume are for generic drugs, and total generic sales were $4.6 billion in 1996. By 2000, brand-name drugs with sales of about $34 billion had gone off patent.

both a brand-name drug and an identical generic drug, so the two have identical ingredients. Generics produced by other firms usually differ in appearance and name from the original product and may have different nonactive ingredients.

Most states have laws that allow (and 13 states require) a pharmacist to switch a prescription from a more expensive brand-name product to a less expensive generic equivalent unless the doctor or patient explicitly prohibits such a substitution. Many consumers, health maintenance organizations, and hospitals switch to the generics if they cost less than the brand-name drug.

What would you expect to happen when a generic enters the market? If consumers view the generic product and the brand-name product as perfect substitutes, entry by many firms will drive down the price—which is the same for both the name-brand drug and the generic drug—to the competitive level (see Chapter 8). Even if consumers view the goods as imperfect substitutes, you'd probably expect the price of the brand-name drug to fall.

Grabowski and Vernon (1992), however, find that entry by generics usually causes brand-name drug prices to rise. They examined 18 major orally administered drug products that faced generic competition between 1983 and 1987. They reported that, on average for each drug, 17 generic brands entered and captured 35% of total sales in the first year. During this period, the brand-name drug price *increased* by an average of 7% (but the average market price fell over 10% because the generic price was only 46% of the price of the brand-name drug).

One explanation for the rise in brand-name prices turns on the different elasticities of two groups of customers. Although some customers are price sensitive and willingly switch to less expensive generic drugs, others do not want to change brands. They prefer the brand-name drug because they are more comfortable with a familiar product, worried that new products may be substandard, or concerned that differences in the inactive ingredients might affect them. Elderly patients in particular are less likely to switch brands. A survey of the American Association of Retired Persons found that people aged 65 and older are 15% less likely than people aged 45 to 64 to request generic versions of a drug from their doctor or pharmacist.

Thus the introduction of generics makes the demand for the brand-name drug *less elastic* rather than more elastic, as usually happens when entry occurs. Before the generics enter, the brand-name drug is sold to both groups of consumers. When the generics become available, price-sensitive consumers stop buying the brand-name drug and switch to whichever generic drug is cheapest. The other consumers with less elastic demand do not switch. After the price-sensitive people switch to the generics, the demand for the brand-name drug is less elastic than before. As a result, the brand-name drug company raises its price after entry.

Thus differences in demands of these two groups explain both why brand-name drugs can charge higher prices than generics and why the price of the brand-name drug may increase after entry. They also explain why some firms sell both a brand-name drug at a relatively high price and an identical generic drug at a lower price so as to price discriminate.

Identifying Groups

Firms use two approaches to divide customers into groups. One method is to divide buyers into groups based on *observable characteristics* of consumers that the firm believes are associated with unusually high or low price elasticities. For example, movie theaters price discriminate using the age of customers. Similarly, some firms charge customers in one country higher prices than those in another country.[9] The antidepression drug Prozac sells for $2.27 in the United States, $1.07 in Canada, $1.08 in the United Kingdom, $0.82 in Australia, and $0.79 in Mexico. Various U.S. firms sell their products for more in Europe than in the United States, as Table 12.2 illustrates. These differences are much greater than can be explained by shipping costs and reflect multimarket price discrimination.

Another approach is to identify and divide consumers on the basis of their *actions*: The firm allows consumers to self-select the group to which they belong. For example, customers may be identified by their willingness to spend time to buy a good at a lower price or to order goods and services in advance of delivery.

Firms use differences in the value customers place on their time to discriminate by using queues (making people wait in line) and other time-intensive methods of selling goods. Store managers who believe that high-wage people are unwilling to "waste their time shopping" may run sales by which consumers who visit the store and pick up the good themselves get a low price while consumers who order over the phone or by mail pay a higher price. This type of price discrimination increases profit if people who put a high value on their time also have less elastic demands for the good.

Table 12.2 **Percentage by Which Europeans Pay More than Americans**			
	Britain	Germany	France
Levi's 501 jeans	74%	87%	60%
Compact disks	51%	20%	45%

Source: Lazich, Robert S., *World Cost of Living Survey*, 2nd Edition, Detroit, Michigan: The Gale Group, 1999.

[9]A firm can charge a higher price for customers in one country than in another if the price differential is too small for many resales between the two countries to occur or if governments enforce import or export restrictions to prevent resales between countries. See **www.awlonline.com/perloff**, "Gray Markets."

Firms draw on a variety of methods to induce consumers to indicate whether they have relatively high or low elasticities of demand. We examine three such approaches.

Coupons

Many firms use discount coupons to multimarket price discriminate. By doing so, they divide customers into two groups, charging those who are willing to use coupons less than those who won't clip coupons. Providing coupons makes sense if people who don't use coupons are less price sensitive on average than those who clip.[10] People who are willing to spend their time clipping coupons buy cereals and other goods at lower prices than those who value their time more. Coupon-using consumers paid $24 billion less than other consumers in the first half of the 1990s. In 1999, 256 billion grocery coupons were distributed in the United States, but only 2% were redeemed.

Airline Tickets

By choosing between two different types of tickets, airline customers indicate whether they are likely to be business travelers or vacationers. Airlines give customers a choice between high-price tickets with no strings attached and low-price fares that must be purchased long in advance and require the traveler to stay over a Saturday night.

Airlines know that many business travelers have little advance warning before they book a flight and are usually unwilling to stay away over a Saturday night. These business travelers have relatively inelastic demand curves: They want to travel at a specific time even if the price is relatively high. In contrast, vacation travelers can usually plan in advance and stay over a Saturday night. Because vacation travelers can drive, take trains or buses, or postpone trips, they have relatively high elasticities of demand for air travel. The choice that airlines give customers ensures that vacationers with relatively elastic demands obtain cheap seats while most business travelers with relatively inelastic demands buy high-price tickets (often more than four times higher than the plan-ahead rate). The expected absolute difference in fares between two passengers on a route is 36% of the airline's average ticket price (Borenstein and Rose, 1994).

Hotel Room Prices

Harris Rosen owns six hotels in Orlando, Florida. Believing that he maximizes his profit by keeping his hotel rooms filled, he cuts the price of a room over the day as necessary. Early in the day, the electronic message board outside his two

[10]As the Internet lowers transaction costs, some coupon clippers trade or sell their coupons to others, using sites such as **www.couponnet.com**. You can obtain discount coupons at **www.supermarkets.com** and **www.coolsavings.com**.

lowest-price hotels shows that a room rents at between $39 and $59. If there are vacancies late in the day, the sign changes to post a rate as low as $29.95.

Customers who are willing to wait until late in the day to book rooms get a lower rate. However, they risk not finding a vacancy at his inexpensive hotels. His hotels average a much higher occupancy rate—96% versus 79%—than those of his competitors, who are less likely to vary their prices over the day.[11]

Welfare Effects of Multimarket Price Discrimination

Multimarket price discrimination results in inefficient production and consumption. As a result, welfare under multimarket price discrimination is lower than that under competition or perfect price discrimination. Welfare may be lower or higher with multimarket price discrimination than with a single-price monopoly, however.

Multimarket Price Discrimination Versus Competition. Consumer surplus is greater and more output is produced with competition (or perfect price discrimination) than with multimarket price discrimination. In Figure 12.4, consumer surplus with multimarket price discrimination is CS_1 (for Group 1 in panel a) and CS_2 (for Group 2 in panel b). Under competition, consumer surplus is the area below the demand curve and above the marginal cost curve: $CS_1 + \pi_1 + DWL_1$ in panel a and $CS_2 + \pi_2 + DWL_2$ in panel b.

Thus multimarket price discrimination transfers some of the competitive consumer surplus, π_1 and π_2, to the monopoly as additional profit and causes the deadweight loss, DWL_1 and DWL_2, of some of the rest of the competitive consumer surplus. The deadweight loss is due to the multimarket-price-discriminating monopoly's charging prices above marginal cost, which results in reduced production from the optimal competitive level.

Multimarket Price Discrimination Versus Single-Price Monopoly. From theory alone, we can't tell whether welfare is higher if the monopoly uses multimarket price discrimination or if it sets a single price. Both types of monopolies set price above marginal cost, so too little is produced relative to competition. Output may rise as the firm starts discriminating if groups that did not buy when the firm charged a single price start buying. In the movie theater example in panel b of Table 12.1, welfare is higher with discrimination than with single-price monopoly because more tickets are sold when the monopoly discriminates (see Solved Problem 12.1).

The closer the multimarket-price-discriminating monopoly comes to perfectly price discriminating (say, by dividing its customers into many groups rather than just two), the more output it produces, so the less the production inefficiency there is. However, unless a multimarket-price-discriminating monopoly sells significantly more output than it would if it had to set a single price, welfare is likely to be lower with discrimination because of consumption inefficiency and time wasted shopping.

---

[11]Presumably, his competitors believe that it is impractical to change prices over the day because the transaction costs are too high, or they think that they can make more money by charging a relatively high price and having higher average levels of vacancies.

These two inefficiencies don't occur with a monopoly that charges all consumers the same price. As a result, consumers place the same marginal value (the single sales price) on the good, so they have no incentive to trade with each other. Similarly, if everyone pays the same price, consumers have no incentive to search for low prices.

Application   TAKING WOMEN TO THE CLEANERS

Under a 1995 law, California dry cleaners, hair salons, and other firms can no longer charge women a higher price than they charge men for the same services. Before passage of this law, prices frequently differed. At one San Francisco firm, cleaning a man's shirt cost $1.85, but cleaning a woman's blouse cost $7.70. One department store offered complimentary hemming for men's slacks and charged $8 to alter men's jackets while charging $15 to hem a skirt and $12 to take in a woman's jacket. Similarly, in 1999, the consumer advocacy group Penn-PIRG charged that female customers paid a price premium at 4 of 14 randomly surveyed dry cleaners and at 18 of 22 hair salons in Pennsylvania. Investigators found that some dry cleaners charged up to twice as much to launder a women's shirt as a man's.

Many firms argue that their price differences are due solely to cost differences. The California law allows firms to charge higher prices for services if they are more costly, difficult, or time consuming, such as cutting longer hair or laundering lace blouses.

For price differences to be due to price discrimination rather than disparities in costs, firms must have market power. A survey by the California state legislature before the law went into effect found that haircutting establishments that charged lower prices were more likely to charge men and women the same price. One possible explanation for why inexpensive firms charge men and women the same price is that these firms have no market power: They provide simple, nearly identical haircuts and act as price takers. In contrast, fancy establishments, whose services are viewed as differing from those of other firms, have market power and can price discriminate.

12.5   TWO-PART TARIFFS

We now turn to two other forms of second-degree price discrimination: *two-part tariffs* in this section and *tie-in sales* in the next one. Both are similar to the type of second-degree price discrimination we examined earlier because the average price per unit varies with the number of units consumers buy.

With a **two-part tariff**, the firm charges a consumer a lump-sum fee (the first tariff) for the right to buy as many units of the good as the consumer wants at a specified price (the second tariff). Because of the lump-sum fee, consumers pay more per unit if they buy a small number of goods than if they buy a larger number (see Math Problem 21 at the end of this chapter).

To get telephone service, you may pay a monthly connection fee and a price per minute of use. Some car rental firms charge a per-day fee and a price per mile driven. To buy season tickets to Oakland Raiders football games, a fan pays a fee of $250 to $4,000 for a "personal seat license," which gives the fan the right to buy season tickets for the next 11 years at a ticket price per game ranging between $40 and $60. The St. Louis Rams, Carolina Panthers, Jacksonville Jaguars, and other teams use similar two-part tariffs.

To profit from two-part tariffs, a firm must have market power, know how demand differs across customers or with the quantity that a single customer buys, and successfully prevent resales. We now examine two results. First, we consider how a firm uses a two-part tariff to extract consumer surplus (as in our previous price discrimination examples). Second, we see how, if the firm cannot vary its two-part tariff across its customers, its profit is greater the more similar the demand curves of its customers are.

We illustrate these two points for a monopoly that knows its customers' demand curves. We start by examining the monopoly's two-part tariff where all its customers have identical demand curves and then look at one where its customers' demand curves differ.

A Two-Part Tariff with Identical Consumers

If all the monopoly's customers are identical, a monopoly that knows its customers' demand curve can set a two-part tariff that has the same two properties as the perfect price discrimination equilibrium. First, the efficient quantity, Q_1, is sold because the price of the last unit equals marginal cost. Second, all consumer surplus is transferred from consumers to the firm.

Suppose that the monopoly has a constant marginal and average cost of $m = \$10$ (no fixed cost), and every consumer has the demand curve D^1 in panel a of Figure 12.5. To maximize its profit, the monopoly charges a price, p, equal to the constant marginal and average cost, $m = \$10$, and just breaks even on each unit sold. By setting price equal to marginal cost, it maximizes the *potential consumer surplus*: the consumer surplus if no lump-sum fee is charged. It charges the largest possible lump-sum fee, $\mathcal{L}$, which is the potential consumer surplus $A_1 + B_1 + C_1 = \$2,450$. Thus its profit is $2,450 times the number of customers.

Had the firm charged a higher per-unit price, it would sell fewer units and hence make a smaller profit. For example, if the monopoly charges $p = \$20$, it sells 60 units, making a profit from its unit sales of $B_1 = (\$20 - \$10)60 = \$600$. It must lower its fee to equal the new potential consumer surplus of $A_1 = \$1,800$, so its total profit per customer is only $2,400. It loses area $C_1 = \$50$ by charging the higher price. Similarly, had the monopoly charged a lower per-unit price, its profit would be lower: It would sell too many units and make a loss on each unit because its price would be below its marginal cost.

Because the monopoly knows the demand curve, it could instead perfectly price discriminate by charging each customer a different price for each unit purchased: the price along the demand curve. Thus this knowledgeable monopoly can capture all potential consumer surplus either by perfectly price discriminating or by setting its optimal two-part tariff.

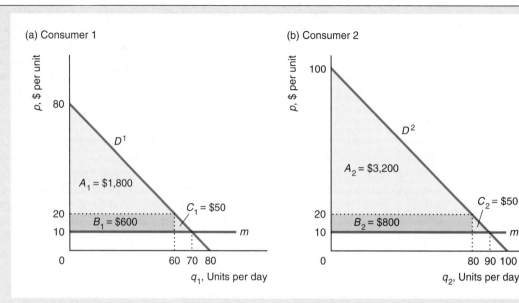

Figure 12.5 Two-Part Tariff. If all consumers have the demand curve in panel a, a monopoly can capture all the consumer surplus with a two-part tariff by which it charges a price, p, equal to the marginal cost, $m = \$10$, for each item and a lump-sum membership fee of $\mathcal{L} = A_1 + B_1 + C_1 = \$2,450$. Now suppose that the monopoly has two customers, Consumer 1 in panel a and Consumer 2 in panel b. If the monopoly can treat its customers differently, it maximizes its profit by setting $p = m = \$10$ and charging Consumer 1 a fee equal to its potential consumer surplus, $A_1 + B_1 + C_1 = \$2,450$, and Consumer 2 a fee of $A_2 + B_2 + C_2 = \$4,050$, for a total profit of \$6,500. If the monopoly must charge all customers the same price, it maximizes its profit at \$5,000 by setting $p = \$20$ and charging both customers a lump-sum fee equal to the potential consumer surplus of Consumer 1, $\mathcal{L} = A_1 = \$1,800$.

If the monopoly does not know its customers' demand curve, it must guess how high a lump-sum fee to set. This fee will almost certainly be less than the potential consumer surplus. If the firm sets its fee above the potential consumer surplus, it loses all its customers.

A Two-Part Tariff with Nonidentical Consumers

Now suppose that there are two customers, Consumer 1 and Consumer 2, with demand curves D_1 and D_2 in panels a and b of Figure 12.5. If the monopoly knows each customer's demand curve and can prevent resales, it can capture all the consumer surplus by varying its two-part tariffs across customers. However, if the monopoly is unable to distinguish between the types of customers or cannot charge consumers different prices, efficiency and profitability fall.

Suppose that the monopoly knows its customers' demand curves. By charging each customer $p = m = \$10$ per unit, the monopoly makes no profit per unit but sells the number of units that maximizes the potential consumer surplus. The monopoly then captures all this potential consumer surplus by charging Consumer 1 a lump-sum fee of $\mathcal{L}_1 = A_1 + B_1 + C_1 = \$2,450$ and Consumer 2 a fee of $\mathcal{L}_2 = A_2 + B_2 + C_2 = \$4,050$. The monopoly's total profit is $\mathcal{L}_1 + \mathcal{L}_2 = \$6,500$. By doing so, the monopoly maximizes its total profit by capturing the maximum potential consumer surplus from both customers.

Now suppose that the monopoly has to charge each consumer the same lump-sum fee, $\mathcal{L}$, and the same per-unit price, p. For example, because of legal restrictions, a telephone company charges all residential customers the same monthly fee and the same fee per call, even though the company knows that consumers' demands vary. As with multimarket price discrimination, the monopoly does not capture all the consumer surplus.

The monopoly charges a lump-sum fee, $\mathcal{L}$, equal to either the potential consumer surplus of Consumer 1, CS_1, or of Consumer 2, CS_2. Because CS_2 is greater than CS_1, both customers buy if the monopoly charges $\mathcal{L} = CS_1$, whereas only Consumer 2 buys if the monopoly charges $\mathcal{L} = CS_2$. The monopoly sets either the low lump-sum fee or the higher one, depending on which produces the greater profit.

Any other lump-sum fee would lower its profit. The monopoly has no customers if it charges more than $\mathcal{L} = CS_2$. If it charges between CS_1 and CS_2, it loses money on Consumer 2 compared to what it could earn by charging CS_2, and it still does not sell to Consumer 1. By charging less than $\mathcal{L} = CS_1$, it earns less per customer and does not gain any additional customers.

In our example, the monopoly maximizes its profit by setting the lower lump-sum fee and charging a price $p = \$20$, which is above marginal cost (see Appendix 12D). Consumer 1 buys 60 units, and Consumer 2 buys 80 units. The monopoly makes $(p - m) = (\$20 - \$10) = \$10$ on each unit, so it earns $B_1 + B_2 = \$600 + \$800 = \$1,400$ from the units it sells. In addition, it gets a fee from both consumers equal to the consumer surplus of Consumer 1, $A_1 = \$1,800$. Thus its total profit is $2 \times \$1,800 + \$1,400 = \$5,000$, which is $\$1,500$ less than if it could set different lump-sum fees for each customer. Consumer 1 has no consumer surplus, but Consumer 2 enjoys a consumer surplus of $\$1,400 (= \$3,200 - \$1,800)$.

Why does the monopoly charge a price above marginal cost when using a two-part tariff? By raising its price, the monopoly earns more per unit from both types of customers but lowers its customers' potential consumer surplus. Thus if the monopoly can capture each customer's potential surplus by charging different lump-sum fees, it sets its price equal to marginal cost. However, if the monopoly cannot capture all the potential consumer surplus because it must charge everyone the same lump-sum fee, the increase in profit from Customer 2 from the higher price more than offsets the reduction in the lump-sum fee (the potential consumer surplus of Customer 1).[12]

---

[12]If the monopoly lowers its price from $\$20$ to the marginal cost of $\$10$, it loses B_1 from Customer 1, but it can raise its lump-sum fee from A_1 to $A_1 + B_1 + C_1$, so its total profit from Customer 1 increases by $C_1 = \$50$. The lump-sum fee it collects from Customer 2 also rises by $B_1 + C_1 = \$650$, but its profit from unit sales falls by $B_2 = \$800$, so its total profit decreases by $\$150$. The loss from Customer 2, $-\$150$, more than offsets the gain from Customer 1, $\$50$. Thus the monopoly makes $\$100$ more by charging a price of $\$20$ rather than $\$10$.

Application   WAREHOUSE STORES

Warehouse clubs, such as Sam's Club, Price-Costco, and BJ's Wholesale Club, use two-part tariffs for their 24 million customers. They set a membership fee to shop at the store and then charge a low price for each item. For example, a Mr. Coffee 12-cup coffeemaker costs $50 at typical discount or department stores but $35 at a warehouse club; Scotch videotape that sells for $2.50 elsewhere is $1.75.

Such two-part tariffs are profitable only if the firm can prevent resales. If customers of such stores could easily resell such goods to their friends, one customer could pay the fixed membership fee, purchase a large number of goods, and then resell them to others so that the store collects only one membership fee. Particularly for relatively inexpensive items such as groceries and underwear, such resales are unlikely to be a practical problem. Apparently, even on larger items such as refrigerators, resales have not been a major problem, as these warehouses continue to sell them.

12.6 | TIE-IN SALES

Another type of nonlinear pricing is a **tie-in sale**, in which customers can buy one product only if they agree to purchase another product as well. There are two forms of tie-in sales.

The first type is a **requirement tie-in sale**, in which customers who buy one product from a firm are required to make all their purchases of another product from that firm. Some firms sell durable machines such as copiers under the condition that customers buy copier services and supplies from them in the future. Because the amount of services and supplies each customer buys differs, the per-unit price of copiers varies across customers.

The second type of tie-in sale is **bundling** (or a *package tie-in sale*), in which two goods are combined so that customers cannot buy either good separately. For example, a Whirlpool refrigerator is sold with shelves, and a Hewlett-Packard ink-jet printer comes in a box that includes both black and color printer cartridges.

Most tie-in sales increase efficiency by lowering transaction costs. Indeed, tie-ins for efficiency purposes are so common that we hardly think about them. Presumably, no one would want to buy a shirt without buttons, so selling shirts with buttons attached lowers transaction costs. Because virtually everyone wants certain basic software, most companies sell computers with this software already installed. Firms also often use tie-in sales to increase profits, as we now illustrate.

Requirement Tie-In Sales

Frequently, a firm cannot tell which customers are going to use its product the most and hence are willing to pay the most for the good. These firms may be able to use a requirement tie-in sale to identify heavy users of the product and charge them more.

Application   **IBM**

In the 1930s, IBM increased its profit by using a requirement tie-in. IBM produced card punch machines, sorters, and tabulating machines (precursors of modern computers) that computed by using punched cards. Rather than selling its card punch machines, IBM leased them under the condition that the lease would terminate if any card not manufactured by IBM were used. (By leasing the equipment, IBM avoided resale problems and forced customers to buy cards from it.) IBM charged customers more per card than other firms would have charged. If we think of this extra payment per card as part of the cost of using the machine, this requirement tie-in resulted in heavy users' paying more for the machines than others did. This tie-in was profitable because heavy users were willing to pay more.[13]

Bundling

Firms that sell two or more goods may use bundling to raise profits. Bundling allows firms that can't directly price discriminate to charge customers different prices. Whether bundling is profitable depends on customers' tastes and the ability to prevent resales.[14]

Imagine that you are in charge of selling season tickets for the local football team. Your stadium can hold all your potential customers, so the marginal cost of selling one more ticket is zero.

Should you bundle tickets for preseason (exhibition) and regular-season games, or should you sell books of tickets for the preseason and the regular season separately?[15] To answer this question, you have to determine how the fans differ in their desires to see preseason and regular-season games.

For simplicity, suppose that there are two customers (or types of customers). These football fans are so fanatical that they are willing to pay to see preseason exhibition games: There's no accounting for tastes!

Whether you should bundle depends on your customers' tastes. It does not pay to bundle in panel a of Table 12.3, in which Fan 1 is willing to pay more for both regular and preseason tickets than Fan 2. Bundling does pay in panel b, in which Fan 1 is willing to pay more for regular-season but less for exhibition tickets than Fan 2.

[13]The U.S. Supreme Court held that IBM's actions violated the antitrust laws because they lessened competition in the (potential) market for tabulating cards. IBM's defense was that its requirement was designed to protect its reputation. IBM claimed that badly made tabulating cards might cause its machines to malfunction and that consumers would falsely blame IBM's equipment. The Court did not accept IBM's argument. The Court apparently did not understand—or at least care about—the price discrimination aspect of IBM's actions.

[14]Preventing resale is particularly easy when a service is included. See **www.awlonline.com/perloff**, "Bundling Hardware with Software and Service."

[15]We assume that you don't want to sell tickets to each game separately. One reason for selling only season tickets is to reduce transaction costs. A second explanation is the same type of bundling argument that we discuss in this section.

Table 12.3 Bundling of Tickets to Football Games

(a) Unprofitable Bundle

	Regular Season	Preseason	Bundle
Fan 1	$2,000	$500	$2,500
Fan 2	$1,400	$100	$1,500
Profit-maximizing price	$1,400	$500	$1,500

(b) Profitable Bundle

	Regular Season	Preseason	Bundle
Fan 1	$1,700	$300	$2,000
Fan 2	$1,500	$500	$2,000
Profit-maximizing price	$1,500	$300	$2,000

To determine whether it pays to bundle, we have to calculate the profit-maximizing unbundled and bundled prices. We start by calculating the profit-maximizing unbundled prices in panel a. If you charge $2,000 for the regular-season tickets, you earn only $2,000 because Fan 2 won't buy tickets. It is more profitable to charge $1,400, sell tickets to both customers, and earn $2,800 for the regular season. By similar reasoning, the profit-maximizing price for the exhibition tickets is $500, at which you sell only to Fan 1 and earn $500. As a result, you earn $3,300 (= $2,800 + $500) if you do not bundle.

If you bundle and charge $2,500, you sell only to Fan 1. Your better option if you bundle is to set a bundle price of $1,500 and sell to both fans, earning $3,000. Nonetheless, you earn $300 more if you sell the tickets separately than if you bundle.

In this first example, in which it doesn't pay to bundle, the same customer who values the regular-season tickets the most also values the preseason tickets the most. In contrast, in panel b, the fan who values the regular-season tickets more values the exhibition season tickets less than the other fan does. Here your profit is higher if you bundle. If you sell the tickets separately, you charge $1,500 for regular-season tickets, earning $3,000 from the two customers, and $300 for preseason tickets, earning $600, for a total of $3,600. By selling a bundle of tickets for all games at $2,000 each, you'd earn $4,000. Thus you earn $400 more by bundling than by selling the tickets separately.

By bundling, you can charge the fans different prices for the two components of the bundle. Fan 1 is paying $1,700 for regular-season tickets and $300 for exhibition tickets, while Fan 2 is paying $1,500 and $500, respectively.[16] If you could per-

---

[16] As with price discrimination, you have to prevent resales for bundling to increase your profit. Someone could make a $198 profit by purchasing the bundle for $2,000, selling Fan 1 the regular-season tickets for $1,699, and selling Fan 2 the preseason tickets for $499. Each fan would prefer attending only one type of game at those prices to paying $2,000 for the bundle.

fectly price discriminate, you'd charge each consumer his or her reservation price for the preseason and regular-season tickets and would make the same amount as you do by bundling.

These examples illustrate that bundling a pair of goods pays only if their demands are *negatively correlated*: Customers who are willing to pay relatively more for regular-season tickets are not willing to pay as much as others for preseason tickets, and vice versa. When a good or service is sold to different people, the price is determined by the purchaser with the *lowest* reservation price. If reservation prices differ substantially across consumers, a monopoly has to charge a relatively low price to make many sales. By bundling when demands are negatively correlated, the monopoly reduces the dispersion in reservation prices, so it can charge more and still sell to a large number of customers.

Application AUTOMATIC SAVINGS

Instead of buying an already assembled automobile—a tie-in sale—you could purchase the parts individually and put the car together yourself. However, doing so would raise the cost substantially. The 1997 Taurus GL sold for $19,000 new but would cost $72,000 if assembled from spare Ford parts today, according to a trade group estimate.

Summary

1. **Why and how firms price discriminate:** A firm can price discriminate if it has market power, knows which customers will pay more for each unit of output, and can prevent customers who pay low prices from reselling to those who pay high prices. A firm earns a higher profit from price discrimination than from uniform pricing because (a) the firm captures some or all of the consumer surplus of customers who are willing to pay more than the uniform price and (b) the firm sells to some people who would not buy at the uniform price.

2. **Perfect price discrimination:** To perfectly price discriminate, a firm must know the maximum amount each customer is willing to pay for each unit of output. If a firm charges customers the maximum each is willing to pay for each unit of output, the monopoly captures all potential consumer surplus and sells the efficient (competitive) level of output. Compared to competition, total welfare is the same, consumers are worse off, and firms are better off under perfect price discrimination.

3. **Quantity discrimination:** Some firms charge customers different prices depending on how many units they purchase. If consumers who want more water have less elastic demands, a water utility can increase its profit by using declining-block pricing, in which the price for the first few gallons of water is higher than that for additional gallons.

4. **Multimarket price discrimination:** A firm that does not have enough information to perfectly price discriminate may know the relative elasticities of demand of groups of its customers. Such a profit-maximizing firm charges groups of consumers prices in proportion to their elasticities of demand, the group of consumers with the least elastic demand paying the highest price. Welfare is less under multimarket price discrimination than under competition or perfect price discrimination but may be greater or less than that under single-price monopoly.

5. **Two-part tariffs:** By charging consumers one fee for the right to buy and a separate price per unit,

Oligopoly and Monopolistic Competition

Anyone can win unless there happens to be a second entry.

—George Ade

When deciding how many Taurus sedans to produce, Ford considers how many Camry and Accord cars Toyota and Honda are likely to sell. Each of these firms closely monitors its rivals' past behavior—the number of cars sold, their pricing, and the cars' features—to predict their future behavior. Indeed, a firm may pay large sums to hire executives and engineers from a rival firm to gain insight into its competitor's decision making and planning.

Firms pay attention to each other's behavior in an **oligopoly**: a small group of firms in a market with substantial barriers to entry. Because relatively few firms compete in such a market, each can influence the price, and hence each affects rival firms. The need to consider the behavior of rival firms makes an oligopoly firm's profit-maximization decision more difficult than that of a monopoly or a competitive firm. A monopoly has no rivals, and a competitive firm ignores the behavior of individual rivals—it considers only the market price and its own costs in choosing its profit-maximizing output.

An oligopoly firm that ignores or inaccurately predicts its rivals' behavior is likely to suffer a loss of profit. As its rivals produce more cars, the price Ford can get for its cars falls. If Ford underestimates how many cars its rivals will produce, Ford may produce too many automobiles and lose money.

Oligopolistic firms may act independently or coordinate their actions. A group of firms that explicitly agree to coordinate their activities is called a **cartel**. These firms may agree on how much each firm will sell or on a common price. By cooperating and behaving like a monopoly, the members of a cartel collectively earn the monopoly profit—the maximum possible profit.

If oligopolistic firms do not collude, they earn lower profits. Nonetheless, because there are relatively few firms in the market, oligopolistic firms that act independently may earn positive economic profits in the long run, unlike competitive firms.

A barrier to entry keeps the number of firms small in an oligopolistic market. If a market has no barriers to entry, firms enter the market until profits are driven to zero. In perfectly competitive markets, enough entry occurs that firms face a horizontal demand curve and are price takers. However, in other markets, even after entry has driven profits to zero, each firm faces a downward-sloping demand curve. Because of this slope, the firm can charge a price above its marginal cost, creating a *market failure*: inefficient (too little) consumption (Chapter 9). **Monopolistic competition** is a market structure in which firms have market power (the ability to raise price profitably above marginal cost) but no additional firm can enter and earn positive profits.

In this chapter, we examine cartelized, oligopolistic, and monopolistically competitive markets in which firms set quantities or prices. As noted in Chapter 11, the monopoly equilibrium is the same whether a monopoly sets price or quantity. Similarly, if colluding oligopolies sell identical products, the cartel equilibrium is the same whether they set quantity or price. The oligopolistic and monopolistically competitive equilibria differ, however, if firms set prices instead of quantities.

IN THIS CHAPTER,

WE EXAMINE

EIGHT MAIN

TOPICS

1. **Market structures:** The number of firms, price, profits, and other properties of markets vary, depending on whether the market is monopolistic, oligopolistic, monopolistically competitive, or competitive.

2. **Game theory:** When there are relatively few firms in a market, firms take into account how their actions affect other firms and how other firms' actions affect them. Economists use a set of tools called *game theory* to analyze conflicts and cooperation between such firms.

3. **Cooperative oligopoly models:** If firms successfully coordinate their actions, they can collectively behave like a monopoly.

4. **Cournot model of noncooperative oligopoly:** In a Cournot model, in which firms choose their output levels without colluding, the market output and firms' profits lie between the competitive and monopoly levels.

5. **Stackelberg model of noncooperative behavior:** In a Stackelberg model, in which a *leader* firm chooses its output level before its identical-cost rivals, market output is greater than if all firms choose their output simultaneously, and the leader makes a higher profit than the other firms.

6. **Comparison of collusive, Cournot, Stackelberg, and competitive equilibria:** Total market output declines from the competitive level to the Stackelberg level to the Cournot level and reaches a minimum with monopoly or collusion.

7. **Monopolistic competition:** When firms can freely enter the market but, in equilibrium, face downward-sloping demand curves, firms charge prices above marginal cost but make no profit.

8. **Bertrand price-setting model:** The oligopoly equilibrium in which firms set prices differs from the quantity-setting equilibrium and depends on the degree of product differentiation.

13.1 | MARKET STRUCTURES

Markets differ according to the number of firms in the market, the ease with which firms may enter and leave the market, and the ability of firms in a market to differentiate their products from those of their rivals. Table 13.1 lists characteristics and properties of competition, monopoly, oligopoly, and monopolistic competition. For each of these market structures, we assume that the firms face many price-taking buyers.

Regardless of market structures, a firm maximizes its profit by setting quantity so that marginal revenue equals marginal cost (row 1 of Table 13.1). The four market structures differ in terms of the market power of firms (ability to set price above marginal cost), ease of entry of new firms, and strategic behavior on the part of firms (taking account of rivals' actions). Monopolies, oligopolies, and

Table 13.1 **Properties of Monopoly, Oligopoly, Monopolistic Competition, and Competition**

	Monopoly	Oligopoly	Monopolistic Competition	Competition
1. Profit-maximization condition	$MR = MC$	$MR = MC$	$MR = MC$	$p = MR = MC$
2. Ability to set price	Price setter	Price setter	Price setter	Price taker
3. Market power	$p > MC$	$p > MC$	$p > MC$	$p = MC$
4. Entry conditions	No entry	Limited entry	Free entry	Free entry
5. Number of firms	1	Few	Few or many	Many
6. Long-run profit	≥ 0	≥ 0	0	0
7. Strategy dependent on individual rival firms' behavior	No (has no rivals)	Yes	Yes	No (cares about market price only)
8. Products	Single product	May be differentiated	May be differentiated	Undifferentiated
9. Example	Local natural gas utility	Automobile manufacturers	Plumbers in a small town	Apple farmers

monopolistically competitive firms are price setters rather than price takers (row 2) because they face downward-sloping demand curves. As a consequence, market failures occur in each of these market structures because price is above marginal revenue and hence above marginal cost (row 3). In contrast, a competitive firm faces a horizontal demand curve, so its price equals its marginal cost.

A monopoly or an oligopoly does not fear entry (row 4) because of insurmountable barriers to entry such as government licenses or patents. These barriers to entry restrict the number of firms so that there is only one firm (*mono-*) in a monopoly and, usually, a few (*oligo-*) in an oligopoly (row 5). The key difference between oligopolistic and monopolistically competitive markets is that firms are free to enter only in a monopolistically competitive market.

In both competitive and monopolistically competitive markets, entry occurs until no new firm can profitably enter (so the marginal firm earns zero profit, row 6). Monopolistically competitive markets have fewer firms than perfectly competitive markets do. Because they have relatively few rivals and hence are large relative to the market, each monopolistically competitive firm faces a downward-sloping demand curve.

Oligopolistic and monopolistically competitive firms pay attention to rival firms' behavior, in contrast to monopolistic or competitive firms (row 7). A monopoly has no rivals. A competitive firm ignores the behavior of individual rivals in choosing its output because the market price tells the firm everything it needs to know about its competitors.

Oligopolistic and monopolistically competitive firms may produce differentiated products (row 8). For example, Camry and Taurus automobiles differ in size, weight, and various other dimensions. In contrast, competitive apple farmers sell undifferentiated (homogeneous) products.

13.2 GAME THEORY

> *Business is a good game—lots of competition and a minimum of rules. You keep score with money.—Nolan Bushnell (founder of Atari, a pioneering electronic game company)*

Unlike a monopoly or a competitive firm, an oligopolistic or monopolistically competitive firm considers how its actions affect its rivals and how rivals' actions will affect it. Each firm forms a **strategy**, which is a battle plan of the actions (such as setting a price or quantity) that it will take to compete with other firms. A fairly simple strategy is to produce 100 units of output regardless of what anyone else does. A more complex strategy is for a firm to produce a small quantity as long as its rival produces a small amount and a large quantity otherwise.

We can think of oligopolies as engaging in a **game**, which is any competition between players (such as firms) in which strategic behavior plays a major role. **Game theory** is a set of tools that economists, political scientists, military analysts, and others use to analyze decision making by players (such as firms) who use strategies. These same tools can be used to analyze oligopolistic games, poker, coin-matching games, tic-tac-toe, elections, and wars.

Although we call the conflict between oligopolists a game, firms do not view this competition as frivolous. These games are serious business. Each firm is interested in achieving the largest possible profit (or payoff) at the end of the game. Typically, one firm's gain comes at the expense of the other firm. Each firm's profit depends on the actions taken by all the firms. For example, if one oligopolistic firm increases its output, the price falls for all firms, affecting the profits of all firms.

When is an oligopolistic market in equilibrium? In describing competitive and monopolistic markets, we said that the market is in equilibrium if no firm has a desire to change its output level given what everyone else is doing. John Nash (1951), a Nobel Prize–winning economist and mathematician, defined an oligopolistic equilibrium similarly: No firm wants to change its strategy given what everyone else is doing. Formally, a set of strategies is a **Nash equilibrium** if, holding the strategies of all other players (firms) constant, no player (firm) can obtain a higher payoff (profit) by choosing a different strategy. In a Nash equilibrium, no firm wants to change its strategy because each firm is using its **best response**—the strategy that maximizes its profit, given its beliefs about its rivals' strategies.

A Single-Period, Two-Firm, Quantity-Setting Game

We illustrate game theory and determine the Nash equilibrium for a **duopoly**: an oligopoly with two (*duo-*) firms. We examine how American Airlines and United Airlines actually compete for customers on flights between Chicago and Los Angeles.[1]

---

[1]This example is based on Brander and Zhang (1990). They reported data for economy and discount passengers taking direct flights between the two cities in the third quarter of 1985. In calculating the profits, we assume that Brander and Zhang's estimate of the firms' constant marginal cost is the same as the firms' relevant long-run average cost.

The total number of passengers flown by these two firms, Q, is the sum of the number of passengers flown on American, q_A, and those flown on United, q_U. These airlines have a great deal of latitude in setting the number of flights and the number of seats per flight. For simplicity in this section, however, we assume that the airlines can pick only a relatively large quantity, 64 units (one unit being 1,000 passengers) per quarter, or a relatively small quantity, 48 units per quarter.

A *profit matrix* (or *payoff matrix*), such as in Table 13.2, shows the strategies the firms may choose and the resulting profits. If American chooses a large quantity, $q_A = 64$ units per quarter, and United chooses a small quantity, $q_U = 48$ units per quarter, the firms' profits are in the cell in the lower left-hand corner of the matrix. In that cell, American's profit (upper-right number) is $5.1 million per quarter, and United's profit (bottom-left number) is $3.8 million per quarter.

Because the firms choose their strategies simultaneously, each firm selects a strategy that maximizes its profit *given what it believes the other firm will do*. Thus the firms are playing a *noncooperative game of imperfect information* in which each firm must choose an action before observing the simultaneous action by its rival.

How can a firm decide its best response to the other firm's strategy if it doesn't know what the other firm will do? The firm rejects any strategy that is strictly dominated by another strategy. Strategy 1 *strictly dominates* Strategy 2 if Strategy 1 produces a profit at least as high as Strategy 2 does, *regardless of the action taken by the rival firm*. If one strategy strictly dominates *all* other strategies, regardless of the actions chosen by rival firms, the firm should choose this **dominant strategy**. Where a firm has a dominant strategy, its belief about its rivals' behavior is irrelevant.

Although firms do not always have dominant strategies, they do have them in this game. To determine American's dominant strategy, American's managers can use the following reasoning:

- *If United chooses the high-output strategy* ($q_U = 64$), *American's high-output strategy maximizes its profit*: Given United's strategy, American's profit is $4.1 million (top-right number in the upper-left cell) with its high-output strategy ($q_A = 64$) and only $3.8 million (top-right number in the upper-right cell) with

---

Table 13.2 Profit Matrix for a Quantity-Setting Game

		✈ **American Airlines**	
		$q_A = 64$	$q_A = 48$
United Airlines	$q_U = 64$	$4.1 / $4.1	$4.1 $5.1 ... $3.8
	$q_U = 48$	$5.1 / $3.8	$5.1 $4.6 ... $4.6

Note: Quantities are in thousands of passengers per quarter; profits are in millions of dollars per quarter.

its low-output strategy ($q_A = 48$). Thus American is better off using a high-output strategy if United chooses its high-output strategy.

■ *If United chooses the low-output strategy ($q_U = 48$), American's high-output strategy maximizes its profit*: Given United's strategy, American's profit is $5.1 million with its high-output strategy and only $4.6 million with its low-output strategy.

■ *Thus the high-output strategy is American's dominant strategy*: Whichever strategy United uses, American's profit is higher if it uses its high-output strategy.

By the same type of reasoning, United's high-output strategy is also a dominant strategy.

Because the high-output strategy is a dominant strategy for both firms, the pair of high-output strategies, $q_A = q_U = 64$, is a Nash equilibrium. We can use the profit matrix to confirm that this pair of strategies is a Nash equilibrium by showing that neither firm wants to change its strategy if it is certain that the other firm will use its high-output strategy. If American knew that United would use its high-output strategy, it still would not switch to its low-output strategy because its profit would fall from $4.1 million to $3.8 million. Similarly, United wouldn't switch if it knew American would use its high-output strategy. Because neither firm wants to change its strategy given that the other firm is playing its Nash equilibrium strategy, this pair of strategies ($q_A = q_U = 64$) is a Nash equilibrium.

Why Firms Do Not Cooperate in a Single-Period Game	In this Nash equilibrium, each firm earns $4.1 million, which is less than the $4.6 million it would make if firms restricted their outputs to $q_A = q_U = 48$. Thus *the sum of the firms' profits is not maximized in this simultaneous-choice, one-period game.*

Many people are surprised the first time they hear this result. Why don't the firms cooperate and use the individually and jointly more profitable low-output strategies, by which each earns a profit of $4.6 million, instead of the $4.1 million in the Nash equilibrium? They don't cooperate due to a lack of trust: Each firm uses the low-output strategy only if the firms have a binding agreement.

Suppose that the two firms meet in advance and agree to restrict their outputs to the lower quantity. If the firms are going to engage in this game only once, each has an incentive to cheat on their agreement. If American believes that United will stick to the agreement and produce $q_U = 48$, American can increase its profit from $4.6 million to $5.1 million by violating the agreement and producing $q_A = 64$. Moreover if American thinks that United will also cheat on the agreement by producing $q_U = 64$, American wants to produce the high output (so that it will earn $4.1 million rather than $3.8 million). By this reasoning, each firm has a substantial profit incentive to cheat on the agreement. In this type of game—called a **prisoners' dilemma** game—all players have dominant strategies that lead to a profit (or other payoff) that is inferior to what they could achieve if they cooperated and pursued alternative strategies.[2]

---

[2]The prisoners' dilemma crops up in virtually every cops-and-robbers show you've seen. The cops arrest Larry and Duncan and put them in separate rooms so that they cannot talk. An assistant district attorney tells Larry, "We have enough evidence to convict you both of a relatively minor crime for which you'll serve a year in prison. If you'll squeal on your partner and he stays silent, we can convict him of a major crime, for which he'll serve five years and you'll go free. If you both confess, you'll each get two years." Meanwhile another assistant district attorney is making Duncan the same offer. By the same reasoning as in the airlines example, both Larry and Duncan confess, even though they are better off if they both keep quiet.

Collusion in Repeated Games

We've just seen that in a single-period prisoners' dilemma game, the two firms produce more than they would if they colluded. Yet cartels do form. What's wrong with this theory, which says that cartels won't occur? One explanation is that firms frequently engage in multiperiod games, in which collusion is more likely than it is in a single-period game.

In a single-period game, one firm cannot punish the other firm for cheating on a cartel agreement. But if the firms meet period after period, a wayward firm can be punished by the other.

Suppose that the single-period prisoners' dilemma game is repeated period after period. In the single-period game, each firm takes its rival's strategy as given and assumes that it cannot affect its rival's strategy. If the same game is played repeatedly, however, firms engage in a **supergame** in which players may devise strategies for this period that depend on rivals' actions in previous periods. For example, a firm may set a low-output level this period only if its rival set a low-output level in the previous period.

In a repeated game, a firm can influence its rival's behavior by *signaling* and *threatening to punish*. One airline could use a low-quantity strategy for a couple of periods to signal to the other firm its desire that the two firms cooperate and produce that low quantity in the future. If the other firm does not respond by lowering its output in future periods, the first firm suffers lower profits for only a couple of periods. However, if the other firm responds to this signal and lowers its quantity, both firms can profitably produce at the low quantity thereafter.

In addition to or instead of signaling, a firm can punish a rival for not restricting output. We can illustrate how firms punish rivals to ensure collusion by using the profit matrix in Table 13.2. Suppose that American announces or somehow indicates to United that it will use the following two-part strategy:

- American will produce the smaller quantity each period as long as United does the same.
- If United produces the larger quantity in period t, American will produce the larger quantity in period $t + 1$ and all subsequent periods.

If United believes that American will follow this strategy, United knows that it will make $4.6 million each period if it produces the lower quantity. Although United can make a higher profit, $5.1 million, in period t by producing the larger quantity, by doing so it lowers its potential profit to $4.1 million in each following period. Thus United's best policy is to produce the lower quantity in each period unless it cares greatly about current profit and little about future profits. If United values future profits nearly as much as current ones, the one-period gain from deviating from the collusive output level does not compensate for the losses from reduced profits in future periods, which is the punishment American will impose. United may take this threat by American seriously because American's best response is to produce the larger quantity if it believes it can't trust United to produce the smaller quantity.[3] Thus if firms play the same game *indefinitely*, they should find it easier to collude.

---

[3]American does not have to punish United forever to induce it to cooperate. All it has to do is punish it for a long enough period that it does not pay for United to deviate from the low-quantity strategy in any period.

Playing the same game many times, however, doesn't necessarily help the firms collude. Suppose, for example, that the firms know that they are going to play the game for T periods. In the last period, they know that they're not going to play again, so they know they can cheat—produce a lot of output—without fear of punishment. As a result, the last period is like a single-period game, and all firms cheat. That makes the $T - 1$ period the last interesting period. By the same reasoning, they'll cheat in $T - 1$. Continuing this type of argument, we conclude that maintaining a cartel will be difficult if the game has a known stopping point. If the players know that the game will end but aren't sure when, cheating is less likely to occur. Collusion is therefore more likely in a game that will continue forever or that will end at an uncertain time.

Application   OLIGOPOLY COMPETITION AMONG GOVERNMENTS

To increase local employment and for other reasons, state governments offer subsidies and tax breaks to attract new businesses. Utah gave Micron Technology $200 million, Illinois showered Sears, Roebuck with $240 million, and New Mexico, using a $1 billion industrial revenue bond issue, won a bidding war against half a dozen other states for an Intel Corporation expansion of its semiconductor plant. In 2000, New Jersey gave three large brokerage houses—Goldman Sachs, Merrill Lynch, and Morgan Stanley—tax incentives worth $200 million to set up offices and move 3,000 jobs to Jersey City, which amounts to $66,667 per job. That payoff pales compared to the $300 million—$200,000 per job created—that Alabama gave Mercedes Benz in 1993.

These state governments may be acting in the best interests of their citizens, but Americans would collectively benefit if state governments were prevented from competing in this way. If only one state government offers a tax break, it can attract a major business at relatively low cost: Any tax break dominates the zero tax break offered elsewhere. Once many governments start bidding against each other for businesses, however, the size of the tax breaks that are needed to attract firms rises. States that were not offering tax breaks originally now have to offer them to prevent a mass exodus of firms.

In the terminology of game theory, the players or states compete in a game in which the strategies are handouts to firms. In the noncooperative Nash equilibrium, all states offer handouts. Collectively, the state governments would benefit by agreeing not to offer handouts. Unfortunately, so far, the state governments have not agreed to collude.

13.3   COOPERATIVE OLIGOPOLY MODELS

We have seen that firms have an incentive to form a cartel in which each firm reduces its output so that firms' individual and collective profits rise. As Adam Smith observed more than two centuries ago, "People of the same trade seldom meet together, even for merriment and diversion, but the conversation ends in a conspiracy against the public, or some contrivance to raise prices." Luckily for consumers, cartels often fail because a government forbids them and because each firm in a cartel has an incentive to cheat on the cartel agreement by producing extra output.

Laws Against Cartels

In the late nineteenth century, cartels (or, as they were called then, *trusts*) were legal and common in the United States. Oil, railroad, sugar, and tobacco trusts raised prices substantially above competitive levels.

In response to the trusts' high prices, the U.S. Congress passed the Sherman Antitrust Act in 1890 and the Federal Trade Commission Act of 1914, which prohibit firms from *explicitly* agreeing to take actions that reduce competition. In particular, cartels that are formed for the purpose of jointly setting price are strictly prohibited. These laws reduce the probability that cartels form by imposing penalties on firms caught colluding. Virtually all industrialized nations have *antitrust laws*—or, as they are known in other countries, *competition policies*—that limit or forbid some or all cartels.

Some cartels persist despite these laws, for three reasons. First, international cartels and cartels within certain countries operate legally. Second, some illegal cartels operate believing that they can avoid detection or that the punishment will be insignificant. Third, some firms are able to coordinate their activity without explicitly colluding and thereby running afoul of competition laws.

Some international cartels organized by countries rather than firms are legal. The Organization of Petroleum Exporting Countries (OPEC) is an international cartel that was formed in 1960 by five major oil-exporting countries: Iran, Iraq, Kuwait, Saudi Arabia, and Venezuela. In 1971, OPEC members agreed to take an active role in setting oil prices.

Many illegal cartels flout the competition laws in major industrial countries. These firms apparently believe that they are unlikely to get caught or that the punishments they face are so negligible that it pays to collude anyway. For example, General Electric (GE) and Westinghouse were charged and punished repeatedly in the first 50 years after the Sherman Act went into effect. The U.S. Department of Justice brought 13 antitrust cases and the Federal Trade Commission filed 3 more against GE and Westinghouse between 1911 and 1952. The government "won" all of the cases by obtaining either a conviction, a *nolo contendere* ("no contest") plea (without admitting guilt, the firms agreed to be punished), or a consent decree by which the firms agreed to stop behaving in certain ways (Walton and Cleveland, 1964).

Small fines fail to discourage cartel behavior. In a recent cartel case involving the $9 billion American carpet industry, a firm with $150 million annual sales agreed with the U.S. Justice Department to plead guilty and pay a fine of $150,000.[4] It is hard to imagine that a fine of one-tenth of 1% of annual sales significantly deters cartel behavior.

American antitrust laws use evidence of conspiracy (such as explicit agreements) rather than the economic effect of monopoly to determine guilt. Charging monopoly-level prices is not necessarily illegal—only the "bad behavior" of explicitly agreeing

---

[4]Drummond, Bob, "Carpet Maker Pleads Guilty," *San Francisco Chronicle*, June 8, 1995:B2.

to raise prices is illegal. As a result, some groups of firms charge monopoly-level prices without violating the competition laws. These firms may *tacitly collude* without meeting by signaling to each other through their actions. Although the firms' actions may not be illegal, they behave much like cartels. For example, MacAvoy (1995) concluded that the major U.S. long-distance telephone companies tacitly colluded; as a result, each firm's Lerner Index (Chapter 11), $(p - MC)/p$, exceeded 60%, which is well above competitive levels. (See **www.awlonline.com/perloff**, "Tacit Collusion in Long-Distance Service.")

Why Cartels Form

We now consider why cartels form, why cartel members have an incentive to deviate from the cartel agreement, and why some cartels succeed where others fail. A cartel forms if members of the cartel believe that they can raise their profits by coordinating their actions. Although cartels usually involve oligopolies, cartels may form in a market that would otherwise be competitive.

If a competitive firm is maximizing its profit, why should joining a cartel increase its profit? The answer involves a subtle argument. When a competitive firm chooses its profit-maximizing output level, it considers how varying its output affects its own profit only. The firm ignores the effect that changing its output level has on other firms' profits. A cartel, by contrast, takes into account how changes in any one firm's output affect the profits of all members of the cartel.

If a competitive firm lowers its output, it raises the market price very slightly—so slightly that the firm ignores the effect not only on other firms' profits but also on its own. If all the identical competitive firms in an industry lower their output by this same amount, however, the market price will change noticeably. Recognizing this effect of collective action, a cartel chooses to produce a smaller market output than is produced by a competitive market.

Figure 13.1 illustrates this difference between a competitive market and a cartel. There are n firms in this market, and no further entry is possible. Panel a shows the marginal and average cost curves of a typical firm. If all firms are price takers, the market supply curve, S, is the horizontal sum of the individual marginal cost curves above minimum average cost, as shown in panel b. At the competitive price, p_c, each price-taking firm produces q_c units of output (where MC intersects the line at p_c in panel a). The market output is $Q_c = nq_c$ (where S intersects the market demand curve in panel b).

Now suppose that the firms form a cartel. Should they reduce their output? At the competitive output, the cartel's marginal cost (which is the competitive industry supply curve, S in panel b) is greater than its marginal revenue, so the cartel's profit rises if it reduces output. The cartel's collective profit rises until output is reduced by enough that its marginal revenue equals its marginal cost at Q_m, the monopoly output. If the profit of the cartel increases, the profit of each of the n members of the cartel also increases. To achieve the cartel output level, each firm must reduce its output to $q_m = Q_m/n$, as panel a shows.

Why must the firms form a cartel to achieve these higher profits? A competitive firm produces q_c, where its marginal cost equals the market price. If only one firm reduces its output, it loses profit because it sells fewer units at essentially the same price. By getting all the firms to lower their output together, the cartel raises the

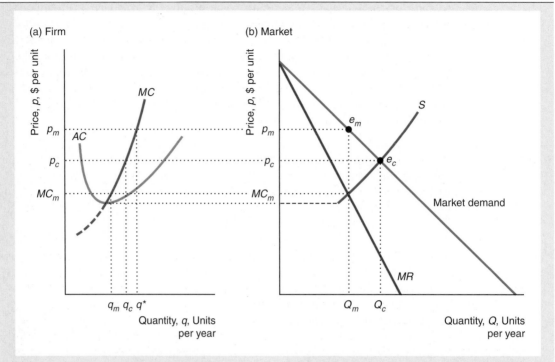

Figure 13.1 Competition Versus Cartel. (a) The marginal cost and average cost of one of the *n* firms in the market are shown. A competitive firm produces q_c units of output, whereas a cartel member produces $q_m < q_c$. At the cartel price, p_m, each cartel member has an incentive to increase its output from q_m to q^* (where the dotted line at p_m intersects the *MC* curve). (b) The competitive equilibrium, e_c, has more output and a lower price than the cartel equilibrium, e_m.

market price and hence individual firms' profits. The less elastic the market demand the potential cartel faces, all else the same, the higher the price the cartel sets (Chapter 11) and the greater the benefit from cartelizing. If the penalty for forming an illegal cartel is relatively low, some unscrupulous businesspeople may succumb to the lure of extra profits and join.

Why Cartels Fail

A thing worth having is a thing worth cheating for.   —W. C. Fields

Cartels fail if noncartel members can supply consumers with large quantities of goods. For example, copper producers formed an international cartel that controlled only about a third of the noncommunist world's copper production and faced additional competition from firms that recycle copper from scrap materials. Because of this competition from noncartel members, the cartel was not successful in raising and keeping copper prices high.

In addition, *each member of a cartel has an incentive to cheat on the cartel agreement.* The owner of a firm may reason, "I joined the cartel to encourage others to reduce their output and increase profits for everyone. I can make more, however, if I cheat on the cartel agreement by producing extra output. I can get away with cheating if the other firms can't tell who's producing the extra output because I'm just one of many firms and because I'll hardly affect the market price." By this reasoning, it is in each firm's best interest for all *other* firms to honor the cartel agreement—thus driving up the market price—while it ignores the agreement and makes extra, profitable sales at the high price.

Figure 13.1 illustrates why firms want to cheat. At the cartel output, q_m in panel a, each cartel member's marginal cost is MC_m. The marginal revenue of a firm that violates the agreement is p_m because it is acting like a price taker with respect to the market price. Because the firm's marginal revenue (price) is above its marginal cost, the firm wants to increase its output. If the firm decides to violate the cartel agreement, it maximizes its profit by increasing its output to q^*, where its marginal cost equals p_m.

As more and more firms leave the cartel, the cartel price falls. The colluding firms act like a dominant firm facing a competitive fringe (Chapter 11). Eventually, if enough firms quit, the cartel collapses.

Maintaining Cartels

To keep firms from violating the cartel agreement, the cartel must be able to detect cheating and punish violators. Further, the members of the cartel must keep their illegal behavior hidden from customers and government agencies.

Detection. Cartels use many techniques to detect cheating. Some cartels, for example, give members the right to inspect each other's books. Similarly, governments often help cartels by reporting bids on government contracts, so that other firms learn if a cartel member bids below the agreed-on cartel price.

Cartels may divide the market by region or by customers, so that a firm that tries to steal another firm's customer is more likely to be detected. The two-country mercury cartel (1928–1972) allocated the Americas to Spain and Europe to Italy.

Other cartels use industry organizations to detect cheating. These organizations collect data on market share by firm and circulate their results. If a firm cheats on a cartel, its share would rise and other firms would know that it cheated.

You may have seen "low price" ads in which local retail stores guarantee to meet or beat the prices of any competitors. You may have thought that such a guarantee assured you of a low price. However, it may be a way for the firm to induce its customers to report cheating on a cartel agreement by other firms (Salop, 1986).

Enforcement. Many methods are used to enforce cartel agreements. For example, GE and Westinghouse, the two major sellers of large steam-turbine generators, included "most-favored-nation clauses" in their contracts. These contracts stated that the seller would not offer a lower price to any other current or future buyer without offering the same price decrease to that buyer. This type of rebate clause creates a penalty for cheating on the cartel: If either company cheats by cutting prices, it has to lower prices to all previous buyers as well. Another means of enforcing a cartel agreement is through threats of violence (see **www.awlonline.com/perloff**, "Bad Bakers").

Application   VITAMIN PRICE FIXING

The U.S. Department of Justice charged that the major international pharmaceutical companies were engaging in a conspiracy to fix the prices of bulk vitamins worldwide during the 1990s. These vitamins are used in dietary supplements, breakfast cereals, other foods and beverages, animal feed, hand creams, and vitamin pills.

According to the Justice Department, senior executives from the world's largest vitamin producers were meeting clandestinely at a European hotel or an executive's home in August or September each year to set market shares for such vitamins as A, B_2, C, and E. The firms allegedly allocated customers and set production quotas, prices, and distribution rules for vitamin ingredients. Firms that exceeded their targets were punished at year's end by being forced to buy excess products from their coconspirators.

The international cartel controlled 90% of the U.S. vitamin market and more than 70% of the global market, thus touching virtually every household in the world. The conspiracy affected more than $5 billion worth of the kind of products found in every U.S. household.

By 1999, senior executives at several pharmaceutical companies had admitted to participating in a nine-year price-fixing cartel for vitamin ingredients. Roche Holding A.G., a Swiss firm with 40% of the world vitamin market, paid a $500 million fine to settle charges with the U.S. Justice Department, and one executive will serve a four-month prison sentence. BASF A.G. of Germany settled similar charges by paying $225 million in fines. Lonza A.G. of Switzerland agreed to pay $10.5 million. In Japan, Takeda Chemical Industries of Osaka agreed to pay $72 million; the Eisai Company of Tokyo, $40 million; and the Daiichi Pharmaceutical Company of Tokyo, $25 million. Rhône-Poulenc of France was also part of the cartel but escaped punishment by providing crucial information to prosecutors. At the same time, executives at Chinook Group, a Canadian company, and Ducoa, a joint venture between DuPont and ConAgra, pleaded guilty to charges that they conspired to fix the prices of animal and human vitamins and divided up U.S. and other markets.

Seven of the largest drug companies also agreed to pay $1.17 billion to settle a class-action lawsuit filed by the world's leading food, beverage, and animal feed companies, including Kellogg, Kraft, and Tyson Foods. The Roche Group alone agreed to pay $632 million. In addition, state class-action suits were filed on behalf of final consumers. Are these fines a bitter enough pill that they will discourage such behavior in the future? That remains to be seen. Roche apparently continued to participate in this cartel even after paying a $14 million fine for its involvement in fixing the price of the food additives citric acid and lysine in 1997.

Government Support. Sometimes governments help create and enforce cartels. For example, U.S., European, and other governments signed an agreement in 1944 to establish a cartel that fixes prices for international airline flights and prevents competition.

Professional baseball teams have been exempted from some U.S. antitrust laws since 1922. As a result, they can use the courts to help enforce certain aspects of their cartel agreement. Major league clubs are able to avoid competing for young athletes by means of a draft and contracts, limit geographic competition between teams, jointly negotiate for television and other rights, and in many other ways act collectively.

Application   **A GOVERNMENT-CREATED CARTEL**

In recent years, a number of governments have created foreign cartels through their trade policies. In 1981, the Reagan administration negotiated voluntary export restraint (VER) agreements whereby Japanese automobile manufacturers would reduce their exports to the United States. The Japanese manufacturers also signed VER agreements with West Germany and Belgium at about the same time.

Why would the Japanese manufacturers "voluntarily" reduce their exports? One explanation is that they were under pressure from both the U.S. and Japanese governments and feared that quotas would be applied. A more likely explanation is that agreeing to the VERs was in their best interests.

Under these agreements, the Japanese manufacturers were to reduce their exports to the United States, thereby forcing American consumers to pay more for domestic and Japanese cars. The VER agreements achieved this goal: Domestic and foreign manufacturers benefited at the expense of American consumers.

If the Japanese car manufacturers were operating independently before 1981, they could increase their collective profit by reducing the number of cars each exported to the United States. They would face the usual problems in trying to agree between themselves to restrict exports. The VERs, then, provided a mechanism for the firms to reduce exports collectively and profitably. By this argument, the Japanese manufacturers wanted firm-specific quotas (if not set too low), which would ensure that no manufacturer cheated on the agreement. Indeed, when the United States allowed the VER agreements to lapse in 1985, the Japanese government—presumably reflecting the sentiments of the car manufacturers—said that it wanted to continue to restrict exports.

Ries (1993) reported that the stock market value of firms in the Japanese automobile industry increased during the VER period by $6.6 billion, of which $2.2 billion was due to the American VER announcement. Scott (1994) estimated that the VERs raised the price of American cars by 5.4% between 1981 and 1983. Using a general-equilibrium trade model, Tarr (1989) concluded that American consumers lost $6.9 billion (in 1984 dollars) because of these export restrictions.

The U.S. government's use of quantity restrictions is bizarre. Foreign and domestic auto manufacturers capture the extra "cartel" profits from the higher prices caused by the VER. Had the U.S. government used tariffs instead, the domestic price would have risen, helping domestic firms, but the extra profits from the increase in price would have gone to the U.S. government through tariff revenues instead of to foreign manufacturers (Chapter 9).

Entry and Cartel Success

Barriers to entry that limit the number of firms help the cartel detect and punish cheating. The fewer the firms in a market, the more likely it is that other firms will know if a given firm cheats and the easier it is to impose costs on that firm. Cartels with a large number of firms are relatively rare, except those involving professional associations. Hay and Kelley (1974) examined Department of Justice price-fixing cases from 1963 to 1972 and found that only 6.5% involved 50 or more conspirators, the average number of firms was 7.25, and nearly half the cases (48%) involved 6 or fewer firms.

When new firms enter their market, cartels frequently fail. For example, when only Italy and Spain sold mercury, they were able to establish and maintain a stable cartel. When a larger group of countries joined them, their attempts to cartelize the world mercury market repeatedly failed (MacKie-Mason and Pindyck, 1986).

Application   BAIL BONDS

The state of Connecticut sets a maximum fee that bail-bond businesses can charge for posting a given size bond (Ayres and Waldfogel, 1994). The bail-bond fee is set at virtually the maximum amount allowed by law in cities with only one active firm (Plainville, 99% of the maximum; Stamford, 99%; and Wallingford, 99%). The price is as high in cities with a duopoly (Ansonia, 99.6%; Meriden, 98%; and New London, 98%). In cities with three or more firms, however, the price falls well below the maximum permitted price, possibly because the difficulty of maintaining a cartel or tacit collusion rises with the number of firms. The fees are only 54% of the maximum in Norwalk with 3 firms, 64% in New Haven with 8 firms, and 78% in Bridgeport with 10 firms.

Mergers

If antitrust or competition laws prevent firms from colluding, they may try to merge instead. Recognizing this potential problem, U.S. laws restrict the ability of firms to merge if the effect would be anticompetitive. Whether the Department of Justice or the Federal Trade Commission (FTC) challenges a proposed merger turns on a large number of issues. One reason why the government limits mergers is that all the firms in a market could combine and form a monopoly.

Then would it not be a good idea to ban all mergers? No, because some mergers result in more efficient production. Formerly separate firms may become more efficient because of greater scale, sharing trade secrets, or closing duplicative retail outlets. For example, when Chase and Chemical banks merged, they closed or combined seven branches in Manhattan that were located within two blocks of other branches.

Application   AIRLINE MERGERS

Kim and Singal (1993) studied price changes from airline mergers during the period 1985–1988 when the government did not contest most airline mergers. Prices increased on routes served by firms that merged relative to those on routes without mergers. Thus the authors concluded that the efficiency gains from the mergers were more than offset by the exercise of increased market power in this market.

13.4 | COURNOT MODEL OF NONCOOPERATIVE OLIGOPOLY

We just used our monopoly and dominant-firm models to analyze markets where oligopoly firms collude. We need new models, however, to explain how oligopolies behave if they act independently.

Although there is only one model of competition and one model of monopoly, there are many models of noncooperative oligopoly behavior. Because strategies matter for oligopolies, many market outcomes are possible. Here we examine two oligopoly models in which firms choose quantities: the Cournot and Stackelberg models.

Which model is appropriate to use depends on the institutional features of a market. If firms set output simultaneously and let the market determine the price, a Cournot model works well. If one firm can set output before other firms, a Stackelberg model is appropriate. Similarly, if oligopolies set price instead of quantity, a Bertrand oligopoly model is relevant. Where the institutional features of a market are not well understood, an economist may try each model to see which best predicts actual behavior in that market.

Antoine-Augustin Cournot introduced the first formal model of oligopoly in 1838. Cournot asked how oligopoly firms behave if they choose how much to produce at the same time. As in the prisoners' dilemma game, the firms are playing a noncooperative game of imperfect information; each firm must choose its output level before knowing what the other firm will choose. Now, however, the firms may choose any output level they want.

To simplify our analysis of the Cournot oligopoly model, we examine a market in which

- There are two firms, and no other firms can enter.
- The firms sell identical (undifferentiated, homogeneous) products.
- The firms compete in a market that lasts for only one period, and the product or service that they sell cannot be stored and sold later.

How much one firm produces directly affects the profit of the other firms, because market price depends on total output. Thus in choosing its strategy to maximize its profit, each firm takes into account its beliefs about the output other firms will sell.

Cournot Model of an Airline Market

We again examine the duopoly market in which United Airlines and American Airlines fly passengers between Chicago and Los Angeles. We assume that no other companies can enter, perhaps because they cannot obtain landing rights at both airports.[5]

---

[5]With the end of deregulation, existing firms were given the right to buy, sell, or rent landing slots. By controlling landing slots, existing firms can make entry difficult. In 1992, a landing slot at Chicago's O'Hare Airport rented for $66,000 per month ("United Wins TWA Lease," *New York Times*, March 20, 1992).

How many passengers does each airline choose to carry? To answer this question, we determine the Nash equilibrium for this model. This Nash equilibrium, in which firms choose quantities, is also called a **Cournot equilibrium**: a set of quantities sold by firms such that, holding the quantities of all other firms constant, no firm can obtain a higher profit by choosing a different quantity.

To determine the Cournot equilibrium, we need to establish how each firm chooses its strategy: the quantity it produces. We start by using the total demand curve for the Chicago–Los Angeles route and a firm's belief about how much its rival will sell to determine the residual demand curve this firm faces. Next, we examine how a firm uses its residual demand curve to determine its best response: the output level that maximizes its profit, given its belief about how much its rival will produce. Finally, we apply this information about both firms' best responses to determine the Cournot equilibrium.

Graphical Approach. The strategy that each firm uses depends on the demand curve it faces and its marginal cost. American Airline's profit-maximizing output depends on how many passengers it believes United will fly. Figure 13.2 illustrates two possibilities.

If American were a monopoly, it wouldn't have to worry about United's strategy. American's demand would be the market demand curve, *D* in panel a. To maximize

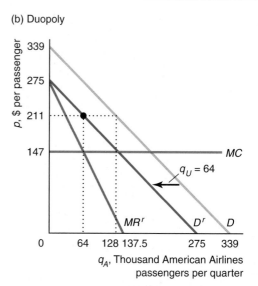

Figure 13.2 American Airlines' Profit-Maximizing Output. (a) If American is a monopoly, it picks its profit-maximizing output, q_A = 96 units (thousand passengers) per quarter, so that its marginal revenue, *MR*, equals its marginal cost, *MC*. (b) If American believes that United will fly q_U = 64 units per quarter, its residual demand curve, D^r, is the market demand curve, *D*, minus q_U. American maximizes its profit at q_A = 64, where its marginal revenue, MR^r, equals *MC*.

its profit, American would set its output so that its marginal revenue curve, MR, intersected its marginal cost curve, MC, which is constant at \$147 per passenger. Panel a shows that the monopoly output is 96 units (thousands of passengers) per quarter and the monopoly price is \$243 per passenger (one way).

Because American competes with United, American must take account of United's behavior when choosing its profit-maximizing output. American's demand is not the entire market demand. If United flies q_U passengers, American transports only the residual demand: the total market demand, Q, minus the q_U passengers: $q_A = Q - q_U$.

Suppose that American believes that United will fly $q_U = 64$. Panel b shows that American's residual demand curve, D^r, is the market demand curve, D, moved to the left by $q_U = 64$. For example, if the price is \$211, the total number of passengers who want to fly is $Q = 128$. If United transports $q_U = 64$, American flies $Q - q_U = 128 - 64 = 64 = q_A$.

What is American's best-response, profit-maximizing output if its managers believe that United will fly q_U passengers? American can think of itself as having a monopoly with respect to the people who don't fly on United, which its residual demand curve, D^r, shows. To maximize its profit, American sets its output so that its marginal revenue corresponding to this residual demand, MR^r, equals its marginal cost. Panel b shows that if $q_U = 64$, American's best response is $q_A = 64$.

By shifting its residual demand curve appropriately, American can calculate its best response to any given q_U using this type of analysis. Figure 13.3 plots American Airline's best-response curve, which shows how many tickets American sells for each possible q_U.[6] As this curve shows, American will sell the monopoly number of tickets, 96, if American thinks United will fly no passengers, $q_U = 0$. The negative slope of the best-response curve shows that American sells fewer tickets, the more people American thinks that United will fly. American sells $q_A = 64$ if it thinks q_U will be 64. American shuts down, $q_A = 0$, if it thinks q_U will be 192 or more, because operating wouldn't be profitable.

Similarly, United's best-response curve shows how many tickets United sells if it thinks American will sell q_A. For example, United sells $q_U = 0$ if it thinks American will sell $q_A = 192$, $q_U = 48$ if $q_A = 96$, $q_U = 64$ if $q_A = 64$, and $q_U = 96$ if $q_A = 0$.

A firm wants to change its behavior if it is selling a quantity that is not on its best-response curve. In a Cournot equilibrium, neither firm wants to change its behavior. Thus in a Cournot equilibrium, each firm is on its best-response curve: Each firm is maximizing its profit, given its correct belief about its rival's output.

These firms' best-response curves intersect at $q_A = q_U = 64$. If American expects United to sell $q_U = 64$, American wants to sell $q_A = 64$. Because this point is on its best-response curve, American doesn't want to change its output from 64. Similarly, if United expects American to sell $q_A = 64$, United doesn't want to change q_U from 64. Thus this pair of outputs is a Cournot (Nash) equilibrium: Given its correct belief about its rival's output, each firm is maximizing its profit, and neither firm wants to change its output.

---

[6]Jargon alert: Some economists refer to the *best-response curve* as the *reaction curve*.

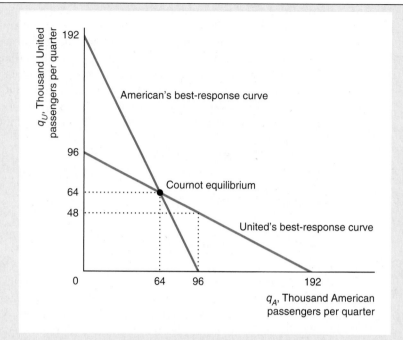

Figure 13.3 American and United's Best-Response Curves. The best-response curves show the output each firm picks to maximize its profit, given its belief about its rival's output. The Cournot equilibrium occurs at the intersection of the best-response curves.

Any pair of outputs other than the pair at an intersection of the best-response functions is *not* a Cournot equilibrium. If either firm is not on its best-response curve, it changes its output to increase its profit. For example, the output pair $q_A = 96$ and $q_U = 0$ is not a Cournot equilibrium. American is perfectly happy producing the monopoly output if United doesn't operate at all: American is on its best-response curve. United, however, would not be happy with this outcome because it is not on United's best-response curve. As its best-response curve shows, if it knows that American will sell $q_A = 96$, United wants to sell $q_U = 48$. Only at $q_A = q_U = 64$ does neither firm want to change its behavior.

Algebraic Approach. We can also use algebra to solve for the Cournot equilibrium for these two airlines. We use estimates of the market demand and firms' marginal costs to determine the equilibrium.

Our estimate of the market demand function is

$$Q = 339 - p, \tag{13.1}$$

where price, p, is the dollar cost of a one-way flight, and total quantity of the two airlines combined, Q, is measured in thousands of passengers flying one way per quarter. Panels a and b of Figure 13.2 show that this market demand curve, D, is a straight line that hits the price axis at $339 and the quantity axis at 339 units (thousands of passengers) per quarter. Each airline has a constant marginal cost, MC, and average cost, AC, of $147 per passenger per flight. Using only this information and our economic model, we can find the Cournot equilibrium for the two airlines.

If American believes that United will fly q_U passengers, American expects to fly only the total market demand minus q_U passengers. At a price of p, the total number of passengers, $Q(p)$, is given by the market demand function, Equation 13.1. Thus the residual demand American faces is

$$q_A = Q(p) - q_U = (339 - p) - q_U.$$

Using algebra, we can rewrite this inverse residual demand function as

$$p = 339 - q_A - q_U. \tag{13.2}$$

In panel b, the linear residual demand, D^r, is parallel to the market demand, D, and lies to the left of D by $q_U = 64$.

If a demand curve is linear, the corresponding marginal revenue curve is twice as steep (Chapter 11). The slope of the residual demand curve, Equation 13.2, is $\Delta p/\Delta q_A = -1$, so the slope of the corresponding marginal revenue curve, MR^r in panel b, is -2. Thus the marginal revenue function is[7]

$$MR^r = 339 - 2q_A - q_U. \tag{13.3}$$

American Airlines' best response—its profit-maximizing output, given q_U—is the output that equates its marginal revenue, Equation 13.3, and its marginal cost:

$$MR^r = 339 - 2q_A - q_U = 147 = MC. \tag{13.4}$$

By rearranging Equation 13.4, we can write American's best-response output, q_A, as a function of q_U:

$$q_A = 96 - \tfrac{1}{2}q_U. \tag{13.5}$$

Figure 13.3 shows American's best-response function, Equation 13.5. According to this best-response function, $q_A = 96$ if $q_U = 0$ and $q_A = 64$ if $q_U = 64$. By the same reasoning, United's best-response function is

$$q_U = 96 - \tfrac{1}{2}q_A. \tag{13.6}$$

A Cournot equilibrium is a pair of quantities, q_A and q_U, such that Equations 13.5 and 13.6 both hold: Each firm is on its best-response curve. This statement is equivalent to saying that the Cournot equilibrium is a point at which the best-response curves cross.

---

[7]American's revenue is $R = pq_A = (339 - q_A - q_U)q_A$. If American treats q_U as a constant and differentiates R with respect to its output, it finds that its marginal revenue is $MR = \partial R/\partial q_A = 339 - 2q_A - q_U$.

One way to determine the Cournot equilibrium is to substitute Equation 13.6 into Equation 13.5,

$$q_A = 96 - \tfrac{1}{2}(96 - \tfrac{1}{2}q_A),$$

and solve for q_A. Doing so, we find that $q_A = 64$ is the Cournot equilibrium quantity for American. Substituting $q_A = 64$ into Equation 13.6, we find that $q_U = 64$ is the Cournot equilibrium quantity for United. As a result, the total output in the Cournot equilibrium is $Q = q_A + q_U = 128$. Setting $Q = 128$ in the market demand Equation 13.1, we learn that the Cournot equilibrium price is $211.

Comparing the Cournot and Cartel Models

The Cournot equilibrium is the only plausible Nash outcome if oligopoly firms set quantities independently in a one-period game. It is possible, however, that the firms could collude—especially if the game is repeated over many periods.

How would American and United behave if they colluded? They would maximize joint profits by producing the monopoly output, 96 units, at the monopoly price, $243 per passenger (panel a of Figure 13.2).

If the airlines collude, they could split the monopoly quantity in many ways. American could act as a monopoly and serve all the passengers, $q_A = 96$ and $q_U = 0$, and possibly give United some of the profits. Or they could reverse roles so that United served everyone: $q_A = 0$ and $q_U = 96$. Or the two airlines could share the passengers in any combination such that the sum of the airlines' passengers equals the monopoly number:

$$q_A + q_U = 96. \tag{13.7}$$

Panel a of Figure 13.4 shows the possible collusive output combinations in Equation 13.7 as a line labeled "Contract curve." Collusive firms could agree (contract) to produce at any of the points along this curve. In the figure, we assume that the collusive firms split the market equally so that $q_A = q_U = 48$.

If the firms were to act as price takers, they would each produce where their residual demand curve intersects their marginal cost curve, so price equals marginal cost of $147. The price-taking equilibrium is $q_A = q_U = 96$. (The Stackelberg equilibrium in the figure is discussed later in this chapter.)

The cartel profits are the highest-possible level of profits the firms can earn. The contract curve shows how the firms split the total monopoly-level profit. Panel b of Figure 13.4 shows the profit possibility frontier, which corresponds to the contract

Figure 13.4 Duopoly Equilibria. (a) The intersection of the best-response curves determines the Cournot equilibrium. The possible cartel equilibria lie on the contract curve. If the firms act as price takers, each firm produces where its residual demand equals its marginal cost. (b) The highest possible profit for the two firms combined is given by the profit possibility frontier. It reflects all the possible collusive equilibria, including the one indicated where the firms split the market equally. All equilibria except collusive ones lie within the profit possibility frontier.

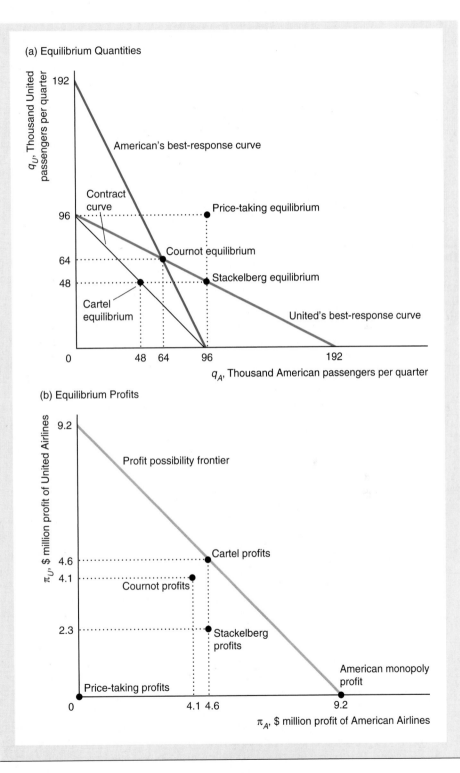

(a) Equilibrium Quantities

q_U, Thousand United passengers per quarter

192

American's best-response curve

Contract curve

96

Price-taking equilibrium

Cournot equilibrium

64

48

Stackelberg equilibrium

Cartel equilibrium

United's best-response curve

0   48 64   96   192

q_A, Thousand American passengers per quarter

(b) Equilibrium Profits

π_U, $ million profit of United Airlines

9.2

Profit possibility frontier

Cartel profits

4.6

4.1

Cournot profits

2.3

Stackelberg profits

American monopoly profit

Price-taking profits

0   4.1 4.6   9.2

π_A, $ million profit of American Airlines

curve. At the upper left of the profit possibility frontier, United is a monopoly and earns the entire monopoly profit of approximately $9.2 million per quarter.[8] At the lower right, American earns the entire monopoly profit. At points in between, they split the profit. Where they split the profit equally, each earns approximately $4.6 million.

In contrast, if the firms act independently, each earns the Cournot profit of approximately $4.1 million. Because the Cournot price, $211, is lower than the cartel price, $243, consumers are better off if the firms act independently than if they collude.

The Cournot equilibrium market quantity predicted by this model, 128, is closer to the actual observed output, 128.6, than is the predicted cartel quantity, 96. Brander and Zhang (1990) reported that they could not reject the hypothesis that American and United are engaged in a Cournot game based on statistical tests.[9]

The Cournot Equilibrium and the Number of Firms

We've just seen that the price to consumers is lower if two firms set output independently than if they collude. The price to consumers is even lower if there are more than two firms acting independently in the market. We now show how the Cournot equilibrium varies with the number of firms.

Each Cournot firm maximizes its profit by operating where its marginal revenue equals its marginal cost. Chapter 11 shows that a firm's marginal revenue depends on the price and the elasticity of demand it faces where it maximizes its profit. The marginal revenue for a typical Cournot firm is $MR = p(1 + 1/\varepsilon_r)$, where ε_r is the elasticity of the residual demand curve the firm faces. Appendix 13A shows that $\varepsilon_r = n\varepsilon$, where ε is the market elasticity of demand and n is the number of firms with identical costs. Thus we can write a typical Cournot firm's profit-maximizing condition as

$$MR = p\left(1 + \frac{1}{n\varepsilon}\right) = MC. \tag{13.8}$$

If $n = 1$, the Cournot firm is a monopoly, and Equation 13.8 is the same as the profit-maximizing monopoly condition, Equation 11.7. The more firms there are, the larger the residual demand elasticity, $n\varepsilon$, a single firm faces. As n grows very large, the residual demand elasticity approaches negative infinity ($-\infty$), and Equation 13.8 becomes $p = MC$, which is the profit-maximizing condition of a price-taking competitive firm.

The Lerner Index, $(p - MC)/p$, is a measure of market power: the firm's ability to raise price above marginal cost. By rearranging the terms in Equation 13.8, we find that a Cournot firm's Lerner Index depends on the elasticity the firm faces:

---

[8]Each firm's profit per passenger is price minus average cost, $p - AC$, so the firm's profit is $\pi = (p - AC)q$, where q is the number of passengers the firm flies. The monopoly price is $243 and the average cost is $147, so the monopoly profit is $\pi = (243 - 147) \times 96$ units per quarter = $9.216 million per quarter.

[9]Because the model described here is a simplified version of the Brander and Zhang (1990) model, the predicted output levels, $q_A = q_U = 64$, differ slightly from theirs. Nonetheless, our predictions are very close to the actual observed outcome, $q_A = 65.9$ and $q_U = 62.7$.

$$\frac{p - MC}{p} = -\frac{1}{n\varepsilon}. \qquad (13.9)$$

Thus a Cournot firm's Lerner Index equals the monopoly level, $-1/\varepsilon$, if there is only one firm: Setting $n = 1$ in Equation 13.9, we obtain the monopoly expression (Equation 11.9). Again, as the number of firms grows large, the residual demand elasticity a firm faces approaches $-\infty$, so the Lerner Index approaches zero, which is the same as with price-taking, competitive firms.

We can illustrate these results using our airlines example. Suppose that other airlines with identical marginal cost, $MC = \$147$, were to fly between Chicago and Los Angeles. Table 13.3 shows how the Cournot equilibrium price and the Lerner Index vary with the number of firms.[10]

As we already know, if there were only one "Cournot" firm, it would produce the monopoly quantity, 96, at the monopoly price, \$243. We also know that each duopoly firm's output is 64, so market output is 128 and price is \$211. The duopoly market elasticity is $\varepsilon = 1.65$, so the residual demand elasticity each duopolist faces is twice as large as the market elasticity, $2\varepsilon = -3.3$.

As the number of firms increases, each firm's output falls toward zero, but total output approaches 192, the quantity on the market demand curve where price equals marginal cost of \$147. Although the market elasticity of demand falls as the

Table 13.3 Cournot Equilibrium Varies with the Number of Firms

Number of Firms, n	Firm Output, q	Market Output, Q	Price, p, \$	Market Elasticity, ε	Residual Demand Elasticity, $n\varepsilon$	Lerner Index, $(p - m)/p = -1/(n\varepsilon)$
1	96	96	243	−2.53	−2.53	0.40
2	64	128	211	−1.65	−3.30	0.30
3	48	144	195	−1.35	−4.06	0.25
4	38.4	154	185.40	−1.21	−4.83	0.21
5	32	160	179	−1.12	−5.59	0.18
6	27.4	165	174.43	−1.06	−6.36	0.16
7	24	168	171	−1.02	−7.13	0.14
8	21.3	171	168.33	−0.99	−7.89	0.13
9	19.2	173	166.20	−0.96	−8.66	0.12
10	17.5	175	164.45	−0.94	−9.42	0.11
50	3.8	188	150.76	−0.80	−40.05	0.02
100	1.9	190	148.90	−0.78	−78.33	0.01
200	1.0	191	147.96	−0.77	−154.89	0.01
∞	~0	192	147	−0.77	−∞	0

[10]In Appendix 13A, we derive the Cournot equilibrium quantity and price for a general linear demand. Given our particular demand curve, Equation 13.1, and marginal cost, \$147, each firm's Cournot equilibrium output is $q = (339 - 147)/(n + 1) = 192/(n + 1)$ and the Cournot market price is $p = (339 + 147n)/(n + 1)$.

number of firms grows, the residual demand curve for each firm becomes increasingly horizontal (perfectly elastic). As a result, the price approaches the marginal cost, $147. Similarly, as the number of firms increases, the Lerner Index approaches the price-taking level of zero.

The table shows that having extra firms in the market benefits consumers. When the number of firms rises from 1 to 4, the price falls by a quarter and the Lerner Index is cut nearly in half. At 10 firms, the price is one-third less than the monopoly level, and the Lerner Index is a quarter of the monopoly level.

Application   **APPLIANCES**

The European market for washing machines, refrigerators, and other appliances has many more firms than the U.S. market. The 5 largest manufacturers—Whirlpool, General Electric, Electrolux (Frigidaire), Maytag, and Raytheon—make 98% of U.S. appliance sales, whereas the top 10 firms in Europe—led by Electrolux, Bosch-Siemens, and Whirlpool—control only 72% of that market. This difference may explain why Whirlpool's American operation has a profit margin (an approximation of the Lerner Index) of 8%, while its European division earns only 4%.

13.5 | STACKELBERG MODEL OF NONCOOPERATIVE BEHAVIOR

In the Cournot model, both firms make their output decisions at the same time. Suppose, however, that one of the firms, called the *leader*, can set its output before its rival, the *follower*, sets its output. This type of game, in which the players make decisions sequentially, arises naturally if one firm enters a market before another.

Would the firm that got to act first have an advantage? Heinrich von Stackelberg showed how to modify the Cournot model to answer this question.

How does the leader decide to set its output? The leader realizes that once it sets its output, the rival firm will use its Cournot best-response curve to pick a best-response output. Thus the leader predicts what the follower will do before the follower acts. Using this knowledge, the leader manipulates the follower, thereby benefiting at the follower's expense.

We illustrate this model using our airlines market example (Appendix 13B analyzes the model mathematically). Although it is difficult to imagine that either American Airlines or United Airlines actually has an advantage that would allow it to act before its rival, we assume (arbitrarily) that American Airlines can act before United Airlines. We first examine how the airlines would behave if they could pick one of only a few quantities. Then we examine the more general problem, in which they can choose any quantity they want.

Stackelberg Game Tree

We illustrate the importance of moving first by using a *game tree*, Figure 13.5. The game tree shows the order of the firms' moves, each firm's possible strategies at the

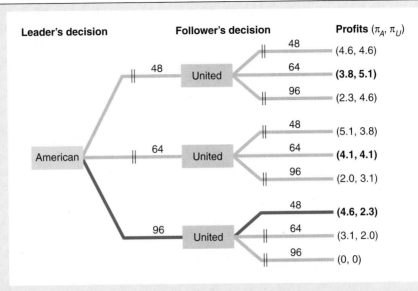

Figure 13.5 Stackelberg Game Tree. American, the leader firm, chooses its output level first. Given American's choice, United, the follower, picks an output level. The profits of the two firms that result from these decisions are shown on the right-hand side of the figure. Two lines through an action line show that the firm rejects that action.

time of its move, and the resulting profits. For simplicity, we assume that each airline can choose one of only three quantities, 48, 64, and 96.

Each line in the decision tree represents an action, and each box is a point of decision by one of the firms. American—the leader—starts by picking one of the three output levels (left side of the figure); then United—the follower—chooses one of the three quantities (middle of the figure), which determines the profits that American and United earn (right side of the figure). For instance, if American picks 64 and then United picks 96, American earns $2.0 million profit per quarter and United earns $3.1 million.

How should American, the leader, pick its output? For each possible quantity it can produce, American predicts what United will do and picks the output level that maximizes its profit.

To determine the strategies the firms use, we work backward from the follower's decision to the leader's. We first ask what United, the follower, would do, given each possible output choice of American, the leader. Then, using this information about United's reasoning, we determine which strategy American chooses.

United, the follower, does not have a dominant strategy. How much output it produces depends on the quantity that American chose. If American chooses 96, United's profit is $2.3 million if its output is 48, $2 million if it produces 64, and $0 if it picks a quantity of 96. Thus if American chose 96, United's best response is 48. The double lines through the other two action lines show that United will not choose those actions.

Using the same reasoning, American determines how United will respond to each of American's possible actions, as the right-hand side of the figure illustrates. Using its predictions of United's responses, American knows that

- If American chooses 48, United will sell 64, so American's profit will be $3.8 million.
- If American chooses 64, United will sell 64, so American's profit will be $4.1 million.
- If American chooses 96, United will sell 48, so American's profit will be $4.6 million.

Thus to maximize its profit, American chooses 96. United responds by selling 48.

This outcome is a Stackelberg (Nash) equilibrium. Given that American Airlines sets its output at 96, United is using a strategy that maximizes its profit, $q_U = 48$, so it doesn't want to change. Similarly, given how United will respond to each possible American output level, American can't make more profit than selling 96.

American, the Stackelberg leader, sells 50% more than the Cournot quantity, 64, and earns $4.6 million, which is 15% more than the Cournot level of profit, $4.1 million. United, the Stackelberg follower, sells a quantity, 48, and earns a profit, $2.3 million, both of which are less than the Cournot levels.

The value to American of being the leader is $0.5 (= $4.6 − $4.1) million, the amount its profit rises over the Cournot level. However, it is worth $1.8 (= $4.1 − $2.3) million to United Airlines not to be the follower.

Given the option to act first, American chooses a large output level to make it in United's best interest to pick a relatively small output level, 48. In this example, if the firms colluded and both produced 48, both would earn $4.6 million, which is what American earns as the leader. Why doesn't American pick the collusive output level, 48, so that both firms can earn the collusive profit? If American did so, it would be in United's best interest to sell 64 and earn $5.1 million, which would reduce American's profit to $3.8 million. Thus American produces a large output to keep United's output low.

Stackelberg Graphical Model

Now suppose that the airlines can choose any output level they want and that American Airlines chooses its output first. How does American decide on its optimal policy now?

American uses its residual demand curve to determine its profit-maximizing output. American knows that when it sets q_A, United will use its Cournot best-response function to pick its best-response q_U. Thus American's residual demand curve, D^r (panel a of Figure 13.6), is the market demand curve, D (panel a) minus the output United will produce as summarized by United's best-response curve (panel b). For example, if American sets $q_A = 192$, United's best response is $q_U = 0$ (as shown by United's best-response curve in panel b). As a result, the residual demand curve and the market demand curve are identical at $q_A = 192$ (panel a).

Similarly, if American set $q_A = 0$, United would choose $q_U = 96$, so the residual demand at $q_A = 0$ is 96 less than demand. The residual demand curve hits the vertical axis, where $q_A = 0$, at $p = 243, which is 96 units to the left of demand at that price. When $q_A = 96$, $q_U = 48$, so the residual demand at $q_A = 96$ is 48 units to the left of the demand.

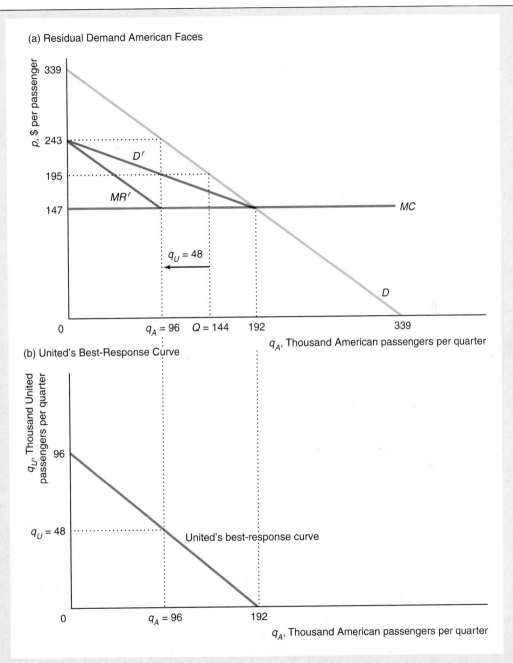

(a) Residual Demand American Faces

(b) United's Best-Response Curve

Figure 13.6 Stackelberg Equilibrium. (a) The residual demand the Stackelberg leader faces is the market demand minus the quantity produced by the follower, q_U, given the leader's quantity, q_A. The leader chooses $q_A = 96$ so that its marginal revenue, MR^r, equals its marginal cost. The total output, $Q = 144$, is the sum of the output of the two firms. (b) The quantity the follower produces is its best response to the leader's output, as given by its Cournot best-response curve.

American chooses its profit-maximizing output, $q_A = 96$, where its marginal revenue curve that corresponds to the residual demand curve, MR^r, equals its marginal cost, \$147. At $q_A = 96$, the price, which is the height of the residual demand curve, is \$195. Total demand at \$195 is $Q = 144$. At that price, United produces $q_U = Q - q_A = 48$, its best response to American's output of $q_A = 96$.

Thus in this Stackelberg equilibrium, the leader produces twice as much as the follower, as Figure 13.6 and panel a of Figure 13.4 show.[11] The total Stackelberg output, 144, is greater than the total Cournot, 128, and collusive, 96, outputs. As a result, the Stackelberg price, \$195, is less than the Cournot, \$211, and collusive, \$243, prices. Thus consumers prefer the Stackelberg equilibrium to the Cournot equilibrium and the Cournot equilibrium to the collusive equilibrium here (and in any market where all firms have identical cost functions).

The combined Stackelberg profit, \$6.9 million, is less than the combined Cournot, \$8 million, and collusive, \$9.2 million, profits, as panel b of Figure 13.4 shows. The Stackelberg leader, though, earns \$4.6 million, which is more than it could earn in a Cournot game, \$4.1 million. Total Stackelberg profit is less than total Cournot profit because the Stackelberg follower, earning \$2.3 million, is much worse off than in the Cournot equilibrium.

Why Moving Sequentially Is Essential

Why don't we get the Stackelberg equilibrium when both firms move simultaneously? Why doesn't one firm—say, American—announce that it will produce the Stackelberg leader output to induce United to produce the Stackelberg follower output level? The answer is that when the firms move simultaneously, United doesn't view American's warning that it will produce a large quantity as a *credible threat*.

If United believed that threat, it would indeed produce the Stackelberg follower output level. But United doesn't believe the threat because it is not in American's best interest to produce that large a quantity of output. If American were to produce the leader level of output and United produced the Cournot level, American's profit would be lower than if it too produced the Cournot level. Because American cannot be sure that United will believe its threat and reduce its output, American will actually produce the Cournot output level.

Indeed, each firm may make the same threat and announce that it wants to be the leader. Because neither firm can be sure that the other will be intimidated and produce the smaller quantity, both produce the Cournot output level. In contrast, when one firm moves first, its threat to produce a large quantity is credible because it has already *committed* to producing the larger quantity, thereby carrying out its threat.

★Strategic Trade Policy

Suppose that two identical firms in two different countries compete in a world market. Both firms act simultaneously, so neither firm can make itself the Stackelberg leader. A government may be tempted to intervene to make its firm a Stackelberg leader. The Japanese and French governments often help their domestic firms com-

---

[11]Here the leader produces the same quantity as a monopoly would, and the follower produces the same quantity as it would in the cartel equilibrium. These relationships are due to the linear demand curve and the constant marginal cost—they do not hold more generally.

pete with international rivals; so do the U.S., British, Canadian, and many other governments. If only one government intervenes, it can make its domestic firm's threat to produce a large quantity of output credible, so foreign rivals will produce the Stackelberg follower level of output (Spencer and Brander, 1983).

Subsidizing an Airline. We'll modify our airline example to illustrate how one country's government can aid its firm. Suppose that United Airlines were based in one country and American Airlines in another. Initially, United and American are in a Cournot equilibrium. Each firm has a marginal cost of $147 and flies 64 thousand passengers (64 units) per quarter at a price of $211.

Now suppose that United's government gives United a $48-per-passenger subsidy, but the other government doesn't help American. As a result, American's marginal cost remains at $147, but United's marginal cost after the subsidy is only $99.

The firms continue to play Cournot, but the playing field is no longer level.[12] How does the Cournot equilibrium change? Your intuition probably tells you that United's output increases relative to that of American, as we now show.

United still acts at the same time as American, so United acts like any Cournot firm and determines its best-response curve. United's best response to any given American output is the output at which its marginal revenue corresponding to its residual demand, MR^r, equals its marginal cost. The subsidy does not affect United's MR^r curve, but it lowers its MC curve, so United produces more output for any given American output after the cost falls.

Panel a of Figure 13.7 illustrates this reasoning. United's residual demand, D^r, lies 64 units to the left of the market demand, D, if American produces 64. The MR^r curve intersects the original marginal cost, $MC^1 = \$147$, at 64 and the new marginal cost, $MC^2 = \$99$, at 88. Thus if we hold American's output constant at 64, United produces more as its marginal cost falls.

Because this reasoning applies for any level of output American picks, United's best-response function in panel b shifts outward as its marginal cost falls.[13] United's best response to any given quantity that American sells is to sell more than at its previous, higher cost. As a result, the Cournot equilibrium shifts from the original e_1, at which both firms sold 64, to e_2, at which United sells 96 and American sells 48. Thus the $48 subsidy to United causes it to sell the Stackelberg leader quantity and American to sell the Stackelberg follower quantity. The subsidy works by convincing American that United will produce large quantities of output.

Using the market demand curve, Equation 13.1, we find that the market price falls from $211 to $195, benefiting consumers. United's profit increases from $4.1 million to $9.2 million, while American's profit falls to $2.3 million. Thus United and consumers gain and American loses from the fall in United's marginal cost.

---

[12]Don't you think that anyone who uses the phrase "level playing field" should have to pay a fine?

[13]United sets the marginal revenue that corresponds to its residual demand curve, MR^r, equal to its new marginal cost, MC:

$$MR^r = 339 - 2q_U - q_A = 99 = MC.$$

Using algebra to rearrange this expression, we find that United's best-response function is

$$q_U = 120 - \tfrac{1}{2}q_A.$$

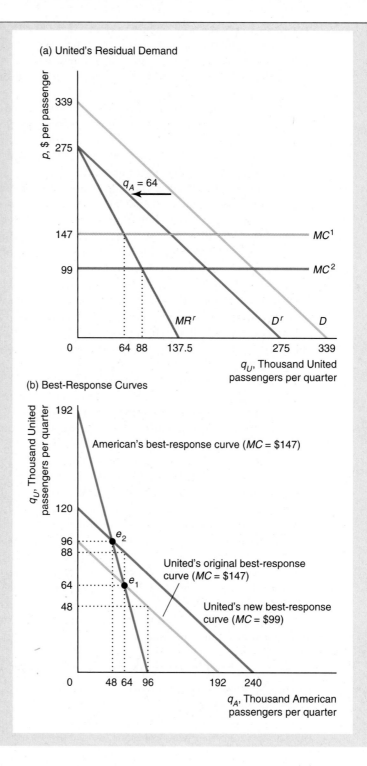

(a) United's Residual Demand

(b) Best-Response Curves

> **Figure 13.7 Effect of a Government Subsidy on a Cournot Equilibrium.** (a) A government subsidy that lowers United's marginal cost from $MC^1 = \$147$ to $MC^2 = \$99$ causes United's best-response output to American's $q_A = 64$ to rise from $q_U = 64$ to 88. (b) If both airlines' marginal costs are $147, the Cournot equilibrium is e_1. If United's marginal cost falls to $99, its best-response function shifts outward. It now sells more tickets in response to any given American output than previously. At the new Cournot equilibrium, e_2, United sells $q_U = 96$, while American sells only $q_A = 48$.

This example illustrates that a government subsidy to one firm *can* lead to the same outcome as in a Stackelberg equilibrium. Would a government *want* to give the subsidy that leads to the Stackelberg outcome?

The answer depends on the government's objective. Suppose that the government is interested in maximizing its domestic firm's profit net of (not including) the government's subsidy. The subsidy is a transfer from some citizens (taxpayers) to others (the owners of United). We assume that the government doesn't care about consumers—which is certainly true if they live in another country.

Table 13.4 shows the effects of various subsidies and a tax (a negative subsidy). If the subsidy is zero, we have the usual Cournot equilibrium. A $48-per-passenger subsidy leads to the same outcome as in the Stackelberg equilibrium and maximizes the government's welfare measure. At a larger subsidy, such as $60, United's profit rises, but by less than the cost of the subsidy to the government. Similarly, at smaller subsidies or taxes, welfare is also lower.

Problems with Intervention. Thus in theory, a government may want to subsidize its domestic firm to make it produce the same output as it would if it were a Stackelberg leader. If such subsidies are to work as desired, however, five conditions must hold.

Table 13.4 Effects of a Subsidy Given to United Airlines

Subsidy, s	United			American	
	q_U	π_U	Welfare, $\pi_U - sq_U$	q_A	π_A
60	104	$10.8	$4.58	44	$1.9
48	96	$9.2	$4.61	48	$2.3
30	84	$7.1	$4.50	54	$2.9
0	64	$4.1	$4.10	64	$4.1
−30	44	$1.9	$3.30	74	$5.5

Notes:
The subsidy is in dollars per passenger (and is a tax if negative).
Output units are in thousands of passengers per quarter.
Profits and welfare (defined as United's profits minus the subsidy)
  are in millions of dollars per quarter.

First, the government must be able to set its subsidy before the firms choose their output levels. The idea behind this intervention is that one firm cannot act before the other, but its government can act first.

Second, the other government must not retaliate. If both governments intervene, instead of having a game of strategies between firms, we have a game of strategies between governments, in which both countries may lose.

Third, the government's actions must be credible. If the foreign firm's country doesn't believe that the government actually will subsidize its domestic firm, the foreign firm produces the Cournot level. Countries have difficulty in committing to long-term policies. For example, during the 1996 Republican presidential primaries, many candidates said that they would reverse President Clinton's trade policies if they were elected.

Fourth, the government must know enough about how firms behave to intervene appropriately. If it doesn't know the demand function and the costs of all firms, the government may set its subsidy at the wrong level.

Fifth, the government must know which game the firms are playing. If they are not engaged in a Cournot game, the government would have to intervene in a different way (see Problem 6 at the end of the chapter).

Many economists who analyze strategic trade policies strongly oppose them because they are difficult to implement and mean-spirited, "beggar thy neighbor" policies. If only one government intervenes, another country's firm is harmed. If both governments intervene, both countries may suffer. For these reasons, the General Agreement on Tariffs and Trade and the World Trade Organization forbade the use of virtually all explicit export subsidies.

Application   AIRBUS AND BOEING

France, Germany, Spain, and the United Kingdom own Airbus, which competes in the widebody aircraft market with Boeing, a U.S. firm. Because of the large sunk costs of starting such a firm, major economies of scale, long product lives of planes, and substantial learning by doing, there may be room for only two firms in this market.

Boeing vehemently complains that the governments that own Airbus provide it with large subsidies that make it difficult for Boeing to compete. Airbus responds that the military contracts Boeing receives from the U.S. government are implicit subsidies.

Using a Cournot model similar to the one we just used to examine subsidies to an airline company, Baldwin and Krugman (1988) examined how a subsidy to Airbus would affect this market under various scenarios. They illustrated that the subsidies benefited consumers worldwide because the Stackelberg price is below the (unsubsidized) Cournot price. Their simulations, however, indicated that U.S. firms were net losers from the subsidy: The fall in Boeing's profits was greater than the increase in the consumer surplus of U.S. airline firms that buy planes. Even more striking, they found that the European countries also lost after paying the subsidy: The subsidy was not set optimally even from the standpoint of the European governments.

Solved Problem 13.1   **If the government charges identical Cournot duopolies a specific tax of τ per unit of output, what is the qualitative effect (direction of change) on the equilibrium quantities and price? Assume that the before-tax best-response functions are linear.**

Answer

1. *Show the initial, before-tax Cournot equilibrium:* We're told that the Cournot firms, labeled Firm A and Firm B on the graph, are identical. As a result, their best-response curves are mirror images of each other, and both firms produce the same quantity, q_1, at the Cournot equilibrium, e_1, where their best-response functions cross.

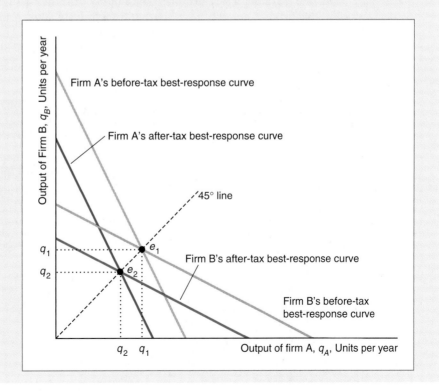

2. *Show how the best-response curves shift in response to the tax*: We've just seen that a subsidy lowers a firm's marginal cost, causing its best-response curve to shift away from the origin. Thus a tax (which is a negative subsidy) raises a firm's marginal cost, causing its best-response curve to shift inward. Because both firms face the same specific tax, marginal costs of both firms rise by the same amount. As a result, both after-tax best-response curves shift toward the origin by the same amount and remain mirror images of each other.

3. *Compare the two Cournot equilibria*: Each firm produces a smaller quantity, q_2, at the new Cournot equilibrium, e_2, than in the original Cournot equilibrium. As a result, total equilibrium quantity falls and the equilibrium price rises.

13.6   COMPARISON OF COLLUSIVE, COURNOT, STACKELBERG, AND COMPETITIVE EQUILIBRIA

The welfare of consumers and firms depends on the market structure, as Table 13.5 shows for our airline example. In this table, the welfare measure is the sum of consumer surplus and the profits of the two firms.

At one extreme, if one firm has a monopoly or if the two firms form a cartel and split the market equally, total output is relatively low, price is high, consumer surplus and welfare are low, and deadweight loss is high. At the other extreme, if American and United act as price takers, output is relatively high, price is low, consumer surplus and welfare are high, and society does not suffer a deadweight loss.

Table 13.5 Comparison of Airline Market Structures

	Monopoly	Cartel	Cournot	Stackelberg	Price Taking
q_A	96	48	64	96	96
q_U	0	48	64	48	96
$Q = q_A + q_U$	96	96	128	144	192
p	$243	$243	$211	$195	$147
π_A	$9.2	$4.6	$4.1	$4.6	$0
π_U	$0	$4.6	$4.1	$2.3	$0
$\Pi = \pi_A + \pi_U$	$9.2	$9.2	$8.2	$6.9	$0
Consumer surplus, CS	$4.6	$4.6	$8.2	$10.4	$18.4
Welfare, $W = CS + \Pi$	$13.8	$13.8	$16.4	$17.3	$18.4
Deadweight loss, DWL	$4.6	$4.6	$2.0	$1.2	$0

Notes:
Passengers are in thousands per quarter.
Price is in dollars per passenger.
Profits, consumer surplus, welfare, and deadweight loss are in millions of dollars per quarter.

The duopoly Cournot and Stackelberg equilibria (in the table, American is the leader) lie between the extreme cases of monopoly or cartel and price taking. The Stackelberg equilibrium is closer to the price-taking equilibrium than the Cournot equilibrium in terms of total output, price, consumer surplus, welfare, and deadweight loss.

We already know that the Cournot equilibrium approaches the price-taking equilibrium as the number of firms grows. Similarly, we can show that the Stackelberg equilibrium approaches the price-taking equilibrium as the number of Stackelberg followers grows. As a result, the differences between the Cournot, Stackelberg, and price-taking market structures shrink as the number of firms grows.

Application   **DEADWEIGHT LOSSES IN THE FOOD AND TOBACCO INDUSTRIES**

Bhuyan and Lopez (1998) estimated the deadweight loss for various U.S. food and tobacco manufacturing oligopolies and monopolistically competitive markets. Most of these industries have deadweight losses that are a relatively small percentage of sales (their prices and quantities are close to competitive levels). However, a few industries, such as cereal and flour and grain mills, have relatively large deadweight losses.

Industry	Loss, $ millions	Share of Sales, %
Cereal	2,192	33
Flour and grain mills	541	26
Poultry and eggs	1,183	8
Roasted coffee	440	7
Cigarettes	1,032	6
All food manufacturing	14,947	5

13.7   **MONOPOLISTIC COMPETITION**

We've assumed that the number of oligopoly firms is fixed because of barriers to entry. As a result, the oligopoly firms (such as the airlines) may earn economic profits. In contrast, monopolistically competitive markets do not have barriers to entry, so firms enter the market until no new firm can enter profitably.

If both competitive and monopolistically competitive firms make zero profits, what distinguishes these two market structures? In contrast to competitive firms (which face horizontal residual demand curves and charge prices equal to marginal cost), monopolistically competitive firms face downward-sloping residual demand curves, so they charge prices above marginal cost. Monopolistically competitive firms face downward-sloping residual demand because they have relatively few rivals or because they sell differentiated products.

The fewer monopolistically competitive firms, the less elastic the residual demand curve each firm faces. As we saw, the elasticity of demand for an individual Cournot firm is $n\varepsilon$, where n is the number of firms and ε is the market elasticity. Thus the fewer the firms in a market, the less elastic the residual demand curve.

When monopolistically competitive firms benefit from economies of scale at high levels of output (the average cost curve is downward sloping), so that each firm is relatively large in comparison to market demand, there is room in the market for only a few firms. In the short run, if fixed costs are large and marginal costs are constant or diminishing, firms have economies of scale (Chapter 7) at all output levels, so there are relatively few firms in the market. In an extreme case with substantial enough economies of scale, the market may have room for only one firm: a natural monopoly (Chapter 11). The number of firms in equilibrium is smaller the greater the economies of scale and the farther to the left the market demand curve.

Monopolistically competitive firms also face downward-sloping residual demand curves if each firm sells a differentiated product. If some consumers believe that Tide laundry detergent is better than Cheer and other brands, Tide won't lose all its sales even if Tide has a slightly higher price than Cheer. Thus Tide faces a downward-sloping demand curve—not a horizontal one.

Monopolistically Competitive Equilibrium

In a monopolistically competitive market, each firm tries to maximize its profit; however, each makes zero economic profit due to entry. Two conditions hold in a monopolistically competitive equilibrium: *Marginal revenue equals marginal cost* (because firms set output to maximize profit), and *price equals average cost* (because firms enter until no further profitable entry is possible).

Figure 13.8 shows a monopolistically competitive market equilibrium. A typical monopolistically competitive firm faces a residual demand curve D^r. To maximize its profit, the firm sets its output, q, where its marginal revenue curve corresponding to the residual demand curve intersects its marginal cost curve: $MR^r = MC$. At that quantity, the firm's average cost curve, AC, is tangent to its residual demand curve. Because the height of the residual demand curve is the price, at the point of tangency, price equals average cost, $p = AC$, and the firm makes zero profit.

If the average cost were less than price at that quantity, firms would make positive profits and entrants would be attracted. If average cost were above price, firms would lose money, so firms would exit until the marginal firm was breaking even.

The smallest quantity at which the average cost curve reaches its minimum is referred to as *full capacity* or **minimum efficient scale**. The firm's full capacity or minimum efficient scale is the quantity at which the firm no longer benefits from economies of scale. Because a monopolistically competitive equilibrium occurs in the downward-sloping section of the average cost curve (where the average cost curve is tangent to the downward-sloping demand curve), a monopolistically competitive firm operates at less than full capacity in the long run.

Fixed Costs and the Number of Firms

The number of firms in a monopolistically competitive equilibrium depends on firms' costs. The larger each firm's fixed cost, the smaller the number of monopolistically competitive firms in the market equilibrium.

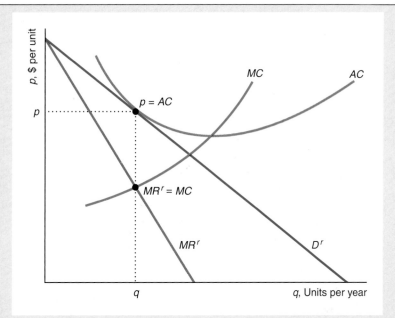

Figure 13.8 Monopolistically Competitive Equilibrium. A monopolistically competitive firm, facing residual demand curve D^r, sets its output where its marginal revenue equals its marginal cost: $MR^r = MC$. Because firms can enter this market, the profit of the firm is driven to zero, so price equals the firm's average cost: $p = AC$.

Although entry is free, if the fixed costs are high, few firms may enter. In the automobile industry, just to develop a new fender costs $8 to $10 million.[14] Developing a new pharmaceutical drug may cost $350 million or more.

We can illustrate this relationship using the airlines example, in which we modify our assumptions about entry and fixed costs. American and United are the only airlines providing service on the Chicago–Los Angeles route. Until now, we have assumed that a barrier to entry—such as an inability to obtain landing rights at both airports—prevented entry and that the firms had no fixed costs. If fixed cost is zero and marginal cost is constant at $147 per passenger, average cost is also constant at $147 per passenger. As we showed earlier, each firm in this oligopolistic market flies $q = 64$ per quarter at a price of $p = \$211$ and makes a profit of $4.1 million per quarter.

---

[14]Treece, James B., "Sometimes, You Gotta Have Size," *Business Week*, Enterprise 1993:200–1. Treece illustrates the role of fixed costs on entry in the following anecdote: "In 1946, steel magnate Henry J. Kaiser boasted to a Detroit dinner gathering that two recent stock offerings had raised a huge $50 million to invest in his budding car company. Suddenly, a voice from the back of the room shot out: 'Give that man one white chip.'"

Now suppose that there are no barriers to entry, but each airline incurs a fixed cost, F, due to airport fees, capital expenditure, or other factors. Each firm's marginal cost remains $147 per passenger, but its average cost,

$$AC = 147 + \frac{F}{q},$$

falls as the number of passengers rises, as panels a and b of Figure 13.9 illustrate for $F = \$2.3$ million.

If there are only two firms in a monopolistically competitive market, what must the fixed costs be so that the two firms earn zero profit? We know that these firms receive a profit of $4.1 million per firm in the absence of fixed costs. As a result, the fixed cost must be $4.1 million per firm for the firms to earn zero profit. With this fixed cost, the monopolistically competitive price and quantity are the same as in the oligopolistic equilibrium, $q = 64$ and $p = \$211$, and the number of firms is the same, but now each firm's profit is zero.

If the fixed cost is only $2.3 million and there are only two firms in the market, each firm makes a profit, as panel a shows. Each duopoly firm faces a residual demand curve (labeled "D^r for 2 firms"), which is the market demand minus its rival's Cournot equilibrium quantity, $q = 64$. Given this residual demand, each firm

Figure 13.9 Monopolistic Competition Among Airlines. (a) If each identical airline has a fixed cost of $2.3 million and there are two firms in the market, each firm flies $q = 64$ units (thousands of passengers) per quarter at a price of $p = \$211$ per passenger and makes a profit of $1.8 million. This profit attracts entry. (b) After a third firm enters, the residual demand curve shifts, so each firm flies $q = 48$ units at $p = \$195$ and makes zero profit, which is the monopolistically competitive equilibrium.

produces $q = 64$, which equates its marginal revenue, MR^r, and its marginal cost, MC. At $q = 64$, the firm's average cost is $AC = \$147 + (\$2.3 \text{ million})/(64 \text{ units}) \approx \$183$, so each firm makes a profit of $\pi = (p - AC)q \approx (\$211 - \$183) \times 64$ units per quarter $\approx \$1.8$ million per quarter.

This substantial economic profit attracts an entrant. The entry of a third firm causes the residual demand for any one firm to shift to the left in panel b. In the new equilibrium, each firm sets $q = 48$ and charges $p = \$195$. At this quantity, each firm's average cost is $\$195$, so the firms break even. No other firms enter because if one did, the residual demand curve would shift even farther to the left and all the firms would lose money. Thus if fixed cost is $\$2.3$ million, there are three firms in the monopolistically competitive equilibrium. This example illustrates a general result: *The lower the fixed costs, the more firms there are in the monopolistically competitive equilibrium.*

Solved Problem 13.2 **What is the monopolistically competitive airline equilibrium if each firm has a fixed cost of $3 million?**

Answer

1. *Determine the number of firms*: We already know that the monopolistically competitive equilibrium has two firms if the fixed cost is $4.1 million and three firms if the fixed cost is $2.3 million. With a fixed cost of $3 million, if there are only two firms in the market, each makes a profit of $1.1 (= $4.1 – 3) million. If another firm enters, though, each firm's loss equals –$0.7 (= 2.3 – 3) million. Thus the monopolistically competitive equilibrium has two firms, each of which earns a positive profit that is too small to attract another firm. This outcome is a monopolistically competitive equilibrium because no other firm wants to enter.

2. *Determine the equilibrium quantities and prices*: We already know that each duopoly firm produces $q = 64$, so $Q = 128$ and $p = \$211$.

Application **ENTRY AND AIRLINE PRICES**

Entry lowers the oligopoly price. When People Express Airlines expanded its operations into 24 new domestic nonstop markets in 1984 and 1985, the incumbent airlines on routes entered by People Express suffered $6.8 million to $12.0 million in pretax losses (Whinston and Collins, 1992). This loss is equivalent to what would occur if incumbents were forced to fly their planes empty for three to five months.

All else the same, prices are higher in oligopolies, in which entry is difficult, than in monopolistically competitive markets, in which entry is relatively easy.

The effect of entry on price is illustrated by comparing airline shuttle flights on the East and West coasts. During much of 1995, shuttle flights between Burbank or Los Angeles in southern California and Oakland or San Francisco in northern California cost $69 (and dipped as low as $39) for the roughly 330-mile trip. At the same time, flying the approximately 230-mile trip between New York and Washington, D.C., or the 190-mile trip between New York and Boston cost $147 on Delta or USAir.

Though there are many differences between these two markets that might account for the higher price on the East Coast, one explanation concerns the number of actual and potential competitors. At least five airlines fly between northern and southern California, and there is always the threat of additional entry, which helps keep the price down in the West. In contrast, at both La Guardia Airport in New York and Reagan National Airport in Washington, the number of landing slots is controlled, effectively guaranteeing that Delta and USAir have a duopoly on that route. As one industry expert observed when asked why Delta and USAir keep their fares higher, "So why should they get in a cat fight when they're both doing well? It isn't like the West Coast shuttle, where anybody can go into that market."

Similarly, European airlines charge much more per mile for domestic flights than U.S. domestic airlines do. Most European countries strictly limit the number of airline companies, whereas entry is relatively easy for many routes in the United States.

13.8 | BERTRAND PRICE-SETTING MODEL

We have examined how oligopolistic and monopolistically competitive firms set quantities to try to maximize their profits. However, many such firms set prices instead of quantities and allow consumers to decide how much to buy. The market equilibrium is different if firms set prices rather than quantities.

In monopolistic and competitive markets, the issue of whether firms set quantities or prices does not arise. Competitive firms have no choice: They cannot affect price and hence can choose only quantity (Chapter 8). The monopoly equilibrium is the same whether the monopoly sets price or quantity (Chapter 11).

In 1883, Joseph Bertrand argued that oligopolies set prices, and then consumers decide how many units to buy. The resulting Nash equilibrium is called a **Bertrand equilibrium**: a set of prices such that no firm can obtain a higher profit by choosing a different price if the other firms continue to charge these prices.

We will show that the price and quantity in a Bertrand equilibrium are different from those in a Cournot equilibrium. We will also show that a Bertrand equilibrium depends on whether firms are producing identical or differentiated products.

Bertrand Equilibrium with Identical Products

We start by examining a price-setting oligopoly in which firms have identical costs and produce identical goods. The resulting Bertrand equilibrium price equals the marginal cost, as in the price-taking equilibrium. To show this result, we use best-response curves to determine the Bertrand equilibrium, as we did in the Cournot model.

Best-Response Curves. Suppose that each of the two price-setting oligopoly firms in a market produces an identical product and faces a constant marginal and average cost of $5 per unit. What is Firm 1's best response—what price should it set—if Firm 2 sets a price of $p_2 = \$10$? If Firm 1 charges more than $10, it makes no sales because consumers will buy from Firm 2. Firm 1 makes a profit of $5 on each unit it sells if it also charges $10 per unit. If the market demand is 200 units and both firms charge the same price, we'd expect Firm 1 to make half the sales, so its profit is $500.

Suppose, however, that Firm 1 slightly undercuts its rival's price by charging $9.99. Because the products are identical, Firm 1 captures the entire market. Firm 1 makes a profit of $4.99 per unit and a total profit of $998. Thus Firm 1's profit is higher if it slightly undercuts its rival's price. By similar reasoning, if Firm 2 charges $8, Firm 1 also charges slightly less than Firm 2.

Now imagine that Firm 2 charges $p_2 = \$5$. If Firm 1 charges more than $5, it makes no sales. The firms split the market and make zero profit if Firm 1 charges $5. If Firm 1 undercuts its rival, it captures the entire market, but it makes a loss on each unit. Thus Firm 1 will undercut only if its rival's price is higher than Firm 1's marginal and average cost of $5. By similar reasoning, if Firm 2 charges less than $5, Firm 1 chooses not to produce.

Figure 13.10 shows that Firm 1's best response is to produce nothing if Firm 2 charges less than $5. Firm 1's best response is $5 if Firm 2 charges $5. If Firm 2 charges prices above $5, Firm 1's best response is to undercut Firm 2's price slightly. Above $5, Firm 1's best-response curve is above the 45° line by the smallest amount possible. (The distance of the best-response curve from the 45° line is exaggerated in the figure for clarity.) By the same reasoning, Firm 2's best-response curve starts at $5 and lies slightly below the 45° line.

The two best-response functions intersect only at e, where each firm charges $5. It does not pay for either firm to change its price as long as the other charges $5, so e is a Nash or Bertrand equilibrium. In this equilibrium, each firm makes zero profit. Thus *the Bertrand equilibrium when firms produce identical products is the same as the price-taking, competitive equilibrium.*

Bertrand Versus Cournot. The Bertrand equilibrium differs substantially from the Cournot equilibrium. We can calculate the Cournot equilibrium price for firms with constant marginal costs of $5 per unit by rearranging Equation 13.8:

$$p = \frac{MC}{1 + 1 / (n\varepsilon)} = \frac{\$5}{1 + 1 / (n\varepsilon)}, \tag{13.10}$$

where n is the number of firms and ε is the market demand elasticity. If the market demand elasticity is $\varepsilon = -1$ and $n = 2$, the Cournot equilibrium price is $\$5/(1 - \frac{1}{2}) = \$10$, which is double the Bertrand equilibrium price.

When firms produce identical products and have a constant marginal cost, the Cournot model is more plausible than the Bertrand. The Bertrand model—unlike the Cournot model—appears inconsistent with real oligopoly markets in at least two ways.

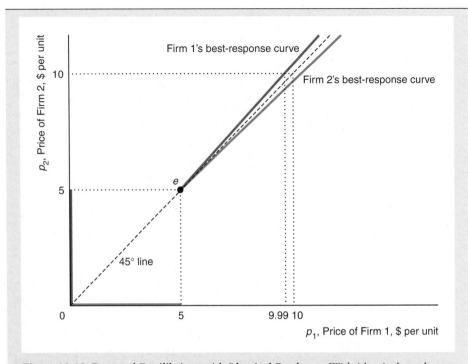

Figure 13.10 Bertrand Equilibrium with Identical Products. With identical products and constant marginal and average costs of $5, Firm 1's best-response curve starts at $5 and then lies slightly above the 45° line. That is, Firm 1 undercuts its rival's price as long as its price remains above $5. The best-response curves intersect at *e*, the Bertrand or Nash equilibrium, where both firms charge $5.

First, the Bertrand model's "competitive" equilibrium price is implausible. If there is only a small number of firms, why would they compete so vigorously that they would make no profit? In contrast, the Cournot equilibrium price with a small number of firms lies between the competitive price and the monopoly price. Because oligopolies typically charge a higher price than competitive firms, the Cournot equilibrium is more plausible.

Second, the Bertrand equilibrium price, which depends only on cost, is insensitive to demand conditions and the number of firms. In contrast, the Cournot equilibrium price, Equation 13.10, depends on the number of firms and demand and cost conditions. In our example, if the number of firms rises from two to three, the Cournot price falls from $10 to $5/(1 − $\frac{1}{3}$) = $7.50, but the Bertrand equilibrium price remains $5. Again, the Cournot model is more plausible because we usually observe market price changing with the number of firms and demand conditions, not just with changes in costs.

As a result, it seems more likely that when firms' products are identical, firms set quantities rather than prices. For these reasons, economists are much more likely to use the Cournot model than the Bertrand model to study markets in which firms produce identical goods.

Bertrand Equilibrium with Differentiated Products

If most markets were characterized by firms producing homogeneous goods, the Bertrand model would probably have been forgotten. Markets with differentiated goods—automobiles, stereos, computers, toothpastes, and spaghetti sauces—however, are extremely common, as is price setting by firms. In such markets, the Bertrand equilibrium is plausible, and the two "problems" of the homogeneous-goods model disappear: Firms set prices above marginal cost, and prices are sensitive to demand conditions.

Indeed, many economists believe that price-setting models are more plausible than quantity-setting models when goods are differentiated. If products are differentiated and firms set prices, then consumers determine quantities. In contrast, if firms set quantities, it is not clear how the prices of the differentiated goods are determined in the market.

We illustrate a Bertrand equilibrium with the differentiated products in the cola market. We use best-response curves in a figure to solve for the equilibrium.

Coke and Pepsi produce similar but not identical products; many consumers prefer one of these products to the other. If the price of Pepsi were to fall slightly relative to that of Coke, some consumers who prefer Coke to Pepsi would not switch. Thus neither firm has to match exactly a price cut by its rival. As a result, neither firm's best-response curve in Figure 13.11 lies along a 45° line through the origin.[15]

The Bertrand best-response curves have different slopes than the Cournot best-response curves in Figure 13.3. The Cournot curves—which plot relationships between quantities—slope downward, showing that a firm produces less the more its rival produces. In Figure 13.11, the Bertrand best-response curves—which plot relationships between prices—slope upward, indicating that a firm charges a higher price the higher the price its rival charges.

If both Pepsi and Coke have a constant marginal cost of $MC_p = MC_c = \$5$, the Bertrand equilibrium, e_1 in Figure 13.11, occurs where the price of each firm is $13 per unit (10 cases). In this Nash equilibrium, each firm sets its best-response price *given the price the other firm is charging*. Neither firm wants to change its price because neither firm can increase its profit by so doing. (See Appendix 13C for a mathematical presentation.)

Differentiating Products

I couldn't believe no one had addressed the mule market.   —Sharon Doherty, president of Vellus Products, on discovering a market niche for mule shampoo and conditioners

The Bertrand model demonstrates that firms can profit from selling differentiated products. If products are homogeneous, Bertrand firms cannot charge above marginal cost. With differentiated products, they can charge prices above marginal

---

[15]The figure is based on Bertrand estimates from Gasmi, Laffont, and Vuong (1992). Their estimated model allows the firms to set both prices and advertising. We assume that the firms' advertising is held constant. The Coke equations are the authors' estimates (with slight rounding). The Pepsi equations are rescaled so that the equilibrium prices of Coke and Pepsi are equal. Quantities are in tens of millions of cases (a case consists of 24 twelve-ounce cans) per quarter, and prices (to retailers) and costs are in real 1982 dollars per 10 cases.

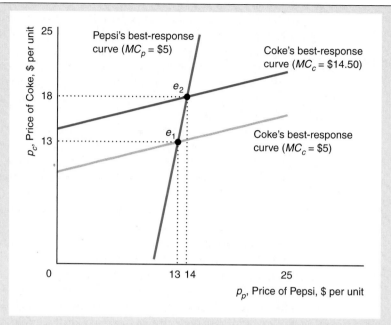

Figure 13.11 Bertrand Equilibrium with Differentiated Products. If both firms have a constant marginal cost of $5, the best-response curves of Coke and Pepsi intersect at e_1, where each sets a price of $13 per unit. If Coke's marginal cost rises to $14.50, its best-response function shifts upward. In the new equilibrium, e_2, Coke charges a higher price, $18, than Pepsi, $14.

cost and make larger profits. Firms aggressively differentiate their products to raise profits. By such differentiation, they affect the average price in a market and welfare.

Economists view products as differentiated if consumers *believe* that they differ. Although few consumers can reliably distinguish Coke from Pepsi in blind taste tests, many consumers strongly prefer buying one product over the other. Conversely, if consumers view products that differ chemically or physically to be identical, the products are homogeneous for the purposes of economic analysis. A firm can differentiate its product from its rivals' by changing a product characteristic consumers view as important (taste or appearance), or the firm can convince consumers that its product differs through advertising and other means, even if the products do not differ physically.

Application   **TOOTHBRUSHES**

Firms constantly add features to their products to differentiate them. Oral-B toothbrushes now have blue bristles that fade to white when it's time to replace the toothbrush, as well as ribbed thumb grips to prevent the brushes from slipping when wet. Johnson & Johnson's pink Good & Plenty Color Youth Glow model has a luminescent grip; Aquafresh Flex features a built-in shock absorber and special handle for "brushing control"; and the Radius toothbrush offers a left-hand grip. For toddlers, some toothbrushes sing, others rattle, and some smell like bananas. In 1999, Oral-B introduced its CrossAction toothbrush, with bristles angled in opposite directions and a thick handle. The brush sells for $4.99, double the price of top-line rivals. To accommodate this proliferation of toothbrushes, the average retail store's toothbrush section is now 4 feet wide.

Product Differentiation and Price. Whether the difference is a nonslip handle or a sneaker pump, if a firm can convince some customers that its brand is superior in some fashion, it can charge a higher price than it could if it sold plain or generic products. Clorox and Bayer are just two examples of firms that charge higher prices for products (bleach and aspirin, respectively) that have an active ingredient that is chemically identical to that of generic brands.

The reason differentiation allows a firm to charge a higher price is that the residual demand curve the firm faces (the market demand minus the quantity supplied by rivals at each price) becomes less elastic. That is, a given decrease in the price charged by a rival lowers the demand for this firm's product by *less*, the less substitutable are the two goods. If consumers view the goods as perfect substitutes, a small drop in the rival's price causes this firm to lose all its sales. If some consumers become convinced that this firm's product is superior in some way, they do not switch to the rival if the rival lowers its price slightly.

Product Differentiation and Welfare. Thus prices are likely to be higher when products are differentiated than when they're identical, all else the same. We also know that welfare falls as the gap between price and marginal cost rises. Does it follow that differentiating products lowers welfare? Not necessarily. Although differentiation leads to higher prices, which harm consumers, differentiation is desirable in its own right. Consumers value having a choice, and some may greatly prefer a new brand to existing ones.

One way to illustrate the importance of this second effect is to consider what the value is of introducing a new, differentiated product. This value reflects how much extra income consumers would require to be as well off without the good as with it.

Application WELFARE GAIN FROM NEW CEREALS

Jerry Hausman (1997) calculated the consumer surplus from General Mills' introducing Apple-Cinnamon Cheerios at $67 million per year, or 26.8¢ per person. Offsetting this gain is the increase in the prices of other cereals that General Mills was already selling, including regular Cheerios and Honey-Nut Cheerios. By introducing the new product, General Mills found it profitable to raise the price of the existing brands slightly because some of their lost sales would go to Apple-Cinnamon Cheerios. Hausman calculated that the profit-maximizing increase in the price of Honey-Nut Cheerios was 8¢ a box and that of Cheerios was 1¢. (Honey-Nut Cheerios is a closer substitute to Apple-Cinnamon Cheerios than regular Cheerios is.) Overall, however, welfare increased because the consumer surplus gains from the new brand outweighs the loss from higher prices.[16]

Summary

1. **Market structures:** Prices, profits, and quantities in a market equilibrium depend on the market's structure. Because profit-maximizing firms set marginal revenue equal to marginal cost, price is above marginal revenue—and hence marginal cost—only if firms face downward-sloping demand curves. In monopoly, oligopoly, and monopolistically competitive markets, firms face downward-sloping demand curves, in contrast to firms in a competitive market. When entry is blocked, as with a monopoly or an oligopoly, firms may earn positive profits; however, when entry is free, as in competition or monopolistic competition, profits are driven toward zero. Noncooperative oligopoly and monopolistically competitive firms, in contrast to competitive and monopoly firms, must pay attention to their rivals.

2. **Game theory:** The set of tools that economists use to analyze conflict and cooperation between firms is called game theory. Each oligopolistic or monopolistically competitive firm adopts a strategy or battle plan of action to compete with other firms. The firms' set of strategies is a Nash equilibrium if, holding the strategies of all other firms constant, no firm can obtain a higher profit by choosing a different strategy.

3. **Cooperative oligopoly models:** If firms successfully collude, they produce the monopoly output and collectively earn the monopoly level of profit. Although their collective profits rise if all firms collude, each individual firm has an incentive to cheat on a cartel arrangement so as to raise its own profit even higher. For cartel prices to remain high, cartel members must be able to detect and prevent cheat-

ing, and noncartel firms must not be able to supply very much output. When antitrust laws or competition policies prevent firms from colluding, firms may try to merge if permitted by law.

4. **Cournot model of noncooperative oligopoly:** If oligopoly firms act independently, the market output and firms' profits lie between the competitive and monopoly levels. In a Cournot model, each oligopoly firm sets its output at the same time. In the Cournot (Nash) equilibrium, each firm produces its best-response output—the output that maximizes its profit—given the output its rival produces. As the number of Cournot firms increases, the Cournot equilibrium price, quantity, and profits approach the price-taking levels.

5. **Stackelberg model of noncooperative behavior:** If one firm, the Stackelberg leader, chooses its output before its rivals, the Stackelberg followers, the leader produces more and earns a higher profit than each identical-cost follower firm. A government may subsidize a domestic oligopoly firm so that it produces the Stackelberg leader quantity, which it sells in an international market.

6. **Comparison of collusive, Cournot, Stackelberg, and competitive equilibria:** Total market output is maximized and price is minimized under competition. For a given number of firms, the Stackelberg equilibrium output exceeds that of the Cournot equilibrium, which exceeds that of the collusive equilibrium (which is the same as a monopoly produces). Correspondingly, the Stackelberg price is less than the Cournot price, which is less than the collusive or monopoly price.

---

[16]Hausman also concluded that the Consumer Price Index (Chapter 5) for cereal overstates inflation by about 20% because it fails to take the benefit of new brands into account.

7. **Monopolistic competition:** In monopolistically competitive markets, after all profitable entry occurs, there are few enough firms in the market that each firm faces a downward-sloping demand curve. Consequently, the firms charge prices above marginal cost. These markets are not perfectly competitive because there are relatively few firms—possibly because of high fixed costs or economies of scale that are large relative to market demand—or because the firms sell differentiated products.

8. **Bertrand price-setting model:** In many oligopolistic or monopolistically competitive markets, firms set prices instead of quantities. If the product is homogeneous and firms set prices, the Bertrand equilibrium price equals marginal cost (which is lower than the Cournot quantity-setting equilibrium price). If the products are differentiated, the Bertrand equilibrium price is above marginal cost. Typically, the markup of price over marginal cost is greater the more the goods are differentiated.

Problems

1. Show the payoff matrix and explain the reasoning in the prisoners' dilemma example involving criminals given in footnote 2 in this chapter. (*Note:* The payoffs are negative because they represent years in jail, which is a bad.)

2. Using a graph and words, explain why an individual firm has an incentive to cheat on a cartel.

3. Two firms are planning to sell 10 or 20 units of their goods and face the following payoff matrix:

		Firm 2	
		10	20
Firm 1	10	30 / 30	35 / 50
	20	60 / 40	20 / 20

a. What is the Nash equilibrium if both firms make their decisions simultaneously? Why? (What strategy does each firm use?)

b. Suppose that Firm 1 can decide first. What is the outcome? Why?

c. Suppose that Firm 2 can decide first. What is the outcome? Why?

4. In 1994, Southwest Airlines' cost-per-available-seat mile was well below that of most of its big rivals and 35% lower than that of the worst performer, USAir. Assuming that Southwest and USAir compete on a route, use a graph to show that their equilibrium quantities differ.

5. Your college is considering renting space in the student union to one or two commercial textbook stores. The rent the college can charge per square foot of space depends on the profit (before rent) of the firms and hence on whether there is a monopoly or a duopoly. Which number of stores is better for the college in terms of rent? Which is better for students? Why?

★6. Suppose that competitive firms in two countries sell in a third country. Each country's supply curve is upward sloping. The government in Country 1 is thinking of taxing or subsidizing its firms to increase national profits (not including the subsidy). The government does not expect the government of Country 2 to retaliate. Using a graph, show that the optimal policy is a tax.

★7. Suppose that two Cournot firms, each located in a different country, sell only in a third country's market. Both governments act to help their domestic firm. Who gains and who loses?

8. In the initial Cournot duopoly equilibrium, both firms have constant marginal costs, m, and no fixed costs, and there is a barrier to entry. Show what happens to the best-response function of firms if both firms now face a fixed cost of F.

9. In the monopolistically competitive airline model, what is the equilibrium if firms face no fixed costs?

10. In a monopolistically competitive market, the government applies a specific tax of $1 per unit of output. What happens to the profit of a typical firm in this market? Does the number of firms in the market change? Why?

11. Does an oligopoly or a monopolistically competitive firm have a supply curve? Why or why not? (*Hint:* See the discussion in Chapter 11 of whether a monopoly has a supply curve.)

12. Will the price be lower if duopoly firms set price or if they set quantity? Under what conditions can you give a definitive answer to this question?

13. Why does differentiating its product allow an oligopoly to charge a higher price?

14. In the initial Bertrand equilibrium, two firms with differentiated products charge the same equilibrium prices. A consumer testing agency praises the product of one firm, causing its demand curve to shift to the right as new customers start buying the product. (The demand curve of the other product is not substantially affected.) Use a graph to illustrate how this new information affects the Bertrand equilibrium. What happens to the equilibrium prices of the two firms?

15. In the Coke and Pepsi example, what is the effect of a specific tax, τ, on the equilibrium prices? (*Hint*: What does the tax do to the firm's marginal cost?)

16. In 1998, California became the first state to adopt rules requiring many sport utility vehicles, pickups, and minivans to meet the same pollution standards as regular cars, effective in 2004. A business group (which may have an incentive to exaggerate) estimates that using the new technology to reduce pollution would increase vehicle prices by as much as $7,000. A spokesperson for the California Air Resources Board, which imposed the mandate, says that the additional materials cost is only about $70 to $270 per vehicle. Suppose that the two major producers are Toyota and Ford, and these firms are price setters with differentiated products. Show the effect of the new regulation. Is it possible that the price for these vehicles will rise by substantially more than marginal cost does?

Math Problems

17. A duopoly faces a market demand of $p = 120 - Q$. Firm 1 has a constant marginal cost of $MC^1 = 20$. Firm 2's constant marginal cost is $MC^2 = 40$. Calculate the output of each firm, market output, and price if there is (a) a collusive equilibrium or (b) a Cournot equilibrium.

18. What is the duopoly Cournot equilibrium if the market demand function is

$$Q = 1{,}000 - 1{,}000p,$$

and each firm's marginal cost is $0.28 per unit?

19. How would the Cournot equilibrium change in the airline example if United's marginal cost were $100 and American's were $200?

20. In the American-United Cournot equilibrium in the chapter, how would the equilibrium outputs change if American's constant marginal cost, m_A, does not equal United's constant marginal cost, m_U? (*Hint*: Modify Equations 13.5 and 13.6 appropriately. Your equilibrium quantities will be functions of m_A and m_U rather than numbers.)

21. What is the equilibrium in the airline example in the chapter if both American and United receive a subsidy of $48 per passenger?

22. The demand the duopoly quantity-setting firms face is

$$p = 90 - 2q_1 - 2q_2.$$

Firm 1 has no marginal cost of production, but Firm 2 has a marginal cost of $30. How much does each firm produce if they move simultaneously? What is the equilibrium price?

23. Using calculus, show how the Cournot equilibrium for n firms given in Appendix 13A changes if each firm faces a fixed cost of F as well as a constant marginal cost per unit.

24. Using calculus, determine the Stackelberg equilibrium with one leader firm and two follower firms if the market demand curve is linear and each firm faces a constant marginal cost, m, and no fixed cost. (*Hint*: See Appendix 13B for the Stackelberg model with one follower.)

25. Suppose that identical duopoly firms have constant marginal costs of $10 per unit. Firm 1 faces a demand function of

$$q_1 = 100 - 2p_1 + p_2,$$

where q_1 is Firm 1's output, p_1 is Firm 1's price, and p_2 is Firm 2's price. Similarly, the demand Firm 2 faces is

$$q_2 = 100 - 2p_2 + p_1.$$

Solve for the Bertrand equilibrium.

26. Solve for the Bertrand equilibrium for the firms described in Problem 25 if both firms have a marginal cost of $0 per unit.

27. Solve for the Bertrand equilibrium for the firms described in Problem 25 if Firm 1's marginal cost is $30 per unit and Firm 2's marginal cost is $10 per unit.

Strategy

A camper awakens to the growl of a hungry bear and sees his friend putting on a pair of running shoes. "You can't outrun a bear," scoffs the camper. His friend coolly replies, "I don't have to. I only have to out-run you!"

Since its inception in the early 1980s, Virgin Atlantic Airways (VAA) has waged a service war with British Airways (BA), taking customers away from BA through an innovative service program. This program—which included massages on flights and free limo service—gave VAA one of the highest customer loyalty ratings in the airlines market. In retaliation, BA tried to sabotage its smaller rival.[1] According to VAA, BA employees spread rumors in the United States and Britain that VAA was in financial trouble so that travel agents would warn potential passengers not to fly VAA. Other dirty tricks perpetrated by BA's staff included tapping into VAA's computers to obtain the names and numbers of passengers, then phoning or meeting VAA passengers and falsely claiming that their flights were delayed or overbooked and offering inducements to fly with BA; breaking into the homes and cars of VAA staff; hiring a consultant to dig up dirt on VAA's owner and plant negative news stories; and withdrawing cooperation between the airlines in plane maintenance and staff training. As a result of British hearings, BA paid VAA £610,000 plus large court costs and admitted to "regrettable incidents." No wonder Richard Branson, chairman of VAA, observed that dealing with BA was "like getting into a bleeding competition with a blood bank."

Fortunately, firms in most markets do not employ such colorful strategies on a regular basis. Nonetheless, they use a wide variety of strategic behaviors. **Strategic behavior** is a set of actions a firm takes to increase its profit, taking into account the possible actions of other firms. A firm may act to alter the beliefs of consumers and other firms, the number of actual and potential firms, the technology the other firms use, and the cost and speed with which a rival can enter the market.

---

[1]London *Times*, September 20, 1984; Nelms, Douglas W., "Defending Its Virtue: A Reluctant Virgin Atlantic Is in Court, Trying to Force British Airways to Do the Honorable Thing," *Air Transport World*, 29(6), July 1992:36; Dwyer, Paula, "British Air: Not Cricket," *Business Week*, January 25, 1993:50–51; "Tactics and Dirty Tricks," *The Economist*, 326, January 16, 1993:21–22; "U.S. Court to Consider Antitrust Case Against British Air," *Reuters European Business Report*, January 3, 1995. An anagram for *British Airways* is "This is war by air."

In this chapter, we focus on **noncooperative strategic behavior**: the set of actions taken by a profit-maximizing firm acting independently of other firms.[2] Conflicts between firms frequently arise because the actions of each profit-maximizing firm affect the profits of other firms.

So far, we've concentrated on one-period games in which firms simultaneously set quantity (Cournot model) or price (Bertrand model). In this chapter, we consider multiperiod or multistage games, in which firms act sequentially. The one multistage game we examined in Chapter 13 is the Stackelberg model, in which the leader firm benefits by choosing its output before the follower firm does. In this chapter, we focus on firms' efforts to limit the number of rivals by deterring rivals from entering a market, though firms may have many other motives for their strategic actions.

In Chapter 13, we noted that, in addition to choosing quantities or setting prices, many firms compete by varying quality or differentiating their products. For example, in response to Burger King ads touting its larger burgers, McDonald's had to decide whether to increase the size of its hamburgers from 1.6 ounces to 2 "full" ounces.[3] Similarly, in response to McDonald's Big Mac success, Burger King introduced the Big King. In this chapter, we see that firms may also compete through advertising campaigns.

IN THIS CHAPTER, WE EXAMINE FOUR MAIN TOPICS

1. **Preventing entry: simultaneous decisions:** When firms make entry decisions simultaneously, firms cannot act strategically to prevent rivals from entering the market.
2. **Preventing entry: sequential decisions:** If an incumbent firm can commit to producing large quantities before another firm decides whether to enter the market, the incumbent may deter entry.
3. **Creating and using cost advantages:** By raising costs to rivals, a firm may be able to deter entry or gain other advantages.
4. **Advertising:** Firms use advertising to increase the demand for their product, possibly at the expense of rival firms.

14.1   PREVENTING ENTRY: SIMULTANEOUS DECISIONS

When new firms enter an oligopolistic market, the profits of existing firms fall, as in the Cournot model in Chapter 13. Using a market that has either one or two firms, we now examine when and how firms behave strategically to prevent entry.

First, we show that neither firm has an advantage that helps it prevent the other firm from entering if both firms *simultaneously* decide whether to enter. Then, in the next section, we examine a market in which one firm, the incumbent, is already in

---

[2]In contrast, *cooperative strategic behavior* is the set of actions taken by firms to increase their profits through coordinating actions and limiting their competitive responses. Cartels (Chapter 13) are examples of cooperative behavior. The distinction between noncooperative and cooperative strategic behavior is not clear cut (see the discussion of tacit collusion in Chapter 13).

[3]Greenberg, Herb, "McDonald's Thinks the Unthinkable: Making Bigger Burgers," *San Francisco Chronicle*, April 18, 1996:D1; Collins, Glenn, "As Business Gets Lean, a Big King Dares Big Mac, *New York Times*, August 28, 1997:C1, C8.

the market and the other firm decides whether to enter. In that market, decisions are *sequential*: The incumbent acts before the potential entrant.

Two firms are considering opening gas stations at a highway rest stop that has no gas stations. There's enough physical space for only two gas stations. The profit or payoff matrix in panel a of Table 14.1 shows that there is enough demand for two stations to operate profitably. In the profit matrix in panel b, there's enough demand for only one station to operate profitably.

Room for Two Firms

According to the payoff matrix in panel a (in which profits are in hundreds of thousands of dollars), both firms can make a profit. The cell in the upper-right corner of the matrix shows the payoffs to the two firms if only Firm 1 enters. Firm 1 earns $3 (upper-right corner of that cell) and the nonentrant, Firm 2, earns $0 (lower left of that cell). Similarly, Firm 2 earns $3 if it is a monopoly (lower-left cell). If both firms enter (lower-right cell), both earn $1. If neither enters (upper-left cell), both earn $0.

Entering the market is a *dominant strategy* (Chapter 13) for both firms. Firm 1 reasons that

- If Firm 2 does not enter, Firm 1 makes $3 by entering and $0 if its does not enter, so entering is Firm 1's best strategy.
- If Firm 2 enters, Firm 1 makes $1 by entering and $0 if it does not enter, so entering is Firm 1's best strategy.

Table 14.1 Simultaneous Entry Game

(a) The market can support two firms.

		Firm 1	
		Do Not Enter	Enter
Firm 2	Do Not Enter	$0 / $0	$0 / $3
	Enter	$3 / $0	$1 / $1

(b) The market can support only one firm.

		Firm 1	
		Do Not Enter	Enter
Firm 2	Do Not Enter	$0 / $0	$0 / $1
	Enter	$1 / $0	-$1 / -$1

Because Firm 1 wants to enter regardless of what Firm 2 does, Firm 1 enters. Using the same reasoning, Firm 2 also enters because that's a dominant strategy. The strategies by which both firms enter constitute a Nash equilibrium: Neither firm wants to change its behavior, given that the other firm enters.

Room for Only One Firm

The firms' strategies change in panel b, where there is enough demand for only one firm to operate profitably.[4] Now if both firms enter, each loses $1. Neither firm has a dominant strategy. What each firm wants to do depends on the other firm's strategy.

Until now, we have examined only games in which firms use a *pure strategy*—each firm chooses an action with certainty—and there is only one Nash equilibrium. Our analysis of the game in panel b differs from these previous games in two ways. First, this game has more than one Nash equilibrium in pure strategies. Second, in addition to using a pure strategy, a firm may employ a *mixed strategy*, in which it chooses between its possible actions with given probabilities.

Pure Strategies. This game has two Nash equilibria in pure strategies: Firm 1 enters and Firm 2 does not, or Firm 2 enters and Firm 1 does not. The equilibrium at which only Firm 1 enters is Nash because neither firm wants to change its behavior. Given that Firm 2 does not enter, Firm 1 does not want to change from entering to staying out of the market. If it changed its behavior, it would go from earning $1 to earning nothing. Similarly, given that Firm 1 enters, Firm 2 does not want to switch its behavior and enter because it would lose $1 instead of making $0. Where only Firm 2 enters is a Nash equilibrium by the same type of reasoning.

How do the players know which (if any) Nash equilibrium will result? They don't. It is difficult to see how the firms choose strategies unless they collude. For example, the firm that enters could pay the other firm to stay out of the market. Without collusion, even discussions between the firms before decisions are made are unlikely to help.

★Mixed Strategies. These pure Nash equilibria are unappealing because they call for identical firms to use different strategies. The firms may use the same strategies if their strategies are mixed. When both firms enter with a probability of one-half—say, if a flipped coin comes up heads—there is a Nash equilibrium in mixed strategies.[5] If both firms use this mixed strategy, each of the four outcomes in the payoff matrix in panel b is equally likely. Firm 1 has a one-fourth chance of earning $1 (upper-right cell), a one-fourth chance of losing $1 (lower-right cell), and a one-half

---

[4]This game is similar to the game of *chicken*: Two foolish people drive toward each other in the middle of a road. As they approach the impact point, each has the option of continuing to drive down the middle of the road or to swerve. Both believe that, if only one driver swerves, that driver loses face (payoff = 0) and the other gains in self-esteem (payoff = 2). If neither swerves, they are maimed or killed (payoff = −1). If both swerve, no harm is done to either (payoff = 1). In Problem 1 at the end of the chapter, you are asked to analyze this game formally.

[5]Probabilities and expected values are discussed in Chapter 17.

chance of earning $0 (upper-left and lower-left cells). Thus Firm 1's expected profit is ($1 × $\frac{1}{4}$) + (–$1 × $\frac{1}{4}$) + ($0 × $\frac{1}{2}$) = $0.

Given that Firm 1 uses this mixed strategy, Firm 2 cannot do better by using a pure strategy. If Firm 2 enters with certainty, it earns $1 half the time and loses $1 the other half, so its expected profit is $0. If it stays out with certainty, Firm 2 earns $0 with certainty (see Appendix 14A). Thus both firms using the mixed strategy or one firm employing one pure strategy of entering and the other firm pursuing the pure strategy of not entering are Nash equilibria.

One important reason for introducing the concept of a mixed strategy is that some games have no pure-strategy Nash equilibria. Every game with a finite number of firms and a finite number of actions, however, has at least one Nash equilibrium, which may involve mixed strategies (Nash, 1950).

Nonetheless, some game theorists argue that mixed strategies are implausible because firms do not flip coins to choose strategies. One response is that firms may only appear to be unpredictable in this way. In this game with no dominant strategies, neither firm has a strong reason to believe that the other will choose a pure strategy. It may think about its rival's behavior as random. In actual games, however, a firm may use some information or reasoning that its rival does not observe in choosing a pure strategy.

Summary of the Simultaneous-Decision Entry Game

In conclusion, if firms make simultaneous entry decisions, their actions depend on the size of the market. If the market is large enough for both firms to make a profit, both firms enter. If the market can support only one firm, there are many possible Nash equilibria, and it is difficult to predict the outcome. *Neither firm can do anything to discourage the other firm from entering because the firms make their decisions simultaneously.*

Solved Problem 14.1
Suppose that Ford and GM are considering entering a new market for electric automobiles and that their profits (in millions of dollars) from entering or staying out of the market are

		GM	
		Enter	*Do Not Enter*
Ford	*Enter*	10 –40	250 0
	Do Not Enter	0 200	0 0

If the firms make their decisions simultaneously, which firms enter? How would your answer change if the government committed to paying GM a lump-sum subsidy of $50 million on the condition that it produce this new type of car?

Answer

1. *Check for dominant strategies and determine the Nash equilibrium*: Given the payoff matrix, Ford always does at least as well by entering the market. If GM enters, Ford earns 10 by entering and 0 by staying out of the market. If GM does not enter, Ford earns 250 if it enters and 0 otherwise. Thus entering is Ford's dominant strategy. GM does not have a dominant strategy. It wants to enter if Ford does not enter (earning 200 rather than 0), and it wants to stay out if Ford enters (earning 0 rather than –40). Because GM knows that Ford will enter (entering is Ford's dominant strategy), GM stays out of the market. Ford's entering and GM's not entering is a Nash equilibrium. Given the other firm's strategy, neither firm wants to change its strategy.

2. *See how the subsidy affects the payoff matrix and dominant strategies*: The subsidy does not affect Ford's payoff, so Ford still has a dominant strategy: It enters the market. With the subsidy, GM's payoffs if it enters increase by 50: GM earns 10 if both enter and 250 if it enters and Ford does not. With the subsidy, entering is a dominant strategy for GM. Thus both firms' entering is a Nash equilibrium.

14.2 | PREVENTING ENTRY: SEQUENTIAL DECISIONS

Additional strategic considerations arise if firms act sequentially. Suppose that an *incumbent* monopoly firm knows that a *potential entrant* is considering entering. These firms make sequential decisions about what actions to take. In the first stage, the incumbent chooses whether to take an action that will prevent the potential entrant from actually entering the market. In the second stage, the potential entrant decides whether to enter, and the firms choose output levels. The incumbent earns the monopoly profit if entry does not occur. If entry occurs, each firm sets its output to maximize its profit—taking account of the possible actions of its rival—and earns a duopoly profit. We assume that the potential entrant will not bother entering if it just breaks even—it enters only if it can make a positive profit.

Whether the incumbent acts to prevent entry depends on the answers to three questions:

- Does it pay for an incumbent to act to prevent entry?
- When can an incumbent prevent entry?
- What strategic acts and threats of future actions can an incumbent use to prevent entry?

We consider these questions in order. First, we examine whether a firm would pay a fee to prevent a rival from entering. Second, we show how the size of the fee depends on the potential rival's fixed cost of entering and the quantity demanded in this market. Third, we demonstrate that a threat of actions by the incumbent deters entry only if the potential rival believes the threat.

| **To Act or Not to Act?** | Whether the incumbent acts to prevent entry depends on whether it *can take actions* that will prevent entry and whether it *pays to take those actions*. We start by assuming that the incumbent can take a strategic action that will prevent the other firm from entering and by asking whether it pays for it to take this action. There are three possibilities: |

- **Blockaded entry:** Market conditions are such that no additional firm can profitably enter the market, even if the incumbent produces the monopoly output—so it is *unnecessary* for the incumbent to act strategically to prevent entry.
- **Deterred entry:** The incumbent acts to prevent an additional firm from entering because it *pays* to do so.
- **Accommodated entry:** Because it *doesn't pay* for the incumbent to prevent entry through strategic action, it does nothing to prevent entry but reduces its output (or price) from the monopoly to duopoly level to maximize its post-entry profit.

Paying to Prevent Entry. We use the gas station example to illustrate these three possibilities. One gas station, the incumbent, is already operating at the rest stop. The incumbent engages in a two-stage game with a potential entrant. In the first stage, the incumbent decides whether to pay the landlord of the rest stop b dollars for the *exclusive right* to be the only gas station at the rest stop. If this amount is paid, the landlord will rent the remaining land only to a restaurant or some other business that does not sell gasoline. If the incumbent doesn't take this strategic action to prevent entry, the potential entrant decides whether or not to enter in the second stage.

Figure 14.1 shows the game tree. In the first stage (left side of the diagram), the incumbent decides whether to pay for exclusive rights (bottom line) or not (top line). In the second stage (middle of the diagram), the potential entrant decides whether or not to enter if entry is possible. The right side of the diagram shows the profit of the incumbent, π_i, and then the profit of the potential entrant, π_e.

The top part of the tree shows what happens if the incumbent doesn't pay b to the landlord. If the other firm does not enter, the incumbent earns the monopoly profit, π_m, and the other firm earns zero. If the other firm enters, both the incumbent and the new firm earn the duopoly profit, π_d.

The bottom part of the tree shows what happens if the incumbent pays b for the exclusive rights. The incumbent earns $\pi_m - b$, and the other firm earns zero. (The landlord may set b so as to capture virtually all the extra profit.)

Entry is *blockaded* if the duopoly profit is negative, $\pi_d < 0$, so entry doesn't pay. The incumbent firm earns the monopoly profit, π_m, without having to pay b for exclusive rights.

If the duopoly profit, π_d, is positive, entry occurs unless the incumbent engages in strategic action to stop it. The incumbent can prevent entry by paying b, but it might not pay for the incumbent to do so. It pays if the incumbent's profit with *deterred* entry, $\pi_m - b$, is greater than the duopoly profit, π_d. However, if the duopoly profit is greater than the profit when the incumbent deters entry, $\pi_d > \pi_m - b$, it is better off with *accommodated* entry.

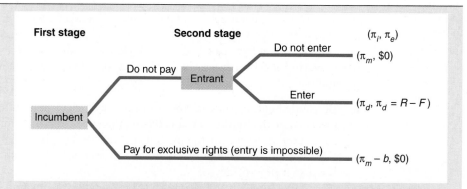

Figure 14.1 Whether an Incumbent Pays to Prevent Entry. If the potential entrant stays out of the market, it makes no profit, $\pi_e = 0$, and the incumbent firm makes the monopoly profit, $\pi_i = \pi_m$. If the potential entrant enters the market, both firms make the duopoly profit, π_d. Entry occurs if the duopoly profit is positive, $\pi_d > 0$. Entry is *blockaded* (does not occur regardless of actions by the incumbent) if the duopoly profit is negative because of low demand or high fixed costs of entering, both of which lower profit. If entry is not blockaded, the incumbent acts to *deter* entry by paying for exclusive rights to be the only firm at the rest stop only if $\pi_m - b > \pi_d$. Otherwise (if $\pi_m - b < \pi_d$), the incumbent *accommodates* entry.

Fixed Costs, Demand, and Blockaded Entry. A second firm can profitably enter this market only if π_d is positive in Figure 14.1. Whether π_d is positive depends on the fixed cost of entering and demand.

Suppose that the firms have no variable cost of production but incur a fixed cost F to enter the market. With two firms in the market, each firm has revenue R and duopoly profit of $\pi_d = R - F$. If revenue is less than the fixed cost of entering, $R < F$, the duopoly profit is negative, $\pi_d < 0$, and the second firm doesn't enter. Even though there is not enough demand, given the fixed cost of entry to support two firms, the incumbent may earn a positive, monopoly profit: $\pi_m > 0$.

Entry is blockaded only if a firm must incur a fixed cost to enter. If $F = 0$, then $R > F$, so an entrant can make a profit even if demand is low: $\pi_d > 0$. With fixed entry costs and demand so low that there's room for only one firm in the market, that firm is a *natural monopoly* (Chapter 11). If demand grows, additional firms can enter profitably. Chapter 13 shows that the number of monopolistically competitive firms in a market depends on how high fixed costs are relative to demand.

Because the incumbent is already in the market, its fixed entry cost is sunk. The incumbent firm ignores its sunk cost in deciding whether to operate. In contrast, the fixed cost of entry is an avoidable cost to the potential entrant, which incurs the cost only if entry takes place.

Whether an incumbent takes strategic action depends on the size of fixed costs and demand conditions, which determine π_m and π_d, and the cost of taking the strategic action, b. If entry is blockaded, there is no need for an incumbent firm to take strategic action. In the rest of this chapter, we concentrate on markets in which entry is not blockaded, so firms consider strategic actions.

GOVERNMENT DETERRENCE

Existing firms often lobby legislatures and regulatory bodies to block entry by potential rivals. Some laws (for example, those regulating taxis and beer distributorships) limit the number of firms in a market, while others (including those pertaining to psychiatric hospitals, lawyers, doctors, and electricians) set up substantial barriers to entry.

Zoning laws are often used to block entry. When Home Depot tried to open a warehouse store in a New Jersey suburb, Pequannock, in 1993–1994, it encountered fierce opposition. A group called Concerned Citizens for Community Preservation posted fliers and signs alleging that Home Depot had a "legacy" of crime and traffic safety violations. One flier ominously warned, "Our kids will be crossing through this deathtrap!" The group's leader, a local attorney, got five experts to write reports and testify at a township planning board meeting to oppose Home Depot's zoning application. Their opposition effort worked: The zoning application was denied.

Then Home Depot tried to open a store in another New Jersey suburb, Bloomfield. Again the firm ran into a citizen's group, headed by the same lawyer. One of its fliers claimed that "over the past three years, 15% of the crime in Clifton has occurred at the Home Depot. 30% of Clifton's car thefts have occurred at Home Depot." But according to the police in neighboring Clifton, this lawyer had obtained a copy of a police department report that said that less than 2% of crime and fewer than 4% of car thefts had occurred at Home Depot in the past three years.

Who was paying for the lawyer and these groups? When Pequannock township officials asked involved residents, they got no answer. In 1995, Home Depot brought a lawsuit charging that Rickel Home Centers, a competitor based in South Plainfield, N.J., had used smear tactics to keep Home Depot from opening the stores in Pequannock and Bloomfield. In a motion that it filed to dismiss Home Depot's suit, Rickel acknowledged its involvement with the formation of the Bloomfield citizens' group.

Rickel had reason to be concerned about Home Depot. With 92 stores in 5 states, Rickel had sales in excess of $680 million a year. It saw Home Depot go from no stores in 1989 to sales of $500 million annually in New Jersey (and national sales of $12.5 billion). It seems likely that a firm would consider it prudent to spend money to try to prevent entry of a potentially effective rival. Following bad publicity from newspaper articles about its strategic actions and the success of Home Depot, Rickel declared bankruptcy in January 1996.

Commitment and Entry Prevention

Imagine that you run the incumbent firm. You may not be able to prevent entry. You can't expect to deter entry merely by telling a potential entrant, "Don't enter! This market ain't big enough for the two of us." The potential entrant will laugh and suggest that your firm exit if it doesn't want to share the market.

If the potential entrant won't agree to stay out of the market just because you've politely asked it to do so, you may be tempted to threaten it. (Actually, you surely wouldn't *threaten*, which is something only a thug would do. You might merely *suggest* that the potential entrant will suffer "adverse consequences" if it enters.) You might announce that your firm will produce such a large quantity if your rival enters that it will lose $100, as the game tree in Figure 14.2 shows.

Unfortunately for you, the potential entrant is almost certain to doubt the veracity of your statement: "Yeah! Right! You'll produce so much output that we'll both lose money. I don't think so." Your rival realizes that, once it enters, you are better off producing a smaller Cournot output so that you'll make a $300 profit instead of suffering a $100 loss.

For a firm's announced strategy to be a **credible threat**, rivals must believe that the firm's strategy is rational in the sense that it is in the firm's best interest to use it.[6] It wouldn't make sense for you to produce large quantities of output and lose money just to punish the other firm after it enters. Once entry occurs, it's too late for you to try to deter your rival. You might as well make the best of the situation and produce only the Cournot amount of output.

We now show that the situation changes if an incumbent can *commit* to producing a large quantity before the potential rival decides to enter. One way a firm can make such a commitment is to sign contracts to sell that amount of output to customers at a future date. By committing to produce a large quantity *whether or not entry occurs*, the incumbent discourages entry. Other firms know they will lose money if they enter because the incumbent is committed to selling a large quantity.

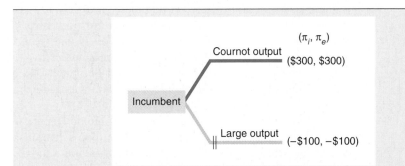

Figure 14.2 Noncredible Threat. The incumbent announces that it will produce such a large amount of output (lower path) if entry occurs that the entrant will lose money. The potential entrant doesn't believe this threat because it is not credible: The incumbent would make a higher profit by accommodating the entrant and the smaller Cournot level of output.

---

[6]No doubt you've been in a restaurant and listened to an exasperated father trying to control his brat with an extreme threat such as, "If you don't behave, you'll have to sit in the car while we eat dinner" or "If you don't behave, you'll never see television again." The kid, of course, does not view such threats as credible and continues to terrorize the restaurant—proving that the kid is a better game theorist than the father.

Because entry does not occur, the incumbent makes a profit even though it produces a large enough quantity that it would make a loss if entry occurred.

Commitment as a Credible Threat. The intuition for why commitment makes a threat credible is that of "burning bridges." If the general burns the bridge behind the army so that it can only advance and not retreat, the army becomes a more fearsome foe (like a cornered animal). Similarly, by limiting its future options, a firm makes itself stronger.[7]

Not all firms can make credible threats, however, because not all firms can make commitments. Typically, for a threat to succeed, a firm must have an advantage that allows it to harm the other firm before that firm can retaliate. Identical firms that act simultaneously cannot credibly threaten each other. A firm may be able to make its threatened behavior believable if firms differ. An important difference is the ability of one firm to act before the other—as could an incumbent firm that got a law passed preventing further entry.

The Cournot and Stackelberg models illustrate these points, as we saw in Chapter 13. In the Stackelberg model, the leader firm chooses its output level before the follower firm and thus has a *first-mover advantage*. Moving first allows the leader to *commit* to producing a relatively large quantity, q_s. Knowing that the leader will definitely produce that large quantity, the follower chooses a relatively small quantity, $q_f < q_s$, as in Figure 13.6.

In contrast, in the Cournot model, in which the two firms choose their output levels simultaneously, neither firm has an advantage over the other: Neither can commit credibly to producing a large quantity. If one firm announced in advance that it was going to produce a large quantity, the other firm would not view that claim as a credible threat (see "Why Moving Sequentially Is Essential" in Chapter 13).

Commitment Options. Suppose that an incumbent can commit to producing a large quantity of output before the potential entrant decides whether to enter. If the incumbent does not make a commitment before its rival enters, entry occurs and the incumbent earns a Cournot duopoly profit. By committing to produce the larger Stackelberg leader quantity before entry occurs, the incumbent makes a larger profit. However, the incumbent may have a better option. Instead of accommodating entry, it may be able to commit to produce such a large quantity (larger than the Stackelberg leader quantity) that the potential entrant decides not to enter because it cannot make a positive profit.

Does the incumbent commit to producing the Stackelberg leader quantity or the larger entry-deterring quantity? The incumbent uses the strategy that maximizes its

---

[7]Some psychologists use the idea of commitment to treat behavioral problems. A psychologist may advise an author with writer's block to set up an irreversible procedure whereby if the author's book is not finished by a certain date, the author's check for $10,000 will be sent to the group the author hates most in the world—be it the Nazi Party, the Ku Klux Klan, or the National Save the Skeets Foundation. Such an irreversible commitment helps the author get the project done by raising the cost of failure. (We can imagine the author as playing a game against the author's own better self.)

profit, as the two game trees in Figure 14.3 illustrate. In each of these, the incumbent can accommodate entry by committing to produce the Stackelberg quantity (upper action), or it can deter entry by producing a larger quantity (which is the smallest quantity such that the potential entrant cannot make a profit).

The incumbent determines its optimal strategy by working backward (Chapter 13). First, the incumbent determines what its rival will do, given that the incumbent takes each of its possible actions believing that its rival will behave rationally. Then the incumbent picks the action that maximizes its profit.

The two panels in Figure 14.3 differ as to the entrant's fixed cost of entering the market. Its fixed cost of entry is $100 in panel a and only $16 in panel b.

In panel a, the incumbent chooses to deter entry. If the incumbent commits to the Stackelberg leader quantity, $q_i = 30$, its rival makes $125 if it enters and $0 otherwise. Thus the rival chooses to enter if the incumbent commits to 30 units (the double line shows that it rejects the no-entry path). If the incumbent commits to

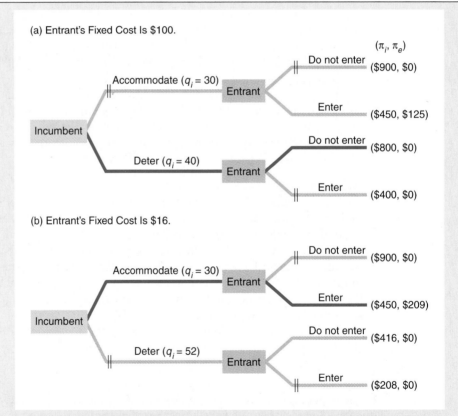

Figure 14.3 Game Trees for the Deterred Entry and Stackelberg Equilibria. (a) When the fixed cost of entry is $100, the incumbent earns more ($800) by deterring entry than by accommodating it ($450). (b) When the fixed cost is only $16, the incumbent's profit is higher ($450) if it accommodates entry than if it deters entry ($416).

producing at least $q_i = 40$, the best the entrant can do if it enters is earn $0, the same amount it would earn if it didn't enter. The rival does not enter.[8]

Thus if the incumbent commits to the Stackelberg quantity, its rival enters and the incumbent earns $450. If the incumbent commits to the larger quantity, its rival does not enter and the incumbent earns $800. Clearly, the incumbent should commit to the larger quantity because it earns a larger profit. However, where the fixed cost of entry is lower, as in panel b, the incumbent's decision is reversed.

Solved Problem 14.2 **In panel b of Figure 14.3, does the incumbent firm make more profit by deterring entry?**

Answer

1. *Determine the best responses of the potential entrant for each possible action by the incumbent firm*: The incumbent firm must first determine how its rival will react to each possible action. If the incumbent produces the smaller output, $q_i = 30$, the potential entrant makes more by entering, $209, than staying out, $0, so it enters. If the incumbent produces the larger output, $q_i = 52$, the best its rival can do is break even, so it does not enter.

2. *Given the best responses of the potential entrant, determine the strategy that maximizes the incumbent's profit*: If the incumbent firm produces the smaller output, its rival enters and the incumbent earns $450. With the larger output, its rival doesn't enter and the incumbent earns $416. Because it prefers $450 to $416, the incumbent commits to the smaller output. By doing so, it accommodates its rival's entry and acts as a Stackelberg leader.

★**Commitment and Fixed Costs**

What causes these two examples to differ? A key factor is the fixed cost of entry. We illustrate the role that fixed cost plays in the incumbent's decision by looking at the demand and cost structure that underlie the game trees in Figure 14.3.

How well the incumbent firm does when facing a potential entrant depends on whether it can commit and how large a fixed entry cost its rival must incur. There are three possibilities if the fixed cost is below the level where entry is blockaded:

■ **Cournot equilibrium:** If the incumbent can't commit—so both firms are on an equal footing—the incumbent produces the Cournot equilibrium quantity.
■ **Stackelberg (accommodated-entry) equilibrium:** If the incumbent can commit and the fixed cost of entry is relatively low, the incumbent commits to the Stackelberg leader quantity (larger than the Cournot quantity).
■ **Deterred-entry equilibrium:** If the incumbent can commit and the fixed cost of entry is relatively high, it commits to a large enough quantity (larger than the Stackelberg quantity) to deter entry.

---

[8]If the incumbent commits to producing more than 40 units, its rival will definitely lose money if it enters, but the incumbent's profit would be lower than if it produced only 40 units.

Table 14.2 **Entrant's Best Response and Profit**

Incumbent's Output, q_i	Entrant's Best Response If $F = 0$, q_e	Entrant's Profit, $R - F$			Incumbent's Profit	
		$F = \$0$	$F = \$16$	$F = \$100$	Entry, π_s	No Entry, π_m
60	0	0	−16*	−100*	0	0
52	4	16	0	−84*	208	416
50	5	25	9	−75*	250	500
40	10	100	84	0	400	800
30	15	225	209	125	450	900
20	20	400	384	300	400	800
10	25	625	609	525	250	500
0	30	900	884	800	0	0

*The entrant's profit if it produces the loss-minimizing output level. Profit is maximized at zero by not entering.

To illustrate these three possibilities, we suppose that the market demand is

$$p = 60 - Q, \tag{14.1}$$

where p is the market price and $Q = q_i + q_e$, the market quantity, is the sum of the incumbent's quantity, q_i, and the entrant's quantity, q_e. The marginal cost of production is zero (for simplicity), but a firm incurs a fixed cost of F to enter the market.

No Fixed Cost. Suppose that the fixed cost of entry is zero. Initially, we also assume that the incumbent firm cannot commit to an output level, so both firms must set their quantities at the same time. The incumbent's best-response function is[9]

$$q_i = 30 - q_e/2. \tag{14.2}$$

and the best-response function of its rival, the potential entrant, is

$$q_e = 30 - q_i/2. \tag{14.3}$$

The second column of Table 14.2 shows the rival's best responses to several of the incumbent's possible output levels.

Solving Equations 14.2 and 14.3, we find that the Cournot equilibrium quantity is $q_i = q_e = 20$.[10] The intersection of the two best-response curves in panel a of Figure 14.4 determines the Cournot equilibrium, e_c.

Now suppose that the incumbent firm can commit to an output level before its rival makes its entry decision. Once the incumbent picks a level of output q_i, the

---

[9]The demand intercept in Equation 14.1 is $a = \$60$, the absolute value of the slope of the demand curve is $b = 1$, the marginal cost is $m = \$0$, and there are two firms, $n = 2$. Substituting these values into Equation 13A.7 in Appendix 13A, the incumbent's best-response function is

$$q_i = (a - m)/(2b) - (n - 1)q_e/2 = 30 - q_e/2.$$

[10]Because both firms are identical, we can set both q_e and q_i equal to q in Equation 14.2 or 14.3 and solve for q. Alternatively, we can substitute the expression for q_e from Equation 14.3 into 14.2, solve for q_i, and then substitute the resulting expression for q_i into Equation 14.3 to obtain q_e.

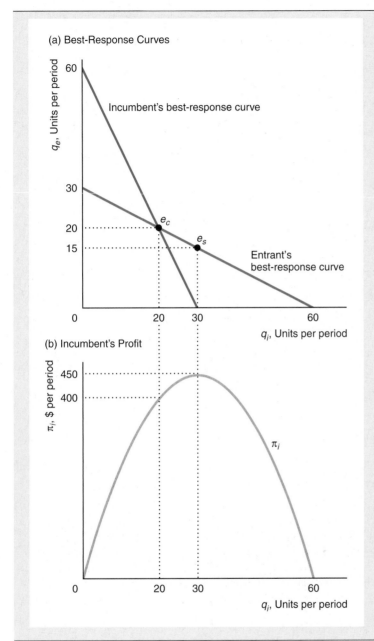

(a) Best-Response Curves

Incumbent's best-response curve

e_c

e_s

Entrant's
best-response curve

q_i, Units per period

(b) Incumbent's Profit

π_i

q_i, Units per period

Figure 14.4 **Cournot and Stackelberg Equilibria.** (a) The Cournot equilibrium, e_c, is determined by the intersection of the best-response curves (where $F = 0$). If the incumbent can commit to a larger quantity, it produces the Stackelberg leader output, 30. (b) The incumbent's profit is maximized at the Stackelberg equilibrium, e_s.

rival uses its best-response curve in panel a of the figure (or column 2 of Table 14.2) to decide how much to produce. Thus by setting its own output, the incumbent determines its rival's output level and hence the total market output. As a result, the incumbent's output level determines its profit, π_s, as panel b of the figure and the next to last (π_s with entry) column in Table 14.2 show.

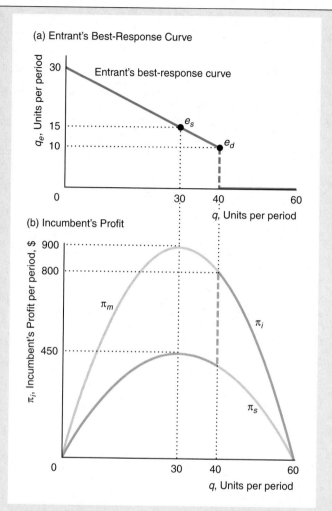

Figure 14.5 Incumbent Commits to a Large Quantity to Deter Entry. (a) Because it must pay a fixed cost of $F = \$100$ to enter, the potential entrant does not enter, and its best-response function is zero if $q_i \geq 40$. (b) The incumbent's profit, π_i (the solid portions of the π_s and π_m curves), is higher at $q_i = 40$, where it deters entry and is a monopoly ($\pi_m = \$900$), than at $q_i = 30$, where it is a Stackelberg leader ($\pi_s = \$450$).

The incumbent maximizes its profit at $450 by committing to producing the Stackelberg leader output of 30 units, as panel b of Figure 14.4 shows. Its rival's best response is to produce the Stackelberg follower quantity, 15 units. By committing to the relatively large Stackelberg leader output, the incumbent increases its profit by $50 over the Cournot level. This additional profit is the result of its commitment, which eliminates its flexibility in the amount of output it can produce.

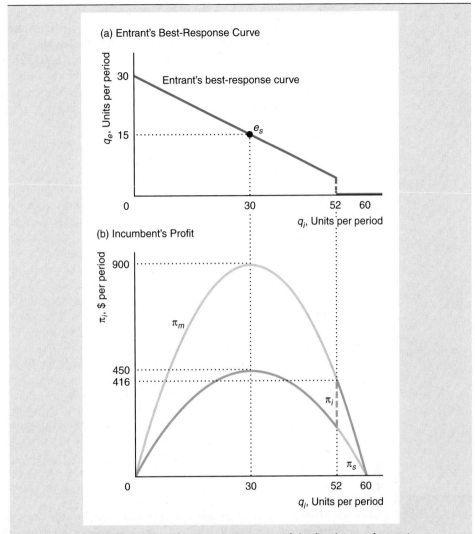

Figure 14.6 Incumbent Loss If It Deters Entry. (a) If the fixed cost of entry is $F = \$16$, the potential entrant does not enter, and its best-response function is zero if $q_i \geq 52$. (b) The incumbent's profit, π_i, is higher at $q_i = 30$ ($\pi_i = \pi_s = \$450$), where it doesn't deter entry, than at $q_i = 30$ ($\pi_i = \pi_d = \$416$), where it deters entry.

Fixed Cost. Now suppose that the rival incurs a fixed cost to enter. If the incumbent firm can commit, it should produce at least the Stackelberg output because that raises its profit above the Cournot level.

Should the incumbent produce even more output and deter the potential entrant from producing at all? The answer depends on the size of the fixed cost. We look first at a relatively large fixed cost, $F = \$100$, and then at a smaller fixed cost, $F = \$16$.

The potential entrant's profit is its revenue minus its fixed cost (because it has no variable cost of production) if it enters and zero if it does not enter.[11] The rival enters only if it makes a profit from entering. Given that the fixed cost of entry is F = $100, the rival enters only if its revenue is at least $100. Table 14.2 shows how the potential entrant's profit varies with the incumbent's output. This table illustrates that the rival shouldn't enter the market if the incumbent produces 40 or more units of output. Similarly, the entrant's best-response curve in panel a of Figure 14.5 is zero when the incumbent's output is 40 or more units.

If the incumbent produces less than 40 units, entry occurs and the incumbent's profit is the solid portion of the π_s curve in panel b. For example, if it produces the Stackelberg leader output of 30 units, it earns $450.

However, if the incumbent increases its output to 40 or more units, it deters entry and is a monopoly. The incumbent's profit is the solid portion of the π_m curve. As panel b shows, the incumbent maximizes its profit at $800 by producing 40 units.

If the incumbent didn't have to worry about entry, it would produce 30 units and earn a profit of $900. Because it fears entry, the incumbent commits to producing more than the monopoly equilibrium quantity to deter entry.

Thus if the potential entrant incurs a sizable fixed cost to enter and the incumbent can commit to a large quantity, it pays for the incumbent to produce more than the Stackelberg leader quantity and deter entry. Does it follow that the incumbent always deters entry as long as there is a fixed cost of entry? No, the incumbent doesn't deter entry if the fixed cost of entry is relatively small.

Suppose that the fixed cost of entry is only F = $16. As Table 14.2 and panel a of Figure 14.6 show, the rival does not enter if the incumbent commits to producing 52 or more units of q_i. If the incumbent commits to selling 52 units to deter entry, its profit is $416. That's less than the $450 it earns if it commits to the Stackelberg quantity, q_i = 30, and accommodates entry. Thus *if the fixed cost is relatively low or zero, the incumbent commits to the Stackelberg leader quantity. If the fixed cost is relatively high, the incumbent commits to a larger output to deter entry.*

Solved Problem 14.3   **Netscape and Microsoft both produce browsers for the Internet. Each firm apparently believes that its software will be successful only if it performs the same tasks as the other firm's software does. Netscape would like to set the standard (determine the tasks the browser can perform), which we call *N*, while Microsoft would like to set its standard, *M*. Suppose that the payoffs to the firms are[12]**

---

[11]The analysis would be similar with a positive variable cost. Indeed, if demand were $p = 100 - Q$ and the marginal cost were constant at $40, the analysis would be identical.

[12]This game is of the same form as the one that game theorists call *the battle of the sexes*. In that game, the husband likes to go to the mountains on vacation, and the wife prefers the ocean, but they both prefer to take their vacations together.

Microsoft

	N Standard	M Standard
N Standard (Netscape)	3 1	-1 -1
M Standard (Netscape)	-1 -1	1 3

What are the pure-strategy Nash equilibria if the firms must pick their standards simultaneously? If Netscape can commit to a standard before Microsoft chooses, what is the Nash equilibrium?

Answer

1. *Determine the pure-strategy Nash equilibria if the firms must decide simultaneously*: There are two Nash equilibria in which both firms choose the same standard. If both choose the N standard, neither firm would change its strategy if it knew that the other was using the N standard. Netscape's profit falls from 3 to −1 if it changes its strategy from N to M, whereas Microsoft's profit falls from 1 to −1 if it makes that change. Similarly, neither firm would change its strategy from the M standard if it believed that the other firm would use the M standard.[13]

2. *Determine the Nash equilibrium if Netscape can commit to a strategy first*: If it can commit first, Netscape chooses the N standard. Netscape knows that, because Microsoft realizes that Netscape is using the N standard, Microsoft chooses the N standard because it makes more (1) than if it chooses the M standard (−1). Thus with a first-mover advantage, Netscape chooses its own standard, which its rival accepts.[14]

---

[13]Each firm may also use a mixed strategy. If Microsoft chooses the N standard with a probability of $\frac{1}{3}$, then Netscape's expected profit is $(3 \times \frac{1}{3}) + (-1 \times \frac{2}{3}) = \frac{1}{3}$ if it chooses the N standard and $(-1 \times \frac{1}{3}) + (1 \times \frac{2}{3}) = \frac{1}{3}$ if it chooses the M standard. Thus Netscape is indifferent as to which strategy it uses if it expects Microsoft to use this mixed strategy. Similarly, if Netscape uses that mixed strategy where it chooses N with a probability of $\frac{2}{3}$ and M with a probability of $\frac{1}{3}$, Microsoft is indifferent.

[14]Netscape was the first mover and had a tremendous advantage over Microsoft with its initial browsers. As the browsers were revised repeatedly, however, the issue of which firm moves first became moot. The U.S. Department of Justice successfully sued Microsoft, claiming that the firm was bundling its browser with its Windows operating system in an attempt to eliminate competitors from the browser market. Thus the Justice Department claimed that the firms' strategies were more complex and involve more products than in this simple example.

14.3 | CREATING AND USING COST ADVANTAGES

We have examined how an incumbent firm obtains a complete barrier to entry (buys exclusive rights or gets the government to intervene) or commits to producing such large quantities that entry doesn't pay. We now examine the types of commitments an incumbent makes in an initial period to lower its marginal cost (relative to that of rivals) in later periods so as to deter entry.

A firm with a lower marginal cost has a larger market share and a higher profit than its higher-cost rival (Chapter 13). If its cost is very low relative to that of potential rivals, a firm can set a price low enough to prevent rivals from entering (Chapter 11). Thus a firm benefits if it can lower its cost relative to that of its rivals or if it can raise its rivals' costs. We look at three techniques an incumbent may use: investing in new equipment, learning by doing, and raising rivals' costs.

Lowering Marginal Cost While Raising Total Cost

Should a monopoly buy a new piece of equipment that lowers its marginal cost but raises its total cost? The answer depends on whether buying the equipment will prevent potential rivals from entering.

A monopoly manufacturing plant currently uses many workers to pack its product into boxes. It can replace these workers with an expensive set of robotic arms. Although the robotic arms raise the monopoly's fixed cost substantially, they lower its marginal cost because it no longer has to hire as many workers.

The monopoly would be enthusiastic about buying this equipment if the labor savings were large enough that its total cost of production would fall. Unfortunately for the monopoly, buying the robotic arms raises its total cost: The monopoly can't sell enough boxes to make the machine pay for itself, given the market demand curve.

Should the monopoly buy the machine anyway? Your response may be, "Is this a trick question? Why should the firm buy a machine that'll cause it to lose money?" Clearly, the firm shouldn't buy the machine if it is sure that it's going to remain a monopoly. However, if the incumbent fears that another firm will enter the market, it may make sense for the incumbent to buy the machine.

Purchasing the robotic equipment is a credible commitment. A potential entrant knows that, the lower the incumbent's marginal cost, the more output the incumbent will produce. The incumbent can deter entry by buying the robotic arms if the incumbent produces so much output that its rival will lose money if it enters.

The game tree in Figure 14.7 illustrates why the incumbent may install the robotic arms to discourage entry even though its total cost rises. (Math Problem 16 at the end of the chapter asks you to use best-response functions to derive the values in this game tree.) The robotic arms cost $1,804, but they lower the marginal cost of manufacturing from $40 to $4.

If the incumbent does not fear entry, it does not buy the machine. Its profit is $900 without the investment and only $500 with it.

If the incumbent fears that a rival is poised to enter, it invests to discourage entry. If the incumbent doesn't buy the robotic arms, the rival enters because it makes $300 by entering and nothing if it stays out of the market. With entry, the incumbent's profit is $400. With the investment, the rival loses $36 if it enters, so it stays out of the market,

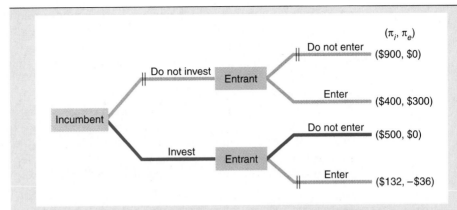

Figure 14.7 **Investment Game Tree.** The incumbent can invest in equipment that lowers its marginal cost. With the lowered marginal cost, it is credible that the incumbent will produce larger quantities of output, which discourages entry. The incumbent's monopoly (no-entry) profit drops from $900 to $500 if it makes the investment because the investment raises its total cost.

losing nothing. Because of the investment, the incumbent earns $500. Nonetheless, earning $500 is better than earning only $400, so the incumbent invests.

Learning by Doing

A firm can often lower its marginal cost of production through *learning by doing*, by which workers and managers become more skilled at their jobs and discover better ways to produce as they gain experience (Chapter 7). Such a firm may want to increase its workers' experience by producing more in the first period so that it can produce at a lower marginal cost than its potential rivals in the second period. The firm produces more output in Period 1 than the quantity that maximizes its profit in that period, ignoring the future. Due to the resulting learning by doing, the incumbent's marginal cost is so low in Period 2 that the potential rival does not enter. (Problem 9 at the end of this chapter asks you to illustrate this result by using a game tree.)

An incumbent's gain from learning by doing depends on the amount by which a firm can lower its cost relative to its rival's and the length of time it takes to learn. The advantage of being in the market first is diminished if learning is extremely rapid *or* extremely slow. If learning is rapid, a late entrant can catch up quickly. When learning is slow, the first firm cannot lower its cost much by accelerating production. Thus learning by doing is most likely to provide a strategic advantage for intermediate rates of learning (Spence, 1981). If the cost advantage from learning by doing is substantial enough, the incumbent may successfully discourage the second firm from entering.

Raising Rivals' Costs

By raising its rivals' variable costs relative to its own, a firm may be able to increase its own profit (Krattenmaker and Salop, 1986; Salop and Sheffman, 1987). A firm can raise rivals' variable costs either directly or indirectly.

Direct Methods. By interfering with its rivals' production or selling methods, a firm can drive up its rivals' costs. The anecdote at the beginning of this chapter about British Airways' alleged treatment of Virgin Atlantic Airways illustrates this approach. Another (particularly sneaky) technique is to buy up all of a rival's product during periods of heavy advertising and return it later, depriving the rival of its extra advertising-induced sales.

By making it difficult for rivals to collect marketing information, a firm may raise their costs. For example, firms sometimes conduct marketing experiments by introducing a new brand or adjusting a price at only a single location. Rival firms can disrupt such an experiment by offering large discounts, engaging in a massive advertising campaign, or otherwise "jamming the signal" (Fudenberg and Tirole, 1986).

Application   HITTING RIVALS WHERE IT HURTS

Firms constantly invent creative new ways to inflict costs on rivals. In May 1995, the U.S. Customs Service raided a warehouse and confiscated 74.5 million large-caliber bullets—enough to fill at least 10 railroad cars—in one of the biggest seizures of ammunition in U.S. history. The accompanying import documents stated that the ammunition came from Russia at a time when the importing firm had a federal permit to import Russian ammunition, but federal investigators claimed that the ammunition was illegally smuggled in from a manufacturer in China. Shooting down the charge as ridiculous, the firm's president said, "We know who caused this problem. It was a competitor." Apparently, he believed that a competitor had called the feds. A month later, the government sheepishly returned the bullets, lending credence to the firm's claims.

In 1999, Coca-Cola and PepsiCo went at each other's throat in Thailand after 5,300 empty reusable Coca-Cola bottles were found stacked in a Pepsi factory in a southern Thai province. Coca-Cola claimed that Pepsi distributors were using underhanded methods to secure a bigger share of the local cola market because the loss of the bottles had sharply raised the cost of restocking shops with Coca-Cola. (Pepsi's Thai distributor denied the charge, claiming that its trucks had brought in assorted brand bottles that were waiting to be sorted.)

Indirect Methods. Firms may also use a variety of indirect methods to raise rivals' costs. Incumbent firms may lobby for a government regulation that disproportionately affects new firms. Many such regulations *grandfather* older firms—that is, exempt them from the law. Some environmental regulations, for example, require new plants to install pollution-control devices but exempt existing factories, thereby raising the relative costs of new firms. From 1884 through 1967, butter manufacturers convinced many state legislatures and the federal government to prohibit coloring margarine to look like butter or to tax yellow-colored margarine (see **www.awlonline.com/perloff**, "Buttering Up Legislatures").

Where one firm produces two products that must be used together and an entrant produces only one of these products, the firm that produces both can impose costs on the other firm. Apple Computer sells computers, operating systems, and peripheral equipment such as hard drives and printers. Some other firms produce only peripheral equipment. If it wants to do so, Apple can repeatedly change its hardware and operating systems for its computers, imposing extra costs on the peripheral manufacturers.

Many antitrust suits charge that incumbent firms buy up market supplies of scarce resources to prevent rivals from using them. For example, it was alleged [in *United States* v. *Aluminum Co. of America*, 148 F.2d 416 (1945)] that, by certain provisions in its contracts with power companies, Alcoa prevented those companies from supplying power to any other firm for the purpose of making aluminum.

In extreme cases, a resource may be an **essential facility**: a scarce resource that a rival must use to survive. Because all the railroad bridges in St. Louis were owned by a group of railroads, the railroads could have prevented entry by rivals by refusing them access to their essential facilities, the bridges. However, the U.S. Supreme Court ruled [in *United States* v. *Terminal Railroad Association of St. Louis*, 224 U.S. 383 (1912)] that the owning group had to provide access to rival railroads on reasonable terms. U.S. courts are apparently more likely to require that access to such facilities be provided if the owners have a monopoly.

Application   PREVENTING CUSTOMERS FROM SWITCHING

If an incumbent firm can make it difficult for its customers to switch to an entrant's brand in the future, it can discourage entry. A case in point involves the customers of Pacific Gas and Electric Company (PG&E), who were told that they'd have to pay a fee to stop buying from PG&E.

When the federal Energy Regulatory Commission ordered electrical utilities to open up their transmission lines to competitors, it left a loophole for utilities that were stuck with high-cost nuclear power plants. If such a utility can show that it will lose revenue from the defection of some wholesale customers to cheaper energy suppliers, the utility can charge the departing customer a fee to help recover the lost revenues.

In 1996, California state regulators acted to block customers from bypassing PG&E—the former monopoly—and buying electricity from less expensive suppliers. Responding to a motion filed by PG&E, the regulators ruled that customers who stopped buying power from PG&E must pay it an exit fee as compensation for lost revenues.

PG&E asked for this help because other suppliers were on the verge of taking away billions of dollars a year of its business. PG&E was vulnerable to this competition because its costs were 40% above the national average (in part because of unusually high costs at the utility's Diablo Canyon nuclear plant). Competitors at the California-Oregon border could buy power from other Western utility companies at about 1¢ per kilowatt hour, which is about one-tenth of PG&E's average retail price.

This ruling clearly helped PG&E by making it difficult for other firms to enter the market and attract customers. You can probably sympathize with PG&E customers. Imagine how you'd feel if someone told you you'd have to pay money to walk out of your economics class early.

Raising All Firms' Costs

In some markets, an incumbent raises the costs of all firms, including its own. An incumbent wants higher costs if its cost is sunk, while its potential rivals' entry costs are still avoidable. Because its costs are sunk, the incumbent is more likely to remain in the market if costs rise than potential entrants are to enter. The incumbent derives a strategic advantage from its sunk-cost commitment: An incumbent is willing to spend more money to keep other firms out of the market than they are willing to spend to get into it (Gilbert, 1979; Salop, 1979), as we now illustrate in Figure 14.8.

Before entry, the incumbent earns a monopoly profit of $\pi_m = \$10$ (million). If entry occurs, the incumbent and entrant together split the total duopoly profits of $\pi_d = \$6$. If the incumbent and entrant share the duopoly profits equally, the entrant would pay up to $\pi_d/2 = \$3$ to enter, whereas the incumbent would pay up to $\pi_m - \pi_d/2 = \$7$ to exclude the potential entrant. Because π_m always exceeds π_d, $\pi_m - \pi_d/2 > \pi_d/2$, so it is always worth more to the monopoly to keep the entrant out than it is worth to the entrant to enter.

Suppose that the incumbent can induce the government to insist on pollution-control devices or other investments that raise the costs of all firms in the market. If the incumbent can raise an entrant's cost as well as its own by $4, the incumbent's profit is $6 if entry does not occur, and it loses $1 if entry occurs. Because the new firm would lose $1 if it were to enter, it does not enter. Thus the incumbent has an incentive to raise costs by $4 to both firms. The incumbent's profit is $6 if it raises costs rather than $3 if it does not.

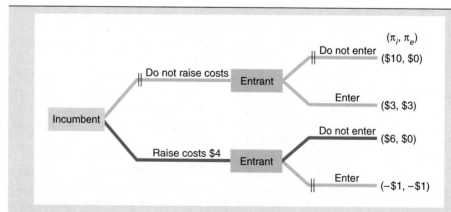

Figure 14.8 Raising-Costs Game Tree. The incumbent induces the government to raise costs to all firms in the market by $4 so as to prevent entry.

Advantages and Disadvantages to Moving First	We've seen how a firm that enters the market first gains an advantage over potential rivals by moving first. The first-mover firm may prevent entry by building a reputation, committing to a large plant, raising costs to potential entrants, or getting an early start on learning by doing.

The downside of entering early is that the cost of entering quickly is higher, the odds of miscalculating demand are greater, and later entrants may build on the pioneer's research to produce a superior product. As the first of a new class of anti-ulcer drugs, Tagamet was extremely successful when it was introduced. However, the second entrant, Zantac, rapidly took the lion's share of the market. Zantac works similarly to Tagamet but has fewer side effects, could be taken less frequently when it was first introduced, and was promoted more effectively.

Such examples of domination by second entrants are unusual. Urban, Carter, and Gaskin (1986) examined 129 successful consumer products and found that the second entrant gained, on average, only three-quarters of the market share of the pioneer and that later entrants captured even smaller shares.

Preventing Entry: Summary	An incumbent firm prefers that no other firm enter its market. If it is lucky, entry is blockaded: Even if this firm acts like a profit-maximizing monopoly, no other firm finds it profitable to enter. Other firms may find entry unprofitable because there is relatively little demand in this market or because entry costs are high.

If there is enough demand to support more than one firm and the incumbent moves first, the incumbent firm may take strategic actions to prevent entry. We examined how an incumbent may buy exclusive rights, lobby governments for laws limiting new entry, make commitments that reduce the incumbent's flexibility in production, and raise costs for all firms or just its rivals. There are many other strategies that firms can use. In fact, many firms admit that entry-preventing strategies are ubiquitous.[15]

Application EVIDENCE ON STRATEGIC ENTRY DETERRENCE

In theory, firms can prevent entry by manipulating price, product variety, reputation, information, scale, or capacity, among other actions. How commonly do they act to restrict entry?

Smiley (1988) surveyed firm managers in most industries about whether they attempted to limit entry by rivals. One might expect that firms that try to prevent entry in ways of questionable legality would be more likely to deny such behavior or refuse to respond to the survey at all. Thus the following responses should probably be viewed as conservative estimates of the frequency with which entry-deterring strategies are used.

Firms were asked whether they employed the following techniques to deter entry:

---

[15]*Ubiquitous* means "all over." This discussion of entry-preventing strategies is all over.

■ **Excess capacity:** Did the firm build a production plant large enough that the firm would be able to meet all expected demand for the new product so as to reduce the attractiveness of entry?

■ **Advertising:** Did the firm advertise and promote the new product intensively so as to create sufficient product loyalty that potential rivals would find entry unattractive?

■ **R&D and patent:** Did the firm acquire patents for all similar products for a new product so as to prevent entry of similar products?

■ **Reputation:** Did the firm signal (using the media or other means) that it would compete especially vigorously against new rivals so as to discourage entry?

■ **Limit pricing:** Did the firm set a price lower than would otherwise be profitable so that a potential competitor would not imitate its new product or would slow its rate of entry?

■ **Learning curve:** Did the firm market products aggressively in early stages to obtain low future costs and discourage entry?

■ **Filling all niches:** Did the firm market so many (similar) products that a new entrant could not find sufficient demand to justify entering?

■ **Hiding profit:** Did the firm move profits to other divisions within the firm to make the attractiveness of entry less apparent?

The table shows the percentage of responding firms that reported using these techniques, depending on whether their product was new or had been in existence for a while. More than half of the respondents thought that entry considerations were at least as important as other strategic marketing and production decisions. Only 13% felt that entry considerations were unimportant.

Strategy	New Products			Existing Products		
	Frequently	*Sometimes*	*Never*	*Frequently*	*Sometimes*	*Never*
Excess capacity	6	58	36	7	63	30
Advertising	32	63	5	24	68	7
R&D and patents	31	52	17	11	67	23
Reputation	10	68	23	8	72	21
Limit pricing (to prevent entry)	2	55	44	7	68	25
Limit pricing (to slow entry)	3	62	35	6	67	27
Learning curve	9	73	18			
Filling all niches				26	67	6
Hiding profits				31	58	12

14.4 | ADVERTISING

In addition to setting prices or quantities, choosing investments, and lobbying governments, firms engage in many other strategic actions to boost their profits. One of the most important is advertising.

Do you feel that you're seeing the same commercial on television over and over? You are. In July 1998, Burger King commercials appeared on national network and cable TV 4,718 times; McDonald's ads, 3,686 times; 1-800-COLLECT commercials, 2,799 times; 10-10-321 promotions, 2,730 times; and Geico Auto Insurance ads, 2,569 times.[16] Even the U.S. Census Bureau got into the TV commercial blitz. The bureau bombarded the viewer with ads—designed to reach each adult at least 36 times, and some people as many as 120 times—urging cooperation with the 2000 census.

Advertising is only one way to promote a product. Other promotional activities include providing free samples and using sales agents. Some promotional tactics are subtle. For example, grocery stores place sugary breakfast cereals on lower shelves so that they are at children's eye level. According to a survey of 27 supermarkets nationwide by the Center for Science in the Public Interest, the average position of 10 child-appealing brands (44% sugar) was on the next-to-bottom shelf, while the average position of 10 adult brands (10% sugar) was on the next-to-top shelf.

Before 1991, media advertising (television, radio, newspaper, and magazine ads) absorbed the major share of marketing budgets. Since 1991, consumer promotions—giveaways, tie-ins, coupons, contests, and the like—have taken the larger share. For example, in the summer of 1994, Frito-Lay put all its marketing dollars into sponsoring country singer Reba McEntire's concert tour.[17]

We begin this discussion by examining advertising (or other promotional activities) by a monopoly, which has no rivals. Then we consider strategic advertising in a duopoly, in which a firm advertises to attract customers from its rival.

Monopoly Advertising

A monopoly advertises to raise its profit. A successful advertising campaign shifts the market demand curve by changing consumers' tastes or informing them about new products. The monopoly may be able to change the tastes of some consumers by telling them that a famous athlete or performer uses the product. Children and teenagers are frequently the targets of such advertising. (See **www.awlonline.com/perloff**, "Smoking Gun Evidence?" for a discussion of cigarette advertising aimed at youths.) If the advertising convinces some consumers that they can't live without the product, the monopoly's demand curve may shift outward and become less elastic at the new equilibrium, at which the firm charges a higher price for its product (see Chapter 11). If the firm informs potential consumers about a new use for the product—for example, "Vaseline petroleum jelly protects lips from chapping"—demand at each price increases.

---

[16]Enrico, Dottie, "On the Spot," *TV Guide*, September 19, 1998:10.

[17]"Wilma! What Happened to the Plain Old Ad?" *Business Week*, 3375, June 6, 1994: 54.

Application   DRUG COMMERCIALS

A major new advertising trend is drug companies' use of commercials aimed directly at the final consumer. The ads urge TV viewers to ask their doctors about specific prescription drugs.

Before 1997, pharmaceutical firms aimed their pitches solely at doctors and pharmacists because any ad had to include detailed information about side effects. In 1997, the U.S. Food and Drug Administration (FDA) relaxed its advertising rules: Ads were acceptable as long as they stuck to FDA-approved usages and advised viewers how to get more details. Soon thereafter, the FDA required disclosure of the most common and serious side effects.

When the rules changes in 1997, drug firms' annual expenditures on ads tripled—to over $60 million each for Pravachol (a cholesterol-lowering drug) and Allegra (which relieves allergy symptoms). Sales growth from 1997 to 1998 was 16% for Pravachol and 105% for Allegra. The roughly $100 million per month expenditures for consumer-targeted advertising in 1998 was almost five times the total only three years earlier.

One of the early direct-to-consumer commercials by Schering-Plough for Claritin, a so-called nonsedating antihistamine, made the drug one of the most requested brand names in a survey of doctors. Sales jumped 40% in the year after airing of TV ads featuring a hot-air balloon drifting to Irving Berlin's "Blue Skies." The company spent an estimated $166 million to advertise Claritin in 1999.

These new promotions are working. According to polls, 80% of patients and doctors have seen drug commercials, 27% of patients who take any prescription drug say they've discussed with their doctors a drug they saw advertised, and 7% said they asked their doctor to prescribe an advertised drug. When patients were asked how they would react if their doctor refused to prescribe such a drug, one-quarter said they'd seek the prescription elsewhere, and 15% said they would consider leaving their doctor. The 10 most heavily advertised drugs accounted for 22% of the total increase in spending by consumers for all drugs in the last five years.

The Decision Whether to Advertise. Even if advertising succeeds in shifting demand, it may not pay for the firm to advertise. If advertising shifts demand outward or makes it less elastic, the firm's *gross profit*, which ignores the cost of advertising, must rise. The firm undertakes this advertising campaign, however, only if it expects its *net profit* (gross profit minus the cost of advertising) to increase.

To illustrate a monopoly's decision making, in Figure 14.9, we return to the Coke and Pepsi example from Chapter 13. Initially, suppose that Coke is a monopoly in the United States. If it does not advertise, it faces the demand curve D^1 (based on the estimates of Gasmi, Laffont, and Vuong, 1992). If Coke advertises at its current level, its demand curve shifts from D^1 to D^2.

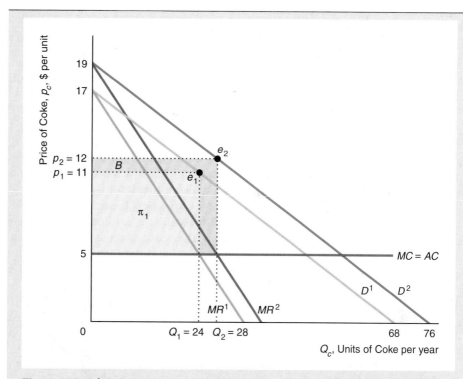

Figure 14.9 **Advertising.** Suppose that Coke were a monopoly. If it does not advertise, its demand curve is D^1. At its actual level of advertising, its demand curve is D^2. Advertising increases Coke's gross profit (ignoring the cost of advertising) from π_1 to $\pi_2 = \pi_1 + B$. Thus if the cost of advertising is less than the benefits from advertising, B, Coke's net profit (gross profit minus the cost of advertising) rises.

Coke's marginal cost, MC, is constant and equals its average cost, AC, at \$5 per unit (10 cases). Before advertising, Coke chooses its output, $Q_1 = 24$ million units, where its marginal cost equals its marginal revenue, MR^1, based on its demand curve, D^1. The profit-maximizing equilibrium is e_1, and the monopoly charges a price of $p_1 = \$11$. The monopoly's profit, π_1, is a box whose height is the difference between the price and the average cost, \$6 (= \$11 − \$5) per unit, and whose length is the quantity, 24 units (tens of millions of cases of twelve-ounce cans).

After its advertising campaign (involving dancing polar bears or whatever) shifts its demand curve to D^2, Coke chooses a higher quantity, $Q_2 = 28$, where the MR^2 and MC curves intersect. In this new equilibrium, e_2, Coke charges $p_2 = \$12$. Despite this higher price, Coke sells more Coke after advertising because of the outward shift of its demand curve.

As a consequence, Coke's gross profit rises more than 36%. Coke's new gross profit is the rectangle $\pi_1 + B$, where the height of the rectangle is the new price minus the average cost, \$7, and the length is the quantity, 28. Thus the benefit, B, to Coke from advertising at this level is the increase in its gross profit. If its cost of advertising is less than B, its net profit rises, and it pays for Coke to advertise at this level rather than not to advertise at all.

How Much to Advertise. In general, how much should a monopoly advertise to maximize its net profit? To answer this question, we consider what happens if the monopoly raises or lowers its advertising expenditures by $1, which is its marginal cost of an additional unit of advertising. If a monopoly spends one more dollar on advertising and its gross profit rises by more than $1, its net profit rises, so the extra advertising pays. In contrast, the monopoly should reduce its advertising if the last dollar of advertising raises its gross profit by less than $1, so its net profit falls. Thus the monopoly's level of advertising maximizes its net profit if the last dollar of advertising increases its gross profit by $1 (see Appendix 14B for an alternative analysis). In short, the rule for setting the profit-maximizing amount of advertising is the same as that for setting the profit-maximizing amount of output: Set advertising or quantity where the marginal benefit (the extra gross profit from one more unit of advertising or the marginal revenue from one more unit of output) equals its marginal cost.

We can illustrate how firms use such marginal analysis to determine how much time to purchase from television stations for infomercials, those interminably long television advertisements sometimes featuring unique (and typically bizarre) plastic products: "Isn't that amazing?! It slices! It dices! . . . But wait! That's not all!" As Figure 14.10 shows, the marginal cost per minute of broadcast time, MC, on small television stations is constant. The firm buys A_1 minutes of advertising time, where its marginal benefit, MB^1, equals its marginal cost.

Application   **O. J. TRIAL EFFECT**

Often a major event such as the Super Bowl affects TV watchers' viewing behavior and the benefits from advertising. A particularly dramatic event was O. J. Simpson's 1995 trial for murder, which many television and radio stations broadcast. The *O. J. Factor* cut the take from infomercials on other television stations. Sales sagged as viewers skipped program-length product pitches to watch trial coverage on weekday mornings.

The reason for the sales slump was that the marginal benefit curve for infomercials shifted. Where every $1,000 spent on commercial time at 12:30 P.M. brought in an average of $2,190 in sales in Charlotte, North Carolina, before the trial, it produced only $1,790 (a drop of 18.3%) during the trial. The comparable figures for San Francisco at 9:30 A.M. were $1,740 and $790, a fall of 54.6%. Thus for a given quantity ($1,000 worth of advertising time), the marginal benefit for San Francisco shifted down by 54.6% from MB^1 to MB^2.

Because the marginal benefit curve shifted, a typical firm reduced the amount of advertising time it purchased from A_1 to A_2, where MB^2 intersects MC. Estimates of average infomercial sales declines due to the Simpson trial ranged from 10% to 60% across cities.

Figure 14.10 **Shifts in the Marginal Benefit of Advertising.** Before the Simpson trial, the marginal benefit of advertising is MB^1. The firm purchases A_1 minutes of advertising time, where MB^1 intersects its marginal cost per minute of broadcast time curve, MC. During the trial, the marginal benefit curve shifts to the left to MB^2. As a result, the firm reduces its purchase of advertising time to A_2.

Strategic Advertising

If there are several firms in a market, each chooses its optimal level of advertising by taking into account the advertising, pricing, and other strategies of its rivals. Advertising by one firm may help or hurt other firms.

Advertising That Helps Rivals. One firm may inform consumers about a new use for its product. By doing so, its advertising may cause demand for its own *and* rival brands to rise. A number of industry groups advertise collectively to increase demand for their product. In recent years, raisin growers (dancing raisins) and milk producers (milk mustache) have joined forces to run successful campaigns.

Application PINK TOOTHBRUSH

Before World War I, only 26% of Americans brushed their teeth. By 1926, in part because of ads like those in Ipana's "pink toothbrush" campaign, which detailed the perils of bleeding gums, the share that brushed rose to 40%. Ipana's advertising helped all manufacturers of toothbrushes and toothpaste.

Advertising That Hurts Rivals. Alternatively, a firm's advertising may increase demand for its product by taking customers from other firms. A firm may use advertising to differentiate its products from those of rivals. The advertising may describe actual physical differences in the products or try to convince customers that essentially identical products differ. If a firm succeeds with this latter type of advertising, the products are sometimes described as *spuriously* differentiated.

Application   SECRET INGREDIENTS

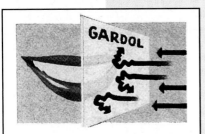

Gardol, Colgate's patented new decay-fighter, forms an invisible shield around your teeth. You can't feel it, taste it, or see it — but Gardol's protection won't rinse off or wear off all day. That's why Colgate's — the only leading toothpaste to contain Gardol — gives the *surest* protection ever offered by any toothpaste!

A firm can raise its profit if it can convince consumers that its product is superior to other brands. From the 1930s through the early 1970s, *secret ingredients* were a mainstay of consumer advertising. These ingredients were given names combining letters and numbers to suggest that they were cooked up in laboratories rather than by Madison Avenue. Dial soap boasted that it contained AT-7. Rinso detergent had solium, Comet included chlorinol, and Bufferin had di-alminate. Among the toothpastes, Colgate had Gardol, Gleem had GL-70, Crest had fluoristan, and Ipana had hexachlorophene and Durenamel ("Bristol-Myers' brand of sodium fluoride and soluble orthophosphate.")

About two decades ago, secret-ingredient claims fell out of favor, and manufacturers asserted that their brands contained *natural* ingredients such as baking soda. In recent years, however, the secret-ingredient approach has been reintroduced to differentiate brands from competitors. Recent ads remind us that Clorets breath-freshening gum and mints contain Actizol. Cheer detergent touts an enzyme called Color Guard, Shade UVA Guard sunscreen lotion has Parasol 1789 and oxybenzone sunblock agents, and Pond's Dramatic Results Skin Smoothing Capsules have Nutrium, "a miraculous oil-free complex."

Empirical Evidence. We do not know from theory alone whether advertising by a firm will help or hurt other firms. At one extreme is cigarette advertising. Roberts and Samuelson (1988) found that cigarette advertising is cooperative: It increases the size of the market but doesn't change market shares substantially.[18] At the other extreme is cola advertising. Gasmi, Laffont, and Vuong (1992) reported that each firm's gain from advertising comes at the expense of its rival. Cola advertising has almost no effect on total market demand. Slade (1995) found results for saltine crackers that lie between these extremes.

---

[18]Note, however, that the Centers for Disease Control and Prevention's evidence suggests that advertising may shift the brand loyalty of youths.

Strategic Advertising Equilibria. Whether advertising hurts or helps rivals may affect the advertising strategies that firms use and the outcome. Table 14.3 shows two possible duopoly games in which firms decide whether to advertise or not.

Advertising only takes customers from rivals in panel a. If only one firm advertises, its advertising lures customers from the other firm. The advertising firm's profit does not rise by as much (from $2 to $3) as the other firm's profit falls (from $2 to $0) because of the cost of advertising. Both firms have a dominant strategy: Advertise. The Nash equilibrium is for both firms to advertise. This game is an example of the prisoners' dilemma. Both firms would be better off if they colluded and agreed not to advertise.

Advertising attracts new customers to both firms in panel b. If only one firm advertises, its profit rises by more ($2 to $4) than that of the other firm ($2 to $3). If both advertise, however, they are better off than if only one advertises or neither advertises. Again, advertising is a dominant strategy for both firms.

In each of these games, both firms advertise. The distinction is that the Nash equilibrium in advertising is the same as the collusive equilibrium when advertising increases the market size (panel b, or the cigarette market). When advertising cannibalizes the sales of other firms in the market (panel a or the cola market), firms are worse off in an equilibrium in which they advertise. Consequently, cola firms would be delighted to have their advertising banned, but cigarette firms oppose an advertising

---

Table 14.3 Advertising Game

(a) Advertising Only Takes Customers from Rivals

		Firm 1	
		Do Not Advertise	Advertise
Firm 2	Do Not Advertise	$2 $2	$0 $3
	Advertise	$3 $0	$1 $1

(b) Advertising Attracts New Customers to the Market

		Firm 1	
		Do Not Advertise	Advertise
Firm 2	Do Not Advertise	$2 $2	$3 $4
	Advertise	$4 $3	$5 $5

ban.[19] In a more general model in which firms set the amount of advertising (rather than just decide whether to advertise or not), the amount of advertising depends critically on whether advertising increases the market size or only steals customers from rivals.

Summary

1. **Preventing entry: simultaneous decisions:** If firms make simultaneous decisions about entering a market, the strategies that they choose depend on the size of the market and possibly on chance. If the market is large enough that two firms can make a profit, both enter. If only one firm can profitably produce, there are many possible Nash equilibria.

2. **Preventing entry: sequential decisions:** If an incumbent firm can commit to producing large quantities before another firm decides whether to enter the market, the incumbent may deter entry. The incumbent has a *first-mover advantage*.

   An incumbent acts to prevent entry only if it pays to do so. In a *blockaded* market, no potential entrant can make a profit, even if the incumbent continues to act as a monopoly, so the incumbent ignores the threat of entry. When there is room for another firm to enter, the incumbent acts to *deter* entry if it is profitable to do so. Otherwise, the incumbent *accommodates* the entrant by doing nothing to prevent entry and reducing its output or price from the monopoly to duopoly level to maximize its postentry profit. Which outcome occurs depends on the cost of entry.

   An incumbent with first-mover advantage prevents entry by making a *credible threat*: It *commits* to taking an action (whether or not entry occurs) that lowers a potential entrant's profit. For example, the incumbent may commit to producing so much output that it will not be profitable for a rival to enter the market, a course the incumbent

follows if the fixed costs of entering are relatively high. Otherwise, if entry costs are low, the incumbent produces a smaller amount that makes it a Stackelberg leader after entry occurs.

3. **Creating and using cost advantages:** A firm with a lower marginal cost has a larger market share and a higher profit than a higher-cost rival. A firm with substantially lower costs may prevent entry by a higher-cost rival. Thus firms benefit from lowering their marginal costs relative to those of rivals. It may pay for a firm to invest in a new technology that raises its total cost of production if such an investment lowers its marginal cost substantially. By lowering its marginal cost, the firm credibly commits to producing relatively large levels of output and thereby discourages entry. Firms may also use learning by doing or various direct and indirect methods so that their costs fall relative to those of their rivals (or so that their rivals' costs rise relatively).

4. **Advertising:** Firms advertise to shift their demand curve outward or to reduce the elasticity of demand they face in equilibrium. Advertising may differentiate a firm's product or inform consumers about new products or new uses for a product. The strategies that firms use in deciding how much to advertise depend on the effect of advertising on rivals' customers. If a firm's advertising increases total market demand, all firms may benefit. Alternatively, if a firm's advertising takes customers from a rival, one firm's gain comes at the expense of the other firm.

---

[19]Since 1997, the cigarette companies, under substantial legal and government pressure, have negotiated various restrictions on their advertising in the United States. However, they have tried to avoid any restrictions on other types of promotional activities, which presumably they planned to use when they could no longer advertise.

Problems

1. Show the payoff matrix for two drivers engaged in the game of chicken (described in footnote 4). Describe the possible Nash equilibria for this game.

2. Modify the payoff matrix in the game of chicken in Problem 1 so that, if neither driver swerves, the payoff is −2. How does that change the equilibria?

3. Suppose that Solved Problem 14.1 were modified so that GM has no subsidy but does have a head start over Ford and can move first. What is the Nash equilibrium? Explain.

4. Suppose that Panasonic and Zenith are the only two firms that can produce a new type of high-definition television. The payoffs (in millions of dollars) from entering this product market are shown in the following payoff matrix:

		Panasonic	
		Enter	*Do Not Enter*
Zenith	*Enter*	−40 / −40	0 / 250
	Do Not Enter	250 / 0	0 / 0

   a. If both firms move simultaneously, does either firm have a dominant strategy? Explain.

   b. What are the Nash equilibria, given that both firms move simultaneously?

   c. If the U.S. government commits to paying Zenith a lump-sum subsidy of $50 million if it enters this market, what is the Nash equilibrium?

   d. If Zenith does not receive a subsidy but has a head start over Panasonic, what is the Nash equilibrium?

5. Suppose that the payoffs two firms face are as shown in the following payoff matrix:

		Firm 1	
		Low Price	*High Price*
Firm 2	*Low Price*	$2 / $0	$1 / $2
	High Price	$0 / $7	$6 / $6

Given these payoffs, Firm 2 wants to match Firm 1's price, but Firm 1 does not want to match Firm 2's price. What, if any, are the pure-strategy Nash equilibria of this game?

★6. What is the mixed-strategy Nash equilibrium for the game in Problem 5?

7. There is an incumbent monopoly in the market. A potential entrant may enter next year. If the incumbent spends b dollars lobbying, it can get the legislature to pass a law that places a lump-sum tax of T on the potential entrant if it enters. If the potential entrant stays out of the market, it makes no profit, $\pi_e = 0$, and the incumbent firm makes the monopoly profit, $\pi_m > 0$, minus the expenditure on lobbying, if any (b or 0). If the potential entrant enters the market, it gets the duopoly profit, $\pi_d > 0$, minus the tax, if any, and the incumbent earns the duopoly profit minus the lobbying costs, if any. Draw the game tree. If the incumbent lobbies, under what conditions (in terms of π_m, π_d, b, or T) will the potential entrant *not* enter? If the potential entrant will not enter when the incumbent lobbies, under what conditions (in terms of π_m, π_d, b, or T) will the incumbent act to deter entry by lobbying?

8. Suppose that you and a friend play a "matching pennies" game in which each of you uncovers a penny. If both pennies show heads or both show tails, you keep both. If one shows heads and the other shows tails, your friend keeps them. Show the payoff matrix. What, if any, is the pure-strategy Nash equilibrium to this game?

9. The more an incumbent firm produces in the first period, the lower its marginal cost in the second period. If a potential entrant expects the incumbent to produce a large quantity in the second period, it does not enter. Draw a game tree to illustrate why an incumbent would produce more in the first period than the single-period profit-maximizing level. Now change the payoffs in the tree to show a situation in which the firm does not increase production in the first period.

10. Before the O.J. Simpson trial, if a firm spent $1,000 on commercial television time at 12:30 P.M. in Charlotte, North Carolina, its sales rose by $2,190. If the firm bought $1,000 of advertising time during the trial, was it advertising optimally? If not, should it have increased or decreased the amount it spent on advertising?

11. If using the Internet allows a monopoly to reduce its cost of advertising, how will the total amount that the firm spends on advertising change?

Math Problems

12. *Review* (Chapter 13): Duopoly quantity-setting firms face the market demand

$$p = 150 - q_1 - q_2.$$

Each firm has a marginal cost of $60 per unit. What is the Cournot equilibrium?

13. *Review* (Chapter 13): In Problem 12, what is the Stackelberg equilibrium when Firm 1 moves first?

14. Given the information in Problems 12 and 13, derive (and draw) the best-response curve for Firm 2 if it has a fixed cost of entry of $100.

15. Given the information in Problems 12–14, what is the optimal strategy for Firm 1, the first mover, to use? What is the equilibrium? Draw the game tree.

16. Using best-response functions, show that the numbers in Figure 14.7 are correct. The market demand is $p = 100 - Q$, where $Q = q_i + q_e$. The potential entrant incurs a fixed cost of $100 to enter, and its constant marginal cost is $40. The incumbent's marginal cost is $40 without investment and $4 if it buys the robotic arms at a cost of $1,804. (*Hint*: Use Equation 12A.7 in Appendix 12A to derive the best-response functions.)

17. The demand a monopoly faces is

$$p = 100 - Q + A^{1/2},$$

where Q is its quantity, p is its price, and A is the level of advertising. Its marginal cost of production is 10, and its cost of a unit of advertising is 1. What is the firm's profit equation? Solve for the firm's profit-maximizing price, quantity, and level of advertising. (*Hint*: See Appendix 14A.)

18. What is the monopoly's profit-maximizing output, Q, and level of advertising, A, if it faces a demand curve of $p = a - bQ + cA^\alpha$, its constant marginal cost of producing output is m, and the cost of a unit of advertising is $1?

★19. Determine the Nash equilibrium where the duopoly firms set price and advertising. The firms face demand curves

$$q_1 = \alpha_1 - \beta_{11}p_1 + \beta_{12}p_2 + \gamma_{11}(A_1)^{1/2} - \gamma_{12}(A_2)^{1/2},$$

$$q_2 = \alpha_2 + \beta_{21}p_1 - \beta_{22}p_2 - \gamma_{21}(A_1)^{1/2} + \gamma_{22}(A_2)^{1/2},$$

where the Greek letter coefficients are positive numbers, p_i is the price, q_i is the quantity, and A_i is the level of advertising of Firm i. Each firm has a constant marginal cost, m, of production, and the marginal cost of advertising is $1.

Factor Markets and Vertical Integration

Work is of two kinds: first, altering the position of matter at or near the earth's surface relative to other matter; second, telling other people to do so.
—Bertrand Russell

To broadcast a television show, a local television station uses a variety of inputs. It builds or leases a studio, purchases or rents transmission equipment, hires labor, and buys or produces its own shows. The firm that owns the station may buy all these inputs from a market or produce some of them itself.

In the past few years, many media and communications companies have merged so that each could provide most of the services needed to bring entertainment into your home. Disney, Time Warner, and other major media firms are **vertically integrated**: They participate in more than one successive stage of the production or distribution of goods or services.

Disney is one of the most vertically integrated firms, with divisions that cover television production, film production, music, publishing, radio, broadcast TV, cable TV, the Internet, theme parks, and retail outlets. Rupert Murdoch's News Corporation's Fox Film Entertainment Group makes movies, TV shows, and animated features (including *The Simpsons*). The Fox network provides Fox-made shows to Fox-owned TV stations and affiliated stations in the United States and Australia. Fox delivers its shows directly via cable stations and satellite dishes around the world through companies that it partially or totally owns, such as fx, fxM, Fox Sports Net, Fox Sports International, ASkyB, and SkyMCI in the United States; BSkyB in the United Kingdom; Star TV, Zee TV, and JSkyB in Asia; Vox in Germany; Foxtel in Australia; and Sky Entertainment Latin American and Canal Fox in Latin America and the Caribbean. The parent company even owns *TV Guide*.

When does a firm buy factors from a market, and when does it produce those factors itself? The answer is that firms vertically integrate if the benefits outweigh the costs. Before we can examine the trade-off between these costs and benefits, we need to analyze how factor markets work.

We show that the factor market equilibrium price depends on the structure of factor markets and the output market. We first look at competitive factor and output markets. We then examine the effect of a monopoly in either or both markets.

We next consider markets in which there is a **monopsony**: the only buyer of a good in a market. A monopsony is the mirror image of a monopoly. Whereas a monopoly sells at a price higher than a competitive industry would charge, a monopsony buys at a lower price than a competitive industry would. Finally, we investigate when a firm vertically integrates to produce inputs itself and when it buys the inputs from a factor market.

IN THIS CHAPTER,

WE EXAMINE

FOUR MAIN

TOPICS

1. **Competitive factor market:** The intersection of the factor supply curve and factor demand curve (which depends on firms' production functions and the market price for output) determines the equilibrium in a competitive factor market.
2. **Effect of monopolies on factor markets:** If firms exercise market power in either factor or output markets, the quantities of inputs and outputs sold fall.
3. **Monopsony:** A monopsony maximizes its profit by paying a price below the competitive level, which creates a deadweight loss for society.
4. **Vertical integration:** A firm may engage in many sequential stages of production itself, perform in only a few stages and relies on markets for others, or use contracts or other means to coordinate its activities with those of other firms, depending on which approach is the most profitable.

15.1 COMPETITIVE FACTOR MARKET

Virtually all firms rely on factor markets for at least some inputs. The firms that buy factors may be competitive price takers or noncompetitive price setters, such as a monopsony. Competitive, monopolistically competitive, oligopolistic, or monopolistic firms sell factors. Here we examine factor markets in which buying and selling firms are competitive price takers. In the next section, we consider noncompetitive factor markets.

Factor markets are competitive when there are many small buyers and sellers. The flower auction in Amsterdam that the Verenigde Bloemenveilingen Aalsmeer cooperative holds daily (Chapter 8) typifies such a competitive market with many sellers and buyers. The sellers supply inputs (flowers in bulk) to buyers, who sell outputs (trimmed flowers in vases, wrapped bouquets) at retail to final customers.

Our earlier analysis of the competitive supply curve applies to factor markets. Chapter 5 derives the supply curve of labor by examining how individuals' choices between labor and leisure depend on tastes and the wage rate. Chapter 8 determines the competitive supply curves of firms in general, including those that produce factors for other firms. Given that we know the supply curve, all we need to do to analyze a competitive factor market is to determine the factor's demand curve.

Short-Run Factor Demand of a Firm

A profit-maximizing firm's demand for a factor of production is downward sloping: The higher the price of an input, the less the firm wants to buy. To understand what is behind a firm's factor demand, we examine a firm that uses capital and labor to produce output from factors. Using the theory of the firm (Chapters 6 and 7), we show how the amount of an input the firm demands depends on the prices of the factors and the price of the final output.

We start by considering the short-run factor demand for labor of a firm that can vary labor but not capital. Then we examine long-run factor demands when both inputs are variable.

In the short run, a firm has a fixed amount of capital, $\overline{K}$, and can vary the number of workers, L, it employs. Will the firm's profit rise if it hires one more worker? The answer depends on whether its revenue or labor costs rise more when output expands.

An extra worker per hour raises the firm's output per hour, q, by the marginal product of labor, $MP_L = \Delta q/\Delta L$ (Chapter 6). How much is that extra output worth to the firm? The extra revenue, R, from the last unit of output is the firm's marginal revenue, $MR = \Delta R/\Delta q$. As a result, the **marginal revenue product of labor** (MRP_L), the extra revenue from hiring one more worker, is[1]

$$MRP_L = MR \times MP_L.$$

For a firm that is a competitive employer of labor, the marginal cost of hiring one more worker per hour is the wage, w. Hiring an extra worker raises the firm's profit if the marginal benefit—the marginal revenue product of labor—is greater than the marginal cost—the wage—from one more worker: $MRP_L > w$. If the marginal revenue product of labor is less than the wage, $MRP_L < w$, the firm can raise its profit by reducing the number of workers it employs. Thus *the firm maximizes its profit by hiring workers until the marginal revenue product of the last worker exactly equals the marginal cost of employing that worker, which is the wage*:

$$MRP_L = w.$$

For now, we restrict our attention to competitive firms. A competitive firm faces an infinitely elastic demand for its output at the market price, p, so its marginal revenue is p (Chapter 8), and its marginal revenue product of labor is

$$MRP_L = p \times MP_L.$$

The marginal revenue product for a competitive firm is also called the *value of the marginal product* because it equals the market price times the marginal product of labor: the market value of the extra output. The competitive firm hires labor to the point at which its marginal revenue product of labor equals the wage:

$$MRP_L = p \times MP_L = w. \tag{15.1}$$

Table 15.1 illustrates the relationship in Equation 15.1. If the firm hires $L = 3$ workers per hour, the marginal product from the third worker is 5 units of output per hour. Because the firm can sell the output at the market price $p = \$3$ per unit, the extra revenue from hiring the third worker is $MRP_L = p \times MP_L = \$3 \times 5 = \$15$. By hiring this worker, the firm increases its profit because the wage of this worker is only $w = \$12$. If the firm hires a fourth worker, the marginal product of labor from this last worker falls to 4, and the marginal revenue product of labor falls to $12. Thus the extra revenue from the last worker exactly equals that worker's wage, so the firm's profit is unchanged. Were the firm to hire a fifth worker, the $MRP_L = \$9$ is less than the wage of $12, so its profit would fall.

---

[1]In the short run, output is a function of only labor, $q(L)$. The price the firm receives from selling q units of output is given by its demand function, $p(q)$. Thus the revenue that the firm receives is $R(L) = p[q(L)]q(L)$. The extra revenue that the firm obtains from using an extra amount of labor services is derived using the chain rule of differentiation:

$$MRP_L \equiv \frac{dR}{dL} = \frac{dR}{dq} \times \frac{dq}{dL} \equiv MR \times MP_L.$$

Table 15.1 Marginal Product of Labor, Marginal Revenue Product of Labor, and Marginal Cost

Labor, L	Marginal Product of Labor, MP_L	Marginal Revenue Product of Labor, $MRP_L = 3MP_L$	Output, q	Marginal Cost, $MC = 12/MP_L$
2	6	$18	13	$2
3	5	$15	18	$2.4
4	4	$12	22	$3
5	3	$9	25	$4
6	2	$6	27	$6

Notes: Wage, w, is $12 per hour of work. Price, p, is $3 per unit of output. Labor is variable, and capital is fixed.

Panel a of Figure 15.1 shows the same relationship. The wage line, $w = \$12$, intersects the MRP_L curve at $L = 4$ workers per hour. *The wage line is the supply of labor the firm faces.* As a competitive buyer of labor services, the firm can hire as many workers as it wants at a constant wage of $12. *The marginal revenue product of labor curve, MRP_L, is the firm's demand curve for labor* when other inputs are fixed. It shows the maximum wage a firm is willing to pay to hire a given number of workers. Thus the intersection of the supply of labor facing the firm and the firm's demand curve for labor, Equation 15.1, determines the profit-maximizing number of workers.

A firm's labor demand curve is usually downward sloping because of the law of diminishing marginal returns (Chapter 6). The marginal product from extra workers, MP_L, of a firm with fixed capital eventually falls as the firm increases the amount of labor it uses. Table 15.1 illustrates that the marginal product of labor falls from 6 for the second worker to 2 for the sixth worker. Because the marginal product of labor declines as more workers are hired, the marginal revenue product of labor (which equals a constant price times the marginal product of labor) or demand curve must slope downward as well.

Profit Maximization Using Labor or Output. Chapter 8 presents another profit-maximization condition: A competitive firm maximizes its profit by operating where the market price, p, equals the marginal cost of an extra unit of output, MC (Equation 8.1). This output profit-maximizing condition is equivalent to the labor profit-maximizing condition in Equation 15.1. Dividing Equation 15.1 by MP_L, we find that

$$p = \frac{w}{MP_L} = MC.$$

As Chapter 7 shows, the marginal cost equals the wage, w, times 1 over the marginal product of labor, which is the extra labor, $\Delta L/\Delta q$, necessary to produce one more unit of output. The marginal cost is the cost of the extra labor, $w\Delta L$, needed to produce the extra output, Δq.

(a) Labor Profit-Maximizing Condition

(b) Output Profit-Maximizing Condition

Figure 15.1 **The Relationship Between Labor Market and Output Market Equilibria.** (a) The firm's profit is maximized at $L = 4$ workers per hour where the wage line, $w = \$12$, crosses the marginal revenue product of labor, MRP_L, curve, which is also the demand curve for labor. (b) The firm's profit is maximized at 22 units of output (produced by 4 workers), for which its marginal cost, $MC = w/MP_L$, curve equals the market price, $p = \$3$.

Table 15.1 illustrates this relationship. The fourth column shows how the amount of output produced varies with the number of workers. Because 3 workers produce 18 units of output and 4 workers produce 22 units of output, the marginal product of the fourth worker is 4 units of output. With a wage of $12, the marginal cost for the last unit of output is $MC = w/MP_L = \$12/4 = \$3$. The market price is also $3, so the firm maximizes its profit by producing 22 units of output, as panel b of Figure 15.1 illustrates.

In summary, the two profit-maximizing equilibria in Figure 15.1 give the same answer: The firm maximizes its profit by hiring 4 workers to produce 22 units of output. Panel a shows that the firm maximizes its profit by hiring 4 workers, for which the marginal benefit or marginal revenue product from the last worker, MRP_L, equals the marginal cost of that worker, w. Panel b shows that the firm maximizes its profit by producing 22 units of output, for which the marginal benefit or marginal revenue from the last unit of output, $p = \$3$, equals the marginal cost of the last unit of output, MC.

How Changes in Wages and Prices Affect Factor Demand. The number of workers a firm hires depends on the wage and the price of the final good, as Equation 15.1 shows. Suppose that the supply of labor shifts so that the wage falls from $w_1 = \$12$ to $w_2 = \$6$ while the market price remains constant at $3. The firm hires more workers because the cost of more labor falls while the incremental revenue from additional output is unchanged. Figure 15.2 shows that a fall in the wage due to a downward shift of the labor supply curve from S^1 to S^2 causes a shift along the labor demand curve D^1 from point *a*, where the firm hires 4 workers, to point *b*, where the firm hires 6 workers per hour.

If the market price falls from $3 to $2, the demand curve for labor shifts downward from D^1 to D^2. Demand D^2 is only $\frac{2}{3} = (2MP_L)/(3MP_L)$ as high as D^1 at any given quantity of labor. If the wage stays constant at $w_1 = \$12$, the firm reduces its demand for workers from 4, point *a*, to 2, point *c*.

Thus a shift in either the market wage or the market price affects the amount of labor that a firm employs. A study of German manufacturing firms (Ross and Zimmerman, 1993) found that changes in the price of the final good—output demand—were more important than changes in relative wages in determining shifts in labor demand.

Figure 15.2 Shift of and Movement Along the Labor Demand Curve. If the market price is $3, the firm's labor demand curve is D^1. A fall in the wage causes a *shift of the supply curve* from S^1 to S^2 and a *shift along the demand curve for labor*. If the wage is $w_1 = \$12$, the firm hires 4 workers per hour, equilibrium point *a*. If the wage falls to $w_2 = \$6$, the firm hires 6 workers, point *b*. A fall in the market price causes a *shift of the demand curve for labor*. A fall in the market price to $2 causes a *shift of the firm's demand curve for labor* from D^1 to D^2. If the wage stays constant at $w_1 = \$12$, the fall in the market price causes a *movement along the supply curve S^1*: The number of workers the firm hires falls from 4, point *a* on D^1 and S^1, to 2, point *c* on D^2 and S^1.

Solved Problem 15.1

How does a competitive firm adjust its demand for labor when the government imposes a specific tax of τ on each unit of output?

Answer

1. *Give Intuition*: The specific tax lowers the price per unit the firm receives, so we can apply the same type of analysis we just used for a fall in the market price.

2. *Show how the tax affects the marginal revenue product of labor*: The marginal revenue product of labor for a competitive firm is the price the firm receives for the good times the marginal product of labor. The tax reduces the price the firm receives. The tax does not affect the relative prices of labor and capital, so it does not affect the marginal product of labor for a given amount of labor, $MP_L(L)$. For a given amount of labor, the marginal revenue product of labor falls from $p \times MP_L(L)$ to $(p - \tau) \times MP_L(L)$. The marginal revenue product of labor curve—the labor demand curve—shifts downward until it is only $(p - \tau)/p$ as high as the original labor demand curve at any quantity of labor.

Application   THREAD MILL

By calculating the marginal revenue product of labor, we can derive the labor demand curve for a Canadian thread mill. The firm has a Cobb-Douglas production function:[2]

$$q = L^{0.6}K^{0.2}. \tag{15.2}$$

Suppose that, in the short run, the mill's capital, K, is fixed at 32 units, so it can increase its output, q, only by increasing the amount of labor, L, it uses. To determine the firm's short-run production function, we set $K = 32$ in Equation 15.2:

$$q = L^{0.6}32^{0.2} = 2L^{0.6}.$$

The extra output or marginal product of labor from the last worker can be determined by using a calculator. We find that the extra output from the last worker when the firm goes from 31 to 32 workers is

$$\Delta q = (2 \times 32^{0.6}) - (2 \times 31^{0.6}) \approx 0.3.$$

The firm can sell its output at $50 per unit. The firm's marginal revenue product of labor at $L = 32$ is

---

[2]This production function is from the estimates of Baldwin and Gorecki (1986). The units of output are chosen appropriately so that the constant multiplier A in the general Cobb-Douglas, $q = AL^{\alpha}K^{\beta}$, equals 1. Chapter 6 reports two significant digits for α and β. We round those numbers to one digit here to simplify the calculations.

$$MRP_L = p \times MP_L = \$50 \times 0.3 = \$15.$$

Thus when the price is $50 and the wage is $15, the firm hires 32 workers.

More generally, the marginal product of labor function, when we hold capital fixed at $K = 32$, is[3]

$$MP_L = 1.2L^{-0.4}.$$

Thus if a competitive thread mill faces a market price of $50, its labor demand curve is

$$MRP_L \equiv p \times MP_L = \$50 \times 1.2L^{-0.4} = \$60L^{-0.4}.$$

Figure 15.3 shows this MRP_L curve or short-run labor demand curve for the firm when capital is fixed at $K = 32$.

Long-Run Factor Demand

In the long run, the firm may vary all of its inputs. Now if the wage of labor rises, the firm adjusts both labor and capital. As a result, the short-run marginal revenue product of labor curve that holds capital fixed is not the firm's long-run labor demand curve. The long-run labor demand curve takes account of changes in the firm's use of capital as the wage rises.

In both the short run and the long run, the labor demand curve is the marginal revenue product curve of labor. In the short run, the firm cannot vary capital, so the short-run MP_L curve and hence the short-run MRP_L curve are relatively steep. In the long run, when the firm can vary all inputs, its long-run MP_L curve and MRP_L curves are flatter.

Figure 15.3 shows the relationship between the long-run and short-run labor demand curves for the thread mill.[4] In the short run, capital is fixed at $K = 32$, the wage is $w = \$15$, and the rental rate of capital is $r = \$5$. The firm hires 32 workers per hour, point *a* on its short-run labor demand curve, where $K = 32$. Using 32

---

[3]We determine the marginal product of labor function holding capital fixed at $K = 32$ by differentiating the short-run production function, $q = 2L^{0.6}$, with respect to labor:

$$MP_L \equiv dq/dL = 0.6 \times 2 \times L^{0.6-1} = 1.2L^{-0.4}.$$

The calculator method, which compares a discrete change from 31 to 32 workers, gives approximately the correct MP_L. Using this exact formula, which is based on an infinitesimal change in labor, we find that the MP_L at $L = 32$ is exactly $0.3 = 1.2(32)^{-0.4}$.

[4]Appendix 15A formally shows that the long-run labor demand and capital demand functions for a Cobb-Douglas production function are functions of the market price, p; the wage rate, w; and the rental rate of capital, r. Substituting the parameters for the Canadian thread mill, $\alpha = 0.6$, $\beta = 0.2$, and $A = 1$, into Equation 15A.8, we find that the firm's long-run labor demand curve is

$$L = (0.6/w)^4(0.2/r)p^5.$$

Its long-run capital demand curve, Equation 15A.9, is

$$K = (0.6/w)^3(0.2/r)^2p^5.$$

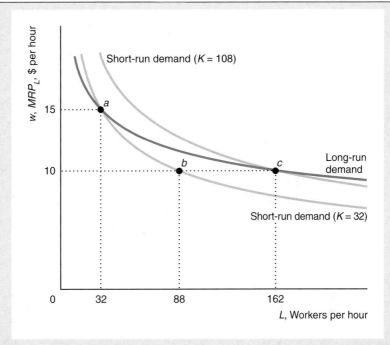

Figure 15.3 Labor Demand of a Thread Mill. If the long-run market price is $50 per unit, the rental rate of capital services is *r* = $5, and the wage is *w* = $15 per hour, a Canadian thread mill hires 32 workers (and uses 32 units of capital) at point *a* on its long-run labor demand curve. In the short run, if capital is fixed at *K* = 32, the firm still hires 32 workers per hour at point *a* on its short-run labor demand curve. If the wage drops to $10 and capital remains fixed at *K* = 32, the firm would hire 88 workers, point *b* on the short-run labor demand curve. In the long run, however, it would increase its capital to *K* = 108 and hire 162 workers, point *c* on the long-run labor demand curve and on the short-run labor demand curve with *K* = 108.

workers and 32 units of capital is profit maximizing in the long run, so point *a* is also on the firm's long-run labor demand curve.

In the short run, if the wage fell to $10, the firm could not increase its capital, so it would hire 88 workers, point *b* on the short-run labor demand curve, where *K* = 32. In the long run, however, the firm would employ more capital and even more labor (because it can sell as much output as it wants at the market price). It would hire 162 workers and use 108 units of capital, which is point *c* on both the long-run labor demand curve and the short-run labor demand curve for *K* = 108.

Factor Market Demand

A factor market demand curve is the sum of the factor demand curves of the various firms that use the input. Determining a factor market demand curve is more difficult than deriving consumers' market demand for a final good. When horizontally summing the demand curves for individual consumers in Chapter 2, we were concerned with only a single market.

Inputs such as labor and capital are used in many output markets, however. Thus, to derive the labor market demand curve, we first determine the labor demand curve for each output market and then sum across output markets to obtain the factor market demand curve.

The Marginal Revenue Product Approach. Earlier we derived the factor demand of a competitive firm that took the output market price as given. The problem we face is that the output market price depends on the factor's price. As the factor's price falls, each firm, taking the original market price as given, uses more of the factor to produce more output. This extra production by all the firms in the market causes the market price to fall. As the market price falls, each firm reduces its output and hence its demand for the input. Thus a fall in an input price causes less of an increase in factor demand than would occur if the market price remained constant, as Figure 15.4 illustrates.

Figure 15.4 Market Demand for Labor. When the output price is $p = \$9$, the individual competitive firm's labor demand curve is $MRP_L(p = \$9)$. If $w = \$25$ per hour, the firm hires 50 workers, point a in panel a, and the 10 firms in the market demand 500 workers, point A on the labor demand curve $D(p = \$9)$ in panel b. If the wage falls to $10, each firm would hire 90 workers, point c, if the market price stayed fixed at $9. The extra output, however, drives the price down to $7, so each firm hires 70 workers, point b. The output market's demand for labor that takes price adjustments into account, D(price varies), goes through points A and B.

At the initial output market price of $9 per unit, the competitive firm's labor demand curve (panel a) is $MRP_L(p = \$9) = \$9 \times MP_L$. When the wage is $25 per hour, the firm hires 50 workers: point *a*. The 10 firms in the market (panel b) demand 500 hours of work: point *A* on the demand curve $D(p = \$9) = 100 \times \$9 \times MP_L$. If the wage falls to $10 while the market price remains fixed at $9, each firm hires 90 workers, point *c*, and all the firms in the market would hire 900 workers, point *C*. However, the extra output drives the price down to $7, so each firm hires 70 workers, point *b*, and the firms collectively demand 700 workers, point *B*. The market labor demand curve for this output market that takes price adjustments into account, *D*(price varies), goes through points *A* and *B*. Thus the output market's demand for labor is steeper than it would be if output prices were fixed.

To derive the labor market demand curve, we need to combine all the demand curves for the various output markets that use labor. We apply the same method as in Chapter 2: We horizontally sum the individual labor demand curves for all the output markets.

An Alternative Approach. For certain types of production functions, it is easier to determine the market demand curve by using the output profit-maximizing equation rather than the marginal revenue product approach. Suppose that calculator manufacturers are competitive and use a fixed-proportions production function, producing each calculator using one microchip and one plastic case. Each plastic case costs p_p, and each microchip costs p_m. What is the calculator market's demand for microchips?

Figure 15.5 shows the demand both for calculators, *Q*, and microchips, *M*. Because the numbers of chips and calculators are equal, $Q = M$, the horizontal axes for chips and calculators are the same.

Because each calculator requires one chip and one case, the marginal cost of producing a calculator is $MC = p_p + p_m$. Each competitive firm operates where the market price equals the marginal cost: $p = p_p + p_m = MC$. As a result, the most that any firm would pay for a silicon chip is $p_m = p - p_p$, the amount left over from selling a calculator after paying for the plastic case. Thus the calculator market's demand curve for microchips lies p_p below the demand curve for calculators, as the figure shows.[5]

Competitive Factor Market Equilibrium

The intersection of the factor market demand curve and the factor market supply curve determines the competitive factor market equilibrium. We've just derived the factor market demand. There's nothing unusual about the factor supply curve. The long-run factor supply curve for each firm is its marginal cost curve above the minimum of its average cost curve, and the factor market supply curve is the horizontal sum of the firm supply curves (Chapter 8). As we've already analyzed competitive market equilibria for markets in general in Chapters 2, 3, 8, and 9, there's no point in repeating the analysis. (Been there. Done that.)

---

[5] The inverse demand function for calculators is a decreasing function of quantity, $p(Q)$. Similarly, the inverse demand function for microchips is $p_m(M)$. Because $Q = M$, we can write the profit-maximization condition as $p(Q) = p_m(M) + p_p$. Thus the demand for chips lies p_p below the demand for calculators: $p_m(M) = p(Q) - p_p$.

Figure 15.5 Demand for Microchips in Calculators. It takes one microchip, which costs p_m, and one plastic case, which costs p_p, to produce a calculator, so the marginal cost of a calculator is $MC = p_m + p_p$. Competitive firms operate where the price of a calculator is $p = p_m + p_p$. Thus the demand curve for a microchip lies p_p below that of a calculator.

Chapter 10 shows that factor prices are equalized across markets. For example, if wages were higher in one industry than in another, workers would shift from the low-wage industry to the high-wage industry until the wages were equalized.

15.2 | EFFECT OF MONOPOLIES ON FACTOR MARKETS

Having examined the factor market equilibrium where competitive firms sell a factor to a competitive output market, we now survey the effects of market power on factor market equilibrium. If firms in the output market *or* the factor market exercise market power by setting price above marginal cost, less of a factor is sold than would be sold if all firms were competitive.

Market Structure and Factor Demands

Factor demand curves vary with market power. As we saw in Chapters 11 and 12, the marginal revenue of a profit-maximizing firm, $MR = p(1 + 1/\varepsilon)$, is a function of the elasticity, ε, of its output demand curve and the market price, p. Thus the firm's marginal revenue product of labor function is

$$MRP_L = p\left(1 + \frac{1}{\varepsilon}\right)MP_L.$$

The labor demand curve is $p \times MP_L$ for a competitive firm because it faces an infinitely elastic demand at the market price, so its marginal revenue equals the market price.

The marginal revenue product of labor or labor demand curve for a competitive market is above that of a monopoly or oligopoly firm. Figure 15.6 shows the market factor demand for a thread mill if it is a competitive firm, one of two identical Cournot quantity-setting firms, or a monopoly.[6]

A monopoly operates in the elastic section of its downward-sloping demand curve (Chapter 11), so its demand elasticity is less than −1 and finite: $-\infty < \varepsilon \le -1$. As a result, at any given price, the monopoly's labor demand, $p(1 + 1/\varepsilon)MP_L$, lies below the labor demand curve, pMP_L, of a competitive firm with an identical marginal product of labor curve.

The elasticity of demand a Cournot firm faces is $n\varepsilon$, where n is the number of identical firms and ε is the market elasticity of demand (Chapter 13). Given that they have the same market demand curve, a duopoly Cournot firm faces twice as elastic a demand curve as a monopoly faces. Consequently, a Cournot duopoly firm's labor demand curve, $p[1 + 1/(2\varepsilon)]MP_L$, lies above that of a monopoly but

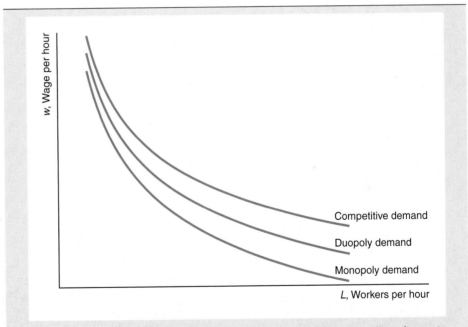

Figure 15.6 How Labor Demand Varies with Market Structure. For all profit-maximizing firms, the labor demand curve is the marginal revenue product of labor: $MRP_L = MR \times MP_L$. Because marginal revenue differs with market structure, so does the MRP_L. At a given wage, a competitive thread firm demands more workers than a Cournot duopoly firm, which demands more workers than a monopoly.

---

[6]In the short run, the thread mill's marginal product function is $MP_L = 1.2L^{-0.4}$. The labor demand is $p \times 1.2L^{-0.4}$ for a competitive firm, $p[1 + 1/(2\varepsilon)] \times 1.2L^{-0.4}$ for one of two identical Cournot duopoly firms, and $p(1 + 1/\varepsilon) \times 1.2L^{-0.4}$ for a monopoly.

below that of a competitive firm. From now on, we concentrate on the competitive and monopoly equilibria because the oligopoly and monopolistically competitive equilibria lie between these polar cases.

A Model of Market Power in Input and Output Markets

When a firm with market power in either the factor or the output market raises its price, the price to final consumers rises. As a result, consumers buy fewer units, so fewer units of the input are demanded. We use a linear example to illustrate how monopolies affect factor market equilibrium. The inverse demand, $p(Q)$, for the final good is

$$p = 80 - Q. \tag{15.3}$$

Figure 15.7 plots this demand curve. An unlimited number of workers can be hired at $20 an hour. Each unit of output, Q, requires one unit of labor, L, and no other factor, so the marginal product of labor is 1.

As a benchmark, we start our analysis with competitive factor and output markets. Then we ask how the factor market equilibrium changes if the output market

Figure 15.7 Effect of Output Market Structure on Labor Market Equilibrium. Because one unit of output is produced with one unit of labor, the marginal product of labor is 1, so the competitive labor demand curve is the same as the output demand curve. If both markets are competitive, the labor market equilibrium is e_1. A monopoly's labor demand curve is identical to its marginal revenue curve. An output monopoly charges final consumers a higher price, so it buys less labor. The new labor equilibrium is e_2. With a labor monopoly (union), the equilibrium is e_3.

is monopolized. Next, we examine a monopolized factor market and a competitive output market. Finally, we investigate the effect of market power in both markets.

Competitive Factor and Output Markets. The intersection of the relevant supply and demand curves determines the competitive equilibria in both input and output markets in Figure 15.7. Because $Q = L$, the figure measures both output and labor on the same horizontal axis.

The marginal product of labor is 1 because one extra worker produces one more unit of output. Thus the competitive market's demand for labor, $MRP_L = p \times MP_L = p$, is identical to the output demand curve. The labor demand function is the same as the output demand function, where we replace p with w and Q with L:

$$w = 80 - L. \tag{15.4}$$

The competitive supply of labor is a horizontal line at $20. Given a competitive output market, the intersection of this supply curve of labor and the competitive demand for labor (Equation 15.4) determines the labor market equilibrium, e_1, where $20 = 80 - L$. Thus the competitive equilibrium amount of labor services is $L_1 = 60$, and the equilibrium wage is $w_1 = \$20$.

The cost of producing a unit of output equals the wage, so the supply curve of output is also horizontal at $20. The intersection of this output supply curve and the output demand curve, Equation 15.3, occurs at $Q_1 = 60$ and $p_1 = \$20$. A competitive firm's average cost, w_1, exactly equals the price at which it sells its good, p_1, so the competitive firm breaks even.

Competitive Factor Market and Monopolized Output Market. Because a monopoly in the output market charges a higher price than a competitive market would, it sells fewer units of output and hires fewer workers. The monopoly faces a competitive labor supply curve that is horizontal at the wage $w_2 = \$20$. Thus the output monopoly's marginal cost is $20 per unit.

The monopoly's marginal revenue curve is twice as steep as the linear output demand curve it faces (Chapter 11):

$$MR_Q = 80 - 2Q.$$

The monopoly maximizes its profit where its marginal revenue equals its marginal cost:

$$MR_Q = 80 - 2Q = 20 = MC.$$

Thus the equilibrium quantity is $Q_2 = 30$. Substituting this quantity into the output demand, Equation 15.3, we find that the equilibrium price is $50. The monopoly makes $p_2 - w_2 = \$50 - \$20 = \$30$ per unit. Its profit is $\pi = \$900$, as the shaded rectangle in Figure 15.7 shows.

Because the monopoly's marginal product of labor is 1, its demand curve for labor equals its marginal revenue curve:

$$MRP_L = MR_Q \times MP_L = MR_Q.$$

We obtain its labor demand function by replacing Q with L and MR_Q with w in its marginal revenue function:

$$w = 80 - 2L.$$

The intersection of the competitive labor supply curve, $w_2 = \$20$, and the monopoly's demand for labor curve determines the labor market equilibrium, e_2, where $80 - 2L = 20$. Thus the equilibrium amount of labor is $L_2 = 30$.

This example illustrates that a monopoly hurts final consumers and drives some sellers of the factor (workers) out of this market. Final consumers pay $30 more per unit than they would pay if the market were competitive. Because of the higher price, consumers buy less output, $Q_2 = 30 < 60 = Q_1$. As a consequence, the monopoly demands less labor than a competitive market does: $L_2 = 30 < 60 = L_1$. If the supply curve of labor were upward sloping, this reduction in demand would also reduce workers' wages.

Application   RECORD PRICES

The exercise of downstream market power substantially raises the price of a CD. The table shows the elements that determined the price of Rod Stewart's *Spanner in the Works* CD. The plastic and various other inputs needed to produce the CD cost Warner Bros. Records, the manufacturer, about half a dollar per disk. Mr.

Steps Involved in Producing Rod Stewart's *Spanner in the Works* CD	Cost, Price, or Markup per CD
1. *Oil is pumped* in Saudia Arabia.	Cost: Fraction of a cent
2. *Benzene is removed* from the oil by a refinery in Pascagoula, Mississippi.	Cost: Fraction of a cent
3. *Benzene is pressed into pellets* of a high-grade, super-clear plastic polycarbonate called Lexan at a plastics factory in Pittsfield, Massachusetts.	Cost: About 1¢
4. *Lexan is pressed into a disk*, and Mr. Stewart's songs are encoded on the CD, which is then coated with aluminum and covered with ultraviolet lacquer by a manufacturer in Oliphant, Pennsylvania.	Cost: 10¢ to 15¢
5. *A plastic case and cover are made* by a printing plant in Louisville, Kentucky.	Cost: 30¢ to 35¢
6. *Mr. Stewart is paid* royalties.	Cost: About $2.50
7. *CDs are assembled and shipped* by Warner Bros. from warehouses in Atlanta, Los Angeles, Chicago, and Philadelphia.	Wholesale price: $10.72 to $11.20 Markup: More than 350%

Source: Strauss, Neil, "Pennies That Add Up to $16.98: Why CDs Cost So Much," *The New York Times*, July 5, 1995: C11.

Stewart was paid royalties of about $2.50 per disk. Warner Bros. set its wholesale price at $10.72 to $11.20, which reflects a markup of more than 2,000% above the cost of the physical inputs and 350% above the marginal costs, including Mr. Stewart's royalty. (However, Time Warner incurs various fixed costs, including more than $1 million to record *Spanner in the Works*.) The CDs were shipped to record chains and independent distributors with a suggested retail price of $16.98. The number of CDs sold would have been substantially higher had the retail price been set closer to $5. Because it sold fewer units at the higher price, Time Warner's demand for Lexan, benzene, oil, and other inputs was reduced.

Monopolized Factor Market and Competitive Output Market. Now suppose that the output market is competitive and that there is a labor monopoly. One possibility is that the workers form a union that acts as a monopoly. Instead, for simplicity, we'll assume that the labor monopoly is the only firm that can supply the workers employed in the output market.[7]

The labor monopoly sets its marginal revenue equal to its marginal cost, which is $20. Because the competitive output market's labor demand curve is the same as the output demand curve, the marginal revenue curve this labor monopoly faces is the same as the marginal revenue curve of an output monopoly, where we replace Q with L:

$$MR_L = 80 - 2L.$$

The labor monopoly operates at e_3 in Figure 15.7, where its marginal revenue equals its marginal cost of $20:

$$80 - 2L = 20.$$

The labor monopoly sells $L_3 = 30$ hours of labor services. Substituting this quantity into the labor demand curve, Equation 15.4, we find that the monopoly wage is $w_3 = \$50$. Because the labor monopoly makes $w_3 - \$20 = \$30$ per hour of labor services and it sells 30 hours, its profit is $\pi = \$900$.

The competitive supply to the output market is horizontal at $w_3 = \$50$. The output equilibrium occurs where this supply curve hits the output demand curve, Equation 15.3: $50 = 80 - Q$. Thus the equilibrium quantity is $Q_3 = 30$. The equilibrium price is the same as the wage, $p_3 = w_3 = \$50$. As a result, the output firms break even.

In our example, in which one unit of labor produces one unit of output, consumers fare the same whether the labor market or the output market is monopolized. Consumers pay $p_2 = p_3 = \$50$ and buy $Q_2 = Q_3 = 30$ units of output. The labor market equilibria are different: The wage is higher if the monopoly is in the labor market rather than the output market. The profit goes to the monopoly regardless of which market is monopolized.

| Application | **UNION MONOPOLY POWER** |

Workers acting collectively within a union can raise their wage much in the same manner as any other monopoly. A union's success in raising the wage depends on the elasticity of demand it faces, members' ability to act collectively, laws, and the share of the labor market that is unionized. Just as the entry of competitive firms reduces the power of a monopoly (Chapter 11), we expect that the markup of the union wage over the nonunion wage will be smaller, the smaller the fraction of the labor market controlled by unions.

---

[7]Many markets have firms that only supply labor to other firms. Manpower, Kelly Services, and Accountemps provide temporary office workers and other employees. Many construction firms supply only skilled craftspeople. Still other firms specialize in providing computer programmers.

The union markup in Britain has fallen over time. The table shows estimates of how much higher British union wages were than nonunion wages in various years for three labor-skill groups.

	1889–1890	1984	1990
Unskilled	25.2%	10.2%	7.2%
Semiskilled	17.4%	10.0%	6.3%
Skilled	19.3%	3.4%	1.5%

In the late nineteenth century, unions were thriving. Union membership more than doubled from 1888 to 1892, rising from 6.2% of the workforce to 13.0%. Most of the workers in the 1889–1890 survey reported in the table were employed in industries in which unions' share of the market was substantially higher (reaching up to 90% in some occupations and industries). Unions engaged in many strikes to demonstrate their market power aggressively.

In recent decades, the union wage markup has fallen. Factors contributing to this decline include legislation that reduced the bargaining strength of trade unions, a drop in the share of union workers from 54% in 1980 to 38% in 1990, and changes in the mix of occupations with strong union representation.

Monopoly in Successive Markets. If the labor and output markets are both monopolized, consumers get hit with a double monopoly markup. The labor monopoly raises the wage, in turn raising the cost of producing the final output. The output monopoly then increases the final price even further.[8]

Figure 15.8 illustrates this double markup. The output monopoly's marginal revenue curve, $MR_Q = 80 - 2Q$, is the same as its labor demand curve, $w = 80 - 2L$. Because the labor demand curve is linear, the labor monopoly's marginal revenue curve is twice as steeply sloped:

$$MR_L = 80 - 4L.$$

The labor monopoly maximizes its profit by setting its marginal revenue equal to its marginal cost: $80 - 4L = 20$. Thus at the labor market equilibrium, e_4, the labor monopoly provides $L_4 = 15$ workers. Substituting this quantity into the labor demand curve, $w = 80 - 2L$, we find that the labor monopoly's equilibrium wage is $w_4 = \$50$. Thus the labor monopoly marks up its wage \$30 above its marginal cost. Its profit is area $B = \$30 \times 15 = \$450$ in the figure.

---

[8]In our example, the labor monopoly has a constant marginal cost of $m = \$20$. It operates where its marginal cost equals its marginal revenue, $w(1 + 1/\varepsilon_L)$, where ε_L is the elasticity of labor demand. As a result, the wage is greater than marginal cost: $w = m\mu_L$, where $\mu_L = 1/(1 + 1/\varepsilon_L) > 1$ is the multiplicative labor monopoly markup. The wage is the output monopoly's marginal cost. The output monopoly further marks up the price: $p = w\mu_Q = m\mu_L\mu_Q$, where $\mu_Q = 1/(1 + 1/\varepsilon_Q) > 1$ is the multiplicative output monopoly markup and ε_Q is the output demand elasticity.

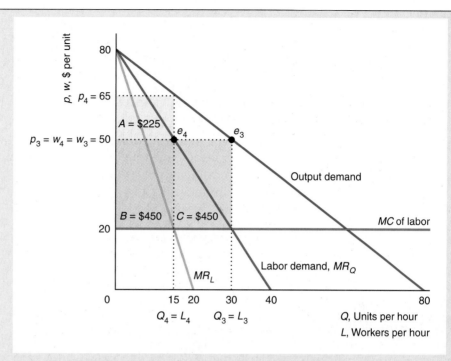

Figure 15.8 Double Monopoly Markup. If there are two successive monopolies, consumers are hit with a double monopoly markup. The labor market equilibrium is e_4, where the wage, w_4, is \$30 above the labor market's marginal and average cost of \$20. The product market monopoly's price, p_4, is \$15 above its marginal cost, w_4. If the labor monopoly integrates vertically, consumers gain ($p_3 < p_4$), and total profit increases from $A + B$ to $B + C$.

To maximize its profit, the output monopoly sets its marginal revenue, $MR_Q = 80 - 2Q$, equal to its marginal cost, $w_4 = \$50$. It sells $Q_4 = 15$ units of output. Substituting this quantity into the output demand curve, we learn that the output monopoly's equilibrium price is $p_4 = \$65$. The output monopoly's markup is \$15 above its marginal cost. Its profit is area $A = \$225$.

This double markup harms consumers. They pay a higher price—\$65 rather than \$50—than they would pay if there were a monopoly in just one market or the other.

<hr />

Solved Problem 15.2

How are consumers affected and how do profits change in the example if the labor monopoly buys the monopoly producer (integrates vertically)?

Answer

1. *Solve for the postmerger equilibrium:* The new merged monopoly's output demand is the market demand, and its marginal revenue from extra output

is $MR_Q = 80 - 2Q$, as Figure 15.8 shows. Now that the firms are one, the former labor monopoly no longer marks up the labor to its production unit. Its marginal cost of an extra unit of output is $20. The monopoly maximizes its profit by setting its marginal cost equal to MR_Q. The resulting output equilibrium is the same as it is when there was a single labor monopoly. Equilibrium output is $Q_3 = 30$ and $p_3 = \$50$. The integrated monopoly's profit is $\$30 \times 30 = \$900$, area $B + C$.

2. *Compare the premerger and postmerger equilibria*: Consumers benefit from this merger. Because the price they pay falls from $p_4 = \$65$ to $p_3 = \$50$, they buy 15 extra units of output. The firms also benefit. The combined profit with two monopolies is areas $A + B = \$675$, which is less than the profit of the integrated firm, areas $B + C = \$900$. The labor monopoly can offer the output monopoly more than it earns as a separate firm and still increase its own profit: The firms can split the extra $225. Thus everyone may gain from a vertical merger that eliminates one of the two monopoly markups.

Application   **BASEBALL SALARIES AND TICKET PRICES**

At a press conference in 1999, the Los Angeles Dodgers announced that they'd signed their star pitcher Kevin Brown to a new $105 million contract. When Mr. Brown was asked what effect his contract would have on ticket prices, he responded, "I have never believed that players' salaries are directly related to ticket prices." The reporters snickered.

Several of these newspaper pundits wrote that Mr. Brown's salary hike would drive up ticket prices to cover the expense. But their prediction doesn't make sense. If fans are willing to pay a higher price, it pays for the team to raise its price even if its players' salaries remain constant. The team sets its ticket price to maximize its profit given market demand and then negotiates with players to see who gets these profits.

A firm's price is determined by the intersection of its marginal revenue curve and its marginal cost curve. When a team raises a player's salary, it increases its fixed cost but not its marginal cost. The player's salary doesn't affect the cost of bringing one more fan to the stadium. Indeed, if there are unfilled seats in the stadium, the marginal cost of the last fan is essentially zero.

Ticket prices rise when a higher salary is paid only if the team hires a new star player, causing the demand curve to shift to the right. If the team has agreed to pay a higher salary to a current player, as in the Dodgers' case, the higher salary should have no effect on ticket prices.

But aren't player payrolls and ticket prices correlated? Sure, but higher ticket prices "cause" higher salaries rather than the other way around. Indeed, the Dodgers raised their 1999 ticket prices before they signed Brown. Teams in cities where the demand is great tend to pay the highest salaries. The New

York Yankees receive nearly $50 million a year in cable television revenue, covering much of their payroll before a single fan enters Yankee Stadium. The next five highest payrolls are paid by teams with new, large stadiums that double as virtual cash registers and provide funds to hire players.

If salaries alone determined ticket prices, then the two teams with the highest salaries, the Yankees and the Baltimore Orioles, should have charged the most for their seats. However, the highest ticket price was set by the Boston Red Sox. The Red Sox increased their average ticket price 16% in 1999 to $23.84, despite having cut player salaries, losing top first baseman Mo Vaughn, and having their archrival New York Yankees (who finished 22 games ahead of the Red Sox in the previous year) sign star pitcher Roger Clemens. Why did the Red Sox raise prices? Their demand curve shifted outward for other reasons: Even at the higher prices, their ticket sales rose by about 36%.

Finally, if higher salaries "cause" higher prices, we'd expect lower salaries to lower the cost of a ticket. Not true. The average player salary fell 5% in 1995, yet the average ticket price rose 2%. Similarly, the Minnesota Twins slashed their payroll by about half in 1999, yet they froze their ticket prices.

15.3 | MONOPSONY

In Chapter 11, we saw that a *monopoly*, a single *seller*, picks a point—a price and a quantity combination—on the market *demand curve* that maximizes its profit. A *monopsony*, a single *buyer* in a market, chooses a price-quantity combination from the industry *supply curve* that maximizes its profit. A monopsony is the mirror image of monopoly, and it exercises its market power by buying at a price *below* the price that competitive buyers would pay.

An American manufacturer of state-of-the-art weapon systems can legally sell only to the federal government. U.S. professional football teams, which act collectively, are the only firms that hire professional football players.[9] In many fisheries, there is only one buyer of fish (or at most a small number of buyers, an *oligopsony*).

Monopsony Profit Maximization

Suppose that a firm is the sole employer in town—a monopsony in the local labor market. The firm uses only one factor, labor (L), to produce a final good. The value the firm places on the last worker it hires is the marginal revenue product of that worker—the value of the extra output the worker produces—which is the height of the firm's labor demand curve for the number of workers the firm employs.

The firm has a downward-sloping demand curve in panel a of Figure 15.9. The firm faces an upward-sloping supply curve of labor: The higher its daily wage, w, the more people want to work for the firm. The firm's *marginal expenditure*—the additional cost of hiring one more worker—depends on the shape of the supply curve.

---

[9]Football players belong to a union that acts collectively, like a monopoly, in an attempt to offset the monopsony market power of the football teams.

Figure 15.9 Monopsony. (a) The marginal expenditure curve—the monopsony's marginal cost of buying one more unit—lies above the upward-sloping market supply curve. The monopsony equilibrium, e_m, occurs where the marginal expenditure curve intersects the monopsony's demand curve. The monopsony buys fewer units at a lower price, w_m = $20, than a competitive market, w_c = $30 ,would. (b) The supply curve is more elastic at the optimum than in (a), so the value that the monopsony places on the last unit (which equals the marginal expenditure of $40) exceeds the price the monopsony pays, w_m = $30, by less than in (a).

The supply curve shows the average expenditure, or wage, the monopsony pays to hire a certain number of workers. For example, the monopsony's average expenditure or wage is $20 if it hires L = 20 workers per day. If the monopsony wants to obtain one more worker, it must raise its wage because the supply curve is upward sloping. Because it pays all workers the same wage, the monopsony must also pay more to each worker it was already employing. Thus the monopsony's marginal expenditure on the last worker is greater than that worker's wage.[10] The marginal expenditure curve in the figure has twice as steep a slope as the linear supply curve.[11]

---

[10]The monopsony's total expenditure is $E = w(L)L$, where $w(L)$ is the wage given by the supply curve. Its marginal expenditure is $ME = dE/dL = w(L) + L[dw(L)/dL]$, where $w(L)$ is the wage paid the last worker and $L[dw(L)/dL]$ is the extra amount the monopsony pays the workers it was already employing. Because the supply curve is upward sloping, $dw(L)/dL > 0$, the marginal expenditure, ME, is greater than the average expenditure, $w(L)$.

[11]Appendix 15B shows that the ME curve is twice as steep as the labor supply curve for any linear labor supply curve.

In contrast, if the firm were a competitive price taker in the labor market, it would face a supply curve that was horizontal at the market wage. Consequently, such a competitive firm's marginal expenditure to hire one more worker would be the market wage.

Any buyer—including a monopsony or a competitive firm—*buys labor services up to the point at which the marginal value of the last unit of a factor equals the firm's marginal expenditure* (Appendix 15B). If the last unit is worth more to the buyer than its marginal expenditure, the buyer purchases another unit. Similarly, if the last unit is less valuable than its marginal expenditure, the buyer purchases one less unit.

The monopsony buys 20 units of the factor. The intersection of its marginal expenditure curve and the demand curve determines the monopsony equilibrium, e_m. The monopsony values the labor services of the last worker at $40 (height of its demand curve), and its marginal expenditure on that unit (height of its marginal expenditure curve) is $40. It pays only $20 (height of the supply curve). In other words, the monopsony values the last unit at $20 more than it actually has to pay.

If the market in Figure 15.9 were competitive, the intersection of the demand curve and the supply curve would determine the competitive equilibrium at e_c, where buyers purchase 30 units at $p_c = \$30$ per unit. Thus the monopsony hires fewer workers, 20 versus 30, than a competitive market would hire and pays a lower wage, $20 versus $30.

Monopsony power is the ability of a single buyer to pay less than the competitive price profitably. The size of the gap between the value the monopsony places on the last worker (the height of its demand curve) and the wage it pays (the height of the supply curve) depends on the elasticity of supply at the monopsony optimum. The markup of the marginal expenditure (which equals the value to the monopsony) over the wage is inversely proportional to the elasticity of supply at the optimum (Appendix 15B):

$$\frac{ME - w}{w} = \frac{1}{\eta}.$$

By comparing panels a and b in Figure 15.9, we see that the less elastic the supply curve is at the optimum, the greater the gap between marginal expenditure and the wage. At the monopsony optimum, the supply curve in panel b of Figure 15.9 is more elastic than the supply curve in panel a.[12] The gap between marginal expenditure and wage is greater in panel a, $ME - w = \$20$, than in panel b, $ME - w = \$10$. Similarly, the markup in panel a, $(ME - w)/w = 20/20 = 1$, is much greater than that in panel b, $(ME - w)/w = 10/30 = \frac{1}{3}$.

---

[12]The supply curve in panel a is $w = L$, while that in panel b is $w = 20 + \frac{1}{2}L$. The elasticity of supply, $\eta = (dL/dw)(w/L)$, at the optimum is $w/L = 20/20 = 1$ in panel a and $2w/L = 2 \times 30/20 = 3$ in panel b. Consequently, the supply curve at the optimum is three times as elastic in panel b as in panel a.

Application   **MONOPSONY WAGE SETTING**

Two examples of monopsony wage setting will illustrate the degree to which a firm can alter prices through the exercise of monopsony power.

Hospitals

In small communities with a single hospital, we expect hospitals to have substantial monopsony power over the nurses they hire. Sullivan (1989) found that the value of a nurse's service to the hospital (the height of the demand or marginal expenditure curve) is 1.79 times what the hospital pays a nurse in the short run (the height of the labor supply curve). However, he estimated that the value of the nurse's service to the wage payment is only 1.26 over a three-year period. Thus hospitals have more monopsony power in the short run than in the long run.

College Sports Scholarships

The National Collegiate Athletic Association (NCAA) controls college athletics. The NCAA effectively limits payments (the value of a scholarship, room and board, and book allowances) to college football players for their athletic services to between $5,000 and $20,000. Thus the NCAA turns colleges into monopsony employers. Brown (1993) estimated that the value to a college of a player who is good enough to be drafted by the pros is more than half a million dollars due to increased ticket sales and television revenues. Thus the value of the services of a star athlete is at least 25 times greater than what the college provides in direct payments.

Welfare Effects of Monopsony

By creating a wedge between the value to the monopsony and the value to the suppliers, the monopsony causes a welfare loss in comparison to a competitive market. In Figure 15.10, sellers lose producer surplus, $D + E$, because the monopsony price, p_m, for a good is below the competitive price, p_c. Area D is a transfer from the sellers to the monopsony and represents the savings of $p_c - p_m$ on the Q_m units the monopsony buys. The monopsony loses C because suppliers sell it less output, Q_m instead of Q_c, at the low price. Thus the deadweight loss of monopsony is $C + E$. This loss is due to the wedge between the value the monopsony places on the Q_m units, the monopoly expenditure ME in the figure, and the price it pays, p_m. The greater the difference between Q_c and Q_m and the larger the gap between ME and p_m, the greater the deadweight loss.

Solved Problem 15.3   **How does the equilibrium in a labor market with a monopsony employer change if a minimum wage is set at the competitive level?**

Answer

1. *Determine the original monopsony equilibrium*: Given the supply curve in the graph, the marginal expenditure curve is ME^1. The intersection of

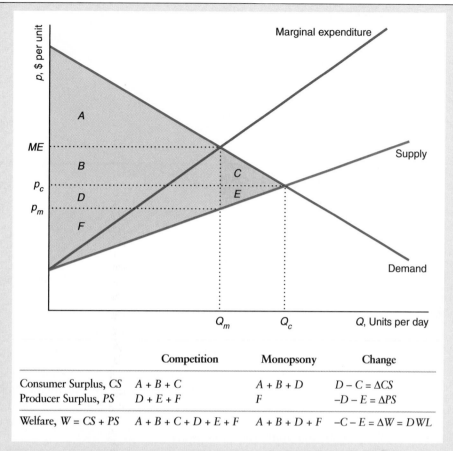

	Competition	Monopsony	Change
Consumer Surplus, CS	$A + B + C$	$A + B + D$	$D - C = \Delta CS$
Producer Surplus, PS	$D + E + F$	F	$-D - E = \Delta PS$
Welfare, $W = CS + PS$	$A + B + C + D + E + F$	$A + B + D + F$	$-C - E = \Delta W = DWL$

Figure 15.10 Welfare Effects of Monopsony. By setting a price, p_m, below the competitive level, p_c, a monopsony causes too little to be sold by the supplying market, thereby reducing welfare.

ME^1 and the demand curve determines the monopsony equilibrium, e_1. The monopsony hires L_1 workers at a wage of w_1.

2. *Determine the effect of the minimum wage on the marginal expenditure curve*: The minimum wage makes the supply curve, as viewed by the monopsony, flat in the range where the minimum wage is above the original supply curve (fewer than L_2 workers). The new marginal expenditure curve, ME^2, is flat where the supply curve is flat. Where the supply curve is upward sloping, ME^2 is the same as ME^1.

3. *Determine the post-minimum-wage equilibrium*: The monopsony operates where its new marginal expenditure curve, ME^2, intersects the demand curve. With the minimum wage, the demand curve crosses the ME^2 curve

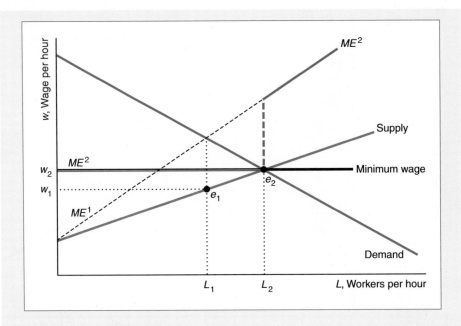

at the end of the flat section. Thus at the new equilibrium, e_2, the monopsony pays the minimum wage, w_2, and employs L_2 workers.

4. *Compare the equilibria*: The post-minimum-wage equilibrium is the same as the competitive equilibrium determined by the intersection of the demand and supply curves. Workers receive a higher wage, and more are employed than in the monopsony equilibrium. The minimum wage helps workers and hurts the monopsony.

Monopsony Price Discrimination

If some consumers have monopsony power while others do not, sellers offer those with monopsony power lower prices. The prices of organ transplants at the Cleveland Clinic, Duke University, and Johns Hopkins hospitals are 29% to 62% lower to health maintenance organizations (HMOs) than to fee-for-service patients, as Table 15.2

Table 15.2 Cost of an Organ Transplant

Transplant	Average Billed Price	Discounted HMO Contract Price
Kidney	$92,700	$50,000–$60,000 (Cleveland Clinic)
Bone marrow	$172,900	$65,000 (Duke University)
Liver	$280,200	$150,000–$200,000 (Johns Hopkins)
Heart	$222,700	$110,000 (Cleveland Clinic)
Lung	$265,100	$130,000 (Cleveland Clinic)

Source: Anders, George, "On Sale Now at Your HMO: Organ Transplants," *Wall Street Journal*, 225(11), January 17, 1995:B1, B5.

shows. One explanation is that the HMOs threaten to take the business of their millions of members to other hospitals unless a hospital offers them a low, fixed-price contract. By getting bids from several hospitals, the HMOs convince each individual hospital that they have a higher elasticity of demand than other patients.

A monopsony may directly price discriminate in much the same way as a monopoly or an oligopoly. For example, suppose that a monopsony employer can hire either of two types of workers. One type is willing to move to any other firm that pays more. The second type is unwilling to move. The employer may pay those who are willing to move more than it pays other workers, all else the same, as the next application illustrates.

Application   MONOPSONY PRICE DISCRIMINATION

Ransom (1993) found that university professors are an exception to the rule in other labor markets that earnings rise with experience. According to statistics from all labor markets, young workers earn 3% more with each year of seniority, and workers with average seniority (about 10 years) earn 2% more for each additional year. A worker with 10 years' experience earns 30% more than a worker of the same age with no experience. In contrast, more than half of doctorate-granting institutions responded in a recent survey that they had hired "new, junior faculty members at a salary above that of some senior faculty members in the same department." Controlling for degree, field, and other factors, faculty with 10 to 14 years of seniority earn about 7% less and those with 30 years of seniority earn 15% less than individuals with less than 2 years of seniority. Salaries decline by about 0.5% per year of seniority.

In most labor markets, earnings rise with experience because workers become more productive as they gain experience or because firms use higher wages for seniority as an incentive that makes employees work hard for years (see Chapter 20). Apparently, only professors who move to a different institution prevent their salaries from falling with seniority. A professor of average seniority gains a 5% to 10% higher salary by moving. Why is academia different?

One possible explanation for the negative effect of seniority is that the best professors change colleges and gain higher salaries, leaving the less productive where they are. However, this explanation appears to be false. Even after Ransom controlled for how many articles faculty members publish (a measure of productivity at research-oriented universities), he found a pronounced negative effect to seniority.

A more plausible explanation is monopsonistic wage discrimination by universities. A professor is more likely to have to move between cities to find a higher-salary job than a worker in other labor markets. A faculty member takes moving costs into account in deciding whether it pays to work in another city for a slightly higher salary. Moving costs are more important for senior than for junior faculty members, because senior faculty members are more likely to be homeowners with children in school and to have other roots in the community.

The upstream activities of mining and refining bauxite are both oligopolistic. Bauxite mines and refineries require large capital investments, have large minimum efficient scales, and face substantial barriers to entry. There were only about 80 alumina refineries worldwide in 1980. Moreover, bauxite is expensive to ship, so the market for bauxite is regional (77% of bauxite imported by the United States in 1976 came from the Caribbean region, while Japan imported close to 90% of its bauxite from Australia and Indonesia). Thus a mine or a refiner has few if any other firms with which it can deal.

To guarantee a steady supply, some refineries sign 20- to 25-year contracts with mines. Because these firms cannot foresee all possible contingencies during such long periods, however, one trading party can inflict substantial costs on the other by refusing to deal with it (say, when prices are unusually high or low). These firms have no alternative uses for bauxite and the plants that mine and refine it.

To avoid the potential for such opportunistic behavior, many firms vertically integrate. Vertically integrated firms mine and refine most of the world's bauxite (91% in 1976).

Avoiding Government Intervention. Firms may also vertically integrate to avoid government price controls, taxes, and regulations. A vertically integrated firm avoids *price controls* by selling to itself. The federal government has set a maximum price that could be charged for steel products on several occasions since World War II. Under such price controls, steel producers did not want to sell as much steel as before the controls took effect. Consequently, they rationed steel, selling their long-time customers only a fraction of what they sold before the controls went into effect.

Because transactions within a company were unaffected by price controls, a buyer who really desired more steel could purchase a steel company and obtain all the steel it wanted (and at least one firm did so). Thus purchasing a steel company allowed firms to avoid price controls. Were it not for the high transaction costs, firms could completely avoid price controls by vertically integrating.

Firms also integrate to lower their *taxes*. Tax rates vary by country, state, and type of product. A vertically integrated firm can shift profits from one of its operations to another simply by changing the *transfer price* at which it sells its internally produced materials from one division to another. By shifting profits from a high-tax jurisdiction to a low-tax jurisdiction, a firm can increase its after-tax profits. The Internal Revenue Service tries to restrict such behavior by requiring that firms use market prices for internal transfers where possible.

Government *regulations* create additional incentives for a firm to integrate vertically (or horizontally) when the profits of only one division of a firm are regulated. When the government restricts the profits that a local telephone company earns on local services but not its profits on other services, such as selling telephones in competition with other suppliers, the telephone company tries to shift profits from its regulated division to its unregulated division.

Extending Market Power. By vertically integrating, a firm may be able to increase its monopoly profits by price discriminating or by monopolizing. The Alcoa example in Chapter 12 shows how a monopoly supplier vertically integrates to prevent resales so that it can price discriminate.

An upstream monopoly supplier of a key input in a production process for a downstream competitive market may be able to boost its profit by vertically integrating forward to monopolize the production industry.[14] Similarly, a vertically integrated firm that supplies itself and others with inputs may be able to restrict essential inputs to potential competitors (see Chapter 14 and **www.awlonline.com/perloff**, "Vertical Integration and Essential Facilities: Barnes & Noble").

Application   **CUTTING OFF OXYGEN**

Under federal antitrust law, the Federal Trade Commission (FTC) challenged two firms that supplied oxygen and oxygen equipment. The firms were formed by doctors who then referred their patients with heart and lung diseases there. In 1993, the companies and the 28 doctors involved agreed to settlements that were to reduce the doctors' financial interest in the businesses.

The doctor-owners comprised 60% of the lung specialists in two California counties. The FTC contended that the doctors had obtained illegal dominance of a market by combining their power to refer patients to a company they jointly owned. Moreover, several of the doctors ran respiratory therapy centers at major hospitals and were able to influence referrals by

---

[14]If the downstream firms use a fixed-proportions production function (as in our earlier examples), a monopoly supplier does not gain additional market power by vertically integrating. See Carlton and Perloff (2000) for the relevant theory and a discussion of the empirical evidence.

hospitals and other doctors. Although such referrals are not necessarily illegal, they could be used to build up market power and to exclude competitors from the market, in violation of the law according to the FTC. Without referrals, another firm could not compete, no matter how good its product or how low its price. Under the settlement, no more than 25% of the lung specialists in the relevant market area could be affiliated with the companies.

A 1993 California law makes such self-referrals a misdemeanor subject to a $5,000 civil penalty. New federal laws also limit such referrals.

Eliminating Market Power. A firm that faces a monopsony buyer or monopoly seller may try to eliminate that market power by vertically integrating. During the Great Depression, farms in a given area could sell their milk only to a single processor, who paid them a low monopsony price. Many farmers banded together to create cooperatives that processed their own milk. As we've seen, everyone may benefit from vertical integration if both buyer and seller have monopoly power.

Summary

1. **Competitive factor market:** Any firm maximizes its profit by choosing the quantity of a factor such that the marginal revenue product (*MRP*) of that factor—the marginal revenue times the marginal product of the factor—equals the factor price. The *MRP* is the firm's factor demand. A competitive firm's marginal revenue is the market price, so its *MRP* is the market price times the marginal product. The firm's long-run factor demand is usually flatter than its short-run demand because it can adjust more factors, thus giving it more flexibility. The market demand for a factor reflects how changes in factor prices affect output prices and hence output levels in product markets.

2. **Effect of monopolies on factor markets:** If firms exercise market power to raise price above marginal cost in an output market or factor market, the quantity demanded by consumers falls. Because the quantity of output and the quantity of inputs are closely related, a reduction in the quantity of an input reduces output, and a reduction in output reduces the demand for inputs.

3. **Monopsony:** A profit-maximizing monopsony—a single buyer—sets its price so that the marginal

value to the monopsony equals its marginal expenditure. Because the monopsony pays a price below the competitive level, fewer units are sold than in a competitive market, producers of factors are worse off, the monopsony earns higher profits than it would if it were a price taker, and society suffers a deadweight loss. A monopsony may also price discriminate.

4. **Vertical integration:** A firm may vertically integrate (participate in more than one successive stage of the production or distribution of goods or services), quasi-vertically integrate (use contracts or other means to control firms with which it has vertical relations), or buy from a factor market. Depending on which is more profitable, a firm vertically integrates and produces an input itself or buys the input from others. Because vertical integration is costly, firms integrate only if there are significant benefits. Five possible benefits from vertically integrating are lowering transaction costs, ensuring a steady supply, avoiding government restrictions, extending market power to another market, and eliminating market power.

Problems

1. What does a competitive firm's labor demand curve look like at quantities of labor such that the marginal product of labor curve is upward sloping or is negative? Why?

2. What effect does an ad valorem tax of α on the revenue of a competitive firm have on that firm's demand for labor?

3. Is a firm more likely to be the victim of opportunistic behavior if it buys parts from (a) a single firm that it will not deal with again next year, (b) a single firm with which it has a long-term relationship, or (c) a market?

4. How does a fall in the rental price of capital affect a firm's demand for labor in the long run?

5. How does a monopoly's demand for labor shift if a competitive fringe (Chapter 11) enters its output market?

6. Does a shift in the supply curve of labor have a greater effect on wages if the output market is competitive or if it is monopolistic?

7. What is a monopoly's demand for labor if it uses a fixed-proportions production function in which each unit of output takes one unit of labor and one of capital?

8. A firm is a monopoly in the output market and a monopsony in the input market. Its only input is the finished good, which it buys from a competitive market with an upward-sloping supply curve. The firm sells the same good to competitive buyers in the output market. Determine its profit-maximizing output. What price does it charge in the output market? What price does it pay to its suppliers?

9. Compare the equilibrium in a market in which a firm is both a monopoly and a monopsony (as in Problem 8) to the competitive equilibrium.

10. Compare the equilibrium quantity and price in two markets: one in which a firm is both a monopsony and a monopoly (as is Problem 8) and one in which the firm buys inputs competitively but has a monopoly in the output market.

11. Compare welfare in a market where a firm that is both a monopsony and a monopoly to welfare in markets in which the firm has a monopsony in the input market but acts as a price taker in the output market.

12. Suppose that the original labor supply curve, S^1, for a monopsony shifts to the right to S^2 if the firm spends \$1,000 in advertising. Under what condition should the monopsony engage in this advertising? (*Hint:* See the monopoly analysis in Chapter 14.)

13. What happens to the monopsony equilibrium if the minimum wage is set slightly above or below the competitive wage?

14. Can a monopsony exercise monopsony power—profitably setting its price below the competitive level—if the supply curve it faces is horizontal?

15. Some health reform proposals call for taxing firms to pay for workers' medical care. How is the incidence of a specific tax per worker shared between competitive firms and workers? How does your answer change if the firm is a monopsony?

16. In 1998, four television networks (including ESPN) agreed to pay \$17.6 billion for eight years of National Football League broadcast rights. In three of the deals, the price was more than double that of the previous contracts. What effect will this deal have on advertising rates and the number of commercials, and why?

17. *Review* (Chapter 12): Discuss the following claim: "Microsoft has a monopoly in the operating system and a near-monopoly in various types of software. It can charge relatively little for the operating system and then price discriminate by charging more for the various software components because people who use them intensively are willing to pay more for the operating system."

Math Problems

18. A competitive firm's production function is $q = L + 2LK + K$. What is its marginal revenue product of labor?

19. Suppose that a firm's production function is $q = L + K$. Can it be a competitive firm? Explain.

20. A firm's production function is Cobb-Douglas:

$Q = AL^{\alpha}K^{\beta}$. What is the firm's marginal revenue product of labor?

21. If the firm in Math Problem 20 is a monopoly that faces a constant elasticity demand curve, what is its marginal revenue product of labor?

22. A monopsony faces a supply curve:

$$p = 10 + Q.$$

What is its marginal expenditure curve?

23. If the monopsony in Problem 22 has a demand curve of

$$p = 50 - Q,$$

what are the equilibrium quantity and price? How does this equilibrium differ from the competitive equilibrium?

Interest Rates, Investments, and Capital Markets

I'd gladly pay you Tuesday for a hamburger today. —Wimpy

This chapter examines *capital* and other *durable goods*: products that are usable for years. Firms use durable goods—such as manufacturing plants, machines, and trucks—to produce and distribute goods and services. Consumers spend one in every eight of their dollars on durable goods such as houses, cars, and refrigerators.

Until now, we have examined the choices between *nondurable* goods and services, which are consumed when they are purchased or soon thereafter. You eat an ice-cream cone or see a movie just after paying for it.

If a firm rents a durable good by the week, it faces a decision similar to buying a nondurable good or service. A firm demands workers' services (or other nondurable input) up to the point at which its *current* marginal cost (the wage) equals its *current* marginal benefit (the marginal revenue product of the workers' services). A firm that rents a durable good, such as a truck, by the month can use the same rule to decide how many trucks to employ per month. The firm rents trucks up to the point at which the *current* marginal rental cost equals its *current* marginal benefit—the marginal revenue product of the trucks.

If the capital good must be bought or built rather than rented, the firm cannot apply this rule on the basis of current costs and benefits alone. (There are many types of capital, such as factories or specialized pieces of equipment, that a firm *cannot* rent.) In deciding whether to build a long-lived factory, a firm must compare the *current* cost of the capital to the *future* higher profits it will make from using the plant.

Often such comparisons involve *stocks* and *flows*. A **stock** is a quantity or value that is measured independently of time. Because a durable good lasts for many periods, its stock is discussed without reference to its use within a particular time period. We say that a firm owns "an apartment building *this* year" (not "an apartment building *per* year"). If a firm buys the apartment house for $500,000, we say that it has a capital stock worth $500,000 today.

A **flow** is a quantity or value that is measured per unit of time. The consumption of nondurable goods, such as the number of ice-cream cones you eat per week, is a flow. Similarly, the stock of a durable good provides a flow of services. A firm's apartment house—its capital stock—provides a flow of housing services (apartments rented per month or year) to tenants. In exchange for these housing services, the firm receives a flow of rental payments from the tenants.

Does it pay for the firm to buy the apartment house? To answer this question, we need to extend our analysis in two ways. First, we must develop a method of comparing a flow of dollars in the future to a dollar today, as we do in this chapter. Second, we need to consider the role of uncertainty about the future (can the firm rent all the apartments each month?), a subject that we discuss in Chapter 17.

IN THIS CHAPTER,

WE EXAMINE

FOUR MAIN

TOPICS

1. **Comparing money today to money in the future:** Interest rates tell us how much more money is worth today than in the future.
2. **Choices over time:** Investing money in a project pays if the return from that investment is greater than that on the best alternative when both returns are expressed on a comparable basis.
3. **Exhaustible resources:** Scarcity, rising costs of extraction, and positive interest rates may cause the price of exhaustible resources like coal and gold to rise exponentially over time.
4. **Capital markets, interest rates, and investments:** Supply and demand in capital markets determine the market rate of interest, which affects how much people invest.

16.1   COMPARING MONEY TODAY TO MONEY IN THE FUTURE

Even if there were no inflation—so a bundle of goods would sell for the same price today, next year, and 100 years from now—most people would still value receiving a dollar today more than a dollar to be received tomorrow. Wouldn't you rather eat a dollar's worth of chocolate today than wait 10 years to eat that same amount of chocolate?

Interest Rates

Because virtually everyone values having a dollar today more than having a dollar in the future, getting someone to loan you a dollar today requires agreeing to pay back more than a dollar in the future. You may have borrowed money to pay for your college education in exchange for a credible promise to repay a greater amount after you graduate. How much more you must pay in the future is specified by an **interest rate**: the percentage more that must be repaid to borrow money for a fixed period of time.[1]

If you put money in a savings account, you are lending the bank your money, which it may in turn loan to someone who wants to buy a car or a house. For the use of your deposited funds for one year, the bank agrees to pay you an interest rate, i, of, say, 4%. That is, the bank promises to return to you $1.04 (= $1 + i$) one year from now for every dollar you loan it. If you put $100 in your savings account, you will have your $100 plus interest of 100×0.04 = $4 for a total of $104 at the end of the year.

Application   USURY

Lending money at interest dates back to at least the Babylon of Hammurabi in 1775 B.C. Today, interest payments are not just widely accepted but required by virtually all lenders. However, some cultures frown on interest.

---

[1] For simplicity, we refer to *the* interest rate throughout this chapter, but in most economies there are many interest rates. For example, a bank charges a higher interest rate to loan you money than it pays you to borrow your money.

The ancient Greek philosopher Aristotle, lawmakers, and at least three of the world's major religions condemned *usury*, which traditionally meant nothing more than lending money for interest. Two common arguments against charging interest are that lenders are getting something for nothing and that one should help one's neighbor without hope of gain.

Islamic societies honor specific injunctions against *riba* (interest). However, a broader Islamic principle—that risk should be shared between borrower and lender—has allowed Muslim lenders to share in any profits from a venture they helped finance. Over the past two decades, some Islamic states, notably Iran and Pakistan, have tried to reimpose the ban, forcing bankers to find ways around it.

In the fifth century, Pope Leo the Great forbade Christian clerics from acting as usurers and warned that laypeople who did so would be guilty of *turpe lucrum*: shameful gain. By 850, Christian clergy called for the excommunication of usurers. By 1179, usurers were to be denied a Christian burial.

Jews, drawing on biblical tradition and Talmudic writings, also condemned usury. Deuteronomy, Chapter 23, holds that "unto foreigners thou mayst lend upon interest but unto thy brother thou shalt not lend." Medieval Christians saw this passage as an excuse to exempt Jews—whom they chose to view as "foreigners"—from their prohibition against usury.

Given the importance of lending to the functioning of an economy, both Jews and Christians loaned money during the Middle Ages. Even royalty borrowed (though when their debts grew large, they tended to expel all the usurers from the land). Reluctantly, the Catholic church relaxed its ban on lending over time as the European economy expanded and the demand for credit rose. According to Jacques Le Goff, a French historian, the thirteenth-century invention of Purgatory helped the development of modern banking. Because usurers no longer expected to go straight to Hell but to linger in Purgatory, moneylenders could hope for redemption—and gained some respectability.

Gradually, a distinction was made between low interest rates, which were viewed as socially acceptable, and high ones. In 1545, England removed the general prohibition on interest charges and set a maximum rate that a lender could legally charge. Charging more than that rate was *usurious*. Other European countries followed suit. Merchant bankers gained social status doing much the same as traditional moneylenders. Governments set up central banks. However, European countries regularly debated moneylending. Regulation of maximum rates on consumer credit persisted in Britain until 1974 and continues in parts of the United States and elsewhere today.

Discount Rate. You may value future consumption more or less than other members of society. If you knew you had a fatal disease that would kill you within two years, you would place less value on payments three or more years in the future than most other people do. We call an individual's personal "interest" rate that person's **discount rate**: a rate reflecting the relative value an individual places on future consumption compared to current consumption.

A person's willingness to borrow or lend depends on whether his or her discount rate is greater or less than the market interest rate. If your discount rate is nearly zero—you view current and future consumption as equally desirable—you would gladly loan money in exchange for a positive interest rate. Similarly, if your discount rate is high—current consumption is much more valuable to you than future consumption—you would be willing to borrow at a lower interest rate. In the following discussion, we assume for simplicity that an individual's discount rate is the same as the market interest rate unless we explicitly state otherwise.

Compounding. If you place $100 in a bank account that pays 4%, at the end of a year, you can take out the interest payment of $4 and leave your $100 in the bank to earn more interest in the future. If you leave your $100 in the bank indefinitely and the interest rate remains constant over time, you will receive a payment of $4 each year. In this way, you can convert your $100 stock into a flow of $4-a-year payments forever.

In contrast, if you leave both your $100 and your $4 interest in the bank, the bank must pay you interest on $104 at end of the second year. The bank owes you interest of $4 on your original deposit of $100 and interest of $4 × 0.04 = $0.16 on your interest from the first year, for a total of $4.16.

Thus at the end of Year 1, your account contains

$$\$104.00 = \$100 \times 1.04 = \$100 \times 1.04^1.$$

By the end of the Year 2, you have

$$\$108.16 = \$104 \times 1.04 = \$100 \times 1.04^2.$$

At the end of Year 3, your account has

$$\$112.49 \approx \$108.16 \times 1.04 = \$100 \times 1.04^3.$$

If we extend this reasoning, by the end of Year t, you have

$$\$100 \times 1.04^t.$$

In general, if you let your interest accumulate in your account, for every dollar you loan the bank, it owes you $1 + i$ dollars after 1 year, $(1 + i) \times (1 + i) = (1 + i)^2$ dollars after 2 years, $(1 + i) \times (1 + i) \times (1 + i) = (1 + i)^3$ after three years, and $(1 + i)^t$ dollars at the end of t years. This accumulation of interest on interest is called *compounding*.

Frequency of Compounding. To get the highest return on your savings account, you need to check both the interest rate and the frequency of compounding. We have assumed that interest is paid only at the end of the year. However, many banks pay interest more frequently than once a year. If you leave your interest in the bank for the entire year, you receive compounded interest—interest on the interest.

If a bank's annual interest rate is $i = 4\%$, but it pays interest two times a year, the bank pays you half a year's interest, $i/2 = 2\%$, after six months. For every dollar in your account, the bank pays you $(1 + i/2) = 1.02$ dollars after six months. If you leave the interest in the bank, at the end of the year, the bank must pay you interest on your original dollar and on the interest you received at the end of the first six months. At the end of the year, the bank owes you $(1 + i/2) \times (1 + i/2) = (1 + i/2)^2 = (1.02)^2 = \$1.0404$, which is your original $1 plus 4.04¢ in interest.

Table 16.1 Interest and the Frequency of Compounding

Frequency of Compounding	Interest Payments on a $10,000 Investment at the End of 1 Year, $	
	4%	18%
Once a year	400.00	1,800.00
Twice a year	404.00	1,881.00
Four times a year	406.04	1,925.19
Daily	408.08	1,971.64
Continuous	408.11	1,972.17

If the bank were to compound your money more frequently, you would earn even more interest. Some banks offer continuous compounding, paying interest at every instant. Such compounding is only slightly better for you than daily compounding. Table 16.1 shows you that the amount you would earn after one year of investing $10,000 at a 4% or at an 18% annual rate of interest depends on the frequency of compounding.

Because most people cannot easily perform such calculations, the 1968 U.S. Truth-in-Lending Act requires lenders to tell borrowers the equivalent noncompounded annual percentage rate (APR) of interest. As the table shows, twice-a-year compounding at 4% has an APR of 4.04%. That is, over a year, an account with a noncompounded interest rate of 4.04% pays you the same interest as a 4% account that was compounded twice during the year.

Thus when considering various loans or interest rates, you should compare the APRs; comparing rates that are compounded at different frequencies can be misleading. If you use credit cards to borrow money, it's particularly important that you compare APRs across accounts because credit card interest rates are usually high. If the interest rate on your card is 18%, a continuously compounded rate has an APR of over 19.7%. If you borrow $10,000 for a year, you'll owe $1,972.17 with continuous compounding, which is 9.6% more than the $1,800 you'd owe with annual compounding. From now on, we assume that compounding takes place annually.

Using Interest Rates to Connect the Present and Future

Interest rates connect the value of the money you put in the bank today, the *present value* (*PV*), and the *future value* (*FV*) that you are later repaid, which is the present value plus interest. Understanding this relationship allows us to evaluate the attractiveness of investments involving payments today for profits in the future and of purchases made today but paid for later. Knowing the interest rate and the present value allows us to calculate the future value. Similarly, we can determine the present value if we know the future value and the interest rate.

Future Value. If you deposit *PV* dollars in the bank today and allow the interest to compound for *t* years, how much money will you have at the end? The future value, *FV*, is the present value times a term that reflects the compounding of the interest payments:

$$FV = PV \times (1 + i)^t. \tag{16.1}$$

Table 16.2 **Future Value, *FV*, to Which $1 Grows by the End of Year *t* at Various Interest Rates, *i*, Compounded Annually, $**					
t, Years	1%	4%	5%	10%	20%
1	1.01	1.04	1.05	1.10	1.20
5	1.05	1.22	1.28	1.61	2.49
10	1.10	1.48	1.63	2.59	6.19
25	1.28	2.67	3.39	10.83	95.40
50	1.64	7.11	11.47	117.39	9,100.44

Note: $FV = (1 + i)^t$, where *FV* is the future value of $1 invested for *t* years at an annual interest rate of *i*.

Table 16.2 shows how much $1 put in the bank today will be worth in the future at various annually compounded interest rates. For example, $1 left in the bank for 50 years will be worth only $1.64 at a 1% interest rate. However, that same investment is worth $7.11 at a 4% interest rate, $117.39 at a 10% rate, and $9,100.44 at a 20% rate.

Application   POWER OF COMPOUNDING

One thousand dollars left to earn interest at 8% a year will grow to $43 quadrillion in 400 years, but the first 100 years are the hardest.
— Sidney Homer, Salomon Brothers analyst

No doubt you've read that the Dutch got a good deal buying Manhattan from the original inhabitants in 1626 for about $24 worth of beads and trinkets.

That conclusion may be wrong. If these native Americans had had the opportunity to sell the beads and invest in tax-free bonds with an APR of 7%, the bond would now be worth over $2 trillion, which is much more than the assessed value of Manhattan Island. On the other hand, if the United States had taken the $7.2 million it paid for the purchase of Alaska from Russia in 1867 and invested in the same type of bonds, that money would now be worth only $50.9 billion, which is much less than Alaska's current value.

Table 16.3 Present Value, *PV*, of a Payment of $1 at the End of Year *t* at Various Interest Rates, *i*, Compounded Annually, $

t, Years	1%	4%	5%	10%	20%
1	0.99	0.96	0.95	0.91	0.83
5	0.95	0.82	0.78	0.62	0.40
10	0.91	0.68	0.61	0.39	0.16
25	0.78	0.38	0.30	0.09	0.01
50	0.61	0.14	0.09	0.009	0.00011

Note: $PV = 1/(1 + i)^t$, where PV is the present value of $1 at the end of year t at an annual interest rate of i.

Present Value. Instead of asking how much a dollar today is worth in the future, we can ask how much a dollar in the future is worth today, given the market interest rate. For example, we may want to know how much money, *PV*, we have to put in the bank today at an interest rate *i* to get a specific amount of money, *FV*, in the future. If we want to have *FV* = $100 at the end of a year and the interest rate is *i* = 4%, then from Equation 16.1 we know that $PV \times 1.04 = \$100$. Dividing both sides of this expression by 1.04, we learn that we need to put *PV* = $100/1.04 = $96.15 in the bank today to have $100 next year.

A more general formula relating money *t* periods in the future to money today is obtained by dividing both sides of Equation 16.1 by $(1 + i)^t$ to obtain

$$PV = \frac{FV}{(1 + i)^t}.$$ (16.2)

This equation tells us what *FV* dollars in year *t* are worth today at an interest *i* compounded annually. Table 16.3 and Figure 16.1 show what $1 in the future is worth today at various interest rates. At high interest rates, money in the future is virtually worthless today: A dollar paid to you in 25 years is worth only 1¢ today at a 20% interest rate.

Stream of Payments

Sometimes we need to deal with payments per period, which are flow measures, rather than a present value or future value, which are stock measures. Often a firm pays for a new factory or an individual pays for a house by making monthly mortgage payments. In deciding whether to purchase the factory or house, the decision maker compares the value of the stock (factory or home) to a flow of payments over time.

Present Value of Payments over Time. One way to make such an evaluation is to use our knowledge of the relationship between present and future value to determine the present value of the stream of payments. To do so, we calculate the present value of each future payment and add.

Payments for a Finite Number of Years. To motivate the general case, we start with a specific example. Suppose that you agree to pay $10 at the end of each year

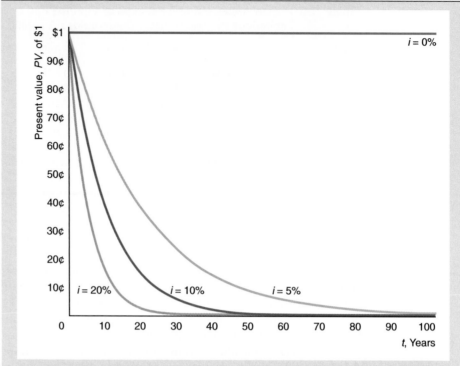

Figure 16.1 Present Value of a Dollar in the Future. The present value of a dollar is lower the farther in the future it is paid. At a given time in the future, the present value is lower when the interest rate is higher.

for three years to repay a debt. If the interest rate is 10%, the present value of this series of payments is

$$PV = \frac{\$10}{1.1} + \frac{\$10}{1.1^2} + \frac{\$10}{1.1^3} \approx \$24.87.$$

More generally, if you make a *future payment* of f per year for t years at an interest rate of i, the present value (stock) of this flow of payments is

$$PV = f\left[\frac{1}{(1+i)^1} + \frac{1}{(1+i)^2} + \cdots + \frac{1}{(1+i)^t}\right]. \tag{16.3}$$

Table 16.4 shows that the present value of a payment of $f = \$10$ a year for five years is $43 at 5%, $38 at 10%, and $30 at 20% annual interest.

Payments Forever. If these payments must be made at the end of each year forever, the present value formula is easier to calculate than Equation 16.3. If you put PV dollars into a bank account earning an interest rate of i, you can get an interest or future payment of $f = i \times PV$ at the end of year. Dividing both sides of this expression by i, we find that to get a payment of f each year forever, you'd have to put

Table 16.4 Present Value, *PV* of a Flow of $10 a Year for *t* Years at Various Interest Rates, *i*, Compounded Annually, $

t, Years	5%	10%	20%
5	43	38	30
10	77	61	42
50	183	99	50*
100	198	100*	50*
∞	200	100	50

*The actual numbers are a fraction of a cent below the rounded numbers in the table. For example, the *PV* at 10% for 100 years is $99.9927.

Note: The payments are made at the end of the year.

$$PV = \frac{f}{i} \qquad (16.4)$$

in the bank. Thus you'd have to deposit $10/i$ in the bank to ensure a future payment of $f = \$10$ forever. (See Appendix 16A for a mathematical derivation.) Using this formula, we determine that the present value of $10 a year forever is $200 at 5%, $100 at 10%, and $50 at 20%.[2]

Solved Problem 16.1 Melody Toyota advertises that it will sell you a 1997 Corolla for $14,000 or lease it to you. To lease it, you must make a down payment of $1,650 and agree to pay $1,800 at the end of each of the next two years. After the last lease payment, you may buy the car for $12,000. If you plan to keep the car until it falls apart (at least a decade) and the interest rate is 10%, which approach has a lower present value of costs?

Answer

1. *Calculate the present value of leasing*: The present value of leasing the car and then buying it is the sum of the down payment of $1,650, the present value of paying $f = \$1,800$ at the end of each year for $t = 2$ years, and the present value of purchasing the car for $FV = \$12,000$ in $t = 2$ years. Equation 16.3 shows the present value of the lease payments to be

$$\$1,800\left(\frac{1}{1.1^1} + \frac{1}{1.1^2}\right) \approx \$3,124.$$

---

[2]This payment-in-perpetuity formula, Equation 16.4, provides a good approximation of a payment for a large but finite number of years. As Table 16.4 shows, at a 5% interest rate, the present value of a payment of $10 a year for 100 years, $198, is close to the present value of a permanent stream of payments, $200. At higher interest rates, this approximation is nearly perfect. At 10%, the present value of payments for 100 years is $99.9927 compared to $100 for perpetual payments. The reason this approximation works better at high rates is that a dollar paid more than 50 or 100 years from now is essentially worthless today, as Table 16.3 shows.

Using Equation 16.2, we find that the present value of buying the car at the end of the lease period is

$$\frac{\$12,000}{1.1^2} \approx \$9,917.$$

Thus the present value of leasing the car and then buying it is approximately

$$\$1,650 + \$3,124 + \$9,917 = \$14,691.$$

2. *Compare leasing to buying the car*: The present value of buying the car is $14,000, which is $691 less than the present value of leasing it.

Future Value of Payments over Time. We just calculated the present value of a stream of payments. This type of computation can help you decide whether to buy something today that you'll pay for over time. Sometimes, however, we want to know about the future value of a stream of payments.

For example, suppose that you want to know how much you'll have in your savings account, FV, at some future time if you save f each year. The first year, you place f dollars in your account. The second year, you add another f and you have the first year's payment plus its accumulated interest, $f(1 + i)^1$. Thus at the end of the second year, your account has $f[1 + (1 + i)^1]$. In the third year, you have the third year's payment, f, plus the current value of the second year's payment, $f(1 + i)$, plus the current value of the first year's payment, $f(1 + i)^2$, for a total of $f[1 + (1 + i) + (1 + i)^2]$. Continuing in this way, we see that, at the end of t years, the account has[3]

$$FV = f[1 + (1 + i)^1 + (1 + i)^2 + \cdots + (1 + i)^t]. \tag{16.5}$$

Application   **SAVING FOR RETIREMENT**

If all goes well, you'll live long enough to retire. Will you live like royalty off your savings, or will you depend on Social Security to provide enough income that you can avoid having to eat dog food to stay alive?

You almost certainly don't want to hear this, but it isn't too early to think about saving for retirement. Thanks to the power of compounding, if you start saving when you're young, you don't have to save as much per year as you would if you start saving when you're middle aged.

Suppose that you plan to work full time from age 22 until you retire at 70 and that you can earn 7% on your retirement savings account. Let's consider two approaches to savings:

■ **Early bird:** You save $3,000 a year for the first 15 years of your working life and then let your savings accumulate interest until you retire.

---

[3]This equation can be written as $FV = f[(1 + i)^0 + (1 + i)^1 + (1 + i)^2 + \cdots + (1 + i)^t]$ because $(1 + i)^0 = 1$.

■ **Late bloomer:** After not saving for the first 15 years, you save $3,000 a year for the next 33 years until retirement.

Which scenario leads to a bigger retirement nest egg? To answer this question, we calculate the future value at retirement of each of these streams of investments.

The early bird adds $3,000 each year for 15 years into a retirement account. Using Equation 16.5, we calculate that the account has

$$\$3,000(1 + 1.07^1 + 1.07^2 + \cdots + 1.07^{14}) = \$75,387$$

at the end of 15 years. This amount then grows as the interest compounds for the next 33 years. Using Equation 16.1, we determine that the fund grows about 9.3 times to

$$\$75,387.07 \times 1.07^{33} = \$703,010$$

by retirement.

The late bloomer makes no investments for 15 years and then invests $3,000 a year until retirement. Again using Equation 16.5, we calculate that the funds at retirement are

$$\$3,000(1 + 1.07 + 1.07^2 + \cdots + 1.07^{32}) = \$356,800.$$

Thus even though the late bloomer contributes to the account for more than twice as long as the early bird, the late bloomer has saved only about half as much at retirement. Indeed, to have roughly the same amount at retirement as the early bird, the late bloomer would have to save nearly $6,000 a year for the 33 years. (By the way, someone who saved $3,000 each year for all 48 years would have $703,010 + $356,800 = $1,059,810 salted away by retirement.)

Inflation and Discounting

So far, we've ignored inflation (implicitly assumed an inflation rate of zero). Now we suppose that general inflation occurs so that *nominal prices*—actual prices that are not adjusted for inflation—rise at a constant rate over time. By adjusting for this rate of inflation (Chapter 5), we can convert nominal prices to *real prices*, which are constant prices that are independent of inflation. To calculate the real present value of future payments, we adjust for inflation and use interest rates to discount future real payments.

To illustrate this process, we calculate the real present value of a payment made next year. First, we adjust for inflation so as to convert next year's nominal payment to a real amount. Then we determine the real interest rate. Finally, we use the real interest rate to convert the real future payment to a real present value.

Adjusting for Inflation. Suppose that the rate of inflation is γ ("gamma") and the nominal amount you pay next year is $\tilde{f}$. This future debt in today's dollars—the real amount you owe—is $f = \tilde{f}/(1 + \gamma)$. If the rate of inflation is $\gamma = 10\%$, a nominal payment of $\tilde{f}$ next year is $\tilde{f}/1.1 \approx 0.909\tilde{f}$ in today's dollars.

Nominal and Real Rates of Interest. To calculate the present value of this future real payment, we discount using an interest rate. Just as we converted the future payments into real values by adjusting for inflation, we convert a nominal interest rate into a real interest rate by adjusting for inflation.

Without inflation, a dollar today is worth $1 + i$ next year, where i is the real interest rate. With an inflation rate of γ, a dollar today is worth $(1 + i)(1 + \gamma)$ nominal dollars tomorrow. If $i = 5\%$ and $\gamma = 10\%$, a dollar today is worth $1.05 \times 1.1 = 1.155$ nominal dollars next year.

Banks pay a nominal interest rate, $\tilde{i}$, rather than a real one. If they're going to get people whose real discount rate is i to save, banks' nominal interest rate must be such that a dollar pays $(1 + i)(1 + \gamma)$ dollars next year. Because $1 + \tilde{i} = (1 + i)(1 + \gamma)$ $= 1 + i + i\gamma + \gamma$, the nominal rate is

$$\tilde{i} = i + i\gamma + \gamma.$$

By rearranging this equation, we see that the real rate of interest depends on the nominal rate of interest and the rate of inflation:

$$i = \frac{\tilde{i} - \gamma}{1 + \gamma}. \qquad (16.6)$$

Equation 16.6 shows that the real rate of interest is less than the nominal rate in the presence of inflation.

If the inflation rate is small, the denominator of Equation 16.6, $1 + \gamma$, is close to 1. As a result, many people approximate the real rate of interest as the nominal rate of interest minus the rate of inflation:

$$\tilde{i} - \gamma.$$

If the nominal rate of interest is 15.5% and the rate of inflation is 10%, the real rate of interest is $(15.5\% - 10\%)/1.1 = 5\%$. The approximation to the real rate, 15.5% $- 10\% = 5.5\%$, is above the true rate by half a percentage point. The lower the rate of inflation, the closer the approximation is to the real rate of interest. If the inflation rate falls to $\gamma = 2\%$ while the nominal rate remains 15.5%, the approximation to the real rate, 13.5%, is above the real rate, 13.24%, by only slightly more than a quarter of a percentage point.

Real Present Value. To obtain the real present value of a payment one year from now, we discount the future real payment of $f = \tilde{f}/(1 + \gamma)$ using the real interest rate:

$$PV = \frac{f}{1 + i} = \frac{\tilde{f}}{(1 + \gamma)(1 + i)}.$$

Thus the real present value is obtained by adjusting for inflation and by discounting using the real interest rate.

Suppose that you sign a contract with a store to pay $100 next year for a tape recorder you get today. The rate of inflation is $\gamma = 10\%$, and the real rate of interest is $i = 5\%$. We calculate the real present value by converting the future payment into real dollars and by using the real interest rate to discount. Next year's nominal payment of $100 is only $100/1.1 ≈ $90.91 in real dollars. Discounting by the real rate of interest, we find that the real present value of that payment is $90.91/1.05 ≈ $86.58.

If everyone anticipates a particular inflation rate, γ, the nominal interest is roughly $i + \gamma$. Suppose, however, that the inflation rate turns out to be higher than the anticipated rate of γ. Such unanticipated inflation helps debtors because it lowers the real cost of future payments that are set in nominal rather than real terms.

Suppose that when you buy the tape recorder, no one expects inflation ($\gamma = 0$), so both you and the store's owner believe that the present value of your future payment is $100/1.05 ≈ $95.24. Immediately after you make the deal, the inflation rate suddenly increases to $\gamma = 10\%$, so the actual present value is only $86.58. Thus because of the unexpected inflation, the present value of what you owe is less than either you or the store owner initially expected.

Application   **WINNING THE LOTTERY**

Lottery: A tax on people who are bad at math.

When Jonnie Ely won the New York State Lottery in 2000, he had his choice of receiving $100 million in 26 annual installments or a lump sum of $44 million ($27 million after taxes). By giving him this choice, New York was acknowledging that money in the future is worth less than money today.

Several states boast that their lottery pays a winner $1 million. This claim is misleading (translation: they lie through their teeth). Typically, a lottery winner gets $50,000 a year for 20 years, which means that the winner receives 20 × $50,000 = 1 million nominal dollars over time. However, after adjustment for inflation and discounting, the real present value of these prize payments over time is much less than $1 million.

What is a payment of $50,000 for 20 years worth today? If the first payment is made today, its real present value is $50,000, regardless of the inflation and interest rates. The later payments need to be adjusted for inflation and discounted to the present to be comparable to this year's payment.

If the rate of inflation is 5% and the real rate of interest is 4%, a $50,000 payment next year is worth only $45,788 ≈ $50,000/(1.05 × 1.04) this year. Generalizing, we determine that the real present value of a dollar t years from now is

$$\frac{1}{(1.05)^t (1.04)^t}.$$

The $(1.05)^t$ term in the denominator adjusts for inflation between now and the year t: It expresses the payment in the future in terms of today's dollars. The $(1.04)^t$ term in the denominator converts the payment in year t to a present value.

At these rates, the real present value of the 20 payments is less than half a million dollars: $491,396. If there were no inflation ($\gamma = 0$), the real present value would be $706,697. With 5% inflation and a real interest rate of 10%, the present value of the prize is only $351,708.[4]

16.2   CHOICES OVER TIME

Earlier chapters discuss how consumers and firms make choices that do not involve time. Often, however, such decisions involve comparisons over time. Individuals and firms must choose between two or more options—such as investments and contracts—that have different present and future values. A land speculator decides whether to sell a plot of land today for $100,000 or next year for $200,000. Margi decides among putting $1,000 into a bank account, buying $1,000 worth of stocks, paying $1,000 for a course in computer programming, and consuming the $1,000 now. MGM, a conglomerate, decides whether to produce a movie that stars a muscle-bound hero who solves the pollution problem by beating up an evil capitalist, to build a new hotel in Reno, to buy a television studio, or to put money in a long-term savings account.

One way to make a choice involving time is to *pick the option with the highest present value.* By borrowing or lending at the market interest rate, we can shift wealth from one period to another. Thus if we choose the option that has the highest present value, we can shift our wealth between periods so that we have more money in every period than we'd have if we made a less attractive choice.

Application   COMPARING TWO CONTRACTS

A professional basketball player is offered contracts by two different teams for playing this year. Both contracts are guaranteed, and payments will be made even if the athlete is injured and cannot play. One team offers him a contract that pays him $1 million today. The other team's contract pays him $500,000 today and $2 million 10 years from now.

Assuming that there is no inflation and that our pro is concerned only about the money, which contract does he accept? Our hero knows that, if he takes the second contract, he will be paid a total of $2.5 million—but most of it won't be available for 10 years. He also knows that if he takes the $1 million today, he can spend it immediately or invest it and have more than $1 million in the future.

He prefers the contract with the higher present value. The present value of the first contract is $1 million.

---

[4]This discussion of lottery prizes is not intended to encourage you to play the lottery. The important thing to remember about a lottery is that the probability of winning if you buy a ticket is almost exactly the same as the probability of winning if you don't buy a ticket: zero.

To calculate the present value of the second contract, he uses the market interest rate. We consider two possible interest rates, 5% and 20%. He can use Equation 16.2 to calculate the present value of the second contract—or hire you to do it for him. For example, you can use a calculator to determine that the present value of $2 million 10 years from now is $2,000,000/(1.05)^{10} \approx $1,227,827 with a 5% interest rate and $2,000,000/(1.2)^{10} \approx $323,011 with a 20% interest rate. Consequently, the present value of the second contract is approximately $1,727,827 at 5% and $823,011 at 20%, as the following calculations show:

Payment	Present Value at 5%	Present Value at 20%
$500,000 today	$500,000	$500,000
$2 million in 10 years	$1,227,827	$323,011
Total	$1,727,827	$823,011

Thus, at an interest rate of 5%, he should definitely take the second contract, which is worth nearly one and three-quarter million dollars today—almost three-quarters of a million dollars more than the present value of the first contract. At an interest rate of 20%, he prefers the contract that pays him $1 million today to the second contract, which is worth only $823,011 today.[5]

Investing

Investment decisions may be made by comparing present values. *A firm makes an investment if the expected return from the investment is greater than the opportunity cost* (Chapter 7). The opportunity cost is the best alternative use of its money, which is what it would earn in the next best use of the money.

Thus to decide whether to make an investment, the firm needs to compare the potential outlay of money to the firm's best alternative. One possibility is that its best alternative is to put the money that it would otherwise spend on this investment in an interest-bearing bank account. We consider two methods for making this comparison: the *net present value* approach and the *internal rate of return* approach.

Net Present Value Approach. A firm has to decide whether to buy a truck for $20,000. Because the opportunity cost is $20,000, the firm should make the investment only if the present value of expected future returns from the truck is greater than $20,000.

More generally, *a firm should make an investment only if the present value of the expected return exceeds the present value of the costs.* If R is the present value of the expected returns to an investment and C is the present value of the costs of the investment, the firm should make the investment if $R > C$.[6]

---

[5]He prefers the second contract for any discount rate less than 14.87%, and he prefers the first contract at any discount rate greater than 14.87%.

[6]This rule holds when future costs and returns are known with certainty and investments can be reversed but cannot be delayed (Dixit and Pindyck, 1994).

This rule is often restated in terms of the net present value, $NPV = R - C$, which is the difference between the present value of the returns, R, and the present value of the costs, C. *A firm should make an investment only if the net present value is positive:*

$$NPV = R - C > 0.$$

Assume that the initial year is $t = 0$, the firm's revenue in year t is R_t, and its cost in year t is C_t. If the last year in which either revenue or cost is nonzero is T, the net present value rule holds that the firm should invest if

$$NPV = R - C$$

$$= \left[R_0 + \frac{R_1}{(1+i)^1} + \frac{R_2}{(1+i)^2} + \cdots + \frac{R_T}{(1+i)^T} \right]$$

$$- \left[C_0 + \frac{C_1}{(1+i)^1} + \frac{C_2}{(1+i)^2} + \cdots + \frac{C_T}{(1+i)^T} \right] > 0.$$

Instead of comparing the present values of the returns and costs, we can examine whether the present value of the *cash flow* in each year (loosely, the annual profit), $\pi_t = R_t - C_t$, is positive. By rearranging the terms in the previous expression, we can rewrite the net present value rule as

$$NPV = \left(R_0 - C_0 \right) + \frac{R_1 - C_1}{(1+i)^1} + \frac{R_2 - C_2}{(1+i)^2} + \cdots + \frac{R_T - C_T}{(1+i)^T}$$

$$= \pi_0 + \frac{\pi_1}{(1+i)^1} + \frac{\pi_2}{(1+i)^2} + \cdots + \frac{\pi_T}{(1+i)^T} > 0. \tag{16.7}$$

This rule does not restrict the firm to making investments only where its cash flow is positive each year. For example, a firm buys a piece of equipment for $100 and spends the first year learning how to use it, so it makes no revenues from the machine and has a negative cash flow that year: $\pi_0 = -100$. The next year, its revenue is $350 and the machine's maintenance cost is $50, so its second year's cash flow is $\pi_1 = \$300$. At the end of that year, the machine wears out, so the annual cash flow from this investment is zero thereafter. Setting the interest rate at 5% in Equation 16.7, we learn that the firm's net present value is

$$NPV = -100 + 300/1.05 \approx \$185.71.$$

Because this net present value is positive, the firm makes the investment.

Solved Problem 16.2

Daniel Snyder, Mortimer Zuckerman, and Fred Drasner bought the Washington Redskins football team and its home stadium for $800 million in 1999. The team's estimated net income for 1999 was $32.8 million. If the new owners believed that they would continue to earn this annual profit (after adjusting for inflation), *f* = $32.8 million, forever, was this investment more lucrative to them than putting the $800 million in a savings account that pays a real interest rate of *i* = 4%?

Answer

Determine the net present value of the team: The net present value of buying the Redskins is positive if the present value of the expected returns, $32.8 million/0.04 = $820 million, minus the present value of the cost, which is the purchase price of $800 million, is positive:

$$NPV = \$820 \text{ million} - \$800 \text{ million} = \$20 \text{ million} > 0.$$

Thus it paid for the investors to buy the Redskins if their best alternative investment paid 4%.

Internal Rate of Return Approach. Whether the net present value of an investment is positive depends on the interest rate. In Solved Problem 16.2, the investors buy the football team, given an interest rate of 4%. However, if the interest rate were 10%, the net present value would be $328 million/0.1 − $800 million = −$472 million, and the investors would not buy the team.

At what discount rate (rate of return) is a firm indifferent between making an investment and not? The **internal rate of return** (*irr*) is the discount rate such that the net present value of an investment is zero. Replacing the interest rate, i, in Equation 16.7 with *irr* and setting the *NPV* equal to zero, we implicitly determine the internal rate of return by solving

$$NPV = \pi_0 + \frac{\pi_1}{1 + irr} + \frac{\pi_2}{(1 + irr)^2} + \cdots + \frac{\pi_T}{(1 + irr)^T} = 0$$

for *irr*.

It is easier to calculate *irr* when the investment pays a steady stream of profit, f, forever and the cost of the investment is PV. The investment's rate of return is found by rearranging Equation 16.4 and replacing i with *irr*:

$$irr = \frac{f}{PV}. \tag{16.8}$$

Instead of using the net present value rule, we can decide whether to invest by comparing the internal rate of return to the interest rate. If the firm is borrowing money to make the investment, *it pays for the firm to borrow to make the investment if the internal rate of return on that investment exceeds that of the next best alternative* (which we assume is the interest rate):[7]

$$irr > i.$$

---

[7]The net present value approach always works. The internal rate of return method is inapplicable if *irr* is not unique. In Solved Problem 16.3, *irr* is unique, and using this approach gives the same answer as the net present value approach.

Solved Problem 16.3 A group of investors can buy the Redskins football team for *PV* = $800 million. They expect an annual real flow of payments (profits) of *f* = $32.8 million forever. If the interest rate is 4%, do they buy the team?

Answer

Determine the internal rate of return to this investment and compare it to the interest rate: Using Equation 16.8, we calculate that the internal rate of return from buying the Redskins is

$$irr = \frac{f}{PV} = \frac{\$32.8 \text{ million}}{\$800 \text{ million}} \approx 4.1$$

Because this rate of return, 4.1%, is greater than the interest rate, 4%, the investors buy the team.

Rate of Return on Bonds

Instead of investing in capital or putting their money in a bank, firms or individuals may invest in a *bond*, a piece of paper issued by a government or a corporation that promises to repay the borrower with a payment stream. The amount borrowed is called the *face value* of the bond. Some bonds have a number of *coupons*. Each year, the holder of the bond clips one coupon, returns it to the issuer, and receives a payment of a fixed amount of money. At the *maturity date* shown on the bond—when no coupons remain—the borrower redeems the bond by returning the face value, the amount borrowed.

Some bonds, *perpetuities*, have no maturity date and the face value is never returned. Instead, the bondholder receives annual payments forever.

For example, last year, Jerome paid *PV* = $2,000 to buy a government-issued bond that guarantees the holder a payment of *f* = $100 a year forever. According to Equation 16.8, the rate of return on Jerome's bond was 5% = $100/$2,000. At the time, banks were paying 5% on comparable accounts and were expected to do so in the future. As a result, Jerome was indifferent between buying a bond and keeping his money in a bank account.

This year, however, because of *unanticipated* inflation, the nominal interest rate that banks paid *unexpectedly* rose to 10%, and everyone expects this new interest rate to persist. If the bonds were to continue to sell for $2,000, the rate of return would remain 5%, so everyone would prefer to keep their money in the bank. Thus if Jerome wants to sell his bond, he must lower the price until the rate of return on the bond reaches 10%. As a result, the present value of Jerome's bond falls to $1,000 = $100/0.1 this year, according to Equation 16.4. In general, a bond's selling price falls from the face value of the bond if the nominal interest rate rises over time (and the price rises if the interest rate falls).

Similarly, the real return to a bond that pays a nominal rate of return varies with the inflation rate. During the high-inflation 1970s and early 1980s, holders of U.S. bonds lost much of their wealth for this reason. Following Canada, Britain, and other countries, the United States in 1997 started offering bonds that adjust for the inflation rate. These bonds are supposed to provide a constant, real rate of return.

Durability

Many firms must decide how durable to make the products they sell or those they produce for their own use. Should they make long-lasting products at a relatively high cost or less-durable goods at a lower cost?

Suppose that the company can vary the quality of a factor (a machine) that it uses in its own production process. If it needs exactly one machine, it must replace the machine when it wears out. Thus *the firm should pick the durability level for the machine that minimizes the present discounted cost of having a machine forever.*

Application **DURABILITY OF TELEPHONE POLES**

Pacific Gas & Electric (PG&E), a western power utility, must decide how durable to make its 132 million wooden utility poles. The poles are a capital stock for PG&E, which uses them to provide a flow of services: supporting power and phone lines year after year. A wooden utility pole provides the same services each year for T years under normal use. After T years, the pole breaks and is replaced because it can't be repaired, but the flow of services must be maintained. Until recently, PG&E used poles with a life span of $T = 25$ years.

The constant marginal cost of manufacturing and installing the poles depends on how long they last, $m(T)$. For an additional cost, the firm can extend the life span of a pole by treating it with chemicals to prevent bug infestations and rot, reinforcing it with metal bands, varying its thickness, or using higher-quality materials. Because the marginal cost increases with the pole's expected life span, a pole that lasts 50 years costs more than one that lasts 25 years: $m(50) > m(25)$.

The replacement cost of a pole that lasts 25 years is $m(25) = \$1,500$. Thus replacing all of PG&E poles today would come to $198 billion—which is more than the cost of many of PG&E's giant power plants.

PG&E believes that it can save money by switching to a longer-lasting pole. The firm picks the duration, T, that minimizes its cost of maintaining its forest of poles. Because the utility keeps the same number of poles in place every year, after a pole wears out at T years, the firm incurs an expense of $m(T)$ to replace it. The present value of providing each pole is the cost of producing it today, $m(T)$, plus the discounted cost of producing another one in T years, $m(T)/(1 + i)^T$, plus the discounted cost of producing another one in $2T$ years, $m(T)/(1 + i)^{2T}$, and so on.

The table shows the present value of the cost of maintaining one pole for the next 100 years, given that the utility faces an interest rate of 5%. Because the cost of producing a pole that lasts for 25 years is $m(25) = \$1,500$, the present value of the cost of providing a pole for the next 100 years is $2,112 (column 2). If the cost of a pole that lasts 50 years were $m(50) = \$1,943$ (column 4), the present value would be the same as that for the 25-year pole. If so, the

	25-Year Pole	50-Year Pole	
Marginal Cost, *m(T)*:	$1,500	$1,650	$1,943
Year			
0	$1,500	$1,650	$1,943
25	443	0	0
50	131	$144	169
75	39	0	0
Present value of the cost of providing a pole for 100 years:	$2,112	$1,794	$2,112

Note: Column 2 does not add to the present value due to rounding.

utility would be indifferent between using poles that last 25 years and poles that last 50 years.

Thus PG&E will not use 50-year poles if the extra cost is greater than $443 = $1,943 − $1,500 but will use them if the difference in cost is less than that. The actual extra cost is less than $150. Thus the present value of the cost of a 50-year pole is only about $1,794 (column 3 of the table). Because using the 50-year poles reduces the present value by $318, or about 15% per pole, the utility wants to use the longer-lasting poles. By so doing, PG&E cuts the present value of the cost of maintaining all its poles for 100 years by about $42 billion. The length of time one maintains a durable good depends on the alternatives and the rate of interest, as www.awlonline.com/perloff, "Durability Solved Problem," demonstrates.

Human Capital

Hard work pays off in the future. Laziness pays off now.   —Steven Wright

Just as a firm considers whether or not to invest in physical capital, individuals decide whether to invest in their own *human capital*. Where a firm chooses the durability of a piece of equipment, some people invest in lengthening their expected life spans by exercising or purchasing medical care. Where a firm buys machinery and other capital to produce more output and increase its future profits, individuals invest in education to raise their productivity and their future earnings.

One of the most important human capital decisions you've had to make is whether to attend college. If you opted to go to college solely for the purpose of increasing your lifetime earnings, have you made a good investment?

Let's look back at your last year of high school. During that year, you have to decide whether to invest in a college education or go directly into the job market. If you venture straight into the job market, we assume that you work from age 18 until you retire at age 70.

If your motivation for attending college is to increase your lifetime earnings, you should start college upon finishing high school so that you can earn a higher salary for as long as possible. Let's assume that you graduate from college in four years, during which time you do not work and you spend $10,000 a year on tuition and other schooling expenses such as books and fees. When you graduate from college, you work from age 22 to 70. Thus the opportunity cost of a college education includes the tuition payments plus the four years of forgone earnings for someone with a high school diploma. The expected benefit is the stream of higher earnings in the future.

Figure 16.2 shows how much the typical person earns with a high school diploma and with a college degree at each age.[8] At age 22, a typical person earns $29,000 with a college degree but only $18,000 with a high school diploma. The college grad's earnings peak at 40 years of age, at $39,000. A high school grad's earnings reach a maximum at 43 years, at $34,000.

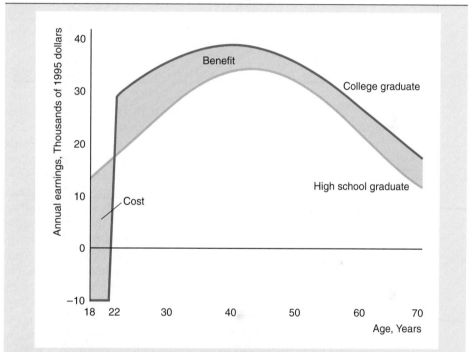

Figure 16.2 Annual Earnings of High School and College Graduates. On the basis of a statistical analysis, the earnings of high school and college graduates vary by age. The cost of getting a college education is four years of forgone earnings (at the rate high school graduates earn) and tuition, which is assumed to be $10,000 a year. The benefit is that the college graduate earns more each year thereafter than a high school graduate.

---

[8]Our figures are based on a statistical analysis of weekly earnings from the March 1995 U.S. *Current Population Survey* that controls for work experience, education, and demographic characteristics but not innate ability. We assume that people are paid for 48 weeks per year and that wages increase at the same rate as inflation, so real earnings are constant over time. No adjustment is made for the greater incidence of unemployment among high school graduates.

Table 16.5 Present Value of Earnings

Discount Rate, %	Present Value, Thousands of 1995 dollars	
	High School	College
0	1,333	1,531
1	1,033	1,170
2	817	911
3	657	720
4	538	578
5	448	471
6	378	388
6.9	329	329
7	324	323
8	281	272
9	246	231
10	218	197

If one stream of earnings is higher than the other at every age, we would pick the higher stream. Because these streams of earnings cross at age 22, we cannot use that method. One way to decide whether investing in a college education pays is to compare the present values at age 18 of the two earnings streams. The present values depend on the interest rate used, as Table 16.5 shows.

If potential college students can borrow money at an interest rate of 0%, money in the future is worth as much as money today, so the present value equals the sum of earnings over time. According to the table, the sum of a college graduate's earnings (including the initial negative earnings) is $1.53 million, which is about 15% more than the earnings of a high school grad. Thus it pays to go to college. The figure also illustrates that attending college pays at a 0% discount rate because the sum of the (negative) cost and (positive) benefit areas—the difference in earnings between going to college and going to work after high school—is positive.

Table 16.5 demonstrates that the present value of earnings for a college grad is greater than that of a high school grad for any interest rate below 6.9%. That is, the average internal rate of return to the college education is 6.9%. Thus income-maximizing people with average characteristics go to college if the real interest rate at which they can borrow or invest is less than 6.9%.[9]

The decision whether to go to college is more complex for people for whom education has a consumption component. Somebody who loves school may go to college even if alternative investments pay more. Someone who hates going to school

---

[9]Real interest rates at which college students can loan money to a bank and the rates at which they can borrow using government loan programs are almost always lower than 6.9%. However, the commercial rates at which they can borrow money from banks may be higher than 6.9%. Some poor people who cannot borrow to pay for college at all—effectively, they face extremely high interest rates—do not go to college, unlike wealthier people with comparable abilities.

invests in a college education only if the financial rewards are much higher than those for alternative investments.

★16.3 | EXHAUSTIBLE RESOURCES

The meek shall inherit the earth, but not the mineral rights. —J. Paul Getty

Discounting plays an important role in decision making about how fast to consume oil, gold, copper, uranium, and other **exhaustible resources**: nonrenewable natural assets that cannot be increased, only depleted. An owner of an exhaustible resource decides when to extract and sell it so as to maximize the present value of the resource. Scarcity of the resource, mining costs, and market structure affect whether the price of such a resource rises or falls over time.

When to Sell an Exhaustible Resource

Suppose that you own a coal mine. In what year do you mine the coal, and in what year do you sell it to maximize the present value of your coal? To illustrate how to answer these questions, we assume that you can sell the coal only this year or next in a competitive market, that the interest rate is i, and that the cost of mining each pound of coal, m, stays constant over time.

Given the last two of these assumptions, the present value of mining a pound of coal is m if you mine this year and $m/(1 + i)$ if you mine next year. As a result, if you're going to sell the coal next year, you're better off mining it next year because you postpone incurring the cost of mining. You mine the coal this year only if you plan to sell it this year.

Now that you have a rule that tells you when to mine the coal—at the last possible moment—your remaining problem is when to sell it. That decision depends on how the price of a pound of coal changes from one year to the next. Suppose that you know that the price of coal will increase from p_1 this year to p_2 next year.

To decide in which year to sell, you compare the present value of selling today to that of selling next year. The present value of your profit per pound of coal is $p_1 - m$ if you sell your coal this year and $(p_2 - m)/(1 + i)$ if you sell it next year. Thus to maximize the present value from selling your coal:

■ *You sell all the coal this year* if the present value of selling this year is greater than the present value of selling next year: $p_1 - m > (p_2 - m)/(1 + i)$.
■ *You sell all the coal next year* if $p_1 - m < (p_2 - m)/(1 + i)$.
■ *You sell the coal in either year* if $p_1 - m = (p_2 - m)/(1 + i)$.

The intuition behind these rules is that storing coal in the ground is like keeping money in the bank. You can sell a pound of coal today, netting $p_1 - m$, invest the money in the bank, and have $(p_1 - m)(1 + i)$ next year. Alternatively, you can keep the coal in the ground for a year and then sell it. If the amount you'll get next year, $p_2 - m$, is less than what you can earn from selling now and keeping the money in a bank account, you sell the coal now. In contrast, if the price of coal is rising so rapidly that the coal will be worth more in the future than wealth left in a bank, you leave your wealth in the mine.

Price of a Scarce Exhaustible Resource

This two-period analysis generalizes to many time periods (Hotelling, 1931). We use a multiperiod analysis to show how the price of an exhaustible resource changes over time.

The resource is sold both this year, year t, and next year, $t + 1$, only if the present value of a pound sold now is the same as the present value of a pound sold next year: $p_t - m = (p_{t+1} - m)/(1 + i)$, where the price is p_t in year t and is p_{t+1} in the following year. Using algebra to rearrange this equation, we obtain an expression that tells us how price changes from one year to the next:

$$p_{t+1} = p_t + i(p_t - m). \tag{16.9}$$

If you're willing to sell the coal in both years, the price next year must exceed the price this year by $i(p_t - m)$, which is the interest payment you'd receive if you sold a pound of coal this year and put the profit in a bank that paid interest at rate i.

The gap between the price and the constant marginal cost of mining grows over time, as Figure 16.3 shows. To see why, we subtract p_t from both sides of Equation 16.9 to obtain an expression for the change in the price from one year to the next:

$$\Delta p \equiv p_{t+1} - p_t = i(p_t - m).$$

This equation shows that the gap between this year's price and next year's price widens as your cash flow this year, $p_t - m$, increases. Thus the price rises over time, and the gap between the price line and the flat marginal cost of mining line grows, as the figure illustrates.

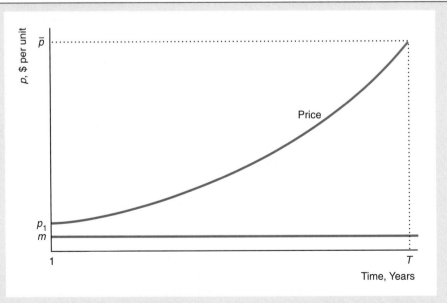

Figure 16.3 Price of an Exhaustible Resource. The price of an exhaustible resource in year $t + 1$ is higher than the price in year t by the interest rate times the difference between the price in year t and the marginal cost of mining, $i(p_t - m)$. Thus the gap between the price line and the marginal cost line, $p_t - m$, grows exponentially with the interest rate.

Although we now understand how price changes over time, we need more information to determine the price in the first year and hence in each subsequent year. Suppose that mine owners know that the government will ban the use of coal in year T (or that a superior substitute will become available that year). They want to price the coal so that all of it is sold by the year T, because any resource that is unsold by then is worthless. The restriction that all the coal is used up by T and Equation 16.9 determine the price in the first year and the increase in the price thereafter.

Price in a Two-Period Example. To illustrate how the price is determined in each year, we assume that there are many identical competitive mines, that no more coal will be sold after the second year because of a government ban, and that the marginal cost of mining is zero in each period. Setting $m = 0$ in Equation 16.9, we learn that the price in the second year equals the price in the first year plus the interest rate times the first-year price:

$$p_2 = p_1 + (i \times p_1) = p_1(1 + i). \qquad (16.10)$$

Thus the price increases with the interest rate from the first year to the second year.

The mine owners face a resource constraint: They can't sell more coal than they have in their mines. The coal they sell in the first year, Q_1, plus the coal they sell in the second year, Q_2, equals the total amount of coal in the mines, Q. The mine owners want to sell all their coal within these two years because any coal they don't sell does them no good.

Suppose that the demand curve for coal is $Q_t = 200 - p_t$ in each year t. If the amount of coal in the ground is less than would be demanded at a zero price, the sum of the amount demanded in both years equals the total amount of coal in the ground:

$$Q_1 + Q_2 = (200 - p_1) + (200 - p_2) = Q.$$

Substituting the expression for p_2 from Equation 16.10 into this resource constraint to obtain $(200 - p_1) + [200 - p_1(1 + i)] = Q$ and rearranging terms, we find that

$$p_1 = (400 - Q)/(2 + i). \qquad (16.11)$$

Thus the first-year price depends on the amount of coal in the ground and the interest rate.

If the mines initially contain $Q = 169$ pounds of coal, p_1 is \$110 at a 10% interest rate and only \$105 at a 20% interest rate, as Table 16.6 shows. At the lower

Table 16.6 Price and Quantity of Coal Reflecting the Amount of Coal and the Interest Rate			
	$Q = 169$		$Q = 400$
	$i = 10\%$	$i = 20\%$	Any i
$p_1 = (400 - Q)/(2 + i)$	\$110	\$105	\$0
$p_2 = p_1(1 + i)$	\$121	\$126	\$0
$\Delta p \equiv p_2 - p_1 = i \times p_1$	11	21	0
$Q_1 = 200 - p_1$	90	95	200
$Q_2 = 200 - p_2$	79	74	200
Share sold in Year 2	47%	44%	50%

interest rate, the difference between the first- and second-year price is smaller ($11 versus $21), so relatively more of the original stock of coal is sold in the second year (47% versus 44%).

Rents. If coal is a scarce good, its competitive price is above the marginal cost of mining the coal ($m = 0$ in our example). How can we reconcile this result with our earlier finding that price equals marginal cost in a competitive market? The answer is that, when coal is scarce, it earns a *rent*: a payment to the owner of an input beyond the minimum necessary for the factor to be supplied (Chapter 8).

The owner of the coal need not be the same person who mines the coal. A miner could pay the owner for the right to take the coal out of the mine. After incurring the marginal cost of mining the coal, m, the miner earns $p_1 - m$. The owner of the mine, however, charges that amount in rent for the right to mine this scarce resource, rather than giving any of this profit to the miner. Even if the owner of the coal and the miner are the same person, the amount beyond the marginal mining cost is a rent to scarcity.

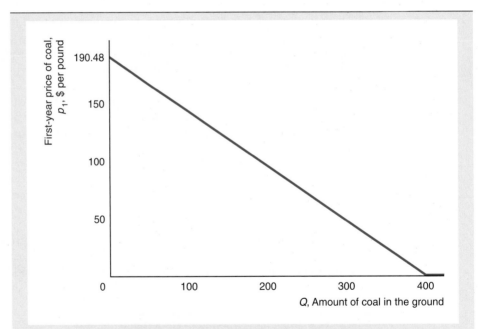

Figure 16.4 First-Year Price in a Two-Period Model. In a two-period model, the price of coal in the first year, p_1, falls as the amount of coal in the ground initially, Q, increases. This figure is based on an interest rate of 10%.

---

[10]Equation 16.11 holds only where coal is scarce: $Q \leq 400$. According to this equation, $p_1 = 0$ when $Q = 400$. If the quantity of coal in the ground is even greater, $Q > 400$, coal is not scarce—people don't want all the coal even if the price is zero—so the price in the first year equals the marginal mining cost of zero. That is, the price is not negative, as Equation 16.11 would imply if it held for quantities greater than 400.

If the coal were not scarce, no rent would be paid, and the price would equal the marginal cost of mining. Given the demand curve in the example, the most coal anyone would buy in a year is 200 pounds, which is the amount demanded at a price of zero. If there is 400 pounds of coal in the ground initially—enough to provide 200 pounds in each year—the coal is not scarce, so the price of coal in both years is zero, as Table 16.6 illustrates.[10] As Figure 16.4 shows, the less coal there is in the ground initially, Q, the higher the initial price of coal.

Rising Prices. Thus according to our theory, the price of an exhaustible resource rises if the resource (1) is scarce, (2) can be mined at a marginal cost that remains constant over time, and (3) is sold in a competitive market. The price of old-growth redwood trees rose as predicted by this theory.

Application   **REDWOOD TREES**

Many of the majestic old-growth redwood trees in America's western forests are several hundred to several thousand years old. If a mature redwood is cut, young redwoods will not grow to a comparable size within our lifetime. Thus an old-growth redwood forest, like fossil fuels, is effectively a nonrenewable resource, even though new redwoods are being created (very slowly). In contrast, many other types of trees, such as those grown as Christmas trees, are quickly replenished and therefore are renewable resources like fish.

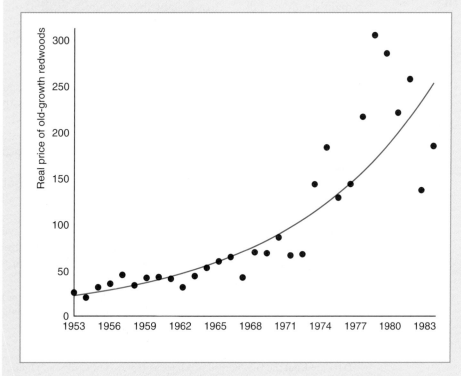

The exponential trend line on the graph shows that the real price of redwoods rose from 1953 to 1983 at an average rate of 8% a year. By the end of this period, virtually no redwood trees were available for sale. The trees either had been harvested or were growing in protected forests. The last remaining privately owned stand was purchased by the U.S. government and the state of California from the Maxxam Corporation in 1996.

The unusually high prices observed in the late 1960s through the 1970s are in large part due to actions of the federal government, which used its power of eminent domain to buy a considerable fraction of all remaining old-growth redwoods for the Redwood National Park at the market price. The government bought 1.7 million million board feet (MBF) in 1968 and 1.4 million MBF in 1978. The latter purchase represented about two and a quarter years of cutting at previous rates. These two government purchases combined equaled 43% of private holdings in 1978 of about 7.3 million MBF. Thus the government purchases were so large that they moved up the time of exhaustion of privately held redwoods by several years, causing the price to jump to the level it would have reached several years later.

Why Price May Be Constant or Fall

If any one of the three conditions we've been assuming—*scarcity*, *constant marginal mining costs*, and *competition*—is not met, the price of an exhaustible resource may remain steady or fall.[11] Most exhaustible resources, such as aluminum, coal, lead, natural gas, silver, and zinc, have had decades-long periods of falling or constant real prices. Indeed, the 1993 index of the real prices of all major minerals and metals was less than half of the 1980 level.

Abundance. As we've already seen, the initial price is set at essentially the marginal cost of mining if the exhaustible resource is not scarce. The gap between the price and the marginal cost grows with the interest rate. If the good is so abundant that the initial gap is zero, the gap does not grow and the price stays constant at the marginal cost. Further, if the gap is initially very small, it has to grow for a long time before the increase becomes noticeable.

Because of abundance, the real prices for many exhaustible resources have remained relatively constant for decades. Moreover, the price falls when the discovery of a large deposit of the resource is announced.

The amount of a resource that can be profitably recovered with current methods is called a *reserve*. Known reserves of some resources are enormous; others are more limited.[12] We have enough silicon (from sand) and magnesium to last virtually for-

---

[11]The following discussion of why prices of exhaustible resources may not rise and the accompanying examples are based on Berck and Roberts (1996) and additional data supplied by these authors. Their paper also shows that pollution and other environmental controls can keep resource prices from rising.

[12]Data are from the U.S. Bureau of Mines as reported in Crowson, Phillip, *Minerals Handbook 1994–95*, New York: Stockton Press, 1994.

ever at the rates we use them; however, known reserves of lead, gold, silver, and zinc will last only about two decades at the 1991–1992 rates of extraction.

Known reserves of aluminum (bauxite) will last 216 years at current rates, and additional reserves are constantly being discovered. Because of this abundance, the real price of aluminum has remained virtually constant for the past 50 years.

Technical Progress. Over long periods of time, steady technical progress has reduced the marginal cost of mining many natural resources and has thereby lowered the price of those exhaustible resources. A large enough drop in the marginal mining cost may more than offset the increase in the price due to the interest rate, so the price falls from one year to the next.[13]

The era spanning the end of the nineteenth century and the beginning of the twentieth century witnessed many advances in mining. As a result of technical

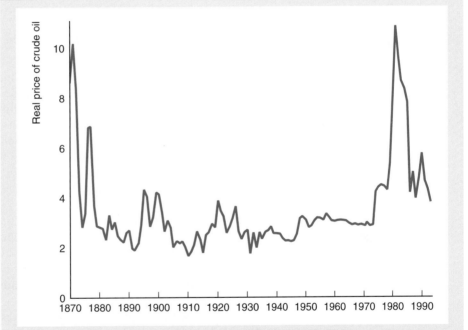

Figure 16.5 **Price of Oil over Time.** The real price index of crude oil fell at the end of the nineteenth century, was relatively constant for many decades, increased rapidly in the late 1970s and early 1980s, then fell back to historical levels.

---

[13]When the marginal cost of mining is constant at m, Equation 16.9 shows that $p_{t+1} = p_t + i(p_t - m)$, so p_{t+1} must be above p_t. If we allow mining costs to vary from year to year, then

$$p_{t+1} = p_t + i(p_t - m_t) + (m_{t+1} - m_t).$$

Thus if the drop in the mining costs, $m_{t+1} - m_t$, is greater than $i(p_t - m)$, the price in p_{t+1} is less than p_t.

progress in mining and discoveries of new supplies, the real prices of many exhaustible resources fell. For example, the real price of aluminum in 1945 was only 12% of the price 50 years earlier. Eventually, as mines play out, prospectors have to dig ever deeper to find resources, causing marginal costs to increase and prices to rise faster than they would with constant marginal costs.

Changing Market Power. Changes in market structure can result in either a rise or a fall in the price of an exhaustible resource. The real price of oil remained virtually constant from 1880 through 1972. But when the Organization of Petroleum Exporting Countries (OPEC) started to act as a cartel in 1973, the price of oil climbed rapidly, as Figure 16.5 shows. At its peak in 1981, the real price of oil was nearly five times higher than its nearly constant level during the period 1880–1972. When Iran and Iraq went to war in 1980, the OPEC cartel began to fall apart and the real price of oil sank to traditional levels, where it remained through the 1990s.

16.4 | CAPITAL MARKETS, INTEREST RATES, AND INVESTMENTS

We've seen that an individual's decision about whether to make an investment depends on the market interest rate. As Figure 16.6 shows, the intersection of the demand and supply of loanable funds determines the equilibrium price or interest rate and the equilibrium quantity of funds in this capital market. In equilibrium, the amount borrowed (demanded) equals the amount loaned (supplied).

Funds are demanded by individuals buying homes or paying for a college education, governments borrowing money to build roads or wage wars, and firms investing in new plants or equipment. The demand curve, D, is downward sloping because more is borrowed as the interest rate falls.

The supply curve reflects loans made by individuals and firms. Many people, when their earnings are relatively high, save money in bank accounts and buy bonds (which they convert back to money for consumption when they retire or during lean times). Firms that have no alternative investments with higher returns may also loan money to banks or others. Higher interest rates induce greater savings by both groups, so the initial supply curve, S^1, is upward sloping.

The initial equilibrium is e_1, with an equilibrium rate of interest of i_1 and an equilibrium quantity of funds loaned and borrowed of Q_1. As usual, this equilibrium changes if any of the variables—such as tastes and government regulations—that affect demand and supply shifts.

Increased Savings, More Investment

The supply curve of funds may shift to the right for many reasons. The government may remove a restriction on investment by foreigners. Or the government may make Individual Retirement Accounts (IRAs) tax exempt until retirement, a policy that induces additional savings at any given interest rate.

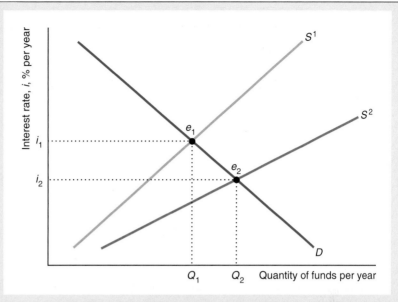

Figure 16.6 Capital Market Equilibrium. The initial equilibrium, e_1, is determined by the intersection of the demand curve for loans, D, and the initial supply curve, S^1. Changes in laws induce more people to save, shifting the supply curve to S^2. The interest rate, i_2, at the new equilibrium, e_2, is lower than the original interest rate, i_1. More funds are loaned than originally: $Q_2 > Q_1$.

Such a change causes the supply curve to shift to the right to S_2 in Figure 16.6. The new equilibrium is e_2, with a lower interest rate, i_2. At the lower interest rate, firms and others undertake investment projects with lower rates of return than before the shift. They borrow more funds, so the new equilibrium is at $Q_2 > Q_1$.

Increased Government Demand, Less Private Investment

Increased borrowing by the government raises the equilibrium interest rate, which discourages—*crowds out*—private investment. Figure 16.7 illustrates this effect. The total demand for funds, D^1 (panel c), is the horizontal sum of the demand from the private sector, D_p (panel a), and the initial demand from the public sector, D_g^1 (panel b). Given the market supply curve of funds S, the initial market equilibrium is e_1, with an equilibrium market interest rate of i_1 and quantity of Q_1.

When the government borrows money to fight a war in a distant land, its demand for funds shifts outward to D_g^2. As a result, the market demand increases to D^2, which is the horizontal sum of D_p and D_g^2. At the new equilibrium, e_2, the market interest rate, i_2, is higher than the initial rate (panel c). The government borrows more than before in equilibrium: $Q_g^2 > Q_g^1$ (panel b). The higher market interest rate, however, causes private investment to fall from Q_p^1 to Q_p^2 (panel a).

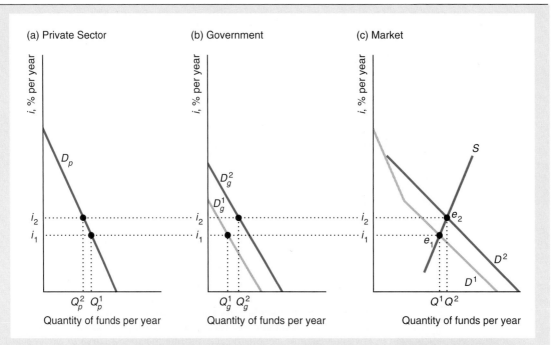

Figure 16.7 How Government Borrowing Squeezes Out Private Investment. (a) Private demand for funds for investment, D_p, remains constant. (b) Government demand for loans increases from D_g^1 to D_g^2 as the government borrows to finance a war. (c) As a result, total demand shifts from D^1 to D^2, and the equilibrium shifts from e_1 to e_2. At the new equilibrium, government borrowing increases, $Q_g^2 > Q_g^1$, while private borrowing falls, $Q_p^2 < Q_p^1$.

Application   TAKING FROM FUTURE GENERATIONS

Blessed are the young, for they shall inherit the national debt. —Herbert Hoover

Most governments are spending money today that they expect your generation and future generations to repay. In the United States, the present value of net taxes (taxes paid minus transfer payments—benefits—received) over a lifetime is $86,300 for someone who was 5 years old in 2000; $144,600 for a 20-year-old; $4,000 for a 60-year-old, and –$101,900 for a 75-year-old. The comparable burden for future generations is expected to be $130,400.

Many other countries face serious generational imbalances. The ratio of the present value of net taxes of future generations to the present value for someone born in 1995 is 2.7 in Japan; 2.3 in Italy; 1.9 in Brazil and Germany; 1.8 in the Netherlands; 1.6 in Argentina, Belgium, Norway, and Portugal; 1.5 in Denmark, France, and the United States; and 1.3 in Australia. In contrast, future generations are expected to pay about the same as current generations in Canada and New Zealand, 20% less in Sweden, and only about 10% as much in Thailand.

About 200,000 Americans turned 65 in 1999, whereas 1.6 million will hit 65 in 2015, when the baby boomers reach retirement age. Consequently, the number of people on Social Security will grow substantially. It is difficult to believe that governments will be able to take from the young to give to the old indefinitely, as the tax burdens on younger generations will become extremely burdensome, and private investments will drop.

Summary

1. **Comparing money today to money in the future:** Inflation aside, most people value money in the future less than money today. An interest rate reflects how much more people value a dollar today than a dollar in the future. To compare a payment made in the future to one made today, we can express the future payment in terms of current dollars by adjusting it using the interest rate. Similarly, a flow of payments over time is related to the present or future value of these payments by the interest rate.

2. **Choices over time:** An individual or a firm may choose between two options with different cash flows over time by picking the one with the higher present value. Similarly, a firm invests in a project if its net present value is positive or its internal rate of return is greater than the interest rate.

3. **Exhaustible resources:** Nonrenewable resources such as coal, gold, and oil are used up over time and cannot be replenished. If these resources are scarce, the marginal cost of mining them is constant or increasing, and the market structure remains unchanged, their prices rise rapidly over time because of positive interest rates. However, if the resources are abundant, the marginal cost of mining falls over time, or the market becomes more competitive, nonrenewable resource prices may remain constant or fall over time.

4. **Capital markets, interest rates, and investments:** Supply and demand in capital markets determine the market rate of interest. A shock that shifts the supply curve to the left or the demand curve to the right raises the interest rate. As the interest rate increases, firms want to make fewer investments.

Problems

1. Some past and current civilizations, believing that interest should not be charged, passed usury laws forbidding it. What are the private and social benefits or costs of allowing interest to be charged?

2. What is the effect of a usury law on the market rate of interest if some potential lenders, hoping that the authorities do not catch them, are still willing to loan money?

3. How does an individual with a zero discount rate compare current and future consumption? How does your answer change if the discount rate is infinite?

4. If the interest rate is near zero, should an individual go to college, given the information in Figure 16.2? State a simple rule for determining whether this individual should go to college in terms of the areas labeled "Benefit" and "Cost" in the figure.

5. Discussing the $350 price of a ticket for one of her concert, Barbra Streisand said, "If you amortize the money over 28 years, it's $12.50 a year. So is it worth $12.50 a year to see me sing? To hear me sing live?"[14] Under what condition is it useful for an individual to apply Ms. Streisand's rule to decide whether to go to the concert? What do we know about the discount rate of a person who made such a purchase?

---

[14]"In Other Words. . ." *San Francisco Chronicle*, January 1, 1995: Sunday Section, p. 3. She divided the $350 ticket price by 28 years to get $12.50 as the payment per year.

Math Problems

6. If you buy a car for $100 down and $100 a year for two more years, what is the present value of these payments at a 5% rate of interest?

7. How much money do you have to put into a bank account that pays 10% interest compounded annually to receive annual payments of $200?

8. What is the present value of $100 paid a year from now and another $100 paid two years from now if the interest rate is i?

9. How much money do you have to put into a bank account that pays 10% interest compounded annually to receive perpetual annual payments of $200 in today's dollars if the rate of inflation is 5%?

10. At a 10% interest rate, do you prefer to buy a phone for $100 or to rent the same phone for $10 a year? Does your answer depend on how long you think the phone will last?

11. What is the present value of a stream of payments of f per year for t years that starts T years from now if the interest rate is i?

12. In 1996, Pacific Gas and Electric sent its customers a comparison showing that a person could save $80 per year in gas, water, and detergent expenses by replacing a traditional clothes washer with a new tumble-action washer. Suppose that the interest rate is 5%. You expect your current washer to die in 5 years. If the cost of a new tumble-action washer is $800, should you replace your washer now or in five years?

13. You plan to buy a used refrigerator this year for $200 and to sell it when you graduate in two years. Assuming that you can get $100 for the refrigerator at that time, there is no inflation, and the interest rate is 5%, what is the true cost (your current outlay minus the resale value in current terms) of the refrigerator to you?

14. You want to buy a room air conditioner. The price of one machine is $200. It costs $20 a year to operate. The price of the other air conditioner is $300, but it costs only $10 a year to operate. Assuming that both machines last 10 years, which is a better deal? (Do you need to do extensive calculations to answer this question?)

15. Which is worth more to you: (a) a $10,000 payment today or (b) a $1,000-per-year higher salary for as long as you work? At what interest rate would (a) be worth more to you than (b)? Does your answer depend on how many years you expect to work?

16. You rent an apartment for two years. You owe a payment of f today and another equal nominal payment next year. If the inflation rate is γ and the real interest rate is i, what is the present value of these rental payments?

17. A firm's profit is π = revenue – labor costs – capital costs. Its capital cost can be stated as its rate of return on capital, rr, times the value of its capital, $p_K K$, where p_K is the price of a unit of capital and K is the number of units of capital. What is the firm's implicit rate of return on its capital?

18. A firm is considering an investment where its cash flow is π_1 = $1 (million), π_2 = –$12, π_3 = $20, and π_t = 0 for all other t. The interest rate is 7%. Use the net present value rule to determine whether the firm should make the investment. Can the firm use the internal rate of return rule to make this decision?

19. You have a barrel of oil that you can sell today for p dollars. Assuming no inflation and no storage cost, how high would the price have to be next year for you to sell the oil next year rather than now?

20. If all the coal in the ground, Q, is to be consumed in two years and the demand for coal is $Q_t = A(p_t)^{-\varepsilon}$ in each year t where ε is a constant demand elasticity, what is the price of coal each year?

Uncertainty

> We must believe in luck. For how else can we explain the success of those we don't like?
> —Jean Cocteau

Life's a series of gambles. Will you receive Social Security when you retire? Will you win the lottery tomorrow? Will your stock increase in value? Will you avoid disease, earthquakes, and fire? In this chapter, we extend the model of decision making by individuals and firms to include uncertainty. We look at how uncertainty affects consumption decisions (Chapters 4 and 5)—such as how much insurance to buy— as well as investment decisions (Chapter 16).

When making decisions about investments and other matters, you consider the possible *outcomes* under various circumstances, or *states of nature*. When deciding about whether to carry a new type of doll, a toy store owner considers how many dolls will be sold if the doll is popular and how many if it is unpopular—two possible outcomes—and how likely these two states of nature are.

Although we cannot know with certainty what the future outcome will be, we may know that some outcomes are more likely than others. When uncertainty can be quantified, it is sometimes called **risk**: The likelihood of each possible outcome is known or can be estimated, and no single possible outcome is certain to occur. All the examples in this chapter concern quantifiable or risky situations.[1]

Consumers and firms modify their decisions about consumption and investment as the degree of risk varies. Indeed, most people are willing to spend money to reduce risk by buying insurance or taking preventive measures. Moreover, most people will choose a riskier investment over a less risky one only if they expect a higher return from the riskier investment.

IN THIS CHAPTER, WE EXAMINE FOUR MAIN TOPICS

1. **Degree of risk:** Probabilities are used to measure the degree of risk and the likely profit from a risky undertaking.
2. **Decision making under uncertainty:** Whether people choose a risky option over a nonrisky one depends on their attitudes toward risk and on the expected payoffs of each option.
3. **Avoiding risk:** People try to reduce their overall risk by not making risky choices, taking actions to lower the likelihood of a disaster, combining offsetting risks, insuring, and in other ways.
4. **Investing under uncertainty:** Whether people make an investment depends on the riskiness of the payoff, the expected return, attitudes toward risk, the interest rate, and whether it is profitable to alter the likelihood of a good outcome.

---

[1]Jargon alert: Many people do not distinguish between the terms *risk* and *uncertainty*. Henceforth, we use these terms interchangeably.

17.1 | DEGREE OF RISK

You are thinking about buying lunch at a new restaurant. There are two possible outcomes: The lunch will or will not taste good to you. Knowing the likelihood of each of these outcomes would help you decide whether to try this new restaurant.

Before we can analyze decision making under uncertainty, we need a way to describe and quantify risk. A particular event—such as eating lunch at a new restaurant—has a number of possible outcomes—say, an enjoyable meal or an unenjoyable meal. Because you don't know whether you will enjoy the meal, eating at this new restaurant is risky. To describe how risky this activity is, we need to quantify the likelihood that each possible outcome occurs.

We can use our estimate of how risky each outcome is to estimate the most likely outcome. We then present measures of risk that reflect how much actual outcomes deviate from the most likely outcome.

Probability

A *probability* is a number between 0 and 1 that indicates the likelihood that a particular outcome will occur. You might, for example, have a 25% probability—a 1 in 4 chance—of enjoying the meal at the restaurant. How do we estimate a probability?

Frequency. If we have a history of the outcomes for an event, we can use the frequency with which a particular outcome occurred as our estimate of the probability. Let n be the number of times one particular outcome occurred during the N total number of times an event occurred. We set our estimate of the probability, θ (theta), equal to the frequency:

$$\theta = n/N.$$

A house either burns or does not burn. If $n = 13$ similar houses burned in your neighborhood of $N = 1,000$ homes last year, you might estimate the probability that your house will burn this year as $\theta = 13/1,000 = 1.3\%$.

Subjective Probability. Often we don't have a history that allows us to calculate the frequency. We use whatever information we have to form a *subjective probability*, which is our best estimate of the likelihood that an outcome will occur. We may use all available information—even information that is not based on a conscious, scientific estimation procedure.

How do you derive a subjective probability about the likelihood that you'll like the new restaurant? You might know that your friend liked the restaurant but your economics professor did not. If you're not sure whether either of these people likes the same food you do, you may estimate the probability that you'll like the restaurant at 50%. However, if you know that your friend usually likes the same type of food you do but you're less sure about whether your professor likes the same type of food, you might put more weight on your friend's report and estimate the probability that you'll like the restaurant as a number greater than half, perhaps 85%.[2]

Probability Distribution. A *probability distribution* relates the probability of occurrence to each possible outcome. Panel a of Figure 17.1 shows a probability distribution over five possible outcomes: zero to four days of rain per month in a relatively dry city. The probability that it rains no days during the month is 10%, as

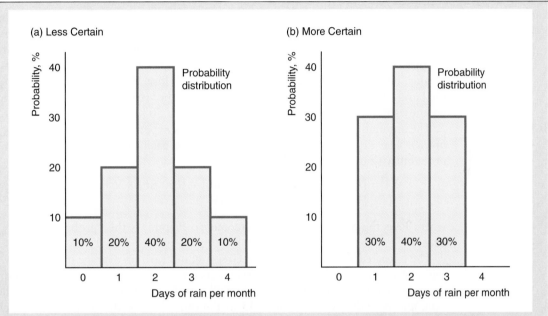

Figure 17.1 Probability Distribution. The probability distribution shows the probability of occurrence for each of the mutually exclusive outcomes. Panel a shows five possible mutually exclusive outcomes. The probability that it rains exactly two days per month is 40%. The probability that it rains five or more days per month is 0%. The probability distributions in panels a and b have the same mean. The variance is smaller in panel b, where the probability distribution is more concentrated around the mean than the distribution in panel a.

---

[2]When events are repeated, we can compare our subjective probabilities to observed frequencies. Your subjective probability (guess) that it rains 50% of the days in January can be compared to the frequency of rain in January during the recorded history for your city. If an event is not going to be repeated, however, it may not be possible to check whether your subjective probability is reasonable or accurate by comparing it to a frequency. You might believe that there's a 75% chance of dry weather tomorrow. If it does rain tomorrow, that doesn't mean you were wrong. Only if you believed that the probability of rain was 0% would observing rain tomorrow prove you wrong.

is the probability of exactly four days of rain. The chance of two rainy days is 40%, and the chance of one or three rainy days is 20% each. The probability that it rains five or more days a month is 0%.

These weather outcomes are *mutually exclusive*—only one of these outcomes can occur at a given time—and *exhaustive*—no other outcomes than those listed are possible. Where outcomes are mutually exclusive and exhaustive, exactly one of these outcomes will occur with certainty, and the probabilities must add up to 100%. For simplicity, we concentrate on situations in which there are only two possible outcomes.

Expected Value

Gregg, a promoter, schedules an outdoor concert for tomorrow.[3] How much money he'll make depends on the weather. If it doesn't rain, his profit or value from the concert is $V = \$15$. (If it will make you happier—and it will certainly make Gregg happier—you can think of the profits in this example as \$15,000 instead of \$15.) If it rains, he'll have to cancel the concert and he'll lose $V = -\$5$, which he must pay the band. Although Gregg does not know what the weather will be with certainty, he knows that the weather department forecasts a 50% chance of rain.

The amount Gregg expects to earn is called his *expected value* (here, his *expected profit*). The expected value, *EV*, is the value of each possible outcome times the probability of that outcome:[4]

$$EV = [Pr(\text{no rain}) \times \text{Value(no rain)}] + [Pr(\text{rain}) \times \text{Value(rain)}]$$
$$= [\tfrac{1}{2} \times \$15] + [\tfrac{1}{2} \times (-\$5)] = \$5,$$

where *Pr* is the probability of an outcome, so *Pr*(rain) is the "probability that rain occurs."

The expected value is the amount Gregg would earn on average if the event were repeated many times. If he puts on such concerts many times over the years and the weather follows historical patterns, he will earn \$15 at half of the concerts without rain, and he will get soaked for –\$5 at the other half of the concerts, at which it rains. Thus he'll earn an average of \$5 per concert over a long period of time.

Solved Problem 17.1

How much more would Gregg expect to earn if he knew that he would obtain perfect information about the probability of rain far enough before the concert that he could book the band only if needed? How much does he gain from having this perfect information?

Answer

1. *Determine how much Gregg would earn if he had perfect information in each state of nature*: If Gregg knew with certainty that it would rain at the

---

[3]My brother Gregg, a successful concert promoter, wants me to inform you that the hero of the following story is some other Gregg who is a concert promoter.

[4]If there are *n* possible outcomes, the value of outcome *i* is V_i, and the probability of that outcome is Pr_i, then the expected value is $EV = Pr_1 V_1 + Pr_2 V_2 + \cdots + Pr_n V_n$.

time of the concert, he would not book the band, so he would make no loss or profit. If Gregg knew that it would not rain, he would hold the concert and make $15.

2. *Determine how much Gregg would expect to earn before he learns with certainty what the weather will be*: Gregg knows that he'll make $15 with a 50% probability and $0 with a 50% probability, so his expected value, given that he'll receive perfect information in time to act on it, is

$$(\tfrac{1}{2} \times \$15) + (\tfrac{1}{2} \times \$0) = \$7.50.$$

3. *His gain from perfect information is the difference between his expected earnings with perfect information and with imperfect information*: Gregg expects to earn $2.50 = $7.50 − $5 more with perfect information than with imperfect information. This answer can be reached more directly. Perfect weather information is valuable to him because he can avoid hiring the band unnecessarily when it rains. (Having information has no value if it doesn't alter behavior.) The *value of this information* is his expected savings from not hiring the band when it rains: $\tfrac{1}{2} \times \$5 = \$2.50$.

Variance and Standard Deviation

If Gregg would earn the same amount—the expected value—whether it rained or not, he would face no risk. We can measure the risk he faces in many different ways. One approach is to look at the degree by which actual outcomes vary from the expected value, *EV*.

The *difference* between his actual earnings and his expected earnings if it does not rain is $10 = $15 − $5. The difference if it does rain is −$10 = −$5 − $5. Because there are two differences—one difference for each state of nature—it is convenient to combine them in a single measure of risk.

One such measure of risk is the *variance*, which measures the spread of the probability distribution. For example, the variance in panel a of Figure 17.1, where the probability distribution ranges from zero to four days of rain per month, is greater than the variance in panel b, where the probability distribution ranges from one to three days of rain per month.

Formally, the variance is the probability-weighted average of the squares of the differences between the observed outcome and the expected value.[5] The variance of the value Gregg obtains from the outdoor concert is

$$\text{Variance} = [Pr(\text{no rain}) \times (\text{Value(no rain)} - EV)^2] + [Pr(\text{rain}) \times (\text{Value(rain)} - EV)^2]$$
$$= [\tfrac{1}{2} \times (\$15 - \$5)^2] + [\tfrac{1}{2} \times (-\$5 - \$5)^2]$$
$$= [\tfrac{1}{2} \times (\$10)^2] + [\tfrac{1}{2} \times (-\$10)^2] = \$100.$$

---

[5] If there are n possible outcomes with an expected value of EV, the value of outcome i is V_i, and the probability of that outcome is Pr_i, then the variance is

$$Pr_1(V_1 - EV)^2 + Pr_2(V_2 - EV)^2 + \cdots + Pr_n(V_n - EV)^2.$$

The variance puts more weight on large deviations from the expected value than on smaller ones.

Table 17.1 Variance and Standard Deviation: Measures of Risk

(a) Outdoor Concert

Outcome	Probability	Value	Difference = Value – $5	Difference^2	Difference^2 × Probability
No rain	$\frac{1}{2}$	$15	$10	$100	$50
Rain	$\frac{1}{2}$	–$5	–$10	$100	$50
				Variance	$100
				Standard Deviation	$10

(b) Indoor Concert

Outcome	Probability	Value	Difference = Value – $5	Difference^2	Difference^2 × Probability
No rain	$\frac{1}{2}$	$10	$5	$25	$12.50
Rain	$\frac{1}{2}$	$0	–$5	$25	$12.50
				Variance	$25
				Standard Deviation	$5

Panel a of Table 17.1 shows how to calculate the variance of the profit from this concert step by step. The first column lists the two outcomes: rain and no rain. The next column gives the probability. The third column shows the value or profit of each outcome. The next column calculates the difference between the values in the third column and the expected value, $EV = \$5$. The following column squares these differences, and the last column multiplies these squared differences by the probabilities in the second column. The sum of these probability weighted differences, $100, is the variance.

Instead of describing risk using the variance, economists and businesspeople often report the *standard deviation*, which is the square root of the variance. The usual symbol for the standard deviation is σ (sigma), so the symbol for variance is σ². For the outdoor concert, the variance is σ² = $100 and the standard deviation is σ = $10.

Holding the expected value constant, the smaller the standard deviation (or variance), the smaller the risk. Panel b of Table 17.1 illustrates that Gregg's expected value of profit is the same if he stages the concert indoors, but the standard deviation of his profit is less. The indoor theater does not hold as many people as the outdoor venue, so the most Gregg can earn if it does not rain is $10. Rain discourages attendance even at the indoor theater, so he just breaks even, earning $0. The expected value of the indoor concert,

$$EV = (\tfrac{1}{2} \times \$10) + (\tfrac{1}{2} \times \$0) = \$5,$$

is the same as that for the outdoor concert. Staging the concert indoors involves less risk, however. As panel b shows, the variance of the profit at the indoor concert is $25, and the corresponding standard deviation is $5.

| 17.2 | **DECISION MAKING UNDER UNCERTAINTY** |

Will Gregg stage an indoor or outdoor concert? To answer such a question, we need to know his attitude toward bearing risk.

Although the indoor and outdoor concerts have the same expected value, the outdoor concert involves more risk. Gregg will earn more with good weather or lose more with bad weather by holding his concert outdoors instead of indoors. He'll book an outdoor concert only if he likes to gamble.

Even if he dislikes risk, Gregg may prefer a riskier option if it has a higher expected value. Suppose that he strikes a new agreement with the band by which he pays only if the weather is good and the concert is held. Gregg's expected value is $7.50, the variance is $56.25, and the standard deviation is $7.50.[6] By holding the concert outdoors instead of inside, Gregg's expected value is higher ($7.50 instead of $5) and the standard deviation is higher ($7.50 instead of $5). He earns the same, $0, from both types of concerts in bad weather. In good weather, he earns more from the outdoor concert. Because he always does as well with an outdoor concert as with an indoor show, Gregg clearly prefers the riskier outdoor concert with its higher expected value.

If he dislikes risk, Gregg won't necessarily stage the concert with the higher expected value. Suppose that his choice is between the indoor concert and an outdoor concert from which he earns $100,015.50 if it doesn't rain and loses $100,005 if it rains. His expected value is greater with the outside concert, $5.25 instead of $5, but he faces much more risk. The standard deviation of the outdoor concert is $100,010.25 compared to $5. Gregg might reasonably opt for the indoor concert with the lower expected value if he dislikes risk. After all, he may be loath to risk losing $100,005 with a 50% probability.

Expected Utility

We can formalize this type of reasoning by extending our model of utility maximization (Chapter 4) to show how people's taste for risk affects their choice among options (investments, career choices, consumption bundles) that differ in both value and risk. If people made choices to maximize expected value, they would always choose the option with the highest expected value regardless of the risks involved. However, most people care about risk as well as expected value. Indeed, most people are *risk averse*—they dislike risk—and will choose a bundle with higher risk only if its expected value is substantially higher than that of a less-risky bundle.

In Chapter 4, we noted that we can describe an individual's preferences over various bundles of goods by using a utility function. John von Neumann and Oskar Morgenstern (1944) suggested an extension of this standard utility-maximizing

---

[6]The expected value is the same as in Solved Problem 17.1: $(\frac{1}{2} \times \$15) + (\frac{1}{2} \times \$0) = \$7.50$. The variance is $\frac{1}{2}(\$15 - \$7.50)^2 + \frac{1}{2}(\$0 - \$7.50)^2 = \$56.25$, so the standard deviation is $7.50.

model that includes risk.[7] In their reformulation, a rational person maximizes *expected utility*. Expected utility is the probability-weighted average of the utility from each possible outcome. For example, Gregg's expected utility, *EU*, from the indoor concert is

$$EU = [Pr(\text{no rain}) \times U(\text{Value(no rain)})] + [Pr(\text{rain}) \times U(\text{Value(rain)})]$$
$$= [\tfrac{1}{2} \times U(\$15)] + [\tfrac{1}{2} \times U(-\$5)],$$

where his utility function, *U*, depends on his earnings. For example, *U*($15) is the amount of utility Gregg gets from $15. (People have preferences over the goods they consume. However for simplicity, we'll say that a person receives utility from earnings or wealth, which can be spent on consumption goods.)

In short, the expected utility calculation is similar to the expected value calculation. Both are weighted averages in which the weights are the probability (Pr) that the state of nature will occur. The difference is that the expected value is the probability-weighted average of the monetary value, whereas the expected utility is the probability-weighted average of the utility from the monetary value.

If we know how an individual's utility increases with wealth, we can determine how that person reacts to risky propositions. We can classify people in terms of their willingness to make a **fair bet**: a wager with an expected value of zero. An example of a fair bet is one in which you pay a dollar if a flipped coin comes up heads and receive a dollar if it comes up tails. Because you expect to win half the time and lose half the time, the expected value of this bet is zero:

$$[\tfrac{1}{2} \times (-\$1)] + [\tfrac{1}{2} \times \$1] = 0.$$

In contrast, a bet in which you pay $1 if you lose the coin flip and receive $2 if you win is an unfair bet that favors you, with an expected value of

$$[\tfrac{1}{2} \times (-\$1)] + [\tfrac{1}{2} \times \$2] = 50¢.$$

Someone who is unwilling to make a fair bet is **risk averse**. A person who is indifferent about making a fair bet is **risk neutral**. A person who is **risk preferring** will make a fair bet.

Risk Aversion

We can use our expected utility model to examine how Irma, who is risk averse, makes a choice under uncertainty. Figure 17.2 shows Irma's utility function. The utility function is concave to the wealth axis, indicating that Irma's utility rises with wealth but at a diminishing rate.[8] She has *diminishing marginal utility of wealth*: The extra pleasure from each extra dollar of wealth is smaller than the pleasure from the previous dollar. An individual whose utility function is concave to the wealth axis is risk averse, as we now illustrate.

---

[7]This approach to handling choice under uncertainty is the most commonly used method. Schoemaker (1982) discusses the logic underlying this approach, the evidence for it, and several variants. Machina (1989) discusses a number of alternative methods. Here we treat utility as a cardinal measure rather than an ordinal measure as we did in Chapters 4 and 5.

[8]Irma's utility from *W* wealth is *U*(*W*). She has positive marginal utility from extra wealth, $dU(W)/dW > 0$; however, her utility increases with wealth at a diminishing rate, $d^2U(W)/dW^2 < 0$.

A *person whose utility function is concave picks the less risky choice if both choices have the same expected value.* Suppose that Irma has an initial wealth of $40 and has two options. One option is to do nothing and keep the $40, so that her utility is U($40) = 120 (point *d* in Figure 17.2) with certainty.

Her other option is to buy a vase. Her wealth is $70 if the vase is a Ming and $10 if it is an imitation. Irma's subjective probability is 50% that it is a genuine Ming vase. Her expected value or wealth remains

$$\$40 = (\tfrac{1}{2} \times \$10) + (\tfrac{1}{2} \times \$70).$$

Thus buying the vase is a fair bet because she has the same expected wealth whether she purchases the vase or not.

Irma prefers the certain wealth from not buying the vase because that option carries less risk. Her utility if the vase is a Ming is U($70) = 140, point *c*. If it's an imitation, her utility is U($10) = 70, point *a*. Thus her expected utility is

$$[\tfrac{1}{2} \times U(\$10)] + [\tfrac{1}{2} \times U(\$70)] = [\tfrac{1}{2} \times 70] + [\tfrac{1}{2} \times 140] = 105.$$

The graph shows that her expected utility is point *b*, the midpoint of a line (called a *chord*) between *a* and *c*.[9]

Because Irma's utility function is concave, her utility from certain wealth, 120 at point *d*, is greater than her expected utility from the risky activity, 105 at point *b*. As a result, she does not buy the vase. Buying this vase, which is a fair bet, increases the risk she faces without changing her expected wealth.

The **risk premium** is the amount that a risk-averse person would pay to avoid taking a risk. The figure shows how much Irma would be willing to pay to avoid this risk. Her certain utility from having a wealth of $26, U($26) = 105, is the same as her expected utility if she buys the vase. Thus Irma would be indifferent between buying the vase and having $26 with certainty. Irma would be willing to pay a risk premium of $14 = $40 − $26 to avoid bearing the risk from buying the vase.

A risk-averse person chooses a riskier option only if it has a sufficiently higher expected value. If Irma were much more confident that the vase were a Ming, her expected value would rise and she'd buy the vase, as Solved Problem 17.2 shows.[10]

---

[9]The chord represents all the possible weighted averages of the utility at point *a* and the utility at point *c*. When the probabilities of the two outcomes are equal, the expected value is the midpoint. If the probability that the vase is a Ming is greater than $\tfrac{1}{2}$, the expected value is closer to point *c*, as Solved Problem 17.2 illustrates.

[10]My colleague Irma Adelman visited an antique store and was offered a vase for $10. In addition to being an outstanding economist, she's an art expert. At first glance, she thought that the vase was a Ming. Turning it over, she found marks on the bottom that convinced her that it was a Ming. Because her subjective probability that the vase was a genuine Ming was very high, she bought it, even though she is risk averse. This lovely Ming vase graced her home until her !#@$! cat broke it.

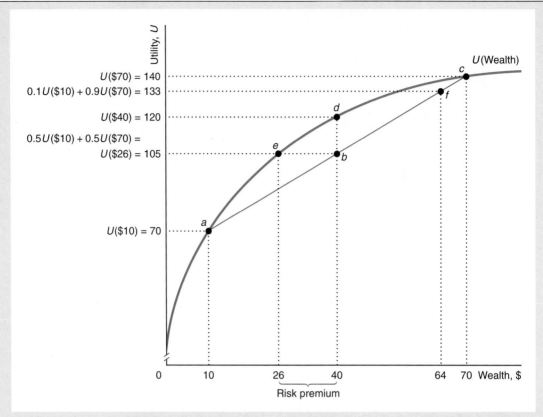

Figure 17.2 Risk Aversion. Initially, Irma's wealth is $40, so her utility is $U(\$40) = 120$, point d. If she buys the vase and it's a Ming, she is at point c, where her utility is $U(\$70) = 140$. If the purchased vase is an imitation, she is at point a, where $U(\$10) = 70$. If her subjective probability that the vase is a Ming is 50%, her expected utility from buying the vase, point b, is $\frac{1}{2}U(\$10) + \frac{1}{2}U(\$70) =$ 105, which is less than her utility with a certain wealth of $40, $U(\$40) = 120$. Thus she does not buy the vase. If Irma's subjective probability that the vase is a Ming is 90%, her expected utility from buying the vase is $0.1U(\$10) + 0.9U(\$70) =$ 133, point f, which is more than her utility with a certain wealth of $40, $U(\$40) = 120$, d, so she buys the vase.

Solved Problem 17.2   Suppose that Irma's subjective probability is 90% that the vase is a Ming. What is her expected wealth if she buys the vase? What is her expected utility? Does she buy the vase?

Answer

1. *Calculate Irma's expected wealth*: Her expected value or wealth is 10% times her wealth if the vase is not a Ming plus 90% times her wealth if the vase is a Ming:

    $$(0.1 \times \$10) + (0.9 \times \$70) = \$64.$$

    In Figure 17.2, $64 is the distance along the wealth axis corresponding to point f.

2. *Calculate Irma's expected utility*: Her expected utility is the probability-weighted average of her utility under the two outcomes:

    $$[0.1 \times U(\$10)] + [0.9 \times U(\$70)] = [0.1 \times 70] + [0.9 \times 140] = 133.$$

    Her expected utility is the height on the utility axis of point f. Point f is nine-tenths of the distance along the line connecting point a to point c.

3. *Compare Irma's expected utility to her certain utility if she does not buy*: Irma's expected utility from buying the vase, 133 (point f), is greater than her certain utility, 120 (point d), if she does not. Thus if Irma is this confident that the vase is a Ming, she buys it. Although the risk is greater from buying than from not buying, her expected wealth is enough higher ($64 instead of $40) that it's worth it to her to take the chance.

Risk Neutrality

Someone who is risk neutral has a constant marginal utility of wealth: Each extra dollar of wealth raises utility by the same amount as the previous dollar. With constant marginal utility of wealth, the utility curve is a straight line in a utility and wealth graph.

Suppose that Irma is risk neutral and has the straight-line utility curve in panel a of Figure 17.3. She would be indifferent between buying the vase and not buying it if her subjective probability is 50% that it is a Ming. Her expected utility from buying the vase is the average of her utility at points a ($10) and c ($70):

$$[\tfrac{1}{2} \times U(\$10)] + [\tfrac{1}{2} \times U(\$70)] = [\tfrac{1}{2} \times 70] + [\tfrac{1}{2} \times 140] = 105.$$

Her expected utility exactly equals her utility with certain wealth of $40 (point b) because the line connecting points a and c lies on the utility function and point b is the midpoint of that line.

Here Irma is indifferent between buying and not buying the vase, a fair bet, because she doesn't care how much risk she faces. Because the expected wealth from both options is $40, she is indifferent between them.

In general, *a risk-neutral person chooses the option with the highest expected value, because maximizing expected value maximizes utility*. A risk-neutral person chooses the riskier option if it has even a slightly higher expected value than the less risky option. Equivalently, the risk premium for a risk-neutral person is zero.

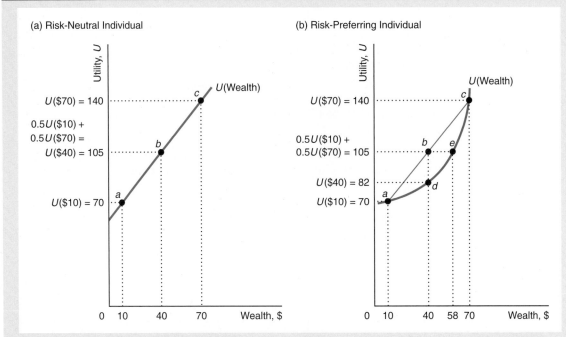

Figure 17.3 Risk Neutrality and Risk Preference. (a) If Irma's utility curve is a straight line, she is risk neutral and is indifferent as to whether or not to make a fair bet. Her expected utility from buying the vase, 105 at *b*, is the same as from a certain wealth of $40 at *d*. (b) If Irma's utility curve is convex to the horizontal axis, Irma has increasing marginal utility to wealth and is risk preferring. She buys the vase because her expected utility from buying the vase, 105 at *b*, is higher than her utility from a certain wealth of $40, 82 at *d*.

Risk Preference

An individual with an increasing marginal utility of wealth is risk preferring: willing to take a fair bet. If Irma has the utility curve in panel b of Figure 17.3, she is risk preferring. Her expected utility from buying the vase, 105 at *b*, is higher then her certain utility if she does not buy the vase, 82 at *d*. Therefore, she buys the vase.

A risk-preferring person is willing to pay for the right to make a fair bet (a negative risk premium). As the figure shows, Irma's expected utility from buying the vase is the same as the utility from a certain wealth of $58. Given her initial wealth of $40, if you offer her the opportunity to buy the vase or offer to give her $18, she is indifferent. With any payment smaller than $18, she prefers to buy the vase.

Application

GAMBLING

Horse sense is something a horse has that prevents him from betting on people.
—Father Mathew

If you ask them, most people say that they don't like bearing risk. Consistent with such statements, they reduce the risk they face by buying insurance. Nonetheless, many of these people engage in games of chance from time to time. Not only do they gamble, but they make unfair bets, in which the expected value of the gamble is negative. That is, if they play the game repeatedly, they are likely to lose money in the long run.

Americans spend about $7 billion on movie tickets, $26 billion on books of all sorts, and $450 billion on groceries, and they wager $630 billion legally. Over two-thirds of them gamble at least once a year, encouraged by the 37 state governments that run lotteries. Seventy percent of British households buy a lottery ticket every week (see **www.awlonline.com/perloff**, "Lotteries").

These bets are unfair. For example, the British government keeps half of the total bet on its lottery. Americans lose at least $50 billion or 7% of the legal bets. A casino's *hold percentage*—the money the casino retains as a percentage of the amount of chips bought—for roulette wheels runs slightly over 20%; for the wheel of fortune about 45%; and for keno, nearly 30%. The house's hold percentage on nickel slot machines is 9.78%, which is twice as much as on dollar machines.

Theories on Why People Gamble Why do people take unfair bets? Some people gamble because they are risk preferring or because they have a compulsion to gamble. However, neither of these observations is likely to explain noncompulsive gambling by most people who exhibit risk-averse behavior in the other aspects of their lives (such as buying insurance). Risk-averse people may make unfair bets for three reasons: They enjoy the game, they have a utility curve with both risk-averse and risk-preferring regions, or they falsely believe that the gamble favors them.

The first explanation is that gambling provides entertainment as well as risk. Risk-averse people insure their property, such as their house, because there's nothing enjoyable about bearing the risk of theft, flooding, and fire. However, these same people may play poker or bet on horse races because they get enough pleasure from playing those games to put up with the financial risk and the expected loss.

The second explanation also involves tastes. Friedman and Savage (1948) suggested that gamblers place a high value on the chance to increase their wealth greatly. The graph shows Sylvia's utility curve, which has the shape that Friedman and Savage described. Sylvia is risk averse with respect to small gambles but risk preferring with respect to bets that allow for large potential

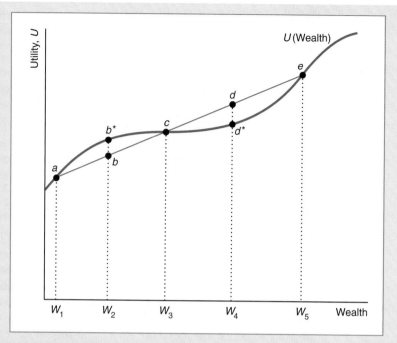

winnings. Sylvia prefers receiving W_2 with certainty to engaging in a bet with an expected value of W_2, where she has an equal probability of receiving wealth W_1 or W_3. Sylvia chooses the certain wealth because her certain utility at b^* is above the expected utility at b. On the other hand, Sylvia prefers a bet with an equal chance of W_2 and W_5 to the certain wealth of W_4, which is the expected value of the bet, because the expected utility at d from the bet is greater than the certain utility at d^*.

The third explanation is that people make mistakes. Either people do not know the true probabilities or cannot properly calculate expected values, so they do not realize that they are participating in an unfair bet.

These three explanations are not mutually exclusive. A person could get entertainment value from gambling *and* have a Friedman-Savage utility *and* be unable to calculate odds correctly.[11]

Evidence on Why People Gamble Evidence supports all three explanations to some degree. People definitely like games of chance. One survey found that 65% of Americans say that they engage in games of chance, even when the

---

[11]Economists, knowing how to calculate expected values and deriving most of their excitement from economic models, apparently are less likely to gamble than are real people. A number of years ago, a meeting of economists was held in Reno, Nevada. Reno hotels charge low room rates on the assumption that they'll make plenty from guests' gambling losses. However, the economists gambled so little that they were asked pointedly not to return.

games involve no money or only trivial sums (Brunk, 1981). That is, they play because they enjoy the games.[12]

Brunk indirectly examined whether the Friedman-Savage explanation or love of the game explains bets. He asked people whether they were dissatisfied with their current income. Presumably, their answers would indicate whether they have increasing marginal utilities of wealth, at least over certain ranges of wealth. Brunk argued that, if the Friedman-Savage explanation is correct, people who were dissatisfied with their incomes would be more likely to buy lottery tickets, after controlling for other individual differences such as education. He expected that this factor would not be an important explanation for social gambling activities such as bingo, which people play because they enjoy the game. He found that people who were dissatisfied with their income were more likely than others to buy lottery tickets but not to engage in social gambling. This evidence is consistent with the Friedman-Savage explanation. Garrett and Sobel (1999) found that the utility functions of people who gamble on the lottery have the shape predicted by Friedman and Savage.

A number of studies show that many people have biased estimates of probabilities and cannot calculate expected values. For example, Golec and Tamarkin (1995) concluded that football bettors tend to make low-probability bets because they are overconfident.

Golec and Tamarkin found that bettors greatly overestimate their probabilities of winning certain types of exotic football bets (an *exotic bet* depends on the outcome of more than one game). In a small survey, gamblers estimated their chance of winning a particular bet at 45% when the objective probability was 20%. Of course, these people may also place exotic bets because they enjoy them more than simple bets.

17.3 AVOIDING RISK

If 75% of all accidents happen within 5 miles of home, why not move 10 miles away?
— Steven Wright

Risk-averse people want to eliminate or reduce risk whether the bet is fair or biased against them. Risk-neutral people avoid unfair bets, and even risk-preferring people avoid very unfair bets.

---

[12]When I was an undergraduate at the University of Chicago, I lived in a dorm and saw overwhelming evidence that the "love of the game" is a powerful force. As the neighborhood provided few forms of entertainment, the dorm's denizens regularly watched the man from the vending company refill the candy machine with fresh candy. He took the old, stale, unpopular bars that remained in the machine and placed them in the "mystery candy" bin. Thanks to our careful study of stocking techniques, we all knew that buying the mystery candy was not a fair bet—who would want unpopular, stale candy bars at the same price as a fresh, popular bar? Nonetheless, one of the dorm dwellers always bought the mystery candy. When asked why, he responded, "I love the excitement of not knowing what'll come out." Life was very boring indeed on the South Side of Chicago.

Individuals can avoid optional risky activities, but often they can't escape risk altogether. Property owners, for instance, always face the possibility that their property will be damaged or stolen or will burn. They may be able to reduce the probability that bad states of nature occur, however.

Just Say No

The simplest way to avoid risk is to abstain from optional risky activities. No one forces you to bet on the lottery, go into a high-risk occupation, or buy stock in a start-up biotech firm. If one brand of a product you use comes with a warranty and an otherwise comparable brand does not, you lower your risk by buying the guaranteed product.

Even when you can't avoid risk altogether, you can take precautions to reduce the probability of bad states of nature or the magnitude of any loss that might occur. For example, you can maintain your car as the manufacturer recommends to reduce the probability that it will break down. By locking your apartment door, you lower the chance that your television will be stolen. Getting rid of your four-year-old collection of newspapers lessens the likelihood that your house will burn. Not only do these actions reduce your risk, but they also raise the expected value of your asset.

Obtain Information

Collecting accurate information before acting is one of the most important ways in which people can reduce risk and increase expected value and expected utility, as Solved Problem 17.1 illustrated. Armed with information, you may avoid a risky choice or you may be able to take actions that reduce the probability of a disaster or the size of the loss.

Before buying a car or refrigerator, many people read *Consumer Reports* to determine how frequently a particular brand is likely to need repairs. By collecting such information before buying, they can reduce the likelihood of making a costly mistake.

Application   **BOND RATINGS**

Investors obtain information about the riskiness of bonds by checking reports on their riskiness, such as the Moody's and Standard & Poor's ratings (see table). These letter-grade ratings reflect whether a bond's issuer has made timely payments in the past, whether the issuer is in danger of becoming bankrupt, and other problems. Bonds of *investment grade* are said to be suitable for purchase by an institutional money manager, who is legally obligated to be a *prudent investor*—one who does not take great risks. Lower-ranked bonds offer unusually high rates of return as inducements for people to buy them. Junk bonds are issued by new firms that have little or no financial history or by established firms that have had severe financial problems, so their Moody's and Standard & Poor's ratings are low. Knowledgeable investors use this information and information about the current rates of return to decide which bonds to buy.

	Moody's	Standard & Poor's
Investment Grade		
Highest quality	Aaa	AAA
High quality	Aa	AA
Upper medium grade	A	A
Medium grade	Baa	BBB
High-Yield or Junk Bonds		
Predominantly speculative	Ba	BB
Low grade	B	B
Default likely	Caa	CCC
Very speculative	Ca	CC
Lowest quality	C	C
Default	—	DDD

Diversify

Although it may sound paradoxical, individuals and firms often reduce their overall risk by making many risky investments instead of only one. This practice is called *risk pooling* or *diversifying*. Your grandparents may have put it this way: "Don't put all your eggs in one basket."

Correlation and Diversification. The extent to which diversification reduces risk depends on the degree to which various events are correlated over states of nature. The degree of correlation ranges from negatively correlated to uncorrelated to positively correlated.[13] If you know that the first event occurs, you know that the probability that the second event occurs is lower if the events are *negatively correlated* and higher if the events are *positively correlated*. The outcomes are *independent* or *uncorrelated* if knowing whether the first event occurs tells you nothing about the probability that the second event occurs.

Diversification can eliminate risk if two events are perfectly negatively correlated. Suppose that two firms are competing for a government contract and have an equal chance of winning. Because only one firm can win, the other must lose, so the two events are *perfectly negatively correlated*. You can buy a share of stock in either firm for $20. The stock of the firm that wins the contract will be worth $40, whereas the stock of the loser will be worth $10. If you buy two shares of the same company,

---

[13]A measure of the *correlation* between two random variables x and y is

$$\rho = E\left(\frac{x - \bar{x}}{\sigma_x} \ \frac{y - \bar{y}}{\sigma_y} \right),$$

where the $E(\cdot)$ means "take the expectation" of the term in parentheses, $\bar{x}$ and $\bar{y}$ are the means, and σ_x and σ_y are the standard deviations of x and y. The two events are said to be uncorrelated if $\rho = 0$.

your shares are going to be worth either $80 or $20 after the contract is awarded. Thus their expected value is

$$\$50 = (\tfrac{1}{2} \times \$80) + (\tfrac{1}{2} \times \$20)$$

with a variance of

$$\$900 = [\tfrac{1}{2} \times (\$80 - \$50)^2] + [\tfrac{1}{2} \times (\$20 - \$50)^2].$$

However, if you buy one share of each, your two shares will be worth $50 no matter which firm wins, and the variance is zero.

Diversification reduces risk even if the two events are imperfectly negatively correlated, uncorrelated, or imperfectly positively correlated. *The more negatively correlated two events are, the more diversification reduces risk.*

Now suppose that the values of the two stocks are uncorrelated. Each of the two firms has a 50% chance of getting a government contract, and whether one firm gets a contract does *not* affect whether the other firm wins one. Because of this independence, the chance that each firm's share is worth $40 is $\tfrac{1}{4}$, the chance that one is worth $40 and the other is worth $10 is $\tfrac{1}{2}$, and the chance that each is worth $10 is $\tfrac{1}{4}$. If you buy one share of each firm, the expected value of these two shares is

$$\$50 = (\tfrac{1}{4} \times \$80) + (\tfrac{1}{2} \times \$50) + (\tfrac{1}{4} \times \$20),$$

and the variance is

$$\$450 = [\tfrac{1}{4} \times (\$80 - \$50)^2] + [\tfrac{1}{2} \times (\$50 - \$50)^2] + [\tfrac{1}{4} \times (\$20 - \$50)^2].$$

The expected value is the same as buying two shares in one firm, but the variance is only half as large. Thus diversification lowers risk when the values are uncorrelated.

In contrast, *diversification does not reduce risk if two events are perfectly positively correlated.* If the government will award contracts either to both firms or to neither firm, the risks are perfectly positively correlated. The expected value of the stocks and the variance are the same whether you buy two shares of one firm or one share of each firm.

Mutual Funds. Individual investors usually do not have the benefit of such detailed information about correlations. They know, however, that the value of the stock of most firms is not perfectly positively correlated with the value of other stocks, so buying stock in several companies tends to reduce risk. Many of these people effectively own shares in a number of companies at once by buying shares in a *mutual fund* of stocks. A mutual fund share is issued by a company that buys stocks in many other companies.

The *Standard & Poor's Composite Index of 500 Stocks* (S&P 500) is a value-weighted average of 500 large firms' stocks, most of them listed on the New York Stock Exchange (NYSE), though some are on the American Stock Exchange or are traded over the counter. The S&P 500 companies constitute only about 7% of all the publicly traded firms in the United States, but they represent approximately 80% of the total value of the U.S. stock market. The *New York Stock Exchange Composite Index* includes more than 1,500 common stocks traded on the NYSE. A number of "total market" funds have been introduced, such as the

Wilshire 5000 Index Portfolio, which initially covered 5,000 stocks but now includes more than 7,200—virtually all of the U.S. stock market in terms of value. The retail assets in total market funds are relatively small: $11.1 billion versus $116.3 billion in S&P 500 index funds. Some other mutual funds are based on bonds or on a mixture of stocks, bonds, and other types of investments.

Mutual funds allow you to reduce the risk associated with uncorrelated price movements across stocks. Suppose that two companies look very similar on the basis of everything you know about them. You have no reason to think that the stock in one firm will increase more in value or be riskier than the stock of the other firm. However, luck may cause one stock to do better than the other. You can reduce this type of random, unsystematic risk by diversifying and buying stock in both firms.

A stock mutual fund, however, has a systematic risk. The prices of all stocks tend to rise when the economy is expanding and to fall when the economy is contracting. By buying a diversified mutual stock fund, you are not able to avoid the systematic risks associated with shifts in the economy that affect all stocks at once.

Application   **LAWS LIMITING DIVERSIFICATION**

To lower risk, insurance companies and various other firms invest in many countries. Laws that limit diversification by insurance companies force these firms to bear extra risk.

In 1994, Hong Kong enacted a law to force general (nonlife) insurers to hold assets in Hong Kong equal to at least 80% of their liabilities. Some legislators claimed that this policy would protect policyholders by keeping the assets of shareholders within Hong Kong. However, this law may have the exact opposite effect, by reducing a firm's ability to diversify and avoid bankruptcy if a major natural disaster strikes Hong Kong.

Insure

> *I detest life-insurance agents; they always argue that I shall some day die, which is not so.*
>   —Stephen Leacock

As we've already seen, a risk-averse person is willing to pay money—a risk premium—to avoid risk. The demand for risk reduction is met by insurance companies, which bear the risk for anyone who buys an insurance policy. Many risk-averse individuals and firms buy insurance; global insurance premiums amounted to nearly $2.2 trillion in 1998.

How Much Insurance Individuals Want. The way insurance works is that a risk-averse person or firm gives money to the insurance company in the good state of nature, and the insurance company transfers money to the policyholder in the bad state of nature. This transaction allows the risk-averse person or firm to shift some or all of the risk to the insurance company.

Because Scott is risk averse, he wants to insure his house, which is worth $80 (thousand). There is a 25% probability that his house will burn next year. If a fire occurs, the house will be worth only $40.

With no insurance, the expected value of his house is

$$(\tfrac{1}{4} \times \$40) + (\tfrac{3}{4} \times \$80) = \$70.$$

Scott faces a good deal of risk. The variance of the value of his house is

$$[\tfrac{1}{4} \times (\$40 - \$70)^2] + [\tfrac{3}{4} \times (\$80 - \$70)^2] = \$300.$$

Now suppose that an insurance company offers a *fair bet*, or **fair insurance**: a bet between an insurer and a policyholder in which the value of the bet to the policyholder is zero. The insurance company offers to let Scott trade $1 in the good state of nature (no fire) for $3 in the bad state of nature (fire).[14] This insurance is fair because the expected value of this insurance to Scott is zero:

$$[\tfrac{1}{4} \times (-\$3)] + (\tfrac{3}{4} \times \$1) = \$0.$$

Because Scott is risk averse, he *fully insures* by buying enough insurance to eliminate his risk altogether. With this amount of insurance, he has the same amount of wealth in either state of nature.

Scott pays the insurance company $10 in the good state of nature and receives $30 in the bad state. In the good state, he has a house worth $80 less the $10 he pays the insurance company, for a net wealth of $70. If the fire occurs, he has a house worth $40 plus a payment from the insurance company of $30, for a net wealth, again, of $70.

Scott's expected value with fair insurance, $70, is the same as his expected value without insurance. The variance he faces drops from $300 without insurance to $0 with insurance. Scott is better off with insurance because he has the same expected value and faces no risk.

Solved Problem 17.3   **The local government assesses a property tax of $4 (thousand) on Scott's house. If the tax is collected whether or not the house burns, how much fair insurance does Scott buy? If the tax is collected only if the house does not burn, how much fair insurance does Scott buy?**

Answer

1. *Determine the after-tax expected value of the house without insurance:* The expected value of the house is

$$\$66 = (\tfrac{1}{4} \times \$36) + (\tfrac{3}{4} \times \$76)$$

---

[14]As a practical matter, the insurance company collects money up front. If the fire doesn't occur, the company keeps the money. If the fire occurs, it gives back the amount paid originally plus additional funds. Scott's insurance company charges him $1 up front for every $4 it will pay him in the bad state. Thus Scott effectively pays $1 in the good state of nature and receives a net payment of $3 in the bad state.

if the tax is always collected and

$$\$67 = (\tfrac{1}{4} \times \$40) + (\tfrac{3}{4} \times \$76)$$

if the tax is collected only in the good state of nature.

2. *Calculate the amount of fair insurance Scott buys if the tax is always collected*: Because Scott is risk averse, he wants to be fully insured so that the after-tax value of his house is the same in both states of nature. If the tax is always collected, Scott pays the insurance company $10 in the good state of nature, so he has $76 − $10 = $66, and receives $30 in the bad state, so he has $36 + $30 = $66. That is, he buys the same amount of insurance as he would without any taxes. The tax has no effect on his insurance decision because he owes that amount regardless of the state of nature.

3. *Calculate the amount of fair insurance Scott buys if the tax is collected only if there is no fire*: If the tax is collected only in the good state of nature, Scott pays the insurance company $9 in the good state ($76 − $9 = $67) and receives $27 in the bad state ($40 + $27 = $67). Thus he has the same after-tax income in both states of nature. Effectively, Scott is partially insured by the tax system, so he purchases less insurance than he otherwise would.

Fairness and Insurance. When fair insurance is offered, risk-averse people fully insure. If insurance companies charge more than the fair-insurance price, individuals buy less insurance.[15]

Because insurance companies do not offer fair insurance, most people do not fully insure. An insurance company could not stay in business if it offered fair insurance. With fair insurance, the insurance company's expected payments would equal the amount the insurance company collects. Because the insurance company has operating expenses—costs of maintaining offices, printing forms, hiring sales agents, and so forth—an insurance firm providing fair insurance would lose money. Insurance companies' rates must be high enough to cover their operating expenses, so the insurance is less than fair to policyholders.

How much can insurance companies charge for insurance? A monopoly insurance company could charge an amount up to the risk premium a person is willing to pay to avoid risk. For example, in Figure 17.2, Irma would be willing to pay up to $14 for an insurance policy that would compensate her if her vase were not a Ming. The more risk averse an individual is, the more a monopoly insurance company can charge. If there are many insurance companies competing for business, the price of an insurance policy is less than the maximum that risk-averse individuals are willing to pay—but still high enough that the firms cover their operating expenses.

---

[15]As Solved Problem 17.3 shows, tax laws may act to offset this problem, so that some insurance may be fair or more than fair after tax.

American Express (AE) recently sent me a letter offering to enroll me in its flight insurance program. If I agree to this plan, AE will charge me $4 for insurance every time I take a scheduled flight. If I die on that flight, AE will pay my family $250,000. (AE also offered much larger amounts of insurance, but I figure there's no point in making myself worth more to my family dead than alive.)

If θ is my probability of dying on a flight, my family's expected value from this bet with AE is

$$[\theta \times \$250,000] + [(1 - \theta) \times (-4)].$$

For this insurance to be fair, this expected value must be zero, which is true if $\theta \approx 0.000016$, or one out of every 62,500 flights has a fatal crash.

I'm not tempted by AE's offer because its insurance is not close to being fair. The chance that I'll die on a flight is much, much less than 0.000016.

How great *is* my danger of being in a fatal airline crash? According to the Air Transport Association, there were no fatalities on a scheduled U.S. commercial airline flight in 1993 or 1998. Over the five years ending in 1998, there were an average of 142 fatalities per year out of an average of 574 million passengers per year. Thus the probability of dying over that five-year period was 0.000000247, or less than 1 in 4 million.

If I randomly choose a seat on a flight each day for 10 years, my probability of *not* being in an accident is 99.91%. If I fly each day for 100 years, my probability of not being in a fatal accident is 99.10%. Indeed, only by flying every day for about 7,690 years would my probability of being in a fatal crash rise as high as 50%. (The greatest risk of an airplane trip for many people is the drive to and from the airport. Indeed, more people are killed by donkeys annually than die in plane crashes.)

Because the chance of being in a fatal crash is 0.000000246, the fair rate to pay for $250,000 of flight insurance is about 6¢. As I see it, AE is offering to charge me 65 times more than the fair rate for this insurance.

I'd have to be incredibly risk averse to be tempted by this offer. Indeed, I wouldn't buy this insurance even if I were that risk averse. Instead, I'd buy general life insurance, which is much less expensive than flight insurance and covers me for death from all types of accidents and diseases.

Insurance Only for Diversifiable Risks. Why is an insurance company willing to sell policies and take on risk? By pooling the risks of many people, the insurance company can lower its risk much below that of any individual. If the probability that one car is stolen is independent of whether other cars are stolen, the risk to an insurance company of insuring one person against theft is much greater than the average risk of insuring many people.

An insurance company sells policies only for risks that it can diversify. If the risks from disasters to its policyholders are highly positively correlated, an insurance company is not well diversified by holding many policies. A war affects all policyholders, so the outcomes that they face are perfectly correlated. Because wars are *nondiversifiable risks*, insurance companies do not offer policies insuring against wars.

Application   NATURAL DISASTERS

In recent years, some insurance companies have started viewing major natural disasters as nondiversifiable risks because such catastrophic events cause many insured people to suffer losses at the same time. As more homes have been built in parts of the country where damage from storms or earthquakes is likely, the size of the potential losses to insurers from nondiversifiable risks has grown.

In the 1990s, insurance companies suffered major losses. Insurers paid $12.5 billion for losses in the 1994 Los Angeles earthquake, $15.5 billion for Hurricane Andrew in 1992 (total damages were $26.5 billion), $1.8 billion for blizzards and tornadoes in 1993, $3.2 billion for damage from Hurricane Fran in 1995, and nearly $1 billion in the aftermath of Hurricane Floyd in 1999. Farmers

Insurance Group reports that it paid out three times as much for the 1994 Los Angeles earthquake as it collected in earthquake premiums over 30 years.

By the end of the twentieth century, insurance companies refused to offer hurricane or earthquake insurance in many parts of the country for these relatively nondiversifiable risks. In 1996, when Nationwide Insurance Company announced that it was sharply curtailing sales of new policies along the Gulf of Mexico and the eastern seaboard from Texas to Maine, a company official explained, "Prudence requires us to diligently manage our exposure to catastrophic losses."

In some of these areas, state-run pools (for example, the Florida Joint Underwriting Association and the California Earthquake Authority) provide households with insurance. However, not only do these policies extend less protection, but their rates are commonly three times more than the previously available commercial rates.

17.4 | INVESTING UNDER UNCERTAINTY

In Chapter 16, we ignored uncertainty when we analyzed how firms take account of discounting in making investment decisions. We now investigate how uncertainty affects the investment decision. In particular, we examine how attitudes toward risk affect individuals' willingness to invest, how people evaluate risky investments that last for many periods, and how investors pay to alter their probabilities of success.

In the following examples, the owner of a monopoly decides whether to open a new retail outlet. Because the firm is a monopoly, the owner's return from the investment does not depend on the actions of other firms. As a result, the owner faces no strategic considerations. The owner knows the cost of the investment but is unsure about how many people will patronize the new store; hence the profits are uncertain.

How Investing Depends on Attitudes Toward Risk

We start by considering a potential investment by the monopoly's owner that has an uncertain payoff this year. The owner must take risk into account but can ignore discounting. Whether the owner invests depends on how risk averse he or she is and on the risks involved.

Risk-Neutral Investing. Chris, the owner of the monopoly, is risk neutral. She maximizes her expected utility by making the investment only if the expected value of the return from the investment is positive.

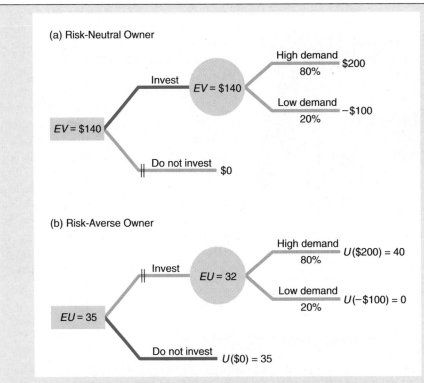

Figure 17.4 Investment Decision Tree with Risk Aversion. The owner of a monopoly must decide whether to invest in a new store. (a) The expected value is $140, so it pays for a risk-neutral owner to invest. (b) The utility from not investing for this risk-averse owner is greater than the expected utility from investing, so the owner does not invest.

To determine whether to invest, Chris uses the *decision tree* in panel a of Figure 17.4. The rectangle, called a *decision node*, indicates that she must make a decision about whether to invest or not. The circle, a *chance node*, denotes that a random process determines the outcome (consistent with the given probabilities). If Chris does not open the new store, she makes $0. If she does open the new store, she expects to make $200 with 80% probability and to lose $100 with 20% probability. The expected value from a new store (see the circle in panel a) is

$$EV = [0.8 \times \$200] + [0.2 \times (-\$100)] = \$140.$$

Because she is risk neutral, she prefers an expected value of $140 to a certain one of $0, so she invests. Thus her expected value in the rectangle is $140.

Risk-Averse Investing. Ken, who is risk averse, faces the same decision as Chris. Ken invests in the new store if his expected utility from investing is greater than his certain utility from not investing. Panel b of Figure 17.4 shows the decision tree for a particular risk-averse utility function. The circle shows that Ken's expected utility from the investment is

$$EU = [0.2 \times U(-\$100)] + [0.8 \times U(\$200)]$$
$$= (0.2 \times 0) + (0.8 \times 40) = 32.$$

The certain utility from not investing is $U(\$0) = 35$. Thus Ken does not invest. As a result, his expected utility (here, certain utility) in the rectangle is 35.

Application   **PREMIUM FOR A RISKIER INVESTMENT**

Risk-averse people will make risky investments only if these investments have an expected return that is sufficiently higher than that of a nonrisky investment such as a U.S. government bond, as Figure 17.2 illustrates.[16] Because most people are risk averse, they will make risky investments only if *the expected rate of return on a risky investment exceeds the rate of return on a nonrisky investment by a risk premium.*

Most stock funds have more nondiversifiable risks—as reflected by a higher standard deviation in returns—than bond funds, even junk bond funds. The table shows that the historical standard deviation varies substantially across a number of diversified stock and bond funds.

Because stocks are riskier than bonds, the rates of return on stocks exceed those on bonds over long periods of time. Over the 20-year period from 1974 through 1993, stocks had higher rates of return than bonds in 13 years in Britain, 12 in France, 11 in the United States, and 14 in Japan. The total annual real rate of return on U.S. stocks averaged 7% between 1926 and 1990,

---

[16]The Tappet brothers (the hosts of National Public Radio's *Car Talk*) offer a risk-free investment. Their Capital Depreciation Fund guarantees a 50% return. You send them $100 and they send you back $50.

compared to 1% on relatively risk-free U.S. Treasury bills (which are short-term bonds). The cumulative nominal rate over a 10-year period ending March 31, 1996, was 269% on an S&P 500 Index Fund, 124% for the Lehman Brothers Government/Corporate Bond Index, 87% for a (low-risk) money market account, and 81% for virtually risk-free U.S. Treasury bills. In comparison, the Consumer Price Index (a measure of inflation) rose by 43% during this period. Because stocks are the riskiest of these assets, we would expect them to provide by far the highest rate of return over the long haul, and they do.

Investment	Standard Deviation	
Japan stock funds	8.3	Riskier→
Gold funds	7.3	
Technology stock funds	5.8	
International stock funds	4.4	
Growth stock funds	4.0	
Standard & Poor's 500 stock funds	3.5	
Stock income funds	3.0	
Balanced funds	2.6	
T. Rowe Price International Bond Fund	2.4	
Junk bond funds	2.2	←Less risky
World income funds	1.9	
Ginnie Mae funds	1.1	

Investing with Uncertainty and Discounting

Now suppose that the uncertain returns or costs from an investment are spread out over time. In Chapter 16, we derived an investment rule by which we know future costs and returns with certainty. We concluded that an investment pays if its *net present value* (calculated by discounting the difference between the return and cost in each future period) is positive.

How does this rule change if the returns are uncertain? A risk-neutral person chooses to invest if the *expected net present value* is positive. We calculate the expected net present value by discounting the difference between expected return and expected cost in each future period.

Sam is risk neutral. His decision tree, Figure 17.5, shows that his cost of investing is C = $25 this year. Next year, he receives uncertain revenues from the investment of $125 with 80% probability or $50 with 20% probability. Thus the expected value of the revenues next year is

$$EV = (0.8 \times \$125) + (0.2 \times \$50) = \$110.$$

With a real interest rate of 10%, the expected present value of the revenues is

$$EPV = \$110/1.1 = \$100.$$

Subtracting the $25 cost incurred this year, Sam determines that his expected net present value is $ENPV = \$75$. As a result, he invests.

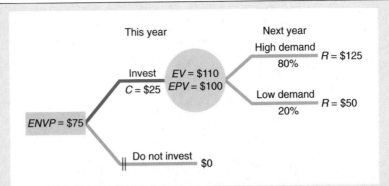

Figure 17.5 Investment Decision Tree with Uncertainty and Discounting. The risk-neutral owner invests if the expected net present value is positive. The expected value, *EV*, of the revenue from the investment next year is $110. With an interest rate of 10%, the expected present value, *EPV*, of the revenue is $100. The expected net present value, *ENPV*, is *EPV* = $100 minus the $25 cost of the investment this year, which is $75. The owner therefore invests.

Investing with Altered Probabilities

We have been assuming that nature dictates the probabilities of various states of nature. Sometimes, however, we can alter the probabilities, though usually at some expense.

Gautam, who is risk neutral, is considering whether to invest in a new store, as Figure 17.6 shows. After investing, he can increase the probability that demand will be high at the new store by advertising at a cost of $50.

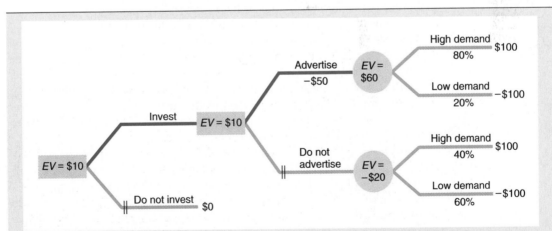

Figure 17.6 Investment Decision Tree with Advertising. By advertising, the risk-neutral owner can alter the probability of high demand. The expected value of the investment is –$20 without advertising and $60 with advertising. Because the cost of advertising is $50, the expected value of investing and advertising is $10 (= $60 – $50). The owner therefore invests and advertises.

If he makes the investment but does not advertise, he has a 40% probability of making $100 and a 60% probability of losing $100. His expected value without advertising is

$$[0.4 \times \$100] + [0.6 \times (-\$100)] = -\$20.$$

Thus if he could not advertise, he would not make this investment.

With advertising, the probability of his making $100 rises to 80%, so his expected value is

$$[0.8 \times \$100] + [0.2 \times (-\$100)] = \$60.$$

His expected value net of the cost of advertising is $10 (= $60 − $50). Thus he is better off investing and advertising than not investing at all or investing without advertising.

Application   LOANS, DEFAULTS, AND USURY LAWS

The following discussion of bank mortgage loans illustrates many of the key ideas of this chapter: measuring risk, diversifying to lower risk, insisting on higher returns for riskier investments, and altering probabilities. It also demonstrates how laws that prevent investors from receiving a risk premium reduce investments.

Banks and other firms (such as credit unions and savings and loans) invest by providing consumers with loans. These loans are risky: Banks worry that their customers will not repay the loans.

Banks know that random bad luck will cause some customers to *default* (fail to repay the money owed). The banks can reduce their risk from such random bad luck by pooling many loans, a form of diversification.

Banks are even more worried about systematic, nondiversifiable risks of default. Research reveals that people who have had trouble repaying loans in the past are more likely than others to default again in the future. Banks could lower their risk by not loaning to these people, but that would substantially reduce the number of loans they could make. Instead, to compensate for the greater risk of default, banks charge people who have weak financial histories or low and unsteady incomes higher mortgage rates.

Banks usually grade borrowers A through D for risk. The table shows how mortgage payments varied by risk class for a typical bank in 1994. People with spotty records of repaying debts pay higher interest rates for mortgages.

Banks also take other steps to alter the odds of a default. They provide smaller loans to relatively bad-risk borrowers by requiring that these people *put more money down*—pay for a larger share of the house in cash—and pay more *points*, which are fees equal to 1% of the loan that are paid up front. By putting more money down and paying more points, a borrower has more to lose and so is less likely to default on the loan.

Borrower's Risk Category	Adjustable Rate, %	Fixed Rate, %	Down Payment, %	Points
A: Clean credit	5.75	8.65	5–20	0–2
B: Clean credit last 12 months but a few missed payments previously	7	11	20–25	3–3.5
C: Clean credit last 12 months but previous possibly serious credit problems	7	11	20–30	3–3.5
D: A serious credit problem last 2 years, such as a foreclosure or bankruptcy	—	14–18	30–60	3–6

Notes: An adjustable-rate mortgage varies with inflation and market conditions; the initial rate is shown here. A fixed-rate mortgage has a nominal interest rate that remains constant for the term of the loan. The down payment is the share of the purchase price that the borrower must pay in cash at the time the house is purchased. A point is an amount of money paid at the start of the mortgage, equal to 1% of the loan.

Source: Ravo, Nick, "Mortgages: Lenders More Forgiving of Poor Credit Records," *The New York Times*, September 3, 1994:34.

Thus when banks are free to set their loan rates and other conditions for loans, people who are poor risks can get loans by paying a relatively higher rate to borrow money. A binding usury law (Chapter 16) that sets a maximum rate that banks can charge forces banks to set the same interest rates for many or all of their customers. In response, banks loan only to relatively low-risk borrowers. High-risk borrowers cannot get loans.

Villegas (1989) compared short-term consumer credit for households in states with usury ceilings and in those without limits. He found that the amount of credit a low-income family has in a state with a usury limit is $1,013 less than that of a comparable household in a state without such a price control. For middle-income households, the difference is $478. There is no significant difference for high-income families.

On the basis of statistical tests, Villegas did not find that households in states with usury laws were able to obtain auto loans at significantly lower interest rates than those in other states. Thus if his results are correct, usury laws hurt poor consumers by limiting their ability to borrow and do not significantly reduce the rate at which wealthier consumers borrow.

Summary

1. **Degree of risk:** A probability measures the likelihood that a particular state of nature occurs. People may use historical frequencies, if available, to calculate a probability. Lacking detailed information, people form subjective estimates of the probability on the basis of available information. The expected value is the probability-weighted average of the values in each state of nature. One widely used measure of risk is the variance (or the standard deviation, which is the square root of the variance). The variance is the probability-weighted average of the squared difference of the value in each state of nature and the expected value.

Application   MICHAEL JORDAN'S POSITIVE EXTERNALITIES

When Michael Jordan was an employee of the Chicago Bulls, he raised sales throughout the National Basketball Association (NBA), creating positive externalities. Controlling for team records, Hausman and Leonard (1997) showed that Jordan's presence increased ticket revenues at away games throughout the league by $2.5 million during the 1991–1992 regular season. (Jordan didn't affect gate receipts for playoff games because they would have sold out even without him.) Local television advertising rev-

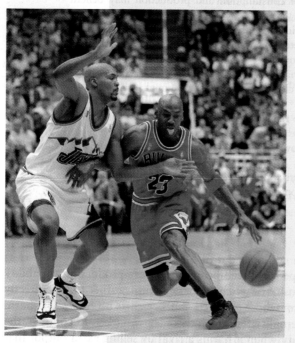

enues also rose by $2.4 million for these games. These increased ticket and local television advertising receipts reflected a positive externality because they went to the home team rather than to Jordan's employer, the Bulls.

Jordan's presence increased national television advertising by $6.6 million during the regular season and by $13.9 million during the playoffs. (Dick Ebersol, the president of NBC Sports, attributed a 15% decline in viewership to his absence in the first post-Jordan playoffs in 1999.) Jordan also boosted the earnings of NBA Properties, which licenses NBA paraphernalia such as clothing and videos, by $15.1 million. National television revenues and NBA Properties' earnings are shared equally by all teams, so most of this increase was a positive externality for other teams. Hausman and Leonard estimated the total value of Jordan's positive externalities at $40.3 million for the 1991–1992 season. (Perhaps less precisely, *Fortune* magazine estimated that Jordan's NBA career contributed $10 billion to the U.S. economy.)

18.2   THE INEFFICIENCY OF COMPETITION WITH EXTERNALITIES

I shot an arrow in the air and it stuck.

Competitive firms and consumers do not have to pay for the harms of their negative externalities, so they create excessive amounts. Similarly, because producers are not compensated for the benefits of a positive externality, too little of such externalities are produced.

To illustrate why externalities lead to nonoptimal production, we examine a (hypothetical) competitive market in which firms produce paper and by-products of the production process—such as air and water pollution—that harm people who live near paper mills. We'll call the pollution *gunk*. Each ton of paper that is produced increases the amount of gunk by one unit, and the only way to decrease the volume of gunk is to reduce the amount of paper manufactured. No less-polluting technologies are available, and it is not possible to locate plants where the gunk bothers no one.

Paper firms do not have to pay for the harm from the pollution they cause. As a result, each firm's **private cost**—the cost of production only, not including externalities—includes its direct costs of labor, energy, and wood pulp but not the indirect costs of the harm from gunk. The true **social cost** is the private cost plus the cost of the harms from externalities.

Supply-and-Demand Analysis	The paper industry is the major industrial source of water pollution. We use a supply-and-demand diagram for the paper market in Figure 18.1 to illustrate that *a competitive market produces excessive pollution because the firms' private cost is less than their social cost*.[2] In the competitive equilibrium, the firms consider only their private costs in making decisions and ignore the harms of the pollution externality they inflict on others. The market supply curve is the aggregate *private marginal cost* curve, MC^p, which is the horizontal sum of the private marginal cost curves of each of the paper manufacturing plants.

The competitive equilibrium, e_c, is determined by the intersection of the market supply curve and the market demand curve for paper. The competitive equilibrium quantity is $Q_c = 105$ tons per day, and the competitive equilibrium price is $p_c = \$240$ per ton.

The firms' *private producer surplus* is the producer surplus of the paper mills based on their *private marginal cost* curve: the area, $F + G + H$, below the market price and above MC^p up to the competitive equilibrium quantity, 105. The competitive equilibrium maximizes the sum of consumer surplus and private producer surplus (Chapter 9). If there were no externality, the sum of consumer surplus and private producer surplus would equal welfare, so competition would maximize welfare.

Because of the pollution, however, the competitive equilibrium does *not* maximize welfare. Competitive firms produce too much gunk because they do not have to pay for the harm from the gunk. This *market failure* (Chapter 9) results from competitive forces that equalize the price and *private marginal cost* rather than *social marginal cost*, which includes both the private costs of production and the externality damage.

For a given amount of paper production, the full cost of one more ton of paper to society, the *social marginal cost* (MC^s), is the cost of manufacturing one more ton of paper to the paper firms plus the additional externality damage to people in the community from producing this last ton of paper. Thus the height of the social marginal cost curve, MC^s, at any given quantity equals the vertical sum of the height of the MC^p curve (the private marginal cost of producing another ton of paper) plus the height of the MC^g curve (the marginal externality damage) at that quantity.

---

[2]Appendix 18A uses algebra to analyze this model and derives the numbers in the figure. These numbers are not based on actual estimates.

	Social Optimum	Private	Change
Consumer surplus, CS	A	$A + B + C + D$	$B + C + D$
Private producer surplus, PS_p	$B + C + F + G$	$F + G + H$	$H - B - C$
Externality cost, C_g	$C + G$	$C + D + E + G + H$	$D + E + H$
Social producer surplus, $PS_s = PS_p - C_g$	$B + F$	$F - C - D - E$	$-B - C - D - E$
Welfare, $W = CS + PS_s$	$A + B + F$	$A + B + F - E$	$-E = DWL$

Figure 18.1 Welfare Effects of Pollution in a Competitive Market. The competitive equilibrium, e_c, is determined by the intersection of the demand curve and the competitive supply or private marginal cost curve, MC^p, which ignores the cost of pollution. The social optimum, e_s, is at the inter- section of the demand curve and the social marginal cost curve, $MC^s = MC^p + MC^g$, where MC^g is the marginal cost of the pollution (gunk). Private producer surplus is based on the MC^p curve, and social producer surplus is based on the MC^s curve.

The social marginal cost curve intersects the demand curve at the socially optimal quantity, $Q_s = 84$. At smaller quantities, the price—the value consumers place on the last unit of the good sold—is higher than the full social marginal cost. There the gain to consumers of paper exceeds the cost of producing an extra unit of output (and hence an extra unit of gunk). At larger quantities, the price is below the social marginal cost, so the gain to consumers is less than the cost of producing an extra unit.

Welfare is the sum of consumer surplus and *social producer surplus*, which is based on the *social marginal cost* curve rather than the *private marginal cost* curve.

Welfare is maximized where price equals social marginal cost. At the social optimum, e_s, welfare equals $A + B + F$: the area between the demand curve and the MC^s curve up to the optimal quantity, 84 tons of paper.

Welfare at the competitive equilibrium, e_c, is lower: $A + B + F - E$, the areas between the demand curve and the MC^s curve up to 105 tons of paper. The area between these curves from 84 to 105, $-E$, is a deadweight loss because the social cost exceeds the value that consumers place on these last 21 tons of paper. *A deadweight loss results because the competitive market equates price with private marginal cost instead of with social marginal cost.*

Welfare is higher at the social optimum than at the competitive equilibrium because the gain from reducing pollution from the competitive to the socially optimal level more than offsets the loss to consumers and producers of the paper. The cost of the pollution to people who live near the factories is the area under the MC^g curve between zero and the quantity produced. By construction, this area is the same as the area between the MC^p and the MC^s curves. The total damage from the gunk is $-C - D - E - G - H$ at the competitive equilibrium and only $-C - G$ at the social optimum. Consequently, the extra pollution damage from producing the competitive output rather than the socially optimal quantity is $-D - E - H$.

The main beneficiaries from producing at the competitive output level rather than at the socially optimal level are the paper buyers, who pay $240 rather than $282 for a ton of paper. Their consumer surplus rises from A to $A + B + C + D$. The corresponding change in private producer surplus is $H - B - C$, which is negative in this figure.

The figure illustrates two main results with respect to negative externalities. First, *a competitive market produces excessive negative externalities.* Because the price of the pollution to the firms is zero, which is less than the marginal cost that the last unit of pollution imposes on society, an unregulated competitive market produces more pollution than is socially optimal.

Second, *the optimal amount of pollution is greater than zero.* Even though pollution is harmful and we'd like to have none of it, we cannot wipe it out without eliminating virtually all production and consumption. Making paper, dishwashers, and televisions creates air and water pollution. Fertilizers used in farming pollute the water supply. Delivery people pollute the air by driving to your home.

Application   **WASTE NOT**

If one person's waste is another's treasure, markets can resolve externality problems without government intervention. More than a decade ago, when Michael R. Daley toured a plant that burned old tires for energy, he learned that the plant paid haulers to remove gypsum, a by-product of the process. He wondered why, because gypsum is a critical component of plaster, toothpaste, paint, and molds for false teeth. Seizing the opportunity, Mr. Daley built a firm, Triad Energy Resources, Inc., near the plant to obtain and resell the gypsum.

Triad now sets up shop next to other corporations and finds uses for their wastes. The firm makes soil additives from C&H Sugar Company's sugarfiltration by-products, fertilizer from Australian wineries and fruit processors' leftover skins and seeds, and fertilizer and fish food from the detritus of Oregon fish processors.

Companies have used this recycling principle for more than two decades in Kalundborg, Denmark. Millennium Exchange Ltd. is a for-profit, Web-based waste exchange. In Tampico, Mexico, 25 companies within a 40-mile radius hire Bechtel Corporation to identify their waste products and to set up exchanges. An increasing number of private developers and economic development agencies are building *eco-industrial parks*, or *eco-parks*, to convert wastes to practical uses. Eco-parks exist or are on the drawing board in California, Connecticut, Mississippi, New Mexico, and Virginia, as well as in Germany, Mexico, and Puerto Rico.

One enterprising American couple, Donald and Winifred Sonner, turned their modest business of making underwear for incarcerated females into a major operation: manufacturing gun-cleaning patches. The Sonners had learned that there is no such thing as "delicate" cycles in prison laundries and that panties were consequently disintegrating. To deal with this problem, the Sonners had started a business supplying prisons with undies made of 5.3-ounce knitted cotton. Today they sell roughly 1.2 million garments to loyal customers at about 125 prisons and mental facilities.

But over a fifth of the material they use to fashion a pair of underwear ends up as waste. As their volume rose and the Sonners' landfill bills mounted, they looked into other uses for the by-product. They first tried mulching the scrap into pillow stuffing, but the knitted material clogged their machine.

Then on a day off, Donald accompanied his son Stephen to a gun store. When he discovered that the store was selling flimsy woven cloth as gun-cleaning patches—squares of cloth that are impregnated with solvent or oil and then reamed down the inside of a gun barrel to clean and lubricate it—Donald had found a use for his much more durable cloth.

The Sonners now sell patches to about 7,000 police departments and chain stores, the FBI, the Special Forces, the State Department, and several other federal agencies that they aren't at liberty to disclose. Because their patch sales now outstrip underwear sales 4 to 1, they have to buy cloth from other companies. The firm's motto is "Manufacturers of Quality Panties & the Finest in Gun-Cleaning Patches."

Reducing Externalities. Because competitive markets produce too many negative externalities, government intervention may provide a social gain. Only within the last several decades, however, have any governments regulated pollution.

In developed countries, public and private expenditures on environmental protection as a percentage of gross domestic product (national income) are 0.9% in Canada, 1.1% in Japan, 1.2% in France, 1.4% in the United Kingdom, 1.5% in Germany, 1.6% in the United States, and 1.9% in the Netherlands (*Eurostat*, 1997). The world's poorest countries spend little, if anything, on pollution control.

Consequently, emissions relative to economic output are higher in developing countries than in Western nations. The Russian Federation emitted 4.7 kg of carbon dioxide (CO_2) per dollar of gross domestic product generated; China, 4.4; India, 2.8; Mexico, 1.2; Australia, 0.8; Canada and the United States, 0.7; the United Kingdom and New Zealand, 0.5; Germany, 0.4; Denmark, 0.3; and France and Japan, 0.2. (World Bank, *1999 World Development Indicators*).

In 1992, representatives from more than 150 countries began negotiating an international emissions reduction policy. An agreement was reached in Kyoto, Japan, in December 1997 that required most industrialized nations to reduce emissions by an average of 5.2% below 1990 levels by 2008–2012. To achieve this goal, the United States, Europe, and Japan need to curb their CO_2 emissions by 31%, 22%, and 35%, respectively, from the levels that would have been attained in the absence of a reduction policy.

If a government has sufficient knowledge about pollution damage, the demand curve, costs, and the production technology, it can force a competitive market to produce the social optimum. The government might control pollution directly by restricting the amount of pollution that firms may produce or by taxing them for pollution they create. A governmental limit on the amount of air or water pollution that may be released is called an *emissions standard*. A tax on air pollution is called an *emissions fee*, and a tax on discharges into the air or waterways is an *effluent charge*.

Frequently, however, a government controls pollution indirectly, through quantity restrictions or taxes on outputs or inputs. Whether the government restricts or taxes outputs or inputs may depend on the nature of the production process.

Emissions Standard. We use the paper mill gunk example in Figure 18.1 to illustrate how a government may use an *emissions standard* to reduce pollution. Here the government can achieve the social optimum by forcing the paper mills to produce no more than 84 units of gunk or paper per day. (Because output and pollution move together in this example, regulating either reduces pollution in the same way.)

Unfortunately, the government usually does not know enough to regulate optimally. For example, to set quantity restrictions on output optimally, the government must know how the marginal social cost curve, the demand for paper curve, and pollution vary with output. The ease with which the government can monitor output and pollution may determine whether it sets an output restriction or a pollution standard.

Even if the government knows enough to set the optimal regulation, it must enforce this regulation to achieve the social optimum. Though the U.S. Environmental Protection Agency (EPA) sets federal smog standards, 33 metropolitan areas—including Baltimore, Boston, Chicago, Houston, Los Angeles, Milwaukee, New York, and Philadelphia—fail to meet these standards.[3]

---

[3]See www.epa.gov/enviro/zipcode.html or www.scorecard.org for details on the environmental risks in your area.

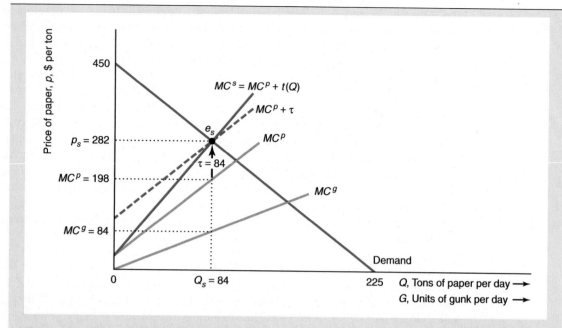

Figure 18.2 Taxes to Control Pollution. Placing a tax on the firms equal to the harm from the gunk, $t(Q) = MC^g$, causes them to internalize the externality, so their private marginal cost is the same as the social marginal cost, MC^s. As a result, the competitive after-tax equilibrium is the same as the social optimum, e_s. Alternatively, applying a specific tax of $\tau = \$84$ per unit, which is the marginal harm from the gunk at $Q_s = 84$, also results in the social optimum.

Emissions Fee. The government may impose costs on polluters by taxing their output or the amount of pollution produced. (Similarly, a law could make a polluter liable for damages in a court.) We use our earlier paper mill example to illustrate the effect of a tax on output.

If the government knows the marginal cost of the gunk, MC^g, it can set the output tax equal to this marginal cost curve: $t(Q) = MC^g$. (We write this tax as $t(Q)$ to show that it varies with output, Q.) Figure 18.2 illustrates the manufacturers' after-tax marginal cost, $MC^s = MC^p + t(Q)$.

The output tax causes a manufacturer to **internalize the externality**: to bear the cost of the harm that one inflicts on others (or to capture the benefit that one provides to others). The after-tax private marginal cost or supply curve is the same as the social marginal cost curve. As a result, the after-tax competitive equilibrium is the social optimum.

Usually, the government sets a specific tax rather than a tax that varies with the amount of pollution, as MC^g does. As Solved Problem 18.1 shows, applying an appropriate specific tax results in the socially optimal level of production.

Solved Problem 18.1 **For the market with pollution in Figure 18.1, what constant, specific tax, τ, on output could the government set to maximize welfare?**

Answer

Set the specific tax equal to the marginal harm of pollution at the socially optimal quantity: At the socially optimal quantity, $Q_s = 84$, the marginal harm from the gunk is $84, as Figure 18.2 shows. If the specific tax is $\tau = \$84$, the after-tax private marginal cost (after-tax competitive supply curve), $MC^p + \tau$, equals the social marginal cost at the socially optimal quantity. As a consequence, the after-tax competitive supply curve intersects the demand curve at the socially optimal quantity. By paying this specific tax, the firms internalize the cost of the externality at the social optimum. All that is required for optimal production is that the tax equals the marginal cost of pollution at the optimum quantity; it need not equal the marginal cost of pollution at other quantities.

Application **TAXES ON FUELS**

Consuming fuels causes pollution. Governments may try to set taxes on fuels so that the people and firms that consume these fuels bear the full social cost, including the harms from pollution. Indeed, one of the reasons that state and federal governments tax fuels is to shift these pollution costs from victims of pollution to consumers of the fuels. (Governments also tax fuels to raise tax revenues—see Chapter 3—and to restrict imports.)

In the United States, before the ban on the use of lead in gasoline, each gallon of gasoline inflicted an estimated 1.08¢ worth of damage from lead, 8.31¢ due to particulates (grit and soot), 1.74¢ from sulfur oxides, 2.14¢ due to ozone, 0.08¢ for reduced visibility, and 2.23¢ as a result of air toxins from motor vehicles (Viscusi, 1992). For many fuels, particulate emissions are the most serious problem. The harms from particulates represent 9% of the price

	Externality Cost as a Percentage of Price	Current Tax as a Percentage of Price
Natural gas	1.1	6.4
Aircraft fuel	12.9	15.5
Gasoline	16.7	16.6
Diesel fuel	50.4	12.9
Heating oils	63.7	14.6
Wood	152.4	0
Coal	528.0	35.9

Note: Data are for 1986. Tax revenues that are returned as subsidies to the use of that form of energy, such as the Highway Trust Fund, are excluded in the tax calculations.

of gasoline, 23% of the price of diesel fuel, 11% of the price of aircraft fuel, and 147% of the price of wood. Mortality losses from sulfur oxide are the major harm from heating oil, with damages that are 53% of price. Damages from coal amount to 464% of price.

The table shows the marginal cost of pollution from one more unit of fuel as a percentage of the price of that unit and the current tax as a percent of price. If the tax is a lower percentage than the externality cost, too much pollution is produced. If the tax is a higher percentage, too little fuel is used. Thus if these estimates are correct, the tax on gasoline roughly equals the marginal harm from pollution,[4] the taxes on natural gas and aircraft fuel are too high, and the taxes on other fuels—particularly coal—are far too low. Indeed, wood is not taxed at all.

Cost-Benefit Analysis

We've used a supply-and-demand analysis to show that *a competitive market produces too much pollution because the price of output equals the marginal private cost rather than the marginal social cost.* By using a cost-benefit analysis, we obtain another interpretation of the pollution problem in terms of the marginal cost and benefit of the pollution itself.

In the cost-benefit diagram, panel a of Figure 18.3 (which corresponds to Figure 18.1), the quantity on the horizontal axis starts at the competitive level, 105 tons, and *decreases to the right* (in contrast to the pattern in most of our graphs). Thus a movement to the right indicates a reduction in paper and gunk, possibly due to a pollution abatement policy. Again, welfare peaks at the socially optimal quantity of output or gunk of 84 tons per day.

The benefit of reducing output is the reduced damage from gunk. The height of the benefit curve at a given quantity is the difference between the pollution harm at that quantity and the harm at the competitive quantity.

The cost of reducing output is that the consumer surplus and private producer surplus fall. The height of the cost curve at a given quantity is the sum of consumer surplus and private producer surplus at that quantity minus the corresponding value at the competitive quantity.

If society reduced output to 63 tons, the quantity at which the total benefit equals the total cost, society would be no better off than it is in the competitive equilibrium. To maximize welfare, we want to set output at 84 tons, the quantity for which the gap between the total benefit and total cost is greatest. At that quantity, the slope of the benefit curve, the marginal benefit, *MB*, equals the slope of the cost curve, the marginal cost, *MC*, as panel b of the figure shows.[5] Thus *welfare is maximized by*

---

[4]Gasoline taxes are not the most efficient way to control auto-related air pollution. Old, ill-maintained cars, which are 10% of all automobiles, cause half the pollution from cars. Removing them from the road would be more cost effective than a gas tax that falls on both heavy and light polluters.

[5]This marginal cost curve, *MC*, reflects the social cost of removing the last unit of paper (gunk), whereas the social marginal cost curve, MC^s, in Figure 18.1 captures the extra cost to society from the last unit of paper (or gunk).

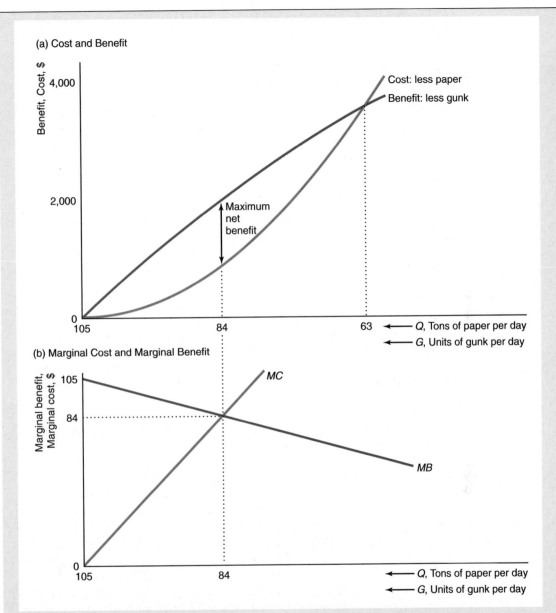

Figure 18.3 Cost-Benefit Analysis of Pollution.
(a) The benefit curve reflects the reduction in harm from pollution as the amount of gunk falls from the competitive level. The cost of reducing the amount of gunk is the fall in output, which reduces consumer surplus and private producer surplus. Welfare is maximized at 84 tons of paper and 84 units of gunk, the quantities at which the difference between the benefit and cost curves, the net benefit, is greatest. (b) The net benefit is maximized where the marginal benefit, *MB*, which is the slope of the benefit curve, equals the marginal cost, *MC*, the slope of the cost curve.

reducing output and pollution until the marginal benefit from less pollution equals the marginal cost of less output.

Application   EMISSIONS STANDARDS FOR OZONE

Ozone, a major pollutant, is formed in the atmosphere through a chemical reaction between reactive organic gases and nitrogen oxides in sunlight. The Clean Air Act of 1990, which set national air-quality standards for major pollutants, mandates that atmospheric ozone levels not rise above 0.12 parts per million (ppm). The California Air Resources Board (CARB) has established an even tighter standard, 0.09 ppm.

The chief costs of reducing ozone are greater expenses of manufacturing and of driving. The main benefits are improved health and increased agricultural production. The health benefits of reducing ozone are greatest in highly populated areas, while the benefits of expanded agricultural yields occur in rural areas. Consequently, the optimal level of ozone differs in urban and agricultural areas.

The benefits of reducing the ozone level have outweighed the costs in Los Angeles over the past several decades. However, the California standards may be too strict even in Los Angeles, which still has the worst air pollution problem in the country. Krupnick and Portney (1991) estimated that reducing the ozone concentration in Los Angeles to the California standard has an annual benefit to human health and materials of about $4 billion, which is much less than the annual cost of about $13 billion.

Although the California standard appears to be too strict for an urban area such as Los Angeles, is it appropriate in an agricultural region? Ozone substantially damages crops. Crop losses due to high ozone levels range from 8.4% for alfalfa hay to 32% for oranges, according to the CARB. The CARB claims that production yields fall for ozone-sensitive crops such as beans, cotton, grapes, lemons, and oranges even at ozone levels as low as 0.09 ppm.

Kim, Helfand, and Howitt (1998) compared the benefits and costs of reducing ozone in the San Joaquin Valley, which produces 60% of California crops and 9% of total U.S. crops in terms of value. The San Joaquin Valley has the second-worst air quality in California, trailing only Los Angeles. The pollution in many San Joaquin Valley counties regularly exceeds both state and national standards. For example, in Kern County, the highest recorded ozone level in 1990 was 0.17 ppm, the 0.09-ppm state standard was surpassed on 120 days that year, and the 0.12-ppm national standard was exceeded on 37 days.

Kim, Helfand, and Howitt estimate that the health benefits from meeting California's 0.09-ppm standard range from $2.58 million to $51.58 million. Achieving the state standard would increase agricultural production, raising consumer surplus by $229 million to $270 million and producer surplus by $297 million to $348 million.

The graph in panel a shows Kim, Helfand, and Howitt's most conservative benefit estimates and their highest cost estimates from reducing ozone concentration levels. The graph in panel b illustrates the corresponding marginal

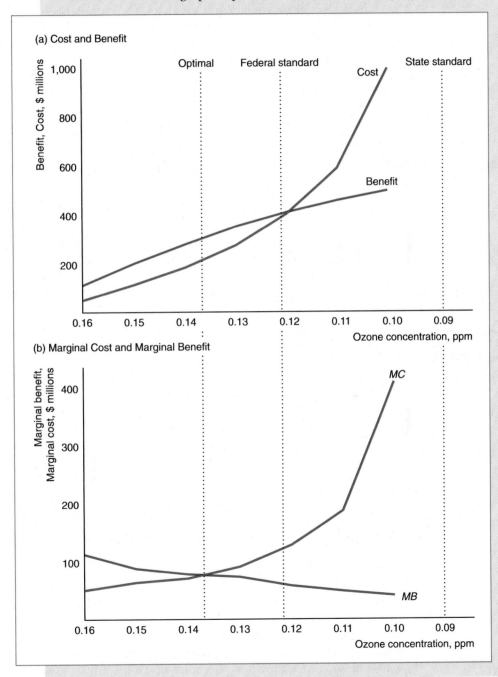

costs and benefits. Welfare is maximized at a concentration level slightly below 0.14 ppm, at which the gap between the benefit and cost curves in panel a is greatest and the marginal benefit equals the marginal cost in panel b.

Thus given these conservative estimates, the state standards are too stringent in this agricultural area. According to the researchers' most likely (as opposed to most conservative) estimates, the federal standards are nearly optimal for this region. Even by these conservative estimates, however, society would benefit from substantially reducing ozone below current levels in many areas of the San Joaquin Valley.

18.3 | MARKET STRUCTURE AND EXTERNALITIES

Two of our main results concerning competitive markets and negative externalities—that too much pollution is produced and that a tax equal to the marginal social cost of the externality solves the problem—do not hold for other market structures. Although a competitive market always produces too many negative externalities, a noncompetitive market may produce more or less than the optimal level of output and pollution. If a tax is set so that firms internalize the externalities, a competitive market produces the social optimum, whereas a noncompetitive market does not.

Monopoly and Externalities

We use the paper-gunk example to illustrate these results. In Figure 18.4, the monopoly equilibrium, e_m, is determined by the intersection of the marginal revenue, MR, and private marginal cost, MC^p, curves. Like the competitive firms, the monopoly ignores the harm its pollution causes, so it considers just its direct, private costs in making decisions.

Output is only 70 tons in the monopoly equilibrium, e_m, which is less than the 84 tons at the social optimum, e_s. Thus this figure illustrates that *the monopoly outcome may be less than the social optimum even with an externality.*

Although the competitive market with an externality always produces more output than the social optimum, a monopoly may produce more than, the same as, or less than the social optimum. The reason that a monopoly may produce too little or too much is that it faces two offsetting effects. The monopoly tends to produce too little output because it sets its price above its marginal cost. But the monopoly tends to produce too much output because its decisions depend on its private marginal cost instead of the social marginal cost.

Which effect dominates depends on the elasticity of demand for the output and on the extent of the marginal damage the pollution causes. If the demand curve is very elastic, the monopoly markup is small. As a result, the monopoly equilibrium is close to the competitive equilibrium, e_c, and greater than the social optimum, e_s. If extra pollution causes little additional harm—MC^g is close to zero at the equilibrium—the social marginal cost essentially equals the private marginal cost, and the monopoly produces less than the social optimum.

Monopoly Versus Competitive Welfare with Externalities

In the absence of externalities, welfare is greater under competition than under monopoly (Chapter 11). With an externality, however, welfare may be greater with monopoly than with competition.

If both monopoly and competitive outputs are greater than the social optimum, welfare must be greater under monopoly because the competitive output is larger than the monopoly output. If the monopoly produces less than the social optimum, we need to check which distortion is greater: the monopoly's producing too little or the competitive market's producing too much.

Welfare is lower at monopoly equilibrium, areas $A + B$, than at the social optimum, $A + B + C$, in Figure 18.4. The deadweight loss of monopoly, C, results from the monopoly's producing less output than is socially optimal.

In the figure, the deadweight loss from monopoly, C, is less than the deadweight loss from competition, D, so welfare is greater under monopoly. The monopoly produces

Figure 18.4 Monopoly, Competition, and Social Optimum with Pollution. At the competitive equilibrium, e_c, more is produced than at the social optimum, e_s. As a result, the deadweight loss in the competitive market is D. The monopoly equilibrium, e_m, is determined by the intersection of the marginal revenue and the private marginal cost, MC^p, curves. The social welfare (based on the marginal social cost, MC^s, curve) under monopoly is $A + B$. Here the deadweight loss of monopoly, C, is less than the deadweight loss under competition, D.

only slightly too little output, whereas competition produces excessive output—and hence far too much gunk.

Solved Problem 18.2   **In Figure 18.4, what is the effect on output, price, and welfare of taxing the monopoly an amount equal to the marginal harm of the externality?**

Answer

1. *Show how the monopoly equilibrium shifts if the firm is taxed*: A tax equal to the marginal cost of the pollution causes the monopoly to internalize the externality and to view the social marginal cost as its private cost. The intersection of the marginal revenue, MR, curve and the social marginal cost, MC^s, curve determines the taxed-monopoly equilibrium, e_t. The tax causes the equilibrium quantity to fall from 70 to 60 and the equilibrium price to rise from $310 to $330.

2. *Determine how this shift affects the deadweight loss of monopoly*: The sum of consumer and producer surplus is only A after the tax, compared to $A + B$ before the tax. Thus welfare falls. The difference between A and welfare at the social optimum, $A + B + C$, is $-(B + C)$, which is the deadweight loss from the taxed monopoly. The tax exacerbates the monopoly's tendency to produce too little output. The deadweight loss increases from C to $B + C$. The monopoly produced too little before the tax. The taxed monopoly produces even less.

Taxing Externalities in Noncompetitive Markets

Many people recommend that the government tax firms an amount equal to the marginal harm of pollution on the grounds that such a tax achieves the social optimum in a competitive market. Solved Problem 18.2 shows that such a tax may lower welfare if applied to a monopoly.[6]

If the government has enough information to determine the social optimum, it can force either a monopolized or a competitive market to produce it. If the social optimum is greater than the unregulated monopoly output, however, the government has to subsidize (rather than tax) the monopoly to get it to produce as much output as is desired.

In short, trying to solve a negative externality problem is more complex in a noncompetitive market than in a competitive market. To achieve a social optimum in a competitive market, the government only has to reduce the externality, possibly by decreasing output. In a noncompetitive market, the government must eliminate problems arising from both externalities *and* the exercise of market power. Thus the gov-

---

[6]The tax definitely lowers welfare if the untaxed monopoly was producing less than the social optimum. If the untaxed monopoly was originally producing more than the social optimum, a tax may cause welfare to increase.

ernment needs more information to regulate a noncompetitive market optimally and may also require more tools, such as a subsidy. To the degree that the problems arising from market power and pollution are offsetting, however, the failure to regulate a noncompetitive market is less harmful than the failure to regulate a competitive market.

18.4 | ALLOCATING PROPERTY RIGHTS TO REDUCE EXTERNALITIES

Instead of controlling externalities directly through emissions fees and emissions standards, the government may take an indirect approach by assigning a **property right**: an exclusive privilege to use an asset. By owning this textbook, you have a property right to read it and to stop others from reading or taking it.

If no one holds a property right for a good or a bad, the good or bad is unlikely to have a price. If you had a property right that assured you of the right to be free from noise pollution, you could get the courts to stop your neighbor from playing loud music. Or you could sell your right, permitting your neighbor to play the music. If you did not have this property right, no one would be willing to pay you a positive price for it.

In earlier chapters, we implicitly assumed that property rights were clearly defined and that no harmful by-products were created, so externalities did not arise. In those chapters, all goods had prices.

For many bads, such as pollution, and for some goods, property rights are not clearly defined. No one has exclusive property rights to the air we breathe. Because of this lack of a price, a polluter's private marginal cost of production is less than the full social marginal cost.

Coase Theorem

According to the *Coase Theorem* (Coase, 1960), the optimal levels of pollution and output can result from bargaining between polluters and their victims if property rights are clearly defined. Coase's contribution is not so much a practical solution to the pollution problem as a demonstration that a lack of clearly defined property rights is the root of the externality problem.

To illustrate the Coase Theorem, we consider two firms, a chemical plant and a boat rental company, that share a small lake. The chemical manufacturer dumps its waste by-products, which smell bad but are otherwise harmless, into the lake. The chemical company can reduce pollution only by restricting its output; it has no other outlet for this waste. The resulting pollution damages the boat rental firm's business. There are other lakes nearby where people can rent boats. Therefore, because they dislike the smell of the chemicals, people rent from this firm only if it charges a low enough price to compensate them fully for the smell.

No Property Rights. These two firms won't negotiate with each other unless property rights are clearly defined. After all, why would the manufacturer reduce its pollution if the boat rental firm has no legal right to clean water? Why would the boat rental firm pay the chemical company not to pollute if the courts may declare that the rental company has a right to be free from pollution?

If the firms do not negotiate, the chemical firm produces the output level that maximizes its profit, ignoring the effect on the boat rental firm. The profit matrix in panel a of Table 18.1 shows that the chemical firm makes $0 if it produces nothing, $10 if it produces 1 ton, and $15 if it produces 2 tons regardless of what the boat rental firm does. Thus the chemical company has a dominant strategy: It produces 2 tons. Knowing that the chemical company will produce 2 tons, the boat rental firm maximizes its profit with 1 boat.

Because nobody else is directly affected by this pollution, we call an outcome *efficient* if it maximizes the sum of the profits of the two firms.[7] The firms maximize their joint profits at $20 when the chemical company produces 1 ton and the boat rental firm rents 1 boat. Thus the no-property-rights equilibrium, with joint profits of $17, is inefficient: Too much pollution is produced.

Property Right to Be Free of Pollution. If a court or the government grants the boat rental firm the property right to be free of pollution, the firm can prevent the chemical company from dumping at all. With no pollution, the boat company rents 2 boats and makes $15. Rather than shut down, the chemical company offers to pay the boat company for the right to dump. The boat rental firm is willing to permit dumping only if it makes at least $15, and it may hold out for more. The largest "bribe" the chemical company is willing to offer for the right to dump is one that leaves it with a positive profit. Panel b of Table 18.1 shows one possible compensation agreement: The chemical company offers the boat rental firm $7 per ton for the right to dump. If the firms agree to this deal, the chemical company's dominant strategy is to produce 1 ton, so the boat rental firm chooses to rent 1 boat. Both firms benefit. Indeed, in this equilibrium, their joint profits are maximized at $20.

In general, the chemical firm pays the boat rental firm between $5 and $10. The boat rental firm wants at least $5 so that its profit when both produce one unit is at least $15—the amount that it makes with no pollution. Any payment larger than $10 would leave the chemical company with a negative profit, so that's the most it is willing to pay. The exact payment outcome depends on the firms' bargaining skills. Because both parties benefit from a deal, they should be able to reach an agreement if transaction costs are low enough that it pays to negotiate.

Property Right to Pollute. Now suppose that the chemical company has the property right to dump in the lake (for example, by paying a pollution tax). Unless the boat rental company pays the chemical company not to pollute, the chemical company produces 2 tons, as in panel a of the table. The boat rental firm may bribe the chemical company to reduce its output so that both firms benefit. Again, the exact deal that is struck depends on their bargaining skills.

Panel c of Table 18.1 shows what happens if the boat rental firm pays the chemical company $6 per ton for each ton less than 2 that it produces. The chemical company's dominant strategy is to produce 1 ton, and the boat rental firm rents 1 boat.

---

[7]Because people who want to rent boats pay sufficiently less as compensation for putting up with the chemicals, they are not harmed by the pollution. Only the boat rental firm is harmed through lower prices.

Table 18.1 Property Rights and Bargaining

(a) No Property Rights

		Boat Rental Firm: Boats Rented per Day		
Chemical Firm: Tons per Day		**0**	**1**	**2**
	0	$0 / $0	$0 / $14	$0 / $15
	1	$10 / $0	$10 / $10	$10 / $5
	2	$15 / $0	$15 / $2	$15 / −$3

(b) Boat Rental Firm Has Property Right: Chemical company pays the boat rental firm $7 per ton for the right to dump

		Boat Rental Firm: Boats Rented per Day		
Chemical Firm: Tons per Day		**0**	**1**	**2**
	0	$0 / $0	$0 / $14	$0 / $15
	1	$3 / $7	$3 / $17	$3 / $12
	2	$1 / $14	$1 / $16	$1 / $11

(c) Chemical Company Has Property Right: Boat rental firm pays the chemical company $6 for each ton by which it reduces its production below 2 tons

		Boat Rental Firm: Boats Rented per Day		
Chemical Firm: Tons per Day		**0**	**1**	**2**
	0	$12 / −$12	$12 / $2	$12 / $3
	1	$16 / −$6	$16 / $4	$16 / −$1
	2	$15 / $0	$15 / $2	$15 / −$3

The equilibrium is efficient as in the previous case. Now, however, the boat rental firm compensates the chemical company rather than the other way around.

To summarize the results from the Coase Theorem:

- If there are no impediments to bargaining, *assigning property rights results in the efficient outcome* at which joint profits are maximized.
- *Efficiency is achieved regardless of who receives the property rights.*
- Who gets the property rights affects the income distribution. *The property rights are valuable.* The party with the property rights may be compensated by the other party.

Problems with the Coase Approach. To achieve the efficient outcome, the two sides must bargain successfully with each other. However, the parties may not be able to bargain successfully for at least three important reasons (Polinsky, 1979).

First, if transaction costs are very high, it might not pay for the two sides to meet. For example, if a manufacturing plant pollutes the air, thousands or even millions of people may be affected. The cost of getting them all together to bargain is prohibitive.

Second, if firms engage in strategic bargaining behavior, an agreement may not be reached. For instance, if one party says, "Give me everything I want" and will not budge, reaching an agreement may be impossible.

Third, if either side lacks information about the costs or benefits of reducing pollution, a nonefficient outcome may occur. It is difficult to know how much to offer the other party and to reach an agreement if you do not know how the polluting activity affects the other party.

For these reasons, Coasian bargaining is likely to occur in relatively few situations. Where bargaining cannot occur, the allocation of property rights affects the amount of pollution.

Markets for Pollution

If high transaction costs preclude bargaining, we may be able to overcome this problem by using a market, which facilitates exchanges between individuals. Starting in the early 1980s, governments experimented with issuing permits to pollute that could be exchanged in a market, often by means of an auction. Today, many firms can buy the right to pollute—much as sinners bought indulgences in the Middle Ages.

Under this system, the government gives firms permits, each of which confers the right to create a certain amount of pollution. Each firm may use its permits or sell them to other firms.

Firms whose products are worth a lot relative to the harm from pollution they create buy rights from firms that have less valuable products. Suppose that the cost in terms of forgone output from eliminating each ton of pollution is $200 at one plant and $300 at another. If the government tells both plants to reduce pollution by 1 ton, the total cost is $500. With tradable permits, the first plant can reduce its pollution by 2 tons and sell its allowance to the second plant, so the total social cost is only $400. The trading maximizes the value of the output for a given amount of pollution damage, thus increasing efficiency.

If the government knew enough, it could assign the optimal amount of pollution to each firm, and no trading would be necessary. By using a market, the government does not have to collect this type of detailed information to achieve efficiency. Its only decision concerns what total amount of pollution to allow.

Application   SULFUR DIOXIDE MARKET

When the U.S. Clean Air Act of 1990 created a market for sulfur dioxide (SO_2) pollution generated by power plants, many environmentalists protested that the legislation was a "license to pollute." However, the reality was otherwise. SO_2 emissions were 10 million tons in 1990. The law set an emissions cap of 8.7 million tons for 1995, when it would take effect. Actual production in 1995 fell nearly 50% to just 5.3 million tons, and at a cost between one-half and one-third that of the traditional standards approach, as firms used smokestack scrubbers (which remove sulfur from exhaust gases) and low-sulfur coal to cut pollution.

Under the law, the EPA issues permits, each of which allows a firm to produce 1 ton of emissions of sulfur dioxide annually, equal to the aggregate emissions cap. Electric utilities that operate the 445 largest and dirtiest coal-fired power plants in the United States received permits in proportion to the amount of fuel they used in a historical period.

A firm producing more pollution than is permitted is fined $2,000 per ton of emissions above its allowance. But at the end of a year, if a company's emissions are less than its allowance, it may sell the remaining allowance to another firm, thus providing the firm with an incentive to reduce emissions. Permits are traded through the Chicago Board of Trade. The EPA holds an annual spot auction for permits that may be used in the current year and an advance auction for permits effective in seven years.

Northeast Utilities and Niagara Mohawk Power donated some of their extra permits to the American Lung Association and an environmental group—thus preventing any other polluter from using them—so as to get a tax deduction equal to the permits' market value.

Permits sell for about $100 to $200 per ton. Environmental groups are encouraging citizens to buy up and retire pollution permits. Want to do so? Go to **cleanairconservancy.org/Markets/le.sulfur.html**. For $10, you can buy the rights to about 200 pounds of SO_2.

The EPA estimated that trading saved utility rate payers $400 million to $600 million a year as of 1994. The U.S. Government Accounting Office projected that the cost of reducing sulfur dioxide emissions by 2001 with this method will be only $2.5 billion annually, compared to $7 billion if every utility had been required to install scrubbers or $4.3 billion if uniform emission rates had been applied to individual power plants.

Canada, Mexico, and several European countries either have or are planning pollution markets. During international negotiations in 1997, the United States pushed hard (but unsuccessfully) for the international trading of pollution rights.

18.5 | COMMON PROPERTY

So far we've examined externalities that arise as an undesired by-product of a production or consumption activity. Another important externality arises with **common property**: resources to which everyone has free access. Unlike private property, for which the owner can *exclude* others from using the property, common property is not subject to such exclusion. For example, anyone can freely enter and enjoy urban parks such as Central Park in New York, Hyde Park in London, and the Boston Common.

Overuse of Common Property

Because people do not have to pay to use common property resources, they are overused. Parks with free entry often become crowded, an outcome that reduces everyone's enjoyment. Similarly, in less-developed economies, the sharing of public lands for hunting, grazing, or growing crops results in the overuse of common property. Other examples of common property problems are common pools, the Internet, roads, and fisheries.

Common Pools. Petroleum, water, and other fluids and gases are often extracted from a common pool. Owners of wells drawing from a common pool compete to remove the substance most rapidly, thereby gaining ownership of the good. This competition creates an externality by lowering fluid pressure, which makes further pumping more difficult. Iraq justified its invasion of Kuwait, which led to the Persian Gulf War in 1991, on the grounds that Kuwait was overexploiting common pools of oil underlying both countries.

The Internet. An important problem—one that may be inconveniencing you—is overcrowding on the Internet. Most users connect to the Internet for a flat fee that does not vary with the number of hours of use. Thus the marginal cost for an extra minute of use (users' time aside) is zero. As a result, serious congestion occurs due to excessive use (see the "Web Fee" application in Chapter 3). Gridlock may prevent people from accessing Web pages or slow traffic to a crawl. Building greater capacity is not an efficient solution because Internet use is likely to continue to grow as long as marginal access is free. Until fees for marginal use are imposed, congestion is likely to persist.

Roads. If you own a car, you have a property right to drive that car. But because you lack a property right to the highway on which you drive, you cannot exclude others from driving on the highway and must share it with them. Each driver, however, claims a temporary property right in a portion of the highway by occupying it (thereby preventing others from occupying the same space). Competition for space on the highway leads to congestion (a negative externality), which slows up every driver.

Fisheries. Many fisheries have common access such that anyone can fish and no one has a property right to a fish until it is caught. Each fisher wants to land a fish before others do to gain the property right to that fish. The lack of clearly defined property rights leads to overfishing. Fishers have an incentive to catch more fish than they would if the fishery were private property.

Suppose that each fisher owns a private lake. Because the property rights are clearly defined, there is no externality. Each owner is careful not to overfish in any one year so as to maintain the stock (or number) of fish in future years.[8]

In contrast, most ocean fisheries are common property. Like polluting manufacturers, ocean fishers look only at their private costs. In calculating these costs, fishers include the cost of boats, other equipment, a crew, and supplies. They do not include the cost that they impose on future generations by decreasing the stock of fish today, which reduces the number of fish in the sea next year. The fewer fish there are, the harder it is to catch any, so reducing the population today raises the cost of catching fish in the future. As a result, fishers do not forgo fishing now to leave fish for the future. The social cost is the private cost plus the externality cost from reduced future populations of fish.

| Application | **EXTENSIVE OVERFISHING** |

The tendency to overfish has diminished many fish populations dramatically because the rate at which fish are being born is lower than the rate at which they are being caught. According to the U.S. National Marine Fisheries Service, at least one-third of the 279 species in federal waters are so extensively overfished that their survival is threatened. Endangered species include the Pacific salmon, bluefin tuna, and the American lobster. One scientific report concluded that New England's second-largest cod-fishing ground was near collapse, endangering the species, because the annual catch was more than double the replenishment level.

To combat overfishing, Congress passed the Sustainable Fisheries Act of 1996, which put fishers and regional regulators under pressure to deal with overfishing. Since then, in an effort to protect cod stocks and allow them to rebuild, many offshore and inshore fishing areas of New England have been closed entirely or restricted to trawling. At the same time, the U.S. Secretary of Commerce slashed allowable catches of major Pacific Coast ocean fish (including black cod, ocean perch, lingcod, dover sole, and various rockfish) by as much as 65% to save these species. The National Marine Fisheries Service estimates that overfishing of cod, haddock, and flounder there had already cost the economy $350 million a year in reduced catch because of the drop in the stock of fish.

Unfortunately, many governments are exacerbating the problem rather than acting to solve it. The UN Food and Agriculture Organization estimates that the global fishing fleet cost $92 billion to operate in 1989 yet brought in only $70 billion in revenues. The difference was made up by government subsidies to fishers and boat builders. The European Union, for instance, has annual subsidies of about $580 million. The Japanese government has extended $19 billion in credit to its fishing industry, much of which won't be paid back.

---

[8]No: A stock of fish is not the same as a fish stock.

Solving the Commons Problem

There are two approaches to ameliorating the commons problem. The first is direct government regulation through either taxation or restriction of access. The second is by clearly defining property rights.

Government Regulation of Commons. Overuse of a common resource occurs because individuals do not bear the full social cost. However, by applying a tax or fee equal to the externality harm that each individual imposes on others, a government forces each person to internalize the externality. For example, governments often charge an entrance fee to a park or a museum. However, if a government sets a tax or fee that is less than the marginal externality harm, it reduces but does not eliminate the externality problem.

Alternatively, the government can restrict access to the commons. One typical approach is to grant access on a first-come, first-served basis. With quotas, people who arrive early gain access. In contrast, with taxes or fees, people who most heavily value the resource or who are wealthier gain access.

Application   **FOR WHOM THE BRIDGE TOLLS**

If anyone can drive across it, a bridge is a common property. Excessive use of a bridge leads to congestion.

The most congested bridge in the United States is the 8.5-mile-long San Francisco–Oakland Bay Bridge in California. Of the 275,000 vehicles that drive across the bridge in a day, 100,000 cross it westbound during the morning peak commuting hours, 6 to 10 A.M. The bridge can handle only about 10,000 commuters per hour in one direction without congestion.

The Bay Bridge morning traffic jam is costly in terms of time, money, and pollution. Drivers frequently wait 20 minutes or more just to get on the bridge. More time is lost crawling across the bridge at low speed. Gasoline is wasted, and tailpipe pollution is 250% greater under these congested conditions than when cars drive at the speed limit. According to some estimates, traffic congestion costs San Francisco Bay Area commuters more than $3 billion annually, or $1,000 per driver in lost productivity and wasted fuel in 1999. In addition, congestion raises vehicle emissions and increases smog.

Starting in 1980, a $1 toll was collected at all hours in only the westbound direction. Imposing a higher toll to cross the bridge during rush hour would reduce congestion by discouraging some current drivers. Rather than drive across the bridge, these people would switch to car pools (three or more people in a car may cross toll free) or to public transit or would not cross at all.

What toll would maximize efficiency by optimally trading off the harm to some travelers versus the gain to other commuters and the reduced pollution? Economists used models employing survey and engineering data to calculate that the optimal peak-hour toll is $3.60. Compared to no toll, the optimal toll would save commuters 20.6 minutes per day by decreasing trips by vehicles with one or two occupants by 9.5%. The benefit from time savings to people who continue to drive minus the loss to people who take other modes of travel is estimated at $55,000 per day. There are additional savings from reduced pollution.

Why have authorities been reluctant to charge a higher toll during peak commuting hours? One explanation is that the travel-time gains from a steeper toll go to those who place a high value on their time and continue to drive across the bridge. But higher tolls harm poorer people, some of whom are discouraged from driving and others of whom continue to drive but value the time savings less than the toll increase. Although the gain to the wealthy is substantially larger than the loss to the poor, no transfer payments from one group to the other are likely. Politicians have hesitated to help wealthier commuters at the expense of harming poorer ones.

This situation has changed, however, as congestion has worsened. Traffic across the bridge rose 23% from 1980 through 1995, so the potential gains from a higher toll have increased over time. Recently, politicians have debated a $3 toll. Estimates of the additional toll revenues from raising the toll from $1 to $3 are $22 million per year above the $40 million that is now collected. Despite these extra revenues, the politicians haven't had the nerve to raise the toll to $3, though they did push it up to $2 in 1998.

Assigning Property Rights. An alternative approach to resolving the commons problem is to assign private property rights. Converting common-access property to private property removes the incentive to overuse it. (See **www.awlonline.com/perloff**, "Claiming Lobster Fisheries," for an example.)

In developing countries over the past century, common agricultural land has been broken up into smaller private farms. Similarly, fish farming on private land is increasingly used as common-access fisheries are depleted.

18.6 | PUBLIC GOODS

We have seen that a competitive market produces too much output when a by-product creates a negative externality or when anyone can use a common property. That same competitive market may produce too little of a good in the presence of a positive externality. Positive externalities and too little production may occur when producers cannot restrict access to a **public good**: a commodity or service whose consumption by one person does not preclude others from also consuming it.

Types of Goods

Previous chapters discussed only *private goods*. *Private goods have the properties of rivalry and exclusion. Rivalry* means that only one person can consume the good: The good is used up in consumption—it is *depletable*. If a second person is to consume a candy bar, the production of a second candy bar is required. *Exclusion* means that others can be prevented from consuming the good. Only the person who owns the candy bar may eat it.

Other types of goods lack rivalry or exclusion or both, as Table 18.2 shows. *Public goods lack rivalry.* Your consumption of a public good does not preclude others from also consuming it. There is no need to ration a public good—everyone can consume it. Indeed, excluding someone from consuming it harms that person without helping other consumers.

All public goods lack rivalry, but only some lack exclusion. Major problems occur when no one can be prevented from consuming a public good. National defense is an important example of a nonexclusive public good. The cost of protecting an extra person is literally zero when all people are protected (no rivalry), and no one in the country can be left unprotected (no exclusion). Clean air is also a public good without exclusion (and air pollution is a *public bad*). If the air is clean, we all benefit. If we clean up the air, we cannot prevent others who live nearby from benefiting from it. A *public good produces a positive externality*, and *excluding anyone from consuming a public good is inefficient.*

Other public goods are exclusive but lack rivalry in consumption. Security guards prevent people who don't have a ticket from entering a concert hall. Until the concert hall is filled, the cost of providing the concert to one extra person is zero. Thus a concert in a hall that is not filled has elements of both a private good (exclusion) and a public good (no rivalry).

Such a concert is a special type of public good, called a *club good*. Although the marginal cost of providing the concert to one more person is zero as long as attendance is less than the seating capacity of the hall, adding another person creates congestion or other externalities that harm concertgoers once the concert hall is filled. Similarly, allowing more people to join a swim club doesn't inflict extra costs until members start getting in each other's way.

In addition to private goods, nonexclusive public goods, and club goods, there are resources with rivalry but without exclusion, such as a common. In an open-access fishery, anyone can fish (no exclusion), but once a fish is caught, no one else can catch it (rivalry).

Many goods differ in the degree to which they have rivalry and exclusion. Many goods are hybrids, with properties of both private and public goods. Telling your friend about something that you learned in a textbook provides a positive externality.

Table 18.2 Rivalry and Exclusion

	Exclusion	*No Exclusion*
Rivalry	*Private good*: candy bar, pencil, aluminum foil	*Common-access resource*: fishery, hunting, highway
No Rivalry	*Public good with exclusion*: cable television, *club good* (concert, tennis club)	*Public good without exclusion*: national defense, aerial spraying of pesticide, clean air

A textbook is often viewed as a private good; however, the information in it is a public good. Because the cost of excluding people from a toll road is less than that of excluding people from an ocean fishery, a toll road may more closely resemble a private good than a fishery does.

Markets for Public Goods

Markets for public goods exist only if nonpurchasers can be excluded from consuming them. Thus markets do not exist for nonexclusive public goods. Usually, if the government does not provide a nonexclusive public good, no one provides it.

Because computer software use is nonrivalrous, computer software is virtually a public good. At almost no extra cost, a copy of the software program that you use can be supplied to another consumer. In countries where exclusion is impossible, computer software is pirated and widely shared, so it is not profitable to produce and sell software. In countries where intellectual property rights to software are protected by preventing piracy, a company such as Microsoft can sell software (very) profitably.

Microsoft makes a fortune by selling its software at a price that is well above its marginal cost, so too few units are sold. Markets tend to produce too little of an exclusive public good because of the lack of rivalry. In the absence of rivalry, the marginal cost of providing a public good to one extra person is (essentially) zero. Firms have no incentive to produce at a zero price. If firms set a price above zero, consumers buy too little of this public good.

Demand for Public Goods. The demand for a private good is different from that for a public good. The social marginal benefit of a private good is the same as the marginal benefit to the individual who consumes that good. The market demand, which is the social marginal benefit curve, for private goods is the *horizontal* sum of the demand curves of each individual (Chapter 2).

In contrast, the social marginal benefit of a public good is the sum of the marginal benefit to each person who consumes the good. Because a public good lacks rivalry, many people can get pleasure from the same unit of output. As a consequence, the *social demand curve* or *willingness-to-pay curve* for a public good is the *vertical* sum of the demand curves of each individual.

We illustrate this vertical summing by deriving the demand for guard services by stores in a mall that want to discourage theft. Guards patrolling the mall provide a service without rivalry: All the stores in the mall are simultaneously protected. Each store's demand for guards reflects its marginal benefit from a reduction in thefts due to the guards. The demand curve for the television store, which stands to lose a lot if thieves strike, is D^1 in Figure 18.5. The ice-cream parlor, which loses less from a theft, demands fewer guards at any given price, D^2.

Because a guard patrolling the mall protects both stores at once, the marginal benefit to society of an additional guard is the sum of the benefit to each store. The social marginal benefit of a fifth guard, $10, is the sum of the marginal benefit to the television store, $8 (the height of D^1 at five guards per hour), and the marginal benefit to the ice-cream store, $2 (the height of D^2 at five guards per hour). Thus the social demand is the vertical sum of the individual demand curves.

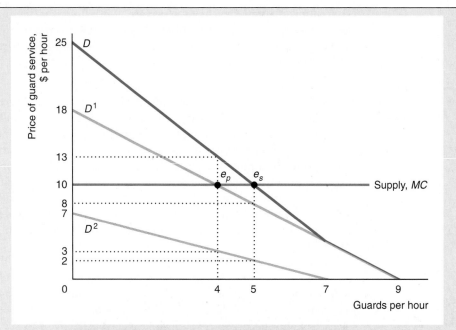

Figure 18.5 Inadequate Provision of a Public Good. Security guards protect both tenants of the mall. If each guard costs $10 per hour, the television store, with demand D^1, is willing to hire four guards per hour. The ice-cream parlor, with demand D^2, is not willing to hire any guards. Thus if everyone acts independently, the equilibrium is e_p. The social demand for this public good is the vertical sum of the individual demand curves, D. Thus the social optimum is e_s, at which five guards are hired.

A competitive market supplies as many guards as the stores want at $10 per hour per guard. At that price, the ice-cream store would not hire any guards on its own. The television store would hire four. If the stores act independently, four guards are hired at the private equilibrium, e_p. The sum of the marginal benefit to the two stores from four guards is $13, which is greater than the $10 marginal cost of an additional guard. If a fifth guard is hired, the social marginal benefit, $10, equals the marginal cost of the last guard. Thus the social equilibrium, e_2, has five guards.

The ice-cream store can get guard services without paying because the guard service is a public good. Acting alone, the television store hires fewer guards than are socially optimal because it ignores the positive externality provided to the ice-cream store, which the television store does not capture. Thus the competitive market for guard services provides too little of this public good.

Free Riding. Many people are unwilling to pay for their share of a public good. They try to get others to pay for it, so they can **free ride**: benefit from the actions of others without paying. That is, they want to benefit from a positive externality.

To illustrate the problem of free riding, we examine a game between two stores in a mall that are deciding whether to hire one guard or none. (For now, we assume that hiring two guards does no more good than hiring one.) The cost of hiring a guard is $10 per hour. The benefit to each store is $8. Because the collective benefit, $16, is greater than the cost of hiring a guard, the optimal solution is to hire the guard.

If the stores act independently, however, they do not achieve this optimal solution. Table 18.3 shows two games. In panel a, each store acts independently and pays $10 to hire a guard on its own or does not hire a guard. If both decide to hire a guard, two guards are hired, but the benefit is still only $8 per store.

In panel b, the stores split the cost of a guard if both firms agree to hire one. If only one firm wants to hire the guard, it must bear the full cost.

In each of these games, the Nash equilibrium is for neither store to hire a guard because of free riding. Each store has a dominant strategy. Regardless of what the other store does, each store is always as well off or better off not to hire a guard. The nonoptimal outcome occurs for the same reason as in other prisoners' dilemma games (Chapter 13): The stores don't do what is best for them collectively when they act independently.

Reducing Free Riding

Governmental or other collective actions can reduce free riding. Methods that may be used include social pressure, mergers, compulsion, and privatization.

Table 18.3 Private Payments for a Public Good

(a) Stores Decide Independently Whether to Hire a Guard

		Television Store	
		Hire	*Do Hot Hire*
Stereo Store	*Hire*	−$2 / −$2	−$2 / $8
	Do Not Hire	$8 / −$2	$0 / $0

(b) Stores Voting to Hire a Guard Split the Cost

		Television Store	
		Hire	*Do Hot Hire*
Stereo Store	*Hire*	$3 / $3	−$2 / $8
	Do Not Hire	$8 / −$2	$0 / $0

Sometimes, especially when the group is small, *social pressure* eliminates free riding. Social pressure results in at least minimal provision of some public goods. Such pressure may cause most firms at a mall to contribute "voluntarily" to a fund to hire security guards.

A direct way to eliminate free riding by firms is for them to *merge* into a single firm and thereby internalize the positive externality. The sum of the benefit to the individual stores equals the benefit to the single firm, so an optimal decision is made to hire guards.

If the independent stores sign a contract that commits them to share the cost of the guards, they achieve the practical advantage from a merger. The question remains, however, as to why they would agree to sign the contract, given the prisoners' dilemma problem. One explanation is that firms are more likely to cooperate in a repeated prisoners' dilemma game (Chapter 13).

Another way to overcome free riding is through *compulsion*. Some outside entity such as the government may dictate a solution to a free-riding problem. For example, the management of a mall with many firms may require tenants to sign a rental contract committing them to pay "taxes" that are assessed through tenants' votes. If the majority votes to hire guards, all must share the cost. Although a firm might be unwilling to pay for the guard service if it has no guarantee that others will also pay, it may vote to assess everyone—including itself—to pay for the service.

With government enforcement—a form of compulsion—milk producers avoided free-rider problems by taxing themselves to produce the "Got Milk?" advertisements. In many cities, the restaurants and hotels tax themselves (or are taxed by the government) to advertise that their city is a place tourists should visit. Thus actions by a group or government may overcome the free-rider problem so that a public service is provided.

Finally, privatization—exclusion—eliminates free riding. A good that would be a public good if anyone could use it becomes a private good if access to it is restricted. An example is water, the use of which is limited by individual meters.

Application   **FREE RIDING ON WATER**

Water is a private good for most households in Perth, Australia: They can consume it only if they pay the price for each unit. Others can be excluded from consuming the water because each household's consumption is individually metered. However, about 10% of the households share meters with one or more other households. Households in duplexes or apartments are likely to share meters. Perth's 20,545 flats have 1,800 meters between them, so on average, 11 households share each meter. Most group-metered households apportion the total bill equally among households.

How would you expect water consumption to vary between individually and collectively metered households? Because of free riding, you might expect households with individual meters to consume less water than households that draw from a common pool. Each member of the common pool has an incentive to free ride on the remaining members. As the household consumes a little more water, it receives all of the marginal benefits but only has to pay $1/n$ fraction of the marginal cost, where there are n households on a meter.

Moreover, you might expect that the incentive to free ride increases with the number of households sharing a meter. Not only is each household's share of the marginal cost smaller, but each household faces less effective social pressure to keep its free riding under control.

Grossman, Pirozzi, and Pope (1993) confirm these predictions. They find that collectively metered households consume 17% more water on average than households with private meters do.

The extra water consumption rises with the number of households sharing a meter. A household in a two-family duplex consumes only 0.05 kiloliter more per year than an individually metered household. Even a household in a block of 10 housing units consumes only 1.3 kiloliters more. However, by the time the number in a housing block reaches 222 members (the largest in the sample), an extra household averages 640 extra kiloliters of water consumption.

Valuing Public Goods

To ensure that a nonexclusive public good is provided, a government usually produces it or compels others to do so. Issues that a government faces in providing such a public good include whether to provide it at all and, if so, how much to provide. To grapple with these questions, the government needs to know the cost—usually the easy part—and the value of the public good to many individuals—the hard part.

The government may try to determine the value that consumers place on the public good through surveys or voting results. One major problem with these methods is that most people do not know how much a public good is worth to them. How much would you pay to maintain the National Archives? How much does reducing air pollution improve your health? How much better do you sleep at night knowing that the army stands ready to protect you?

Even if people know how much they value a public good, they have an incentive to lie on a survey. Those who value the good greatly and want the government to provide it may exaggerate the value of the benefit. Similarly, people who place a low value on it may report too low a value—possibly even a negative one—to discourage government action.

Rather than rely on surveys, a government may have citizens vote directly on public goods. Suppose that a separate, majority-rule vote is held on whether to install a traffic signal—a public good—at each of several street corners. If a signal is installed, all voters are taxed equally to pay for it. An individual will vote to install a signal if the value of the signal to that voter is at least as much as the tax each must pay for the signal.

Whether the majority votes for the signal depends on the preferences of the *median voter*: the person with respect to whom half the populace values the project less and half values the project more. If the median voter wants to install a signal, then at least half the voters agree, so the vote carries. Similarly, if the median voter is against the project, at least half the voters are against it, so the vote fails.

It is *efficient* to install the signal if the value of the signal to society is at least as great as its cost. Does majority voting result in efficiency? The following examples illustrate that efficiency is not ensured.

Each signal costs $300 to install. There are three voters, so each individual votes for the signal only if that person thinks that the signal is worth at least $100, which is the tax each person pays if the signal is installed. Table 18.4 shows the value that each voter places on installing a signal at each of three intersections.

For each of the proposed signals, Hayley is the median voter, so her views signal the outcome. If Hayley, the median voter, likes the signal, then she and Asa, a majority, vote for it. Otherwise, Nancy and Hayley vote against it. The majority favors installing a signal at corners *A* and *C* and are against doing so at corner *B*. It would be efficient to install the signal at corner *A*, where the social value is $300, and at corner *B*, where the social value is $375, because each value exceeds the cost of $300.

At corner *A*, the citizens vote for the signal, and that outcome is efficient. The other two votes lead to inefficient outcomes. No signal is installed at corner *B*, where society values the signal at more than $300, but a signal is installed at corner *C*, where voters value the signal at less than $300.

The problem with yes-no votes is that they ignore the intensity of preferences. A voter indicates only whether or not the project is worth more or less than a certain amount. Thus such *majority voting fails to value the public good fully and hence does not guarantee that it is efficiently provided.*[9]

Table 18.4 Voting on $300 Traffic Signals

	Value to Each Voter, $			Value to	Outcome
Signal Location	Nancy	Hayley	Asa	Society, $	of Vote*
Corner *A*	50	100	150	300	Yes
Corner *B*	50	75	250	375	No
Corner *C*	50	100	110	260	Yes

*An individual votes to install a signal at a particular corner if and only if that person thinks that the signal is worth at least $100, the tax that individual must pay if the signal is installed.

---

[9]Although voting does not reveal how much a public good is worth, Tideman and Tullock (1976) and other economists have devised taxing methods that can sometimes induce people to reveal their true valuations. However, these methods are rarely used.

Summary

1. **Externalities:** An externality occurs when a consumer's well-being or a firm's production capabilities are directly affected by the actions of other consumers or firms rather than indirectly affected through changes in prices. An externality that harms others is a negative externality, and one that helps others is a positive externality. Some externalities benefit one group while harming another.

2. **The inefficiency of competition with externalities:** Because producers do not pay for a negative externality such as pollution, the private costs are less than the social costs. As a consequence, competitive markets produce more negative externalities than are optimal. If the only way to cut externalities is to decrease output, the optimal solution is to set output where the marginal benefit from reducing the externality equals the marginal cost to consumers and producers from less output. It is usually optimal to have some negative externalities, because eliminating all of them requires eliminating desirable outputs and consumption activities as well. If the government has sufficient information about demand, production cost, and the harm from the externality, it can use taxes or quotas to force the competitive market to produce the social optimum. It may tax or limit the negative externality, or it may tax or limit output.

3. **Market structure and externalities:** Although a competitive market produces excessive output and negative externalities, a noncompetitive market may produce more or less than the optimal level. With a negative externality, a noncompetitive equilibrium may be closer than a competitive equilibrium to the social optimum. A tax equal to the marginal social harm of a negative externality—which results in the social optimum when applied to a competitive market—may lower welfare when applied to a noncompetitive market.

4. **Allocating property rights to reduce externalities:** Externalities arise because property rights are not clearly defined. According to the Coase Theorem, allocating property rights to *either* of two parties results in an efficient outcome if the parties can bargain. The assignment of the property rights, however, affects income distribution, as the rights are valuable. Unfortunately, bargaining is usually not practical, especially when many people are involved. In such cases, markets for permits to produce externalities may overcome the externality problem.

5. **Common property:** Externalities are a problem with common property, which is a resource to which everyone has free access. Common property resources are overexploited. For example, if anyone can drive on a highway, too many people are likely to do so because they ignore the externality—delays due to congestion—that they impose on others. Taxes and quotas may reduce or eliminate overuse.

6. **Public goods:** Public goods lack rivalry. Once a public good is provided to anyone, it can be provided to others at no additional cost. Excluding anyone from consuming a public good is inefficient. Markets provide too little of a nonexclusive public good. A government faces challenges in providing the optimal amount because it is difficult to determine how much people value the public good.

Problems

1. Why is zero pollution not the best solution for society? Can there be too little pollution? Why or why not?

2. In the paper market example in the text, what are the optimal emissions fee and the optimal tax on output (assuming that only one fee or tax is applied)?

3. In Figure 18.2, the government may optimally regulate the paper market using a tax on output. A technological change drives down the private marginal cost of production. Discuss the welfare implications if the output tax is unchanged.

4. Suppose that the only way to reduce pollution from paper production is to reduce output. The

government imposes a tax equal to the marginal harm from the pollution on the monopoly producer. Show that the tax may raise welfare.

5. Which allocation of property rights leads to the highest possible welfare level if firms cannot bargain with each other in Table 18.1?

6. Are broadcast television and cable television public goods? Is exclusion possible? If either is a public good, why is it privately provided?

7. Do publishers sell the optimal number of intermediate microeconomics textbooks? Discuss in terms of public goods, rivalry, and exclusion.

8. Analyze the following extract. Is garbage a positive or negative externality? Why is a market solution practical here?

Garbage in Philadelphia is undesirable of course. Since the turn of the century, however, hog farmers in New Jersey have been feeding Philadelphia garbage to their pigs. Philadelphia saves $3 million a year and reduces its garbage mound by allowing New Jersey farmers to pick up leftover food scraps for their porcine recyclers. The city pays $1.9 million to the New Jersey pig farmers for picking up the waste each year, which is about $79 a ton. Otherwise, the city would have to pay $125 a ton for curbside recycling of the same food waste.[10]

9. In granting patents, governments give inventors monopoly rights to sell their invention for a fixed period of time. We know that monopolies set too high a price. Why, then, might a government reasonably grant patents? (*Hint*: Discuss in terms of the public good nature of information.)

10. In 1994, the state of Connecticut announced that commercial fleet operators would get a tax break if they converted vehicles from ozone-producing gasoline to what the state said were cleaner fuels such as natural gas and electricity. For every dollar spent on the conversion of their fleets or building alternative fueling stations, operators could deduct 50¢ from their corporate tax. Is this approach likely to be a cost-effective way to control pollution?

Math Problems

11. Using the numerical example in Appendix 18A, determine the social optimum if the marginal harm of gunk is $MC^g = \$84$ (instead of Equation 18A.3). Is there a shortcut that would allow you to solve this problem without algebra?

★12. Using the numerical example of the model of the paper market in Appendix 18A, derive the equations for the benefit, cost, marginal benefit, and marginal cost curves in Figure 18.3.

13. Suppose that the inverse demand curve for paper is $p = 200 - Q$, the private marginal cost (unregulated competitive market supply) is $MC^p = 80 + Q$, and the marginal harm from gunk is $MC^g = Q$.
    a. What is the unregulated competitive equilibrium?
    b. What is the social optimum? What specific tax (per unit of output or gunk) results in the social optimum?
    c. What is the unregulated monopoly equilibrium?

d. How would you optimally regulate the monopoly? What is the resulting equilibrium?

14. Let $H = \bar{G} - G$ be the amount that gunk, G, is reduced from the competitive level, $\bar{G}$. The benefit of reducing gunk is $B(H) = AH^\alpha$. The cost is $C(H) = H^\beta$. If the benefit is increasing but at a diminishing rate in H, and the cost is rising at an increasing rate in H, what are the possible ranges of values for A, α, and B?

15. Applying the model in math Problem 14, use calculus to determine the optimal level of H.

16. Two tenants of a mall are protected by the guard service, q. The number of guards per hour demanded by the television store is $q_1 = a_1 + b_1 p$, where p is the price of one hour of guard services. The ice-cream store's demand is $q_2 = a_2 + b_2 p$. What is the social demand for this service?

---

[10]"What's for Dinner?" *San Francisco Chronicle*, May 1, 1994:A15.

Asymmetric Information

> *The buyer needs a hundred eyes, the seller not one.*
>
> —George Herbert (1651)

So far we've examined models in which everyone is equally knowledgeable or equally ignorant. In the competitive model, everyone knows all relevant facts. In the uncertainty models in Chapter 17, the companies that sell insurance and the people who buy it are equally uncertain about future events. In contrast, in this chapter's models, people have **asymmetric information**: One party to a transaction knows a material fact that the other party does not. For example, the seller knows the quality of a product and the buyer does not.

The more informed party may exploit the less informed party. Such *opportunistic behavior* due to asymmetric information leads to market failures, destroying many desirable properties of competitive markets. In a competitive market in which everyone has full information, consumers can buy whatever quality good they want at its marginal cost. In contrast, when firms have information that consumers lack—when information is asymmetric—firms may sell only the lowest-quality good, the price may be above marginal cost, or other problems may occur.

If consumers do not know the quality of a good they are considering buying, some firms may try to sell them a dud at the price of a superior good. However, knowing that the chance of buying schlock is high, consumers may be unwilling to pay much for goods of unknown quality. As a result, firms that make high-quality products may not be able to sell them at prices anywhere near their cost of production. In other words, *bad products drive good ones out of the market.* The market failure is that the market for a good-quality product is reduced or eliminated, even though (knowledgeable) consumers value the high-quality product at more than the cost of producing it.

If consumers (unlike sellers) do not know how prices vary across firms, *firms may gain market power and set prices above marginal cost.* Suppose that you go to Store A to buy a television set. If you know that Store B is charging $299 for that set, you are willing to pay Store A at most $299 (or perhaps a little more to avoid having to go to Store B). *Knowledge is power.* However, if you don't know Store B's price for that set, Store A might sell you a television for much more than $299. *Ignorance costs.* This market failure results in a deadweight loss because price is set above marginal cost.

Market failures due to asymmetric information can be eliminated if consumers can inexpensively determine the quality of a product or learn the prices that various stores charge. In many markets, however, obtaining this information is prohibitively expensive.

IN THIS CHAPTER,

WE EXAMINE

SIX MAIN

TOPICS

1. **Problems due to asymmetric information:** Informed people take advantage of uninformed people.
2. **Responses to adverse selection:** To reduce the harms from adverse selection—an informed person's benefiting from trading with an uninformed person who does not know about a characteristic of the informed person—government actions or contracts between involved parties may be used to prevent opportunistic behavior, or the information asymmetry may be reduced or eliminated.
3. **How ignorance about quality drives out high-quality goods:** If consumers cannot distinguish between good and bad products before purchase, it is possible that only bad products will be sold.
4. **Price discrimination due to false beliefs about quality:** If some consumers incorrectly think that quality varies across identical products, a firm may price discriminate.
5. **Market power from price ignorance:** Consumers' ignorance about the price that each firm charges gives firms market power.
6. **Problems arising from ignorance when hiring:** Attempts to eliminate information asymmetries in hiring may raise or lower social welfare.

19.1 PROBLEMS DUE TO ASYMMETRIC INFORMATION

When both parties to a transaction have equally limited information, neither has an advantage over the other. If a roadside vendor sells a box of oranges to a passing motorist and neither person knows the quality of the oranges, neither has an advantage because both are operating with equal uncertainty.

In contrast, asymmetric information leads to problems of *opportunism*, whereby the informed person benefits at the expense of the person with less information. If only the vendor knows that the oranges are of low quality, the vendor may allege that the oranges are of high quality and charge a premium price for them.

The two major types of opportunistic behavior are *adverse selection* and *moral hazard*. **Adverse selection** is opportunism characterized by an informed person's benefiting from trading or otherwise contracting with a less informed person who does not know about an *unobserved characteristic* of the informed person. For example, people who buy life insurance policies are better informed about their own health than insurance companies are. If an insurance company offers to insure people against death for 10 years at a fixed rate, a disproportionately large share of unhealthy people will buy this policy. Because of this adverse selection, the insurance company will pay off on more policies than it would pay if healthy and unhealthy people bought the policy in proportion to their share in the population.

Similarly, if one firm starts offering an unusually generous maternity leave to mothers of newborn children, a disproportionate number of women planning to become mothers in the near future will apply for employment with that firm. The intention to have children is known to potential employees but not to the firm. As a result, the cost of this benefit is greater to the firm than its cost would be if the employees were a random sample of the entire population.

Adverse selection creates a market failure by reducing the size of a market or eliminating it, thereby preventing desirable transactions. Insurance companies have to charge higher rates for insurance due to adverse selection or choose not to offer insurance at all. Very few older people, regardless of their health, buy term life insurance because the rates are extremely high because of adverse selection. A parental leave benefit's higher cost due to adverse selection may discourage firms from offering the benefit, a decision that hurts both employees who are new parents (because they lose the benefit) and the firm (because it cannot use a benefit that would otherwise allow it to pay a lower wage).

Moral hazard is opportunism characterized by an informed person's taking advantage of a less-informed person through an *unobserved action*. An employee may *shirk*—fail to fulfill job responsibilities—if not monitored by the employer. An employer who observes shirking can prevent it. Similarly, insured people tend to take unobserved actions—engage in risky behaviors—that increase the probability of large claims against insurance companies, or they fail to take reasonable precautions that would reduce the likelihood of such claims. An insured homeowner may fail to remove fire hazards such as piles of old newspapers. Some insured motorists drive more recklessly than they would without insurance. Moral hazards such as shirking, failure to take care, and reckless behavior reduce output or increase accidents, which are market failures that harm society.

Not all moral hazards, despite the pejorative name, are entirely harmful. Pregnant women with health insurance make more prenatal doctor visits. Although the extra cost from these visits is a moral hazard to insurance companies, society benefits from healthier mothers and babies.

The distinction between adverse selection and moral hazard—between unobserved characteristics and unobserved actions—is not always simple. A life insurance company may face unusually high risks if it insures George and Marge, who, unknown to the company, skydive. George will skydive whether or not he has life insurance. Knowing the risks of skydiving, he's more likely to buy life insurance than other, similar people are. His unobserved characteristic—his love of plunging toward the earth at high speed—leads to adverse selection. Marge will skydive only if she has life insurance. Her unobserved action is a moral hazard for the insurance company.

This chapter focuses on adverse selection and unobserved characteristics. We identify the problems that arise from adverse selection and discuss how they can sometimes be solved. Chapter 20 concentrates on moral hazard problems due to unobserved actions and on the use of contracts to deal with them.

19.2 RESPONSES TO ADVERSE SELECTION

Responses to adverse selection problems increase welfare in some markets, but they may do more harm than good in others. The two main methods for solving adverse selection problems are to *restrict opportunistic behavior* and to *equalize information*.

Controlling Opportunistic Behavior Through Universal Coverage

Adverse selection can be prevented if informed people have no choice. For example, a government can avoid adverse selection by providing insurance to everyone or by mandating that everyone buy insurance. Many states require that every driver carry auto insurance. They thereby reduce the adverse selection that would arise from having a disproportionate number of bad drivers buy insurance.

Similarly, firms often provide health insurance to all employees as a benefit, rather than paying a higher wage and letting employees decide whether to buy such insurance on their own. By doing so, firms reduce adverse selection problems for their insurance carriers: Both healthy and unhealthy people are covered. As a result, firms can buy medical insurance for their workers at a lower cost per person than workers could obtain on their own (because relatively more unhealthy individuals buy insurance).

Equalizing Information

Either informed or uninformed parties can eliminate information asymmetries. **Screening** is an action taken by an uninformed person to determine the information possessed by informed people. A buyer may test-drive (screen) several used cars to determine which one starts and handles the best. **Signaling** is an action taken by an informed person to send information to a less-informed person. A firm may send a signal—such as widely distributing a favorable report on its product by an independent testing agency—to try to convince buyers that its product is of high quality. In some markets, government agencies or nonprofit organizations such as Consumers Union also provide consumers with information.

Screening. Uninformed people may try to eliminate their disadvantage by screening to gather information on the hidden characteristics of informed people. If the originally uninformed people obtain better information, they may refuse to sign a contract or insist on changes in contract clauses or in the price of a good.

Insurance companies try to reduce adverse selection problems by learning the health history of their potential customers—for example, by requiring medical exams. A life insurance company uses such information to better estimate the probability that it will have to pay off on a policy. The firm can then decide not to insure high-risk individuals or can charge high-risk people a higher premium as compensation for the extra risk.

It is costly to collect information on how healthy a person is and on whether that individual has dangerous habits (such as smoking and drinking). As a result, insurance companies collect information only up to the point at which the marginal benefit from extra information equals the marginal cost of obtaining it. Over time, insurance companies have increasingly concluded that it pays to collect information about whether individuals exercise, have a family history of dying young, or engage in potentially life-threatening activities. If individuals but not insurance companies know about these

"Good—very good! You qualify for our dental plan with no deductible whatsoever!"

characteristics, individuals can better predict whether they'll die young, and adverse selection occurs.

To reduce the risk of adverse selection, life insurance companies no longer rely solely on information about age and general health in determining risk. They now also look into individuals' smoking and drinking habits and occupations and even their hobbies. Indeed, some hobbies or activities greatly affect the probability that an individual will die from an accident. Various sports add $100 to $2,500 in annual premiums for each $100,000 of life insurance.

Steve Potter, a 40-year-old managing director at an executive recruiting firm, prepared to climb Mount Everest by buying a $2 million life insurance policy. His firm took out an additional $1 million on his life. Although Prudential Insurance Company of America would offer a typical healthy 40-year-old a $1 million policy for $1,000, the company wanted $6,000 to cover the adventurous Mr. Potter.

Signaling. Signaling is used primarily by informed parties to try to eliminate adverse selection. If a buyer cannot tell a high-quality good or service from one of low quality, the buyer is unwilling to pay top dollar for the better good. Informed sellers of better goods and services may signal to potential buyers that their products are of high quality.

Likewise, potential employees use a variety of signals to convince firms of their abilities. For a job interview, serious candidates arrive on time, dress appropriately, don't chew gum, document their training and achievements, and show that they worked for long periods at other firms. Similarly, an applicant for life insurance could have a physical examination and then present an insurance company with a written statement from the doctor to signal good health.

Only people who believe that they can show that they are better than others want to send a signal. Moreover, signaling solves an information problem only if the signals are accurate. For example, if it is easy for people to find an unscrupulous doctor who will report falsely that they are in good health, insurance companies won't rely on such signals. Here screening may work better, and the insurance firms may require that potential customers go to a designated doctor for a checkup.

19.3 | HOW IGNORANCE ABOUT QUALITY DRIVES OUT HIGH-QUALITY GOODS

We now examine markets in which asymmetric information causes major problems due to adverse selection. In most of these situations, buyers know less than sellers.

Consumers often have trouble determining the quality of goods and services. Most people don't know how to judge the abilities of a professional such as a doctor, a lawyer, a plumber, an electrician, or an economist. Many of us have no reliable information about whether the processed foods we eat are safe. Is it safer to fly in a Boeing 747 than in a McDonnell Douglas DC-10?

Consumer ignorance about quality leads to a less-efficient use of resources than would occur if everyone had perfect information. Here we first show how limited consumer information leads to adverse selection. We demonstrate that adverse selection occurs whether or not a seller can alter the quality of the good. We then discuss how to ameliorate—though not necessarily eliminate—the adverse selection problem.

Lemons Market with Fixed Quality

Anagram for General Motors: or great lemons

When buyers cannot judge a product's quality before purchasing it, low-quality products—*lemons*—may drive high-quality products out of the market (Akerlof, 1970). This situation is common in used-car markets: Owners of lemons are more likely to sell their cars, leading to adverse selection.

Cars that appear to be identical on the outside often differ substantially in the number of repairs they will need. Some cars—*lemons*—are cursed. They have a variety of insidious problems that become apparent to the owner only after the car has been driven for a while. In contrast, the seller of a used car knows from experience whether the car is a lemon. We assume that the seller cannot alter the quality of the used car—at least not practically.

Suppose that there are many potential buyers for used cars. All are willing to pay $1,000 for a lemon and $2,000 for a good used car: The demand curve for lemons, D^L, is horizontal at $1,000 in panel a of Figure 19.1, and the demand curve for good cars, D^G, is horizontal at $2,000 in panel b.

Although the number of potential buyers is virtually unlimited, only 1,000 owners of lemons and 1,000 owners of good cars are willing to sell. The *reservation price* of owners of lemons—the lowest price at which they will sell their cars—is $750. Consequently, the supply curve for lemons, S^L in panel a, is horizontal at $750 up to 1,000 cars, where it becomes vertical (no more cars are for sale at any price). The reservation price of owners of high-quality used cars is v, which is less than $2,000. Panel b shows two possible values of v. If $v = $1,250, the supply curve for good cars, S^1, is horizontal at $1,250 up to 1,000 cars and then becomes vertical. If $v = $1,750, the supply curve is S^2.

Symmetric Information. If both sellers and buyers know the quality of all the used cars before any sales take place, all the cars are sold, and good cars sell for more than lemons. In panel a of Figure 19.1, the intersection of the lemons demand curve D^L and the lemons supply curve S^L determines the equilibrium at e in the lemons market, where 1,000 lemons sell for $1,000 each. Regardless of whether the supply curve for good cars is S^1 or S^2 in panel b, the equilibrium in the good-car market is E, where 1,000 good cars sell for $2,000 each.

This market is efficient because the goods go to the people who value them the most. All current owners, who value the cars less than the potential buyers, sell their cars.

More generally, all buyers and sellers may have symmetric information by being equally informed or equally uninformed. *All the cars are sold if everyone has the same information.* It does not matter whether they all have full information or all lack information—it's the equality of information that matters. However, *the amount of information they have affects the price at which the cars sell.* With full information, good

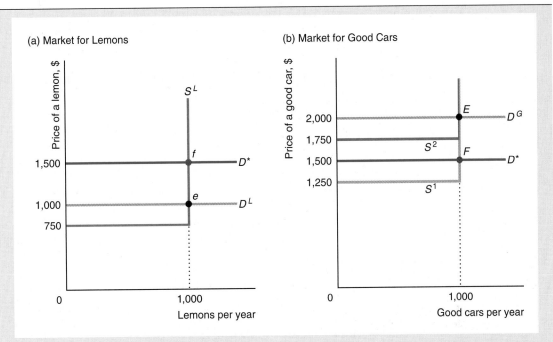

Figure 19.1 Markets for Lemons and Good Cars. If everyone has full information, the equilibrium in the lemons market is *e* (1,000 cars sold for $1,000 each), and the equilibrium in the good-car market is *E* (1,000 cars sold for $2,000 each). If buyers can't tell quality before buying but assume that equal numbers of the two types of cars are for sale, their demand in both markets is D^*, which is horizontal at $1,500. If the good car owners' reservation price is $1,250, the supply curve for good cars is S^1, and 1,000 good cars (point *F*) and 1,000 lemons (point *f*) sell for $1,500 each. If their reservation price is $1,750, the supply curve is S^2. No good cars are sold; 1,000 lemons sell for $1,000 each (point *e*).

cars sell for $2,000 and lemons for $1,000. If no one can tell a lemon from a good car at the time of purchase, both types of cars sell for the same price.

Suppose that everyone is risk neutral (Chapter 17) and no one can identify the lemons: Buyers *and* sellers are equally ignorant. A buyer has an equal chance of buying a lemon or a good car. The expected value (Chapter 17) of a used car is

$$\$1,500 = (\tfrac{1}{2} \times \$1,000) + (\tfrac{1}{2} \times \$2,000).$$

A risk-neutral buyer would pay $1,500 for a car of unknown quality. Because sellers cannot distinguish between the cars either, sellers accept this amount and sell all the cars.[1] Thus this market is efficient because the cars go to people who value them more than their original owners.

Sellers of good-quality cars are implicitly subsidizing sellers of lemons. If only lemons were sold, they would sell for $1,000. The presence of good-quality cars

[1]Risk-neutral sellers place an expected value of $(\tfrac{1}{2} \times \$750) + \tfrac{1}{2}v = \$375 + \tfrac{1}{2}v < \$1,375$ (because $v < \$2,000$) on a car of unknown quality, so they are willing to sell their cars for $1,500.

raises the price received by sellers of lemons. Similarly, if only good cars were sold, their owners would obtain $2,000. The presence of lemons lowers the price that sellers of good cars receive.

Asymmetric Information. If sellers know the quality but buyers do not, this market may be inefficient: The better-quality cars may not be sold even though buyers value good cars more than sellers do. The equilibrium in this market depends on whether the value that the owners of good cars place on their cars, v, is greater or less than the expected value of buyers, $1,500. *There are two possible equilibria: All cars sell at the average price, or only lemons sell for a price equal to the value that buyers place on lemons.*

Initially, we assume that the sellers of good cars value their cars at $v = \$1,250$, which is less than buyers' expected value, so sellers are willing to sell their cars. The equilibrium in the good-car market is determined by the intersection of S^1 and D^G at F, where 1,000 good cars sell at $1,500. Similarly, owners of lemons, who value their cars at only $750, are happy to sell them for $1,500 each. The new equilibrium in the lemons market is f.

Thus all cars sell at the same price. Consequently, *asymmetric information does not cause an efficiency problem, but it does have equity implications.* Sellers of lemons benefit and sellers of good cars suffer from consumers' inability to distinguish quality. Consumers who buy the good cars get a bargain, and buyers of lemons are left with a sour taste in their mouths.

Now suppose that the sellers of good cars place a value of $v = \$1,750$ on their cars and thus are unwilling to sell them for $1,500. As a result, the *lemons drive good cars out of the market.* Buyers realize that, at any price less than $1,750, they can buy only lemons. Consequently, in equilibrium, the 1,000 lemons sell for the expected (and actual) price of $1,000, and no good cars change hands. This equilibrium is inefficient because high-quality cars remain in the hands of people who value them less than potential buyers do.

In summary, if buyers have less information about product quality than sellers do, the result might be a lemons problem in which high-quality cars do not sell even though potential buyers value the cars more than their current owners do. If so, the asymmetric information causes a competitive market to lose its desirable efficiency and welfare properties. The lemons problem does not occur if the information is symmetric. If buyers and sellers of used cars know the quality of the cars, each car sells for its true value in a perfectly competitive market. If, as with new cars, neither buyers nor sellers can identify lemons, both good cars and lemons sell at a price equal to the expected value rather than at their (unknown) true values.

Solved Problem 19.1   Suppose that everyone in our used-car example is risk neutral, potential car buyers value lemons at $1,000 and good used cars at $2,000, the reservation price of lemon owners is $750, and the reservation price of owners of high-quality used cars is $1,750. The share of current owners who have lemons is θ [in our previous example, the share was $\theta = \frac{1}{2} = 1,000/(1,000 + 1,000)$]. For what values of θ do all the potential sellers sell their used cars? Describe the equilibrium.

Answer

1. *Determine how much buyers are willing to pay if all cars are sold*: Because buyers are risk neutral, if they believe that the probability of getting a lemon is θ, the most they are willing to pay for a car of unknown quality is

$$p = [\$2,000 \times (1 - \theta)] + (\$1,000 \times \theta) = \$2,000 - (\$1,000 \times \theta). \quad (19.1)$$

For example, $p = \$1,500$ if $\theta = \frac{1}{2}$ and $p = \$1,750$ if $\theta = \frac{1}{4}$.

2. *Solve for the values of θ such that all the cars are sold, and describe the equilibrium*: All owners will sell if the market price is \$1,750 or more. Using Equation 19.1, we know that the market (equilibrium) price is \$1,750 or more if a quarter or fewer of the used cars are lemons, $\theta \leq \frac{1}{4}$. Thus for $\theta \leq \frac{1}{4}$, all the cars are sold at the price given in Equation 19.1.

Lemons Market with Variable Quality

Many firms can vary the quality of their products. If consumers cannot identify high-quality goods before purchase, they pay the same for all goods regardless of quality. Because the price that firms receive for top-quality goods is the same as that for schlock, they do not produce top-quality goods. Such an outcome is inefficient if consumers are willing to pay sufficiently more for top-quality goods.

This unwillingness to produce high-quality products is due to an externality: *A firm does not completely capture the benefits from raising the quality of its product.* By selling a better product than what other firms offer, a seller raises the average quality in the market, so buyers are willing to pay more for all products. As a result, the high-quality seller shares the benefits from its high-quality product with sellers of low-quality products by raising the average price to all. *The social value of raising the quality*, as reflected by the increased revenues shared by all firms, *is greater than the private value*, which is only the higher revenue received by the firm with the good product.

To illustrate, suppose that it costs \$10 to produce a low-quality book bag and \$20 to produce a high-quality bag, consumers cannot distinguish between the products before purchase, there are no repeat purchases, and consumers value the bags at their cost of production. The five firms in the market produce 100 bags each. A firm produces only high-quality or only low-quality bags.

If all five firms make a low-quality bag, consumers pay \$10 per bag. If one firm makes a high-quality bag and all the others make low-quality bags, the expected value per bag to consumers is

$$\$12 = (\$10 \times \tfrac{4}{5}) + (\$20 \times \tfrac{1}{5}).$$

Thus if one firm raises the quality of its product, all firms benefit because the bags sell for \$12 instead of \$10. The high-quality firm receives only a fraction of the total benefit from raising quality. It gets \$2 extra per high-quality bag sold, which is less than the extra \$10 it costs to make the better bag. The other \$8 is shared by the other firms. Because the high-quality firm incurs all the expenses of raising quality, \$10 extra per bag, and reaps only a fraction, \$2, of the benefits, it opts not to produce the high-quality bags. Thus *due to asymmetric information, the firms do not produce high-quality goods even though consumers are willing to pay for the extra quality.*

Limiting Lemons

In some markets, it is possible to avoid problems stemming from consumer ignorance. Laws might provide protection against being sold a lemon, consumers might screen by collecting the information themselves, the government or another third party might supply reliable information, or sellers might send credible signals.

Laws to Prevent Opportunism. Product liability laws protect consumers from being stuck with nonfunctional or dangerous products. Moreover, many state supreme courts have concluded that products are sold with an implicit understanding that they will safely perform their intended function. If they do not, consumers can sue the seller even in the absence of product liability laws. If consumers can rely on explicit or implicit product liability laws to force a manufacturer to make good on defective products, they need not worry about adverse selection.

An inherent problem with legal recourse, however, is that the transaction costs of going to court are very high. Moreover, state laws may be less effective than federal regulations in protecting consumers with respect to cars that are lemons.

Application   RECYCLING LEMONS

Daniel Garcia of Virginia bought a Dodge Caravan that leaked when it rained. The Chrysler Corporation repurchased his minivan when he sued under his state's lemon law. Soon thereafter, Karen Melvin of Minneapolis, Minnesota, adopted the same unusual driving practice as Daniel Garcia: taking a towel along with the car keys on rainy days. That's not surprising, as she had bought Daniel Garcia's former Caravan. She too sued Chrysler and sold the company the minivan. Then Wade Wilson of Champaign, Illinois, purchased this lemon.

Such cases led consumer advocates to seek uniform laws to prevent cars identified as lemons in one state from being sold without warning in another state. Today, all states have lemon laws, though they differ as to what they require dealers and manufacturers to do with returned vehicles.

In 12 states, firms are not required to tell a prospective car buyer that a car was previously returned as a lemon (see **www.autopedia.com/html/ Hotlinks_Lemon.html**). Only Alabama, California, Connecticut, the District of Columbia, Florida, Indiana, Iowa, Louisiana, Maryland, New Jersey, New York, South Dakota, Utah, Vermont, Washington, and Wisconsin require that a vehicle be labeled a lemon on its title. California, Idaho, and New Hampshire alone insist that titles be carried over from other states. In the United States, you can discover whether you are buying someone else's lemon by paying a small fee at **www.carfax.com** to uncover a used vehicle's original title.

If you live in Europe, you have fewer protections. The situation is slowly improving: A relatively weak European directive (The Consumer's

Guarantees) takes effect in 2002 that forces retailers to fix defects appearing within two years in a new car or one year in a used car and that makes manufacturers' guarantees binding for the first time.

The enforcement of lemon laws is often lax. Florida, which requires reports on lemons, found that automakers had reported only 12% of the 3,412 vehicles that were repurchased in the state between 1992 and 1994.

Regardless of where you live, remember: Buyer beware!

Consumer Screening. Consumers can avoid the lemons problem if they can obtain reliable information about quality (screen). When a consumer's cost of securing information is less than the private benefits, consumers obtain the information and markets function smoothly. However, if the cost exceeds the benefit, they do not gather the information and the market is inefficient. Consumers buy information from experts or infer product quality from sellers' reputations.

For many goods, consumers can buy reliable information from *objective experts*. For example, you can pay to have a mechanic appraise a used car. If the mechanic can reliably determine whether the car is a lemon, the information asymmetry is eliminated.

In some markets, consumers learn of a firm's *reputation* from other consumers or from observation. Consumers can avoid the adverse selection problem by buying only from firms that have reputations for providing high-quality goods. Consumers know that a used-car firm that expects repeat purchases has a strong incentive not to sell defective products.

Generally, in markets in which the same consumers and firms trade regularly, a reputation is easy to establish. In markets in which consumers buy a good only once, such as in tourist areas, firms cannot establish reputations as easily.

Third-Party Comparisons. Some nonprofit organizations, such as consumer groups, and for-profit firms publish expert comparisons of brands. To the degree that this information is credible, it may reduce adverse selection by enabling consumers to avoid buying low-quality goods.

If an outside organization is to provide believable information, it must convince consumers that it is trustworthy and is not deceiving them. Consumers Union, which publishes the product evaluation guide *Consumer Reports*, tries to establish its trustworthiness by refusing to accept advertising or other payments from firms.

Unfortunately, expert information is undersupplied because information is a *public good* (nonrivalrous and only sometimes exclusive—see Chapter 18). Consumers Union does not capture the full value of its information through sales of *Consumer Reports* because buyers lend their copies to friends, libraries stock the magazine, and newspapers report on its findings. As result, Consumers Union conducts less research than is socially optimal.

Standards and Certification. The government, consumer groups, industry groups, and others provide information based on a **standard**: a metric or scale for evaluating the quality of a particular product. For example, the R-value of insulation—a standard—tells how effectively insulation works. Consumers learn of a brand's quality through **certification**: a report that a particular product meets or exceeds a given standard level.

Many industry groups set their own standards and get an outside group or firm, such as Underwriters' Laboratories (UL) or Factory Mutual Engineering Corporation (FMEC), to certify that their products meet specified standard levels. For example, by setting standards for the size of the thread on a screw, we ensure that screws work in products regardless of brand.

When standard and certification programs inexpensively and completely inform consumers about the relative quality of all goods in a market and do not restrict the goods available, the programs are socially desirable. Some of these programs have harmful effects, however.

Standard and certification programs that provide degraded information, for instance, may mislead consumers. Many standards use only a high- versus low-quality rating even though quality varies continuously. Such standards encourage the manufacture of products that have either the lowest-possible quality (and cost of production) or the minimum quality level necessary to obtain the top rating.

If standard and certification programs restrict salable goods and services to those that are certified, such programs may also have anticompetitive effects. Many governments license only professionals and craftspeople who meet some minimum standards. People without a license are not allowed to practice their profession or craft. In most states, dozens, if not hundreds, of categories of professionals, craftspeople, and others are licensed, including electricians, plumbers, dentists, psychologists, contractors, and beauticians.

The restrictions raise the average quality in the industry by eliminating low-quality goods and services. They drive up prices to consumers for two reasons. First, the number of people providing services is reduced because the restrictions eliminate some potential suppliers. Second, consumers are unable to obtain lower-quality and less-expensive goods or services. As a result, welfare may go up or down, depending on whether the increased-quality effect or the higher-price effect dominates. Whether such restrictions can be set properly and cost-effectively by government agencies is widely debated.

Moreover, licensing and mandatory standards and certification are often used for anticompetitive purposes such as erecting entry barriers to new firms and products. Doctors, lawyers, electricians, and other professionals establish their own licensing standards under government auspices. Frequently, these groups set standards that prevent entry of professionals from other states or those who have just finished their education so as to keep the wages of currently licensed professionals high. Such licensing is socially harmful because it excludes qualified professionals and raises consumers' costs. (Unfortunately, economists have not been clever enough to get their profession licensed so that they can act anticompetitively to limit supply and raise their earnings.)

Signaling by Firms. Producers of high-quality goods often try to signal to consumers that their products are of better quality than those of their rivals. If consumers believe their signals, these firms can charge higher prices for their goods. But if the signals are to be effective, they must be credible.

Firms use brand names as a signal of quality. For example, some farms brand their produce, while rivals sell their produce without labels. Shoppers may rely on this signal and choose only fruits and vegetables with brand labels. Presumably, a firm uses a brand name to enable buyers to identify its product only if the item's quality is better than that of a typical unbranded product.

Some firms provide guarantees or warranties as signals to convince consumers that their products are of high quality. Consumer durables such as cars and refrigerators commonly come with guarantees or warranties. Virtually all new cars have warranties. Moreover, one-third of used cars purchased from dealers include warranties (Genesove, 1993).

Signals solve the adverse selection problem only when consumers view them as credible (only high-quality firms find their use profitable). Smart consumers may place little confidence in unsubstantiated claims by firms. Would you believe that a used car runs well just because an ad tells you so? Legally enforceable guarantees and warranties are more credible than advertising alone.

Signaling will not solve an adverse selection problem if it is unprofitable for high-quality firms to signal or if both high- and low-quality firms send the same signal. For example, if a firm's overhead costs are very high, it may not pay for the firm to provide a guarantee to signal the high quality of its product. Another possibility is that both low- and high-quality firms signal. If so, the signal is worthless to consumers. Both low-quality and high-quality fruit and vegetable firms can use trademarks in tourist areas, where there are few repeat purchases. Similarly, all firms may provide guarantees for inexpensive goods, for which transaction costs are usually too high for consumers to use guarantees. (See **www.awlonline.com/perloff**, "Wholesale Market for Cherries," for an example of how firms use sorting of their products to signal quality.)

Application   **COLLEGE GUARANTEE**

Students at Middlesex Community College in New Jersey are now guaranteed. A firm that hires a graduate from one of Middlesex's vocational programs and discovers that he or she lacks the necessary skills can send that worker back to Middlesex for retraining. Flora Mancuso Edwards, the president of the college, says, "We warranty the expertise of our students to be absolutely fit for the purposes for which the education was intended."

The first school to offer such a guarantee was Henry Ford Community College in Dearborn, Michigan. This idea has spread to schools not only in New Jersey but also in Pennsylvania, Illinois, and Texas.

In the first eight years of the Henry Ford program, only one student returned for more classes. Some observers maintain that the guarantee motivates the school to stay on top of its program and keep it current with industry practices. But critics wonder how many people know about the guarantee and hence question whether it has any effect.

19.4 | PRICE DISCRIMINATION DUE TO FALSE BELIEFS ABOUT QUALITY

We've seen that bad products can drive out good products if consumers cannot distinguish lemons from good-quality products at the time of purchase. The market outcome also changes if consumers falsely believe that identical products differ in quality. Consumers pay more for a product that they believe is of higher quality.

If some consumers know that two products are identical while others believe that they differ in quality, a firm can profitably price discriminate. The firm takes advantage of the less informed customers by charging them a high price for the allegedly superior product. The firm does not want to charge informed customers this same high price. Doing so would reduce profit because the resulting fall in sales would be greater than the gain from the higher price on sales that are made.

Asymmetric information on the part of some, but not all, consumers makes price discrimination possible. However, if all customers are informed or all are uninformed about the quality of different products, firms charge a single price.

By intentionally increasing consumer uncertainty, a firm may be better able to exploit ignorant consumers and earn a higher profit (Salop, 1977). One way in which firms confuse consumers is to create *noise* by selling virtually the same product under various brand names. Similarly, firms sometimes sell a product under their own brand name at a relatively high price and supply grocery or discount stores with a virtually identical product that is sold at a lower price under a *private-label* (house or store) brand. For example, the same bakery produces Wonder Bread and similar house brands for various grocery stores.

Brand proliferation pays if the cost of producing multiple brands is relatively low and the share of consumers who are willing to buy the higher-price product is relatively large. Otherwise, the firm makes a higher profit by selling a single product at a moderate price than by selling one brand at a low price and another at a high price.

Over time, as consumers have become familiar with private-label brands and recognized their quality, firms have reaped less advantage in maintaining multiple brands for many products. Indeed, private-label products are rapidly gaining market share.[2] Since 1991, the share of consumers who are familiar with store-brand products has risen from 86% to 91%, and the percentage of consumers who regularly buy the store brand has increased from 77% to 83%. Of consumers who have bought premium private-label items, 90% have rated the products equal to or better than national brands and plan to buy private-label products in the future. In 1999, the upscale Saks Fifth Avenue chain, recognizing this trend, announced that it would focus on private-label brands.

---

[2]Krumrei, Doug, "Brand Ho! Bakery Industry Trends for 1996," *Bakery Production and Marketing*, May 15, 1996; and Palmer, Eric, "New Vigor in Bread," *Milling & Baking News*, December 5, 1995.

Application | MULTIPLE BRAND NAMES

By selling the same product under more than one brand name, firms can charge ignorant consumers higher prices. For decades, outside firms have manufactured products that Sears, Roebuck & Company sells under its house brand names, Kenmore, Die-Hard, and Craftsman. Amana refrigerators are sold under their own brand name and under the Kenmore brand name. Similarly, Whirlpool sells its own washers and driers, but Sears also markets these products under the Kenmore name.

Frequently, the Kenmore product is identical to or even superior to the brand-name product and costs less. Knowledgeable consumers realizing that the two brands are identical except for the label, buy the Sears brand at the lower price. But customers who falsely believe that the name brand is better than the Kenmore product pay more for the name brand.

Similarly, a car manufacturer (or a group of manufacturers working collectively) sells cars that are nearly physically identical—at least in terms of their inner workings—under different brand names. The Ford Taurus and Mercury Sable are automotive twins, as are the Toyota Camry and Lexus ES 300. Indeed, triplets and quadruplets are observed: The Dodge Colt, Mitsubishi Mirage, Plymouth Colt, and Eagle Summit cars are virtual clones.

Twins often have very different prices. Consumers can save $1,124 by purchasing an Olds 98 Regency rather than its twin, the Buick Park Avenue. Even the rich can save a bundle if they don't mind a different grille and headlights: The $152,400 long-wheelbase Bentley Brookland costs $25,800 less than the similar $178,200 Rolls-Royce Silver Spur III.

19.5 | MARKET POWER FROM PRICE IGNORANCE

We've just seen that consumer ignorance about quality can keep high-quality goods out of markets or lead to price discrimination. Consumer ignorance about how prices vary across firms has yet another effect: It gives firms market power. As a result, firms have an incentive to make it difficult for consumers to collect information about prices. For this reason, some stores won't quote prices over the phone.

We now examine why asymmetric information about prices leads to noncompetitive pricing in a market that would otherwise be competitive. Suppose that many stores in a town sell the same good. If consumers have *full information* about prices, all stores charge the full-information competitive price, p^*. If one store were to raise its price above p^*, the store would lose all its business. Each store faces a residual demand curve that is horizontal at the going market price and has no market power.

In contrast, if consumers have *limited information* about the price that firms charge for a product, one store can charge more than others and not lose all its customers.

Customers who do not know that the product is available for less elsewhere keep buying from the high-price store.[3] Thus each store faces a downward-sloping residual demand curve and has some market power.

Tourist-Trap Model

We now show that, if there is a single price in such a market, it is higher than p^*. You arrive in a small town near the site of the discovery of gold in California. Souvenir shops crowd the street. Wandering by one of these stores, you see that it sells the town's distinctive snowy: a plastic ball filled with water and imitation snow featuring a model of the Donner party. You instantly decide that you must buy at least one of these tasteful mementos—perhaps more if the price is low enough. Your bus will leave very soon, so you can't check the price at each shop to find the lowest price. Moreover, determining which shop has the lowest price won't be useful to you in the future because you do not intend to return anytime soon.

Let's assume that you and other tourists have a guidebook that reports how many souvenir shops charge each possible price for the snowy, but the guidebook does not state the price at any particular shop.[4] There are many tourists in your position, each with an identical demand function.

It costs each tourist c in time and expenses to visit a shop to check the price or buy a snowy. Thus if the price is p, the cost of buying a snowy at the first shop you visit is $p + c$. If you go to two souvenir shops before buying at the second shop, the cost of the snowy is $p + 2c$.

When Price Is Not Competitive. Will all souvenir shops charge the same price? If so, what price will they charge? We start by considering whether each shop charges the full-information, competitive price, p^*.

The full-information, competitive price is the equilibrium price only if no firm has an incentive to charge a different price. No firm would charge less than p^*, which equals marginal cost, because it would lose money on each sale.

However, a firm could gain by charging a higher price than p^*, so p^* is *not* an equilibrium price. If all other shops charge p^*, a firm can profitably charge $p_1 = p^* + \varepsilon$, where ε, a small positive number, is the shop's price markup. Suppose that you walk into this shop and learn that it sells the snowy for p_1. You know from your guidebook that all other souvenir shops charge only p^*. You say to yourself, "How unfortunate [or other words to that effect], I've wandered into the only expensive

---

[3]A grave example concerns the ripping off of the dying and the survivors of the dead. A cremation arranged through a memorial society—which typically charges a nominal enrollment fee of $10 to $25—costs $400 to $600, compared with $1,500 to $2,000 for the same service when it is arranged through a mortuary. Consumers who know about memorial societies—which get competitive bids from mortuaries—can obtain a relatively low price. The less knowledgeable people who deal directly with mortuaries pay more. Rowland, Mary, "Shedding Light on a Dark Subject," *New York Times*, July 24, 1994:13.

[4]We make this assumption about the guidebook to keep the presentation as simple as possible. This assumption is not necessary to obtain the following result.

shop in town." Annoyed, you consider going elsewhere. Nonetheless, you do not go to another shop if this shop's markup, $\varepsilon = p_1 - p^*$, is less than c, the cost of going to another shop.

As a result, it pays for this shop to raise its price by an amount that is just slightly less than the cost of an additional search, thereby deviating from the proposed equilibrium where all other shops charge p^*. Thus *if consumers have limited information about price, an equilibrium in which all firms charge the full-information, competitive price is impossible.*

Monopoly Price. We've seen that the market price cannot be lower than or equal to the full-information, competitive price. Can there be an equilibrium in which all stores charge the same price and that price is higher than the competitive price? In particular, can we have an equilibrium when all shops charge $p_1 = p^* + \varepsilon$? No, shops would deviate from this proposed equilibrium for the same reason that they deviated from charging the competitive price. A shop can profitably raise its price to $p_2 = p_1 + \varepsilon = p^* + 2\varepsilon$. Again, it does not pay for a tourist who is unlucky enough to enter that shop to go to another shop as long as $\varepsilon < c$. Thus p_1 is not the equilibrium price. By repeating this reasoning, we can reject other possible equilibrium prices that are above p^* and less than the monopoly price, p_m.

However, the monopoly price may be an equilibrium price. No firm wants to raise its price above the monopoly level because its profit would fall due to reduced sales. When tourists learn the price at a particular souvenir shop, they decide how many snowies to buy. If the price is set too high, the shop's lost sales more than offset the higher price, so its profit falls. Thus although the shop can charge a higher price without losing all its sales, it chooses not to do so.

The only remaining question is whether a shop would like to charge a lower price than p_m if all other shops charge that price. If not, p_m is an equilibrium price.

Should a shop reduce its price below p_m by less than c? If it does so, it does not pay for consumers to search for this low-price firm. The shop makes less on each sale, so its profits must fall. Thus a shop should not deviate by charging a price that is only slightly less than p_m.

Does it pay for a shop to drop its price below p_m by more than c? If there are few shops, consumers may search for this low-price shop. Although the shop makes less per sale than the high-price shops, its profits may be higher because of greater sales volume. If there are many shops, however, consumers do not search for the low-price shop because their chances of finding it are low. As a result, when the presence of a large number of shops makes searching for a low-price shop impractical, no firm lowers its price, so p_m is the equilibrium price. Thus *when consumers have asymmetric information and when search costs and the number of firms are large, the only possible single-price equilibrium is at the monopoly price.*

If the single-price equilibrium at p_m can be broken by a firm charging a low price, there is no single-price equilibrium. Either there is no equilibrium or there is an equilibrium in which prices vary across shops (see Stiglitz, 1979, or Carlton and Perloff, 2000). Multiple-price equilibria are common.

Solved Problem 19.2   Initially, there are many souvenir shops, each of which charges p_m (because consumers do not know the shops' prices), and buyers' search costs are c. If the government pays for half of consumers' search costs, can there be a single-price equilibrium at a price less than p_m?

Answer

Show that the argument we used to reject a single-price equilibrium at any price except the monopoly price did not depend on the size of the search cost: If all other stores charge any single price p, where $p^* \le p < p_m$, a firm profits from raising its price. As long as it raises its price by no more than $c/2$ (the new cost of search to a consumer), unlucky consumers who stop at this deviant store do not search further. This profitable deviation shows that the proposed single-price equilibrium is not an equilibrium. Again, the only possible single-price equilibrium is at p_m.[5]

Advertising and Prices

The U.S. Federal Trade Commission (FTC), a consumer protection agency, opposes groups that want to forbid price advertising; the FTC argues that advertising about price benefits consumers. If a firm informs consumers about its unusually low price, it may be able to gain enough extra customers to more than offset its loss from the lower price. If low-price stores advertise their prices and attract many customers, they can break the monopoly-price equilibrium that occurs when consumers must search store by store for low prices. The more successful the advertising, the larger these stores grow and the lower the average price in the market. If enough consumers become informed, all stores may charge the low price. Thus without advertising, no store may find it profitable to charge low prices, but with advertising, all stores may charge low prices.

Application   **ADVERTISING LOWERS PRICES**

Many studies by FTC economists and others show that allowing stores to advertise their prices lowers the average price that consumers pay for products such as drugs, eyeglasses, liquor, toys, and gasoline. Years ago, some states banned the advertising of eyeglass prices. Benham (1972) found that banning all advertising raised prices by 28% relative to the prices in states without bans. The price difference was negligible, however, between states that allowed advertising and those that banned only price advertising.

---

[5]If the search cost is low enough, however, the single-price equilibrium at p_m can be broken profitably by charging a low price so that only a multiple-price equilibrium is possible. If the search cost falls to zero, consumers have full information, so the only possible equilibrium is at the full-information, competitive price.

A subsequent FTC study on eyeglass advertising (Bond, Kwoka, Phelan, and Whitten, 1980) found that prices were lower in cities that allowed advertising than in those that banned it. In cities without advertising bans, even optometrists who did not advertise charged an average of $20 less for an exam and glasses than their counterparts in cities that banned advertising. Moreover, this study found that eyeglass quality was the same in cities with and without the ban.

Because advertising can lower prices in a market, professional groups try to ban it. Until Supreme Court decisions stopped them, medical, dental, and legal organizations blocked advertising, claiming that it was unprofessional. Today, many of these professionals advertise in newspapers and the Yellow Pages and on radio and television. Some law firms issue press releases after trial victories, mail brochures to prospective clients, and hire public relations firms to help penetrate the market. Schroeter, Smith, and Cox (1987) found that the cost of legal services for simple wills and uncontested bankruptcy proceedings fell with advertising.

19.6 | PROBLEMS ARISING FROM IGNORANCE WHEN HIRING

Asymmetric information is frequently a problem in labor markets. Prospective employees may have less information about working conditions than firms do. Firms may have less information about potential employees' abilities than the workers do.

Information asymmetries in labor markets lower welfare below the full-information level. Workers may signal and firms may screen to reduce the asymmetry in information about workers' abilities. Signaling and screening may raise or lower welfare, as we now consider.

Information About Employment Risks

Firms typically have more information than workers about job safety. This asymmetric information may lead to less than optimal levels of safety (Viscusi, 1979).

Prospective employees who do not know the injury rate at individual firms may know the average injury rates in an industry because these data are reported by the U.S. Bureau of Labor Statistics. People will work in a risky industry only if they are paid more than they would earn in less-risky industries.

Each firm must consider how safe to make its plant. Extra safety is costly. Safety investments—sprinkler systems, color-coded switches, fire extinguishers—by one firm provide an externality to other firms: That firm's lower incidence of accidents reduces the wage that all firms in the industry must pay. *Because each firm bears the full cost of its safety investments but derives only some of the benefits, the firms underinvest in safety.*

The prisoners' dilemma game in Table 19.1, which is played by the only two firms in an industry, illustrates this result. In the Nash equilibrium (upper left), neither firm invests and each earns $200.

An investment by only one firm raises safety levels at its plant. Workers in the industry do not know that safety has improved only at the plant of the investing

Table 19.1 Safety Investment Game

		Firm 2	
		No Investment	*Investment*
Firm 1	*No Investment*	$200 $200	$250 $100
	Investment	$100 $250	$225 $225

firm. They realize only that it is safer to work in this industry, so both firms pay lower wages. The loss from the investment is greater than the wage savings, so the profit falls to $100 for the firm that invests. The wage savings causes its rival's profit to rise to $250.

If both firms invest (lower right), both earn $225, which is more than they would earn in the Nash equilibrium. However, investment by both firms is not an equilibrium, as each firm has an incentive to deviate.

This prisoners' dilemma would not occur if workers knew how safe each firm was. Only the firm that invested in safety would be able to pay a lower wage if workers knew the accident rate by firms. There would be no externality. Thus a firm that can credibly convince workers that it is a relatively safe place to work can overcome this asymmetric information problem.[6]

In this example, the underinvestment problem could be avoided if the government provided the information, if the government set safety standards that would force both firms to invest, or if unions effectively lobbied both firms for higher levels of safety. For the government or unions to provide these useful functions practically, however, their cost of gathering the necessary information would have to be relatively low.

Cheap Talk

Honesty is the best policy—when there is money in it.   —Mark Twain

We now consider situations in which workers have more information about their ability than firms do. We look first at inexpensive signals sent by workers, then at expensive signals sent by workers, and finally at screening by firms.

When an informed person voluntarily provides information to an uninformed person, the informed person engages in **cheap talk**: unsubstantiated claims or statements (see Farrell and Rabin, 1996). People use cheap talk to distinguish themselves or their attributes at low cost. Even though informed people may lie when it suits them, it

---

[6]Because this information is a public good, others may obtain this information if the firm provides it to employees. The cost to the firm of having others, such as government regulators, obtain this information may exceed the lower-wage benefit from providing it to workers.

is often in their and everyone else's best interest for them to tell the truth. Nothing stops me from advertising that I have a chimpanzee for sale, but doing so serves no purpose if I actually want to sell my DVD player. One advantage of cheap talk, if it is effective, is that it is a less-expensive method of signaling ability to a potential employer than paying to have that ability tested.

Suppose that a firm plans to hire Cyndi to do one of two jobs. The demanding job requires someone with high ability. The undemanding job can be done better by someone of low ability because the job bores more able people, who then perform poorly.

Cyndi knows whether her ability level is high or low, but the firm is unsure. It initially thinks that either level is equally likely. Panel a of Table 19.2 shows the payoffs to Cyndi and the firm under various possibilities.[7] If Cyndi has high ability, she enjoys the demanding job: Her payoff is 3. If she has low ability, she finds the demanding job too stressful—her payoff is only 1—but she can handle the undemanding job. The payoff to the firm is greater if Cyndi is properly matched to the job: She is given the demanding job if she has high ability and the undemanding job if she has low ability.

Table 19.2 Employee-Employer Payoffs

(a) *When Cheap Talk Works*

		Job That the Firm Gives to Cyndi	
		Demanding	Undemanding
Cyndi's Ability	High	3 2	1 1
	Low	1 1	2 4

(b) *When Cheap Talk Fails*

		Job That the Firm Gives to Cyndi	
		Demanding	Undemanding
Cyndi's Ability	High	3 2	1 1
	Low	3 1	2 4

---

[7]Previously, we used a 2 × 2 matrix to show a simultaneous-move game (as in Table 19.1), in which both parties choose an action at the same time. Here only the firm can make a move. Cyndi does not take an action: She cannot choose her ability level.

We can view this example as a two-stage game. In the first stage, Cyndi tells the firm something. In the second stage, the firm decides which job she gets.

Cyndi could make many possible statements about her ability. For simplicity, though, we assume that she says either "My ability is high" or "My ability is low." This two-stage game has an equilibrium in which Cyndi tells the truth and the firm, believing her, assigns her to the appropriate job. If she claims to have high ability, the firm gives her the demanding job.

If the firm reacts to her cheap talk in this manner, Cyndi has no incentive to lie. If she did lie, the firm would make a mistake, and a mistake would be bad for both parties. Cyndi and the firm want the same outcomes, so cheap talk works.

In many other situations, however, cheap talk does not work. Given the payoffs in panel b, Cyndi and the firm do not want the same outcomes. The firm still wants Cyndi in the demanding job if she has high ability and in the undemanding job otherwise. But Cyndi wants the demanding job regardless of her ability. So she claims to have high ability regardless of the truth. Knowing her incentives, the firm views her statement as meaningless babbling—her statement does not change the firm's view that her ability is equally likely to be high or low.

Given that belief, the firm gives her the undemanding job, for which its expected payoff is higher. The firm's expected payoff is $(\frac{1}{2} \times 1) + (\frac{1}{2} \times 4) = 2.5$ if it gives her the undemanding job and $(\frac{1}{2} \times 2) + (\frac{1}{2} \times 1) = 1.5$ if it assigns her to the demanding job. Thus given the firm's asymmetric information, the outcome is inefficient if Cyndi has high ability.

When the interests of the firm and the individual diverge, cheap talk does not provide a credible signal. Here an individual has to send a more expensive signal to be believed. We now examine such a signal.

Education as a Signal

No doubt you've been told that one good reason to go to college is to get a good job. Going to college may get you a better job because you obtain valuable training. Another possibility is that a college degree may land you a good job because it serves as a signal to employers about your ability. If high-ability people are more likely to go to college than low-ability people, schooling signals ability to employers (Spence, 1974).

To illustrate how such signaling works, we'll make the extreme assumptions that graduating from an appropriate school serves as the signal and that schooling provides no training that is useful to firms (Stiglitz, 1975). High-ability workers are θ share of the workforce, and low-ability workers are $1 - \theta$ share. The value of output that a high-ability worker produces for a firm is worth w_h, and that of a low-ability worker is w_l (over their careers). If competitive employers knew workers' ability levels, they would pay this value of the marginal product to each worker, so a high-ability worker receives w_h and a low-ability worker earns w_l.

We assume that employers cannot directly determine a worker's skill level. For example, when production is a group effort—such as in an assembly line—a firm cannot determine the productivity of a single employee.

Two types of equilibria are possible, depending on whether or not employers can distinguish high-ability workers from others. If employers have no way of telling workers apart, the outcome is a **pooling equilibrium**: Dissimilar people are treated (paid) alike or behave alike. Employers pay all workers the average wage:

$$\bar{w} = \theta w_h + (1 - \theta)w_l. \tag{19.2}$$

Risk-neutral, competitive firms expect to break even because they underpay high-ability people by enough to offset the losses from overpaying low-ability workers.

We assume that high-ability individuals can get a degree by spending c to attend a school and that low-ability people cannot graduate from the school (or that the cost of doing so is prohibitively high). If high-ability people graduate and low-ability people do not, a degree is a signal of ability to employers. Given such a clear signal, the outcome is a **separating equilibrium**: One type of people takes actions (such as sending a signal) that allow them to be differentiated from other types of people. Here a successful signal causes high-ability workers to receive w_h and the others to receive w_l, so wages vary with ability.

We now examine whether a pooling or a separating equilibrium is possible. We consider whether anyone would want to change behavior in an equilibrium. If no one wants to change, the equilibrium is feasible.

Separating Equilibrium. In a separating equilibrium, high-ability people pay c to get a degree and are employed at a wage of w_h, while low-ability individuals do not get a degree and work for a wage of w_l. The low-ability people have no choice, as they can't get a degree. High-ability individuals have the option of not going to school. Without a degree, however, they are viewed as low ability once hired, and they receive w_l. If they go to school, their net earnings are $w_h - c$. Thus it pays for a high-ability person to go to school if

$$w_h - c > w_l.$$

Rearranging terms in this expression, we find that a high-ability person chooses to get a degree if

$$w_h - w_l > c. \tag{19.3}$$

Equation 19.3 says that the benefit from graduating, the extra pay $w_h - w_l$, exceeds the cost of schooling, c. If Equation 19.3 holds, no worker wants to change behavior, so a separating equilibrium is feasible.

Suppose that $c = \$15,000$ and that high-ability workers are twice as productive as others: $w_h = \$40,000$ and $w_l = \$20,000$. Here the benefit to a high-ability worker from graduating, $w_h - w_l = \$20,000$, exceeds the cost by $5,000. Thus no one wants to change behavior in this separating equilibrium.

Pooling Equilibrium. In a pooling equilibrium, all workers are paid the average wage from Equation 19.2, $\bar{w}$. Again, because low-ability people cannot graduate, they have no choice. A high-ability person must choose whether or not to go to school. Without a degree, that individual is paid the average wage. With a degree, the worker is paid w_h. It does not pay for the high-ability person to graduate if the benefit from graduating, the extra pay $w_h - \bar{w}$, is less than the cost of schooling:

$$w_h - \bar{w} < c. \tag{19.4}$$

Thus if Equation 19.4 holds, no worker wants to change behavior, so a pooling equilibrium persists.

For example, if w_h = $40,000, w_l = $20,000, and $\theta = \frac{1}{2}$, then

$$\bar{w} = (\tfrac{1}{2} \times \$40,000) + (\tfrac{1}{2} \times \$20,000) = \$30,000.$$

If the cost of going to school is c = $15,000, the benefit to a high-ability person from graduating, $w_h - \bar{w}$ = $10,000 is less than the cost, so a high-ability individual does not want to go school. As a result, there is a pooling equilibrium.

Solved Problem 19.3

For what values of θ is a pooling equilibrium possible in general? In particular, if c = $15,000, w_h = $40,000, and w_l = $20,000, for what values of θ is a pooling equilibrium possible?

Answer

1. *Determine the values of θ for which it pays for a high-ability person to go to school*: From Equation 19.4, we know that a high-ability individual does not go to school if $w_h - \bar{w} < c$. Using Equation 19.2, we substitute for $\bar{w}$ in Equation 19.4 and rearrange terms to find that high-ability people do not go to school if

$$w_h - [\theta w_h + (1 - \theta)w_l] < c,$$

or

$$\theta > 1 - \frac{c}{w_h - w_1}. \tag{19.5}$$

If almost everyone has high ability, so θ is large, a high-ability person does not go to school. The intuition is that, as the share of high-ability workers, θ, gets large (close to 1), the average wage approaches w_h (Equation 19.2), so there is little benefit, $w_h - \bar{w}$, in going to school.

2. *Solve for the possible values of θ for the specific parameters*: If we substitute c = $15,000, w_h = $40,000, and w_l = $20,000 into Equation 19.5, we find that high-ability people do not go to school—a pooling equilibrium is possible—if $\theta > \frac{1}{4}$.

Unique or Multiple Equilibria. Depending on differences in abilities, the cost of schooling, and the share of high-ability workers, only one type of equilibrium may be possible or both may be possible. In the following examples, using Figure 19.2, w_h = $40,000 and w_l = $20,000.

Only a pooling equilibrium is possible if schooling is very costly: $c > w_h - w_l$ = $20,000, so Equation 19.3 does not hold. A horizontal line in Figure 19.2 shows where $c = w_h - w_l$ = $20,000. Only a pooling equilibrium is feasible above that line, $c > $20,000, because it does not pay for high-ability workers to go to school.

Equation 19.5 shows that, if there are few high-ability people (relative to the cost and earnings differential), only a separating equilibrium is possible. The figure

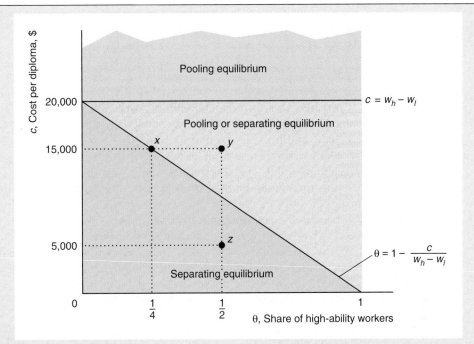

Figure 19.2 Pooling and Separating Equilibria.
If firms know workers' abilities, high-ability workers are paid w_h = \$40,000 and low-ability workers get w_l = \$20,000. The type of equilibrium depends on the cost of schooling, c, and the share of high-ability workers, θ. If $c >$ \$20,000, only a pooling equilibrium, in which everyone gets the average wage, is possible. If there are relatively few high-ability people, $\theta < 1 - c/$ \$20,000, only a separating equilibrium is possible. Between the horizontal and sloped lines, either type of equilibrium may occur.

shows a sloped line where $\theta = 1 - c/(w_h - w_l)$. Below that line, $\theta < 1 - c/(w_h - w_l)$, relatively few people have high ability, so the average wage, $\bar{w}$, is low. A pooling equilibrium is not possible because high-ability workers would want to signal. Thus below this line, only a separating equilibrium is possible. Above this line, Equation 19.5 holds, so a pooling equilibrium is possible. (The answer to Solved Problem 19.3 shows that no one wants to change behavior in a pooling equilibrium if $c =$ \$15,000 and $\theta > \frac{1}{4}$, which are points to the right of x in the figure, such as y.)

Below the horizontal line where the cost of signaling is less than \$20,000 and above the sloped line where there are relatively many high-ability workers, either equilibrium may occur. For example, where $c =$ \$15,000 and $\theta = \frac{1}{2}$, Equations 19.3 and 19.4 (or equivalently, Equation 19.5) hold, so both a separating equilibrium and a pooling equilibrium are possible. In the pooling equilibrium, no one wants to change behavior, so this equilibrium is possible. Similarly, no one wants to change behavior in a separating equilibrium.

A government could ensure that one or the other of these equilibria occurs. It achieves a pooling equilibrium by banning schooling (and other possible signals). Alternatively, the government creates a separating equilibrium by subsidizing schooling for some high-ability people. Once some individuals start to signal, so that firms pay either a low or high wage (not a pooling wage), it pays for other high-ability people to signal.

Efficiency. In our example of a separating equilibrium, high-ability people get an otherwise useless education solely to show that they differ from low-ability people. An education is privately useful to the high-ability workers if it serves as a signal that gets them higher net pay. In our extreme example, education is socially inefficient because it is costly and provides no useful training.

Signaling changes the distribution of wages: Instead of everyone's getting the average wage, high-ability workers receive more pay than low-ability workers. Nonetheless, the total amount that firms pay is the same, so firms make zero expected profits in both equilibria.[8] Moreover, everyone is employed in both the pooling and the screening equilibrium, so total output is the same.

Everyone may be worse off in a separating equilibrium. At point y in Figure 19.2 ($w_h = \$40,000$, $w_l = \$20,000$, $c = \$15,000$, and $\theta = \frac{1}{2}$), either a pooling equilibrium or a separating equilibrium is possible. In the pooling equilibrium, each worker is paid $\bar{w} = \$30,000$ and there is no wasteful signaling. In the separating equilibrium, high-ability workers make $w_h - c = \$25,000$ and low-ability workers make $w_l = \$20,000$.

Here high-ability people earn less in the separating equilibrium, $25,000, than they would in a pooling equilibrium, $30,000. Nonetheless, if anyone signals, all high-ability workers will want to send a signal to prevent their wage from falling to that of a low-ability worker. The reason socially undesirable signaling happens is that the private return to signaling—high-ability workers net an extra $5,000 [$= (w_h - c) - w_l = \$25,000 - \$20,000$]—exceeds the net social return to signaling. The gross social return to the signal is zero—the signal changes only the distribution of wages—and the net social return is negative because the signal is costly.

This inefficient expenditure on education is due to asymmetric information and the desire of high-ability workers to signal their ability. Here the government can increase total social wealth by banning wasteful signaling. Both low-ability and high-ability people benefit from such a ban.

In other cases, however, high-ability people do not want a ban. At point z (where $\theta = \frac{1}{2}$ and $c = \$5,000$), only a separating equilibrium is possible without government intervention. In this equilibrium, high-ability workers earn $w_h - c = \$35,000$ and low-ability workers make $w_l = \$20,000$. If the government bans signaling, both types of workers earn $30,000 in the resulting pooling equilibrium, so high-ability workers are harmed, losing $5,000 each. So even though the ban raises total output (wasteful signaling is eliminated), high-ability workers oppose the ban.

In this example, efficiency can always be increased by banning signaling because signaling is unproductive. However, some signaling is socially efficient because it increases total output. Education may raise output because its signal results in a better

---

[8]Firms pay high-ability workers more than low-ability workers in a separating equilibrium, but the average amount they pay per worker is $\bar{w}$, the same as in a pooling equilibrium.

matching of workers and jobs or because it provides useful training as well as serving as a signal. Education also may make people better citizens. In conclusion, *total social output falls with signaling if signaling is socially unproductive but may rise with signaling if signaling also raises productivity or serves some other desirable purpose.* See **www.awlonline.com/perloff**, "Wages Rise with Education," for evidence that signaling raises wages.

Screening in Hiring

Firms screen prospective workers in many ways. An employer may base hiring on an individual's characteristic that the employer believes is correlated with ability, such as how a person dresses or speaks. Or, a firm may use a test. Further, some employers engage in *statistical discrimination*, believing that an individual's gender, race, religion, or ethnicity is a proxy for ability.

Interviews and Tests. Most societies accept the use of interviews and tests by potential employers. Firms commonly use interviews and tests as screening devices to assess abilities. If such screening devices are accurate, the firm benefits by selecting superior workers and assigning them to appropriate tasks. However, as with signaling, these costly activities are inefficient if they do not increase output. In the United States, the use of hiring tests may be challenged and rejected by the courts if the employer cannot demonstrate that the tests accurately measure skills or abilities required on the job.

Statistical Discrimination. If employers think that people of a certain gender, race, religion, or ethnicity have higher ability on average than others, they may engage in *statistical discrimination* (Aigner and Cain, 1977) and hire only such people. Employers may engage in this practice even if they know that the correlation between these factors and ability is imperfect.

Figure 19.3 illustrates one employer's belief that members of race 1 have, on average, lower ability than members of race 2. The figure shows that the employer believes that some members of the first race have higher ability than some members of the second race: Part of the race 1 curve lies to the right of part of the race 2 curve. Still, because the employer believes that a group characteristic, race, is an (imperfect) indicator of individual ability, the employer hires only people of race 2 if enough of them are available.

The employer may claim not to be prejudiced but to be concerned only with maximizing profit.[9] Nonetheless, this employer's actions harm members of race 1 as much as they would if they were due to racial hatred.

It may be very difficult to eliminate statistical discrimination even though ability distributions are identical across races. If all employers share the belief that members of race 1 have such low ability that it is not worth hiring them, people of that race are never hired, so employers never learn that their beliefs are incorrect. Thus

---

[9]Not all employment discrimination is due to statistical discrimination. Other common sources of discrimination are prejudice (Becker, 1971) and the exercise of monopsony power (Madden, 1973).

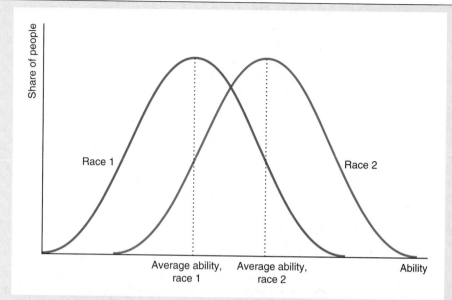

Figure 19.3 **Statistical Discrimination.** This figure shows the beliefs of an employer who thinks that people of race 1 have less ability on average than people of race 2. This employer hires only people of race 2, even though the employer believes that some members of race 1 have greater ability than some members of race 2. Because this employer never employs members of race 1, the employer may never learn that workers of both races have equal ability.

false beliefs can persist indefinitely. Such discrimination lowers social output if it keeps skilled members of race 1 from performing certain jobs.

However, statistical discrimination may be based on true differences between groups. For example, insurance companies offer lower auto insurance rates to young women than to young men because young men are more likely, *on average*, to have an accident. The companies report that this practice lowers their costs of providing insurance by reducing moral hazard. Nonetheless, this practice penalizes young men who are unusually safe drivers and benefits young women who are unusually reckless drivers.

Summary

1. **Problems due to asymmetric information:** Asymmetric information causes market failures when informed parties engage in opportunistic behavior at the expense of uninformed parties. The resulting failures include the elimination of markets and pricing above marginal cost. Two types of problems arise from opportunism.

Adverse selection is opportunism whereby only informed parties who have an unobserved characteristic that allows them to benefit from a deal agree to it, to the detriment of a less-informed party. Moral hazard is opportunism whereby an informed party takes advantage of a less-informed party through an unobserved action.

2. **Responses to adverse selection:** Avoiding adverse selection problems requires restricting the opportunistic behavior or eliminating the information asymmetry. To prevent the opportunism that occurs when information is asymmetric, governments may intervene in markets or the people involved may write contracts that restrict the behavior of informed people. To eliminate or reduce information asymmetries, uninformed people screen to determine the information of informed people, informed people send signals to uninformed people, or third parties such as the government provide information.

3. **How ignorance about quality drives out high-quality goods:** If consumers cannot distinguish between good and bad products before purchase, bad products may drive good ones out of the market. This lemons problem is due to adverse selection. Methods of dealing with the lemons problem include laws limiting opportunism, consumer screening (such as by using experts or relying on firms' reputations), the provision of information by third parties such as government agencies or consumer groups, and signaling by firms (including establishing brand names and providing guarantees or warranties).

4. **Price discrimination due to false beliefs about quality:** Firms may price discriminate if some consumers incorrectly think that quality varies across identical products. Because only some consumers collect information about quality, only those consumers know whether the quality differs between products in some markets. Firms can exploit ignorant consumers by creating noise: selling the same good under two different brand names at different prices.

5. **Market power from price ignorance:** If consumers do not know how prices vary across firms, a firm can raise its price without losing all its customers. As a consequence, consumers' ignorance about price creates market power. In a market that would be competitive with full information, consumer ignorance about price may lead to a monopoly price or a distribution of prices.

6. **Problems arising from ignorance when hiring:** Companies use signaling and screening to try to eliminate information asymmetries in hiring. Where prospective employees and firms share common interests—such as assigning the right worker to the right task—everyone benefits from eliminating the information asymmetry by having informed job candidates honestly tell the firms— through *cheap talk*—about their abilities. When the two parties do not share common interests, cheap talk does not work. Potential employees may inform employers about their abilities by using expensive signals such as a college degree. If these signals are unproductive (as when education serves only as a signal and provides no training), they may be privately beneficial but socially harmful. If the signals are productive (as when education provides training or leads to greater output due to more fitting job assignments), they may be both privately and socially beneficial. Firms may also screen. Job interviews, objective tests, and other screening devices that lead to a better matching of workers and jobs may be socially beneficial. Screening by statistical discrimination, however, is harmful to discriminated-against groups. Employers who discriminate on the basis of a particular group characteristic may never learn that their discrimination is based on false beliefs because they never test these beliefs.

Problems

1. Some states prohibit insurance companies from using car owners' home addresses to set auto insurance rates. Why do insurance companies use home addresses? What are the efficiency and equity implications of forbidding such practices?

2. The state of California set up its own earthquake insurance program for homeowners in 1997. The rates vary by ZIP code, depending on the proximity of the nearest fault line. However, critics claim that the people who set the rates ignored soil type. Some houses rest on bedrock; others sit on unstable soil. What are the implications of such rate setting?

3. You want to determine whether there is a lemons problem in the market for single-engine airplanes.

Can you use any of the following information to help answer this question? If so, how?

a. Repair rates for original-owner planes versus planes that have been resold

b. The fraction of planes resold in each year after purchase

4. If you buy a new car and try to sell it in the first year—indeed, in the first few days after you buy it—the price that you get is substantially less than the original price. Use Akerlof's lemons model to give one explanation for why.

5. Use Akerlof's lemons model to explain why restaurants that cater to tourists are likely to serve low-quality meals. Tourists will not return to this area, and they have no information about the relative quality of the food at various restaurants, but they can determine the relative price by looking at menus posted outside each restaurant.

6. A firm spends a great deal of money in advertising to inform consumers of the brand name of its mushrooms. Should consumers conclude that its mushrooms are likely to be of higher quality than unbranded mushrooms? Why or why not?

7. Explain how a monopoly firm can act like a noisy monopoly by advertising sales in newspapers or magazines or through other media that only some of its customers see.

8. In the signaling model, suppose that firms can pay c^* to have a worker's ability determined through a test. Does it pay for a firm to make this expenditure?

9. When is statistical discrimination privately inefficient? When is it socially inefficient? Does it always harm members of the discriminated-against group?

10. Certain universities do not give letter grades. One rationale is that eliminating the letter-grade system reduces the pressure on students, thus enabling them to do better in school. Why might this policy help or hurt students?

11. Some firms are willing to hire only high school graduates. On the basis of past experience or statistical evidence, these companies believe that high school graduates perform better than nongraduates, on average. How does this hiring behavior compare to statistical discrimination by employers on the basis of race or gender? Discuss the equity and efficiency implications of this practice.

Math Problems

12. There are many buyers who value high-quality used cars at the full-information market price of p_1 and lemons at p_2. There are a limited number of potential sellers who value high-quality cars at $v_1 \leq p_1$ and lemons at $v_2 \leq p_2$. Everyone is risk neutral. The share of lemons among all the used cars that might potentially be sold is θ. Under what conditions are all cars sold? When are only lemons sold? Are there any conditions under which no cars are sold?

13. Suppose that the buyers in Problem 12 incur a transaction cost of $200 to purchase a car. This transaction cost is the value of their time to find a car. What is the equilibrium? Is it possible that no cars are sold?

14. Suppose that you are given w_h, w_l, and θ in the signaling model in the chapter. For what value of c are both a pooling equilibrium and a separating

equilibrium possible? For what value of c are both types of equilibria possible and high-ability workers have a higher net earnings in a separating equilibrium than in a pooling equilibrium?

15. Education is a continuous variable, where e_h is the years of schooling of a high-ability worker and e_l is the years of schooling of a lower-ability worker. The cost per period of education for these types of workers is c_h and c_l, respectively, where $c_l > c_h$. The wages they receive if employers can tell them apart are w_h and w_l. Under what conditions is a separating equilibrium possible? How much education will each type of worker get?

16. In Problem 15, under what conditions is a pooling equilibrium possible?

17. In Problems 15 and 16, describe the equilibrium if $c_l \leq c_h$.

Contracts and Moral Hazards

The contracts of at least 33 major league baseball players have incentive clauses providing a bonus if that player is named the Most Valuable Player in a Division Series. Unfortunately, no such award is given for a Division Series.[1]

An employee cruises the Internet for jokes instead of working when the boss is not watching. A driver of a rental car takes it off the highway and ruins the suspension. The dentist caps your tooth, not because you need it, but because he wants a new stereo.

Each of these examples illustrates an inefficient use of resources due to a *moral hazard*, whereby an informed person takes advantage of a less-informed person, often through an *unobserved action* (Chapter 19). In this chapter, we examine how to design contracts that *eliminate inefficiencies* due to moral hazard problems *without shifting risk to people who hate bearing it*—or contracts that at least reach a good compromise between these two goals.

For example, insurance companies face a trade-off between reducing moral hazards and increasing the risk of insurance buyers. Because an insurance company pools risks, it acts as though it is risk neutral (Chapter 17). The firm offers insurance contracts to risk-averse homeowners so that they can reduce their exposure to risk. If homeowners can buy full insurance so that they will suffer no loss if a fire occurs, some of them fail to take reasonable precautions. They store flammable liquids and old newspapers in their houses, increasing the chance of a catastrophic fire.

A contract that avoids this moral hazard problem specifies that the insurance company will not pay in the event of a fire if the company can show that the policyholders stored flammable materials in their home. If this approach is impractical, however, the insurance company might offer a contract that provides incomplete insurance, covering only a fraction of the damage from a fire. The less complete the coverage, the greater the incentive for policyholders to avoid dangerous activities but the greater the risk that the risk-averse homeowners must bear.

To illustrate methods of controlling moral hazards and the trade-off between moral hazards and risk, we focus in this chapter on contracts between a principal—such as an employer—and an agent—such as an employee. The *principal* contracts with the *agent* to take some *action* that benefits the principal. Until now, we have

---

[1]FitzGerald, Tom, "Top of the Sixth," *San Francisco Chronicle*, January 31, 1997:C6.

assumed that firms can produce efficiently. However, if a principal cannot practically monitor an agent all the time, the agent may steal, not work hard, or engage in other opportunistic behavior that lowers productivity.[2]

Opportunistic behavior by an informed agent harms a less-informed principal. Sometimes the losses are so great that both parties would be better off if both had full information and opportunistic behavior were impossible.

IN THIS CHAPTER,

WE EXAMINE

SEVEN MAIN

TOPICS

1. **Principal-agent problem:** How an uninformed principal contracts with an informed agent determines whether moral hazards occur and how risks are shared.
2. **Production efficiency:** How much the agent produces depends on the type of contract used and the ability of the principal to monitor the agent's actions.
3. **Trade-off between efficiency in production and in risk bearing:** A principal and an agent may agree to a contract that does not eliminate moral hazards or optimally share risk but strikes a balance between these two objectives.
4. **Payments linked to production or profit:** Employees work harder if they are rewarded for greater individual or group productivity.
5. **Monitoring:** Employees work harder if an employer monitors their behavior and makes it worthwhile for them to keep from being fired.
6. **Checks on principals:** As a restraint against taking advantage of employees, an employer may agree to contractual commitments that make it in the employer's best interest to tell employees the truth.
7. **Contract choice:** By observing which type of contract an agent picks when offered a choice, a principal may obtain enough information to reduce moral hazards.

20.1   PRINCIPAL-AGENT PROBLEM

When you contract with people whose actions you cannot observe or evaluate, they may take advantage of you. If you pay someone by the hour to prepare your tax return, you do not know whether that person worked all the hours billed. If you retain a lawyer to represent you in a suit arising from an accident, you do not know whether the settlement the lawyer recommends is in your best interest or the lawyer's.

Of course, many people behave honorably even if they have opportunities to exploit others. Many people also honestly believe that they are putting in a full day's work even when they are not working as hard as they might. Aiko, who manages Pat's printing shop, is paid an hourly wage. She works every hour she is supposed to, even though Pat rarely checks on her. Nonetheless, Aiko may not be spending her time as effectively as possible. She politely (but impersonally) asks everyone who enters the shop, "May I help you?" If she were to receive the appropriate financial incentives—say, a share of the shop's profit—she would memorize the names of her customers, greet them enthusiastically by name when they enter the store, and check with nearby businesses to find out whether they would be interested in new services.

---

[2]Sometimes the principal's problem is not so much one of monitoring as one of legally verifying that opportunistic behavior occurred. For example, an insurance company (principal) might be able to determine that the homeowner (agent) engaged in arson but might have trouble proving it.

A Model

We can describe many principal-agent interactions using the following model. This model stresses that the output or profit from this relationship and the risk borne by the two parties depend on the actions of the agent and the state of nature.

In a typical principal-agent relationship, the principal, Paul, owns some property (such as a firm) or has a property right (such as the right to sue for damages from an injury). Paul hires or contracts with an agent, Amy, to take some action a that increases the value of his property or that produces profit, π, from using his property.

The principal and the agent need each other. If Paul hires Amy to run his ice-cream shop, Amy needs Paul's shop and Paul needs Amy's efforts to sell ice cream. The profit from the ice cream sold, π, depends on the number of hours, a, that Amy works. The profit may also depend on the outcome of a random variable, θ, that represents the *state of nature*:

$$\pi = \pi(a, \theta).$$

For example, profit may depend on whether the ice-cream machine breaks, $\theta = 1$, or does not break, $\theta = 0$. Or it may depend on whether it is a hot day, θ = the temperature.

In extreme cases, the profit function depends only on the agent's actions or only on the state of nature. At one extreme, profit depends only on the agent's action, $\pi = \pi(a)$, if there is only one state of nature: no uncertainty due to random events. In our example, the profit function has this form if demand does not vary with weather and if the ice-cream machine is reliable.

At the other extreme, profit depends only on the state of nature, $\pi = \pi(\theta)$, such as in an insurance market in which profit or value depends only on the state of nature and not on the actions of an agent. For instance, a couple buys insurance against rain on the day of their marriage. The value they place on their outdoor wedding ceremony is $\pi(\theta)$, which depends only on the weather, θ, because no actions are involved.

Types of Contracts

A verbal contract isn't worth the paper it's written on.   —Samuel Goldwyn

Where a formal market exists, the principal may deal impersonally with an anonymous agent by buying a good at the market price. In this chapter, we focus on situations for which either a formal market does not exist or a principal and an agent agree on a customized contract that is designed to reduce opportunism.

A contract between a principal and an agent determines how the outcome of their partnership (such as the profit or output) is split between them. Three common types of contracts are fixed-fee, hire, and contingent contracts.

In a *fixed-fee contract*, the payment to the agent, F, is independent of the agent's actions, a, the state of nature, θ, or the outcome, π. The principal keeps the *residual profit*, $\pi(a, \theta) - F$. Alternatively, the principal may get a fixed amount and the agent may receive the residual profit. For example, the agent may pay a fixed rent for the right to use the principal's property.[3]

---

[3]Jefferson Hope says in the Sherlock Holmes mystery *A Study in Scarlet*, "I applied at a cab-owner's office, and soon got employment. I was to bring a certain sum a week to the owner, and whatever was over that I might keep for myself."

In a *hire contract*, the payment to the agent depends on the agent's actions as they are observed by the principal. Two common types of hire contracts pay employees an *hourly rate*—a wage per hour—or a *piece rate*—a payment per unit of output produced. If w is the wage per hour (or the price per piece of output) and Amy works a hours (or produces a units of output), then Paul pays Amy wa and keeps the residual profit $\pi(a, \theta) - wa$.

In a *contingent contract*, the payoff to each person depends on the state of nature, which may not be known to the parties at the time they write the contract. For example, Penn agrees to pay Alexis a higher amount to fix his roof if it is raining than if it is not.

One type of contingent contract is a *splitting* or *sharing contract*, where the payoff to each person is a fraction of the total profit (which is observable). Alain sells Pamela's house for her for $\pi(a, \theta)$ for a commission of 7% on the sales price. He receives $0.07\pi(a, \theta)$, and she keeps $0.93\pi(a, \theta)$.

Efficiency

The type of contract selected depends on what the parties can observe. A principal is more likely to use a hire contract if the principal can easily monitor the agent's actions. A contingent contract may be chosen if the state of nature can be observed after the work is completed. A fixed-fee contract does not depend on observing anything, so it can always be used.

Ideally, the principal and agent agree to an **efficient contract**: an agreement with provisions that ensure that no party can be made better off without harming the other party. Using an efficient contract results in *efficiency in production* and *efficiency in risk sharing*.

Efficiency in production requires that the principal's and agent's combined value (profits, payoffs), π, is maximized. We say that production is efficient if Amy manages Paul's firm so that the sum of their profits cannot be increased. In our examples, the moral hazard hurts the principal by more than it helps the agent, so total profit falls. Thus achieving efficiency in production requires preventing the moral hazard.

Efficiency in risk bearing requires that risk sharing is optimal in that the person who least minds facing risk—the risk-neutral or less-risk-averse person—bears more of the risk. In Chapter 17, we saw that risk-averse people are willing to pay a risk premium to avoid risk, whereas risk-neutral people do not care if they face fair risk or not. Suppose that Arlene is risk averse and is willing to pay a risk premium of $100 to avoid a particular risk. Peter is risk neutral and would bear the risk without a premium. Arlene and Peter can strike a deal whereby Peter agrees to bear *all* of Arlene's risk in exchange for a payment between $0 and $100. For simplicity, we concentrate on situations in which one party is risk averse and the other is risk neutral. (Generally, if both parties are risk averse, with one more risk averse than the other, both can be made better off if the less-risk-averse person bears more but not all of the risk.)

If everyone has full information—there is no uncertainty and no asymmetric information—efficiency can be achieved. The principal contracts with the agent to perform a task for some specified reward and observes whether or not the agent completes the task properly before paying, so no moral hazard problem arises.

Throughout the rest of this chapter, we examine what happens when the parties do not have full information. Production inefficiency is more likely when either the agent has more information than the principal or both parties are uncertain about the state of nature.

When the agent has more information than the principal and there is no risk because there is only one state of nature, contracts are used to achieve efficiency in production by conveying adequate information to the principal to eliminate moral hazard problems. Alternatively, incentives in the contract may discourage the informed person from engaging in opportunistic behavior. The contracts do not have to address efficiency in risk bearing because there is no risk.

Given that they face both asymmetric information and risk, the parties try to contract to achieve efficiency in production and efficiency in risk bearing. Often, however, both objectives cannot be achieved, so the parties must trade off between them.

20.2 | PRODUCTION EFFICIENCY

The contract that an agent and principal use affects production efficiency. In the following example, production efficiency is achieved by maximizing *total* or *joint profit*: the sum of the principal's and the agent's individual profits. To isolate the production issues from risk bearing, we initially assume that there is only one state of nature, so the parties face no risk due to random events: Total profit, $\pi(a)$, is solely a function of the agent's action, a.

Efficient Contract

To be efficient and to maximize joint profit, the contract that a principal offers to an agent must have two properties. First, the contract must provide a large enough payoff that the agent is willing to *participate* in the contract. We know that the principal's payoff is adequate to ensure the principal's participation because the principal offers the contract.

Second, the contract must be **incentive compatible** in that it provides inducements such that the agent wants to perform the assigned task rather than engage in opportunistic behavior. That is, it is in the agent's best interest to take an action that maximizes joint profit. If the contract is not incentive compatible—so the agent tries to maximize personal profit rather than joint profit—efficiency can be achieved only if the principal monitors the agent and forces the agent to act so as to maximize joint profit.

We use an example to illustrate why some types of contracts lead to efficiency and others do not. Paula, the principal, owns a store called Buy-A-Duck (located near a canal) that sells wood carvings of ducks. Arthur, the agent, manages the store. Paula and Arthur's joint profit is

$$\pi(a) = R(a) - 12a,$$

where $R(a)$ is the sales revenue from selling a carvings, and $12a$ is the cost of the carvings. It costs Arthur $12 to obtain and sell each duck, including the amount he pays a local carver and the opportunity value (best alternative use) of his time.

Because Arthur bears the full marginal cost of selling one more carving, he wants to sell the joint-profit-maximizing output only if he also gets the full marginal benefit from selling one more duck. To determine the joint-profit-maximizing solution, we can ask what Arthur would do if he owned the shop and received all the profit so that he would have an incentive to maximize total profit.

How many ducks must Arthur sell to maximize the parties' joint profit? As panel a of Figure 20.1 shows, he would maximize profit by selling 12 carvings, for which his marginal revenue curve, *MR*, intersects his marginal cost curve, *MC* = $12, at the equilibrium point e.[4] Panel b shows that total profit, π, reaches a maximum of $72 at point *E*.

Which types of contracts lead to production efficiency? To answer this question, we first examine which contracts yield that outcome when both parties have full information and then consider which contracts bring the desired result when the principal is relatively uninformed. It is important to remember that we are considering a special case: Contracts that work here may not work in some other settings, whereas contracts that do not work here may be effective elsewhere.

Full Information

Suppose that both Paula and Arthur have full information. Each knows the actions Arthur takes—the number of carvings sold—and the effect of those actions on profit. Because she has full information, Paula can dictate exactly what Arthur is to do. Are there incentive-compatible contracts that do not require such monitoring and supervision? To answer this question, we consider four kinds of contracts: a fixed-fee rental contract, a hire contract, and two types of contingent contracts.

Fixed-Fee Rental Contract. If Arthur contracts to rent the store from Paula for a fixed fee, *F*, joint profit is maximized. Arthur earns a residual profit equal to the joint profit minus the fixed rent he pays Paula, $\pi(a) - F$. Because the amount Paula makes is fixed, Arthur gets the entire marginal profit from selling one more duck. As a consequence, the amount, *a*, that maximizes Arthur's profit, $\pi(a) - F$, also maximizes joint profit, $\pi(a)$.

In Figure 20.1, Arthur pays Paula *F* = $48 rent. This fixed payment does not affect his marginal cost. As a result, he maximizes his profit after paying the rent, $\pi - \$48$, by equating his marginal revenue to his marginal cost: *MR* = *MC* = 12 at point *e* in panel a.

Because Arthur pays the same fixed rent no matter how many units he sells, the agent's profit curve in panel b lies $48 below the joint-profit curve at every quantity. As a result, Arthur's net profit curve peaks (at point *E**) at the same quantity, 12, where the joint profit curve peaks (at *E*). Thus the fixed-fee rental contract is incentive compatible. Arthur participates in this contract because he earns $24 after paying for the rent and the carvings (point *E**).

Hire Contract. Now suppose that Paula contracts to pay Arthur for each carving he sells. If she pays him $12 per carving, Arthur just breaks even on each sale. He is indifferent between participating and not. Even if he chooses to participate, he does not sell the joint-profit-maximizing number of carvings unless Paula supervises him. If she does supervise him, she instructs him to sell 12 carvings, and she gets all the joint profit of $72.

---

[4]The demand curve is $p = 24 - \frac{1}{2}a$, where *p* is the price and *a* is the number of carved ducks sold. Revenue is $R = 24a - \frac{1}{2}a^2$, and marginal revenue is $MR = 24 - a$. Profit is maximized where $MR = 24 - a = 12 = MC$ or $a = 12$.

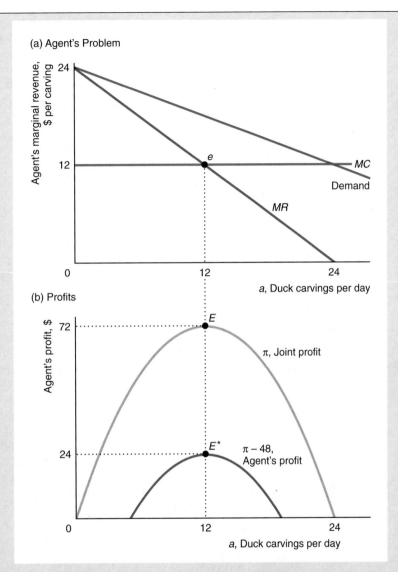

Figure 20.1 Maximizing Joint Profit When the Agent Gets the Residual Profit. (a) If the agent, Arthur, gets all the joint profit, π, he maximizes his profit by selling 12 carvings at *e*, where the marginal revenue curve intersects his marginal cost curve: *MR* = *MC* = 12. If he pays the principal, Paula, a fixed rent of $48, he maximizes his profit by selling 12 carvings. (A fixed rent does not affect either his marginal revenue or his marginal cost.) (b) Joint profit at 12 carvings is $72, point *E*. If Arthur pays a rent of $48 to Paula, Arthur's profit is π – $48. By selling 12 carvings and maximizing joint profit, Arthur also maximizes his profit.

For Arthur to want to participate and to sell carvings without supervision, he must receive more than $12 per carving. If Paula pays Arthur $14 per carving, for example, he makes a profit of $2 per carving. He now has an incentive to sell as many carvings as he can, which does not maximize joint profit, so this contract is not incentive compatible.

Even if the contract calls for Arthur to get $14 per carving and for Paula to control how many carvings he sells, joint profit is not maximized. Paula keeps the revenue minus what she pays Arthur, $14 times the number of carvings,

$$R(a) - 14a.$$

Thus her objective differs from the joint-profit-maximizing objective, $\pi = R(a) - 12a$. Joint profit is maximized when marginal revenue equals the marginal cost of $12. Because Paula's marginal cost, $14, is larger, she directs Arthur to sell fewer than the optimal number of carvings.[5]

Revenue-Sharing Contract. If Paula and Arthur use a *contingent contract* whereby they share the *revenue*, joint profit is not maximized. Suppose that Arthur receives three-quarters of the revenue, $\frac{3}{4}R$, and Paula gets the rest, $\frac{1}{4}R$. Panel a of Figure 20.2 shows the marginal revenue that Arthur obtains from selling an extra carving, $MR^* = \frac{3}{4}MR$. He maximizes his profit at $24 by selling 8 carvings, for which $MR^* = MC$ at e^*. Paula gets the remaining profit of $40, which is the difference between their total profit from selling 8 ducks per day, $\pi = \$64$, and Arthur's profit.

Thus their joint profit in panel b at $a = 8$ is $64, which is $8 less than the maximum possible profit of $72 (point E). Arthur has an incentive to sell fewer than the optimal number of ducks because he bears the full marginal cost of each carving he sells, $12, but gets only three-quarters of the marginal revenue.[6]

Profit-Sharing Contract. Paula and Arthur may instead use a *contingent contract* by which they divide the *economic profit*, π. If they can agree that the true marginal and average cost is $12 per carving (which includes Arthur's opportunity cost of time), the contract is incentive compatible because Arthur wants to sell the optimal number of carvings. Only by maximizing total profit can he maximize his share of profit. As Figure 20.3 illustrates, Arthur receives one-third of the joint profit and chooses to produce the level of output, $a = 12$, that maximizes joint profit.[7] Arthur earns $24, so he is willing to participate.

---

[5]Paula maximizes $R - 14a = (24a - \frac{1}{2}a^2) - 14a = 10a - \frac{1}{2}a^2$. Setting the derivative with respect to a equal to zero, $10 - a = 0$, we find that she maximizes her profit by selling 10 carvings. Joint profit is only $70 at 10 carvings, compared to $72 at the optimal 12 carvings.

[6]Even if Paula controls how many carvings are sold, joint profit is not maximized. Because the amount she makes, $\frac{1}{4}R$, depends only on revenue and not on the cost of obtaining the carvings, she wants the revenue-maximizing quantity sold. Revenue is maximized where marginal revenue is zero at $a = 24$ (panel a). Arthur would not participate if the contract granted him only three-quarters of the revenue but required him to sell 24 carvings because he would lose money.

[7]Arthur gets one-third of profit, $\frac{1}{3}\pi = \frac{1}{3}(R - C) = \frac{1}{3}R - \frac{1}{3}C$, where R is revenue and C is cost. He maximizes his profit where $\frac{1}{3}MR = \frac{1}{3}MC$. Although he gets only one-third of the marginal revenue, $\frac{1}{3}MR$, he bears only one-third of the marginal cost. Dividing both sides of the equation by $\frac{1}{3}$, we find that this condition is the same as the one for maximizing total profit: $MR = MC$.

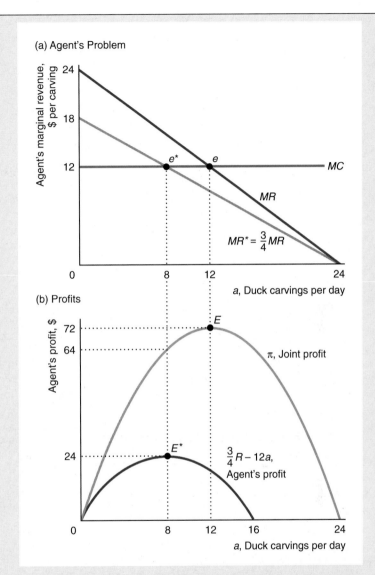

Figure 20.2 Why Revenue Sharing Reduces Agent's Efforts. (a) Joint profit is maximized at 12 carvings, where $MR = MC = 12$ at equilibrium point e. If Arthur gets three-quarters of the revenue and Paula gets the rest, Arthur maximizes his profit by selling 8 carvings, where his new marginal revenue curve $MR^* = \frac{3}{4}MR$ equals his marginal cost at point e^*. (b) Joint profit reaches a maximum of $72 at E, where they sell 12 carvings per day. If they split the revenue, Arthur sells 8 ducks per day and gets $24 at E^*, and Paula receives the residual, $40 (= $64 − $24).

The second column of Table 20.1 summarizes our analysis. Whether efficiency in production is achieved depends on the type of contract the principal and the agent

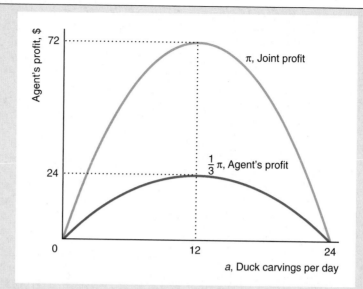

Figure 20.3 Why Profit Sharing Is Efficient. If the agent, Arthur, gets a third of the joint profit, he maximizes his profit, $\frac{1}{3}\pi$, by maximizing joint profit, π.

use. If the principal has full information (knows the agent's actions), the principal achieves production efficiency without having to supervise by using one of the incentive-compatible contracts: fixed-fee rental or profit-sharing.

Table 20.1 Production Efficiency and Moral Hazard Problems for Buy-A-Duck

	Full Information	Asymmetric Information	
Contract	Production Efficiency	Production Efficiency	Moral Hazard Problem
Fixed-fee rental contract			
Rent (to principal)	Yes	Yes	No
Hire contract, per unit pay			
Pay equals marginal cost	No[a]	No[b]	Yes
Pay is greater than marginal cost	No[c]	No	Yes
Contingent contract			
Share revenue	No	No[b]	Yes
Share profit	Yes	No[b]	Yes

[a]The agent may not participate and has no incentive to sell the optimal number of carvings. Efficiency can be achieved only if the principal supervises.
[b]Unless the agent steals all the revenue (or profit) from an extra sale, inefficiency results.
[c]The agent sells too many or the principal directs the agent to sell too few carvings.

Solved Problem 20.1

Zhihua and Pu are partners in a store in which they do all the work. They split the store's *business profit* equally (ignoring the opportunity cost of their own time in calculating this profit). Does their business-profit-sharing contract give them an incentive to maximize their joint economic profit if neither can force the other to work? (*Hint:* Imagine Zhihua's thought process if it's late Saturday night and Zhihua, who is alone in the store, is debating whether to keep the store open a little later or go out on the town.)

Answer *Show that each partner has an incentive to work too few hours.* A partner who works an extra hour bears the full opportunity cost of this extra hour but gets only half the marginal benefit from the extra business profit. The opportunity cost of extra time spent at the store is the partner's best alternative use of time. A partner could earn money working for someone else or use the time to have fun. Because a partner bears the full marginal cost but gets only half the marginal benefit (the extra business profit) from an extra hour of work, each partner works only up to the point at which the marginal cost equals half the marginal benefit. Thus each has an incentive to put in less effort than the level that maximizes their joint profit, where the marginal cost equals the marginal benefit.[8]

Asymmetric Information

Now suppose that the principal, Paula, has less information than the agent, Arthur. She cannot observe the number of carvings he sells or the revenue. Due to this asymmetric information, Arthur can steal from Paula without her detecting the theft.

As Table 20.1 shows, with asymmetric information, *the only contract that results in production efficiency and no moral hazard problem is the one whereby the principal gets a fixed rent.* All the other contracts result in inefficiency, and Arthur has an opportunity to take advantage of Paula.

Fixed-Fee Rental Contract. Arthur pays Paula the fixed rent that she is due because Paula would know if she were paid less. Arthur receives the residual profit, joint profit minus the fixed rent, so he wants to sell the joint-profit-maximizing number of carvings.

---

[8]When I was in graduate school, I shared an apartment with a fellow who was madly in love with a woman who lived in another city. They agreed to split the costs of their long-distance phone calls equally, regardless of who placed the call. This agreement led to very long conversations. Whichever of them was enjoying the call more apparently figured that he or she would get the full marginal benefit of one more minute of talking while having to pay only half the marginal cost. What I learned from this experience was not to open our phone bill so as to avoid being shocked by its size.

Hire Contract. If Paula offers to pay Arthur the actual marginal cost of $12 per carving and he is honest, he may refuse to participate in the contract because he makes no profit. Even if he participates, he has no incentive to sell the optimal number of carvings.

If he is dishonest, he may underreport sales and pocket some of the extra revenue. Unless he can steal all the extra revenue from an additional sale, he sells less than the joint-profit-maximizing quantity.

If Paula pays him more than the actual marginal cost per carving, he has an incentive to sell too many carvings, whether or not he steals. If he also steals, he has an even greater incentive to sell too many carvings.

Revenue-Sharing Contract. Even with full information, the revenue-sharing contract is inefficient. Asymmetric information adds a moral hazard problem: The agent may steal from the principal. If Arthur can steal a larger share of the revenues than the contract specifies, he has less of an incentive to underproduce than he does with full information. Indeed, if the agent can steal all the extra revenue from an additional sale, the agent acts efficiently to maximize joint profit, all of which the agent keeps.

Profit-Sharing Contract. If they use a contingent contract by which they agree to split the economic profit, Arthur has to report both the revenue and the cost to Paula so that they may calculate their shares. If he can overreport cost or underreport revenue, he has an incentive to produce a nonoptimal quantity. Only if Arthur can appropriate all the profit does he produce efficiently.

Application   **CONTRACTS AND PRODUCTIVITY IN AGRICULTURE**

In agriculture, landowners (principals) contract with farmers (agents) to work their land. Farmers may work on their own land (the principal and agent are the same person), work on land rented from a landowner (fixed-fee rental contract), work as employees for a time rate or a piece rate (hire contract), or sharecrop (contingent contract). A sharecropper splits the output (crop) with the landowner at the end of the growing season.[9]

Our analysis tells us that farmers' willingness to work hard depends on the type of contract that is used. Farmers who keep all the marginal profit from additional work—those who own the land or rent it for a fixed fee—work hard and maximize (joint) profit. Sharecroppers, who bear the full marginal cost of working an extra hour and get only a fraction of the extra revenue, put in too little effort. Hired farmworkers who are paid by the hour may not work hard unless they are very carefully supervised. That is, they may engage in **shirking**: a moral hazard in which agents do not provide all the services they are paid to provide.

---

[9]If a farmer is someone who is out standing in his field, a sharecropper is someone who is out standing in someone else's field.

These predictions about contract type and agent effort were tested by using data on farmers in the Philippines. Foster and Rosenzweig (1994) could not directly monitor the work effort—any more than most landowners can. Rather, they ingeniously measured the effort indirectly. They contended that the harder people work, the more they eat and the more they use up body mass (defined as weight divided by height squared), holding calorie intake constant.

Foster and Rosenzweig estimated the effect of each compensation method on body mass and consumption (after adjusting for gender, age, type of activity, and other factors). They found that people who work for themselves or are paid by the piece use up 10% more body mass, holding calorie consumption constant, than time-rate workers and 13% more than sharecroppers. Foster and Rosenzweig also discovered that piece-rate workers consume 25% more calories per day and that people who work on their own farm consume 16% more than time-rate workers.

20.3 | TRADE-OFF BETWEEN EFFICIENCY IN PRODUCTION AND IN RISK BEARING

Writing an efficient contract is extremely difficult if the agent knows more than the principal, the principal never learns the truth, and both face risk. Usually, a contract does not achieve efficiency in production *and* in risk bearing. Contract clauses that increase efficiency in production may reduce efficiency in risk bearing, and vice versa. If these goals are incompatible, the parties may write imperfect contracts that reach a compromise between the two objectives. To illustrate the trade-offs involved, we consider a common situation in which it is difficult to achieve efficiency: contracting with an expert such as a lawyer.

We illustrate how contracts affect the outcome by using an example in which Pam, the principal, is injured in a traffic accident and is a plaintiff in a lawsuit, and Alfredo, the agent, is her lawyer. Pam faces uncertainty due to risk and to asymmetric information. The jury award at the conclusion of the trial, $\pi(a, \theta)$, depends on a, the number of hours Alfredo works before the trial, and θ, the state of nature due to the (unknown) attitudes of the jury. All else the same, the more time Alfredo spends working on the case, a, the larger the amount, π, that the jury is likely to award. Pam never learns the jury's attitudes, θ, so she cannot accurately judge

Alfredo's efforts even after the trial. For example, if she loses the case, she doesn't know whether she lost because Alfredo didn't work hard (low a) or because the case was weak and the jury was prejudiced against her (bad θ).

Contracts and Efficiency

How hard Alfredo works depends on his attitudes toward risk and his knowledge of the payoff for his trial preparations. For any hour that he does not devote to Pam's case, Alfredo can work on other cases. The most lucrative of these forgone opportunities is his marginal cost of working on Pam's case.

The beneficiary of the extra payoff that results if Alfredo works harder depends on his contract with Pam. If Alfredo is risk neutral and gets the entire marginal benefit from any extra work, he puts in the optimal number of hours that maximizes their expected joint payoff. Alfredo collects the marginal benefit from the extra work and bears the marginal cost, so he sets his expected marginal benefit equal to his marginal cost, thus maximizing the expected joint payoff.

The choice of various possible contracts between Pam and Alfredo affects whether efficiency in production or in risk bearing is achieved. They choose among fixed-fee, hire (hourly wage), and contingent contracts. Table 20.2 summarizes the outcomes under each of these contracts.

Lawyer Gets a Fixed Fee. If Pam pays Alfredo a fixed fee, F, he gets paid the same no matter how much he works. Thus he has little incentive to work hard on this case, and production is inefficient.[10] Production efficiency could be achieved only if Pam could monitor Alfredo and force him to act optimally. Most individual plaintiffs, however, cannot monitor a lawyer and thus cannot determine whether the lawyer is behaving appropriately or not.

Whether the fixed-fee contract leads to efficiency in risk bearing depends on the attitudes toward risk on the part of the principal and the agent. Pam, the principal, bears all the risk. Alfredo's pay, F, is certain, while Pam's net payoff, $\pi(a, \theta) - F$, varies with the unknown state of nature, θ.

Table 20.2 Efficiency of Client-Lawyer Contracts

Type of Contract	Fixed Fee to Lawyer	Fixed Payment to Client	Lawyer Paid by the Hour	Contingent Contract
Lawyer's payoff	F	$\pi(a, \theta) - F$	wa	$\alpha\pi(a, \theta)$
Client's payoff	$\pi(a, \theta) - F$	F	$\pi(a, \theta) - wa$	$(1 - \alpha)\pi(a, \theta)$
Production efficiency	No*	Yes	No*	No*
Who bears risk	Client	Lawyer	Client	Shared

*Production efficiency is possible if the client can monitor and enforce optimal effort by the lawyer.

[10]His main incentive to work hard is to establish a reputation as a good lawyer so as to attract future clients. For simplicity, we will ignore this effect, as it applies for all types of contracts.

A lawyer who handles many similar cases may be less risk averse than an individual client whose financial future depends on a single case. If Alfredo has many cases like Pam's and if Pam's future rests on the outcome of this suit, their choice of this type of contract leads to inefficiency in both production and risk bearing. Not only is Alfredo not working hard enough, but Pam bears the risk even though she is more risk averse than Alfredo.

In contrast suppose that Alfredo is a self-employed lawyer working on a major case for Pam, who runs a large insurance company with many similar cases. Alfredo is risk averse and Pam is risk neutral (because she is able to pool many similar cases). Here having the principal bear all the risk is efficient. If the insurance company can monitor Alfredo's behavior, it is even possible to achieve production efficiency. Indeed, many insurance companies employ lawyers in this manner.

Plaintiff Gets a Fixed Payment. Instead, the two parties could agree to a contract by which Alfredo could pay Pam a fixed amount of money, F, for the right to try the case and collect the entire verdict less the payment to Pam, $\pi(a, \theta) - F$. With such a contract, Alfredo has an incentive to put in the optimal number of hours. He works until his marginal cost—the opportunity cost of his time—equals the marginal benefit—the extra amount he gets if he wins at trial. Because he has already paid Pam, all extra amounts earned at trial go to Alfredo.

Under this contract, Alfredo bears all the risk related to the outcome of the trial. No matter how risk averse Pam is, she may hesitate to agree to such a contract. Because she is not an expert on the law, she cannot easily predict the jury's likely verdict. Thus she does not know how large a fixed fee she should insist on receiving. There is no practical way in which Alfredo's superior information about the likely outcome of the trial can be credibly revealed to her. She suspects that it is in his best interest to tell her that the likely payout is lower than he truly believes.[11]

Lawyer Is Hired by the Hour. In complicated cases, a lawyer's output is not easily measured, so it is not practical to pay the attorney by the piece. Pam could pay Alfredo a wage of w per hour for the a hours that he works. Doing so would create the potential for a serious moral hazard problem unless Pam could monitor Alfredo to determine how many hours he works. If she could not, Alfredo could bill her for more hours than he actually worked.[12] Even if Pam could observe how many hours he works, she would not know whether Alfredo worked effectively and whether the

---

[11]Alfredo may be hesitant to offer Pam a fixed fee. How well they do in court depends on the merits of her case. At least initially, Alfredo does not know how good a case she has. Initially, she has an incentive to try to convince him that the case is very strong. Moreover, a lawyer may worry that if he pays the plaintiff a fixed fee, she will not fully cooperate in preparing the case (an issue that we've ignored in our example, in which only the actions of the lawyer matter).

[12]A lawyer dies in an accident and goes to heaven. A host of angels greet him with a banner that reads, "Welcome Oldest Man!" The lawyer is puzzled: "Why do you think I'm the oldest man who ever lived? I was only 47 when I died." One of the angels replied, "You can't fool us; you were at least 152 when you died. We saw how many hours you billed!"

work was necessary. Thus it would be difficult, if not impossible, for Pam to monitor Alfredo's work.

Here Pam bears all the risk. Alfredo's earnings, wa, are determined before the outcome is known. Pam's return, $\pi(a, \theta) - wa$, varies with the state of nature and is unknown before the verdict.

Fee Is Contingent. Some lawyers offer plaintiffs a contract whereby the lawyer works for "free"—receiving no hourly payment—in exchange for splitting the compensation awarded in court or in a settlement before trial. The lawyer receives a **contingent fee**: a payment to a lawyer that is a share of the award in a court case (usually after legal expenses are deducted) if the client wins and nothing if the client loses. If the lawyer's share of the award is α and the jury awards $\pi(a, \theta)$, the lawyer receives $\alpha\pi(a, \theta)$ and the principal gets $(1 - \alpha)\pi(a, \theta)$. This approach is attractive to many plaintiffs because they cannot monitor how hard the lawyer works and are unable or unwilling to make payments before the trial is completed.

How they split the award affects the amount of risk each bears. If Alfredo gets one-quarter of the award, $\alpha = \frac{1}{4}$, and Pam gets three-quarters, Pam bears more risk than Alfredo does. Suppose that the award is either 0 or 40 with equal probability. Alfredo receives either 0 or 10, so his average award is 5. His variance (Chapter 17) is

$$\sigma_a^2 = \tfrac{1}{2}(0 - 5)^2 + \tfrac{1}{2}(10 - 5)^2 = 25.$$

Pam makes either 0 or 30, so her average award is 15 and her variance is

$$\sigma_p^2 = \tfrac{1}{2}(0 - 15)^2 + \tfrac{1}{2}(30 - 15)^2 = 225.$$

Thus the variance in Pam's payoff is greater than Alfredo's.

Whether splitting the risk in this way is desirable turns on how risk averse each party is. If one is risk neutral and the other is risk averse, it is efficient for the risk-neutral person to bear all the risk. If they are equally risk averse, a splitting rule where $\alpha = \frac{1}{2}$ and they face equal risk may be optimal.[13]

A sharing contract encourages shirking: Alfredo is likely to put in too little effort. He bears the full cost of his labors—the forgone use of his time—but gets only α share of the returns from this effort. Thus this contract results in production inefficiency and may or may not lead to inefficient risk bearing.

Choosing the Best Contract

Which contract is best depends on the parties' attitudes toward risk, the degree of risk, the difficulty in monitoring, and other factors. If Alfredo is risk neutral, they can achieve both efficiency goals if Alfredo gives Pam a fixed fee. He has the incentive to put in the optimal amount of work and does not mind bearing the risk.

However, if Alfredo is risk averse and Pam is risk neutral, they may not be able to achieve both objectives. Contracts by which Alfredo receives a fixed fee or a wage rate cause Pam to bear all the risk and lead to inefficiency in production because Alfredo has too little incentive to work hard.

---

[13]If Pam and Alfredo split the award equally and each receives either 0 or 20, each has a variance of $\tfrac{1}{2}(0 - 10)^2 + \tfrac{1}{2}(20 - 10)^2 = 100$.

Often when the parties find that they cannot achieve both objectives, they choose a contract that attains neither goal. For example, they may use a contingent contract that fails to achieve efficiency in production and may not achieve efficiency in risk bearing. The contingent contract strikes a compromise between the two goals. Alfredo has more of an incentive to work if he splits the payoff than he has if he receives a fixed fee. He is less likely to work excessive hours with the contingent fee than he would work if he were paid by the hour. Moreover, neither party has to bear all the risk—they share it under the contingent contract.

Lawyers usually work for a fixed fee only if the task or case is very simple, such as writing a will or handling an uncontested divorce. The client has some idea of whether the work is done satisfactorily, so monitoring is relatively easy and little risk is involved.

In riskier situations, the other types of contracts are more commonly used. When the lawyer is relatively risk averse or when the principal is very concerned that the lawyer works hard, an hourly wage may be used.

Contingent fee arrangements are particularly common for plaintiffs' lawyers who specialize in auto accidents, medical malpractice, product liability, and other *torts*: wrongful acts in which a person's body, property, or reputation is harmed and for which the injured party is entitled to compensation. Because these plaintiffs' lawyers can typically pool risks across clients, they are less concerned than their clients about risk. As a consequence, these attorneys are willing to accept contingent fees (and might agree to pay a fixed fee to the plaintiff). Moreover, accident victims often lack the resources to pay for a lawyer's time before winning at trial, so they often prefer contingent contracts.

Application　LAWYERS' CONTINGENT FEES

Plaintiffs' lawyers receive contingent fees in most tort cases involving personal injury and medical malpractice in the United States. Kakalik and Pace (1986) report that most tort plaintiffs pay lawyers a contingent fee by which the lawyer gets a percentage of the compensation, usually after other legal expenses are deducted. Only 2% of individual plaintiffs in state courts and 6% in federal courts pay on an hourly basis, and only 1% pay on another basis such as a fixed fee. Most plaintiffs that are organizations also use contingent fees, but 12% of them in state courts and 15% in federal courts pay their lawyers by the hour. Lawyers' contingent fees usually range from 20% to 50%. Rates of 33% and 40% are particularly common.

Some jurisdictions restrict these fees. California limits medical malpractice contingent fees to 40% of the first $50,000 of compensation, one-third of the next $50,000, 25% of the next $100,000, and 10% of anything over $200,000. All provinces of Canada except Ontario permit contingent fees; most European countries ban them. In England and Wales, American-style contingent-fee contracts between lawyers and clients are unenforceable against the client. However, the Courts and Legal Services Act of 1990 permits contingent contracts whereby the lawyer receives no payment if the case is lost but is entitled to normal costs plus a percentage markup with a win.

Solved Problem 20.2

Gary's demand for medical services (visits to his doctor) depends on his health. Half the time his health is good and his demand is D^1 on the graph. When his health is less good, his demand is D^2. Without medical insurance, he pays $50 a visit. Because Gary is risk averse, he wants to buy medical insurance. With full insurance,

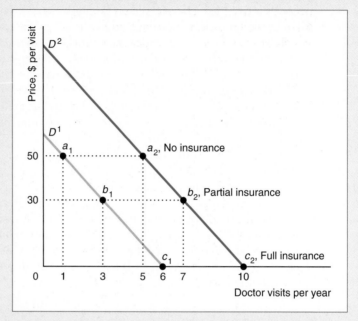

Gary pays a fixed fee at the beginning of the year, and the insurance company pays the full cost of any visit. Alternatively, with a contingent contract, Gary pays a smaller premium at the beginning of the year, and the insurance company covers only $20 per visit and Gary pays the remaining $30. How likely is a moral hazard problem to occur with each of these contracts? What is Gary's risk (variance of his medical costs) with each type of insurance? Compare the contracts in terms of the trade-offs between risk and moral hazards.

Answer

1. *Describe the moral hazard for each demand curve for each contract*: If Gary's health is good, he increases from 1 visit, a_1, with no insurance (where he pays $50 a visit) to 6 visits, c_1, with full insurance (where he pays nothing per visit). Similarly, if his health is poor, he increases his visits from 5, a_2, to 10, c_2. Thus regardless of his health, he makes five extra visits a year with full insurance. These extra visits are the moral hazard. With a contingent contract whereby Gary pays $30 a visit, the moral hazard is less because he makes only two extra visits instead of five (the difference between the number of visits at b_1 and a_1 and between b_2 and a_2).

2. *Calculate the variance of Gary's medical expenses with each level of insurance*: Without insurance, his average number of visits is 3 [= $(\frac{1}{2} \times 1) + (\frac{1}{2} \times 5)$],

so his average annual medical cost is \$150. Thus the variance of his medical expenses without insurance is

$$\sigma_n^2 = \tfrac{1}{2}[(1 \times \$50) - \$150]^2 + \tfrac{1}{2}[(5 \times 50) - \$150]^2$$
$$= \tfrac{1}{2}(\$50 - \$150)^2 + \tfrac{1}{2}(\$250 - \$150)^2$$
$$= \$10,000.$$

If he has full insurance, he makes a single fixed payment each year, so his payments do not vary with his health: His variance is $\sigma_f^2 = 0$. Finally, with partial insurance, he averages 5 visits with an average cost of \$150, and his variance is

$$\sigma_p^2 = \tfrac{1}{2}(\$90 - \$150)^2 + \tfrac{1}{2}(\$210 - \$150)^2 = \$3,600.$$

Thus $\sigma_n^2 > \sigma_p^2 > \sigma_f^2$.

3. *Discuss the trade-offs*: Because Gary is risk averse, efficiency in risk bearing requires that the insurance company bear all the risk, as with full insurance. Full insurance, however, results in the largest moral hazard. Without insurance, there is no moral hazard but Gary bears all the risk. The contingent contract is a compromise whereby both the moral hazard and the degree of risk lie between the extremes.

20.4 PAYMENTS LINKED TO PRODUCTION OR PROFIT

We now examine how additional clauses are added to a contract to eliminate or reduce moral hazards. For simplicity, we ignore risk bearing. We focus on employer-employee contracts. Under most such contracts, employees are paid by the hour or given a fixed salary. The problem with such agreements is that the workers are not directly rewarded for productive, profit-enhancing actions, so they tend to shirk. Here rewarding agents for productive activities leads to greater efficiency.

There are two main ways to reward productive effort directly. One method is to link pay to a worker's individual output. Another is to link a worker's pay to the firm's output or profitability. However, employers who cannot monitor workers do not use incentive-compatible contracts.

Piece-Rate Hire Contracts

One direct approach to getting employees to work hard is to pay them by the *piece*—the output they produce—rather than by *time*—the number of hours they work. Piece rates are usually effective in increasing output, but they are not practical in all markets.

Greater Effort. Piece rates—by explicitly rewarding productivity—provide a greater incentive to employees to work hard than hourly wages do. For example, Billikopf (1995) found that employees who are paid by the piece prune a vineyard in only 19 hours of work per acre compared to 26 hours for employees paid by the hour.

The increase in joint profit due to this greater productivity may be shared between the firm and the employees. As the following application illustrates, many workers, because they earn more with piece rates than they would earn with hourly pay, are pleased to be paid by the piece.

Application   **PLEASED TO BE PAID BY THE PIECE**

Mike Darrah sweeps up shards of broken glass from Safelite Glass's repair shop floor, lifts heavy replacement windshields onto car frames and wrestles them into position, and then carefully seals the rims. He hardly pauses between tasks. He doesn't want to. He is an enthusiastic participant in Safelite's performance pay plan, which pays him in proportion to how much he accomplishes.

When Mr. Darrah started as a glass installer in 1994, he earned $7.50 an hour and could expect wage increases up to about $12 when he mastered the craft. In 1996, under the incentive system, he averaged $20 an hour. "I'd rather skip the coffee and get paid," he said. His annual take-home pay had roughly doubled without his working much overtime.

Safelite pays workers by the piece, with a guaranteed wage floor. In a typical month, two-thirds of the workers earn more than this guaranteed minimum, and in the long run, almost all do. Workers average 15% above the guaranteed minimum. That workers like this new program is shown by the drop in the absenteeism rate by 61%, which benefits Safelite, a firm that depends on timely, high-quality service.

According to Edward Lazear, a Stanford Business School economist who studied this transition to piecework from traditional wage-and-benefits compensation, the hourly output of glass installers rose 41% over the 18 months during the phase-in period for this program. The company received about half this gain in higher profits. The 41% increase is divided into two parts. Slightly more than half is due to increased productivity on the part of existing workers; the rest is due to the departure of less motivated workers, who were quickly replaced by eager beavers.

The workers who stayed, like Mr. Darrah, are pleased with their increased earnings. Likewise, Safelite relishes its higher profits, which stem from greater output per worker, lower turnover, and higher quality. Turnover in this industry can be 50% to 60% annually, but Safelite benefited from a disproportionate number of good workers staying.

By forcing employees to pay for making repairs for flawed installations, Safelite ensures that quality does not fall as employees rush to produce output. After jobs are completed, the company surveys 1 out of every 10 customers by phone, and each installer gets a monthly performance report. Before this performance pay system was instituted, the percentage of customers who were "very satisfied" was in the mid-80s; now this percentage is in the mid-90s.

Problems with Piece Rates. Piece rates are not always practical. There are three chief difficulties with this system: measuring output, eliciting the desired behavior, and persuading workers to accept piece rates.

Paying piece rates is practical only if the employer can easily measure the output produced, such as the number of pieces of fruit picked or windshields installed. Employers do not use piece rates to compensate teachers, managers, and others whose output is difficult to measure. Thus piece rates are more common for blue-collar jobs than for white-collar jobs. Roughly 15% of the labor force receives pay based on individual productivity, but most piecework is concentrated in a handful of low-paying industries such as agriculture (in which about a third of workers are paid by the piece) and apparel manufacturing or is confined to sales personnel, individual contractors, and other similar occupations.

Piece rates backfire if they encourage undesirable behavior. Sears, Roebuck & Company used to reward auto shop employees on the basis of the size of customers' repair bills. This system apparently led to overbilling of customers, which resulted in government actions and lawsuits.[14]

Some workers object to piece rates because they do not like to work hard or because they are concerned that firms will ratchet down workers' compensation after a while by lowering the pay per piece. In addition, piecework has a negative connotation in many people's minds because of its association with sweatshops, where workers toiled at repetitive tasks for 12 or more hours a day.

Contingent Contract Rewards Linked to a Firm's Success

Although companies can use piece rates with workers who produce easily measured output, they need alternative incentive schemes for managers, corporate directors, and others whose productivity is difficult to quantify, especially those who work as part of a team. Such workers may be rewarded if their team or the firm does well in general. Frequently, year-end bonuses are based on increases in the firm's profit or the value of its stock.

A common type of incentive is a lump-sum year-end bonus based on the firm's performance or that of a group of workers within the firm. Another incentive is a stock option, which gives managers (and increasingly other workers) the option of buying a certain number of shares of stock in the firm at a prespecified *exercise price*. If the stock's market price exceeds the exercise price during that period, an employee can exercise the option—buy the stock—and then sell it at the market price, in this way making an immediate profit. But if the stock's price stays below the exercise price, the option is worthless. Beyond motivating employees to work hard, these incentives also act as *golden handcuffs*: a deterrent to taking a job at a competing firm and forfeiting the stock option.

Application   **INCREASING USE OF INCENTIVES**

More and more employment contracts contain individual and group incentives. A 1998 survey of more than 1,000 employers found that 72% had at least one incentive plan in 1998, up from 61% in 1996. The percentage of

---

[14]Buchholz, Barbara B., "The Bonus Isn't Reserved for Big Shots Anymore," *New York Times*, October 27, 1996.

Fortune 1000 companies that offered bonus pay plans for hourly employees rose from 26% in 1993 to 37% in 1997. Hourly employees' bonuses are typically 3% to 8% of their base salary, middle managers receive 10% to 17%, and many executives receive 100% or more. Other countries also use incentives (see **www.awlonline.com/perloff**, "Australian Compensation").

Share option grants accounted for a record 53.3% of the compensation given by the top 100 U.S. companies in 1998, compared to 26% in 1994 and 2% in the mid-1980s. In 1998, the typical boss of one of the United States' top 200 firms made a pretax profit of $8.3 million by exercising executive share options and had total unrealized profits on stock options of nearly $50 million.

The rest of the world is starting to use American-style executive remuneration. A 1998 study at more than 2,000 leading companies around the world found that roughly two-thirds of these CEOs' earnings were due to share options and other incentives and bonuses in the United States, compared to a little over 40% in the United Kingdom, 30% in Canada, and slightly less than 20% in France.

Apparently, firms benefit substantially from offering such bonuses. In one study of 70 companies, directors of firms rated in the top 25% in performance had $257,000 each in stock, while the directors of the worst 25% held just $49,000.

20.5   MONITORING

When using piece rates and rewarding workers for the success of the firm rather than individual output are not feasible, employers usually pay fixed-fee salaries or hourly wages. Employees who are paid a fixed salary have little incentive to work hard if the employer cannot observe shirking. If an employer pays employees by the hour but cannot observe how many hours they work, employees may inflate the number of hours they report working.

A firm can reduce such shirking by intensively supervising or monitoring its workers. Monitoring eliminates the asymmetric information problem: Both the employee and the employer know how hard the employee works. If the cost of monitoring workers is low enough, it pays to prevent shirking by carefully monitoring and firing employees who do not work hard.

Firms have experimented with various means of lowering the cost of monitoring. Requiring employees to punch a time clock and installing videocameras to record the work effort are examples of firms' attempts to use capital to monitor job performance.[15] Similarly, by installing assembly lines that force employees to work at a pace dictated by the firm, employers can control employees' work rate.

According to a recent survey by the American Management Association, nearly two-thirds of employers record employees' voice mail, e-mail, or phone calls;

---

[15]Jackson, Maggie, "Most Firms Spy on Employees, Survey Finds," *San Francisco Chronicle*, May 23,1997:B1.

review computer files; or videotape workers. A quarter of the firms that use surveillance don't tell their employees. The most common types of surveillance are tallying phone numbers called and recording the duration of the calls (37%), videotaping employees' work (16%), storing and reviewing e-mail (15%), storing and reviewing computer files (14%), and taping and reviewing phone conversations (10%). Monitoring and surveillance are most common in the financial sector, in which 81% of firms use these techniques. Rather than watching all employees all the time, companies usually monitor selected workers using spot checks.

For some jobs, however, monitoring is counterproductive or not cost effective. Monitoring may lower employees' morale, in turn reducing productivity. Several years ago, Northwest Airlines took the doors off bathroom stalls to prevent workers from slacking off there.[16] When new management eliminated this policy (and made many other changes as well), productivity increased.

It is usually impractical for firms to monitor how hard salespeople work if they spend most of their time away from the main office. As telecommuting increases, monitoring workers may become increasingly difficult.

When direct monitoring is very costly, firms may use various financial incentives, which we now consider, to reduce the amount of monitoring that is necessary. Each of these incentives—bonding, deferred payments, and efficiency (unusually high) wages—acts as a *hostage* for good behavior (Williamson, 1983). Workers who are caught shirking or engaging in other undesirable acts not only lose their jobs but give up the hostage too. The more valuable the hostage, the less monitoring the firm needs to use to deter bad behavior.

Bonding

A direct approach to ensuring good behavior by agents is to require that they deposit funds guaranteeing their good behavior, just as a landlord requires tenants to post security deposits to ensure that they will not damage an apartment. An employer may require an employee to provide a performance *bond*, an amount of money that will be given to the principal if the agent fails to complete certain duties or achieve certain goals. Typically, the agent *posts* (leaves) this bond with the principal or another party, such as an insurance company, before starting the job.

Many couriers who transport valuable shipments (such as jewels) or guards who watch over them have to post bonds against theft and other moral hazards. Similarly, bonds may be used to keep employees from quitting immediately after receiving costly training (Salop and Salop, 1976). Academics who take a sabbatical—a leave of absence that is supposed to be devoted to training or other activities that increase their future productivity—must typically sign an agreement to pay the college or university a certain sum if they quit within a year after returning from their sabbatical. Most of the other approaches we will examine as strategies for controlling shirking can be viewed as forms of bonding.

Bonding to Prevent Shirking. Some employers require a worker to post a bond that is forfeited if the employee is discovered shirking. For example, a professional athlete

---

[16]Garcia, Kenneth J., "Multimillionaire's Run for His Money," *San Francisco Chronicle*, April 17, 1997:A1, A4.

faces a specified fine (the equivalent of a bond) for skipping a meeting or game. The higher the bond, the less frequently the employer needs to monitor to prevent shirking.

Suppose that the value that a worker puts on the gain from taking it easy on the job is G dollars. If a worker's only potential punishment for shirking is dismissal if caught, some workers will shirk.

Suppose, however, that the worker must post a bond of B dollars that the worker forfeits if caught not working. Given the firm's level of monitoring, the probability that a worker is caught is θ. Thus a worker who shirks expects to lose θB.[17] A risk-neutral worker chooses not to shirk if the certain gain from shirking, G, is less than or equal to the expected penalty, θB, from forfeiting the bond if caught: $G \leq \theta B$. Thus the minimum bond that discourages stealing is

$$B = \frac{G}{\theta}. \tag{20.1}$$

Equation 20.1 shows that the bond must be larger, the higher the value that the employee places on shirking and the lower the probability that the worker is caught.

Trade-Off Between Bonds and Monitoring. Thus the larger the bond, the less monitoring is necessary to prevent shirking. Suppose that a worker places a value of $G =$ $1,000 a year on shirking. A bond that is large enough to discourage shirking is $1,000 if the probability of being caught is 100%, $2,000 at 50%, $5,000 at 20%, $10,000 at 10%, and $20,000 if the probability of being caught is only 5%.

Solved Problem 20.3
Workers post bonds of B that are forfeited if they are caught stealing (but no other punishment is imposed). Each extra unit of monitoring, M, raises the probability that a firm catches a worker who steals, θ, by 5%. A unit of M costs $10. A worker can steal a piece of equipment and resell it for its full value of G dollars. What is the optimal M that the firm uses if it believes that workers are risk neutral? In particular, if $B =$ $5,000 and $G =$ $500, what is the optimal M?

Answer

1. *Determine how many units of monitoring are necessary to deter stealing*: The least amount of monitoring that deters stealing is the amount at which a worker's gain from stealing equals the worker's expected loss if caught. A worker is just deterred from stealing when the gain, G, equals the expected penalty, θB. Thus the worker is deterred when the probability of being caught is $\theta = G/B$. The number of units of monitoring effort is $M = \theta/0.05$, because each extra unit of monitoring raises θ by 5%.

2. *Determine whether monitoring is cost effective*: It pays for the firm to pay for M units of monitoring only if the expected benefit to the firm is greater

---

[17]The expected penalty is $\theta B + (1 - \theta)0 = \theta B$, where the first term on the left-hand side is the probability of being caught times the fine of B and the second term is the probability of not being caught and facing no fine.

than the cost of monitoring, $10 \times M$. The expected benefit if stealing is prevented is G, so monitoring pays if $G > \$10 \times M$, or $G/M > \$10$.

3. *Solve for the optimal monitoring in the special case*: The optimal level of monitoring is

$$M = \frac{\theta}{0.05} = \frac{G/B}{0.05} = \frac{500/5,000}{0.05} = \frac{0.1}{0.05} = 2.$$

It pays to engage in this level of monitoring because $G/M = \$500/2 = \$250 > \$10$.

Problems with Bonding. Employers like the bond-posting solution because it reduces the amount of employee monitoring necessary to discourage moral hazards such as shirking and thievery. Nonetheless, firms use explicit bonding only occasionally to prevent stealing, and they rarely use it to prevent shirking.

Two major problems are inherent in posting bonds. First, to capture a bond, an unscrupulous employer might falsely accuse an employee of stealing. An employee who fears such employer opportunism might be unwilling to post a bond. One possible solution to this problem is for the firm to develop a reputation for not behaving in this manner. Another possible approach is for the firm to make the grounds for forfeiture of the bond objective and thus verifiable by others.

A second problem with bonds is that workers may not have enough wealth to post them. In our example, if the worker could steal $10,000, and if the probability of being caught were only 5%, shirking would be deterred only if a risk-neutral worker were required to post a bond of at least $200,000.

Principals and agents use bonds when these two problems are avoidable. Bonds are more common in contracts between firms than in those between an employer and employees. Moreover, firms have fewer problems than typical employees do in raising funds to post bonds.

Construction contractors sometimes post bonds to guarantee that they will satisfactorily finish their work by a given date. It is easy to verify whether the contract has been completed on time, so there is relatively little chance of opportunistic behavior by the principal.

Deferred Payments

Effectively, firms can post bonds for their employees through the use of deferred payments. For example, a firm pays new workers a low wage for some initial period of employment. Then, over time, workers who are caught shirking are fired, and those who remain get higher wages. In another form of deferred wages, the firm provides a pension that rewards only hard workers who stay with the firm until retirement. *Deferred payments serve the same function as bonds*. They raise the cost of being fired, so less monitoring is necessary to deter shirking.

Workers care about the present value (see Chapter 16) of their earnings stream over their lifetime. A firm may offer its workers one of two wage payment schemes. In the first, the firm pays w per year for each year that the worker is employed by the firm. In the second arrangement, the starting wage is less than w but rises over the years to a wage that exceeds w.

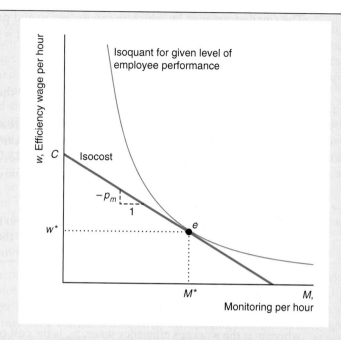

Figure 20.4 Trade-Off Between Efficiency Wage and Monitoring. By paying an efficiency wage that is above a worker's best alternative, an employer can reduce its level of monitoring and still prevent shirking. The isoquant curve shows the combinations of efficiency wage, w, and monitoring, M, that produce a given level of employee performance. The employer sets the efficiency wage and the amount of monitoring to minimize its labor cost of producing where the straight-line isocost line is tangent to the isoquant.

Thus to discourage shirking, firms have to raise their efficiency wage even higher, and even more unemployment results. See **www.awlonline.com/perloff**, "Deferred Payments Versus Efficiency Wages in Fast-Food Restaurants."

After-the-Fact Monitoring

So far we've concentrated on monitoring by employers looking for bad behavior as it occurs. If shirking or other bad behavior is detected after the fact, the offending employee is fired or otherwise disciplined. This punishment discourages shirking in the future.

Punishment. It is often very difficult to monitor bad behavior when it occurs but relatively easy to determine it after the fact. As long as a contract holds off payment until after the principal checks for bad behavior, after-the-fact monitoring discourages bad behavior. For example, an employer can check the quality of an employee's work. If it is substandard, the employer can force the employee to make it right (as in the Safelite Glass example).

Insurance companies frequently use this approach in contracts with their customers. Insurance firms try to avoid extreme moral hazard problems by offering contracts that do not cover spectacularly reckless, stupid, or malicious behavior. If an insurance company determines after the fact that a claim is based on reckless behavior rather than chance, the firm refuses to pay.

For example, an insurance company will not pay damages for a traffic accident if the insured driver is shown to have been drunk at the time. A house insurance company disallows claims due to an explosion that is found to result from an illegal activity such as making crack cocaine. It will certainly disallow claims by arsonists who torch their own homes or businesses. Life insurance companies may refuse to pay benefits to the family of someone who commits suicide (as in the play *Death of a Salesman*).

Application   ABUSING LEASED CARS

Because drivers of fleet automobiles such as rental cars do not own them, they do not bear all the cost from neglecting or abusing the vehicles, resulting in a moral hazard problem. These vehicles are driven harder and farther and depreciate faster than owner-operated vehicles.

Using data from sales at used-car auctions, Dunham (1996), after controlling for mileage, found that fleet vehicles (not including taxis or police cars) depreciate 10% to 13% more rapidly than owner-driven vehicles.[21] The average auction price for a Pontiac 6000 is $5,200 for a fleet car and $6,500 for a nonfleet car. This $1,300 difference, which is one-fourth of the fleet car's price, reflects the increased depreciation of fleet cars.

To deal with this moral hazard, an automobile-leasing firm commonly writes contracts—open-ended leases—in which the driver's final payment for the vehicle depends on the selling price of the car. In this way, the contract makes the leasing driver responsible for at least some of the harm done to the car, to encourage the lessee to take greater care of the vehicle. Given the difference in auction prices, however, such leases apparently are not the full solution to this moral hazard.

No Punishment. Finding out about moral hazards after they occur is too late if wrongdoers cannot be punished at that time. Indeed, there's no point in monitoring after the fact if punishment is then impossible or impractical. Although it's upsetting to find that you've been victimized, there's nothing you can do beyond trying to prevent the situation from happening again.

---

[21]According to the National Public Radio show *Car Talk*—one of the world's most reliable sources of information—police cars have very few miles on them, but their engines are quickly shot because cops spend untold hours sitting in their cruisers in front of donut shops with the engine running and the air conditioner on high.

Application   SAVINGS AND LOANS MORAL HAZARDS

Moral hazard played an important role in causing the bankruptcies of many savings and loans (S&Ls) in the late 1980s and early 1990s. Individuals are willing to put their money into an S&L because they know that federal or state agencies insure their deposits against an S&L failure.

To prevent S&Ls from engaging in moral hazards that lead to bankruptcies, government agencies had traditionally required these institutions to invest primarily in relatively safe, local residential mortgage loans. In the early 1980s, however, government rules changed to allow S&Ls to make investments in other assets. It was hoped that giving S&Ls leeway to diversify their portfolio of investments would reduce investment risks. With this change, the percentage of investments in nontraditional assets by federally insured S&Ls increased from 11.5% in 1982 to 20.2% in 1985.

To keep S&Ls from engaging in extremely risky behavior or committing fraud, the government agencies examined their records. Unfortunately, just when S&Ls were given greater latitude in investment, such monitoring decreased. The number of examinations of S&Ls fell from 3,210 in 1980 to 2,347 in 1984, and the examinations per billion dollars of assets dropped from 5.4 to 2.4.

After the rules changed, many S&L managers started making extremely risky investments, including buying junk bonds. They reasoned that they'd make a lot of money if these investments paid off. If the investments failed and the S&L went bankrupt, the managers believed—correctly—that they could walk away with impunity. They anticipated that the federal government would make good on the losses and not punish them (unless fraud was involved—and apparently not always then). The combination of government insurance, greater freedom to invest, and slack monitoring created a moral hazard problem from bad investments.

The fastest-growing S&Ls tended to be those that took the largest risks. Whereas S&Ls that grew less than 15% in 1984 had 68% of their assets in traditional residential mortgages and mortgage-backed securities, only 53% of the assets in S&Ls growing at more than 50% were in traditional assets. Moreover, the investments of S&Ls that were soon to fail were different from other's. In 1985, soon-to-fail S&Ls had more commercial (rather than residential) mortgage loans, 13.4% versus 8.1%; more land loans, 7.7% versus 1.2%; more commercial loans (including junk bonds), 2.2% versus 1.3%; and more direct equity (stock) investments, 5.0% versus 1.7%. Many S&Ls that had invested heavily in these risky investments went into bankruptcy when the investments failed.

To bail out the failed S&Ls, the federal government made extremely large payouts—much larger than those of earlier periods. In 1979, the federal government had to dispose of only three failed S&Ls by liquidating their assets—about 0.1% of all S&L assets—or finding a new owner. In 1988, however, the federal government had to deal with 205 disposals, representing 7.45% of all S&L assets.

The present discounted value of the government's cost for 1988 alone was $38 billion. Government estimates in 1999 were that the S&L debacle had cost taxpayers $165 billion, or about $1,650 per household.

To minimize future moral hazard problems among S&Ls, the government insurers raised the capital requirements that govern how much money the owners and managers must provide. A capital requirement acts like an insurance deductible. It forces S&L managers and owners to put more of their own money (and less of account holders' money) at risk when making investments. As a consequence, S&L operators are likely to invest more conservatively.

20.6 | CHECKS ON PRINCIPALS

To this point, we have concentrated on situations in which the employee knows more than the employer. Sometimes, however, the employer may have asymmetric information and engage in opportunistic behavior.

Because employers often pay employees after work is completed, employers have many opportunities to exploit workers. For example, a dishonest employer can underpay after falsely claiming that a worker took time off or that some of the worker's output was substandard. The employer can decrease piece rates over time, after employees are committed to this payment system. Employers who provide bonuses can underreport the firm's output or profit. An employer can dock earnings, claim that an employee bond was forfeited, or refuse to make deferred payments such as pensions after dishonestly claiming that a monitored worker engaged in bad behavior. Efficient contracts prevent or reduce such moral hazard problems created by employers as well as those caused by employees.

Requiring that a firm post a bond can be an effective method of deterring the firm's opportunistic behavior. For example, a firm may post bonds to ensure that it has the means of paying current wages and future pensions.

Another strategy for preventing a firm from acting opportunistically is to eliminate asymmetric information by requiring the employer to reveal relevant information to employees. For example, an employer can provide access to such information by allowing employee representatives to sit on the company board—from which vantage point they can monitor the firm's behavior. To induce workers to agree to profit sharing, a firm may provide workers with information about the company's profit by allowing them (or an independent auditor) to check its accounts. Alternatively, the firm may argue that its stock closely mirrors its profit and suggest that the known stock price be used for incentive payments.

As another means of conveying information to employees, firms may seek to establish a good reputation. For instance, a firm may publicize that it does not make a practice of firing senior employees to avoid paying pensions. The better the firm's reputation, the more likely workers are to accept a deferred payment scheme, which deters shirking.

When firms find these approaches infeasible, they may use inefficient contracts that might, for example, stipulate payments to employees on the basis of easily observed revenues rather than less reliable profit reports. The next application discusses a particularly damaging but common type of inefficient contract.

Application   PERFORMANCE TERMINATION CONTRACTS

During economic downturns—recessions and depressions—demand for a firm's product falls. Many firms respond by laying off workers and reducing production rather than by lowering wages and keeping everyone employed (Hall and Lilien, 1979). The graph shows that real private U.S. hourly earnings remained relatively constant over the period 1987–1996 even as the unemployment rate fluctuated substantially.

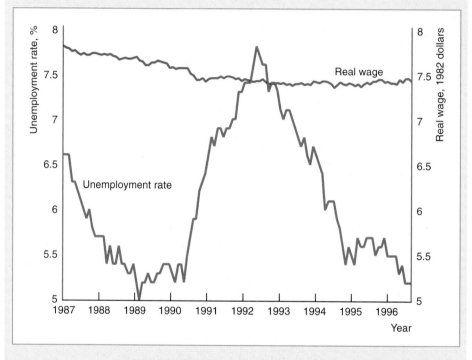

If both sides agreed to it, a wage reduction policy would benefit firms and workers alike. Workers would earn more than they would if they were laid off. Because the firm's costs would fall, it could sell more during the downturn than it otherwise could, so its profits would be higher than they would be if there were layoffs. Firms that provide relatively low wages and then share profits with employees achieve this type of wage flexibility.

Why then are wage reductions less common than layoffs? One explanation involves asymmetric information: Workers, unlike the firm, don't know whether the firm is actually facing a downturn, so they don't agree to wage cuts. In short, they don't trust the firm to tell them the truth. They fear that the firm will falsely claim that economic conditions are bad to justify a wage cut. If the firm has to lay off workers—an action that hurts the firm as well as the workers—the firm is more likely to be telling the truth about economic conditions.

We illustrate this reasoning in the following matrix, which shows the payoffs if wages are reduced during downturns. The value of output produced by

Wage Cut

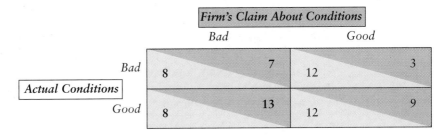

each worker is $21 during good times and $15 during bad times. The firm pays employees $12 per hour if it reports that economic conditions are good and $8 if it says that conditions are bad. If economic conditions are bad, the firm earns more by reporting these bad conditions, $7, than it earns if it says that conditions are good, $3. Similarly, if conditions are good, the firm earns more if it claims that conditions are bad, $13, than if it says that they are good, $9. Thus regardless of the true state, the firm always claims that conditions are bad.

To shield themselves from such systematic lying, employees may insist that the firm lay off workers whenever it says that conditions are bad. This requirement provides the firm with an incentive to report the true conditions. In the next matrix, the firm must lay off workers for half of each period if it announces that times are bad, causing the value of output to fall by one-third. Because they now work only half the time, workers earn only half as much, $6,

Worker Layoff (for Half of Any Period the Firm Claims Is Bad)

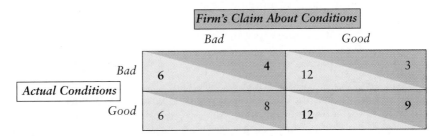

as they earn during good times, $12. If conditions are bad, the firm makes more by telling the truth, $4, than by claiming that conditions are good, $3. In good times, the firm makes more by announcing that conditions are good, $9, than by claiming that they are bad, $8. Thus the firm reports conditions truthfully.

With the wage-cut contract in which the firm always says that conditions are bad, workers earn $8 regardless of actual conditions. If economic conditions are good half the time, the firm earns an average of $10 = ($\frac{1}{2}$ × $7) + ($\frac{1}{2}$ × $13). Under the contract that requires layoffs, the workers earn an average of $9 = (\frac{1}{2} \times \$6) + (\frac{1}{2} \times \$12)$ and the firm earns an average of $\$6.50 = (\frac{1}{2} \times \$4) + (\frac{1}{2} \times \$9)$.

Therefore, the firm prefers the wage-cut contract and the workers favor the layoff contract. However, if the workers could observe actual conditions, both parties would prefer the wage-cut contract. Workers would earn an average of $\$10 = (\frac{1}{2} \times \$8) + (\frac{1}{2} \times \$12)$, and the firm would earn $\$8 = (\frac{1}{2} \times \$7) + (\frac{1}{2} \times \$9)$. With the layoff contract, total payoffs are lower because of lost production. Thus socially inefficient layoffs may be used because of the need to keep relatively well-informed firms honest.

20.7 | CONTRACT CHOICE

We have examined how to construct a single contract so as to prevent moral hazards. Often, however, a principal gives an agent a choice of contract. By observing the agent's choice, the principal obtains enough information to prevent agent opportunism.

Firms want to avoid hiring workers who will shirk. Employers know that not all workers shirk, even when given an opportunity to do so. So rather than focusing on stopping lazy workers from shirking, an employer may concentrate on hiring only industrious people. With this approach, the firm seeks to avoid *moral hazard* problems by preventing *adverse selection*, whereby lazy employees falsely assert that they are hardworking.

As discussed in Chapter 19, employees may *signal* to employers that they are productive. For example, if only nonshirking employees agree to work long hours, a commitment to work long hours serves as a reliable signal. In addition, employees can signal by developing a reputation as hard workers. To the degree that employers can rely on this reputation, sorting is achieved.

When workers cannot credibly signal, firms may try to *screen out* bad workers. One way in which firms can determine which prospective employees will work hard and which will shirk is to give them a choice of contracts. If job candidates who are hard workers select a contingent contract whereby their pay depends on how hard they work and if job applicants who are lazy workers choose a fixed-fee contract, the firm can tell the applicants apart by their choices.

Suppose that a firm wants to hire a salesperson who will run its Cleveland office and that the potential employees are risk neutral. A hardworking salesperson can sell $100,000 worth of goods a year, but a lazy one can sell only $60,000 worth (see Table 20.3). A hard worker can earn $30,000 from other firms, so the firm considers using a contingent contract that pays a salesperson a 30% commission on sales.

If the firm succeeds in hiring a hard worker, the salesperson makes $30,000 = $100,000 × 0.30. The firm's share of sales is $70,000. The firm has no costs of production (for simplicity), but maintaining this branch office costs the firm $50,000 a year. The firm's profit is therefore $20,000. If the firm hires a lazy salesperson under the same contract, the salesperson makes $18,000, the firm's share of sales is $42,000, and the firm loses $8,000 after paying for the office.

Table 20.3 Firm's Spreadsheet

	Contingent Contract (30% of Sales), $	Fixed-Fee Contract ($25,000 Salary), $
Hard Worker		
Sales	100,000	100,000
– Salesperson's pay	–30,000	–25,000
= Firm's net revenue	70,000	75,000
– Office expenses	–50,000	–50,000
= Firm's profit	20,000	25,000
Lazy Worker		
Sales	60,000	60,000
– Salesperson's pay	–18,000	–25,000
= Firm's net revenue	42,000	35,000
– Office expenses	–50,000	–50,000
= Firm's profit	–8,000	–15,000

Thus the firm wants to hire only a hard worker. Unfortunately, the firm does not know in advance whether a potential employee is a hard worker. To acquire this information, the firm offers a potential employee a choice of contracts:

■ *Contingent contract:* No salary and 30% of sales
■ *Fixed-fee contract:* Annual salary of $25,000, regardless of sales

A prospective employee who doesn't mind hard work would earn $5,000 more by choosing the contingent contract. In contrast, a lazy candidate would make $7,000 more from a salary than from commissions. If an applicant chooses the fixed-fee contract, the firm knows that the person does not intend to work hard and decides not to hire that person.

The firm learns what it needs to know by offering this contract choice as long as the lazy applicant does not pretend to be a hard worker by choosing the contingent contract. Under the contingent contract, the lazy person makes only $18,000, but that offer may dominate others available in the market. If this pair of contracts fails to sort workers, the firm may try different pairs. If all these choices fail to sort, the firm must use other means to prevent shirking.

Summary

1. **Principal-agent problem:** A principal contracts with an agent to perform some task. The size of their joint profit depends on any assets that the principal contributes, the actions of the agent, and the state of nature. If the principal cannot observe the agent's actions, the agent may engage in opportunistic behavior. This moral hazard reduces the joint profit. An efficient contract leads to efficiency in production (joint profit is maximized by eliminating moral hazards) and efficiency in risk bearing (the less-risk-averse party bears more of the risk). Three common types of contracts are *fixed-fee contracts*, whereby one party pays the other a fixed fee and the other

keeps the rest of the profits; *hire contracts*, by which the principal pays the agent a wage or by the piece of output produced; and *contingent contracts*, wherein the payoffs vary with the amount of output produced or in some other way. Because a contract that reduces the moral hazard may increase the risk for a relatively risk-averse person, a contract is chosen to achieve the best trade-off between the twin goals of efficiency in production and in risk bearing.

2. **Production efficiency:** Whether efficiency in production is achieved depends on the contract that the principal and the agent use and the degree to which their information is asymmetric. For the agent to put forth the optimal level of effort in our example, the agent must get the full marginal profit from that effort or the principal must monitor the agent. When the parties have full information, an agent with a fixed-fee rental or profit-sharing contract gets the entire marginal profit and produces optimally without monitoring. If the principal cannot monitor the agent or does not observe profit and cost, only a fixed-fee rental contract prevents moral hazard problems and achieves production efficiency.

3. **Trade-off between efficiency in production and in risk bearing:** A principal and an agent may agree to a contract that strikes a balance between reducing moral hazards and allocating risk optimally. Contracts that eliminate moral hazards require the agent to bear the risk. If the agent is more risk averse than the principal, the parties may trade off a reduction in production efficiency to lower risk for the agent.

4. **Payments linked to production or profit:** To reduce shirking, employers may reward employees for greater individual or group productivity. Piece rates, which reward faster individual work, are practical only when individual output can be easily measured and the quality of work is not critical. Bonuses and stock options that reward workers for increases in group effort provide less of an incentive than piece rates but still may reduce shirking.

5. **Monitoring:** Because of asymmetric information, an employer must normally monitor workers' efforts to prevent shirking. Less monitoring is necessary as the employee's interest in keeping the job increases. The employer may require the employee to post a large bond that is forfeited if the employee is caught shirking, stealing, or otherwise misbehaving. If an employee cannot afford to post a bond, the employer may use deferred payments or efficiency wages—unusually high wages—to make it worthwhile for the employee to keep the job. Employers may also be able to prevent shirking by engaging in after-the-fact monitoring. However, such monitoring works only if bad behavior can be punished after the fact.

6. **Checks on principals:** Often both agents and principals can engage in opportunistic behavior. If a firm must reveal its actions to its employees, it is less likely to be able to take advantage of the employees. To convey information, an employer may let employees participate in decision-making meetings or audit the company's books. Alternatively, an employer may make commitments so that it is in the employer's best interest to tell employees the truth. These commitments, such as laying off workers rather than reducing wages during downturns, may reduce moral hazards but lead to nonoptimal production.

7. **Contract choice:** A principal may be able to obtain valuable information from an agent by offering a choice of contracts. Employers avoid moral hazard problems by preventing adverse selection. For example, they may present potential employees with a choice of contracts, prompting hardworking job applicants to choose one contract and lazy candidates to choose another.

Problems

1. In the duck-carving example with full information (which the second column of Table 20.1 summarizes), is a contract efficient if it requires that Paula give Arthur a fixed-fee salary of $168 and leaves all decisions to Arthur? If so, why? If not, are there any additional steps that Paula can take to ensure that Arthur sells the optimal number of carvings?

2. The state of California set up its own earthquake insurance program in 1997. Because the state agency in charge has few staff members, it will pay private insurance carriers to handle claims for earthquake damage. These insurance firms will receive 9% of each approved claim. Is this compensation scheme likely to lead to opportunistic behavior by insurance companies? What would be a better way to handle the compensation?

3. Two students are given an assignment to produce a joint report for which they will both get the same grade. What problems, if any, are likely to arise?

4. In the duck-carving example with limited information (summarized in the second and third columns of Table 20.1), is a fixed-fee contract efficient? If so, why? If not, are there any additional steps that Paula can take to ensure efficiency?

5. A health insurance company tries to prevent the moral hazard of "excessive" dentist visits by limiting the visits per person per year to a specific number. How does such a restriction affect moral hazard and risk bearing? Show in a graph.

6. Some sellers offer to buy back a good later at some prespecified price. Why would a firm make such a commitment?

7. Traditionally, doctors have been paid on a fee-for-service basis. Now doctors are increasingly paid on a capitated basis (they get paid for treating a patient for a year, regardless of how much treatment is required). In this arrangement, doctors form a group and sign a capitation contract whereby they take turns seeing a given patient. What are the implications of this change in compensation for moral hazards and for risk bearing?

8. Fourteen states have laws that limit a franchisor's ability to terminate a franchise agreement. What effects would such laws have on production efficiency and risk bearing?

9. A promoter arranges for many different restaurants to set up booths to sell Cajun-Creole food at a fair. Appropriate music and other entertainment are provided. Customers can buy food using only "Cajun Cash," which is scrip with the same denominations as actual cash sold by the promoter at the fair. Why aren't the food booths allowed to sell food directly for cash?

10. Many law firms consist of partners who share profits. On being made a partner, a lawyer must post a bond, a large payment to the firm that will be forfeited on bad behavior. Why?

11. According to a 1997 flyer from Schwab *AdvisorSource*, "Most personal investment managers base their fees on a percentage of assets managed. We believe this is in your best interest because your manager is paid for investment management, not solely on the basis of trading commissions charged to your account. You can be assured your manager's investment decisions are guided by one primary goal—increasing your assets." Is this policy in a customer's best interest?

12. Explain why full employment may be inconsistent with no shirking.

Math Problems

13. Suppose that a textbook author is paid a royalty of α share of the revenue from sales where the revenue is $R = pq$, p is the competitive market price for textbooks, and q is the number of copies of this textbook (which is similar to others on the market) sold. The publisher's cost of printing and distributing the book is $C(q)$. Determine the equilibrium, and compare it to the outcome that maximizes the sum of the payment to the author plus the firm's profit. Answer using both math and a graph.

14. Suppose now that the textbook publisher in Problem 13 faces a downward-sloping demand curve. The revenue is $R(Q)$, and the publisher's cost of printing and distributing the book is $C(Q)$. Compare the equilibria for the following compensation methods in which the author receives the same total compensation from each method:
    a. The author is paid a lump sum, $\mathcal{L}$.
    b. The author is paid α share of the revenue.
    c. The author receives a lump-sum payment and a share of the revenue.

Why do you think that authors are usually paid a share of revenue?

15. In Solved Problem 20.3, a firm calculated the optimal level of monitoring to prevent stealing. If $G = \$500$ and $\theta = 20\%$, what is the minimum bond that deters stealing?

16. In Problem 15, suppose that, for each extra $1,000 of bonding that the firm requires a worker to post, the firm must pay that worker $10 more per period to get the worker to work for the firm. What is the minimum bond that deters stealing?

CHAPTER APPENDIXES

Appendix 2A: Regressions

Economists use a *regression* to estimate economic relationships such as demand curves and supply curves. A regression analysis allows us to answer three types of questions:

- How can we best fit an economic relationship to actual data?
- How confident are we in our results?
- How can we determine the effect of a change in one variable on another if many other variables are changing at the same time?

Estimating Economic Relations

We use a demand curve example to illustrate how regressions can answer these questions. The points in Figure 2A.1 show eight years of data on Nancy's annual purchases of candy bars, q, and the prices, p, she paid.[1] For example, in the year when candy bars cost 20¢, Nancy bought q_2 candy bars.

Because we assume that Nancy's tastes and income did not change during this period, we write her demand for candy bars as a function of the price of candy bars and unobservable random effects. We believe that her demand curve is linear and want to estimate the demand function:

$$q = a + bp + e,$$

where a and b are coefficients we want to determine and e is an error term. This *error term* captures random effects that are not otherwise reflected in our function. For instance, in one year, Nancy broke up with her longtime boyfriend and ate more candy bars than usual, resulting in a relatively large positive error term for that year.

The data points in the figure exhibit a generally downward-sloping relationship between quantity and price, but the points do not lie strictly on a line because of the error terms. There are many possible ways in which we could draw a line through these data points.

The way we fit the line in the figure is to use the standard criterion that our estimates *minimize the sum of squared residuals*, where a residual, $e = q - \hat{q}$, is the difference between an actual quantity, q, and the fitted or predicted quantity on the

---

[1]We use a lowercase q for the quantity demanded for an individual instead of the uppercase Q that we use for a market. Notice that we violated the rule economists usually follow of putting quantity on the horizontal axis and price on the vertical axis. We are now looking at this relationship as statisticians who put the independent or explanatory variable, price, on the horizontal axis and the dependent variable, quantity, on the vertical axis.

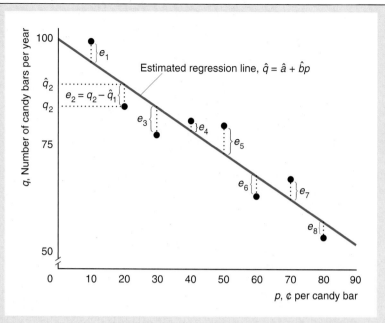

Figure 2A.1 Regression. The circles show data on how many candy bars Nancy bought in a year at several different prices. The regression line minimizes the sum of the squared residuals, e_1 through e_8.

estimated line, $\hat{q}$. That is, we choose estimated coefficients $\hat{a}$ and $\hat{b}$ so that the estimated quantities from the regression line,

$$\hat{q} = \hat{a} + \hat{b}p,$$

make the sum of the squared residuals, $e_1^2 + e_2^2 + \cdots + e_8^2$, as small as possible. By summing the square of the residuals instead of the residuals themselves, we treat the effects of a positive or negative error symmetrically and give greater weight to large errors than to small ones.[2] In the figure, the regression line is

$$\hat{q} = 99.4 - 0.49p,$$

where $\hat{a} = 99.4$ is the intercept of the estimated line and $\hat{b} = -0.49$ is the slope of the line.

Confidence in Our Estimates

Because the data reflect random errors, so do the estimated coefficients. Our estimate of Nancy's demand curve depends on the *sample* of data we use. If we were to use data from a different set of years, our estimates, $\hat{a}$ and $\hat{b}$, of the true coefficients, a and b, would differ.

---

[2]Using calculus, we can derive the $\hat{a}$ and $\hat{b}$ that minimize the sum of squared residuals. The estimate of the slope coefficient is a weighted average of the observed quantities, $\hat{b} = \Sigma_i w_i q_i$, where $w_i = (p_i - \bar{p}) / \Sigma_i (p_i - \bar{p})^2$, $\bar{p}$ is the average of the observed prices, and Σ_i indicates the sum over each observation i. The estimate of the intercept, $\hat{a}$, is the average of the observed quantities.

If we had many estimates of the true parameter based on many samples, the estimates would be distributed around the true coefficient. These estimates are *unbiased* in the sense that the average of the estimates would equal the true coefficients.

Computer programs that calculate regression lines report a *standard error* for each coefficient, which is an estimate of the dispersion of the estimated coefficients around the true coefficient. In our example, a computer program reports

$$\hat{q} = 99.4 - 0.49p,$$
$$(3.99) \quad (0.08)$$

where, below each estimated coefficient, its estimated standard error appears between parentheses.

The smaller the estimated standard error, the more precise the estimate, and the more likely it is to be close to the true value. As a rough rule of thumb, there is a 95% probability that the interval that is within two standard errors of the estimated coefficient contains the true coefficient.[3] Using this rule, the *confidence interval* for the slope coefficient, $\hat{b}$, ranges from $-0.49 - (2 \times 0.08) = -0.65$ to $-0.49 + (2 \times 0.08) = -0.33$.

If zero were to lie within the confidence interval for $\hat{b}$, we would conclude that we cannot reject the hypothesis that the price has no effect on the quantity demanded. In our case, however, the entire confidence interval contains negative values, so we are reasonably sure that the higher the price, the less Nancy demands.

Multiple Regression

We can also estimate relationships involving more than one explanatory variable using a *multiple regression*. For example, Moschini and Meilke (1992) estimate a pork demand function, Equation 2.2, in which the quantity demanded is a function of income, Y, and the prices of pork, p, beef, p_b, and chicken, p_c:

$$Q = 171 - 20p + 20p_b + 3p_c + 2Y.$$

The multiple regression is able to separate the effects of the various explanatory variables. The coefficient 20 on the p variable says that an increase in the price of pork by $1 per kg lowers the quantity demanded by 20 million kg per year, holding the effects of the other prices and income constant.

Appendix 3A: Effects of a Specific Tax on Equilibrium

The government collects a specific or unit tax, τ, from sellers, so sellers receive $p - \tau$ when consumers pay p. We now determine the effect of the tax on the equilibrium.

In the new equilibrium, the price that consumers pay is determined by the intersection of supply and demand after taxes:

$$D(p) - S(p - \tau) = 0, \tag{3A.1}$$

---

[3]The confidence interval is the coefficient plus or minus 1.96 times its standard error for large samples (at least hundreds of observations) in which the coefficients are normally distributed. For smaller samples, the confidence interval tends to be larger.

where the supply equals demand equation is written in implicit function form (the right-hand side of the equation is zero).

We determine the effect of a small tax on price by totally differentiating Equation 3A.1 with respect to p and τ:

$$\frac{dS}{dp}\,d\tau + \left(\frac{dD}{dp} - \frac{dS}{dp}\right)dp = 0.$$

Rearranging terms, it follows that the change in the price that consumers pay with respect to a change in the tax is

$$\frac{dp}{d\tau} = \frac{dS/dp}{dS/dp - dD/dp} \qquad (3A.2)$$

We know that $dD/dp < 0$ from the Law of Demand. If the supply curve slopes up, $dS/dp > 0$, then $dp/d\tau > 0$. The higher the tax, the greater the price consumers pay. If $dS/dp < 0$, the direction of change is ambiguous.

By multiplying both the numerator and denominator of the right-hand side of Equation 3A.2 by p/Q, we can express this derivative in terms of elasticities:

$$\frac{dp}{d\tau} = \frac{(dS/dp)(p/Q)}{(dS/dp)(p/Q) - (dD/dP)(p/Q)} = \frac{\eta}{\eta - \varepsilon}$$

where the last equality follows because dS/dp and dD/dp are the changes in the quantities supplied and demanded as price changes and the consumer and producer prices are identical when $\tau = 0$. The change in price, Δp, equals $[\eta/(\eta - \varepsilon)]\Delta\tau$. This expression holds for any size change in $\Delta\tau$ if both the demand and supply curves are linear or have constant elasticity at each point. The expression only holds for small changes $\Delta\tau$ for other curves.

To determine the effect on quantity, we can combine the price result from Equation 3A.2 with information from either the demand or supply curve. Differentiating the demand function with respect to τ, we know that

$$\frac{dQ}{d\tau} = \frac{dD}{dp}\frac{dp}{d\tau} = \frac{(dD/dP)(dS/dp)}{dS/dp - dD/dP}$$

which is negative if the supply curve is upward sloping.

Appendix 4A: Utility and Indifference Curves

We now use calculus to examine the relationship between utility and indifference curves and some properties of indifference curves. Suppose that Lisa's utility function is $U(B, Z)$, where B is the number of burritos and Z is the number of pizzas. Lisa's marginal utility for burritos, MU_B, is the amount of extra pleasure she would get from extra burritos, holding her consumption of pizza constant. Formally, her marginal utility for burritos, B, is the partial derivative of utility, $U(B, Z)$, with respect to B holding Z constant:

$$MU_B(B, Z) = \lim_{\Delta B \to 0} \frac{U(B + \Delta B, Z) - U(B, Z)}{\Delta B} = \frac{\partial U(B, Z)}{\partial B}.$$

By assumption, marginal utility is always nonnegative: A little more of a good makes you better off or at least doesn't harm you. The marginal utility depends on the current levels of B and Z.

Which combinations of B and Z leave Lisa with a given level of pleasure, say, $\bar{U}$? We can write those combinations as

$$\bar{U} = U(B, Z). \tag{4A.1}$$

Equation 4A.1 is the equation for an indifference curve with utility level $\bar{U}$.

We can express the slope of an indifference curve—the marginal rate of substitution, *MRS*—in terms of the marginal utilities. The slope of the indifference curve is found by determining the changes in B and P that leave utility unchanged. Totally differentiating Equation 4A.1, we find that

$$d\bar{U} = 0 = \frac{\partial U(B, Z)}{\partial B} dB + \frac{\partial U(B, Z)}{\partial Z} dZ \equiv MU_B \, dB + MU_Z \, dZ. \tag{A4.2}$$

This equation says that a little extra utility, MU_B, times the change in B, dB, plus the extra utility, MU_Z, times the change in Z, dZ, must add to zero. If we increase one of the goods, we must decrease the other to hold utility constant so that we stay on the same indifference curve. In Equation 4A.2, $d\bar{U} = 0$ because we are holding utility constant so that we stay on the same indifference curve. Rearranging the terms in Equation 4A.2, we find that

$$\frac{dB}{dZ} = -\frac{MU_Z}{MU_B}.$$

The slope of the indifference curve is the negative of the ratio of the marginal utilities.

Suppose that Lisa has the following utility function, known as a *Cobb-Douglas utility function*:

$$U(B, Z) = AB^\alpha Z^\beta. \tag{A4.3}$$

Her marginal utility of burritos is

$$MU_B(B, Z) = \alpha AB^{\alpha-1}Z^\beta = \alpha \frac{U(B, Z)}{B},$$

and her marginal utility of pizza is

$$MU_Z(B, Z) = \beta AB^\alpha Z^{\beta-1} = \beta \frac{U(B, Z)}{Z}.$$

Suppose that $\alpha = \beta = \frac{1}{2}$ and $A = 20$. If $B = Z = 4$, then $U(4, 4) = 80$ and $MU_B(4, 4) = MU_Z(4, 4) = 10$. If $B = 1$ and $Z = 4$, however, $U(1, 4) = 40$, $MU_B(1, 4) = 20$, and $MU_Z(1, 4) = 5$. The extra pleasure that Lisa gets from an extra burrito is greater, the fewer burritos she initially has, all else the same.

The slope of her indifference curve is

$$MRS = \frac{dB}{dZ} = -\frac{MU_Z}{MU_B} = -\frac{\beta AB^\alpha Z^{\beta-1}}{\alpha AB^{\alpha-1}Z^\beta} = -\frac{\beta B}{\alpha Z}.$$

The slope of the indifference curve differs with the levels of B and Z. If $\alpha = \beta = \frac{1}{2}$, $B = 4$, and $Z = 1$, $MRS(4, 1) = -(\frac{1}{2} \times 4)/(\frac{1}{2} \times 1) = -4$. At $B = Z = 4$, $MRS(4, 4) = -1$.

Appendix 4B: Maximizing Utility

Lisa's objective is to maximize her utility, $U(B, Z)$, subject to (s.t.) a budget constraint:

$$\max_{B,Z} U(B, Z)$$

$$\text{s.t.} \quad Y = p_B B + p_Z Z, \tag{4B.1}$$

where B is the number of burritos she buys at price p_B, Z is the number of pizzas she buys at price p_Z, Y is her income, and $Y = p_B B + p_Z Z$ is her budget constraint (her spending on burritos and pizza can't exceed her income). The mathematical statement of her problem shows that her *control variables* (what she chooses) are B and Z, which appear under the "max" term in the equation. We assume that Lisa has no control over the prices she faces or her budget.

One way to solve this type of constrained maximization problem is to use the Lagrangian method, in which we convert the constrained problem in Equation 4B.1 into an unconstrained problem:

$$\max_{B,Z,\lambda} \mathcal{L} = U(B, Z) - \lambda(p_B B + p_Z Z - Y), \tag{4B.2}$$

where λ is called the Lagrange multiplier. With normal-shaped utility functions, the values of B, Z, and λ that maximize this unconstrained problem are the same as the values that maximize the original constrained problem.

The advantage of changing the problem to an unconstrained problem is that we know how to maximize it using standard calculus techniques. We need to derive first-order conditions of Equation 4B.2 with respect to the three control variables, B, Z, and λ:[4]

$$\frac{\partial \mathcal{L}}{\partial B} = MU_B(B, Z) - \lambda p_B = 0, \tag{4B.3}$$

---

[4]To make our presentation as simple as possible, we assume that we have an interior solution, B and Z are infinitely divisible, and $U(B, Z)$ is continuously differentiable at least twice (so that the second-order condition is well defined). The first-order conditions give us the necessary conditions for an interior solution in which positive quantities of both goods are consumed. We assume that the second-order (sufficient) conditions hold, which is true if the utility function is quasiconcave or if the indifference curves are convex to the origin. That is, we assume that Lisa is maximizing rather than minimizing her utility when she chooses the levels of B and Z given by the first-order conditions.

$$\frac{\partial \mathscr{L}}{\partial Z} = MU_Z(B, Z) - \lambda p_Z = 0, \tag{4B.4}$$

$$\frac{\partial \mathscr{L}}{\partial \lambda} = Y - p_B B - p_Z Z = 0, \tag{4B.5}$$

where $MU_B(B, Z) \equiv \partial U(B, Z)/\partial B$ is the partial derivative of utility with respect to B (the marginal utility of B) and $MU_Z(B, Z)$ is the marginal utility of Z. Equation 4B.5 is the budget constraint. Equations 4B.3 and 4B.4 say that the marginal utility of each good equals its price times λ.

What is λ? If we equate Equations 4B.3 and 4B.4 and rearrange terms, we find that

$$\lambda = \frac{MU_B}{p_B} = \frac{MU_Z}{p_Z}. \tag{4B.6}$$

Because the Lagrangian multiplier, λ, equals the marginal utility of each good divided by its price, λ equals the extra pleasure one gets from one's last dollar of expenditures. Equivalently, λ is the value of loosening the budget constraint by one dollar.[5] Equation 4B.6 tells us that, to maximize her utility, Lisa should pick a B and Z so that, if she got one more dollar, spending that dollar on B or on Z would give her the same extra utility.

There is an alternative interpretation of this condition for maximizing utility. Taking the ratio of Equations 4B.3 and 4B.4 (or rearranging 4B.6), we find that

$$\frac{MU_Z}{MU_B} = \frac{p_Z}{p_B}. \tag{4B.7}$$

The left-hand side of Equation 4B.7 is the absolute value of the marginal rate of substitution, $MRS = -MU_Z/MU_B$, and the right-hand side is the absolute value of the marginal rate of transformation, $MRT = -p_Z/p_B$. Thus the calculus approach gives us the same condition for an optimum that we derived using graphs. The indifference curve should be tangent to the budget constraint: The slope of the indifference curve, MRS, should equal the slope of the budget constraint, MRT.

---

[5]Differentiating utility with respect to Y, we find that

$$\frac{dU}{dY} = MU_B(B, Z)\frac{dB}{dY} + MU_Z(B, Z)\frac{dZ}{dY}.$$

Substituting from Equation 4B.6 into this expression, we obtain

$$\frac{dU}{dY} = \lambda p_B \frac{dB}{dY} + \lambda p_Z \frac{dZ}{dY} = \lambda \frac{p_B\, dB + p_Z\, dZ}{dY}.$$

Totally differentiating the budget constraint, we learn that

$$dY = p_B\, dB + p_Z\, dZ.$$

Substituting this expression into the previous expression gives us

$$\frac{dU}{dY} = \frac{\lambda p_B\, dB + \lambda p_Z\, dZ}{p_B\, dB + p_Z\, dZ} = \lambda.$$

Thus λ equals the extra utility one gets from one more dollar of income.

For example, suppose that the utility is Cobb-Douglas, as in Equation 4A.3: $U = AB^{\alpha}Z^{\beta}$. The first-order condition, Equation 4B.5, the budget constraint, stays the same, and Equations 4B.3 and 4B.4 become

$$\frac{\partial \mathscr{L}}{\partial B} = \alpha \frac{U(B, Z)}{B} - \lambda p_B = 0, \tag{4B.8}$$

$$\frac{\partial \mathscr{L}}{\partial Z} = \beta \frac{U(B, Z)}{Z} - \lambda p_Z = 0. \tag{4B.9}$$

Using Equations 4B.8 and 4B.9, we can write Equation 4B.6 as

$$\lambda = \alpha \frac{U(B, Z)}{p_B B} = \beta \frac{U(B, Z)}{p_Z Z}.$$

Taking the ratio of Equations 4B.8 and 4B.9 and rearranging terms, we find that

$$\beta p_B B = \alpha p_Z Z. \tag{4B.10}$$

Substituting $Y - p_B B$ for $p_Z Z$, using Equation 4B.5, into Equation 4B.10 and rearranging terms, we get

$$B = \frac{\alpha}{\alpha + \beta} \frac{Y}{p_B}. \tag{4B.11}$$

Similarly, by substituting Equation 4B.11 into Equation 4B.10, we find that

$$Z = \frac{\beta}{\alpha + \beta} \frac{Y}{p_Z}. \tag{4.B12}$$

Thus knowing the utility function, we can solve the expression for the B and Z that maximize utility in terms of income and prices.

Equations 4B.11 and 4B.12 are the consumer's demand curves for B and Z, respectively. (We derive demand curves using graphs in Chapter 5.)

If $\alpha = \beta = \frac{1}{2}$, $A = 20$, $Y = 80$, and $p_Z = p_B = 10$, then $B = Z = 4$ and the value of loosening the budget constraint is $\lambda = MU_B/p_B = MU_Z/p_Z = 10/10 = 1$. If p_B rises to 40, then $Z = 4$, $B = 1$, and $\lambda = 20/40 = 5/10 = \frac{1}{2}$.

Appendix 5A: The Slutsky Equation

The total effect on the quantity demanded when the price of a good rises equals the sum of the substitution and income effects. The Slutsky equation (named after its discoverer, the Russian economist Eugene Slutsky) explicitly shows the relationship among the price elasticity of demand, ε, the pure substitution elasticity of demand, ε^*, and the income elasticity of demand, ξ:

Total effect	=	substitution effect	+	income effect
ε	=	ε^*	+	$(-\theta\xi)$

where θ is the budget share of this good: the amount spent on this good divided by the total budget.

We now sketch the derivation of the Slutsky equation (for a formal derivation, see a graduate microeconomics textbook such as Varian, 1992). The total effect, $\Delta q/\Delta p$, is the change in the quantity demanded, Δq, for a given change in the good's price, Δp. The substitution effect is the change in quantity demanded for a change in price, holding utility constant, which we label $(\Delta q/\Delta p)_{U\ constant}$.

A change in the price affects how much the consumer can buy and acts like a change in income. The income effect is the change in quantity as income changes times the change in income as price changes, $(\Delta q/\Delta Y)(\Delta Y/\Delta p)$, where ΔY is the change in income. The change in income from a change in price is $\Delta Y/\Delta p = -q$. For example, if price rises by \$1, income falls by the number of units purchased. From this last result, the income effect is $-q(\Delta q/\Delta Y)$.

Using these expressions, we write the identity that the total effect equals the substitution plus the income effect as

$$\Delta q/\Delta p = (\Delta q/\Delta p)_{U\ constant} - q(\Delta q/\Delta Y).$$

Multiplying this equation through by p/q, multiplying the last term by Y/Y, and rearranging terms, we obtain

$$\frac{\Delta q}{\Delta p}\frac{p}{q} = \left(\frac{\Delta q}{\Delta p}\right)_{U\ constant}\frac{p}{q} - \frac{\Delta q}{\Delta Y}\frac{Y}{q}\frac{pq}{Y}.$$

Substituting, $\varepsilon = (\Delta q/\Delta p)(p/q)$, $\varepsilon^* = (\Delta q/\Delta p)_{U\ constant}(p/q)$, $\xi = (\Delta q/\Delta Y)(Y/q)$, and $\theta = pq/Y$ into this last expression, we have the Slutsky equation:

$$\varepsilon = \varepsilon^* - \theta\xi.$$

Appendix 5B: Labor-Leisure Model

Jackie's utility, U, is a function,

$$U = U(Y, L), \tag{5B.1}$$

of her leisure, L, and her income, Y, which she uses to buy all other goods and services. Jackie maximizes her utility, Equation 5B.1, subject to two constraints. The first, imposed by the clock, is that the number of hours she works, H, equals her total hours in a day minus her hours of leisure:

$$H = 24 - L. \tag{5B.2}$$

The second constraint is that her earned income (earnings), Y, equals her wage, w, times the hours she works:

$$Y = wH. \tag{5B.3}$$

For now, we assume that her unearned income is zero.

Although we can maximize Equation 5B.1 subject to Equations 5B.2 and 5B.3 using Lagrangian techniques, it is easier to do so by substitution. By substituting

Equations 5B.2 and 5B.3 into Equation 5B.1, we can convert this constrained problem into an unconstrained maximization problem:

$$\max_{H} U = U(wH, 24 - H). \tag{5B.4}$$

By using the chain rule of differentiation, we find that the first-order condition for an interior maximum to the problem in Equation 5B.4 is

$$\frac{dU}{dH} = MU_Y w - MU_L = 0,$$

where MU_Y, the marginal utility of goods or income, is the partial derivative of utility with respect to income, $\partial U/\partial Y$, and MU_L, the marginal utility of leisure, is the partial derivative with respect to leisure, $\partial U/\partial L$.[6] This expression can be rewritten as $w = MU_L/MU_Y$.

If we use the terminology from Chapter 4, to maximize her utility, Jackie must set her marginal rate of substitution of income for leisure, $MRS = -MU_L/MU_Y$, equal to her marginal rate of transformation of income for leisure, $MRT = -w$, in the market:

$$MRS = -\frac{MU_L}{MU_Y} = -w = MRT.$$

Suppose that Jackie's utility is

$$U = Y^\alpha L^{1-\alpha} = (wH)^\alpha (24 - H)^{1-\alpha},$$

which is a Cobb-Douglas utility function (Appendix 4A). Differentiating this utility function with respect to H, setting the derivative equal to zero, and rearranging terms, we find that $H = 24\alpha$. With this particular utility function, an individual works a fixed number of hours regardless of the wage. If $\alpha = \frac{1}{2}$, the individual works 12 hours a day whether the wage is 50¢ an hour or $500 an hour.

Appendix 6A: Properties of Marginal and Average Product Curves

We can use calculus to show that the MP_L curve crosses the AP_L curve at its peak. Because capital is fixed, we can write the production function solely in terms of labor: $q = f(L)$. In the figure, $df/dL > 0$ and $d^2f/dL^2 < 0$. Thus $MP_L = dq/dL = df/dL > 0$ and $AP_L = q/L = f(L)/L > 0$. A necessary condition to identify the amount of labor where the AP_L curve reaches a maximum is that the derivative of AP_L with respect to L equals zero:

$$\frac{dAP_L}{dL} = \left(\frac{dq}{dL} - \frac{q}{L}\right)\frac{1}{L} = 0.$$

---

[6]The second-order condition for an interior maximum is

$$\frac{d^2U}{dH^2} = \frac{\partial^2U}{\partial Y^2}w^2 - 2\frac{\partial^2U}{\partial Y\,\partial L}w + \frac{\partial^2U}{\partial L^2} < 0.$$

(At the L determined by this first-order condition, AP_L is maximized if the second-order condition is negative: $d^2AP_L/dL^2 = d^2f/dL^2 < 0$.) From the first-order condition, $MP_L = dq/dL = q/L = AP_L$ at the peak of the AP_L curve.

Appendix 6B: Cobb-Douglas Production Function

Economists frequently estimate production functions. The Cobb-Douglas production function (named after its inventors, Charles W. Cobb, a mathematician, and Paul H. Douglas, an economist and U.S. senator) is probably the most commonly estimated one. Examples of estimated Cobb-Douglas production functions include the Norwegian printing firm's production function (Griliches and Ringstad, 1971) and the various Canadian manufacturing firms' production functions (Baldwin and Gorecki, 1986) discussed in Chapter 6.

The Cobb-Douglas production function is

$$q = AL^\alpha K^\beta. \tag{6B.1}$$

Economists use statistical means to estimate A, α, and β, which determine the exact shape of the production function. The larger A is, the more output the firm gets from a given amount of labor and capital. A 1% increase in labor, holding capital constant, causes an α% increase in output. Similarly, a 1% increase in capital, holding labor constant, causes a β% increase in output.

For a Canadian thread mill, $\alpha = 0.64$ and $\beta = 0.18$ (Baldwin and Gorecki, 1986). Thus a 1% increase in labor, holding capital fixed, causes output to increase by 0.64%, and a 1% increase in capital causes only a 0.18% increase in output.

The α term tells us the relationship between the average product of labor and the marginal product of labor. By differentiating the Cobb-Douglas production function with respect to L, holding K constant, we find that the marginal product of labor is

$$MP_L = \frac{\partial q}{\partial L} = \alpha AL^{\alpha-1}K^\beta = \alpha \frac{AL^\alpha K^\beta}{L} = \alpha \frac{q}{L}.$$

The marginal product of labor equals α times the average product of labor, $AP_L = q/L$. Thus a Canadian thread mill's marginal product of labor is about two-thirds, 0.64, of its average product of labor. Using similar reasoning, the marginal product of capital is $MP_K = \beta q/K$.

The marginal rate of technical substitution is $MRTS = MP_L/MP_K = (\alpha q/L)/(\beta q/K) = (\alpha/\beta)K/L$. For a Canadian thread mill, $MRTS = (0.64/0.18)K/L \approx 3.56K/L$.

Appendix 7A: Minimum of the Average Cost Curve

To determine the output level q where the average cost curve, $AC(q)$, reaches its minimum, we set the derivative of average cost with respect to q equal to zero:

$$\frac{dAC(q)}{dq} = \frac{d(C(q)/q)}{dq} = \left(\frac{dC(q)}{dq} - \frac{C(q)}{q} \right) \frac{1}{q} = 0.$$

This condition holds at the output q where $dC(q)/dq = C(q)/q$, or $MC = AC$. If the second-order condition holds at that q, the average cost curve reaches its minimum at that quantity. The second-order condition requires that the average cost curve be falling to the left of this q and rising to the right.

Appendix 7B: Norwegian Printing Firm's Short-Run Cost Curves

We can use math to derive the various short-run cost curves for a typical Norwegian printing firm. Based on the estimates of Griliches and Ringstad (1971), its production function is

$$q = 1.52L^{0.6}K^{0.4},$$

where labor, L, is measured in years of work (2,000 hours of work per year), K is the number of units of capital, and q is the amount of output that can be sold for 200 kroner (kr).

In the short run, the firm's capital is fixed at $\overline{K} = 100$. If the rental rate of a unit of capital is 8 kr, the fixed cost, F, is 800 kr. The figure in Chapter 7's application "Short-Run Cost Curves for a Printing Firm" shows that the average fixed cost,

$$AFC = F/q = 800/q,$$

falls as output increases.

We can use the production function to derive the variable cost. First, we determine how output and labor are related. Setting capital, K, at 100 units in the production function, we find that the output produced in the short run is solely a function of labor:

$$q = 1.52L^{0.6}100^{0.4} \approx 9.59L^{0.6}.$$

Rearranging this expression, we can write the number of workers per year, L, needed to produce q units of output, as a function solely of output:

$$L(q) = \left(\frac{q}{1.52 \times 100^{0.4}}\right)^{\frac{1}{0.6}} \approx 0.023q^{1.67}. \tag{7B.1}$$

Now that we know how labor and output are related, we can calculate variable cost directly. The only variable input is labor, so if the wage is 24 kr, the firm's variable cost is

$$VC(q) = wL(q) = 24L(q).$$

Substituting for $L(q)$ using Equation 7B.1, we see how variable cost varies with output:

$$VC(q) = 24L(q) = 24\left(\frac{q}{1.52 \times 100^{0.4}}\right)^{\frac{1}{0.6}} \approx 0.55q^{1.67}. \tag{7B.2}$$

Using this expression for variable cost, we can construct the other cost measures.

We obtain the average variable cost as a function of output, $AVC(q)$, by dividing both sides of Equation 7B.2 by q:

$$AVC(q) = \frac{VC(q)}{q} = \frac{24L(q)}{q} \approx 24\left(\frac{0.023q^{1.67}}{q}\right) = 0.55q^{0.67}.$$

As the figure shows, the average variable cost is strictly increasing.

To obtain the equation for marginal cost as a function of output, we differentiate the variable cost, $VC(q)$, with respect to output:

$$MC(q) = \frac{dVC(q)}{dq} \approx \frac{d(0.55q^{1.67})}{dq} = 1.67 \times 0.55q^{0.67} \approx 0.92q^{0.67}.$$

Thus to construct all the cost measures of the printing firm, we need only the production function and the prices of the inputs.

Appendix 7C: Minimizing Cost

We can use calculus to derive the cost minimization conditions, Equations 7.6 and 7.7, discussed in the chapter. The problem the firm faces in the long run is to choose the level of labor, L, and capital, K, that will minimize the cost of producing a particular level of output, $\bar{q}$, given a wage of w and a rental rate of capital of r.

The relationship between inputs and output is summarized in the firm's production function: $q = f(L, K)$. The marginal product of labor, which is the extra output the firm produces from a little more labor, holding capital constant, is $MP_L(L, K) = \partial f(L, K)/\partial L$, which is positive. There are diminishing marginal returns to labor, however, so the marginal product of labor falls as labor increases: $\partial MP_L(L, K)/\partial L = \partial^2 f(L, K)/\partial L^2 < 0$. The marginal product of capital has the same properties: $\partial f(L, K)/\partial K > 0$ and $\partial MP_K(L, K)/\partial K < 0$.

The firm's problem is to minimize its cost, C, of production, through its choice of labor and capital,

$$\min_{L,K} C = wL + rK,$$

subject to the constraint that a given amount of output, $\bar{q}$, is to be produced:

$$f(L, K) = \bar{q}. \tag{7C.1}$$

Equation 7C.1 is the $\bar{q}$ isoquant.

We can change this constrained minimization problem into an unconstrained problem by using the Lagrangian technique. The firm's unconstrained problem is to minimize the Lagrangian, $\mathcal{L}$, through its choice of labor, capital, and the Lagrange multiplier, λ:

$$\min_{L,K,\lambda} \mathcal{L} = wL + rK - \lambda(f(L, K) - \bar{q}).$$

The necessary conditions for a minimum are obtained by differentiating $\mathscr{L}$ with respect to L, K, and λ and setting the derivatives equal to zero:

$$\partial \mathscr{L}/\partial L = w - \lambda MP_L(L, K) = 0, \tag{7C.2}$$

$$\partial \mathscr{L}/\partial K = r - \lambda MP_K(L, K) = 0, \tag{7C.3}$$

$$\partial \mathscr{L}/\partial \lambda = f(L, K) - \overline{q} = 0. \tag{7C.4}$$

We can rewrite Equations 7C.2 and 7C.3 as $w = \lambda MP_L(L, K)$ and $r = \lambda MP_K(L, K)$. Taking the ratio of these two expressions, we obtain

$$\frac{w}{r} = \frac{MP_L(L, K)}{MP_K(L, K)} = MRTS, \tag{7C.5}$$

which is the same as Equation 7.6. This condition states that cost is minimized when the rate at which firms can exchange capital for labor in the market, w/r, is the same as the rate at which capital can be substituted for labor along an isoquant. That is, the isocost line is tangent to the isoquant.

We can rewrite Equation 7C.5 to obtain the expression

$$\frac{MP_L(L, K)}{w} = \frac{MP_K(L, K)}{r}.$$

This equation tells us that the last dollar spent on labor should produce as much extra output as the last dollar spent on capital; otherwise, the amount of factors used should be adjusted.

We can rearrange Equations 7C.2 and 7C.3 to obtain an expression for the Lagrangian multiplier:

$$\lambda = \frac{w}{MP_L(L, K)} = \frac{r}{MP_K(L, K)}. \tag{7C.6}$$

Equation 7C.6 says that the Lagrangian multiplier, λ, equals the ratio of the factor price to the marginal product for each factor. The marginal product for a factor is the extra amount of output one gets by increasing that factor slightly, so the reciprocal of the marginal product is the extra input it takes to produce an extra unit of output. By multiplying the reciprocal of the marginal product by the factor cost, we learn the extra cost of producing an extra unit of output by using more of this factor. Thus the Lagrangian multiplier equals the marginal cost of production: It measures how much the cost increases if we produce one more unit of output.

If a firm has a Cobb-Douglas production function, $Q = AL^\alpha K^\beta$, the marginal product of capital is $MP_K = \beta q/K$ and the marginal product of labor is $MP_L = \alpha q/L$ (see Appendix 6B), so the $MRTS$ is $\alpha K/(\beta L)$. Thus the tangency condition, Equation 7C.5, requires that

$$\frac{w}{r} = \frac{\alpha K}{\beta L}. \tag{7C.7}$$

Using algebra, we can rewrite Equation 7C.7 as

$$K = \frac{\beta w}{\alpha R} L,$$ (7C.8)

which is the expansion path for a Cobb-Douglas production function and given w and r. According to Equation 7C.8, the expansion path of a firm with a Cobb-Douglas production function is an upward-sloping straight line through the origin with a slope of $\beta w/(\alpha r)$.

Appendix 8A: The Elasticity of the Residual Demand Curve

Here we derive the expression for the elasticity of the residual demand curve given in Equation 8.2. Differentiating the residual demand (Equation 8.1),

$$D^r(p) = D(p) - S^o(p),$$

with respect to p, we obtain

$$\frac{dD^r}{dp} = \frac{dD}{dp} - \frac{dS^o}{dp}.$$

Because the firms are identical, the quantity produced by each is $q = Q/n$, and the total quantity produced by all the other firms is $Q_o = (n - 1)q$. Multiplying both sides of the expression by p/q and multiplying and dividing the first term on the right-hand side by Q/Q and the second term by Q_o/Q_o, this expression may be rewritten as

$$\frac{dD^r}{dp} \frac{p}{q} = \frac{dD}{dp} \frac{p}{Q} \frac{Q}{q} - \frac{dS^o}{dp} \frac{p}{Q_o} \frac{Q_o}{q},$$

where $q = D^r(p)$, $Q = D(p)$, and $Q_o = S^o(p)$. This expression can in turn be rewritten as Equation 8.2,

$$\varepsilon_i = n\varepsilon - (n - 1)\eta_o,$$

by noting that $Q/q = n$, $Q_o/q = (n - 1)$, $(dD^r/dp)(p/q) = \varepsilon_i$, $(dD/dp)(p/Q) = \varepsilon$, and $(dS^o/dp)(p/Q_o) = \eta_o$.

Appendix 8B: Profit Maximization

In general, a firm maximizes its profit, $\pi(q) = R(q) - C(q)$, by its choice of output q. A *necessary condition* for a maximum at a positive level of output is found by differentiating profit with respect to q and setting the derivative equal to zero:

$$\frac{d\pi}{dq} = \frac{dR(q^*)}{dq} - \frac{dC(q^*)}{dq} = 0.$$ (8B.1)

where q^* is the profit-maximizing output. Because $dR(q)/dq$ is the marginal revenue, $MR(q)$, and $dC(q)/dq$ is the marginal cost, $MC(q)$, Equation 8B.1 says that marginal revenue equals marginal cost at q^*:

$$MR(q^*) = MC(q^*). \tag{8B.2}$$

A *sufficient condition* for profit to be maximized at $q^* > 0$ is that the second-order condition holds:

$$\frac{d^2\pi}{dq^2} = \frac{d^2R(q^*)}{dq^2} - \frac{d^2C(q^*)}{dq^2} = \frac{dMR(q^*)}{dq} - \frac{dMC(q^*)}{dq} < 0. \tag{8B.3}$$

Equation 8B.3 can be rewritten as

$$\frac{dMR(q^*)}{dq} < \frac{dMC(q^*)}{dq}. \tag{8B.4}$$

Thus a sufficient condition for a maximum is that the slope of the marginal revenue curve is less than that of the marginal cost curve and that the MC curve cuts the MR curve from below at q^*.

For a competitive firm, $\pi(q) = pq - C(q)$, so the necessary condition for profit to be maximized, Equation 8B.1 or 8B.2, can be written as

$$p = MC(q^*). \tag{8B.5}$$

Equation 8B.5 says that a profit-maximizing, competitive firm sets its output at q^* where its marginal cost equals its price.

Because a competitive firm's marginal revenue, p, is a constant, $dMR/dq = dp/dq = 0$. Thus the sufficient condition for profit to be maximized, Equation 8B.4, can be rewritten as

$$0 < \frac{dMC(q^*)}{dq} \tag{8B.6}$$

for a competitive firm. Equation 8B.6 shows that a sufficient condition for a competitive firm to be maximizing its profit at q^* is that its marginal cost curve is upward sloping at the equilibrium quantity.

Appendix 9A: Demand Elasticities and Surplus

If the demand curve is linear, as in Figure 9.2, the lost consumer surplus, area $B + C$, equals the sum of the area of a rectangle, $Q\Delta p$, with length Q and height Δp, plus the area of a triangle, $\frac{1}{2}\Delta Q\Delta p$, of length ΔQ and height Δp. We can approximate any demand curve with a straight line, so that $\Delta CS = Q\Delta p + \frac{1}{2}\Delta Q\Delta p$ is a reasonable approximation to the true change in consumer surplus. We can rewrite this expression for ΔCS as

$$\Delta p\left(Q + \tfrac{1}{2}\Delta Q\right) = Q\Delta p\left[1 + \tfrac{1}{2}\left(\frac{\Delta Q}{Q}\frac{p}{\Delta p}\right)\frac{\Delta p}{p}\right]$$

$$= (pQ)\frac{\Delta p}{p}\left(1 + \tfrac{1}{2}\varepsilon\frac{\Delta p}{p}\right)$$

$$= Rx\left(1 + \tfrac{1}{2}\varepsilon\,x\right),$$

where $x = \Delta p/p$ is the percentage increase in the price, R (= pQ) is the total revenue from the sale of good Q, and ε is the elasticity of demand. (This equation is used to calculate the last column in Table 9.1.)

Appendix 11A: Relationship Between a Linear Demand Curve and Its Marginal Revenue Curve

When the demand curve is linear, its marginal revenue curve is twice as steep and hits the horizontal axis at half the quantity of the demand curve. A linear demand curve can be written generally as

$$p = a - bQ.$$

The monopoly's revenues are quadratic, $R = pQ = aQ - bQ^2$. Differentiating revenue with respect to quantity, we find that the marginal revenue, $dR(Q)/dQ$, is linear,

$$MR = a - 2bQ.$$

The demand and MR curves hit the price axis at a. The slope of the demand curve, $dp/dQ = -b$, is half (in absolute value) the slope of the marginal revenue curve, $dMR/dQ = -2b$. The MR curve hits the quantity axis at half the distance, $a/(2b)$, of the demand curve, a/b.

Appendix 11B: Incidence of a Specific Tax on a Monopoly

In a monopolized market, the incidence of a specific tax falling on consumers can exceed 100%: The price may rise by an amount greater than the tax. To demonstrate this possibility, we examine a market where the demand curve has a constant elasticity of ε and the marginal cost is constant at $MC = m$.

Suppose that the inverse demand curve the monopoly faces is

$$p = Q^{1/\varepsilon}. \tag{11B.1}$$

The monopoly's revenue is $R = pQ = Q^{1+1/\varepsilon}$. By differentiating, we learn that the monopoly's marginal revenue is $MR = (1 + 1/\varepsilon)Q^{1/\varepsilon}$.

To maximize its profit, the monopoly operates where its marginal revenue equals its marginal cost:

$$MR = (1 + 1/\varepsilon)Q^{1/\varepsilon} = m = MC.$$

Solving this equation for the profit-maximizing output, we find that $Q = [m/(1 + 1/\varepsilon)]^\varepsilon$. Substituting that value of Q into Equation 11B.1, we find that

$$p = m/(1 + 1/\varepsilon)$$

A specific tax of τ per unit raises the marginal cost to $m + \tau$, so that the monopoly price increases to

$$p_t = (m + \tau)/(1 + 1/\varepsilon).$$

Consequently, the increase in price is $\tau/(1 + 1/\varepsilon)$. The incidence of the tax that falls on consumers is $\Delta p/\Delta \tau = [\tau/(1 + 1/\varepsilon)]/\tau = 1/(1 + 1/\varepsilon) > 1$, because $\varepsilon < -1$ (a monopoly never operates in the inelastic portion of its demand curve).

Appendix 12A: Perfect Price Discrimination

A perfectly price-discriminating monopoly charges each customer the reservation price $p = D(Q)$, where $D(Q)$ is the inverse demand function and Q is total output. The discriminating monopoly's revenue, R, is the area under the demand curve up to the quantity, Q, it sells:

$$R = \int_0^Q D(z)\,dz,$$

where z is a placeholder for quantity. Its objective is to maximize its profit through its choice of Q:

$$\max_Q \pi = \int_0^Q D(z)\,dz - C(Q). \tag{12A.1}$$

Its first-order condition for a maximum is found by differentiating Equation 12A.1 to obtain

$$\frac{d\pi}{dQ} = D(Q) - \frac{dC(Q)}{dQ} = 0. \tag{12A.2}$$

According to Equation 12A.2, the discriminating monopoly sells units up to the quantity, Q, where the reservation price for the last unit, $D(Q)$, equals its marginal cost, $dC(Q)/dQ$. (This quantity is $Q_c = Q_d$ in Figure 12.2.)

For this solution to maximize profits, the second-order condition must hold: $d^2\pi/dQ^2 = dD(Q)/dQ - d^2C(Q)/dQ^2 < 0$. Thus the second-order condition holds if the marginal cost curve has a nonnegative slope (because the demand curve has a negative slope). More generally, the second-order condition holds if the demand curve has a greater (absolute) slope than the marginal cost curve.

The perfectly price-discriminating monopoly's profit is

$$\pi = \int_0^Q D(z)\,dz - C(Q).$$

For example, if $D(Q) = a - bQ$,

$$\pi = \int_0^Q (a - bz)\,dz - C(Q) = aQ - \frac{b}{2}Q^2 - C(Q). \qquad (12A.3)$$

The monopoly finds the output that maximizes the profit by setting the derivative of the profit in Equation 12A.3 equal to zero:

$$a - bQ - \frac{dC(Q)}{dQ} = 0.$$

By rearranging terms, we find that $D(Q) = a - bQ = dC(Q)/dQ = MC$, as in Equation 12A.2. Thus the monopoly produces the quantity at which the demand curve hits the marginal cost curve.

Appendix 12B: Quantity Discrimination

In the block-pricing example in the chapter, we assume that the utility monopoly faces an inverse demand curve $p = \$90 - Q$ and that its marginal and average cost is $m = \$30$. Consequently, the quantity-discounting utility's profit is

$$\pi = p(Q_1)Q_1 + p(Q_2)(Q_2 - Q_1) - mQ_2$$
$$= (90 - Q_1)Q_1 + (90 - Q_2)(Q_2 - Q_1) - 30Q_2,$$

where Q_1 is the largest quantity for which the first-block rate, $p_1 = \$90 - Q_1$, is charged and Q_2 is the total quantity a consumer purchases. The utility chooses Q_1 and Q_2 to maximize its profit. It sets the derivative of profit with respect to Q_1 equal to zero, $Q_2 - 2Q_1 = 0$, and the derivative of profit with respect to Q_2 equal to zero, $Q_1 - 2Q_2 + 60 = 0$. By solving these two equations, the utility determines its profit-maximizing quantities, $Q_1 = 20$ and $Q_2 = 40$. The corresponding block prices are $p_1 = \$90 - \$20 = \$70$ and $p_2 = \$50$.

Appendix 12C: Multimarket Price Discrimination

Suppose that a monopoly can divide its customers into two groups, as in Figure 12.4. It sells Q_1 to the first group and earns revenues of $R_1(Q_1)$, and it sells Q_2 units to the second group and earns $R_2(Q_2)$. Its cost of producing total output $Q = Q_1 + Q_2$ units is $C(Q)$. The monopoly can maximize its profit through its choice of prices or quantities to each group. We examine its problem when it chooses quantities:

$$\max_{Q_1, Q_2} \pi = R_1(Q_1) + R_2(Q_2) - C(Q_1 + Q_2). \qquad (12C.1)$$

The first-order conditions corresponding to Equation 12C.1 are obtained by differentiating with respect to Q_1 and Q_2 and setting the partial derivative equal to zero:

$$\frac{\partial \pi}{\partial Q_1} = \frac{dR_1(Q_1)}{dQ_1} - \frac{dC(Q)}{dQ}\frac{\partial Q}{\partial Q_1} = 0, \tag{12C.2}$$

$$\frac{\partial \pi}{\partial Q_2} = \frac{dR_2(Q_2)}{dQ_2} - \frac{dC(Q)}{dQ}\frac{\partial Q}{\partial Q_2} = 0. \tag{12C.3}$$

Equation 12C.2 says that the marginal revenue from sales to the first group, $MR^1 = dR_1(Q_1)/dQ_1$, should equal the marginal cost of producing the last unit of total output, $MC = dC(Q)/dQ$, because $\partial Q/\partial Q_1 = 1$. Similarly, Equation 12C.3 says that the marginal revenue from the second group, MR^2, should also equal the marginal cost. By combining Equations 12C.2 and 12C.3, we find that the two marginal revenues are equal where the monopoly is profit maximizing:

$$MR^1 = MR^2 = MC.$$

Appendix 12D: Two-Part Tariffs

In the example of a two-part tariff with nonidentical consumers, the demand curves for Consumers 1 and 2 are $q_1 = 80 - p$ and $q_2 = 100 - p$. The consumer surplus for Consumer 1 is $CS_1 = \frac{1}{2}(80 - p)q_1 = \frac{1}{2}(80 - p)^2$. Similarly, $CS_2 = \frac{1}{2}(100 - p)^2$. If the monopoly charges the lower fee, $\mathcal{L} = CS_1$, it sells to both consumers and its profit is

$$\pi = 2\mathcal{L} + (p - m)(q_1 + q_2) = (80 - p)^2 + (p - 10)(180 - 2p).$$

Setting the derivative of π with respect to p equal to zero, we find that the profit-maximizing price is $p = 20$. The monopoly charges a fee of $\mathcal{L} = CS_1 = \$1,800$ and makes a profit of $\$5,000$. If the monopoly charges the higher fee, $\mathcal{L} = CS_2$, it sells only to Consumer 2, and its profit is

$$\pi = \mathcal{L} + (p - m)q_2 = \frac{1}{2}(100 - p)^2 + (p - 10)(100 - p).$$

The monopoly's profit-maximizing price is $p = 10$, and its profit is $\mathcal{L} = CS_2 = \$4,050$. Thus the monopoly makes more by setting $\mathcal{L} = CS_1$ and selling to both customers.

Appendix 13A: Cournot Equilibrium

Here we use calculus to determine the Cournot equilibrium for n identical oligopolistic firms. We first solve for the equilibrium using general demand and cost functions, which are identical for all firms. Then we apply this general solution to a linear example. Finally, using the linear example, we determine the equilibrium when two firms have different marginal costs.

General Model

Suppose that the market demand function is $p(Q)$ and that each firm's cost function is the same $C(q_i)$. To analyze a Cournot market of identical firms, we first examine the behavior of a representative firm. Firm 1 tries to maximize its profits through its choice of q_1:

$$\max_{q_1} \pi_1(q_1, q_2, \ldots, q_n) = q_1 p(q_1 + q_2 + \ldots + q_n) - C(q_1), \qquad (13A.1)$$

where $q_1 + q_2 + \cdots + q_n = Q$, the total market output. Firm 1 takes the outputs of the other firms as fixed. If Firm 1 changes its output by a small amount, the price changes by $(dp(Q)/dQ)(dQ/dq_1) = dp(Q)/dQ$. Its necessary condition to maximize profit (first-order condition) is found by differentiating profit in Equation 13A.1 and setting the result equal to zero. After we rearrange terms, this necessary condition is

$$MR = p(Q) + q_1 \frac{dp(Q)}{dQ} = \frac{dC(q_1)}{dq_1} = MC, \qquad (13A.2)$$

or marginal revenue equals marginal cost. Equation 13A.2 specifies the firm's best-response function: the optimal q_1 for any given output of other firms.

The marginal revenue expression can be rewritten as $p[1 + (q_1/p)(dp/dQ)]$. Multiplying and dividing the last term by n, noting that $Q = nq_1$ (given that all firms are identical), and observing that ε, the market elasticity of demand, is $(dQ/dp)(p/Q)$, we can rewrite Equation 13A.2 as

$$p\left(1 + \frac{1}{n\varepsilon}\right) = \frac{dC(q_1)}{dq_1}. \qquad (13A.3)$$

The left-hand side of Equation 13A.3 expresses Firm 1's marginal revenue in terms of the elasticity of demand of its residual demand curve, $n\varepsilon$, which is the number of firms, n, times the market demand elasticity, ε. Holding ε constant, the more firms, the more elastic the residual demand curve, and hence the closer a firm's marginal revenue to the price.

We can rearrange Equation 13A.3 to obtain an expression for the Lerner Index, $(p - MC)/p$, in terms of the market demand elasticity and the number of firms:

$$\frac{p - MC}{p} = -\frac{1}{n\varepsilon}. \qquad (13A.4)$$

The larger the Lerner Index, the greater the firm's market power. As Equation 13A.4 shows, if we hold the market elasticity constant and increase the number of firms, the Lerner Index falls. As n approaches ∞, the elasticity any one firm faces approaches $-\infty$, so the Lerner Index approaches 0 and the market is competitive.

Linear Example

Now suppose that the market demand is linear,

$$p = a - bQ,$$

and each firm's marginal cost is m, a constant, and it has no fixed cost. Firm 1, a typical firm, maximizes its profits through its choice of q_1:

$$\max_{q_1} \pi_1(q_1, q_2, \cdots, q_n) = q_1[a - b(q_1 + q_2 + \cdots + q_n)] - mq_1. \qquad (13A.5)$$

Setting the derivative of profit with respect to q_1, holding the output levels of the other firms fixed, equal to zero, and rearranging terms, we find that the necessary condition for Firm 1 to maximize its profit is

$$MR = a - b(2q_1 + q_2 + \cdots + q_n) = m = MC. \tag{13A.6}$$

Because all firms have the same cost function, $q_2 = q_3 = \cdots = q_n \equiv q$ in equilibrium. Substituting this expression into Equation 13A.6, we find that the first firm's best-response function is

$$q_1 = R_1(q_2, \ldots, q_n) = \frac{a - m}{2b} - \frac{n - 1}{2} q. \tag{13A.7}$$

The other firms' best-response functions are derived similarly.

All these best-response functions must hold simultaneously. The intersection of the best-response functions determines the Cournot equilibrium. Setting $q_1 = q$ in Equation 13A.7 and solving for q, we find that the Cournot equilibrium output for each firm is

$$q = \frac{a - m}{(n + 1)b}. \tag{13A.8}$$

Total market output, $Q = nq$, equals $n(a - m)/[(n + 1)b]$. The corresponding price is obtained by substituting this expression for market output into the demand function:

$$p = \frac{a + nm}{n + 1}. \tag{13A.9}$$

Setting $n = 1$ in Equations 13A.8 and 13A.9 yields the monopoly quantity and price. As n becomes large, each firm's quantity approaches zero, total output approaches $(a - m)/b$, and price approaches m, which are the competitive levels. In Equation 13A.9, the Lerner Index is

$$\frac{p - MC}{p} = \frac{a - m}{a + nm}.$$

As n grows large, the denominator goes to ∞, so the Lerner Index goes to 0, and there is no market power.

Different Costs

In the linear example with two firms, how does the equilibrium change if the firms have different marginal costs? The marginal cost of Firm 1 is m_1, and that of Firm 2 is m_2. Firm 1 chooses output to maximize its profit:

$$\max_{q_1} \pi_1(q_1, q_2) = q_1[a - b(q_1 + q_2)] - m_1 q_1. \tag{13A.10}$$

Setting the derivative of Firm 1's profit with respect to q_1, holding q_2 fixed, equal to zero, and rearranging terms, we find that the necessary condition for Firm 1 to maximize its profit is $MR_1 = a - b(2q_1 + q_2) = m_1 = MC$. Using algebra, we can rearrange this expression to obtain Firm 1's best-response function:

$$q_1 = \frac{q - m_1 - bq_2}{2b}. \tag{13A.11}$$

By similar reasoning, Firm 2's best-response function is

$$q_2 = \frac{a - m_2 - bq_1}{2b}. \tag{13A.12}$$

To determine the equilibrium, we solve Equations 13A.11 and 13A.12 simultaneously for q_1 and q_2:

$$q_1 = \frac{a - 2m_1 + m_2}{3b}, \tag{13A.13}$$

$$q_2 = \frac{a - 2m_2 + m_1}{3b}. \tag{13A.14}$$

By inspecting Equations 13A.13 and 13A.14, we find that the firm with the smaller marginal cost has the larger equilibrium output. Similarly, the low-cost firm has a higher profit. If m_1 is less than m_2, then

$$\pi_1 = \frac{(a + m_2 - 2m_1)^2}{9b} > \frac{(a + m_1 - 2m_2)^2}{9b} = \pi_2.$$

Appendix 13B: Stackelberg Equilibrium

We use calculus to derive the Stackelberg equilibrium for the linear example given in Appendix 13A with two firms that have the same marginal cost, m. Because Firm 1, the Stackelberg leader, chooses its output first, it knows that Firm 2, the follower, will choose its output using its best-response function, which is (see Equation 13A.7, where $n = 2$)

$$q_2 = R_2(q_1) = \frac{a - m}{2b} - \frac{1}{2}q_1. \tag{13B.1}$$

The Stackelberg leader's profit, $\pi_1(q_1 + q_2)$, can be written as $\pi_1(q_1 + R_2(q_1))$, where we've replaced the follower's output with its best-response function. The Stackelberg leader maximizes its profit by taking the best-response function as given:

$$\max_{q_1} \pi_1(q_1, R_2(q_1)) = q_1\left[a - b\left(q_1 + \frac{a - m}{2b} - \frac{1}{2}q_1\right)\right] - mq_1. \tag{13B.2}$$

Setting the derivative of Firm 1's profit (in Equation 13B.2) with respect to q_1 equal to zero and solving for q_1, we find that the profit-maximizing output of the leader is

$$q_1 = \frac{a - m}{2b}. \tag{13B.3}$$

Substituting the expression for q_1 in Equation 13B.3 into Equation 13B.1, we obtain the equilibrium output of the follower:

$$q_2 = \frac{a - m}{4b}.$$

Appendix 13C: Bertrand Equilibrium

We can use math to determine the cola market Bertrand equilibrium discussed in the chapter. First, we determine the best-response functions each firm faces. Then we equate the best-response functions to determine the equilibrium prices for the two firms.

Coke's best-response function tells us the price Coke charges that maximizes its profit as a function of the price Pepsi charges. We use the demand curve for Coke to derive the best-response function.

The reason Coke's price depends on Pepsi's price is that the quantity of Coke demanded, q_c, depends on the price of Coke, p_c, and the price of Pepsi, p_p. Coke's demand curve is

$$q_c = 58 - 4p_c + 2p_p. \tag{13C.1}$$

Partially differentiating Equation 13C.1 with respect to p_c (that is, holding the price of Pepsi fixed), we find that the change in quantity for every dollar change in price is $\partial q_c / \partial p_c = -4$, so a \$1-per-unit increase in the price of Coke causes the quantity of Coke demanded to fall by 4 units. Similarly, the demand for Coke rises by 2 units if the price of Pepsi rises by \$1, while the price of Coke remains constant: $\partial q_c / \partial p_p = 2$.

If Coke faces a constant marginal and average cost of m per unit, its profit is

$$\pi_c = (p_c - m)q_c = (p_c - m)(50 - 4p_c + 2p_p), \tag{13C.2}$$

where $p_c - m$ is Coke's profit per unit. To determine Coke's profit-maximizing price (holding Pepsi's price fixed), we set the partial derivative of the profit function, Equation 13C.2, with respect to the price of Coke equal to zero,

$$\frac{\partial \pi_c}{\partial p_c} = q_c + (p_c - m)\frac{\partial q_c}{\partial p_c} = q_c - 4(p_c - m) = 0, \tag{13C.3}$$

and solve for p_c as a function of p_p and m to find Coke's best-response function:

$$p_c = 7.25 + 0.25p_p + 0.5m. \tag{13C.4}$$

Equation 13C.4 shows that Coke's best-response price is 25¢ higher for every extra dollar that Pepsi charges and 50¢ higher for every extra dollar of Coke's marginal cost.

If Coke's average and marginal cost of production is \$5 per unit, its best-response function is

$$p_c = 9.75 + 0.25p_p, \tag{13C.5}$$

as Figure 13.11 shows. If $p_p = \$13$, then Coke's best response is to set $p_c = \$13$.

Using the same approach, we find that Pepsi's best-response function (for $m = \$5$) is

$$p_p = 10.4 + 0.2p_c. \tag{13C.6}$$

The intersection of Coke's and Pepsi's best-response functions (Equations 13C.5 and 13C.6) determines the Nash equilibrium. By substituting Pepsi's best-response function, Equation 13C.6, for p_p in Coke's best-response function, Equation 13C.5, we find that

$$p_c = 9.75 + 0.25(10.4 + 0.2p_c).$$

Solving this equation for p_c, we determine that the equilibrium price of Coke is \$13. Substituting $p_c = \$13$ into Equation 13C.6, we discover that the equilibrium price of Pepsi is also \$13.

Appendix 14A: Mixed Strategies

In the simultaneous-entry game in Table 14.1, the firms may use mixed strategies where each firm may enter (or not) with equal probability. Why would a firm pick a mixed strategy where its probability of entering is one-half?

Because the payoff matrix is symmetrical, we can look for an equilibrium in which each firm has the same probability of entering. If Firm 1 uses a mixed strategy, it must be willing to use either of the pure strategies, so it must be indifferent between staying out and entering. Thus the probability that Firm 2 enters, α, must be such that Firm 1's expected profit from staying out, $E\pi_n^1$, equals its expected profit from entering, $E\pi_e^1$:

$$E\pi_n^1 = 0(1 - \alpha) + 0\alpha = 1(1 - \alpha) + (-1)\alpha = E\pi_e^1.$$

For the expected profits to be equal, it must be true that $E\pi_e^1 = 1(1 - \alpha) + (-1)\alpha = 0$, so $\alpha = \frac{1}{2}$. Similarly, Firm 2 uses a mixed strategy if it thinks that the probability that Firm 1 enters is $\frac{1}{2}$. (In general, firms' mixed strategies can differ, and the probability that a firm chooses a strategy need not equal one-half.)

Appendix 14B: Profit-Maximizing Advertising and Production

To maximize its profit, a monopoly must optimally set its advertising, A, and quantity, Q. Suppose that advertising affects only current sales, so the demand curve the monopoly faces is

$$p = p(Q, A).$$

As a result, the firm's revenue is

$$R = p(Q, A)Q = R(Q, A).$$

The firm's cost of production is the function $C(Q)$. Its cost of advertising is A, because each unit of advertising costs \$1 (we chose the units of measure appropriately). Thus its total cost is $C(Q) + A$.

The monopoly maximizes its profit through its choice of quantity and advertising:

$$\max_{Q,A} \pi = R(Q, A) - C(Q) - A. \tag{14B.1}$$

Its necessary (first-order) conditions are found by differentiating the profit function in Equation 14B.1 with respect to Q and A in turn:

$$\frac{\partial \pi(Q, A)}{\partial Q} = \frac{\partial R(Q, A)}{\partial Q} - \frac{dC(Q)}{dQ} = 0, \tag{14B.2}$$

$$\frac{\partial \pi(Q, A)}{\partial A} = \frac{\partial R(Q, A)}{\partial A} - 1 = 0. \tag{14B.3}$$

The profit-maximizing output and advertising levels are the Q^* and A^* that simultaneously satisfy Equations 14B.2 and 14B.3. Equation 14B.2 says that output should be chosen so that the marginal revenue, $\partial R(Q,A)/(\partial Q)$, equals the marginal cost, $dC(Q)/(dQ)$. Equation 14B.3 says that the monopoly advertises to the point where its marginal revenue from the last unit of advertising, $\partial R(Q, A)/(\partial A)$, equals the marginal cost of the last unit of advertising, \$1.

Appendix 15A: Factor Demands

If a competitive firm hires L units of labor at a wage rate of w and K units of capital at a rental rate of r, it can produce $q = f(L, K)$ units of output. The firm sells its output at the market price of p. The firm picks L and K to maximize its profit:

$$\max_{L,K} \pi = pq - (wL + rK) = pf(L, K) - (wL + rK). \tag{15A.1}$$

Thus the firm's revenue, pq, and cost both depend on L and K, so its profit depends on L and K.

Profit is maximized by setting the partial derivatives of profit (in Equation 15A.1) with respect to L and K equal to zero:

$$\frac{\partial \pi}{\partial L} = pMP_L - w = 0, \tag{15A.2}$$

$$\frac{\partial \pi}{\partial L} = pMP_K - r = 0, \tag{15A.3}$$

where $MP_L = \partial f(L, K)/\partial L$, the marginal product of labor, is the partial derivative of the production function with respect to L, and $MP_K = \partial f(L, K)/\partial K$ is the marginal product of capital. Solving Equations 15A.2 and 15A.3 simultaneously produces the factor demand equations.

Rearranging Equations 15A.2 and 15A.3, we can write these factor demand equations as

$$MRP_L \equiv pMP_L = w,$$

$$MRP_K \equiv pMP_K = r.$$

Thus the firm maximizes its profit when it picks its inputs such that the marginal revenue product of labor equals the wage and the marginal revenue product of capital equals the rental rate of capital. For these conditions to produce a maximum, the second-order conditions must also hold. These second-order conditions say that the MRP_L and MRP_K curves slope downward.

If the production function is Cobb-Douglas, $q = AL^\alpha K^\beta$, then Equations 15A.2 and 15A.3 are

$$\frac{\partial \pi}{\partial L} = p\alpha AL^{\alpha-1}K^\beta - w = 0,$$

$$\frac{\partial \pi}{\partial K} = p\beta AL^\alpha K^{\beta-1} - r = 0.$$

Solving these equations for L and K, we find that the factor demand functions are

$$L = \left(\frac{\alpha}{w}\right)^{(1-\beta)/\delta}\left(\frac{\beta}{r}\right)^{\beta/\delta}(Ap)^{1/\delta}, \tag{15A.4}$$

$$K = \left(\frac{\alpha}{w}\right)^{\alpha/\delta}\left(\frac{\beta}{r}\right)^{(1-\alpha)/\delta}(Ap)^{1/\delta}, \tag{15A.5}$$

where $\delta = 1 - \alpha - \beta$. By differentiating Equations 15A.4 and 15A.5, we can show that the demand for each factor decreases with w or r and increases with p.

If the Cobb-Douglas production function has constant returns to scale, $\delta = 0$, then Equations 15A.4 and 15A.5 are not helpful. The problem is that with constant returns to scale, a competitive firm with a Cobb-Douglas production function does not care how much it produces (and hence how many inputs it uses) as long as the market price and input prices are consistent with zero profit.

A competitive firm with a Cobb-Douglas production function pays labor the value of its marginal product, $w = p \times MP_L = p \times \alpha AL^{\alpha-1}K^\beta = \alpha pQ/L$. As a result, the share of the firm's revenues that is paid to labor is $\omega_L = wL/(pQ) = \alpha$. Similarly, $\omega_K = rK/(pQ) = \beta$. Thus with a Cobb-Douglas production function, the shares of labor and of capital are fixed and independent of prices.

Appendix 15B: Monopsony

If only one firm can hire labor in a town, the firm is a monopsony. It chooses how much labor to hire to maximize its profit,

$$\pi = p(Q(L))Q(L) - w(L)L,$$

where $Q(L)$ is the production function, the amount of output produced using L hours of labor, and $w(L)$ is the labor supply curve, which shows how the wage varies with the amount of labor the firm hires. The firm maximizes its profit by setting the derivative of profit with respect to labor equal to zero (if the second-order condition holds):

$$\left(p + Q(L)\frac{\mathrm{d}p}{\mathrm{d}Q}\right)\frac{\mathrm{d}Q}{\mathrm{d}L} - w(L) - \frac{\mathrm{d}w}{\mathrm{d}L}L = 0. \tag{15B.1}$$

Rearranging terms in Equation 15B.1, we find that the maximization condition is that the marginal revenue product of labor,

$$MRP_L = p \times MPL = \left(p + Q(L)\frac{\mathrm{d}p}{\mathrm{d}Q}\right)\frac{\mathrm{d}Q}{\mathrm{d}L} = p\left(1 + \frac{1}{\varepsilon}\right)\frac{\mathrm{d}Q}{\mathrm{d}L},$$

equals the marginal expenditure,

$$ME = w(L) + \frac{\mathrm{d}w}{\mathrm{d}L}L = w(L)\left(1 + \frac{w}{L}\frac{\mathrm{d}w}{\mathrm{d}L}\right) = w(L)\left(1 + \frac{1}{\eta}\right), \tag{15B.2}$$

where η is the supply elasticity of labor.

If the supply curve is linear, $w(L) = g + hL$, the monopsony's expenditure is $E = w(L)L = gL + hL^2$, and the monopsony's marginal expenditure is $ME = \mathrm{d}E/\mathrm{d}L = g + 2hL$. Thus the slope of the marginal expenditure curve, $2h$, is twice as great as that of the supply curve, h.

By rearranging the terms in Equation 15B.2, we find that

$$\frac{ME - w}{w} = \frac{1}{\eta}.$$

Thus the markup of the marginal expenditure (and the value to the monopsony) to the wage, $(ME - w)/w$, is inversely proportional to the elasticity of supply. If the firm is a price taker, so η is infinite, the wage equals the marginal expenditure.

Appendix 16A: Perpetuity

We derive Equation 16.4, $PV = f/i$, which gives the present value, PV, of a stream of payments f that lasts forever if the interest rate is i. Using Equation 16.3, where the number of periods is infinite, we know that the present value is

$$PV = \frac{f}{1 + i} + \frac{f}{(1 + i)^2} + \frac{f}{(1 + i)^3} + \cdots. \tag{16A.1}$$

Factoring Equation 16A.1, we can factor $1/(1 + i)$ out and rewrite the equation as

$$PV = \frac{1}{1 + i}\left[f + \frac{f}{1 + i} + \frac{f}{(1 + i)^2} + \frac{f}{(1 + i)^3} + \cdots\right]. \tag{16A.2}$$

The term in the brackets in Equation 16A.2 is $f + PV$ as given in Equation 16A.1. When we make this substitution, Equation 16A.2 becomes

$$PV = \frac{1}{1+i}(f + PV). \tag{16A.3}$$

Rearranging terms in Equation 16A.3, we obtain Equation 16A.4:

$$PV = \frac{f}{i}.$$

Appendix 18A: Welfare Effects of Pollution in a Competitive Market

We now show the welfare effects of a negative externality in a competitive market where demand and marginal costs are linear, as in Figure 18.1. The inverse demand curve is

$$p = a - bQ, \tag{18A.1}$$

where p is the price of the output and Q is the quantity. The private marginal cost is the competitive supply curve if pollution is an externality:

$$MC^p = c + dQ. \tag{18A.2}$$

The marginal cost to people exposed to the pollution (gunk) is

$$MC^g = eQ. \tag{18A.3}$$

Equation 18A.3 shows that there is no pollution harm if output is zero and that the marginal harm increases linearly with output. The social marginal cost is the sum of the private marginal cost and the marginal cost of the externality:

$$MC^s = c + (d + e)Q. \tag{18A.4}$$

The intersection of the demand curve, Equation 18A.1, and the supply curve, Equation 18A.2, determines the competitive equilibrium where pollution is an externality:

$$p_c = a - bQ_c = c + dQ_c = MC^p. \tag{18A.5}$$

If we solve Equation 18A.5 for Q, the competitive equilibrium quantity is

$$Q_c = \frac{a - c}{b + d}.$$

Substituting this quantity into the demand curve, we find that the competitive price is $p_c = a - b(a - c)/(b + d)$.

If the externality is taxed at a rate equal to its marginal cost, so the externality is internalized, the market produces the social optimum. We find the social optimum by setting p in Equation 18A.1 equal to MC^s in Equation 18A.4 and solving for the resulting quantity:

$$Q_s = \frac{a - c}{b + d + e}.$$

The corresponding price is $p_s = a - b(a - c)/(b + d + e)$.

If output is sold only by a monopoly, the monopoly's revenue is found by multiplying both sides of Equation 18A.1 by quantity: $R = aQ - bQ^2$. Differentiating with respect to quantity, we find that the monopoly's marginal revenue is

$$MR = a - 2bQ. \tag{18A.6}$$

If the monopoly is unregulated, its equilibrium is found by setting MR, Equation 18A.6, equal to private marginal cost, Equation 18A.2, and solving for output:

$$Q_m = \frac{a - c}{2b + d}.$$

The corresponding price is $p_m = a - b(a - c)/(2b + d)$. If the monopoly internalizes the externality due to a tax equal to MC^g, the equilibrium quantity is

$$Q_m^* = \frac{a - c}{2b + d + e}.$$

The price is $p_m^* = a - b(a - c)/(2b + d + e)$.

In Figure 18.1, $a = 450$, $b = 2$, $c = 30$, $d = 2$, and $e = 1$. Substituting these values into the equations, we solve for the following equilibrium values:

	Quantity	Price
Competition	105	240
Social optimum (competition with a tax)	84	282
Monopoly	70	310
Monopoly with a tax	60	330

Appendix 20A: Nonshirking Condition

An efficiency wage acts like a bond to prevent shirking. An employee who never shirks is not fired and earns the efficiency wage, w. A fired worker goes elsewhere and earns the lower, going wage, $\underline{w}$. The expected value to a shirking employee is

$$\theta \underline{w} + (1 - \theta)w + G,$$

where the first term is the probability of being caught shirking, θ, times earnings elsewhere if caught and fired; the second term is the probability of not being caught times the efficiency wage; and the third term, G, is the value a worker derives from shirking. The worker chooses not to shirk if the certain high wage from not shirking exceeds the expected return from shirking:

$$w \geq (1 - \theta)w + \theta \underline{w} + G,$$

which simplifies to Equation 20.2, $\theta(w - \underline{w}) \geq G$. That is, a risk-neutral worker does not shirk if the expected loss from being fired is greater than or equal to the gain from shirking.

ANSWERS TO SELECTED PROBLEMS

I know the answer! The answer lies within the heart of all mankind! The answer is twelve? I think I'm in the wrong building.

—Charles Schultz

Chapter 2

8. The law would create a price ceiling (at 110% of the pre-emergency price). Because the supply curve shifts substantially to the left during the emergency, the price control will create a shortage: A smaller quantity will be supplied at the ceiling price than will be demanded.

9. A ban has no effect if foreigners supply nothing at the pre-ban, equilibrium price. Thus if imports occur only at prices above those actually observed, a ban has no practical effect.

14. The statement "Talk is cheap because supply exceeds demand" makes sense if we interpret it to mean that the *quantity supplied* of talk exceeds the *quantity demanded* at a price of zero. Imagine a downward-sloping demand curve that hits the horizontal, quantity axis to the left of where the upward-sloping supply curve hits the axis.

16. The demand curve for pork is $Q = 171 - 20p + 20p_b + 3p_c + 2Y$, where quantity is measured in millions of kg per year and income is measured in thousands of dollars per year. As a result, a ΔY change in income causes the quantity demanded to change by $\Delta Q = 2\Delta Y$. That is, a $1,000 increase in income causes the quantity demanded to increase by 2 million kg per year, and a $100 increase in income causes the quantity demanded to increase by a tenth as much, 0.2 million kg per year.

19. In equilibrium, the quantity demanded, $Q = a - bp$, equals the quantity supplied, $Q = c + ep$, so

$$a - bp = c + ep.$$

By solving this equation for p, we find that the equilibrium price is $p = (a - c)/(b + e)$. By substituting this expression for p into either the demand curve or the supply curve, we find that the equilibrium quantity is $Q = (ae + bc)/(b + e)$.

Chapter 3

1. According to Equation 3.1, the elasticity of demand is ε = (percentage change in quantity demanded) ÷ (percentage change in price) = –3% ÷ 2% = –1.5.

5. A binding rent control law results in excess demand in the short run and transfers wealth from landlords to renters by reducing the rent paid. In the long run, the supply curve of apartments shifts to the left and quality falls as landlords convert some existing apartments to condominiums, allow other units to deteriorate, and build fewer new units than they would without the law. As a consequence, the excess demand may be greater in the long run than in the short run.

11. We showed that, in a competitive market, the effect of a specific tax is the same whether it is placed on suppliers or demanders. Thus if the market for milk is competitive, consumers will pay the same price in equilibrium regardless of whether the government taxes consumers or stores.

14. The elasticity of demand is (slope) $\times$ (p/Q) = $(\Delta Q/\Delta p)(p/Q)$ = (–9.5 thousand metric tons per year per cent) $\times$ (45¢/1,275 thousand metric tons per year) $\approx$ –0.34. That is, for every 1% fall in the price, a third of a percent more coconut oil is demanded. The cross-price elasticity of demand for coconut oil with respect to the price of palm oil is $(\Delta Q/\Delta p_p)(p_p/Q)$ = 16.2 × (31/1,275) $\approx$ 0.39.

16. Because the linear supply function is $Q = g + hp$, a change in price of Δp causes a $\Delta Q = h\Delta p$ change in quantity. Thus $\Delta Q/\Delta p = h$, and the elasticity of supply is $\eta = (\Delta Q/\Delta p)(p/Q) = hp/Q$. By substituting for Q using the supply function, we find that $\eta = hp/(g + hp)$. By using the supply function to substitute for p, we learn that $\eta = (Q - g)/Q$.

20. By dividing both the numerator and the denominator of the right-hand side of Equation 3.7 by η, we can rewrite that incidence equation as

$$\frac{\eta}{\eta - \varepsilon} = \frac{1}{1 - \varepsilon / \eta}.$$

As η goes to infinity, ε/η goes to zero, so the incidence approaches 1.

21. Differentiating quantity, $Q(p(\tau))$, with respect to the specific tax τ, we learn that the change in quantity as the tax changes is $dQ/d\tau = (dQ/dp)(dp/d\tau)$. Multiplying and dividing this expression by p/Q, we find that the change in quantity as the tax changes is $\varepsilon(Q/p)(dp/d\tau)$. Thus the closer ε is to zero, the less the quantity falls, all else the same. The tax causes revenue to change by

$$\frac{dR}{d\tau} = \left(Q + p\frac{dQ}{dp} \right)\frac{dp}{d\tau} = (1 + \varepsilon)Q\frac{dp}{d\tau}.$$

The closer ε is to zero, the larger the tax revenue effect.

Chapter 4

2. See www.awlonline.com/perloff, Chapter 4.

4. If the neutral product is on the vertical axis, the indifference curves are parallel vertical lines.

9. Suppose that Dale purchases two goods at prices p_1 and p_2. If her original income is Y, the intercept of the budget line on the Good 1 axis (where the consumer buys only Good 1) is Y/p_1. Similarly, the intercept is Y/p_2 on the Good 2 axis. A 50% income tax lowers income to half its original level, $Y/2$. As a result, the budget line shifts inward toward the origin. The intercepts on the Good 1 and Good 2 axes are $Y/(2p_1)$ and $Y/(2p_2)$, respectively. The opportunity set shrinks by the area between the original budget line and the new line.

17. If we plot B on the vertical axis and Z on the horizontal axis, the slope of Steve's indifference curve is $-MU_Z/MU_B = -2$. The marginal utility from one extra unit of Z is twice that from one extra unit of B. Thus if the price of Z is less than twice as much as that of B, Steve buys only Z (the optimal bundle is on the Z axis at Y/p_Z, where Y is his income and p_Z is the price of Z). If the price of Z is more than twice that of B, Steve buys only B. If the price of Z is exactly twice as much as that of B, he is indifferent

between buying any bundle along his budget line.

20. Using Equations 4B.11 and 4B.12, we find that the necessary conditions for a utility maximum are $B = \alpha Y/[2(\alpha + \beta)]$ and $Z = \beta Y/(\alpha + \beta)$.

Chapter 5

4. An opera performance must be a normal good for Don because he views the only other good he buys as an inferior good. To show this result in a graph, draw a figure similar to Figure 5.3, but relabel the vertical "Housing" axis as "Opera performances." Don's equilibrium will be in the upper-left quadrant at a point like a in Figure 5.3.

7. The CPI accurately reflects the true cost of living because Bessie does not substitute between the goods as the relative prices change.

9. On the graph on the next page, L^f is the budget line at the factory store and L^o is the constraint at the outlet store. At the factory store, the consumer maximum occurs at e_f on indifference curve I^f. Suppose that we increase the income of a consumer who shops at the outlet store to Y^*, so that the resulting budget line L^* is tangent to the indifference curve I^f. The consumer would buy Bundle e^*. That is, the pure substitution effect (the movement from e_f to e^*) causes the consumer to buy relatively more firsts. The total effect (the movement from e_f to e_o) reflects both the substitution effect (firsts are now relatively less expensive) and the income effect (the consumer is worse off after paying for shipping).

★23. The consumer's budget constraint is

$$p_1 q_1 + p_2 q_2 + \cdots + p_n q_n = Y,$$

where Y is income and p_i is the price and q_i is the quantity of Good i. Differentiating with respect to Y, we find that

$$p_1 \frac{dq_1}{dY} + p_2 \frac{dq_2}{dY} + \cdots + p_n \frac{dq_n}{dY} = \frac{dY}{dY} = 1.$$

Multiplying and dividing each term by $q_i Y$, we rewrite this last equation as

$$\frac{p_1 q_1}{Y} \frac{dq_1}{dY} \frac{Y}{q_1} + \frac{p_2 q_2}{Y} \frac{dq_2}{dY} \frac{Y}{q_2}$$

$$+ \cdots + \frac{p_n q_n}{Y} \frac{dq_n}{dY} \frac{Y}{q_n} = 1,$$

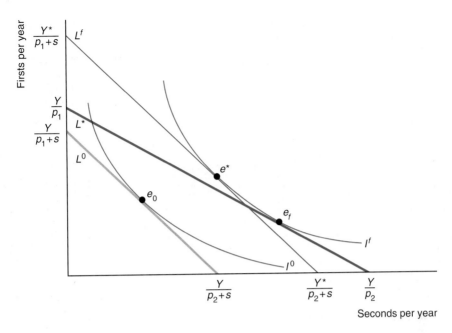

or

$$\omega_1\eta_1 + \omega_2\eta_2 + \cdots + \omega_n\eta_n = 1,$$

where η_i, the income elasticity for each Good i, equals $(dq_i/dY)(Y/q_i)$, and the budget share of Good i is $\omega_i = p_iq_i/Y$. That is, the weighted sum of the income elasticities equals 1. For this equation to hold, at least one of the goods must have a positive income elasticity; hence not all the goods can be inferior.

Chapter 6

1. One worker produces one unit of output, two workers produce two units of output, and n workers produce n units of output. Thus the total product of labor equals the number of workers: $q = L$. The total product of labor curve is a straight line with a slope of 1. Because we are told that each extra worker produces one more unit of output, we know that the marginal product of labor, $\Delta q/\Delta L$, is 1. By dividing both sides of the production function, $q = L$, by L, we find that the average product of labor, q/L, is 1.

6. The isoquant looks like the "right angle" ones in panel b of Figure 6.3 because the firm cannot substitute between disks and machines but must use them in equal proportions: one disk and one hour of machine services.

12. Not enough information is given to answer this question. If we assume that Japanese and American firms have identical production functions and produce using the same ratio of factors during good times, Japanese firms will have a lower average product of labor during recessions because they are less likely to lay off workers. However, it is not clear how Japanese and American firms expand output during good times (do they hire the same number of extra workers?). As a result, we cannot predict which country has the higher average product of labor.

16. The production function is $q = L^{3/4}K^{1/4}$. (a) As a result, the average product of labor, holding capital fixed at $\bar{K}$, is $AP_L = q/L = L^{-1/4}\bar{K}^{1/4} = (\bar{K}/L)^{1/4}$. (b) The marginal product of labor is $MP_L = dq/dL = \frac{3}{4}(\bar{K}/L)^{1/4}$. (c) If we double both inputs, output doubles to $(2L)^{3/4}(2K)^{1/4} = 2L^{3/4}K^{1/4} = 2q$, where q is the original output level. Thus this production function has constant returns to scale.

18. Using Equation 6.3, we know that the marginal rate of technical substitution is $MRTS = MP_L/MP_K = \frac{2}{3}$.

21. The marginal product of labor of Firm 1 is only 90% of the marginal product of labor of Firm 2 for a particular level of inputs. Using calculus, we find that the MP_L of Firm 1 is $\partial q_1/\partial L = 0.9\partial f(L, K)/\partial L = 0.9\partial q_2/\partial L$.

Chapter 7

1. If the plane cannot be resold, its purchase price is a sunk cost, which is unaffected by the number of times the plane is flown. Consequently, the average cost per flight falls with the number of flights, but the total cost of owning and operating the plane rises because of extra consumption of gasoline and maintenance. Thus the more frequently someone has reason to fly, the more likely that flying one's own plane costs less per flight than a ticket on a commercial airline. However, by making extra ("unnecessary") trips, Mr. Agassi raises his total cost of owning and operating the airplane.

4. The total cost of building a 1-cubic-foot crate is $6. It costs four times as much to build an 8-cubic-foot crate, $24. In general, as the height of a cube increases, the total cost of building it rises with the square of the height, but the volume increases with the cube of the height. Thus the cost per unit of volume falls.

5. You produce your output, exam points, using as inputs the time spent on Question 1, t_1, and the time spent on Question 2, t_2. If you have diminishing marginal returns to extra time on each problem, your isoquants have the usual shapes: They curve away from the origin. You face a constraint that you may spend no more than 60 minutes on the two questions: $60 = t_1 + t_2$. The slope of the 60-minute isocost curve is –1: For every extra minute you spend on Question 1, you have one less minute to spend on Question 2. To maximize your test score, given that you can spend no more than 60 minutes on the exam, you want to pick the highest isoquant that is tangent to your 60-minute isocost curve. At the tangency, the slope of your isocost curve, –1, equals the slope of your isoquant, $-MP_1/MP_2$. That is, your score on the exam is maximized when $MP_1 = MP_2$, where the last minute spent on Question 1 would increase your score by as much as spending it on Question 2 would. Therefore, you've allocated your time on the exam wisely if you are indifferent as to which question to work on during the last minute of the exam.

15. Let w be the cost of a unit of L and r be the cost of a unit of K. Because the two inputs are perfect substitutes in the production process, the firm uses only the less expensive of the two inputs.

Therefore, the long-run cost function is $C(q) = wq$ if $w \leq r$; otherwise, it is $C(q) = rq$.

21. The average cost of producing one unit is α (regardless of the value of β). If $\beta = 0$, the average cost does not change with volume. If learning by doing increases with volume, $\beta < 0$, so the average cost falls with volume. Here the average cost falls exponentially (a smooth curve that asymptotically approaches the quantity axis).

Chapter 8

2. Suppose that a U-shaped marginal cost curve cuts a competitive firm's demand curve (price line) from above at q_1 and from below at q_2. By increasing output to $q_2 + 1$, the firm earns extra profit because the last unit sells for price p, which is greater than the marginal cost of that last unit. Indeed, the price exceeds the marginal cost of all units between q_1 and q_2, so it is more profitable to produce q_2 than q_1. Thus the firm should either produce q_2 or shut down (if it is making a loss at q_2). We can derive this result using calculus. The second-order condition, Equation 8B.3, for a competitive firm requires that marginal cost cut the demand line from below at q^*, the profit-maximizing quantity: $dMC(q^*)/dq > 0$.

8. The shutdown notice reduces the firm's flexibility, which matters in an uncertain market. If conditions suddenly change, the firm may have to operate at a loss for six months before it can shut down. This potential extra expense of shutting down may discourage some firms from entering the market initially.

16. The competitive firm's marginal cost function is found by differentiating its cost function with respect to quantity: $dC(q)/dq = b + 2cq + 3dq^2$. The firm's necessary profit-maximizing condition is $p = MC = b + 2cq + 3dq^2$. The firm solves this equation for q for a specific price to determine its profit-maximizing output.

Chapter 9

4. If the tax is based on *economic* profit, the tax has no long-run effect because the firms make zero economic profit. If the tax is based on *business* profit and business profit is greater than economic

profit, the profit tax raises firms' after-tax costs and results in fewer firms in the market. The exact effect of the tax depends on why business profit is less than economic profit. For example, if the government ignores opportunity labor cost but includes all capital cost in computing profit, firms will substitute toward labor and away from capital.

8. Solved Problem 8.3 shows the long-run effect of a lump-sum tax in a competitive market. Consumer surplus falls by more than tax revenue increases, and producer surplus remains zero, so welfare falls.

16. The consumer surplus at a price of 30 is 450 = $\frac{1}{2}(30 \times 30)$.

Chapter 10

1. A tax is a negative subsidy. Thus we can use the same analysis as in Solved Problem 10.1 to answer this question (reversing the signs of the effects).

15. Amos's marginal rate of substitution is $MRS_a = [\alpha/(1 - \alpha)]H_a/G_a$, and Elise's is $MRS_e = [\beta/(1 - \beta)] H_e/G_e$.

★16. Along the contract curve, the two marginal rates of substitution are equal: $MRS_a = MRS_e$. Thus to find the contract curve, we equate the right-hand sides of the expressions for MRS_a and MRS_e from the answer to Problem 15. Using the information about the endowments and some algebra, we can write the (quadratic) formula for the contract curve as

$$(\beta - \alpha)G_aH_a + \beta(\alpha - 1)50G_a + \alpha(1 - \beta)100H_a = 0.$$

Chapter 11

3. Because the government takes a percentage of before-tax economic profit, the quantity that maximizes the monopoly's before-tax profit also maximizes its after-tax profit. Using calculus, we have the following: The before-tax profit is $\pi_B = R(Q) - C(Q)$, and the after-tax profit is $\pi_A = (1 - \gamma)[R(Q) - C(Q)]$. For both, the first-order condition is marginal revenue equals marginal cost: $R'(Q) = C'(Q)$. (See Figure 20.3.)

6. Yes. As the electric power utility application illustrates, the demand curve could cut the average cost

curve only in its downward-sloping section. Consequently, the average cost is strictly downward sloping in the relevant region.

16. The graph shows that the dominant firm–competitive fringe equilibrium, e_{df}, lies between the competitive equilibrium, e_c, and the monopoly equilibrium, e_m. The supply of the fringe erodes but does not eliminate the dominant firm's market power. The dominant firm still faces a downward-sloping residual demand curve—hence it retains some market power—but the residual demand curve lies below and is flatter than the market demand curve for the monopoly. Because the residual demand curve is flatter, the dominant firm faces a more elastic demand than the monopoly; hence the dominant firm sets a lower price. At this lower price, consumers demand more, and collectively, the dominant firm and the fringe produce more than the monopoly did alone. Thus consumers benefit from the entry of the fringe, and some but not all of the deadweight loss under monopoly is eliminated.

★17. Suppose that the monopoly faces a constant-elasticity demand curve, with elasticity ε, and has a constant marginal cost, m, and that the government imposes a specific tax of τ. The monopoly sets its price such that $p = (m + \tau)/(1 + 1/\varepsilon)$. Thus $dp/d\tau = 1/(1 + 1/\varepsilon) > 1$.

Chapter 12

2. This policy allows the firm to maximize its profit by price discriminating if people who put a lower value on their time (are willing to drive to the store and move their purchases themselves) have a higher elasticity of demand than people who want to order over the phone and have the goods delivered.

3. The colleges may be providing scholarships as a form of charity, or they may be price discriminating by lowering the final price to less wealthy families (with presumably higher elasticities of demand).

10. This law delays entry by new firms. The patent holder has decided that it does not pay to sell both its name-brand drug and its own generic (otherwise, it would do so). Thus the law delays the introduction of generics for several years. When entry occurs, the price of generics will fall below the current price of the name brand. The price of the name-brand drug may rise or fall (see the application in the chapter).

17. The inverse demand curve in Japan is $p_J = 3,500 - \frac{1}{2}Q_J$, and the one in the United States is $p_{US} = 4,500 - Q_{US}$. Thus the corresponding marginal revenue in Japan is $MR_J = 3,500 - Q_J$. Setting that expression equal to m, we find that the optimal $Q_J = 3,500 - m$. Similarly, $Q_{US} = 2,250 - \frac{1}{2}m$. If $m = 500$, then the optimal outputs are $Q_J = 3,000$ and $Q_{US} = 2,000$. The profit in Japan is $(p_J - m)Q_J = (\$2,000 - \$500) \times 3,000 = \$4.5$ million, and the U.S. profit is \$4 million. The deadweight loss is greater in Japan, \$2.25 million ($= \frac{1}{2} \times \$1,500 \times 3,000$), than in the United States, \$2 million ($= \frac{1}{2} \times \$2,000 \times 2,000$).

Chapter 13

1. The payoff matrix in this prisoners' dilemma game is

If Duncan stays silent, Larry gets 0 if he squeals and –1 (a year in jail) if he stays silent. If Duncan confesses, Larry gets –2 if he squeals and –5 if he does not. Thus Larry is better off squealing in either case, so squealing is his dominant strategy. By the same reasoning, squealing is also Duncan's dominant strategy. As a result, the Nash equilibrium is for both to confess.

5. The monopoly will make more profit than the duopoly will, so the monopoly is willing to pay the college more rent. Although granting monopoly rights may be attractive to the college in terms of higher rent, students will suffer (lose consumer surplus) because of the higher prices.

★6. Effectively, the government changes the domestic industry into a dominant firm facing a competitive fringe (as given by the supply curve in the other exporting country). The government sets the tax so that the domestic industry produces the same output level as a dominant firm would. (You can show this analysis using a graph similar to Figure 11.14.)

★7. Don't be silly: This problem is too difficult. For an answer, see Karp and Perloff (1995).

12. Given that the duopolies produce identical goods, the equilibrium price is lower if the duopolies set price rather than quantity. If the goods are heterogeneous, we cannot answer this question definitively.

13. By differentiating its product, a firm makes the residual demand curve it faces less elastic everywhere. For example, no consumer will buy from that firm if its rival charges less and the goods are homogeneous. In contrast, some consumers who prefer this firm's product to that of its rival will still buy from this firm even if its rival charges less. As the chapter shows, a firm sets a higher price, the lower the elasticity of demand at the equilibrium.

		Duncan	
		Squeal	Stay silent
Larry	Squeal	-2 -2	0 –5
	Stay silent	–5 0	–1 –1

15. Firm 1 wants to maximize its profit:

$$\pi_1 = (p_1 - 10)q_1 = (p_1 - 10)(100 - 2p_1 + p_2).$$

Its first-order condition is $d\pi_1/dp_1 = 100 - 4p_1 + p_2 + 20 = 0$, so its best-response function is $p_1 = 30 + \frac{1}{4}p_2$. Similarly, Firm 2's best-response function is $p_2 = 30 + \frac{1}{4}p_1$. Solving, the Bertrand-Nash equilibrium prices are $p_1 = p_2 = 40$. Each firm produces 60 units.

18. The inverse demand curve is $p = 1 - 0.001Q$. The first firm's profit is $\pi_1 = [1 - 0.001(q_1 + q_2)]q_1 - 0.28q_1$. Its first-order condition is $d\pi_1/dq_1 = 1 - 0.001(2q_1 + q_2) - 0.28 = 0$. If we rearrange the terms, the first firm's best-response function is $q_1 = 360 - \frac{1}{2}q_2$. Similarly, the second firm's best-response function is $q_2 = 360 - \frac{1}{2}q_1$. By substituting one of these best-response functions into the other, we learn that the Cournot-Nash equilibrium occurs at $q_1 = q_2 = 240$, so the equilibrium price is 52¢.

22. Using Equations 13A.13 and 13A.14, we find that the equilibrium quantities are $q_1 = (a - 2m_1 + m_2)/3b = (90 + 30)/6 = 20$ and $q_2 = (90 - 60)/6 = 5$. As a result, the equilibrium price is $p = 90 - 20 - 5 = 65$.

Chapter 14

3. Allowing GM to enter first does not change the outcome of this game. Because Ford has a dominant strategy and enters regardless of GM's action, GM chooses not to enter even if it can act first.

★6. Let the probability that a firm sets a low price be α for Firm 1 and β for Firm 2. If the firms choose their prices independently, then $\alpha\beta$ is the probability that both set a low price, $(1 - \alpha)(1 - \beta)$ is the probability that both set a high price, $\alpha(1 - \beta)$ is the probability that Firm 1 prices low and Firm 2 prices high, and $(1 - \alpha)\beta$ is the probability that Firm 1 prices high and Firm 2 prices low. Firm 2's expected payoff, $E(\pi_2)$, is

$$E(\pi_2) = 2\alpha\beta + (0)\alpha(1 - \beta)$$
$$+ (1 - \alpha)\beta + 6(1 - \alpha)(1 - \beta)$$
$$= (6 - 6\alpha) - (5 - 7\alpha)\beta.$$

Similarly, Firm 1's expected payoff is

$$E(\pi_1) = (0)\alpha\beta + 7\alpha(1 - \beta)$$
$$+ 2(1 - \alpha)\beta + 6(1 - \alpha)(1 - \beta)$$
$$= (6 - 4\beta) + (1 - 3\beta)\alpha.$$

Each firm forms a belief about its rival's behavior. For example, suppose that Firm 1 believes that Firm 2 will choose a low price with a probability $\hat{\beta}$. If $\hat{\beta}$ is less than $\frac{1}{3}$ (Firm 2 is relatively unlikely to choose a low price), it pays for Firm 1 to choose the low price because the second term in $E(\pi_1)$, $(1 - 3\hat{\beta})\alpha$, is positive, so that as α increases, $E(\pi_1)$ increases. Because the highest possible α is 1, Firm 1 chooses the low price with certainty. Similarly, if Firm 1 believes $\hat{\beta}$ is greater than $\frac{1}{3}$, it sets a high price with certainty ($\alpha = 0$).

If Firm 2 believes that Firm 1 thinks $\hat{\beta}$ is slightly below $\frac{1}{3}$, Firm 2 believes that Firm 1 will choose a low price with certainty, and hence Firm 2 will also choose a low price. That outcome, $\beta = 1$, however, is not consistent with Firm 1's expectation that $\hat{\beta}$ is a fraction. Indeed, it is only rational for Firm 2 to believe that Firm 1 believes Firm 2 will use a mixed strategy if Firm 1's belief about Firm 2 makes Firm 1 unpredictable. That is, Firm 1 uses a mixed strategy only if it is *indifferent* between setting a high or a low price. It is only indifferent if it believes $\hat{\beta}$ is exactly $\frac{1}{3}$. By similar reasoning, Firm 2 will use a mixed strategy only if its belief is that Firm 1 chooses a low price with probability $\hat{\alpha} = \frac{5}{7}$. Thus the only possible Nash equilibrium is $\alpha = \frac{5}{7}$ and $\beta = \frac{1}{3}$.

10. The firm's marginal revenue exceeded its marginal cost, so the firm should have increased its advertising.

12. In the Cournot equilibrium (see Chapter 13), $q_i = (a - m)/(3b) = (150 - 60)/3 = 30$, $Q = 60$, $p = 90$.

13. In the Stackelberg equilibrium (see Chapter 13) in which Firm 1 moves first, $q_1 = (a - m)/(2b) = (150 - 60)/2 = 45$, $q_2 = (a - m)/(4b) = (150 - 60)/4 = 22.5$, $Q = 45$, and $p = 82.5$.

Chapter 15

2. Before the tax, the competitive firm's labor demand was $p \times MP_L$. After the tax, the firm's effective price is $(1 - \alpha)p$, so its labor demand becomes $(1 - \alpha)p \times MP_L$.

18. The competitive firm's marginal revenue of labor is $\partial q/\partial L = 1 + 2K$, so its $MRP_L = p(1 + 2K)$.

20. The answer is given in Appendix 15A.

Chapter 16

3. An individual with a zero discount rate views current and future consumption as equally attractive. An individual with an infinite discount rate cares only about current consumption and puts no value on future consumption.

9. If the interest rate is set in real terms, putting $2,000 in the bank today results in an annual flow of $200 in real terms. If the interest rate is set in nominal terms, the real payment will shrink over time, so you cannot receive a real payment of $200 annually. (If the nominal rate were set at 15.5%, an initial $2,000 investment would ensure an annual flow of $200 in real terms.)

16. The real payment this year is the same as the nominal payment: $f = \tilde{f}$. The real payment next year is obtained by adjusting the nominal payment for inflation: $f = \tilde{f}/(1 + \tau) = \tilde{f}/1.1$. Thus the real present value of the two payments is this year's real payment plus next year's real payment discounted by the real interest rate: $f + f/(1 + i) = \tilde{f} + \tilde{f}/[(1 + \gamma)(1 + i)]$, which is less than $2\tilde{f}$ because nominal future payments are worth less than current ones because of both inflation and discounting.

17. *Hint:* Set profit equal to zero and solve for *irr*.

18. Solving for *irr*, we find that *irr* equals 1 or 9. This approach fails to give us a unique solution, so we should use the *NPV* approach instead.

Chapter 17

2. As the graph shows, Irma's expected utility of 133 at point f (where her expected wealth is $64) is the same as her utility from a certain wealth of Y.

3. The expected punishment for violating traffic laws is θV, where θ is the probability of being caught and fined and V is the fine. If people care only about the expected punishment (there's no additional psychological pain from the experience), increasing the expected punishment by increasing θ or V works equally well in discouraging bad behavior. The government prefers to increase the fine, V, which is costless, rather than to raise θ, which is costly due to the extra police, district attorneys, and courts required.

11. Assuming that the painting is not insured against fire, its expected value is

$$\$550 = (0.2 \times \$1,000) + (0.1 \times \$0) + (0.7 \times \$500).$$

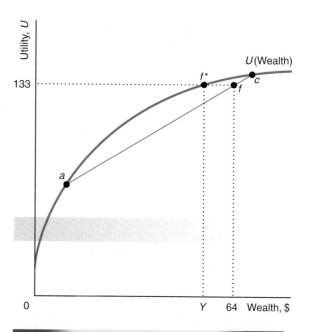

Chapter 18

2. A specific tax of $64 per ton of output or per unit of emissions (gunk) leads to the social optimum.

5. Granting the chemical company the right to dump 1 ton per day results in that firm's dumping 1 ton and the boat company's maintaining one boat, which maximizes joint profit at $20.

11. Use the model in Appendix 18A to determine the equilibrium if the marginal harm of gunk is $MC^g = \$84$ (instead of Equation 18A.3). We care only about the marginal harm of gunk at the social optimum, which we know is $MC^g = \$84$ (because it is the same at every level of output). That is the same marginal cost as in the table at the end of Appendix 18A. Thus the social optimum is the same as in that example (and no algebra is necessary). Using algebra, we set the demand curve equal to the new social marginal cost, $MC^2 = c + dQ + 84$, and we find that the socially optimal quantity is $Q_s = (a - c - 84)/(b + d) = (450 - 30 - 84)/(2 + 2) = 84$.

Chapter 19

2. Because insurance costs do not vary with soil type, buying insurance is unattractive for houses on good soil and relatively attractive for houses on bad soil. These incentives create a moral hazard

problem: Relatively more homeowners with houses on poor soil buy insurance, so the state insurance agency will face disproportionately many bad outcomes in the next earthquake.

6. Brand names allow consumers to identify a particular company's product in the future. If a mushroom company expects to remain in business over time, it would be foolish to brand its product if its mushrooms are of inferior quality. (Just ask Babar's grandfather.) Thus all else the same, we would expect branded mushrooms to be of higher quality than unbranded ones.

12. Because buyers are risk neutral, if they believe that the probability of getting a lemon is θ, the most they are willing to pay for a car of unknown quality is $p = p_1(1 - \theta) + p_2\theta$. If p is greater than both v_1 and v_2, all cars are sold. If $v_1 > p > v_2$, only lemons are sold. If p were less than both v_1 and v_2, no cars would be sold. However, we know that $v_2 < p_2$ and $p_2 < p$, so owners of lemons are certainly willing to sell them. (If sellers bear a transaction cost of c and $p < v_2 + c$, no cars are sold.)

Chapter 20

1. If Paula pays Arthur a fixed-fee salary of $168, Arthur has no incentive to buy any carvings for resale, as the $12 per carving cost comes out of his pocket. Thus Arthur sells no carvings if he receives a fixed salary and can sell as many or as few carvings as he wants. The contract is not incentive compatible. For Arthur to behave efficiently, this fixed-fee contract must be modified. For example, the contract could specify that Arthur gets a salary of $168 and that he must obtain and sell 12 carvings. Paula must monitor his behavior. (Paula's residual profit is the joint profit minus $168, so she gets the marginal profit from each additional sale and wants to sell the joint-profit-maximizing number of carvings.) Arthur makes $24 = $168 – $144, so he is willing to participate. Joint profit is maximized at $72, and Paula gets the maximum possible residual profit of $48.

6. By making this commitment, the company may be trying to assure customers who cannot judge how quickly the product will deteriorate that the product is durable enough to maintain at least a certain value in the future. The firm is trying to eliminate asymmetric information to increase the demand for its product.

9. Presumably, the promoter collects a percentage of the revenue at each restaurant. If customers can pay cash, the restaurants may lie to the promoter as to the amount of food they sold. The scrip makes such opportunistic behavior difficult.

15. The minimum bond that deters stealing is $2,500.

DEFINITIONS

I hate definitions.

—Benjamin Disraeli

adverse selection: opportunism characterized by an informed person's benefiting from trading or otherwise contracting with a less informed person who does not know about an unobserved characteristic of the informed person. (19)

asymmetric information: situation in which one party to a transaction knows a material fact that the other party does not. (19)

average cost (*AC*): the total cost divided by the units of output produced: $AC = C/q$. (7)

average fixed cost (*AFC*): the fixed cost divided by the units of output produced: $AFC = F/q$. (7)

average product of labor (*AP$_L$*): the ratio of output, q, to the number of workers, L, used to produce that output: $AP_L = q/L$. (6)

average variable cost (*AVC*): the variable cost divided by the units of output produced: $AVC = VC/q$. (7)

bad: something for which less is preferred to more, such as pollution. (4)

barrier to entry: an explicit restriction or a cost that applies only to potential new firms—existing firms are not subject to the restriction or do not bear the cost. (9)

Bertrand equilibrium: a *Nash equilibrium* in prices; a set of prices such that no firm can obtain a higher profit by choosing a different price if the other firms continue to charge these prices. (13)

best response: the strategy that maximizes a firm's profit, given its beliefs about its rivals' strategies. (13)

budget line (or *budget constraint*): the bundles of goods that can be bought if the entire budget is spent on those goods at given prices. (4)

bundling (*package tie-in sale*): a type of tie-in sale in which two goods are combined so that customers cannot buy either good separately. (12)

cartel: a group of firms that explicitly agree to coordinate their activities. (13)

certification: a report that a particular product meets or exceeds a given *standard* level. (19)

cheap talk: unsubstantiated claims or statements. (19)

common property: resources to which everyone has free access. (18)

comparative advantage: the ability to produce a good at a lower opportunity cost than someone else. (10)

competitive fringe (or *fringe*): small, price-taking firms that compete with a *dominant firm*. (11)

constant returns to scale (*CRS*): property of a production function whereby all inputs are increased by a certain percentage, output increases by that same percentage. (6)

consumer surplus (*CS*): the monetary difference between what a consumer is willing to pay for the quantity of the good purchased and what the good actually costs. (9)

contingent fee: a payment to a lawyer that is a share of the award in a court case (usually after legal expenses are deducted) if the client wins and nothing if the client loses. (20)

contract curve: the set of all Pareto-efficient bundles. (10)

cost (*total cost*, *C*): the sum of a firm's variable cost and fixed cost: $C = VC + F$. (7)

Cournot equilibrium: a *Nash equilibrium* in quantities; a set of quantities sold by firms such that, holding the quantities of all other firms constant, no firm can obtain a higher profit by choosing a different quantity. (13)

credible threat: an announcement that a firm will use a strategy harmful to its rival that the rivals believe because the firm's strategy is rational in the sense that it is in the firm's best interest to use it. (14)

cross-price elasticity of demand: the percentage change in the *quantity demanded* in response to a given percentage change in the price of another good. (3)

deadweight loss (*DWL*): the net reduction in welfare from losses of surplus by one group that are not offset by a gain to another group from an action that alters a market equilibrium. (9)

decreasing returns to scale (*DRS*): property of a production function whereby output increases less than in proportion to an equal percentage increase in all inputs. (6)

demand curve: the *quantity demanded* at each possible price, holding constant the other factors that influence purchases. (2)

discount rate: a rate reflecting the relative value an individual places on future consumption compared to current consumption. (16)

diseconomies of scale: property of a cost function whereby the average cost of production rises when output increases. (7)

dominant firm: a price-setting firm that competes with price-taking firms in a *competitive fringe*. (11)

dominant strategy: a strategy that strictly dominates (gives higher profits than) all other strategies, regardless of the actions chosen by rival firms. (13)

duopoly: an oligopoly with two firms. (13)

durable good: a product that is usable for years. (7)

economic cost (*opportunity cost*): the value of the best alternative use of a resource. (7)

economic profit: revenue minus *economic cost*. (8)

economically efficient: minimizing the cost of producing a specified amount of output. (7)

economies of scale: property of a cost function whereby the average cost of production falls as output expands. (7)

economies of scope: situation in which it is less expensive to produce goods jointly than separately. (7)

efficiency in production: situation in which the principal's and agent's combined value (profits, payoffs), π, is maximized. (20)

efficiency in risk bearing: a situation in which risk sharing is optimal in that the person who least minds facing risk—the risk-neutral or less risk-averse person—bears more of the risk. (20)

efficiency wage: an unusually high wage that a firm pays workers as an incentive to avoid shirking. (20)

efficient contract: an agreement with provisions that ensure that no party can be made better off without harming the other party. (20)

efficient production (*technological efficiency*): situation in which the current level of output cannot be produced with fewer inputs, given existing knowledge about technology and the organization of production. (6)

elasticity: the percentage change in a variable in response to a given percentage change in another variable. (3)

endowment: an initial allocation of goods. (10)

Engel curve: the relationship between the quantity demanded of a single good and income, holding prices constant. (5)

equilibrium: a situation in which no one wants to change his or her behavior. (2)

essential facility: a scarce resource that a rival must use to survive. (14)

excess demand: the amount by which the *quantity demanded* exceeds the *quantity supplied* at a specified price. (2)

excess supply: the amount by which the *quantity supplied* is greater than the *quantity demanded* at a specified price. (2)

exhaustible resources: nonrenewable natural assets that cannot be increased, only depleted. (16)

expansion path: the cost-minimizing combination of labor and capital for each output level. (7)

externality: the direct effect of the actions of a person or firm on another person's well-being or a firm's production capability rather than an indirect effect through changes in prices. (18)

fair bet: a wager with an expected value of zero. (17)

fair insurance: a bet between an insurer and a policy-holder in which the value of the bet to the policy-holder is zero. (17)

firm: an organization that converts inputs such as labor, materials, energy, and capital into outputs, the goods and services that it sells. (6)

fixed cost (*F*): a production expense that does not vary with output. (7)

fixed input: a factor of production that cannot be varied practically in the short run. (6)

flow: a quantity or value that is measured per unit of time. (16)

free ride: to benefit from the actions of others without paying. (18)

game: any competition between players (firms) in which strategic behavior plays a major role. (13)

game theory: a set of tools that economists, political scientists, military analysts, and others use to analyze decisionmaking by players that use strategies. (13)

general-equilibrium analysis: the study of how equilibrium is determined in all markets simultaneously. (10)

Giffen good: a commodity for which a decrease in its price causes the quantity demanded to fall. (5)

good: a commodity for which more is preferred to less, at least at some levels of consumption. (4)

incentive compatible: referring to a contract's provision of inducements such that the agent wants to perform the assigned task rather than engage in opportunistic behavior. (20)

incidence of a tax on consumers: the share of the tax that falls on consumers. (3)

income effect: the change in the quantity of a good a consumer demands because of a change in income, holding prices constant. (5)

income elasticity of demand (or *income elasticity*): the percentage change in the *quantity demanded* in response to a given percentage change in income. (3)

increasing returns to scale (*IRS*): property of a production function whereby output rises more than in proportion to an equal increase in all inputs. (6)

indifference curve: the set of all bundles of goods that a consumer views as being equally desirable. (4)

indifference map (or *preference map*): a complete set of indifference curves that summarize a consumer's tastes or preferences. (4)

inferior good: a commodity of which less is demanded as income rises. (5)

interest rate: the percentage more that must be repaid to borrow money for a fixed period of time. (16)

internalize the externality: to bear the cost of the harm that one inflicts on others (or to capture the benefit that one provides to others). (18)

internal rate of return (*irr*): the discount rate that results in a net present value of an investment of zero. (16)

isocost line: all the combinations of inputs that require the same (*iso-*) total expenditure (*cost*). (7)

isoquant: a curve that shows the efficient combinations of labor and capital that can produce a single (*iso-*) level of output (*quant*ity). (6)

Law of Demand: consumers demand more of a good the lower its price, holding constant tastes, the prices of other goods, and other factors that influence consumption. (2)

learning by doing: the productive skills and knowledge that workers and managers gain from experience. (7)

Lerner Index: the ratio of the difference between price and marginal cost to the price: $(p - MC)/p$. (11)

limited liability: condition whereby the personal assets of the owners of the corporation cannot be taken to pay a corporation's debts if it goes into bankruptcy. (6)

long run: a lengthy enough period of time that all inputs can be varied. (6)

marginal cost (*MC*): the amount by which a firm's cost changes if the firm produces one more unit of output. (7)

marginal product of labor (MP_L): the change in total output, Δq, resulting from using an extra unit of labor, ΔL, holding other factors constant: $MP_L = \Delta q/\Delta L$. (6)

marginal profit: the change in profit a firm gets from selling one more unit of output. (8)

marginal rate of substitution (*MRS*): the maximum amount of one good a consumer will sacrifice to obtain one more unit of another good. (4)

marginal rate of transformation (*MRT*): the trade-off the market imposes on the consumer in terms of the amount of one good the consumer must give up to obtain more of the other good. (4)

marginal revenue (*MR*): the change in revenue a firm gets from selling one more unit of output. (8)

marginal revenue product of labor (MRP_L): the extra revenue from hiring one more worker. (15)

marginal utility: the extra utility that a consumer gets from consuming the last unit of a good. (4)

market: an exchange mechanism that allows buyers to trade with sellers. (1)

market failure: inefficient production or consumption, often because a price exceeds marginal cost. (9)

market power: the ability of a firm to charge a price above marginal cost and earn a positive profit. (11)

market structure: the number of firms in the market, the ease with which firms can enter and leave the market, and the ability of firms to differentiate their products from those of their rivals. (8)

microeconomics: the study of how individuals and firms make themselves as well off as possible in a world of scarcity and the consequences of those individual decisions for markets and the entire economy. (1)

minimum efficient scale (*full capacity*): the smallest quantity at which the average cost curve reaches its minimum. (13)

model: a description of the relationship between two or more economic variables. (1)

monopolistic competition: a market structure in which firms have market power but no additional firm can enter and earn positive profits. (13)

monopoly: the only supplier of a good for which there is no close substitute. (11)

monopsony: the only buyer of a good in a given market. (15)

moral hazard: opportunism characterized by an informed person's taking advantage of a less-informed person through an unobserved action. (19)

multimarket price discrimination (*third-degree price discrimination*): a situation in which a firm charges different groups of customers different prices but charges a given customer the same price for every unit of output sold. (12)

Nash equilibrium: a set of strategies such that, holding the strategies of all other firms constant, no firm can obtain a higher profit by choosing a different strategy. (13)

natural monopoly: situation in which one firm can produce the total output of the market at lower cost than several firms could. (11)

noncooperative strategic behavior: the set of actions taken by a profit-maximizing firm acting independently of other firms. (14)

nonuniform pricing: charging consumers different prices for the same product or charging a single customer a price that depends on the number of units the customer buys. (12)

normal good: a commodity of which as much or more is demanded as income rises. (5)

normative statement: a conclusion as to whether something is good or bad. (1)

oligopoly: a small group of firms in a market with substantial barriers to entry. (13)

opportunistic behavior: taking advantage of someone when circumstances permit. (15)

opportunity cost (*economic cost*): the value of the best alternative use of a resource. (7)

opportunity set: all the bundles a consumer can buy, including all the bundles inside the budget constraint and on the budget constraint. (4)

Pareto efficient: describing an allocation of goods or services such that any reallocation harms at least one person. (10)

partial-equilibrium analysis: an examination of equilibrium and changes in equilibrium in one market in isolation. (10)

patent: an exclusive right granted to the inventor to sell a new and useful product, process, substance, or design for a fixed period of time. (11)

perfect complements: goods that a consumer is interested in consuming only in fixed proportions. (4)

perfect price discrimination (*first-degree price discrimination*): situation in which a firm sells each unit at the maximum amount any customer is willing to pay for it, so prices differ across customers and a given customer may pay more for some units than for others. (12)

perfect substitutes: goods that a consumer is completely indifferent as to which to consume. (4)

pooling equilibrium: an equilibrium in which dissimilar people are treated (paid) alike or behave alike. (19)

positive statement: a testable hypothesis about cause and effect. (1)

price discrimination: practice in which a firm charges consumers different prices for the same good. (12)

price elasticity of demand (or *elasticity of demand*, ε): the percentage change in the *quantity demanded* in response to a given percentage change in the price. (3)

price elasticity of supply (or *elasticity of supply*, η): the percentage change in the *quantity supplied* in response to a given percentage change in the price. (3)

prisoners' dilemma: a game in which all players have dominant strategies that result in profits (or other payoffs) that are inferior to what they could achieve if they used cooperative strategies. (13)

private cost: the cost of production only, not including *externalities*. (18)

producer surplus (*PS*): the difference between the amount for which a good sells and the minimum amount necessary for the seller to be willing to produce the good. (9)

production function: the relationship between the quantities of inputs used and the maximum quantity of output that can be produced, given current knowledge about technology and organization. (6)

production possibility frontier: the maximum amount of outputs that can be produced from a fixed amount of input. (7)

profit (π): the difference between revenues, R, and costs, C: $\pi = R - C$. (6)

property right: the exclusive privilege to use an asset. (18)

public good: a commodity or service whose consumption by one person does not preclude others from also consuming it. (18)

quantity demanded: the amount of a good that consumers are willing to buy at a given price, holding constant the other factors that influence purchases. (2)

quantity discrimination (*second-degree price discrimination*): situation in which a firm charges a different price for large quantities than for small quantities but all customers who buy a given quantity pay the same price. (12)

quantity supplied: the amount of a good that firms *want* to sell at a given price, holding constant other factors that influence firms' supply decisions, such as costs and government actions. (2)

quota: the limit that a government sets on the quantity of a foreign-produced good that may be imported. (2)

rent: a payment to the owner of an input beyond the minimum necessary for the factor to be supplied. (8)

rent seeking: efforts and expenditures to gain a rent or a profit from government actions. (9)

requirement tie-in sale: a tie-in sale in which customers who buy one product from a firm are required to make all their purchases of another product from that firm. (13)

reservation price: the maximum amount a person would be willing to pay for a unit of output. (13)

residual demand curve: the market demand that is not met by other sellers at any given price. (11)

residual supply curve: The market supply that is not met by demanders in other sectors at any given wage. (10)

risk: situation in which the likelihood of each possible outcome is known or can be estimated and no single possible outcome is certain to occur. (17)

risk averse: unwilling to make a fair bet. (17)

risk neutral: indifferent about making a fair bet. (17)

risk preferring: willing to make a fair bet. (17)

risk premium: the amount that a risk-averse person would pay to avoid taking a risk. (17)

screening: an action taken by an uninformed person to determine the information possessed by informed people. (19)

separating equilibrium: an equilibrium in which one type of people takes actions (such as sending a *signal*) that allows them to be differentiated from other types of people. (19)

shirking: a *moral hazard* in which agents do not provide all the services they are paid to provide. (20)

shortage: a persistent excess demand. (2)

short run: a period of time so brief that at least one factor of production cannot be varied practically. (6)

signaling: an action taken by an informed person to send information to an uninformed person. (19)

social cost: the private cost plus the cost of the harms from *externalities*. (18)

standard: a metric or scale for evaluating the quality of a particular product. (19)

stock: a quantity or value that is measured independently of time. (16)

strategic behavior: a set of actions a firm takes to increase its profit, taking into account the possible actions of other firms. (14)

strategy: a battle plan of the actions a firm plans to take to compete with other firms. (13)

substitution effect: the change in the quantity of a good that a consumer demands when the good's price changes, holding other prices and the consumer's *utility* constant. (5)

supergame: a game that is played repeatedly, allowing players to devise strategies for one period that depend on rivals' actions in previous periods. (13)

sunk cost: an expenditure that cannot be recovered. (7)

supply curve: the *quantity supplied* at each possible price, holding constant the other factors that influence firms' supply decisions. (2)

tariff (*duty*): a tax on only imported goods. (9)

technical progress: an advance in knowledge that allows more output to be produced with the same level of inputs. (6)

technological efficiency (*efficient production*): property of a production function such that the current level of output cannot be produced with fewer inputs, given existing knowledge about technology and the organization of production. (6)

tie-in sale: a type of nonlinear pricing in which customers can buy one product only if they agree to buy another product as well. (12)

total cost (*C*): the sum of a firm's variable cost and fixed cost: $C = VC + F$. (7)

total product of labor: the amount of output (or total product) that can be produced by a given amount of labor. (6)

transaction costs: the expenses of finding a trading partner and making a trade for a good or service beyond the price paid for that good or service. (2)

two-part tariff: a pricing system in which the firm charges a consumer a lump-sum fee (the first tariff or price) for the right to buy as many units of the good as the consumer wants at a specified price (the second tariff). (12)

utility: a set of numerical values that reflect the relative rankings of various bundles of goods. (4)

utility function: the relationship between *utility* values and every possible bundle of goods. (4)

variable cost (*VC*): a production expense that changes with the quantity of output produced. (7)

variable input: a factor of production whose quantity can be changed readily by the firm during the relevant time period. (6)

vertically integrated: describing a firm that participates in more than one successive stage of the production or distribution of goods or services. (15)

REFERENCES

Adelaja, Adesoji O., "Price Changes, Supply Elasticities, Industry Organization, and Dairy Output Distribution," *American Journal of Agricultural Economics*, 73(1), February 1991:89–102.

Aigner, Dennis J., and Glen G. Cain, "Statistical Theories of Discrimination in Labor Markets," *Industrial and Labor Relations Review*, 30(2), January 1977:175–187.

Akerlof, George A., "The Market for 'Lemons': Quality Uncertainty and the Market Mechanism," *Quarterly Journal of Economics*, 84(3), August 1970:488–500.

Akerlof, George A., "Labor Contacts as Partial Gift Exchanges," *Quarterly Journal of Economics*, 97(4), November 1982:543–569.

Akridge, Jay T., and Thomas W. Hertel, "Multiproduct Cost Relationship for Retail Fertilizer Plants," *American Journal of Agricultural Economics*, 68(4), November 1986:928–938.

Allingham, M. G., "Progression and Leisure," *American Economic Review*, 62(3), June 1972:447–450.

Anderson, Keith B., and Michael R. Metzger, *Petroleum Tariffs as a Source of Government Revenues*. Washington, D.C.: Bureau of Economics, Federal Trade Commission, 1991.

Arrow, Kenneth, *Social Choice and Individual Values*. New York: Wiley, 1951.

Ayres, Ian, and Joel Waldfogel, "A Market Test for Race Discrimination in Bail Setting," *Stanford Law Review*, 46(5), May 1994:987–1047.

Baldwin, John R., and Paul K. Gorecki, *The Role of Scale in Canada/U.S. Productivity Differences in the Manufacturing Sector, 1970–1979*. Toronto: University of Toronto Press, 1986.

Baldwin, Robert E., and Paul R. Krugman, "Industrial Policy and International Competition in Wide Bodied Jet Aircraft," in Robert E. Baldwin, ed., *Trade Policy Issues and Empirical Analysis*. Chicago: University of Chicago Press, 1988.

Barlow, R., and G. R. Sparks, "A Note on Progression and Leisure," *American Economic Review*, 54(4), June 1964:372–377.

Battalio, Raymond, John H. Kagel, and Carl Kogut, "Experimental Confirmation of the Existence of a Giffen Good," *American Economic Review*, 81(3), September 1991:961–970.

Becker, Gary S., *The Economics of Discrimination*, 2nd ed. Chicago: University of Chicago Press, 1971.

Benham, Lee, "The Effect of Advertising on the Price of Eyeglasses," *Journal of Law and Economics*, 15(2), October 1972:337–352.

Berck, Peter, and Michael Roberts, "Natural Resource Prices: Will They Ever Turn Up?" *Journal of Environmental Economics and Management*, 31(1), July 1996:65–78.

Besley, Timothy J., and Harvey S. Rosen, "Sales Taxes and Prices: An Empirical Analysis," *National Tax Journal*, 52(2), June 1999:157–178.

Bhuyan, Sanjib, and Rigoberto A. Lopez, "What Determines Welfare Losses from Oligopoly Power in the Food and Tobacco Industries?" *Agricultural and Resource Economics Review*, 27(2), October 1998:258–265.

Billikopf, Gregory Encina, "High Piece-Rate Wages Do Not Reduce Hours Worked," *California Agriculture*, 49(1), January–February 1995:17–18.

Blanciforti, Laura Ann, "The Almost Ideal Demand System Incorporating Habits: An Analysis of Expenditures on Food and Aggregate Commodity Groups." Doctoral thesis, University of California, Davis, 1982.

Bond, Ronald S., John E. Kwoka Jr., John J. Phelan, and Ira Taylor Whitten, *Staff Report on Effects of Restrictions on Advertising and Commercial Practice in the Professions: The Case of Optometry*. Washington, D.C.: Bureau of Economics, Federal Trade Commission, 1980.

Bordley, Robert F., and James B. McDonald, "Estimating Aggregate Automotive Income Elasticities from the Population Income-Share Elasticity," *Journal of Business and Economic Statistics*, 11(2), April 1993:209–214.

Borenstein, Severin, and Nancy L. Rose, "Competition and Price Dispersion in the U.S. Airline Industry," *Journal of Political Economy*, 102(4), August 1994:653–683.

Boskin, Michael J., Ellen R. Dulberger, Robert J. Gordon, Zvi Griliches, and Dale W. Jorgenson, "The CPI Commission: Findings and Recommendations," *American Economic Review*, 87(2), May 1997:78–93.

Boyd, Roy, and Barry J. Seldon, "Revenue and Land-Use Effects of Proposed Changes in Sin Taxes: A General

Equilibrium Perspective," *Land Economics*, 67(3), August 1991:365–374.

Brander, James A., and Anming Zhang, "Market Conduct in the Airline Industry: An Empirical Investigation," *Rand Journal of Economics*, 21(4), Winter 1990:567–583.

Brander, James A., and M. Scott Taylor, "The Simple Economics of Easter Island: A Ricardo-Malthus Model of Renewable Resource Use," *American Economic Review*, 88(1), March 1998:119–138.

Brown, Deborah J., and Lee F. Schrader, "Cholesterol Information and Shell Egg Consumption," *American Journal of Agricultural Economics*, 72(3), August 1990:548–555.

Brown, Robert W., "An Estimate of the Rent Generated by a Premium College Football Player," *Economic Inquiry*, 31(4), October 1993:671–684.

Brownlee, Oswald, and George Perry, "The Effects of the 1965 Federal Excise Tax Reductions on Prices," *National Tax Journal*, 20(3), September 1967:235–249.

Brunk, Gregory G., "A Test of the Friedman-Savage Gambling Model," *Quarterly Journal of Economics*, 96(2), May 1981:341–348.

Buschena, David E., and Jeffrey M. Perloff, "The Creation of Dominant Firm Market Power in the Coconut Oil Export Market," *American Journal of Agricultural Economics*, 73(4), November 1991:1000–1008.

Card, David, and Alan B. Krueger, *Myth and Measurement: The New Economics of the Minimum Wage*. Princeton, N.J.: Princeton University Press, 1995.

Carlson, Steven, "An Overview of Food Stamp Cashout Research in the Food and Nutrition Service," in Nancy Fasciano, Darryl Hall, and Harold Beebout, eds., *New Directions in Food Stamp Policy Research*. Alexandria, Va.: U.S. Department of Agriculture, Food and Nutrition Service, 1993.

Carlton, Dennis W., and Jeffrey M. Perloff, *Modern Industrial Organization*, 3rd ed. Reading, Mass.: Addison Wesley Longman, 2000.

Castillo-Freeman, Alida, and Richard B. Freeman, "When the Minimum Wage Really Bites: The Effect of the U.S.-Level Minimum on Puerto Rico," in George J. Borjas and Richard B. Freeman, eds., *Immigration and the Work Force: Economic Consequences for the United States and Source Areas*. Chicago: University of Chicago Press, 1992.

Caves, Richard E., and David R. Barton, *Technical Efficiency in U.S. Manufacturing Industries*. Cambridge, Mass.: MIT Press, 1990.

Christensen, Laurits R., and William H. Greene, "Economies of Scale in U.S. Electric Power Generation," *Journal of Political Economy*, 84(4, pt. 1), August 1976:655–676.

Coase, Ronald H., "The Nature of the Firm," *Economica*, 4(16), November 1937:386–405.

Coase, Ronald H., "The Problem of Social Cost," *Journal of Law and Economics*, 3, October 1960:1–44.

Davies, J. E., "Competition, Contestability and the Liner Shipping Market," *Journal of Transport Economics and Policy*, 20(3), September 1986:299–312.

Deacon, Robert T., and Jon Sonstelie, "The Welfare Costs of Rationing by Waiting," *Economic Inquiry*, 27(2), April 1989:179–196.

Delipalla, Sophia, and Michael Keen, "The Comparison Between Ad Valorem and Specific Taxation Under Imperfect Competition," *Journal of Public Economics*, 49(3), December 1992:351–367.

de Melo, Jaime, and David Tarr, *A General Equilibrium Analysis of U.S. Foreign Trade Policy*. Cambridge, Mass.: MIT Press, 1992.

Diewert, W. Edwin, and Alice O. Nakamura, eds., *Essays in Index Number Theory*, Vol. 1. New York: North Holland, 1993.

Dixit, Avinash K., and Robert S. Pindyck, *Investment Under Uncertainty*. Princeton, N.J.: Princeton University Press, 1994.

Dunham, Wayne R., *Moral Hazard and the Market for Used Automobiles*. Economic Analysis Group Discussion Paper 96-4. Washington, D.C.: U.S. Department of Justice, Antitrust Division, 1996.

Dunn, L. F., "Quantifying Nonpecuniary Returns," *Journal of Human Resources*, 2(3), Summer 1977:347–359.

Dunn, L. F., "An Empirical Indifference Function for Income and Leisure," *Review of Economics and Statistics*, 60(4), November 1978:533–540.

Dunn, L. F., "Measurement of Internal Income-Leisure Tradeoffs," *Quarterly Journal of Economics*, 93(3), August 1979:373–393.

Dunne, Timothy, Mark Roberts, and Larry Samuelson, "Patterns of Firm Entry and Exit in U.S. Manufacturing Industries," *Rand Journal of Economics*, 19(4), Winter 1988:495–515.

Eastwood, David B., and John A. Craven, "Food Demand and Savings in a Complete, Extended, Linear Expenditure System," *American Journal of Agricultural Economics*, 63(3), August 1981:544–549.

Edell, Richard J., and Pravin P. Varaiya, "Providing Internet Access: What We Learn from the INDEX Trial," www.index.berkeley.edu/reports/99-010W, April 1999.

Exxon Company, U.S.A., *Competition in the Petroleum Industry*. Submission to the U.S. Senate Judiciary Subcommittee on Antitrust and Monopoly, January 21, 1975.

Farrell, Joseph, and Matthew Rabin, "Cheap Talk," *Journal of Economic Perspectives*, 10(3), Summer 1996:103–118.

Fasciano, Nancy, Daryl Hall, and Harold Beebout, eds., *New Directions in Food Stamp Policy Research*. Alexandria, Va.: U.S. Department of Agriculture, Food and Nutrition Service, 1993.

Fisher, Franklin M., "The Social Cost of Monopoly and Regulation: Posner Reconsidered," *Journal of Political Economy*, 93(2), April 1985:410–416.

Foster, Andrew D., and Mark R. Rosenzweig, "A Test for Moral Hazard in the Labor Market: Contractual Arrangements, Effort, and Health," *Review of Economics and Statistics*, 76(2), May 1994:213–227.

Fraker, Thomas M., "The Effects of Food Stamps on Food Consumption: A Review of the Literature," in Nancy Fasciano, Darryl Hall, and Harold Beebout, eds., *Current Perspectives on Food Stamp Program Participation*. Alexandria, Va.: U.S. Department of Agriculture, Food and Nutrition Service, 1990.

Frech, H. E., III, and William C. Lee, "The Welfare Cost of Rationing-by-Queuing Across Markets: Theory and Estimates from the U.S. Gasoline Crisis," *Quarterly Journal of Economics*, 102(1), February 1987:97–108.

French, Ben C., and Gordon A. King, "Demand and Price-Markup Functions for Canned Cling Peaches and Fruit Cocktail," *Western Journal of Agricultural Economics*, 11(1), July 1986:8–18.

Friedlaender, Ann F., Clifford Winston, and Kung Wang, "Costs, Technology, and Productivity in the U.S. Automobile Industry," *Bell Journal of Economics and Management Science*, 14(1), Spring 1983:1–20.

Friedman, Milton, and Leonard J. Savage, "The Utility Analysis of Choices Involving Risk," *Journal of Political Economy*, 56(4), August 1948:279–304.

Fudenberg, Drew, and Jean Tirole, "A 'Signal-Jamming' Theory of Predation," *Rand Journal of Economics*, 17(3), Autumn 1986:366–376.

Fullerton, Don, "On the Possibility of an Inverse Relationship Between Tax Rates and Government Revenues," *Journal of Public Economy*, 19(1), October 1982:3–22.

Gallini, Nancy T., "Demand for Gasoline in Canada," *Canadian Journal of Economics*, 16(2), May 1983:299–324.

Garrett, Thomas A., and Russell S. Sobel, "Gamblers Favor Skewness, Not Risk: Further Evidence from United States' Lottery Games," *Economics Letters*, 63(1), April 1999:85–90.

Gasmi, Farid, Jean-Jacques Laffont, and Quang H. Vuong, "Econometric Analysis of Collusive Behavior in a Soft-Drink Market," *Journal of Economics and Management Strategy*, 1(2), Summer 1992, 277–311.

Genesove, David, "Adverse Selection in the Wholesale Used Car Market," *Journal of Political Economy*, 101(4), August 1993:644–665.

Gilbert, Richard J., "Patents, Sleeping Patents, and Entry Deterrence," in Steven C. Salop, ed., *Strategy, Predation, and Antitrust Analysis*. Washington, D.C.: Federal Trade Commission, 1979.

Globerman, Steven, "A Policy Analysis of Hospital Waiting Lists," *Journal of Policy Analysis and Management*, 10(2), Spring 1991:247–262.

Golec, Joseph, and Maurry Tamarkin, "Do Bettors Prefer Long Shots Because They Are Risk Lovers, or Are They Just Overconfident?" *Journal of Risk and Uncertainty*, 11(1), July 1995:51–64.

Goolsbee, Austan, "In a World Without Borders: The Impact of Taxes on Internet Commerce," Working Paper No. 6863, National Bureau of Economic Research, www.nber.org/papers/w6863, December 1998.

Grabowski, Henry G., and John M. Vernon, "Brand Loyalty, Entry, and Price Competition in Pharmaceuticals After the 1984 Drug Act," *Journal of Law and Economics*, 35(2), October 1992:331–350.

Griliches, Zvi, and Vidar Ringstad, *Economies of Scale and the Form of the Production Function: An Econometric Study of Norwegian Manufacturing Establishment Data*. Amsterdam: North Holland, 1971.

Grossman, Michael, and Frank Chaloupka, "Demand for Cocaine by Young Adults: A Rational Addiction Approach," *Journal of Health Economics*, 17(4), August 1998:427–474.

Grossman, Philip J., Marco Pirozzi, and Jeff Pope, "An Empirical Test of Free-Rider Behaviour," *Australian Economic Papers*, 32(60), June 1993:152–160.

Gruber, Harald, "The Learning Curve in the Production of Semiconductor Memory Chips," *Applied Economics*, 24(8), August 1992:885–894.

Guillickson, William, and Michael J. Harper, "Multifactor Productivity in U.S. Manufacturing, 1949–83," *Monthly Labor Review*, 110(10), October 1987:18–28.

Hall, Robert E., and David M. Lilien, "Efficient Wage Bargains Under Uncertain Supply and Demand," *American Economic Review*, 69(5), December 1979:868–879.

Hamilton, Stephen F., "The Comparative Efficiency of Ad Valorem and Specific Taxes Under Monopoly and Monopsony," *Economics Letters*, 63(2), May 1999:235–238.

Hatton, T. J., G. R. Boyer, and R. E. Bailey, "The Union Wage Effect in Late Nineteenth Century Britain," *Economica*, 61(244), November 1994:435–456.

Hausman, Jerry A., "Valuation of New Goods Under Perfect and Imperfect Competition," in Timothy F. Bresnahan and Robert J. Gordon, eds., *The Economics of New Goods*, National Bureau of Economic Research Studies in Income and Wealth, Vol. 58. Chicago: University of Chicago Press, 1997.

Hausman, Jerry A., and Gregory K. Leonard, "Superstars in the NBA: Economic Value and Policy," *Journal of Labor Economics*, 14(4), October 1997:586–624.

Hay, George A., and Daniel Kelley, "An Empirical Survey of Price-Fixing Conspiracies," *Journal of Law and Economics*, 17(1), April 1974:13–38.

Head, J. G., "A Note on Progression and Leisure: Comment," *American Economic Review*, 56(1), March 1966:172–179.

Hennart, Jean-François, "Upstream Vertical Integration in the Aluminum and Tin Industries," *Journal of Economic Behavior and Organization*, 9(3), April 1988:281–299.

Holt, Matthew, "A Multimarket Bounded Price Variation Model Under Rational Expectations: Corn and Soybeans in the United States," *American Journal of Agricultural Economics*, 74(1), February 1992:10–20.

Hotelling, Harold, "The Economics of Exhaustible Resources," *Journal of Political Economy*, 39(2), April 1931:137–175.

Jha, Raghbendra, M. N. Murty, Satya Paul, and Balbir S. Sahni, "Cost Structure of the Indian Cement Industry," *Journal of Economics Studies*, 8(4), 1991:59–67.

Kakalik, J.S, and N.M. Pace, *Costs and Compensation Paid in Tort Litigation*. Santa Monica, Calif.: RAND Corporation, Institute for Civil Justice, 1986.

Kalirajan, K.P., and M.B. Obwona, "Frontier Production Function: The Stochastic Coefficient Approach," *Oxford Bulletin of Economics and Statistics*, 56(1), 1994:87–96.

Karp, Larry S., and Jeffrey M. Perloff, "The Failure of Strategic Industrial Policies Due to the Manipulation by Firms," *International Review of Economics and Finance*, 4(1), 1995:1–16.

Keeler, Theodore E., Teh-Wei Hu, Paul G. Barnett, and Willard G. Manning, "Taxation, Regulation, and Addiction: A Demand Function for Cigarettes Based on Time-Series Evidence," *Journal of Health Economics*, 12(1), April 1993:1–18.

Kennickell, Arthur B., and R. Louise Woodburn, "Consistent Weight Design for 1989, 1992, and 1995 SCPs, and the Distribution of Wealth," working paper, Board of Governors of the Federal Reserve System, August 1997.

Kim, E. Han, and Vijay Singal, "Mergers and Market Power: Evidence from the Airline Industry," *American Economic Review*, 83(3), June 1993:549–569.

Kim, H. Youn, "Economies of Scale and Scope in Multiproduct Firms: Evidence from U.S. Railroads," *Applied Economics*, 19(6), June 1987:733–741.

Kim, Hongjin, Gloria E. Helfand, and Richard E. Howitt, "An Economic Analysis of Ozone Control in California's San Joaquin Valley," *Journal of Agricultural and Resource Economics*, 23(1), July 1998:55–70.

Krattenmaker, Thomas G., and Steven C. Salop, "Anticompetitive Exclusion: Raising Rivals' Costs to Achieve Power over Price," *Yale Law Journal*, 96(2), December 1986:209–293.

Krupnick, A. J., and Paul R. Portney, "Controlling Urban Air Pollution: A Benefit-Cost Assessment," *Science*, 252, April 1991:522–528.

Lenard, Thomas M., "The Efficiency Costs of the Postal Monopoly: The Case of Third-Class Mail," *Journal of Regulatory Economics*, 6(4), December 1994:421–431.

Leslie, Phillip J., "A Structural Econometric Analysis of Price Discrimination in Broadway Theatre," working paper, University of California, Los Angeles, November 15, 1997.

Levin, Richard C., Alvin K. Klevorick, Richard R. Nelson, and Sidney G. Winter, "Appropriating the Returns from Industrial Research and Development," *Brookings Papers on Economic Activity*, 3(Special Issue on Microeconomics), 1987:783–820.

Lopez, Rigoberto A., and Emilio Pagoulatos, "Rent Seeking and the Welfare Cost of Trade Barriers," *Public Choice*, 79(1–2), April 1994:149–160.

MacAvoy, Paul W., "Tacit Collusion Under Regulation in the Pricing of Interstate Long-Distance Services," *Journal of Economics and Management Strategy*, 4(2), Summer 1995:147–185.

MacCrimmon, Kenneth R., and M. Toda, "The Experimental Determination of Indifference Curves," *Review of Economic Studies*, 56(3), July 1969:433–451.

Machina, Mark, "Dynamic Consistency and Non-Expected Utility Models of Choice Under Uncertainty," *Journal of Economic Literature*, 27(4), December 1989:1622–1668.

MacKie-Mason, Jeffrey K., and Robert S. Pindyck, "Cartel Theory and Cartel Experience in International Minerals Markets," in R. L. Gordon, H. D. Jacoby, and M. B. Zimmerman, eds., *Energy: Markets and Regulation: Essays in Honor of M. A. Adelman*. Cambridge, Mass.: MIT Press, 1986.

MaCurdy, Thomas, David Green, and Harry Paarsch, "Assessing Empirical Approaches for Analyzing Taxes and Labor Supply," *Journal of Human Resources*, 25(3), Summer 1990:415–490.

Madden, Janice F., *The Economics of Sex Discrimination*. Lexington, Mass.: Heath, 1973.

Maddock, Rodney, Elkin Castano, and Frank Vella, "Estimating Electricity Demand: The Cost of Linearizing the Budget Constraint," *Review of Economics and Statistics*, 74(2), May 1992:350–354.

Moffitt, Robert, "Estimating the Value of an In-Kind Transfer: The Case of Food Stamps," *Econometrica*, 57(2), March 1989:385–409.

Moschini, Giancarlo, and Karl D. Meilke, "Production Subsidy and Countervailing Duties in Vertically Related Markets: The Hog-Pork Case Between Canada and the United States," *American Journal of Agricultural Economics*, 74(4), November 1992:951–961.

Nash, John F., "Equilibrium Points in *n*-Person Games," *Proceedings of the National Academy of Sciences*, 36, 1950:48–49.

Nash, John F., "Non-Cooperative Games," *Annals of Mathematics*, 54(2), July 1951:286–295.

Nemoto, Jiro, Yasuo Nakanishi, and Seishi Madono, "Scale Economies and Over-Capitalization in Japanese

Electric Utilities," *International Economic Review*, 34(2), May 1993:431–440.

Norman, G., "Economies of Scale in the Cement Industry," *Journal of Industrial Economics*, 27(4), June 1979:317–337.

Panzar, John C., and Robert D. Willig, "Economies of Scale in Multi-Output Production," *Quarterly Journal of Economics*, 91(3), August 1977:481–493.

Panzar, John C., and Robert D. Willig, "Economies of Scope," *American Economic Review*, 71(2), May 1981:268–272.

Perry, Martin K., "Forward Integration by Alcoa: 1888–1930," *Journal of Industrial Economics*, 29(1), September 1980:37–53.

Perry, Martin K., "Vertical Integration: Determinants and Effects," in Richard Schmalensee and Robert D. Willig, eds., *Handbook of Industrial Organization*. New York: North Holland, 1989.

Polinsky, A. Mitchell, "Controlling Externalities and Protecting Entitlements: Property Right, Liability Rule, and Tax-Subsidy Approaches," *Journal of Legal Studies*, 8(1), January 1979:1–48.

Pollak, Robert A., *The Theory of the Cost-of-Living Index*. New York: Oxford University Press, 1989.

Posner, Richard A., "The Social Cost of Monopoly and Regulation," *Journal of Political Economy*, 83(4), August 1975:807–827.

Pratten, Clifford F., "The Manufacture of Pins," *Journal of Economic Literature*, 18(1), March 1980:93–96.

Ransom, Michael R., "Seniority and Monopsony in the Academic Labor Market," *American Economic Review*, 83(1), March 1993:221–233.

Rawls, John, *A Theory of Justice*. New York: Oxford University Press, 1971.

Ries, John C., "Windfall Profits and Vertical Relationships: Who Gained in the Japanese Auto Industry from VERs?" *Journal of Industrial Economics*, 41(3), September 1993:259–276.

Roberts, Mark J., and Larry Samuelson, "An Empirical Analysis of Dynamic Nonprice Competition in an Oligopolistic Industry," *Rand Journal of Economics*, 19(2), Summer 1988:200–220.

Robidoux, Benoît, and John Lester, "Econometric Estimates of Scale Economies in Canadian Manufacturing," Working Paper No. 88-4, Canadian Department of Finance, 1988.

Robidoux, Benoît, and John Lester, "Econometric Estimates of Scale Economies in Canadian Manufacturing," *Applied Economics*, 24(1), January 1992:113–122.

Ross, David R., and Klaus F. Zimmermann, "Evaluating Reported Determinants of Labor Demand," *Labour Economics*, 1(1), June 1993:71–84.

Rousseas, S. W., and A. G. Hart, "Experimental Verification of a Composite Indifference Map," *Journal of Political Economy*, 59(4), August 1951:288–318.

Salop, Joanne, and Steven C. Salop, "Self-Selection and Turnover in the Labor Market," *Quarterly Journal of Economics*, 90(4), November 1976:619–627.

Salop, Steven C., "The Noisy Monopolist: Imperfect Information, Price Dispersion, and Price Discrimination," *Review of Economic Studies*, 44(3), October 1977:393–406.

Salop, Steven C., "Strategic Entry Deterrence," *American Economic Review*, 69(2), May 1979:335–338.

Salop, Steven C., "Practices That (Credibly) Facilitate Oligopoly Coordination," in Joseph E. Stiglitz and G. Frank Mathewson, eds., *New Developments in the Analysis of Market Structure*. Cambridge, Mass.: MIT Press, 1986.

Salop, Steven C., and David T. Sheffman, "Cost-Raising Strategies," *Journal of Industrial Economics*, 36(1), September 1987:19–34.

Schoemaker, Paul J. H., "The Expected Utility Model: Its Variants, Purposes, Evidence and Limitation," *Journal of Economic Literature*, 20(2), June 1982:529–563.

Schroeter, John R., Scott L. Smith, and Steven R. Cox, "Advertising and Competition in Routine Legal Service Markets: An Empirical Investigation, *Journal of Industrial Economics*, 36(1), September 1987:49–60.

Scott, Robert E., "The Effects of Protection on a Domestic Oligopoly: The Case of the U.S. Auto Market," *Journal of Policy Modeling*, 16(3), June 1994:299–325.

Shapiro, Carl, and Joseph E. Stiglitz, "Equilibrium Unemployment as a Worker Discipline Device," *American Economic Review*, 74(3), June 1984:434–444.

Shea, John, "Do Supply Curves Slope Up?" *Quarterly Journal of Economics*, 108(1), February 1993:1–32.

Shoesmith, Gary L. "Economies of Scale and Scope in Petroleum Refining," *Applied Economics*, 20(12), December 1988:1643–1652.

Skeath, Susan E., and Gregory A. Trandel, "A Pareto Comparison of Ad Valorem and Unit Taxes in Noncompetitive Environments," *Journal of Public Economics*, 53(1), January 1994:53–71.

Slade, Margaret E., "Product Rivalry with Multiple Strategic Weapons: An Analysis of Price and Advertising Competition," *Journal of Economics and Management Strategy*," 4(3), Fall 1995:224–276.

Smiley, Robert, "Empirical Evidence on Strategic Entry Deterrence," *International Journal of Industrial Organization*, 6(2), June 1988:167–180.

Spence, A. Michael, *Market Signaling*. Cambridge, Mass.: Harvard University Press, 1974.

Spence, A. Michael, "The Learning Curve and Competition," *Bell Journal of Economics and Management Science*, 12(1), 1981:49–70.

Spencer, Barbara J., and James A. Brander, "International R&D Rivalry and Industrial Strategy," *Review of Economic Studies*, 50(4), October 1983:707–722.

Stewart, Mark B., "Union Wage Differentials in an Era of Declining Unionization," *Oxford Bulletin of Economics and Statistics*, 57(2), May 1995:143–166.

Stiglitz, Joseph E., "The Theory of 'Screening,' Education, and the Distribution of Income," *American Economic Review*, 65(3), June 1975:283–300.

Stiglitz, Joseph E., "Equilibrium in Product Markets with Imperfect Information," *American Economic Review*, 69(2), May 1979:339–345.

Stiglitz, Joseph E., "The Causes and Consequences of the Dependence of Quality on Price," *Journal of Economic Literature*, 25(1), March 1987:1–48.

Stuart, Charles, "Swedish Tax Rates, Labor Supply, and Tax Revenues," *Journal of Political Economy*, 89(5), October 1981:1020–1038.

Stuart, Charles, "Welfare Costs per Dollar of Additional Tax Revenue in the United States," *American Economic Review*, 74(3), June 1984:352–362.

Sullivan, Daniel, "Monopsony Power in the Market for Nurses," *Journal of Law and Economics*, 32(2, pt. 2) October 1989:S135–S178.

Tarr, David G., *A General Equilibrium Analysis of the Welfare and Employment Effects of U.S. Quotas in Textiles, Autos and Steel.* Washington, D.C.: Bureau of Economics Staff Report, Federal Trade Commission, 1989.

Taube, Paul M., and Don N. MacDonald, "A Dynamic Almost Ideal Demand System Incorporating Consumer Expectations," *Managerial and Decision Economics*, 12(3), June 1991:197–206.

Terrell, Katherine, "Technical Change and Factor Bias in Polish Industry (1962–1983)," *Review of Economics and Statistics*, 75(4), November 1993:741–747.

Tideman, T. Nicholaus, and Gordon Tullock, "A New and Superior Process for Making Social Choices," *Journal of Political Economy*, 84(6), December 1976:1145–1159.

Timmer, C. Peter, "Choice of Technique in Rice Milling on Java," in Carl K. Eicher and John M. Staatz, eds., *Agricultural Development in the Third World.* Baltimore: Johns Hopkins University Press, 1984.

Tullock, G., "The Welfare Cost of Tariffs, Monopolies, and Theft," *Western Economic Journal*, 5(3), June 1967:224–232.

Urban, Glen L., Theresa Carter, and Steven Gaskin, "Market Share Rewards to Pioneering Brands: An Empirical Analysis and Strategic Implications," *Management Science*, 32(6), June 1986:645–659.

Vandermeulen, Daniel C., "Upward Sloping Demand Curves Without the Giffen Paradox," *American Economic Review*, 62(3), June 1972:453–458.

Van Ravenstein, Ad, and Hans Vijlbrief, "Welfare Cost of Higher Tax Rates: An Empirical Laffer Curve for the Netherlands," *De Economist*, 136(2), 1988:205–219.

Varian, Hal R., "Measuring the Deadweight Cost of DUP and Rent-Seeking Activities," *Economics and Politics*, 1(1), Spring 1989:81–95.

Varian, Hal R., *Microeconomic Analysis*, 3rd ed. New York: Norton, 1992.

Varian, Hal R., "Estimating the Demand for Bandwidth," www.sims.berkeley.edu/~hal/papers/wtp/wtp.pdf, August 1999.

Villegas, Daniel J., "The Impact of Usury Ceilings on Consumer Credit," *Southern Economic Journal*, 56(1), July 1989:126–141.

Viscusi, W. Kip, *Employment Hazards*. Cambridge, Mass.: Harvard University Press, 1979.

Viscusi, W. Kip, *Pricing Environmental Risks*. Policy Study No. 112. St. Louis, Mo.: Center for the Study of American Business, Washington University, 1992.

von Neumann, John, and Oskar Morgenstern, *Theory of Games and Economic Behavior*. Princeton, N.J.: Princeton University Press, 1944.

Waldfogel, Joel, "The Deadweight Loss of Christmas," *American Economic Review*, 83(5), December 1993:1328–1336.

Walton, Clarence C., and Frederick W. Cleveland, *Corporations on Trial: The Electric Cases*. Belmont, Calif.: Wadsworth, 1964.

Whinston, Michael D., and Scott C. Collins, "Entry and Competitive Structure in Deregulated Airline Markets: An Event Study Analysis of People Express," *Rand Journal of Economics*, 23(4), Winter 1992:445–462.

Williamson, Oliver E., *Markets and Hierarchies: Analysis and Antitrust Implications*. New York: Free Press, 1975.

Williamson, Oliver E., "Credible Commitments: Using Hostages to Support Exchange," *American Economic Review*, 73(4), September 1983:519–540.

Willis, Robert J., "A New Approach to the Economic Theory of Fertility Behavior," *Journal of Political Economy*, 81(2, pt. 2), March–April 1973:S14–S64.

Womer, N. Keith, and J. Wayne Patterson, "Estimation and Testing of Learning Curves," *Journal of Business and Economic Statistics*, 1(4), October 1983:265–272.

Yellen, Janet L., "Efficiency Wage Models of Unemployment," *American Economic Review*, 74(2), May 1984:200–205.

SOURCES FOR APPLICATIONS

Chapter 1

Oregon Decides Which Medical Treatments to Provide: MacKenzie, Bill, "Rationing Helps Poor in Oregon Get Care," *Newsday*, April 22, 1993:44; "State's Expanded Medicaid Program to Begin with Managed Care Component," *BNA Pension and Benefits Reporter*, 21(7), February 14, 1994:391; "ADA Analyses of the Oregon Health Care Plan," *Issues in Law and Medicine*, March 22, 1994; "Oregon's Failed Experiment," *Detroit News*, January 14, 1999:A8.

Tax on Fast-Food Containers: Kinzer, Stephen, "Germany Upholds Tax on Fast-Food Containers," *New York Times*, August 22, 1994.

Income Threshold Model and China: "Next in Line: Chinese Consumers," *Economist*, 326(7795), January 23, 1993:66–67; Pelline, Jeff, "U.S. Businesses Pour into China," *San Francisco Chronicle*, May 17, 1994:B1–B2; *China Statistical Yearbook* (Beijing: China Statistical Publishing House, 1998).

Putting Saturn in Orbit: Edwards, Martin, "We're Not Dealing: Fixed-Price Sales Find Fans," *Business Journal of North Carolina*, 7(33), November 30, 1992:20; Jedlicka, Dan, "Saturn Becomes a Star: GM's Newest Baby Has Won Buyers' Trust," *Chicago Sun-Times*, December 2, 1992:Auto Times, 3; Pelline, Jeff, "No-Dicker Stickers for New Cars," *San Francisco Chronicle*, April 15, 1993:D1; Pelline, Jeff, "GM Sold on New Pricing," *San Francisco Chronicle*, July 2, 1993:D1; "Automakers Urge Dealers to Quit Haggling," *Plain Dealer*, February 20, 1994:43K; Glover, Mark, "There's No Haggling over GM Sales Jump," *Sacramento Bee*, February 4, 1994:D1; Martin, Tim, "'No-Dicker' Sticker Has Mixed Success," *Nashville Tennessean*, April 12, 1994; Levy, Michael, "Auto Sales Undergoing a Revolution: New Pricing, Mega-Dealerships Change Business," *Buffalo News*, April 24, 1994:Business, 15; Kenzie, Jim, "Saturn Homecoming Celebrated First Decade," *Toronto Star*, August 14, 1999; Kaltenheuser, Skip, "At Car Dealers, a No-Haggle Policy Sets Off a Battle," *New York Times*, August 29, 1999:4; Flavelle, Dana, "Tiny, Tough Cynthia Trudell in Driver's Seat," *Toronto Star*, September 11, 1999.

Chapter 2

Aggregating the Demand for Cling Peaches: French and King (1986).

American Steel Quotas: Crandall, Robert W., "The Effects of U.S. Trade Protection for Autos and Steel," *Brookings Papers on Economic Activity*, 1, 1987:271–288; Burnham, James B., *American Steel and International Trade: The Challenge of Globalization*, Center for the Study of American Business Contemporary Issues Series 95 (Center for the Study of American Business Contemporary Issues, September 1999); Mitchell, Alison, "By a Wide Margin, the House Votes Steel Import Curb," *New York Times*, March 18, 1999:A1, C23.

Gas Lines: "Saxbe Warns Gas Stations," *Los Angeles Times*, January 8, 1974:(I)16; "Waiting in Line? Gasoline Burns Too," *Los Angeles Times*, February 8, 1974:(I)22; "Psst! Let's Get Tanked at Old Phil's," *Los Angeles Times*, February 11, 1974:(I)21; "Favoritism in Sale of Gasoline Banned," *Los Angeles Times*, February 13, 1974:(I)1; "52 Cities Have No Lines at the Pumps," *Los Angeles Times*, February 13, 1974:(I)15; David Shaw, "Motorists Besiege Open Gas Stations; Fistfights Break Out," *Los Angeles Times*, February 17, 1974:(I)1; "L.A. Cars Sparkle in Fuel Crisis," *Los Angeles Times*, February 17, 1974:(I)30.

Minimum Wage Law in Puerto Rico: Perloff, Harvey S., *Puerto Rico's Economic Future* (Chicago: University of Chicago Press, 1950) [my dad]; Reynolds, Lloyd G., Peter Gregory, and Luz M. Torruellas, *Wages, Productivity, and Industrialization in Puerto Rico* (Homewood, Ill.: Irwin, 1965); Castillo-Freeman and Freeman (1992); *Handbook of U.S. Labor Statistics* (Washington, D.C.: U.S. Department of Labor, 1999).

Chapter 3

Web Fees: Edell and Varaiya (1999); Varian (1999); Ahmad, Nadia, "Internet Fees Alter Network Use," *Daily Californian*, May 21, 1999:1, 3; www.index.berkeley.edu/reports/99-01w.

Demanding Rail Safety: "Rail Safety: Costing Lives," *Economist*, 324(7776), September 12, 1992:66.

Discouraging Smoking: Keeler, Hu, Barnett, and Manning (1993); "A Tax We Can Live With," *University of California at Berkeley Wellness Letter*, 9(9), June 1993:7; Passell, Peter, "Doing Well by Doing Good," *New York Times*, December 24, 1992:C2; Koretz, Gene, "Add $2 to the Cost of a Pack of Cigarettes . . . ," *Business Week*, March 15, 1993:18;

A–53

"Tobacco: Armageddon and Appalachia," *Economist*, 32(7820), July 17, 1993:25; "In Canada, They're Cutting Sin Taxes," *Business Week*, February 21, 1994:44; Farrell, Christopher, "This Sin Tax Is Win-Win," *Business Week*, April 11, 1994:31; Marshall, Jonathan, "Smokers Paying Their Way," *San Francisco Chronicle*, August 29, 1994:D1, D3; Marshall, Jonathan, "Life Is Very Good for Silicon Valley Residents," *San Francisco Chronicle*, January 13, 1997:B3; Grossman, Michael, "Health Economics," *NBER Reporter*, Winter 1998:1–5; www.ash.org.

Gasoline Taxes as a Revenue Source: Gallini (1983); "Energy Taxes: Coming Soon, to a Station Near You," *Economist*, 326(7793), January 3, 1993:24; Viviano, Frank, "High Gas Tax a Way of Life in Europe," *San Francisco Chronicle*, January 22, 1993:A1; Hebert, H. Josef, "Examining the Surge in Gas Prices," *Rocky Mountain News*, May 3, 1996:34A; Kessler, Glenn, "Running on Empty," *Newsday*, May 8, 1996:A3; *Energy Prices and Taxes* (Washington, D.C.: International Energy Agency, 1999); *Consumption Tax Trends* (Geneva: Organization for Economic Cooperation and Development, 1999).

Incidence of Federal Ad Valorem Tax: Brownlee and Perry (1967).

Chapter 4

Indifference Curves Between Food and Clothing: Eastwood and Craven (1981).

Taxes and Internet Shopping: Goolsbee (1998); Emert, Carol, "Retailers Step Up Drive for Net Taxes," *San Francisco Chronicle*, December 15, 1999:C1, C5.

Food Stamp Experiment: Moffitt (1989); Fraker (1990); Fasciano, Hall, and Beebout (1993); Carlson (1993).

Chapter 5

Income Elasticities of Demand for Cars: Bordley and McDonald (1993).

Why the Wealthy Buy More Houses: Johnston, David Cay, "Mortgage Tax Break: Who Gets What," *New York Times*, June 10, 1999:sec.3: 5; Taube and MacDonald (1991).

Does Inflation Hurt?: Passell, Peter, "Every Second Counts Even More," *New York Times*, June 28, 1998:9, based on a paper by W. Michael Cox and Richard Alm.

The Total CPI Bias: Hausman (1997); "Who's Afraid of the Big Bad Deficit?" *Economist*, 336(7934), September 30, 1995:25–26; Uchitelle, Louis, "Balancing Quantity, Quality and Inflation," *New York Times*, December 18, 1996:C1, C6; Marshall, Jonathan, "Figuring Inflation Is a Truly Tough Job," *San Francisco Chronicle*, December 9, 1996:C1, C2; Boskin et al. (1997); *Statistical Abstract of the United States* (Washington, D.C.: U.S. Bureau of the Census, 1999); White, Alan G., "Measurement Biases in Consumer Price Indexes," *International Statistical Review*, 67(3), December 1999:301–325.

Leisure-Income Choices of Textile Workers: Dunn (1977, 1978, 1979).

Estimated Labor Supply Curves: Killingsworth, Mark R., *Labor Supply* (Cambridge, England: Cambridge University Press, 1983); MaCurdy, Green, and Paarsch (1990).

Effects of Tax Cuts: Stuart (1981, 1984); Fullerton (1982); Van Ravestein and Vijlbrief (1988).

Chapter 6

Malthus and Mass Starvation: Tweeten, Luther, *Farm Policy Analysis* (Boulder, Colo.: Westview Press, 1989); Duvick, Donald N., "Genetic Contributions to Advances in Yield of U.S. Maize," *Maydica*, 37(1), 1992:69–79; Crossette, "How to Fix a Crowded World: Add People," *New York Times*, November 2, 1997:sec.4: 1, 3; Brander and Taylor (1998); Phillips, Michael M., "Greenspan Credits New Technology for Helping Farmers Weather Crisis," *Wall Street Journal*, March 17, 1999; *Statistical Abstract of the United States* (Washington, D.C.: U.S. Bureau of the Census, 1999); *FAO Quarterly Bulletin of Statistics* (New York: United Nations, 1999).

A Semiconductor Integrated Circuit Isoquant: Nile Hatch, personal communications; Roy Mallory, personal communications.

Returns to Scale in Manufacturing: Baldwin and Gorecki (1986).

German Versus British Productivity: Rattner, Steven, "A Tale of Two Ford Plants," *New York Times*, October 13, 1981:D1, D4.

Nonneutral Technical Change in Pin Manufacturing: Pratten (1980).

Automobile Manufacturing Innovations: "The Secrets of the Production Line," *Economist*, 325(7781), October 17, 1992:5; Nash, Nathaniel C., "Putting Porsche in the Pink," *New York Times*, January 1, 1996:17.

Chapter 7

Opportunity Cost of Waiting Time: Globerman (1991).

Swarthmore College's Cost of Capital: Passell, Peter, "One Top College's Price Tag: Why So Low, and So High?" *New York Times*, July 27, 1994:A1.

Internet Firms' Fixed Costs: Friedman, Thomas L., "Foreign Affairs: Amazon.you," *New York Times*, February 26, 1999; Friedman, Thomas L., "Foreign Affairs: KillingGoliath.com," *New York Times*, March 9, 1999; De Jonge, Peter, "Riding the Wild, Perilous Waters of Amazon.com," *New York Times*, March 14, 1999; and Banda, P. Solomon "University Professor Challenges Amazon.com from His Home," Associated Press, March 16, 1999; www.newswatch.org/mediacritic/mar99/990310m1.html.

Short-Run Cost Curves for a Printing Firm: Griliches and Ringstad (1971).

Rice Milling on Java: Timmer (1984).

Average Cost of Cement Firms: Norman (1979); Jha, Murty, Paul, and Sahni (1991).

Long-Run Cost Curves in Printing and Oil Pipelines: Griliches and Ringstad (1971); Exxon (1975).

Choosing an Ink-Jet or a Laser Printer: Various advertisements.

Learning by Doing in Computer Chips: Gruber (1992).

Dead End: "Jay Meatier's Newsreel: Death Warmed Over," *U.S. News and World Report*, 123(12), September 29, 1997:12.

Chapter 8

Breaking Even on Christmas Trees: "How They Do It: Breaking Even in a Seasonal Business," *New York Times*, December 25, 1993:21.

Shutting Down Oil Wells: Salpukas, Agis, "Low Prices Have Sapped Little Oil Producers," *New York Times*, April 3, 1999:B1, B4.

Threat of Entry in Shipping: Davies (1986).

The Naked Truth About Costs and Entry: "Branded Flesh," *Economist*, August 14, 1999:56.

Upward-Sloping Long-Run Supply Curve for Cotton: International Cotton Advisory Committee, *Survey of the Cost of Production of Raw Cotton*, September 1992:5; *Cotton: World Statistics*, April 1993:4–5. The figure shows the supply of the major producing countries for which we have cost information. The only large producers for whom cost data are missing are India and China.

Slope of Long-Run Market Supply Curves: Shea (1993).

Chapter 9

Consumer Surplus from Television: Delsol, Michel, "Would You Give Up TV for a Million Bucks?" *TV Guide*, October 10, 1992:11.

Deadweight Loss of Christmas: Waldfogel (1993).

Taxicab Medallions: Fisher, Ian, "A Bumpier Ride for New York Taxis," *New York Times*, October 6, 1991:7; Marshall, Jonathan, "Cab Companies Haled into Court," *San Francisco Chronicle*, July 1, 1993:A1, A11; Fragin, Sheryl, "Taxi!" *Atlantic Monthly*, May 1994:30f; Yeh, Emerald, and Christine McMurry, "Are San Francisco Cabs a Bit Too Rare?" *San Francisco Chronicle*, September 15, 1996: 4; Bowman, Catherine, "Why San Francisco Taxis Are Catch as Catch Can," *San Francisco Chronicle*, September 16, 1995:A1, A11; Harrington, Kathleen, "Bottom Line: 300 More Cabs Needed," *San Francisco Chronicle*, July 28, 1998:A19; Coliver, Victoria, "Taxi Turmoil," *San Francisco Examiner*, June 13, 1999:B1, B7; Epstein, Edward, "S.F. Tax Deal Rejected by Board of Supervisors," *San Francisco Chronicle*, April 13, 1999:A16.

Discriminating Against Groups: "It's Soul Food at Africa Hut," *San Francisco Chronicle*, June 8, 1994:C1.

Barriers to Protect Our Way of Life: Epstein, Edward, "New Coffee Bars Banned in Castro, Upper Market," *San Francisco Chronicle*, April 15, 1997:A13, A15; Lane, Lea, "Bermuda Seeks to Shake Off Doldrums," *Business and Management Practices*, 212(7), April 21, 1997:4–5; McCann, John, "Scots Publicans Try to Call Time on 'Superpubs,'" *Scotsman*, May 8, 1998:10.

International Cost of Agricultural Subsidies: *Agricultural Policies, Markets and Trade: Monitoring and Outlook* (Geneva: Organization for Economic Cooperation and Development, 1994–1999); Andrews, Edmund L., "No Agreement on Reducing Europe Farm Subsidies," *New York Times*, February 27, 1999:B1, B2.

Japanese Nontariff Barriers: "Japan's Protection Racket," *Economist*, January 7, 1995:58; Sazanami, Yoko, Shujiro Urata, and Hiroki Kawai, *Measuring the Costs of Protection in Japan* (Washington, D.C.: Institute for International Economics, 1995). The reported numbers are probably upper bounds on the true losses, as they do not fully control for quality differences in Japanese and imported goods.

Chapter 10

Sin Taxes: Boyd and Seldon (1991).

Living-Wage Laws: De Bare, Ilana, "Living-Wage Wildfire," *San Francisco Chronicle*, April 9, 1999:B1, B2; Sinton, Peter, "'Living Wage': Effects on Firms," *San Francisco Chronicle*, May 5, 1999:B3; Reich, Michael, Peter Hall, and Fiona Hsu, "Living Wages and the San Francisco Economy," working paper, University of California, Berkeley, June 1999; Leung, Shirley, and Sheila Muto, "As 'Living Wage' Gains Momentum, a Look at How It Has Done So Far," *Wall Street Journal Interactive Edition*, December 15, 1999.

Auto Trade Barriers: "Caveat Emptor," *Economist*, August 27, 1994:43; "A Car Buyer's Heaven in a Borderless Europe," *New York Times*, January 17, 1996:C1, C4; Griffiths, John, "Car Price Disparities Highlighted," *Financial Times*, January 7, 1999:2.

Wealth Distribution in the United States: Nasar, Sylvia, "The Rich Get Richer, but Never the Same Way Twice," *New York Times*, August 16, 1992:3; Golan, Elise, and Mark Nord, "How Government Assistance Affects Income," *Food Review*, 21(1), January–April 1998:2–7; Johnston, David Cay, "Gap Between Rich and Poor Bigger than Ever," *San Francisco Examiner*, September 5, 1999:B4; "*Forbes*' List of the Wealthy Finds Richest Even Richer," *San Francisco Chronicle*, September 24, 1999:A2.

Chapter 11

Humana Hospitals: Frantz, Douglas, "Congress Probes Hospital Costs—$9 Tylenols, $118 Heat Pads," *San Francisco Chronicle*, October 18, 1991:A2. The elasticities in the table were calculated by assuming that Humana sets the price of each good independently and operates where its marginal revenue equals its marginal cost: $MR = p(1 + 1/\varepsilon) = MC$. By rearranging this expression, we discover that $\varepsilon = p/(MC - p)$. (If the hospital sets prices of several goods and services simultaneously, we should use a more complex formula.)

Airport Monopolies: Sinton, Peter, "Airport Shops Cut Prices: A Move to Subdue Fear of Gouging," *San Francisco Chronicle*, February 15, 1995:C1.

Deadweight Loss of the U.S. Postal Service: Lenard (1994).

Electric Power Utilities: Christensen and Greene (1976).

Government Sales of Monopolies: Matier, Phillip, and Andrew Ross, "City Tow Kowtows to S.F. and Coughs Up More Cash," *San Francisco Chronicle*, February 18, 1994:A17; Bryant, Adam, "In a Bill's Shipbuilding Provision, Some See a Floating Pork Barrel," *New York Times*, October 11, 1997:A1, B2; McNeil, Donald G., "Crossed Wires in South Africa," *New York Times*, December 17, 1997:C1, C8; Kopytoff, Verne G., "Coke, Pepsi Waging Bidding Battle in California," *San Francisco Chronicle*, November 30, 1999:C4.

A Drug Patent: Berndt, Ernst R., Linda T. Bui, David Reiley, and Glen L. Urban, "The Roles of Marketing, Product Quality, and Price Competition in the Growth and Composition of the U.S. Anti-Ulcer Drug Industry," Working paper 19-94, May 1994; Berndt, Ernst R., Linda T. Bui, David Reiley, and Glen L. Urban, "Information, Marketing and Pricing in the U.S. Anti-Ulcer Drug Market." Unpublished manuscript, 1995; Suslow, Valerie Y., "Measuring Quality Change in Pharmaceutical Markets: Hedonic Price Indexes for Anti-Ulcer Drugs," in Robert B. Helms, ed., *Competitive Strategies in the Pharmaceutical Industry* (Washington, D.C.: AEI Press, 1996); "Ulcer Drug's Price About to Drop," *San Francisco Chronicle*, May 11, 1994:D1; Milt Freudenheim, "New Drug Era Begins as Tagamet Patent Ends," *New York Times*, May 17, 1994:C4; "Having an Ulcer Is Getting a Lot Cheaper," *Business Week*, May 9, 1994:30; Day, Kathleen, "Putting a Price on a Pill," *Washington Post*, March 21, 1993. When the firm had a monopoly, its name was SmithKline Beckman. Through a merger it became SmithKline Beecham and will soon be Glaxo SmithKline. The graph shows an inverse linear demand curve of the form $p = a - bQ$. Such a demand curve has an elasticity of $\varepsilon = -(1/b)(p/Q)$. If the elasticity of demand is $-1.11 = -(1/b)(0.75/1.3)$ where $p = 0.75$ and $Q = 1.3$, then $b = 0.52$. Solving $p = 0.75 = a - 0.52 \times 1.3$, we find that $a = 1.43$. The height of the triangle $A + B + C$ is $\$1.355 = \$1.43 - \$0.075$, and its length is approximately 2.61 million doses, so its area is $\frac{1}{2}(\$1.355 \times 2.61) \approx \$1.77$ million per day.

Monopoly in Names: Mullins, Andrew, "Network: Nominet Set to De-Mutualise," *Independent*, July 5, 1999:Features, 12; "Network Solutions' 2nd-Quarter Profit Soars," *Washington Post*, July 23, 1999:E2; Clausing, Jeri, "A Planned Internet Yellow Pages Draws Federal Scrutiny," *New York Times*, July 26, 1999:C1, C8; "Gordian Knotwork," *Economist*, July 31, 1999:58–59; Kaplan, Karen, "Two Schools of Thought at Work in Effort to Expand Domain Names," *Los Angeles Times*, August 5, 1999:C8; "Hey, Buddy, I Got a Potent Domain Name Here," *Los Angeles Times*, August 5, 1999:C8; Cook, John, "The Way We Live Now: 8-22-99," *New York Times*, August 22, 1999:sec.6: 18; Clausing, Jeri, "First out of Starting Gate," *New York Times*, August 23, 1999:C3; Sinton, Peter, "Virtual Vineyard Swallows Up Wine.com," *San Francisco Chronicle*, September 14, 1999:D1; Clausing, Jeri, "Deal Is Reached to Open Internet Registration," *New York Times*, September 29, 1999:C12; "Domain Name Democracy?" *PC Magazine*, November 16, 1999:34.

Chapter 12

Disneyland Pricing: Disneyland.

A Hot Sale of Coke: Hays, Constance L., "Variable-Price Coke Machine Being Tested," *New York Times*, October 28, 1999:C1.

Tagamet Revisited: See Chapter 11, "A Drug Patent" for the sources and the assumptions used in this analysis for 1983, the last year Tagamet had a monopoly on this type of anti-ulcer drug. In our calculations, we assume that there is no fixed cost so that average cost equals marginal cost equals 7.5¢ per dose. The estimated welfare numbers reported here are sensitive to the assumed shape of the estimated demand curve. Most drug companies charge hospitals and other organizations lower prices than pharmacies, so they do not behave as single-price monopolies. However, for simplicity, our analysis compares single-price monopoly to perfect price discrimination among pharmacy customers.

Generics and Brand-Name Loyalty: "Generics, the Impact at the Grass Roots," *Drug Topics Supplement*, 1994; Caves, Richard E., Michael D. Whinston, and Mark A. Hurwitz, "Patent Expiration, Entry, and Competition in the U. S. Pharmaceutical Industry: An Exploratory Analysis," *Brookings Papers on Economic Activity*, 7 (Special Issue on Microeconomics), 1991:1–48; Frank, Richard G., and Davis S. Salkever, "Pricing, Patent Loss and the Market for Pharmaceuticals," *Southern Economic Journal*, 59(2), October 1992:165–179; Grabowski and Vernon (1992); Freudenheim, Milt, "Cleaning Out the Medicine Cabinet," *New York Times*, September 11, 1997:C1.

Getting Consumers to Identify Themselves: Borenstein and Rose (1994); McDowell, Edwin, "His Goal: No Room at the Inns," *New York Times*, November 23, 1995:C1.

Taking Women to the Cleaners: Burdman, Pamela, "New Law Not Likely to Cut Women's Costs," *San Francisco Chronicle*, October 21, 1995:A1; California Legislature, Assembly Office of Research, letter to Assembly member Jackie Speier, March 17, 1993; Marder, Dianna, "Hair-Care Differential: Women Pay Premium," *Philadelphia Inquirer*, March 10, 1999:D1, D8.

Warehouse Stores: "Should You Join a Warehouse Club?" *Consumer Reports*, May 1995:330–333.

IBM: *IBM v. United States*, 298 U.S. 131 (1936).

Automatic Savings: Wald, Matthew L., "Consumers May Be Losers in a Verdict on Auto Parts," *New York Times*, October 17, 1999:Business, 10.

Chapter 13

Oligopoly Competition Among Governments: Clark, Don, "New Mexico Gets Huge Intel Plant," *San Francisco Chronicle*, April 1, 1993:C1; Holmes, Thomas J., "Analyzing a Proposal to Ban State Tax Breaks to Businesses," *Quarterly Review*, Federal Reserve Bank of Minneapolis, 19(2), Spring 1995:29–39; "Helping Handouts," *Economist*, 337(7945), December 16, 1995:73; Myerson, Allen R., "O Governor, Won't You Buy Me a Mercedes Plant?" *New York Times*, September 1, 1996:sec.3: 1, 10; Weissman, Dan, "New Jersey Approves Tax Breaks to Lure Giant Brokerages," *Newark Star-Ledger*, January 12, 2000. This behavior occurs in other countries as well: Britain's government gave Ford $129 million to build Jaguar cars at Castle Bromwich, near Birmingham, England, rather than in Detroit.

Vitamin Price Fixing: Barboza, David, "Settlements Seen in Vitamin Pricing," *New York Times*, May 20, 1999:A1, C23; Segal, David, "Big fines for Fixing Vitamin Prices," *San Francisco Chronicle*, May 21, 1999:A3; Labaton, Stephen, with David Barboza, "U.S. Outlines How Makers of Vitamins Fixed Global Prices," *New York Times*, May 21, 1999:A1, C6; Andrews, Edmund L., "Roche Officers Say Scandal Is a Surprise," *New York Times*, May 22, 1999:B1, B5; Barboza, David, "3 Drug Makers Agree to Settle U.S. Charges," *New York Times*, September 10, 1999:C1, C7; Barboza, David, "$1.1 Billion to Settle Suit on Vitamins," *New York Times*, November 4, 1999:C1, C2.

A Government-Created Cartel: Tarr (1989); Ries (1993); Scott (1994).

Bail Bonds: Ayres and Waldfogel (1994).

Airline Mergers: Kim and Singal (1993).

Appliances: Rehfeld, Barry, "Where Whirlpool Flies, and Maytag Sputters," *New York Times*, January 3, 1993:5.

Airbus and Boeing: Baldwin and Krugman (1988); Tagliabue, John, "Airbus Tries to Fly in a New Formation," *New York Times*, May 2, 1996:C1. In the first quarter of 1996, Airbus had 40.2% of orders for new planes, Boeing had 56.4%, and McDonnell Douglas had 3.4%. When Boeing announced in 1997 that it wanted to acquire the (unprofitable) McDonnell Douglas Corporation, the U.S. government approved the merger, but the European Community initially objected on the grounds the merger would benefit Boeing at the expense of Airbus.

Deadweight Losses in the Food and Tobacco Industries: Bhuyan and Lopez (1998).

Entry and Airline Prices: Whinston and Collins (1992); McDowell, Edwin, "Shuttles in the Northeast Keep Fares Up," *New York Times*, May 8, 1995:C4.

Toothbrushes: Carton, Barbara, "Dental Persuasion: Fear of Droopy Gums Starts a Brush Rush," *Wall Street Journal*, April 12, 1996:A1, A10; "'Build a Better Mousetrap' Is No Claptrap," *Business Week*, February 1, 1999:47. I'm grateful to one of my students who showed me one of these articles. She said she felt so gullible after reading it that she immediately replaced her name-brand toothbrush with the cheapest generic brush she could find.

Welfare Gain from New Cereals: Hausman (1997).

Chapter 14

Government Deterrence: De Lisser, Eleena, and Anita Sharpe, "Stealth Warfare," *Wall Street Journal*, August 18, 1995:A1, A5; Cory, James M., "Rickel Woes Are Self-Made," *Home Improvement Market*, February 1996:13.

Hitting Rivals Where It Hurts: Burdman, Pamela, and Charles Burress, "75 Million Rounds Seized in Santa Clara Ammo Raid," *San Francisco Chronicle*, May 4, 1995:A1, A13; Wallace, Bill, "Feds Return All Ammo from Raid: Santa Clara Firm Won't Sue over Botched Bust," *San Francisco Chronicle*, June 14, 1995:A19; "Cola Makers Battling for Thai Market Share," *Journal of Commerce*, May 28, 1999:3A.

Preventing Customers from Switching: Salpukas, Agis, "Electric Utilities Ordered to Open Distribution Systems to Rivals," *San Francisco Chronicle*, April 25, 1996:A3; Marshall, Jonathan, "Regulators Give PG&E a Big Win," *San Francisco Chronicle*, April 11, 1996:D1.

Evidence on Strategic Entry Deterrence: Smiley (1988).

Drug Commercials: Hall, Carl T., "Magic Elixir for Drug Sales," *San Francisco Chronicle*, March 12, 1998:E1, E12; Freudenheim, Milt, "Influencing Doctor's Orders," *New York Times*, November 17, 1998:C1, C8; Rosenblatt, Robert A., "Drug Firms' TV Ads Fuel Rise in Costs and Demand," *Los Angeles Times*, November 26, 1999:A1, A9; Stolberg, Sheryl Gay, "Want a New Drug? Plenty to Choose from on TV," *New York Times*, January 23, 2000:5.

O. J. Trial Effect: Elliott, Stuart, "Advertising: The 'O. J. Factor' Takes a Toll on Producers of Infomercials," *New York Times*, March 24, 1995:C4.

Pink Toothbrush: "50 Years Ago . . . ," *Consumer Reports*, January 1986.

Secret Ingredients: Elliott, Stuart, "Advertising," *New York Times*, April 28, 1994:C7.

Chapter 15

Thread Mill: Baldwin and Gorecki (1986).

CD Prices: Strauss, Neil, "Pennies That Add Up to $16.98: Why CDs Cost So Much," *New York Times*, July 5, 1995:B1, B6.

Union Monopoly Power: Hatton, Boyer, and Bailey's (1994) estimates for 1889–1890 are based on data for individual workers, controlling statistically for age, skill level, industry, and other worker characteristics. Stewart's (1995) estimates for 1984 and 1990 reflect a comparison between union and nonunion firms that controls for firm attributes.

Baseball Salaries and Ticket Prices: Shaikin, Bill, "Experts Say Demand, Not Higher Salaries, Drives Up Baseball Ticket Prices," *Los Angeles Times*, April 1, 1999.

Monopsony Wage Setting: Sullivan (1989); Brown (1993).

Monopsony Price Discrimination: Ransom (1993).

Outsourcing: "The Outing of Outsourcing," *Economist*, 337(7942), November 25, 1995:57–58; Sessler, Amy, "Outside, Looking Up," *Boston Globe*, April 21, 1999:D1, D4.

Aluminum: Hennart (1988).

Cutting Off Oxygen: Pear, Robert, "U.S. Uses Antitrust Law over Doctors' Ventures," *New York Times*, November 3, 1993:A16; Barnum, Alex, "East Bay Doctors Settle with FTC," *San Francisco Chronicle*, November 4, 1993:B1–B2.

Chapter 16

Usury: "Usury: The Lender's Long Lament," *Economist*, 329(7843), December 24, 1993:103–105; "Usury," *New Columbia Encyclopedia* (New York: Columbia University Press, 1975); "Usury," *Encyclopaedia Britannica*, 1997; "Damned Usurers," *Economist*, December 31, 1999:90.

Power of Compounding: Huntley, Helen, Kim Norris, and Robert Trigaux, "An Early Lesson in Investing for the Long Term," *St. Petersburg Times*, March 14, 1994:Business 3.

Winning the Lottery: "Baby Sitter from Chile Is Winner of Record $197 Million in Lottery," *San Francisco Chronicle*, April 16, 1999:A2.

Durability of Telephone Poles: Marshall, Jonathan, "PG&E Cultivates Its Forest," *San Francisco Chronicle*, May 5, 1995:D1.

Redwood Trees: Berck, Peter, and William R. Bentley, "Hotelling's Theory, Enhancement, and the Taking of the Redwood National Park," *American Journal of Agricultural Economics*, 79(2), May 1997:287–298; Peter Berck, personal communications.

Taking from Future Generations: Kotlikoff, Laurence J., and Willi Leibfritz, "An International Comparison of Generational Accounts," in Auerbach, Alan J., Laurence J. Kotlikoff, and Willi Leibfritz, *Generational Accounting Around the World* (Chicago: University of Chicago Press, 1999); *Economist*, December 23, 1999:37 (OECD data). The net tax calculations presume a growth rate of 1.5% and an interest rate of 5%.

Chapter 17

Gambling: Friedman and Savage (1948); Brunk (1981); Golec and Tamarkin (1995); Gurdon, Meghan Cox, "British Accuse Their Lottery of Robbing the Poor to Give to the Rich," *San Francisco Chronicle*, November 25, 1995:D1; Coll, Steve, "Chances Are Brits Have Bet on It," *San Francisco Examiner*, July 10, 1994: 4; Pollack, Andrew, "In the Gaming Industry, the House Can Have Bad Luck, Too," *New York Times*, July 25, 1999:Business, 4; Garrett and Sobel (1999); Will, George, "Government's Hand in Surge of Gambling," *San Francisco Chronicle*, June 28, 1999:A21.

Bond Ratings: Moody's; Standard & Poor's.

Laws Limiting Diversification: "Asian Insurance Concentrating," *Economist*, May 7, 1994:87.

Flight Insurance: American Express; Air Transport Association.

Natural Disasters: Treaster, Joseph B., "Insurer Curbing Sales of Policies in Storm Areas," *New York Times*, October 10,1996:A1, C4; Treaster, Joseph B., "Headed for Trouble," *New York Times*, September 18, 1998:B1, B14; "The New Protection Game," *Consumer Reports*, January 1999:16–19; Treaster, Joseph B., "Why Insurers Shrink from Earthquake Risk," *New York Times*, November 21, 1999:sec.3: 1, 13.

Premium for a Riskier Investment: "The Cost of Looking," *Economist*, 328(7828), September 11, 1993:74; Eaton, Leslie, "Assessing a Fund's Risk Is Part Math, Part Art," *New York Times*, April 2, 1995:sec.3: 9.

Loans, Defaults, and Usury Laws: Villegas (1989); Ravo, Nick, "Mortgages Lenders More Forgiving of Poor Credit Records," *New York Times*, September 3, 1994:27.

Chapter 18

Michael Jordan's Positive Externalities: Hausman and Leonard (1997); *Harper's Index*, 1999; Wise, Mike, "NBC Focuses on the Story Lines," *New York Times*, May 9, 1999.

Waste Not: Deutsch, Claudia H., "Letting Little Go to Waste: An Enterprise Evolves from the Byproducts of Industry," *New York Times*, March 17, 1999:C1, C8; Sterba, James P., "How a Panty Line Turned into Profits in the Gun Business," *Wall Street Journal*, April 1, 1999:1, 8 (I thank Peter von Allmen for pointing out this example).

Taxes on Fuels: Viscusi (1992); Barnum, Alex, "Potent Smog Fighter—Cleaner Gas," *San Francisco Chronicle*, February 15, 1996:A1, A15; Viscusi, W. Kip, and Wesley A. Magat, "Interim Draft Report on Efficient Energy Pricing," EPA Project on Economic Research for Long-Term Environmental Risks and Pollution Prevention, April 17, 1992, as reported in Viscusi (1992). The reported estimates of the harm from pollution are midpoints of estimated ranges. Estimates of the harm from gasoline vary from 3% to 31% of its price. The range of the estimates for coal is even greater, between 21% and 1,035% of price.

Emissions Standards for Ozone: Krupnick and Portney (1991); Kim, Helfand, and Howitt (1998); Gloria Helfand, personal communication. Valuing health benefits is particularly difficult. Epidemiological studies find a relationship between ozone concentrations and respiratory problems. Using surveys, economists ascertain individuals' willingness to pay to avoid these respiratory ailments. By combining these two types of information, researchers estimate the monetary value of reducing ozone to avoid respiratory trouble.

Sulfur Dioxide Market: Burtraw, Dallas, "Trading Emissions to Clean the Air: Exchanges Few but Savings Many," *Resources*, 122, Winter 1996:3–6; Passell, Peter, "For Utilities, New Clean-Air Plan," *New York Times*, November 18, 1994:C1, C6; Wald, Matthew L., "Acid-Rain Pollution Credits Are Not Enticing Utilities," *New York Times*, June 5, 1995:C11; Passell, Peter, "Economic Scene," *New York Times*, January 4, 1996:C2; Rensberger, Boyce, "Clean Air Sale," *Washington Post*, August 8, 1999:W7; Edwards, Randall, "Dear Santa: Please Bring Me Sulfur Dioxide for Christmas," *Columbus Dispatch*, December 19, 1999:4D.

Extensive Overfishing: Swardson, Anne, "Once Bountiful, the Seas Slowly Empty," *San Francisco Chronicle*, October 3, 1994:A10, A12; "The Economics of the Sea," *Economist*, 334(7906), March 18, 1995:48; "One-Third of Valuable U.S. Fish Species Depleted," *San Francisco Chronicle*, October 7, 1997:A5; Clifford, Frank, "Fishing Limits on Key Species Take Effect," *Los Angeles Times*, January 1, 1998:A29; "New England Fisherman Fear Catch Limits for Cod," *San Francisco Chronicle*, December 7, 1998:A4; Molyneaux, Paul, "Drastic Measures to Save Cod Are Discussed in New England," *New York Times*, March 7, 1999:35.

For Whom the Bridge Tolls: Geoghegan, Jacqueline M., "The Road Not Taken: Environmental Congestion Pricing on the San Francisco–Oakland Bay Bridge," doctoral dissertation, University of California, Berkeley, 1995; Geoghegan, Jacqueline M., Barbara Kanninen, and Craig Mohn, "The Bridge Not Taken: Optimal, Equilibrium Congestion Pricing for the San Francisco–Oakland Bay Bridge," paper presented to the Association of Environmental and Resource Economists at the Allied Social Science Meetings, San Francisco, January 1996; Brazil, Eric, "$3 Bay Bridge Toll Faces Rough Ride," *San Francisco Examiner*, November 20, 1994:A1, A12; Nolte, Carl, "Bay Bridge—All Grit, No Glory," *San Francisco Chronicle*, November 11, 1996:A1, A13; Goulder, Lawrence H., "Time to Get Serious About

Traffic," *San Francisco Chronicle*, January 22, 1999:A23.

Free Riding on Water: Grossman, Pirozzi, and Pope (1993).

Chapter 19

Risky Hobbies: Cropper, Carol Marie, "Risk Takers Pay Dearly: It's the Danger of Living Fearlessly," *New York Times*, April 2, 1995:sec.3: 11.

Recycling Lemons: Adelson, Andrea, "Pushing Lemons over State Lines," *New York Times*, August 27, 1996:C1, C4; Ruppert, James, "Motoring: Case of Lemon Aid," *Independent*, September 18, 1999:Features, 10.

College Guarantee: McLarin, Kimberly, "If a Graduate Fails, Return to Sender," *New York Times*, November 26, 1994:9.

Multiple Brand Names: Schuon, Marshall, "Twins, Triplets and Other Siblings," *New York Times*, November 7, 1993:sec.1:27.

Advertising Lowers Prices: Benham (1972); Bond, Kwoka, Phelan, and Whitten (1980); Schroeter, Smith, and Cox (1987).

Chapter 20

Contracts and Productivity in Agriculture: Foster and Rosenzweig (1994).

Lawyers' Contingent Fees: Kakalik and Pace (1986); Gravelle, Hugh, and Michael Waterson, "No Win, No Fee: Some Economics of Contingent Legal Fees," *Economic Journal*, 103(420), September 1993:1205–1220.

Pleased to Be Paid by the Piece: Passell, Peter, "Paid by the Widget, and Proud," *New York Times*, June 16, 1996:sec.3: 1.

Increasing Use of Incentives: Stobaugh, Robert B., "More and More, Directors Are Owners," *New York Times*, January 1, 1995:Business, 9; Buchholz, Barbara B., "The Bonus Isn't Reserved for Big Shots Anymore," *New York Times*, October 27, 1996; Wells, Susan J., "Pay Is Rising, Thanks to Sweeteners in a Tight Labor Market," *New York Times*, August 30, 1998:11; "Share and Share Unalike," *Economist*, August 7, 1999:18–20; "Business This Week," *Economist*, September 18, 1999:7.

Abusing Leased Cars: Dunham (1996); *Car Talk*, National Public Radio, May 1997.

Savings and Loans Moral Hazards: White, Lawrence J., *The S&L Debacle* (New York: Oxford University Press, 1991); Labaton, Stephen, "The Debacle That Buried Washington," *New York Times*, November 22, 1998:sec.3: 1, 12.

Performance Termination Contracts: Hall and Lilien (1979).

CREDITS

INDEX

Accommodated entry, 471
Ade, George, 416
Ad valorem tariff, 296
Ad valorem tax. *See also* Taxes
    effects of, 67–68
    explanation of, 59
    specific vs., 67–68
    welfare effects of, 362–363
Adverse selection
    effects of, 638–639
    explanation of, 638, A-40
    responses to, 639–641, 665
Advertising
    function of, 491, 498
    investment tree with, 597–598
    monopoly, 491–495
    price and, 654–655
    profit maximization in,
        A-25–A-26
    strategic, 495–498
Africa, 155
Agents, 677–678. *See also* Principal-
    agent problems
Agriculture industry
    population growth and, 154
    price floors and, 289–292
    productivity in, 154–155,
        678–679
    subsidies paid in, 293
Aibo (Sony), 398–400
Airbus, 448–449
Airline industry
    Airbus and, 448, 449
    competition within, 417–419
    Cournot model and, 431–436,
        440
    entry and prices in, 455–456
    fare differences in, 404
    government intervention in,
        445–449
    market structure and, 450, 451
    mergers in, 430–431
    monopolistic competition in,
        453–456
    Stackelberg model and, 440–447

strategic behavior used in, 465
Airports
    duopoly and, 456
    monopolies at, 355–356
Alcohol, taxes on, 310–311
Allegra, 492
Allen, Woody, 305
Allocation
    decisions regarding, 2–3
    price as determinant of, 3
    of resources, 1
AltaVista, 379
Aluminum industry, 531–532
Amana, 651
Amazon.com, 183
American Airlines, 419–422,
    431–438, 440–447, 453
American Express, 592
America Online (AOL), 50
Annual percentage rate (APR) of
    interest, 541
Antitrust legislation, 424–425
Apple Computers, 487
Appliance market, 440
Arrow, Kenneth, 337–338
Asymmetric information
    contracts and, 677–678
    explanation of, 637, A-40
    ignorance when hiring and,
        655–664
    market power from ignorance
        and, 651–655
    price discrimination and quality
        and, 650–651
    problems due to, 638–639, 664
    quality of goods and, 641–649
    responses to adverse selection
        and, 639–641
Australia
    aluminum, 532
    agricultural subsidies in, 293
    cotton, 253
    imports, 295
    News Corporation, 501
    pollution in, 609

tax burden in, 568
    water, 632–633
Automobiles/automobile industry
    abuse of leased cars and, 695
    income elasticities of demand for,
        116–117
    lemons and, 642–647
    manufacturing innovations in,
        172
    multiple brand names and, 651
    tie-in sales and, 413
    trade barriers and, 330–331, 429
Average cost curves
    explanation of, 185
    minimum of, A-11–A-12
    shape of, 188–189, 207–208
    taxes and, 189
Average costs
    explanation of, 182–183, A-40
    natural monopolies and, 365
    taxes and, 190
Average fixed costs (AFC), 182, A-40
Average product curves, A-10–A-11
Average product of labor, 150, A-40
Average revenue
    elasticity of demand and, 347
    explanation of, 344, 345
Average variable cost curve
    explanation of, 185–186
    taxes and, 190
Average variable costs, 182, A-40

Bad, A-40
Bail bonds, 430
Baltimore Orioles, 523
Banks, 598
Bargaining ability, 319
Barriers to entry. *See* Entry barriers
Barriers to exit. *See* Exit
Baseball teams
    antitrust laws and, 429
    player contracts and, 667
    salaries and, 521
BASF A.G., 428
Bentham, Jeremy, 84, 338

Bermuda, 286
Bertrand, Joseph, 456
Bertrand equilibrium
　best-response curves and, 457
　cola market and, A-24–A-25
　Cournot vs., 457–458
　with differentiated products,
　　459–461
　explanation of, 456–457, A-40
Best response
　Bertrand equilibrium and, 457
　Cournot equilibrium and,
　　432–435, 459
　explanation of, 419, 463, A-40
BJ's Warehouse Club, 410
Blockaded entry, 471
Block-pricing schedules, 396
Boeing, 448, 449
Bonding
　explanation of, 689
　monitoring vs., 690
　to prevent shirking, 689–690
　problems with, 691
Bonds
　explanation of, 554
　rate of return on, 554–555, 596
　rating measures for, 586–587
Boston Red Sox, 523
Bowlin, Linda, 183
Bowlin, Lyle, 183
Brand names
　loyalty to, 401–403
　multiple, 651
　to signal quality, 649
Branson, Richard, 465
Bridges, 626–627
British Airways, 465, 486
British Telecom, 368
Brown, Kevin, 520
Budget constraint
　effect of change in income on
　　consumption and, 90–91
　effect of change in price on
　　consumption and, 89–90
　explanation of, 74, 87–88, 103
　purchasing fractional quantities
　　and, 89
　slope of, 89
Budget line, 88, A-40
Bundling
　explanation of, 410, 411, A-40
　pros and cons of, 411–413
Burger King, 466, 491
Burns, George, 283
Bushnell, Nolan, 419

Business license fee, 190–191
Business profit, 228

Canada
　agricultural subsidies in, 293
　chair demand in, 227
　cigarette tax in, 63
　demand elasticity for gasoline in,
　　58, 66
　health care in, 179
　inflation bonds, 554
　job termination laws in, 287
　labor supply curve in, 137
　lime firm in 233–235, 237, 239,
　　241–242, 244–246
　pollution in, 608, 609, 623
　rates of returns in manufacturing
　　industries in, 166–168
　shape of average cost curves in
　　manufacturing in, 207
　shipping to, 249
　tax burden in, 568
　vegetable mill in, 240–241
　water in, 304
Capital
　explanation of, 143
　human, 556–559
　as input, 146
Capital costs
　actual and historical costs and,
　　180
　allocated over time, 179–180
　explanation of, 179
　nonprofit institutions and, 180
Capital equipment, 213–214
Capital markets
　equilibrium and, 566, 567
　supply and demand in, 569
Cartels
　Cournot model vs., 436–438
　entry and success of, 430
　explanation of, 416, A-40
　failure of, 426–427
　formation of, 425–426
　government-created, 429
　laws against, 424–425
　maintaining, 427–429
Cash flow, 552
CD prices, 516
Cement firms, 207–208
Certification, 648, A-40
Cheap talk, 656–658, A-40
China, 5
Chinook Group, 428
Christmas presents, 279–28

Christmas trees, 229–230
Chrysler Corporation, 646
Cigarettes. See Tobacco industry
City Tow, 368
Claritin, 492
Clean Air Act of 1990, 614, 623
Clemens, Roger, 523
Cleveland Clinic, 526
Clinton, Bill, 448
Clothing, 83
Coal mines, 559–562
Coase Theorem, 619–622
Cobb-Douglas production function
　returns to scale and, 165–166
　use of, 507, A-11
Coca-Cola, 368, 391, 459, 460, 486,
　　492–494, A-24, A-25
Cocteau, Jean, 571
Cola advertising, 496
Cola market, 459, 460, A-24–A-25
College education
　guarantees on, 649
　salaries and, 556–559
　as signal, 658–663
Common property
　access restrictions to, 626
　assigning property rights to,
　　627
　explanation of, 602, 624, 635,
　　A-40
　government regulation of, 626
　overuse of, 624–625
Comparative advantage
　benefits of trade and, 325
　explanation of, 324, A-40
　marginal rate of transformation
　　and, 324–325
　number of producers and,
　　326–327
　production possibility frontier
　　and, 323, 324
Competition. See also Monopolistic
　　competition
　efficiency of, 322–323
　explanation of, 224, 262
　horizontal demand curve and,
　　224–227
　to maximize welfare, 276–280,
　　302
　multimarket price discrimination
　　vs., 405
　obtaining efficient allocation
　　using, 322–323
　perfect, 227–228
　price taking and, 224

properties of, 418
Competition in long run
  explanation of, 246, 262–263
  long-run competitive equilibrium
    and, 256–259
  long-run competitive profit
    maximization and, 246
  long-run firm supply curve and,
    246–247
  long-run market supply curve
    and, 248–256
  zero profit and, 259–262
Competition in short run
  explanation of, 262
  profit maximization and,
    233–238
  short-run competitive equilibrium
    and, 244–246
  short-run market supply curve
    and, 241–243
  short-run supply curve and,
    239–241
Competitive equilibrium
  in competitive markets, 320–322
  consumption efficiency and, 328
  government policies and, 280
  long-run, 256–259
  monopolistic vs., 452
  short-run, 244–246
Competitive exchange, 319–320, 340
Competitive factor market
  equilibria and, 511–512
  explanation of, 502, 534
  factor market demand and,
    509–511
  long-run factor demand and,
    508–509
  short-run factor demand of firm
    and, 502–506
Competitive fringe
  dominant firms and, 379–380
  explanation of, 379, A-40
Competitive markets
  cartels vs., 425, 426
  competitive equilibrium in,
    320–322
  efficiency of competition in,
    322–323
  explanation of, 42, 225
  feedback between, 307–311
  importance of, 227–228
  welfare effects of pollution in,
    605–607, A-29–A-30
Completeness property, 75

Compounding
  explanation of, 540
  frequency of, 540–541
  power of, 542
Computer chips, 217
ConAgra, 428
Constant-elasticity demand curve, 52
Constant returns to scale (CRS), 164,
  A-40
Constrained consumer choice
  explanation of, 74, 92, 103–104
  food stamps and, 99–102
  more is better and, 97–98
  optimal bundles and, 92–97
Consumer choice
  budget constraint and, 87–91
  constrained, 74, 92–103
  food stamps and, 99–102
  more is better and, 97–98
  optimal bundle and, 92–97
  overview of, 73–74
  preferences and, 74–83
  utility and, 84–87
Consumer ignorance
  about product quality, 641–642
  market power from, 651–655
Consumer Price Index (CPI)
  adjustments of, 126–128
  calculation of, 124–125
  explanation of, 123
  inflation estimates and, 105
  substitution bias and, 129–130
  in United States, 123–124
Consumer Reports, 586, 647
Consumers
  identifying groups of, 403–405
  preferences of, 75–76
  two-part tariffs with identical,
    407–408
  two-part tariffs with nonidentical,
    408–409
Consumer's optimum, 94
Consumer surplus
  calculation of, 461–462
  effect of price change on,
    269–272
  explanation of, 267, A-40
  measurement of, 267–268
  from television, 269
  two-part tariffs and, 407, 408
Consumer theory
  cost-of-living adjustments and,
    123–130
  derived demand curves and,
    106–108

  derived labor supply curves and,
    130–140
  income change and demand
    curves and, 109–117
  overview of, 105
  price change effects and,
    117–123
Consumer welfare
  demand curve to measure,
    266–269
  effect of price change on consumer
    surplus and, 269–272
  explanation of, 266, 302
Contingent contracts
  efficiency and, 682
  explanation of, 670, 674
  for lawyers, 683
  success of firm and, 687
Contingent fee, A-40
Contract curves
  bargaining and, 319
  explanation of, 318, 319, A-40
Contracts
  in agriculture, 678–679
  asymmetric information and,
    677–678
  choice of, 682–683, 700, 702
  comparison of, 550–551
  efficient, 671–672, 680–682
  full information and, 672–676
  incentives in, 687–688
  linked to production, 685–687
  linked to profit, 687–688
  performance termination,
    698–700
  production efficiency and,
    671–672
  types of, 669–670
Cooperative oligopolies
  entry and cartel success and, 430
  explanation of, 423–424, 462
  failure of cartels and, 426–427
  formation of cartels and,
    425–426
  laws against cartels and, 424–425
  maintaining cartels and, 427–429
  mergers and, 430–431
Corn market, 307–310
Corporations, 145
Cost advantages
  explanation of, 498
  learning by doing and, 485
  lowering marginal cost while
    raising total cost and,
    484–485

moving first and, 489
raising all firms' costs and, 488
raising rivals' costs and, 485–488
Cost-benefit analysis, 612–616
Cost-of-living adjustments (COLAs)
effects of inflation adjustments and, 126
explanation of, 123, 140
inflation indexes and, 123–125
Costs
average, 182–183
capital, 179–180
economic, 178, 179
explanation of, A-40
fixed, 181–182
long-run, 193–217 (*See also* Long-run costs)
marginal, 182
measuring, 178–180, 220
minimizing, A-13–A-15
short-run, 181–193 (*See also* Short-run costs)
total, 182
Cotton industry, 252–253
Coupon-using consumers, 404
Cournot equilibrium
Bertrand vs., 457–458
determination of, 432–438
explanation of, 432, 450, 451, 462, A-40
for identical oligopolistic firms, A-20–A-23
number of firms and, 438–440
Cournot model of noncooperative oligopoly
airline industry and, 431–436, 445
cartel model vs., 436–438
entry prevention and, 475, 477, 479
explanation of, 431, 462
Craftsman, 651
Credible threat
commitment as, 475
explanation of, 474, A-40
Crematoriums, 220
Cross-price elasticity of demand, 54–55, A-40

Daiichi Pharmaceutical Company, 428
Daley, Michael R., 607
Darrah, Mike, 686
Deadweight loss
of Christmas presents, 279–280

explanation of, 277–278, A-41
in food and tobacco industries, 451
of monopolies, 358, 372, 383
perfect price discrimination and, 393
of U.S. Postal Service, 359–360
Decision making
expected utility and, 577–578
risk aversion and, 578–580
risk neutrality and, 581–582
risk preference and, 582
under uncertainty, 577, 600
Decreasing returns to scale (DRS), 165, A-41
Deferred payments, 691–692
Delta Airlines, 456
Demand
cross-price elasticity of, 54–55
excess, 29
explanation of, 13, 15, 43
government policies and, 35–41
income elasticity of, 53–54
price elasticity of, 48–50
for public goods, 629–630
Demand curves
application of, 20–21
causes of shift in, 17
combining individual, 20–21
deriving, 106–108, 140
downward-sloping linear, 51–52
effects of price change on, 117–123
effects of shift in, 30–31, 381
elasticity along, 50–53
explanation of, 15–16, A-41
factor market, 509–510
for Giffen good, 121
horizontal, 52, 53, 224–227
income change and, 109–117, 140
for leisure, 130–132
marginal revenue vs., 345–346, A-17
residual, 226, 227, 379–380, A-44
shape of, 46–48, 70, 352–353
vertical, 52–53
what can be shown by, 16–20, 27
Denmark, 568
Department of Justice, 428, 430
Deterred entry
commitment and, 477, 480
explanation of, 471
incumbent loss and, 481

Die-Hard, 651
Differentiated products, 459–461
Discount coupons, 404
Discounting, 596–597
Discount rate, 539–540, A-41
Discrimination
gender, 406
against groups, 284–285
statistical, 663–664
Diseconomies of scale, 206, A-41
Disequilibrium, 29
Disney, 501
Disneyland, 386–387
Diversification
correlation and, 587–588
laws limiting, 589
mutual funds and, 588–589
Doherty, Sharon, 459
Domain names, 378–379
Dominant firm
competitive fringe and, 379–380
explanation of, 379, A-41
Dominant strategy
explanation of, 420, A-41
market entry as, 467, 468
quantity-setting games and, 420, 421
Drug Price Competition and Patent Term Restoration Act of 1984, 372
Drugs.com, 379
Ducoa, 428
Duke University Hospital, 526
Duopoly
bail-bond business and, 430
explanation of, 419, 436, A-41
landing spots at airports and, 456
Nash equilibrium for, 417–419
DuPont, 428
Durable goods
decisions regarding, 555–556
explanation of, A-41
function of, 537

E-commerce, 183
Economically efficient, 177, A-41
Economic cost, 178, 228, A-41
Economic profit, 228–229, A-41
Economic theories, 6–7
Economies of scale, 206–207, A-41
Economies of scope, A-41
Edgeworth, Francis Ysidro, 315
Edgeworth box, 315, 316
Education. *See* College education
Edwards, Flora Mancuso, 649

Efficiency
  of competition, 322–323
  consumption, 328
  equity vs., 339–340
  government policies and, 331,
    334–335
  higher education and, 662–663
  principal-agent problems and,
    670–671
  in production, 670, A-41 (*See
    also* Production efficiency)
  in risk bearing, 670, A-41
  technological, 146
Efficiency wages, 692–694, A-41
Efficient contracts
  elements of, 671–672
  explanation of, 670, A-41
Einstein, Albert, 4
Eisai Company, 428
Elasticity. *See also* Price elasticity of
    demand; Price elasticity of supply
  cross-price, 54–55
  explanation of, 48, A-41
  income, 53–54
  of residual demand curve, A-15
  specific tax effects and, 60–61
  surplus and demand, A-16–A-17
  tax incidence and, 63–65
Electric power utilities. *See also*
    Utilities, public
  durability of utility poles and,
    555–556
  as natural monopolies, 365–366
  regulation of, 372, 377
Electronic Data Systems, 530
Ely, Jonnie, 549
Emissions reduction, 608–609
Employment
  ignorance when hiring and,
    655–664
  screening in hiring and,
    663–664
Employment risk, 655–656
Enderbery, Keppel, 295
Endowments
  in Edgeworth box, 316
  explanation of, 315, A-41
Engel curve, 109, 110, A-41
Entry
  airline industry and, 453–456
  barriers to, 248–249, 285,
    367–368, 430
  ease of, 250
  market supply and, 248–249,
    251–252

  in selected industries, 250
  zero profit with free, 259–260
  zero profit with limited, 260–262
Entry barriers
  airline industry and, 453–456
  cartels and, 430
  effects of, 285
  explanation of, A-40
  long-run market supply curve
    and, 248–249
  monopolies and, 367–368
Entry prevention
  commitment and fixed costs and,
    477–483
  decisions to act or not act and,
    471–477
  effects of, 489
  evidence on, 489–490
  sequential decisions and,
    470–483, 498
  simultaneous decisions and,
    466–470, 498
Environmental protection, 608–609.
    See also Pollution; Pollution
    control
Environmental Protection Agency
    (EPA), 623
Equilibrium. *See also* General
    Equilibrium; Market
    equilibrium
  capital market, 566, 567
  comparisons between, 450–452
  competitive factor market,
    511–512
  Cournot, 432–440, 462
  effects of specific tax on, A-3–A-4
  explanation of, 27, A-41
  general, 306–314, 340 (*See also*
    General equilibrium)
  long-run competitive, 256–259
  monopolistic vs. competitive,
    452
  Nash, 419–421, 423, 436, 469
  perfect price discrimination, 391
  pooling, 659–661
  sales tax and, 66–67
  separating, 659, 661–662
  shocking the, 13, 30–32, 43, 47
  short-run competitive, 244–246
  Stackelberg, 442–444
  types of, 462
  unique or multiple, 660–661
Equilibrium price, 27
Equilibrium quantity, 27

Equity
  efficiency vs., 339–340
  social welfare functions and,
    338–339
  voting and, 336–338
Essential facility, 487, A-41
Europe. *See also specific countries*
  agricultural subsidies in, 293
  appliance market in, 440
  automobile trade in, 330–331
  demand elasticity for gasoline in,
    66
  gasoline taxes in, 66
  marginal tax rate in, 140
  pollution markets in, 623
  product defect protections in,
    646–647
Excess demand, 29, A-41
Excess supply, 29, A-41
Exhaustible resources
  constant or falling prices for,
    564–566
  explanation of, 559, 569, A-41
  price of, 560–564
  when to sell, 559
Exit
  ease of, 250
  market supply and, 248–249
  raising barriers to, 286–287
  in selected industries, 250
Expansion paths
  explanation of, 202, A-41
  long-run cost curve and, 203,
    204
  short-run and long-run, 214
Expected utility, 577–578
Expected value, 574–575
Explicit costs, 178
Externalities
  allocating property rights to
    reduce, 619–623, 635
  cost-benefit analysis and,
    612–616
  explanation of, 602, 603, 635,
    A-41
  inefficiency of competition with,
    604–605, 635
  internalizing, 610, 611, A-42
  market structure and, 616, 635
  monopolies and, 616–618
  supply-and-demand analysis and,
    605–611
  types of, 603

Factor demands, A-26–A-27
Factor markets
    competitive, 502-512
    effects of monopolies on,
        512–519
Factor prices
    long-run costs and, 200–202
    short-run supply curve and,
        240–241
Factory Mutual Engineering
    Corporation (FMEC), 648
Fair bet, 590, A-41
Fair insurance
    explanation of, 590, A-41
    risk aversion and, 591–592
Fair Labor Standards Act of 1938,
    40
Federal Express, 355
Federal Trade Commission Act of
    1914, 424
Federal Trade Commission (FTC),
    430, 533, 534, 654, 655
Fields, W. C., 426
Firms
    excluding specific groups from
        owning, 284–285
    explanation of, 144, A-41
    management of, 145, 174
    ownership of, 145, 174
    profit maximization by, 146
    restrictions on number of,
        281–284
First-degree price discrimination. See
    Perfect price discrimination
First Theorem of Welfare Economics,
    320
Fishing, 624–625
Fixed costs
    average, 182
    entry prevention and, 472,
        477–482
    explanation of, 181, A-41
    of Internet firms, 183
    number of firms and, 452–455
Fixed-fee contracts
    efficiency and, 680–681
    explanation of, 669
Fixed input, 147, A-41
Fix-fee rental contracts
    asymmetric information and, 677
    explanation of, 672, 676
Flight insurance, 592
Flow, 537, A-41
Flynn, Errol, 92
Food, 83

Food and Drug Administration
    (FDA), 492
Food industry, 451
Food stamps
    cash preferred to, 100–101
    reasons for issuing, 102
Food Stamps Program, 99
Ford, Henry, 173
Ford Motor Company, 170–171, 416
Fox Film Entertainment Group, 501
France
    cigarette tax in, 63
    gasoline taxes in, 66
    patents, 369
    sales of monopolies in, 368
    tax burden in, 568
Franchise tax, 190–191
Franklin, Benjamin, 296
Free riding
    explanation of, 630–631, A-41
    reduction of, 631–632
    on water, 632–633
Free trade. See also Trade; Trade
    policies
    ban on imports vs., 296
    loss from eliminating, 297
    quotas vs., 300–301
    tariffs vs., 296–300
Fuel taxes, 611
Future value
    explanation of, 541–543
    of payments over time, 546–547

Gambling, 583–585
Games
    collusion in repeated, 422–423
    cooperation in single-period,
        421
    explanation of, 419, A-41
    prisoners' dilemma, 421, 422
    single-period, two-firm quantity-
        setting, 421, 436
Game theory, 419, 462, A-41
Game trees
    for deterred entry and Stackelberg
        equilibria, 476
    investment, 485
    raising-costs, 488
    Stackelberg, 440–442
Garcia, Daniel, 646
Gasoline
    pollution control and taxes on,
        611
    price controls on, 36–38
    tax revenue from, 65–66

GATT, 369
Geico Auto Insurance, 491
Gender, price discrimination and,
    406
General Electric (GE), 424, 427
General equilibrium
    explanation of, 306–307, 340
    feedback between competitive
        markets and, 307–311
    minimum wages with incomplete
        coverage and, 311–313
General-equilibrium analysis, 307,
    A-42
General Mills, 461–462
General Motors, 9–12
Generic brands, 401–403
Germany
    Airbus and, 448–449
    automobile manufacturing in,
        173
    gasoline taxes in, 66
    labor supply curve in, 137
    patents in, 369
    pollution in, 608, 609
    productivity in, 170–171
    tax burden in, 568
    tax on fast-food containers in, 4
Getty, J. Paul, 559
Ghiradelli Chocolate Company,
    143–144
Giffen good
    explanation of, 121, A-42
    illustration of, 120
Goldman Sachs, 423
Goods. See also Normal goods;
    Public goods
    cost of producing multiple,
        218–220
    demand curve and essential, 53
    durable, 537, 555–556
    explanation of, A-42
    inferior, 113–115, 119–121
    private, 627
    quality and, 665
Government policies. See also
    Income tax; Sales tax; Taxes
    airline industry and, 445–449
    cartels and, 424–425, 428–429
    causing demand to differ from
        supply, 35–37
    demand and, 13, 14
    effects of, 32, 43
    efficiency and, 331, 334–335
    entry blocking and, 473
    for environmental protection, 611

excluding specific groups from owning firms, 284–285
gas price controls and, 37–39
to limit diversification, 589
mergers and, 430
minimum wages and, 40
raising entry and exit costs, 285–287
regarding trade, 295–302 (*See also* Trade policies)
restricting number of firms, 281–284
setting price ceiling, 293–295
setting price floor, 289–292
steel imports and, 34, 35
supply and, 13 21, 25–26, 32–34
that create monopolies, 367–372, 381
that reduce monopolies, 372–381
vertical integration and, 532–533
why supply need not equal demand and, 41
Great Britain. *See also* United Kingdom
productivity in, 170–171
sales of monopolies in, 368
Gypsum, 607

Hausman, Jerry, 461–462
Henry Ford Community College, 649
Herbert, George, 637
Hire contracts
asymmetric information and, 678
explanation of, 670, 672–674
Hiring
ignorance when, 655–665
screening in, 663–664
HMOs, 526–527
Home Depot, 473
Home sales, 122–123
Hong Kong, 589
Hoover, Herbert, 568
Horizontal demand curves
derivation of, 226–227
explanation of, 52, 53
reasons for, 224–226
Hotel room prices, 404–405
Humana hospitals, 354
Human capital, 556–559

IBM, 411
Iceland, 293
Imperfect substitutes, 82
Implicit costs, 178
Import policies. *See* Trade policies

Incentive compatible, 671, A-42
Income
demand and, 14
demand curves and change in, 109–117
effect on consumption of change in, 90–91
Income-consumption curves
explanation of, 109, 110
income elasticities and, 113–114
Income effects
explanation of, 117, 119, 133, A-42
home sales and, 122–123
with inferior good, 119–121
with normal good, 117–119
wage change and, 133–135
Income elasticity of demand
for automobiles, 116–117
explanation of, 53–54, 112–113, A-42
income change and, 115–116
income-consumption curve and, 113, 114
normal goods and, 114–115
Income tax. *See also* Taxes
effects of cuts in, 139–140
labor supply and, 138–139
Income threshold model, 4–5
Increasing returns to scale (IRS), 164–165, A-42
Indifference curves
curvature of, 80–83
explanation of, 77–79, A-42
between food and clothing, 83
food stamps and, 100, 101
impossible, 79
optimal bundles on, 92, 93, 95, 97
trade decisions and, 315, 317, 318
utility and, 85, A-4–A-6
willingness to substitute and, 80
Indifference maps, A-42. *See also* Preference maps
Inferior goods
explanation of, 113, 114–115, A-42
illustration of, 115
income and substitution effects with, 119–121
Inflation
adjustments for, 126, 547–550
lottery payments and, 549–550
nominal prices and, 125, 126,

547
rate of return on bonds and, 554–555
Inflation indexes. *See also* Consumer Price Index (CPI)
calculating, 124–125
constant utility and, 127, 128
real vs. nominal prices and, 123–124
Innovation
in automobile manufacturing, 173
organizational change and, 172–173
technical, 171–172
Input markets, 514–520
Inputs
categories of, 146
explanation of, 144
labor, 143, 146
long-run market supply and, 253–256
material, 143, 146
substitutability of, 158, 159, 161–164
time and variability of, 147–148
Insurance
adverse selection and, 638–641
after-the-fact monitoring and, 695
for diversifiable risks, 592–593
flight, 592
moral hazards and, 667
risk avoidance and, 589–590
universal coverage and, 639–640
Intel Corporation, 423
Interest rates
compounding and, 540–542
discount rate and, 539–540
explanation of, 538, A-42
future value and, 541–542
nominal and real, 548
present value and, 543
usury and, 538–539
Internalize the externality, 610, 611, A-42
Internal rate of return, 553, 554, A-42
Internal Revenue Service, 533
Internet. *See also* E-commerce
domain names and, 378–379
fees for use of, 50
fixed costs for business on, 183
taxes and shopping on, 96

Internet Tax Freedom Act of 1998, 96
Investing/investments
  with altered probabilities, 597–599
  durability and, 555–556
  government demand and, 567, 568
  human capital and, 556–559
  internal rate of return and, 553, 554
  net present value and, 551–552
  rate of return on bonds and, 554–555
  risk-averse, 596
  risk-neutral, 594–596
  under uncertainty, 593–598
  with uncertainty and discounting, 596–597
Investment decision trees, 597
Ipana, 495
Ipderdome, 378
Ireland, 63
Isocost lines
  cost information and, 194–196
  explanation of, 194, A-42
  isoquant lines and, 196–199
Isoquants
  explanation of, 155–156
  isocost lines and, 196–199
  properties of, 156–157
  semiconductor integrated circuit, 159–161
  shape of, 157–159, 161, 162
  substitutability of inputs and, 161–162
Isowelfare curves, 335, 336
Italy, 66

Japan
  agricultural subsidies in, 293
  automobile industry in, 173, 429
  gasoline taxes in, 66
  nontariff barriers in, 300–301
  outsourcing in, 530
  pollution in, 608, 609
  rice imports in, 33
  sales tax in, 59
Java, 199–200
Job termination laws, 287
Johns Hopkins Hospital, 526
Jordan, Michael, 604

Kellogg, 428
Kenmore, 651

Kennedy, John F., 138
Kessler, David A., 14
Kraft, 428

Labor inputs, 143, 146
Labor-leisure model, A-9–A-10
Labor supply curves
  demographic groups and, 136–137
  deriving, 130–140
  explanation of, 132, 140
  income and substitution effects and, 133–134
  income tax rates and, 138–140
  labor-leisure choice and, 130–132, 135–136
  shape of, 136–137
Labor unions, 517–518
Larder, Ring, 99
Last-dollar rule, 196, 198
Law of Demand
  explanation of, 16, 19, 23, A-42
  Giffen goods and, 121
Lazear, Edward, 686
Learning by doing
  in computer chips, 217
  cost advantages and, 485
  costs and, 214–217
  explanation of, 214, A-42
Leased cars, 695
Leisure
  choice between income and, 135–136
  choice between labor and, 130–132
Lemon laws, 646, 647
Lemons
  asymmetric information and, 644
  explanation of, 642
  limiting, 646–649
  symmetric information and, 642–644
  variable quality and, 645–646
Lerner Index
  of Cournot firm, 438–440
  explanation of, 353–354, A-42
  telephone companies and, 425
Lime market, 233–239, 241–245
Limited liability, 145, A-42
Lincoln, Abraham, 73
Living-wage laws, 313
Long run
  competition in, 262–263
  explanation of, 147, A-42
  lower costs in, 209–217

short run vs., 46, 58–59, 71
Long-run average costs, 209–210
Long-run competitive equilibrium, 256–259
Long-run cost curves
  estimation of, 208–209
  expansion path and, 202, 203
  in oil pipelines, 211–213
  in printing firms, 210–211
  shape of, 204–207
Long-run costs
  capital equipment purchases and, 213–214
  combining cost and production information and, 196–199
  expansion paths and, 214
  explanation of, 193, 220
  factor price changes and, 200–202
  input choice and, 193–194
  isocost line and, 194–196
  learning by doing and, 214–217
  output and, 202–204
Long-run factor demand, 508–509
Long-run firm supply curves, 246–247
Long-run market supply curves
  for cotton, 252–253
  explanation of, 248
  with firms that differ, 252
  with identical firms and free entry, 251–252
  with limited entry, 252
  role of entry and exit and, 248–250
  slope of, 256
  when input prices vary with output, 253–256
Long-run production
  explanation of, 155
  isoquants and, 155–161
  substituting inputs and, 161–164
Lonza A.G., 428
Los Angeles Dodgers, 520–521
Lotteries, 549–550
Lower costs in the long run, 220
Lowest-isocost rule, 196

MacIver, Eric, 379
Malthus, Thomas, 154
Marginal cost curves
  explanation of, 185, 187–188
  paper industry and, 605–607
  shift in, 356, 357
  taxes and, 189

Marginal costs
  cartels and, 427
  explanation of, 182, 231, A-42
  monopolistically competitive
    equilibrium and, 452
  natural monopolies and, 365–366
  raising total costs while lowering,
    484–485
Marginal expenditure, 521, 522
Marginal product curves, A-10–A-11
Marginal product of labor
  explanation of, 149–150, A-42
  substitutability of inputs and,
    163–164
Marginal profit, 230–232, A-42
Marginal rate of substitution (MRS)
  diminishing, 80
  explanation of, 80–82, A-42
  product mix and, 328, 329
  utility and, 85–87
Marginal rate of technical
    substitution (MRTS)
  along isoquant, 162, 163
  explanation of, 161
  marginal products and, 163–164
Marginal rate of transformation,
  326–327
Marginal rate of transformation
  (MRT), 89, A-42
Marginal revenue
  cartels and, 427
  explanation of, 231, A-42
  monopolies and, 344–348
  monopolistically competitive
    equilibrium and, 452
  perfect price discrimination and,
    390–391
  price elasticity of demand and,
    346–348
Marginal revenue curve
  linear demand curve and, A-17
  for monopolies, 345–348
Marginal revenue product of labor
  for competitive firms, 502–503,
    510–511
  explanation of, 502, A-42
Marginal tax rate
  cuts in, 138, 139
  in various countries, 139–140
Marginal utility, 85, 86, 87, A-42
Marginal value, 267
Marginal willingness to pay,
  266–267
Market clearing price, 29
Market equilibrium

  explanation of, 13, 27, 43
  forces leading to, 28–30
  using graphs to determine, 27
  using math to determine, 27–28
Market failure
  asymmetric information and,
    637
  explanation of, 279, A-42
Market power
  explanation of, 352, 380–381,
    A-42
  government actions that reduce,
    372–381
  in input and output markets,
    514–520
  Lerner Index and, 353–354
  price discrimination and, 387
  from price ignorance, 651–655,
    665
  shape of demand curve and,
    352–353
  sources of, 354–356
  vertical integration and, 533,
    534
Markets
  explanation of, 3, A-42
  perfectly competitive, 42, 225
  spillover effect between, 307
Market structure
  competitive, 223, 224 (*See also*
    Competition)
  explanation of, 417, 462, A-42
  factor demands and, 512–514
  prices of exhaustible resources
    and, 566
  types of, 417–418
Marriott Corporation, 355–356
Mass starvation, 154–155
Material inputs, 143, 146
McCarthy, Charlie, 143
McDonald's, 4, 248, 285, 354, 355,
  466, 491
Medicaid, 2–3, 7–8
Melvin, Karen, 646
Mercedes Benz, 423
Mergers
  airline, 430–431
  government policies and, 430
Merrill Lynch, 423
Mexico
  agricultural subsidies in, 293
  cigarette tax in, 63
  pollution markets in, 623
MGM, 550
Microeconomic models

  application of, 1, 9–12
  used by individuals and
    governments, 8–9
Microeconomics
  allocation decisions and, 2–4
  explanation of, 1–2, 12, A-42
Micron Technology, 423
Middlesex Community College,
  649
Mill, John Stuart, 84
Minimum efficient scale, 452, A-43
Minimum wage
  with incomplete coverage,
    311–313
  in Puerto Rico, 40
  unemployment and, 39–40
Minimum wage laws, 311–313
Minnesota Twins, 523
Mixed strategies, 468–469, A-25
Models
  economic theories and, 6–7
  explanation of, 4, 12, A-43
  function of, 1
  positive vs. normative statements
    and, 7–8
  as simplifications by assumption,
    5–6
Monitoring
  after-the-fact, 694–695
  bonding and, 689–691
  deferred payments and, 691–692
  effects of, 689
  efficiency wages and, 692–694
  explanation of, 688–689, 702
Monopolies
  cost advantages that create,
    364–367, 381
  demand curve shifts and, 356,
    357
  explanation of, 42, 343, A-43
  externalities and, 616–618
  factor markets and, 512–520,
    534
  government actions that create,
    367–372, 381
  government actions that reduce,
    372–381
  historical background of, 343
  incidence of specific tax on,
    A-17–A-18
  market power and, 352–356
  multimarket price discrimination
    vs. single-price, 405–406
  in names, 378–379
  natural, 364–366

pricing and, 348, 372–374, 383, 653
profit maximizing advertising and production in, A-25–A-26
properties of, 417–418
shutdown decisions and, 350
welfare effects of, 357–363, 381
Monopolistic competition
competitive firms vs., 451–452
equilibrium and, 452, 453
explanation of, 416, 463, A-43
fixed costs and number of firms and, 452–455
properties of, 418
Monopoly advertising, 491–495
Monopoly profit maximization
explanation of, 380
graphical approach to, 349–350
marginal revenue and, 344–348
mathematical approach to, 350, 351
price and quantity choice and, 348–349
Monopsony
explanation of, 501, 521, A-43
price discrimination and, 526–528
profit maximization and, 521–524, A-27–A-28
welfare effects of, 524–526
Moody's ratings, 586–587
Moral hazards. See also Contracts
effects of, 639
explanation of, 638, 667, A-43
leased cars and, 695
savings and loan, 696–697
Moratoriums, 286
More-is-better property, 75–76
Morgan Stanley, 423
Mortgage loans, 598
Motorola, 530
Movie theater pricing, 385–386
Multimarket price discrimination
explanation of, 389, 397–398, 413, A-43
identifying consumer groups and, 403–405
with two groups, 398–401, A-19–A-20
welfare effects of, 405–406
Multiple regression, A-1–A-3
Mutual funds, 588–589, 595

Nash, John, 419
Nash equilibrium. See also Bertrand

equilibrium; Cournot equilibrium
advertising and, 497
explanation of, 419, A-43
mixed strategy and, 469
quantity-setting games and, 419–421
single-period games and, 421, 436
state governments and, 423
National Governors Association (NGA), 96
Natural disasters, 593
Natural monopoly, 364–366, A-43
The Netherlands
flower market in, 502
marginal tax rate in, 140
pollution in, 608, 609
tax burden in, 568
Net present value, 551–552
Network Solutions, Inc., 378
New York Stock Exchange Composite Index, 588
New York Yankees, 523
New Zealand
agricultural subsidies in, 293
cigarette taxes in, 63
pollution in, 609
tax burden in, 568
Niagara Mohawk Power, 623
Nixon, Richard, 36
Nominal prices
explanation of, 123, 547
inflation and, 125, 126, 547
real vs., 123–124, 548
Nominet, 378
Noncooperative strategic behavior
advertising and, 491–498
creating and using cost advantages and, 484–490
explanation of, 466, A-43
preventing entry and sequential decisions and, 470–483
preventing entry and simultaneous decisions and, 466–470
Nonneutral technical changes, 171, 172
Nonsatiation, 75, 315
Nonshirking condition, A-30
Nonuniform pricing. See also Price discrimination; Tie-in sales; Two-part tariffs
explanation of, 383, 384, A-43
types of, 389

Normal goods
determination of, 114–115
explanation of, 112, A-43
illustration of, 115
income and substitution effects with, 117–119
Normative statements, 7, 8, A-43
Northeast Utilities, 623
Norway
cigarette tax in, 63
printing firms in, 210–211, A-12–A-13
tax burden in, 568

Octel Network Services, 530
Oil industry
demand elasticities and, 58
import policy and, 295–300
long-run cost curves for pipelines and, 211–213
shutdown decisions and, 243
O.J. Simpson Trial, 494
Oligopolies
cooperative, 424–430, 462
Cournot model of noncooperative, 431–440, 462
explanation of, 42, 416, A-43
properties of, 417–418
1-800-COLLECT commercials, 491
Opportunistic behavior
explanation of, 637, 638, A-43
by informed agents, 668
laws to prevent, 646
universal coverage and, 639–640
Opportunity costs
explanation of, 178, 228, A-43
investments and, 551
of waiting time, 179
Opportunity set, 88, A-43
Optimal bundles
on convex sections of indifference curves, 96
corner solution and, 93–95
explanation of, 92, 94
interior solution and, 94
Optimal price regulation, 348, 372–374
Oral-B toothbrushes, 460–461
Orben, Robert, 602
Ordinal preferences, 84–85
Oregon, 2–3, 7–8
Organizational change, 172–173

Organization for Economic Cooperation and Development (OECD), 293
Organization of Petroleum Exporting Countries (OPEC)
  function of, 424
  oil supplies and, 36, 37, 58
Organ transplants, 526–527
Orwell, George, 335
Output
  categories of, 146
  cumulative, 214
  explanation of, 144
  long-run cost and, 202–204
  long-run market supply and, 253–256
  profit maximization using, 504–505
  relationship between labor and, 148–149
  welfare and competitive, 276–280
Output decision
  explanation of, 230–232
  long-run, 246
  short-run, 233–236
Output markets, 514–520
Outsourcing, 529–530
Overfishing, 625
Oxygen equipment, 533–534
Ozone, 614–616

Pacific Gas & Electric Company, 487–488, 555–556
Package tie-in sale, 410
Paper industry, 605–607, 609–610, 612, 613
Pareto efficient
  competitive equilibrium as, 322, 323
  explanation of, A-43
  government policy and, 334–335
  trading between two people and, 315, 340
Partial-equilibrium analysis
  bias in, 310
  explanation of, 306, A-43
Partnerships, 145
Patents
  alternatives to, 372
  drug, 369–371
  explanation of, 343, 368, A-43
  length of, 368–369
  research and, 369
Payments
  deferred, 691–692

future value over time of, 546–547
inflation and, 547–550
linked to production or profit, 685–688, 702
present value over time of, 543–546
PC Magazine, 388
Penn-PIRG, 406
People Express Airlines, 455–456
Pepsi, 368, 459, 460, 486, 492, A-24, A-25
Perfect complements, 82, A-43
Perfectly competitive markets. *See* Competitive markets
Perfectly elastic demand curves, 52
Perfectly inelastic demand curves, 51
Perfect price discrimination
  effects of, 391–394
  explanation of, 389, 413, A-43
  function of, 389–391, A-18–A-19
  transaction costs and, 395
Perfect substitutes, 81, 82, A-43
Performance termination contracts, 698–700
Perpetuities, 554, A-28–A-29
Peter, Laurence J., 46
Pharmaceutical companies, 428, 492
Piece-rate hire contracts, 685–687
Pin manufacturing, 172
Poland, 171–172
Pollution
  cost-benefit analysis of, 612–616
  markets for, 622–623
  paper industry as source of, 605–607
  property rights and, 619–622
  social optimum and, 617
  sulfur dioxide, 623
  welfare effects of, 605–607, A-29–A-30
Pollution control
  emissions standards and, 614–616
  expenditures for, 608–609
  taxes on fuels for, 611
Pooling equilibrium, 659–661, A-43
Pork market, 47–52, 54–57, 60, 61, 63, 64, 66, 67
Pornography market, 250
Positive monotonic transformation, 85*n*
Positive statements, 7, A-43
Potter, Steve, 641
Pravachol, 492

Preference maps
  explanation of, 76–77
  indifference curves and, 77–83
  willingness to substitute and, 80
Preferences
  explanation of, 74–75, 102
  indifference curves and, 80–83
  marginal rate of substitution and, 80
  ordinal, 84–85
  properties of consumer, 75–76
Prescription drugs, 369–371, 401–403
Present value
  choice over time and, 550–559
  of earnings, 558
  explanation of, 543
  net, 551–552
  of net taxes, 568–569
  of payments over time, 543–545
  real, 548–549
Price ceilings
  effects of, 36–38
  explanation of, 35
  supply-and-demand model and, 41
  welfare effects of, 293–295
Price change
  effect on consumer surplus of, 269–272
  effect on consumption and, 89–90
  effect on demand curves of, 117–123
  effects of, 140
  factor demand and, 505–506
  long-run costs and factor, 200–202
Price-consumption curve, 108
Price-Costco, 410
Price discrimination
  conditions for, 387
  due to false beliefs about quality, 650, 651, 665
  elements of, 388
  explanation of, 383, 413, A-43
  gender and, 406
  monopsony, 526–528
  multimarket, 389, 397–406, 413, A-19–A-20
  perfect, 389–395, 413
  positive effects of, 384–387
  quantity discrimination as, 389, 396, 397, 413

resale limitation or prevention
    and, 387, 388
types of, 389
Price elasticity of demand
    explanation of, 48–50, 53,
        A-43
    marginal revenue and, 346–348
    over time, 58
Price elasticity of supply
    explanation of, 56–58, A-43
    over time, 58
Price floor
    effects of, 39–40
    explanation of, 35
    supply-and-demand model and,
        41
    welfare effects of, 289–292
Price/pricing. *See also* Price
        discrimination; Quantity
        discrimination
    advertising and, 654–655
    allocation determined by, 3
    block, 396
    demand and, 14, 16, 18–19
    determination of, 4
    full-information competitive,
        652–653
    marginal revenue and, 344–345
    nonuniform, 383
    overview of, 383–384
    product differentiation and, 461
    sensitivity of quantity demanded
        to, 48–55, 71
    sensitivity of quantity supplied to,
        56–58
    supply and, 22–23
Price setters, 42, 417
Price takers
    explanation of, 223, 224, 450,
        451
    properties of, 224–225, 436
Principal-agent problems
    efficiency and, 670–671
    example of, 669
    explanation of, 668
    types of, 701–702
    types of contracts and, 669–670
Principals
    checks on, 697, 702
    contracts between agents and,
        667–668
Printing firms
    long-run cost curves in, 210–211
    short-run cost curves in,
        A-12–A-13

Prisoners' dilemma, 421, 422, 655,
        A-43
Private costs
    explanation of, 605, A-43
    pollution and, 605, 612
Probability
    explanation of, 572
    frequency and, 572
    gambling and, 583–585
    subjective, 572–573
Probability distribution, 573–574
Producer surplus
    explanation of, 273, A-43
    supply curve to measure,
        273–274
    use of, 274
Producer welfare
    explanation of, 273, 302
    supply curve to measure producer
        surplus and, 273–274
    use of, 274
Production
    factors of, 146
    long-run, 155–164, 174
    payments linked to, 685–687,
        702
    short-run, 148–155, 174
    trading and, 340
Production efficiency
    asymmetric information and,
        677–678
    efficient contracts and, 671–672
    explanation of, 146, 702, A-41
    full information and, 672–677
    requirements for, 670–671
    risk bearing and, 679–685, 702
Production functions
    average cost curves and,
        188–189
    Cobb-Douglas, 165–166
    explanation of, 147, 174, A-43
    marginal cost curves and,
        187–188
    variable cost curves and,
        186–187
Production possibility frontier
    comparative advantage and,
        323–326
    explanation of, 218–219, A-44
    marginal rate of transformation
        and, 326–327
Productivity
    agricultural, 154–155, 678–679
    German vs. British, 170–171
    organizational change and, 172,

        173
    relative, 169–170
    technical change and, 174
    technical progress and, 171–172
    variations in, 169, 170
Product mix, 328, 329
Product of labor
    average and, 149, 150
    extra labor and, 150–152
    marginal, 149–150, 152
    total, 149, 150, 152, 153
Profit
    business, 228
    explanation of, 146, A-44
    marginal, 230–231, A-42
    payments linked to, 687–688,
        702
Profit matrix, 420
Profit maximization
    in advertising and production,
        A-25–A-26
    airline industry and, 432–434
    conditions for, A-15–A-16
    explanation of, 146, 262
    long-run competitive, 246
    method of, 228–230
    monopoly, 344–351, 380
    monopsony, 520–524
    output rules and, 230–232
    quantity and price and, 239
    short-run competitive, 233–238
    shutdown rules and, 232–233
    using labor or output, 504–505
Profit-sharing contracts
    asymmetric information and, 678
    explanation of, 674–676
Property rights
    common property and,
        624–627
    explanation of, 602, 619, A-44
    reducing externalities by
        allocating, 619–623
Prozac, 403
Prudential Insurance Company of
        America, 641
Public goods
    explanation of, 602–603, 627,
        635, A-44
    markets for, 629–631
    reduction of free riding and,
        631–633
    types of, 627–629
    value of, 633–634
Publilius Syrus, 383
Puerto Rico, 40

Quality
  consumer ignorance and, 641–642
  lemons market with fixed,
    642–645
  lemons market with variable,
    645–646
  price discrimination due to false
    beliefs about, 650–651
Quantity demanded
  effect of prices on, 16
  explanation of, 15, A-44
  sensitivity of, 46, 48–55, 71
Quantity discrimination
  explanation of, 389, 396, 397,
    413, A-44
  utility monopoly and, 396, 397,
    A-19
Quantity-setting games, 419–421
Quantity supplied
  explanation of, 22, A-44
  sensitivity of, 46, 56–58, 71
Quasi-vertical integration, 529
Quotas
  effects of, 300
  explanation of, 290, A-44

Rail safety, 55
Raising-costs game tree, 488
Rastelli, Umberto, 66
Rate of return
  on bonds, 554–555
  internal, 553, 554
Rawls, John, 339
Reagan, Ronald, 35, 138
Real prices
  explanation of, 123, 547
  nominal vs., 123–124
Record prices, 516
Redwood trees, 563–564
Regression analysis, A-1–A-3
Relative productivity, 169–170
Rent
  exhaustible resources and, 562
  explanation of, 562, A-44
Rent seeking, 301–302, A-44
Repeated games, 422–423
Requirement tie-in sale
  example of, 411
  explanation of, 410, A-44
Resales, 387, 388
Reservation price, A-44
Residual demand curves
  competitive fringe and, 379–380
  elasticity of, A-15
  explanation of, 226, 227, A-44

Residual supply curves, 312, A-44
Retirement savings, 546–547
Returns to scale
  constant, 164–165
  decreasing, 165
  explanation of, 174
  increasing, 164–165
  in manufacturing, 166–168
  variations in, 168, 169
Revenue-sharing contracts
  asymmetric information and, 678
  explanation of, 674, 675
Rhône-Poulenc, 428
Rice milling, 199–200
Rickel Home Centers, 473
Risk. *See also* Uncertainty
  degree of, 572, 599
  expected value and, 574–575
  explanation of, A-44
  information about employment,
    655–656
  investing and attitudes toward,
    594–596
  natural disasters as
    nondiversifiable risk, 593
  probability and, 572–574
  trade-off between moral hazard
    and, 667
  variance and standard deviation
    and, 575–576
Risk aversion
  collecting information and,
    586–587
  diversification and, 587–588
  explanation of, 578–580,
    585–586, 600, A-44
  gambling and, 583, 584
  insurance and, 589–593
  mutual funds and, 588–589
  saying no and, 586
Risk bearing
  efficiency in, 670, A-41
  tradeoff between efficiency in
    production and, 679–685
Risk neutrality, 581–582, A-44
Risk preference, 582, A-44
Risk premium, 579, A-44
Roche Group, 428
Roche Holding A.G., 428
Rosen, Harris, 404–405
Russell, Bertrand, 501

Safelite Glass, 686
Salaries. *See also* Wages
  of baseball players, 521–522

college education and, 556–559
  fixed, 688
  of university professors, 527–528
Sales tax. *See also* Taxes
  ad valorem tax and, 59, 67–68
  on cigarettes, 62–63
  effects of, 46, 59, 71
  equilibrium and, 60–63, 66–67
  tax incidence and, 63–65
  types of, 59–60
  welfare effects of, 287–288
Sam's Club, 410
San Francisco-Oakland Bay Bridge,
  626–627
Savings and loans, 696–697
Saxbe, William B., 38
Screening
  equalizing information and,
    640–641
  explanation of, 640, A-44
Sears, Roebuck & Company, 423,
  651, 687
Second-degree price discrimination.
  See Quantity discrimination
Second Theorem of Welfare
  Economics, 320
Secret ingredients, 496
Seita, 368
Semiconductor integrated circuits,
  159–161
Separating equilibrium, 659,
  661–662, A-44
Sequential entry decisions
  actions by incumbents and,
    471–473
  commitment and entry prevention
    and, 473–477
  commitment and fixed costs and,
    477–483
  explanation of, 470
7-Eleven stores
Shareholders, 145
Sharing contracts, 670
Shaw, George Bernard, 223
Sherman Antitrust Act of 1890, 424
Shipping industry, 249
Shirking
  bonding to prevent, 689–690
  efficiency wages and, 692–693
  explanation of, 688, A-44
Shocking the equilibrium
  explanation of, 13, 30, 43
  shift in demand curve and,
    30–31, 47
  shift in supply curve and, 31, 47

Shortage, A-44
Short run
  competition in, 262
  explanation of, 147, A-44
  long run vs., 46, 58–59, 71
Short-run average cost curves,
  209–210
Short-run competitive equilibrium
  effects of tax on, 245–246
  explanation of, 244
  in lime market, 244–245
Short-run cost curves
  explanation of, 183–186
  for printing firm, 189, A-12–A-13
  production functions and,
    186–189
Short-run costs
  effects of taxes on, 189–191
  expansion paths and, 214
  explanation of, 181, 192–193,
    220
  measures of, 181–183
  taxes and, 189–192
Short-run factor demand, 502–506
Short-run production
  average product of labor and,
    150
  explanation of, 148
  graphing product curves and,
    150–153
  law of diminishing marginal
    returns and, 153–154
  marginal product of labor and,
    149–150
  total product and, 148–149
Short-run supply curve
  factor prices and, 240–241
  market, 241–243
  tracing out, 239
Shutdown decision
  explanation of, 230, 232–233
  long-run, 246
  monopoly, 350
  short-run, 236–238
Signaling
  brand names as, 649
  college education as, 658–663
  equalizing information and, 641
  explanation of, 640, A-44
Simon, William F., 38
Simpson, O. J., 494
Simultaneous entry decisions
  effects of, 469
  explanation of, 466–467
  room for one firm and, 468–469

room for two firms and,
  467–468
Single-period games, 421, 436
Sin taxes, 310–311
Slutsky, Eugene, A-8
Slutsky equation, A-8–A-9
Smith, Adam, 423–424
SmithKline Beckman, 369–371,
  393–394
Smoking, cigarette. See Tobacco
  industry
Social costs
  explanation of, 605, A-44
  of pollution, 605–607, 612
Social welfare, 338–339
Sole proprietorships, 145
Sonner, Donald, 608
Sonner, Winifred, 608
Sony, 398–400
South Africa, 368
Soybean market, 307–310
Spain, 448–449
Specific tariffs, 296
Specific tax. See also Taxes
  ad valorem vs., 67–68
  effect on equilibrium of, A-3–A-4
  effects of, 60, 66–67
  elasticities and, 60–61
  explanation of, 60
  on monopolies, A-17–A-18
  tax incidence of, 63–65
Splitting contracts, 670
Stackelberg, Heinrich von, 440
Stackelberg equilibrium
  entry prevention and, 475–477,
    479
  explanation of, 440, 450, 451,
    462
  game tree and, 440–442
  graphical model and, 442–444
  sequential moves and, 444
  strategic trade policy and,
    444–449
  use of, 431, A-23–A-24
Standard deviation, 576
Standard & Poor's Composite Index
  of 500 Stocks, 588
Standard & Poor's ratings, 586–587
Standards, 647–648, A-44
State governments, 423
Statistical discrimination, 663–664
Steel imports, 34, 35
Stock
  explanation of, 537, A-44
  rate of return on, 596

Stoppard, Tom, 155
Strategic advertising
  effects of, 497–498
  empirical evidence on, 496
  that helps rivals, 495
  that hurts rivals, 496
Strategic behavior, 465, A-44. See
  also Cartels; Noncooperative
  strategic behavior
Strategy
  dominant, 420, 467, 468
  explanation of, 419, A-44
  mixed, 468–469, A-25
  pure, 468
Subjective probability, 572–573
Subsidies, 292, 293
Substitution effects
  explanation of, 117, 119, A-44
  with inferior good, 119–121
  with normal good, 117–119
  wage change and, 133–135
Sulfur dioxide market, 623
Sunk costs, 180, A-44
Supergame, 422, A-44
Supply
  explanation of, 13, 21, 43
  government policies and, 35–41
  vertical integration and, 531
Supply-and-demand analysis,
  605–611
Supply-and-demand model, 13,
  41–43
Supply curves. See also Labor supply
  curves
  capital market and, 566–567
  causes of shift in, 23
  effect of import policies on,
    25–26
  effects of shift in, 31
  elasticity along, 57–59
  explanation of, 22, A-44
  government policies that shift,
    32–35
  long-run firm, 246–247
  long-run market, 248–256
  measurement of producer surplus
    using, 273–274
  policies that shift, 280–303 (See
    also Government policies)
  residual, 312
  shapes of, 46–48, 70
  short-run firm, 239–241
  short-run market, 241–243
  what can be show by, 22–24, 27
Supply function, 24

Surplus
  demand elasticities and,
    A-16–A-17
  government responses to, 292
Sustainable Fisheries Act of 1996,
    625
Swarthmore College, 180
Sweden
  cigarette tax in, 63
  energy production in, 220
  marginal tax rate in, 140
  tax burden in, 568
Switzerland, 293
Symmetric information, 642–643

Tagamet, 369, 371, 393, 489
Takeda Chemical Industries, 428
Tangency rule, 196–197
Tariffs. *See also* Taxes; Two-part
    tariffs
  effects of, 298–300
  explanation of, 295, A-44
  resale prevention and, 388
  taxes vs., 297
  two-part, 384, 413–414, A-20
  types of, 296–297
Taxes. *See also* Ad valorem tax;
    Income tax; Sales tax; Tariffs;
    Specific tax
  in Canada, 179
  effect on short-run costs,
    189–192
  on externalities in noncompetitive
    markets, 618–619
  on fast-food containers in
    Germany, 4
  franchise, 190–191
  fuel, 611
  Internet shopping and, 96
  mortgage payments and,
    122–123
  present value of net, 568–569
  short-run equilibrium and,
    245–246
  sin, 310–311
  tariffs vs., 297
  vertical integration and, 533
  welfare effects of, 362–363
Taxicabs, 281–284
Tax incidence
  elasticities and, 63–65
  explanation of, 63, A-42
Technical progress
  explanation of, 171, A-44
  nonneutral, 171, 172

Technological efficiency, 146, A-44
Telephone companies, 425
Telephone poles, 555–556
Television, 269
Telkom, 368
10-10-321 commercials, 491
Textile workers, 135–136
Thales, 343
Third-degree price discrimination.
    See Multimarket price
    discrimination
Thread mill, 507–509
Ticket prices, baseball, 522
Tie-in sales
  bundling as, 411–413
  explanation of, 406, 410, 414,
    A-45
  requirement, 410, 411
  types of, 410
Time Warner, 501
Tobacco industry
  advertising and, 496
  deadweight losses in, 451
  taxes and, 62–63, 310–311
Toothbrushes, 460–461, 495
Toothpaste, 496
TopsyTail, 529–530
Torts, 683
Total costs
  explanation of, 182, A-45
  lowering marginal costs while
    raising, 484–485
Total product of labor
  explanation of, 148–149, A-45
  labor change and effects to, 150
Trade
  bargaining ability and, 319
  benefits of, 325
  effects of, 314–135, 340
  endowments and, 315
  mutually beneficial, 315–318
  production and, 323–330
Trade-offs, 2
Trade policies. *See also* Tariffs
  automobile exports and, 429
  free trade vs. ban on imports, 296
  free trade vs. quota, 300–301
  free trade vs. tariff, 296–300
  overview of, 295–296
  rent seeking and, 301–302
  Stackelberg model and strategic,
    444–449
  supply curve and, 25–26
Transaction costs
  explanation of, 42–43, A-45

perfect price discrimination and,
    395
  vertical integration and, 531
Transitivity property, 75
Triad Energy Resources, Inc.,
    607–608
Trusts. *See* Cartels
Truth-in-Lending Act, 541
Twain, Mark, 656
Two-part tariffs
  explanation of, 384, 406–407,
    413–414, A-45
  with identical consumers,
    407–408
  with nonidentical consumers,
    408–409, A-20
  warehouse stores and, 410
Tyson Foods, 428

Uncertainty. *See also* Risk
  decision making under, 577–583,
    600 (*See also* Decision
    making)
  investing under, 593–598, 600
Underwriters' Laboratories (UL), 648
Unemployment
  efficiency wages and, 693–694
  minimum wage and, 39–40
Unitary elasticity, 52
United Airlines, 419–422, 431–438,
    440–447, 453
United Kingdom
  Airbus and, 448–449
  British Airways, 465, 486
  British Telecom, 368
  cigarette tax in, 63
  gasoline tax in, 66
  inflation bonds, 554
  internet registrar in, 379
  job termination laws in, 287
  labor supply curves and, 136–137
  New Corporation, 501
  patents in, 369
  pin manufacturing, 172
  pollution in, 608, 609
  productivity in, 170–171
  rail safety in, 55
  sales of monopolies in, 368
  unions, 519
United Parcel Service, 355
United States
  Consumer Price Index in,
    123–124
  firms in, 144, 145
  gasoline taxes in, 66

labor supply curves and, 136–137
sales of monopolies in, 368
wealth distribution in, 331
United States v. Aluminum Co. of America, 487
United States v. Terminal Railroad Association of St. Louis, 487
U.S. Customs Service, 486
U.S. Postal Service (USPS), 129, 354, 355, 359–360
U.S. Steel, 144
USAir, 456
Usury, 538–539
Utilities, public
  block pricing by, 396, 397
  as monopolies, 364–367
  regulation of, 372, 377
Utility
  expected, 577–578
  explanation of, 74, 83, 102–103, A-45
  indifference curves and, 85
  marginal, 85
  marginal rates of substitution and, 86–87
  maximization of, A-6–A-8
  ordinal preferences and, 84–85
Utility curves, A-4–A-6
Utility function
  explanation of, 83–84, A-45
  risk aversion and, 578–579
Utility maximization, 315
Utility poles, 555–556
Utility possibility frontier (UPF), 335, 336

Variable cost curve
  average, 185–186
  explanation of, 185
  shape of, 186–187
Variable costs
  explanation of, 181–182, A-45
  raising rivals', 485–488
Variable input, 147, 148, A-45
Variance, 575–576
Vaughn, Mo, 522
Vegetable oil mill, 240–241, 257
Vertical demand curve, 52–53
Vertical integration
  degree of, 529
  explanation of, 501, 534, A-45
  outsourcing and, 529–530
  produce or buy and, 530–534
  quasi-, 529
  resales and, 388
  stages of production and, 528–529
Virgin Atlantic Airways, 465, 486
Vitamin industry, 428
Voluntary export restraint (VER) agreements, 429
Voting
  government policies and, 335–338
  on public goods, 633–634

Wages. *See also* Salaries
  based on piecework, 685–687
  efficiency, 692–694
  factor demand and change in, 505–506

Wage setting, 524
Warehouse clubs, 410
Water, 632–633
Watson, Thomas J., 246
Welfare
  consumer, 266–272, 302
  explanation of, 265
  import policy and, 295
  maximized by competition, 276–280, 302
  monopolies and, 357–363, 381, 617–618
  monopsony and, 524
  multimarket price discrimination and, 405–406
  producer, 273–276, 302
  product differentiation and, 461
  sales tax and, 287–288
Westinghouse, 424, 427
Wheat market, 225
Wilshire 5000 Index Portfolio, 589
Wilson, Wade, 646
World War II, 36
Wright, Samuel W., 172
Wright, Steven, 8, 87, 556, 585

Xerox Corporation, 354, 530

Zantac, 369, 489
Zero profit
  explanation of, 263
  with free entry, 259–260
  with limited entry, 260–262
  profit maximization and, 262
Zinsser, William, 1

Applications on the Perloff Companion Web Site

Chapter 3
Condoms
Incidence of Tax on Restaurant
   Meals
Specific Taxes

Chapter 4
Substitution Effects in Canada

Chapter 5
Christmas Price Index
International Comparison of
   Substitution and Income Effects
Quality Improvements, New
   Products, and the CPI
Wealth of Developing Countries

Chapter 6
Does That Compute Down on the
   Farm?
Just-in-Time Delivery and
   Productivity
More Productive Death
Rolls-Royce

Chapter 7
Cost of Caring for Parents
Cost of Names
Depreciation
Quality and Factor Proportions
Tax Rules

Chapter 8
Changes in Banking

Chapter 9
Cheaper Gas
Occupational Licenses
Trucking
Unions and Guilds
Wal-Mart in Germany
Zoning

Chapter 10
U.S. Minimum Wage Laws and
   Teenagers

Chapter 11
Banking Market Power
Deregulating Energy
Ending the Monopoly in
   Telephone Service
Near Monopolies

Chapter 12
Bundling Hardware with Software
   and Service
Gray Markets

International Price Discrimination
Mixed Bundling
Product Differentiation 1
Product Differentiation 2
Tailoring Credit Cards
The Supreme Court's View on
   Tie-in Sales
Using Information to Perfectly
   Price Discriminate

Chapter 13
Bad Bakers
Designer Glasses
Economists Prevent Collusion
Insurance Price Wars
Tacit Collusion in Long-Distance
   Service

Chapter 14
Advertising Expenditures
Advertising Targets
Brand-Switching Advertising
Buttering Up Legislatures
Celebrities
Electric Utilities
Generic Milk Promotions
Nonprice Strategies
Phone Companies
Restroom Advertising
Smoking-Gun Evidence?
Trade

Chapter 15
Life Cycle of a Firm
Piggish Vertical Integration
Vertical Integration and Essential
   Facilities: Barnes & Noble
Vertical Integration of Auto
   Manufacturers

Chapter 16
Buying Versus Renting a Phone
Consumed Investments
Costs of Gold Mining
Dam
Price of Aluminum over Time
Rates of Return on Paintings,
   Prints, and Coins
Recycling
Reserves of Natural Resources
Taking from Future Generations

Chapter 17
Acceptable Risk
Diversification Traps
International Risks

Lotteries
Risky Hobbies and Occupations
Risky Jobs Pay (Slightly) More
S&P 500 Funds
Socially Irresponsible Mutual Fund

Chapter 18
Claiming Lobster Fisheries
Commons and Highways
Education as a Public Good
International Pollution-Control
   Expenditures
Quantity Controls on Pig Pollution
Taxing Coal
Trash and Pollution Markets

Chapter 19
Commercial Free Speech vs.
   Strength Wars
Consumer ValueStar
Everyone Talks about the Weather
Keeping Consumers Ignorant
Labeling Laws
Price Dispersion
Rent-to-Own Stores
Taking Candy from Babies and
   Their Parents
Wages Rise with Education
Wholesale Market for Cherries
Wholesale Used-Car Auctions

Chapter 20
Australian Compensation
BMW Incentives
Bonding by British Trading
   Companies
Deferred Payments Versus
   Efficiency Wages in Fast-Food
   Restaurants
Effectiveness of Monitoring
Efficiency Wage and Supervision in
   Petrochemical Firms
High-Tech Stock Options
Incentives for Financial Advisors
Inspiring Directors
Medical Partnerships
Piece Rates at Lincoln Electric
Sharing Textbook Revenue
Teachers' Incentives